FAULT LINES

FAULT LINES

EXPIRATION DATE
EARTHQUAKE WEATHER

TIM POWERS

GUILD**A**MERICA
B O O K S

EXPIRATION DATE Copyright © 1996 by Tim Powers
Printing History: Tor Hardcover January 1996

EARTHQUAKE WEATHER Copyright © 1997 by
Tim Powers
Printing History: Tor Hardcover October 1997

Published by arrangement with:
Tor Books
Tom Doherty Associates, Inc.
175 Fifth Avenue
New York, New York 10010

Tor® is a registered trademark of Tom Doherty Associates, Inc.

ISBN # 1-56865-497-9

Visit our website at *http://www.sfbc.com*
Visit Tor's website at *http://www.Tor.com*

Printed in the United States of America.

For Serena
again, and still, and always

And with thanks to Chris Arena, Bonnie Badenoch, John Bierer, Jim Blaylock, Russ Galen, Tom Gilchrist, Doug Goulet, Ann James, Delphine Josephe, Dorothea Kenny, Jim Crooks, Phil Mays, David Masesan, Kitty Myshkin, David Perry, Celene Pierce, Brendan and Regina Powers, Richard Powers, Serena Powers, Fred Ramer, Randal Robb, Jacques Sadoul, Marv Torrez, Rex Torrez, and Greg Wade.

CONTENTS

Her wanton spirits look out
At every joint and motive of her body.
O, these encounterers, so glib of tongue,
That give a coasting welcome ere it comes,
And wide unclasp the table of their thoughts
To every ticklish reader, set them down
For sluttish spoils of opportunity
And daughters of the game.

—William Shakespeare,
Troilus and Cressida

My brain I'll prove the female to my soul,
My soul the father, and these two beget
A generation of still-breeding thoughts;
And these same thoughts people this little world,
In humors like the people of this world . . .
Thus play I in one person many people,
And none contented . . .

—William Shakespeare,
Richard II

So long as you do not die and rise again,
You are a stranger to the dark earth.

—Goethe

EXPIRATION DATE

BOOK ONE

Open up that
Golden Gate

*TRENTON, NJ—Thomas A. Edison, the inventor of the light bulb,
whose honors have included having a New Jersey town and college
named after him, received a college degree Sunday, 61 years after
his death.*

*Thomas Edison State College conferred on its namesake a bach-
elor of science degree for lifetime achievement.*

—The Associated Press,
Monday, October 26, 1992

CHAPTER 1

"But I don't want to go among mad people," Alice remarked.
"Oh, you can't help that," said the Cat: "we're all mad here. I'm mad. You're mad."
"How do you know I'm mad?" said Alice.
"You must be," said the Cat, "or you wouldn't have come here."
— Lewis Carroll,
Alice's Adventures in Wonderland

When he was little, say four or five, the living room had been as dim as a church all the time, with curtains pulled across the broad windows, and everywhere there had been the kind of big dark wooden furniture that's got stylized leaves and grapes and claws carved into it. Now the curtains had been taken down, and through the windows Kootie could see the lawn—more gold than green in the early-evening light, and streaked with the lengthening shadows of the sycamores—and the living room was painted white now and had hardly any furniture in it besides white wood chairs and a glass-topped coffee table.

The mantel over the fireplace was white now too, but the old black bust of Dante still stood on it, the only relic of his parents' previous taste in furnishings. Dante Allah Hairy, he used to think its name was.

Kootie leaned out of his chair and switched on the pole lamp. Off to his left, his blue nylon knapsack was slumped against the front door, and ahead of him and above him Dante's eyes were gleaming like black olives. Kootie hiked himself out of the chair and crossed to the fireplace.

He knew that he wasn't allowed to touch the Dante. He had always known that, and the rule had never been a difficult one to obey. He was eleven now, and no longer imagined that the black-painted head and shoulders were just the visible top of a whole little body concealed inside the brick fireplace-front—and he realized these days that the rustlings that woke him at night were nothing more than the breeze in the boughs outside his bedroom window, and not the Dante whispering to itself all alone in the dark living room—but it was still a nasty-looking thing, with its scowling hollow-cheeked face and the way its black finish was shiny on the high spots, as if generations of people had spent a lot of time rubbing it.

Kootie reached up and touched its nose.

Nothing happened. The nose was cool and slick. Kootie put one hand under the thing's chin and the other hand behind its head and then carefully lifted it down and set it on the white stone slab of the hearth.

He sat down cross-legged beside it and thought of Sidney Greenstreet in *The Maltese Falcon*, sweating furiously, hacking with a penknife at the black-painted statue of the falcon; Kootie had no idea what might be inside the Dante, but he thought the best way to get at it would be to simply shatter the thing. He had glimpsed the unpainted white base of the bust just now, and had seen that it was only plaster.

But breaking it would be the irrevocable step.

He had packed shirts, socks, underwear, sweatsuit, a jacket, and a baseball cap in his knapsack, and he had nearly three hundred dollars in twenties in his pocket, along with his Swiss army knife, but he wouldn't be *committed* to running away until he broke the bust of Dante.

Broke it and took away whatever might be inside it. He hoped he'd find gold—Krugerrands, say, or those little flat blocks like dominoes.

It occurred to him, now, that even if the bust was nothing but solid plaster all through, as useless as Greenstreet's black bird had turned out to be, he would still have to break it. The Dante was the . . . what, flag, emblem, totem pole of what his parents had all along been trying to make Kootie into.

With a trembling finger, he pushed the bust over backward. It clunked on the stone, staring at the ceiling now, but it didn't break.

He exhaled, both relieved and disappointed.

Dirty mummy-stuff, he thought. Meditation, and the big tunnel with all the souls drifting toward the famous white light. His parents had lots of pictures of that. Pyramids and the Book of Thoth and reincarnation and messages from these "old soul" guys called Mahatmas.

The Mahatmas were dead, but they would supposedly still come around to tell you how to be a perfect dead guy like they were. But they were coy—Kootie had never seen one at all, even after hours of sitting and trying to make his mind a blank, and even his parents only claimed to have *glimpsed* the old boys, who always apparently snuck out through the kitchen door if you tried to get a good look at them. Mostly you could tell that they'd been around only by the things they'd rearrange—books on the shelves, cups in the kitchen. If you had left a handful of change on the dresser, you'd find they'd sorted the coins and stacked them. Sometimes with the dates in order.

At about the age when his friends were figuring out that Santa Claus was a fake, Kootie had stopped believing in the Mahatmas and all the rest of it; later he'd had a shock when he learned in school that there really had been a guy named Mahatma Gandhi, but a friend of his who saw the movie *Gandhi* told him that Gandhi was just a regular person, a politician in India who was skinny and bald and wore diapers all the time.

Kootie wasn't allowed to *see* movies . . . or watch TV, or even eat meat, though he often sneaked off to McDonald's for a Big Mac, and then had to chew gum afterward to get rid of the smell.

Kootie wanted to be an astronomer when he grew up, but his parents weren't going to let him go to college. He wasn't sure if he'd even be allowed to go to all four years of high school. His parents told him he was a *chela*, just as they were, and that his duty in life was to . . . well, it was hard to say, really; to get squared away with these dead guys. Be their "new Krishnamurti"—carry their message to the world. Be prepared for when you died and found yourself in that big tunnel.

And in the meantime, no TV or movies or meat, and when he grew up he wasn't supposed to get married or ever have sex at all—not because of AIDS, but because the Mahatmas were down on it. Well, he thought, they *would* be, wouldn't they, being dead and probably wearing diapers and busy all the time rearranging people's coffee cups. Shoot.

But the worst thing his parents had ever done to him they did on the day he was born—they *named* him after one of these Mahatmas, a dead guy who had to go and have the name Koot Hoomie. Growing up named Koot Hoomie Parganas, with the inevitable nickname Kootie, had been . . . well, he had seen a lot of fat kids or stuttering kids get teased mercilessly in school, but he always wished he could trade places with them if in exchange he could have a name like *Steve* or *Jim* or *Bill*.

He lifted the Dante in both hands to a height of about four inches, and let it fall. *Clunk!* But it still didn't break.

He believed his parents worshipped the thing. Sometimes after he had gone off to bed and was supposedly asleep, he had sneaked back and peeked into the living room and seen them bowing in front of it and mumbling, and at certain times of the year—Christmas, for example, and Halloween, which was only about a week away—his mother would knit little hats and collars for Dante. She always had to make them new, too, couldn't use last year's, though she saved all of them.

And his parents always insisted to Kootie—nervously, he thought—

that the previous owner of the house had coincidentally been named
Don Tay (or sometimes *Om* Tay) and that's why the drunks or crazy
people who called on the phone sometimes at night seemed to be asking
to talk to the statue.

Terminator 2. "Peewee's Playhouse." Mario Brothers and Tetris on the
Nintendo. Big Macs and the occasional furtive Marlboro. College, even-
tually, and maybe even just finishing high school. Astronomy. *Friends.*
All that, on the one hand.

Rajma, khatte chhole, masoor dal, moong dal, chana dal, which were
all just different kinds of cooked beans. On the other hand. Along with
Mahatmas, and start some kind of new theosophical order (instead of
go to college), and don't have a girlfriend.

As if he ever could.

You think it's bad that Melvin touched you and gave you his cooties?
We've *got a Kootie in our* class.

His jaw was clenched so tight that his teeth ached, and tears were being
squeezed out of his closed eyes, but he lifted the Dante over his head
with both hands—paused—and then smashed it down onto the hearth.

With a muffled *crack* it broke into a hundred powdery white pieces,
some tumbling away onto the tan carpet.

He opened his eyes, and for several seconds while his heart pounded
and he didn't breathe, he just stared down at the scattered floury rubble.
At last he let himself exhale, and he slowly stretched out his hand.

At first glance the mess seemed to consist entirely of angular lumps
of plaster; but when he tremblingly brushed through the litter, he found
a brick-shaped piece, about the size of two decks of cards glued together
front-to-back. He picked it up—it was heavy, and its surface *gave* a
little when he squeezed it, cracking the clinging plaster and exhaling a
puff of fine white dust.

He glanced over his shoulder at the front door, and tried to imagine
what his parents would do if they were to walk in right now, and see
this. They might very well, he thought, go completely insane.

Hastily he started tugging at the stiffly flexible stuff that encased the
object; when he got a corner unfolded and was able to see the inner
surface of the covering he realized that it was some sort of patterned
silk handkerchief, stiffened by the plaster.

Once he'd got the corner loose, it was easy—in two seconds he had
peeled the white-crusted cloth away, and was holding up a little glass
brick. The surfaces of it were rippled but gleamingly smooth, and its
translucent depths were as cloudy as smoky quartz.

He held it up to the light from the window—

And the air seemed to vibrate, as if a huge gong had been struck in the sky and was ringing, and shaking the earth, with some subsonic note too profoundly low to be sensed by living ears.

All day the hot Santa Ana winds had been combing the dry grasses down the slopes of the San Bernardino Mountains, moving west like an airy tide across the miles-separated semi-desert towns of Fontana and Upland, over the San Jose Hills and into the Los Angeles basin, where they swept the smog blanket out to sea and let the inhabitants see the peaks of Mount Wilson and Mount Baldy, hallucinatorily clear against a startlingly blue sky.

Palm trees bowed and nodded over old residential streets and threw down dry fronds to bounce dustily off of parked cars; and red-brick roof tiles, loosened by the summer's rains and sun, skittered free of ancient cement moorings, cartwheeled over rain gutters, and shattered on driveways that were, as often as not, two weathered lines of concrete with a strip of grass growing between. The steady background bump-and-hiss of the wind was punctuated by the hoarse shouts of crows trying to fly upwind.

Downtown, in the streets around the East L.A. Interchange where the northbound 5 breaks apart into the Golden State and Santa Monica and Hollywood Freeways, the hot wind had all day long been shaking the big slow RTD buses on their shocks as they groaned along the sun-softened asphalt, and the usual reeks of diesel smoke and ozone and the faint strawberry-sweetness of garbage were today replaced with the incongruous spice of faraway sage and baked Mojave stone.

For just a moment now as the sun was setting, redly silhouetting trees and oil tanks on the western hills around Santa Monica, a higher-than-usual number of cars swerved in their freeway lanes, or jumped downtown curbs to collide with light poles or newspaper stands, or rolled forward at stoplights to clank against the bumpers of the cars ahead; and many of the homeless people in East L.A. And Florence and Inglewood cowered behind their shopping carts and shouted about Jesus or the FBI or the Devil or unfathomable personal deities; and for a few moments up on Mulholland Drive all the westbound cars drifted right and then left and then right again, as if the drivers were all rocking to the same song on the radio.

In an alley behind a ramshackle apartment building down in Long Beach, a fat, shirtless old man shivered suddenly and dropped the handle of the battered dolly he had been angling toward an open garage, and the refrigerator he'd been carting slammed to the pavement, pinning his foot; his gasping shouts and curses brought a heavyset young woman running, and after she'd helped him hike the refrigerator off of his foot, he demanded breathlessly that she run upstairs and draw a bath for him, a *cold* one.

And on Broadway the neon signs were coming on and darkening the sky—the names of the shops were often Japanese or Korean, though the rest of the lettering was generally in Spanish—and many of the people in the hurrying crowds below glanced uneasily at the starless heavens. On the sidewalk under the marquee of the old Million Dollar Theater a man in a ragged nylon jacket and baggy camouflage pants had clenched his teeth against a scream and was now leaning against one of the old ornate lampposts.

His left arm, which had been cold all day despite the hot air that was dewing his forehead with sweat, was warm now, and of its own volition was pointing west. With his grubby right hand he pushed back the bill of his baseball cap, and he squinted in that direction, at the close wall of the theater, as if he might be able to see through it and for miles beyond the bricks of it, out past Hollywood, toward Beverly Hills, looking for—

—An abruptly arrived thing, a new and godalmighty smoke, a switched-on beacon somewhere out toward where the sun had just set.

"Get a life," he whispered to himself. "God, *get* a life!"

He pushed himself away from the pole. Walking through the crowd was awkward with his arm stuck straight out, though the people he passed didn't give him a glance, and when he got on an RTD bus at Third Street he had to shuffle down the crowded aisle sideways.

And for most of the night all the crickets were silent in the dark yards and in the hallways of empty office buildings and in the curbside grasses, as if the same quiet footstep had startled all of them.

CHAPTER 2

".. . when she next peeped out, the Fish-Footman was gone, and the other was sitting on the ground near the door, staring stupidly up into the sky."
—Lewis Carroll,
Alice's Adventures in Wonderland

Kootie trudged back up the quiet dimness of Loma Vista Drive toward home. He was walking more slowly than he had been a few minutes ago on Sunset Boulevard, and now that he had got his breath back he realized that he was limping, and that his side hurt worse than ever. Probably that punch in the stomach had cracked a rib.

Tomorrow must be trash day—all the wheeled green plastic trash cans were out along the curbs. His neighbors' houses, which he had always scornfully thought looked like 1950s-style Japanese restaurants, were hidden behind the trees, but he knew that behind the ARMED RESPONSE signs on the lawns they were probably all dark at this hour. He was sure that dawn couldn't be far off.

He leaned against one of the trash cans and tried to ignore the hard pounding of his heart, and the tight chill in his belly that was making his hands sweat and shake. He could claim that burglars had got in, and kidnapped him because he had seen them, because he was a *witness* who could identify them in a *lineup*; they had panicked, say, and grabbed him and fled after doing nothing more than break the Dante. Kootie had managed to escape . . . after a fight, which would be how come his left eye was swelling shut and his rib was perhaps broken.

He tried to believe the burglar story, which he would probably have to tell to some policeman—he tried to imagine the fictitious burglars, what they had said, what their car had looked like; and after a few moments he was horrified to realize that the tone of the whole thing just rang with kid-ingenuity, like the ''concerto'' he had composed on the piano a year ago, which had sounded every bit as good and dramatic as Tchaikovsky to him at the time, but later was somehow just meandering and emphatic.

A kid just couldn't see the difference. It was like being color-blind or something, or preferring Frazetta to all those blobby old paintings of haystacks and French people in rowboats.

A grown-up would probably have been able to tell that Lumpy and Daryl weren't nice guys. *Well, shit, Koot my man, you can stay in my garage—it's right down here, nothing fancy but it's got a bed and a refrigerator—and you can work for me detailing cars.*

It had sounded all right.

And then *pow* behind a Dumpster, and hard hands turning out his pockets while his knapsack was dragged off his back and all his carefully folded clothes were flung out onto the littered pavement, and a moment later Kootie was alone in the alley, snuffling and choking as quietly as he could and shoving his clothes back into the broken knapsack.

The glass brick had slid under the Dumpster, and he had had to practically get down on his face and crawl to retrieve it.

At least he could still return that. And his parents *had* to take him back. He didn't care what punishment they would give him, just so that he could soon be in his own room again, in his own bed. Last night he had dreamed of going to college, of getting a "B.S.," which in the dream had meant something besides *bullshit.* The dream had given him the (stupid!) determination to finally put his (stupid!) running-away scheme into actual (stupid!) action.

He hoped he never dreamed again.

He pushed away from the trash can and resumed limping up the street, from one silent pool of agitated street light to the next. Go to bed and put it off until morning, he thought miserably. They might think I've spent the night at Courtney's house, and . . . No. There was the busted Dante to raise the alarm. Still, sneak into bed and deal with everything tomorrow morning.

The curb by his own driveway was bare—no trash cans. That wasn't reassuring. His mom and dad must be too upset to think of taking down the cans. But maybe they were off in the car right now, looking for him, and he'd be able to—

No. As he started limping up the white cement driveway he saw their Mercedes against the lights of the kitchen. And the leaves of the peach tree to the right of the house were yellowly lit, so his bedroom light was on too.

Shit, he thought with despairing defiance. Shit shit *shit*, and I don't care who knows it. At least there's no police cars. At the moment.

He tiptoed across the grass around to the garage on the north side of the house. The laundry-room door was open, spilling light across the lawn, and he crouched up to it and peered inside.

The gleaming white metal cubes of the washer and dryer, with the colorful Wisk and Clorox 2 boxes on the shelf over them, were so achingly familiar a sight that he had to blink back tears. He stepped in and walked quietly, heel-and-toe, into the kitchen.

He could see into the living room—and there were two elegantly dressed people standing by the fireplace, a man and a woman, and only after a moment did he recognize them as his mom and dad.

His dad was wearing . . . a black *tuxedo*, with a ruffled white shirt, and his mother had on a puffy white dress with clouds of lace at the wrists and the low neckline. The two of them were just standing there, staring at different corners of the room.

In the first moment of frozen bewilderment Kootie forgot about wanting to cry. Could they have put on these crazily formal clothes just to greet him when he returned? His father's hair was *styled*, obviously blow-dryered up, and . . . and the hair was all black now, not gray at all.

Kootie took a deep breath and stepped out onto the deep tan carpet. "Mom?" he said quietly.

His mother looked much slimmer in the dress, and he noticed with disbelief that she was actually wearing eye makeup. Her calm gaze shifted to the ceiling.

"Mom," Kootie repeated, a little louder. He was oddly reluctant to speak in a normal tone.

His father turned toward the kitchen—and then kept turning, finally fixing his gaze on a chair by the hallway arch.

"I'm sorry," Kootie whimpered, horrified by this grotesque punishment. "*Talk* to me, it fell and broke so I ran away, I've got the glass thing that was inside it—"

His mother raised her white-sleeved arms, and Kootie stumbled forward, sobbing now—but she was turning around, and her arms were out to the sides now as if she was doing a dance in slow motion. Kootie jerked to a stop on the carpet, abruptly very frightened.

"*Stop it!*" he screamed shrilly. "*Don't!*"

"*Fuck is that?*" came a hoarse shout from down the hall.

Kootie heard something heavy fall over, and then clumping footsteps in the hall—then a homeless-looking man in a ragged nylon wind breaker was standing there scowling crazily at him. The big man's whiskery face was round under a grimy baseball cap, and his eyes seemed tiny. He blinked in evident surprise at the slow-moving figures of Kootie's parents, but quickly focused again on the boy.

"Kid, come here," the man said, taking a quick step into the living room. He was reaching for Kootie with his right hand—because his left hand, his whole left arm, was gone, with just an empty sleeve folded and pinned-up there.

Kootie bolted to the left into the green-lit atrium, skidding and almost falling on the sudden smooth marble floor, and though he clearly saw the two figures who were sitting in chairs against the lattice wall he didn't stop running; he had seen the figures vividly but he hit the backyard door with all his weight—it slammed open and he was running across the dark grass so fast that he seemed to be falling straight down from a height.

His hands and feet found the crossboards in the back fence and he was over it and tearing through ivy in darkness, getting up before he even knew he had fallen—he scrambled over a redwood fence and then was just running away full tilt down some quiet street.

His eyes must have been guiding his feet on automatic pilot, for he didn't fall; but in his head all he could see was the two figures sitting in the chairs in the atrium, *duct-taped* into the chairs at neck and wrist and ankle—his overweight mother and his gray-haired father, mouths gaping and toothless, eyes just empty blood-streaked sockets, hands clawed and clutching the chair arms in obvious death.

CHAPTER 3

"... Just look along the road, and tell me if you can see either of them."
"I see nobody on the road," said Alice.
"I only wish I had such eyes," the King remarked in a fretful tone. "To be able to see Nobody! And at that distance too! Why, it's as much as I can do to see real people, by this light!"

—Lewis Carroll,
Through the Looking-Glass

Pete Sullivan opened his eyes after the flash, but seconds went by as he watched a patch of sky through the screened window of the van, and he didn't hear any thunder. He sat up in the narrow bed and wondered whether silent flashes behind one's eyes were a symptom of impending stroke; he had been unaccountably jumpy tonight, and he had played a terrible game of pool in the bar here after work, flinching and clumsy with the cue stick.

The thought of incipient stroke wasn't alarming him, and he realized that he didn't really believe it. He swung his bare feet to the carpeted floorboards and stood up—years ago he had replaced the van's stock roof with a camper top that raised the ceiling two and a half feet, so he was able to stand without bumping the top of his head—and he leaned on the little sink counter and stared out through the open window at the Arizona night.

Tonto Basin was down inside a ring of towering cumulus clouds tonight, and as he watched, one of the clouds was lit for an instant from inside; and a moment later a vivid fork of lightning flashed to the east, over the southern peaks of the Mogollon Rim.

Sullivan waited, but no thunder followed.

The breeze through the screen smelled like the autumn evenings of his boyhood in California, a cool smell of rain-wet rocks, and suddenly the stale old-clothes and propane-refrigerator air inside the van was confining by contrast—he pulled on a pair of jeans and some socks, stepped into his steel-toed black shoes, and slid the door open.

When he was outside and standing on the gravel of O'Hara's back parking lot, he could hear the noise from the bar's open back door— Garth Brooks on the jukebox and the click of pool shots and the shaking racket of drink and talk.

He had taken a couple of steps out across the lot, looking up vainly for stars in the cloudy night sky, when a Honda station wagon spoke to him.

"Warning," it said. The bar's bright back-door light gleamed on the car's hood. *"You are too close to the vehicle—step back."* Sullivan stepped back. *"Thank you,"* said the car.

The thing's voice had been just barely civil.

Sullivan plodded back to the van for cigarettes and a lighter. When he was back out on the gravel, the Honda was quiet until he clicked his lighter; then the car again warned him that he was too close to the vehicle.

He inhaled on the cigarette and blew out a plume of smoke that trailed away on the breeze. "Too close for what?" he asked.

"Step back," said the car.

"What vehicle?" Sullivan asked. "You? Or is there somebody else around? Maybe we both ought to step back."

"Warning," the thing was saying, speaking over him. *"You are too close to the vehicle. Step back."*

"What'll you do if I don't?"

"It'll go off like a fire siren, Pete," came a voice from behind Sullivan. "What are you teasing a car for?"

It was Morrie the bartender, and out here in the fresh air Sullivan thought he could smell the beer stains on the man's apron. "He started it, Morrie."

"It started it. It's a *car.* You've got a call."

Sullivan imagined picking up the bar phone and hearing the flat mechanical voice telling him that he was standing too close to a vehicle. "The power station?"

"Didn't say. Maybe it's some local dad pissed about his daughter being messed with."

Morrie had turned and was crunching back toward the lit doorway, and Sullivan tucked in his T-shirt and followed him. It wouldn't be some citizen of this little desert town—Sullivan was one of the apparently few tramp electricians who didn't get drunk every night and use his eight-hundred-a-week paycheck to sway the local girls.

Besides, he'd only been in town this season for a week. Last Friday he'd been bending conduit pipe and pulling wires at the Palo Verde Nuclear Generating Station a hundred miles west of here—and during this last week at the Roosevelt Station, outside of town, there had been too much overtime for him to do anything more than work, come back here to gulp a couple of Cokes and shoot a couple of games of pool, and sleep.

The noise of conversation increased when he walked in through the back door after Morrie, and Sullivan squinted in the sudden glare of overhead lights and neon beer signs. He walked to the bar, and Morrie was already behind it and tilting a plastic cup under the Coke tap. The telephone was on the bar with the receiver lying beside it.

Sullivan picked it up. "Hello."

"Pete? God, you're a creature of habit—every year working the same places at the same seasons." She sounded angry.

It was his twin sister, and his hand tightened on the receiver. "Sukie, what—"

"Shut up and listen. I'm at a hotel in Delaware, and the front desk just called me. They say somebody hit my car in the lot, and they want me to go down and give 'em insurance information. I—"

"Sukie, I don't—"

"Shut *up!* I woke up on bar-time, Pete! I was bolt upright a second before the phone rang, and then I felt the plastic of the receiver before my hand hit it! I could feel my pupils tighten up a second before I turned on the lamp! Nobody hit my car, I'll bet my life on it! She's *found* me, and she'll find you—she'll have people at the desk here waiting for me, and she's got people out there where you are, you *know* she does. And you know what she wants us *for*, too, unless you've managed to forget *everything*. *I'm* looking Commander Hold-'Em in the *eye* right now, if you care; this is for *you*. Go straight out of there, right now, and drive and—this call is through the goddamn front desk, I know they're listening—go to the place where we hid—a thing, some things, okay? In a garage? It's what you're gonna need if she's—wanting us again. For *any* purpose."

"I can't—"

"Do you know the thing I'm talking about?"

"I think so, the . . . where you can't hardly walk for all the palm fronds on the pavement, right? And you've got to crawl under low branches? Is the . . . thing still there?"

"*I've* never moved it."

"But I can't just walk away here, Sukie, I'd have to . . . God, go to

Radiation Control and get a Whole Body Count, that takes twenty
minutes right there, and for my paycheck—"

"*Walk away, Pete!* It's just a job."

"It's the Arizona Public Service," Sullivan told her evenly, "that's
Edison-owned, just like all the utilities are—the east coast is all Con
Ed, and the West Coast is California Edison, and even Niagara up there
is on the Edison grid. It's all Edison, coast to coast. I'd never work for
any of the utilities again."

"*A.O.P., dude.*"

"Sukie, maybe somebody *did* hit your car," he began, then realized
that he was talking to a dead phone. He hung it up and pushed it toward
Morrie.

"Sukie?" the bartender said.

"My sister. Somebody ran into her car and she wants to make a
federal case out of it." Sullivan was remembering how awkwardly he'd
played pool earlier in the evening, and he was annoyed to notice that
his hands were trembling. He pushed away the Coke. "Give me a shot
of Wild Turkey and a Coors chaser, would you?"

Morrie raised his eyebrows, but hiked up the bottle of bourbon without remarking on the fact that this would be the first real drink Sullivan
had ever ordered in the place.

Sullivan sat down at one of the stools and slugged back the bourbon
and then chased it with a long sip of cold beer. It made him feel closer
to his sister, and he resented that almost enough to push the drinks away.

But not quite. He waved the emptied shot glass at Morrie and had
another sip of the beer.

I'm looking Commander Hold-'Em in the eye *right now, if you care.*

Commander Hold-'Em was Sukie's name for the Grim Reaper—Sullivan believed she'd derived it from the name of some poker game that
she always lost at—and it was also what she had always called whatever
gun she carried. For several years, in the old days in L.A., it had been
a .45 Derringer with two hollow-point bullets in it. Commander Hold-
'Em would certainly still be something as effective today. Sullivan wondered if she would kill herself before even going down to the front desk
and making *sure* that the call had been a trap. Maybe she would. Maybe
she had just been waiting, all these years, for a good enough excuse to
blow her goddamned head off. And of course not neglect to call him
first.

And you know what she wants us *for, too, unless you've managed to
forget* everything.

For a moment Sullivan found himself remembering an enigmatic image from his recurrent adolescent nightmare: three cans of Hires Root

Beer, sitting in beach sand, unopened forever . . . a man's voice saying, *You're not Speedy Alka-Seltzer—*

And he shuddered and thrust the thought away. He lifted his glass and took such a huge slug of beer that his throat ached sharply, and he had to sit rigid until the swallow had finally gone down. At last he could breathe again.

Now he could feel the sudden cold of the beer in his stomach. At least it had driven away the momentary memory. God, he thought, I'm turning into Sukie.

A.O.P., dude.

She'd been good at driving the L.A. freeways drunk—she always said that if you started to weave in your lane, you could cover it by accelerating as you corrected, and nobody would know you'd been out of control; it had become a motto of theirs—*Accelerate Outta Problems.*

Morrie finally refilled the shot glass; Sullivan nodded and took a cautious sip. I was *never* any good at shooting pool, he thought. Or else I've always been fairly good at it, but I was just jumpy when I was playing earlier tonight. I can't accelerate out of this town, out of this job. Probably she made the whole thing up—giggling in a house somewhere right now, not in Delaware and not even owning a gun anymore—just to wreck my life one more time.

No way it'll happen.

He took a moderate swallow of the beer. I *could* just *resign* from this job, he thought. If I turn in my resignation to the general foreman, it won't be held against me. Tramp electricians are always getting "a case of red-ass" and moving on. I'd just have to sign out, and get a Whole Body Count, wearing paper pyjamas and lying in the aluminum coffin while the counter box inches over me, measuring the rems of radiation I've picked up this year; then drive to California and retrieve the . . . the *mask,* and move on, to Nevada or somewhere. There's always utilities work for someone who's still in good with Edison.

But if Sukie's just jerking me around, why should I bother?

And if she's *not,* he thought, then there'll be people waiting for me to show up at the station, as she said. In fact, if bad guys were listening in on our call, at the front desk of her hypothetical hotel, then they'd have heard Morrie answer the phone here the way he always does, *O'Hara's in Roosevelt, Morrie speaking.*

It's a half-hour's drive from the Roosevelt Nuclear Generating Station to O'Hara's . . . if you're not in a tearing hurry.

Sullivan bolted the rest of the bourbon and the beer and walked out of the bar. Morrie would add the cost of the drinks to the rent on the parking space in the back lot.

As he trudged across the obliquely lit gravel, the sight of the familiar, homely old van slowed his pace. He could just climb in, pull the doors shut behind him and lock it and get back into the fold-out bed, and tomorrow morning at eight be driving through the gate at the Roosevelt Station, waving his badge at the guard who knew him anyway, and then happily spend all morning tightening conduit bolts that would have to be ripped out and done again after the foreman noticed that the inspection date on all the torque wrenches had expired a week ago. Assured, meaningless, union work, at thirty dollars an hour. Where would he find another trade like it?

He jumped in surprise, and an instant later the Honda said *"Warning—you are too close to the vehicle."* The breeze was suddenly cold on his forehead, and his heart was pounding. *"Step back,"* the thing went on. He stepped back. *"Thank you."*

Bar-time. It had not just been clumsiness at the pool table. He was definitely on bar-time again.

I woke up on bar-time, Pete!

That's what the Sullivan twins had called the phenomenon when they'd first noticed it, early in their years of working for Loretta deLarava in L.A.—Sukie had got the term from California bars that keep their clocks set about ten minutes fast, so as to be able to get all the drinks off the tables by the legal shut-down time of 2 A.M., and drinkers experience 2 A.M. a little while before it actually occurs. The twins had spent a lot of nights in bars, though Pete drank only Cokes and the occasional beer, and he could still vividly see Sukie, wearing dark glasses at some dark corner table, sucking a cigarette and asking someone, *One-thirty? Is that real time or bar-time?*

Sullivan stood beside the van now, his hand on the driver's-side door handle.

Finally he unlocked the door and climbed in. The engine started at the first twist of the key, and Sullivan let it warm up for only a few seconds before clanking the van into gear and steering it out toward the road that would take him south to Claypool and the 60 Highway that stretched away west.

The sky flashed again, twice; and though he had rolled the window down as he drove past the glaringly lit front entrance of O'Hara's and then picked up speed on the paved road, he still heard no following thunder.

He touched the brake pedal an instant before the brake lights of the car ahead came on; and then he saw the next jagged spear of lightning clearly because he had already glanced toward where it would be.

Bar-time for sure. He sighed and kept driving.

Everyone experiences bar-time occasionally, usually in the half-conscious hypnagogic stage of drifting into or out of sleep—when the noise that jolts one awake, whether it's an alarm or a bell or a shout, is anticipated, is *led up to,* by the plot of the interrupted dream; or when some background noise like the hum of a refrigerator compressor or an air conditioner becomes intrusive only in the instant before it shuts off.

The Sullivan twins had spent countless hours on bar-time during the eighties—it had seemed that they were always reaching for a telephone just before it would start to ring, and appearing in indoor snapshots with their eyes closed because they had anticipated the flash. Eventually they had figured out that it was just one more weird consequence of working for Loretta deLarava, but the pay had been good enough to make it, too, just a minor annoyance.

Pay. Sullivan glanced at his fuel gauge and wondered if he would ever be able to get his last paycheck from the power station. Probably not, if Sukie had been right about deLarava being after them. Could he get a job as a lighting technician again?

Probably not, if deLarava was still in any aspect of the film business. Great.

Worry about it all later, he told himself, after you've got to Hollywood and fetched the mask—if it's still in that weird garage, if somebody hasn't planed off that hill and put up condominiums there.

Without taking his eyes from the highway rushing past in his headlights, he fumbled in the broad tray on the console beside him, found a tape cassette, and slid it into the dashboard slot; and as the adventurous first notes of Men At Work's "A Land Down Under" came shaking out of the speakers behind him, he tried to feel braced and confident. The intrepid traveler, he thought, the self-reliant nomad; movin' on, able to handle anything from a blown head gasket to a drunk with a knife in a roadside bar; and always squinting off at the horizon like the Marlboro man.

But he shivered and gripped the wheel with both hands. All the way out to Hollywood? The oil in the van hadn't been changed for four thousand miles, and the brakes needed bleeding.

Sukie had frequently, and apparently helplessly, made up nonsense lyrics for songs, and when the tape ended he found himself humming the sold "Beverly Hillbillies" tune, and unreeling random lyrics in his mind:

> Sister said, "Pete, run away from there."
> She said, "California is the place you ought to be,"
> So he cranked the poor old van, and he drove to Galilee.

On the night of his sixteenth birthday he had borrowed his foster-father's car and gone tearing around a dark shopping-center parking lot, and then the security guards had chased him for miles in their fake cop car, and at the end of the chase the furious guards had threatened to charge him with all kinds of crimes; nothing had come of it, and the only one of the wild charges he could remember now was *Intercity flight to avoid apprehension.*

And now here he was, twenty-four years later, his black hair streaked with gray at the temples, forlornly wondering how even an inter*state* flight could possibly let him avoid apprehension.

In the rearview mirror he saw the back window flash white, and this time thunder came rolling and booming across the desert, past him and on ahead into the darkness, followed a moment later by thrashing rain.

He switched on the windshield wipers. Her real name had been Elizabeth, but she'd somehow got her nickname from Bobby Darin's "Mack the Knife"—the song had briefly referred to a woman named Sukie Tawdry. His vision blurred with tears and he found that he was weeping, harshly and resentfully, for the twin sister who had been lost to him long before tonight.

The unfamiliar liberation of drink made him want to stomp on the accelerator—*A.O.P., dude*—and hammer the flat front of the van relentlessly through the desert air; but he remembered that this first rain would free up oil on the surface of the highway, slicking everything, and he let the speedometer needle drift back down to forty.

There was, after all, no hurry. DeLarava would want to do her work on Halloween, and that was still five days off.

CHAPTER 4

It was all very well to say "Drink me," but the wise little Alice was not going to do that in a hurry. "No, I'll look first," she said, "and see whether it's marked 'poison' or not"...

—Lewis Carroll,
Alice's Adventures in Wonderland

Lumpy and Daryl had not found Kootie's bag of quarters in the knapsack's side pocket, and in an all-night drugstore farther up Fairfax he had bought a cheap pair of sunglasses to conceal his swelling discolored eye. That left a little more than six dollars.

Kootie was sitting on a bus bench now, just because he had been too tired to walk one more block. Maybe it didn't matter—maybe all the bus benches in the whole city looked like this one; or, worse, appeared normal to normal people but would all look like this to *him.*

The bench was black, with a big white skull and crossbones painted on it, along with the words DON'T SMOKE DEATH CIGARETTES.

And he had seen packs of these Death cigarettes at the drugstore. The packs were black, with the same skull and crossbones for a logo. Could that actually be a brand name? What could possibly be in the packs? Little white lengths of finger bones, he thought, stained with dried blood at one end to show you where the filter is.

He was shivering in his heavy flannel shirt. The sunlight was warm enough when it was shining on him, but in the shade like this the air was still nighttime air—chilly, and thin enough to get in between the teeth of a zipper. Maybe when the sun got up over the tops of the storefront buildings this strange night would finally be all the way gone, and the bus bench would be stenciled with some normal colorful ad.

Maybe he could go home, and his mom and dad would be there.

(in their wedding clothes, those two had to have been his real mom

*and dad, not the bodies duct-taped into the chairs in the atrium, the
bodies with their eyes—)*

He was shaking now, and he leaned back, gripping his elbows tightly,
and forced the shuddering breaths into his lungs and back out. Perhaps
he was having a heart attack. That would probably be the best thing
that could happen. He wished his feet could reach the ground so that
he could brace them on the pavement.

Back up on Sunset, hours ago when the sky had still been middle-
of-the-night dark, he had tried several times to call the police. Maybe
in the daytime he'd be able to find a telephone that worked right. Maybe
maybe maybe.

The shivering had stopped, and he cautiously took a deep breath as
if probing to see if a fit of hiccups had finally gone away. When he
exhaled, he relaxed, and he discovered that his toes could reach the
pavement.

He brushed back his black curly hair and stood up; and when he had
walked several yards to be able to stand in a patch of sunlight, he
discovered that he was hungry. He could afford breakfast, but probably
not much after that.

"You waiting for the 217 bus, kid?"

Kootie glanced up at the old man who had spoken to him. "No," he
said quickly. "No, I'm . . . walking to school today." He shoved his
hands in his pockets and hurried on south down the Fairfax sidewalk,
forcing himself not to glance fearfully back over his shoulder.

That guy *looked* normal, Kootie told himself. He might have been
just a man on his way to work, curious about this kid out by himself at
dawn here.

But Kootie remembered some of the people he'd met during this long,
alarming night. An old woman pushing a shopping cart across a bright-
lit supermarket parking lot had shouted to him, calling him Al, and when
he had hurried away from her she had started crying; her echoing sobs
had been much louder than her shouting, and he'd still been able to
hear her when he was a block away. Later, ducking away from an old
man that had seemed to be following him, he had interrupted a young
bum, his pants down around his ankles, defecating behind some trash
cans . . . and Kootie shook his head now to drive away the memory of
seeing *rocks and bottlecaps* coming out of the embarrassed guy's butt
and clattering on the asphalt. And one woman had pulled up to the curb
in a gleaming XKE Jaguar and rolled down the passenger-side window
and called out to him, "You're too young to smoke! I'll give you a
hundred dollars for your cigar!" That time *he'd* started crying, because
even though he couldn't understand what she'd meant, he had wanted

to run to the nice car and beg the pretty lady for help, but her eyes and lips and teeth had been so glitteringly bright that he could only hurry away, down an alley too clogged with trash cans and stacks of wooden pallets for her car to follow.

Behind him now he heard the familiar puff of air brakes and the roar of a bus engine, and a moment later the big black-and-white RTD bus had gone grinding and sighing past on his left. Kootie distantly hoped that the old man had got aboard, and was going to some job that he liked, and that to him this city was still the malls-and-movie-billboards place Kootie remembered living in.

He watched the bus move ponderously through the lanes of morning traffic—what was down in that direction? The Farmer's Market, Kootie recalled, and that Jewish delicatessen where a big friendly man behind the fish counter had once given him samples of smoked whitefish and salmon—and Kootie saw a police car turn north from Beverly.

There was a pair of pay telephones in front of a minimart ahead of him, and he slanted his pace to the right, toward them, walking just fast enough so that he could be standing there holding a receiver to his ear when the police car would be driving past at his back. When he got to the phone he even went so far as to drop one of his precious quarters into the slot. I need time to think, he told himself.

He was imagining waving down the police car, or the next one that came by. He would let himself just hang on to the door handle and cry, and tell the officers everything, and they would all go back to Kootie's house on Loma Vista Drive. He would wait in the car with one of the cops while the man's partner checked out the house. Or else they'd radio for another car to go to the house, and they'd take Kootie "downtown."

And then what? Several times during his long night's trek he had paused to close his eyes and try to believe that his parents weren't dead, that he had just hallucinated all that terrible stuff about them being dressed up for a wedding in the living room and at the same time sitting murdered in the atrium, and about the one-armed hobo rushing up the hall and trying to grab him; and he had tried to believe too that the glass brick in his shirt pocket had nothing to do with the people he was encountering; and he hadn't once been able to believe either thing.

Could he believe them now, now that the sun had cleared the rooftops of the shop buildings across the street and all these distracted, ordinary strangers were busily going to work?

He could do an easy test. With a trembling finger he punched the 9 button once and the 1 button twice. I can still change my mind, he told himself nervously. I can still just run away from this phone—jeez, walk, even.

There was a click in the earpiece, and then a man's blurry voice: "... and I told him to just go fuck himself. What do you think of that? I don' gotta . . ." The voice faded, and Kootie was listening to the background murmur—laughter, mumbling, glasses clinking, someone singing. He could just barely hear a child's voice reciting, over and over again, "In most gardens they make the beds too soft—so that theIowers are always asleep."

Kootie's chest was empty and cold. "Hello," he said, in a voice that might have been too loud because he had to talk over the sudden ringing in his ears, "hello, I was trying to get the emergency police number—" It could still be all right, he thought tensely, *all* the L.A.-area phones could be crossed-up in this way—but even just in his head, just unspoken, the thought had a shrilly frightened tone. "Who have I reached, please?"

For a moment there was just the distant clatter and slurred speech, and then a woman's voice, choking and thick, wailed, "Al? Al, thank God, where are you gonna meet me tonight? That supermarket parking lot again? Al, my legs've swelled up like *sausages,* and I need—"

Kootie hung up the phone without dropping it, and he was able a moment later to walk easily away down the Fairfax sidewalk; but he was surprised that the air wasn't coagulating into the invisible molasses that, in nightmares, kept him from being able to drag one foot ahead of the other.

It was all real. The sun was up, and he was wide awake, and that voice on the phone had been the voice of the old crazy woman he'd run away from in the parking lot, hours ago. His parents really were dead, obviously killed because he had broken the Dante and taken away the glass brick.

Kootie had killed them.

And even though the police wouldn't ever believe that, they would make Kootie do things—like what? Identify the bodies? No, they wouldn't force a *kid* to do that, would they? But he'd still have to make probably a million *statements*, which would either be true and sound crazy, or be lies and sound like a kid's lies; and eventually he'd be put into a foster home somewhere. And how would the telephones behave *there*? What sort of person would be in charge of the place, or soon come visiting? And if by then they'd decided he was crazy, they might have him in restraints, strapped down on his bed.

He recoiled away from a memory of duct tape.

If he just got rid of the glass brick, would all this stuff stop happening? But who would eventually *find* it, and why had his parents kept it hidden?

He remembered a Robert Louis Stevenson story about a devil in a bottle—it could get you anything you wanted, but if you died owning it you'd go to hell—and if you wanted to get rid of it you had to sell it for less than you'd paid for it, or it would come back to you even if you threw it into the ocean.

Was this thing worth money, could he *sell* it? Was *it* a "cigar"? If so, he could have got a hundred dollars for it from the Jaguar woman last night. It seemed to him that a hundred dollars was a good deal less than what he had paid for it.

There was a low, white-painted cinder-block wall around the little parking lot of a strip shopping center ahead of him, and he crossed to it and hiked himself up to sit on the coping. He glanced around at the wide, busy intersection and the sidewalks to make sure no one was paying any particular attention to him, and then he unbuttoned the pocket of his heavy flannel shirt and lifted out the glass brick. It seemed to *click*, very faintly deep inside, when he turned it in his hand.

This was the first time he'd looked at it in sunlight. It was rectangular, but bumpy and wavy on its surfaces, and even when he held it up to the sun he couldn't see anything in its cloudy depths. He ran a finger around its narrow side—and felt a seam. He peered at the side surfaces and saw that a tiny straight crack went all the way around, dividing the brick into two equal halves.

The two guys that had robbed him so long ago last night had taken his Swiss army knife, so he worked a fingernail into the groove and twisted, and only managed to tear off a strip of his nail. By holding the glass thing between his palms, though, with his fingers gripped tightly over the edges, he was able to pry hard enough to feel the two glass sections move against each other, and to be sure that the thing *could* be opened.

He pressed it firmly together again and took off his backpack to tuck the brick safely down among his tumbled clothes. He pulled the flap down over it all and then, since the plastic buckles had been broken last night, carefully tied the straps tight before putting the backpack on again. Maybe people wouldn't be able to sense the glass thing so easily now.

Like a gun, he thought dully, or a grenade or blasting caps or something. It's like they had a *gun* in the house and never told their kid even what a gun is. It's their *own* fault I somehow accidentally got them killed by playing with it.

If I open it—what? A devil might come out. A *devil* might *actually* come out. It wouldn't matter whether or not I believe in devils, or that my friends and the teachers in school don't. People in 1900 didn't think that radium could hurt you, just carrying a chip of it in your pocket like a lucky rock, and then one day their legs fell off and they died of cancer. Not believing something is no help if you turn out to be wrong.

He heard the short *byoop* of a motorcycle cop's siren and looked up nervously—but the cop was stopping way out in the intersection, and, as Kootie watched, he climbed off the blue-flashing bike and put down the kickstand and began directing traffic with broad slow gestures. The traffic signals had gone completely out sometime during the last few minutes, weren't even flashing red; and then even when the policeman waved for the southbound lanes to move forward, the cars and trucks and buses stayed backed up for another several minutes because nearly every driver had stalled and had to start up again.

As Kootie crossed Beverly, the sound of grinding starter motors was echoing among the lanes behind him like power saws.

CHAPTER 5

"Then you keep moving around, I suppose?" said Alice.
"Exactly so," said the Hatter: "as the things get used up."
"But what happens when you come to the beginning again?" Alice
ventured to ask.
"Suppose we change the subject," the March Hare interrupted . . .
—Lewis Carroll,
Alice's Adventures in Wonderland

One of them had finally been for real.

It had been two hours since the Greyhound bus had pulled out of the dawn-streaked yard of the Albuquerque station, subsequently finding the I-40 highway and cranking its way up through the dry rock Zuni Mountains, downshifting to follow the twisting highway among the ancient lava beds, and booming down the western slope to roar right through Gallup without stopping; but when the bus finally swung off the I-40 at the little town of Houck, just over the border into Arizona, Angelica Anthem Elizalde simply kept her seat while most of the other passengers shuffled past her down the aisle to catch some fresh morning air and maybe a quick cup of coffee during the fifteen-minute stop.

She looked out her window. Though it was now eight-thirty, the bus was still casting a yards-long shadow, and the shadow pointed west. She shivered, but tucked her ladies' magazine into the pocket of the seat in front of her.

She had hoped to distract herself with its colorful pages, but had run aground on an almost hysterically cheerful article about how to cook squash, with a sidebar that addressed "Twelve Important Squash Questions"; and then she had been forced out of the pages again by a multiple-choice "Creativity Test," which gave high marks to the hypothetical housewife who, confronted with two mismatched socks after all the laundry had been put away, elected to (C) make hand puppets of them rather than (A) throw them away or (B) use them for dusting.

None of the listed answers had been anything like "burn them," "eat them," "bury them in the backyard," or "save them in case one night you answer the door to a stranger with bare, mismatched feet."

Elizalde managed a tight smile. She flexed her hands and wondered what work she would find to do in Los Angeles. Typist, again? Waitress, again? *Panhandler, bag lady, prostitute, a patient in one of the county mental hospitals in which she'd done her residency—*

—a felon locked up in the Sybil Brand Institute for Women—

She quickly fetched up the magazine out of the seat pocket and stared hard at a photograph of some happy family having fun around a swing set (—probably all of them models, really, who had never seen each other before lining up there for the picture—) and she thought again about turning back. Get off the bus at Flagstaff, she told herself, and catch the 474 bus, take it all the way back to Oklahoma City, be there by eight-thirty tonight. Go back to the big truck stop under the Petro water tower, tell the manager at the Iron Skillet that you were *too* sick to call *in* sick when you failed to show up for the waitress shift last night.

Get back on that old heartland merry-go-round.

For nearly two years she had been traveling, far from Los Angeles, working in restaurants and bars and small offices, along the Erie Canal from the Appalachians to Buffalo, and up and down the Ohio River from Pittsburgh to Cairo, and, most recently, along the Canadian River in Oklahoma. She'd celebrated her thirty-fourth birthday with half a dozen of the Iron Skillet waitresses in the bar at O'Connell's in Norman, twenty minutes south of Oklahoma City.

At least L.A. would be fairly warm, even now, in October, four days before Halloween. The Mexican street vendors in the Boyle Heights area might already be selling *El Día de los Muertos* candy, the white stylized skulls and skeletons—

(*—Shut up!—*)

Again she forced herself to stare at the family in the magazine photo, and she tried to believe that it really was a family, that they were genuinely enjoying some—

(*—long-lost—*)

(*—Shut up!—*)

weekend in the backyard, oblivious of this photographer—

. . . It didn't word. The adults and kids in the photograph just looked like models, strangers to each other.

Elizalde remembered driving the L.A. Freeways at night, snatching an occasional glance to the side at some yellow-lit kitchen window in a passing apartment building, and always for one moment desperately envying the lives of whatever people lived there. She had always imagined hammered-copper roosters on the kitchen wall, a TV in the next room with "Cheers" getting innocent laughs, children sitting cross-legged on the carpet—

(—Shut up.)

That had never really worked, either. Maybe those apartments had all been vacant, with the lights left on. She folded the magazine and put it back.

A few moments later she jumped, and looked toward the front of the bus just before the first returning passenger stepped aboard, rocking the bus on the shocks. Elizalde sighed. No, she couldn't go back to Oklahoma.

For about twelve hours now she had been doing this, reacting to noises and jolts just before they happened. She'd been in bed when it started, and she'd awakened in her darkened apartment just before the clock radio had blared on. At first she had thought some mental clock had been keeping track of the time while she'd slept—she'd found herself remembering her grandmother's saying, *Es como los brujos, duerme con los ojos abiertos*: He is like the witches, and sleeps with his eyes open—but the effect had continued as she'd proceeded to get ready for work, so that she'd flinched before water had come out of the shower head, and dropped her hair dryer because it had seemed to quiver animately in her hand just as she was about to push the On button.

Then she had begun blinking her eyes even before the tears welled up in them. She'd sat down on her bathroom floor and just sobbed with fright, for in the same way that she'd seemed to be anticipating physical events, she had now been afraid that an idea was about to surface in her mind, an idea that she had been strenuously avoiding for two years. Before she'd been able to distract herself, the idea had hit her: *maybe she had not, after all, had a psychotic schizophrenic episode in her Los Angeles clinic in 1990.*

And, bleakly, she had known that she would have to go back there and find out. Find out if

One of them had finally been for real.

Everybody was getting back on the bus now, and the driver had the engine idling. Elizalde let her head sink back against the high, padded seat, and she thought she might at last be able to get some sleep, during the twelve hours it would take the bus to plow on through Flagstaff and Kingman and Barstow to, finally, Los Angeles.

After all, it seemed that nothing could sneak up on her.
Soy como las brujas, duermo con mis ojos abiertos.

Pete Sullivan clanked the gearshift into neutral and gunned the engine
to keep it from stalling. He was stopped in what was supposed to be
the fast lane of the 101, a mile or so short of the tunnel where the
northbound Santa Ana Freeway would merge in. God only knew when
he would get to Hollywood.

Though it was a non-holiday Friday morning, even on the westbound
60 the traffic had been jammed up—fully stopped much of the time,
and occasionally speeding up and opening out in front of him for just
enough moments to let him imagine that the congestion was behind him,
before the red brake lights would all start glaring again ahead of him.

In the driver's seat of his van he was above most of the other drivers,
and during the course of an hour, while his foot had moved back and
forth from the brake to the gas pedal, he had watched the towers of Los
Angeles rise ahead of him in the brassy light. The towers had been
scrimmed to dim silhouettes by the smog, as if they were faded shapes
in a photograph that's been left out too long in the sun—or, he had
thought, as if the city has had its picture taken so many times that the
cumulative loss of images had begun to visibly diminish it.

Like deLarava's ghosts, he had thought. Maybe the whole city has
died, but is too distracted to have realized it yet.

The towers were clearer now, and it was disorienting to see big buildings that he didn't recognize—one of the new ones was a tall tan-stone
cylinder, like a stylized sculpture of a rocket ship, and he wondered
uneasily if he would still be able to find his way around the city's streets.

His window was open to the diesel-reeking air, and he looked down
over his elbow at the center divider, which in the old days had generally
just been a featureless blur rushing past. Flowering weeds, and even a
couple of midget palm trees, were pushing up out of cracks in the concrete, and curled around them and the many Budweiser cans was an
apparently constant web of brown tape from broken stereo cassettes;
there were even a lot of *peaches* for some reason, bruised but unbitten,
as if some citizen of this no-man's-land had left them there like Hansel
and Gretel's bread crumbs.

Sullivan wondered what cassettes these were that drivers had so prod-
igally pitched out their windows, and he grinned nervously at the temptation to open the door and salvage some of the tape. It would be a
cinch to clean it and wind it onto a fresh cassette-half. Would it all be
the same kind of music, perhaps even all copies of the same tape? It
occurred to him that the center divider looked like a miles-long shrine

to primitive-but-urban gods; and he shivered and turned his attention back to the pickup truck in front of him, in the bed of which two Mexican girls were listlessly brushing their long black hair.

About an hour ago he had stopped peering ahead to see what wreck or freeway construction would be causing the traffic jam—apparently the freeways just snarled up without any definable cause these days, like the turbulence that would sometimes inexplicably shake a sump pipe at a power station even when all the air had been bled out of it.

In Los Angeles space is time, he thought—you don't say *I'm thirty miles from downtown*, you say *I'm half an hour from it*. If unpredictable turbulence has become a real, constant factor in traffic, then all the maps and clocks are broken (like the Mad Hatter's butter-clogged watch!) and you can only make a hazy guess about how far it might be from one point to another.

I'm a hundred years from Venice Beach, he thought, and a thousand miles from Christmas Eve of 1986. Better draw up a chart.

He pushed the thought away and concentrated on the traffic.

The Brew 102 brewery proved to be gone. 102 had been the only beer Sullivan had ever encountered that had sediment in it, but he found that he missed the old black-and-yellow sign, and he was further disoriented to see half a dozen helicopters parked on the wide roof of a building on the other side of the freeway. With the glittering rocket still ahead of him, the whole place was looking like a poster for some 1930s science-fiction movie.

When he eventually gunned the van up the off-ramp at Hollywood Boulevard, though, there were beat-up old couches under the palm trees in the freeway border area, and a dispirited-looking group of ragged black men, their hair in ropy dreadlocks, were slouching there in the shade. He half expected to see chickens running around their skinny ankles, and a fire in a split oil drum behind them.

The clocks and maps are smashed and ripped to bits, he thought. Even though it was the *best* butter.

He drove west on Hollywood Boulevard, cautiously pleased to see that though the names of many businesses had changed—there was no Howard Johnson's restaurant at Hollywood and Vine anymore—most of the actual buildings he remembered had survived.

It seemed to him that it had always been like this, in the area from Franklin south to Melrose and beyond. Every building looked as if it had originally been used for something else. Even here on Hollywood Boulevard, the odd top corners of the storefronts were frequently broken or bent, showing old brick underneath, and between buildings he could see brick alcoves, way up and far back, dating from God knew when. Tiny ironwork balconies still stuck out on second and third floors, with probably nothing behind them anymore but empty offices.

Now that he was nearly there—only one turn remaining, a right onto Laurel Canyon once he'd got out past this tourist area of the boulevard—he was in no hurry to get to the ruins he and his sister had explored on that spring day in '86. At Wilcox he impulsively decided to turn north—and when he'd made the turn he saw that the Shelton Apartments had been torn down, replaced by some sprawling new pink apartment building.

He pulled the van over to the curb and switched off the engine for the first time since stopping for eggs and bacon in Blythe, four hours ago. Then for several minutes, while he lit a cigarette and stared across the street at the new four-story building, he tried to remember the old Shelton.

Like the Lido and the Mayfair, both of which were still standing a block farther up the street, the Shelton had had one of those big signs on the roof, separate ornate letters in line, supported by a lattice of steel beams, and had had a lot of the decorative cornices and balconies that architects never seemed to bother with anymore. The only eccentricities of this new place, the HOLLYWOOD STUDIO CLUB APARTMENTS, were inset windows and an apparent blanket policy of having all corners be rounded. A banner across the top announced $777 MOVES YOU IN! Probably not a bad price around here, he thought absently, these days. It had been while filming a documentary in the lobby of the old Shelton in the winter of '84 that he and his sister had finally got a strong clue about what Loretta deLarava really did.

DeLarava had hired the twins right out of college ten years earlier, and they'd been working for her ever since as "gaffers"—lighting technicians. DeLarava produced short-subject films—in-house instruction pieces for businesses, nontimely human-interest bits for news programs, the occasional commercial—and for twelve years the twins had spent their days driving to what seemed like every corner of Los Angeles, to lay cables and set up Genie lifts and hang lights over some beach or office floor or sidewalk.

DeLarava had been a disconcerting boss. One of the first jobs the twins worked on with her had been a short film about the vandalizing of Houdini's grave in Brooklyn in 1975—and deLarava had been the first to cover the event because it hadn't even occurred before she arrived. It had been deLarava *herself* who shattered the stone bust of Houdini in the Machpelah Cemetery and took a mummified thumb out of a hollow inside it, and who had dug two plaster hands out of the soil in front of the grave. The twins had of course not even been tempted to turn their new boss in to the authorities—but, apparently on a drunken whim, Sukie had stolen the thumb and the hands from deLarava's luggage on the drive back to the airport.

DeLarava had cried when she'd discovered the loss, and ransacked the car, and had even had to make new airline reservations because she insisted on driving back to the cemetery to look for the items, but Sukie had not ever admitted to the theft.

From the beginning Sukie had taken a perverse pleasure in tormenting their boss, and certainly deLarava was an easy target. The fat old woman always wore a rubber band around her scalp, with her hair brushed down over it to keep it from showing, and after Sukie had discovered the habit she made a point of finding opportunities to bump the woman's head, dislodging the rubber band so that it sprang to the top of her head, making a wreck of her hair. And deLarava's clothes always had Velcro closures instead of buttons or zippers, and Sukie frequently managed to get the old woman's shoes or jackets attached to upholstered chairs or textured wallpaper, so that deLarava had to pull herself loose with an embarrassing tearing sound. And once, after a minute or so of silence during a drive, Sukie had glanced brightly at the old woman and said, "Yeah? Go on—? You were saying something about a picnic?"—acting as if their boss had just begun a sentence and then forgotten it— but deLarava had reacted with such fright to the disorienting gambit that Sukie had never tried that particular trick again.

At the Shelton they'd been filming in the lobby and in an upstairs hallway, and of course Pete and Sukie had arrived three hours before the rest of the crew to locate a 220-volt power source in the old building and set up the hydraulic lifts and hang the key lights. Sullivan remembered now that for an outdoor shot of the hotel they'd rented battery-powered lights made by a company called Frizzolini, and that Sukie had kept saying that deLarava had better be careful of getting her hair all frizzied. Possibly Sukie had been drunk already.

DeLarava herself had arrived early for that shoot. She would have been in her mid-fifties then, and for once she had been looking her age. She had always smoked some kind of clove-flavored Indonesian cigarettes that made a room smell as though someone were baking a glazed ham nearby, and on this morning her chubby hands had been shaking as she'd lit each one off the butt of the last, sparks dropping unnoticed onto the carpet, and her pendulous cheeks had quivered when she inhaled. She had brought with her a whole hatbox full of props to distribute around the shooting area; Sullivan remembered pocket watches, a couple of diamond rings, even a feather boa, in addition to the usual antique, still-sealed bottles of liquor.

The project had been a short morbid piece on the suicides that had taken place in the old building; perhaps the film had been done on spec, for Sullivan couldn't now recall any particular client for the job, and he couldn't remember it having gone through the post-production or screening steps. Incongruously, they had been filming it on Christmas Eve. The old woman had never let a Christmas Eve or a Halloween go by without filming something, somewhere.

Sullivan wondered uneasily what she might have scheduled for this upcoming Saturday.

DeLarava had been interested in only two of the suicides that had taken place at the Shelton. The first was a woman called Jenny Dolly— around the turn of the century Jenny Dolly and her twin sister Rosie were a celebrated dance team, renowned for their beauty; but Jenny's face had been horribly scarred in a car crash in 1933, and she had hanged herself in her apartment here in 1941. The other suicide had been the actress Clara Blandick, who, one day in 1962, had got her hair fixed up and had carefully done her makeup and put on a formal gown and then pulled a plastic bag over her head and smothered herself. She was chiefly remembered for having played Auntie Em in the 1939 version of *The Wizard of Oz.*

Auntie Em, Auntie Em, thought Sullivan now as he puffed on his cigarette, echoing in his head the mocking voice of the Wicked Witch of the West in the movie.

And, he thought as he squinted through the smoke, a twin sister who killed herself. How're you doing, Sukie?

The shoot had been what gaffers called a bad-hang day. The lights had been plagued with "ghosting," the lamps glowing dimly even when the big old dimmer boxes indicated no power being transmitted, which called for a lot of laborious checks of the light board and all the cable connections; and then when the cameras were finally running, the shoot had repeatedly been interrupted by power surges and blackouts.

Apparently a lot of people had died at the Shelton, he thought now.

Live and learn.

DeLarava had kept looking at her watch, though the clock on the lobby wall was accurate. Twice Pete had peered at her watch as she glanced at it, and both times it had been wrong—*differently* wrong: once it would read, say, 6:30, and a few minutes later it would be indicating something like 12:35. At one point he had called Sukie over to one of the malfunctioning lights and in a low voice had told her about their boss's erratic watch.

Sukie had followed deLarava around the carpeted lobby for a few minutes after that, ostensibly to ask about the placing of the props and the fill lights, and then she had come back to where Pete was still crouched over the flickering lamp; and she had told him in a whisper that no matter which way deLarava was facing, the hour hand of her watch always wobbled around to point up Wilcox—north. It was a compass.

Shortly after that the music had started up. DeLarava had liked to have taped music playing before the cameras started running, even *during* takes for which the soundtrack would be entirely dubbed in later—she said it helped establish the mood—and the music was always something contemporary with the period the film was dealing with. Today it was Glenn Miller's "Tuxedo Junction," and she had decided to start it up early.

As the audiotape reels started rotating and the first notes came razoring out of the speaker grilles, deLarava had turned away from the twins and fumbled something out of her purse. She was clearly trying to conceal it, but both of the twins saw that she was holding a drinking straw—one of the striped ones marketed for children, with a flexible neck and some kind of flavor capsule inside it to make plain milk taste like chocolate or strawberry.

Sullivan pitched his cigarette out the window and started up the van's engine. Stopped ahead of him was a battered old blue-painted school bus with the back doors open, and inside it, on wooden shelves and on the floor, were crates of bananas and tortillas and garlic and long, dried red chili peppers. A mobile third-world grocery store, he thought, a hundred feet from the Hollywood Boulevard sidewalk.

It reminded him of lunch, and he wondered if Musso and Frank's was still in business, a block or two west. He steered the van around the stopped bus and drove up Wilcox to make a U-turn back to the boulevard. Over the tops of the old apartment buildings in front of him he could see the Capitol Records building, designed long ago to look like a stack of vinyl records with a needle touching the top disk.

Vinyl records, he thought. The clocks and maps are definitely broken.

CHAPTER 6

"I dare say you never even spoke to Time!"

"Perhaps not," Alice cautiously replied: "but I know I have to beat time when I learn music."

"Ah! that accounts for it," said the Hatter. "He won't stand beating. Now, if you only kept on good terms with him, he'd do almost anything you liked with the clock."

—Lewis Carroll,
Alice's Adventures in Wonderland

Musso and Frank's Grill, Hollywood's oldest restaurant, was still in business on the north side of the boulevard at Cherokee, and Sullivan parked around the corner and walked in through the double wood-and-glass doors and crossed to one of the booths under the eternal autumn-scene mural and the high ceiling. The Tuesday special was corned beef and cabbage, but he sentimentally ordered a sardine sandwich and a Coors.

This had been his and Sukie's secret hideout; their friends and co-workers had hung out in trendier places like the City Café and the Café Figaro on Melrose, or the Ivy down on Robertson.

In fact, he and Sukie had driven here in 1984 for dinner right after the Christmas Eve shoot at the Shelton, and during the drive Sukie had been loudly singing gibberish Christmas carols—*O car-bo-lic faith-less, poi-son-ously pregnant . . . O rum key, O ru-um key to O-bliv-i-on . . . Com-mander Hold-'Em, bone dry king of a-angels . . .* —and of course the old schoolyard song they'd got in trouble for singing in some foster home when they'd been seven, *We three kings of Orient are, trying to smoke a rubber cigar; it was loaded, it exploded . . .*

As soon as they'd got to the restaurant and been seated, Sukie had ordered a double Jack Daniel's, and Pete, though he had wanted a beer, had wound up with a Coke, because when the waiter had walked up to their booth Pete had been leaning forward and saying, "Coke?"

After the waiter had left, Sukie had grinned and said, "Coke what?"

Pete had waved vaguely. "What she was doing. Loretta, our dignified boss, snorting a straw along the old hotel wallpaper! Old cocaine mixed up in the dust, do you think?"

In reply Sukie had resumed singing some badly remembered lines from "We Wish You a Merry Christmas"—*"We won't go until we got some, we won't go until we got some, we won't go until we got some, so trot 'em out now."*

"What the hell, Suke," Pete had said, bewildered by her manic cheer.

"I figure that's what the Sodomites and—what would you call 'em, Gomorrites?—were singing outside of Lot's house, you know? In the Bible, when all of Lot's neighbors wanted to bugger the angels that were visiting him. Loretta wouldn't go today until she got some, and she did get some—she sucked 'em up through that straw." The drinks had arrived then, and Sukie had drained hers in one long swallow and mutely signaled for another.

"Got some what?" Pete had said after a halfhearted sip of his Coke. "Angels? Angel dust? What?"

"*Ghosts,*" Sukie had said impatiently. "What did you think? She snorted up a whole pile of ghosts today—did you see how much younger she looked when she finally got into her car and split? She looked thirty years old tonight, a *youthful* thirty, and she looked a god-damn *hundred* this morning. We somehow made it possible for her to draw a whole lot of ghosts out of the walls of that place and then snort 'em up her nose."

Pete hadn't wanted to start discussing ghosts with his sister. "She's a, something like a necrophiliac voyeur," he said. "There's probably a single word for it. She likes to go shoot films at cemeteries and places where people have died, and kind of rub her fingers in the dirt, we've noticed that in her before. Hell, I suppose there's somebody somewhere who watches the tape of Jack Ruby shooting Oswald, over and over again. Getting off on . . . what, the thought that somebody really did die here. Creepy, but probably harmless, right? But I'm afraid she's going flat-out *crazy* now. Where does that leave our jobs? I mean, there she was, crouched over and snuffling along with a *straw*, as if some dead lady's perfume might still be in the wallpaper!"

"Pete," said Sukie, "I don't mean perfume, and I don't mean *metaphorical* ghosts. I mean there were real essences of dead people in that place, and she *consumed* them in some literal way, like a whale eating plankton."

Pete stared at her. "Are you saying," he asked carefully after a moment, "that you think she actually *believes* that?"

"God, you're an idiot sometimes. I'm saying that's what happened. She's *right* to believe it, she *did* eat a bunch of ghosts. Didn't she change, visibly, between eight this morning and nine tonight?"

Pete tried to smile derisively, but gave it up and let his face relax into a frown. "She did get something out of it," he admitted. "But come on, *ghosts*?"

The word hadn't sounded ludicrous in this dark wooden booth at Musso and Frank's.

"And," he found himself going on, "she is often . . . prettier and cheerier, after a shoot. Still damn fat." He laughed uncertainly. "Do you suppose that's what she's been doing, all along? She never used a *straw* before. That we ever noticed, anyway."

"I'm sure she'd have liked it better if we hadn't seen her do that—but she obviously needed it too bad to be subtle this time. I bet she usually sucks 'em in through those damned cigarettes of hers—maybe ghosts are drawn to that clove smell, like kids to hot cookies. It *was* a flavored straw, you noticed."

Sukie's fresh drink arrived. Pete drained it himself, and Sukie glanced at her watch and then at the clock on the wall, and she asked for two more.

For a full minute neither of them spoke.

Pete was feeling the bourbon hit his fragile alertness like static muddying up an AM radio signal. "And of course it would have something to do with bar-time," he said finally. "Ghosts are . . . if there *are* ghosts, they're certainly a very derailed crowd, in terms of time."

"Of course. And the electrical problems. We always have electrical problems, and she still not only doesn't fire us, but pays us way too much."

"We don't *always* have electrical problems," Pete said irritably. Then he made himself think about what Sukie had said. "Now you're saying it has to be *us*? Specifically Pete and Sukie?"

"She acts like it, doesn't she? Has she ever once hired anyone else? Those props, those watches and things, those were lures; but for some reason she needs *us* to make her able to hook 'em. Did you keep on looking at her watch?"

"Not after the first business," he said glumly. Of course Sukie would have, once he'd told her about it.

"When we finally got started filming, the hour hand was pointing straight to the section of wall she took her straw to, every time, and it wasn't north anymore."

Pete grinned weakly. "Compass needles point to ghosts?"

"Evidence of the old glazzies, droogie," she said, quoting the movie *A Clockwork Orange*. *Glazzies*, he recalled, meant eyes. "Let's get some menus," she went on. "I may as well eat while I drink, and she'll want her precious twins all peppy and full of vitamins tomorrow."

Her precious twins, Pete thought now as he finished his sardine sandwich and drank off the last of the Coors alone in the booth on this sunny but cold morning eight years later.

The twins had continued working for deLarava, for precisely another two years, after that Christmas Eve; and Pete had eventually come to believe that Sukie was right about what deLarava had been doing at their shooting locations.

Neither of them, though, had seriously considered quitting. *What the hell*, Sukie had remarked more than once when she'd been drunk; *it's just exorcism, right? I mean, she inhales the ghosts and then they're gone—obviously, since she never goes back and does a shoot at the same place twice. We're exorcists, like that priest in that movie. And we didn't take no vows of poverty.*

No indeed, thought Sullivan now. DeLarava paid us damn well. And if she hadn't tried to get us

car-bo-lic faithless, poi-so-nously pregnant

to do that muscle beach feature in Venice, on

bone dry king of angels

Christmas Eve in 1986,

won't go until we got one, so dredge him out now

we'd probably be working for her still, to this day.

He frowned intently at the check, tossed thirteen dollars onto the Formica table and walked quickly out of the restaurant into the chilly October breeze.

It had been *early* in 1986 when they had hidden the mask in the ruins up on Laurel Canyon Boulevard. Just a dried thumb and two plaster hands, but Sukie always referred to the set as "the mask."

Sullivan steered the van back onto Hollywood Boulevard, heading west again; there was still only the one more turn ahead. On the south side of the street stood a new McDonald's restaurant that looked like an incongruously space-age Grecian temple, but at least the Chinese Theater was still there in all its battered black and red byzantine splendor at Highland.

The boulevard narrowed after that, as it flowed west between big old apartment buildings and broad lawns, and around Fairfax the pavement of the eastbound lane was entirely ripped up for repairs, but the sun hung still a little short of noon in the empty blue sky when Sullivan reached Laurel Canyon Boulevard and turned right, up the hill.

The curling road had only one lane each way, and no shoulder at all between the pavement and the greenery hanging over bowed chain-link fencing, and he had to drive a good quarter of a mile past the place before he found a wider spot where the van could plausibly be parked without getting clipped by a passing car. And then the walk back down the hill was a series of lateral hops from the asphalt into the tall curbside grass every time a car came looming at him from around a corner ahead. Already he was sweating.

Even after six years he recognized the section of chain-link fence he was looking for, and when he stopped and hooked his fingers through it and peered up the wooded slope beyond, he saw that the ruins had not been cleared away. Nearly hidden under shaggy palm trees and oaks, the broad stone stairway swept up to the terrace at the top of the hill, and even from out here on the street he could see many of the broken pillars and sagging brick walls.

He was breathing deeply, and wondering almost resentfully why no one *had* planed this off and put up condos or something. The real estate must be worth a fortune. At last he unhooked his fingers and stepped back.

Several NO TRESPASSING signs were hung on the fence, but it was widely split at one point, and among the tall weeds beyond he could see empty twelve-pack beer cartons and a couple of blankets and even a sort of little tent made from an upended shopping cart. Sullivan glanced up and down the road, and at a moment when no cars were in sight he ducked through the gap and sprinted to the shade of the nearest palm tree. He picked his way through a dense hedge of blue-flowered vinca, and after a few seconds noticed that he wasn't walking on dirt anymore—the soles of his black leather shoes were brushing dust and drifts of leaves off of paving stones that had been laid in the 1920s.

The stairs were broad between the low corniced walls, but were thickly littered with bricks and chunks of masonry and the brown palm fronds that had been falling untended for five decades; and sycamore branches hung so low in places that he practically had to crawl from step to step. When he had scrambled up to the second landing he paused to catch his breath. The air was still and silent and fragrant with eucalyptus, as if Laurel Canyon Boulevard and all of Hollywood were very far away. He couldn't even hear any birds or insects.

A row of once-white marble pillars supporting nothing anymore ran along the top of a wall across the stairs from him, and below the wall a dead stone fountain poked up from a bank of dried leaves; the ruined architecture all looked Greek, or at least Mediterranean, and it occurred to him that time didn't seem to pass here—or, rather, seemed already to have passed and left this place behind. Probably that's why they don't tear it all down, he thought. It's too late.

He was now three-quarters of the way up the dusty, overgrown slope. To his right was a little stone bridge over a dry streambed, and though both of the wide cement railings still arched over the gully, the middle six feet of the bridge's floor had long ago fallen away. A weathered two-by-six beam spanned the gap, and he remembered that in 1986, at least, the beam had been sturdy enough to bear his weight.

He discovered that it still was, though it was springy and he had to stretch his arms out to the sides to keep his balance. On the far side he paused to wipe the dusty sweat off his face; he thought about lighting a cigarette, but looked around at all the dry brush and glumly decided he'd better not.

Then he froze—someone was moving around below him, clumsily, through the litter on one of the clogged side terraces. Sullivan couldn't hope to see the person through the shaggy greenery below, but in the weighty silence he could hear someone mumbling and scuffling around.

One of the bums that live here, he thought. It doesn't sound like a cop or a caretaker; still, the bum might draw the attention of such people, and I don't want to get kicked out of here myself before I retrieve the mask. They might fix the fence, or even post guards, before I could get back. This place is a historical landmark, after all, though nobody seems to pay any attention to it.

He tiptoed through the fieldstone arch ahead of him and picked his way up a side stairway, which, being narrower, was relatively clear of debris. His fast breathing sounded loud in the still air.

There was another arch at the top, and he paused under it, for he was at the broad main terrace of the hill now, and he'd be visible crossing the cement pavement that stretched between the jungle below and the odd house in front of him.

The pavement was clear up here, and he let himself light a cigarette. Sukie, he recalled, had brought a flask, on that . . . March? . . . day in '86. That's right, March—it had been Good Friday afternoon, which had seemed like a good day for burials.

At first the two of them had thought that *this* house—this narrow two-story building, brick below and stuccoed above, with castle-like crenellations along the roof as if the owner were ready to hire archers to repel attack from below—must be Houdini's mansion, and they'd been surprised that the famed magician would live in such a little place. Later they'd learned that this was just the servants' quarters. Houdini's mansion had stood a hundred yards off to the south, and had burned down in the thirties. But this was nevertheless a part of the old Houdini estate. It would do fine as a place to hide the mask. "Hide a thumb in a place where there's already a lot of its thumbprints," Sukie had said.

Sullivan now stared uneasily at the house. The doors and windows were all covered with weathered sheets of plywood, but on the tiny upstairs balcony sat a flowerpot with a *green* plant growing in it. Had there been rain in L.A. recently? The palm fronds he'd climbed over below had been dry as mummies. Was some homeless person *living* in this place?

He decided to hide here for a little while and see if the noises on the slope had been heard and might draw someone out onto the balcony.

Sullivan recalled that he and Sukie had nearly killed themselves struggling up the slope six years ago, for they'd been "on bar-time big time," as Sukie had said—they'd been feeling the roughness of a step underfoot before the shoe actually touched it, and the bark of a tree limb a second before the hand grasped it. But Sukie had been full of hectic cheer, chatting graciously with imaginary guests and singing misunderstood snatches from Handel's *Messiah*. Sullivan had been constantly whispering at her to shut up.

No one seemed to be home in the little castle. Sullivan relaxed and sucked on his cigarette, and he looked up at the brushy slope beyond the house. The upper slope had advanced visibly since his previous visit—broken dirt was piled up right to the stones of the arch at the south end of the house now, and a section of ornate marble railing stuck up crookedly above and behind the arch like a bleached rib cage exposed by a cemetery landslide.

He jumped suddenly, and as his cigarette hit the pavement he heard a voice from the stairway he'd just climbed: "By the hair of my chinny-chin-chin—"

Sullivan crouched behind the house side of the arch as the voice went on, "I'll huff and I'll puff and I'll eat you, billy-goat-gruff."

It's that bum, he thought nervously. He's following me, and of course my gun is locked up back in the van.

Then he grinned at his momentary panic. Just a bum, he told himself. Forget him and go get the mask from the garage, which luckily is still standing. Sullivan stretched out his leg and stepped on the smoldering cigarette, but he was trembling, for the *billy-goat-gruff* remark had reminded him of the troll that had lived under a bridge in that old children's story. Maybe, he thought as he made himself maintain his grin,

I shouldn't have walked across that board over the broken bridge back there.

He straightened up and stepped out into the sunlight and began walking across the old cement, careful not to kick any stray rocks.

The open-arched garage was a strange structure too, entirely fronted with tiny inset stones and with two broad castle-like merlons on the roof; the inside walls were all stonework as well, and the back wall was concave, as though to provide good acoustics.

After only a few steps he whipped his head back around to the left and saw a skinny old woman come shuffling around the corner of the house. Her white dress looked as if it had been elegant before someone had spent years sleeping, and apparently doing engine work, in it, but all she was wearing on her stained feet was a broken pair of plastic zoris. The soles flapped on the cement as she hunched toward him.

"I suppose you don't want to lose your name?" she was calling anxiously.

Then Sullivan heard the bum scuffling quickly to the top of the stairs behind him. "Blow your house down!" he was cawing.

Sullivan broke into a run for the garage; he stomped and skidded inside and in an instant was crouched in the shadows against the back wall, digging in the loose dry dirt with his hands. It seemed to him that the dirt was colder than it had any right to be.

"Where the *fuck*," he was keening to himself, just as he felt the plywood board he and Sukie had laid over Houdini's mask. He paused, even though he could hear the bum wheezing his way across the driveway toward the garage. It's not Houdini buried here, Sullivan reminded himself, it's not even his ghost. He took a deep breath and lifted the board away in a shower of powdery dirt.

And he saw that the life-size plaster hands and the little cloth Bull Durham sack were still in the hole. If the bum *was* just a bum, Sullivan could probably chase him away by waving the plaster hands like clubs.

Even in his panic he grimaced with distaste as he tucked the sack into his shirt pocket, and then he made himself snatch up the plaster hands, and he turned toward the light of the entrance.

The bum from the hill slope was standing there, visible at last, and Sullivan saw that he did have hair on his chin; lots of it, white and matted. The man had his hands in the pockets of an enormous ragged overcoat, and he was rocking his head and peering in Sullivan's direction.

Sullivan's heart was pounding, for the man was clearly puzzled to see him. "What do you want?" Sullivan ventured. "How did you get in here?"

"I saw a guy—come in here," mumbled the old man, "couldn'a had a hall pass, aren't they—I forget. Where'd he go, anyway? I think he's the guy that stole my . . . my Buick." He was scuffling backward in confusion now. "I'm still pissed about that Buick."

"He came in here," said Sullivan, trying to keep the shakiness out of his voice. "I ate him. And I'm still hungry." He could smell the old man now, the well-remembered tang of raw cheap wine oozing out through dead pores.

"Jesus God!" the old man exclaimed shrilly, his brown-mottled eyes wide. "*Ate*—him! I help out around here, ask anybody, I fold the news-papers—" He was flapping his shaky hands. "—rearrange the rocks and—branches, you know? Make it all neater." He bared teeth that seemed to be made of the same bad stuff as his eyes. "You can't eat *me*, not right on top of *him*."

Sullivan jerked his head toward the slope and the ruined stairs. "Go, then."

Nodding as rapidly as a pair of wind-up chattering teeth, the old man turned and began limping rapidly back toward the stairs.

Sullivan stepped out into the light, his heart pounding against the little bag in his pocket. The old woman had stopped a few yards away and was gaping at him uncertainly.

"I . . . was keeping your plant watered," she said. "In most gardens they make the beds too soft—so that the flowers are always asleep."

Sullivan recognized the line as something from the *Alice in Wonderland* books. So many of them had read and somehow remembered them. Sukie had aways said that the Alice books were the Old and New Testaments for ghosts—which Pete had never understood; after all, Lewis Carroll hadn't been dead yet when he'd written them.

"Fine," Sullivan told the old woman, making a vaguely papal gesture with one of the hands. "Carry on."

The old man had by now scrambled some distance down the side stairway, and in a birdy old voice was calling, "I got away-ay! I got away-ay!" in the *nyah nyah nyah-nyah-nah!* cadence of spiteful chil-dren.

Sullivan glanced back in distaste, then turned and looked past the old woman at the driveway that curled away down the hill to Laurel Canyon Boulevard. Best to leave *that* way, he thought. I haven't heard any sirens, and it's less important, now, that I not be seen. At least now I've *got* the goddamn things.

"Excuse me," he said, and stepped around the woman.

After a few moments, as he was trudging down the driveway, she called after him, "Are you animal, vegetable, or mineral?"

That was what the Lion had asked Alice, in *Through the Looking-Glass.* "It's a fabulous monster!" he called back, quoting what the Unicorn had answered about Alice.

Don't I wish, he thought.

CHAPTER 7

"I ca'n't help it," said Alice very meekly: "I'm growing."
"You've no right to grow here," said the Dormouse.
—Lewis Carroll,
Alice's Adventures in Wonderland

The van shook every time a car drove past it, but after carefully laying the plaster hands and the little bag with the dried thumb in it on the front seat, Sullivan climbed in the back and tossed the sheets and blanket and cushions off the unmade bed. The bed could be disassembled and partially telescoped to become a U-shaped booth with a little table in the middle, but when it was extended out like this, the boards under the booth-seat cushions could be lifted off, exposing a few cubic feet of unevident space. He hooked his finger through the hole in the forward board and levered it up out of its frame.

Inside the booth-seat box lay a couple of square, limp-plastic rectangles connected by two foot-and-a-half-long ribbons, and a gray canvas fanny-pack containing his .45 semi-automatic Colt and a couple of spare magazines.

He lifted out the fanny pack and hefted it. He hadn't shot the .45 since an afternoon of target practice in the desert outside Tucson with some of the other tramp electricians a couple of years ago, but he did remember cleaning it afterward, and buying a fresh box of hardball rounds and reloading all three magazines.

The strung-together plastic rectangles were meant to be worn around the neck while traveling, with one rectangle lying on the chest and the other back between the shoulder blades—right now he had about six and a half thousand dollars in hundreds in the one, and his union papers in the other. Sullivan always thought of the pair as his ''scapular,'' because the linked flat wallets looked like one of those front-and-back medallions Catholics wear to keep from going to hell. He was always vaguely embarrassed to wear it.

He glanced toward the front of the van, where the three pieces of Houdini's "mask" lay on the passenger seat.

What would he put away in the seat box, and what would he keep out?

If he was going to drive straight back to Arizona and try to save his job at the Roosevelt Nuclear Generating Station, he would peel off a couple of hundred dollars to comfortably cover gas and food, and leave the rest of the cash hidden in the seat box here, along with the loaded gun, which was a felony to take across state borders; and the mask would be most effective where it was, out in the open. But if he was going to stay in Los Angeles for a while he'd have to allow for the possibility of being separated from, or even abandoning, the van—he'd want to have the cash and the gun *on* him, and the mask would have to be hidden from the sort of people who might get into the van and ransack it.

Another car drove past on Laurel Canyon Boulevard, and the van rocked on its shocks.

Stay in Los Angeles? he asked himself, startled even to have had the thought. Why would I do that? *She* works here, Loretta deLarava, and she probably still lives aboard the *Queen Mary* in Long Beach and commutes right up through the middle of the whole city every day.

I'd be crazy to do anything but leave the mask on the front seat and drive . . . anywhere. If I'm screwed with the Edison network I can still get electrician work, in Santa Fe or Kansas City or Memphis or any damn place. I could be a plain old handyman in any city in the whole country, doing low-profile electric, as well as cement work and drywall and carpentry and plumbing. An independent small-time contractor, getting paid under the table most of the time and fabricating expenses to show to the IRS on the jobs where I'd have to accept checks.

And if I scoot out of here right now, I *might* not even be screwed with Edison.

Sukie's nonsense Christmas carols were still droning in the back of his head, and he found himself thinking about the last time he'd seen her, at the shoot at Venice Beach on Christmas Eve in '86. He had somehow not ever been to Venice before—he was certain—and of course he had not been there since.

But on that overcast winter morning he had *recognized* the place. Driving around in one of deLarava's vans, he had several times found himself knowing what he would see when he rounded the next corner:

a gray old clapboard house with flowers growing in a window box, the traffic circle, the row of chipped Corinthian pillars lining Windward Avenue.

On this Christmas Eve of '86, big red plastic lanterns and garlands of fake pine boughs had been strung around the tops of the pillars and along the traffic-signal cables overhead, and the sidewalks had been crowded with last-minute Christmas shoppers and children, and dogs on leashes, and there had seemed to be a car in every curbside parking slot—but the pavements in his flickering memory had been empty and stark white under a harsh summer sun, and in his memory the shadows in the gaping windows and behind the bone-white colonnades were impenetrably black, all as silent and still as a streetscape in some particularly ominous De Chirico painting.

Under an overcast sky the real, winter ocean had been gray, with streaks of foam on the faces of the waves, but luckily deLarava had not wanted to actually go out onto the sand. Sukie was already drunk and wearing sunglasses, and Pete had been shaking as he set up the lights along the sidewalk.

They'd been supposed to be doing a short subject on the bodybuilders who apparently spent all their days lifting weights in the little fenced-in yard by the pavilion at the bottom of Windward Avenue, but deLarava's props had been old—a rented 1957 Buick, a *Gigi* movie poster to hang in a shop window—and she had had something else, too, that she'd carried in a shoebox.

(Sullivan was shaking now, holding the scapular and the gun.

(Idaho, he thought desperately, up in the Pelouse area where they grow lentils instead of potatoes. It'll be snowing soon now, and people always need electrical work done when it gets real cold. Or, what the hell, all the way out to the east coast, way out to Sag Harbor at the far end of Long Island—there was a lot of repair work of all sorts to be done during the off season, and you could hardly get farther away from Los Angeles.)

But helplessly he found himself remembering the moment on that chilly morning when deLarava had put down the shoebox on a truck fender, and Sukie had found an opportunity to peek inside it—and then had screamed and flung it away from her onto the sidewalk.

Pete had already spun around in sudden fright, and he'd expected to see something like a dead rat, or even a mummified baby, roll out of the box; but what had come spilling out of the box, tumbling across the looping electrical cables on the beachfront sidewalk, had been a well-remembered brown leather wallet and ring of keys and, somehow worst of all, three cans of Hires Root Beer. One of the cans rolled up against Pete's shoes, spraying a tiny jet of brown foam.

He and Sukie had simply fled then, mindlessly, running away up Windward Avenue. He had eventually stopped, winded, at a gas station somewhere up on Washington Boulevard, and had taken a cab to their apartment, and then driven his car to his bank, where he had cashed out his savings account. To this day he didn't know or care where Sukie had run to. Pete had been in Oregon by the next afternoon. Sukie had eventually tracked him down through union records, and they had talked on the phone a few times, but they'd never knowingly been in the same state at the same time again.

And now deLarava apparently wanted them back again. Sukie had obviously believed that the old woman intended to try the Venice "exorcism" again, with Pete and Sukie again present—voluntarily or not.

Sullivan tried to think of some other explanation. Maybe deLarava *didn't* want the twins back, hadn't thought about them in years, and Sukie's car had simply been hit by some random drunk, and the sudden onset of bar-time was caused by something that had nothing to do with deLarava; or deLarava might indeed want the twins back, but just to do the sort of work they'd done for her before, nothing to do with Venice; or she did want to do the Venice one again, but wouldn't be able to, now, because Sukie had killed herself. The old lady would be unable to do it unless she got a new pair of twins.

He bared his teeth and exhaled sharply. She might try to do it again, with some other pair of twins. Probably on Halloween, four days from now. Halloween was even better than Christmas, probably, for her purpose.

Well, he thought, in any case, I'm out of it. It has nothing to do with (—*a Hires Root Beer can rolling against his foot, wasting itself spraying a thin needle of foam out onto the sandy sidewalk*—) me.

For five full minutes, while cars roared past outside the van, he just crouched over the open underseat box.

Finally, with trembling fingers, he unbuttoned his shirt and draped the ribbons of the scapular over his head and onto his shoulders. After he had rebuttoned the shirt he flipped the black web belt of the fanny pack around his waist and snapped the buckle shut. Then he straightened up to go fetch the plaster hands so that he could put them away and reassemble the bed. The thumb in the Bull Durham sack he could carry in his shirt pocket.

CHAPTER 8

"How are you getting on?" said the Cat, as soon as there was mouth
enough for it to speak with.

—Lewis Carroll,
Alice's Adventures in Wonderland

Kootie awoke instantly when he heard someone scramble over the
wooden fence downstairs, but he didn't move, only opened his eyes.
The scuffed planks of the balcony floor were warm under his unbruised
cheek; by the shadow of the big old banana tree he judged the time to
be about four in the afternoon.

He had found this enclosed courtyard at about noon; somewhere south
of Olympic he'd picked his way down an alley between a pair of gray
two-story stucco-fronted buildings that had no doubt housed businesses
once but were featureless now, with their windows painted over; a
wooden fence in the back of one of the buildings was missing a board,
leaving a gap big enough for Kootie to scrape through.

Towering green schefflera and banana and avocado trees shaded the
yard he had found himself in, and he'd decided that the building might
once have been apartments—this hidden side was green-painted clapboard with decoratively framed doors and windows, and wooden steps
leading up to a long, roofed balcony. Someone had stored a dozen big
Coca-Cola vending machines back here, but Kootie didn't think anyone
would be coming back for them soon. He doubted that anyone had
looked in on this little yard since about 1970. It was a relief to be able
to take the adult-size sunglasses off his nose and tuck them into his
pocket.

He had climbed the rickety old stairs to the balcony, and then had
just lain down and gone to sleep, without even taking off his knapsack.

And he had slept deeply—but when he awoke he remembered everything that had happened to him during the last twenty hours.

He could hear the faint scuff of the person downstairs walking across the little yard now, but there was another sound that he couldn't identify: a recurrent raspy hiss, as though the person were pausing here and there to slowly rub two sheets of coarse paper together.

For several seconds Kootie just lay on the boards of the balcony and listened. Probably, he told himself, this person down in the yard won't climb the steps to this balcony. A grown-up would worry that the stairs might break under his weight. Probably he'll go away soon.

Kootie lifted his head and looked down over the balcony edge—and swallowed his instinctive shout of horror, and made himself keep breathing slowly.

In the yard, hunched and bent-kneed, the ragged man in camouflage pants was moving slowly across the stepping-stones, his single arm swinging like the clumped legs of a hovering wasp. The baseball cap kept Kootie from seeing the man's face, but he knew it was the round, pale, whiskered face with the little eyes that didn't seem to have sockets behind them to sit in.

Kootie's ears were ringing shrilly.

This was the man who had tried to grab him in the living room of Kootie's house last night—*Hey, kid, come here.* This was almost certainly the man who had murdered Kootie's parents. And now he was here.

The rasping sound the man was making, Kootie realized now, was *sniffing*—long, whistling inhalations. He was carefully seining the air with his nose as he made his slow way across the yard; and every few seconds he would jerk heavily, as if an invisible cord tied around his chest were being tugged.

Kootie ducked back out of sight, his heart knocking fast. He's been following me, Kootie thought. Or following the glass brick. What does the thing do, leave a trail in the air, like tire tracks in mud?

He is going to come up the stairs.

Then Kootie twitched, startled, and an instant later the bum began talking. "You came in here through the fence," said the bum in a high, clear voice, "and you didn't leave by that means. And I don't think you have a key to any of these doors, and I don't think you can fly." He laughed softly. "Therefore you're still here."

Kootie looked toward the far end of the balcony; it ended at a railing just past the farthest door, with no other set of stairs.

I can jump, he thought tensely. I can climb over the railing and hang from as low a place as I can hold on to, and then drop. Scramble out of the yard through the fence before this guy can even get back down the stairs, and then just run until . . . until I get to the ocean, or the Sierras, or until I drop dead.

"Let me tell you a parable," said the man below, still audibly shuffling across the leafy yard. "Once upon a time a man killed another man, and then he was . . . *sorry*, and wanted to be *forgiven*. So he went to the dead man's grave, and dug him up, and when he opened the casket he saw that the man inside it was himself, smiling at the joke.

"Hah!"

The balcony shook as a muscular hand grabbed the vertical rail-post in front of Kootie's eyes, and two shod feet loudly scuffled for traction on the planks, inches from Kootie's own feet; and the round face had poked up above the balcony floor and the bum's little black eyes were staring straight into Kootie's.

Kootie had rolled back against the wall, but now couldn't move, or breathe, or think.

The inches-away mouth opened among the patchy whiskers, opened very wide, and out of it grated a million-voice roar like a stadium when a player hits a home run.

Then Kootie had kicked himself up and was running for the far end of the balcony, but behind him he heard the fast booming scuffle of the man scrambling up onto the planks, and before Kootie reached the rail his head was rocked as the bum snatched at his curly hair.

Kootie sprang, slapped the balcony rail with the sole of his left Reebok, and was airborne.

Banana leaves were whipping his face, and he tried to grab a branch but only managed to skin his palm and go into a spinning fall. His knapsack and the base of his spine hit the hard dirt in almost the same instant that his feet did, and his head was full of the coppery taste of pennies as he scrambled on all fours, unable to work his lungs, toward the fence.

By the time he reached the alley he could at least wring awful whooping and gagging sounds out of his chest, and could even get up onto his feet, and he hopped and hunched and sobbed his way to the street sidewalk.

A pickup truck with its bed full of lawnmowers and fat burlap sacks was groaning past in the slow lane, and Kootie forced his numbed and shaking legs to run—and after a few pounding seconds he managed to collide with the truck's tailgate, his knees on the bumper and his arms wrapped around the two upright metal tubes of a power-mower handle. At least his feet were off the ground.

But the truck's old brakes were squealing now, and Kootie was being pushed against the tailgate as the battered vehicle ground to a halt. He used the momentum to help him climb into the truck bed, and then, kneeling on a burlap sack that reeked of gasoline and the stale-beer smell of old cut grass, he waved urgently at the rearview mirror. "Go," Kootie croaked, "start up, *go!*"

Through the dusty rear window he could see that the Mexican driver had put his elbow up on the back of the seat and was looking back at him. He was waving too, and mouthing something, no doubt ordering Kootie to get out of the truck.

Kootie looked back, toward the alley, and saw the one-armed bum stride out from between the two gray buildings into the brassy late-afternoon sunlight, smiling broadly straight at him.

Kootie sprang over the burlap sacks and banged his fist on the truck's back window, and he managed to scream: "Go! *Vaya! Ahora! Es el diablo!*"

The driver might not have heard him, but Kootie could see that the man was looking past Kootie now, at the advancing bum; then the driver had turned back to the wheel and the truck lurched forward, swerving into the left lane and picking up some speed.

Kootie peered behind them through the swaying fence of lawnmower handles and weed whips. The bum had slowed to a strolling pace on the receding sidewalk, and waved at Kootie just before the intervening cars and trucks hid him from view.

Kootie sat back against a spare tire, hoping the driver would not stop for at least several blocks. When he stretched out his legs his right ankle gave him a momentary twinge of pain; he tugged up the cuff and saw that it was already visibly thicker than the left ankle.

The ankle felt hot, too, but his stomach was suddenly icy with alarm. Am I gonna be *limping* for a while? he thought. How fast can I *limp*?

Five minutes later the driver of the pickup truck turned in to a Chevron station. He opened the driver's-side door and got out, and as he un-screwed the truck's gas cap he nodded to Kootie and then jerked his head sideways, obviously indicating that this was as far as he meant to take his young passenger.

Kootie nodded humbly and climbed over the tailgate. His right ankle took his weight well enough, but had flared with pain when he'd rotated it in climbing down.

"Uh, thanks for the ride," Kootie said. He fished the sunglasses out of his pocket and pushed them onto his nose.

"Sí," said the man, unhooking the gas-pump nozzle and clanking up the lever. *"Buena suerte."* He began pumping gas into the tank.

Kootie knew that those Spanish words meant *good luck.* The sunlight was slanting straight down the east-west lanes of the street, and the shadows of the cars were lengthening.

Kootie was more upset about what he had to do now than he was by his injured ankle. "Uh," the boy said quickly, *"lo siento, pero . . . tiene usted algunas cambio? Yo tengo hambre, y no tengo una casa."* Kootie wished he had paid more attention in Spanish class; what he had tried to say was, *I'm sorry, but do you have any change? I'm hungry and I don't have a house.*

His face was cold, and he had no idea whether he was blushing or had gone pale.

The man stared at him expressionlessly, leaning against the gas nozzle's accordioned black rubber sleeve and squeezing the big aluminum trigger. Kootie could faintly hear gasoline sloshing in the filler pipe, though the air smelled of fried rice and sesame oil from a Chinese restaurant across the street. Eventually the gas pump clicked off, and the man hung up the nozzle and stumped away to the cashier to pay. Kootie just stood miserably by the back bumper of the truck.

When the man came back he handed Kootie a five-dollar bill. *"Buena suerte,"* he said again, turning away and getting back into his truck.

"Thanks," said Kootie. *"Gracias."* He looked back to the west, and as the truck clattered into gear behind him and rocked back out onto the street, Kootie stood on the oil-stained concrete and wondered where the one-armed bum was right now. Somewhere to the west, for sure.

Kootie started walking eastward down the sidewalk. His ankle didn't hurt if he kept his right heel off the ground and walked tiptoe.

Sleep, he thought dazedly—where? There's no way I can go to sleep, stop moving. He'll catch up. Maybe I could sleep on a train—"hop a freight."

Right.

Can I hide?

Most of the buildings in L.A. were low—three stories or shorter—and he looked around at the rooftops. Every one of them seemed to have a smaller house on top, in behind the old insulators and chimneys.

He's only got one arm, Kootie thought; maybe I can climb somewhere that he can't get to.

Right. With my sprained ankle?

Kootie was walking fairly briskly, and it seemed to him that he was just barely keeping ahead of panic.

He had passed many empty lots. He could describe the typical one now—fenced in with chain-link, with a few shaggy palm trees and a derelict car, and lines of weeds tracing lightning-bolt patterns across the old asphalt. Maybe he could get into a lot, and be ready to wake up and run when he heard the one-armed bum climbing the fence.

At the intersection ahead of him a man in an old denim jacket was standing on the sidewalk with a dog beside him. The dog was some kind of black German-shepherd mix, and the man was holding a white cardboard sign. When Kootie limped up beside them the dog began wagging its tail, and Kootie stooped to catch his breath and pat the dog on the head.

"*Bueno perro,*" Kootie told the man. He could now see that the hand-lettered sign read, in big black letters, WILL WORK FOR FOOD—HOMELESS VIETNAM VET.

"*Sí,*" the man said. "Uh . . . *cómo se dice* . . . *perro* is dog, right?"

"Right," Kootie said. "Nice dog. You speak English."

"Yeah. You got no accent."

"I'm Indian, not Mexican. India Indian. Anyway, I was born here."

The man he was talking to could have been of any race at all, almost of any age at all. His short-cropped white hair was as curly as Kootie's, and his skin was dark enough so that he might be Mexican or Indian or black or even just very tanned. His lean face was deeply lined around the mouth and the vaguely Asian eyes, but Kootie couldn't tell if that was a result of age or just exposure to lots of weather.

"Where do you two live?" Kootie found himself asking.

"Nowhere, Jacko," the man said absently, watching the traffic over Kootie's head. "Why, where do you live?"

Kootie patted the dog's head again and blinked back tears of exhaustion, glad of the sunglasses. "Same place."

The man looked down again and focused on Kootie. "Really? *Here?*"

Kootie blinked up at him and tried to understand the question. "If it was *here*, how could it be nowhere?"

"Hah. You'd be surprised. Act cool, now, okay?"

The light had turned red, and a big battered blue Suburban truck had stopped at the crosswalk lines. The driver leaned across the seat and cranked down the passenger-side window. "Nice dog," he said through a ragged mustache. "How you all doing?"

"Not so good," said the white-haired man standing beside Kootie. "My son and I and the dog been standing out here all day waitin' for someone who needs some kind of work done, and we'd like to be able to stay in a motel, tomorrow being Sunday and us wantin' to get a shower before church, you know? We're just six bucks short right now.''

Kootie rolled his eyes anxiously behind the sunglasses. Tomorrow was Wednesday, not Sunday.

''Shit,'' said the driver. Then, just as the light turned green, he tossed a balled-up bill out the window. ''Make it count!'' he yelled as he gunned away across the intersection.

The white-haired man had caught the bill and uncrumpled it—it was a five. He grinned down at Kootie, exposing uneven yellow teeth. ''Good job. So whatta you, a runaway?''

Kootie glanced nervously back up the street to the west. ''My parents are dead.''

''Some kind of foster home? Go back to wherever it is, Jacko.''

''There isn't any place at all.''

''There isn't, huh?'' The man was watching traffic, but he glanced down at Kootie. ''Well there *was* a place, I believe, a day or two ago. That's a Stussy shirt, and those Reeboks are new. Where were you plannin' to sleep? Any old where? You get fucked up bad around here, Jacko, trust me. Whole streets of chickenhawks looking for your sort. Nastiness, know what I mean?'' He squinted around, then sighed. ''You wanna move in with Fred and me for a couple of days?''

Kootie understood that Fred was the dog, and that helped; still he said quickly, ''I don't have any money at all.''

''Bullshit you don't, you got two bucks just in the last couple of seconds. Fred takes twenty percent, okay? Let's work this corner for another ten minutes, and then we can move up to Silver Lake.''

Kootie tried to figure where Silver Lake was from here. ''That's a long walk, isn't it?''

''Fuck walk, and in fact fuck talk, we got a red light coming up again here. I got a car, and Fred and I keep moving. Trust me, you be doin' yourself a favor to ride along with us.''

Kootie looked desperately at the dog's wide grin and brown eyes, and he thought about *keep moving*, and then he blurted, ''Okay.'' He stuck out his hand. ''I'm Kootie.''

The man clasped Kootie's hand in his own dry, callused palm. ''*Kootie?* No kidding. I'm Rightful Glory Mayo. Known as Raffle.'' Then, more loudly, he said, ''Can we wash your car windows, ma'am? My boy and I haven't had anything to eat all day.''

Raffle didn't even have a squirt bottle or a newspaper to wash windows with, but the woman in the Nissan gave them a dollar anyway.

''That's another forty cents you got, Kootie,'' said Raffle as the light turned green. "You know, we might do better if you ditched the shades—makes you look like a pint-size doper."

Kootie took off the sunglasses and looked mutely up at Raffle. He had no idea what color his eye socket was, but it was swollen enough to perceptibly narrow his vision.

"Well now, little man," Raffle said, "you've had a busy day or two, haven't you? Yeah, keep the shades—people will think I gave you that, otherwise."

Kootie nodded and put the glasses back on—but not before he had nervously looked westward again.

CHAPTER 9

"I only took the regular course."

"What was that?" inquired Alice.

"Reeling and Writing, of course, to begin with," the Mock Turtle replied; "and then the different branches of Arithmetic—Ambition, Distraction, Uglification, and Derision."

—Lewis Carroll,
Alice's Adventures in Wonderland

Raffle was obviously pleased with the money they made during the next ten minutes, and he dug a laundry marking pen out of the pocket of his topmost shirt and, under the words HOMELESS VIETNAM VET, he added WITH MOTHERLESS SON.

"We gonna make booyah bucks on this," said Raffle with satisfaction. "We probably be sleepin' in motels every night."

Kootie thought of sleeping on wheels. "I don't mind a car," he said, struggling to keep the impatience out of his voice. He still hadn't seen the one-armed man, but he could imagine him watching from behind some wall.

"Good attitude," Raffle said. "Hey, we should be shifting locations—you want a beer?"

Kootie blinked. "I'm only eleven."

"Well, I'll drink it if you don't want it. Come on."

They walked across the street to a little liquor store, Fred following closely on their heels, and Raffle bought a bottle of Corona in a narrow paper bag.

"Let's head for the car," he said as they walked back out onto the sidewalk.

The car was a twenty-year-old mustard-colored Ford Maverick parked behind a nearby laundromat, and the back seat was piled with clothes and Maxell floppy-disk boxes and at least a dozen gray plastic video-cassette rewinders. Fred hopped up onto the clutter when Raffle unlocked the door, and he and Kootie sat in the front seats.

Raffle levered the cap off the beer bottle against the underside of the dashboard. In an affectedly deep voice, he said, "What's your name, boy?"

Catching on that Raffle was pretending to be someone else, Kootie said, "Mayo. Uh, Jacko Mayo."

"Very good." Raffle took a long sip of the beer. "We used to live in La Mirada, that's forty-five minutes south of here on the 5, okay? Four-bedroom house, only place you ever lived. I used to be a car mechanic, but your mom was a legal secretary and she made the real money, but she didn't have health insurance and when she got cancer we lost everything, and then she died. Nobody's likely to ask you for anything more than that, but if it ever comes up, just start crying. Can you cry if you have to?"

Kootie thought about it. "Easy."

"Great. Now are we black or white or Mexican or Indian or what?"

"To work for both of us? I'd just say—" He shrugged. "—we're Angelenos. We just . . . grew up out of the sidewalks."

"Good. Don't remember no old days at all." Raffle tilted up the bottle and drained the last of the beer. "Now, there's some . . . things you're gonna have to just get used to seeing, okay? Like if you suddenly moved to . . . Borneo or Australia or somewhere, they might do stuff that you were always taught was bad, but it's okay there, right? I mean, as long as they don't say *you've* got to do 'em. *You* just consider it higher education."

"Right," said Kootie cautiously.

"Okay. There's a little nail in the ashtray, lemme have it, hm?"

Kootie found the nail and handed it to the man.

Raffle put the point of the nail into a little dimple in the base of the glass beer bottle, and then he picked up an old shoe from between the seats and whacked the head of the nail with it; the point was now inside the bottle, though the bottle hadn't broken, and Raffle twisted it back out, then blew through the hole.

"All us good Dagwood-type dads smoke pipes," he said. Then he reached under the seat and dragged up a box of Chore Boy scrubbing pads and prized a little cushion of steel wool out of the box. He tore off a bristly shred of the stuff and tucked it like a little bird's nest into the neck of the bottle, and then replaced the rest of the pad and pushed the box back under the seat.

"If you see a one-time," Raffle said, "don't change your expression or look around, but slap me on the leg."

Kootie remembered reading in the newspaper that *one-time* was a street term for policeman. "Is this," he faltered, "some kind of—no offense—dope thing?"

"Just say yo," Raffle agreed. Out of a hole in the double thickness of his shirt cuff he dug a tiny fragment of what seemed to be white stone, like a piece off one of the ones Kootie's father had spread around the plants in the atrium pots, and Raffle carefully laid it in the nest of steel wool at the top of the empty beer bottle.

Raffle slouched down in the seat and held the bottle up to the textured plastic head liner, which Kootie now noticed was dotted with scorch marks, and the man put his mouth to the little hole he'd punched in the bottle's base; then he flicked a long orange-plastic Cricket lighter and held the flame to the piece of rock as he sucked.

Kootie looked away as the bottle began to fill with pale smoke. His heart was pounding, but he didn't see any "one-times," and in just a couple of seconds Raffle had opened the door and rolled the bottle away across the parking lot.

Raffle exhaled, and Kootie smelled burned steel wool and a faint chemical tang. "Never hang on to a pipe," Raffle told him hoarsely as he began grinding the starter motor. "There's always another at the next liquor store."

"*Dagwood* probably saved 'em," said Kootie bravely.

Raffle laughed as the engine finally caught and he clanked the transmission into reverse. "Yeah," he said, still hoarse. "He probably had all kinds of oak pipe racks, full of cans and bottles. Blondie would dust 'em, and sometimes break one of the bottles and make him real mad—*I had that Corona broke in perfect, you bitch!*"

Kootie laughed nervously. Raffle made a left turn onto Fourth Street and angled into the far right lane to get on the southbound 110 Freeway.

"I thought we were going to Silver Lake," said Kootie. "Isn't that north?"

"Detour for medical supplies."

They got off three miles south at the Vernon Avenue exit, and Raffle parked in the empty lot of a burned-out gas station.

"The plan's this," he said as he rolled up the driver's-side window. "Me and Fred will be gone for twenty minutes or so. You keep the doors locked, and if anybody tries to mess with you, just lean on the horn until they go away, right? A one-time, roll the window down and smile and say you're waitin' for your dad. When we get back, it's dinnertime.''

Kootie nodded, and Raffle grinned and got out of the car. He folded the seat forward so that Fred could scramble out onto the pavement, and then the door was shut and locked and the two of them had gone loping away down the sidewalk and around a corner.

Kootie realized that Raffle was going to go spend some of the afternoon's income on more drugs, but he never even considered getting out of the car and walking away. He remembered watching the riots on TV six months ago, and he imagined that the people around here would break his face off with bricks if they so much as saw him on the sidewalk.

He wondered what kind of food Raffle generally ate. Kootie was ready to eat just about anything at all.

He hiked up on the car seat and looked around. Dimly in the bay of the ruined gas station he could see the brown shell of a burned-up car, still raised up off the floor on the hydraulic lift; Kootie wondered if the owner had ever come by to see if any progress was being made on whatever repairs he'd brought the car in for. The tall palm trees along the sidewalks were black silhouettes against the darkening sky, and lights had begun to come on in shop windows up and down the street. Raffle's car smelled like unbathed dog, and Kootie wished he were allowed to roll down the windows. Big speakers were playing music somewhere not too far away, but all Kootie could hear was the pounding bass and a lot of angry, rhythmic shouting.

He sat back down. The one-armed bum would no doubt show up here, tracing the smell or warped refraction or abraded air or whatever effect it was that the glass-brick thing left as a track, but Kootie and his new friend—friends, plural, counting the dog—would be long gone.

He flipped the straps of the knapsack off of his shoulders and dragged it around onto his lap and unknotted the straps. Then he dug around among the clothes until he found the glass brick.

He lifted it out and turned it against the windshield, trying to see the fading daylight through the murky glass depths. The brick still clicked faintly when he turned it, as though there was something hard and transparent inside. He rocked it in time to the incomprehensible music from outside. *Tick, tick, tick.*

He was pretty sure he should just pitch it—toss it into the wrecked gas station and let the wrecked bum find it. Or the lady he'd seen in the Jaguar last night—*"a hundred dollars for your cigar"*—she could come and get it, and have her tires rotated and burned up, as long as she was here.

He gripped the glass thing in his palms the way he had on the Fairfax sidewalk this morning; again he could feel the halves of it shift when he pulled at it, and he looked nervously at the street, but none of the cars driving by stalled.

Prying hard and rocking the halves away from each other, he soon had them almost completely separated. One more tug, and the thing would be opened.

He thought again of the Robert Louis Stevenson story, the one about the demon in the bottle. Here by the burned-out gas station, though, in Raffle's car full of Raffle's litter, on this alien street, it no longer seemed likely that some kind of old-world monster would erupt out of the little glass box.

He lifted off the top half.

And nothing happened. Inside it, laid into a fitted cavity in the glass was . . . a test tube? A glass vial, with a tapered black-rubber stopper. He put the halves of the glass brick down on his lap and lifted out the vial.

He could see that it was empty. He found that he was disappointed, and he wondered what the vial might once have contained. Somebody's blood, mummy dust, gold nuggets with a curse on them?

He twisted out the stopper and sniffed the vial.

CHAPTER 10

Alice caught the baby with some difficulty, as it was a queer-shaped little creature, and held out its arms and legs in all directions, "just like a star-fish," thought Alice. The poor little thing was snorting like a steam-engine when she caught it, and kept doubling itself up and straightening itself out again, so that altogether, for the first minute or two, it was as much as she could do to hold it.

—Lewis Carroll,
Alice's Adventures in Wonderland

As if he had plugged in the wires for the second of a pair of stereo speakers—as if he'd attached the wires when the second stereo channel was not only working but had its volume cranked up high—Kootie's head was abruptly *doubly* hit by the the ongoing music from outside now; and he found himself somehow jolted, shocked, by the mere fact of being able to hear.

Dropping the vial, he grabbed the steering wheel and gripped it hard, gritting his teeth, cold with sudden sweat, for he was falling with terrible speed through some kind of gulf—his eyes were wide open and he was aware that he was seeing the dashboard and the motionless windshield wipers and the shadowed sidewalk beyond the glass, but in his head things clanged and flashed as they hurtled incomprehensibly past, voices shouted, and his heart thudded with love and terror and triumph and mirth and rage and shame all mixed together so finely that they seemed to constitute life itself, the way rainbow colors on a fast-spinning disk all blur into white.

It wasn't stopping. It was getting faster.

Blood burst out of his nose and he pitched sideways across the passenger seat onto his right shoulder, twitching and whimpering, his eyes wide open but rolled so far back into his head that he couldn't see anything outside the boundaries of his own skull.

Pete Sullivan jackknifed up out of the little bed and scrambled for the front seat—but when he yanked the curtain back from the windshield he saw that the van was *not* careering down some hill. He almost shouted with relief; still, he tumbled himself into the driver's seat and tromped hard on the emergency brake.

Ahead of him, beyond a motionless curb, half a dozen boys in baggy shorts and T-shirts were strolling aimlessly across a broad lawn. Their shadows were long, and the grass glowed a golden green in the last rays of sunlight.

Sullivan's heart was pounding, and he made himself wait nearly a full minute before lighting a cigarette, because he knew his hands were shaking too badly to hang on to one.

At last he was able to get one lit and suck in a lungful of smoke. He'd had a bad dream—hardly surprising!—something about . . . trains? Electricity? Sudden noise after a long silence . . .

Machinery. His work at the nuclear power plant, at the other utilities? The whole Edison network—Con Ed, Southern California Edison . . .

He took another long drag on the cigarette and then stubbed it out. The van was in shadow now, definitely not moving, and the sky was darkening toward evening. He breathed slowly and evenly until his heartbeat had slowed down to normal. Should he go find something to eat, or try to get some more sleep?

He had driven the van back down Laurel Canyon Boulevard and parked it here in the La Cienega Park lot, south of Wilshire. He had pulled the curtains over the little windows in the back and dragged the rings of the long shade across the curtain rod over the windshield and behind the rearview mirror, and had then locked up and crawled into the bed. He had apparently slept for several hours.

The boys in the park were at the top of a low green hill now, their laughing faces lit in chiaroscuro by the departing sun. Griffith's hour, Sullivan thought.

He fumbled in his pocket now for his keys. No way sleep, after that jolt. Dinner, then—but a drink somewhere first.

On the Greyhound bus, Angelica Anthem Elizalde had been dreaming of the ranch in Norco where she had spent her childhood.

Her family had raised chickens, and it had been Angelica's job to scatter chicken scratch in the yard for the birds. Wild chickens that a neighbor had abandoned used to roost in the trees at night, and bustle around with the domesticated birds during the day. All of the chickens, and a dozen cats and a couple of goats as well, had liked to congregate around the trail of dry dog food Angelica's mother would spread by the driveway every morning. The half-dozen dogs had never seemed to mind.

It had always been her grandfather whose job it was to kill the chickens—he would grab a chicken by the neck and then give it a hard overhand whirl as if he had meant to see how far he could throw it but forgot to let go, and the bird's neck would be broken. Angelica's mother had tried it one time when the old man had been in jail, and the creature hadn't died. The chicken had done everything *but* die. It was screaming, and flapping and clawing, and feathers flew everywhere as her mother tried lashing it around again—and again. All the kids were crying. Finally they had got an axe from the shed, a very dull old axe, and her mother had managed to kill the chicken by smashing its skull. The meat had been tough.

For the occasional turkey they would cut a hole in a gunny sack—her mother always called them guinea sacks—and hang the bird in it upside down from a tree limb, and then cut the bird's throat, standing well back. The sack was to keep its wings restrained—a turkey could hurt you if it hit you with a wing.

One Easter her father had trucked home a live pig, and they had killed it and butchered it and cooked it in a pit the men dug in the yard—the giant vat of carnitas had lasted for days, even with all the neighbors helping to eat it. For weeks before that, her mother had saved eggshells whole by pricking the ends with a hatpin and blowing the egg out; she had painted the eggshells and filled them with confetti, and the kids ran around all morning breaking them over each other's heads, until their hair and their church clothes looked like abstract pointillist paintings.

One of them had finally been for real—late in the afternoon her brother had broken a real, ripe, fertilized egg over Angelica's head, and when she had felt warm wetness on her scalp, and had reached up to wipe it off, she had found herself holding a spasming little naked red monster, its eyes closed and its embryonic beak opening and shutting.

Her dream had violently shifted gears then—suddenly there was clanging and lights, and train whistles howling in fog, and someone was nearly insane with terror.

With a jolt she was awake, sitting up stiffly in the padded bus seat, biting her lip and tasting the iron of her own blood.

It's . . . 1992, she told herself harshly. You're on a bus to Los Angeles and the bus is not out of control. Look out the window—the bus is staying in its lane and not going more than sixty.

You're *not* dead.

She looked up, beyond the rushing darkening lanes, to the flat desert that was shifting by so much more slowly. Probably the bus was somewhere around Victorville by now, still an easy sixty miles out of L.A.

On her panicked late-afternoon drive out of Los Angeles two years ago she had seen a Highway Patrol car behind her, just south of Victorville, and she had meticulously pulled off and let him go on by, and had had a hamburger at a Burger King alongside the freeway. Then she had driven the next dozen miles northeast on a side road paralleling the freeway, to let the cop get far ahead. Even on the side road she had stopped for a while, at a weird roadside lot among the Joshua trees where a white-bearded old man had assembled a collection of old casino signs, and big plywood caricatures of a cowboy and a hula dancer, and assortments of empty bottles hung on the bare limbs of scrawny sycamores, out here in the middle of the desert. Out of sympathy for another outcast, she had bought from him a book of poems he'd written and had published locally.

Now, biting her nails aboard a rushing Greyhound bus, she wondered if the old man was still there, wondered if Southern California still had room for such people.

Or for herself. She and the old man at the ramshackle roadside museum had both at least been alive.

The man known as Sherman Oaks screamed when the heat scalded his left arm, and he fell to his knees in the lush ice plant of the shadowy freeway island at the junction of the 10 and the 110.

After a few choking moments he was able to stand up and breathe; but his heart was pounding, and his left arm, still hot but at least not burning now, was pointed stiffly south. His right palm and the knees of his baggy pants were greenly wet from having crushed the ice plant. Beyond the thickly leaved branches of the bordering oleander bushes, the flickering tracks of car headlights continued to sweep around this enclosed park-like area as they followed the arc of the on-ramp onto the southbound 110.

He ate it, he thought numbly. *The kid ate it, or it ate him.*

But I'll eat who's left.

He had come here to check his ghost traps. The trap right in front of him had caught one, but the ghost seemed to have fled when he had screamed. Sherman Oaks decided to leave the trap here—the ghost would come back to it in a few hours, or else another ghost would come. Sometimes he was able to bottle five or six from just one trap.

He had knocked the trap over when he had fallen, and now he righted it: a hand-lettered cardboard sign that read, SIT ON A POTATO PAN, OTIS. Other traps he had set up in this secret arbor included several more homemade signs—THE NOON SEX ALERT RELAXES NO ONE HT, and GO HANG A SALAMI, I'M A LASAGNA HOG—and scatterings of jigsaw-puzzle pieces on patches of clear dirt. Better-known palindromes, such as *Madam, I'm Adam*, didn't catch the attention of the wispy ghosts, and heavier items such as broken dishes seemed to be beyond the power of their frail ectoplasmic muscles to rearrange; but the Potato Pan and the Sex Alert and the Lasagna palindromes kept them confounded for hours, or even days, in wonderment at the way the sentences read the same backward as forward; and the ghosts would linger even longer trying to assemble the jigsaw puzzles.

Real, living homeless people seldom came here, knowing that this isolated patch of greenery was haunted, so he sometimes dropped a big handful of change among the jigsaw pieces—that trick would hold ghosts probably till the end of the world, for they not only felt compelled to put the puzzle together but also to count and stack the money; and apparently their short-term memories were no good, because they always lost count and had to start over. Sometimes, when he arrived with his little glass bottles, the ghosts would faintly ask him for help in counting the coins.

And then he would scoop the ghosts in and stopper the bottles tight. (It was awkward, using just his right hand; but sometimes he had actually seemed able to *nudge them along* a little with his missing left!) He had always known that he had to use glass containers—the ghosts had to be able to see out, even if it was only as far as the inside lining of a pocket, or they rotted away and turned to poison in the container.

He had his makeshift traps all over the city. In RTD yards under the Santa Monica Freeway, ghosts would climb aboard the doorless old hulks of city buses and then just sit in the seats, evidently waiting for a driver to come and take them somewhere; and they often hung around deserted pay telephones, as if waiting for a call; and sometimes in the empty cracked concrete lots he would just paint a big bull's-eye, and the things would gather there, presumably to see what sort of missile might eventually hit the target. Even spiderwebs often caught the very new ones.

Sometimes he got so many bottles filled that even his stash boxes wouldn't hold any more, and he could sell the surplus. The dope dealers that catered to the wealthy Benedict Canyon crowd would pay him two or three hundred dollars per bottle—cash and no questions and not even an excitation test with a magnetic compass, because they had known him long enough to be sure he wouldn't just sell them an empty bottle. The dealers siphoned each ghost into a quantity of nitrous oxide and then sealed the mix into a little pressurized glass cartridge, and eventually some rich customer would fill a balloon with it and then inhale the whole thing.

The cylinders were known as *smokes* or *cigars*, slang terms of the old-timers who attracted ghosts with aromatic pipe tobacco or cherry-flavored cigars, and then inhaled the disintegrating things right along with the tobacco smoke. *Take a snort of Mr. Nicotinus, walk with the Maduro Man.* It had been considered a gourmet high, in the days before health and social concerns had made tobacco use déclassé. Nitrous oxide was the preferred mixer now, even though the hit tended to be less "digestible," lumpy with unbroken memories.

Sherman Oaks favored ghosts raw and uncut—not pureed in the bowl of a pipe or the cherry of a cigar, or minced up in a chilled soup of nitrous oxide; he liked them fresh and whole, like live oysters.

He opened his mouth now and exhaled slowly, emptying his lungs, hearing the faint roar of all the ghosts he had eaten over the years or decades.

The Bony Express, all the fractalized trinities of Mr. Nicotinus.

To his left the towers of downtown, among which he could still pick out the old City Hall, the Security Bank building and the Arco Towers, were featureless and depthless silhouettes against a darkening sky stained bronze by the returned smog, but the cooling evening breeze down here in the freeway island somehow still carried, along with the scents of jasmine and crushed iceplant, a whiff of yesterday's desert sage smell.

His lungs were empty.

Now Sherman Oaks inhaled deeply—but the kid was too far away. That old gardening truck had apparently kept right on going; he should have got the license number. But his left arm, still uncomfortably warm, was at least pointing toward the nearest loop of the track the kid was leaving. West of here.

The actual flesh-and-blood left arm was gone—lost long ago, he assumed from the smooth, uninflamed scar tissue that covered the stump at the shoulder. The loss of the limb had no doubt been a dramatic incident, but it had happened back in the old life that he knew only through vague and unhelpful fragments of dreams. He couldn't now even remember what name he might once have had; he had chosen

"Sherman Oaks" just because that was the district of Los Angeles he'd been in when awareness had returned to him.

But he still *felt* a left arm. Sometimes the phantom hand at the end of it would feel so tightly clenched into a fist that the imaginary muscles would cramp painfully, and sometimes the "arm" felt cold and wet. When someone died nearby, though, he felt a little tingle of warmth, as if a cigarette ash had been tapped off onto the phantom skin; and if the ghost was trapped somehow, snagged on or in something, the phantom arm would warm up and point to it.

And even though he knew that there was not really any arm attached to the shoulder, Sherman Oaks found it awkward to walk through doorways or down bus aisles when the phantom limb was thrust out in that way. At other times the missing hand would for whole days at a time seem to be clutching his chest, and he would have to sleep on his back, which he hated to do because he always started snoring and woke himself up.

He squinted around at the darkening grove. He knew he should check the other traps, but he wanted to find the kid before someone else did; obviously Koot Hoomie Parganas had not yet reached puberty—that was why the boy couldn't absorb the super-smoke that he was overlapped with, even if he had actually inhaled it now. The unabsorbed ghost would continue to be conspicuous.

Sherman Oaks lifted his head at a sudden rustling sound. With muffled cursing and a snapping of oleander branches, someone was clumsily breaking into his preserve. Sherman Oaks tiptoed toward the intruder, but relaxed when he heard the mumbled words: "Goddamn spirochetes can't hear yourself think in a can of tuna fish. Yo bay-*bee*! Gotcha where they want 'em if it's New York minutes in a three-o'clock food show." And Oaks could smell him, the sharp reek of unmetabolized cheap wine.

Oaks stepped out into a clearing, intentionally stamping his feet. The stranger goggled at him in vast confusion.

"Get out of here," Oaks told him. "Or I'll eat you too."

"Yes, boss," quavered the stranger, toppling over backward and then swimming awkwardly back toward the oleander border, doing a thrashing backstroke across the ice plant. "Just lookin' to get my ashes hauled."

You got your ashes hauled years ago, thought Oaks as he watched the ludicrous figure disappear back onto the freeway shoulder.

But Oaks was uneasy. Even this sort of creature, the creepy old ghosts who had accumulated physical substance—from bugs and sick animals, and spilled blood and spit and jizz, and even from each other, sometimes—might go lurching after the boy, in their idiot intrusive way.

They always seemed to find clothes to wear, and they could panhandle for money to buy liquor, but Sherman Oaks could recognize them instantly by their disjointed babbling and the way the liquor, unaffected by their lifeless token guts, bubbled out of their pores still redolent with unmetabolized ethanol.

They couldn't eat organic stuff, because it would just rot inside them; so they mindlessly ate . . . rocks, and bottle caps, and marbles, and bits of crumbled asphalt they found in the gutters of old streets. Sherman Oaks had to smile, remembering the time a truck full of live chickens had overturned on the Pasadena Freeway, freeing a couple of dozen chickens who took up messy residence on one of the freeway islands. Passing motorists had started bringing bags of corn along with them on the way to work, and throwing the bags out onto the island as they drove past. Several of the big old solid ghosts had mistaken the corn kernels for gravel, and had eaten it, and then a couple of weeks later had been totally bewildered by the green corn shoots sprouting from every orifice of their squatter's-rights bodies, even out from behind their eyeballs.

To hell with the ghost traps, thought Sherman Oaks. I can go hungry for one night. I've got to track down that kid, and that big unabsorbed ghost, before somebody else does.

The sky was purple now, darkening to black, and the *Queen Mary* was a vast chandelier of lights only a quarter of a mile away across Long Beach Harbor, throwing glittering gold tracks across the choppy water to where Solomon Shadroe stood on the deck of his forty-six-foot Alaskan trawler.

His boat was moored at a slip in the crowded Downtown Long Beach Marina, by the mouth of the Los Angeles River, and though most of the owners of the neighboring boats only rocked the decks on weekends, Shadroe had been a "live-aboard" at the marina for seventeen years. He owned a twenty-unit apartment building near the beach a mile and a half east of here, and even though his girlfriend lived there he hadn't spent the night on land since 1975.

He swiveled his big gray head back toward the shore. He had no sense of smell anymore, but he knew that something heavy must have happened not too far away—half an hour ago he had felt the punch of a big psychic shift somewhere in the city, even harder than the one that had knocked him down in the alley yesterday evening, when he'd been moving the refrigerator. And all of the stuffed pigs in his stateroom and galley and pilothouse had started burping and kept it up for a full ten minutes, as if their little battery-driven hearts would break.

A few years ago it had rained hard on Halloween night, and he had climbed into his skewed old car and rushed to a Montgomery Ward's and bought a dozen little stuffed-pig dolls that were supposed to oink if you "GENTLY PET MY HEAD," as the legend had read on the boxes; actually the sound they made was a prolonged burp. As soon as he had got back to the boat he had pulled them all out of their boxes and stood them on the deck, and they had soaked in the Halloween rain all night. To this day they still had the old-bacon mustiness of Halloween rain.

Now they were his watchdogs. Watchpigs.

Shadroe limped back to the stern transom and stared past the lights of the Long Beach Convention Center, trying to see the towers of Los Angeles.

He had been ashore today, dollying a second used Frigidaire to a vacant apartment on the ground floor of his building—the refrigerator he'd tried to install yesterday had fallen onto his foot, possibly breaking something in his ankle and certainly breaking the refrigerator's coils, and right there was a hundred dollars blown and the trouble of hiring somebody to take the damned inert machine away—and through an open window in another apartment he had caught a blare of familiar music. It was the theme song of the old fifties situation comedy "Ghost of a Chance," and when he had stopped to ask the tenant about it he had learned that Channel 13 was running that show again, every afternoon at three—by popular demand.

The sea breeze was suddenly chillier on his immobile face, and he realized that he was crying. He couldn't taste the tears, but he knew that if he could, they would taste like cinnamon.

One night, and it looked like being soon, he would go ashore and stretch out and take a nap on the beach. Just so there was no one around. He really didn't want anyone else to get hurt.

And miles away to the northwest, out on the dark face of the Pacific, fish were jumping out of the water—mackerel and bonita leaping high in the cold air and slapping back down onto the waves, and sprays of smelt and anchovies bursting up like scattershot; fishermen working the offshore reefs noticed the unusual phenomenon, but being on the surface of the ocean they couldn't see that the pattern was moving, rolling east across the choppy face of the sea, as if some thing were making its underwater way toward Venice Beach, and the fish were unwilling to share the water with it.

Jesus, Jacko did you get beat up again?''

Someone was shaking the boy awake, and for a few moments he

thought it was his parents, wanting to know what had happened to the friend he'd been playing with that afternoon. "He was swimming in the creek," he muttered blurrily, sitting up and rubbing his eyes. "And he went under the water and just never came up again. I waited and waited, but it was getting dark, so I came home." He knew that his parents were upset—horrified!—that he had calmly eaten dinner and gone to bed without even bothering to mention the drowning.

He wanted to explain, but . . .

"Little man, you might be more trouble than you're worth."

A dog was licking the boy's face—and abruptly, as if across a vast gulf, the boy remembered that the dog's name was Fred; and then he remembered that his own name was Koot Hootie Parganas, not . . . Al?

His own memories flooded back, reclaiming his mind. He remembered that this was 1992, and that he was eleven years old, and until last night had lived in Beverly Hills—briefly he saw again the one-armed bum in his parents' living room, and his parents' blood-streaked bodies taped into chairs—and he knew that he was sitting in the car that belonged to his new friend, Raffle; and finally he remembered that he had opened his parents' secret glass vial, and had sniffed whatever had been in it right up into his nose.

His forehead was icy with sudden sweat, and he grabbed the handle of the passenger-side window crank, thinking he was about to throw up; then Fred clambered into the back seat, and leaned between the two front seats to lick Kootie's cheek again. Oddly, that made the boy feel better. He just breathed deeply, and alternately clenched and opened his hands. Whatever had happened to him was slowing down, tapering off.

"I'm okay," he said carefully. "Nightmare. Hi, Fred."

"*Hello, Kootie,*" said Raffle in a falsetto voice, and after a moment Kootie realized that the man was speaking for the dog. "Fred don't know to call you Jacko," explained Raffle in his own voice.

The boy managed a fragile smile.

Memories from a past life? he wondered. Visions? Maybe there was LSD in that vial!

But these were just forlorn, wishful notions. He knew with intimate immediacy what had happened.

He had inhaled some kind of ghost, the ghost of an old man who had lived a long time ago, and Kootie had briefly lost his own consciousness in the sudden onslaught of all the piled-up memories as the old man's whole life had flashed before Kootie's eyes. *Kootie* had not ever watched a playmate drown—that had been one of the earliest of the old man's memories.

A shout of "Gee-haw!" and the snap of a whip as the driver kept

the six-horse team moving, tugging a barge along the Milan canal, and
the warm summer breeze up from the busy canal basin reeked of tanning
hides and fresh-brewing beer . . .

Kootie forced the vision down. Milan was the name of a place in
Italy, but this had been in . . . Ohio?

and a caravan of covered wagons, which he knew were about to head
west, to find gold in California . . .

Kootie coughed harshly, spraying blood onto the dashboard.

"Oh, dammit, Jacko. You sick? I don't need a sick kid. . . ."

"No," said Kootie, suddenly afraid that the man might order him out
of the car right here. "I'm fine." He leaned forward and swiped at the
blood drops with his sleeve. "Like I said, it was just a nightmare." He
closed his eyes carefully, but the intrusive memories seemed to have
trickled to a stop. Only the last few, the chronologically earliest ones,
had hit him slowly enough to be comprehensible. "Are we gonna do
some more business tonight?"

After a few moments Raffle gave him a doubtful smile. "Well, okay,
yeah, I believe we will. After dark, and until ten o'clock, at least, a
homeless dad-and-son tableau has gotta be worth booyah, out west of
the 405 where the guilty rich folks live. You want to eat?"

Kootie realized that in fact he was very hungry. "Oh, yes, please,"
he said.

"Great." Raffle got out of the car, walked around to the front, and
lifted the hood. "I trust you like Mexican cuisine," he called.

"Love it!" Kootie called back, hoping nothing was wrong with the
car. His parents had often taken him to Mexican restaurants, though of
course they had made sure he ordered only vegetarian things like chiles
rellenos, not cooked in lard. He was picturing bowls of corn chips and
chunky red salsa on a table, and he wanted to get there very soon.

Now Raffle was coming back and getting inside, but he had not closed
the hood, and he was carrying a foil-wrapped package which, Kootie
realized when the man sat down and began gingerly unwrapping it, was
hot and smelled like chili and cilantro.

"Burritos," Raffle said. "I buy these cold in the morning and drive
around all day with 'em wedged in between the manifold and the carb.
Plenty hot by dinnertime."

Newspapers from underfoot turned out to be informal place mats, and
silverware was a couple of plastic forks from the console tray; unlike
Raffle's "pipes," the forks had obviously not ever been considered
disposable.

Kootie made himself stop imagining a hot plate with a couple of
enchiladas swimming in red sauce and melted cheese. This burrito was

hot, at least; and the spices nearly concealed the faint taste of motor oil and exhaust fumes.

He wondered if the ghostly intruder in his head was aware of the events happening out here in Kootie's world; and for just a moment he had the impression of . . . of someone profoundly horrified in a long-feared hell. Kootie found himself picturing walking quickly past a cemetery at night, and being afraid to sleep for more than an hour at a time, and, somehow, sitting crouched on the cowcatcher of an old locomotive racing through a cold night.

Kootie shuddered, and after that he just concentrated on the burrito, and on thwarting the dog's cheerful interest in the food, and on the shadows on the dark street outside the car windows.

CHAPTER 11

"You may not have lived much under the sea—" ("I haven't," said Alice)—
"and perhaps you were never even introduced to a lobster—" (Alice began
to say "I once tasted—"but checked herself hastily, and said, "No,
never")—"so you can have no idea what a delightful thing a Lobster-
Quadrille is!"

—Lewis Carroll,
Alice's Adventures in Wonderland

In Wilmington the glow of dawn was held back by the yellow flares of the Naval Fuel Reserve burn, huge flames gouting out of towering pipes at the top of a futuristic structure of white metal scaffolding and glaring sodium-vapor lights; below it and inland, on the residential streets around Avalon and B Street, shaggy palm trees screened the old Spanish-style houses from some of the all-night glare.

Pete Sullivan tilted a pan of boiling water over his McDonald's cup and watched the instant-coffee crystals foam brown when the water hit them. When the cup was nearly full he put the pan back on the tiny propane stove and turned off the burner.

As he sipped the coffee, he switched off the overhead light and then pulled back the curtain and looked out through the van's side window at this Los Angeles morning.

The money-scapular was pasted to his sweaty chest, for he hadn't known this area well enough to sleep comfortably with a window open.

Last night he had driven aimlessly south from his early-evening nap stop at La Cienega Park, and only after he'd found himself getting off the 405 at Long Beach Boulevard did he consciously realize that he must have come down here to look at the *Queen Mary.*

To put that off, he had resolved to have something good for dinner first, and then had been shocked to find that the Joe Jost's bar and restaurant on Third Street was gone. He'd made do with a pitcher of beer and a cold ham sandwich at some pizza parlor, disconsolately thinking of the Polish sausage sandwiches and the pickled eggs and the pretzels-with-peppers that Joe Jost's used to have.

At last he had got back into the van and driven down Magnolia all the way to the empty south end of Queen's Highway and stopped in the left lane, by the chain-link fence; he had slapped his shirt pocket to be sure he still had the dried thumb in the Bull Durham sack, and then he'd got out and stood on the cooling asphalt and stared through the fence, across the nearly empty parking lot, at the *Queen Mary.*

Her three canted stacks, vividly red in the floodlights, had stood up behind and above the trees and the fake-Tudor spires of the ''London-towne'' shopping area, and he had wondered if Loretta deLarava was at home in her castle tonight.

The breeze had been cold out in the dark by the far fence, but he had been glad of his distance and anonymity—even if deLarava had been standing out on the high port docking wing and looking out this way, she couldn't have sensed him, not with the thumb in his pocket and the plaster hands in the van right behind him. Houdini's mask was only in effect draped around him right now; he wasn't really wearing it, wasn't a decoy-Houdini as the wearer of the mask was intended to be; but even so the mask would blur his psychic silhouette, fragment it like an image in a shattered mirror.

You've hurt my family enough, he had thought at her. *Fully, fully enough. Let us rest in peace.*

The beer had made him sleepy, and, after eventually getting back in the van, he had driven only a little distance west, across the Cerritos Channel and up Henry Ford Avenue to Alameda, which was called B Street down here in lower Wilmington, before pulling over to a curb and turning the engine off and locking up.

The rattling roar of a low helicopter swept past overhead now, and for an instant he glimpsed the vertical white beam of a searchlight sweeping across the yards and rooftops and alleys. Somewhere nearby a rooster crowed hoarsely, and was echoed by another one farther away.

Sullivan wondered if Los Angeles had ever been really synchronized with the time and space and *scale* of the real world. Even finding a men's room, he remembered now as he sipped this first cup of coffee, had often been an adventure. Once in a Chinese restaurant he had trudged down a straight and very long flight of stairs to get to one, and then discovered that a number of doors led out of the tiny, white-tiled subterranean room—he had made sure to remember which doorway he had come in through, so that he wouldn't leave by the wrong one and wind up in some unknown restaurant or bakery or laundry, blocks from where he had started; and one time in a crowded little low-ceilinged Mexican restaurant on Sixth he had pushed his way through the REST ROOMS door to find himself in a cavernous dark warehouse or something, as big as an airplane hangar, empty except for a collection of old earthmoving tractors in the middle distance—looking behind him he had seen that the restaurant was just a plywood box, attached to the street-side wall, inside the inexplicably enormous room. His Spanish had not been good enough to frame a question about it, and Sukie had been irritably drunk, and when he'd gone back a month or so later the place had been closed.

He lit a cigarette now and wondered if Sukie really had, actually, killed herself.

Remotely he remembered how close the two of them had become—after their father

died

when they were seven years old—during the years they'd spent in several foster homes. They had never had a "psychic link" or anything like that, but the world was so coldly divided between *us two* and *all of them* that the twins could read each other's moods instantly, even over the phone, and either one of them could unthinkingly and correctly order for the other at any restaurant, and the random letters on passing license plates would always suggest identical words to each of them.

Now Sukie was probably dead, and still his first response to the thought was *Good riddance.* He was surprised and uncomfortable with the vehemence of the thought.

The twins had begun to differ when they were going to Hollywood High School, and it had become clear that the money their father had left them would be used up before they would finish college in about 1974. Sukie had never been interested in boyfriends, and she resented Pete spending money and time on things like dances. And the girls Pete went out with always dumped him before long, so the whole effort of trying to pursue romances really had seemed like a costly waste.

Eventually he had got a clue to why the girls had always dumped him.

He and Sukie had supported themselves through their last years in City College with jobs at pizza parlors and miniature golf courses and pet stores, but even after they'd graduated and got hired by Loretta deLarava for substantial salaries, they had continued to be roommates. Sukie continued to have no interest in the sex that was opposite to her, and Pete had continued to have meager success in pursuing the sex that was opposite to him.

And then in the summer of '86, Pete had got engaged.

Judy Nording was a film editor who had done postproduction work for deLarava since the late seventies, and Pete had got into the habit of drifting past the editing rooms when she would be working. Somehow he had known that he'd be wise to do this visiting when Sukie was off on some solo errand.

Judy had been two years younger than Pete, but she had made him feel naive and stodgy and *incurious*—she not only knew everything about editing and mixing, but also knew nearly as much as he did about lights and colored gels and generator trucks and on-site electrical problems. And she was tall and slim, and when he strolled into her office she had a casual way of shoving her chair back and throwing one long blue-jeaned leg over the editing bench, with her ankle between the rewind posts, and the tight denim that sheathed her calf glowing in the glare from the light well. Her long blond hair was generally tied back in a braid.

He had been fascinated when she'd shown him things like the xenongas projection bulbs that worked under eight atmospheres of pressure, and that burned so hot that they reconfigured ordinary air into ozone, which had to be piped up through the ceiling by exhaust fans; and she had taken him down to the wide Foley stage in front of the screen in the projection room, and shown him the dozen floor-sections that could be lifted away to expose yards-wide movable wooden trays, so that the actors who were dubbing English dialogue onto foreign movies could audibly plod through sand while they spoke their lines onto the new soundtrack, or walk clickingly over marble, or even, if the last partition was lifted away, slosh noisily through a pool of water.

She had lived with half-a-dozen other young people in an old three-story Victorian house off Melrose, near the studio; even in '86 the house and yard had been fenced in with chain-link and barbed wire. Eventually Judy had given Pete a key to the front gate.

Sukie had been furious when he first spent the night there—but as it became clear that her brother and Judy Nording were actually likely to get married, Sukie had apparently changed her mind about the woman, taking her out for "girl-lunches" and shopping expeditions.

Pete had been naively pleased that the two women were getting along, and he was seeing Judy every night.

Then one evening at Miceli's, an Italian restaurant off Hollywood Boulevard, Judy had been inexplicably cold and abrupt with him; he had not been able to demand or plead or wheedle the reason from her, and after he had sulkily driven her home and gone back to his and Sukie's apartment, he had shut himself into his room with a bottle of Sukie's Wild Turkey bourbon and had laboriously and painstakingly written a maudlin sonnet to his suddenly hostile fiancée. At about two in the morning he had opened the door, thrown all the drafts of the sonnet into the kitchen wastebasket, and lurched off to bed.

The next morning he had been awakened at about ten by intermittent laughter, and a harsh voice droning on and on, outside his bedroom window, in the alley; but he had not opened his eyes and dragged himself out of bed until he had recognized the lines the voice was reciting. Then, his face cold with nausea and disoriented horror, he had reeled to the window and squinted out.

Apparently Sukie had taken out the trash.

Some ragged old man had found the drafts of Pete's sonnet in the Dumpster and, in mock-theatrical tones and with exaggerated grimacings, was reading the verses to an audience of about half a dozen unkempt men and women, who were bracing themselves on their shopping carts to keep from falling down with laughter.

Pete hadn't been able to work up the peremptory tone to tell them to go away, and neither could he bear to go back to bed and listen to more of the recital, so he had defeatedly set about showering and shaving and making coffee. He had eventually got to deLarava's studio at about noon—to discover that Judy Nording had quit. When he rushed to her house he was told that she had packed up her bed and stereo and books in a U-Haul trailer and had simply driven away. By nightfall he had established that none of her friends, nor even her parents in Northridge, would admit to knowing where she might have gone.

Upon hearing of it, Sukie had denounced Nording as a teasing, fickle bitch and probable sociopath; and under her indignation she had been obviously pleased and relieved.

In November, Pete had located Judy Nording—she'd been working for a news station in Seattle, and he had flown up there and surprised her on her front doorstep one rainy evening when she was returning from the studio. She had burst out sobbing at the sight of him, and he had walked her to a bar across the street. Over a calming gin-and-tonic she had stiffly apologized for disappearing the way she had done, but insisted that she had had no choice, after finding out about his previous marriages, and his children, and his bisexuality. Sukie had told her all of it, Nording had assured him—Sukie had taken her to one last lunch and had shown her the wedding announcements, pictures of the many kids, and had even brought along a man who'd been one of Pete's ill-treated gay lovers. Sukie, Nording explained, had felt that she ought to know.

Now, sitting on the narrow bed in his van six years later, Sullivan winced as he remembered that *he had not been able to convince Nording that Sukie's stories had been lies.* It hadn't really mattered anymore, for Nording was by that time involved with some guy at the station, and Pete himself had begun dating a young woman who worked in a Westwood restaurant—but though he had laughed, and spoken earnestly, and shouted, and thrown a handful of change onto the table and waved at the telephone, during the course of a long half hour in that Seattle bar, he had *not* been able to convince Judy Nording that he really was single, childless, and heterosexual.

Pete had been glad Sukie hadn't gone on to attribute to him something like heroin dealing, or murder, for Nording would probably have believed those things too, and called the police on him.

He had flown back down to Los Angeles later that night. Nothing about the scene he'd then had with Sukie in their shared apartment had gone the way he had indignantly planned. Sukie had cried, and told him why she had chased Judy away, and, hanging on to his jacket sleeve as he struggled toward the front door, had kept on telling him.

He gulped the last of the hot coffee, and decided against another cup. Sukie had always had a couple of cups of coffee first thing in the morning, and then followed them with two or three cold beers "to keep anything from catching up."

He could see now that Sukie had been an alcoholic by the time they'd got out of college in '75. By the early eighties, when the twins had been working for Loretta deLarava for a while, they had been known to some of their friends as "Teet and Toot"—Pete was "Teet," for teetotaller, and Sukie was "Toot" for off-on-a-toot.

He was sure that he must have tried on a number of occasions to talk her into at least cutting back on her drinking, but this morning he could remember only one time. During a break at a shoot somewhere in Redondo Beach, years before she would wreck his engagement to Judy Nording, he had timidly suggested that one more slug from her bourbon-filled thermos bottle might be enough for the day, or at least for the rest of the morning, and she had said, "What you don't know can't hurt you." She had given him a strange look then—a sort of doubtful smile, with her eyebrows hiked up in the center and down at the outer edges, as if affectionately forgiving him for having asked a naively rude question, one that could have elicited a devastating answer.

He stubbed his cigarette out in a little tin ashtray on the narrow sink, then stood up and pulled his pants on. Later today he'd have to get a shower in some college gym, but right now he wanted to find some early breakfast at a place with an accessible men's room . . . and then have a look around the city.

He put on his shoes and a shirt and ducked between the front seats to pull back the windshield curtain. The windows of the houses on this street were still dark, though the dawn was beginning to fade the orange glow of the flares crowning the Naval Fuel Reserve.

As he sat down in the driver's seat and switched on the engine, he was suddenly, deeply certain that Sukie had indeed killed herself three nights ago. His heartbeat didn't speed up, and all he did was light another cigarette as he fluttered the gas pedal to keep the cold engine running, but quietly and all at once he had realized that for decades she had been wanting to be dead—maybe ever since their father died, in 1959.

A.O.P., dude. Accelerate Outta Problems. She hadn't exactly accelerated out of that one. It had taken her thirty-two years.

And now Sukie was a ghost. Sullivan hoped she would rest quietly and asleep, and not be searched out and snorted up by some East Coast deLarava, nor stay up, awake and agitated, and eventually grow by slow accretion into one of the lurching, imbecilic creatures such as he had seen at the Houdini ruins yesterday.

He let off on the gas pedal. The engine seemed to be running smoothly. He turned on the lights, squinted at the green radiance of the gauges, then clanked the engine into gear and nosed the van away from the curb into the still street. May as well head up to Sunset and see if Tiny Naylor's is still there, he thought.

In the Greyhound bus station on Seventh, Angelica Anthem Elizalde stood by the glass doors off to the street side of the ticket counter, down at the end where the word BOLETOS was printed very big over the small word TICKETS on the overhead sign.

For the last several hours she had tried to nap in one or another of the cagelike chairs, or peered out the doors at the empty nighttime street, or paced the shiny linoleum floor while humbled families gathered around Gate 8, to eventually all pile aboard some bus bound for God knew where, and then after half an hour or so be replaced by more shuffling, apologetic, fugitive families. Their luggage was old thrift-store suitcases, and cardboard boxes hastily sealed with glossy brown tape, and woven-nylon sausage bags so stained that they might plausibly have contained actual sausages; Elizalde kept expecting to see goats on rope leashes, too, and wicker cages full of live chickens.

After some time she had convinced herself that the hands of the clock on the wall did move, but she had been wearily sure that they moved with supernatural slowness. Without believing it very much at all, she had played with the thought that she had died on the bus, that the jolt that had waked her up as they'd been passing through Victorville had been a massive cerebral hemorrhage, and everything she had experienced since that moment was only after-death hallucination; in that case yesterday's eerie sensation of momentarily anticipating events had probably been pre-stroke phenomena. This fluorescently bright bus station boarding area, with its cage-chairs and its chrome-and-tile restrooms and its jarringly jaunty posters of rocketing buses, would be the antechamber of Hell. This night would never end, and eventually she would defeatedly join one of the crowds of departing families and go away with them to whatever lightless tenements and government-project housing Hell consisted of. (She could offer her apologies to Frank Rocha in discorporate person.)

But now, standing by the glass doors that faced Seventh, she could see that the sodium-yellow-stained blackness of the sky had begun to glow a deep blue in the east; white lights shone now in the liquor store across the street—presumably the employees were preparing for the dawn rush—and a couple of the hotel-room windows above the store were luminous amber rectangles. Los Angeles was wearily getting up, she thought, shambling to the bathroom, lip-smacking the false teeth into place, strapping on the prosthetic limbs . . .

A whisper of cool breeze breathed between the aluminum doorframes into the stale atmosphere of the bus station, and somehow even down here south of Beverly and west of the L.A. River, it carried a scent of newly opened morning glories.

The day, the staring Western day, is born, she thought. *Awake, for morning in the bowl of night/ has fired the shot that puts the stars to flight.*

She jumped, and then the public-address speakers snapped on to announce another departure.

With a rueful sigh she abandoned the notion that she was dead. Another few cups of vending-machine coffee, and then it would be time to start walking.

Lobsters and crabs had begun crawling out of the Venice Beach surf at dawn.

Under the brightening tangerine and spun-metal sky, the streets were still in dimness, and for a silent few moments at six-thirty a ripple of deeper shadows stepped across the uneven city blocks as the streetlights sensed the approaching day and one by one winked out. NO PARKING signs had kept the curbs of Main and Pacific clear all night, but on the side streets, and in the tiny dirt lots between houses, cars sat parked at whatever crooked angles had let them fit, and motorcycles leaned on their kickstands right up against walls and fence posts and car fenders.

On the rust-streaked walls of the old buildings, the little iron diamonds of earthquake-reinforcement bolts studded the old stucco. The painted Corinthian columns of the porticoed shop fronts facing Windward Avenue were faded in the half-light, and the littered expanse of the street was empty except for an occasional shapeless figure trudging along or stolidly pushing a trash-filled shopping cart. Occasional early-morning joggers, always flanked by at least one bounding dog, scuffed down the middle of the street toward the open lots facing the narrow lane that was Ocean Front Walk.

The lots were ringed with empty metal-pipe frameworks and cages that would be occupied with vendors' booths later in the morning, and the only color in the scene now was the vividly shaded and highlighted graffiti that was gradually engulfing the once-red Dumpsters lined up against the building walls.

Out past the stark volleyball poles and the cement bike trails was the open beach, not taking clear footprints now but showing clearly the sharp broken-star prints of bird feet and the crumble-edged footprints of joggers who had been out when the dew had still clung to the sand.

The waves were low and the blue ocean stretched out to the brightening horizon, undimmed by any fog. A jet rising steeply into the sky from LAX to the south was a dark splinter, with a point of white light at the wingtip shining as bright as Venus in the dawn sky. Fishing boats moved past in the middle distance as silently and slowly as the minute hand of a watch, and a fat pelican bobbed on the waves a hundred yards offshore.

And crabs and lobsters were climbing over the sprawled and trailing piles of coppery kelp. Seagulls shouted and glided low over the spectacle, their cries ringing emptily in the chilly air, and sandpipers swiveled their pencil beaks and high-stepped away along the surf edge. A shaggy golden retriever and a Great Dane had stopped to bark at the armored animals who had come clambering and antennae-waving up the sand, and the owners of the dogs stopped to peer and back away. More lobsters and crabs were tumbling up in the low waves, and the ones

who had come out first were already up above the flat brown dampness
and were floundering in the dry sand. A John Deere tractor had been
chugging up the beach from the direction of the pier and the lifeguard
headquarters, dragging a leveler across the night-randomized dunes and
gullies, but the driver had put the engine into neutral and let the tires
drag to a halt when he noticed the leggy exodus.

Then a wave began to mount, out on the face of the water.

It was a green hump against the horizon, rather than a line, more like
the bow-swell of an invisible tanker aiming to make landfall here than
a wave rolling in to crash indiscriminately along the whole length of
the Santa Monica Bay coastline. Only when the pelican was lifted on
it, and squawked and spread his wings at his sudden elevation, did the
people on the beach look up, and then they hastily moved back up the
flat beach toward the gray monolith of the Recreation Center.

The tall green swell grew taller, seeming to gather up all the visible
water as it swept silently toward the shore. As the wave crested, and
finally began to break apart into spray at the curling top edge and roar-
ingly exhale as it leaned forward against the resistance of the air, a long
form was visible rolling inside the solid water—and when the wave
boomingly crashed on the sand, surged far up the slope in hissing foam
and then was sucked away back to the receding sea, a big steely *thing*
had been left behind on the brown, bubbling sand.

It shifted and settled, and then didn't move.

It was a fish. That much was agreed upon by the half-dozen people
who timidly approached after the thing had lain inert on the sand for a
full minute and no further big waves gathered out at sea—but the fish
was twenty or thirty feet long and as thick as a thigh-high stack of
mattresses, and its body and head were covered with bony plates rather
than scales. No one in the knot of spectators could even guess what
species it might be. It appeared to be dead, but it looked so like some
monster from the pages of an illustrated book on the Cretaceous period
that no one approached the thing within twenty feet. Even the dogs
stayed away from it, and made do with bounding away to bark busily
at the fleeing lobsters and crabs.

For a while, water leaked out of the fish's blunt face from between
its open, armored jaws, but now there was no motion at all to the creature.

An old woman in a parka stared for a while, then backed away from
the big and vaguely repulsive spectacle. "I'll go get someone," she said
querulously. "A lifeguard, or someone."

"Yeah," called a young man. "Maybe he can do CPR on it."

Up the slope, on the dry sand closer to the sidewalks and the handball courts and the sea-facing row of shops and cafés and blocky old apartment buildings, the panicky crabs and lobsters were turning in disoriented circles and waving their claws in the air.

BOOK TWO

Get a Life

Father got a lot of amusement out of lighting firecrackers, throwing them at our bare feet and making us dance when they exploded. He had it all his way one Fourth. After that we ganged up and made him take off his own shoes and stockings and do his dancing on the lawn while we three lighted firecrackers at his feet.
        —Charles Edison,
            The New York Times, September 26, 1926

CHAPTER 12

"And what does it live on?"
  "Weak tea with cream in it."
  A new difficulty came into Alice's head. "Supposing it couldn't find any?" she suggested.
  "Then it would die, of course."
  "But that must happen very often," Alice remarked thoughtfully.
  "It always happens," said the Gnat.

—Lewis Carroll,
Through the Looking-Glass

The sky was still pale with dawn when Solomon Shadroe turned his old gray Chevy Nova left from Ocean Boulevard onto Twenty-First Place and immediately turned left again into the parking lot of his apartment building. From long practice he was able to do the maneuver smoothly, in spite of the the car's rear end swinging out wide. The locator pins holding the rear axle to the springs had broken off long ago, and so the rear axle was no longer parallel to the front one; when driving straight ahead down a straight lane, the car was always at an angle to the center line, like a planing blade moving along a level board.

The three-story building dated from the 1920s, and had once been a hospital. The rooms were mismatched in size, and over the years he had cut out new windows and doors, laid two new floors across the elevator shaft to make three closets, and hung new partitions or torn old ones out, so no styles matched and no hallway and few rooms had the same flooring from one end to the other; but rents were low, and the place was shaded with big old untrimmed palm and carob trees, and the peeling stucco front was largely covered with purple-flowering bougainvillea. Any tenants that stayed long, and he had some who had been here for a decade or more, were the sort that would generally do their own repairs; the old-timers called the place Solville, and seemed to take obscure pride in having weathered countless roof leaks, power failures, and stern inspections by the city.

Shadroe parked on his customary patch of oil-stained dirt, clambered out of the old car, and limped ponderously to his office, pausing to crouch and pick up the newspaper in front of the door.

Inside, he turned on the old black-and-white TV set. While it warmed up he listened to the birds in the trees outside his office window—the mockingbirds seemed to be shrilling *cheeseburger, cheeseburger, cheeseburger*, and the doves were softly saying *Curaçao, Curaçao, Curaçao*.

Curaçao was some orange-flavored liqueur, he believed. He couldn't recall ever having drunk any, and it probably wouldn't complement a cheeseburger, but for a moment he envied all the people who had the option of choosing that breakfast, and who would be able to taste it.

He sighed, picked up a cellophane bag, and shook half-a-dozen Eat-'Em-&-Weep balls—red-hot cinnamon jawbreaker candies—into a coffeepot, filled it with water from the faucet he had piped in last year, and put it on a hot plate to brew; then he lowered his considerable bulk into his easy chair and unfolded the newspaper.

The front section he read cursorily—Ross Perot was back in the presidential race, claiming that he had only dropped out three months ago because Bush's people were supposedly planning to wreck his daughter's wedding; "Electrified Rail Lines Would Energize Edison's Profits"; a Bel-Air couple named Parganas had been found tortured and killed in their home, and police were searching for their son, whose name Shadroe didn't bother to puzzle out but seemed to be something like Patootie, poor kid; country singer Roger Miller had died at fifty-six—that was too bad, Shadroe had met him a few times in the sixties, and he'd seemed like a nice guy. He was about to toss it and pick up the Metro section when he noticed something in a little box on the front page:

FANS SEARCHING FOR "SPOOKY" FROM OLD SITCOM

Attention Baby-Boomers! It worked for Father Knows Best *and* Leave It to Beaver *and* Gilligan's Island, *didn't it?*

Plans are afoot for another reunion show!

Led by independent television producer Loretta deLarava, fans of the situation comedy Ghost of a Chance, *which ran from 1955 to 1960 on CBS, are searching for the only elusive—and, some would say, the only indispensable—actor from the old show. They've been unable to locate Nicky Bradshaw, who played Spooky, the teenage ghost whose madcap antics kept the dull-witted Johnson family hopping. In the thirty-two years since the show's cancellation, the "Spooky" character has taken a place in pop mythology comparable to "Eddie Haskell" (Ken Osmond, Leave it to Beaver), "Aunt Bee" (Frances Bavier, The Andy Griffith Show) and "Hop Sing" (Victor Sen Yung, Bonanza).*

Bradshaw, godson to the late filmmaker Arthur Patrick Sullivan, had been a child actor before Ghost of a Chance *propelled him into millions of American living rooms, but he left showbiz in the mid 1960s to become an attorney. He disappeared in 1975, apparently under the cloud of some minor legal infractions on which he was due to be arraigned.*

The police have had no luck in locating Bradshaw, but deLarava is certain that Spooky's many fans can succeed where the law can't! DeLarava wants to assure Bradshaw that most of the charges (all having to do with receiving stolen goods— for shame, Spooky!) have been dropped, and that his salary for doing the Ghost of a Chance Reunion Show *will easily offset all lingering penalties. And—she adds with a twinkle in her eye—who knows? This reunion show just might develop into a whole new series!*

There was also the telephone number of a Find Spooky hotline.

Solomon Shadroe put down the front section of the paper and, with a steady hand, poured some of his Eat-'Em-&-Weep tea into a coffee cup. The dissolved candies gave the stuff the bright red color of transmission fluid. After a long sip he chewed up a couple of fresh ones out of the bag. The jawbreakers, and the tea he brewed from them, were all he had eaten and drunk for seventeen years. He never turned on the light when he went to the bathroom here, nor in the head on his boat.

Heavy footsteps clumped overhead, letting him know that Johanna was up. He reached across the table for his long-handled broom and, squinting upward to find an undented section of the plaster, thumped the end of the broom against the ceiling. Faintly he heard her yell some acknowledgment.

He put the broom down and fished a little flat can of Goudie Scottish snuff out of a pile of receipts on the desk. He twisted the cap until the holes in the rim were lined up, then shook some of the brown powder onto the back of his hand and effortlully snorted it up his nose. He couldn't smell or taste the stuff anymore, of course, but it was still a comforting habit.

He glanced at the three stuffed pigs he had set up on the empty bookshelves in here. They weren't burping right now, at least.

Can she find me, he thought. I live on water . . . but she lives right over there on the *Queen Mary*. I make Johanna do all the shopping, and anyway deLarava wouldn't be likely to recognize me these days. And she'd have a hard time tracking me—when I do drive, my car always points off to the left of wherever I'm really going. Still, I'd better take some measures. It would be hard at my age and in my condition to find another slip for the boat, and it'd probably be impossible ever again to get out to the Hollywood Cemetery and visit the old man's grave— though even now I don't dare sweep the dust and leaves off the marker.

When the knock came at the door he clomped his uninjured foot twice on the floor, and Johanna let herself in.

Shadroe inhaled. "Draw me a bath, sweetie," he said levelly, "and put ice in it." Again he drew air into his lungs. "Today I gotta start re-wiring the units, and then I think I'll re-pipe the downstairs ones so the water's going north instead of south." His voice had gone reedy, and he paused to take in more air. "If I can find the ladder, I think I'll rearrange all the TV antennas later in the week."

Johanna brushed back her long black hair. "What for you wanna do that, lover?" The seams of her orange leotards had burst at the hips, and she scratched at a bulge of tattooed skin. "After the painting men the other month—your tenants are gonna go crazy."

"Tell 'em . . . tell 'em November rent's on me. They've put up with worse." *Gasp.* "As to why—look at this." He bent down with a grunt and picked up the front section of the paper. "Here," he whispered, pointing out the article. "I need to change the hydraulic and electro- magnetic . . ." *Gasp.* ". . . *fingerprint* of this place again."

She read it slowly, moving her lips. "Oh, baby!" she finally said in dismay. She crossed to his chair and knelt and hugged him. He patted her hair three times and then let his hand drop. "Why can't she forget about you?"

"I'm the only one," he said patiently, "who knows who she is."

"Couldn't you . . . *blackmail* her? Say you've put the eddivence in a box in a bank, and if you die the noosepapers will get it?"

"—I suppose," said Shadroe, staring at the dark TV screen. It was set on CBS, channel 2, with the brightness turned all the way down to blessedly featureless black. "But nobody thought it was . . . murder, even at the time." He yawned so widely that pink tears ran down his gray cheeks. "What I *should* do," he went on, "is go to her office when she's there''—he paused to inhale again—''and then take a nap in the waiting room.''

"Oh, baby, no! All those innocent people!"

Too exhausted to speak anymore, Shadroe just waved his hand dismissingly.

CHAPTER 13

"If I wasn't real," Alice said—half laughing through her tears, it
all seemed so ridiculous—"I shouldn't be able to cry."
"I hope you don't suppose those are real *tears?"* Tweedledum
interrupted in a tone of great contempt.

—Lewis Carroll,
Through the Looking-Glass

If you follow the Long Beach Freeway south from the 405, the old
woman thought, you're behind L.A.'s scenes. To your left is a scattered
line of bowing tan grasshoppers that are oil-well pumping units, with
the machined-straight Los Angeles River beyond, and to your right, train
tracks parallel you across a narrow expanse of scrub-brush dirt. High-
voltage cables are strung from the points of big steel asterisks atop the
power poles, and the fenced-in yards beyond the tracks are crowded
with unmoored boxcars. It's all just supply, with no dressing-up. Even
when the freeway breaks up and you're on Harbor Scenic Drive, the
lanes are scary with roaring trucks pulling big semitrailers, and the horizon to your right is clawed with the skeletal towers of the quayside
cranes. The air smells of crude oil, though by now you can probably
see the ocean.

Loretta deLarava sighed and wondered, not for the first time, what
the stark logo on the cranes stood for—ITS was stenciled in giant black
letters on each of them, easily readable across the water from where she
stood high up on the Promenade Deck of the *Queen Mary.*

Its? she thought. *What's?* Will *it* be coming back for its branded
children one of these days? She imagined some foghorn call throbbing
in from the sea, and the cranes all ponderously lifting their cagelike
arms in obedient worship.

She gripped the rail of the open deck and looked straight down. A hundred feet below her, the narrow channel between the *Queen Mary* and the concrete dock was bridged by mooring lines and electric cables and orange hoses wide enough for a kid to crawl through. Down there to her left the dock crowded right up against the black cliff of the hull, and the morning shift was unloading boxes from trucks. Faintly, over the shouts of the seagulls, she could hear the men's impatient voices, not far enough away below.

The mechanics of supply and waste disposal, she thought. Always there, if you look.

She turned away from the southward view and looked along the worn teak deck, and she took another bite of the half pound of walnut fudge she'd just bought. In a few hours the deck would be crowded with tourists, all wearing shorts even in October, with their noisy kids, stumbling around dripping ice cream on the deck and gaping at the glassed-in displays of the first-class staterooms and wondering what the bidets were for. They wouldn't recognize elegance, she thought, if it walked up and bit them in the ass.

During World War II the *Queen Mary* had been a troopship, and the first-class swimming pool had been drained and stacked with bunks, all the way up to the arched ceiling. Before that, in the thirties, the ceiling had been lined with mother-of-pearl, so that guests seemed to be swimming under a magically glittering sky; but the top shelf of soldiers had picked it all away, and now the ceiling was just white tile.

She tried to imagine the ship crowded with men in army uniforms, and trestle tables and folding chairs jamming the pillared first-class dining room under the tall mural of the Atlantic, on which two little crystal ships day by day were supposed to trace the paths of the *Queen Mary* and the *Queen Elizabeth*. The crystal ships had probably been stopped in those days, with around-the-clock shifts of soldiers inattentively eating Spam below.

The unconsidered life, she thought as she took another bite of the fudge, is not worth living. And in spite of herself she wondered if the soldiers would have considered her.

The tourists didn't. The tourists didn't know that she lived aboard, on B Deck, in one of the nicest staterooms; they just thought she was another of themselves, fatter than most. And sometimes older.

Such tourists as might be around on this upcoming Saturday would at least see her in a position of some importance, when she would be directing the filming of her *Ship of Ghosts* feature aboard the ship.

Her scalp itched, and she scratched carefully over her ear.

It was time to be starting for the studio. She wrapped up the end of the fudge-brick in the waxed paper it had been served on, tucked it into her big canvas purse, and started walking toward the elevators. She had of course been careful to leave the door of her stateroom not-quite-closed, so that a push would open it, and today there was a big, diamond-studded 18-carat gold bangle on the bedside table, right where the light from the porthole would show it off. Attractive to a thief, and too heavy for a ghost. And the doors of the Lexus in the parking lot were unlocked, with the key in the ignition. Maybe today she would wind up having to rent a car to drive to work in—there was an Avis counter in the lobby area of the ship.

On Halloween of 1967 the *Queen Mary* had made her last departure from England; and for these past twenty-five years the world's grandest ocean liner had been moored at the Port of Los Angeles in Long Beach, a hotel and tourist attraction now. The Cunard line had sold her to the city for 3.2 million dollars, and had insisted that the boilers be removed so that the ship could never again sail under her own power.

Under another name Loretta deLarava had sailed aboard her in 1958, and had once danced with Robert Mitchum in the exclusive Verandah Grill at the stern, where you never ordered from the menu; the head waiter, Colin Kitching, would find you at lunch and ask what you'd like for dinner, and you could order anything you could think of, and they'd have it ready by eight.

The Verandah Grill now served hamburgers and Cokes and beer, and anybody on earth could get in. The tables and benches now were contoured sheets of vinyl-covered particleboard, and the floor was hard black rubber, with a herringbone pattern of bumps on it so people wouldn't slip on the french fries.

Her Lexus had not been stolen; and unfortunately the car telephone beeped at her while she was still on the Long Beach Freeway, within sight of the usual litter of old pickup trucks parked in the dirt by the river to her right and the usual half-dozen men on the banks with their fishing poles. DeLarava sometimes fished off the stern of the *Queen Mary*, late at night, and ate raw the big opal-eye perch and sea bass she occasionally hauled all the way up the side of the ship, but it never seemed to help. And these weary old men fishing in the poisoned Los Angeles River just seemed to mock her efforts.

She was soon crying as she held the telephone receiver to her ear, though her face as she stared through the windshield at the cars ahead of her was effortfully expressionless. More wrinkles she didn't need. She could only speak haltingly as she steered with her left hand.

"Are you still there?" buzzed the voice from the phone.

"I'm here, Neal." Why did the best vegetarian restaurant in Los Angeles have to have that name?

"So they're going to meet us for lunch at Nowhere at one," he went on. "Table for Obstadt, okay? They like the *Queen Mary* ghost show; be ready to defend this reunion-show concept, though, the 'Ghost of a Chance' thing, I don't think they view it as feasible yet." There was a click on the line. "You've got another call, Loretta—that's all I had. See you at Nowhere, at one."

"Right." The line clicked on Obstadt's end. DeLarava sniffed hard and blinked, then pushed a button on the back of the phone. "Hello?"

Over the background static of a portable telephone, she heard a steady echoing splashing. Whoever was calling her was doing so while urinating!

"Hi," came a voice, "is this Loretta deLarava?"

"Who is *this?*"

"Ms. deLarava? This is Ayres out in Venice Beach, and I don't know if this one is worth your time, but—"

"Are you *pissing* as you speak to me, Mr. Ayres?"

The noise abruptly stuttered to a stop. "No," Ayres said breathlessly. "No, of course not. Of course not."

"Good. What did you want to speak to me about?"

"Um. Oh, yeah—this may not be the kind of thing you told me to watch for, but a big goddamn fish just washed up on the beach this morning. It's about twenty feet long, apparently dead, and nobody can figure out what the hell kind of fish it is. And a bunch of lobsters and crabs crawled up out of the ocean at about the same time—they're still running around, some of 'em have got into the shops and the tennis courts. People are freaked."

DeLarava's heart was pounding, and all thought of Ayres's discourtesy was forgotten. That would have to be *him*, causing that, she thought. Coming back out of the ocean these . . . thirty-three years later. Of course this new damned smoke would finally be the beacon that would lead him ashore. And if *Pete* Sullivan is in town, that would also have helped draw him out.

"Thanks, Bernie," she croaked. She hung up the phone and began signaling for a lane change. She hadn't needed to ask *where* at Venice Beach.

She would have to call the studio and have them send a news crew to Venice, and then scoot south on the 405 to pick up Joey Webb at his creepy Signal Hill apartment. Good thing he never went anywhere.

She wasn't ready for this. Here was the old man coming out of the sea already—and Halloween was only three days off. It would definitely have to be *this* year, *this* Halloween. Would Joey *do*, would he be mask enough, all by himself? He'd probably be okay today, when she'd just be trying to see where the old man went, but what might happen on Saturday? Damn Sukie Sullivan anyway. Paranoid lush.

DeLarava's scalp was itching again, under the rubber band that encircled it under her brushed-over hair, and when she scratched, the rubber band slipped upward and jumped to the top of her head, where it sat slackly holding her hair up in an effect that she knew from past experience looked like a miniature thatched hut. She couldn't pull the rubber band back down into place before she got off the freeway—it took two hands, and she would want to fix her hair too.

She had started wearing a rubber band around her scalp when she turned forty (*in 1966!*), as a measure to keep her facial skin pulled taut. It had perhaps never worked very well for that purpose, but she had noticed that the cerebral constriction of it seemed to keep her thoughts aligned, keep her personality from fragmenting into half a dozen frightened little girls. And when old triumphs began (irrationally!) to shake up silty clouds of guilt and shame in her thoughts, a rubber band or two around her skull helped to slow the involuntary tears.

But fresh tears were leaking out of her eyes now. At least I've got an excuse to miss the Nowhere lunch, she thought. *Alert businesswoman, consummate professional; had to go cover the story of the crabs terrorizing Venice.* And maybe my stateroom will be robbed today.

In '46, when she'd had her other name and had still been waiting tables in Fort Worth, her little rented house had been broken into. The burglars had emptied her jewelry box onto the bed, and had flung her best clothes onto the floor, and had even left a greasy handprint on her not-yet-paid-off radio—*but they had not taken anything at all.* Obviously she had had nothing, perhaps *had been* nothing, worth their attention.

The unconsidered life is not worth living. She had got consideration a number of times since then; she'd been robbed of diamonds, Krugerrands, fine cars—and she had gone to bed with a number of men, especially during her brief period of fame, and had even briefly been . . .

She shied away from memories of her marriage, and of a starkly sunny summer afternoon at Venice Beach.

But none of it had ever been enough to *confirm* her.

She knew it was Houdini's fault.

The southbound 405 was crowded, and she had to slow down to a full stop in the right lane. She sat there expressionlessly leaking tears for a full minute before the cars ahead of her began to move, and only then, too late to fix it, did she remember her disordered hair. She glanced at the driver of a Volkswagen trundling along in the lane to her left, and wondered if he was puzzled by her unusual coif, but he was oblivious of her. That didn't help at all.

The day after the day after tomorrow would be her seventy-seventh birthday. She had been born on Halloween in Grace Hospital in Detroit at 1:26 in the afternoon, in, apparently, the very instant that the famous magician and escape artist Harry Houdini was expiring in the same hospital.

And she had been robbed of her birth-ghosts, the psychic shells of herself that had been thrown off in the stress and fright of being born. Those shells should have been instantly reabsorbed, like the virtual photons that electrons are always throwing off and then recapturing . . . but they had been caught by someone else, and so she had been tumbled out into this busy world with only a fraction of her proper *self*. The loss had to be connected with Houdini's death.

DeLarava hit the brake pedal again as taillights flashed red in front of her, and she thought about what Sukie Sullivan had said to her brother Pete on the telephone on Friday night, just before she'd shot her own drunken head off: *Go to the place where we hid—a thing, some things, okay? In a garage? It's what you're gonna need . . .* And Pete had said, *Where you can't hardly walk for all the palm fronds on the pavement, right? And you've got to crawl under low branches? Is it still there?* And Sukie had replied, *I've never moved it.*

DeLarava was sure that they'd been talking about Houdini's mask— the severed thumb and the plaster hands. The loss of them at Kennedy Airport in '75 had not been a random, tragic luggage theft after all— the twins had snatched the package, and hidden it from her. That, and the theft of her birth-ghosts, had been the only robberies that had ever hurt her.

A garage, she thought as she signaled for a lane change to the left, with palm fronds on the pavement and low branches around it. That could be nearly anywhere—and if Pete has recovered the thumb and the hands, there's no use in me finding the garage now anyway. And if he's carrying them with him, then he's masked and I can't track him.

At least not by psychic means.

But the old man is apparently out of the sea now, or at least emerging. Maybe I can catch him and eat him even without Pete being present as a lure. And though my twin set is broken, I ought to be able to get by, just with the help of Joey Webb. A real bag-full-of-broken-mirror schizophrenic is nearly as good a mask as a pair of twins.

And maybe this . . . this *lobster quadrille* will even draw Nicky Bradshaw out of hiding, him being the old man's godson and all, and the

old man having got him his start in show business. Maybe I could have
Bradshaw gassed or knocked unconscious. Do people dream, when
they're unconscious? If so, I could probably be on hand to get live
footage of one godalmighty fireball in Venice. It'd certainly be a more
valuable bit of film to peddle to the networks than this feature on the
lobsters and the dead fish.

It might even be possible for me to catch Nicky's ghost. I wonder
how that one would taste, it having been in effect carried in a locket
around his neck for seventeen years.

Neal Obstadt's offices were on the roof of the Hopkins Building on the
corner of Beverly Glen and Wilshire, ten stories above the Westwood
sidewalks and overlooking the tan blocks of the UCLA buildings to the
west and the green lawns of the Los Angeles Country Club to the east.
The walls of his consulting room were sectional cement slabs paneled
with Burmese teak, but there was no roof, just a collapsible vinyl awning
that was rolled back this morning to let the chilly breeze flutter the
papers on the desk. Obstadt was slouched sideways in his thronelike
chair, squinting up at an airliner slanting west across the blue sky.

"Loretta's a clown," he said without looking away from the plane.
"Trying to eat the ghost of Jonah or somebody out of those fishes she
hooks up from that puddle around the *Queen Mary*."

The black-bearded man across the desk from him opened his mouth,
but Obstadt held up a hand.

"Got to think," Obstadt said. "I need . . . what I need is a fresh
viewpoint."

He pulled open a drawer and lifted out of it a thing that looked like
a small black fire extinguisher. From his pocket he fished a thumb-sized
glass cartridge, and he looked at the label hand-Dremled onto the side:
HENRIETTA HEWITT—9-5-92.

"Was last month a good vintage?" he asked absently as he laid the
cartridge into a slot in the nozzle at the top of the black cylinder and
then twisted a screw at the base of the slot until he heard a muffled hiss
inside the cylinder. A plastic tube like a straw stuck out from the top
of the nozzle, and he leaned forward over the desk to get his lips around
it.

He exhaled through his nose for several seconds, then pressed a button on the side of the nozzle and inhaled deeply.

All at once:

*Yellowed curtains flapping in an old wood-framed window with peel-
ing white paint, hip and wrist lanced with flaring hot pain against the
dusty carpet and the weight of the whole noisy planet crushing her*

sunken chest; only newspapers for years now on the big leather recliner by the TV, no one will find me, who'll feed Mee-mow and Moozh; Edna and Sam both moved away, back East, having had weddings of their own, but a string of Christmases before that with smells of pine and roasting turkey, and bright-painted metal toys; and their births, wailing little creatures wet and red-faced after the hours of anxious, joyful, expanding pain—(nothing like this constricting agony that was smashing her out of existence now like a locomotive rolling a fragmenting car in front of it)—and breath-catching nakedness under sweaty sheets in a palm-shaded Pasadena bungalow, a wedding in 1922, drunk, and driving the boxy new Ford around and around the little graveled traffic circle at Wilshire and Western; long hair easier to brush when the air carried the sulfur smell of smudge pots burning in the orange groves in the winter, and a schoolhouse and pet ducks in the flat farmlands out home in the San Fernando Valley, dolls made of wood and cloth, and smells of cabbage and talcum powder and sour milk; pain and being squeezed and choking and bright light—ejected out into the cold!—and now there was nothing but a little girl falling and falling down a deep black hole, forever.

Obstadt exhaled slowly, aware again of the sun on his bare forearms, the breeze tickling between the coarse gray hairs. He uncrossed his legs and sat up straight, his man's body still feeling strange to him for a moment or two. And, he thought, I now weigh one three-thousandth of an ounce more than I did a minute ago.

He took a deep breath of the chilly morning air. The memories were fading—an old woman dying of a heart attack, after kids and a long life. He knew that the details would filter into his dreams . . . along with the details of all the others. Nice not to have a wino or a crackhead for once.

"Loretta's a clown," he repeated hoarsely, dragging his attention back across the vicarious decades. "She wins chips in this low-level game, but never cashes 'em in to move up to a bigger table; though she'd obviously like to, with her Velcro and her vegetarianism."

He rubbed his fists over his gray crew cut, knuckling his scalp. "Still," he went on, "some big chips do sometimes slide across her table, and she's all excited about one now." He stood up and stretched, flexing his broad shoulders. "I'm going to take it away from her." He thought of brightly painted toys under Christmas trees. "Children," he said thoughtfully. "Does Loretta have any, biological or adopted? Find out, and find them if she does. Keep monitoring her calls." He looked at Canov. "What have you got on Topper?"

"Spooky," Canov corrected him. "Nicholas Bradshaw. I think the courts still have warrants out on him. We're pretty sure he's dead."

"Loretta's pretty sure he's not."

Canov made a tossing gesture with one hand. "Or she's trying to fake somebody out by *pretending* she thinks so. He does seem to be reliably dead. We got a broad spectrum of media out to do resonance tests at the houses he lived in, and in his old law office in Seal Beach, and they found no ringing lifelines that worked out to be him. The one that seems to be *his* thuds dead at around 1975, when he disappeared."

"What kind of *mediums*?" Obstadt hated faggoty overprecise language.

Canov shrugged. "Hispanic *brujas*, a team of psychics from USC, autistic kids, ghost-sniffing dogs, even; a renegade Catholic priest, two Buddhist monks; we fed LSD to some poker players and had them do sixty or seventy hands of seven-stud with a Tarot deck in the law office one night. We had some blind fencers in, and videotaped 'em, watching for spontaneous disengages, but we didn't see any dowsing effects. And all the EM stuff, TV sets and current and compasses, behave normally."

"Okay, so he's dead," said Obstadt, "and his ghost hasn't been hanging out at the places you checked. Is it wandering around?"

"Not if he died anywhere locally—it looks like he just dispersed, or was eaten. He published an as-told-to book in 1962, *Spooked*, but no copy we've found in libraries or bookstores or junk stores has any fly-specks on it at all, and we located a dozen copies of his high-school yearbooks, all of them with clean pages where his picture is. His parents were both cremated—Neptune Society—but his godfather's buried at the Hollywood Cemetery next to Paramount Studios, and we keep scattering dirt on the old man's marker, but the only time it's cleaned off is when the maintenance people do it."

Obstadt nodded. " 'Kay." He stood up and crossed the carpeted floor to an east-facing window. "And right now go to Venice, will you? Check out this business with the fish and the lobsters."

CHAPTER 14

"I should like to buy an egg, please," she said timidly.
"How do you sell them?"

—Lewis Carroll,
Through the Looking-Glass

One of them had finally been for real. Maybe.

Angelica Anthem Elizalde stood in the center of the tiny *botánica* shop and stared resentfully at the morbid items for sale. On one wall were hung a hundred little cellophane bags of dried herbs, along with crude cloth "voodoo dolls" that cost two dollars apiece; on the opposite wall, on shelves, were ranked dozens of little bottles with labels like ABRE CAMINO and LE DE VETE DE AQUÍ—"Road Opener" oil and "Stay Away Law" oil—and aerosol spray cans labeled ST. MICHAEL THE ARCHANGEL and HIGH JOHN THE CONQUEROR (*"Spray all areas of your surroundings. Make the sign of the Cross. Repeat spraying as necessary"*). In the glass case by the cash register were a lot of books with colored pictures of Jesus and Our Lady of Guadalupe and the Devil on the covers—one, called *Conjuro del Tobaco,* by Guillermo Ceniza-Bendiga, was apparently a handbook on how to tell the future by watching the ash on cigars.

She had sat in the bus station on Seventh Street until dawn, and then stashed her canvas bag in a locker and walked east, over the Fourth Street bridge into the old Boyle Heights area of L.A., where she'd grown up after the move from Norco. When the police had brought bloodied Mexicans into Lincoln Heights Receiving Hospital, just a few blocks up Soto here, they'd always just called the area Hollenbeck Division, but Elizalde had liked the words *Boyle Heights*, and she had always tried to focus on the old Craftsman and Victorian houses on the narrow streets, and not on the bars and liquor stores and *ropa usada* used clothing stores.

And she had always been somehow personally embarrassed by *botánica* shops like this one.

The two young women behind the counter were conversing in fast, colloquial Spanish, ignoring Elizalde.

Elizalde frowned, not sure how she felt about being mistaken for an Anglo; but she just blinked around impatiently and gave no indication that she understood what was being said. One of the women assured the other that the tourist would soon get bored and leave; the other resumed the topic of laundry, reminding her friend that Saturday was Halloween and that she had better not leave her clothing out if it rained that night: *"La ropa estará mojado en te espiritu, y olada mal por meses"*—The clothes will be soaked in ghost-tea, and stink for months.

This is the vein, all right, Elizalde thought dourly. All the creepy stuff that I was brought up to believe was orthodox Roman Catholicism.

She remembered her surprise when a fellow student at UCLA had mentioned being a Roman Catholic. Elizalde had asked him how an intelligent person could really believe, for example, that rolling a raw egg over a child would cure fever—and then she'd been humiliated when he'd assured her that there was nothing like that in Catholic doctrine, and asked her where she had got such an idea.

She had of course chosen to laugh it off as a joke, rather than tell him the truth: that her mother had viewed taking Communion at church, and curing afflictions by rolling eggs over sick people—or by burning cornflowers, or eating papers with incantations scrawled on them—as all part of the same faith.

A plastic lighter and an open pack of Marlboros lay on the glass counter; and Elizalde, reminded by the cigar-ash book of a trick her grandmother used to perform, impulsively laid a dime on the counter and took one of the cigarettes. The women stopped talking and stared at her, but didn't object when she lit it.

She puffed rapidly, not inhaling, and when she had a half-inch of ash she tapped it off onto the glass and with a fingertip rapidly smeared it into the shape of a six-pointed Star of David. Then she puffed hard at the cigarette for a full half-minute, while the two women on the other side of the counter watched cautiously. Elizalde wiped her right hand hard down the flank of her jeans.

Finally she tapped the long ash into her dry palm; she squeezed it, rubbed it around with her fingers, and pressed her hand down onto the center of the star.

If this was done correctly, with the heel of the hand imprinting a beardlike semicircle and the curled-under fingernails scraping clean spaces that looked like shadowed eye sockets and then jiggling across the ash forehead, the result was a face that was plausibly that of Jesus, identifiable by the beard and a sketchy crown of thorns. Elizalde's grandmother had reduced grown men to tears with the apparently miraculous image.

Elizalde lifted her hand away—it had worked well enough.

One of the women crossed herself, and the other opened her mouth as if to say something—but then the ash pattern on the glass started to move.

Elizalde had glanced down when the women's eyes had gone wide and they'd stepped back, and at first she'd thought a draft was messing up her crude picture; but the ash image was *re-forming* itself. The jagged streaks that had been the crown of thorns became straggly lines like unruly bangs, and the broad smear of beard crowded up and became the jowls of a fat face. The ash around the eye gaps arranged itself in a finely striated pattern, representing baggy wrinkles.

Fleetingly it occurred to Elizalde that her palms were too damp now to do the trick again. The blood was singing in her ears, and she gripped the metal edge of the display case because she her sense of balance was gone.

She recognized the face. It was Frank Rocha, one of the patients who had died during that last group-therapy session at Elizalde's clinic on Halloween night two years ago.

Then the blur of the picture's mouth coalesced into clarity like solid curds forming in vinegared milk—and the mouth opened, and began moving. It was of course silent, and Elizalde couldn't read lips, but she convulsively slapped her hand across the ash image, nearly hard enough to break the glass.

Her expression when she looked up at the two women must have been wild, for they backed up against the pay telephone on the back wall.

Elizalde dropped the cigarette onto the linoleum floor and ground it out with the toe of her sneaker. *"Yo volveré,"* she said, *"quando usted no está tan ocupado."* I'll be back when you're not so busy.

She turned and strode out of the *botánica* onto the Soto Street sidewalk. The morning air was cold in her open, panting mouth, but she could feel a trickle of sweat run down her left-side ribs.

That *really was* Frank Rocha's face, she thought. God!

Her own face was as cold as if she had been caught in some horrifying crime, and she wanted to hide from this street, from this city, from the very sky.

She still had the letter from Frank Rocha in her wallet, in the hip pocket of these very jeans. She wanted to throw it away, throw the whole wallet away, every bit of ID.

One of them was finally for real, she insisted to herself even as she was furiously shaking her head and nearly sprinting away from the incriminating counter in the *botánica*. That last . . . *séance,* two years ago, actually fucking *worked.* It *did*! Dr. Alden, drunken old asshole, was *right* to make me resign. I should have listened to him, listened to the damned nurses, even though they were all wrong in their *reasons* for criticizing me. I *killed* those three patients who died in that clinic conference room, and I'm *responsible* for the ones who were injured, and the ones who are probably still in one or another of the state mental hospitals.

Angelica Elizalde vividly remembered the two times she had been called in to Dr. Alden's office.

"Come in," he had told her when she had walked down the hall to his ostentatiously book-lined cubicle. "Do please close the door, Dr. Elizalde, and sit down."

Alden had been the chief of the attending staff at the county hospital on Santa Fe in Huntington Park; he was a political appointee with unkempt hair and cigarette-stained fingers, and drunk half the time. Elizalde had been thirty-two years old, a psychiatrist with the title of "Director of Medical Education for Psychiatric Training." She had been at the county hospital for two years at that time, and in '90 was making $65,000 a year.

And she had felt that she earned it. After her internship she had stayed on at the county hospital for genuinely altruistic reasons, not just because it was the path of least resistance—the third-world-like situation provided experience that a more gentrified area couldn't give her, and she had wanted to help the sort of people who ordinarily wouldn't have access to psychiatric care.

Alden had reached across his cluttered desk to hand her a folded letter. "The charge nurse charged in here this morning with this," he said, smiling awkwardly. "You'd better read it."

The letter from the charge nurse to Alden had been a denunciation of Elizalde and her techniques; it concluded with, "Nurses and staff have lost confidence in Dr. Elizalde and would not feel comfortable carrying out her orders in the future."

Elizalde had known that every hospital is virtually run by the nurses, and that no chief of staff could afford to displease them; but she had looked up at Alden defiantly. "My patients get better. Ask the nurses themselves how my patients do, compared with those of the other doctors.''

Alden's mouth was still kinked in a forced smile, but he was frowning now. ''No. I don't need to ask them. You must know as well as I do that your methods have no place in a modern hospital. Voodoo dolls! Ouija boards! And how many of those candles have you got on your shelves in there, the tall ones with . . . *saints,* and, and *God,* and the *Virgin Mary* painted on them? It's not helpful to—a *white-bearded* God, *Caucasian, a man,* leaning out of the clouds and holding a scepter! And Rastafari paraphernalia, Santeria stuff! Your office smells like a church, and looks like some kind of ignorant Mexican fortune-teller's tent!''

Abruptly Elizalde wondered if she should have brought along a witness. In an even voice she said, ''These methods are no more—''

''Voodoo dolls, Dr. Elizalde! I can't believe you credit such—''

''I *don't* credit them, any more than I credit Rorschach blots as really being pictures of monsters!'' She had made herself take a deep breath then. ''Really. Listen. By having patients do readings with cards and planchettes I get them to be unself-consciously objective—about themselves, their spouses, parents, children. The readings let me see, without the patients having to *tell* me, the problems that deeply concern them, traumas that they subconsciously know should be exposed. A lot of people *can't do* the abstraction needed to see things in blots, or—or see motivations in situational sketches that look like old storyboards from 'Leave It to Beaver.' But if they've grown *up* with *these* symbols, they—''

''The subject is closed,'' Alden said tremulously. ''I order you to resume the standard psychiatric routines.''

Elizalde knew what that meant—see each patient for ten minutes at a visit, during which time she would be expected to do nothing more than look at the patient's chart, ask the patient how he or she was doing, assess the medications and perhaps tweak the prescription a little; nothing more than maintenance, generally by means of Thorazine.

She had left his office without another word, but she had not obeyed him. While the other psychiatrists' offices had all looked alike—the metal desk, the announcements taped to the walls, the particleboard bookcase, the toys in the corner for patients' children—Elizalde's office had gone on looking like a *bruja*'s den, with the religious *veladoro* candles on the shelves, pictures of Jesus and Mary and filthy old St. Lazar on the walls, and Ouija boards and crystal balls holding down the papers on the desk. She had even had, and frequently used to good effect, one of those giant black 8-balls, in the little window at the base of which messages like *Good Luck* and *True Love* would float to the surface when the thing was turned upside down. A simple "What do you think that's referring to, for you?"—with any of these admittedly morbid toys—had often unlocked important fears and resentments.

Some of the other members of the psychiatric team had frequently talked about raising "spiritual awareness" in their patients, and had liked to use the blurry jargon of New Age mysticism, but even they found Elizalde's use of spiritualism vulgar and demeaningly utilitarian— especially since Elizalde insisted that there was not a particle of instrinsic *truth* behind *any* sort of spiritualism.

Too, she had not been inclined to come up with the trendy sorts of diagnoses. It had been popular among psychiatrists then to uncover hitherto-unsuspected childhood memories of sexual abuse, just as ten years earlier all the patients had been diagnosed as having "anger" that needed to "be worked through." Elizalde was sure that guilt and shame were the next emotions that patients would be encouraged to rid themselves of.

She herself thought that guilt and shame were often healthy and appropriate responses to one's past behavior.

And so she had again been called in to Alden's office.

This time he had simply asked her to submit her resignation. He assured her that if she did not resign, she'd be "put on the shitlist" with the Peer Review Organization and the National Register of Physicians—suspended from taking any Medicare or Medicaid patients, and thus unhirable at any hospital in the country.

He had given her the rest of the day off to think about it, and she had paced up and down the living room of her Los Feliz house, determined to call "60 Minutes" and the *Los Angeles Times*; she would expose the county psychiatric system, rout the self-righteous nurses, get Alden's job. But by the next morning she had realized that she would not be able to win this fight—and at last she had driven to the hospital and mutely handed in her resignation.

Then she had gone into private practice. She found a chiropractor who agreed to let her rent his storefront Alvarado Street office on Tuesdays, and she worked as a secretary for a downtown law firm the rest of the week.

Her Tuesday psychiatric business had been slow at first—two or three patients, sometimes a fifty-minute group "séance"—but good results earned referrals for her from local businesses and even from the county, and within six months she had moved into an office of her own, between a credit dentist and a car-insurance office on Beverly. Soon she'd had to hire a receptionist to help out with correspondence and billing the insurance companies.

Finally, on Halloween night in 1990, she had held the last of her séance sessions. And it had been for real.

Elizalde had been walking west on the Whittier Boulevard sidewalk for the last several blocks, having fled Soto Street, and now she stopped.

In 1990, Frank Rocha had been living in a little bungalow-style house just north of MacArthur Park. Elizalde had called on him twice, in the determined, I-make-housecalls spirit she'd had at the time, and she thought she could find the place again.

He had had a wife, and . . . two daughters?

Standing on the sidewalk in the morning sun, Elizalde was snapping her fingers with controlled, fearful excitement. She knew that her two years of aimless wandering around the country had been just postponement; or not postponement but preparation, getting her strength back, for . . .

For the perilous and almost certainly pointless ordeal of making amends.

Amado Street, it had been. She would be able to find it once she had got to MacArthur Park. She took a deep breath, and then began walking, looking for a bus stop.

CHAPTER 15

"When the sands are all dry he is gay as a lark,
And will talk in contemptuous tones of the Shark:
But, when the tide rises and sharks are around,
His voice has a timid and tremulous sound."
—Lewis Carroll,
Alice's Adventures in Wonderland

Since this was in effect breakfast, Pete Sullivan had ordered a Coors Light with his menudo. The beer was finished by the time the waiter carried the bowl of tripe stew to his corner table, so he waved the empty glass at the man.

"Another Coors," noted the waiter, nodding. From the moment Sullivan had sat down, the man had proudly insisted on speaking English. "That was *unleaded*, right?"

"Right," said Sullivan. "Right," he repeated quietly as the waiter walked back to the counter. Unleaded, he thought. That's the only kind of gasoline they sell now, so people with old vehicles like mine have to dump little jugs of lead substitute into the tank every time they fill up. Probably the term *unleaded* for light beer will still be in use long after leaded gasoline is forgotten, and everyone will assume that it's a corruption of some old beer term. *Uhnledden*, he thought blurrily. *The original light beer, brewed since the Middle Ages in the ancient German village of Bad Fahrting.*

There were two or three plastic bottles of shampoo now alongside the bottles of lead substitute in the box under the sink in his van, and he imagined strolling into the men's gym at City College up on Vermont and pouring the wrong stuff onto his head in the shower. He could claim it was a delousing measure. It probably would *work* as a delousing measure. But what would he tell the gas-station attendant when he poured shampoo into the gas tank?

The shampoo had been only ninety-nine cents a bottle—logically— at the Arab-run ninety-nine-cent store he'd stopped at on Western. The ubiquitous little L.A. strip malls seemed to be all ninety-nine-cent stores now, as they had seemed to be all Mexican-style barbecue chicken places in the eighties.

Tiny Naylor's was gone, and so he had driven on down Sunset past the various coffee shops that he still thought of as *the chicken-hawk place, the A.A. and N.A. place, the rock-'n'-roll place, the punk-rock-hell place.* God knew what sorts of crowds they attracted now. Ben Frank's was still by the La Cienega intersection, and he remembered that it had been such a hangout for the long-hair-and-granny-glasses types in the sixties that the casting call ad for the Monkees' TV show had said, "Ben Frank's types wanted."

He had turned south on Highland and then east again on Melrose— and discovered that Melrose Avenue, though still animated, had died. He remembered when Flip, the huge used-clothing store, had burned in '83 or '84, and had then had an epic fire sale out on the sidewalk— kimonos and tuxedos and fedoras, all selling cheap in the hot sun and the loud rock music. Now there was a Gap clothing store, just like you'd see in any mall. In the early eighties, savvy Japanese had been scouring Melrose for old leather jackets and jukeboxes, and nervous tourists would drive by to look at the punks with green mohawks; now the funny hairstyles looked as if they'd been done at the Beverly Center. Like a government-subsidized avant-garde, Sullivan had thought as he'd tooled his old van down the crowded avenue, affluent disenfranchisement is just galvanic twitching in a dead frog's leg.

Once safely past the neighborhood of deLarava's studio, he had turned south on Western and driven down to Wilshire and followed it farther east, past the marooned Art Deco relics of the Wiltern Building and the Bullocks Wilshire, to Hoover Street; east of Hoover, Wilshire slants through MacArthur Park (Sullivan's father had always stubbornly gone on calling it Westlake Park, as it had been called before World War II, but today Sullivan sped through to Alvarado without thinking about the old man), and Sullivan recalled that the boulevard would end a mile or so ahead, just past the Harbor Freeway.

Here in this triangle between the Harbor and Hollywood Freeways were the narrow streets and old houses of the area known as the Temple-Beaudry district. Over on the far side of the freeways, on the hill above downtown L.A., the grand Victorian houses of Bunker Hill had stood until thirty years ago. Anonymous office towers stood there now; and on this side Sullivan saw new cleared lots and construction, and he knew that Temple-Beaudry would soon go the same way.

He had got off Wilshire and driven around through the pepper-tree-shaded streets, and had eventually found this place—a tiny Mexican restaurant called Los Tres Jesuses. Presumably it was owned by three guys who each had the common Hispanic first name Jesus—pronounced *Hey-soos*, and usually, perhaps out of reverence, replaced with the nickname Chui—pronounced Chewy. "The Three Chewies" had sounded to him like a good place to get breakfast.

Snap, Crackle, and Pop, he thought now as he took a sip of his second cold beer. Manny, Moe, and Flapjack. Larry, Moe, and Culero. Sukie had called people *culero* sometimes—it meant, roughly, coward.

He picked up his spoon and dipped it into the hot menudo. Even the steam from it, sharp with garlic and onion and cilantro, was strengthening; in a few minutes he had eaten it all, chewed up every white rectangle of tripe and mopped up the last of the red, beefy broth with tortillas.

He wiped his forehead with the paper napkin and waved the second emptied bottle of beer at the waiter. He put it down and shook a cigarette out of the pack, and as he struck a match he noticed that the tin ashtray on the table had a crude felt-pen drawing of a skull in the dish of it, with, carefully lettered around the rim, the words L.A. CIGAR—TOO TRAGICAL.

It was a palindrome—L.A. cigar both ways, with toot in the middle.

Startled an instant in advance, he dropped the burning match onto the drawn skull, and the ashtray glared for a moment with a silent puff of flame, as if someone had previously poured a film of high-proof brandy into it.

The flame was out instantly, and the faint whiff of . . . bacon? . . . was gone as soon as Sullivan caught a trace of it.

Suddenly he was nervous—but a moment later all that happened was that a car alarm started up in the lot behind the bar. *Beep . . . beep . . . beep . . .* He smiled wryly—*Que culero*, he thought—but his hand was almost twitching with impatience for the third beer.

Then the bartender began clanging a spoon against a glass between the beats of the car horn: *beep*-clang-*beep*-clang-*beep . . .*

For a moment it was the Anvil Chorus from *Il Trovatore* . . . and with that the memories of his father had caught him.

You couldn't count on motors, their father had told Sukie and Pete a hundred times, sitting over chili sizes at Ptomaine Tommy's down on Broadway, or in line for the Cyclone Racer roller coaster way out at at the Pike in Long Beach, or just driving the new Studebaker up Mulholland Drive along the crest of the Santa Monica Mountains to Topanga Canyon and back. *The camera had to be cranked at a steady speed even when you were crouched on a platform bolted to the front of a car spinning out around a turn, or on a boat in the Bering Sea when it was so cold that the oil in the camera was near to freezing solid. Some guys tried to use the second hand of a watch to keep rolling that foot of film per second, but Karl Brown told me the trick of humming the Anvil Chorus in your head—if you got that tune really tromping, they could swing you on a sling in a high wind from the top of a twenty-story building and you'd still have that crank turning sixteen frames a second as steady as a metronome in somebody's parlor.*

Their father had been Arthur Patrick Sullivan—known as A.P. or ''Apie,'' apparently because he liked to do feats of strength and had hair growing thickly on the backs of his shoulders—and he had started in the movie business in 1915, working as a cameraman and film technician in Cecil B. DeMille's barn at Vine and Selma in Hollywood. His bosses in those early days had been DeMille, Jesse Lasky, and Samuel Goldfish, who was soon to change his name to Goldwyn—but the infant movie business was chaotic, and Apie Sullivan had eventually become a producer and director at 20th Century Fox. For a cresting decade or so he had made feature films with stars like Tyrone Power and Don Ameche and Alice Faye; but it had been obvious to the twins that he had been happiest in the days before sound stages and artificial set lighting. *They'd say "We're losing the light" when the sun would start to set,* he had often told the twins, *but that was Griffith's magic hour, that hour when the sun was just over the trees, and the buildings and the actors would be lit from the side with that gold glow.*

The 1920s had been their father's magic hour.

By the time the twins were born, in 1952, the old man had been on his third marriage, had subsided into doing documentaries and freelance editing, and was supplementing his income by buying and selling real estate out in Riverside and Orange County; but he had never moved out of the old Spanish-style house in Brentwood, and he had sometimes hung out at Hillcrest Country Club with Danny Kaye and George Jessel, and had been proud that he could still occasionally get jobs in show business for the children of various old friends.

The waiter brought the third Coors Light, and Pete took a long sip from the neck of the bottle. Drinking in the morning, he thought.

Beth, as Sukie had been known until college, had always claimed to remember their mother, who died a year after the twins' birth. Pete had never believed her.

When the twins were seven, their father had got engaged to be married again. Kelley Keith had been thirty-three years old to their father's sixty-one, but she was a genuine actress, having had a few supporting roles in films like *We're Not Married* and *Vampire Over London*, and the twins had been impressed with her contemporary career as they had never been with their father's old movies. And she had been slim and blond with a chipmunk overbite and laugh-crinkled eyes, and Pete had been desperate not to let Beth know that he had fallen in love—he was certain—with their stepmother-to-be.

The four of them had seemed, to the twins at least, to do everything together—wading in the tide pools at Morro Bay to find tiny octopuses and to nervously stick their bare toes into the clustered grasping fingers of sea anemones, hiking through the pine woods around their father's cabin in Lake Arrowhead, having grand lunches at the giant-hat-shaped Brown Derby on Wilshire. . . . Their father always ordered raw oysters and steak tartare, and kept promising the twins that they'd be getting new brothers and sisters before too long.

The wedding was held in April of 1959, at St. Alban's Church on Hilgard. Sukie—Elizabeth—had been sulking for weeks and refused to be the flower girl, and in the end it had been Shirley Temple's little girl, Lori Black, who carried the bouquet of lilacs. The reception was at Chasen's, and Pete could still remember Andy Devine raucously singing "At the Codfish Ball."

And then, one afternoon that summer, their father and his new bride had driven out to Venice Beach for a picnic. The twins had *not* been along for this outing. Their white-haired father had reportedly gone swimming, doing his always-self-consciously-athletic "Australian Crawl" way out past the surf line, and he had apparently gotten a stomach cramp. And he had drowned.

Pete tilted the bottle up for another slug of cold beer.

After their father's death, Kelley Keith had just disappeared. She had simply packed up all her belongings and moved, and no one had been able to say where to.

Story of my life, Pete Sullivan thought now with no particular bitterness. Later he'd heard a rumor that she had gone to Mexico with a lot of their father's money. Then he'd heard that she had got in a car crash down there and died.

And so the twins had been put into the first of what was to be a succession of foster homes. And eventually there had been Hollywood High, and City College and no money, and then the jobs with deLarava.

DeLarava probably has the license number of my van, Sullivan thought now as he swirled the last inch of beer in the bottle. Could she somehow have the cops looking for it?

He remembered a joke his father had liked to tell:

What do you make your shoes out of?
Hide.
Hide? Why should I hide?
No, hide! Hide! The cow's outside!
Well, let her in, I'm not afraid.

I'm afraid, Sullivan thought. *Yo soy culero.*

He had seen a pay telephone on the back wall by the restroom doors, and now he slid a couple of quarters from the scatter of change on the table and stood up. See if you can't establish a solider home base, he thought as he walked steadily to the phone. Clausewitz's first piano concerto.

Be there, Steve, he thought as he punched in the remembered number. Don't have moved.

He heard only one ring before someone picked it up at the other end. "Hello?"

"Hi," Sullivan said cautiously, "is Steve Lauter there please?"

"This is Steve. Hey, this sounds like Pete Sullivan! Is that you, man?"

"Or an unreasonable facsimile." Steve had been working at some credit union in the eighties. Sullivan wondered if he was about to leave for work. "Listen, I'm in L.A. for a couple of days, I was thinking we should get together."

"I can have a case of Classic Coke on the premises when you get here," said Steve heartily. "Where are you staying?"

"Well," said Sullivan, grateful that Steve had so readily provided a cue, "I'm sleeping in my van. It's got a bed in it, and a stove—"

"No, you stay here. I insist. How soon can you be here?"

Sullivan recalled that Steve had been married, and he wanted to shave and shower before showing up at his old friend's door. "Aren't you working today?"

"I get Wednesdays off. I was just going to mow the lawn today."

"Well, I've got a couple of errands to run," Sullivan said, "people to see. This afternoon? I'll give you a call first. Are you still off Washington and Crenshaw?"

"Naw, man, I moved west of the 405, in Sawtelle where the cops don't pull you over if you're in a decent car. Let me give you the address, I'm at—"

"I'll get it when I call you back," Sullivan interrupted. "And I'll watch the speed limits on the way, I don't think I'm in a decent car."

"Make it soon, Pete."

"You bet. I'll bring some . . . Michelob, right?"

"It's Amstel Light these days, but I've got plenty."

"I'll bring some anyway."

"Are *you* drinking now? Old Teet himself?"

"Only when it's sunny out."

Steve laughed, a little nervously. "That's every day, here, boy, you know that. I'll be by the phone when you call."

After he had hung up, Sullivan stood beside the phone in the dark hallway. His mouth tasted of menudo and beer, and he wished he hadn't left his cigarettes out on the table, for there was another call to make. A siren wailed past outside, and he slid his other quarter into the slot. He remembered the studio number too.

After two rings, "Chapel Productions," said a woman's voice.

Good Lord, he thought, that's new. "Could I talk to Loretta deLarava, please. This is Donahue at Raleigh." He wondered if deLarava still used Raleigh for special postproduction work, and if Donahue was still there.

He had no intention of speaking to deLarava, and was ready to hang up if she came on the line, but the woman said, "Ms. deLarava is at lunch—no, that's right, she's doing a timely in Venice. Might be a while."

Sullivan's face was chilly with sweat again, and he glanced at the men's-room door, measuring the distance to it—but the surge of nausea passed. "Okay," he said, breathing shallowly, "I'll try later."

He juggled the receiver back onto the hook and swayed back to his table. Sitting down, he lifted the bottle and drank the last of the beer.

Order another? he thought. No. Can't A.O.P. in these narrow old streets, and you sure don't need a drunk-driving arrest. What the hell is she doing in Venice *today*? Halloween's three days off. At worst, this is just a reconnaissance scouting trip for what she'll be doing then— and maybe something timely really *is* happening there.

He thought about driving out there to see, and discovered that he could not.

CHAPTER 16

"I'm sure I didn't mean—" Alice *was beginning, but the Red Queen interrupted her impatiently.*
"That's just what I complain of! You should *have meant! What do you suppose is the use of a child without any meaning?"*
— Lewis Carroll,
Through the Looking-Glass

Sometimes *Kootie would be kind to the poor things, putting wooden croutons in the soup so that there would be something they could eat at the dinner table; but today, when he was trying to inoculate his children, he didn't want the things around, so he was smoking a cigar made of paper and horsehair. It tasted horrible, but at least there were no indistinct forms hunching around the gate.*

His children weren't cooperating—Kootie had got them out on the lawn barefoot, and he was throwing little Chinese firecrackers to make the children dance away from their exploded footprints, but they were crying; and when he set up a pole with coins at the top, his son Tommy couldn't climb it, and Kootie had to rub rosin on the boy's knees and shout at him before he managed it.

It hadn't been easy for Kootie to learn these tricks—he was deaf, and had to bite *the telephone receiver in order to hear by bone conduction. Now in the dream he was biting one of the firecrackers, lighting it as if it was one of the awful cigars, and when it went off it jolted him awake.*

His warm, furry pillow was awake too—Fred had scrambled up at the noise, and Kootie sat up on the pile of videocasette rewinders in the back seat of Raffle's car. Outside, bright morning sun lit the tops of old office buildings. Kootie straightened the sunglasses on his nose.

"*That* roused the sleepyheads," said Raffle from the driver's seat.

"Backfire, sorry." He revved the engine, and the whole car shook. "You were both twitching in your sleep," Raffle went on. Kootie watched the back of his gray head bob in time with the laboring engine. "I always wonder what city dogs dream about. Can't be chasing rabbits, they've never seen a rabbit. Screwing, probably. I always used to want to do it with my wife doggie-style, but I could never get her to come out in the yard."

Raffle was laughing now as he hefted the bottle of Corona beer he'd bought late last night, and he wedged it under the dashboard and popped off the cap.

Kootie pulled one of the rewinders out from under himself, and as he dug in his pocket for a dime he peered out through the dusty back window and tried to remember what part of L.A. they were in now. He saw narrow shops with battered black iron accordion gates across their doors, drifts of litter in the gutters and against the buildings, and ragged black men wrapped in blankets sitting against the grimy brick and stucco walls.

He nervously pulled a dime out of his pocket and remembered that Raffle had called this area "the Nickel"—Fifth Street, skid row, just a block away from the lights and multilingual crowds of Broadway.

Raffle was chugging the warm beer, and Kootie was nauseated by the smell of it first thing in the morning, on top of the smells of Fred and last night's burritos. He bent over the gray plastic box of the rewinder and began using the dime to twist out the screws in the base of it. By the time Raffle had used the empty bottle as a pipe—needling the stuffy air with the astringent tang of crack cocaine and hot steel wool—and opened the car door to spin it out into the street, Kootie had worked the back off the machine and was trying to jam the blunt dime edge into the screw heads of the electric motor inside.

Raffle glanced back at him before putting the car in gear. "What *you* been snortin', Koot me boy?" he asked cheerfully as he steered out away from the curb. "A little *crank* up the nose to wake you up?"

"Nothing," said Kootie quickly, thinking of the ghost he'd inhaled at twilight yesterday. The ghost had surely been responsible for his peculiar dreams. *Kootie* certainly didn't have any children.

"Huh. Regular speed freak you are." The engine was popping and coughing, but Raffle was goosing the car forward down the curbside lane, tapping his foot rapidly on the gas pedal. "A speed freak, you leave him alone with a screwdriver and come back and find your stereo all over the apartment in pieces. This crack now, it's nothin' for kids, you understand, but it's harmless compared to speed." The light was green at Broadway, but he had to wait for pedestrians to wobble past before turning north. "Thing about speed, a guy cooks it up in a secret factory out in Twentynine Palms or somewhere, in the desert, you know? And if he's paranoid, which he usually is, with good reason, the paranoia gets in the speed, and when you snort it you wind up feeling what he felt when he was cooking it. You get his personality. They should have those priests make it, up here at St. Vibiana Cathedral on Second Street—spike the stuff with some sanka-titty."

For a moment Kootie pictured a breast that was heavy with decaf coffee, then realized that Raffle must have meant *sanctity*. Outside the car, the Broadway sidewalk was already crowded with bums and businessmen of, apparently, every nationality the world had to offer; all of them seemed busy, with concerns that Kootie couldn't imagine. How long, the boy thought unhappily, can I live out here on the streets like this?

The narrow ground-floor shops were all shoestores and Asian restaurants and—of all things—travel agencies, but above the restless heads of the crowd stood antique iron lampposts with frosted glass globes, and fire-escape balconies zigzagging up the dignified brick faces of the smog-darkened buildings.

He looked down at the machine in his lap—and suddenly he didn't know what it was. Without deciding to, he found himself asking, "What does this thing do?"

Raffle glanced into the back seat. "Nothing, anymore, I guess. It's a video rewinder, was. To rewind movies, so you don't have to wear out your VCR."

"Movies?" Kootie stared at the plastic box and tried to imagine reels of cellulose nitrate film small enough to fit inside it. Then, "VCR," he repeated thoughtfully. Video-something, apparently. Video-cathode-rectifier, video-camera-receiver?

"Where did you grow up, boy?" said Raffle. "It hooks up to your TV set, and you rent movies to watch on it."

Kootie's heart was pounding, and he took off his sunglasses and ducked his head to peer out ahead, through the windshield, at the remote glass towers that intersected the yellow sky to the north. "What," he asked shakily, "has been the greatest invention since—" He caught himself. "—oh, say, in the twentieth century?" he finished.

He could see Raffle scratch the gray stubble on his brown chin. "Oh, I reckon . . . the thermos."

Kootie blinked. "The *thermos?* You mean like thermos bottles?"

"Sure," said Raffle expansively. "Hot things, it keeps hot. And cold things, them it keeps cold."

"Well," said Kootie helplessly, "yes . . ."

Raffle lifted his hands from the steering wheel for a moment to spread them in mystification. "So how does it *know*?"

Raffle was laughing again, and when Fred whined and licked his right ear he rolled down the driver's-side window so the dog could poke his head out from the backseat. Kootie leaned forward and took deep breaths of the chilly diesel-and-fish-oil-scented breeze.

"Where are we headed?" he asked.

"Civic Center, I think, wander around Spring and Grand and all, catch some of the effluent citizens who're on a break from jury duty or waiting in line for the matinee of *Phantom of the Opera*. Good guilt either way. And first a stop at the Market up here, get some good fresh tamales to put under the hood for dinner. There's Chinese too, but it don't last so good on the manifold."

"Tamales sound fine," said Kootie. "Uh . . . can I buy some fire-crackers?"

"*Fire*crackers?" exclaimed Raffle. "On top of my felonies you want to . . . *purchase illegal explosives*?" Kootie had started to stammer an apology, but Raffle went on, "Sure, the boy can have firecrackers. And for breakfast, how about a slice of pepperoni pizza? *Let's have another cup of coffeee*," he sang raucously, "*let's have another pizza pie*."

Kootie smiled uncertainly and nodded as Fred's tail thumped repeat-edly against his cheek. Between two of the thumps he managed to get his sunglasses back on.

The first part of the morning was heady, nervous fun. Raffle parked the car on Third Street, and with Fred tagging right along they walked in the open front of the Grand Central Market, past the shoeshine stands on the sidewalk to the wide dim interior, where big live fish slapped on butchers' blocks and gray-haired little old women wolfed noodles from paper bowls with chopsticks and haggled over vegetables the like of which Kootie had never seen before. Raffle handled his party's pur-chases, joking in broken Spanish with the Hispanic fellow at the tamale counter and pausing for mumbled exchanges with a couple of overly made-up women who seemed to be just wandering around and whom Kootie took for hostesses.

Back out on the sunny sidewalk, Kootie and Raffle nibbled slices of hot pizza wrapped in waxed paper as they walked back to the car, while Fred trotted alongside carrying the bag of tamales in his mouth. Raffle had tucked a little flat square package into Kootie's shirt pocket in the market, and when they got to the car and Raffle bent over the hood,

Kootie dug the package out and saw the Chinese dragon printed on the wrapper and realized it was his firecrackers. He tucked it into the hip pocket of his jeans.

Firecrackers, he thought bewilderedly. What do I want firecrackers for?

Kootie wondered if his dream was still clinging to him; all morning he had been flinching at voices and car horns and the whacks of the butchers' cleavers in the market, and until Raffle hoisted up the car hood Kootie was blankly staring at the low, sharp-edged cars that blundered incongruously through the lanes on this floor of the echoing valley between the buildings; the cars looked as though they'd been built to fly.

But when the hood had creaked up, Kootie leaned in over the fender and peered at the black engine. He could recognize the radiator, and vaguely the block, but he wondered why there were so many fan belts.

"Gimme the daily bread, Fred," muttered Raffle to the dog, who relinquished the bag he'd been carrying.

Beside the left wheel well a roll of aluminum foil was tucked in behind some square translucent box that appeared to have green water in it, and Raffle unrolled a yard of foil and wrapped the tamales tightly, then tucked them in under the air filter.

Kootie was delighted with the notion. "Automotive cuisine," he said. "They should design the engine with a box there, for baking."

"And hang a string from the radiator cap," Raffle agreed, "so you could steam ess-cargo." He patted the crumpled silvery bulge. "Think that's gonna stay wedged in there?"

Kootie didn't answer. He had just looked up into an enormous color photograph of his own face, and for a dizzy moment he couldn't guess the distance or the size of the thing. He blinked and bobbed his head, and then the image fell into its proper scale.

Behind Raffle and way above his head, in a wide metal bracket on the second floor of the building they'd parked in front of, a billboard had been hung—its bright and unfaded colors made it stand out from the weathered beer and cigarette signs around it.

The right third of it was a huge color blowup of Kootie's own fifth-grade school photo. And the words on the billboard were in Spanish, but the meaning was clear:

RECOMPENSA DINERO POR ESTE NINO PERDIDO,
SE LLAMA CUT HUMI
LA ULTIMO VES QUE LO VI LUNES, 26 DE OCTUBRE,
EN BULEVA SUNSET

$20,000 LLAMA (213) JKL KOOT $20,000
NO PREGUNTAS

Kootie began whistling, and he shuffled to the driver's-side door and pulled it open, letting the thumb-button on the handle snap out loudly. "Want me to drive?" he asked with a broad smile.

CHAPTER 17

Alice thought to herself "I never should try to remember my name in the middle of an accident! ..."

—Lewis Carroll,
Through the Looking-Glass

Raffle was frowning at him in puzzlement over the top of the hood. "No, Jacko," he said, slamming it down. "Nor do I want Fred to drive. Get in on your own side."

"I can scoot across." Kootie got in the car and then hiked and dragged himself over the console into the passenger seat, so that Raffle's attention would be drawn *down* at him rather than *up* toward the billboard. Kootie's face was chilly with sweat, and his T-shirt was wet under the heavy flannel shirt. He was whistling again to hold the older man's attention, whistling Raffle's *another pizza pie* tune because he couldn't think of anything else; he knew that with his bad ankle he wouldn't be able to outrun Raffle, if it came to that.

But now Raffle had coaxed the dog into the backseat, and had got in himself and closed the door. "Are all little kids as crazy as you?"

Kootie was glad that his sunglasses were hiding the alarm that must still be shining in his eyes. "I'm not a little kid," he said, hoping his heartbeat would slow down once the car got moving. "I'm an eighty-four-year-old . . . midget."

"Mayor of the Munchkin City," recited Raffle in a high, solemn voice as he cranked the starter, "in the county of the land of Oz." The engine caught, and the car shook.

"*Fol*low the *yel*low brick *road*," quacked Kootie.

Raffle clanked the car into gear, nosed it forward, and steered it north again on Broadway. Kootie ruffled Fred's fur and stole a glance back at the receding white rectangle that was the billboard, and he wondered who was offering the $20,000 "*recompensa.*" One last quote from *The Wizard of Oz* occurred to him. "I don't think we're in Kansas anymore, Toto," he told Fred softly and self-consciously.

In the next two blocks they crossed over an invisible thermocline border, from hot, colorful third-world agitation into an area of tall, clean gray buildings, and streets with young trees planted along the sidewalks at measured intervals, and new cars and men in dark suits.

They turned left on Beverly and then parked in a broad pay lot off Hope Street. "We'll make booyah more than the seven bucks it costs to park here," said Raffle confidently as they piled out of the car and he opened the trunk to get his WILL WORK FOR FOOD—HOMELESS VIETNAM VET WITH MOTHERLESS SON sign; "so it's no problem parking on credick." (Kootie guessed that Raffle had derived his pronunciation of *credit* from the way people generally said *credit cards.*) The whoosh of trucks on the Hollywood Freeway, muffled by the tall hedge of the shoulder at the north end of the lot, was like low random surf on the lee side of a jetty.

They had slept in the car last night, and Kootie had noticed that Raffle slept only a few hours between medication runs. He hoped that tonight they might crash for a while in a motel—the sight of the Ahmanson Theater and the Mark Taper Forum and the Dorothy Chandler Pavilion, standing as imposing as foreign capitol buildings on the wide, elevated, tree-shaded plaza across the interscection of Temple and Hope, reminded him of the Los Angeles he used to live in, and he yearned for the gracious luxury of a shower.

Kootie limped across the asphalt of the parking lot, holding the end of the belt that was Fred's leash. The dog lunged at a couple of prancing pigeons, and Kootie tried to hop after him but turned his bad ankle and went painfully to his knees on the pavement. For a moment the world went from color to black-and-white.

"You're just gettin' beat to bits, Jacko," said Raffle sympathetically as he helped the boy back up to his feet. "Here, I'll take Fred."

Kootie wasn't crying, though the pain in his ankle was like a razory-high violin note, and he was sure blood must be trickling down his shin under his pants. "Okay," he managed to gasp, blindly handing Raffle the end of the belt.

As soon as Kootie was able to breathe smoothly he spoke, to show that he was okay.

"What 'work' do we do," he asked, "for food?"

The people who had given them stray one-dollar bills and pocket-warmed handfuls of change yesterday and last night had clearly been just paying an urban toll, but here he could imagine getting a *twenty* or two, and being given some actual *task*.

They stopped at the Temple Street curb. "Well," said Raffle, squinting around at the wide, clean streets, "you gotta *anticipate*. It's no good saying 'I gotta go buy my gardening tools back out of hock' if the guy turns out to *have* gardening tools. The basic trick is 'Gimme forty bucks right now and I'll be at the address in a couple of hours,' see? With you along it should be easy. 'My boy's sick, I just need thirty bucks to stash him in a motel bed, and then I'll be right over.' A cough or two from you, and the guy's some kind of monster if he don't cooperate."

The light changed, and they crossed Temple, Fred tugging eagerly at the leash in Raffle's knobby fist.

"So we don't do any actual *work* at all," Kootie said, relieved in spite of himself.

"Work is whatever you do that gets you a nice time, Jacko," Raffle said, "and you gotta figure out how to get the most for the least. Food, shelter, drink, dope. Some guys take a lot of R and R in jail, they don't mind those orange jumpsuits, but that ain't for me—my outstanding warrants are under different names, every one. In jail, speaking of your video rewinder, they start the movies at eight, but bedtime is nine, so you always miss the end of the movie. Could you live like that? And if you even smoke a cigarette—and one cigarette, in trade, costs you anywhere from four to eight items from the commissary, like soap or candy bars—a guy hiding in the air-conditioning vent or somewhere tells on you, and then on the loudspeaker, 'Mayo, report to the front watch, and put out that cigarette.' You get a write-up, and gotta spend four hours scrubbing the toilets or something. Get two or three write-ups and you get a major—you don't get your early release date. The *good* life is this out here."

Kootie shrugged bewilderedly. "I'm sold," he said.

They were stopped now at the Hope Street corner curb, waiting for the east-west light to change, and several men in suits and a woman in a coffee-colored dress had drifted up beside them, chattering about whoever was singing the Phantom role today.

The words *I'm sold* went on ringing in Kootie's head as he stared to his right, back north across Temple.

The sky and the houses on the Echo Park hills and the greenery of the Hollywood Freeway shoulder all faded into a blurry two-dimensional frame surrounding the white, white billboard with the black lettering and the livid color photograph.

Kootie was icy cold inside his heavy flannel shirt. His ears were ringing as if with the explosions of the dreamed firecrackers, and he wondered if he would be able to run, able to work his muscles at all. It had not occurred to him that there might be more than one of the billboards—this affront had the disorienting dreamlike intrusiveness of supernatural pursuit.

The billboard was in English here, three blocks north of the first one:

CASH REWARD FOR THIS MISSING BOY:
NAMED KOOT HOOMIE
LAST SEEN MONDAY, OCTOBER THE 26TH,
ON SUNSET BOULEVARD
$20,000 CALL (213) JKL-KOOT $20,000
NO QUESTIONS ASKED

Kootie swung his head around to blink up at Raffle.

Raffle was staring at the billboard, and now looked down at Kootie with no expression on his weathered brown face.

The little green figure was glowing now in the screened box below the traffic signal across Hope, and the people beside Kootie stepped out into the crosswalk. Kootie found himself following them, staring at the crude silhouette in the box and hearing Raffle's step and Fred's jangling chain coming right along behind him.

"You'd get eight thousand," said Raffle quietly. "After my cut and Fred's."

"Damn Ford," said Kootie helplessly.

"We can get a Cadillac," said Raffle. "Hell, we can get a Winnebago with two bathrooms."

"I can't . . . go to them," Kootie said, involuntarily. *Why not?* he asked himself—I surely can't live in a damn *car* forever. Then he heard himself saying, "They'll eat me and kill you."

Kootie stepped up the curb, helplessly letting the theater goers hurry on ahead, and turned to face Raffle.

Raffle was frowning in puzzlement. "*Eat* you?" he said. "And kill *me*?"

"Not you," Kootie said, speaking voluntarily now. "He was talking to me—he meant kill *me*."

"That's what he meant, huh?" Now Raffle was grinning and nodding. "*I* get it, Jacko—you really *are* crazy. Your nice clothes and nice manners—you're the escaped schizo kid of some rich people, and they want you back so you can take your Thorazine or lithium, right? I'll be *rescuing* you."

Kootie, entirely himself for the moment, stared at the man and wondered how fit Raffle was. "I can just run, here." His heart thumping in his chest.

"You got a bad ankle. I'd catch you."

"I'll say I don't know you, you're trying to molest me."

"I'll point at the billboard."

Kootie looked past Raffle at the momentarily empty sidewalk and street. "Let's let these cops decide."

When Raffle turned around, Kootie hopped up the stairs and broke into a sprint across the broad flat acropolis-like plaza, toward the curved brown wall below the flared white turret of the Mark Taper Forum; a walkway crossed the shallow pool around the building, and he focused on that. The tall glass façade of the Dorothy Chandler Pavilion was too far away.

Behind him he heard a yelp as Raffle collided with Fred, and then he heard the big man's shoes scuffling up the steps; but Kootie was running full tilt, ignoring for now the pounding blaze of pain in his ankle, and when he crossed the moat and skidded around the circular brown wall of the Mark Taper Forum he couldn't hear his pursuers.

Then he could. Fred's claws were clattering on the smooth concrete and Raffle's shoes were slapping closer. Kootie was more hopping than running now, and his face was icy with sweat—in a moment they'd catch him, and there was no one around who would help, everybody would want a piece of the $20,000.

Caught. Jagged memories crashed in on him—whipping his horse as he drove home at night past a cemetery while unsold newspapers tumbled in the back of the cart as insubstantial fingers plucked at the pages; crashing through the dark woods at Port Huron, pursued by the ghost of a recently dead steamship captain; fleeing west to California under the "mask" of a total eclipse of the sun in 1878, leaving no trail, sitting uncomfortably on a cushion on the cowcatcher of the racing Union Pacific locomotive, day after day, as it crested the mounting slopes toward the snowy peaks of the Sierras . . .

And too he remembered *expiring* in the bedroom of the mansion in Llewellyn Park in October of 1931, breathing out his last breath—into a glass test tube.

Anyone could eat him now, inhale him, *inspire* the essence of him. In his tiny glass confinement he had been taken to Detroit, and then eventually back out to California, and this prepubescent boy had inhaled him; the boy wasn't mature enough to *digest* him, unmake him and violate him and put his disassembled pieces to use for alien goals . . . but the people pursuing him *could,* and *would.*

If they caught him.

At this moment the boy was just a shoved-aside passenger in his young body, and the old man turned on the dog that came bounding around the curve of white wall.

No more than *two* other people at the *worst*, thought Raffle, at the *very* worst, and that'll still leave sixty-six hundred for me, since dumb Jacko is forfeiting his share, making me run after him like this; I can knock him down and then start yelling *Rightful Glory Mayo! Rightful Glory Mayo!*—no, no jail names here, use the real name—what the hell *is* the real name?—and then tell 'em to call 911, this kid's having a prophylactic fit, swallowing his tongue. I can take off my shoe and stick it in the kid's mouth so he can't talk, say it's a first-aid measure.

Raffle sprinted across the walkway over the shallow pool and skidded around the curved wall of the Mark Taper only a few seconds after Kootie had, and practically on Fred's tail—just as a deep *thump* buffeted the morning air.

And he clopped to a frozen halt, slapping the wall to push himself back.

The wall was wet with spattered blood that was still *hot,* and through a fine, turbulent crimson spray he stared at the portly old man, dressed in a black coat and battered black hat, who was gaping at him wide-eyed. Thinking *gunshot*, Raffle glanced down for Kootie's body, but saw instead the exploded, bloody dog-skeleton of Fred.

Kootie was nowhere to be seen.

The old man half turned away, and then suddenly whirled and *sprang* at Raffle, whipping up one long leg and punching him hard in the ear with the toe of a hairy black shoe; the impact rocked Raffle's head, and he scuffled dizzily back a couple of steps, catching himself on the pool railing.

The old man's mouth sprang open, and though more blood spilled out between the uneven teeth, he was able to say, *"Let's see you capture me now, you sons of bitches."*

Raffle remembered the boy having said something like *Kill you and eat me*, and for this one twanging, stretched-out second Raffle was able to believe that this old man had *eaten* Kootie, and was now ready to kill *him*, ready to blow him up the way he'd apparently blown up the dog.

And an instant later Raffle had leaped the railing and was running away, splashing through the shallow pool, back toward the steps and the car and the smoggy familiar anonymity of the scratch-and-scuffle life south of the 10 Freeway.

*   *   *

The figure of the old man walked unsteadily to the stairs on the west side of the elevated plaza. A few of the people in line for Phantom tickets nudged their companions and stared curiously at the shapeless black hat, and at the black coat, which was coming apart at the shoulders as the arms swung at the figure's sides.

The well-dressed people in line had seen the boy run that way, pursued by the bum, and they'd seen the bum come running back, across the pool and right on past to the stairs, in a fright; but this old man was walking calmly enough, and there hadn't been any screams or cries for help. And the old man was disappearing down the parking garage stairs now, at a slow, labored pace. Clearly whatever had happened was over now.

The old man had thrown Kootie right out of his own body, into a pitch dark room that Kootie somehow knew was "Room 5 in the laboratory at West Orange."

The boy was panting quickly and shallowly, with a whimper at the top of each expiration. He wasn't thinking anything at all, and he could feel a tugging in his eyes as his pupils dilated frantically in the blackness.

As he slowly moved across the wooden floor, sliding his bare feet gently, he passed through static memories that were strung through the stale air like spiderwebs.

There was another boy in this room—no, just the faded ghost of a boy, a five-year-old, who dimly saw this dark room as the bottom of a dark creek in Milan, Ohio. He had drowned a very long time ago, in 1852, while he and his friend Al had been swimming. In the terror of being under the water and unable to get back up to the surface, in the terror of actually sucking water into his lungs, he had jumped—right out of his body!—and clung to his friend on the bank above. And he had gone on clinging to his friend for years, while Al had done things and moved around and eventually grown up into an adult.

Kootie shuffled forward, out of the standing wave that was the boy's ghost, and he was aware of Al himself now, who as a boy had simply walked home after his friend had disappeared under the water and not come back up; Al had had dinner with his mother and father and eventually gone to bed, without remarking on the incident at the creek—and he had been bewildered when his parents had shaken him awake hours later, demanding to know where he had last seen his friend. Everyone in town, apparently, was out with torches, searching for the boy. Al had patiently explained what had happened at the creek . . . and had been further bewildered by the horror in the faces of his mother and father,

*by their shocked incredulity that he would just walk away from his
drowning friend.*

As far as Al had been concerned, he had carried his friend home.

*And in this room, thirty-seven years later, the friend had finally left
Al.*

*Al was forty-two by then, though he had never forgotten the drowning.
In this dark, locked room he had been working with Dickson on a secret
new project, the Kineto-phonograph, and late on a spring night in 1889
the two of them had tried the thing out. It was supposed to be a masking
measure—and actually, as such, it had worked pretty well.*

*Dickson had set up a white screen on one wall, while Al had started
up the big wood-and-brass machine on the other side of the room; as
the machine whirred and buzzed, the screen glowed for a moment with
blank white light, and then Al's image appeared—already portly, with
the resolute chin set now on a thick neck, the graying hair slicked back
from the high, pale forehead—and then the image began to speak.*

*And the ghost of the drowned boy, confronted with an apparently
split host, sprang away from Al and* ignited *in confusion.*

Abruptly Kootie was back in his own body and remembered who he
was, but he couldn't *see*—there was some hot, wet *framework* all over
him. Shuddering violently, he reached up and clawed it off; it tore sog-
gily as he dragged it over his head, but when he had flung it onto the
railing of the cement steps he could see that it had been a sort of full-
torso mask: the now-collapsed head of an old man with a coarse black-
fur coat attached to the neck, and limp white fleshy hands lying askew
at the ends of the sleeves. It smelled like a wet dog.

Kootie was shaking violently. The morning breeze in the stairwell
was chilly on his face and in his wet hair, and he realized numbly that
the slickness on his hands and face was blood, a whole lot of
somebody's *blood.* Profoundly needing to *get away* from whatever had
happened here, he stumbled further down the steps into the dim artificial
light, unzipping his heavy flannel shirt. His throat was open, but he
hadn't started breathing again yet.

Standing on the concrete floor at the foot of the steps, he pulled off
the heavy shirt, which was slick with more of the blood; the nylon lining
was clean, though, and he wiped his face thoroughly and rubbed his
hair with it. Then he pushed the sticky curls back off his forehead, wiped
his hands on the last clean patch of quilted nylon, and flung the sodden
bundle away behind him. His backpack had fallen to the concrete floor,
but at this moment it was just one more blood-soaked encumbrance to
be shed.

The shirt he had on underneath was a thin, short-sleeved polo shirt, but at least it had been shielded from the blood. He scuffed black furry slippers off of his Reeboks, wincing at the sight of the red smears on the white sneakers. *Good enough!* his mind was screaming. *Get out of here!*

He ran back up the steps, hopping over the collapsed organic framework, and when he was back up on the pavement he hopped over a low retaining wall, down to the Hope Street sidewalk.

He was walking away fast, with a hop in every stride.

The brief vision of normal life that the Music Center had kindled in him was forgotten—his brain was still recoiling from having been violated by another personality, but his nervous system had turned his steps firmly south, toward hiding places. The shaking of his heartbeat had started his lungs working again, and he was breathing in fast gasps with a nearly inaudible whistling in his lungs.

The old man's memories were still intolerably ringing in his head, and at every other step he exhaled sharply and shook his head, for along with the immediate clinging smells of dog and blood he could feel in the back of his nose the acrid reek of burned hair.

The little boy's ghost had exploded in an instantaneous white flash halfway between Al and the movie screen, charring the screen and putting a calamitous halt to the world's first motion picture, which, ahead of its time, had been a talkie.

A combusty.

Later, Al had explained the bandages over his burns as just the result of a crucible happening to blow up while he'd been near it, but of course the press had played it up.

The New York Times *headline for April 21, 1889, had read, EDISON BURNED BUT BUSY.*

CHAPTER 18

However, when they had been running half an hour or so, and were quite dry again, the Dodo suddenly called out "The race is over!" and they all crowded round it, panting, and asking "But who has won?"

—Lewis Carroll,
Alice's Adventures in Wonderland

Even on this Wednesday morning in October the Santa Monica Bay beaches were crowded—with surfers in black and turquoise wet suits paddling out across the unbroken blue of the deep water or skating in across the curling jade-green faces of the waves, and blankets and umbrellas and glossy brown bodies thickly dotting the pale sand, and cars and vans and bicycles glinting in the sun on the black asphalt of the parking lots.

On the mile and a half of narrow grassy park on the bluffs above Palisades Beach Road, just north of the Santa Monica Pier, the villages of tents and old refrigerator boxes had drawn a crowd of tourists to mingle gingerly with the resident homeless people, for there was some kind of spontaneous revival meeting going on throughout the whole stretch of Sleeping-bag Town. Six or eight old women abandoned their aluminum-can-filled shopping carts to hop bowlegged across the grass, growling *brrrm-brrrm* in imitation of motorcycle engines or howling like police sirens; then all paused at once and, even though they were yards and yards apart and separated by dozens of people, all shouted in unison, "Stop! You're on a one-way road to Hell!" Ragged old men, evidently caught up in some kind of primitive Eucharistic hysteria, babbled requests that someone take their flesh and eat it; then all at the same instant fell to their knees and began swallowing stones and fistfuls of mud. Several tourists got sick. On the indoor merry-go-round at the

Santa Monica Pier, children were crying and protesting that they didn't like the scary faces in the air.

A mile to the south, at Ocean Park, surfing was disrupted when nearly a hundred people went clumsily thrashing out into the water, shouting to each other and urgently calling out "Sister Aimee! Sister Aimee!" to some apparently imaginary swimmer in peril.

And south of that, at Venice Beach, several trucks and a skip-loader had been driven around the Pavilion and down onto the sand, where, with police clearing the way, they slowly pushed their way through the crowd that had gathered around the big dead fish.

The thing was clearly dead—it was beginning to smell bad, and the crowd tended to be denser downwind of the fat woman who was feverishly puffing on one clove-scented cigarette after another.

None of the exhibitionist bodybuilders in the little fenced-in workout area had bothered to set down their barbells and get up off the padded benches to go look at the fish. And the girls in Day-Glo sunglasses and neon spandex went on splitting the crowd on Ocean Front Walk as they swept through on in-line skates, and the jugglers and musicians stayed by their money-strewn hats or guitar cases. Attention can be briefly diverted by some kind of freak wonder, thought Canov as he leaned against one of the concrete pillars on the concrete stage, but these people know it'll eventually swing back to them.

From up on the stage he could see the signs on the storefronts above the heads of the crowd—MICK'S SUBS, PITBULL GYM FITNESS WEAR, CANDY WORLD/MUSCLE BEACH CAFE/HOT DOGS/PIZZA—and blocks away to the north, up by Windward, he could see the ranks of tentlike booths selling towels and sunglasses and hats and T-shirts and temporary tattoos. The direct sunlight was hot up here on the stage, though when he'd sidled over here through patches of shade he'd noticed that the breeze, bravely spicy with the smells of Polish sausage and sunblock, was nevertheless chilly. The LAPD officers ambling in pairs along the sidewalks were wearing blue shorts and T-shirts, but they'd probably been wearing sweats a few hours ago.

Canov wished he'd had time to change before driving out here, but deLarava had told somebody on the phone that she intended to come straight here herself, and Obstadt had ordered Canov to get to Venice quickly. Now here he was, dressed for the office, and his charcoal suit and black beard probably made him look like some kind of terrorist.

A massive concrete structure on broad pillars overhung the stage on which Canov was standing, and when he'd walked up to the thing and climbed up the high steps, he'd thought it was probably supposed to abstractly represent a man bent over a barbell; and behind it, squatting between it and Ocean Front, was a big gray garage structure that was shaped like a barbell sitting on one of those machines in an automated bowling alley that returned your ball to you. To Canov it all looked like some kind of surreal fascist physical-fitness temple in an old Leni Riefenstal documentary.

He turned his attention back out to the beach. DeLarava's film crew had begun piling their lights and microphone booms back into their van. Apparently they were about to leave—Canov stood up on tiptoes in his Gucci shoes to make sure.

Why the hell, Loretta deLarava thought as she plodded heavily away from the fish, down toward the booming surf, are so many people out on the beach? Did *he* draw them, as cover?

Her shoes had come unfastened, with sand clogging the patches of Velcro, and she couldn't refasten them without a comfortable chair to be sitting in. And the white sun, reflecting needles off the sea and an oven glow upward from the sand, was a physical weight—she was sweating under her white linen sheath dress.

She paused and twisted around without moving her feet, blinking when the salty breeze threw a veil of her hair across her face. I should wear the rubber band on *top* of my hair, she thought. "Come here, Joey," she called irritably.

Her bent little old assistant, ludicrous here on the beach in his boots and khaki jacket, crab-stepped away from the crowd down to where she was standing on the firmer damp sand. *He* never sweated.

"You're on a one-way road to Hell," he said, in a shrilly mocking imitation of a woman's voice. "*She* knew enough," he went on in his own voice, "to keep radio electricians around to screw. Total-immersion baptism to renounce the devils, and then she made sure to resurface under the spiderweb of radar-foxing moves. Rotor-fax devils," he droned then, apparently caught in one of his conversational spirals, "Dover-taxed pixels, white cliffs of image too totally turned-on for any signal *to* show. Too too too, Teet and Toot, tea for two."

DeLarava sucked on the stub of her cigarette so hard that sparks flew away down the beach, but there was no taste of ghost in the smoke. "What about Teet and Toot? Go on."

Joey Webb blinked at her. "They were here once, you said."

Perhaps he was lucid now. "Can you sense them, either of them? Can you sense their *father*?"

"Me sense a person?" Joey said, his voice unfortunately taking on his skitzy singsong tone again, "Aimee Semple McPherson swam out to sea here, and everybody thought she drowned. Two divers *did* drown, trying to save her, and she had to carry those ghosts forever, after that.''

DeLarava had wanted Joey Webb to sift news of old Apie Sullivan's ghost from the turbulent psychic breezes, but he appeared to be hung up on Aimee Semple McPherson, the evangelist who had disappeared in the surf off Ocean Park in 1926; it had been big news at the time, but later the newspapers had discovered that she had just ducked away to spend a couple of weeks in anonymous seclusion with an electrician from her gospel radio station.

DeLarava sighed. Even as a film shoot, today's expedition had pretty much been a failure. The generator truck from the Teamster's Union had got stuck in the sand a couple of hundred feet short of the fish, so that cables had had to be run where people were sure to trip over them, and then there had been trouble with the Mole-phase lights, the tic-tac-toe squares of nine 5600-Kelvin lamps that were supposed to provide daylight-colored illumination to fill the shadows on people's faces; the lights had alternately flared and faded, and finally deLarava had told the cameraman to just shoot the bystanders with their eye sockets and cheek hollows gaping like caverns. God knew what the fish would come out looking like on the film.

Hours ago Animal Control had sent a truck out to haul away the fish, but a bystander claimed that the dead monster was a *coelacanth*, some sort of living fossil from the Carboniferous Age, uncommon anywhere and never found in the Pacific Ocean. The Department of Fish and Game had arrived after that, and some professors had driven down from UCLA and were still arguing with anyone who planned to even touch the damned thing.

The news story, such as it was, was in the can, and deLarava had sent one of her people back to the studio with it, but she didn't want to leave the beach without learning whether old Sullivan's ghost had emerged from the sea yet—and if so, *where he was.* She wouldn't dare try to eat him until Saturday, but she could safely catch him in a jar now.

For what must have been the hundredth time, she glanced at her watch, but the compass needle was still jittering unreliably, pointing more or less at the concrete block of handball courts, which was north of her. Before the camera had started rolling she had stumped her way through the crowd around the site, peering constantly at her watch, but each of the six times the needle had pointed away from north it had been indicating some nearby grinning or frowning old lunatic in junk-store clothes—accreted, hardened old ghosts, whose stunted fields wouldn't even be detectable if they'd step back a yard or two.

Apie Sullivan's ghost would be indistinguishable from a death-new one, and *strong*, preserved for all these past thirty-three years in the grounded stasis of the sea. But tracking a new ghost, she thought now as she watched the quivering needle, is like trying to spot a helicopter in a city—you "hear" 'em from all kinds of false directions; they aren't truly at any "where" yet, and they're subject to "echoes."

But I'm not even getting any echoes. And Joey Webb isn't sensing him, and he would—Joey thinks they're angels or spirits or something, but he does reliably sense ghosts. Joey would know it if he was here.

And he's not here.

DeLarava dug in her purse and pulled out her wallet. "Joey," she said, "are you listening to me? I want you to stay here, rent a room at a motel or something, can you do that?" She slid a sheaf of twenties and hundreds out of the wallet and held it out toward him.

"Which motel?" said old Joey alertly, taking the money. "What name will he be using?"

"He's not going to stay at a motel, you—" She threw her cigarette away toward the waves, and coughed harshly, tasting clove in the back of her throat. "*He'll* be just a little wispy shred, like the cellophane from a cigarette pack, but not reflecting. Track him with a compass—he'll be dazed, wandering. Buy a jar of orange marmalade, dump out the marmalade but leave some smears in it for him to smell, and if you find him, catch him in it." She stared at the crazy old man anxiously. "Can you do all this?"

"Oh, *do* it, sure," he said with a careless wave. He shoved the bills inside his shirt. "What do you want me to tell him?"

"Don't *talk* to him," deLarava wailed, nearly crying with exhaustion and frustration. "Don't unscrew the lid after you've caught him. Just wrap him in your coat or something and call me, okay?"

"*O*kay, o*kay*. Sheesh."

"You won't let him get past you? He mustn't get inland of Pacific Avenue, I can't afford to lose him in the maze of the city."

Joey stood up straight and squinted at her. "He shall not pass."

This would have to do. "Call me when you're checked in," she said clearly, then turned and began striding heavily up the sand slope, shoving her way between the bystanders.

When she had elbowed her way to the clearing in the center of the crowd, she paused by the thigh-high hulk of the coppery fish and looked down into its big, dulled eye. A living fossil, one of the UCLA professors had called this monstrosity. Hardly a living one, she thought. Though some of us still are.

She was on the north side of the dead thing, and she looked at her watch—but the compass needle pointed away behind her, northward.

She sighed and began pushing her way back out of the crowd. This was a waste of time, she thought. But maybe my billboards will have elicited a call about the Parganas kid. And I parked the Lexus way up on Main here—maybe somebody will have broken into it.

Sweat had run down from Canov's styled hair into his beard, and he scratched at it before it could work down his neck to his white collar. He was glad to see that deLarava was finally leaving, for a dozen children in swimsuits had climbed up onto the open-air stage that he'd chosen as a lookout post, and they'd started some skipping and singing game.

A big dead fish, Canov thought as he carefully stepped down the cement block stairs to the pavement. What can I tell Obstadt, besides that she hung around and looked at it and filmed it? This one's bigger than the ones she hooks and hauls up to the *Queen Mary* deck on dark nights, but she didn't catch this one, and she surely didn't eat it. Maybe she's just interested in fish. And the crabs and lobsters have all been picked up, or managed to return to the sea. I can't even bring him one, not that Obstadt would have any use for it, being a strict vegetarian.

"Can I buy a smoke off you, man?"

Canov turned away from the beach. A tanned young man who had been standing over by the volleyball nets had walked across the gray pavement to the stage, and now stood with one hand extended and the other digging in the pocket of his cutoff jeans. Canov thought he looked too healthy to be wanting nicotine.

"I haven't found any," said Canov. If it *was* a cigarette the man wanted, this answer ought to disconcert him.

But instead of protesting that he didn't want a cigarette picked up off the sidewalk, the young man shook his head ruefully. "They're out today, though, aren't they?" he said, his voice just loud enough for Canov to hear it over the rap music shouting out of the black portable stereos on the sidelines of the volleyball games. "You can almost smell how they died."

Canov, never a user of the stuff known as "smokes" and "cigars," just shrugged. "I can smell that that fish died," he said inanely.

The young man glanced disinterestedly down toward the crowd by the shore. "Dead fish, yeah. Well, see you." And he began jogging away barefoot toward the bike path, doubtless searching for some other out-of-place-looking person standing around.

Police had cleared another path through the crowd, and now a pickup truck with a cherry-picker crane in its bed had been driven down onto the sand, and Canov could see men in overalls trying to roll the fish over onto a long board. A big flatbed tow truck was parked nearby, and he wondered idly who had won custody of the creature.

He sighed and began walking over. Obstadt would probably want to know.

The fish was to be driven to an oceanography lab at UCLA. When the creature had been covered with a tarpaulin and roped down on the long bed of the tow truck, the driver slowly backed the truck out the way it had come, around the north side of the pavilion; the *beep, beep, beep* of the reverse-gear horn was drowned out at one point by metallic squealing, as one of the back wheels pinched and then flattened a blue-and-white trash can that had RECYCLE*RECICLE*RECYCLE*RECICLE sten-ciled endlessly around it, but eventually all four wheels were on pavement again, and the driver muscled the stick shift into first gear and began inching the big laboring old truck toward the Ocean Front curb, as policemen waved dozens of nearly naked people out of the way.

At last the truck reached Windward; and when the traffic thinned, out past Main, it drove up Venice Boulevard to Lincoln, and then turned north, toward the Santa Monica Freeway.

On the freeways, there you feel free.

As the truck ascended the on-ramp, grinding with measured punctu-ation up through the gears, the purple-flowered oleanders along the shoulder waved their leafy branches in a sudden gust; and sunlight flashed in the rushing air where there was no chrome or glass reflecting it, as if the ghosts of dozens of angular old cars accompanied the la-boring truck.

In the steamy dimness under the flapping tarpaulin the jaws of the dead coelacanth creaked open, and a shrill faint whistling piped out of the throat as reversed peristalsis drove gases out of the creature's stom-ach. The whistling ran up and down the musical scale in a rough ap-proximation of the first nine notes of "Begin the Beguine," and then a tiny gray translucency wobbled out of the open mouth, past the teeth, like a baby jellyfish moving through clear water.

A puff of smoke that didn't disperse at its edges, the thing climbed down over the plates of the fish's lower jaw, clung for a moment to the shaking corrugated aluminum surface of the truck bed, then sprang up into the agitated dimness toward the close tent-roof of the tarpaulin. The wind sluicing along the sides of the dead fish caught the wisp and whirled it back and out under the flapping tarpaulin edge into the open air, where hot, rushing diesel updrafts lifted it above the roaring trucks and cars and vans to spin invisibly in the harsh sunlight.

Traffic behind the flatbed truck slowed then, for suddenly the truck appeared to be throwing off pieces of itself: a glimpsed rushing surface of metal here, a whirling black tire there, glitters of chrome appearing first on one side of the truck and then the other, as if some way-ultraviolet light were illuminating bits of otherwise invisible vehicles secretly sharing the freeway. Then windshields were darkened in a moment of shadow as a long-winged yellow biplane roared past overhead, low over the traffic, with the figure of a man dimly visible standing on the top wing.

After no more than two seconds the plane flickered and disappeared, but before winking out of visibility it had banked on the inland wind, as if headed northeast, toward Hollywood.

CHAPTER 19

"But then," thought Alice, "shall I never *get any older than I am now?
That'll be a comfort, one way—never to be an old woman—but then—
always to have lessons to learn! Oh, I shouldn't like* that*!"*
—Lewis Carroll,
Alice's Adventures in Wonderland

Back in his Olive Street office after court, well in time for a healthful
lunch, J. Francis Strube tossed his briefcase onto the long oak credenza
and slumped his oversized frame into the padded leather McKie chair
behind his desk.

He had an appointment this afternoon, some guy whose wife was
divorcing him. The man had sounded almost apologetic on the phone,
clearly reluctant to hire an attorney because he hoped his wife would
abandon the divorce action and come back to him. Strube would sym-
pathize during this first consultation, let the guy ramble and emote and
probably weep; during later sessions Strube could begin to raise his
eyebrows over the man's willingness to let the wife take so much stuff.
Strube would interject, *Oh, she'll need it because she'll be doing a lot
of* entertaining, *eh?*—delivered in a tone that would make Strube seem
like a sympathetically angered friend. *Well, if you want to let her have
everything . . .*

Eventually Strube could get a man to refuse to part with a vacuum
cleaner that he might never have actually used, or possibly ever even
seen.

It took more time, but Strube preferred nurturing rapacity in these
timid clients to flattering the egos of the villains who just wanted to
ditch the old wife and marry the twenty-year-old *sex . . . pot.* For the
latter sort Strube would have to say, in tones of polite surprise, things

like *You're* fifty*? Good Lord, you don't look a day over forty.* And, *How did you put up with this for so long?*

Anyway, the timid ones needed attorneys. What they initially wanted, like first-time Driving Under the Influence offenders, was to appear in court in humble *pro per*, not realizing that judges had all been attorneys once, and planned to be again after they retired, and wanted to make of these fools examples of how badly unrepresented people fared.

In a courthouse hallway this morning another attorney had told Strube a riddle.

Question: What do a lawyer and a sperm cell have in common?

Strube pursed his lips and leaned forward to pick up the newspaper that Charlotte had left on the desk. The telephone rang, but Charlotte would get it. Strube made it a point never to answer the phone on spec.

He waited, but the intercom didn't buzz. That was good, she was fielding whatever it was. He let himself start to read.

He saw that Ross Perot was claiming to have backed out of the presidential race only because of threats from the Bush-campaign people. He smiled. Strube never voted, but he liked to see things shaken up. "Time for a Change!" was a political slogan that always appealed to him. He was about to flip the front page when he noticed the box at the bottom.

FANS SEARCHING FOR "SPOOKY"
FROM OLD SITCOM

Strube read the story quickly, peripherally aware that his heartbeat was speeding up. When he had finished it, he pushed a button on the intercom.

"Charlotte!" he squeaked. "Get in here and look at this." No, he thought immediately, she might try to get the credit herself. "Wait, get me—" he began again, but she had already opened his office door and was staring in at him curiously.

She was wearing another of the anonymous dark jacket-and-skirt combinations to which she had been confining herself ever since he'd made a blundering pass at her six months ago. "Look at what?" she asked.

"Perot says Bush was going to wreck his daughter's wedding," he said absently, folding the paper and pushing it aside. "Did you read about that? Say, get me the telephone number of . . ." What had been the name of the damned snuff? Ouchie? "Goudie! Goudie Scottish Snuff, uh, Company. G-O-U-D-I-E. It's in San Francisco."

"Snuff?"

Strube raised the back of his pudgy hand to his nose and sniffed loudly. "Snuff. Like lords and ladies used to do. Powdered tobacco."

"Do you want me to call them?"

"No, just get me the number."

Charlotte nodded, mystified, and walked back out to the reception desk, closing his office door behind her.

If Nicky Bradshaw's still alive, thought Strube excitedly, he's gotta still be doing that snuff; and it's a clue I'll bet not a lot of people remember. And I'll bet nobody but me remembers the actual brand name. God knows I ordered it often enough.

Strube stood up and walked quickly across the carpet to the window overlooking Olive, and he stared down at the gleaming multicolored car roofs rippling through the lanes like beetles. Strube had a new BMW himself, but from up here it could look no different from any of the cars below him now. He was a member of Sports Club LA on Sepulveda—he had even got occasional business from his ad in the club's networking newsletter—and he was proud of his healthful diet regimen, years having passed since he had last eaten real eggs or bacon or butter or sour cream; and his apartment on Sunset was expensive, but . . .

Aside from his suits and the sectional furniture and some signed sailing prints on the walls, the apartment was pretty bare—in truth, about half of his worldly goods were in the goddamn credenza here in the office, along with the ceiling fan that he'd never taken out of its box and the routed cherrywood decoupaged J. FRANCIS STRUBE name plaque that a client had handcrafted for him and that he'd been embarrassed to put out on his desk because people might think he represented hippie dopers.

But he *could* be . . . the attorney who located Spooky.

Answer: Each of them has one chance in two million of becoming a human being.

Of becoming somebody.

It seemed to him now that, when he was twenty and twenty-one, he had mailed orders to the Goudie Snuff Company as often as he had mailed solicitation letters to the people whose names and addresses had appeared on the thrice-weekly foreclosure lists.

He had worked as a legal secretary for Nicholas Bradshaw in '74 and '75, in Seal Beach. Bradshaw had handled mostly bankruptcy cases, which often came around to involving divorce and child custody, and young Strube had proved to have a natural knack for the tactics of family breakup.

Strube had planned to go into show-business law—after law school he had let his mousy brown hair grow long and had worn crazy little granny glasses, and he had gone to work for Bradshaw mainly because Bradshaw had once been an actor—but somewhere along the line Bradshaw had developed an aversion to the TV and movie business; and without a contact, an in, access, Strube hadn't been able to get any of the industry's law firms to consider taking him on.

Then after Bradshaw had just ... *up and disappeared* ... in '75, Strube had been left without any job at all. He had hastily gone to work for a divorce and personal-injury attorney, and passed the bar in '81. At last in '88 had been able to open his own practice ... but he was still just disassembling families.

The intercom buzzed, and Strube walked back to his desk and pushed the button. "Yeah, Charlotte." He wrote down the 415-area number she read to him. At least Goudie was still in business.

Back in '74 and '75, Bradshaw had kept a box of snuff cans in his desk, and when he had paperwork to do he would open the box and lay out half a dozen cans, like a buffet, and sniff a bit of this one, a couple of snorts of that one, and a chaser of another. He had gone through so much of the stuff that he found it easiest to have his legal secretary order directly from the company.

Strube punched the number into the telephone.

Bradshaw had paid young Strube a generous weekly salary, and never cared what hour Strube came into the office or went home, as long as the work got done, and he had been lavish with bonuses—and, too, he'd always been paranoid, afraid of being findable, always varying his schedule and never divulging, even to Strube, his home address or phone number; wherever he was now, he clearly didn't want to be found. But ...

"Goudie Snuff Company," chirped a voice from the phone.

"Hi, my name is J. Francis Strube. I'm in Los Angeles and I'm marketing a line of—" What, he thought nervously. "—traditional Scottish products, tartan sweaters and walking sticks and so on, and I'd like to buy a copy of your mailing list."

Angelica Anthem Elizalde slumped wearily in the RTD bus seat with her forehead against the cool window, and she watched the shops and old houses of Sixth Street, fogged by her breath on the glass, swing past in the sunlight outside.

She wondered if people still used the word *chicana,* and she wondered when and where she had stopped being one. The women in the seats around her were happily chatting in Spanish, and twice they had referred to her as *"la Angla sonalienta al lado de la ventana"*—the sleepy Anglo lady by the window. Elizalde had wanted to smile and, in Spanish, say something back about the long Greyhound ride across the desert yesterday, then had realized that she no longer had the vocabulary.

Elizalde's mother had always told her that she looked *mestizo*—European Spanish, rather than *indigena*. Her face was long and angular and pale, like a saint in an El Greco painting, and in her Oklahoma Levi jeans and her old Graceland sweatshirt she probably did look Anglo. It occurred to her that she probably even spoke with a bit of an Oklahoma accent now.

At one point during the long night at the Greyhound station—waiting for the dawn, not able to afford a taxi and not wanting to walk anywhere on the menacing dark streets—she had washed her face in the ladies' room, and had stared in the mirror at the vertical grooves in her cheeks and the lines around her eyes. Her face looked older than her thirty-four years, though the rest of her was somehow still as trim and taut as she'd been in her twenties—or even in her teens.

Immature? she wondered now as she watched the old houses sweep past outside the bus window. Say—she smiled nervously—arrested adolescent.

It seemed to her now that there had been something naively Quixotic about her psychiatric career and her stubbornly terminal argument with Dr. Alden. In her private practice, in her own clinic, she had been able to make her own rules—and then had just fled the state and changed her name when the whole arrangement had blown up.

(Almost literally blown up—the fire department had managed to save the building.)

She had never married, nor ever had children. In idly psychoanalyzing herself, she had once decided that her "morbid dread" of pregnancy derived from the time when, at the age of three, she had climbed into an old milk can in the living room in Norco and got stuck—and, to hear her mother describe the event in later years, lost her mind. It was a three-foot-tall, forty-quart metal can that her parents had kept in the corner and tossed spare change into, and when toddler Angelica got stuck inside it, she had apparently had a severe claustrophobic reaction. After her father had failed to pull her out, and had failed to break the can open with a hammer (all of this no doubt compounding little Angelica's terror), Angelica's grandmother had been summoned from the house across the street. The old woman, who had luckily done midwifing for half a century, ordered Angelica's father to turn the can upside down, and then had delivered the toddler out of the can as though she were guiding a newborn baby out of the womb, head first and then one shoulder at a time. The afterbirth had been a shower of pennies and nickels and dimes.

Her mother had always told her how, apparently out of regret for having caused so much trouble, baby Angelica must have awakened late that night and gone into the dark living room and gathered up all the spilled coins, separated them out by denomination, and then ranked them in stacks on a table; and her mother had forever insisted, with obviously sincere astonishment and pride, that the baby had even arranged the coins in chronological order of mint date, with the oldest coins on top.

Angelica had never believed that she had got up and moved the coins at all, but even as a child she had known better than to say so to her mother, who would probably have called the grandmother over again to do some distressing kind of homespun exorcism. Perhaps as a child Angelica had known that there were some borders that it was best not to include in one's maps. If so, she had recently learned it again.

The women in the bus seats around her this morning had no such compunctions. One woman was cautioning the others against leaving the living-room drapes open at night this weekend, and Elizalde at first assumed that it was a precaution against being shot in a drive-by shooting; and it might have been, partly, but after a few moments she understood that it was mainly to keep from calling to oneself the attention of the witches that would surely be flying around in *calabazas y bolos fuegos*, gourds and fireballs. Another woman said that she would be smoking cornhusk cigarettes every night for the next week or so; and one old grandmother in the very back seat said she'd be going out to Santa Monica on Friday night to feed her *"piedra iman"* in the sand and seawater. When Angelica Elizalde had been growing up, a *piedra iman* was a magnet; perhaps the term now meant something else.

Mundane borders too were commonplace with these ladies—secure in the supposed secrecy of the Spanish language, they casually traded adventure stories of how they'd stolen across the California-Mexico border, and a couple of them even discussed holiday plans to travel back and forth across it again to visit relatives in Mazatlán and Guadalajara, and they traded bits of advice for dealing with the *coyotes* who guided parties north across the broken wasteland of gullies and arroyos into the border cities of the United States.

Altogether they made Elizalde feel . . . incompetent and unworldly, a frightened fugitive with an out-of-date tourist's map.

It should, she thought wearily, be the other way around. These women were housemaids, paid stingily in cash under the table, and they lived in the neighborhoods around Rampart and Union and the east end of Wilshire, where the families who were crowded into the shabby apartments did "hot bed" sleeping, in shifts, and Sunday dawns no doubt found these women stirring steaming pots of menudo for their hungover husbands, who would have towels beside them to mop the sweat off their faces as they ate the spicy stuff. Elizalde had gone to college, and medical school, and had thought she had moved *up*, out of this world; now she wished she could trade places with any one of these women.

On the south side of the street, a sign over the bay door of a onetime gas station read CARREDIOS, and—in the few seconds it took her to realize that it was just a badly spaced and misspelled attempt at CAR RADIOS—she read it as *carre dios*, which would mean something like the god of the course, the god of the run; and she had fleetingly thought of getting off the bus and going in there and lighting a candle.

She would have to be getting off soon anyway. Alvarado was the next stop. She sat up and tugged at the cord over the window, hearing the faint *bong* from the front of the bus, then got stiffly to her feet. Only a few blocks south of here was the office she had rented on Tuesdays, when she had first gone into private practice. Frank Rocha had been one of her patients even back in those early days, and later he had attended the group "seances" when she had opened her clinic up on Beverly.

She grabbed one of the upright steel poles as the bus squealed to a stop. What on earth, she thought helplessly as she let go and shuffled toward the opened back doors, do I think I'm going to *do* here? If his widow and kids even still live in that house? Apologize? Offer to . . . *help*? What money I've got I do need.

The letter in her wallet seemed to be heavy, seemed to be almost pulling her pants down on that side.

Do yardwork? Tune up the car engine?

Madam, she thought, suppressing a hysterical giggle, *I accidentally ran over your cat, and I want to replace it.*

Fine, but how good are you at catching mice?

She stepped down to the curb. Apologize, I guess. I can at least give her that, I can let her know that her husband's death has shattered me, that I'm aware that I was responsible for it, that I haven't been blithely forgetful of it.

As the doors hissed shut and the bus pulled away from the curb in a cloud of diesel smoke, Elizalde looked across across the lanes of Sixth Street at the receding green lawn of MacArthur Park. She sighed and turned away, toward a ripped-up construction site where, according to signs on the plywood hoardings, city workers were digging tunnels for the proposed Metro Rail; and she started trudging that way, north up the Alvarado sidewalk.

*   *   *

She recognized Rocha's house by the willow tree in the front yard. It must have had deep roots, for its narrow leaves were still green, while the lawn had not only died but gone entirely away, leaving only bare dirt with a couple of bright orange plastic tricycles knocked over on it. The old wood-frame house was painted navy blue now, with a red trim that Elizalde thought looked jarring.

Under these twittery surface impressions her mind was spinning. How on earth could she dare approach Mrs. Rocha?

How could she not? Only two nights ago, when she had weirdly begun reacting to events a second before the events happened, she had finally decided to *confront* whatever it was that had happened in her clinic on Halloween two years ago; and part of confronting it, as far as she could see, had to be facing the victims of it. Trying to make amends.

But she herself was a victim of it! Walking wounded! How would this ordeal—subjecting herself to this unthinkable meeting—be making amends to *Angelica Anthem Elizalde*?

Just to . . . *apologize*? No one would be better off.

But she was shuffling up the concrete walk toward the front porch. And when she had stepped up to the front door, she rapped on the frame of the screen. Brassy mariachi music was blaring inside.

Peering through the mesh of the screen door, she could see the blue-and-pink flicker of a television reflecting in framed pictures on a living-room wall. The music and the colors both ceased at the same instant.

The gray-haired woman who appeared behind the screen stared at Elizalde for a moment, and then said something fast in Spanish.

"Perdón," said Elizalde, as light-headed as if she'd just bolted a stiff drink on her empty stomach, *"estoy buscando por Señora Rocha?"*

"Ahora me llamo Señora Gonzalvez." Her last name was now Gonzalvez, but this was apparently Frank Rocha's widow. Elizalde didn't recognize her, but after all she had seen the woman only once before, three or four years ago. She didn't recall her hair being gray then.

"Me llamo Elizalde, Angelica Anthem Elizalde. Necesito—"

The woman's eyes were wide, and she echoed "Elizalde!" slowly, almost reverently.

"Sí. Por favor, necesito hablar con usted. Lo siento mucho. Me hace falto . . . explicar que yo estaba . . . tratando de hacer—"

"Un momento." The woman disappeared back into the dimness of the living room, and Elizalde could hear her moving things, a shuffling sound like books being rearranged on a table.

Un momento? Elizalde blinked at the again-vacant rectangle of the screen door. One of us isn't understanding the other, she thought helplessly. This woman can't be Frank Rocha's widow, or else I can't have made it clear who I am—otherwise, surely, she wouldn't have just walked away.

"Escúsame?" she called. This was ridiculous. Her heart was thudding in her rib cage like fists hitting a punching bag, and her mouth was dry and tasted of metal. Hel*lo-o*, she thought crazily, wondering if she might start giggling. I'm responsible for the death of *somebody's* husband around here . . . !

She curled her fingers around the door handle, and after a moment pulled it open against the resistance of creaking hinges.

On the mantel against the far wall an *ofrenda* had been set up, an altar, a figured silk scarf laid across a little embroidered cushion with framed photographs set up on it and around it, and two stylized, fancifully painted wooden skulls at either end of the display, like bookends. Preparation for El Día de los Muertos, the day of the dead. On the wall over it was hung a heart-shaped frame, its interior occupied by a gold-colored crucifix and a small clock face. She noted that the time was nearly noon.

She stepped inside, letting the screen door slap closed behind her.

Abruptly startled, she blinked her eyes shut—and a flash of red through her closed eyelids, and then a little mechanical whirring sound, let her know that the woman had taken her picture with an instamatic camera. To add to the *ofrenda*? wondered Elizalde in bewilderment as she opened her eyes and blinked at the woman's silhouette. But I'm not dead. . . .

Then her knees and the palms of her hands hit the carpet as a tremendous, stunning *bang* shook the room, and she was up and spinning and punching the screen door aside as another gunshot bruised her eardrums; she had clenched her eyes shut an instant before the shot, and so the splinters from the struck oak doorframe just stung her eyelids.

She felt one of her sneaker soles slap the porch boards—and then the porch had hit her again, and she was falling, and the dirt of the yard slammed against her hip and elbow as another *bang* crashed behind her and a plume of white dust sprang up from the sidewalk.

Rolling to her feet, she sprinted slantways across the barren yard and pelted away back south down the Amado Street sidewalk. She had to run in a slapping, flat-footed gait, for her feet kept feeling the impacts with the pavement before they actually occurred.

A one-story travel-agency building, apparently closed, loomed at the corner on her left, and she skidded around its wall tightly enough to have knocked over anyone who might have been walking up on the other side—but the sidewalk, the whole narrow street, was empty.

In an alley-fronting parking lot across the street an old lime-green couch was propped against the back wall of another retail-looking building, and she crossed the street toward it—forcing herself to shuffle along, to stroll, rather than flail and stamp and wheeze as she had been doing.

Her lungs felt seared, and the back of her head tingled in anticipation of savage pursuit, but nobody had yelled or audibly begun running across the asphalt by the time she stepped up the curb and crossed to the couch.

She thought she could hide behind it, crouch in the cool shadow of it, until dark, and then creep away. Her teeth were clenched, and her face was cold with shame. *Why did I go there?* she was screaming in her head, *why did I rip open her old wounds, and mine, and*—She remembered the shots, and rolling on the dirt, and running so clumsily, and she opened her eyes wide with the effort of forcing those things out of her attention, concentrating instead on the blue sky behind the shaggy palm trees and the telephone wires and the whirling crows.

Dizzy, she looked down and put her hand on the couch. The couch arm was fibrous and oily under her hand—*gristly*—but she realized that she had felt the texture of it only when she had actually touched it. The weird anticipation of sensations had apparently stopped when she had been crossing the street.

"Did you leave that here?" piped a close young man's voice, speaking in English.

Elizalde looked up guiltily. The back door of the building had been standing open, and now a fat white man with a scruffy beard was leaning out of it. He was wearing cutoff jeans, and his belly was stretching a stained example of the sleeveless undershirts she had always thought of as wife-beater T-shirts.

She realized that she had forgotten what he had asked her. "I'm sorry?"

He peered up and down the alley. "Did you hear gunshots just now?"

"A truck was backfiring on Amado," said Elizalde, keeping her voice casual.

The fat man nodded. "So is it yours?"

"The truck?" Her face was suddenly hot, and she knew she was either blushing or pale, for she had almost said, *The gun?*

"The couch," he said impatiently. "Did you put it here?"

"Oh," Elizalde said, "no. I was just looking at it."

"Somebody dumped it here. We find all kinds of crap back here. People think they can unload any old junk." He eyed the couch with disfavor. "Probably some big old black lady gave birth on it. And her mother before that. We got better furniture inside, if you got any money.''

Elizalde blinked at him, trickles of disgust beginning to puddle in the scraped, blown-out emptiness of her mind. And where were *you* born, she thought—on a culture dish in a VD lab, I'd judge. But all she said was, ''Furniture?''

''Yeah, secondhand. And books, kitchenware, *ropa usada*. Had Jackie Onassis in here the other day.''

Elizalde had caught her breath at last, and she could smell beer on him. She nodded and made herself smile as she stepped past him into the store. ''Yeah, she was telling me about it.''

Inside were racks of pitiful clothes, bright cheap blouses and sun hats and colorful pants, that seemed still to carry an optimistic whiff, long stale now, of their original purchases at sunny swap meets and canvas-tent beachside stands. And there were shelves of books—hardcover jun-ior-college texts, paperback science fiction and romances—and rows of family-battered Formica and particleboard-and-wood-veneer tables, cov-ered with ceramic ashtrays and wrecked food processors and, somehow, a lot of fondue pots. A white-glass vase had been knocked over on one table, spilling a sheaf of dried flowers. My *quinceniera* bouquet, she thought as she looked at them. Withered roses, and husks of lilies, and a stiffened spray of forgive-me-nots.

''Begin life anew,'' advised the drunk bearded man, who had fol-lowed her back inside.

Life a-old, she thought. This was an accumulation of the crumbled shells of lives, collapsed when the owners had become absent, piled here now like broken cast-off snakeskins, some pieces still big enough to show outlines of departed personalities.

Well, Elizalde thought, I'm kind of a broken personality myself. I should hide in here for a while, at least long enough to see if cop sirens go past on the street outside, or angry Rochas or Gonzalvezes come bursting in. If they do, I'll just drape myself over one of these fine tables and be as inconspicuous as a skeleton hiding in a scrimshaw shop.

But nobody did come in at all, and the traffic outside was uneventful. The sunny October Los Angeles day had apparently swallowed up the gunshots without a ripple and was rolling on. Elizalde bought a Rastafari knitted tam—red, gold, black, and green—big enough to tuck her long black hair up into, and a tan size-fourteen Harve Benard jumpsuit that had no doubt had an interesting history. Three dollars paid for the whole bundle at the counter by the street door, and the bearded man didn't even remark on it when Elizalde swept the hat forward over her head and then pulled the jumpsuit on right over her jeans and sweatshirt.

After she had pushed open the door and walked a block back south toward Sixth Street, she realized that she had taken on the humbled, slope-shouldered gait she remembered in many of her patients; and she was pleased at the instinctive mimicry, during the few moments it took her to realize that it was not mimickry at all, but natural.

CHAPTER 20

"Don't keep him waiting, child! Why, his time is worth a thousand pounds a minute!"

—Lewis Carroll,
Through the Looking-Glass

Hunching and hopping along the walkway that flanked the Ahmanson Theater, moving in and out of the fleeting shade of the strips of decorative roof so narrow and so far overhead that they could serve as shelter only against a preternaturally straight-falling rain, Sherman Oaks followed his missing, pointing arm. The nonexistent arm was so hot that the rest of him felt chilly, as if he were reaching out the door of an air-conditioned bar in Death Valley, out into the harsh sunlight. And he was sniffing vigorously, for the boy Koot Hoomie Parganas had moved through this place not long ago, and he could strongly smell the big ghost that the boy carried.

Run, he read in the impressions still shaking in the air, a long run, fleeing under a masked sun on the front of a train, running . . . on all fours? With long nails clicking on pavement! What the hell?

His missing arm practically dragged him around the moat that encircled the giant wedding cake of the Mark Taper Forum, and then the stair railing across the pavement ahead of him seemed to be the only focused thing in the landscape; everything else, even the incongruous ragged pile of raw meat by the Taper's entry doors, was a blur. He was close!

At the top of the stairs he came to a full stop, and then cautiously peered down—and his heart began pounding still harder, for a *dead old man* was sprawled down there on the blood-smeared concrete stairs.

I should get right out of here, he thought—hop over this deceased old party and continue on the kid's trail.

But as he shuffled down the steps he realized that the thing on the stairs was not actually a man; it was a limply collapsed dummy, stitched into a coarse black coat of badly woven fur. But the imbecilically distorted face, and the white hands, seemed to be made of flesh—and the spattered and smeared blood looked real. It *smelled* real.

Oaks paused to crouch over the crumpled shell. He emptied his lungs through his open mouth, hearing the faint outraged stadium roar of all the ghosts he had inhaled over the years; and then he inhaled deeply, flaring his nostrils and tilting his head back and swelling his chest.

He caught the flat muskiness of ectoplasm, the protean junk that squirted out of mediums to lend substance to ghosts . . . but he smelled real flesh, too, and real blood.

Dog flesh, he realized as he sucked up more of the charged air. Dog blood.

No wonder he had caught an impression moments ago of running on all fours! Someone had vaporized a *dog* to get substance for filling out a figure too big and solid for ectoplasm alone. And a prepubescent kid wouldn't be able to provide much ectoplasm anyway.

The big ghost had done this, had made this thing. Why? The ghost must have perceived itself to be in some emergency, for this would have been a very stressful move.

Oaks stared down at the flat head of the thing. This would have to be a portrait of the big ghost that the kid was carrying: white hair, a pouchy and wrinkled face . . .

Who the hell was it? Probably someone famous, certainly someone powerful, to judge by the huge psychic field that his ghost projected. The face, broad and big-chinned and dominant even deflated on the steps here, looked vaguely familiar to Oaks . . . but from a *long* time ago. Briefly and uneasily, Oaks wondered how old he himself might be, really; but he pushed the question away and thought about the ghost who had left this thing here.

Whoever it was, he had died at the Parganas house on Loma Vista two nights ago—or at least that's where and when his spanking-new ghost had appeared, blazing in the psychic sky like a nova—and the Parganas couple had chosen to die horribly rather than tell Oaks anything at all.

Oaks stared at the blood on the steps here, and he remembered following the powerful new ghost's beacon all the way across town to that house in Beverly Hills on Monday night. By the time Oaks had got there the ghost was gone, headed south, but Oaks had stayed to find out who it had been, and who had taken it away, in the hope of avoiding this weary labor of following every step of the thing's trail. He remembered his useless torturing of the middle-aged man and woman in that garden-type patio off the living room. As soon as he had taped the two of them into the chairs and started questioning them, they had gone into some kind of defensive trance; and Oaks, fearful of being caught there, had got angry and had cut them more and more savagely, and after he had finally cut out their very eyes he had realized that they had died at some point.

After that, still angry, he had set about searching the house. And then the kid had come home—very late, not far short of dawn—and when Oaks had gone into the living room the dead couple's ghosts had been standing in there! Blinking around stupidly, but as solid as you could ask for, and them only an hour dead at the most!

He should have known right then that the big ghost had come back, and that it was the big ghost's promiscuous field that had lit up the two silly new ghosts in their wedding clothes. But the trail had been looped right back onto itself at that point, and too grossly powerful for Oaks to comprehend that it had doubled when the kid entered the scene. And anyway, the kid had taken off like an arrow out of a bow; and the boy had run out of the house *through* that garden patio, which could only have speeded him up still more.

Oaks hopped over the bloody mess on the stairs and stepped down to the cement-floored landing—apparently this was a parking level—but after a couple of steps he froze.

His phantom left arm wasn't pointing anymore; it had flopped nervelessly, and he couldn't feel anything at all in it. He tried to work the hand—usually when the arm was down by his side he could rasp the fingers against the hairy skin of his thigh, whether or not he happened to be wearing long pants—but the nonexistent fingers sensed nothing now but, perhaps, a faint cool breeze sluicing between them. The trail was gone.

Had the ghost freed itself from the kid and evaporated? That would be bad—Oaks was getting thin, and for the last thirty or forty hours he had been passing up the chance to eat smaller ghosts, in his anxiety not to miss this big feast. Or had the kid somehow all at once attained *puberty* this morning, enabling him to eat and digest the ghost himself?

Oaks's face was chilly with alarm—but after a moment he relaxed a little. Whatever had happened here, whatever it was that had provoked the ghost into whipping up this ectoplasmic mannikin . . . *the whole event must have been a terrible shock to the kid, too.* In his terror the boy might very well have just *clathrated* the ghost, convulsively enclosed it within his own psyche but not assimilated it—encysted the thing, shoved it down, walled it up tightly inside himself.

That could happen, Oaks knew; and if it had, the locked-in ghost wouldn't be detectable from the outside.

Like that one time when Houdini . . .

The fleeting thought was gone, leaving only an association: Jonah and the whale. Sherman Oaks hurried back up the stairs, stepping carelessly right on the limp face this time, and when he was back up on the pavement he hopped over a retaining wall by the valet-parking driveway and strode away south on the Hope Street sidewalk.

Houdini? Jonah and the whale? God knew what memory had started to surface there—something from the time before he had come into this present continuity-of-consciousness three years ago, in the district of Sherman Oaks, from which he had whimsically taken this present name. Again he wondered, briefly and uneasily, how old he might really be, and when and how he might have lost his left arm.

To his right, across the street, the elevated pools around the Metropolitan Water District building reflected the watery blue sky. Oaks calculated that the time could hardly be even an hour past noon, but the pale sun had already begun to recede, having come as far up above the southern horizon as it cared to in this season. North was behind him, and the thought prompted him to sneak a glance down at the pommel of the survival knife he wore inside his pants.

When he had stolen the knife, its hollow hilt had been full of things like fishhooks and matches. He had replaced that stuff with reliable compact ghost lures—a nickel with a nail welded to the back so that it could be hammered into a wooden floor, where it would confound the patient efforts of ghosts to pick it up, and some pennies stamped with the Lincoln profile smoking a pipe, another surefire ghost-attention holder—but he had valued the screw-on pommel, which had a powerful magnetic compass bobbing around in its glass dome.

But right now the compass was pointing firmly, uselessly, north. And his gone left arm was still sensing nothing at all. The ghost was effectively hidden inside the boy's mind now—Oaks was sure that that was what had happened—and, at least for as long as the ghost *remained* concealed, Oaks would have to track Koot Hoomie Parganas without any psychic beacons or Hansel-and-Gretel trails at all. And *now,* when he found the boy, he would probably have to *kill* him to get the big ghost out and eat it—and of course eat the boy's ghost too, as a garnish. A parsley child.

It occurred to Sherman Oaks that he might be smart to get to a telephone—and damn quick.

He walked faster, and then began jogging, hoping that in spite of his stained windbreaker and camouflage pants he looked like someone getting exercise and not like somebody in murderous pursuit.

Clouds as solid and white as sculptured marble were shifting across the blue vault of the sky, south from the San Fernando Valley and down the track of the Hollywood Freeway, graying the woods and lawns of Griffith Park and tarnishing the flat water of the Silverlake Reservoir. Chilly shade swept over the freeway lanes and across the area of wide dirt lots and isolated old Victorian houses west of the Pasadena Freeway, and the squat wild palms shook their shaggy heads in the wind. Pedestrians around Third and Sixth Streets began to move more quickly . . . though one toiling small figure on the Witmer Street sidewalk didn't increase its pace.

Kootie was limping worse than ever, but he made himself keep moving. Raffle had been meticulous about divvying up their panhandling income, and Kootie had a pocketful of change as well as forty-six dollars in bills— eventually he would get on a bus, and then get on another, and eventually, ideally, sleep on one, and then tomorrow think of some durable sanctuary (—*church, stow away on a ship, hide somewhere on a "big rig eighteen-wheeler," go to the police, hide in a*—). But right now he needed the sensation of motion—of ground being covered— that only working his legs and abrading the soles of his shoes could give him.

Kootie had stopped being angry at Raffle, and was instead panicked and dismayed at having lost the only person in Los Angeles, in the *world*, who'd cared to help him. Kootie was certain that if he hadn't been such a stupid *kid*, he could somehow have talked Raffle out of turning him in, and they could right now have been driving to get Raffle's dope somewhere, happy in the car, with Fred licking their faces. Kootie winced as he stepped down off a high curb, and he wondered what Fred was doing now; probably right this minute Fred was sharing Kootie's own personal heated-up tamale with Raffle in some safe parking lot.

Kootie's pelvis and right hip ached, as if he'd recently tried doing one of those Russian crouch-and-kick dances and then finished with a full butt-to-the-floor split—but he was trying not to think about it, for the mysterious muscle strain was a result of whatever had gone on during the time he had been blacked out at the Music Center, when the ghost of the old man had been in control of his body.

God only knew what the old man had done. Fallen awkwardly? Karate-kicked somebody? Kootie would have expected more dignity from *Thomas Alva Edison.*

There it was, he had thought about it. The ghost had been *Edison*—as in the SCE logo, painted on the doors of the Halloween-colored black-and-orange trucks, Southern California Edison—the guy that invented the lightbulb. Kootie's parents had always told him not to play with lightbulbs, that there was a poisonous "noble gas" in them; in school he had found out that they'd been thinking of neon lights, and that neon wasn't poisonous anyway. But there had been a poison in the glass brick hidden in the Dante statue, for sure.

Noble gas my ass, he thought defiantly as he blinked away tears. You old . . . *shithead!* What were you doing in that test tube inside the glass brick anyway?

Duh, he thought, replying for the absent Edison, *I dunno.*

You got my mom and dad killed! And now everybody wants to kill me too.

Duh. Sorry.

Moron.

Kootie remembered the face on the top of the bloody framework he had pulled off of himself, but a shudder torqued through him, almost making him miss his footing on the cracked sidewalk. It was apparently far too soon to think about that episode, and he found that he had focused his eyes on the stucco walls, bright orange even in the shadow of the clouds, of a ninety-nine cent store on the corner ahead of him. Two pay telephones were perched under metal hoods on a post by the parking-lot curb.

Al, he thought nervously, quoting the old woman who had moaned to him out of the pay-phone receiver on Fairfax this morning, *where am I gonna meet you tonight?*

Al. Alva. Thomas Alva Edison. And in the hallucination he'd had—

Again he shied away from the memory of being dislocated out of his own body—but he was sure that it had been the Edison ghost that the old woman had been trying to talk to. She had known the name—the nickname!—of the ghost Kootie had been carrying around. To the people who live in the magical alleys of the world, Kootie thought, that ghost must have been sticking out like a sore thumb.

But the ghost was gone now! Kootie had left it torn and deflated on the steps at the—

Involuntarily he exhaled, hard enough to have blown out a whole birthday-cake-full of candles, if one had been here. (Raffle had told him that in these neighborhoods they generally hung paper-skinned figures from trees on kids' birthdays, and then beat the things with sticks until they split apart, at which point the kids would scramble for the little cellophane-wrapped hard candies that spilled onto the dirt from the broken paper abdomens.)

The ghost was gone now, that was the important thing. Maybe telephones would work, for Kootie, now.

He flexed the fingers of his right hand and slowly reached down and dug in his jeans pocket for a quarter. Who would he call?

The police, for sure.

Kootie's teeth were cold, and he realized that he was smiling. He would call the police, and the one-armed bum wouldn't follow him anymore, not after the bum stumbled across the—

After the bum came to the end of the ghost's trail.

And then Kootie would be put in . . . *some* kind of home, finally, with showers and bathrooms and beds and food. Eventually he'd be adopted, by some family. He'd be able to see any movies he wanted to see. . . .

His teeth were still cold, but he was sobbing now, to his own horror and astonishment. I want my *own* family, he thought, I want my own house and my own mom and dad. Maybe they aren't dead—*(in those bloody chairs)*—of course they aren't dead, they were standing in the living room in formal clothes *(ignoring me in such a scary way)* and probably they're the ones that hired the billboards and posted the reward!

He needed to know, he needed to throw himself somewhere *now*, and he ran to the telephones even though the pain of running wrung whimpers through his clenched teeth.

When he had rolled the quarter into the slot, he punched in 911.

After two rings, a woman's voice said, calmly, "Nine-one-one operator, is this an emergency?"

"I'm Koot Hoomie Parganas," said Kootie quickly. "My parents were—were robbed and beaten up, real bad, night before last, and there's billboards with my picture on 'em, and a reward—" Kootie was suddenly dizzy, and he actually had to clutch the receiver tightly to keep from falling. He swung around on the pivot of his good heel until his shoulder hit the phone's aluminum cowl. When he had straightened up he had a quick impression that someone was behind him, wanting to use the phone, but he looked around and saw no one near him. "—A reward," he went on, "that's being offered for me. My mom and dad live on Loma Vista Street in Beverly Hills and there was—"

A man's voice interrupted him. "Parganas?" the man said altertly. *"Yes."*

"Just a sec. Hey," the man said away from the phone, "it's the Parganas kid!" More loudly, he added, "It's Koot Hoomie!"

The phone at the other end was put down with a clunk on something hard. In the background Kootie could hear a lot of people talking, and a clatter like a cafeteria. He heard glass break, and a voice mumble "Fuck."

There was a rattling on the line as someone picked up the distant phone. "Koot Hoomie?"

It was his mother's voice! She *was* alive! He was sobbing again, but he managed to say, clearly, *"Mom, come and get me."*

There was a moment of relative silence, broken only by mumbling and clattering at the other end; then, "Kethoomba!" his mother exclaimed. (Was she drunk? Was everybody *drinking* there in the dispatcher's office?) Kootie remembered that Kethoomba was the Tibetan pronunciation of the name of the mahatma his parents had named him after. She had never called Kootie that. "Gelugpa," she went on, "yellow-hatted monk! Come and get me!"

"Gimme that phone," said someone in the background. "Master!" came the quavering voice of Kootie's father. "We'll be out front!" Quietly, as if speaking off to the side of the receiver, Kootie's father asked someone, "Where are we?"

"Fock you," came a thick-voiced reply.

"Dad," shouted Kootie. "It's me, Kootie! I need you to come get me! I'm at—" He poked his head out into the breeze and tried to see a street sign. He couldn't see one up or down the gray street. "They trace these calls, ask the dispatcher where I'm calling from. Have 'em send a cop car here quick."

"Don't go outside!" called his father to someone in the noisy room. "Cop cars!" Then, breathily, back into the mouthpiece: *"Kootie?"*

"Yes, Dad! Are you all drunk? Listen—"

"No, *you* listen, young man. You *broke the Dante*—don' interrupt— you broke the, the Dante, let the light shine out before anything was prepared—well, it's your *son*, if you mus' know—"

Then Kootie's mother was on the line again. "Kootie! Put the master back on!"

Kootie was crying harder now. Something was terribly wrong. "There's nobody here but me, Mom. What's the matter with you? I'm lost, and that guy—there's bad guys following me—"

"We need the master to pick 's up!" his mother interrupted, her voice slurred but loud. "Put 'im on!"

"He's not here!" wailed Kootie; his ear was wet with wind-driven tears or sweat, and chilly because he was now holding the phone several inches away from his head. "*I* called. *My* name is Koot Hoomie, re-member? I'm *alone!*"

"You killed us!" his mother yelled. "You broke the Dante, you couldn't wait, and then the . . . *forces of darkness!* . . . found us, and killed us! I'm *dead*, your father's *dead*, because you disobeyed us! And now the master hasn't called! You're *bad*, Kootie, you're *ba-a-ad.*"

"She's right, son," interjected Kootie's father. "Iss your fault we're dead and Kethoomba's off somewhere. Get over here *now.*"

Kootie couldn't imagine the room his parents were in—it sounded like some kind of bar—but he was suddenly certain of what they were wearing. The same formal wedding clothes.

In the background there, a little girl was reciting a poem about how some flower beds were too soft . . . and then a hoarse woman's voice said, "Tell him to put Al on, will ya?"

Kootie hung up the phone. The wind was colder on this street now, and the sky's gray glow made opaque smoke of the windshields on the passing cars.

His quarter clattered into the coin-return slot. Apparently there was no charge on 911 calls.

And ten blocks east of Kootie, leaning against bamboo-pattern wallpaper at the back of a steamy Thai takeout restaurant, Sherman Oaks pressed another pay-telephone receiver to his ear.

At the other end of the line, a man answered, recited the number Oaks had called, and said, "What category?"

"I don't know," said Oaks, "Missing Persons? It's about that kid, Koot Hoomie Parganas, the one on the billboards."

"Koot Hoomie sightings, eh?" Oaks could hear the rippling clicking of a computer keyboard. "You speak English," the operator noted.

The remark irritated Oaks. Probably he had always spoken English. "Most people don't?"

"Been getting a lot of Kootie calls from illegal immigrants: '*Tengo el nino, pero no estoy en el pais legalimente.*' Got the kid, but got no green card. Looking for a second party to pick up the reward. There must be fifty curly-haired stray kids locked in garages in L.A. right now. One of 'em might even be the right one, though he hasn't been turned in yet, or this category would be closed out. Okay, what? You've got him, you know where he is? We've got a bonded outfit checking all reasonable claims, and a representative can be anywhere in the greater Los Angeles area within ten minutes."

"What I've got," Oaks said, "is a counter-offer." He looked around at the other people in the tiny white-lit restaurant—they all seemed to be occupied with their takeout bags and cardboard cartons, and even the obtrusive smells of cilantro and chili peppers seemed to combine with the staccato voices and the sizzle of beef and shrimp on the griddle to provide a screen of privacy for the phone. "You know smoke? Cigar? The Maduro Man?"

"It's a different category, but I can call it up."

"Well, I can put up—" Oaks paused to pull his attention away from the bright agitation of the restaurant, and he ran a mental inventory of the three major caches he kept, hidden out there in corners of the dark city; he pictured the dusty boxes of empty-looking but tightly sealed jars and bottles and old crack vials—he even had a matched pair, an elderly matrimonial suicide pact, locked up in the two snap-lid receptacles of a clear plastic contact-lens case. "I can put up *a thousand doses* of L.A. cigar, in exchange for the kid. Even wholesale that's a lot more than twenty grand."

He heard more keyboard clicking. "Yeah, it is." The man sighed. "Well, for that we'd need a guarantor, somebody we've got listed, who can put up forty grand. Counter-offers have to be double, house policy. If we get that, we'll go ahead and list it under the Parganas heading. But the guarantor would have to do all the other work, like maybe putting a trap on the reward-number phone and being ready to intercept anybody who, you know, might already have the kid and be trying to get the original reward. I don't have to tell you that hours count in this one. Minutes, even."

"I know."

Oaks looked down at the compass in the pommel of his knife—right now it was pointing up in the direction of Dodger Stadium, which was plain old north, but a few minutes ago it had joggled wildly and then, for what must have been nearly a full minute, pointed emphatically west. After that it had wobbled back to north, and he hadn't seen it deviate from that normal reading since.

During it all, he had felt no heat in his absent arm—but the compass had clearly registered a brief re-emergence of the big ghost; and the ghost had been in the excited state, too, for ghosts didn't cast the huge magnetic fields when they were in their normal quiescent ground state. It *was* clathrated in the boy's psyche, and not dissipated or eaten. Oaks was achingly anxious to get off the phone and resume his jogging pursuit—westward!—but this insurance was worth a minute's delay.

"So who's your guarantor?" the man on the phone was asking him. "Or do you have forty grand yourself, to put up instead of your smoke?"

"No, not me. Uh . . ." The street dealers he ordinarily sold to wouldn't have this kind of money ready to hand. He would have to go higher up. "You got a Neal Obstadt listed?" Oaks asked. "Under gambling, probably, I think that's his main business."

"Yeah, I got Obstadt." *(Clickety-click.)* "What do I tell him? Even for him, forty ain't just lunch money."

Oaks had heard Obstadt described as a heavy user, a good customer who was generally able to score the best specimens in the dealers' stocks. "Tell him it's from the guy named Sherman Oaks, the producer who brought you such hits as—I hope you're taping this?"

"Always got a loop going."

"Such hits as Henrietta Hewitt, the old lady who died on September fifth and whose kids were named Edna and Sam." It was a fairly long shot, but old Henrietta had been the best ghost Oaks had bottled lately, and anyway Obstadt might very well recognize Oaks's name and reputation. He might not, but the possibility of changing the Parganas listing was definitely worth this delay.

"I'll play it for him. I imagine he'll want to tape your voice himself, as your receipt for the money, if he goes for it. Are you at a number?"

"No, I'll call back in an hour. But if he authorizes it, you can list it on the board right now, can't you?"

"Yup. As soon as he says okay, it's on, and the . . . *mere mercenary details* are between you and him."

"Go," said Oaks, and hung up the phone.

Immediately he wondered if he was making a costly mistake. He could easily get to all of his stashes within a hopping hour or two, but turning it all over to Obstadt's people would leave Oaks with approximately nothing. He might even have to kill a few street people to make up the full thousand bottled doses. But of course he wouldn't have to cough up the smoke unless he received the Parganas boy, and the big ghost inside the boy was clearly worth a thousand ordinary bottled dead folk. The nightly fresh catches in his traps would keep Oaks going until he could build up reserve stocks again.

He could feel his missing arm again, but it was just clutching his chest, and it was as uselessly cold as if it were cradling a bag of ice. He actually looked down at his grubby shirtfront, and was remotely surprised not to see the fabric bunched by the clawed fingers. His compass was still pointing north—either the ghost was in the normal catatonic ground state, or was reimprisoned inside the boy's psyche, or both.

The burning-plastic smells of sizzling shrimp and cilantro helped propel him across the linoleum floor and out onto the Figueroa sidewalk.

Oaks despised the processes of biological ingestion and digestion and elimination, and he generally lived on crackers, and bean soup fingered up cold and solid right out of a can, and water from unguarded hoses and faucets. His real sustenance was his ghosts, snorted up raw and new and vibrant from a hand-lettered palindrome or a pile of scattered coins, or—occasional serendipitous luxuries!—furtively inhaled in hospital corridors or from a body freshly tumbled on the street.

He remembered stalking the halls of County Hospital during the war, when every one of the hundreds of windows had been painted black in case of a Japanese air raid, and the ghosts of newly dead patients were too fearful to dissipate normally, and instead huddled in the corners of the halls, always faintly asking him, as he swept them into his bottles, "Are the Japs out there?" . . . And the maternity ward at Hollywood Presbyterian Hospital, where he had often been able to inhale the fresh-cast virtual ghosts thrown off by newborn infants in the stress of birth. . . .

But it was now getting on to forty-eight hours since he had last "got a life"—which had been *before* he'd gone to the Parganas house. He hadn't even bothered to consume the ghosts of Kootie's parents after he killed them, so confident had he been that the big ghost must still be nearby; he had not wanted to waste the chase-time by pausing to eat those two minor items.

Out on the sidewalk he realized that the day had turned cold, and that the gray light would be diminishing toward evening before too long. Already the zigzag neon sign of a shoe store across the street was glowing yellow against the ash-colored wall. An orange-and-black SCE truck roared past, and he flinched away—from the roaring of it.

Those two minor items. Oaks would have been grateful for one such minor item right now. One lungful of real soul food, to keep away the Bony Express.

For he could feel the unrest of the ghosts he had consumed in the past. When he was forced to fast, they all became agitated, and his exhalations were more and more audibly wheezy with their less and less distant roars, as if they were all riding toward him—the Bony Express!—ever closer, over the midnight black hills of the unmapped borderlands of his mind, toward the lonely middle-of-nowhere campfire that was his consciousness.

His phantom left hand had crawled down his chest and now gripped his abdomen, squeezing so hard that Oaks was wincing as he hurried west along the Sixth Street sidewalk. He thought of making a detour, catching a bus up to—which stash was he nearest to?—the rooftop air-conditioning shed over the hair salon on Bellevue; but the thought of how strongly the compass needle had pointed west only a few minutes ago, and the memory of the collapsed face on the parking garage stairs at the Music Center, made him keep on putting one foot ahead of the other on the westward-leading sidewalk.

Mouth-to-mouth unsuscitation, with Koot Hoomie Parganas's body still twitching under him in protest at being so newly dead, and the two souls, the boy's and the big ghost, blasting hotly down Oaks's windpipe to his starving lungs.

Soon, he thought.

CHAPTER 21

"The little fishes of the sea,
They sent an answer back to me."
—Lewis Carroll,
Through the Looking-Glass

The sun was under the skirts of the dark clouds now, showing briefly on the western edge of the world before disappearing below the silhouetted hills of Pacific Palisades. Pete Sullivan was sitting by the leaded-glass window of Kendall's Sport Time Bar, and the long, horizontal rays of sunlight glowed red in the depths of the Guinness stout in the glass on the polished table.

He was waiting for his order of appetizers—fried mozzarella with marinara sauce, and Buffalo chicken wings with celery and blue-cheese dressing—but he had got the stout in the meantime because a teacher at City College had once told him that Guinness contained all the nutrients required to sustain human life. It was thick and brown and rich, though, and he planned to switch to Coors Light as soon as he had emptied this glass and thus fulfilled his health duties. And this bar somehow didn't have any smoking area at all, so his next cigarette would have to wait until he got back into the van. A healthful evening all around.

Television sets were hung at several places in the darkness under the ceiling beams, but each one seemed to be tuned to a different channel, and the ones with the sound turned up loud weren't the ones closest to Sullivan. On the nearest screen he watched presidential candidate Bill Clinton moving his lips, while what he heard was whining electrical machinery and mechanical thumping from a farther speaker. Sullivan looked away.

His hands were still sticky from having washed them with Gojo hand-cleaning jelly at the tiny sink in the van. This morning, after driving around to pick up supplies, he had found an unfenced dirt lot east of Alameda, among the windowless plastic-works and foundries by the train tracks and the cement-walled Los Angeles River, and he had done some work on the poor old van.

The sun had still been glaring out of a clear October sky, and he had taken off his shirt and scapular and popped a beer from a fresh twelve-pack before opening the van's back doors and dragging out his tools.

The tire pressures were low, so he hooked up a little electric air pump to the battery with his jumper cables, and crouched beside each tire in turn, puffing a cigarette and sipping the chilly beer, and watched to make sure the cable clamps didn't touch each other as the pump wobbled and vibrated on the adobe dirt. Then he crawled under the van and dumped the oil, conscientiously draining the old black stuff into the kind of sealable plastic container that could be taken to an oil-recycling center, though unless someone was watching he intended to leave the container right there in the middle of the field. A new oil filter, new spark plugs, and six quarts of Valvoline 20-50-weight oil finished the job.

L.A. air in the tires, he thought, and fresh oil in the engine. Nothing with any memories of fleeing Arizona—of driving to Houdini's wrecked old place—of fearfully crossing borders. And he remembered the old notion that after some number of years every cell in a human body had been replaced, every atom, so that the body is just a wave form moving through time, incorporating just for a little while the stuff of each day; only the wave itself, and none of the transient physical bits, makes the whole trip. Even a scar would be no more significant than a wobble still visible in an ocean wave long after the wave had passed the obstruction that caused it, while the water molecules that had actually *sustained* the impact were left comfortably far behind.

A.O.P., Sullivan thought now as he sipped his cloying Guinness. Accelerate Outta Problems. He had always been uneasy watching people *dig in*—the newlyweds committing themselves to a mortgage and a roof and plumbing, the brave entrepreneur leasing a building and getting boxes and boxes of letterhead printed up. Sullivan had owned the van for five years now, but he had owned other vehicles before that, and he would own others after the van met whatever its eventual terminal problem would turn out to be; the very books on the shelf over the top bunk were a wave form—paperbacks that were bought new, became bent and ruptured and yellowed, and eventually served as ragged whiskbrooms that went out with the trash they swept up, to be replaced by new paperbacks.

Sullivan had once read some Greek philosopher quoted to the effect that no man can step into the same river twice, because it's never again the same river, and he's never again the same man.

Thank God for that, Sullivan thought now as he beckoned to the waitress. On the nearest television screen, in front of some shabby house draped in yellow police-line tape, a concerned-looking newsman was frowning into the camera and opening and closing his mouth, seeming, because another set was turned up loud on a different channel, to be barking like a dog while someone kept saying, "Speak!"

Sullivan looked back down at the table. It was better with just the sound. Today he had set up his portable radio and casette deck on the van floor, and on the noon news he had heard that some giant prehistoric fish had washed up on the shore at Venice Beach, and that lobsters had crawled out of the ocean and terrified people on the shore.

So there *had* been a timely at Venice. That was immensely reassuring. DeLarava's motive in going there *had* been just for a news story, and nothing to do with . . . anything else.

You're not Speedy Alka-Seltzer, you won't dissolve.

He cut off the intrusive remembered sentence before he could distinguish the voice that had *(long ago)* spoken it. Better to dissolve, he thought.

"And could I switch to a Coors Light now," he said aloud, for the waitress had brought the two steaming plates to his table, and lukewarm stout wasn't at all the thing for washing down garlic and Tabasco and blue cheese. "In fact," he added, "could I have two of them."

One of them to drink in memory of the surely dissolved ghost of Sukie, he thought.

Now that his head was ringing slightly with alcohol, he was comfortably sure that the wave form that had been his sister was safely dispersed and flattened out, and not carrying on past the death of the body that had maintained it. DeLarava only went to Venice today because her job happened to take her there, he told himself, and all the ghosts are laid.

Let it all dissolve. Scarf this hasty late lunch or early dinner, call Steve and go over to his house for a few more beers, and then just get out of L.A. All the old dirty shit is cleaned out of the van's works, and you've surely cleared all the old guilts and uncertainties out of your soul just by coming back here and looking around at the outgrown home town.

Veni, vidi, exii, he thought, quoting another motto of Sukie's. I came, I saw, I left.

The sound vibrating out of the nearest speaker was some kind of mulitudinous roar like a crowded stadium, but on the nearest screen he could now see a beach, breezy basketball courts, a crowd of people in swimming suits standing and craning their necks . . . a brightly sunlit scene, not live.

Jarringly, it was Venice Beach—but obviously this was just a recap of the prehistoric fish story. Perhaps this film clip was deLarava's work. Sullivan's two beers arrived then, and with one of the chilly glasses clamped in his palm he was able to keep on looking up at the TV screen.

And a deep slug of cold beer helped him hang on to his mood of serenity. I *can look* at films of Venice Beach now, he thought steadily. All the old ghosts are laid.

As soon as the televised scene was replaced by a view of some new car leaning fast around rural roads, he drained the beer and took the other one with him as he got up—the food could wait—and walked back through the crowded tables to the hallway where the telephones and the rest rooms were.

He dropped a handful of change on the wood floor, retrieved most of it and thumbed a quarter into the pay-phone slot, then punched in the remembered number.

Above belt-level wainscoting the wallpaper was furry red velvet— and it fleetingly occurred to him that in spite of the beamed ceiling and the etched glass partitions around the booths, this place was probably too new for deLarava to find it worthwhile snuffling a straw in these corners.

The phone at the other end was ringing, and then it was picked up. "That you, Pete?" came a gasping voice.

"Sure is. Steve? I'm—"

"Where are you calling from, man?" Away from the phone he snapped, "I'm fine, dammit!" to someone.

"Well, I'm in a bar—in Westwood, I think, on Wilshire. A 'sports bar,' with TV sets hung all over the place, every one on a different channel. Loud. I can't wait to get to your place. And I don't think I'll be spending the night after all. I gotta get back to Arizona—"

"Okay, listen, I just this second dumped a whole panful of Beans Jaime dip all over myself, and it's *damn hot.* I've got to get back in the shower. Stay there for another half hour or so, okay?"

"No problem, I've got some snacks—"

"Cool. That's good then. Shit, this stuff is like napalm! How's—I meant to ask, how's Sukie?"

Sullivan was glad that he had thought to bring a beer with him. After chugging a series of gulps, he gasped, "Fine. No, she's—well, I think she's dead."

"Jesus. You *think*?" After a pause, Steve said, "I always liked her. Well! Do something sentimental for me? Have a Kahlua and milk for me, in her memory, will you do that? Promise?"

It had been Sukie's favored breakfast drink. Sullivan nodded dutifully, imagining dumping Kahlua and milk into his stomach on top of the Guinness. He realized that Steve couldn't hear a nod, and said, "Okay, Steve. So what's your address? I don't need directions, I've got a Thomas Brothers guide."

Steve gave him an address on La Grange Avenue, and Sullivan hung up and returned to his table.

The fried mozzarella had cooled off, but the Buffalo wings were still hot, and he dipped them in the marinara sauce as often as in the blue-cheese dressing. When the waitress came by again he ordered two more beers . . . and a Kahlua and milk, though he resolved to let the drink stand as a gesture rather than drink it.

He got hungrier as he diminished the fresh beers and ate the snacks, and after gnawing at the chicken bones he began chewing up the re-hardened mozzarella. Just as he was considering ordering something else, maybe the Nachos Grande, the waitress walked up and told him he had a call at the bar.

He blinked up at her. "I doubt it," he said. "Who did they ask for?"

"A guy drinking a Kahlua and milk. You haven't touched it, but I figure you're who they want."

That has to be Steve, somehow, Sullivan thought uneasily as he pushed back his chair and weaved his way between the tables to the bar, on which a white telephone sat with the receiver lying next to it. He was reminded of the call he'd got at O'Hara's, back in Roosevelt, the call from Sukie that had started this pointless—no, this *cathartic*—odyssey, and after he had nervously picked up the receiver and said "Hello?" he was relieved to find that the voice on the other end was not Sukie's again. Then he realized that he hadn't listened to what this woman had said.

"What?"

"I said, is this Pete Sullivan," she said angrily.

"Yes. Are you somebody at Steve's house? I—"

"This is Steve's wife, and I'm at a pay phone. He *scalded* himself dumping that dip on his leg! And in his hair! *Intentionally!* To have an excuse to give me a shopping list and get out of the house so I could call you from somewhere where those men wouldn't hear! Here's his note for you, his 'shopping list': *Pete—Call me back and say you cannot make it over to my house, please, Pete. And don't say on the line where you're going, and get out of there. Whatever it is, they want you alive.*

I've got a wife and kids. Good luck, but don't call me again ever after this next call. That's his note, okay? This is the third damn *sports* bar on Wilshire that I've called, and now I've got to go to some store and buy some more frijoles and Jack cheese and stuff, even though I know we're not going to be making more Beans Jaime, thank God, just so this shopping trip will look genuine to those men! They'll leave when you call and tell them you can't come over, so call. And then just leave us alone!''

"Okay," he said softly, though she had hung up. The waitress was standing nearby, watching him, so he smiled at her and said, "Can I make a local call?" When she shrugged and nodded, he went on, "And could I have another Coors Light."

Again he punched in Steve's number; and again Steve answered it quickly. "Steve," Sullivan said, "this is Pete. I'm calling from a different bar, I'm up on Hollywood Boulevard now. Listen, man, I just won't be able to make it by tonight. And, ah, I'm gonna be leaving town—I'll catch you next trip, okay? Next year some time, probably."

As he carried his fresh beer back toward his table he wondered, without being able to care very much, if Steve's regrets had sounded any more sincere to "those men" than they had to Pete.

He was looking down and carefully watching each of his shoes in turn catch his forward-moving weight, for his spine was as tense as if he were walking along the top of a high wall.

He sat down heavily in his chair at last, and, just in case, hid the glass of Kahlua and milk under his tented napkin.

Those would be deLarava's men, he thought dully.

And I can drink all night long, or run to the van and drive to Alaska, and it won't change the obvious fact that she *is* planning, again, to—

He inhaled, drained the beer, and then dizzily exhaled.

—She is again planning to consume my father's ghost. For some reason she can't just let him rest in peace.

She went to Venice today because of the fish business, sure, but the fishes must have been acting up because my father's ghost is coming back out of the sea; right there in Venice, where he drowned thirty-three years ago. Right back where it *start*ed from, he sang in his head.

DeLarava would like to have me—alive—as a lure. Not as part of a mask, the way Sukie and I used to work, but, for *this* one, as a lure.

With a shudder of revulsion, Sullivan remembered how fat and youthful and happy deLarava always was after sucking in some ghost through one of her sparking clove cigarettes.

Presumably one ghost was as good as another . . . so why was she again going after his father's? On that Christmas Eve in 1986, Pete and

Sukie had both been uneasy with the fact of being physically present in Venice Beach, especially with deLarava, for it had been in the Venice surf that their father had drowned in 1959, when the twins had been seven—but it wasn't until well after noon, in the instant when Sukie had spilled the contents of the shoebox deLarava had brought along, that he and Sukie had known what ghost was indeed that day's particular quarry. DeLarava had probably been hoping to consummate the inhalation without the twins even suspecting, but the exposed wallet and key ring had been, horribly and unmistakably, their father's.

The old man had drowned, and they hadn't been there. And then Loretta deLarava had tried to eat the old man's ghost, and—as Pete Sullivan had realized only after having driven far up the featureless Interstate 5 toward San Francisco, and as Sukie must have realized at some point during her own flight—*they had fled without taking away the wallet and the keys.*

Sullivan held the cold beer glass tightly to keep his hands from shaking, and his face was cold and sweaty. In that instant he completely understood, and completely envied, Sukie's suicide.

She'd had to do it. How could you hide forever in a bottle?—unless you became transparent yourself. Dissolved (—like Speedy Alka-Seltzer—) so that you were a waveform propagated all the way out beyond any scraps of physical material, even compass needles, that might move in response to the fact of you and thus betray your presence.

(He couldn't think about the three cans of Hires Root Beer that had also fallen out of the shoebox, one of which had rolled right up to his foot and sprayed a tiny forlorn jet of ancient brown pop across his shoe, but) he knew in the tightening back of his throat that he and his sister had betrayed their father on *that* day, that *chilly winter of 1986* day, by running mindlessly away and leaving the tokens of their father's ghost in deLarava's hands.

But I'm still alive, he thought, and I'm back in L.A. I've got to save him from her. And I can't possibly face him.

"—the ghosts of dead family members," said a placid male voice from one of the television speakers, "but police investigators speculate that the apparently supernatural effects were caused by some electrical or gas-powered apparatus that may have exploded and caught fire, causing the blaze that gutted the psychiatric clinic and killed three of Dr. Elizalde's patients. Several others still to this day remain hospitalized for psychological trauma sustained during that Halloween tragedy."

Sullivan looked up at the nearest screen, but saw only football players running across a green field. He pushed his chair back and turned around, and on one of the farther sets saw a blond man in a suit standing behind a news-show podium. As Sullivan watched, the studio set was replaced with a still photo of a slim, dark-haired woman standing with raised eyebrows and an open mouth in a doorway. Her eyes were shut.

That looks like a bar-time snapshot, Sullivan thought as a chill prickled the back of his neck. Whoever this woman is, she seems to have anticipated the flash.

"And today," the newsman's voice went on, "nearly two years after that scam-gone-wrong, Dr. Elizalde is reportedly back in Los Angeles. Police say that this morning she went to the Amado Street house of Margarita Gonzalvez, the widow of one of the patients who died in the so-called séance—and drew a handgun and fired four shots! Mrs. Gonzalvez was able to snap this photograph of Elizalde shortly before the discredited psychiatrist allegedly began shooting. Police are investigating reports that Elizalde may subsequently have bought a disguise and stolen a car."

The scene changed back to the newscaster in the studio, who had now been joined by another blond man in a suit. " 'Physician, heal thyself,' " said the newcomer solemnly. "A tragic story of misplaced faith, Tom."

"Certainly is, Ed," agreed the grave newscaster. "Though medical authorities now believe that many of the folk remedies dispensed at these *curanderias* and *hierverias* can actually be beneficial. It's the charlatans who prey on credulity, and exaggerate the reasonable claims, who give the whole field a bad name."

The newsmen were apparently segueing into a topical Halloween-related story about the upcoming Day of the Dead celebrations in the local Hispanic communities, and shortly they switched to film clips of stylized papier-mâché skulls waving on poles, and dancing people wearing black and white face makeup and wreaths of marigolds. Sullivan turned back to his table, frowning at the spooklike figure of the napkin-draped drink. The dead woman's drink, the suicide's drink. He wasn't going to touch it.

Apparently this psychiatrist's catastrophic "so-called séance" had been big news two years ago. Sullivan never read newspapers, so he hadn't heard about it.

She held a séance at her psychiatric clinic, he thought; on Halloween, a dangerous night even for a séance that might not have been meant to get real supernatural effects. And something sure enough happened— the surviving patients apparently saw "dead family members," and then there were fires and explosions or something, and three of her patients died. (Of course the police would assume that the disaster was caused by some kind of goofy "apparatus" blowing up.)

If she *is* on bar-time, as that photo implies, it's certainly no wonder—she's now got ghosts guilt-linked to her, like all of us ghost-sensitives.

Sullivan had gathered from the news story that Dr. Elizalde had fled Los Angeles after the fire and the deaths. Why had she come back now, at another Halloween? Not to shoot at that widow, it seemed to him—if there was shooting, it was probably aimed at Elizalde. Elizalde probably came back here in some idiot attempt to . . . *set things right.*

Apologize to all of them, living and dead.

But . . .

It sounds to me as though she really *can* raise ghosts, he thought. Whether she's happy with it or not, it sounds as though she's a genuine, if accidentally ordained, medium.

She could probably raise the ghost of my father, and I could—insulated from him, at a *medium* distance, speaking through a screen like a shameful penitent in a confessional—warn him.

His heart was beating faster. Elizalde, he thought. Remember the name.

She'll be hiding now, but I'll bet she won't leave L.A. until after Halloween, until after her Quixotic amends are impossible again. She'll be hiding, but I'll bet I can find her.

He smiled bleakly into his empty beer glass.

After all, she's one of us.

Outside, in the westbound left lane of Wilshire Boulevard, a 1960 Cadillac Fleetwood slowed to a stop at the Westwood intersection.

Behind the wheel, Neal Obstadt could see that all the other drivers had their headlights on, so he reached out carefully and switched on his own. He liked to be the last.

A cellular telephone was wedged under his jaw, and in his right hand he held a Druid Circle oatmeal cookie from Trader Joe's. "You don't need to be fretting about overcosts, Loretta," he said absently into the phone. "Your location accountant's an anal-retentive, and the production reports always balance. You've got the insurance and permissions. Worry about something else, if you've got to worry."

Obstadt had had various business dealings with deLarava for years, and he knew that this anxiety was what she called "checking the gates"—a cameraman's term for a last-minute, finicky checking of the lens for dust or hair. Still, he could hear her sniffling—and she'd been crying on the phone this morning, too—and it occurred to him that this agitation was out of proportion for the modest ghosts-on-the-*Queen-Mary* shoot she had scheduled for Saturday.

"You having a bad hair day, Loretta?" he asked. "Your big manhunt suffer a setback?" The light turned green, and he accelerated west, toward the elevated arch of the 405.

"What did you have to do with that?" shrilled her voice out of the phone. "He isn't *really* leaving the state, *is* he?"

Obstadt blinked, and smiled as he took a bite of the cookie. "Who, Topper?" he said around the mouthful. "Spooky, I mean—your Nicky Bradshaw. He left the state? I had nothing to do with it, I swear. I never even liked the show."

"Oh, *Bradshaw*," she said, her quick anger deflating. "My . . . *man-hunts* are doing just fine, thank you. I've got one snatch working right now that's going to be costing me *twenty grand.*"

"Good for you, kid, the big time at last." Obstadt glanced at the taped-shut Marlboro carton on the seat beside him. Twenty grand for a washed-up old prehistoric *fish*? he thought. Or did you give up on the fish? *I'm* spending *forty* grand to finance a snatch, buy the access to somebody else's snatch—but forty grand for a thousand primo smokes is the bargain of a lifetime. Jeez, though, cash!—in a cigarette carton that I've got to hand to some guy from the phone exchange, just for rerouting their reward listing of that missing Sockit Hoomie boy! The exchange people are reliable, but who, really, is this Sherman Oaks person? His *ass*'ll be smoke, if he hoses me on this. "So who is it that slipped through your fingers tonight?" Obstadt said into the phone.

"If everybody minded their own business," sniffed deLarava, "the world would go round a deal faster than it does."

Obstadt suspected that her line was a quote from one of the Alice-in-Wonderland books. Loretta liked old smokes that had hung around hotel lobbies for decades; Obstadt preferred them fresh. It was the old ones that quoted Alice all the time. Among the solid old bum-smokes on the street, the Alice stuff seemed almost to be scripture.

He was driving between the broad dark lawns of the Veterans Administration grounds now, with the Federal Building to his left and the cemetery to his right.

"Is it that fish?" he asked, taking another bite of the cookie. "Did you get outbid by the fish-market man at Canter's?" So much for your bid to be the Fisher Queen, he thought—in spite of all your vegetarianism, and your "youth treatments," and your Velcro instead of buttons and topologically compromising buttonholes.

"What are you eating?" deLarava demanded. "Don't speak while you're chewing, you're getting crumbs in my ear."

"Through the *phone*? I doubt it, Loretta." Obstadt was laughing, and in fact spraying crumbs onto his lap. "It's probably dead fleas. Don't you wear a flea collar under your hair?"

"Jesus, it's sand! Grains of sand! Has he been whispering to me while I napped? But I'll eat him—"

The line clicked. She had hung up.

He replaced the phone in the console cradle, and his smile unkinked as he drove under the freeway overpass, the cemetery behind him now. You spend all day at the beach, Loretta, he thought, you shouldn't be surprised to find sand in your ear.

Loretta was crazy, beyond any doubt. But—

Something big had happened last night, at around sundown; he had had to excuse himself from dinner at Rusty's Hacienda in Glendale and go stand on the sidewalk and just breathe deeply and stare at the pavement, for all the ghosts he'd snorted up over the years were clamoring so riotously in his mind that he couldn't hear anything else; the Santa Ana wind had strewn the lanes of Western Avenue with palm fronds, and Obstadt had squinted almost fearfully southwest, over the dark hills of Griffith Park, wondering who it was that had so abruptly arrived on the west coast psychscape.

The intensity had faded—but now the street-smokes were all jabbering and eating dirt, and some kind of dinosaur had washed up in Venice, and deLarava couldn't stop crying.

Loretta's a clown, he had said this morning. *She wins chips in this low-level game, but never cashes 'em in to move up to a bigger table; still, some big chips do sometimes slide across her table; and she's all excited about one now.*

He stomped the gas pedal furiously to the floor, and bared his teeth at the sudden roar of the engine as acceleration weighted him back against the seat.

The fish? he thought; some Jonah *inside* the fish? The guy that maybe left the state? Nicky Bradshaw?

Who?

CHAPTER 22

*The snoring got more distinct every minute, and sounded more like a tune:
at last she could even make out words...*

—Lewis Carroll,
Through the Looking-Glass

And way out east at the other end of Wilshire, out where multicolored
plastic pennants fluttered along nylon lines strung above used-car lots,
where old brownstone apartment buildings still stood on the small grassy
hills, their lower walls blazing even in the failing daylight with bright
Mexican murals, where neglected laundry flapped on clotheslines in the
grassless courtyards of faded apartment complexes built in the 1960s,
Kootie stepped up a curb, limped across the sidewalk away from the
red glow of a Miller Beer sign in a corner bar window, and rocked to
a halt against the bar's gritty stucco wall.

He was still intermittently talking to himself, and during the walking
of these last several blocks he had even begun moving his lips and
whispering the dialogue.

"I can't walk anymore," he panted. "I think I've ruined my foot—
they're probably gonna have to just cut it off and put a wooden one
on."

"Duh," he said thickly then, speaking for the absent ghost of Thomas
Alva Edison, which he was certain he had left behind in a mess on the
stairs at the Music Center, "well, I got wooden teeth. No, that was
George Washington—well, I got a wooden head."

"I *saw* your head," Kootie whispered, his voice shaky even now as
he remembered that shocking period of dislocation. "It was made out
of old strips of beef fat." He mouthed the last two words with, it fleetingly occurred to him, as much revulsion as his vegetarian parents would
have done. He jumped hastily to the next thought: "I'm gonna go in

this bar—no, not to get a *cocktail*, you stupid old *fart!*—I'm gonna get somebody to call the cops for me.''

Kootie was still holding the quarter that the pay telephone had given back to him two hours ago. He had been gripping it between his first two fingers and tapping it against the palm of his hand as he had walked. The rhythm of the tapping had been unconsidered and irregular, but now, probably because he had a purpose for the coin again, the tapping was forcefully repetitive.

"I don' wanna go in the bar," he said in his dopy-old-Edison voice, and in fact Kootie didn't want to step in there. The memory was still too fresh of the lunatic phone call with—with what, exactly? The ghosts of his parents? It had been that, or it had been a hallucination. And his parents had seemed to be in a bar.

But if somebody *else* made the telephone call . . .

(He found himself picturing carbon; *black grains in a tiny cell at first, with a soft iron diaphragm that would alternately compress and release the carbon grains, thus changing the conductivity; but the grains tended to* pack, *so that after a while the conductivity was stuck at one level . . .*)

If somebody else made the call it might go through, and not just be routed again to that bar from hell.

That call an hour ago had *started* to get through—Kootie was sure now that the first voice he had heard had really been the 911 operator, for after he had walked away from the pay phone he had seen a police car drive past slowly in the right-hand eastbound lane of what had proved to be Sixth Street. Kootie had wanted to go flag him down, but had found himself hurrying away across the parking lot instead, and pushing open the glass door of the ninety-nine cent store, where he had then gone to the back aisle and crouched behind a shelf of candles in tall glasses with decals of saints stuck on the outsides.

He must have been afraid, still, of facing the police and deciding which sort of crazy story to tell them.

And then the shop manager had yelled at him, demanded to know what the boy was doing there, and in his feverish embarrassment Kootie had bought a bagful of stuff he hadn't wanted, just to placate the man: a box of Miraculous Insecticide Chalk, a blister-pack roll of 35-millimeter film, and a Hershey bar with almonds. They were all things displayed right at the checkout counter. The bag was crumpled up now, jammed inside his lightweight shirt.

When he had finally left the store and resumed limping east, away from the fading light, he had pretended that the imaginary ghost of Edison took the blame for Kootie having hidden from the police car.

Duh, sorry, he had had the ghost say, *but I can't let the cops catch me—I've got library books that have been overdue since 1931!*

Now Kootie forced himself to push away from the wall and walk toward the bar's front door. He was chilly in the smoky evening breeze with just the polo shirt on, and he hoped the bar's interior would be warm.

(A glass lamp-chimney, blackened with smoke. When the black stuff, which was carbon, was scraped off, it could be pressed into the shape of a little button, and that button could be attached to the metal disk. In another room you could bite the instrument it was connected to, and, through your teeth and the bones of your skull, hear the clearer, louder tones.)

Kootie pulled open the door with his left hand, for the fingers of his right were still rapidly thumping the quarter into the tight skin of his palm. *Tap . . . tap . . . tap . . . tap-tap-tap . . . tap . . . tap . . . tap . . .*

An outward-bursting pressure of warm air ruffled his curly hair— stale air, scented with beer and cigarette smoke and sweaty shirts, and shaking with recorded mariachi guitar and the click and rattle of pool balls breaking across bald green felt. Yellow light shone in the linoleum under his Reeboks' soles as he shuffled to the nearest of the two empty barstools. The bartender was squinting impassively down at him over a bushy mustache.

"Do you have a telephone?" Kootie asked, grateful that his voice was steady. "I'd like to have someone make a call for me."

The man just stared. The men on the barstools around him were probably staring too, but Kootie was afraid to look any of them in the face. They'll recognize me from those billboards, he thought, and turn me in. But isn't that what I want?

"Teléfono," he said, and in desperate pantomime he raised his left hand in front of his chin as if holding an empty Coke bottle to blow hoots on, while he held his right hand up beside his head, the fingers extended toward his ear. "Hel-*lo*?" he said, speaking into the space above his left hand. "Hel-*lo*-o?"

His left hand was still twitching with the coin, and belatedly he realized that the rhythm it had been beating against his palm was the Morse code for SOS; and at the same time he noticed that he was miming using one of those old candlestick-and-hook telephones, like in a Laurel and Hardy movie.

SOS? he thought to himself—and then, instinctively and inward, he thought: *What is it, what's wrong?*

An instant later he had to grab the padded vinyl seat of the barstool to keep from falling over.

Kootie's mouth opened, and for several whole seconds a series of wordless but conversational-tone cat warbles yowled and yipped out of his throat; finally, after his forehead was hot and wet with the effort of resisting it and he had inadvertently blown his nose on his chin, he just stopped fighting the phenomenon and let his whole chest and face relax into passivity.

"Duh," came his voice then, clear at last. *"Du-u-h,"* it said again, prolonging the syllable, indignantly *quoting* it. Then he was looking up at the bartender. "Thanks, boys," said Kootie's voice, "but never mind. All a mistake, sorry to have wasted your time. Here, have a round of beers on me." After a pause, Kootie's voice went on, "Kid, put some money on the bar."

Catching on that he was being addressed—by his own throat!—Kootie hastily dug into the pocket of his jeans and, without taking out his roll of bills, peeled one off and pulled it out. It was a five; probably not enough for very many beers, but the next bill might be a twenty. He reached up and laid it on the surface of the bar, then ducked his head and wiped his chin on his shoulder.

"Lord, boy, a fiver?" said his mouth. "I bet they don't get many orangutans in here. Who are these fellas, anyway, son? Mexicans? Tell 'em in Mexican that this was a misunderstanding, and we're leaving."

"Uhhh," said Kootie, testing his own control of his voice. *"Lo siento, pero no yo soy aquí. Eso dinero es para cervezas. Salud. Y ahora, adiós."*

"Oh," he heard himself add, "and get matches, will you?"

"Uh, y para mi, fosforos, por favor? Mechas? Como para cigarros?"

After another long several seconds, the bartender reached out and pushed a book of matches forward to the edge of the bar.

Kootie reached up and took it. *"Gracias."*

Then he could almost feel a hand grab his collar and yank him away from the bar, toward the door.

(But even with the pressed carbon disk, if you were relying on just the current set up in the wire, there was clarity but no reach; all you had was a little standing system. To fix that, the changing current in the wire had to be just the cue for changes that would be mirrored big-scale in an induction coil. Then the signal could be carried just about anywhere.)

"Trolley-car lines," Kootie heard himself say as he pushed open the door and stepped out into the cold evening again. Standing on the curb, he waited for the headlights of the cars in the eastbound lanes to sweep past, and then he limped out across the asphalt to stand on the double yellow painted lines in the middle of the street. His head bent forward to look at the pavement under his feet. His mouth opened again, and "Find us a set of streetcar lines," he said.

"There aren't any," he answered—hoarsely, for he had forgotten to inhale after the involuntary remark. He took a deep breath and then went on, "There haven't been streetcars in L.A. for years."

"Damn. The tracks make a nice house of mirrors."

Trucks were roaring past only inches from Kootie's toes, and the glaring headlights against the dark backdrop of the neighborhood made him feel like a dog crouching on the center divider of a freeway; and briefly he wondered how Fred was.

His attention was roughly shoved away from the thought. "After this next juggernaut, go," said his own voice as he watched the oncoming westbound traffic. "Have they always been this *loud*?"

"Sure," Kootie answered as he skipped and hopped across the lanes after a big-wheel pickup had ripplingly growled past.

On the north sidewalk at last, Kootie limped east, his back to the blurred smear of red over the western hills under the clouds. Of course he knew now that he had not lost Edison's ghost after all, and he suspected that he had known it ever since he had involuntarily hidden from the slow-moving police car two hours ago; but the old man's ghost was not shoving Kootie out of his body now, and so the boy wasn't experiencing the soul-vertigo that had so shattered him at the Music Center.

Actually, he was glad that the old man was with him.

"Well now," said his voice gruffly, "did you get the firecrackers?"

Kootie's face went cold. Had those firecrackers been *important*? Surely he had lost them along with everything else that had been in the knapsack or in the pockets of his heavy shirt—but then he slapped the hip pocket of his jeans, and felt the flat square package.

"Yes, sir!"

"Good boy. Haul 'em out and we'll squelch pursuit."

Kootie hooked out the package and began peeling off the thin waxed paper. The things were illegal, so he looked around furtively, but the TV repair shop they were stopped in front of was closed, and none of the gleaming car roofs moving past in the street had police light bars. "Why would an orangutan go into a bar?" he asked absently.

"Sounds like a riddle. You know why the skeleton didn't go to the dance?" Kootie realized that his mouth was smiling.

"No, sir."

"He had no body to go with. Hardy-har-har. How much is a beer these days?" Kootie's hands had peeled off the paper, and now his fingers were gently prizing the firecracker fuses apart. Kootie didn't believe he was doing it himself.

"I don't know. A dollar."

"Whoa! I'd make my own. The joke is, you see, an orangutan goes into a bar and orders a beer, and he gives the bartender a five-dollar bill. The bartender figures, shoot, what do orangutans know about money, so he gives the ape a nickel in change. So the creature's sitting there drinking its beer, kind of moody, and the bartender's polishing glasses, and after a while the bartender says, just making conversation, you know, 'We don't get many orangutans in here.' And the orangutan says, 'At four-ninety-five a beer, I'm not surprised.' "

Kootie's laugh was short because he was out of breath, but he tried to make it sound sincere.

"Don't like jokes, hey," said the Edison ghost grumpily with Kootie's mouth and throat. "Maybe you think it's funny having to pay four-ninety-five for a *beer*. Or whatever you said it was. Maybe you think it's funny that somebody could be trying for an *hour* to tell you what you got to do, but your intellectual grippers ain't capable of grasping any Morse except plain old SOS! Both times I proposed marriage, I did it by tapping in Morse on the girl's hand, so as not to alert anyone around. Where *would* we be, if the ladies had thought I was just . . . testing their reflexes? I knew Morse when I was fifteen! Damn me! How *old* are you?"

Kootie managed to pronounce the word "Eleven." Then, momentarily holding on to control of his throat, he went on, defiantly, "How old are *you*?" What with being unfairly yelled at, on top of exhaustion and everything else, Kootie was, to his humiliation, starting to cry.

"No business of yours, sonny." Edison sniffed with Kootie's nose. "But I was a year short of seventy when I bet Henry Ford I could kick a globe off a chandelier in a New York hotel, I'll tell you that for nothing. Quit that crying! A chandelier on the ceiling! Did it, too. Did you see me kick that guy back there? What the hell have we got here?" Kootie's hands shook the nest of firecrackers.

"F-fire—"Kootie began, and then Edison finished the word for him: "Firecrackers. That's right. Good boy. Sorry I was rude—I shouldn't put on airs, I didn't get my B.S. until I was well past eighty-four. Eighty-four. Four-ninety-five! Oh well, we'll make our own, once we've got some breathing time. Breathing time. Hah."

Two black people were striding along the sidewalk toward where Kootie stood, a man in black jeans and a black shirt and a woman wearing what seemed to be a lot of blankets, and Kootie hoped Edison would stop talking until the couple had passed.

But he didn't. "You like graveyards, son?" Kootie shook his head. "I got no fondness for 'em either, but you can learn things there." Air was sucked haltingly into Kootie's lungs. "From the restless ghosts—in case the bad day comes, in spite of all your precautions, and you're one yourself."

The black couple stared at him as they passed, clearly imagining that this was a crazy boy.

"Leave no tracks, that's the ticket. I did all my early research in a lab on a train. Take your shoes off. Daily train between Port Huron and Detroit; in '61 I got a job as newsboy on board of it, so I could have a laboratory that couldn't be located." He sniffed. "Not easily, anyway. One fellow did find me, even though I was motivating fast on steel rails, but I gave him the slip, sold him my masks instead of myself. Take off your shoes, damn it!"

Kootie had not really stopped crying, and now he sobbed, "Me? Why? It's cold—" Then he had suddenly bent forward at the waist, and had to put weight on his bad ankle to keep from falling. *"Don't!"* He sat down on the concrete and then began defeatedly tugging at the shoelaces. "Okay! Don't push!" His hand opened, dropping the firecrackers.

Edison inhaled harshly, his breath hitching with sobs, and Kootie's voice said, brokenly, "Sorry, son. It's (*sniff*) important we get this done quick." Kootie had pulled off both his shoes. The concrete was cold against his butt through his jeans. "Socks too," wept Edison. "Quit *crying*, will you? This is . . . ludicrous."

Kootie let Edison work his numbing hands, stuffing the socks into the shoes and then tying the laces together and draping the shoes around his neck. He straightened carefully and leaned against the window of the TV repair shop. He half hoped the window would break, but even with Thomas Edison in his head he didn't weigh enough.

"Your furt's hoot," spoke Edison, interrupting Kootie's breathing. "Excuse me. Your *foot is hurt.* I'll let you get up by yourself. Grab the firecrackers."

Too tired to give a sarcastic reply, Kootie struggled to his feet, closing his fist on the firecrackers as he got up. Standing again, he shivered in his flimsy shirt.

"Now," said Edison, "we're going to run up this street here to our left—we're going to do that *after* you start to—no, I'd better do it—after *I* start dropping lit firecrackers on your feet."

At that, Kootie began hiccuping, and after a moment he realized that he was actually laughing. "I can't go to the cops," he said. "I got a one-armed murderer following me around—and a dope fiend cooking me dinner on a car engine, and my parents—and anyway, now *Thomas Alva Edison* is gonna chase me up a street barefoot throwing *illegal explosives* at my feet. And I'm eleven years old. But I can't go to the cops, hunh.''

''I liked that trick of cooking on the engine.'' Edison had made Kootie's hands cup around the matchbook and strike a flame. ''I'm saving your life, son,'' he said, ''and my . . . my . . . soul? Something of mine.'' He held one of the lit firecrackers until the sparking fuse had nearly disappeared into the tiny cardboard cylinder. Then, ''Jump!'' he said merrily as he let go of it.

Kootie got his foot away from the thing, but when it went off with a sharp little bang his toes were stung by the exploded shreds of paper.

He opened his mouth to protest, but Edison had lit two more. Kootie's head jerked as Edison cried, ''Run!,'' and then Kootie was bounding up the narrower street's shadowed sidewalk, both feet stinging now.

''Fucking—crazy man!'' the boy gasped as another firecracker went off right in front of the toes that had already been peppered.

The next one Edison didn't let go of; he held it between his fingers, and the rap of its detonation banged Kootie's fingers as painfully as if he'd hit them with a hammer. ''What the damn hell—'' Kootie yiped, still leaping and scampering.

''Watch your language, boy! You'll have the recording angels hopping to their typewriters! Keep a clean mouth!''

''Sorreee!''

In the back of his mind, Kootie was aware that Edison's children had hated this, too, having their footsteps disattached from the ground; for an instant he caught an image of a girl and two boys hopping on a lawn as exploding firecrackers stippled their shins with green fragments of grass, and fleetingly he glimpsed how strenuous it had been to get Tommy Junior to shinny up a pole and grab the coins laid on the top— how Edison had finally had to rub rosin on the inside of the boy's knees so that he could get traction. It had had to be done, though, the children needed to be insulated every so often, for their own good.

He was hopping awkwardly, and the whoops of his breath burned his throat and nose. At least no one was out on this street at the moment; to his left, beyond a chain-link fence that he grabbed at again and again to keep his balance, dusty old hulks of cars sat in a closed bodywork lot, and the little houses on the opposite side of the street were dark.

One of Kootie's bouncing shoes had caught him a good clunk under the chin, and his ankle was flaring with pain, when Edison finally let him duck around a Dumpster in an empty parking lot and sit down on a fallen telephone pole to catch his breath. The nearest streetlight had gone out when Kootie had pranced past beneath it, and now as he sat and panted he watched the light's glow on the nearest cinder-block wall fade through red toward black.

Kootie's mouth hissed and flapped as he and Edison both tried to use it at once. Kootie rolled his eyes and relaxed, then listened to Edison gasp out, quietly, "If I was your father—I'd wash out your mouth—with soap."

Kootie had heard the phrase before, but this time he got a clear impression of a father actually doing that to a son, and he shuddered at the picture. Kootie's own father had not ever punished him physically, always instead discussing each error with him in a "helpful dialogue," after which the transgression was respected as having contributed to a "learning experience" that would build his "self-esteem."

"Well, that's plain *bullshit*," Edison went on in a halting whisper, apparently having caught Kootie's thought. "When I was six years old I burned down my father's barn—I was trying to . . . ditch a playmate who'd been following me around for a year or so, of course at that age I didn't know about tricks like blowing up your footprints with firecrackers!" He wheezed, apparently laughing. "*Oh,* no! Burned to the ground, my father's barn did, and my *little friend* was still no more ditched than my shadow was. What was I saying? Oh—so I burned down the barn, and do you think *my* father *discussed* it with me, called it a—what was it?"

"A learning experience," said Kootie dully. "No, I suppose he didn't."

"I'll say. He invited all the neighbors and their children to come watch, and then he damn well whipped the daylights out of me, right there in the Milan town square!"

Kootie sniffed, and from across all the subsequent years of the old man's accumulated experiences, a trace of that long-ago boy's remembered despair and fear and humiliation brushed Kootie's mind.

For a long moment neither of them spoke. Then Kootie whispered, "Can I put my shoes and socks back on now?"

"Yes, son." He sighed. "That *was* for your own good, you know. We'll do better evasion tricks when we get the time, but the gunpowder cakewalk will probably have foxed your—what was it? one-armed murderer?—for a while. Slow him down, at least." Kootie's hand wavered out, palm down and fingers spread, and then just wobbled back to the splintery surface of the wooden pole. "You're tired, aren't you? We'll find some place to sleep, after we've taken one or two more precautions. This looks like a big city, we'll be able to do something. Before all this started up, I had the impression I was in Los Angeles—is that where we are?"

"Yes, sir," said Kootie. "Not in the best part of it."

"Better for our purposes, maybe. Let's move east a couple of blocks here, and keep our eyes open."

"Which way's east?"

"Turn right at that light. Need directions, always ask a ghost."

CHAPTER 23

"I have tasted eggs, certainly," said Alice, who was a very truthful child; "but little girls eat eggs quite as much as serpents do, you know."

"I don't believe it," said the Pigeon; "but if they do, why, then they're a kind of serpent: that's all I can say."

—Lewis Carroll,
Alice's Adventures in Wonderland

In the office on the ground floor of his apartment building, Solomon Shadroe had finally stopped staring at the horizontal white line on the television screen, and had plodded to his desk to resume doing the month's-end paperwork.

He didn't like the line being there on the screen at all, but at least it had stopped flaring and wiggling.

At last he pushed his chair back from his desk; he had finished writing the October checks and had then laboriously calculated the balance left in the account. As he stared at the worn blotter it occurred to him that pencil shavings looked like scraps of garlic and onion skins—his desk looked as though someone had been chopping together a *battuto*.

Garlic and onions—he remembered liking them, though he couldn't remember anymore what they had tasted like. Something like fresh sweat, he thought as he stood up, and a fast hot pulse.

His cup of Eat-'Em-&-Weep tea was lukewarm, but he drank off the last inch of it, tilting the cup to get the last sticky red drops. He put the cup down on the cover of the old ledger-style checkbook and took a can of Goudie snuff out of the desk drawer.

As he tapped out a pile of the brown powder onto his thumb-knuckle and raised it to his nose, he looked at the high built-in shelf on which sat three of his stuffed pigs. They had been burping away like bad boys during the half-minute when the line on the TV screen had been acting up, but—he looked again to make sure—the line was still motionless, and the pigs were quiet now. Johanna had the radio on, and the only noises in the office were the rolling urgencies of Bruce Springsteen's "Dancing in the Dark."

"Too loud?" asked Johanna from the couch where she lay reading a ladies' magazine.

Shadroe took a deep breath as he inhaled the snuff. "No. Just finished it up. Utility bills eating me alive. Gonna feed the beasties now." He got to his feet and plodded to the shelves.

"Oh good. Beasties!" she called to the screened window. "Din din din!"

Shadroe pried two white paper plates out of a torn cellophane wrapper and laid them on the coffee table. Onto one he shook a handful of Happy Cat food pellets from a box on a chair. Then he dug a handful of smooth pebbles out of his shirt pocket and spread them on the other plate.

He had taken Johanna to the Orange County fair this summer, and in one of the exhibit halls his attention had been caught by a display called the "Banquet of Rock Foods Collection." The display had been an eclectic meal laid out on a lace tablecloth: on one plate sat a hamburger, pickles, french fries, olives, and what might have been a slice of pâté; on another sat a stack of pancakes with some jagged fragments of butter on top, with a sunny-side-up egg and two slices of underdone bacon alongside. There had been other things too, a narrow roast turkey with ruffled paper socks on the ends of the drumsticks, a thin slice of toast, a boiled egg in an egg cup. The thing was, they were all rocks. Somebody had scoured deserts all over the west to find pieces of rocks that looked like food items.

He had wondered at the time if any raggedy old derelict had ever sat down at the table and tucked a napkin into his outermost grimy shirt. There had been a relish jar, Shadroe recalled, filled with tiny cubes of green glass—a spry old ghost could probably wolf down a spoonful of that before being hauled away.

In the months since, he had been putting out *two* plates at night— one with catfood for the possums, as always, and one with delectable looking rocks for the poor hungry old wandering ghosts. The rocks were often gone when he came back from the boat in the morning. In a catalogue recently he had seen a set of Mikasa Parklane crystal candies for a sale price of eighteen bucks, and he meant to get some to dole out during the cold nights around Christmas.

He had once read that Chinese people bury raw eggs in mud, and then dig them up years later and eat them. When he thought about that he was just glad that he couldn't remember taste, but apparently *Loretta deLarava* was not so fastidious—*she* didn't mind eating things that had long ago lost their freshness.

In his head he made up a lyric for the pounding Springsteen song:

> *Did your face catch* fire *once?*
> *Did they use a tire iron to put it out?*

It had been in 1962, on the set of *Haunted House Party*, that he had first met *Loretta deLarava.*

He'd been trying to make the shift from being a teen TV star to getting young-adult movie roles, but couldn't seem to shake the Spooky persona he'd acquired during the five years of "Ghost of a Chance." (People would keep asking to see him do the Spooky Spin, the dancelike whirl that, on the show, had always preceded his disappearing into thin air.) This was the fourth movie he'd worked in since CBS had canceled the series, and like the first three it had been a low-budget tongue-in-cheek horror picture, filmed at a pace almost as fast as TV work.

The novice production assistant had probably been about thirty years old, though it was hard to be sure—she was already overweight even then, and her jaw and nose were noticeably misshapen even after evident reconstructive surgery. *(Did they use a tire iron to put it out?)* Her name was deLarava—she claimed that it had originally been two words but had been inadvertently combined into one, like DeMille's, by a careless ad-copy writer. She had quickly outgrown the modest PA chores—somebody else had had to be found to make the coffee and drive to fetch paper clips and saber-saw blades, for, within days of starting, deLarava was filling out time cards and writing the daily production reports. Her credentials were hazy, but clearly she had had experience on a movie set.

"Sun's down," said Shadroe after putting the plates outside and coming back in and closing the door. "Draw me a bath, will you—" He paused to inhale. "—sweetie?"

Johanna put down the magazine and sat up. She glanced at the television screen, but the line was still steady and motionless. "Not ice?"

"Ice," he said firmly. "A lot of it." He looked at the TV too, and sighed. Can't wait till my alma mater actually goes nova, he thought. "Ice every night," he went on in his labored voice. "Until Halloween's past. Anybody from the building," he added. "Should come knocking. Tell 'em I walked to the store, unless. There's actual blood or fire."

" 'Sol,' " said Johanna in a drawling imitation of a tenant they'd had for a while, " 'I heard a *noise?*—in the *parking* lot?—so I shoveled your mailbox full of *dirt.*' "

The tenant had thought he'd smelled gas from a neighboring apartment, and, unable to reach Shadroe, had in a panic broken out all the windows in his own apartment. In the years since that tenant had left, Shadroe and Johanna had endlessly amplified on the man's possible responses to emergencies.

"Heh heh," said Shadroe levelly.

The couch springs twanged as Johanna levered herself up, and then the floorboards creaked as she padded barefoot to the next room; after a few seconds he heard water booming into the big old claw-footed cast-iron bathtub he had installed in there a couple of years ago. He used to take makeshift showers at dawn out behind the garages, holding a lawn sprinkler over his head, but a tenant had seen him one time and complained to the police—even though Shadroe had always been wearing jockey shorts when he did it—and anyhow he had had to stop.

Now he was wondering if even cold baths would work for much longer. He didn't speak to people face-on anymore, even if he'd just chewed up an Eat-'Em-&-Weep ball, because of the way they would flinch at his breath; and he knew that his ankle, onto which he had squarely dropped that refrigerator two days ago, couldn't possibly ever heal. He had wrapped it up tight with an Ace bandage, but it still hurt, and he wondered if he would be around long enough to get so tired of it that he would just saw the whole foot off.

He was only fifty-two years old . . . or would have been, if he had still had any right to birthdays. At least he wasn't a ghost.

Loretta deLarava obviously wanted to finish him off now—as she had smashed him seventeen years ago—after having taken aim at him all the way back in '62, on the set of *Haunted House Party*.

She had known who he was—Nicky Bradshaw, star of "Ghost of a Chance," godson to Apie Sullivan—but he had not realized who *she* was until that summer night when unseasonable rain had actually put rushing water in the L.A. River bed all the way up by the Fourth Street bridge, and the shooting of some zombie scene had had to be postponed.

Everybody had been sitting around in the big, chilly brick warehouse in which the indoor sets had been built, and deLarava had kept looking at her watch. That was natural enough, since by that time she was practically the second assistant director on the picture, but after a while she had lit up a corncob pipe full of some vanilla-scented tobacco and gone wandering out into the rain. He had heard her whistling old tunes out there, specifically "Stormy Weather," and when she had come back in she had ditched the pipe and had seemed to be stoned. At the time he had assumed that she'd been hiding the smell of grass or hash under the vanilla . . .

Though in fact she had seemed *wired*, as if on cocaine or an amphetamine. As soon as she'd got back inside and shaken back her wet hair she had started talking nonstop in her hoarse, fake British accent—rambling on about her genius-plus IQ, and telling fragments of anecdotes that clearly had no point except to illustrate how competent she was, equal to any challenges and a master of subtle revenge upon anyone who might foolishly dismiss her as unimportant.

The monologue had sat awkwardly with the crew and the youthful actors, all of whom had until then thought pretty highly of her. Bradshaw had been napping in a nest of rags in the costuming room, but the change in the tone of the conversation woke him, and he had wandered sleepily out into the big room.

"I was married once," deLarava was saying airily. "He was a very powerful figure in . . . an industry I'm not at liberty to name. He gave me everything I asked for, we had a big estate in Brentwood and a whole fleet of classic cars! But he couldn't give me the gift I demand of a man—that I be the most important person in his life. His two children . . . *occupied that spot*." (One of the crew wearily asked her what she had done about that, and deLarava simpered.) "We went on a picnic," she said, "and I fixed potato salad just the way he liked it, with olives and red onions and celery seed, but I used a jar of mayonnaise that had been sitting out opened for a few days. And he had an appointment later that afternoon. Oh yes," she went on as though someone had asked, "the most important appointment of his life. His precious children pigged down a lot of the potato salad too."

("Jesus," someone muttered. "Did they all *die*?")

(The question brought deLarava back from the spicy pleasures of the memory.) "Hm? Oh no, they didn't . . . *die*. But for a while they definitely had nothing to think about except when Nurse . . . Nurse Loretta might find the time to attend to their sickbeds! I can assure you!" Her British accent had been broadening out to sound more Texan, and was practically a drawl when she added, "*That* time they really *were* pooped-out puppies."

At that moment Bradshaw realized who she was. Her appearance had changed drastically in the intervening three years, but when he forgot the hoarseness and the affected accent he knew the voice even an instant before the *pooped-out puppies* phrase—which he had heard her say a number of times—confirmed it. Then she looked up and saw him, and her eyes widened and then narrowed momentarily as she visibly became aware that she had been recognized.

It's Kelley Keith, he thought in that first moment of surprise; it's my godfather's widow . . . fat and disfigured now . . .

Only then did he consider what she had just said. *The most important appointment of his life.* And he remembered that the autopsy of Arthur Patrick Sullivan had mentioned spoiled potato salad in his stomach as the cause of the cramp that had caused him to drown, out past the surf line on that summer day in Venice in 1959.

Bradshaw had backed away without changing his sleepy expression . . . but he'd known that she wasn't fooled. She was aware that he—alone!—had recognized her, and that he alone had understood her oblique and inadvertent admission of murder.

After *Haunted House Party* was in the can, he had finally stopped trying to chase his earlier success in show business. He had enrolled in the UCLA law school, and two years later passed the California bar and moved to Seal Beach to practice real-estate law.

Sometimes during the ensuing decade he had wondered if the advent of Loretta deLarava had scared him away from the movies . . . and then he had always recalled the artistic merits of *Haunted House Party*, and had wryly dismissed the suspicion.

He had stayed away from Hollywood, though, and had gradually stopped seeing his friends in the industry; and even so, he was careful to keep his home address and phone number a secret, and to vary the route he took to his office, and to come and go there on no set schedule. He kept a gun in his office and car and bedside table. Superstitiously, he never ate potato salad.

And in fact it wasn't potato salad that she finally got him with, in 1975. It was a spinach salad with hot bacon dressing, and lots of exotic mushrooms.

When Johanna returned to her magazine, Shadroe, who hadn't called himself Nicholas Bradshaw since his "death" in '75, took one more look at the static television screen and then stumped into the little room where the tub was, and by the glare of the bare overhead lightbulb he stared with distaste down at the dozens of ice cubes floating in the gray water—like broken glass in a tub of mercury.

The sooner he took his bath and got out, the sooner he could be in his car and driving west on Ocean Boulevard to the marina, where he would climb aboard his boat and spend the long hours of darkness sitting

and staring at another TV set switched to CBS with the brightness control turned down just far enough to black out the picture, watching the
white line that would certainly be on that screen too, and listening for
the burping croaks of his pigs.

Like every other night.

CHAPTER 24

"That's the effect of living backwards," the Queen said kindly: "it always makes one a little giddy at first—"

"Living backwards!" Alice repeated in great astonishment. "I never heard of such a thing!"

"—but there's one great advantage in it, that one's memory works both ways."

—Lewis Carroll,
Through the Looking-Glass

At the northwest corner of MacArthur Park, crouched under a pyracantha bush in the shadow of the statue of General MacArthur, Kootie watched as his fingers opened his bag of purchases from ninety-nine-cent store on Sixth Street. The box of insecticide proved to be MIRACULOUS INSECTICIDE CHALK—MADE IN CHINA, and inside it were two sticks of white chalk with Chinese writing stamped into them. An instruction sheet on flimsy paper was all written in Chinese figures, and Kootie leaned out of the shadow of the statue's base as his hands held the paper up close to his eyes in the leaf-filtered radiance of a streetlight.

" *'Directions for use . . .'* " he heard his own voice say thoughtfully. Kootie started to interrupt, "You read Chinese—?" but Edison took over again and finished, " '*. . . On floor, use enclosed chalk to write "Bugs, kill yourselves forthwith."* ' "

Then Edison was laughing an old man's laugh with Kootie's boy's voice, and he flipped the paper over. "Kidding," Edison said. On this side the directions were in English. " *'The chalk is more effective to use at night,'* " Edison read, and Kootie could see that he was reading it correctly this time. "Well, that's handy, eh? *'Draw several parallel lines each two to three centimeters apart across the track which the insect used to take . . .'* I like 'used to,' as if the job's already done.

Well,'' he said, folding up the instructions, ''this will do some good, though it's a child's version of a device I set up in the Western Union office in '64 in Cincinnati, and later in Boston—a series of plates hooked up to a battery. That was for night work, too—I told everybody it was for rats or roaches or whatever they'd believe, but it was to get some rest from the damn ghosts.''

Kootie caught a brief glimpse of memory: a big dark room in what had once been a downtown Cincinnati restaurant, copper wire connections arcing and popping all night, the harsh smell of the leaky batteries, and morose, transparent ectoplasmic figures huddled in the corners far away from the stinging metal plates.

Kootie's hands waved. ''Get us back out to the sidewalk, will you boy?''

Kootie tucked the bag back into his shirt and then obediently straightened up and walked across the grass and stepped up to the sidewalk. He started to brush dirt off his pants, but found that he was crouching to draw a circle all the way around himself on the concrete with the stick of chalk. His lips twitched, and then Edison used them to say, ''I'd better let you do it; spit in the circle. If I try it you'll do something else at the same moment and we'll wind up with spit all down our chin.''

Our chin? thought Kootie—but he did spit on the sidewalk before straightening up.

''Very well, *your* chin,'' said Edison. ''Now crouch again and let me draw some lines.''

Kootie squatted down, and then watched as his hand drew a maze of lines around the circle: parallel lines, spirals, radii from the circle's edge—until this section of sidewalk looked, Kootie thought, like the site of some hopscotch Olympics. Cars hissed past in front of him in the street beyond the curb, but the only close sounds were the click-and-scratch of the chalk and his own eager breath.

The chalk was being worn down to a stump as cartoon eyes were added, and more wheels were drawn, and crosshatch squares were carefully colored in. The production was a couple of yards wide now.

Kootie shivered. It was cold out here, and he didn't like having his arm stretched out for so long. ''Will you be done when that stick of chalk is used up?'' he asked hopefully. There had been two sticks of the chalk in the yellow-and-orange box, and he hoped Edison wasn't going to need the other one as well.

He was about to repeat his question when Edison spoke instead: ''What? What is it now?''

''How much of that stuff have you got to draw?''

''Stuff . . .'' Kootie's head was swung this way and that, and he had the impression that Edison was even more bewildered than he was by the convoluted designs he'd drawn on the sidewalk.

"Did *I*—" Edison began. He took a deep breath. "Yes. *There*. That'll stop any ghosts or ghost hunters who might pick up my trail."

As Kootie presumed to straighten up, he could feel his recent memories being ransacked. "And," Edison went on, "it might slow down your . . . *one-armed murderer*. Now—how much does a dinner cost around here? *Oaffg*—Never mind, what I meant was, let's find some place to eat." Kootie's head tilted to look down, and again their gaze swept the lunatic drawing. "After that we can come back here and— see if we've caught something to put in your film canister."

Only now did Kootie realize that his purchases at the ninety-nine cent-store might not have been his own idea; and he wondered why Edison apparently wanted to catch a ghost. But the notion of dinner was compelling.

"I've been smelling barbecue for a while," he ventured.

"Good lad, I'm not getting anything . . . *olfactory,* myself. Lead the way, by all means—it's never a good idea to turn your back on your nose."

The thrilling blend of onion and peppers and lemon on the breeze seemed to carry at least the promise of warmth, and Kootie was briskly rubbing his arms above the elbows as he followed the smells across the Park View intersection and around a corner, to a doorway under a red neon sign that read JUMBO'S BURGOO & MOP TROTTER. Even from out on the street Kootie could hear laughter and raised voices from within.

"It's food," Edison assured him. "Southern stuff."

(Again Kootie got a memory flash—Spanish moss hanging from old live oaks along the banks of the Caloosahatchee as he chugged upriver in an old sloop, the winter house in Fort Myers among the towering bamboo and tropical fruit trees, cornmeal-dipped fried catfish served alongside corn on the cob that had crinkly hairpins stuck in the ends for handles . . .)

"And without any sense of smell I won't be able to *taste* any of it," Edison went on in an aggrieved voice as Kootie pulled open the screen door and stepped into the place. "I'd much rather have stayed deaf instead."

Redwood picnic tables were lined up on the flagstone floor, with a counter along one side of the room—ORDER at the near end, PICKUP at the other—and in the kitchen beyond that, Kootie could just see the tops of big shiny steel ovens. Framed hand-painted menus swung in the hot air above the counter, and the other three walls, dark old brickwork, were crowded with black-and-white photos that all seemed to be autographed. The cooks and the countermen and all the men and women and children at the tables were black, but for the first time since losing Raffle and Fred, Kootie didn't feel like an excluded fugitive.

"What can we do for you, little mon?" rumbled a voice above Kootie's head. Looking up, he saw the broad, red-eyed face of a counterman staring down at him.

"I'm going to have—" began Kootie, from habit wondering what sort of pulses and grains and vegetables they might serve here; then he finished defiantly, *"meat!"*

"Meat you shall have," the man said agreeably, nodding. "Of what subcategory and method of preparation?"

"Barbecue pork ribs," said Edison while Kootie was still trying to read the menu through the dark lenses of his sunglasses, "and the turnip and mustard greens with bacon dumplings—" ("Please," interjected Kootie breathlessly, just to be polite.) "And a big mug of beer—" ("N-n-no," Kootie managed to interrupt, "I'm too young, I'll just have a large Coke!") "And," Edison went on—(*"Not"* said Kootie, who could see what was coming)—"a cigar," finished Edison in defeat, "dammit."

The black man was frowning and nodding. "Yes, *sir,"* he said. "Nothing wrong with *you."* He was tapping keys on the cash register, which hummed and spat out a receipt. "Seven dollars and a quarter, that comes to."

Kootie gave the man a ten-dollar bill, keeping his mouth and throat firmly closed against Edison's outraged grunting.

The man gave him his change. "It'll be at the far end of the counter there, in just a minute. Do you think you can keep the number *twenty-two* in mind? Can you remember it even now?"

"Twenty-two," said Kootie. "Sure. Why?"

"Because that's the number that one of us up here will call, when your supper is ready for you to pick up. I can't see why that shouldn't be satisfactory to everybody concerned, can you?"

"No, sir," said Kootie. He limped to a table that was occupied only at one end by a couple of old men playing dominoes, and he wondered if he might ever get used to everyone thinking that he was crazy; then he wondered what schemes Edison might come up with for finding a place to sleep tonight, and to make money tomorrow. Remembering the chalk drawing, he hoped the old man's ghost wasn't going senile.

When his number was called and he went up to get his tray, his gaze was caught by a polished wooden box on the counter. A metal rod, hinged at the bottom, ran up the front of it, and a piece of paper had been taped to the rod, with L.A. CIGAR—TOO TRAGICAL hand-lettered vertically on the paper. On the counter in front of the box was a cardboard bowl of peppermints.

Kootie's gaze was snagged on the lettering. He read it downward, and then upward, and it was the same letters either way. This seemed important, this proof that moving backward could be the same as forward, that the last letter of a sentence could be not only identical to the lead-off capital letter but the very same thing. . . .

He realized that he had been standing here, holding the tray with the steaming plates on it and staring at the vertical words, for at least several seconds. He made himself look away and breathe deeply. "What," he whispered, "is it?"

"That's a cigar lighter," rumbled his throat as he crossed to his table and sat back down. "Well," he answered, "you didn't get a cigar, so forget about it."

Kootie made both of them focus on the food.

The ribs were drenched in a hot sauce that reeked of tomato and onion and cider vinegar, and he gnawed every shred of meat off the bones and was glad of the napkin dispenser on the table. The greens only got nibbled, because Edison couldn't taste them and Kootie found them strong and rank, but he did eat most of the dumplings.

A mouthful of Coke ran down his chin onto his shirt when Edison opened his mouth to whisper, "My God, it's *fly paper!*"

Then Kootie watched his hands untuck his shirt to get at the bag and pull out of it the box of film. The film cartridge itself was dumped out onto the table, and Kootie's fingers snatched up the empty black plastic canister. Kootie was about to point out that the film was in the yellow metal thing, but Edison hissed, "That fella's going to light a cigarette!" Sure enough, one of the old men at the table had taken out of his pocket a pack of Kools and was shaking one out.

Kootie's head snapped forward, and then he couldn't tell if it was intentional or not when he drooled some Coke into the empty plastic film container.

"Get to the cigar lighter before he does," Edison whispered. "Go, or I'll motivate for you, this is too lucky a chance to waste."

His legs already twitching impatiently, Kootie pushed back the bench, got to his feet and wobbled over to the wooden box on the counter. *How does it work?* he thought.

Edison whispered, "*Don't* work it—act like you just came over here to get a mint."

Kootie started to say *Okay*, but had got no farther than the "Oke—" when the ceiling lights dimmed and the air was suddenly cold; and he was distantly grateful when he felt his knees lock, for sudden dizziness had made the field of his vision dwindle like a receding movie screen. He thought he sensed someone big standing behind him, but he couldn't turn around.

" 'Kay," he managed to whisper.

Kootie watched his own hands. His left hand picked up one of the mints, and he could feel its powdery dry surface, like a big aspirin, even though he wasn't controlling the fingers—(It's like the opposite of when your hand's asleep, he thought)—and his right hand brought up the plastic container to catch the mint deftly when his left hand dropped it. Then his right hand slowly scraped the edge of the container up the metal rod at the front of the cigar-lighter box, as if trying to scratch off the taped-on paper.

Then the ceiling lights brightened again and all three of the cash registers began clicking and buzzing. Edison had capped the little container as quickly as if he had caught a bee in it. "Grab a mint," he made Kootie whisper. "Grab a whole handful, like you're just a greedy boy."

Kootie dizzily obeyed, and walked back to his table when his left foot began to slide in that direction. As he sat down, heavily, he heard one of the countermen demanding to know why all the registers were going through their cash-out cycles.

"Let's go before they figure it out," Edison said softly. "Leave a tip?" put in Kootie. "They didn't bring it to the table," Edison pointed out impatiently.

As he rode his scissoring legs out of the restaurant, Kootie managed to wave one shaky hand at the counterman.

The night outside was colder now, and the headlights of the faceless cars seemed to glow more hotly as they swept past. Edison, forgetful of Kootie's hurt ankle, was making him hurry, and the result was a bobbing, prancing gait. He had stuffed the plastic container into his front jeans pocket, but his left hand still clutched the mints.

"Did*jjj*—" began Kootie, but Edison clamped his teeth shut, then said, "Don't speak of it. I lit up the whole area—we've got to get clear of it."

Kootie was hurrying west on Wilshire, away from the spot where Edison had drawn the chalk patterns on the park sidewalk by the statue, and he caught a thought that might or might not have been his own: *A stupid use for chalk—that was just stupid—a* ghost's *idea of a ghost trap.* Apparently the "flypaper" on the cigar lighter had been better.

Edison made Kootie glance up at a streetlight as he shuffled past under it, and Kootie understood that the old man was glad to see that the light didn't go out to mark their passage.

Ionic. From nowhere the word had come into Kootie's mind, and at first he thought of marble pillars with curled scroll-like tops. (Doric, Ionic, and Corinthian. Doric columns had just a flat brick at the top, and Corinthian ones had lots of carved grapes and leaves.) Then the notion of pillars disappeared, and he pictured a clump of little balls, with much tinier balls orbiting rapidly around the clump; when the tiny balls were stripped away, the clump—the nucleus—had a powerful electric charge. If it was moving, it threw electromagnetic waves.

These were not Kootie's thoughts, and they didn't feel like Edison's either. "Ionaco," Kootie said out loud.

And suddenly the gleam of moonlight shining on the fender of a parked car ahead of them was not just a reflection, but an angular white shape, a thing; and Kootie's perception of *scale* was gone—the white shape seemed to be much farther away than the car.

The shape was rotating, growing against the suddenly flat backdrop of the city night, and it was . . . an open Greek *E*, a white spider lying sideways, a white hand with fragmenting fingers . . .

It was moving upward and growing larger, or closer.

It was a side-lit white face, an older man's face—with a white ascot knotted under the chin; and as Kootie stared, gaping and disoriented, the lines of a formal old claw-hammer coat coalesced out of the shadows under the face, and an unregarded background shadow that might have been a building was now a top hat. Cars on the street were just blurs of darkness, moving past as slowly as moon shadows.

Kootie thought the image was some kind of black-and-white still projection—the light on it didn't correspond to the direction of the moon or the nearest streetlight—until the white mouth opened and moved, and Kootie heard the words, "I only have one left." The voice was low, and reverberated as if speaking in a room instead of out here on the street, and the lips didn't move in synch with the sounds.

The figure still seemed to be some kind of black-and-white hologram.

Neither Kootie nor Edison had kept the boy's body moving. Halted, Kootie was aware of sweat on his forehead chilly in the night breeze. "One what?" asked Edison wearily.

"Belt." The ghost, for Kootie was sure that's what this thing was, opened its coat, and Kootie saw that the figure wore, as a sort of bulky cummerbund, a belt made of bundled wire. A little flashlight bulb glowed over the buckle. "Fifty-eight dollars and fifty cents, even now."

"We don't need a belt," Edison said; but, "What does it do?" asked

Kootie. It was heady for the boy to realize that, on this night, he would believe nearly any answer the ghost might give.

"Well," said the ghost in its oddly contained and unsynchronized voice, "it *could* have cured Bright's disease and intestinal cancer. But it banishes paralysis and restores lost hair color and stops attacks of homicide. It's called the I-ON-A-CO, like the boy said. It's a degaussing device—you can sleep safely, if you're wearing it."

"I don't have fifty-eight dollars," Kootie said. For the first time since hurrying out of Jumbo's whatever-it-had-been, he opened his hand. "I've got mints, though."

The ghost came into clearer focus, and a tinge of color touched its white face. "Out of respect for Thomas Alva Edison," it said, and its words matched its lip movements now, "I'll take the mints in lieu of the money."

"He'd rather have had the mints in any case," said Edison grumpily. "And you never thought that *I* might want 'em."

"Is it okay," said Kootie before Edison could go on, "if I hold a couple out for Mr. Edison?"

"Well . . . a *couple*," allowed the ghost.

Edison again took over Kootie's tongue. "You have the advantage of me, sir. Your name was—?"

"Call me Gaylord." Pink-tinged hands appeared in front of the coat, and the two-dimensional fingers managed to unfasten the buckle—but when the ghost tried to pull the belt from around itself, the heavy cables fell through its insubstantial flesh, and clattered on the pavement; one of the hands wobbled forward, though, palm-up, and Kootie poured the mints into the hand, which was able to hold them. Kootie was careful to hold back two of them.

Kootie's hand slapped to his own face, and his mouth caught the pair of mints and chewed them up furiously. Then, only because it was his own mouth talking, he was able to understand the mumbled words "Pick up your damned belt and let's go."

Kootie crouched and took hold of the belt. The heavy metal bands of it were as cold as the night air, not warmed as if someone had been wearing it. As he straightened and swung it around his waist he noticed that it must have weighed five or six pounds, and he wondered how the ghost had managed to carry it.

When he looked around, he saw that he was alone on the sidewalk, and that the dark street with its population of rushing cars had regained its depth and noise, and no longer seemed to be a moving picture projected onto a flat screen.

Edison had swallowed the chewed-up mints. "I said let's go."

Kootie started forward again, trying to figure out the working of the buckle as he limped along. "This is pretty neat, actually," he said.

"Poor doomed old things," said his voice then, softly, and Kootie just listened. "God knows where *we* are, the *real* us. Heaven or hell, I suppose, or simply gone—in any case, probably not even aware of these lonely scramblings and idiot ruminations back here." Kootie's hand had pulled the capped black plastic film canister out of his pocket, and now shook the thing beside his ear. "I wonder who this poor beggar was. I invented a telephone, once."

Edison seemed to have paused, and Kootie put in, "I thought that was Alexander Graham Bell."

"I wasn't talking about that telephone. *Bell!*—all he had was Reis's old magnetotelephone, a stone-age circuit with 'make and break' contact interruption, good enough for tones but lousy for consonants. Showing off in front of the King of South America or somebody at the Centennial Exhibition in '76, with his voice not hardly carrying along the wire from one end of a building to the other. He recited Hamlet's soliloquy— 'For in that sleep of death what dreams may come/When we have shuffled off this mortal coil . . .' Two years later, with my carbon transmitter and *induction* coil, I held a loud-and-clear conversation with the Western Union boys across a hundred and seven miles, New York to Philadelphia!" Kootie snorted, to his own startlement. " 'Physicists and sphinxes in majestical mists!' A test phrase, that was, for checking the transmission of *sibilant syllables*. Think all that was easy? And *Bell* could *hear*! He had a very soft job of it."

Again he held the black container up to Kootie's ear and shook it; the mint rattled inside. Then he put it back in Kootie's pocket. "Nymph," he said softly, apparently to the night sky, "in thy orisons, be all my sins remembered."

Kootie's footsteps had turned left, south down a side street, and the high reinforced windows of the buildings were dark. Up ahead on the right was a chain-link fence with some yawning lot beyond it. Kootie was rubbing his arms again in the chill, and he hoped Edison was feeling it too, and realizing that they'd need to find a safe place to sleep before long.

It occurred to him that Edison had not explained the telephone *he* had invented.

CHAPTER 25

There was a short silence after this, and then the Knight went on again.
"I'm a great hand at inventing things. Now, I daresay you noticed, the
last time you picked me up, that I was looking rather thoughtful?"
"You were *a little grave," said Alice.*

—Lewis Carroll,
Through the Looking-Glass

In the glare of the streetlight at the southeast corner of Park View and Wilshire, glittering flies were darting around in the chilly air like metal shavings at a machine shop. Sherman Oaks waved them away from his face, keeping his mouth closed and breathing whistlingly through squinched nostrils, for the flies were harkening to the multitude-roar of his exhalations, and on this night of all nights he was not going to condescend to consume such trash even accidentally.

He had called the exchange back a couple of hours ago, and the router had told him that Neal Obstadt had agreed to putting up forty grand for the fugitive Parganas boy against Oaks's pledged thousand doses of smoke.

The lady who had put up the $20,000-reward billboards had been eliminated from the exchange listings, and replaced by Obstadt.

As a receipt, the router had played for Oaks Obstadt's authorization message: *Yeah, tell this Al Segundo or Glen Dale or whoever he is that I'll fade him—but if he hoses me on the smokes, his own ass is smoke.*

Sherman Oaks had irritably got off the phone and resumed his anxious search of the streets around Union and Wilshire—

And then about an hour ago a glance at his knife-pommel compass had shown the needle pointing west so hard that it didn't wobble at all, and moved only to correct for his own motion.

He had immediately thrashed his imaginary left arm in a furious circle, but the only blinks of heat it felt were weak and distant and *fleeting*—human lives flickering out uselessly, in deaths that simply tossed the ghosts up to dissolve in the air. Naive psychics were impressed when occasionally they sensed this routine event, but Oaks was only interested in the coagulant ghosts that hung around and got snagged on something.

He hadn't been able to sense the big one. It must still have been contained in the boy. But at least it was still distinct and unassimilated, and at the moment it was in its excited state, for his compass needle was pointing at it.

He had hurried west—and at Park View Street his compass had gone crazy.

Someone, almost certainly the big ghost working the boy's hands, had drawn a lunatic ghost lure in chalk on the sidewalk, and had spat in the center of it; and now all the broken-down ghost fragments that inhabited the houseflies around the MacArthur Park lake had swarmed out and were circling the intricate chalk marks as if trying to follow some prescribed hopscotch pattern in their flight. The ones that landed on the chalk lines seemed to be dying.

The flies alone wouldn't have hampered Oaks too badly, for their charges were very weak even in excited swarms like this; but when he stood on the Park View curb and looked down at the compass at his belt, he saw that the needle was jigging and sweeping back and forth across nearly ninety degrees of the compass face. From at least Sixth Street in the north to Seventh in the south, the city blocks ahead were *waked up*. Every ghost in every building was agitated and clamoring. Office workers tomorrow would probably be seeing magnetically induced distortions on the screens of their computer monitors, and if they'd left their purses in their desks they'd find that their automatic teller cards were demagnetized and no longer worked. And even hours from now the offices would still be chilly with the cold spots where the ghosts had drawn up their energies.

The big ghost must have stepped *way* out, at some point in this neighborhood, and just damn *flashed* the ghost populace, mooned them. That would energize and urgently draw every spirit lingering nearby. God knew why the big ghost had done it, for it couldn't eat any ghosts itself.

What, thought Oaks uneasily. You just wanted somebody to chat with? Or did you do it simply to fox my radar this way?

Sherman Oaks felt tense, nearly brittle, and he kept calling to mind the collapsed, hijacked-flesh face he had seen on the steps to the parking level at the Music Center this afternoon. Who the hell *was* that, who *is* this big ghost?

The threads of association trailed away back into the blankness that was his life before the awakening of consciousness in the district of Sherman Oaks three years ago.

But he shook his head sharply. Enough idle chatter, he told himself, quit dishing the applesauce. If the compass is temporarily foxed, that only means that you're back on a limited-to-visual footing. Get your footing moving—you know you're on the right track, and you know he's close.

"So what was the telephone *you* invented?" Kootie asked tiredly. He had walked down the side street, away from the streaking headlights of Wilshire, and was now staring through a chain-link fence at an enclosed paved yard that was shadowed from the intermittent moonlight by surrounding buildings.

"Well, I had to stop work on it. I found I was able to call people who hadn't died yet. What do you suppose this is?"

"*Hadn't* died?" Suddenly Kootie was uncomfortable with this conversation. "It's an empty lot."

"With, for once, no barbed wire on the fence. And it's got a couple of old cars in there, that look like they've been there since Ford first rolled them off the production line. Damn Ford anyway."

Kootie remembered having said *Damn Ford* when Raffle had seen the reward-for-this-boy billboard at the Music Center; and he realized that it must have been Edison talking then, and that he had been referring to Henry Ford, rather than to Raffle's car.

Kootie found that he had curled his fingers through the chain link, and was looking up and down the empty sidewalk.

"What did Ford do to you?" he asked.

He wasn't really surprised when he began helplessly climbing the fence, but he had certainly not expected the old man to be so agile. "Ow!" Kootie exclaimed breathlessly at one point, "watch the right ankle!—Oh, sorry." The street was silent except for the rush of cars back on Wilshire and the immediate thrashing clang of the shaken chain-link.

Astride the crossbar at the top, Kootie's body paused to catch its breath. "When I was dying," said Edison, "Ford made my son catch my last breath in a test tube for him." In deference to Kootie's ankle, he didn't just jump, but climbed down the other side.

At last unhooking his fingers from the chain-link, Kootie hurried across the cracked pavement of the enclosed lot to the nearest of the abandoned cars. Shaggy night-blooming jasmine bushes overhung the car, and crumpled plastic bags had been shrink-wrapped by Monday's wind right onto the heavy leafy clusters, like butterflies captured in midflight poses against the fronts of car radiators.

When Kootie was crouched behind the fender, Edison went on in a whisper, "Oh, he meant well—just like he did when he built an exact replica of my Menlo Park lab, for his 'Light's Golden Jubilee' in 1929, the fiftieth anniversary of my incandescent lamp. That must have confused a whole nation of ghosts and ghost trackers—Ford reconstructed the entire lab, even using actual planks from my old buildings, with the old dynamos and half-built stock-ticker machines on the benches inside, and all the old tools. And he even erected a duplicate of the boarding-house across the street! And he trucked in genuine red New Jersey clay, for the soil around the buildings! And there *was* a villain hanging around me in those days, trying to hook out my soul—I fed the fellow a poisoned apple!—and it was against such people that Ford was trying to protect me. Oh, it's hard to fault the . . . the generous, sentimental old fool, even now, now that I'm hiding in an empty lot in Los Angeles in . . . what year is it?"

"1992," said Kootie.

"*Good . . . God.* I died sixty-one years ago." Kootie had stopped panting after the exertion of climbing the fence, but now he was breathing hard again. "And I rattled my last breath into a test tube, which my son Charles then stopped up and *obediently* gave to Henry Ford." Kootie found himself staring at his hands and shaking his head. "Where did *you* get it?"

Into the ensuing silence, Kootie said, flatly, "My parents had it. Hidden inside a bust of Dante. They've had it forever. Had it."

"Inside *Dante*, eh? Just like I'm inside *your* head now. I guess I'm your built-in Virgil, though I've got to admit I don't really know the neighborhood. I wonder when we get to El Paradisio? Huh. Sounds like a Mexican speakeasy."

"So Ford was trying to protect you."

"In his blundering way. Yeah, from ghosts and ghost hunters both—I stood out like a spiritualist bonfire. And—" Kootie's shoulders shrugged. "It was to *honor* me, too. A replica of the great man's lab, the great man's actual last breath! He was pleased to see his friends get *accolades.* He'd have been tickled to death—as it were—to know that I finally got a B.S." Kootie could feel his pulse thumping faster in his chest. "And not an honorary one, either—it was earned! The faculty examined seventeen portfolios of my research! And this was at *Thomas A. Edison State College*—if you please!—in Trenton, New Jersey."

"I . . . *dreamed* about that," said Kootie softly, "Sunday night." It, the thought of college, was the spur that finally made me put my runaway plan into action, he thought. Which has turned out to have put a lot of other stuff into action, too. "I must have been picking it up from you, you all worked up in the bust in the living room."

The laugh that came out of his mouth then was embarrassed. "I guess I *was* excited about it myself. A little. Not that I put any stock in academic honors." He shrugged again. "The news was all over the party line."

"Yeah," said Kootie, "I met some old lady that wanted to talk to you. Probably had a graduation present for you." Kootie sighed, feeling bad about dead people. "What are you gonna do with the ghost in the film can?"

Kootie could feel that Edison's mood was down too, and had been for the last several minutes; probably Kootie's own melancholy was largely induced in his surrounding mind by the suggestion from Edison's frail, contained ghost.

"The ghost in the film can," said Edison. "If he hasn't died in there yet, we could talk to *him* on my telephone. If we had my telephone with us I could work it. You might be able to as well—you strike me as another boy who's carrying around some solid guilty link with a dead person or two, hm?"

"I . . . guess I am." Kootie was too desolated and exhausted, here in the dark empty lot, to cry.

"There now, son, I don't mean to stir it up." Edison had Kootie sit down, leaning back against the car body. The wind was rustling softly in the fronds of a stocky wild palm on the far side of the car, and the only sound on the breeze was the rapid *pop-pop-pop* of semiautomatic gunfire, comfortably far away.

"My telephone," Edison said. "I got the ghost-telephone idea when a spiritualist paid Marconi to buy my Lehigh Valley grasshopper telegraph patents for him. It was originally a scheme to make two-way telegraphy possible on a moving train, by an induction current between plates on the train and telegraph wires overhead, with regularly spaced dispatcher stations along the way, hence 'grasshopper.' *But* . . . they got a lot of random clicking, some bits of which turned out to be . . . oh, you know, idiot clowning: *Shave and a haircut, two bits,* and *Hey Rube,* and the beats of the *Lohengrin* wedding march and popular songs. Even so, I didn't figure it out until the spiritualist bought the patents." He yawned. "Up, son, I've got to set up the apparatus for our our night's worth of six signals."

Kootie didn't want to do any more work. Why was it always *his* muscles and joints that took the wear and tear? "What's a six signal? I bet we don't need it."

"Tramp telegraphers have to tap out a signal every hour, all night long. Called a 'six signal.' It's to show that you're still awake, alert, ready to participate. I used to just hook up a clock to a rotary saw blade, so it sent the signals *for* me, right on time, while I napped. *Up*, lad, it won't take but a few moments."

Kootie struggled to his feet one more time, and then he took out the chalk and, crouching, drew a big oval all the way around the car, which, he now saw, was a wrecked old Dodge Dart, of God knew what color under the dust of years. This time he drew arrows radiating out from the circumference, and he spit several times outside the wobbly chalk line.

"That'll make it seem that we're up and about, in a number of places," said Edison, "and for the night I can clathrate myself inside your head again—voluntarily this time!—with all hatches battened down. Then we'll be as damn hard to find as a gray hat in a rock pile." It seemed to Kootie that this simile had been derived from experience. "And we should sleep, and we should sleep."

Edison used Kootie's fingers to probe the car-door lock with a bit of wire he found on the pavement, but after a while he swore and tossed it away and just had Kootie punch in the wind-wing window with a chunk of concrete. Kootie's arm was just barely long enough for his stretched-out fingers to reach the lock-post button.

Kootie stepped back and opened the door—wincing at the echoing screech of the ancient hinges—and then he leaned inside, breathing shallowly in musty air that somehow nevertheless had a flavor of new houses.

The seats and floor of the car proved to be stacked with dozens of ancient gallon paint cans that someone had once halfheartedly covered with a stiffened drop cloth, and Kootie had to lift some of the cans out and set them down on the pavement just to have room to sit with his legs stretched out. He didn't know if the old man could feel the aching, stinging fatigue in his shoulders and knees—and in his hip, which pain he now remembered that the old man was responsible for—but Edison didn't argue when Kootie suggested that this was enough, and that they could sleep sitting up.

Kootie pulled the door closed—slowly, so that it wouldn't squeal again. The broken wind-wing wasn't letting in much fresh air, so he wrestled with the door's crank handle and managed to open the passenger-side window several inches, enough to probably keep the fumes of mummified paint from overcoming him during the night. That done, he bent the old drop cloth snugly around his shoulders and shifted around until he found a position in which he could relax without setting off any big twinges of pain.

The empty lot was unlit, and it was very dark inside the old car.

Sometimes his father had come into Kootie's room at bedtime and had haltingly and awkwardly tried to talk to the boy. Once, after Kootie had supposedly gone to sleep, he had heard his father, back out in the kitchen with his mother, dejectedly refer to the conversations as "quality time." Still, it had been comforting, in its way.

"So you fixed up this phone," he ventured now, speaking quietly in the close shelter.

"Hm? Oh, yes, that I did. Do you remember the story of Rumpelstiltskin? Your parents must have told it to you."

No. Kootie's parents had told him all about Rama and Koot Hoomie and Zorro-Aster and Jiddu Krishnamurti (in whose holy-man footsteps he had been intended to follow), and about self-realization and meditation, and the doings of various Egyptian holy men. But at least he had heard about Rumpelstiltskin in school. Thank God for school. "Sure," he said now, sleepily.

"Well, you remember that the little man didn't want anybody to know what his name was. That's important if a person is like you and me—misfortunate enough to be tethered by a stout leash of responsibility to somebody who's in the ghost world; it's like we've got one foot outside of time, isn't it, so that we react to noises and jolts just a split instant before they actually happen."

"You've had that happen too," said Kootie faintly, slumping farther down in the warming seat.

"Ever since I watched a playmate drown in a creek when I was five, son. So have a lot of unhappy people. And that . . . *antenna* we carry around makes us stand out to ghosts. They're drawn to us, and without meaning any harm they can attach themselves to us and sympathetically induce the collapse of *our* time lines—kill us, like a parasite that kills its host.

"People like you and me, if we manage to live long, have generally had a *wanderjahr*, a time of wandering around untraceably, often luckily giving a fake name and fake birth date, while we get the time to figure out what the hell's going on. I was a plug telegrapher when I was sixteen, that's like an apprentice, and for years I rode trains all over this country, because there was always ready work for any class of telegrapher during the Civil War. Blavatsky was doing her wander-time around then too: Europe, Mexico, Tibet. What you learn, if you're lucky, is that you need a mask if you're going to deal up close with ghosts.

You can't let them get a handle on *you*, not anything. Real name and real birth date, especially. Those are solid handles.''

Edison blew a chuckle out of Kootie's mouth. ''One time in the early seventies I had to go to City Hall in Newark to pay real-estate taxes—last day, big fine if I didn't—and the fellow behind the desk was one of the big solidified ghosts, who had managed the no doubt difficult task of scraping together enough alertness to hold a county job, and he asked me what my name was. Hah! I had to pretend I couldn't remember! And pay the fine! My own name! Everybody in line thought I was an imbecile.''

Kootie yawned so widely that tears ran down his cheeks, and it interrupted Edison's monologue. ''So who did you call that was still alive?'' he asked. ''That must be embarrassing—*'Hi, George, what are you doing there? Did you just this morning die or something?'* ''

Breath whickered out of his nostrils as Edison laughed softly. ''That's just about exactly how it went. In 1921 I had got the spirit phone working: it required summoning back the ghost of my dead playmate—by then I had managed to cauterize the bit of him that had been stuck to me, sort of the way I'm stuck to you right now—and energizing him in a strong electromagnetic field. He was still my antenna. And then his augmented charge was amplified dramatically with an induction coil, and then he was . . . the operator.

''I was trying to call a man named William Sawyer, who had died forty years earlier; Sawyer was an electrical inventor who claimed to have come up with the electric lamp before I did, and wanted me to buy him out. I told him to go to hell, I just left him in the dust, and then he came around to my place when I was giving an exhibition, right after Christmas in, it must have been, '79. Sawyer came drunk, yelling and shouting that it was all fake, and he broke a vacuum pump and stole *eight* of the electric lamps, which I didn't have a lot of in those days. In the years after that, I had some opportunities to help him—and I didn't do it. I hadn't forgotten the theft and the vandalism, you see, and whenever I was asked about him I made sure to drip—I mean, made sure to drop—some unflattering statements about him. He turned into a drunk, and wound up killing a man, and he died before he could go to prison. So, forty years later, I was trying to get him on the phone to . . .'' Kootie's hands lifted.

''. . . Apologize?''

After a few seconds of silence, Edison said, softly, ''Yep.'' He exhaled. ''But you get a crowd on that line, it's a *party line*, and everybody wants to talk. When they heard who was calling, somebody picked up, and I found myself talking to a mathematician who I had fired the day before! I was flabbergasted, and I said something like, 'Lord, Tom, did you kill yourself today?' All he wanted to do was recite poems to me, so I hung up and went round to his house. It developed that he had had a nervous breakdown, but had not in fact died. So I hired him back. But I had learned that people can sometimes throw ghosts in moments of high stress, and those ghosts can sometimes wander away just exactly the same as though the people had died. They *are* the same.''

"So . . . you quit work on the phone because of that?''

Suddenly agitated, Edison said, ''Those aren't the *people*, the people you harmed, those ghosts. It's like trying to make amends to somebody's car, after they've parked it and walked away. Blavatsky was right when she claimed that the spirits called up by mediums are just animate shells. You can talk to the ghost of your dead uncle Bob, but Uncle Bob himself doesn't know anything about it. Chesterton said that, I believe.'' He shook Kootie's head. ''What you've got to do is somehow *rehire* the sons of bitches.''

Rehire my mom and dad? thought Kootie. ''But . . . they're dead. What do you do about that?''

For nearly a whole minute there was silence.

Then, quietly, ''Don't look at me, son, I'm one of 'em myself. Go to sleep now.''

A fleeting impression of a candle being blown out and a door being closed, and then Kootie was alone in his own head again. Before loneliness could creep up on him he closed his eyes, and he was instantly asleep.

Beyond the dust-crusted glass of the car's windows, out on the sidewalk past the end of the lot and the chain-link fence, a silhouette came shuffling along from the direction of Wilshire Boulevard. Only one arm swung as it ambled along, though the torso rocked as though another arm were swinging alongside too. The head was turning to look one way and another, with frequent pauses to glance down at the figure's waist, but the silhouette registered no change in its pace as it walked on down the sidewalk, past the lot, and disappeared to the south.

CHAPTER 26

". . . I wonder what'll become of my name when I go in? I shouldn't like to lose it at all—because they'd have to give me another, and it would be almost certain to be an ugly one. But then the fun would be, trying to find the creature that had got my old name! That's just like the advertisements, you know, when people lose dogs—'answers to the name of "Dash": had on a brass collar'—just fancy calling everything you met 'Alice,' till one of them answered! Only they wouldn't answer at all, if they were wise."

> —Lewis Carroll,
> Through the Looking-Glass

By eleven o'clock in the morning, Hollywood Boulevard was a crowded tourist street again, and it was the signs overhead—movie marquees, names of ethnic fast-food restaurants, huge red Coca-Cola logos, and the giant infantry soldier over the army-surplus store—that caught the eye. But when Sullivan had driven down the boulevard at dawn, it had been the pavements that he had watched; empty lanes still blocked by last night's police barricades, litter in the gutters, and solitary junkies and long-night male and female prostitutes shambling wearily toward unimaginable refuges in the gray shadows.

Sullivan turned down Cherokee, parked his van in the lot on the south side of Miceli's and switched off the engine, and for a few minutes he just sat in the van and smoked a cigarette and sipped at a freshly popped can of beer. Thank God for the propane refrigerator, he thought.

Just because he had parked here didn't mean he had to eat at Miceli's. He remembered a Love's barbecue place on Hollywood Boulevard just a block or two away. He could even restart the van and go eat at Canter's, or Lawry's. What he *should* do, in fact, was get a to-go sandwich somewhere; he had no business blowing his finite money in sit-down restaurants.

It had been here at Miceli's, on that rainy night in the fall of '86, that he had had his last dinner with Julie Nording; the dinner at which she had been so distant and cold, after which he had gone back to the apartment he'd shared with Sukie, and had got drunk and written his ill-fated sonnet.

You're here to exorcise the ghost, he told himself comfortably as the cold beer uncoiled in his stomach. Prove to yourself that there's no more power to sting in those old memories—

And then he winced and took a deep swallow of the beer, for he remembered his real ghosts: Sukie, who for years had been so close a companion that the two of them were almost one person, their love for each other so deeply implicit that it could be unspoken, ignored, and finally forgotten; and his father, whose wallet and key ring *(and three Hires Root Beer cans)* he and Sukie had intolerably left behind when they had mindlessly fled deLarava's shoot in Venice Beach on Christmas Eve of 1986.

He had spent this morning at City College. He had showered and washed his hair in the cologne-reeking men's gym, setting his clothes and "scapular" and fanny pack on a bench he could see from the broad tile floor where the showerheads were mounted against the tile wall, so that he wouldn't have to rent an authorized padlock for the brief use of a locker, and possibly have to show some ID; and then he had got dressed again and reluctantly walked over to the library.

He'd made his way upstairs to the reference section, a maze of tall shelves full of ranked orange plastic file folders stuffed with newspapers and magazines, and endless sets of leather-bound volumes with titles like *Current Digest of the Soviet Press* and *Regional Studies*, and with some help he managed to find the long metal cabinets of drawers where the microfilm was kept.

He'd pried out the boxed spool of the *Los Angeles Times* from July to December of 1990 and carried it to a projector in one of the reading booths. Once the film was properly threaded and rolling, he sat for several minutes watching July newspaper pages trundle past on the glowing screen—advertisements, comics, and all—until he inadvertently discovered that there was a fast-forward setting on the control knob. At last he found the first of November. (President Bush had "had it" with Saddam Hussein; the governor's race between Wilson and Feinstein was still too close to call.)

The Elizalde story was at the bottom corner of the front page: THREE DEAD IN CLINIC BLAZE. According to the text, a firebomb had been detonated in Dr. Angelica Anthem Elizalde's psychiatric clinic on Beverly Boulevard at 8:40 P.M. on Halloween night. The resulting three-alarm fire brought fifty firefighters, from Los Angeles, Vernon, and Huntington Park, who put the the fire out in forty-five minutes. Dr. Elizalde, 32, had suffered second-degree burns while trying to extinguish one of the patients who had caught fire; altogether, three of her patients had died, though only that one had died of burns; and five more were hospitalized with unspecified traumas. Police and the Fire Department were investigating the incident.

Sullivan had fast-forwarded the microfilm to the November 2 issue. The story was still on the front page—now Dr. Elizalde had been arrested and charged with manslaughter. Several of the survivors of her Wednesday-night group-therapy session had told police that Elizalde had been conducting a séance when the disaster had struck, and that hideous apparitions had materialized in the air; and they claimed that one of the patients, a man named Frank Rocha, had spontaneously burst into flames. Fire investigators noted that Rocha's body had been *incinerated.* Police theorized that Elizalde had installed machinery to simulate the appearance of ghosts, and that this machinery had exploded during the fraudulent psychic performance . . . though they admitted that no traces of any such machinery had been found.

The November 3 issue had moved the story to the front page of the second section, where it eclipsed the "Cotton Club" murder trial, which had apparently been hot news in 1990. Elizalde had raised her $50,000 bail, and then had apparently disappeared.

The descriptions of the Halloween-night séance were fuller now, and more lurid—the surviving patients claimed that ropes of ectoplasm had burst from the bodies of many present, and that spirits of eviscerated babies, and of screaming women and babbling old men, had then formed in the air over their heads; and Frank Rocha had exploded into white-hot flames. It was now revealed that several of the patients who had had to be hospitalized were in fact confined in psychiatric wards with acute psychotic reactions.

In the issue of November 4 it was confirmed that Elizalde had disappeared; police sources commented that until her arraignment they would not issue a bench warrant. Included in the article were quotes from an interview that the *L.A. Weekly* had done with Elizalde two months previous to what was now being referred to as the Día del Muerte Séance. "I find it effective," she was quoted as having said, "to use the trappings of the so-called 'occult' in eliciting responses from credulous patients. It has no more intrinsic value than the psychiatrist's cliché couch or the stained-glass windows in a church—it's simply *conducive.*" Police were still speculating that she had decided to enhance the effect by somehow staging dangerous, faked supernatural phenomena.

Sullivan had tucked the microfilm spool back into its box and returned it to the drawer, and then located the cited issue of *L.A. Weekly*—an actual paper copy, not microfilm—and turned the pages to the interview.

There had been a photograph of Dr. Elizalde in her consulting room, and, looking at it in the library this morning, Sullivan had winced. She was strikingly good-looking, with long black hair and big dark eyes, but she looked more like a gypsy fortune-teller than a psychiatrist: the photographer had caught her smilingly underlit over a glowing crystal ball the size of a melon, and behind her he could see saint-candles and all kinds of primitive little statues on shelves, and a framed print of Our Lady of Guadalupe.

The interview itself had not been so bad. He had made notes of some of her statements:

On ghosts: "*Well, of course when a person dies, actually that person is gone; a TV set that was used only to view PBS is no different from one that never showed anything but Sunday morning televangelists, once the two sets have been disassembled—they're both equal in their total absence now. But all of us who are still* around *have* hooks *in the* memories *of these dead people, unresolved resentments and guilts, and these things don't stop being true, and being motivational, just because the person that caused them is dead, has stopped existing. By having my patients strongly pretend—oh hell, briefly* believe—*that they can* communicate *with the dead collaborators in their pasts, I let them forgive, or ask for forgiveness—'give the pain to God'—and achieve peace. My patients don't* forget *the old wrongs endured or committed, but the memories of them being actively, cripplingly poisonous. My methods facilitate this by letting the patients* literalize *the old ghosts.* [ans. to quest.:] *No, I don't believe in ghosts at all. I'm a rational materialist atheist. By the charged term 'God' I mean objectivity.* [ans. to quest.:] *My patients are free to. I don't preach.*

On men in her life: "*No, I—(laughter) physician heal thyself!—I think I'm still reacting against the machismo image of my father and my brothers. My father drank—I was thirteen when I figured out that his drinking was worst around February and March, when he'd get his vacation pay and his tax refunds—and he'd beat up my mother; and even on the farm out in Norco he always had to have steak and salad and a baked potato and a couple of glasses of wine at dinner, and silverware, while the rest of the family got rice and beans. And my brothers and their friends were . . . oh, you know, khaki pants, polished black shoes, Pendleton shirts buttoned only at the top button with white*

T-shirts underneath, hairnets with the gather-point in the middle of the forehead like a black spidery caste mark. Tough—all the firstborn boys are Something-Junior, and the fathers always had them out on the front lawn in a boxing ring made with a garden hose, sparring like fighting-cocks. And the boys and girls were supposed to get married and have kids as soon as possible. I've reacted against the whole establishment I was raised in, there—I'm not Catholic, I don't drink, and I don't seem to be attracted much to men. Oh—and not to women at all!—let me add. (Laughter.)"

On why the crystal ball (if she's so materialistic): "The stasis of the clarity, the clarity of the stasis—people look deeply for ghosts in pools where the agitation has passed. Tide pools seem to be the best, actually, literally, in eliciting the meditation that brings the old spirits to the surface; the sea is the sink of ghosts . . . that is, in the superstitious mind, mind you. Seriously, patients seem to find their ghosts more accessible in the shallow depths of actual ocean water. It's been worth field trips. Eventually I'd like to move my clinic to some location on the beach— not to where there's surf, you see, but pools of ordered, quieted sea-water."

In the City College library, Sullivan had leaned back in his plastic chair and imagined the statements of a psychiatrist in some bucolic culture about a thousand years from now, when guns had survived as nothing but inert, storied relics: *Because of the legends still adhering to the objects known as "Smith and Wessons," I find that valuable shocks can be administered by pressing the "muzzle" of one such object against a patient's temple, and then ritualistically pulling the "trigger." I have here a specimen that has been perfectly preserved through the millennia . . . now, watch the patient . . .*

BOOM.

Boom indeed, he thought now two hours later in the Miceli's parking lot, as he finished his beer and dropped the cigarette butt inside the can. One of her patients must have been a ghost-connected person who acted as a primer, the charge being Halloween night and the hollow-point slug being a whole shitload of actual, angry, idiot ghosts. And the main target seemed to have been one of her patients who had died but hadn't re-alized it yet, so that he threw posthumous shock-shells when his lifeline collapsed, igniting his overdue-for-the-grave body. And then two others died of heart attacks or something, and everybody else just plain went crazy.

That must have been some night, Sullivan thought now as he levered open the van's driver's-side door and stepped down to the pavement in the chilly morning air. Well, maybe she's learned better now; here she is back in town, and, unless I miss my guess, the reason she's come back is to make amends—to a more literal sort of ghost than any she was willing to acknowledge when she gave that interview.

If I can *find* Dr. Angelica Anthem Elizalde, he thought, maybe she could be talked into doing another séance. She knows how, and I've got Houdini's mask, which has got to be big enough for both of us to hide behind. We could both deal with our ghosts *from behind the mask*, like Catholics confessing through the anonymizing screen in a confessional.

As he trudged up the sidewalk beside the brick wall of Miceli's, he wondered if Elizalde felt differently about the Catholic Church now. Or about drinking.

Or even about men, he thought as he pushed open the door and stepped inside.

Sullivan was sitting alone at a table down the hall from the entry and just taking a solid sip of Coors when someone tapped him on the shoulder.

He choked and blew beer out through his nose—and he dropped the glass, for his right hand had slapped his shirt pocket for the bag with the severed thumb in it and his left hand had darted to the loop on the fanny pack that would open the thing with one yank, exposing the grip of the .45 inside.

"Jesus, dude," came a startled, anxious voice, and a man stepped widely around from behind him, smiling and showing his hands self-deprecatingly. "Sorry!"

Sullivan recognized him—it was an old college friend named Buddy Schenk. "I spilled my friend's drink, sorry," Schenk said, looking over Sullivan's shoulder. "Could he have another? Uh—and I'll have one too." Schenk looked down at Sullivan. "Okay if I sit?"

Sullivan was coughing hard, but could inhale only with strangled, whooping gasps. He waved at the chair across from him and nodded.

"Beer in the morning," said Schenk awkwardly as he sat down. "You're getting as bad as your sister. And you're jumpy! You went off like a rattrap! About gave me a heart attack! What are you so jumpy for?" He had unfolded a paper napkin from the table and was mopping up the foamy beer and pushing aside the curls of broken glass.

Sullivan tried to inhale quietly, and was humiliated to find that he couldn't. His eyes were watering and his nose stung. "Hi—Buddy," he managed to choke.

My God, I am nervous, he thought. If I'd known I was so scared of deLarava I would have sat with my back to a wall.

He wished he could smell something besides beer, for suddenly he wanted to seine the garlicky air for the scent of clove cigarettes.

The waiter who had earlier taken Sullivan's order for a meatball sandwich walked up then, and swept the soaked napkin and the broken glass into a towel.

After the man had walked away, Sullivan said, "Buddy, you asshole," mostly to test his voice; and he could speak now. "It's good to see you."

Sullivan discovered that he meant it. This was his third day back in Los Angeles, and until this moment he had felt more locked out of the bloodstream of the place than the most postcard-oriented tourist. It was a new Los Angeles, not his city anymore—the freeways didn't work nowadays, Joe Jost's was gone, Melrose Avenue was ruined, Steve Lauter had moved across the 405 and had guns pointed at his head, and the people Sullivan was most concerned about were dead people.

"Well, it's good to see you too, man," Buddy said. The waiter brought two glasses and beer bottles to the table, another Coors for Sullivan and of course a Budweiser for Buddy. "How's Twat?"

Sullivan smiled uncertainly, not sure if he'd misheard his friend or if the question was some vulgar variation on *How's business?* He looked over his shoulder and took a sip of beer carefully. "Hm?"

"Sorry, *Toot.* We used to call you two Twit and Twat sometimes."

Sullivan's momentary cheer was deflating, and he had another gulp of beer. "I never . . . heard that," he said.

"Well, you wouldn't have. Hey, it was all a long time ago, right? College days. We were all kids." Buddy laughed reminiscently. "Everybody figured Sukie had an incestuous thing for you, was that true?"

"I'm sure I'd have noticed." Sullivan said it with a blink and a derisive snort, but he found himself gulping some more of the beer. The glass was nearly empty, and he poured into it the rest of the beer in the bottle.

The old shock was still a cold tingling in his ribs. (He had read that the weight of the Earth's atmosphere on a person was fourteen pounds on every square inch of skin, and he thought he could feel every bit of the weight right now.) Sukie had been like the poor lonely ghosts, hopelessly trying to find that *better half.*

Old Buddy sure has a winning line of remember-whens, he thought.

"She's dead," Sullivan said abruptly, wanting to put a final cold riposte to Buddy's thoughtless needling before it went any further. "Sukie—Elizabeth—killed herself. Monday night."

Buddy frowned. "Really? Jesus, I'm sorry, man. What the hell have you—that's why you're alone. Were you with her? I'm real sorry."

Sullivan sighed and looked around at the Pompeii-style murals on the high walls. Why had he come here? "No I wasn't with her, she was in another state. I'm just in town for . . . business and pleasure."

"Sex and danger," agreed Buddy cheerfully, apparently having got over his dismay at the news of Sukie's suicide. Sullivan remembered now that for the few months that Buddy had stayed with them in '82, he'd always remarked, upon going out in the evening, *Off for another night of sex and danger!*—and when he'd drag back in later he'd every time shrug and say, *No sex. Lotta danger.*

"No sex," Buddy said now, grinning, "lotta danger. Right?"

"That's it, Buddy."

"You're having lunch, right? Lemme join you, it's on me and we'll eat ourselves sick, okay? Whatever you ordered already is just the first course. We'll drink to poor . . . Sukie. I'm supposed to be meeting a guy at noon, but I'll call him and put it off till three or so."

Sullivan was already tired of Buddy Schenk. "I can't be staying long—"

"Bullshit, you're staying long enough to eat, no?" Buddy was already pushing back his chair. "Order me a small pepperoni-and-onion pizza, and another beer, when you get your refill, okay?" He was calling the last words over his shoulder, striding away to the hallway where the telephone was.

"Okay," said Sullivan, alone in the dining room again.

He was agitated by the conversation about Sukie. And the insult to himself! *Twit* and Twat! And he was sure that he and Sukie hadn't picked up the Teet and Toot nicknames until . . . the early eighties, at the earliest. So much for the *we were all kids* disclaimer. It's not just thoughtless—why is he jabbing at me this morning?

Sullivan tried to recall when he'd last seen Buddy. Had Sullivan said or done something rude? Sukie might have. Sukie could probably be counted on to have.

His beer was gone, and he looked around for the waiter. A pepperoni-and-onion pizza, he thought, and another Bud and maybe two more Coorses. It's always been Bud for Buddy.

Even the waiter had known it.

Sullivan's hands were cold and clumsy, and when he accidentally banged his fingers on the edge of the table they seemed to *ring*, like a tuning fork.

How had the waiter known it?

Oh hell, Buddy had probably been in here for a while, and this one hadn't been his first. Or maybe he was a regular, these days. Sullivan breathed deeply and wished he had gone somewhere else for lunch.

Why was Buddy hanging around drinking beer at Miceli's when he had a noon appointment somewhere? Miceli's wasn't the sort of place one ducked into for a quick beer.

Maybe the appointment was for lunch right here *at* Miceli's, and Buddy had arrived early to drink up some nerve.

Through the high window overlooking Cherokee, a beam of morning sunlight lanced down onto the tabletop and gleamed on a stray sliver of broken glass.

Sullivan had certainly jumped, when Buddy had tapped him on the shoulder; grabbed not only for the gun but for Houdini's mummified thumb, too. What had he been afraid of? Well—that deLarava had found him.

Maybe deLarava *had* found him. Who was Buddy calling?

Jesus, he thought, taking a deep breath. Where's that waiter? You need a couple of beers bad, boy. Pa-ra-noia strikes deep. You meet one of your old friends in one of your old hangouts . . .

Both of which deLarava would have been aware of, just as she'd been aware of Steve Lauter. Maybe there was no one I knew at Musso and Frank's, day before yesterday, just because that was Sukie's and my personal place. We never went there with anybody else, so deLarava wouldn't have known to plant an "old friend" informer there.

If Buddy's here to betray me, he might very well want to pick a fight, to justify it to himself.

Sullivan stood up, walked around the table and sat down in Buddy's chair, facing the entry.

Are you seriously saying, he asked himself as his fingers tingled and he took quick breaths, that you believe deLarava has planted an old friend at each of your old hangouts? Restaurants, bars, parks, theaters, bookstores? (Do I have that many old friends? Maybe the roster is filled out with strangers who've each got a picture of me in their pockets.)

Oh, this really is paranoia, boy—when you start imagining that everybody in the city has nothing in mind but finding *you*; imagining that you're the most important little man in Los Angeles.

But I *might* be, to Loretta deLarava. If she really wants to capture and eat my father's ghost. And she has money and power, and the paranoid insect-energy to put them to directed use.

O'Hara's in Roosevelt, Morrie speaking, he thought, remembering his flight out of Arizona on Monday night, after Sukie's call. He had calculated then that it would take less than half an hour for bad guys to get from the nuclear plant to O'Hara's.

He thought: How quickly can they get here, today?

Warning—you are too close to the vehicle.

Sullivan was out of the chair and walking toward the front door and feeling in his pocket for the keys to the van.

"Pete! Hey, where you going, man?"

Sullivan pushed open the door and stepped out into the chilly morning sunlight. Behind him he heard Buddy yell, "Goddammit," and heard Buddy's feet pounding on the wooden floor.

Sullivan was running too.

He had the van key between his thumb and forefinger by the time he slammed into the driver's-side door, and he didn't let himself look behind him until he had piled inside and twisted the key in the ignition.

Buddy had run to a white Toyota parked two slots away; he had the door open and was scrambling in.

Sullivan jerked the gearshift into reverse and goosed the van out of the parking slot, swinging the rear end toward Buddy's Toyota; the Toyota backed out too, so Sullivan bared his teeth and just stomped the gas pedal to the floor.

With a jarring metallic *bam* the van stopped, and Sullivan could hear glass tinkling to the pavement as the back of his head bounced off the padded headrest. Luckily the van hadn't stalled. He reached forward and clanked the gearshift all the way over into low and tromped on the gas again.

Metal squeaked and popped, and then he was free of the smashed Toyota. He glanced into the driver's-side mirror as he swung the wheel toward the exit, and he flinched as he saw Buddy step out and throw something; a moment later he heard a crack against his door and saw wet strings and tiny white fragments fly away ahead of him. Then he was rocking down the driveway out onto Cherokee amid screeching rubber and car horns, and wrenching the van around to the left to gun away down the street south, away from Hollywood Boulevard. He slapped the gearshift lever up into Drive.

He caught a green light and turned left again on Selma, and then drove with his left hand while he dug the Bull Durham sack out of his shirt pocket. Feeling like a cowboy rolling a smoke one-handed, he shook the dried thumb into his palm and tossed the sack away, then drove holding the thumb out in front of his face, his knuckles against the windshield. It felt like a segment of a greasy tree branch, but he clung to it gratefully.

Out of the silvery liquid glare of the cold sunlight, a big gold Honda motorcycle was cruising toward him in the oncoming lane; he couldn't see the rider behind the gleaming windshield and fairing, but the passenger was a rail-thin old woman sitting up high against the sissy bar, her gray hair streaming behind, unconfined by any sort of helmet . . . and she was wearing a blue-and-white bandanna tied right over her eyes.

Her head was swiveling around, tilted back as though she was trying to smell or hear something. Sullivan inched the thumb across the inside of the windshield to keep it blocking the line from her blindfolded face to his own.

Sweat stung his eyes, and he forced himself not to tromp on the accelerator now; the Honda could outmaneuver him anywhere, even if he got out and ran. (The shadows of wheeling, shouting crows flickered over the lanes.) And it was probably only one of a number of vehicles trolling between Highland and Cahuenga right now.

God, he prayed desperately as a tree and a parking lot trundled past outside his steamy window, let me get clear of this and I swear I'll *learn*. I won't blunder into predictable patterns again, *trust me*.

The 101 Freeway was only a couple of big blocks ahead, and he ached for the breezy freedom of its wide gray lanes.

Keening behind his clenched teeth, he pulled over to the Selma Avenue curb and put the engine into Park.

He sprang out of the driver's seat and scrambled into the back, tossing the mattress off the folded-out bed. Buddy would even now be telling them that Sullivan was in a brown Dodge van, but they'd recognize him even sooner if he didn't have the full mask working. They would already have been given his name, his birth date, *too much of what was himself.* When he and Sukie had worked together they had been a good pair of mirror images, being twins, and so there had been no solid figure for a ghost or a tracker to focus on; but now he was alone, discrete, quantified, discontinuous. Identifiable.

He had to grip the thumb between his teeth to bend over and lift the plaster hands out of the compartment under the bed, and he was gagging as he hopped forward and slid back into the driver's seat. He laid one plaster hand on the dashboard and grotesquely stuck the other upright between his legs as he put the van back into gear and carefully pulled out away from the curb.

The Honda had looped back, and now was passing him on the left. The riders hadn't had time to have talked to Buddy, but the old woman swung her head around to blindly face Sullivan, and peripherally he could see the frown creasing her forehead.

She's sensing a psychic blur, he thought; a mix of Houdini's birth and life, and my own. She won't be catching any echoes of Houdini's death, because the old magician was masked for that event, and got away clean even though he died on perilous Halloween. She'll be wondering if I'm a schizophrenic, or on acid—what it is that makes the driver of this vehicle such a psychic sackful of broken mirror. (He even felt a little different—his jacket seemed looser and lighter, though he didn't dare look down at himself right now.)

He groped through his mind for any remembered prayer—*Our Father . . . ? Hail Mary . . . ?*—but came up with nothing but a stanza of verse from one of the Alice-in-Wonderland books, a bit Sukie had liked to recite:

> *"The sea was wet as wet could be,*
> *The sands were dry as dry.*
> *You could not see a cloud because*
> *No cloud was in the sky:*
> *No birds were flying overhead—*
> *There were no birds to fly."*

The motorcycle drifted past outside his window and pulled in ahead of him; through the close glass of the windshield he could hear the bass drumbeat of the motorcycle's exhaust pipes, and through the fluttering gray hair he could see the old woman's jaw twisted back toward him; but he kept a steady, moderate pressure on the gas pedal, though his legs felt like electrified bags of water. Was the driver of one of these cars around him seeing some signal from the old woman? Was he about to be cut off? They wanted him alive, but only so that deLarava could use him as lure for his father's ghost.

In a hoarse voice he quoted more of the Alice scripture, thinking of Sukie and mentally hearing her remembered recitation of it:

> *"Still she haunts me, phantomwise,*
> *Alice moving under skies*
> *Never seen by waking eyes."*

The brake lights flashed on the transom of the gold motorcycle—but its rider leaned the heavy bike around in a U-turn and then accelerated back toward Cherokee, the diminishing roar of its engine rising and falling as the rider clicked rapidly up through the gears. Sullivan's jacket was heavy and tight again.

He spat the old brown thumb out onto the dashboard and gagged hoarsely, squinting to be able to see ahead through tears of nausea.

He turned left on Wilcox, and then right onto the crowded lanes of eastbound Hollywood Boulevard. Don't puke on yourself, he thought as he squinted at the cars glinting in the sunlight ahead of him. It looks like you got away this time. Now stay away. Hide. Buddy will have described the van, and might even have got the license number.

The thought of Buddy reminded him of the missile his old friend had thrown at the van as Sullivan had committed hit-and-run. Stopped at a red light, Sullivan now rolled down the driver's-side window and craned his neck to look at the outside of the door.

A branching pattern of viscous wetness was splattered from the door handle to the front headlight. It was clear stuff mottled with yellow and dotted with angular bits of white, and half a dozen vertical trickles had already run down the fender from the initial horizontal streaking.

Buddy's missile had been a raw egg.

The schoolboy-prankishness of the gesture was disarming. He egged my van, Sullivan thought; after I smashed the front end of his car! How could he have been colluding with deLarava at one moment and doing something as goofy as this in the next? I must have been wrong—poor Buddy wasn't guilty of anything but beery tactlessness back there in the restaurant, and then he must really have been calling some business associate when he went to the phone. I should go back, and apologize, and agree to pay for getting his car fixed. This was *pure* paranoia. Even the people on the motorcycle had probably just been—

No. Sullivan remembered the old woman sitting high up against the sissy bar, blindfolded against visual distractions and sniffing the breeze, and he couldn't make himself believe that the pair on the Honda had been random passersby.

He kept driving straight ahead.

East of Vine, the street stopped seeming to be Hollywood Boulevard, and was just another Los Angeles street, with office buildings and and CD stores and boarded-up theaters, and red-and-yellow-blooming wild lantana bushes crouched in the squares of curbside dirt; but when he glanced out of his open window he saw, a smoky mile to the north against the green Griffith Park hills, the old white HOLLYWOOD sign— and for just a moment, to his still-watering eyes, it had seemed to read HALLOWEEN.

Not for two days yet, he thought, and he spat again to get rid of the taste of Houdini's thumb. I've got about thirty-six hours.

Just past Van Ness he turned right onto the 101 southbound. The freeway was wide open and cars were moving along rapidly for once, and he gunned down the ramp with the gas pedal to the floor so as to be up to speed when he merged into the right lane.

A. O. fucking P., he thought as he took his first deep breath in at least five minutes. *On the freeways, there you feel free.*

He remembered now, now that he was at long last experiencing it again, the always-downstream rush of driving along open fast-moving freeway lanes. Up here above the surface streets, above them even if the freeway was sluicing through a valley, the real world off to the sides was reduced to a two-dimensional projection of sketchy hills and skyscraper silhouettes, and you dealt with the *names* of places, spelled out in reflector-studded white on the big green signs that swept past overhead, rather than with the grimy stop-and-go places themselves; even the spidery calligraphy of gang graffiti markers, looping across the signs in defiance of barbed wire and precarious perches and rushing traffic below, were formal *symbols* of senseless-killing neighborhoods, rather than the neighborhoods themselves.

Other drivers were just glimpsed heads in the gleaming solidity of rushing cars in this world of lanes and connectors; space and time were abridged, and a moment's inattention could have you blinking at unfamiliar street names in Orange County or Pomona.

Sullivan had to find a place to stay, a place with a garage. After this, he couldn't keep living in the van out on the streets. And he wanted to be close to deLarava, without putting himself in the way of her possibly stumbling across him.

Just short of the towers of downtown he turned south on the Harbor Freeway, toward Long Beach and the Los Angeles Harbor . . . and the *Queen Mary.*

CHAPTER 27

"If it had grown up," she said to herself, *"it would have made a dreadfully ugly child: but it makes rather a handsome pig, I think."*
—Lewis Carroll,
Alice's Adventures in Wonderland

Francis Strube's black leather electric office chair was acting up. It was made by the McKie Company, which was supposed to manufacture the best race-car seats, and he had punched the button on the "comfort console" to pump up the lower-back region, but it had inflated out grossly, to the size of a watermelon, and in order to sit back with his shoulders against the top of the chair he had to push out his chest and belly like a pouter pigeon.

Ludicrous. He leaned forward instead, dividing his attention between the flimsy sheets of fax paper in his hand and the man in the seat across the desk. The Goudie Snuff people—after extorting a thousand dollars out of him!—had printed out their mailing list in some kind of minimalist dot-matrix, and Strube was afraid he'd have to get Charlotte to puzzle it out for him.

"But," said the client uncertainly, "would that be best for them?"

Strube looked up at him. What dreary aspect of the man's divorce case had they been discussing? Damn the chair. He pushed the "deflate" button several times, but the leather-covered swelling behind his kidneys didn't diminish; if anything, it swelled more. But he put patient concern in his voice as he asked, "Best for whom?"

"Whom we're talking about, Mr. Strube! Heather and Krystle!"

These, Strube recalled, were the man's daughters. He remembered now that custody of the children had been the topic at hand.

"Well, of *course* it would be best for *them*," Strube said, indicating by his tone that he was way ahead of the man, and had not lost track of the conversation at all. "Our *primary* concern is the well-being of Heather and Krystle." Strube had made a bad impression early on, when, having only read the girls' names on the information form, he had pronounced the second one to rhyme with *gristle* rather than *Bristol.*

"But," went on the father of the girls, waving his hands bewilderedly, "you want me to demand alternating custody of the girls, a week with me and then a week with Debi, and then a week with me again? How would that work? They'd have to pack their clothes and . . . and toothbrushes and schoolbooks and . . . I don't even know what all. Every weekend! Would Debi be supposed to feed their goldfish, every other week? They wouldn't even know what was in the refrigerator half the time. The girls, I mean."

Rather than the goldfish, thought Strube. I follow you. "It's your right—and it's to their benefit," he said soothingly. "For two weeks out of every month they'd be living with you, in a normal, nurturing environment, away from that woman's influences."

He let his gaze fall back to where the fax sheets lay in a patch of slanting sunlight on the desk. Most of the customers for Goudie snuff were shops, but there were a couple that seemed to be residential addresses. He noticed one on Civic Center Drive in Santa Ana, and drew a checkmark beside it. Santa Ana was just an hour away, down in Orange County—that could easily be where Nicky Bradshaw was hiding out these days. Strube reminded himself that he would have to scout all the likely addresses, and actually *see* Bradshaw at one of them; he wouldn't get the credit for having *found Spooky* if he just sent in half a dozen likely addresses.

And here was one in Long Beach. Why did so many people need to have snuff mailed right to their houses?

" 'That woman' is my wife," protested the client.

"For a while," Strube answered absently. Here was another address, in Southgate. How did somebody in Southgate afford a luxury item like Scottish snuff? "You did come in here for a divorce, you'll recall."

"Only because she filed! *I* didn't want a divorce! The girls staying a week with me, and then a week with her—this is fantastic!"

Strube looked up. "Well, you won't be paying child support for half the time. Besides, the arrangement won't last for very long. Your girls will hate it, and it'll wear Debi down, and then you can press for total custody." To hell with your girls, he thought; it'll protract the proceedings, and I'm paid by the hour.

The thought was suddenly depressing, and he remembered yesterday's riddle about the lawyer and the sperm cell. He realized that he was hunched over the desk like some kind of centipede.

He spread his Nautilus-broadened shoulders inside the Armani jacket, and leaned back, lifting his chin.

And from the back of the McKie chair burst a sharp, yiping fart-sound. A wordless cry escaped his astonished client.

Still sitting up straight, though he could feel the sudden heat in his face, Strube said, "That will be all for today."

"But—about the division of property—"

"That will be all for today," Strube repeated. He would press for a Substitution of Attorney tomorrow.

One chance in two million of becoming a human being. He could work with the studios, handle prestige cases for famous clients. *Swimming pools—movie stars.* He could start by representing Bradshaw.

The client had stood up. "What time . . . ?"

"Miss Meredith will schedule an appointment." I knew him in '74 and '75, which was more than ten years after he quit showbiz, Strube thought. I'm likelier to recognize him than any of his old Hollywood crowd is.

He maintained his stiff pose until the man had left the office. Then he let himself slump. He could check the Santa Ana address today.

Maybe even the Long Beach one too.

Loretta deLarava was crying again, and it was taking her forever to eat her ham-and-cheese sandwich. She was in a window-side booth in the Promenade Café; out through the glass, across the blue water of the Pacific Terrace Harbor she could see the low skyline of Long Beach, with the boat-filled Downtown Long Beach Marina spread like a bristly carpet of confetti around the foot of it.

She preferred to eat in the employees' cafeteria on C Deck, four decks down, back by the stern; but she couldn't make herself go there anymore.

When the *Queen Mary* had been an oceangoing ship, that C Deck auxiliary room had been the men's crew's bar, called the Pig and Whistle, and she liked the airy brightness of the present-day cafeteria, with the young men and ladies in the tour-guide uniforms chatting and carrying trays to the white tables, and the absence of obnoxious tourists. But yesterday, and the day before too, when deLarava had gone there, she had found herself in a low dark hall, with dartboards on the walls and long wooden tables and benches crowded with men, some in aprons and some in black ties and formal jackets. The men at the nearest table had looked up from their pint glasses of dark beer and stared at her in wonderment. She hadn't been able to hear anything over the throbbing, droning vibration that seemed to come up through the floor, and she'd realized that it was the sound of the ship's propellers three decks directly below her.

It had been the old Pig and Whistle that she'd seen, as it had been in . . . the sixties? Hell, the thirties?

And late last night she had left her stateroom and followed uncarpeted stairs all the way down to D Deck, and stood by the closed-up crew's galley by the bow and looked aft down the long, dim service alley, known to the crew in the old days as the Burma Road, that was said to stretch all the way back to the old bedroom service pantry and the hulking machinery of the lift motors by the stern. From far away in that dimness she had heard a lonely clashing and rattling, and when she had nerved herself up to walk some distance along the red-painted metal floor, between widely separated walls that were green up to belt height and beige above, hurrying from one bare bulb hung among the pipes and valves overhead to the next, she had seen tiny figures moving rapidly in one of the far distant patches of yellow light; children in red uniforms with caps—she had peered at them around the edge of a massive steel sliding door, and eventually she had realized that they were the ghosts of bellboys on roller skates, still skating up and down the old Burma Road on long-ago-urgent errands.

She had hurried away, and climbed the stairs back to her stateroom on B Deck, and locked the door and shivered in her bed under the dogged-shut porthole for hours before getting to sleep.

The sandwich was actually very good, with tomato and basil in among the ham and cheese, and she made herself take another bite.

The man sitting across the table from her was holding a pencil poised over the wide white cardboard storyboards. "You okay, Loretta?"

"Sure, Gene," she mumbled around the food in her mouth. She waved her free hand vaguely. "Stress. Listen, we've also got to get a lot of footage of the belowdecks areas—the crew's quarters, the section up by the bow where the service men were bunked during the war— it'd be a good contrast, you know? To all the glamour of the top decks."

"Well," he said, sipping nervously at a Coors Light, "I guess you can edit to a balance in postproduction—but we cleared it with the Disney people for just the engine-room tour and the pool and the staterooms and the salons. There might not be accessible power sources down in the catacombs, and God knows what their routines are—they might tell us it's too late to set it all up. It'd only be giving them two days' warning, if you want to get everything in the can Saturday."

"Well, we can at least do stills down there. A still photographer, and me, and my assistant carrying a portable stereo—that shouldn't disrupt any employees."

"You don't need music to shoot stills, Loretta. And how are you going to use stills?"

DeLarava had looked past him and seen Ayres standing by the cash register. She waved, and said, "I've got to talk to this guy, Gene. Do what you can, okay?"

The man stood up, taking the storyboards with him. "Okay. If the PR guy's in his office I'll talk to him now, on my way out. I'll call you and let you know what he says. Tomorrow I'll be at the studio all day, and I'll be back here Saturday, early, to make sure they rope off the areas from the tourists. I still don't see why we had to *film* on Halloween. A weekday would have been less crowded."

"Will you not be questioning my *decisions*, Gene? You gentlemen all work for *me*."

Gene left as Ayres walked up, shrugging as they passed each other, and deLarava was crying again; she wanted to scratch her scalp, but didn't dare, because she had stretched *three* rubber bands over it this morning. She had felt she had to, after the dream that had somehow left her to wake up crouched over the toilet in the stateroom's bathroom, whispering to the water in the bowl.

Ayres sat down and promptly drank off the last inch of the Coors Light. "Your old boy Joey Webb is crazy," he said. "He's out at all hours on the beach with a metal detector and a jar of orange marmalade, singing that 'Ed Sullivan' song from *Bye Bye Birdie*."

"*Ed* Sullivan? The moron. He's not supposed to be looking for *Ed* Sullivan."

"Could I have another of these, please?" said Ayres to a passing waitress. To deLarava he said, quietly, "I found out some things about the Parganas couple."

"Okay . . . ?"

"Well, they were crazy too. The old man, named Jiddu K. Parganas, was born in 1929. His parents announced that he was the *jagadguru*, which is apparently like a messiah, okay? The World Teacher. Theosophical stuff. There was a guy he was named for, named Jiddu Krishnamurti, who was supposed to be it, but he shined the job on in '28. He got tired of the spirit world, he said, seeing ghosts crowding up the beaches all the time. Great stuff, hm? But *our* Jiddu, the one born a year later, didn't work out too well. When he was twenty he got arrested for having burglarized the old house of Henry Ford, who had died two years earlier. The Ford executors hushed it up, but apparently Jiddu got away with a glass test tube. The Ford people hoked up another one to replace it, and nowadays the fake is on display in the Ford Museum in Greenfield Village in Michigan.''

DeLarava's heart was pounding, and tears were again leaking out of her eyes. "Fake of . . . what?"

"It's supposed to contain Edison's last breath."

"*Edison?*" My God, deLarava thought, no wonder the psychic gain is cranked up so high around here since Monday! No wonder Apie is coming out of the sea, and every ghost in town needs only a sneeze to set it frolicking. I *guessed* that the Monday-night torture-murder wasn't a coincidence, and that the kid had run away with *someone* heavy—but *Edison!*

"Yeah," said Ayres blandly, "the guy that invented the lightbulb. Anyway, Jiddu married a rich Indian woman who was also into this spiritual stuff, and they seem to have formed a sort of splinter cult of their own, just the two of them. They bought the house in Beverly Hills, where they were killed Monday night. The police are aware of the place—they've had to answer a lot of complaints from the Parganases and their neighbors. A lot of drunks and bums used to come around demanding to talk to somebody named *Dante* or *Don Tay.*"

"That would have been the mask," said deLarava softly. "They kept it in a hollowed-out copy of *The Divine Comedy* or something." She waved at Ayres. "Never mind. Go on."

"Some comedy. Their kid, this Koot Hoomie that you're looking for, was born in '81. His teachers say that he was okay, considering that his parents were trying to raise him to be some kind of Hindoo holy man. Have you got any calls?"

"Hundreds," she said. "People have grabbed every stray kid in L.A. except Koot Hoomie Parganas." She thought of the boy out there in the alleys and parking lots somewhere, eating out of Dumpsters and sleeping all alone under hedges . . . and last night's dream came back to her, forcefully.

She was crying again. "I've got to get some air," she said, blundering up out of her chair. "Tell Joey Webb to keep looking—and tell him to keep an eye on the *canals.*"

The sea was too full of imagined ghosts, waked up and opposing her, and the carpeted corridors and long splendid galleries seemed suddenly bristly with hostile ectoplasm accumulated like nicotine stains over the decades, so she fled to the Windsor Salon on R Deck.

She liked the Windsor Salon because it had *hanging chandeliers*, not the lights-on-columns that stood everywhere else in the ship, big Art Deco mushrooms with glowing mica-shade caps. The Windsor Salon had been built after the *Queen Mary* had been permanently moored in Long Beach, had in fact been built in the space of one of the now-useless funnels, and so it could afford the luxury of ceiling lights that would have swung and broken if the ship had been out at sea.

No parties of tourists were being shown through the room at the moment, so she collapsed into one of the convention-hotel chairs and buried her face in her hands.

She had dreamed of a group of little girls who were camping out on a dark plain. At first they had played games around the small fire they had kindled up—a make-believe tea party, charades, hopscotch on lines toed across the gray dust—but then the noises from the darkness beyond the ring of firelight had made them huddle together. Roars and shouts of subhuman fury had echoed from unseen hills, and the drumbeat of racing hooves and the hard flutter of flags had shaken in the cold wind.

Perhaps the girls had gathered together in this always-dark wasteland because they all had the same name—Kelley. They had formed a ring now, holding hands to contain their campfire and chattering with tearful, nervous, false cheer, until one of the girls noticed that her companions weren't real—they were all just mirrors set up closely together in the dirt, reflecting back to her her own pale, dirt-smeared face.

And her sudden terror made the face change—the nose was turned up, and became fleshier, the skin around the eyes became pouched and coarse, and the chin receded away, leaving the mouth a long, grinning slit. Kelley had known what this was. She was turning into a pig.

Loretta had driven herself up out of the well of sleep then, and discovered that she was kneeling on the tile floor of the little bathroom, crouching over the toilet and calling down, down, down into the dark so that Kelley might find her way back up out of the deep hole she'd fallen into.

There were no parking lines painted on the weathered checkerboard of cracked concrete and asphalt behind the apartment building, so Sullivan just parked the van in the shade of a big shaggy old carob tree. He dug around among the faded papers on the dashboard until he found Houdini's thumb, unpleasantly spitty and dusty now, and then he groped below the passenger seat and retrieved the Bull Durham sack and pushed the thumb back into it.

With the sack in his shirt pocket and his gun snugged in under his belt, he pushed open the door and stepped down onto the broken pavement. Green carob pods were scattered under the overhanging tree branches, and he could see the little V-shaped cuts in the pods where early-morning wild parrots had bitten out the seeds.

This would be the fourth apartment building he checked out. When he had come down off the freeway at Seventh Street in Long Beach, he had quickly confirmed his suspicion that motels never had garages, and then he'd driven around randomly through the run-down residential streets west of Pacific and south of Fourth, looking for rental signs.

He had stopped and looked at five places already, and, no doubt because of his stated preference for paying in cash, only a couple of the landlords had seemed concerned about his murky, out-of-state, unverifiable references. He thought he would probably take the last one he had looked at, a $700-a-month studio apartment in a shabby complex on Cerritos Avenue, but he had decided to look at a few more before laying out his money.

He was down on Twenty-first Place now, right next to Bluff Park and only half a block from the harbor shore, and he had just decided that any of these beachfront rentals would be too expensive, when he had driven past this rambling old officelike structure. He wouldn't even have thought it was an apartment building if it hadn't had an APT FOR RENT sign propped above the row of black metal mailboxes. It looked promisingly low-rent.

Sullivan walked across the pavement now toward the back side of the building, and soon he was scuffing on plain packed dirt. Along the building's back wall, between two windowless doors, someone had set up a row of bookshelves, on which sat dozens of mismatched pots with dry plants curling out of them, and off to his left plastic chairs sat around a claw-footed iron bathtub that had been made into a table by having a piece of plywood laid over it. He stared at the doors and wondered if he should just knock at one of them.

He jumped; and then, "Who parked all cattywampus?" came a hoarse call from behind him.

Sullivan turned around and saw a fat, bald-headed old man in plastic sandals limping across the asphalt from around the street-side corner of the building. The man wore no shirt at all, and his suntanned belly overhung the wide-legged shorts that flapped around his skinny legs.

"Are you talking about my van?" asked Sullivan.

"Well, if that's your van," the old man said weakly; he inhaled and then went on, "then I guess I'm talking about it." Again he rasped air into his lungs. "Ya damn birdbrain."

"I'm here to speak to the manager of these apartments," Sullivan said stiffly.

"I'm the manager. My name's Mr. Shadroe."

Sullivan stared at him. "You are?" He was afraid this might be just some bum making fun of him. "Well, I want to rent an apartment."

"I don't *need* to . . . *rent* an apartment." Shadroe waved at the van. "If that leaks oil, you'll have to . . . park it on the street." The old man's face was shiny with sweat, but somehow he smelled spicy, like cinnamon.

"It doesn't leak oil," Sullivan said. "I'm looking for an apartment in this area; how much is the one you've got?"

"You on SDI or some—kinda methadone treatment? I won't take you if you are, and I—don't care if it's legal for me to say so. And I won't have children here."

"None of those things," Sullivan assured him. "And if I decide I want the place I can pay you right now, first and last month's rent, in cash."

"That's illegal, too. The first and last. Gotta call the last month's rent a *deposit* nowadays. But I'll take it. Six hundred a month, utilities are included . . .'cause the whole building's on one bill. That's twelve hundred, plus a *real* deposit of . . . three hundred dollars. Fifteen. Hundred, altogether. Let's go into my office and I can . . . give you a receipt and the key." Talking seemed to be an effort for the man, and Sullivan wondered if he was asthmatic or had emphysema.

Shadroe had already turned away toward one of the two doors, and Sullivan stepped after him. "I'd," he said laughing in spite of himself, "I'd like to see the place first."

Shadroe had fished a huge, bristling key chain from his shorts pocket and was unlocking the door. "It's got a new refrigerator—in it, I hooked it up myself yesterday. I do all my—own electrical and plumbing. What do you do?"

"Do? Oh, I'm a bartender." Sullivan had heard that bartenders tended to be reliable tenants.

Shadroe had pushed the door open, and now waved Sullivan toward the dark interior. "That's honest work, boy," he said. "You don't need to be ashamed."

"Thanks."

Sullivan followed him into a long, narrow room dimly lit by foliage-blocked windows. A battered couch sat against one of the long walls and a desk stood across from it under the windows; over the couch were rows of bookshelves like the ones outside, empty except for stacks of old *People* magazines and, on the top shelf, three water-stained pink stuffed toys. A television set was humming faintly on a table, though its screen was black.

Shadroe pulled out the desk chair and sat down heavily. "Here's a rental agreement," he said, tugging a sheet of paper out of a stack. "No pets either. What are those shoes? Army-man shoes?"

Sullivan was wearing the standard shoes worn by tramp electricians, black leather with steel-reinforced toes. "Just work shoes," he said, puzzled. "Good for standing in," he added, feeling like an idiot.

"They gotta go. I got wood floors, and you'll be boomin' around all night—nobody get any sleep—I get complaints about it. Get yourself some *Wallabees,*" he said with a look of pained earnestness. "The soles are *foam rubber.*"

The rental agreement was a Xerox copy, and the bottom half of it hadn't printed clearly. Shadroe began laboriously filling in the missing paragraphs in ink. Sullivan just sat helplessly and watched the old man squint and frown as his spotty brown hand worked the pen heavily across the paper.

The old man's cinnamon smell was stronger in here, and staler. The room was silent except for the scratching of the pen and the faint hum of the television set, and Sullivan's hairline was suddenly damp with sweat.

He found himself thinking of the containment areas of nuclear generating plants, where the pressure was kept slightly below normal to keep radioactive dust from escaping; and of computer labs kept under higher-than-normal pressure to keep ordinary dust out. Some pressure was wrong in this dingy office.

I don't want to stay here, he thought. I'm not *going* to stay here.

"While you're doing that," he said unsteadily, "I might go outside and look around at the place."

"I'll be done here. In a second."

"No, really, I'll be right outside."

Sullivan walked carefully to the door and stepped out into the sunlight, and then he hurried across the patchwork pavement to his van, taking deep breaths of the clean sea air.

That apartment back up on Cerritos looks good, he told himself. (This place is only half a block from the beach, and I could probably see the *Queen Mary* across the water from the cul-de-sac right beyond the driveway, but) I certainly couldn't count on getting anything done here, not with this terrible Shadroe guy blundering around.

He unlocked the van door, carefully so as not to touch the drying egg-smear, and climbed in. Mr. Shadroe was probably still sitting back there in the office, carefully writing out the missing paragraphs of the rental agreement; not even breathing as his clumsy fingers worked the pen.

Sullivan pulled the door closed, but paused with the key halfway extended toward the ignition. The man hadn't been breathing.

Shadroe had *inhaled* a number of times, in order to talk, but he had not been breathing. Sullivan was suddenly, viscerally sure that that's what had so upset him in there—he had been standing next to a walking vapor lock, the pressure of a living soul in the vacuum of a dead body.

What are you telling me? he asked himself; that Mr. Shadroe is a *dead* guy? If so, I should *definitely* get out of here, fast, before some shock causes him to throw stress-shells, and his overdrawn lifeline collapses and he goes off like a goddamn firebomb, like the patient at Elizalde's Día del Muerte séance.

Still uncomfortable with the idea, he put the key into the ignition.

Shadroe could be alive, he thought—he could just have been breathing very low, very quietly. Oh yeah? he answered himself immediately. When he inhaled in order to *speak*, it sounded like somebody dragging a tree branch through a mail slot.

Maybe he's just one of the old solidified ghosts, a man-shaped pile of animated litter, who drifted down here to be near the ocean, as Elizalde in her interview, unaware of how literally she was speaking, noted that the poor old creatures like to do. (*"Tide pools seem to be the best, actually, in eliciting the meditation that brings the old spirits to the surface . . ."*) But Shadroe didn't quite talk crazily enough, and a ghost wouldn't be able to deal with the paperwork of running an apartment building; collecting rents, paying taxes and license and utility bills.

Okay, so what if he *is* one of the rare people who can continue to occupy and operate their bodies after they've died? What's it to me?

Sullivan twisted the key, and the engine started right up, without even a touch of his foot on the gas pedal.

I wonder how long he's been dead, he thought. If his death was recent, like during the last day or so, he probably hasn't even noticed it himself yet; but if he's been hanging on for a while, he must have figured out measures to avoid the collapse: he must not ever sleep, for example, and I'll bet he spends a lot of time out on the ocean.

(*". . . patients seem to find their ghosts more accessible in the shallow depths of actual ocean water. It's been worth field trips."*)

He didn't want to think, right now, about what Elizalde had said in the interview.

What would that blind witch on the Honda see, he wondered instead, if she were to come around here? With a dead guy up and walking around all over this building and grounds, insulting people's vehicles and shoes, this whole place must look like a patch of dry rot, psychically.

This place *would* be good cover.

And the location is perfect for me. And six hundred a month, with utilities included—and a new refrigerator!—is pretty good.

Sullivan sighed, and switched off the engine and got out of the van. When he had walked back across the yard and stepped into the office, Shadroe was still at work on the rental agreement. Sullivan sat down on the couch to wait, stoically enduring the psychically stressed atmosphere.

(*"Eventually I'd like to move my clinic to some location on the beach—not to where there's surf, you see, but pools of ordered, quieted seawater."*)

"If you'll take cash right now," he said unsteadily, "I'd like to start moving my stuff in this afternoon."

"If you right now got the time," said Shadroe, without looking up. "I right now got the key."

Sullivan had the time. He was suddenly in no hurry to go find Angelica Anthem Elizalde, for he was pretty sure that he knew where she would be.

At the canals at Venice Beach.

CHAPTER 28

"I can't go no lower," said the Hatter: "I'm on the floor, as it is."
—Lewis Carroll,
Alice's Adventures in Wonderland

Sitting in a bus seat by a sunny window, warmed by the noon glare through the glass and by the oversized fleece-lined denim jacket he had bought at a thrift store on Slauson, Kootie was too sleepy and comfortable to worry. He was sure that the last two days and three nights had aged his face way beyond that picture on the billboards, and, especially with the sunglasses, he was sure he must look like a teenager. The denim jacket even smelled like stale beer.

Keeping his face maturely expressionless, he cocked an eyebrow out the window at the *pollo* stands and the 1950s-futuristic car washes along Crenshaw Boulevard. He would be transferring at Manchester to catch another RTD bus to the Dockweiler State Beach at Playa del Rey.

The boy had awakened at dawn, his eyes already open and stinging in the ancient paint fumes in the abandoned car, and he had recognized the stiff drop cloth under his chin, and the split and faded dashboard in front of him; he had clearly remembered breaking the wind-wing window the night before, and opening the door and climbing in.

But he hadn't recognized the city dimly visible beyond the dusty windshield this morning.

Cables and wires were strung so densely against the sky overhead that for one sleepy moment he had thought he was under some kind of war-surplus submarine-catching net; then he had seen that the wires were higher than he had thought, and separate, strung haphazardly from telegraph poles and bulky insulators on the high roofs of all the old buildings. And even through the grime on the glass he could see that they *were* old buildings—imposing brick structures with arched windows at the top and jutting cornices.

He knew he'd have to prove himself here, in spite of being virtually broke and so terribly young—here in Boston, his first *big city*—

Boston?

He reached a hand out from under the drop cloth and opened the door. It squeaked out on its rusty hinges and let in a gust of fresh morning air that smelled distantly of what he knew must be coal smoke and horse manure—and then Kootie was glad he was sitting down, for he was suddenly so dizzy that he grabbed the edge of the seat.

"You're," croaked his own voice, "don't tell me—Kootie." After a moment he said, voluntarily, "Right." Then his voice went on, thickly, "I was dreaming. This isn't Boston, is it? Nor New Jersey yet. It's . . . Los Angeles." His eyes closed and his hands came up and rubbed his eye sockets. "Sorry," said his voice as his right hand sprang away from the painful swelling around his right eye.

When he looked around again, it was typical backstreet Los Angeles that he saw and smelled around him: low stuccoed buildings and palm trees, and the smells of diesel exhaust and gardenias; above a three-story building a couple of blocks away, crows were diving over the condenser fans of a big rooftop air-conditioner shed and then lofting up on the hot air drafts, over and over again. Only a few wires drooped overhead from the telephone poles.

The night air had been cold, and Kootie's nose was stuffed—after he sniffed, his jammed-up sinuses emitted an almost ultrasonic *wheee*, like the flash attachment on a camera recharging.

"All this running around is doing you no good at all, son," Edison had croaked then. "And I'm not getting any fresher out here. To hell with New Jersey. Let's get to the sea. I'll be able to just go into the seawater, safely, and be gone; and you'll be free of me, free to go be a normal boy."

Kootie had not said anything then, as he climbed stiffly out of the car, stretched as well as he could with the heavy I-ON-A-CO cable belt constricting his waist, and limped toward the lot fence; but he thought the old Edison ghost could probably tell that Kootie didn't want to lose him.

Where will I go?" asked Kootie softly now as he clambered painfully down the steps of the bus exit and hopped to the Manchester sidewalk. "I'll need money."

All at once, into the muted early-afternoon air, "*You're young!*" shouted Edison with Kootie's shrill voice. "You're still *alive*! You can send and receive as fast as any of them!'' Kootie was hobbling away from the bus stop as quickly as he could, not looking at any of the faces around him, his own face burning with embarrassed horror and all feelings of maturity completely blown away.

He caught a breath and choked out, ''Shut up!''—but Edison used the rest of the breath to yell, ''Skedaddle to the Boston office of Western Union! I've got to get to New Jersey anyway, to pick up my diploma!'' Kootie was sweating now in the chilly breeze, and he had clenched his teeth against his own squawking voice, but Edison kept yelling anyway: ''The usual job! Napping during night work, with the ghost repellers popping and the gizmo sending your sixing signals on the hour!''

Kootie tried to shout *Be quiet!* but Edison was trying to say something more, and the resulting scream was something like ''*Baklava!*'' (which was a kind of pastry Kootie's parents had sometimes brought home for him).

Kootie was just crying and running blindly in despair now, blundering against pedestrians and light poles, and he wasn't aware of slapping footsteps behind him until a pair of hands clasped his shoulders and yanked him back to a stop.

''Kid,'' said a man's concerned voice, ''what's the matter? Was somebody *bothering* you? Where do you live? My wife and I can drive you home.''

Kootie turned into the man's arms and sobbed against a wool sweater. ''The beach,'' he hiccuped; ''the police—I don't know where I've got to go. I'm lost, mister.'' Blessedly, Edison seemed to have withdrawn.

''Well, you're okay now, I promise. I hopped out of our car at the light when I saw you running—my wife is driving around the block. Let's go back and catch her at the corner, away from all these people here.''

Kootie was happy to do as the man said. Several of the people behind him on the corner were laughing, and somebody called out a filthy suggestion about what he should do once he had skedaddled to New Jersey and picked up his ''*dip*shit *dip*loma.'' It horrified Kootie to think that adults could be the same as kids; and now even Edison was drunk or had gone crazy or something.

As he walked along quickly beside the man who had stopped him, Kootie looked up at his rescuer. The man had short blond hair and round, wire-rim glasses, and he looked tanned and fit, as if he played tennis. He still had one hand on Kootie's right shoulder, and Kootie reached up and clasped the man's wrist.

''Here she is, kid,'' the man said kindly as a shiny new teal-blue minivan came nosing up to the Manchester curb. "Are you hungry? We can stop for a bite to eat if you like."

The passenger door had swung open, and a dark-haired young woman in shorts had one knee up and was leaning across the seat and smiling uncertainly. "Well, hi there, kiddo," she said as Kootie let go of the man's wrist and hurried to the minivan.

"Hi, ma'am," Kootie said, pausing humbly on the curb. "Your husband said you could give me a ride."

She laughed. "Hop in then."

Kootie hiked himself up, and then climbed around the console to crouch behind the passenger seat as the man got in and closed the door. The interior of the minivan smelled like a new pair of dress shoes straight out of the Buster Brown box.

"Let's head toward the 405, Eleanor," the man said, "just to get moving. And if you see a Denny's—did you want something to eat, uh, young man?" The minivan started forward, and Kootie sat down on the blue-carpeted floor.

"My name's Koot Hoomie," he said breathlessly, having decided to trust these people. "I'm called Kootie. Yes, please, about eating—but some kind of takeout would be better. I get screaming fits sometimes. You saw. It's not like I'm crazy, or anything." He tried to remember the name of the ailment that made some people yell terrible things, but couldn't. All he could think of was *Failure to Thrive*, which an infant cousin of his had reportedly died of. Kootie probably had that too. "It's that syndrome," he finished lamely.

"Tourette's, probably," the man said. "I'm Bill Fussel, and this is my wife, Eleanor. Have you had any sleep, Kootie? There are blankets back there."

"No thanks," said Kootie absently, "I slept in an old car last night." Get to the beach, he thought; let crazy Edison jump into the sea, and then these nice people can adopt me. "Can we go to the beach? Any beach. I want to . . . wade out in the water, I guess." He tried to think of a plausible reason for it, and decided that anything he came up with would sound like a kid lie. Then, "My parents died Monday night," he found himself saying to the back of Mr. Fussel's head. "In our religion it's a purifying ritual. We're Hindus."

He had no idea whether it had been Edison or himself that had said it, nor if any of it was true. I suppose we might have been Hindus, he thought. In school I always just put down *Protestant.*

"A beach?" said Mr. Fussel. "I guess we could go out to Hermosa or Redondo. Elly, why don't we stop somewhere and you can call your mom and let her know we'll be a little late."

For a moment no one spoke, and the quiet burr of the engine was the only sound inside the minivan.

"Okay," said Mrs. Fussel.

"Where does your mom live?" asked Kootie, again not sure it was himself who had spoken.

"Riverside," said Mrs. Fussel quickly.

"Where in Riverside? I used to live there."

"Lamppost and Riverside Drive," Mrs. Fussel said, and Kootie saw her dart a harried glance at her husband.

Now Kootie knew it was Edison speaking for him, for with no intention at all he found himself saying, "There are no such streets in Riverside." Kootie didn't know if there were or not, and certainly Edison didn't either. *Why are you being rude?* he thought hard at the Edison ghost in his mind.

"I guess she knows where her mother lives," Mr. Fussel began in a stern voice, but Kootie was interrupting:

"Very well, name for me any five big streets in Riverside."

"We don't go there a lot—" said Mrs. Fussel weakly.

Mr. Fussel turned around in his seat and faced Kootie. He was frowning. "What's the matter, Kootie? Do you want us to drive you back to that corner and let you out?"

"Yes," Kootie's voice said firmly, and then Edison kept Kootie's jaw clamped shut so that his *No!* came out as just a prolonged "Nnnnn!"

"That's a dangerous neighborhood," Mr. Fussel said.

"Then let me out—dammit!—right—here! Kootie, let me talk! It's kidnapping if you people keep me in this vehicle!"

Mrs. Fussel spoke up. "Let's let him out and forget the whole thing."

"Eleanor, he's sick, listen to him! It would be the same as murder if we left him out on these streets. It's our duty to call the police." The man had got up out of the passenger seat and turned swayingly to face Kootie. "And even if we have to call in the police, we'll still get the twenty thousand dollars."

Kootie spun toward the sliding door in the side of the van, but before he could grab the handle the man had lunged at him and whacked him hard in the chest with his open palm, and Kootie jackknifed sideways onto the back seat; he was gasping, trying to suck air into his lungs and get his legs onto the floor so that he could spring toward Mrs. Fussel and perhaps wrench at the steering wheel, but Mr. Fussel gave him a stunning slap across the face and then strapped the seat belt across him, and pulled the strap tight through the buckle, with Kootie's arms under the woven fabric. The boy could thrash back and forth, but his arms were pinioned. He was squinting in the new brightness, for the man had knocked his sunglasses off.

"If you," Kootie gasped, his heart hammering, "let me go—I won't tell the police—that you hit me—and tied me up."

Mr. Fussel had to duck his head to stand in the back of the minivan, and now he rocked on his feet and slapped the ceiling to keep his balance. "Drive carefully!" he shouted at his wife. "If a cop pulls us over right now we're fucked!"

Kootie could hear Mrs. Fussel crying. "Don't talk like that in front of the boy! I'm pulling over, and you're going to let him out!"

"Do as she says," Edison grated, "or I'll say you gave me the shiner, too. Kept me for days."

Mr. Fussel was pale. For a moment he looked as though he might hit Kootie again; then he disappeared behind the rear seat and began clanking around among some metal objects. When he reappeared he was peeling a strip off a silvery roll of duct tape.

A sudden intrusive vision: *two stark figures strapped into chairs with duct tape, eye sockets bloody and empty . . .*

Edison was blown aside in Kootie's mind as the boy screamed with all the force of his aching lungs, clenching his fists and his eyes and whipping his head back and forth, dimly aware of the minivan slewing as the noise battered the carpeted interior—but the strip of tape scraped in between Kootie's jaws and then more tape was being wound roughly around the back of his head, over his chin, around his bucking head again and over his upper lip.

Kootie was breathing whistlingly, messily, through his nose. He heard tape rip, and then Mr. Fussel was taping Kootie's elbows and forearms to the seat belt.

Against the tape that his teeth were grinding at, Kootie was grunting and huffing, and after two or three blind, impacted seconds he realized that his lips and tongue were trying to form words; they couldn't, around the tape, but he could *feel* what his mouth was trying to say:

Stop it! Stop it! Listen to me, boy! You might *die even if you calm down and stay alert, watch for a chance to run, but you'll* certainly *die if you keep thrashing and screaming like a big baby! Come on, son, be a man!*

Kootie let the mania carry him for one more second, howling out of him to swamp Edison's words in a torrent of unreasoning noise; finally the muffled scream wobbled away to silence, leaving his lungs empty and aching. He raised his shoulders in an exaggerated shrug, held it for a moment, and then let them slump back down—and the panic fell away from him, leaving him almost calm, though the pounding of his heart was visibly twitching his shirt collar.

Kootie was motionless now, but as tense as a flexed fencing foil. He told himself that Edison was right; he had to stay alert. Nobody was going to kill him right here in these people's minivan; eventually someone would have to cut him free of this seat, and he could pretend to be asleep when they did, and then jump for freedom in the instant that the tape was cut.

He was in control of himself again, coldly and deeply angry at the Fussels and already ashamed at having gone to pieces in front of them.

And so he was surprised when he began weeping. His head jerked down and he was wailing "*Hoo-hoo-hoo*" behind the tape, on and on, even though he could feel drool moving toward the corner of his distended mouth.

"*For . . . God's sake,* William," said Mrs. Fussel in a shrill monotone. "Have you gone crazy? You can't—"

"Pull over," the man said, blundering back up toward the front of the van. "I'll drive. *This is the kid,* El, it's Koot Hoomie Parganas and he's obviously an escaped nut! They'll put him back in restraints as soon as we turn him over to them! I'll . . . bite my arm, and say he did it. Or better, we'll buy a cheap knife, and I'll cut myself. He's dangerous, we *had* to tape him up. And it's *twenty thousand goddamn dollars.*"

Kootie kept up his *hoo-hoo*ing, and did it louder when Mrs. Fussel turned the wheel to the right to pull over; and then he felt his drooling mouth try to grin around the tape as the three of them were jolted by the right front tire going up over the curb. Edison's *enjoying* this, Kootie thought.

Mr. Fussel slapped him across the face—it didn't sting much this time, through the tape. "Shut up or I'll run a loop of tape over your nose," the man whispered.

Edison winked Kootie's good eye at Mr. Fussel. Kootie hoped Edison knew what he was doing here.

The Fussels found a place to park in a lot somewhere—the windshield faced a close cinder-block wall so that no passersby would see the bound and gagged boy in the back of the minivan—and then Mr. Fussel picked some quarters out of a dish on the console and climbed out, locking the passenger door behind him.

After several seconds of no sound but the quiet burr of the idling engine, Mrs. Fussel turned around in the driver's seat.

"He's a nice man," she said. Kootie could almost believe she was talking to herself. "We want to have children ourselves."

Kootie stared at the floor, afraid Edison would give her a sardonic look.

"Neither of us knows how to deal with . . . a child with problems," she went on, "a runaway, a *violent* runaway. We don't believe in hitting children. This was like when you have to hit someone who's drowning, if you want to save them. Can you understand? If you tell the people from the hospital—or wherever it is that you live—if you tell them Bill hit you, we'll have to tell them *why* he hit you, won't we? Trying to bite, and yelling obscenities. That means nasty words," she explained earnestly.

Kootie forgot not to stare at her.

"Your parents were murdered," she said.

He nodded expressionlessly.

"Oh, good! That you knew it, I mean, that I wasn't breaking the news to you. And I guess someone hit you in the eye. You've had a bad time, but I want you to realize that today really *is* the first day of your, of the rest of your—wait, you were living at home, weren't you? The story in the paper said that. You weren't in a hospital. Who's put up this reward for you?"

Kootie widened his eyes at her.

"Relatives?"

Kootie shook his head, slowly.

"You don't think it was the people that murdered your *parents*, do you?"

Kootie nodded furiously. "Mm-hmmm," he grunted.

"Oh, I'm sure that's not true."

Kootie rolled his eyes and then stared hard at her.

After a moment her expression of concern wilted into dismay. "Oh, shit. Oh shit. Twenty thousand dollars? You were a *witness*!"

Close enough. Rocking his head back and humming loudly was as close as Kootie could come to conveying congratulations.

She was saying "Sorry! Sorry! Sorry!" as she got out of the seat and stepped over the console, and then she was prying with her fingernails at the tape edges around his wrists.

The tape wasn't peeling up at all, and Kootie didn't waste hope imagining that she'd free him. He wasn't surprised when keys rattled against the outside of the passenger door and the lock clunked and then Mr. Fussel was leaning in.

"What are you *doing*, El? Get away from—"

"He's a witness, Bill! The people that killed his parents are—are the ones you just called! Did you tell them where we are? Let's get out of here right now!'' She hurried back up front to the driver's seat and grabbed the gearshift lever.

Mr. Fussel gripped her hand. "Where'd you get all that, El? He can't even talk. These people sounded okay."

"Then let's drive somewhere and let Goaty talk to us, and you can call them back if we're *sure* it's all right."

"*Mm-hmm!*" put in Kootie as loudly as he could.

"El, they'll be here in ten minutes. We can talk to them right here, this is a public place, he'll be safe. It's his safety I'm concerned with; what if we have an accident driving? We're both upset—"

"An accident? I won't have an accident. They can—"

"They're bringing *cash*, El! We can't expect them to be driving all over L.A. with that kind of cash, in these kinds of neighborhoods!"

"You're worried about *them*? They killed his—"

The minivan shook as something collided gently but firmly with the rear end, and then there were simultaneous knocks against the driver's and passenger's windows. Even from the back seat Kootie could see the blunt metal cylinders of silencers through the glass.

That wasn't ten minutes, thought Kootie.

A voice spoke quietly from outside. "Roll down the windows right now or we'll kill you both."

Both of the Fussels hastily pressed buttons on their armrests, and the windows buzzed down.

"The boy's in the back seat," Mr. Fussel said eagerly.

A hand came in through the open window and pushed Mr. Fussel's head aside, and then a stranger peered in. Behind mirror sunglasses and a drooping mustache, he was nothing more than a pale, narrow face.

"He's taped in," the face noted. "Good. You two get out."

"Sure," Mr. Fussel said. "Come on, El, get out. You guys are gonna take the van? Fine! We won't report it stolen until—what, tomorrow? Would that be okay? Is the money in something we can carry inconspicuously?"

The face had withdrawn, but Kootie heard the voice say, "You'll have no problems with it."

Mrs. Fussel was sobbing quietly. "Bill, you idiot," she said, but she opened her door and got out at the same time her husband did.

A fat man in a green turtleneck sweater got in where she had been, and the man with the mirror sunglasses got in on the passenger side. The doors were pulled closed, and the minivan rocked as the obstruction was moved from behind it, and then the fat man had put the engine into reverse and was backing out. He glanced incuriously at Kootie.

"Check the tape on the kid," he said to his companion.

When the man in the sunglasses stepped into the back of the van, Kootie didn't make any noises, but tried to catch his eye. The man just tugged at the seat belt, though, and then found the roll of tape and bound Kootie's ankles together and taped them sideways to the seat leg, without looking at Kootie's face.

Somehow Kootie was still just tense, no more than if he were one of only a couple of kids left standing at a spelling bee. After the man had returned to the front seat and fastened his seat belt, Kootie wondered what had happened to the Fussels. He supposed that they were dead already, shot behind some Dumpster. It was easy for him to avoid picturing the two of them. He looked at the backs of his captors' heads and tried to figure out who the two men could be. They didn't look like associates of the raggedy one-armed man.

Kootie was surprised, and cautiously pleased, with his own coolness in this scary situation . . . until he realized that it was based on a confidence that Thomas Alva Edison would think of some way to get him out of it; then he remembered that Edison seemed to have gone crazy, and in a few minutes tears of pure fright were rolling warmly along the top edges of the duct tape on Kootie's cheeks as the minivan rocked through traffic.

They may not mean to kill me, he thought. Certainly not yet. Our destination might be miles from here, and—

He tried to think of any other comforting thoughts.

—And there'll probably be a lot of traffic lights, he told himself forlornly.

CHAPTER 29

"I don't like the look of it at all," said the King: "however, it may kiss my hand, if it likes."

—Lewis Carroll,
Alice's Adventures in Wonderland

Sullivan had driven up the 405 past LAX airport, past one of the government-sanctioned freeway-side murals (this one portraying a lot of gigantic self-righteous-looking joggers that made him think better of the fugitive graffiti taggers with their crude territory markers), and then he followed the empty new sunlit lanes of the 90 freeway out to where it came down and narrowed and became a surface street, Lincoln Boulevard, among new condominium buildings and old used-camper lots.

The plaster hands were on the passenger seat and the Bull Durham sack was in his shirt pocket, above the sun-and-body-heated bulk of his .45 in the canvas fanny pack. He had bought a triple-A map at a gas station and studied it hard, and he had only nerved himself up to come to Venice by vowing to stay entirely out of sight of the ocean.

The canals, thin blue lines on the map, were only half a fingernail inland from the black line that indicated the shore, and it was in the surf off this little stretch of beach that his father had drowned in '59— and it was from there that he and Sukie had fled in '86, leaving Loretta deLarava in possession of their father's wallet and keys and the three cans of . . .

Nothing looked familiar, for he had been here only that one time, in '86. He managed to miss North Venice Boulevard, and had to loop back through narrow streets where summer rental houses crowded right up to the curbs, and parked cars left hardly any room for traffic, and then when he came upon North Venice again he saw that it was a one-way street aimed straight out at the now-near ocean; and though he was ready to just put the van in reverse and honk his way backward a couple of blocks, he saw a stretch of empty curb right around the corner of North Venice and Pacific, and he was able to pull in and park without having to focus past the back bumper of the Volkswagen in the space ahead of him.

He didn't want to be Peter Sullivan here at all, even if nobody was looking for him—presumably his father's ghost was in the sea only a block away, and that was enough of a presence to shame him into assuming every shred of disguise possible.

So he tied an old bandanna around the plaster hands and took them with him when he got out and locked the van. The sea breeze had cleared the coastal sky of smog, but it was chilly, and he was glad of his old leather flight jacket.

Two quarters in the parking meter bought him an hour's worth of time, and he turned his back on the soft boom of the surf and stalked across Pacific with the hands clamped against his ribs and his hands jammed in his pockets. The plaster hands were heavy, but at a 7-Eleven store an hour ago he had bought six lightbulbs and stuffed them into his jacket pockets, and he didn't want to risk breaking any of them by shifting the awkward bundle under his arm. He stepped carefully up the high curb at the north side of Pacific.

Almost there anyway, he told himself as he peered ahead.

He was in a wide, raised parking lot between the North and South Venice Boulevards, and past the far curb of South, just this side of a windowless gray cement building, he could see a railing paralleling the street, and another that slanted away down, out of sight. There was a gap there between rows of buildings, and it clearly wasn't a street.

He crossed the parking lot and hobbled stiffly across South Venice, and when he had got to the railing and the top of the descending walkway, he stopped. He had found the westernmost of the canals, and he was relieved to see that it didn't look familiar at all.

Below him, fifty feet across and stretching straight away to an arched bridge in the middle distance, the water was still, reflecting the eucalyptus and bamboo and lime trees along the banks. The canal walls were yard-high brickworks of slate-gray half-moons below empty sidewalks, and the houses set back from the water looked tranquil in the faintly brassy October sunlight. He could see a broad side-channel in the east bank a block ahead, but this ramp from South Venice led down to the west bank, and apparently the only way to walk along that side-canal would be to go past it on this side, cross the bridge, and then come back.

By the time he had walked halfway down the ramp toward the canal-bank level, he had left behind the gasping sea breeze and all of the sounds of the beach-city traffic, and all he could hear was bees in the bushes and wind chimes and a distant grumbling of ducks.

He had never cared to read up on this particular seaside town, but from things people had said over the years he had gathered that it had been built in the first years of the century as a mock-up of the original Italian Venice; the canals had been more extensive then, and there had even been gliding gondolas poled by gondoliers with Italian accents. The notion hadn't caught on, though, and the place had fallen into decrepitude, and in the years after World War II it had been a seedy, shacky beatnik colony, with rocking oil pumps between the houses on the banks of the stagnating canals.

He was walking along the sidewalk now, and he'd gone far enough so that he could look down the cross canal. Another footbridge arched over the blue-sky-reflecting water in that direction, framed by tall palm trees, and a solider-looking bridge farther down looked as though it could accommodate cars.

City-planning types had moved to have the canals filled in, but the residents had protested effectively, and the canals were saved. The neat brickwork of the banks was clearly a modern addition, and many of the houses had the stucco anonymity or the custom Tudor look of new buildings, though there were still dozens of the old, comfortably weather-beaten California bungalow-style houses set in among ancient untrimmed palm trees and overhanging shingle roofs.

Two women and a collie were walking toward him along the sidewalk he was on, and though neither of the women looked particularly like the pictures he'd seen of Elizalde, he dug with his free hand into the pocket of his jacket and pulled out one of the lightbulbs and the paper 7-Eleven bag.

Sullivan noticed a brown plastic owl on a fence post, and it reminded him that he had seen another one on a roof peak behind him. Ahead, now, he spied still another, swinging on a string from a tree branch. And he could hear several sets of jangling wind chimes—maybe Elizalde was right about ghosts being drawn to places like this, and the residents had set out these things as scarecrows. Scareghosts.

"Afternoon," he said as he passed the ladies and the dog.

When they were behind him he slid the lightbulb into the bag and crouched over the pavement. He glanced back at the two women, and then swung the bag in an arc onto the cement, popping the bulb.

Both of the women jumped in surprise—*right after* the noise.

"Excuse me," he said sheepishly, nodding and waving at them.

He straightened and kept walking, tucking the jingling bag back into his pocket.

The white-painted wooden footbridge was steep, and he paused at the crest to shift the Houdini hands to his left side. He was sweating, and wishing now that he'd left the things in the van.

The water below him was clear, and he could see rocks in it but no fish. There had been fish—

He was halfway up the sidewalk of the branch canal, staring at a bleached steer skull on the wall of an old wooden house (another scare-ghost!), and he had no recollection of having descended from the bridge or walking this far up.

Aside from the two women he had seen, who had since disappeared, there seemed to be no one out walking along the canals this afternoon. He looked around. Even the houses all seemed to have been evacuated—he hadn't even seen a cat. (His heart was knocking inside his chest.) The water was too still, the houses by the canal were too low, crouching under the tall legs of the palm trunks, and the silence wasn't *nice* anymore—it was the silence of a dark yard when all the crickets suddenly stop chirping at once.

Elizalde wasn't here, and he didn't want to meet whatever might be.

Without noticing it he had already passed the footbridge on this canal branch, but the wider bridge was still ahead of him, and as he started toward it he saw a car mount it from the islanded side, pause at the crest, and then nose down the far slope—slowly, for the arch was so steep that the driver couldn't be able to see the pavement ahead of him.

Just *A.O.P.*, dude, Sullivan thought.

He was clutching the plaster hands with both of his own hands as he walked now, and it was all he could do not to break into a run. He didn't look back to make sure nothing was crawling out of the canal behind him, because he was sure that if he did, he would have to *keep on* looking back as he fled this place, would have to *walk backward* toward the bridge that led away to the normal city channels that were asphalt and not water, and something would manifest itself ahead of him, and then just wait for him to back into it.

His eyebrows itched with sweat, and he was breathing fast and shallow.

This is just a funk, he thought, a fit of nerves. There are other canals here *(Are there?)* and Elizalde might be on the sidewalk of the next one over, or the one beyond that; she might be stark naked and waving her arms and riding a goddamn *unicycle*, but you won't see her because you're panicking here.

So be it. She couldn't have helped me anyway. I'll find *some other* way to warn my father's ghost (this trip out here was an idiotic long shot) after I drive out of this damned town and find a place to relax and chug a couple of fast, cold beers.

His right shoulder was brushing against vines and bricks as he strode toward the bridge, and he realized that he was crowding the fences of the houses, avoiding the bank—horrified, in fact, at the thought of falling into the shallow water.

the way all sounds echo like metallic groans underwater

He must have just dropped the plaster hands. He was running, and his unimpeded hands were clenched into fists, pumping the air as his legs pounded under him. From the shoulder of his jacket he heard a snap, and then another, as if stitches were being broken.

At the foot of the bridge he stopped, and let his breathing slow down. This bridge was part of a street, Dell Street, and he could hear cars sighing past on South Venice Boulevard ahead. Even if something audibly swirled the water of the canal now, he felt that he could sprint and be in the middle of the boulevard before his first squirted tears of fright would have had time to hit the pavement.

With a careful, measured tread he walked up the slope of the bridge, and he paused at the crest. Ahead of him on the right side of the street was the grandest yet of the neo-Tudor buildings, a place with gables and stained-glass windows and an inset tower with antique chimney pots on its shingled funnel roof. He was wondering if it might be a restaurant, with a bar and a men's room, when in the bright stillness he heard something splashing furtively in the water under the bridge.

All he did was exhale all the air out of his lungs, and then rest his hands on the coping of the bridge and look down over the edge.

There was someone crouched down there, beside a small white fiberglass rowboat that had been drawn up onto the gravel slope beside the bridge abutment; the figure was wearing a tan jumpsuit and a many-colored knitted tam that concealed the hair, but Sullivan could see by the flexed curve of the hips and the long legs that it was a woman. Blinking and peering more closely, he saw that the woman wasn't looking at the boat, but at the barred storm drain that the boat was moored to. She was swirling her hand in the water and calling softly through the grating, as if to someone in the tunnel on the other side of the steel bars.

"Frank?" she said. "Frank, don't hide from me."

Sullivan's heart was pounding again, and belatedly he wondered if he had *really* wanted to find this Elizalde woman.

For that had to be who this was. Still, he silently reached up to his coat pocket (the pocket flap felt rough, like cloth instead of leather) and fished out a lightbulb. Holding it by the threaded metal base, he swung the glass bulb at the stone coping of the bridge.

"*Yah!*" shouted the woman below, scrambling up and splashing one foot into the water; and the bulb popped against the coping.

She turned a scared glance up at him, and a moment later she had ducked under the bridge, out of his sight.

"Wait!" yelled Sullivan, hurrying down the landward slope of the bridge. "Doctor—" No, he thought, don't yell her last name out here, that won't reassure her. "Angelica!"

She had splashed under the bridge and was back up in the sunlight on the bank on the west side, striding away from him, obviously ready to break into a run at any sound of pursuit. A couple of ducks on the bank hurried into the water, out of her way.

"We can help each other!" he called after her, not stepping down from the bridge onto the sidewalk. "Please, you're trying to get in touch with this Frank guy, and I need to get in touch with my father!" She was still hurrying away, her long legs taking her farther away with every stride. She wouldn't even look back. "Lady," Sullivan yelled in despair, "*I need your help!*"

That at least stopped her, though she still didn't turn around.

He opened his mouth to say something else, but she spoke first, in a low, hoarse voice that carried perfectly to his ears but would probably have been inaudible ten feet back: "Go away. My help is poison."

Here I am in Venice Beach, he thought. "Well, so's mine. Maybe we cancel out."

When she turned around she was pushing the knitted cap back from her face, and then she rubbed her hand down her forehead and jaw as if she had a headache or was very tired. "You know who I am," she said. "Don't say *your* name here, and don't say mine again." She waved him to silence when he opened his mouth, then went on, "You can follow me to the big parking lot, if you like. Don't get close to me."

She walked back, past the foot of the bridge, and started up Dell Street, walking next to the slack-rope fence of the white Tudor house Sullivan had thought was a restaurant. When she had passed it and was halfway to the stop sign at South Venice, he started forward from the bottom of the bridge.

After a few steps, he stopped in confusion and looked down at his own legs.

He was wearing . . . someone else's pants, somehow. Instead of the blue jeans he had pulled on in the gym at City College this morning, he was wearing formal gray wool trousers. With cuffs. He crouched to touch them, and two more snaps popped loose from the sleeve of his coat, and then the sleeve was disattached, hanging down over his hand. The sleeve was wool too—he slapped dizzily at his sides—the whole garment was, and it was a suit coat. He couldn't help looking back, to see if his leather jacket might somehow be lying on the bridge behind him. It wasn't.

He pulled the sleeve off with his other hand. The upper edge was hemmed, with metal snaps sewed on. He gripped the cuff of the other sleeve and tugged, and that sleeve came off too, with a popping of snaps. (He noted that he was now wearing a long-sleeved white shirt, no longer the plaid flannel he remembered.) The coat was convertible, it could be worn with the sleeves long or short.

Why, he wondered, would anyone want a short-sleeved formal coat?

Well, it occurred to him, a magician might. To show that he didn't have anything up his sleeves. Houdini was a magician, wasn't he? Maybe I didn't lose the mask after all—maybe I'm wearing it.

He breathed deeply, and watched the ducks paddling out across the water. He was still nervous, but the sense of imposed isolation, of being the only moving thing on a microscope slide, had moved on past him.

He looked at his hands, and in the middle of this dream-logic afternoon he wasn't very surprised, or even very scared, to see (though the sight did speed up his heartbeat) that his hands were different. The fingers were thicker, the nails trimmed rather than bitten, and the thumbs were longer. There were a few small scars on the knuckles, but the scars he remembered were gone.

He lifted the hands and ran the fingers through his hair, and immediately his arms tingled with goose bumps: for his hair felt kinky and wiry, not straight and fine as it normally did. But it was falling back into limp strands as he disordered it, and he could now feel again the constriction of creased leather around his elbows.

When he lowered his arms he found himself catching the sudden weight of the plaster hands; he gripped them firmly and slung them safely under his left arm. A lightbulb broke with a muffled pop in the pocket of his leather jacket, but he didn't need the lightbulbs anymore.

"Um!" he said loudly, to catch Elizalde's attention. "Hey, lady!"

She stopped and looked back, and his first thought was that she was a much shorter person than he had originally thought. Then he realized that this was a different woman—plumper than Elizalde, and with curly dark hair unconfined by any sort of hat, and wearing a long skirt.

But it had to be Elizalde. "Look at yourself," he said—quickly, for the skirt was already becoming transparent.

The woman looked down at her own legs, which were now again zipped into the tan jumpsuit. And though Sullivan had not blinked nor seen her figure shift at all against the background of pavement and distant buildings, she was taller, as if she had suddenly moved away.

He hurried up the narrow sunlit street toward her, and she let him get within ten feet of her before she stepped back.

"You saw that?" he asked.

Elizalde's olive complexion had gone very pale at some point in the last minute. She looked at the lumpy bandanna Sullivan was carrying. "You're not another damned *ghost*, are you?" she asked.

"No, I'm as alive as you are. Did you see—"

"Yes," she interrupted, "both of us. God, I hate this stuff. Let's not talk until we've got the street between us and the canals."

He followed her as she jaywalked across the one-way inland-bound lanes of South Venice. On the far side she stepped up the curb but then walked on the dirt between the curb and the sidewalk, toward Pacific Avenue. Sullivan followed her lead, stepping over weed clumps and Taco Bell bags and bottles in brown paper bags. *Avoiding marked channels*, he thought.

They walked into the parking lot through a gap in the low wall. A red sign on a pole by the exit read WRONG WAY—STOP—SEVERE TIRE DAMAGE; and someone had crookedly stenciled SMOKE under the STOP.

"There's a canal running under this parking lot," Sullivan ventured to say when they had walked out onto the broad cement face of it, ringed at a distance by light poles and low apartment buildings and shaggy eucalyptus trees in the chilly afternoon sun.

"I can run in any direction from here," said Elizalde shortly; "so can you. And anyway, we're between two oppositely one-way streets, one facing the sea and one away. It should make us hard to fix. And you've got a powerful mask, haven't you? Big enough for two, as we saw."

"Someone . . . *focused* on us back there, didn't they?" said Sullivan. "And the mask came on full strength. Maybe because there *were* two of us, our fields overlapping, there beside your . . . 'stasis of clarity, clarity of stasis.' "

Elizalde was sweating. Her jumpsuit was bulky and lumpy, and he realized, belatedly, that she must be wearing another outfit under it. She stared at him. "That's something I said, in that interview in *L.A. Weekly.* Who are you? Quick."

"I'm Peter Sullivan, I'm an electrical engineer and I used to work in film, which might give you some clues. I've been out of town, too, traveling everywhere in the country except California." He was breathless again. "Hiding from all this, from somebody who died. Well, I told you it was my father, didn't I? But this Halloween is—is gonna be a heavy one. I'll tell you frankly, there are people after me; but I'm sure you're smart enough to know that there'll be people looking for you too. I think you and I should work together, pool our resources. I've got this mask. And I've found a safe place to live, a waterfront apartment building that's in a sort of psychic pea-soup fog."

She wasn't looking convinced. Her dark eyes were still narrowed with suspicion and hostility.

"And I know this city real well," he went on lamely.

Her voice was stiff when she answered him. "I too am familiar with *Nuestra Señora la Reina de los Angeles*," she said.

I get it, he thought wearily. You're Mexican, you've got a blood-in-the-soil, soil-in-the-blood kinship with the place, and you don't need a gringo sidekick. Our Lady Queen of the Angels, he thought; and it reminded him of the garbled lyrics of one of Sukie's Christmas carols: *Commander Hold-'Em, bone-dry king of angels. . . .* Death, Sukie had meant, the Grim Reaper. In this kind of crisis, here in L.A., suddenly and very deeply he missed his twin sister, who had gone away with Commander Hold-'Em.

"Lady," he said, almost hopelessly, "I need a partner. I think you do too."

She frowned past him at the cars crossing in both directions over on Pacific Avenue . . . and abruptly he knew that she was going to refuse, politely but firmly, and just go away. Probably she wouldn't come back here, probably she'd go looking for Frank somewhere else, where Sullivan would never find her.

"Don't decide right now," he said hastily, "no, don't even speak. I'll speak. I'll be at Bluff Park in Long Beach tonight at eight. That's wide open, you can drive by in a cab, in a disguise, and if you don't like the look of it you can go right on past, can't you? Or, if you like, you can run away in the meantime, be in San Diego by then, be hiding up a tree somewhere. I'll be at Bluff Park. At eight. Tonight. Goodbye."

He turned his back on her and walked quickly away, toward Pacific and his van and, somewhere not too many minutes distant, some dark bar with a men's room.

O rum key, O ru-um key to O-bliv-ion, he sang in his head.

CHAPTER 30

"How cheerfully he seems to grin,
How neatly spreads his claws,
And welcomes little fishes in,
With gently smiling jaws!"
—Lewis Carroll,
Alice's Adventures in
Wonderland

But I swallowed him, thought Kootie dully for the dozenth time.

He was lying awkwardly across the back seat of the van, on his left shoulder, which had gone numb. His whole spine ached every time the van leaned around a corner.

I swallowed him, like the whale swallowed Jonah. (Well, I inhaled him, actually.) But can I throw up the ghost? Cough him out? Or will they really have to cut me open to get it? It's in my *head*!

At the Music Center yesterday Edison had said, *They'll kill you and eat me.* Was that really what was going to turn out to be true?

The driver had looped a pair of headphones over his bald scalp, and from time to time he spoke into a tiny microphone that stuck out under his chin. The other man had found KLSX on the radio, and his head was jogging to some old rock song from before Kootie's time.

Kootie was shocked again by their indifference. Were they *used to* driving little boys off to be killed?

All at once his right elbow was pressed painfully into his ribs against the sudden restraint of the seat belt—the minivan was slowing. Kootie discovered that he couldn't sit up again, with his feet tied together to the sidepost of the seat. He tried to push himself up, but his left arm was as numb and uselessly limp as if it belonged to someone else.

"Low gear, and slow," said the man in the passenger seat, "and keep the wheels dead straight."

"I've driven up a ramp before," said the driver.

A grating clank jarred the minivan. The pressure against Kootie's ribs and right elbow was abruptly gone, and he was rocked back against the seat—the minivan had moved slowly forward, and the front end was mounting some incline; a ramp, apparently. Kootie couldn't see the windshield, but the men's heads were in shadow now, and the interior of the minivan was darker.

"As soon as the front wheels are over the lip, give it a boost, to clear the oil pan—then brake hard as soon as the back wheels are in."

"I've *driven* up a *ramp* before."

The motor gunned briefly and the front end of the minivan dropped, and Kootie was again flung against the taut seat belt.

The driver switched off the engine, ratcheted up the parking brake, and opened the door—it clunked against something, and the metal echoes told Kootie that the van had been driven up into the back of a truck, like the ambulance in *Die Hard.*

Both of the men climbed out of the Fussels' van, shuffled to the back of the truck, and then Kootie heard them hop down to some pavement. After that, with an abrupt dimming of the already-shadowy light into complete darkness, he heard some heavily clanging metal things tossed inside and the clattering rumble of the sliding back door being pulled down.

Kootie's eyes were wide, and his straining to see something in the pitch blackness only made imaginary rainbow pinwheels spin in his vision.

They could have left me a light, he thought. He was clinging to the sense of the words, for his breathing and his heartbeat were very fast, and (even more than starting to thrash and scream with not any particle of control at all) he was afraid he would wet his pants. *A flashlight left on, I could have paid for the batteries. The van's headlights, they could have jumped the van battery later from the truck battery. A fucking Zippo lighter!—left flaming and wedged in the console somewhere.*

Usually Kootie was uncomfortable using bad words, but today in this total darkness he clung to it. *One fucking Zippo lighter,* he thought again. Above the tape, the skin over his cheekbones was cold and stiff with tears.

He waited for Edison to yell at him . . . but he caught nothing from the old man. Perhaps he had deserted Kootie too. Maybe now these men would let him go, if Edison had gone . . . ? Kid-stuff nonsense.

The truck's engine started up now—it was louder than the minivan's had been. Through the padded seat under him Kootie felt the jar as the truck was put into gear, and then the whole mobile room was moving forward, with the minivan rocking inside it.

And a moment later Kootie jumped, for suddenly, silently, there was a dim light in one corner of the truck—outside the minivan, up by the right front bumper, a moving yellow glow. Then he could hear dragging footsteps—heavy, an adult—on the metal floor.

The minivan door was pulled open on that side, and a face leaned in, waveringly lit from below by a flashlight strung to swing around the person's neck. The glittering little eyes were like spitty sunflower seeds stuck onto the white skin under the eyebrows.

"Let me tell you a parable," said the voice Kootie remembered. "A man walking down the road saw another man in a field, holding a live pig upside-down over his head under the branches of an apple tree. 'What are you doing?' asked the first man. 'Feeding apples to my pig,' said the second man. 'Doesn't it take a long time, doing it that way?' asked the first man. And the man in the field said, 'What's time to a pig?' "

Kootie's eyes were wide and he was just moaning into the clotted tape between his jaws. The whole truck seemed to be dropping away into some dark abyss, hopelessly far below the lost sunlit streets of L.A.

Mindlessly, Kootie shouted against the duct tape gag—

"Al! Help me, Al!"

Sherman Oaks had called the exchange again at 4 P.M., and at last the operator had had something to say besides *Nothing yet, dude.* The man had given Oaks a telephone number and had suggested that he call it at his earliest possible convenience. Oaks used his last quarter to call the number.

"Where are you?" some man asked as soon as Oaks had identified himself. "We got a van and a truck circling each other down in Inglewood, and if they have to drive around much longer, the man says your tithe goes up to fifteen percent."

"I'm at Slauson and Central, by the trainyards," Oaks said.

"Truck'll be there in . . . six or seven minutes. It's an Edison truck, black and orange—"

"What?"

"SCE—what we could get quick. Is that a problem? The truck's not stolen; the driver's real Edison, but he's on the network barter, and he was right in the area where they picked up the van. After we talked to him, he just called in Code Seven or something."

Oaks groped to find a reason for his inordinate dismay, and found one. "I need a big boxy truck, with ramps, that you can drive a car into! I've got no use for some damn boom or crane thing—" He was working up genuine outrage now. This *was* wrong. "I'll pay no tithe at *all* for some damn—"

"Jeez, man, this is the kind you want. Edison's got all kinds of vehicles, not just those repair things."

"... Oh," said Oaks, feeling like a cloud chamber in which the vacuum had just been violated, so that rain was condensing inside. "Okay. It's just that ..."

"Sure. Now listen, there's a gun in the back of the truck, along with the stuff you asked for. The driver insisted that this scenario be set up so it could look like a hijacking if anything goes wrong, okay? Don't touch the gun, it's got smeary untraceable fingerprints on it right now."

"But there *is* a knife there, too? I need a knife—" I can't kill the boy with a noisy *gun*, Oaks thought.

"Your knife's there too. Try to relax, will you? Get in touch with your Inner Child." The line went dead, and Oaks hung up.

He took a deep breath and let it out slowly, trying not to hear the shrill voices in the exhalation.

Outer child you mean, he thought—it's the Inner Old Man I want to ... *get in touch* with.

In an *Edison* truck! The shudder that accompanied the thought bewildered him.

He bent and with his one hand picked up the cardboard box at his feet, then stepped away from the pay telephone to let one of the impatient crack-cocaine dealers get to it.

The box rattled in his hand. Tithe, he thought bitterly. It's like taxing waitresses' tips—the man taking the cut can be trusted to overestimate the actual take. In the box Oaks had packed ten little glass vials, which was supposed to represent a tenth of the garden-fresh ghosts he would collect during the upcoming month. He had brought it along in advance this way to "show humble."

He had stuck each vial into a condom. Obstadt had probably never seen the raw product before, and he would doubtless imagine that this eccentric packaging was standard in the trade. Nine of the vials were in Ramses condoms, but one was in a Trojan.

Safe sexorcism. The Trojan hearse. Oaks had no intention of paying any more tithe. If Obstadt was still just a dilettante, well, he could take up an interest in fine wines or something; if by this time he was actually riding piggyback on the Maduro Man, though, he would be in the same jam that Oaks had been in in 1929.

(This morning Oaks had begun to remember events from before 1989;

and he had concluded that he was a good deal older than he had thought.)

After hurriedly gathering up the thousand smokes and handing them over to one of Obstadt's men, and then packing up these ten, he had had only four unlabeled ones left to inhale himself: four miserable, vicious, short-lived gang boys, as luck would have it, the sort of bottled lives he ordinarily disdained as *pieces-a-shit*. They hadn't done much to hold back the tumultuous army of the Bony Express, clamoring and shouting in Oaks's head.

In the turbulence, old memories were being shaken free of the river-bed of his mind, and wobbling up to the surface *(like the unsavory old corpse that had bobbed up in the Yarra River in Melbourne in 1910, right after the manacled Harry Houdini had been dropped into the river for one of his celebrated escapes; and it had been a natural, if distaste-ful, mistake to pounce on the ragged old thing, imagining that it was Houdini freshly dead at last).*

He remembered living in Los Angeles in the 1920s, when neon light-ing was so new and exotic that its ethereal colored glow was mainly used to decorate innovative churches—the "Mighty I AM" cathedral, and Aimee Semple MacPherson's giant-flying-saucer-shaped Angelus Temple on Glendale Boulevard. Under some other name, Oaks had been a follower of all kinds of spiritualist leaders, even joining William Dud-ley Pelley's pro-Nazi "Legion of Silver Shirts"—though when, as re-quired in the Silver Shirts, he had been asked to give the exact date and time of his birth, he had given false ones. Actually, he had not known what his real birth date might be; and so, lest he might give the correct date and time unconsciously, he had been careful to give the published birth figures of a randomly chosen movie star.

(It had been Ramon Novarro, and Oaks had occasionally wondered, though never with remorse, if Novarro's brutal death in the early hours of Halloween, 1969, might have been a long-delayed consequence of that lie.)

And in 1929 he had somehow inhaled a ghost that had been stored in an opaque container; and the stinking lifeless thing had choked his mind, blocked his psychic gullet, rendered him unable to inhale any more ghosts at all. (He thought of the collapsed face he had seen yes-terday on the steps down to the parking level at the Music Center up on Temple.)

Oaks knew that he had got past that catastrophe somehow. (A suicide attempt? Something about his missing arm? The memories were like smoke on a breeze.) Some psychic Heimlich maneuver.

The Edison truck had pulled up then, and a man in bright new blue jeans and a Tabasco T-shirt had opened the passenger-side door and hopped down to the pavement.

"Oaks?" he said. When Oaks nodded, he went on, "Here she is. Driver'll pull into an alley and let the van aboard, and then you got half an hour of drive-around time. More than that, and your monthly rate increases. What's in the box?"

Oaks held out the cardboard box on the fingertips of his one hand, like a waiter. "Next month's payment, in advance."

The man took it. "Okay, thanks—I'll see he gets it."

A new Chrysler had pulled in behind the truck, and the man carried the box to it and got in.

Oaks had looked bleakly at the orange and black and yellow truck— Halloween colors!—then sighed and walked around to the back as the Chrysler drove away. When he'd pulled up the sliding back door, he'd been grudgingly pleased to see the things he'd asked for laid out on the aluminum floor: a flashlight, twine and duct tape, and a Buck hunting knife. In the front right corner he could see the gun the driver had apparently insisted on, a shiny short-barreled revolver. Won't be needing that, Oaks had thought as he'd grabbed the doorframe, put one foot on the bumper, and boosted himself up.

CHAPTER 31

And once she had really frightened her old nurse by shouting suddenly in her ear, "Nurse! Do let's pretend that I'm a hungry hyaena, and you're a bone!"

—Lewis Carroll,
Through the Looking-Glass

Even by straining all his muscles, all together or against one piece of restraining tape at a time, Kootie had failed to break or even stretch his bonds; though he could reach his fingers into the pockets of his jeans.

The flashlight swung wildly as the man climbed over the passenger seat and leaned down over Kootie. He reached out slowly with his one arm, closed his fingers in Kootie's curly hair, and then lifted the boy back up to a sitting position. Then he sat down on the console, facing Kootie, and stared into the boy's eyes.

Kootie helplessly stared back. The one-armed man's round, smooth face was lit from beneath by the flashlight, making a snouty protuberance of his nose, and his tiny eyes gleamed.

"No ectoplasm left, hey?" the man said. "No dog-mannikin today?" He smiled. "Your mouth is taped shut. You'll be having trouble expiring, just through your nose that way. Here." He leaned forward, and Kootie wasn't aware that the man had a knife until he felt the narrow cold back of it slide up over the skin of his jaw and across his cheek almost to his ear, with a sound like a zipper opening.

Kootie blew out through his mouth, and the flap of tape swung away from his mouth like a door. He thought of saying something—*Thank you? What do you want?*—but just breathed deeply through his open mouth.

"My compass needle points north," the man said. "Your smoke is clathrated. You need to unclamp, open up."

He lowered his chin, pushing the flashlight to the side, and he held his right hand out so that it was silhouetted against the disk of yellow light high up on the riveted truck wall. Squinting up sideways at the projection, the man wiggled his fingers and said, with playful eagerness, "What would you say to a . . . *rhinoceros*?" He bunched the fingers then, and said, "Clowns are always a favorite with little boys." The thumb now made a loop with the forefinger, while the other fingers stuck out. "Do you know what roosters say? They say *cock-a-doodle-doo!*"

Kootie realized belatedly that the man was doing some kind of shadow show for him. He blinked in frozen bewilderment.

"Helpful and fun, but not very exciting," the man concluded, lowering his arm and letting the flashlight swing free so that it underlit his face again. "What could be more *exciting* for a lonely little angel than a flight *up* the hill to where the rich people live? Aboard a charming conveyance indeed! I believe I can provide a snapshot of that."

He stared into Kootie's eyes again, and hummed and bobbed his round head until the spectacle of it began to blur from sheer monotony. In spite of his rigid breathlessness, Kootie thought he might go to sleep.

All at once the motion of the truck became jerky and clanging and *upward*, and the seat under him was hard wood. He opened his eyes, and jumped against his restraints.

Cloudy daylight through glass windows lit the interior of a trolley car climbing a steep track up a hill. Kootie's seat was upright, though, and when he looked around he saw that the trolley car had been *built* for the slope—the floor, seats, and windows were stepped, a sawtooth pattern on the diagonal chassis. A city skyline out of an old black-and-white photograph hung in the sky outside.

There was a little boy wearing shorts and a corduroy cap sitting in the window seat next to Kootie, and he was staring past Kootie at someone across the aisle. Kootie followed the boy's gaze, and flinched to see the round-faced man sitting there, still wearing stained old bum clothes but with two arms and two hands now.

"Where is the gentleman you boys came with?" he asked.

The boy beside Kootie spoke. "In heaven; send thither to see; if your messenger find him not there, seek him i' the other place yourself. But, indeed, if you find him not within this month, you shall nose him as you go up the stairs into the lobby."

"Hamlet to Claudius," the man said, nodding. "Showing as a youngster, then, eh? Why not?" He smiled at the boy. "What's the matter, don't you like my pan?"

"Not much," the boy said.

The man chuckled. From under his windbreaker he pulled a pencil that was a foot long and as wide around as a sausage, and with his other hand he pulled out a giant pad of ruled white paper. "At the top of the hill I'll fill out the adoption papers on both you lads," he said affectionately.

The boy next to Kootie shook his head firmly. "I have a snapshot myself," he said.

Then the whole length of the cable car fell to level, silently, the front end down and the back end up, though none of the three passengers were jarred at all. It was just that the seats and floor were all lined up horizontally now, like a normal car. The gray sunlight had abruptly faded to darkness outside the windows, and flames had sprung up in little lamps on the paneled walls.

The car was longer and broader now, chugging along across some invisible nighttime plain. The man with the little eyes was sitting several rows ahead now, and he was wearing a ruffled white shirt and a gray cutaway coat. In the aisle next to him stood a tall black man—his clothes were as elegantly cut, but seemed to be made of broad teak-colored leaves stitched together.

From behind Kootie came a boy's voice: "Newspapers, apples, sandwiches, molasses, peanuts!" Kootie turned around awkwardly in the seat belt that was still taped to his wrists, and saw the boy in the corduroy cap. A big wicker basket was slung over the boy's arm now, and he was slowly pacing up the length of the car, looking straight at the two men at the far end.

"Where are we?" Kootie whispered when the boy was beside him.

"An hour out of Detroit," the boy said without looking down, "two hours yet to Port Huron. Sit tight, Kootie. Newspapers, peanuts!" he went on more loudly. There were only the four people in the train car.

The man who now had two arms was staring at the boy. "I *remember* this!" he said softly. "*You* were *him*? Christ, what *year* was this?"

For a moment the boy with the basket paused, and Kootie sensed surprise on his part too. Then, "Apples, sandwiches, newspapers!" he called, resuming his walk up the aisle. The train car smelled of new shoes fresh out of the box.

The man got to his feet, bracing himself on the back of the seat in front of him against the train's motion. "Well enough, I'll blow down your straw barricades. Uh . . . papers?" he said, smiling and holding out his two arms.

The boy lifted out a pile of newspapers and laid them in the man's hands. The man turned to the open window and tossed the stack out into the windy blackness outside.

When he straightened up, he said, "Pay this boy, Nicotinus."

The black man handed the boy some coins.

"Magazines," the man said then. He took the stack of magazines that the boy lifted out of the basket, and threw them too out the window. "Pay the boy, Nicotinus."

Kootie sat on his wooden seat, his wrists moored in the stocks of the anachronistic woven-nylon seat belt, and watched as all the wares in the boy's basket were dealt with in the same way, item by item, sandwich by bag of peanuts.

Through it all the black man was staring intently at the man who kept repeating, "Pay the boy, Nicotinus."

When the basket was empty, it too went out the window in exchange for a handful of clinking coins. The boy put his filled hand into his pocket, then took it out and put his fist to his mouth for just a moment, as if eating one of the coins.

For a moment the boy stood empty-handed, facing away from Kootie, while the train rattled through the night and the glassed-in lamp-flames flared. Then he took off his shoes and coat and hat, and, barefoot, lifted them up and laid them in the man's hands.

The man's round face smiled, though his tiny eyes didn't narrow at all. He turned and pitched the clothes out the window, and then he said, "Pay the boy, Nicotinus."

The boy held out his hand one more time—and the black man seized it and threw the boy to the wooden floor.

Kootie was slammed sideways across the back seat of the minivan with a man's weight on top of him crushing his ribs, and he was choking and gagging on a bulky plastic cylinder that had somehow got into his mouth; the flashlight was jammed between their bodies somewhere, and he could see nothing in the darkness. He knew the man's face was right above his own because of the harsh hot breaths battering at his right ear and eyelashes.

Something was repeatedly punching him in the side over the steel-cable belt, audibly tearing the denim jacket. He knew it must be the blade of the knife, being stopped by the metal coils of the I-ON-A-CO belt; but the stabs were wild, and he was sure that the next one wouldn't be another blunted impact but a cold plunge into his guts.

He shoved his tongue against the flat bottom of the plastic cylinder in his mouth, but before he could spit it out to scream and bite, his jaws involuntarily clamped tight around the thing.

At the same moment, *No, Kootie!* shouted a voice in his head; it was

Edison—and the boy train-vendor in the hallucinations had been Edison too. *I'll do this!*

At that moment the knife blade grated off of the top edge of the belt cable and the point of it stabbed against the bone of one of his ribs. Kootie sagged in ringing shock.

But an instant later he had inhaled deeply through his whistling nostrils, and then his head was whipped around to face the man who was killing him, and his lower teeth popped the lid off the plastic cylinder.

And he blew a hard exhalation straight up into the man's wide-open mouth.

The man drove a knee solidly into Kootie's stomach, so that Kootie's long exhalation ended in a sharp, yelping wheeze—but the man had jackknifed off the seat, boomed hard against the sliding door as the flashlight whirled around his tumbling body like a crazy firefly, and then he had bounced onto his belly across the console, kicking his legs in the empty air so that Kootie heard popping tendons rather than impacts. A moment later Kootie cringed to hear him vomiting so hard and loud that the terrified boy thought the man must be splitting open his face, popgunning his eyeballs, his sinus and nose bones cracking out to fall onto the carpeted floorboards.

Kootie's left hand was gently slapping his ribs, and when his fingers found the knife grip they held on and then carefully pulled the blade out of the hole it had punched in the denim. Kootie winced and whimpered to feel the point pull out of his flesh and the edge violin across the coils of the belt, but he just held still, knowing it was Edison that was working his hand.

Kootie lay half on his side across the seat, and he could feel hot blood roll wet down across his stomach from his cut left rib. He nearly jumped when he felt wet steel slide past his right wrist, and then that hand had twisted and was free, and had snatched the knife.

At last he spat out the emptied cylinder, and he was sobbing with urgent claustrophobic fright. "Get me out of here, mister!" he whimpered. "Oh, please, mister, get me *out of here!*"

He was anxious to be just a cooperative passenger in his own body now—gratefully he felt his right hand cut free his left wrist, and then he was sitting up and bending over to cut the tape around his ankles.

The one-armed man had heaved himself forward with each abdomen-abrading retch, and now his feet boomed against the van's ceiling as he toppled over the console to the floor. *"Edison!"* he said loudly, grating out the syllables like cinder blocks. *"Wast—thee—agayn?"*

Kootie didn't know whether it was himself or Edison that worked the door handle and pulled back the minivan's sliding side door. He stepped out, down to the floor of the truck, rocking as if he were aboard a boat, and he groped his way in darkness to the rippling, sectional metal wall that was the truck's door.

The cut in his side was just a point of tingling chill, but he could feel blood weighing down the folds of his shirt over his belt, and a hot trickle ran down the inside of his leg.

"Kootie!" he gasped. *"Breathe slower!* You're going to make us faint."

Kootie's mouth snapped shut, and he made himself count four heartbeats for every inhalation, and four for every exhalation.

Without his volition his right hand went to his side and pressed against the cut.

Behind him he heard feet thumping and scraping—inside the minivan, the one-armed man was up.

With his left hand Kootie slapped hurriedly at the ribbed inner surface of the truck's door until he found a blocky steel lever, and he braced himself on his good foot and heaved the lever upward.

Dazzling sunlight flooded the truck's interior as the door clattered upward, folding along its track overhead. Without his sunglasses, the day outside seemed terribly bright.

Pavement was rushing past down there beyond the toes of his Reeboks, and he was squinting out at the windshields of oncoming cars; a low office building and a red-roofed Pizza Hut were swinging past off to his left. The people in the cars might be gaping, pointing at him, but their windshields were just blank patches of reflected blue sky.

Kootie glanced behind him, into the dimness of the truck's interior, and he could see the one-armed man crawling down out of the minivan headfirst, onto the truck floor. *Breathe slower!* Kootie reminded himself.

"What do I do, Mr. Edison?" Kootie cried, his voice not echoing now but breezing away in the open air.

He sensed no answer; and when he tried to let the ghost take control of his body again, he had to grab the bottom edge of the half-raised door, for his knees had simply buckled and he would have fallen out of the truck.

He had to step back then, for the truck was slowing down.

Kootie freed his bloody hand from his side and waved it broadly at the cars following the truck, mouthing *Slow down, I'm getting out! Don't run over me!* and pointing down at the street. He glanced down past his shoes—the street was still moving by awfully fast, and his belly and an instant later his neck quailed like shaken ice water.

You'll tumble, he thought; even if he slows a lot more than this, you won't be able to land running fast enough, and you'll tumble like a

Raggedy Andy doll. He imagined his skull socking the pavement, his elbows snapping backward, shinbones split and telescoped . . .

He couldn't do it. But if he waited another couple of seconds, the one-armed man would be on him again.

Then, with an abrupt hallucinatory burst of glaring red and blue flashes on his retinas, a gleaming black-and-white police car had surged into the gap between the truck's bumper and the car behind. A half-second segment of siren shocked his ears, and Kootie swayed backward again as the truck slowed still more, and Kootie saw the front end of the police car dip as it braked to avoid hitting the truck.

And Kootie jumped.

His kneecaps banged the hood of the police car, and his palms and forehead smacked the windshield, cracking it with a muffled creak; in nearly the same instant, with a boom that shook the very air, the windshield crystallized into an opaque white honeycomb as a hole was punched through it next to Kootie's bloody right hand.

Kootie's right hip and shoulder hit the windshield then, and the glass gave beneath him like starched white canvas. And another boom rocked the world as a hole was punched through the wrecked webwork of glass near his upraised left knee; the windshield dissolved into a spray of little green cubes, and he was sitting on the dashboard.

He whipped his head around to squint ahead at the truck. The one-armed man's face was right above the truck-bed floor, and in his one hand wobbled the silver muzzle of a gun. As Kootie stared, a hammer-stroke of glare eclipsed the gun, and he felt a jolt in the police car as the boom of the gunshot rolled over him.

The police car was screeching to a halt now, slewing sideways, but Kootie was able to hang on to the rounded inside edges of the dash-board, and though he was rocked back and forth he was not thrown off; even when the car behind rear-ended the police car with a squeal and bang and tinkle of broken glass, he just lifted his shoulders and dug in with his butt and let his chin roll down and up.

The police car was stopped at last. The orange-and-black Southern California Edison truck was wobbling to the curb against further braking and honking horns from behind, and Kootie scrambled to the fender and hopped down to the asphalt. The pavement under his feet was so steady, and he was so torqued, that he had to take several hopping steps to keep from falling over.

A couple of people had got out of stopped cars and were hurrying up. "Has someone got . . . change for a telephone call?" Kootie shouted, to his own surprise.

"Here you go, kid," said a woman absently, handing him a quarter.

She was staring past him, at whatever was going on with the police and the one-armed man.

"Thank you," Kootie said. He was wobbling dizzily as he stepped up the curb, and a man in a business suit called something to him. "Man back there," Kootie yelled, "bleeding bad. Where's a telephone?"

The man pointed at a liquor store and said, "Dial nine-one-one!"

Sure, thought Kootie wildly as he wobbled onward through the cold sunlight. Nine-one-one. I'd get to talk to my mom and dad again, drunk as fig beetles by now; Edison could shoot the breeze with the fat lady from the supermarket parking lot. At least I'd get my quarter back.

He glanced back, but the doors of the police car hadn't opened, and, blinking against the silvery glare of the sunlight, Kootie couldn't see the one-armed man. He wished he hadn't lost the sunglasses.

"Where are we going?" he whispered, with timid hope, when he had limped around the corner of the liquor store and was facing a long alley with Dumpsters and old mattresses shored up against the graffiti-fouled walls.

"Anywhere relatively private," Edison said, and Kootie exhaled and began sweating with relief—the old man was not only back, but seemed to be sensible again, and would now take care of everything. "Keep pressing your hand hard against the cut, it'll slow the bleeding. I need to get a look at this wound, and then we'll go buy whatever sort of stuff we need to get you repaired. And some liquor. I really don't think we can get by, here, without some liquor."

"Shit, no," said Kootie, stumbling forward down the alley.

His face was cold and sweaty, but he smiled, for Edison apparently wasn't going to scold him for his language this time.

CHAPTER 32

"... How puzzling all these changes are! I'm never sure what I'm going to be, from one minute to another! However, I've got back to my right size: the next thing is, to get into that beautiful garden—how is that to be done, I wonder?"

—Lewis Carroll,
Alice's Adventures in Wonderland

Dios te guarde tan linda," said Angelica Elizalde softly into the sea breeze.

She had taken off her sneakers in order to wade out in the low, breakwater-tamed surf of Los Angeles Harbor. The lights of the *Queen Mary* rippled across the dark water, and Elizalde shivered now when she looked at the vast old ship out there by San Pedro.

She had walked down to this narrow stretch of beach from the bus stop at Cherry and Seventh, and she was still putting off the decision of whether or not to meet the Peter Sullivan person up in the parking lot on the bluff. She glanced at her watch and saw that she still had half an hour in which to decide.

She paused and looked back up the shore. A hundred yards west of her, the Mexican women's fire still fluttered and threw sparks on the breeze. She might just plod back there and talk to them some more. The bruises on her knees and hip were aching in the cold, and it would be nice to sit by the fire, among people who could hear her secrets and not consider her insane.

Elizalde had walked up to the fire when the sun was still a flattened red coal in the molten western sky, and in her exhaustion her Spanish had effortlessly come back to her, so that she was able to return the greetings of the women and make small talk.

She had smiled at the toddler daughter of one, and the woman had touched the girl's forehead and quickly said, *"Dios te guarde tan linda"*—God keep you pretty baby. Elizalde had remembered her grandmother doing the same whenever a stranger looked at one of the children. It was to deflect *mal ojo*, the evil eye. But Elizalde also remembered that it was a routine precaution, and she smiled at the mother too, and crossed herself. Only after the mother had smiled back, and Elizalde had accepted the gestured offer of a seat on the sand beside the fire, had she felt hypocritical.

Veladoros, devotional candles in tall glasses, ringed the fire; and Elizalde soon learned that these women were here waiting for midnight, when, it then being the Friday before *El Día de los Muertos*, they would bathe their *piedras imanes* in the seawater.

Elizalde realized that she had not misunderstood the word yesterday—it did mean magnets. Her new friend Dolores untied her handkerchief and showed her her own, a doughnut-sized magnet from a stereo speaker. The best ones, Elizalde had gathered, were the little ones from old telephones—stubby cylinders, no bigger than a dime in cross section, that looked like the smoking "snakes" that her brothers had always lit on Cinco de Mayo and the Fourth of July.

Witches used the magnets as part of the ritual that transformed them into animals, she learned, but *piedra imanes* were good things to have around the house to attract good luck and deflect spells. The magnets needed to be fed—by tossing them into dirt or sand so that they became bristly with iron filings—and it was a good idea to immerse them in the sea on this one Friday every year.

As she'd sat there and listened to the gossip and the jokes and the occasional scolding of one of the children for playing too close to the fire, Elizalde had lain back against a blanket over an ice chest, and from time to time had made such answers and remarks as she imagined her grandmother would have.

And she heard stories—about a man in Montebello who had to wear sunglasses all the time, because one night he had left his eyes in a dish of water in his garage and taken a cat's eyes to see with while he made a midnight cocaine buy, and returned at dawn to find that the dog had eaten the eyes in the dish, leaving the man stuck with the vertical-pupiled, golden-irised cat's eyes for the rest of his life (Elizalde had commented that, in fairness, the cat should have been given the dog's eyes); about how raw eggs could be used to draw fevers, and how if the fevers had been very bad the egg would be hard-cooked afterward; about *los duendes*, dwarves who had once been angels too slow in trying to follow Lucifer to Hell, and so were locked out of Heaven and Hell both, and, with no longer any place in the universe, just wandered around the world enviously ruining human undertakings.

Elizalde had already heard stories about *La Llorona*—the Weeping Lady—the ghost of a woman who had thrown her children into a rushing flood to drown, and then repented it, and forever wandered along beaches and riverbanks at night, mourning their deaths and looking for living children to steal in replacement. As a child, Elizalde had heard the story as having occurred in San Juan Capistrano, with the children drowned in the San Juan Creek; but, in the years since, she had also heard it as having occurred in just about every town that had a large Hispanic community, with the children reputedly thrown into every body of water from the Rio Grande to the San Francisco Bay. There was even an Aztec goddess, Tonantzin, who was supposed to have gone weeping through Nahuatl villages and stealing infants from their cradles, leaving stone sacrificial knives where the children had lain.

These women that Elizalde had met tonight told a different version. Aboard the *Queen Mary*, they whispered, lived a *bruja* who had somehow lost all her children in the moment of her own birth, and then drowned her husband in the sea; and now she wandered weeping everywhere, night and day, eating *los difuntos*, ghosts, in an unending attempt to fill the void left by those losses. She had eaten so many that she was now very fat, and they called her *La Llorona Atacado,* the Stuffed Weeping Lady.

Elizalde wondered what character of folklore she herself might fit the role of. Surely there was the story of a girl baptized once conventionally with water and once with a fertilized egg, who endured a second birth (out of a milk can!) in a shower of coins, and who fled her home to wander along far rivers, in a foredoomed attempt to avoid the ghosts of the poor people who had come to her for help, and whom she had let die.

What would the girl in that story do next, having journeyed all the way back to her home village?

She looked again at her watch. Ten of eight.

She turned her plodding steps across the sand toward the steel stairs that led up the bluff to the parking lot. It was time to meet Peter Sullivan.

Sullivan had parked the van in a dark corner of the lot, and had walked away from it to smoke a cigarette in the spotlight of yellow glare at the foot of a light pole a couple of hundred feet away. Moths fluttered around the glass of the lamp a dozen feet above his head, flickering and winking in and out of the light like remote, silent meteors.

He had arrived at Bluff Park early, and had made a sandwich in the van with some groceries he'd bought after his flight from Venice; and though there were still three or four cans of beer in the little propane refrigerator, he had been drinking Coke for the last couple of hours. He always felt that Sukie was in a sense *somewhere nearby* when he was drunk, and anyway he wanted to be alert if the Elizalde psychiatrist actually showed up.

He was watching the cars sweeping past on Ocean Boulevard, and wondering if he shouldn't just get in the van and head back to Solville—which, he had learned, was the name given by the other tenants to the apartment building he had moved into today.

Now that he was sober again—hungover, possibly—teaming up with this Elizalde woman didn't seem like such a good idea. If she was unbalanced, which it sounded like she had every right to be, she might just lead deLarava to him. How could he take her to Solville, expose that perfect blind spot to her, when she might be crazy? He remembered his first sight of her in Venice—crouched in the mud below the canal sidewalk—wearing two sets of clothes—talking into a storm drain—!

He took a last deep drag on the cigarette, then patted his jeans pocket for the van keys.

And Elizalde touched his shoulder.

Sullivan knew that he had felt the touch an instant before it had happened, and he knew it was her; but he stood without turning around, still staring out at the cars passing on Ocean Boulevard, and he exhaled the cigarette smoke in a long, nearly whistling exhalation as a slow snowfall of dead moths spun down through the yellow light to patter almost inaudibly on the asphalt.

He dropped the cigarette among the lifeless little bodies, stepped on it, and then turned to face her, smiling wryly. "Hi," he said.

She sighed. "Hi. What do we do now?"

"Talk. But not out here where we might draw attention, like we did this afternoon. That's my van over in that corner."

"Those . . . hands are in it?"

"Yeah. If they become *my* hands again, we'll know somebody's looking at us again."

They began walking across the asphalt away from the light, their swinging fingertips separated by three feet of chilly night air. Enough light reached the boxy old vehicle for it to be clearly visible.

To his own annoyance, Sullivan found himself wishing that he had washed it. "Somebody egged my van," he said gruffly. "Makes it look like I threw up out the window."

"While you were going backward real fast," she agreed, stopping to stare at the dried smear. "When and how did that happen?"

"Today." He led her around the front of the van to the side doors. "A guy, an old friend of mine, tried to turn me over to a woman who wants to eat my father's ghost; I think she wants to capture me, use me as a live lure. The old friend threw an egg at me as I was driving out of there." He unlocked the forward of the two side doors and swung it open. The light was still on inside—the battery could sustain a light or two for a full day without getting too weak to turn the motor over. "Beer and Coke in the little fridge there, if you like."

Elizalde looked at him intently for a moment, then stepped lithely up into the van.

She leaned one hip on the counter around the sink, and Sullivan noticed to his embarrassment that the bed was still extended, and unmade. I must not really have meant to meet her, he thought defensively.

"Sorry," he said. "I wasn't anticipating company." And what is *that* supposed to mean? he asked himself. He threw her a helpless glance as he climbed up and pulled the door closed.

"You've got to wash off the egg," she said, and for a moment he thought she had meant *on your face*. Then he realized that she meant the egg on the outside of the driver's door.

"Is it important?"

"I think it's a marker," she said, "and more than a visible marker. Like a magical homing device. Raw eggs have all kinds of uses in magic. I should get out of this van right now, and walk away, mask or no mask. You should too, in a different direction."

Sullivan sat down on the bed. "I've got a place we can go where the psychic static will drown out the egg's signal. I'm pretty sure. Anyway, there's certainly a hose at this place, we can wash it off." She didn't seem crazy, and he was tired of spinning through his own circular thought-paths over and over again. "I think we should stick together."

"That's what Peter Sullivan thinks, huh." She stepped around him and sat down in the passenger seat, watching him over her shoulder. "Okay, for a while. But let's at least be a moving target." She looked forward, out through the windshield, and stiffened.

Sullivan stood up and hurried to the driver's seat with the key.

Outside in the parking lot, several people were standing on the asphalt a few yards away from the front bumper, shifting awkwardly and peering. Sullivan knew that he and Elizalde had been alone in the parking lot a few moments earlier.

"Ghosts," he said shortly, starting the engine. "Fresh ones, lit up by our overlapping auras." He switched on the headlights, and the figures covered their pale faces with their lean, translucent hands.

He tapped the horn ring to give them a toot, and the figures began shuffling obediently to the side. One, a little girl, was moving more slowly than the rest, and when he had clanked the engine into gear he had to spin the steering wheel to angle around her.

"Damn little kid," he said, momentarily short of breath. The way clear at last, he accelerated toward the Ocean Boulevard driveway.

Elizalde pulled the seat belt across her shoulder and clicked the metal tongue of it into the slot by the console. "I saw her as an old woman," she said quietly.

He shrugged. "I guess each of 'em is all the ages they ever were. He or she was, I mean. Each one is—"

"I got you. Put on your seat belt."

"The place is right here," he said, pushing down the lever to signal for a left turn.

The first faucet Sullivan found, on the end of a foot-tall pipe standing in weeds at the corner of the Solville lot, just sucked air indefinitely when the tap was opened. He walked across the dark lot to another, ascertained that it worked, and then drove the van over and parked it. He carried a big sponge out to scrub the outside of the driver's door, and then had to go back inside for a can of Comet, but at last all the chips and strips of dried egg had been sluiced off the van, and he locked it up.

Elizalde carried a beer in from the van to Sullivan's apartment, and when she popped it open foam dripped on the red-painted wooden floor. The only light in the living room was from flame-shaped white bulbs in a yard-sale chandelier in the corner, and Sullivan berated himself for not having thought to buy a lamp somewhere today. At least there were electrical outlets—Sullivan noticed that Shadroe had put six of them in this room alone.

Sullivan had carried the plaster hands inside, and he laid them against the door as though they were holding it closed.

"This is your safe place?" Elizalde's voice echoed in the empty room. She twisted the rod on the venetian blinds over the window until the slats were vertical, then walked to the far wall and ran her long fingers over a patched section where Shadroe had apparently once filled in a doorway. "What makes it safe?"

"The landlord's dead." Sullivan leaned against another wall and let himself slide down until he was sitting on the floor. "He walks around and talks, and he's in his original body and he's not . . . you know, *retarded*—he's not a ghost, it's still his actual *self* inside the head he carries around. I believe he's been dead for quite a while, and therefore he must know it, and be taking steps to keep from departing this . . .''

"Vale of tears."

"To use the technical term," Sullivan agreed. "The place must be a terrible patch of static, psychically. The reason I think he's aware of his situation is that he's made it a terrible patch physically, too, a confusing ground-grid. All the original doors and windows seem to have been rearranged, and you can see from outside that the wiring is something out of Rube Goldberg. I can't wait to start plugging things in."

"Running water can be a betrayer too."

"And he's messed that up. I noticed earlier today that the toilet's hooked up to the *hot* water. I could probably make coffee in the tank of it."

"And have steamed buns in the morning," she said.

Her smile was slight, but it softened the lean plane of her jaw and warmed her haunted dark eyes.

"Hot cross buns," added Sullivan lamely. "Speaking of which, do you want to order a pizza or something?"

"You don't seem to have a phone," she said, nodding toward an empty jack box at the base of one wall. "And I don't think we should leave this . . . compound again tonight. Do you have anything to eat in your van?"

"Makings of a sandwich or two," he said. "Canned soup. A bag of M&M's."

"I've missed California cuisine," she said.

"You were out of town, I gather," he said cautiously.

"Oklahoma most recently. I took a Greyhound bus back here, got in late Tuesday night. Drove through the Mojave Desert. Did you ever notice that there are a lot of *ranches*, out in the middle of the desert?"

"I wonder what they raise."

"Rocks, probably." She leaned against the wall across from him. " 'Look out, those big rocks can be mean.' And on cold nights they put gravel in incubators. And, 'Damn! Last night a fox got in and carried off a bunch of our fattest rocks!' "

" 'Early frost'll kill all these nice quartzes.' "

She actually laughed, two contralto syllables. "Don't get excited now," she said, "but your dead man's got the heat turned all the way up in here, and not a thermostat in sight." She unzipped the front of her jumpsuit and pulled down the shoulders, revealing a wrinkled Graceland sweatshirt; and when she pulled the jumpsuit down over her hips and sat down to bunch it down to her ankles, he saw that she was wearing faded blue jeans.

She began untying the laces of her sneakers, and Sullivan made himself look away from her long legs in the tight denim.

"I hope you don't trust everybody," he said.

Out of the top of her right sneaker she pulled a little leather cylinder with a white plastic nozzle at the top. It had a key ring at the base of it, and with the ring around her first finger she opened her hand to show it to him. "CN mace," she said with a chillier smile. "In case the soup is bland. I don't trust anybody . . . very far."

Sullivan discarded the idea of taking offense. "Good." He straightened his legs out across the floor and hooked a finger through the loop at the corner of the fanny pack that was hanging on his left hip; then, not knowing whether he was being honest with her or showing off, he pulled on the loop—the zippers whirred open as the front of the canvas pack pulled away, exposing the grip of the .45 under the Velcro cross-straps.

Her face was blank, but she echoed, "Good."

She had taken her shoes and socks off and pulled the jumpsuit free of her ankles and tossed it aside. She stretched her legs, wiggling her toes in the air.

"But," Sullivan went on. He unsnapped the belt and pulled it from around his waist, and then slid the fanny pack across the floor toward the door. "I've decided to trust *you.*"

She stared at him expressionlessly for a long moment, but then she spun the leather-sleeved cylinder away. It bumped the heavy pack six feet away from where she sat, and she said softly, "All right. Are we partners, then? Do we shake on it?"

On his hands and knees he crossed the floor to her. They shook hands, and he crawled back to his wall and sat down again.

"Partners," he said.

"What do you know about ghosts?"

To business, he thought. "People eat them," he began at random. "They can be drawn out of walls or beds or empty air, made detectable, by playing period music and setting out props like movie posters; when they're excited that way, magnetic compasses will point to 'em, and the air around tends to get cold because they've assumed the energy out of it. They like candy and liquor, though they can't digest either one, and if they get waked up and start wandering around loose they mainly eat things like broken glass and dry twigs and rocks. They—"

"Produce from the Mojave ranches."

"Amber fields of stone," he agreed. "They're frail little wisps of smoke when they're new, or if they've been secluded and undisturbed. Unaroused, unexcited. The way you eat them is to inhale them. But if they wander around they begin to accrete actual stuff, physical mass, dirt and leaves and dog shit and what have you—"

"What have *you*," she said, politely but with a shudder, "I *insist.*"

"—and they grow into solid, human-looking things. They find old clothes, and they can talk well enough to panhandle change for liquor. They don't have new thoughts, and tend to go on and on about old grievances. A lot of the street lunatics you see—maybe most of 'em— are this kind of hardened ghost. They're no good to eat when they get like that. I worked for a woman who stayed young by finding and eating ghosts that had been preserved in the frail state, in old libraries and hotels and restaurants. She lives on water, aboard the *Queen Mary*—"

"I just heard about her! And she drowned her husband in the sea."

Sullivan crawled across the floor again and picked up Elizalde's beer. "I never heard of her having a husband. May I?"

Elizalde had one eyebrow cocked. "Help yourself, partner. I just wanted a sip to cut the dust."

Sullivan took a deep swallow of the chilly beer. Then he sat down next to her, setting the can down on the floor between them.

"What do you know about séances?" he asked breathlessly. "Summoning specific ghosts?"

She picked up the can and finished the beer before answering him. "I know a turkey can hurt you if he hits you with a wing—you've got to have 'em bagged up tight in a guinea sack. Excuse me. With ghosts, you'd be smart to have some restraints in place, before you call them. They do come when you call, sometimes. Séances are dangerous— sometimes one of them is for real." She yawned, with another shudder at the end of it, and then she glanced at the two white hands braced against the door. Sullivan was thinking of the ghosts they'd seen in the parking lot a few minutes ago, and he guessed that she was too. "I'm not hungry," she said in a low voice.

He knew what she was thinking: *Let's not open the door.* "Me either," he said.

"You've got your leather jacket for a pillow, and I can ball up my jumpsuit. Let's go to sleep, and discuss this stuff when the sun's up, hmm? We can even . . . leave the light on."

"Okay." He stood up and took off the jacket, but then crouched and folded it on the floor just a couple of feet from her, and stretched himself out parallel to the wall.

She had leaned toward the window to pick up the jumpsuit, and then she stared at him for several seconds. The gun and the mace spray were islands out in the middle of the floor.

At last she sighed and stretched out beside him, frowning uncertainly as she set the empty beer can on the floor between them. "You . . . read the whole interview?" she said as she slowly lowered her head to the bunched-up jumpsuit. She was looking away from him, facing the wall. "The interview of me, in *L.A. Weekly?*"

Sullivan remembered reading, *I've reacted against the whole establishment I was raised in, there—I'm* not *Catholic, I* don't *drink, and I* don't *seem to be attracted much to men.*

And he remembered Judy Nording, and Sukie, and his sonnet that had wound up so publicly in the trash. I suppose I've reacted too, he thought. "Yes," he said gently.

As he closed his eyes and drifted toward sleep, he thought: Still, Doctor, you did try a couple of sips of beer.

BOOK THREE

Hide, Hide, the Cow's Outside!

I don't claim that our personalities pass on to another existence or sphere. I don't claim anything because I don't know anything about the subject; for that matter, no human being knows. But I do claim that it is possible to construct an apparatus which will be so delicate that if there are personalities in another existence or sphere who wish to get in touch with us in this existence or sphere, this apparatus will at least give them better opportunity to express themselves than the tilting tables and raps and ouija boards and mediums and the other crude methods now purported to be the only means of communication.

—Thomas Alva Edison,
Scientific American, October 30, 1920

CHAPTER 33

"But it's no use now," thought poor Alice, *"to pretend to be two people!*
Why, there's hardly enough of me left to make one *respectable person!"*
—Lewis Carroll,
Alice's Adventures in Wonderland

Kootie woke up when a black man nudged his foot with a bristly push broom. The boy straightened up stiffly in the orange plastic chair and blinked around at the silent chrome banks of clothes dryers, and he realized that he and the black man were the only people in the laundromat now. Whenever he had blinked out of his fitful naps during the long night, there had been at least a couple of women with sleepy children wearily clanking the change machine and loading bright-colored clothing into the washing machines in the fluorescent white glare, but they had all gone home. The parking lot out beyond the window wall was gray with morning light now, and apparently today's customers had not yet marshaled their laundry.

"My mom will be back soon," Kootie said automatically, "she had to go back home for the bedspreads." He had said this many times during the night, when someone would shake him awake to ask him if he was okay, and they had always nodded and gone back to folding their clothes into their plastic baskets.

But it didn't work this morning. "I should charge you rent," said the black man gently. "Sun's up, boy."

Kootie slid down out of the seat and pulled his new sunglasses out of his jacket pocket. "Sorry, mister."

"You wouldn't know anything about some chalk drawings somebody did on the outside of the building, would you?"

Kootie put on the sunglasses before he looked up at the man. "No."

The man stared at him for a moment, then crinkled his eyes in what might have been a smile. "Oh well. At least it wasn't gang-marks from our Kompton Tray-Fifty-Seven Budlong Baby Dipshits or whoever they are today. And at least it was just chalk."

Kootie's head was stuffed and throbbing. "Are the chalk markings still there?"

"I hosed 'em off just now." Again he gave Kootie the wry near-smile. "Figured I'd let you know."

Kootie started to stretch, but he hitched and pulled his right arm back when the cut over his rib flared hotly in protest. "Okay, thanks."

He limped across the white linoleum, around the wheeled hanger-carts, to the glass doors, and as soon as he had pushed them open and stepped outside, he missed the stale detergent-scented air of the laundromat, for the dawn breeze was chilly, and harsh with the damp old-coins smell of sticky trash-can bottoms.

A half-pint bottle of 151-proof Bacardi rum had cost him sixteen dollars yesterday afternoon—six for the bottle, and a ten-dollar fee for the woman who had gone in and bought it for him. By her gangly coltish figure Kootie had judged her to be only a few years older than himself, but her tanned face, under the lipstick and eyeliner and flatteringly acne-like sores, had been as seamed and lined as a patch of sunbaked mud. Edison had made Kootie tear the ten-dollar bill jaggedly into two pieces before giving one half of it to the woman prior to the purchase; he had laughingly said that this made her his indentured servant, but neither Kootie nor the woman had understood him. He had wordlessly given her the other half of the bill after she had delivered the bottle.

Edison had already had Kootie buy a roll of adhesive tape and a box each of butterfly bandages and "Sterile Non-Stick Pads," and then in a patch of late-afternoon sunlight behind a hedge on a side street off Vermont, Edison had pulled up Kootie's shirt to look at their wound, which had still been perceptibly leaking blood even though Kootie had been keeping his fist or his elbow pressed against it almost without a break since he had got away from the Southern California Edison truck half an hour earlier.

It was a V-shaped cut too big for him to be able to cover with his thumb, and Kootie had begun whimpering as soon as Edison started swabbing at it with a rum-soaked pad, so Edison had made Kootie swallow a mouthful of the rum. The taste was surprising—like what Kootie would have expected from film developer or antifreeze—but it did make his head seem to swell up and buzz, and it distracted him from the pain as Edison thoroughly cleaned the cut and then dried the edges, pulled them together, and fastened them shut with the I-shaped butterfly bandages.

Then, with a pad taped over the closed and cleaned cut, Edison had had a sip of the rum himself. When Kootie had floundered back over the hedge and started down the sidewalk, he had seemed to be walking on the deck of a boat, and Edison steered him into a *taquería* to eat some enchiladas and salsa and drink several cups of Coke. After that Kootie had been sober but sleepy, and they had found the laundromat, had furtively marked up the wall outside it, and finally had gone in to nap in one of the seats. The nap had continued, with interruptions, all night.

He shivered now in the morning breeze and shoved his hands into his pockets. He knew he must be sober, but the pavement still didn't seem firmly moored.

He felt his mouth open involuntarily, and he wearily braced himself for forcing it shut against some crazy outburst, but Edison just used it to to say, grumpily, "Where are we now?"

"Walking on Western," said Kootie, quietly even though there were no other pedestrians on the sidewalk. "Looking for a bus to take us to a beach."

"*Final discorporation* is on my agenda today, is that it? Why did we have to go outside so early? It's cold. It was warm back in that automat."

Each spoken syllable was an effort, and Kootie wished Edison wouldn't use so many of them. "They washed the chalk off the wall," he said hoarsely. Cars were rumbling past at his left, and his voice wasn't loud, but he knew Edison could hear him.

"Ah! Then you're a clever lad to have got away quickly." Kootie's mouth opened very wide then, so that the cold air got all the way in to his back teeth, and he was afraid Edison was going to bellow something that would be audible to any early-morning workers who might already be in these shadowed tax offices and closed movie-rental shops—but it was just a jaw-creaking yawn. "I shouldn't stay out here, in my excited state, like this. Compasses will be wagging. I'll go back to sleep. Holler for me if you—*mff!*"

Kootie had stumbled on a high curb and fallen to his knees.

"What's the matter?" said Edison too loudly. Kootie took the ending *r* sound and prolonged it into a groan that rose to a wail. "Don't *talk* so much," Kootie said despairingly. "I can't breathe when you do." He sniffed. "I bet we didn't get one full half hour of sleep last night without somebody waking us up to ask us something, or yelling at their kids or dropping baby bottles." He tried to struggle back to his feet, and wound up resting his forehead on the sidewalk. "I can still taste those enchiladas," he whispered to the faint trowel lines in the surface of the pavement. "And the rum."

"This won't do," came Edison's voice out of Kootie's raw throat. Kootie's arms and legs flexed and then acted in coordination, and he got his feet under himself and straightened all the way back up. Slanting morning sunlight lanced needles of reflected white glare off of car windshields into his watering eyes.

"You're just not used to the catnap system," said Edison kindly. "I can go for weeks on a couple of interrupted hours a night. *You* go to sleep, now—I'll take the wheel for the next couple of miles."

"Can we do that?" asked Kootie. He left his mouth loose for Edison's reply, but had to close it when he felt himself starting to drool.

"Certainly. What you do is stand still for a moment here, and close your eyes—then in half a minute or so I'll open your eyes but you'll already have started to go to sleep, get it? You'll go ahead and relax, and you won't fall. I'll hold us up, and walk and talk. Okay?" Kootie nodded. "Close your eyes, now, and relax."

Kootie did, and he let himself fall away toward sleep, only peripherally aware of still being up in the air, and of the daylight when his eyes were eventually opened again. It was like falling asleep in a tree house over a busy street.

And his confused memories and worries wandered outside the yard of his control and began bickering among themselves, and assumed color and voices and became disjointed dreams.

His gray-haired father was at the front door of their Beverly Hills house, arguing with someone from the school district again. Sometimes Kootie's parents would keep him home from school when science classes prompted him to ask difficult questions on topics like the actual properties of crystals and the literal meanings of words like *energy* and *dimension.*

"We're saving it for the boy," his father was saying angrily. "We're not selfish here. In my youth I had the clear opportunity to become a nearly perfect *jagadguru,* but I sacrificed that ambition, I unfitted myself by committing a theft, so that the boy could become the *jagadguru* perfectly, in psychic yin-and-yang twinhood with one who was the greatest of the unredeemed seers. The unredeemed one won't be able to accompany our boy to godhood, but he will be able to achieve redemption for himself by serving as the boy's guide through the astral regions. Right now the guide must wait—masked in the boy's *persona* ikon, as he will eventually occupy a place in the boy's *persona.* In order for the union to be seamless, it must occur after the boy has achieved puberty.''

Kootie had heard his father say much the same thing to his mother, on the nights Kootie had tiptoed back up the hall after his bedtime. It all had to do with the Dante statue, and the drunks and crazy people who wanted to talk to Don Tay.

His father waved ineffectually. ''Clear off, or I'll have no choice but to summon the police.''

But now Kootie could see the man standing grinning on the front doorstep, and it was the one-armed man with the tiny black unrecessed eyes.

Kootie flinched, and the dream shifted—he was lying in the back seat of a car, half asleep, rocking gently with the shock absorbers on the undulating highway and watching the door handle gleam in reflected oblique light when the occasional streetlamp swept past out in the darkness. He was relaxed, slumped in the tobacco-scented leather upholstery—this wasn't Raffle's Maverick, nor the old marooned Dodge Dart he had slept in on Wednesday night, nor the Fussels' minivan. He was too warm and comfortable to shift around and look at the interior, but he didn't have to. He knew it was a Model T Ford. The driver was definitely his father, though sometimes that was Jiddu Parganas and sometimes it was Thomas Edison.

Kootie smiled sleepily. He didn't know where they were driving to, and he didn't need to know.

But suddenly there was a screech of brakes, and Kootie was thrown forward into the back of the front seat—he hit it with his open palms and the toes of his sneakers.

The dream impact jolted him out of sleep, and so he was awake when his palms and the toes of his sneakers hit the cinder-block wall an instant later; using the momentum of the leap he had found himself making, he flung one leg over the top of the wall, and before he boosted himself up and dropped into the dirt lot on the other side, he glanced behind him.

The glance made him scramble the rest of the way over the wall and land running, and he was across the lot and over a chain-link fence before he had taken and exhaled two fast breaths, and then he was pelting away down a palm-shaded alley, looking for some narrow L-turn that would put still more angles and distance between himself and the Western Avenue sidewalk.

A pickup truck had been pulled in to the curb, and five men in sleeveless white undershirts had hopped out of the bed of it to corner him;

but what had driven the fatigue out of his muscles was a glimpse of the bag-thing one of the men was carrying.

It was a coarse burlap sack, flopping open at the top to show the clumps of hair it was stuffed with, and a battered Raiders baseball cap had been attached to the rim and was bobbing up and down as the man carrying it stepped up the curb; but the sack was rippling as if a wind were buffeting it, and harsh laughter was shouting out of the loose flaps. As Kootie had scrambled over the wall, the bag had called to him, *"Tu sabes quien trae las llaves, Chavez!"* and barked out another terrible laugh.

Kootie was beginning to limp now on his weak ankle, and his cut rib was aching hotly. He crossed a street of old houses and hurried down another alley, ceaselessly glancing over his shoulder and ready to duck behind one of the old parked cars if he glimpsed the bumper of a pickup truck rounding the corner.

"What was that?" he asked finally in a grating whisper, and even just forming the question squeezed tears of fright out of his eyes.

Even Edison's voice was unsteady. "Local witch-boys," he panted. "They tracked us with a compass, I've got to assume. I'm going to go under, clathrate, so they can't track me. Holler if you need me—"

"But what was that?"

"Ahhh." Kootie's shoulders were raised and lowered. "They . . . got a ghost, captured one, and had it animate the trash in that bag, apparently. It's got no legs, so it can't run away . . . but . . . well, you heard it? I was afraid you did. It can talk. Cheerful thing, hmm?" The bravura tone of Edison's last remark was hollow.

"It woke me up."

"Yes, I felt you wake up in the instant before we hit the wall. It's like hearing the tiny snap of a live switch opening, just before the collapsing electric field makes a big spark arc across the gap, isn't it?"

"Just like that."

Kootie was still walking quickly, and he could tell that it was himself placing one foot in front of the other now. "Where do I go now?" he asked, ashamed of the pleading note in his voice.

"God, boy—just walk straight away from here, fast. As soon as I'm under consciousness you should start looking for someplace to hide for a while—behind a hedge, or go upstairs in some office building, or hide in a boring section of the library."

"Okay," said Kootie, clenching his teeth and looking ahead to the next street. "Don't hide too deep, okay?"

"I'll be not even as far away as your nose."

CHAPTER 34

" 'Bring it here! Let me sup!'
It is easy to set such a dish on the table.
'Take the dish-cover up!'
Ah, that is so hard that I fear I'm unable!"
—Lewis Carroll,
Through the Looking-Glass

Sherman Oaks sat shivering in the early-morning sunlight on a wall beside the parking lot of an A.M. P.M. minimart. His companions, two ragged middle-aged men who were passing back and forth a bottle of Night Train in a paper bag, were ghosts, old enough and solid enough to throw shadows and to contain fortified wine without obviously leaking. They were pointing at a skinny lady in shorts and high heels at the street corner, and laughing *("FM shoes, 'fuck me' shoes, hyuck-hyuck-hyuck"),* but Oaks just clutched his elbows and shivered and stared down at the litter of paper cups and beer cans below his dangling feet.

He was starving. The four *piece-a-shit* ghosts he had inhaled yesterday were all the sustenance he had had for more than three days, and the Bony Express was a shrill chorus in his head and a seeping of blood from the corners of his fingernails.

He hadn't slept last night. He hadn't even been able to stop moving—walking along sidewalks, riding buses, climbing the ivied grades of freeway shoulders. During the course of the long night he had found his way to a couple of his secluded ghost traps, but though the creatures had been there, hovering bewilderedly around the palindromes and the jigsaw-puzzle pieces, he hadn't been able to sniff them all the way up into his head; they had gone in through his nostrils smoothly enough, but just bumped around inside his lungs until he had to exhale, and then they were back out on the dirt again, stupidly demanding to know what had happened. He had even inhaled over one of the antismoke crowd's L.A. CIGAR—TOO TRAGICAL ashtrays in an all-night doughnut shop, and got nothing but ashes up his nose.

He was jammed up.

The "big ghost" that had been shining over the magical landscape of Los Angeles for the past four days had been the ghost of *Thomas Alva Edison.* It had been *Edison's* face on the collapsed ectoplasm figure at the Music Center, the day before yesterday. And now Edison had *(again!)* fed Oaks a rotted ghost—and it had jammed him up, and he was starving.

Oaks looked up at the sky, and he remembered mornings when he had snorted his fill the night before, and had had more unopened vials ready to hand. I'd like it always to be six o'clock on a summer morning, he thought, and I'm in a sleeping bag on some inaccessible balcony or behind a remote hedge, and my feet are warm but my arms and head are out in the cool breeze and I'm sweating with a sort of disattached, unspecific worry, and I've got hours yet to just lie there and listen to the traffic and the parrots flying past overhead.

The police would be after him. He had run away from that confusion in Inglewood yesterday afternoon, but his shots had probably hit both of the cops in that patrol car, and his fingerprints were all over the inside of the SCE truck, and the van in the back of it. And the police probably still had his fingerprints on file; he now remembered that he had held several custodial jobs in hospitals, during the fifties and sixties, catching fresh death-ghosts and lots of the tasty, elusive birth-ghosts.

He'd have to get rid of the revolver—a "ballistics team" would be able to tell that it was the weapon that had fired on the police car. Oaks should have no trouble finding some street person who would take it in trade for some other (certainly less desirable) sort of gun.

But the police, unfortunately, weren't his main problem.

He twitched, and turned to the ghost sitting nearest him on his left. The man was breaking off fragments of mortar from between the cinder blocks of the wall, and eating them.

"You'll choke," Oaks rasped.

"Hyuck-hyuck. Choke on *this*," said the ghost, without any gesture.

"*I'm* choking," said Oaks. "If you choke on one of those rocks, a Heimlich maneuver could unblock it, right? How can I unblock a spoiled *ghost* from my *mind*-pipe? Do *you* know?"

The ghost wrinkled his spotty forehead in a frown, and then began counting off points on the fingers of one hand. "Okay, you got stones in your ears and a magnet up your nose, right? And toads have got a stone in their heads. The Venerable Bead. And plenty of people have got shrapnel and metal plates in them, and steel hips. Check it out. Learnest Hand Hemingway used to save the shrapnel that came out of his legs and put it in little bowls so that his friends could take the bits as souvenirs; and eat them, of course, to get a bit of Hemingway.'' He smiled. ''Everything is a Learnest experience. The golden rule to be ingot at the College of Fortuitous Knox. Fort You-It-Us Knocks.'' (The unattained pun made the intended spelling clear.) ''It's important to feel good about yourself. This morning I met somebody I really like—me.''

''That's good,'' said Oaks hopelessly. ''Tell him hello from me, if you ever run into him again.''

There was apparently no help to be had from the ghosts themselves. Oaks was choked, and the only way *he* knew how to unjam himself was likely to kill him. This time. Instead of just costing him another limb.

He could remember all kinds of things now. He remembered that Thomas Alva Edison had choked him this way once before—or at least once before—in 1929. Small surprise that the flattened face on the Music Center parking-level stairs had looked familiar! No wonder the *Edison* logo on the side of the truck had upset him! He should have paid attention to his forebodings. Thomas Alva Edison had never been any good for him.

As the shock-loosened memories had come arrowing up to the surface of his mind, one right after another, during his endless odyssey last night, Oaks had learned that he had always been an ambitious fellow, setting his sights on the most powerful people around and then trying to catch them unguarded so that he could snatch out of their heads their potent ghosts.

He had pursued the famous escape artist Harry Houdini for at least sixteen years—fruitlessly. Houdini had evaded every trap, had been effectively masked, psychically inaccessible, at every face-to-face confrontation. Houdini had even given protection to his friends: there had been a writer of horror stories in Rhode Island to whom Houdini had given his own severed thumb in June of 1924; Houdini had had his plaster mask-hands made by then, and could assume them and make them flesh any time he liked, and so he didn't need the original-issue thumb anymore, and besides, Houdini had probably known that he himself was only a couple of years from death at that point. In Los Angeles, Houdini had even picked up some kind of electric belt for this writer friend, an electromagnetic device that could supposedly cure all kinds of ailments, including Bright's disease and cancer—which pair of illnesses the writer died of in 1937, in fact, for he had been skeptical of the belt and disgusted by the thumb, and had got rid of them.

Houdini himself had been untouchable, a genuine escape artist . . . even though Oaks had eventually managed to arrange his physical death on a Halloween. It had been useless, for even in the moment of his dying Houdini had eluded him. Trying to catch Houdini had always been like trying to cross-examine an echo, wound an image in a mirror, sniff out a rose in an unlighted gallery of photographs of flowers.

Houdini's parents must have known right from his birth that their son had a conspicuous soul, for they had taken quick, drastic steps to hamper access to it. Confusingly, they had given him the name *Erik*, which was the same name they'd given to their first son, who had died of a fall while still a baby; and within weeks of Houdini's birth they had moved from Budapest to London to goddamn *Appleton, Wisconsin!*—and given an inaccurate birth date for him.

Slippery name, vast distance from his birthplace, and a bogus birthday. Worthless coordinates.

And the boy had compounded the snarling of his lifeline by running away at the age of twelve to be an itinerant boot polisher for the U.S. Cavalry. When that proved to be an unreliable career, he had just drifted, riding freight trains around the Midwest—begging, doing manual labor on farms, and learning magic from circus sideshows. With no real name or address or nativity date, his soul had no ready *handles*, and such ghost fanciers as might have been intrigued by the weirdly powerful boy were no doubt left holding a metaphorical empty coat while the boy himself was safely asleep in a probably literal outward-bound boxcar.

Sherman Oaks had certainly been pursuing Houdini by 1900, when the magician was twenty-six years old (Oaks had no clue as to how old he himself might have been), but Oaks had not ever managed to get Houdini's soul squarely in his sights.

In the moment of opening up the jaws of his mind for the kill, for the forcible extraction of another self from its living body, his plain physical vision always became a superfluous blur, and he relied on the sensed identity coordinates of the other self, like a pilot making an instrument landing by following a homing beam in bad weather.

Just when he would be zeroing in on the thing that was "Houdini," it became something else, and the real Houdini would be gone.

Once, in Paris in 1901, Oaks had psychically traced Houdini to a sidewalk café—but when Oaks walked up to the place with a gun in his pocket, seven bald men at the tables in front simultaneously took off their hats and bowed their heads, revealing the seven letters H-O-U-D-I-N-I painted one apiece on their shining scalps, and that grotesque assembly was the only "Houdini" that was present.

Always in his stage act Houdini was untraceably switching places with his wife (whom he had taken care to marry in three different ceremonies); another favorite trick was escaping out of a big milk can that was filled with water and padlocked shut—so that each escape was confusingly like a reexperienced birth. *(Slippery!)* In Boston in the fall of 1911, Oaks had been closing in on Houdini—the magician was weakened with a fever and haunted by dreams of his dead older brother—when suddenly the magician's psychic ground-signal was extinguished; Oaks had panicked, and expended far too much energy trying to find the ghost, and then, recuperating in defeat afterward, learned that the magician had had himself *chained inside the belly of a dead sea monster* during the eclipsed period. (The creature had been washed up dead on a Cape Cod beach, and was described as "a cross between a whale and an octopus.")

In the 1920s Oaks had got closer. Houdini had begun a new career as an exposer of phony spiritualist mediums who weren't entirely phony, and ghosts themselves had begun to threaten him. The famous Boston medium Margery gave a séance near Christmas of '24, and the ghost of her dead brother Walter announced that Houdini had less than a year to live. Houdini lived out the year, but on Halloween of '25, he was stricken with a "severe cold," and after a brief, restless sleep stayed up all night. Oaks had managed to get into Houdini's hotel room, but the sick magician had climbed out the window and disappeared until showing up protected at the Syracuse train station the next day.

On the following Halloween, in 1926, Oaks had managed to end the chase. Houdini's wife Bess got ptomaine poisoning from rat excrement that Oaks had managed to put into her dinner, and the magician had to travel without her masking presence. On October 11, in Albany, a ghost had been coached to walk translucently out onto the stage where a manacled Houdini was being hoisted into the air by his bound ankles and lowered into his Water Cell, a glass-sided tank from which he was supposed to escape; the ghost got itself caught in the pulleys, and Houdini was joltingly dropped a foot before the rope retightened, and a bone in his left ankle was broken. Houdini didn't try to complete that trick, but bravely went on with the rest of his act. Then, on October 22 at the Princess Theatre in Montreal, a blurry-minded religious student was induced to visit the magician in his dressing room and try Houdini's claim to be able to withstand the hardest punches; the student struck without giving Houdini any warning so that he could brace himself, and the four solid blows ruptured the magician's appendix.

Houdini of course didn't stop performing. He finished the run in Montreal the next day, and on the twenty-fourth he opened at the Garrick

Theater in Detroit. But Oaks had known that the man was dying now. That night Houdini was admitted to Grace Hospital, diagnosed with streptococcal peritonitis.

And so Oaks had got what might have been the first of his janitorial jobs at a hospital. It took Houdini a week longer to die, and in that time Oaks managed to snag a few fresh ghosts—but when Houdini finally did die, at 1:26 P.M., he died masked. Oaks was ready to catch him, and strained numbingly hard after Houdini's ghost when the magician died, but the old magician had been as slick as ever, and his ghost had darted away from Oaks's grasp in a flicker of false memories and counterfeit dates and assumed identities.

Oaks had seized and devoured a splash of fresh ghosts—but they had nothing to do with Houdini. Later he learned that a baby girl had been born in the same instant as Houdini's death, and he realized that what he had caught was the natal explosion of stress-thrown ghost-shells emitted by the newborn infant.

It had been tasty, but it had not been Houdini.

Spiritually depleted by the decades of that useless pursuit, Oaks had gone hungrily after the other psychically conspicuous figure of the time—Thomas Alva Edison. And he had had no luck there either.

Sherman Oaks boosted himself down off the cinder-block wall and shambled across the parking lot.

At some weary point last night he had got on a bus. He had dozed off, and when he'd snapped awake he had been sitting in a moving streetcar, one of the old long-gone Red Car Line, and he had passively ridden it south to the Long Beach Pike on the shore of Long Beach Harbor. He had got out of the streetcar and dazedly walked up and down the arc-lit midway, among the tattoo parlors and the baseball-pitch booths, startled repeatedly by the ratcheting clank of the Ferris-wheel chain and the *snap-clang* of .22 rounds being fired at steel ducks in the shooting gallery. The only lighted construct against the blackness of ocean had been the Cyclone Racer roller coaster—the *Queen Mary* had still been somewhere on the other side of the world, steaming across the sunlit face of the Atlantic.

On the street in front of him this morning he was seeing Marlboro billboards with slogans in Spanish, and Nissans and the boxy new black-and-white RTD diesel buses; the Mexican teenagers at the corner were wearing untucked black T-shirts and baggy pants with the crotches at their knees, and from the open window of a passing Chevy Blazer boomed some Pearl Jam song. He was living in 1992 again—the bus trip last night had been a brief tour through long-lost snapshots, requickened memories.

Yesterday, in the minivan in the back of the truck, he had animated one of the memories that had been tumbling back into him since Monday night—a moving-picture snapshot of the old Angel's Flight cable car that used to climb the hill from Third Street to Bunker Hill in downtown Los Angeles, until it was torn down for redevelopment schemes in the sixties. He had projected the hallucination to help awaken the clathrated ghost inside the boy, *excite* the ghost like an atom in a laser tube, so that Oaks would be sure of sucking the big old ghost out, along with the boy's trivial ghost, when he would finally succeed in killing the boy. And then Edison's ghost had countered by animating a relevant and defensive snapshot-memory of its own.

As much as it had been a shock to Oaks to realize that it was a memory they happened to have in common, it must also have been a shock to the ghost of Thomas Edison.

Oaks had gone after the world-famous inventor in late 1926—but the memory that the Edison ghost had projected had shown Oaks trying to get that ghost at a far earlier time, when Edison had been an anonymous but obviously strong-spirited boy selling snacks and papers on a train somewhere near Detroit.

Oaks thought about that now. In that surprisingly *shared* memory the boy Edison had been . . . twelve? Fifteen? God, that would have to have been in the early 1860s, during the Civil War! Oaks had been an *adult* . . . a hundred and thirty years ago!

How old *am* I? wondered Oaks bewilderedly. How long have I been *at* this?

Well, I was no more successful with damnable Edison in 1929 than I was on that train during the Civil War.

Or in the truck yesterday.

As soon as he had recovered from the loss of Houdini's ghost, Oaks had made his way to Edison's home in East Orange, New Jersey; and then down the coast to the "Seminole Lodge" on the Caloosahatchee River in Fort Myers, Florida, where Edison and his wife spent the winters.

Edison had been eighty years old then. He had retired from the Edison Phonograph Company only weeks earlier, leaving it in the hands of his son Charles, and was planning to devote his remaining years to the development of a hybrid of domestic goldenrod weeds that would yield latex for rubber, to break the monopoly of the British Malayan rubber forests.

The old man might as well have been *made* of rubber, for all the dent Oaks had been able to put in him during the next couple of years.

Edison had invented motion pictures, and voice-recording, and telephones, largely for their value as psychic masks, and with a transformer and an induction coil and a lightning rod with some child's toy hung on it he could have ghosts flashing past as rapidly as the steel ducks in the Pike shooting gallery, confounding any efforts to draw a bead on the real spirit of Edison behind all the decoys.

But Oaks had managed to sneak carbon tetrachloride into the old man's coffee in the summer of 1929, and as the kidneys began to fail and the doctors speculated about diabetes, the psychic defenses had weakened too; like the van der Waals force that lets an atom's nucleus have a faint magnetic effect when its surrounding neutralizing electrons are grossly low in energy, the old man's exhaustion was letting his real *self* gleam through the cloud of distracting spectral bit-players and simulations.

Oaks had begun to move in—but Edison's friend Henry Ford had moved more quickly. As an exhibit in his Ford Museum, in Dearborn Michigan, he had built a *precise duplicate of Edison's old Menlo Park laboratory.* It couldn't even be dismissed as a replica, for he had used actual boards and old dynamos and even *dirt* from the original. And Edison *visited* the place, and was emotionally *moved* by it, thus grievously fragmenting his psychic locus.

Ford had arranged a gala "Golden Jubilee of Light" to be celebrated on the 21st of October at the Dearborn museum. Oaks had *met* Edison—along with Ford and President Hoover!—at a railway station near Detroit, and in Edison's honor the whole party had transferred to a restored, Civil War–vintage wood-burning locomotive.

In the instant when Oaks was poised to kill Edison and inhale the man's ghost—and then escape somehow—a period-costumed trainboy had walked down the aisle of the railway car, carrying a basket of traveler's items for sale. Edison, sensing Oaks's momentarily imminent attack, snatched the basket from the boy—and then the eighty-two-year-old inventor tottered a few steps down the aisle, weakly calling, "Candy, apples, sandwiches, newspapers!"

And so the image in Oaks's psychic sights was fragmented in the instant of his striking; there were suddenly two Edisons in the car, or else perhaps two boys and no Edison at all. Oaks managed to keep from uselessly, blindly firing the gun in his pocket, but he was unable to restrain his long-prepared psychic inhalation.

Edison had been ready for him, too. He must have set up this replay of the remembered train scenario as a trap. The old man smashed a doctored apple against a wooden seat back and shoved the split fruit into Oaks's face, and Oaks helplessly inhaled the confined, spoiled ghost that had been put into it.

Oaks had been . . . *jammed up.*

Not yet sure what had happened to him, knowing only that he had failed to get Edison, Oaks had stumbled off the antique train at Dearborn and disappeared into the crowd.

And he had discovered that he couldn't eat ghosts anymore—and that he *needed* to. The Bony Express had begun to assail his identity inside his head, and he could feel himself fragmenting as their power increased and his own declined.

Desperately reasoning that what Edison had done, Edison could undo, he had tried to get an audience with the great man—after all, he hadn't done anything obviously overt on the train, and he had actually worked for a while at Edison's Kinetoscope studio in the Bronx in the early nineteen-teens, to make pocket money and calculate countermasking techniques, while keeping up his pursuit of Houdini—but Ford and Charles Edison had kept him away, and kept Edison secluded and effectively masked.

And so Oaks had returned to Los Angeles in despair, to commit suicide while he "still had a *sui* to *cide*," as he had grimly told himself.

The method he chose was sentimental. He went to his stash box, a rented locker in a South Alameda warehouse in those days, and selected a choice smoke he'd been saving—and then he drew it into a hypodermic needle and injected the five cc's of potent air into the big vein inside his right elbow.

He expected the air bubble to cause an embolism and stop his heart.

Instead, the ghost he had injected, perceiving itself to be in a host that was about to fragment into death, spontaneously combusted in idiot terror.

The detonation had blown most of the flesh off of the bones of Oaks's arm, and the doctors at Central Receiving Hospital on Sixth Street had amputated the limb at the shoulder.

Oaks had been put in the charity ward, with drunks and bar-fight casualties, and when he woke up after the surgery it wasn't long before one of his wardmates expired of an infected knife wound.

And Oaks caught the ghost; ate it, assumed it, got a life. The explosion had cost him his arm, but it had also unblocked his psychic windpipe.

* * *

He could do *that* again, any time; bottle one of the palindrome-confounded ghosts, bum a needle somewhere, and then shoot the lively ghost into his . . . leg, this time? *Right* arm? And then be missing *two* limbs. And what was to prevent the ghost from being propelled the short distance to his *heart* before it blew up?

Oaks was twitching with the urge to try once more to inhale a ghost. Maybe it would work now—now that the sun was up, now that he'd remembered all these things, now that his goddamn teeth ached so fiercely from being clenched that he couldn't see why they didn't crumble to rotten sand between his jawbones, which seemed intent on crashing *through* one another—maybe that's why he was clamping them shut, because otherwise they'd stretch *apart* just as forcefully, swing all the way around and bite his head off—

No. He had proved that it didn't work anymore, he couldn't ingest ghosts the way he was right now. He would shoot one into a vein if he had to, before the Bony Express could crash in through the walls of his identity and made a shattered crack-webbed *crazed* imbecile of him . . .

But first he would see if Edison couldn't undo what Edison could do. At least Edison was a ghost now, without the resources he'd had as a living person; and he didn't have Henry Ford protecting him anymore.

Just some kid. Some *bleeding* kid.

Oaks sighed, flinching at the multitude of outraged and impatient voices that shook his breath. His trembling left hand wobbled to the compass-pommel of his knife, and brushed the bulk of the revolver under his untucked shirt. Three more shots in it. One for himself, if everything worked out as badly as it could and even a ghost injected right into a vein didn't unjam him.

But I found the kid once, he thought dully. I can find him again. And I *can* make Edison tell me how to get unjammed.

And then I can eat him at last.

Oaks reached his hand into the pocket of his baggy camouflage pants and dug out his money. He had a five and three ones and about three dollars in change. Enough for bus fare south, and a can of bean soup.

Better make it two cans, he thought. Tomorrow's Halloween. This might be a demanding twenty-four hours, and already you feel like shit.

CHAPTER 35

"There's nothing like eating hay when you're faint," he remarked to her,
as he munched away.
"I should think throwing cold water over you would be better," Alice
suggested: *"—or some sal-volatile."*
"I didn't say there was nothing better,*" the King replied. "I said there
was nothing* like *it."*

—Lewis Carroll,
Through the Looking-Glass

Rubbers," said Neal Obstadt, using a pencil to push a tightly latex-
sleeved vial across his desk. The roof of his penthouse office was folded
back again, but the breeze out of the blue sky was chilly, and a couple
of infrared space heaters had been rolled in and now glowed like giant
open-walled toasters in the corners. "Why do they pack 'em in rubbers?"

The vial was empty. All ten of the ghosts Sherman Oaks had paid as
his November tithe had been compressed and sealed inside glass car-
tridges, along with some nitrous oxide for flavor, but Obstadt had kept
one of the vials to roll around on his desk.

"The guys in the lab say they don't," said Canov impatiently. "They
say it must be some kind of special gift wrap. Listen, I've got two urgent
things. You said to monitor deLarava's calls. She—"

Obstadt looked up sharply. "She's said something? What?"

"No, nothing that seems to be important. She's talked to that Webb
guy in Venice, but he still hasn't sensed the ghost she's apparently got
cornered there, the one that drove all those sea creatures onto the beach
Wednesday morning. Mainly she's busy setting up for her shoot on the
Queen Mary tomorrow. But we—"

"Gift wrap," Obstadt interrupted. "*Gift* wrap. Is it sarcasm? Disre-

spect? I've snorted nine of 'em already, and they've been primo, every
one. A diorama of Los Angeles citizens. No complaints about the mer-
chandise, and I'm a connoisseur. Still, *rubbers*. What do you think?
Does he mean *Go fuck yourself?* Go fuck yourself *safely*?''

"*She has a telephone line we weren't aware of.* Her listed office lines,
and the phones in her stateroom on the *Queen Mary*—'' Canov paused
to peer nervously down at Obstadt, but Obstadt was staring at him with
no expression. "She got another,'' Canov blurted. "JKL-KOOT, that's
the number—''

"On those billboards. The famous Parganas kid.'' Obstadt tried to
think. "I'm like a cat,'' he said absently, "I've got nine lives.'' *Nine*
of them he had snorted up, since yesterday afternoon! No wonder he
couldn't think—he was awash in other people's memories, and the Los
Angeles he pictured outside didn't have freeways yet, and Truman or
Eisenhower or somebody was president. "The Parganas kid! Are the
cops still buying that Edison driver's hijack story?''

"It looks like it. He's been let go, after questioning, anyway.''

"Why does Loretta want that kid? Why did Paco Rivera want him,
why *really*?'' He waved his hand. "I know, his name was Sherman
Oaks. A joke. We assumed it was Oaks that murdered the kid's parents,
and that he wanted to kill the kid because he could identify him; but
. . . They both got away, right? Yesterday? Oaks and the Parganas kid?''

"Not together.''

"And *Loretta* wants the kid, too?''

After a pause, Canov shrugged. "Yes.''

Obstadt stuck his pencil into the opened vial and lifted it up. "The
big smoke that hit town Monday night . . .'' he said thoughtfully, whirling the vial around the pencil shaft. "Oaks would have been . . . *terribly*
. . . aware of that. How old is the kid?''

"Eleven.''

"Not puberty yet, probably.'' He was nodding. "The *kid* has got to
have the *big ghost*. Either he's carrying it, or he's inhaled it and it's
grafted onto him, not assimilated. That's why Loretta wants him, and
why Sherman Oaks wanted him. Oaks can't have *got* the ghost yet, or
not as of yesterday afternoon, anyway, or the kid would be dead, not
running around.''

Obstadt looked up from the spinning, condom-sheathed vial, and
smiled at Canov. "Your guys *caught* the kid yesterday! Took him away
from that yuppie couple, the dead Fussels! And you *gave* the kid to
Sherman Oaks!'' Obstadt was speaking in a wondering tone, still smiling, his eyes wide. "And if you had done what I told you, monitored
fucking all of Loretta's phone lines, *I'd* have the kid, *I'd* have the big

ghost, which is probably goddamn *Einstein* or somebody, do you realize that?'' Obstadt was still smiling, but it was all teeth, and he was panting and his face was red.

Almost a whisper: ''Yes, sir.''

''Good. Good.'' Obstadt knew that Canov must be aching to say, *But you got a thousand and ten smokes! How big can this one* be *in comparison?* You weren't there, Obstadt thought, Canov my boy—you weren't there Monday night, you weren't *aware,* anyway, when that wave swept across L.A. and every streetlight dimmed in obeisance, every car radio whirled off into lunatic frequencies, and every congealed-ghost street bum fell down hollering.

''There's another thing,'' said Canov in a strangled tone. ''You told me to check out any kids deLarava might have. No, she doesn't seem to have any—but she's looking for this Peter Sullivan, and she's got a description of the van he's driving, and the license number. He used to work for her, along with a twin sister of his named Elizabeth who everybody called Sukie, who killed herself in Delaware Monday night.''

''She did? Now, why—''

''Listen! The Sullivan twins were orphans, their father was a movie producer named Arthur Patrick Sullivan, okay? He drowned *in Venice* in 1959. Now Sullivan the Elder was the godfather of this Nicky Bradshaw character—''

''Who Loretta's also looking for, right. Spooky, in that old TV show.''

''And . . . and Sullivan the Elder had just got married to a starlet named Kelley Keith. He drowned, while she was on the beach watching, and then she took a lot of his money and disappeared.''

''In '59,'' said Obstadt thoughtfully. ''He drowned at Venice, and now Loretta's . . . after the son, and the godson, and a big-time ghost that apparently came out of the sea . . . in Venice.''

''And she was obviously after the daughter too, but she killed herself. Clearly you follow my thinking.''

''Okay!'' Obstadt opened his desk drawer and took out the glass cartridge that contained the last of Sherman Oaks's tithe ghosts. The lab boys had painted a blue band around it to distinguish it from the others—the vial its smoke had come in had been tucked into a different kind of condom: Trojan, while the others were all Ramses. How do the lab boys know? he wondered. Nobody should be an expert at recognizing different kinds of *rubbers*.

Trojan—it reminded Obstadt of something, but Canov was speaking again.

''Loretta deLarava is almost certainly Kelley Keith,'' he was saying, ''and she seems to be unwilling to have that fact known.''

"Maybe she's got crimes still outstanding," mused Obstadt aloud, "hell, maybe she killed the old movie producer! Any number of possibilities. Whatever it is, we can use it to crowbar her, and she would be a useful employee. Meanwhile! *Tomorrow* is Halloween. Get all your men out—find the Parganas kid, and this Peter Sullivan, and Oaks, and bring 'em all to me. Alive, if that's easily convenient, but their fresh ghosts in glass jars would be fine. Better, in a lot of ways."

"But the Sullivan guy is masked, deLarava said so; he ditched one of her top sniffers outside of Miceli's yesterday. And the big ghost and the kid can mask each other, and Sherman Oaks is nothing *but* a walking mask—he's got no name or birth date, and the ghosts *inside* him probably have more personality definition than *he* does. We'd never catch their ghosts in vials, they'd be everywhere, like a flashlight beam through a kaleidoscope."

"I don't care," said Obstadt, opening another drawer and lifting out the thermoslike inhaler. "I want Oaks out of the picture, by which I mean dead. He's not just a dealer, he's fallen into the product and become a junkie, a heavy smoker, a rival. And I want deLarava working for me, severely subservient to me." He laid the glass cartridge into the slot at the top of the inhaler. "Do you know why water in a bucket hollows out and climbs the walls and gets shallower when you spin the bucket real fast?"

Canov blinked. "Uh, centrifugal force."

"No. Because there's other *stuff around*, for it to be spinning in relation *to*; the room, the city, the world. If the bucket of water was the only thing in the universe, if it *was* the universe, the water would be still, and you couldn't tell if it was spinning or not. Spinning compared to *what*? The question wouldn't have any meaning."

"Okay," said Canov in a cautious tone.

"So—" So I'm tired of being hollowed out, thought Obstadt, and of climbing the walls, and of getting shallow. I'm tired of not being the only person in the universe. "So I need to *contain* them, don't I? As long as they're existing at all. DeLarava I can contain by just *owning* her."

"She's doing her shoot aboard the *Queen Mary* tomorrow," Canov reminded him, "the Halloween thing, about ghosts on the ship. Anything about that?"

"Ummm . . . wait, on that. I don't think there's anything much on the *Queen Mary* right now. Let's see how you do at finding these people before sundown tonight, hm?"

"Okay." Canov visibly shifted his weight from one foot to the other, and he scratched his beard. "I'm sorry about not finding the other phone line sooner—we—"

"Get out of my sight," said Obstadt gently, with a smile.

After Canov had tottered out the door, Obstadt leaned back in his chair and looked up into the cold blue vault of the sky, wishing that the tiny crucifix of a jet would creep across it, just to break up the monotony of it.

Then he sighed and twisted the valve on the inhaler. He heard the hiss as the pressure from the punctured cartridge filled the inside of the cylinder, and then he lifted the tube to his lips.

The hit was cold with nitrous oxide, but nausea-sweat sprang out on his forehead at the hard, static *absence* of the rotted thing that rode the rushing incoming stench and wedged itself hopelessly sideways in the breech of his mind. The back of Obstadt's head hit the carpet as his chair went over backward, and then his knees banged against a bookcase and clattered sideways to the floor, and he was convulsing all alone on the carpet under the high blue sky.

CHAPTER 36

"I love my love with an H," Alice couldn't help beginning, *"because
he is Happy. I hate him with an H, because he is Hideous. . . ."*
　　　　　　　　　　　　　　　　　—Lewis Carroll,
　　　　　　　　　　　　　　　　　Through the Looking-Glass

At eye-height on one of the glass shelves was a white bas-relief of
Jesus done in reverse, with the face indented into a plaster block, the
nose the deepest part—as if, Elizalde thought, Jesus had passed out face-
first into a bowl of meringue. Someone had at some time reached into
the hollow of the face to paint the eyes with painstaking lack of skill,
and as Elizalde shuffled across the linoleum floor the head gave the
illusion of being convex rather than concave, and seemed to swivel to
keep the moronic eyes fixed on her.

What household out there, she asked herself nervously, is decorated
to *near* perfection, lacking only this fine *objet d'art* to make it complete?

*Frank Rocha's house had been full of things like that—prints of Our
Lady of Guadalupe, tortured Jesuses painted luridly on black velvet.*
Elizalde nervously touched the bulge of her wallet in her back pocket.

The old woman behind the counter smiled at her and said, *"Buenas
días, mi hija. Cómo puedo ayudarte?"*

"Quiero hacer reparaciones a un amigo muerto," said Elizalde. How
easy it was to express the idea, *I want to make amends to a dead friend,*
in Spanish!

The woman nodded understandingly, and bent to slide open the back
of a display case. Elizalde set down her grocery bag and clasped her
hands together to still their trembling. Already she had stopped at a tiny
corner grocery store and bought eggs and Sugar Babies and a pint of
Myers rum and a cheap plastic compass with stickum on the back so

that it could be glued to a windshield; and in another *botánica* she had bought a selection of herbs in cellophane packets, and oils in little square bottles, that she had been assured *habría ojos abrir del polvo*, would open eyes out of the dust—all of it had been set out on the counter in response to her request for something that would call up the dead.

Out of the display arrangement of stones and garish books and cheap metal medallions, the old woman now lifted a plastic bag that contained a sprig of dried leaves: YERBA BUENA, read the hand-lettered sticker on the bag, and Elizalde didn't even have to sniff it, just had to look at the dusty, alligator-bumpy leaves, to be surrounded by the remembered smell of mint; and, for the first time, she realized that the Spanish name meant *good herb*—over the generations her family had smoothed and elided the words to something that she would have spelled *yerra vuena*, which she had always taken to mean something like "fortunate error," with the noun given an unusual feminine suffix.

"Incapácita las alarmas del humo en su apartamento," the woman told her—quietly, though they were alone in the shop. *"Hace un te cargado, con muchas hojas; anade algún licor, tequila o ron, y déjalo cocinar hasta que está seco, y deja las hojas cocinar hasta que están secas, y humando y quemadas. Habla al humo."*

Elizalde nodded as she memorized the instructions—*disable smoke alarms in the apartment, make a strong mint tea with booze in it, then cook it dry and let the leaves smoke, and talk to the smoke.*

Jesus, she thought; and then in spite of herself she glanced at the disquieting bas-relief-in-reverse, which still seemed to be turned toward her, staring.

I still like "fortunate error," she thought helplessly as she took the bag from the woman and handed her a couple of dollar bills. She tucked the dried mint into the bag with her other purchases, thanked the woman, and shuffled out of the store. Bells hung on the doorframe rang a minor chord out into the sunlight as she stepped down to the Beverly Boulevard sidewalk.

Two young boys whirled past her on bicycles, giggling, one of them riding with one hand on the handlebars and the other clutching the metal box of a car stereo. Looking in the direction they'd come from, she saw a blue scatter of car-window glass on the sidewalk, and a white-haired old woman wrapped in a curtain scooping up the bits of glass and eating them.

Up ahead of her on the other side of Beverly was the two-story, fifties-vintage building where she had rented her psychiatric office. She could see a vertical edge of it from here, and a corner of glowing green neon—it was still standing, apparently still occupied.

Well, she thought with a shudder of nausea, the fire trucks did get there damn quick.

Elizalde had rented a suite there for only a couple of months *(before that final night, two years ago tomorrow)*—a tiny reception room, her office, a bathroom, and the big conference room with windows looking out over Beverly *(the glass of which had burst out in the intense heat of the flames)*.

At her Wednesday-night séances she would have the six or eight of her patients sit around the conference table, and after lighting a dozen or so candles on the shelves she would turn out the lights and have everyone hold hands. They took turns "sharing with the dead"—reliving old disagreements, talking with the dead sometimes, crying and praying sometimes—and Elizalde had tried to insist that if someone felt the need to say *Fuck you, fuck you* to the group and then storm out of the room, that it at least be done quietly.

Frank Rocha had always tried to get the seat next to Elizalde, and the palm of his hand was often damp and trembling. At the penultimate séance, a week before Halloween, he had passed her a folded note.

She had tucked it into her pocket, and only read it later, at home.

It had been painstakingly handwritten, and some misguided idea of formality had led him to draw quotation marks around nearly every noun (. . . *my "love" for you . . . the lack of "understanding" from my "wife" . . . my concern for your "needs" and "wants" . . . my "efforts" to make a "life" for you and me . . . the "honor" of "marrying" you . . .*), which gave the thing an unintended tone of sarcasm. Elizalde had telephoned him at his job the next day and, as gently as she had been able, had told him that what he had proposed was impossible.

But she had cried over the note, alone in her living room late that Wednesday night, and she had kept it in her wallet through all the subsequent horrors and flight and migration.

Elizalde hadn't wanted to leave the Long Beach apartment this morning—or at worst go any farther outside than to where Sullivan had parked the van, to fetch his meager food and some instant coffee and then hurry back inside—until the dawning of Sunday morning, when Halloween would safely be passed. But when Sullivan had begun to speculate on things that they ought to go buy before sundown today, his own readiness to be talked out of leaving Solville was so palpable that she had pretended to be unaware of it, and she'd made herself agree brightly to his proposed shopping trip. New socks and underwear, she noted, would be a necessity.

The apartment's toilet had indeed proved to be hooked up to the hot-water pipe—the bathroom window was steamy. They took turns showering and getting back into yesterday's unfresh clothes, and by the time they had moved the plaster hands away from the door and opened it to the fresh Friday-morning breeze, Sullivan was tight-lipped and grumpy and Elizalde was brittle with imitation cheer.

Sullivan had furtively switched license plates with a pickup truck in the Solville parking lot, and then the two of them had driven off north into the skyline-spiked brown haze of Los Angeles, Sullivan to buy some "electronics" and Elizalde to cruise the *botánicas* and *hierverias* for any likely-looking séance aids.

"I think that, in addition to being wisps of *stuff*, ghosts are an electromagnetic phenomenon," Sullivan had said nervously as he steered the van along the middle lane of the Harbor Freeway, "something like radio waves. When they *focus* somewhere, like they do when something energizes them and wakes them up, gets them into their excited state, they're located—a particle rather than a wave, for our purposes, or maybe a standing wave with perceptible nodes, sort of low-profile ball lightning—and they're detectably magnetic. Sometimes strongly so." Sullivan had been sweating. "I've seen them around the step-up transformers at power plants out in the desert, just a bunch of indistinct guys standing around blinking on the concrete, and if there's enough of them their magnetic field can interfere with the power readouts. What I'm going to . . . *try* to do is scrounge together some gear that'll isolate an individual ghost's signal, step it up, and hook it to a speaker. Meanwhile, you can pick up whatever sort of voodoo stuff it is that . . ."

He had paused then, at least having the grace to be embarrassed. . . . *that you used when you killed your patients two years ago*, she had thought, mentally finishing his sentence for him.

She had given him a hooded gaze under one raised eyebrow. "You just be sure you get some spare big-amp fuses for your *electronics, gabacho*," she'd said quietly.

He had pursed his lips and nodded, clearly intimidated by her supposed connections to some vast, secret, potent *brujeria folklórica*.

Now, standing on the sidewalk in her stale clothes and stringy long hair, among the baby carriages and beer signs, watching the progress of all the old beat Torinos and Fairlanes with defeated suspensions and screeching power-steering belts, she wondered if she could accomplish anything at all.

Sullivan had told her about "bar-time," and had explained that experiencing it was one of the consequences of being a spiritual antenna, with a psychic guilt-link to some dead person or persons; when hungry ghosts or ghost hunters focused their attention on her, she couldn't help but put some of her spiritual weight on her "one foot in the grave," so that she lived just a fraction of a second outside of time, *ahead* of time. He said it happened to all ghost-bound people.

And Sullivan had told her how dormant ghosts could be excited into fitful agitation by people such as themselves, and had told her how to spot the elusive creatures, once that had happened.

She had been careful not to make any of the moves that would rouse the things—she had not whistled any old Beatles tunes (Sullivan had told her that "The Long and Winding Road" was particularly evocative), nor, in this neighborhood, Santana's "Oye Como Va"; she'd been careful not to pick up stray coins on the pavement, especially very shiny ones; and she had not stared into the eyes of the faces, faded to washes of pink and blue, in the photos taped up in the windows of the little hairstyling salons, for Sullivan had told her that frightened new ghosts would cling to those paper eyes and then wait to meet and hold on to an unguarded gaze.

She *had* bought the compass, though. Sullivan had told her that when a compass needle pointed in some direction besides north, it was very likely pointing at one of the awakened ghosts. She had kept it in her pocket and glanced at it frequently—and at one point during her shopping stroll she had walked wide around a dusty old Volkswagen sitting on flat tires in a parking lot, averting her eyes as she skirted it; and a few minutes later she had crossed Beverly to avoid the open front door of a corner bar; because the needle had swung away from north to point at these things.

Sullivan had told her to wait for him by the video games in the RAPHAEL'S LIQUOR store at the corner of Lucas Avenue, and now she started angling through the crowd in that direction. It would be better for her to be waiting for him inside than for him to have to idle in the parking lot in the conspicuous van. Her bag of purchases was heavy enough now, and her hip and shoulder still ached from her fall on the Amado Street sidewalk two days ago; and she was walking awkwardly, for she had tucked the thing that Sullivan swore was *Houdini's dried thumb* into the high top of her left shoe, to balance the can of mace in her right one.

Un buen santo te encomiendas, she thought, quoting an old saying of her grandmother's. A fine patron saint you've got.

At a red light, she leaned her elbow on the little steel cowl over the signal-change button on a curbside traffic-light pole—and then gasped with dizziness and heard the thump of the seat of her jeans and the grocery bag hitting the sidewalk in the instant before her vision jumped with the jar of the impact.

People were staring at her, and she thought she heard *borracha!*—drunk!—as she scrambled back up to her feet; the light box on the pole across the street had finally begun flashing WALK, and she hoisted her bag in both arms and marched between the lines of the crosswalk toward the opposite curb, sweat of embarrassment chilly on her forehead. Not until she heard a wet *plop* on the pavement by her foot, and looked down just in time to see an egg from her torn bag hit the asphalt, did she realize that she was on bar-time again.

She stepped up the curb so carefully that any bar-time effect was imperceptible, and then she crossed the sidewalk and leaned against the brick wall of a *mariscos* restaurant, panting in the steamy squid-and-salsa-scented air that was humming out of a window fan.

It could be just Sullivan nearby, she told herself nervously; he said we can have that effect when we're together, our antenna fields overlapped and making "interference fringes"—it happened with him and his twin sister all the time, he said. Or it could be Frank Rocha, resonating in the sidewalk in forlorn response to the scuff of my sneakers (though the dried thumb in my shoe should be keeping any spiritoids from *recognizing* me). Maybe I just got *confused*, and *thought* I heard the egg break on the street before it really did; I haven't had a decent night's sleep, a decent meal, in—

But of course she was standing right across the street now from 15415 Beverly. She looked up, slowly and sullenly; the two-story building had been repainted, but she couldn't recall now anyway whether the fire had streaked the outside walls with soot. The windows of what had been her conference room had glass in them again, and between the glass and the curtains hung a green neon sign reading PSYCHIC—PALM READER.

Good luck to you, she thought bitterly to the present tenant. You'll never host as good a show as I did.

On that final Wednesday evening, that Halloween night, Frank Rocha had arrived very drunk. A week had passed since the night when she had read his clumsy letter, and, mostly out of guilt and uncertainty, she had let him stay at the meeting in spite of his condition. At one point early in the evening he had taken his hand out of hers, and had fumbled at something inside his leather jacket; after a muffled *snap!*, he had shuddered and coughed briefly, then returned his hand to hers, and the séance had proceeded. The smoke from the candles and incense had covered any smell of cordite, and Frank Rocha had continued to mumble and weep—no one present had realized that he was now dead, that he had neatly shot himself squarely through the heart with a tiny .22 revolver.

Later, in the darkness, he had again pulled his hand free, but this time it had been to squeeze her thigh under the table; not wanting to hurt his feelings, she had thought for a while before reaching down and firmly pushing his hand away. Luckily she had had her face averted from him.

With a blast of scorching air that hit her like a mailbag dropped from a train, Frank Rocha's body had exploded into white fire. Elizalde and the person who had been sitting on the other side of him were ignited into flame themselves and tumbled away in a screaming tangle of bodies and folding chairs, and everyone was dazzled to blindness by the man-sized, magnesium-bright torch that had been Frank Rocha.

And then the séance had started to be for real.

Elizalde looked away from the white building across the street and made herself take deep, slow breaths.

Hoping to reassure herself, she dug the plastic compass out of her jeans pocket and looked at it—

But it was pointing southeast, straight ahead down Beverly toward the Civic Center.

The compass needle didn't wobble in synch with any of the cars or pedestrians she could see. Unlike the readings she had got earlier at the abandoned Volkswagen and the barroom door, this one seemed to be some distance away.

There's a . . . a *ghost* down that way, she thought carefully, trying to assimilate the idea. A big one.

A furniture truck made a ponderous low-gear left turn onto the boulevard from Belmont Avenue, and little Toyotas and big old *La Bamba* boat cars rattled along the painted asphalt, up toward Hollywood or down toward City Hall, and crows and pigeons flapped around the traffic lights or pecked at litter on the sidewalks in the chilly sunlight . . . but there was a big *ghost* awake and walking around somewhere down Beverly in the direction of the Harbor Freeway.

The ghosts had arrived at the séance sometime during the confused moments when curtains were being torn down from the windows and bundled around the people who had been set afire; Frank Rocha himself was a roaring white pyre that no one could get close to.

Half of Elizalde's hair had been burned off, and after she'd been extinguished herself she had scorched her hands and face in a useless attempt to throw a curtain over Frank Rocha, but what she today remembered most vividly was the agony of listening to the shattering, withering screams.

The hallway doors had opened, and a lot of people had begun to come in who didn't even seem to notice the fire; and they hadn't *walked* in, but seemed to glide, or float, or flicker like bad animation. The light had been wrong on most of them—the shadows on their faces had not been aligned with the flaring corpse on the floor, and when their faces had happened to turn toward it, the incongruously steady shadows had abruptly looked like holes.

Others appeared from the ceiling—several of these were oversized infants, impossibly floating in midair, with the purple umbilical cords still swinging from their bellies, and their huge faces were red and their mouths hideously wide as they howled like tornadoes.

Bloody, mewling embryonic chicks pecked and clawed at Elizalde's scorched scalp, and fell into her face when she tried to cuff them off.

Instead of running for the ghost-crowded doors, everyone had seemed to be scrambling to the corners, down on their hands and knees to be below the churning burnt-pork-reeking smoke. The clothing burst away from three of her patients, two women and a man, to release long fleshy snakes, which lifted like pythons as they grew, and then dented and swelled to form grimacing human faces on the bulbous ends.

The faces on the flesh-snake bulbs, and the shadow-pied faces of the intruding ghosts, and the red faces of the giant infants, and the blood-and-smoke-and-tear-streaked faces of Elizalde's patients, all were shouting and screaming and babbling and praying and crying and laughing, while Frank Rocha blazed away like a blast furnace in the middle of the floor. By the time his unbearably bright body had shifted and rolled over and then fallen through the floor, the big windows had all popped and disintegrated into whirling crystalline jigsaw pieces and spun away into the darkness, and people had begun to climb out, hang from the sill, and drop to the flower bed below. Elizalde had dragged one unconscious woman to the window, and had then somehow hoisted the inert body over her shoulder and climbed out; the jump nearly broke her neck and her knees and her jaw, but when the fire trucks had come squealing across the parking lot Elizalde had been doing CPR on the unconscious patient.

Elizalde blinked now, and realized that she had been standing for some length of time on the curb, shivering and sweating in the cold diesel breeze.

That was all two years ago, she told herself. What are you going to do right now?

She decided to backtrack up Belmont and then walk on down to Lucas along some other street; Houdini's thumb was still there tickling her, down behind her sweaty anklebone, but something had paid attention to her a few moments ago, and she didn't want to blunder into some supernatural event. She turned around and walked into the mariachi-jukebox noise of the *mariscos* place and bought a couple of fish tacos wrapped in wax paper just so as to be able to wheedle from the counterman a plastic bag big enough to slide her ruptured grocery bag into.

The next block up was Goulet Street, gray old bungalow houses that had mostly been fenced in and converted to body shops and tire outlets after some long-ago zoning change. As she hurried along the sidewalk past the sagging fences, a young man stepped up from beside a parked car and asked her what he could get her, and half a block later another man nodded at her and made whip-snapping gestures, but she knew that they were both just crack-cocaine dealers, and she shrugged and shook her head at each of them and kept walking.

On the morning after the séance, she had been remanded from the hospital into the custody of the police, charged with manslaughter; she spent that night in jail, and on the following day, Friday, she had put up the $50,000 bail—and then had calmly driven her trusty little Honda right out across the Mojave Desert, out of California. She hadn't had a clue as to what had happened at her therapy session—she had known only two things about it: that Frank Rocha and two of the other patients had died, and—of course—that she herself had had a psychotic episode, suffered a severe schizophrenic perceptual disorder. She had been sure that she had briefly gone crazy—and she had not doubted that diagnosis until this last Monday night.

Walking along the Goulet Street sidewalk now, she wondered if she might have been better off when she had thought she was crazy.

At Lucas she turned right, and then turned right again into a narrow street that curved past the the rear doors of a liquor store and a laundry, back to Beverly. RAPHAEL'S LIQUOR was across the Beverly intersection, and she was hurrying, hoping Sullivan wasn't parked there yet.

But the compass was still in her hand, and she glanced at it. The needle was pointing behind her, which was north.

Good old reliable north, she thought. She sighed, and felt the tension unkink from her shoulders—whatever had been going on was apparently over—but she glanced at it again to reassure herself, and saw the needle swing and then hold steady.

Grit crunched under her toes as she spun around to look back. A hunched, dwarfed figure was lurching toward her from around the corner of the liquor store.

Duende! she thought as she twisted to get her balance leaned back the other way; it's one of those malevolent half-damned angels the women on the beach told me about last night!

Then she had crouched and made a short hop to get her footing and was striding away toward Beverly, in her retinas burning the glimpsed image of a gaunt face behind glittering sunglasses under a bobbing straw cowboy hat.

But a battered, primer-paint-red pickup truck had turned up from Beverly, its engine gunning as the body rocked on bad shocks, and she knew that the half-dozen mustached men in wife-beater T-shirts crouching in the back were part of whatever was going on here.

Elizalde sprinted to the back wall of the laundry, leaning on it and hiking up her left foot to dig out the can of mace; but the men in the truck were ignoring her.

She looked back—the *duende* had turned and was hurrying away north, but it was limping and clutching its side, and making no speed. The truck sped past Elizalde and then past the *duende*, and made a sharp right, bouncing up over the curb. The men in the back vaulted out and grabbed the dwarfish figure, whose only resistance was weak blows with pale little fists.

The hat spun away as the men lifted the small person by the shoulders and ankles, and then the oversized sunglasses fell off and she realized that the men's prey was just a little boy.

Even as she realized it, she was running back there, clutching the bag in her left arm, her right hand thumbing the cap of the mace spray around to the ready position.

"*Déjalo marchar!*" she was shouting. "*Qué estás haciendo? Voy a llamar a policía!*"

One of the men who wasn't holding the boy spun toward her with a big brown hand raised back across his shoulder to hit her, and she aimed the little spray can at his face and pushed the button.

The burst of mist hit him in the face, and he just sat down hard on the asphalt; she turned the can toward the men holding the boy and pushed the button again, sweeping it across their faces and the backs of their heads alike, and then she stepped over the spasming, coughing bodies and shot a squirt into the open passenger-side window of the truck.

A quacking voice from the bed of the truck called, "*No me chingues, Juan Dominguez!*"—but she didn't see anyone back there, only some

kind of cloth bag with a black Raiders cap on it. The *bag* seemed to
have spoken, in merry malevolence.

The boy had been dropped, and had rolled away but not stood up;
Elizalde's own eyes were stinging and her nose burned, but she bent
down to spray whatever might be left in the can directly into the faces
of the two men who had only fallen onto their hands and knees. They
exhaled like head-shot pigs and collapsed.

Elizalde dropped the emptied can and hooked her right hand under
the boy's armpit and hoisted him up to his feet. She was still clutching
her bag of supplies in the crook of her left arm.

"Gotta run, kiddo," she said. "Fast as you can, okay? *Corre con-
migo, bien?* Just across the street. I'll stay with you, but you've got to
motivate with your feet. *Vayamos!*"

He nodded, and she noticed for the first time the faded bruise around
his left eye. Not stopping to retrieve the hat and the sunglasses, she
frog-marched him back around the liquor store to the Lucas Avenue
sidewalk and started down it toward the stoplight.

Across the wide, busy street she could see the dusty brown box that
was Sullivan's van.

She looked behind her—there was no sign of the pickup truck.

The boy seemed to be able to walk, and she let go of him to dig the
compass out of her pocket. The needle was pointed straight east. The
ghost's still ahead of us, she thought nervously; then she held it out in
front of them, and the needle swung back toward north.

She moved it around, to be sure—and it was consistently pointing *at
the boy who was lurching along beside her.*

She knew that she would change her pace, one way or the other,
when she gave that new fact a moment's thought—so she instantly
gripped the compass between her teeth and began to walk faster, dragging the boy along, lest she might otherwise stop, or ditch him and just
flat-out run.

This *boy* is the ghost, she told herself; Sullivan said they can accumulate mass from organic litter, and eventually look like solid street
people.

But Elizalde couldn't believe it. For a moment she pulled her attention
away from the sidewalk pedestrians they were passing, and craned her
neck to look down into his pinched, pale face—and she couldn't believe
that a restless ghost could have made those clear brown eyes, now pel-
lucidly deep with fear, out of gutter puddles and sidewalk spit and tamale husks. And his eye socket was bruised! Surely the bogus flesh of
those scarecrows couldn't incorporate working capillaries and circulat-

ing blood! He must have a ghost . . . *on* him, somehow, like an infestation of lice.

A *big* ghost, she reminded herself uneasily, remembering how steadily the compass needle had pointed at it from blocks away.

She still couldn't see the red pickup truck, behind or ahead. Apparently the mace had worked.

They had nearly reached the corner. She spat the compass into her shopping bag. "What's your name?" she asked, wondering if she would even get a response.

"The kid's in shock," said the boy huskily, his voice jerking with their fast steps. "Better you don't know *his* name. Call me . . . Al."

"I'm Angelica," she said. Better you don't know my last name, she thought. "A friend of mine is in that brown van across the street. See it?" She still had her hand under his arm, so she just jerked her chin in the direction of the van. "Our plan is to get out of here, back to a safe place where nobody can find us. I think you should come with us."

"You've got that compass," said the boy grimly. "I've been *in* a 'van,' and I can scream these lungs pretty loud."

"We're not going to kidnap you," said Elizalde.

They shuffled to a rocking halt at the Lucas corner, panting and waiting for the light to turn green. Elizalde was still looking around for pursuit. "I don't even know if my friend would want another person along," she said. She shook her head sharply, wondering if it could even be noon yet. "But I think you should come with us. The compass—anybody in the whole city who knows about this stuff can track you."

The boy nodded. At least he was standing beside her, and hadn't pulled away from her hand. "Yeah," he said. "That is true, sister. And if I put my light back under the bushel basket, if I—*step out of the center-ring spotlight*, here, this kid will collapse like a sack of coal. So you've got a place that's safe? Even for *us*? How are you planning on degaussing me? This damned electric belt's not worth *one* mint."

Hebephrenic schizophrenia? wondered Elizalde; *or one of the dissociative reactions of hysterical neurosis?* MPD would probably be the trendy analysis these days—multiple personality disorder.

She floundered for a response. What had he said? Degaussing? Elizalde had heard that term used in connection with battleships, and she thought it had something to do with radar. "I don't know about that. But my friend does—he's an electrical engineer."

This seemed to make the boy angry. "Oh, an *electrical engineer*! All mathematics, I daresay, equations on paper to match the paper diploma

on his wall! Never any dirt under his fingernails! Maybe he thinks he's
the only one around here with a *college degree*!''

Elizalde blinked down at the boy in bewilderment. ''I—I'm sure he
doesn't—I have a college degree, as a matter of fact—'' Good Lord,
she thought, why am I bragging? Because of my rumpled old clothes
and dirty hair? Bragging to a traumatized street kid? ''But none of that's
important here—''

''B.S.,'' said the boy now, with clear and inexplicable pride. ''Let's
go meet your electrical engineer.''

''Shit, yes,'' said Elizalde. The light turned green, and they started
walking.

CHAPTER 37

"But that's not your fault," the Rose added kindly. *"You're beginning to fade, you know—and then one ca'n't help one's petals getting a little untidy."*
   Alice didn't like this idea at all . . .

—Lewis Carroll,
Through the Looking-Glass

Sullivan had seen Elizalde crossing the street, and when he saw that the reason she was moving slowly was because she was helping a limping *kid* along, he swore and got out of the van.

He had noticed the onset of bar-time as he'd been driving, five or ten minutes ago, when he reflexively tapped the brake in the instant before the nose of a car appreared out of an alley ahead of him; he had then tested it by blindly sliding a random cassette into the tape player, cranking the volume all the way up, and then turning on the player—he had not only cringed involuntarily, but had even recognized the opening of the Stones' "Sympathy for the Devil," just before the first percussive yell had come booming out of the speakers. He had switched the set off then, wondering anxiously what was causing the psychic focus on him, and if it was on Elizalde too.

And now here she was with some kid.

He met them by the traffic-light pole at the corner, and he took the shopping bag from her. "Say goodbye to your little friend," he said. "We've gotta go *now*. Bar-time, you feel it?"

"Yes, I do," she said, smiling. "Other people out here probably do too. Act natural, like you *don't* feel it."

She was right. He smiled stiffly back at her and hefted the bag. "So, did you get your shopping done? All ready to go?"

Two teenage Mexican boys swaggered up to them, one of them muttering, *"Vamos a probar la mosca en leche, porqué no?"* Then one of them asked her, in English, "Lady, can I have a dollar for a pack of cigarettes?"

"*Porqué no?*" echoed Elizalde with a mocking grin. She reached into her pocket with the hand that wasn't supporting the sick-looking boy, and handed over a dollar.

"I need cigarettes too!" piped up the other teenager.

"You can share his," said Elizalde, turning to Sullivan. "We're ready to go," she told him.

We're *not* taking this sick kid along with us! he thought. "No," he said, still holding his smile but speaking firmly. "Little Billy's got to go home."

"Auntie Alden won't take him today," she said, "and it's getting very late."

Sullivan blew out a breath and let his shoulders sag. He looked at the boy. "I suppose you *do* want to come along."

The boy had a cocky grin on his face. "Sure, plug. On your own, you might get careless and open a switch without turning off the current first."

Sullivan couldn't help frowning. He had spent the morning at an old barn of a shop on Eighth Street called Garmon's Pan-Electronics, and he wondered if this boy knew that, somehow. Was the boy's remark the twang of a snapped trap-wire?

"I told him you're an electrical engineer," said Elizalde in a harried voice. "Let's *go!*"

After a tense, anguished pause: "Okay!" Sullivan said, and turned and began marching his companions back across the liquor-store parking lot toward the van. "The collapsing magnetic field," he told the boy, in answer to the boy's disquieting remark, "will induce a huge voltage that'll arc across the switch, right?" Why, he wondered, am I bothering to prove anything to a kid?

"Don't say it just to please me," the boy told him.

When they had climbed into the van and pulled the doors closed, Sullivan and Elizalde sat up front, and the boy sat in the back on the still-unmade bed.

"Why did you give that guy a buck?" asked Sullivan irritably as he started the engine and yanked the gearshift into drive.

"He might have been Elijah," Elizalde said wearily. "Elijah wanders around the Earth in disguise, you know, asking for help, and if you don't help him you get in trouble at the Last Judgment."

"Yeah?" Sullivan made a fast left turn onto Lucas going south, planning to catch the Harbor Freeway from Bixel off Wilshire. "Well, the *other* guy was probably Elijah, the guy you *didn't* give a buck to. Who's our new friend, by the way?"

"Call me Al," spoke up the boy from the back of the van. "No, my name's Kootie—" The voice sounded scared now. "—where are we going? It's all right, Kootie, you remember how I didn't trust the Fussels? These people are square. I'm glad you're back with us, son. I was worried about you."

Sullivan shot Elizalde a furious glance.

"He's magnetic," she said. She seemed near tears. "Compasses point to him. And I used up my mace spray on a crowd of bad guys who were trying to force him into a truck."

"It's okay," Sullivan said. "That's good, I'm glad you did. I wish I'd been there to help." Good God, he thought. "Did you get some likely . . . groceries?"

"I think so." She sighed deeply. "Did you hear what those two *vatos* said? They described you and me as *la mosca en leche*. That means fly-in-milk—like 'salt-and-pepper,' you know, a mixed-race couple. They thought I was a Mexican."

Sullivan glanced at her. "You *are* a Mexican."

"I know. But it's nice that they could tell. How did you do, did you get some good electronic stuff?"

Sullivan was looking into the driver's mirror on the outside of the door. A new Lincoln had sped up to make the light at Beverly, and it was now swerving into the right lane as if to pass him. He was glad of the distraction, for he didn't want to talk about the ragtag equipment he'd bought.

"Not bad," he said absently, "considering I didn't know what I wanted." When the Lincoln was alongside, Sullivan pressed the brake firmly, and the big car shot ahead. "They had some old carborundum-element bulbs there cheap, so I bought a few, and I got an old Ford coil for fifty bucks, and a Langmuir gauge." He made a show of peering ahead with concern.

But the Lincoln ahead had actually *slowed*, and now another one just like it was speeding up from behind. "Other stuff," he added—nearly in a whisper, for something really did seem to be going on here. His palms were suddenly damp on the wheel.

There was a cross street to the right ahead, and he waited until the last instant to touch the brake and whip the wheel around to cut directly across the right-hand lane; the tires were screeching, and a bar-time jolt of vertigo made him open the sharp turn a little wider before the van could roll over, and then he had stamped the gas pedal and they were roaring down the old residential street.

A glance in the mirror showed him the second Lincoln coming up fast behind him. He could hear the roar of the car's engine.

"Bad guys," he said breathlessly. "Fasten your belts—kid, get down somewhere. I'm gonna try to outrun 'em. They want us alive."

The other Lincoln had somehow looped back, and was now rushing up behind the nearer one, which was swerving to pass Sullivan on the left. Sullivan jerked the wheel that way to cut the car off, and he kept his foot hard on the gas pedal.

A loud, rapid popping began, and the van shuddered and rang and shook as splinters whined around the seats. Sullivan snatched his foot off the gas and stomped the brake; Elizalde tumbled against the dashboard as the front end dropped and the tires screamed, and then as the van slewed and ground to a halt, and rocked back, he slammed it into reverse and gave it full throttle again.

The closer Lincoln had driven up a curb and run over a trash can. Sullivan had to hunch around to watch the other one through the narrow frames of the back windows, for the door mirror had been blown out; the van's rear end was whipping wildly back and forth as Sullivan fought the wheel, and he heard five or six more shots, but then the second Lincoln too had driven up onto a lawn to get out of Sullivan's lunatic way, and the van surged back-end foremost right out into the middle of Lucas Avenue.

A hard, smashing impact punched the van, and as Sullivan's chin clunked the top of the seat back he heard two more crashes a little farther away. The van was stalled, and he clanked it into neutral and cranked at the starter. Feathers were flying around the stove and the bed in the back, where he had last seen the kid. At last the engine caught.

Sullivan threw the shift into Drive again and turned around to face out the starred windshield, and he hit the gas and the van sped away down Lucas with only a diminishing clatter of glass and metal in its wake.

Sullivan drove quickly but with desperate concentration, yanking the wheel back and forth to pass cars, and pushing his way through red lights while looking frantically back and forth and leaning on the horn.

When he was sure that he had at least momentarily lost any pursuit, he took a right turn, and then an immediate left into a service alley behind a row of street-facing stores. There was an empty parking space between two trucks, but his sweaty hands were trembling so badly that he had to back and fill for a full minute before he had got the vehicle into the space and pushed the gearshift lever into park.

"Kid," Sullivan croaked, too shaky even to turn around, "are you all right?" His mouth was dry and tasted like old pennies.

In the sudden quiet, over the low rumble of the idling engine, he could now hear the boy sobbing; but the boy's voice strangled the sobs long enough to choke out, "No worse than I was before."

" '*They want us alive,*' " said Elizalde from where she was crumpled under the dashboard. She climbed back up into the seat and shook glass out of her disordered black hair. "I'm glad you've got these guys figured out, you asshole."

"Are you hit?" Sullivan asked her, his voice pitched too high. "They were shooting at us. Am *I* hit?" He spread his hands and looked down at himself, then shuffled his feet around to see them. He didn't see any blood, or feel any particular pain or numbness anywhere.

"No," said Elizalde after looking herself over. "What do we do now?"

"You—you left your jumpsuit in Solville. Get a jacket of mine from the closet in the back, and a T-shirt or something for the kid. Disguises. I got a baseball cap back there you can tuck your hair up into. You two take a bus back, you'll look like a mother and son. I'll drive the van, and—I don't know, take backstreets or something. I think I'll be out of trouble once I get on the freeway, but you'd be safer traveling in something besides this van."

"Why don't we all take the bus?" asked Elizalde. "Abandon the van?"

"He'd have to abandon the stuff he bought," said the boy, who was still sniffling, "and a couple of these things aren't useless rubbish."

"Thanks, sonny," said Sullivan, not happy that the kid had been examining his purchases. Then, to Elizalde, he said, "Oh—here." He unsnapped the fanny-pack belt and pulled it free of his waist. "Have you ever shot a .45?"

"No. I don't believe in guns."

"Oh, they do exist, trust me." He pulled the loop and the zippers sprang open, exposing the grip of the pistol under two straps. "See? Here's one now."

"I saw it last night, remember? I *meant* I don't *like* them."

"Oh, *like* them," said Sullivan as he popped the snap on the straps and drew the pistol out of the holster sewed inside the fanny pack. Pointing the pistol at the ceiling, he managed to push the magazine-release button beside the trigger guard, but missed catching the magazine as it slid out of the grip. It clunked on the floorboards and he let it lie there. "*I* don't *like* 'em. I don't *like* dental surgery, either, or motorcycle helmets, or prostate examinations."

He pulled the slide back, and the stubby bullet that had been in the chamber flicked out and bounced off Elizalde's forehead.

"Ow," she said.

"Sorry."

"That's a Colt," said the boy, who had shuffled up behind Sullivan's seat. "Army issue since 1911."

"Right," said Sullivan, peripherally beginning to wonder who the hell this boy was.

The slide was locked back, exposing the shiny barrel, and he tripped the slide release and it snapped forward, hooding the barrel again. He held the gun out toward her, grip first and barrel up, and after a long moment she took it.

"It's unloaded now," he said, "but of course you always assume it is loaded. Go ahead and shoot it through the floor—hold it with both hands. Jesus, not that way! Your thumbs have got to be around the *side*; that slide on the top comes back, hard, and if you've got your thumb over the back of it that way . . . well, you'll have another severed thumb to stick in your shoe."

She rearranged her hands, then pointed the pistol at the floor. Her finger visibly tightened on the trigger for several seconds—and then there was an abrupt, tiny *click* as the hammer snapped down.

Elizalde exhaled sharply.

"Nothing to it, hey?" said Sullivan. "Now, it's got a fair recoil, so get the barrel back down in line with your target before you take your second shot. The gun recocks itself, so all you've got to do is pull the trigger again. And again, if you need to. You'll have seven rounds in the magazine and one in the chamber, eight in all. If you *hit* a guy with one of 'em, you'll knock him down for sure."

She took hold of the slide with her left hand and tried to pull it back as Sullivan had done; she got it halfway back against the compression of the spring, and had to let go.

"Try it again," said Sullivan, "but instead of pulling the slide back with your left hand, just hold it steady, and push the gun forward with your right." He was nervous about having the pistol unloaded for so many seconds, but wanted her to have as much sketchy familiarity with it as might be possible.

This time she managed to cock it, and again dry-fired it at the floor.

"Good." Sullivan retrieved the fallen magazine and slid it up into the grip until it clicked, then jacked a round into the chamber and released the magazine again to tuck into the top of it the bullet that had bounced off Elizalde's forehead. He slid the magazine into the grip again and clicked the safety up.

"Cocked and locked," he said, handing it back to her carefully. "This fan-shaped ridged thing behind the trigger is the safety; pop it down, and then all you've got to do is pull the trigger. Keep it in the fanny pack, under the jacket, and don't let the kid play with it."

Sullivan's chest felt hollow, and he was sweating with misgivings about this. He could have set up the pistol with the chamber empty, but he wasn't confident that she'd be able to work the slide in a panicky second; and he could have left the hammer down, along with the safety engaged, but that would require that she remember two moves, and have the time for them, in that hypothetical panicky second.

"You still got money?" he asked her.

"Three or four of the twenties, and some ones and some change."

"Fine. Grab the clothes and scoot." To his own surprise, his head bobbed forward as if to kiss her; but he caught himself and leaned back.

She blinked. "Right." To the boy, she said, "Is your name Kootie or Al?"

The boy's mouth twitched, but finally he said, "Kootie."

"All right, Kootie, let's outfit ourselves and then get the hell out of here."

In the dim living room of Joey Webb's motel room off Grand Boulevard in Venice, Loretta deLarava sat on the bed and blotted her tears with a silk handkerchief. Obstadt's man Canov had put her on hold, and she had been sitting here now for *ten minutes* it seemed like, and the room reeked because Joey Webb, suspicious in an unfamiliar environment, had resumed his old precaution of hiding half-eaten Big Macs and Egg McMuffins behind the furniture.

"Hello, Loretta," said Obstadt at last. His voice was echoing and weak.

"Neal, I *know* about it, so don't even waste a moment with lies. Why are you trying to impede me? You had your people try to *kill* Sullivan and the Parganas boy an hour ago! You should thank God that they got away. Now I want you to help me find them—and they'd better not be dead!—or I'll call the police about the incident. I want, immediately, all the information you have—"

Obstadt inhaled loudly, and coughed. "Shut up, Loretta."

"You can't tell *me* to shut up! I can call spirits from the vasty deep—"

"Me too, babe, but do they come when you call? Face it, Loretta, nobody gives the least particle of a rat's ass about your . . . *magical prowess.*"

Over the line she heard a familiar metallic splashing. The man was urinating! He had *begun* urinating during the conversation! He was going on in his new, labored voice: "You work for me, now, Miss Keith— sorry, Mrs. Sullivan—oh hell, I guess I know you well enough to just call you *Kelley*, don't I?"

DeLarava just sat perfectly still, her damp handkerchief in front of her eyes.

"I know you're busy tomorrow," Obstadt said, "so I'll drive down and say . . . 'Hi!' . . . at your ghost shoot on the *Queen Mary.* I need to quiz you about a problem that can arise in this ghost-eating business. And you'll tell me everything you know.''

The line went dead. Slowly she lowered the phone back down onto the cradle. Then her hands flew to her temples and pressed inward, helping the rubber bands constrict her skull and keep the pieces of her mind from flying away like a flock of baby chicks when the shadow of the hawk was sweeping the ground.

"The egged van was at the canals yesterday,'' remarked Webb, who was sitting cross-legged on top of the TV set.

She dragged her attention away from the stark fact that her false identity had been blown. (If Obstadt talked, and Nicky Bradshaw stepped forward and talked, she could conceivably be arraigned for murder; and, even worse, everyone would see through the deLarava personality to the fragmented fraud that was Kelley Keith; and even if Obstadt told no one, *he* knew, *he* could—intolerably—see it.)

"The van,'' she said dully; then she blinked. "The *egged* van, Pete's van! You didn't call me? He was *here in Venice*? What was he doing?''

"Relax, ma'am! He wasn't here. He must have loaned the van to a friend. This was a curly-haired shorter guy in a fancy coat with breakaway sleeves.''

"Breakaway sleeves . . . ? Oh, Jesus, that was *Houdini* you saw! It was Sullivan wearing *my* goddamn *Houdini* mask!''

"That was Pete Sullivan? This guy didn't look anything like your pictures of him.'' Webb frowned in thought. "Not at first, anyway. He did get taller.''

"Damn it, it was him, trust me. What was he doing?''

"Oh. Oh, chatting up a bird. A-sparkin' and a-spoonin', I'm assumin'. Mex gal. She got taller too, after a while. She was trying to reason with a guy who was in love with her, a sulking man hiding in a drainage pipe. But when Neat Pete showed up with his joke dinner jacket and fine white hands, she decided to chat with him instead. They stood in a parking lot that was in a traffic whirlpool, so I couldn't intuit what they said. Dig this—there was a Venice Farmer's Market in that very parking lot this morning! I bought various vegetable items. I will cook a *ratatouille*.''

"Shut up, Joey, I'm trying to think.'' Who on earth, she wondered, could this "Mex gal'' be? Not just someone he met by chance, if the two of them took the precaution of talking in an eye of traffic. And the mask seems to have covered her too, giving her the appearance of some other person, which undoubtedly would have been Houdini's wife, Bess! *(What a mask!)* (May thieving Sukie Sullivan's ghost be snorted up by a shit-eating rat!) Was Pete in Venice looking for his father's ghost? Did he *find* Apie's ghost? What—

"Ratatouille," said Webb, "is an eggplant-based vegetable medley. I tried to write MISTER ELEGANT once on a T-shirt, and it was days before I realized that I'd got it wrong, and I'd been walking around labeled MISTER EGGPLANT."

"Shut *up,* Joey." The Parganas kid, she thought, and Pete, and the "Mex gal," will be running scared now, keeping low; but maybe I can still get a line on Nicky Bradshaw. I'll have to check my answering machine, see if there have been any Find Spooky calls.

*And and and—*Obstadt's coming to the shoot on the *Queen Mary* tomorrow. He wants to know about some "problem that can arise with this ghost-eating business." (How vulgar of him to speak plainly about it!) I'll have to watch for a weakness in him, and be ready to assert myself. There'll be high voltage, and steep companionways—and the whole damned ocean, right over any rail.

"You don't seem to be *getting ahold* of anybody, do you?" Webb said, smiling and shaking his head.

"Joey, *shut* the fuck *up* and get *out* of my stinking *face,* will you?" She levered her bulk off of the bed and swung herself toward the door of the motel room. "Keep looking for *Arthur Patrick* Sullivan. He's got to be here, or be coming ashore in the next twelve hours—you haven't left this area, and you'd have sensed him if he was *awake* anywhere within several blocks of here, wouldn't you?"

"Like American Bandstand." Webb hopped down from atop the TV set, agile as an old monkey. "He can't have got past the walls of my awareness," he said, nodding mechanically. "Unless someone opened the gate to a Trojan horse. A Trojan sea horse, that would be, locally."

"A Trojan . . . sea horse." Her face was suddenly cold, and a moment later the marrow in her ribs tingled.

"Oh my God that *fish,* that goddamn *fish!*" she whispered. "Could Apie have been hiding inside that fish?" *I am in control of nothing at all,* she thought dazedly.

Webb gave her a look that momentarily seemed lucid. "If so, he's gone."

"If so," she said, pressing her temples again, "he's in L.A. somewhere." She was panting, clutching at straws. "He'll probably try to find Pete."

"Oh well then," said Webb with a shrug and a grin. "Find one and you've found them both, right? It's that simple!"

"That simple," echoed deLarava, still panting. Tears were spilling down her shaking cheeks again, and she blundered out the door.

CHAPTER 38

"What else had you to learn?"
"Well, there was Mystery," the Mock Turtle replied, *counting off the subjects on his flappers,—"Mystery, ancient and modern, with Seaography..."*
—Lewis Carroll,
Alice's Adventures in Wonderland

Sullivan had parked the van in the shade under one of the shaggy carob trees at the back of the Solville parking lot, and then he had got out and looked the old vehicle over.

The back end was a wreck. The right rear corner of the body, from the smashed taillights down, was crumpled sharply inward and streaked and flecked with blue paint. Apparently it had been a blue car that had hit them when he had reversed out onto Lucas. The doors were still folded-looking and flecked with white from having hit Buddy Schenk's Honda in the Miceli's lot yesterday, and the bumper, diagonal now, looked like a huge spoon that had been mauled in a garbage disposal.

In addition to all this, he could see four little-finger-sized holes in and around the back doors, ringed with bright metal where the paint had been blown off.

Forcing open the left-side back door, he had found that the little propane refrigerator had stopped two 9-millimeter slugs, and he had disconnected the appliance and laid the beer and Cokes and sandwich supplies out on the grass to carry in to the apartment; the sink cabinet had a hole punched through it and the sink itself was dented; and a solid ricochet off of the chassis of the field frequency modulator he'd just bought had ripped open one of his pillows, the deformed slug ending up shallowly embedded in the low headboard. One of the back-door windows was holed, and the slug had apparently passed through the interior of the van and exited through the windshield; and one perfectly round, deep dent in the back fender might have been put there by a bullet. And of course the driver's-side mirror was now a half-dozen fragments dangling from some kind of rubber gasket.

These were the extent of the damage, and he shivered with queasy gratitude when he thought of the boy having been crouched on the van floor in the middle of the fusillade, and of Elizalde's head nearly having been in the way of the one that had punched through the windshield. They had been lucky.

Sullivan had made several trips to the apartment to stack his electronic gear in a corner with Elizalde's bag of witch fetishes beside it, and put the drinks and the sandwich things into the refrigerator. Finally he had locked the van up and covered the whole vehicle with an unfolded old rust-stained parachute, trying to drape it as neatly as he could in anticipation of Mr. Shadroe's probable disapproval.

Now he was sitting on a yellow fire hydrant out by the curb across Twenty-first Place, holding one of Houdini's plaster hands and watching the corner of Ocean Boulevard. There was a bus stop at Cherry, just around the corner. Clouds like chunks of broken concrete were shifting across the sky, and the tone of his thoughts changed with the alternating light and shade.

In shadow: They've been caught, Houdini's thumb can't deflect the attention the boy was drawing; they're being tortured, disloyal Angelica is leading bad guys here, I should be farther away from the building so I can hide when I see the terrible Lincolns turn onto Twenty-first Place.

In sunlight: Buses take forever, what with transfers and all, and Angelica is a godsend, how nice to have such challenging and intelligent company if you've got to be in a mess like this, even if this séance attempt *doesn't* work; and even the kid, Shake Booty or whatever his name is, is probably going to turn out to be interesting.

It's been an hour just since I came to sit out here, he thought finally—and then he heard a deliberate scuffing on the sidewalk behind him.

His first thought as he hopped off the hydrant and turned around was that he didn't have his gun—but it was Elizalde and the boy who were walking toward him from the cul-de-sac at the seaward end of Twenty-first. The boy was carrying a big white bag with KFC in red on the side of it.

"You stopped for food?" Sullivan demanded, glancing around even as he stepped forward; he had meant it to sound angry, but he found that he was laughing, and he hugged Elizalde. She returned the hug at first, but then pulled away.

"Sorry," he said, stepping back himself.

"It's not you," she said. "Just use your left arm."

He clasped his left arm around her shoulders and pulled her close to himself, her head under his chin.

When they turned to walk across the street to the old apartment building, she nodded toward the white plaster hand that Sullivan was holding in his right hand. "I just don't like strangers' hands on me," she said.

"I don't like people with the wrong number of hands," said the boy.

Sullivan looked dubiously at the boy, and then at the Kentucky Fried Chicken bag the boy was carrying, and he tried to think of some pun about *finger-lickin' good*; he couldn't, and made do with saying, "Let's get in out of the rain," though of course it wasn't raining.

When they had got inside the apartment and dead-bolted the door and propped the Houdini hands against it, the boy set the bag on the painted wooden floor and said, "Has either of you two got any medical experience?"

"I'm a doctor," said Elizalde cautiously. "A real one, an M.D."

"Excellent." The boy shrugged carefully out of his torn denim jacket and began stiffly pulling his filthy polo shirt off over his head.

Sullivan raised his eyebrows and glanced at Elizalde. Under the shirt, against his skin, the boy was wearing some kind of belt made of wire cables, with a glowing light at the front.

"What are your names?" came his voice from inside the shirt.

Sullivan was grinning and frowning at the same time. "Peter Sullivan, Your Honor," he said, sitting down in the corner beside his boxes. He had opened all the windows when he had carried the things in here earlier, but the heat was still turned on full, and the air above about shoulder height was wiltingly hot.

"Angelica Elizalde."

"This kid is—I'm called Koot Hoomie Parganas." The boy had got the shirt off, and Sullivan could see a bloodstained bandage taped over his ribs on the right side, just above the grotesque belt. "A man cut us with a knife yesterday afternoon. We treated it with high-proof rum, and it doesn't seem to be infected, but the bleeding won't quite stop."

Elizalde knelt in front of him and pulled back the edge of the bandage—the boy's mouth tightened, but he stood still.

"Well," said Elizalde in a voice that sounded irritated, even embarrassed, "you ought to have had some stitches. Too late now, you'll have a dueling scar. But it looks clean enough. We should use something besides liquor to prevent infection, though."

"Well, fix it right," Koot Hoomie said. "This is a good little fellow, my boy is, and he's been put through a lot."

" 'Fix it right,' " echoed Elizalde, still on her knees beside the boy.

She sighed. "Fix it right." After a pause she shot a hostile glance at Sullivan, and then said, "Peter, would you fetch me a—damn it, an unbroken egg from my grocery bag?"

Wordlessly Sullivan leaned over from where he was sitting and hooked the bag closer to himself, dug around among the herb packets and oil bottles until he found the opened carton of eggs, and lifted one out. He got to his hands and knees to hand it across to her, then sat back down.

"Thank you. Lie down on the floor, please, Kootie."

Kootie sat down on the wooden floor and then gingerly stretched out on his back. "Should I take off the belt?"

"What's it for?" asked Sullivan quietly.

"Degaussing," said Elizalde.

"No," said Sullivan. "Leave it on."

Elizalde leaned over the boy and rolled the egg gently over his stomach, around the wound and over the bandage, and in a soft voice she recited, *"Sana, sana, cola de rana, tira un pedito para ahora y mañana."* She spoke the words with fastidious precision, like a society hostess picking up fouled ashtrays.

Sullivan shifted uneasily and pushed away the bullet-dented field frequency modulator so that he could lean back against the wall. "You're sure this isn't a job for an emergency room?"

Elizalde gave him an opaque stare. *"La cura es peor que la enfermedad*—the cure would be worse than the injury, he wouldn't be safe half an hour in any kind of public hospital. Kootie is staying with us. *Donde comen dos, comen tres."*

Sullivan was able to work out that that one meant something like "Three can live as cheaply as two." He thought it was a bad idea, but he shrugged and struggled to his feet, up into the hot air layer, and walked into the open kitchen.

"There you go, Kootie," he heard Elizalde say. "You can get up now. We'll bury the egg outside, after the sun goes down."

Elizalde and the boy were both standing again, and Kootie was experimentally stretching his right arm and wincing.

"Voodoo," said the boy gruffly. "As useless as the hodgepodge of old radio parts Petey bought."

Sullivan turned away to open the refrigerator. "Kootie," he said, pulling a Coors Light out of the depleted twelve-pack carton, "I notice that you refer to yourself in the first person singular, the third person, and the first person plural. Is there a—" He popped the tab and took a deep sip of the beer, raising his eyebrows at the boy over the top of the can. "—reason for that?"

"That's beer, isn't it?" said Kootie, pressing his side and wincing. "Which costs a dollar a can? Aren't you going to offer any to the lady and me?"

"Angelica," said Sullivan, "would you like a beer?"

"Just a Coke, please," she said.

"A Coke for you too, sonny," Sullivan told Kootie, turning back toward the refrigerator. "You're too young for beer."

"I'll start to answer your question," said Kootie sternly, "by telling you that one of us is eighty-four years old."

Sullivan had put down his beer and taken out two cans of Coke. "Well it's not me, and it's not you, and I doubt if it's Angelica. Anyway, you can't divvy it up among people socialistically that way. You gotta accumulate the age yourself."

Kootie slapped his bare chest and grinned at him. "I *meant* one of *us*. First person plural."

A knock sounded at the door then, and all three of them jumped. Sullivan had dropped the cans and spun toward the door, but he looked back toward Elizalde when he heard the fast *snap-clank* of the .45 being chambered. An ejected bullet clicked off the wall, for she hadn't needed to cock it, but it was ready to fire and her thumbs were out of the way of the slide.

He sidled to the window, ready to drop to the floor to give her a clear field of fire, and pushed down one slat of the venetian blinds.

And he sighed, sagging with relief. "It's just the landlord," he whispered, for the window beyond the blinds was open. He wondered if Shadroe had heard the gun being chambered.

Elizalde engaged the safety before shoving the gun back into the fanny-pack holster and zipping it shut.

Sullivan unbolted the door and pulled it open. Gray-haired old Shadroe pushed his way inside even as Sullivan was saying, "Sorry, I'm having some friends over right now—"

"I'm a friend," Shadroe said grimly. He was wearing no shirt, and his vast suntanned belly overhung his stovepipe-legged shorts. His squinty eyes took in Elizalde and Kootie, and then fixed on Sullivan. "Your name's *Peter Sullivan*," he said, slowly, as if he meant to help Sullivan learn the syllables by heart. "It was on the . . . rental agreement."

"Yes."

"It's a common enough name—" Shadroe paused to inhale. "Wouldn't you have thought so yourself?"

"Yes . . . ?" said Sullivan, mystified.

"Well, not today. I'm your godbrother."

Sullivan wondered how far away the nearest liquor store might be. "I suppose so, Mr. Shadroe, but you and I are going to have to discuss God and brotherhood later, okay? Right now I'm—"

Shadroe pointed one grimy finger at the also-shirtless Kootie. "It's him, isn't it? My pigs were—starting to *smoke*. I had to pull the batteries out of 'em—and I sent my honey pie to my boat—to take the batteries out of the pigs aboard there. Burn the boat down, otherwise." He turned an angrily earnest gaze on Sullivan. "I want you all," he said. "To come to my office, and see. What your boy has done to my television set."

Sullivan was shaking his head, exhaustion and impatience propelling him toward something like panic. Shadroe reeked of cinnamon again, and his upper lip was dusted with brown powder, as if he'd been snorting Nestle's Quik, and Sullivan wondered if the crazy old man would even hear anything he might say.

"The boy hasn't been out of this room," Sullivan said loudly and with exaggerated patience. "Whatever's wrong with your TV—"

"Is it 'godbrother'?" Shadroe interrupted. "What I mean is, your *father*." Sullivan coughed in disgust and tried to think of the words to convince Shadroe that Sullivan was not his son, but the old man raised his hand for silence. "Was my *godfather*," he went on, completing his sentence. "My real name is Nicholas Bradshaw. Loretta deLarava is after my. Ass."

Sullivan realized that he had been almost writhing with insulted impatience, and that he was now absolutely still. "Oh," he said into the silence of the room. "Really?" He studied the old man's battered, pouchy face, and with a chill realized that this *could* very well be Nicholas Bradshaw. "Jesus. Uh . . . how've you been?"

"Not so good," said Bradshaw heavily. "I died in 1975."

The statement rocked Sullivan, who had not even been completely convinced that the man *was* dead, and in any case had only been supposing that he'd been dead for a year or two at the most.

"*Amanita phalloides* mushrooms," Bradshaw said, "in a salad I ate. You have bad abdominal seizures twelve . . . hours after you eat it. Phalloidin, one of the several poisons. In the mushrooms. And then you feel fine for a week or two. DeLarava called me during the week. Couldn't help gloating. It was too late by then—for me to do anything. *Alphaamanitine* already at work. So I got all my money in cash, and hid it. And then I got very drunk, on my boat. Very drunk. Tore up six telephones, ate the magnets—to keep my ghost in. And I climbed into the refrigerator." His stressful breathing was filling the hot living room with the smell of cinnamon and old garbage. "A week later, I climbed out—dead, but still up and walking."

Elizalde walked to the kitchen counter, put down the egg, and picked up Sullivan's beer. After she had tipped it to her lips and drained it, she dropped the can to clang on the floor, and held out her right hand. "I'm Angelica Anthem Elizalde," she said. "The *police* are after *my* ass."

Shadroe shook her hand, grinning squintingly at Sullivan. "I'm gonna steal your *señori*ter, Peter," he said, his solemnity apparently forgotten. "What are you people doing here? Hiding here? I won't have that. You'll lead deLarava and the police to me and my honey pie." He was still smiling, still shaking Elizalde's hand. "Your van is an eyesore, even under the parachute. I can't understand people who have no pride at all."

Sullivan blinked at the man's random-fire style, but gathered that he was on the verge of being evicted. He tried to remember Nicky Bradshaw, who had been a sort of remote older cousin when Pete and Elizabeth had been growing up. Their father had always seemed to like Nicky, and of course had got him the Spooky part in "Ghost of a Chance."

"Listen to me, Nicky, we're going to try to build an apparatus, set up a séance, to talk to dead people, to ghosts," he said quickly. "To get *specific* ones, *clearly*, not the whole jabbering crowd. I want to talk to my father, to warn him that deLarava is devoting all her resources to finding him and eating him, tomorrow, on Halloween."

And then an idea burst into Sullivan's head, and suddenly he thought the séance scheme might work after all. "*You* should be the one to talk to him, Nicky, to warn him—he always liked you!" Sullivan's heart was still pounding. I might need to buy another part or two, he thought excitedly. This changes everything.

"You should talk to him yourself, Peter," said Elizalde, who was standing beside him.

"No no," Sullivan said eagerly, "the main thing here isn't what I'd prefer, it's what will work! This is a huge stroke of luck! He'll listen to Nicky more seriously than he'd listen to me, Nicky's twelve years older than I am. Aren't you, Nicky? He always took you seriously."

Bradshaw just stared at him, looking in fact a hundred years old these days. "I'd like to talk to him," he said. "But you should be the one—to warn him. You're his son."

"And he's your father," Elizalde said.

Sullivan didn't look at her. "That's not the *point* here," he snapped impatiently, "what *matters*—"

"And," Elizalde went on, almost gently, "Nicky presumably isn't linked to your father by a consuming guilt, the way you clearly are."

"You're the antenna," agreed Kootie. "The variable capacitor that's fused at the right frequency adjustment."

Sullivan clenched his fists, and he could feel his face getting red. "But the machinery *won't work* if it's—"

For a moment no one spoke, and the only sound was a faint fizzing from one of the cans of Coke that he'd dropped when Bradshaw had knocked on the door. Sullivan's forehead was misted with sweat. *You're not Speedy Alka-Seltzer*, he thought, *you won't dissolve.*

"You weren't going to do it," said Elizalde, smiling. "You were going to go through the motions, set it all up so plausibly that nobody, certainly not *yourself*, could accuse you of not having done your best. But there was going to be some factor that you were going to forget, something no one could blame you for not having thought of."

Sullivan's chest was hollow with dismayed wonderment. "A condensing lens," he said softly.

"A condensing lens?" said Kootie. "Like in a movie projector, between the carbon arc and the aperture?"

Sullivan ignored him.

Without a condensing lens set up between the Langmuir gauge and the brush discharge in the carborundum bulb, the signal couldn't possibly be picked up by the quartz filament inside the gauge.

But wouldn't he have *thought* of that, as soon as he saw the weakness and dispersion of the flickering blue brush sparks in the bulb? Even if Elizalde hadn't said what she had just said?

In this moment of unprepared insight, while his bones shivered with an icy chill in spite of the hot air and the sweat on his face, he was bleakly sure he would *not* have thought of it, or would at least have contrived to set the lens up incorrectly.

He wouldn't be able to do it wrong now, now that he was aware of the temptation.

But maybe it *still* won't work! The thought was almost a prayer.

Kootie limped forward and held his right hand up to Bradshaw. "Pleased to meet you, Mr. Bradshaw," he said. "I'm two people at the moment—one of 'em is known as Kootie—"

"That's an I-ON-A-CO belt you got on," said Bradshaw, shaking the boy's hand. "They don't work. You got it from Wilshire?"

"We *were* on Wilshire," said the boy in a surprised tone, and it occurred to Sullivan that this was the first time the voice had really sounded like a little boy's. "Right by MacArthur Park!"

"I meant H. Gaylord Wilshire himself," said Bradshaw. "That was his original tract. From Park View to Benton, and Sixth down to Seventh. My godfather bought one of those fool belts. From him, in the twenties. What's old man Wilshire like, these days?''

''Insubstantial,'' said the boy, and his voice was controlled and hard again. ''But I didn't get to introduce my other self.'' He looked around at the other three people in the room. ''I'm Thomas Alva Edison,'' he said, ''and I promise you *I* can get your ghost telephone working, even if Petey here can't.''

Sullivan was relieved that everyone was staring at the boy now, and he went back to the refrigerator and took the second-last beer and popped it open. I shouldn't have said *condensing lens*, he thought bitterly. I should have blinked at her in surprise, and then acted insulted. *Edison.* I'm *sure*. No doubt the kid *is* a ghost, or has one on him, but I'll bet every ghost that knows anything about electricity claims to have been Thomas Edison.

''Cart all your crap to my office,'' said Bradshaw wearily. ''You can set up your gizmo there. It's the most masked room in this whole masked block. Electric every which way, water running uphill and roundabout—even hologram pictures in a saltwater aquarium under black light. And bring your bag of fried chicken, Mr. Edison—Johanna loves that stuff. Did you get Original Recipe—or the new crunchy stuff?''

''Original Recipe,'' said Elizalde over her shoulder as she stepped past Sullivan and opened the refrigerator.

''Good,'' said Bradshaw. ''That's what she likes. I hope you brought enough.''

An hour later Sullivan was sitting cross-legged on the dusty rug in Bradshaw's dim office, staring idly at the featureless white glow of the old man's TV screen and gnawing a cold chicken wing.

Bradshaw's ''honey pie,'' a heavy young woman in tight leotards and a baggy wool sweater, had burst in shortly after they'd carried all the supplies to the office, and after the introductions *(Johanna, this is Thomas Edison—Mr. Edison, my honey pie Johanna)* she had told Bradshaw that ''the pigs on the boat were just burping, not smoking yet.''

After that, Johanna and Elizalde had gone out again in Bradshaw's car to buy supplies—bandages, hydrogen peroxide, a secondhand portable movie projector, a pint of tequila for Elizalde, more beer and more Kentucky Fried Chicken, and a box of sidewalk chalk, which Kootie had insisted on.

When they had got back Elizalde had cleaned the cut in Kootie's side and secured it with the bandages and put on a more expert-looking dressing, and then they had torn open the KFC bags.

The chicken was now gone, and Sullivan had had several of the beers.

He tossed the chicken bone onto his newspaper place mat and took a sip of his latest beer. "Angelica," he said, "could you pass me that muffin?"

Elizalde looked at him coldly. "Why do you call it a *muffin*?"

He stared back at her. "Well, it's . . . a little round thing made out of dough."

"So's your head, but I don't call *it* a *muffin*. This is a *roll*." She picked it up and leaned across the newspapers to hold it out. "Don't get drunk for this," she added.

"Keep the roll," he said. "I had my heart set on a muffin."

"I wish *I* could get drunk," said Bradshaw grumpily. He had crunched up a succession of red cinnamon balls as the others had passed around the chicken and mashed potatoes and gravy, and now he poured himself another glass of whatever it was that he was drinking—some red fluid that also reeked of cinnamon. "My pigs and TV are useless while Mr. Edison's here."

Sullivan had decided not to ask about the smoking pigs, but he waved his beer at the white-glowing television. "What're you watching?"

"Channel Two," said Bradshaw, "CBS, my old alma mater."

"I'll bet I could mess with it and get you a better picture." Sullivan felt tightly tensed, as if any move he made would break something in the cluttered office.

"It's not on for the picture," wheezed Bradshaw. "Ghosts are an electrical brouhaha in the fifty-five-megahertz range—and Channel Two is the—closest channel to that. The brightness control on that set is—turned all the way to black, right now—believe it or not."

"That's awfully shortwave," commented the boy who claimed to be Edison.

"You're a shortwave critter," Bradshaw said. "And a damn big one. Even if you were a dozen miles away—you'd still show up on the screen here as a—white band. But standing here you're hogging the whole show. We could have the ghost of—goddamn Godzilla standing right outside, and I wouldn't have a clue."

"Don't you people have a telephone to build?" asked Elizalde.

Sullivan looked irritably across the newspapers at her—but then with a flush of sympathy he realized that she was as tense as he was. He remembered how she had bravely pretended to be eager to go witch-craft-shopping this morning, when he had been ready to sit holed up in the apartment all weekend; and for a moment, before he sighed and got to his feet, he felt a flicker of pitying love for her, and of disgust with himself.

"Yeah," he said. "Household current should be enough—I bought a train-set transformer, and there's the Ford coil."

Elizalde had got up too, and was lifting candles and herb packets and tiny bottles of oil out of her shopping bag.

"What did you have in mind?" asked Kootie, who was sitting crouched like a bird up on the back of the old couch. "Let's be speedy, it's less than twelve hours to midnight, and I want to be clathrated damn deep, out of range of any magnets, when church bells are ringing the first strokes of Halloween."

"You're not Speedy Alka-Seltzer, you won't dissolve! I'll race you into the water!" It had been a man's voice that had said it, calling happily. Sullivan remembered the two Coke cans he had dropped on the floor back in the apartment, and he didn't want to remember whose voice it had been that had said, *"I'll race you into the water!"*

"A bulb with a carborundum button instead of a filament," he said loudly, "charged, with the eventual brush of electric discharge . . . focused through a goddamn *condensing lens* . . . onto the quartz filament, which we'll blacken with soot, inside a Langmuir gauge. It'll work like the vanes in a radiometer, wiggle in response to the light coming through the lens. We can break a thermometer to get a drop of mercury to put in the gauge, and then we can evacuate it to a good enough rarefication with a hose connected to the sink faucet. . . ."

But the twins had been feeling nauseated ever since eating the potato salad at lunch, and were queasy even at the smell of the Coppertone lotion, and they had decided to stay out of the surf and just lie on the towels, on the solid bumpy mattress of the sand.

Kootie had been listening as Sullivan had been describing his proposed device, and he now interrupted: "You don't want a magnet in the receiver. This is such a sensitive thing you're talking about that an actual *magnet* in the same room would draw the voices of all the ghosts in Los Angeles. We'll have enough trouble with fields caused by the changing electrical charges. Use chalk, I had the ladies buy some." He paused, and then said, "We still have some of the Miraculous Insecticide Chalk, Mr Edison. That won't do, Kootie, this has to be round, like a cylinder. Good thought, though."

"Chalk?" asked Sullivan, trying to concentrate.

Their father had shrugged, and his remark about Speedy Alka-Seltzer had hung in the air as he turned away from them, toward the foam-streaked waves, and young Pete had been able to see the frail white hair on the backs of his father's shoulders fluffing in the ocean breeze.

"The friction of a piece of wet chalk varies with changes in its electric charge," Kootie said. "Without a charge it's toothy and has lots of friction, but it's instantly slick when there's a current. . . ."

The three cans of Hires Root Beer were laid out like artillery shells, awaiting their father's return from his swim. There was one for him, and one each for Pete and Elizabeth. Their stepmom had explained that she didn't drink soda pop, so there were only three cans.

". . . A spring connected to the center of the diaphragm," Kootie was saying, drawing with his hands in the stale dim air, "with the other end pressed against the side of the rotating chalk cylinder. The fluctuations in the current from your Ford coil will change the mechanical resistance of the chalk, so the needle will wiggle, you see, as the chalk rapidly changes from slick to scratchy, and the wiggle will be conveyed to the diaphragm."

"It sounds goofy," quavered Sullivan, forcing himself to pay attention to what Kootie was saying, and not to the intrusive, unstoppable, intolerably resurrected memory.

"It works," said Kootie flatly. "A young man named George Bernard Shaw happened to be working for me in London in '79, and maybe you've read his description of my electromotograph receiver in his book *The Irrational Knot.*"

Sullivan shivered, for he was suddenly sure that the ghost this boy carried was, in fact, Thomas Edison. Sullivan's voice was humble as he said, "I'll take your word for it."

But he didn't add, "sir." Aside from police officers, there was only one man he had ever called "sir."

Their stepmother didn't even bother to act very surprised when Pete and Elizabeth screamed at her that their father was in trouble out in the water. The old man had swum out through the waves in his usual briskly athletic Australian crawl, but he was floundering and waving now, way out beyond the surf line, and their stepmother had only got to her feet and shaded her eyes to watch.

". . . and the carborundum bulb should be sensitive enough to pick the ghost up," Sullivan was saying, "and reflect his presence in the brush discharge. He should easily be able to vary it, so it's a *signal* that's going through the lens into the Langmuir viscosity gauge . . ."

Sullivan blinked stinging sweat out of his eyes.

Their stepmother hadn't eaten any of the potato salad, and she seemed to be fine; but she wouldn't even take one step across the dry sand toward the water, and so the twins had gone running down to the surf all by themselves, even though cramps were wringing their stomachs. . . .

Kootie had asked Sullivan a question, and he struggled to remember what it had been. "Oh," he said finally, "right. We'll have primed the quartz filament with a ground vibration, set it ringing by waving a magnet past the little swiveling iron armature in the gauge, and then I guess we get rid of the magnet, outside the building. The quartz starts from a peak tone, and then the vibration will damp down as the quartz loses its initial . . . its initial *ping*. We'll gradually lose volume, but even with the damping radiometer effects of the signal it's getting from the focused light, and from friction with the trace of mercury gas in the gauge, the sustaining vibration should last a good while."

Both of the twins had paused when they were chest deep and wobbling on tiptoe in the cold, surging water. But Elizabeth let the buoyancy take her, and began dog-paddling out toward their distant suffering father; while Pete, frightened of the deep water that was frightening their father, and of the clenching pain in his abdomen, had turned and floundered back toward shore.

"You're the antenna," said Kootie, who was now looking down at him curiously from his perch on the couch back, "but you'll need a homing beacon too, a lure."

And after a while Elizabeth had dragged herself back, exhausted and sick and alone.

"I'm that as well," said Sullivan bleakly. "I'm still his son."

They had not of course opened the three Hires cans, though the twins were destined to glimpse the cans again twenty-seven years later . . . again in Venice.

And Sullivan's face went cold—the memory of Kelley Keith's face blandly observing the drowning of her husband had overlaid memories of deLarava's face, and at long, long last he realized that they were the same woman.

"Nicky!" he said, so unsteadily that Elizalde shot him a look of spontaneous concern. "Loretta deLarava is Kelley Keith!"

"Shoot," said Bradshaw. "I've known that since 1962."

"When we were ten? You could have told us!"

"You'd have wanted to go back to her?"

Sullivan remembered the pretty young face looking speculatively out at the old man drowning beyond the waves. "Jesus, no."

"She killed your father," said Bradshaw. "Just like she killed me. And now she wants to erase both guilts. Both reproaches, both awarenesses. If we're gone, see, it can be not true. For her."

"She, no, he *drowned*, she didn't *kill* him—"

"She fed you and your sister and your father. Poisoned potato salad. All in the golden afternoon."

Kootie bounced impatiently down off the couch, and as he began pacing the floor he picked up Sullivan's pack of Marlboros. Now he shook one out and, with it hanging on his lower lip, slapped his pants pockets. "Somebody got a match?"

"It's the kid's lungs!" protested Elizalde.

"One cigarette?" said Kootie's voice. "I hardly think—It's all right, Mrs. Elizalde, I've smoked Marlboros before. Really? Well, she's right, you shouldn't. Don't let me catch you with one of these in your hand again!" He took the cigarette out of his mouth and put it back in the pack. "You started it, you were working my hands. Don't argue with your elders, the lady was right. I was out of line . . . dammit." He turned a squinting gaze on Sullivan. "I think your plan will work. It's better than mine was, in some ways. I like the carborundum bulb to focus just the one signal—it just *might* eliminate the party-line crowd. Let's get busy."

Bradshaw volunteered to clear off the top of his desk, and soon Kootie and Sullivan were laying out globes and boxes and wires across the scarred mahogany surface. Bradshaw even dragged a couple of old rotary-dial telephones out of a cupboard for them to cannibalize. Twice Sullivan went out to the van, once for tools and once to disconnect and tote back the battery so as to have some solid 12-volt direct current, and at one point, while he was doing some fast, penciled calculations on the desktop, Elizalde stepped up behind him and briefly squeezed his shoulder. She'd been intermittently busy with something in the little added-on kitchen, and the stale cinnamon air in the office was getting sharp with the steamy fumes of mint and hot tequila.

As his fingers and brain followed the inevitable chessboard logic of potentials and resistances and magnetic fields, Sullivan's mind was a ringing ground zero after the detonation of his hitherto-entombed memories, with frightened thoughts darting among the raw, broken ruins of his psyche.

I was there when he drowned! The Christmas shoot in '86 was not *the first time I was ever at Venice Beach—no wonder I kept seeing déjà-vu sunlit overlays of the Venice scene projected onto those gray winter streets and sidewalks. I had* been there *when he drowned on that summer day in '59, and Loretta deLarava is Kelley Keith, our stepmother, and she killed him, she poisoned him and watched my father die! I was there—I watched my father die! At least Sukie tried to swim out and save him—I gave up, ran away, back to the towels.*

O car-bolic faithless, he sang in his head, echoing Sukie's old misremembered Christmas carol.

He was suddenly sure that Sukie had all along remembered some of that day, possibly a lot of it. Her drinking *("What you can't remember can't hurt you"),* her celibacy, and her final feverish attempt to force Pete into bed and have sex with him after he had confronted her with the lies she had told to Judy Nording—even her eventual suicide—must, it seemed to him now as he screwed the Ford coil onto the surface of the desk, have been results of her remembering that day.

By midafternoon the assembly had been wired and screwed down and propped up across the desktop, and the carborundum bulb was plugged in. Edison pointed out that when the evacuated bulb warmed up, the line of its brushy interior discharge would be sensitive to the motion of any person in the room, so they ran wires around the doorway and into Bradshaw's little fluorescent-lit kitchen, and set up the chalk-cylinder speaker assembly on the counter by the sink, with a rewired old telephone on a TV table in the middle of the floor. Sullivan had ceremoniously slid a kitchen chair up in front of it.

Elizalde had made a steaming, eye-watering tea of mint leaves and tequila in a saucepan on the old white-enameled stove, and had turned off the flame when all the liquid had boiled away and the leaves had cooked nearly dry. She and Johanna were standing by the stove, hemmed in by the wires trailing across the worn linoleum floor.

Elizalde's eyes were big and empty when she looked up at Sullivan, and he thought he must look the same way. "When you're ready," she said, "Johanna and I will go light the candles in the other room, and splash the *vente aquí* oil around. Then we should disconnect any smoke alarms, and I'll turn on this stove burner again, high, under this pot of *yerra vuena.* You want to be talking into the smoke from it."

Sullivan had been making sure to take each emptied beer can to the trash before furtively opening the next, so that Elizalde wouldn't be able to count them. *O rum key, O ru-um key to O-bliv-ion,* he sang shrilly in his head.

He took the latest beer into the office, which was very dark now that Bradshaw had unplugged the television set and carried it out to one of the garages, and he pried the can open quietly as he checked the discharge in the carborundum bulb. The bulb had indeed warmed up, and the ghostly blue wisp of electrons was curling against the inside of the glass, silently shifting its position as he moved across the carpet.

"I guess we're ready," he said, sidling back into the bright lit kitchen past Bradshaw, who was standing in the doorway.

CHAPTER 39

"She must be sent as a message by the telegraph—"
—Lewis Carroll,
Through the Looking-Glass

I don't remember the old man's number," Bradshaw said. "We could call the reference desk at a library, from a regular phone, I guess."

"I know the number," said Sullivan.

Running and running, he thought, running with Sukie since 1959, and then running extra fast and alone since 1986. All over the country. To wind up here, now, in this shabby kitchen, staring at a gutted old black bakelite telephone. "It's April Fool's Day, 1898."

He looked at Elizalde. "My father's birthday. That and his full name will be his telephone number." He looked down at the rotary dial on the telephone. The old man would be summoned by dialing April the first, 1898, A-R-T-H-U-R—P-A-T-R-I-C-K—S-U-L-L-I-V-A-N.

Slowly, looking at the rotary dial, he read off, "411898, 2784877287425-78554826."

"A lot of numbers," said Kootie, and Sullivan thought it might actually be the boy talking.

"It's very long distance," he said.

"I remember I always thought God's phone number was Et cum spiri 2-2-oh," said Elizalde nervously. "From the Latin mass, you know? *Et cum spiritu tuo.*"

"You can call Him after I'm done talking to my dad."

"Can magical calls out of here be traced?" asked Bradshaw suddenly.

Kootie cleared his throat. "Sure," he said. The boy was sitting up on the kitchen counter beside the chalk cylinder, which had been mounted on the stripped frame of an electric pencil sharpener; he was pale, and his narrow chest was rising and falling visibly. Sweat was running in shiny lines down over his stomach, and the bandage over his ribs on the right side was spotted with fresh blood. "You've got—what, three? four?—antennas sitting around in this kitchen, and they do broadcast as well as receive."

"Don't worry, Nicky," said Sullivan, "we'll use a scrambler. Angelica, could I have Houdini's thumb?" When she had dug the thing out of her shoe and passed it to him, he laid it on the table beside the telephone. "We can dial with this."

"It would be good if we could make a test call first," Kootie said thoughtfully. "Anybody got any dead people they got to get a message to?"

Visibly tensing before she moved, Elizalde stepped forward away from the stove, placing her sneakers carefully among the looped wires, and sat down in the chair. "There's a guy I took money from," she said steadily, "and I didn't do the work he paid for."

Kootie hopped down from the counter. "You know his number?"

"Yes."

"But you'll need a lure," he said, "remember? A 'homing beacon.' "

She leaned sideways to pull her wallet out of her hip pocket, and then she dug a tattered, folded note out of it. "This is in his handwriting," she said. "His *emotional* handwriting." She looked over at Johanna by the stove. "Could you light the candles and . . . smear the oil over the door lintel, or whatever's required?"

"Better than you, maybe," said Johanna with a merry smile.

Elizalde looked at Sullivan. "Drop the dime."

He was grateful to her for going first. "Okay. Kootie, turn up that fire."

Sullivan stepped past Bradshaw into the dark office, and while Johanna struck matches to the candles on the shelves and shook out the oil and muttered rhymes under her breath, he dug out of his pocket the magnet they had pulled from the old telephone. He crouched beside the upright Langmuir gauge and waved the magnet past the tiny iron armature, and heard the faint contained *ting* as it rocked against the dangling quartz filament. Then he opened the outside door, sprinted out through the glaring sunlight to the covered van and set the magnet down on the asphalt beside it.

Seven seconds later he was back in the kitchen, panting in the hot fumes of cinnamon and mint.

Kootie had connected the modified pencil sharpener, and the speaker was resonating with a flat sound like a sustained exhalation; the mint in the saucepan was steaming and sputtering.

Elizalde took the receiver off the hook, then picked up Houdini's thumb and began dialing the telephone; somehow the speaker behind her made a fluttering sound in synchronization with the rattle of the dial. Belatedly Sullivan realized that privacy would not be possible here, and he took a hasty sip of the beer to cool his heated face.

Elizalde was still dialing numbers into the telephone, but already a whispering voice was rasping out of the speaker.

"Cosa mala nunca muere," it said. *"Me entiendes, Mendez?"*

Sullivan felt moving air on his sweaty scalp at the back of his head, and he realized that his hair was actually standing on end.

"It's the damned crowd effect," said Kootie irritably, "that can't be your man yet." He frowned at Elizalde. "Do you recognize this voice?" Then Kootie's eyes were wide, and he spoke with a scared boy's intonation: *"It's that laughing bag!"*

Elizalde's hand sprang away from the dial, and Houdini's thumb landed in the sink. "Jesus, he's right," she said. "The cloth bag in the truck bed!"

Sullivan didn't know what they were talking about. "What did it just say?"

"It said, a—a bad thing never dies," said Elizalde rapidly, hugging herself, "and then it said, 'You understand?' " She threw Sullivan a frightened look. "Can't I quit this and just go away?"

He spread his hands. "Can't *I?*" he asked, really hoping that she would find some way to say *yes.*

But she was rubbing her eyes with the heels of her hands; and then she said, "Could you bring that thumb back here?"

As Sullivan stepped over to the sink, Bradshaw growled, "Is this somebody you two *(gasp)* tracked in on your shoes?" The mint leaves in the pot on the fire were smoking and popping now.

Kootie shrugged. "It's . . . yes, something, somebody, that was paying attention to me this morning, and it would have seen Mrs. Elizalde."

"Miss," said Elizalde.

"Let a dead guy clear the line for you," Shadroe said. He stumped into the kitchen—carelessly stepping all over the wires, his bare belly swinging ahead of him—and he took the receiver and blew sharply into the mouthpiece. "Hello?" he said. "Hello?" Then he dialed *Operator,* twice.

He set the receiver back down beside the telephone. "Try it now."

Sullivan had fetched the thumb, and handed it to her, and she began shakily dialing again. It took nearly a full minute for her to dial all the

numbers of her man's birth date and full name, but Bradshaw's breath
had apparently chased away any stray ghosts.

At last she was finished dialing, and she hesitantly picked up the
receiver.

A musical buzz sounded from the speaker by the sink; it stopped, and
then began again, stopped, and began again.

"My God," said Sullivan softly. "It's *ringing!*"

"Cultural conditioning," muttered Kootie. "It's what everybody ex-
pects, even the man she's calling."

"Who is that?" came a startled voice from the speaker, and Sullivan
was peripherally impressed with the fidelity of Edison's chalk speaker.

"Frank?" said Elizalde into the mouthpiece. "It's me, it's Angelica."

"Angelica!" The initial surprise in the voice gave way to petulance:
"Angelica, where are you? Who is this old man?"

Sullivan saw Elizalde glance bewilderedly from Bradshaw to Kootie.
"Who do you mean, Frank?"

*"He comes in your clinic every day! He does the séances all wrong,
reading palms of people's hands, and . . .* taking liberties *with the pretty
women!"*

"Oh, that would be—that's not my clinic anymore, Frank, I don't—"

*"I saw you today, from here, from the window. You fell on the curb
when I saw you coming. I live here, and I waved, but you didn't come
in."*

"I'm sorry, Frank, I—"

*"You didn't come in—you don't respect me anymore—you never did
respect me! I didn't speak to you in the sewer, and I shouldn't speak
to you now. You didn't come visit me after I hurt myself in your clinic.
You have other boyfriends now, in your fine house, and you've never
once thought of me."*

Elizalde's face was contorted, but her voice was strong. "Frank,"
she said, "I failed you. I'm sorry. Do you remember why you came to
my clinic, why you were sent there?"

*"Uh . . . well, because I always had to keep checking over and over
again if my shoes were tied and if I locked doors and turned off the
headlights on my car, even in the daytime—and I went to bed and didn't
come out for a month—and I tried to kill myself. And then after I got
out of the hospital they said I should be your outpatient."*

"I failed to help you, and I'm terribly sorry. I haven't had any boyfriends. I've been hiding, running. And every day I've been thinking
about what I did to you, how I let you down, and wishing I could go
back and make it right."

"You can make it right—right now! We can get married, like I said in my note—"

The mint had flared up in the pan. Sullivan took the pan off the fire and clanged the lid onto it for a moment to snuff the flames.

"No, Frank," said Elizalde. "You're dead now. I think you know that, don't you? Things like marriage are behind you now. You didn't *hurt* yourself in my clinic that night, you *killed* yourself. You remember when you went to bed and stayed there for a month—you weren't supposed to *relax* yet, then, it wasn't time for that yet. It's time now. You're dead. Go to sleep, and sleep so deeply that . . . there won't be room or light for any dreams."

For several long seconds the kitchen was silent except for the background hissing of the speaker, and Sullivan saw Kootie glance speculatively at the spinning chalk cylinder.

Then the voice came back. *"I've thought I might be dead,"* it said quietly. *"Are you sure, Angelica?"*

"I am sure. I'm sorry."

"You've thought about me? Been sorry?"

"You've been behind all the thoughts I've had. I came back here to ask you to forgive me."

"Ah." Again there was silence for a few seconds. *"Goodbye, Angelica. Vaya con Dios."*

"Do you forgive me?"

The hissing went on for a full minute before Bradshaw shifted his weight on his feet and cleared his throat; and finally the speaker began making a dull rattle, which ceased when Elizalde reached out and pressed the hang-up button on the telephone cradle.

Sullivan tipped up his can of beer to avoid having to meet anyone's eye, and he could hear Bradshaw's knees creak as he shifted his weight again. The mint smoke was billowing thickly under the low ceiling.

Elizalde pushed back the chair and stood up. "I fucking don't—" she began in a choking voice—

And the musical buzz started up from the speaker by the sink; it stopped, and then started again.

She bent to snatch up the receiver again. "Hello?"

From the chalk-and-pencil-sharpener speaker behind her a cultured man's voice said, *"Could I speak to Don Tay, please?"*

"That's for me," said Kootie, stepping forward and sitting down in the chair. Elizalde mutely handed him the receiver. He cleared his throat. "This is Thomas Edison," he said.

The voice on the speaker exhaled sharply. *"For God's sake, this is an open line! Use elementary caution, will you? My son—"*

"—Is safe," said Kootie. His face was composed, but tears had begun to run down his cheeks. "We've got the line masked and deviled on this end."

"God, and you're speaking physically! *With his voice! What—in hell—did we do?"* Louder now, the voice called, *"Kootie! Can you hear me, boy?"*

Kootie's reddening face relaxed into a grimace and he burst into tears. "I'm here, Dad, but don't yell or—or the speaker might break, we've got it hooked up to a pencil sharpener. Mr. Edison is taking good care of me, don't worry. But Dad! Tell Mom I didn't mean to do it! I'm the one that should be dead! I tried to tell you before, but you were b-both d-d-drunk!" His head was down and his stiff poise was gone, and he was just sobbing.

Elizalde got on her knees beside him and put her arm around his bare narrow shoulders and rocked him gently.

"Boy, boy," said the voice on the speaker shakily, *"we're fragmented here, we blur and break, and some of the pieces you talk to may be minimal. Your mother has gone on ahead, and perhaps has . . . found the white light, who knows? She told me to make you understand that she loves you, and I love you, and you were . . ."*—the voice was still loud, but blurring— *"mot to vlame for what haphened. Ee-bay areful-kay. Isten-lay oo-tay Om-Tay . . ."*

Gradually the hissing background had been becoming textured with clinking and mumbling, and Sullivan thought he heard a voice in the middle distance say, *Te explico, Federico?*

"I love you!—Dad?" said Kootie loudly into the receiver; then he fumbled at the telephone until he had found and pushed the disconnect button. The speaker clicked and resonated hollowly, and faintly a woman's voice said, *"If you would like to make a call, please hang up and dial again."*

Elizalde helped Kootie out of the chair, and to Sullivan she seemed to be hurrying the weeping boy, clearing the way so that he could finally call *his* father. She's a psychiatrist, Sullivan thought. She probably figures this is all good therapy, all this awful idiot pathos.

As he sat down on the warmed chair seat he noticed that Edison was letting Kootie cry, not taking over the boy's body again. Sullivan frowned—he knew the fused quartz filament would hold its initial vibration for quite a while in the rarefied mercury-vapor atmosphere inside the gauge, but it had to be picking up noise, random interference, to judge by the way the crowd effect kept creeping in.

But there was nothing Edison would have been able to do about it. At least the speaker was giving out only an even hiss right now.

Sullivan held out his open palm like a surgeon in the middle of an operation. "Thumb?"

Over Kootie's shaking shoulder, Elizalde gave him a glance of exhausted pique. *"Thumb,"* she said, slapping Houdini's black thumb into his hand.

Sullivan began dialing. *Hide, hide,* he thought, *the cow's outside? Or, Dad, I'm sorry I wasn't out there treading water beside you, even if it would just have been to drown with you.* Or simply, *Dad, where have you been? What on earth am I supposed to do now?*

He dialed the last numbers of SULLIVAN and laid the thumb down. The speaker beside the sink buzzed as the woman's voice came back on the line. *"What number were you trying to reach?"*

Her tone was palpably sarcastic now—and with a sudden emptiness in his chest he realized that, for the second time in four days, he was talking on the telephone to his twin sister, Sukie.

Impulsively he replied in a falsetto imitation of Judy Garland: "Oh, Auntie Em, I'm frightened!"

And Sukie came back quickly enough to override his last couple of syllables with *"Auntie Em! Auntie Em!"* in the sneering tones of the Wicked Witch of the West.

Sullivan sneaked a glance to the side. Everyone in the smoky kitchen, including fat Johanna in the office doorway, was staring at him; even Kootie had stopped crying in order to gape.

"He put her in a Leyden jar," Sukie went on in a singsong voice, *"and there he kept her near yet far."*

What? thought Sullivan bewideredly. Put who in a Leyden jar? Auntie Em, in that crystal ball in the movie? A Leyden jar was an early kind of capacitor for storing a static electric charge. "What the hell, Sukie?" he said.

"This root beer will not pass away, Pete. Have you drained it yet?"

"—Yes." The blood was thudding in his ears, and he felt as though he were standing behind his own body, leaning over its defeat-slumped shoulder. "At least *you* swam *out.*"

"We will not regret the past nor wish to shut the door on it. You should have drank more.

> *" 'We are but older children, dear,*
> *Who fret to find our bedtime near.' "*

"That's from *Alice,*" said Sullivan.

"Through the Looking-Glass, *actually,*" Sukie said.

"Why do—you all—quote those books so much?"

"They're not nonsense here, Pete. The little girl who falls down the deep well that's lined with bookshelves and pictures—call it 'your whole life flashing before your eyes'—the collapse of all the events of your timeline, down to an idiot unlocated point that occupies no space—the Alice books are an automortography. And then you're in a place where your . . . 'physical size' is a wildly irrational variable, and distance and speed are problematical. And you can't help but go among mad people."

The volume was perceptibly diminishing; the vibrations of the quartz filament in the Langmuir gauge in the other room were becoming increasingly randomized.

"I—" said Sullivan, "wanted to talk to Dad, actually. . . ."

"He doesn't want to talk to you, actually. You're just going to have to be a little soldier about this. Lewis Carroll wasn't dead, but he knew a little girl who did die—he had taken photographs of her, and he caught her ghost in a Leyden jar, just like Ben Franklin used to do. She told Lewis Carroll all those stories, and he wrote 'em down." She paused then, and when she spoke again her voice was gentler. *"You're probably looking Commander Hold-'Em in the eye right now, aren't you?"*

Sullivan was. (He felt even further removed from his seated body than he had a few minutes ago, and he knew that, if Elizalde refused to give him back the .45, he could easily find something else—hell, he could walk in two minutes from here to the ocean, and just swim out.) His father had not forgotten nor forgiven. Over the reeks of burnt mint and Bradshaw's cinnamon-and-rot breath and his own beery sour sweat, Sullivan could smell Coppertone lotion and mayonnaise and the terrible sea.

"If you care," he whispered.

"I've got to take a moment to say . . . good. But! It's just that he doesn't want to talk to anyone over this open line, Pete. He wants you to go pick him up. He says Nicky Bradshaw will know where he is, he has apparently dreamed about Nicky. Dream a little dream of me . . . not." Her voice was definitely fading now.

"Beth," he said loudly, "I ran away from you too, can you—"

At the same time she was saying, *"I worked hard to ruin your whole life, Pete, can you—"*

With their old skill of each knowing what the other was about to say, they paused—Sullivan smiled, and he thought that Sukie was smiling somewhere too—and then they said, in perfect unison, "Forgive me?"

After a pause, *"How could I possibly not?"* they both said.

Sukie's voice faded away into the increasing hiss of the speaker; for a few seconds everyone in the kitchen heard a dog barking somewhere deep in the amplified abyss, and then the roaring hiss was all there was. For some reason Kootie whispered "Fred?" and began crying again.

Sullivan hung up the telephone. He lifted his head and looked at Bradshaw's impassive, squinting face. "I need to go pick up my father," he said hoarsely. "Apparently you know where he would be."

"Turn off your telephone," whined Bradshaw aggressively. "Every psychic from San Fran to San Clam is probably picking all this up."

Sullivan stood up and pushed the sweaty hair back from his forehead. "True. Hell, it's probably been breaking in on TV sets and radios," he said, "like CB transmissions." He walked stiffly into the dark office and crouched to unplug the transformer from the wall socket. The air in here was sharp with the oily, metallic, but somehow also organic-smelling reek of ozone.

Bradshaw had followed him, and now swung open the outside door. Late-afternoon sunlight and the cold sea breeze swept into the room, and Elizalde and Kootie and Johanna shuffled blinking out of the smoky kitchen onto the office carpet.

Sullivan twisted the cable clamps off the van battery's terminals, and then began disconnecting the wires that linked the components of their makeshift device. "We're off the air," he remarked.

"If I'm supposed to know where he is," said Bradshaw, "then he must be at his grave in—the Hollywood Cemetery. I've been visiting the grave ever since he died—even after *I* died."

Nettled, Sullivan just nodded his head. "That's fine. Hollywood Cemetery, I know where that is, on Santa Monica, right over the fence from Paramount Studios. Straight up the Harbor Freeway to the 101. I should easily be back before dark." He would even have time to stop at Max Henry's on Melrose for a shot or two of Wild Turkey and a couple of chilly Coorses, before going on, north a block, to—to the cemetery.

It occurred to Sullivan that he had not been within the walls of that cemetery since the day of his father's funeral, in 1959. "Uh," he asked awkwardly, "where's his . . . grave marker?"

"North end of the lake—by Jayne Mansfield's *cenotaph*—that means empty grave—she's buried somewhere else."

"Okay. Now I wonder if I could borrow your—"

"Explain to him," interrupted Bradshaw, "that I couldn't come along. Tell him I'm waiting here, and I—*(gasp)*—I've missed him." He raised his hand as if fending off an argument. "And you can't drive that van."

"No, I was just going to ask if—"

"No," Bradshaw insisted, "the van is out. It's a . . . a disgrace. Take

my car, it's a Chevy Nova. Full tank of gas. It drives a little sideways—
but that'll help keep anyone from being able to see—which way you're
going.''

"Great," said Sullivan, wishing he had a beer in his hand right now.
"That's a good idea, thanks." He squinted through the open doorway
at Elizalde, who had walked out across the asphalt and was taking deep
breaths of the fresh air. "Angelica," he called, "can I have back the
. . . machine in the fanny pack?"

She gave him an opaque look—she probably couldn't see him in the
dim interior—and then she walked back and stepped up inside. "What
is Commander Hold-'Em?" she asked quietly.

"My sister's slang for death, the Grim Reaper. Is it back in the apartment?"

"You've *named* the gun that?"

Psychiatrists! he thought. "No," he said patiently. "I was talking
about the gun, and then you asked a question about my sister's term for
death and I answered you, and then I was talking about the gun again.
Which I still am. Could I have it?"

"You showed me how to use it," she said. Her brown eyes were still
unreadable.

"I remember. After you said you didn't believe in them." Suddenly
he was sure that her patient, Frank, had killed himself with a gun.

"Kootie would be safer here," she said, "in this masked area, with
Bradshaw or Shadroe or whoever your 'godbrother' is."

"I agree," said Sullivan, who thought he could see where this was
going. "And so would the famous Dr. Elizalde, whose face I saw on
the network news, night before last."

"I'm coming with you," she said. "Don't worry, I won't intrude on
you and your father."

Bradshaw started to speak, but Sullivan cut him off with the chopping
gesture. "Why?" Sullivan asked her.

"Because you should have a gun along with you when you go there,"
Elizalde told him, "and I won't let you go by yourself with a gun,
because I think you're still 'looking Commander Hold-'Em in the
eye.'" She was staring straight at him, and she raised her eyebrows
now. "That is to say, I think you might kill yourself."

"No," interjected Bradshaw worriedly, "I won't take responsibility
for the kid. I told you no kids."

"I won't be any trouble, mister," said Kootie, "just—"

"That's . . . hysterical," Sullivan said to Elizalde. "Give me the goddamn gun."

"No." Elizalde jumped out into the yard and sprinted across the asphalt; when she was ten yards away, she turned and shaded her face with her hand to look back at him. She lifted the hem of her untucked old sweatshirt, and he saw that she was wearing the fanny pack. "If you try to take it from me, I will shoot you in the leg."

His face hot, Sullivan stepped down out of the office. "With a .45? You may as well shoot me in the chest, Angelica!"

Her hand was under the flapping hem of her sweatshirt. "All right. At least you won't die a suicide, and go to Hell."

He stopped, and grinned tiredly at her. "*Whaa?* Is this a psychiatric thing or a Catholic thing?"

"It's me not wanting you *dead*, asshole! Why won't you let me come along?"

Sullivan had lost his indignity somehow, and he shrugged. "Come along, then. I hope you don't mind if I stop for a drink on the way."

"Your sister drank, I gather?"

His exhausted grin widened. "You want to make something out of it?"

"I've got to make something out of *something*."

Bradshaw stepped down to the pavement behind Sullivan. "Take the kid!" he wheezed. "With you!" He seemed to be at a loss for words then. "On Long Beach sands," he said finally. "I can connect nothing with nothing."

Sullivan turned around. "What's the matter with you, Nicky? Kootie can stay in our apartment. He won't be any trouble. He'll probably just take a nap."

"Sure, mister," said Kootie. "I didn't get a lot of sleep last night anyway; I could use a nap. I won't be any trouble, mister."

Bradshaw just shook his head. After a moment he shook himself and dug into the pocket of his ludicrous old shorts, and then tossed a ring of keys to Sullivan. "Gray Chevy Nova right behind you," he said. "The blinkers don't work right—the emergency flashers come on if you try to signal. Use hand signals, okay?"

Sullivan frowned. "Okay. I guess we'll *for sure* be back before dark."

Bradshaw nodded bleakly. "Leave a dollar in the ashtray for gas."

CHAPTER 40

"It's only the Red King snoring," said Tweedledee.
"Come and look at him!" the brothers cried, and they each took one of
Alice's hands, and led her up to where the King was sleeping.
"Isn't he a lovely sight?" said Tweedledum.
Alice couldn't say honestly that he was.

—Lewis Carroll,
Through the Looking-Glass

The cemetery in the late afternoon was full of ghosts, and at first Sullivan and Elizalde tried to avoid them.

Even before they parked Bradshaw's goofy car, while they were still hardly past the office, they saw semitransparent figures clustered around the big white sculpture of a winged man sexually assaulting a woman. The smoky figures might have been attempting to stop the winged man, or help him subdue the woman, or just conceal the atrocity from the street.

Sullivan swore softly and looked for a place to park. The broad lawns he remembered out front along Santa Monica Boulevard were gone, those spaces now stacked full of shops—a Mexican market and a Chinese restaurant shouldering right up to the east side of the ivied stone buildings of the cemetery entrance, muffler and bodywork shops to the west—but there was still a sense of isolation here inside, in this silent, far-stretching landscape of old sycamores and palms and canted gravestones. Looking through Bradshaw's windshield at the ghosts that could hold their shapes in this still air, Sullivan wished the noise and smoke and spastic motion of the boulevard could intrude their vital agitations here.

Elizalde had Houdini's plaster right hand in her lap, and Sullivan was gripping the left one between his knees; the dried thumb was in his shirt pocket.

Past the ghosts was a crossroads, and he turned left onto the narrow paved lane and parked. "The lake's ahead of us," he said, hefting Houdini's plaster hand. "Let's *walk* up to it—the noise of the engine might spook him—" He winced at the unintended pun. "—and anyway, this car keeps looking like it's in the process of running off onto the grass."

Actually, he simply didn't want to get there. His father's ghost was to *meet* him? Would it be a translucent figure like the ones climbing on the statue?

I was only seven years old! he thought, with no conviction. *It was thirty-three years ago! How can I—still—be to blame?*

Still, he was profoundly sorry that he had let Elizalde talk him out of the preliminary drinks, and remotely glad that she was holding the gun.

"Okay." Elizalde seemed subdued as she climbed out of the car, and the double slam of the doors rang hollowly in the quiet groves. "Do normal people see that crowd by the entrance?"

"No," said Sullivan. "They're just visible to specimens like you and me."

Looking north, Sullivan could see the distant white letters of the HOL-LYWOOD sign standing on the dark hills, and the words *holy wood* flickered through his mind. To the south across the stone-studded hillocky lawn, past the farthest palms, was the back wall of Paramount Studios, with the red Paramount logo visible on the water tower beyond the air-conditioning ducts.

"It's . . . somewhere ahead of us," said Sullivan, starting forward. He glanced to his left, remembering that Carl Switzer was buried right there by the road somewhere. Switzer had been "Alfalfa" in the old Our Gang comedies, and had been shot to death in January of '59. Alfalfa's grave had been only five months old when Arthur Patrick Sullivan was buried, and the twins, big fans of the Our Gang shows, had found the still-bright marker while silently wandering around the grounds before their father's graveside service. Neither of them had said anything as they had stared down at Switzer's glassy-smooth stone marker. It had been obvious that anybody at all could die, at any time.

"This is very pretty," said Elizalde, scuffing along next to him and holding Houdini's plaster right hand like a flashlight.

"It's morbid," snapped Sullivan. "Burying a bunch of *dead bodies*, and putting a fancy marker over each one so the survivors will know where to go and cry. What if the markers got rearranged? You'd be weeping over some stranger. *Not* some stranger, even, some cast-off dead *body* of a stranger, like a pile of fingernail clippings or old shoes, or the dust from inside an electric razor. What's the difference between coming out *here* to think about dead Uncle Irving, and thinking about him in your own living room? Okay, here you can sit on the grass and be only six feet above his inert old body. Would it be better if you could dig a hole, and sit only *one* foot above it?'' He was shaking. "Everybody should be cremated, and the ashes should be tossed in the sea with no fanfare at all.''

"It's a sign of respect,'' said Elizalde angrily. "And it's a real, tangible link. Think of the Shroud of Turin! Where would we be if they had cremated Jesus?''

"I don't know—we'd have the Ashtray of Turin.''

She swung Houdini's plaster hand and hit Sullivan hard in the shoulder. One of the fingers flew off and bounced in the coarse green grass.

Sullivan had let out a sharp *Hah!* at the impact, and he sidestepped onto the grass to keep his balance. "Goddammit,'' he whispered, rubbing his shoulder as he stepped back down to the asphalt, keeping away from her, "give me back the fucking .45, will you? If you go trying to make some theatrical gesture with *that*, you'll kill someone.'' He noticed the gap in the hand, and looked around until he spotted the finger. "Oh, good work,'' he said, stepping across and bending to pick it up. "It didn't half cost my dead sister and I any trouble to get hold of these things, go ahead and bust 'em up, by all means.''

"I'm sorry,'' she said. "We can glue it. I'm tired, I didn't mean it to be more than a tap. But you weren't saying what you believed, just what you *wished* you believed—that dead people go away and stay away, canceled. Are these ghosts or not?''

He thought her question was rhetorical until she repeated it in an urgent whisper. Then he stopped fiddling with the plaster finger and looked ahead.

"Uh,'' he said, "my guess is ghosts.''

Three fat men in tuxedos were walking toward them, a hundred feet ahead, where the road was unpaved; the man in the middle had his arms around his companions' shoulders, and they were all walking in step, but no dust at all was being kicked up, and their steps made no sounds in the still air. Their mouths gaped in wide, silent smiles.

"Let's slant south, toward Paramount,'' said Sullivan.

He and Elizalde set off diagonally across the grass to their right with a purposeful air.

The sun was low over the mausoleum along the distant Gower Street border of the cemetery—the shadows of the palm trees stretched for dozens of yards across the gold-glowing grass.

Griffith's magic hour, Sullivan thought with a shiver.

Flat markers stippled the low luminous hills in meandering ranks, like stepping-stones, and some graves were bordered with ankle-high sections of scalloped pink concrete, and the interior space of these was consistently filled with broken white stones; a few, the graves of little children, had plastic dinosaurs and toy cars and miniature soldiers set up on the stones to make pitiful dioramas.

Mausoleums like ornate WPA powerhouse relay stations stood along the dirt road ahead of them, and the brassy sunlight shone on the wingless eagle atop the Harrison Gray Otis monument; Sullivan was sure that the eagle had had wings in 1959. The cypresses around them rustled in the gentle breeze and threw down dry leaves.

Sullivan and Elizalde had by now wandered into a marshy area, back by the corrugated-aluminum walls and broken windows of the Paramount buildings, that seemed to be all babies' graves, the markers sunken and blurred with silt.

Houdini's maimed hand was shaking in Elizalde's fists. "We've passed those ghosts," she whispered. "Let's get to the lake."

At that moment a wailing laugh erupted from somewhere far off among the trees and gravestones behind them. Elizalde's free hand was cold and tight in Sullivan's.

They hurried back to the dirt road, and over it, onto a descending slope of shadowed grass. Ahead of them was a long lake, with stone stairs at the north end and, at the south end, tall white pillars and a marble pedestal rising out of the dark water. A white sarcophagus lay on the pedestal.

"Douglas Fairbanks, Senior," panted Sullivan as he and Elizalde hurried along the marge of the narrow lake.

Human shapes made out of dried leaves were dancing silently in the shadows of the stairs, and curled sections of dry palm fronds swam and bobbed their fibrous necks out on the dark face of the water.

"Just up the hill and across the next road," Sullivan said, "is the other lake, the one my father—"

He couldn't finish the sentence, and just pulled her along.

Nicholas Bradshaw had been standing for several minutes, watching Kootie breathe in his sleep as he lay curled on the wooden floor, before he crouched and shook the boy's shoulder.

The boy's eyes opened, but Bradshaw was sure that the alert, cautious intelligence in the gaze was Thomas Edison's.

"A car went by twice," said Bradshaw, "slow. I don't think it was bad guys—but it did make me think you'd be—safer back in the office."

Kootie got lithely to his feet and glanced at the blinds, which glowed orange around the slats. "They're not back yet."

"No," said Bradshaw. The empty living room echoed hollowly, and he didn't like to talk in here.

"The boy's asleep," said Kootie. "I suppose I can be out in the air for a few minutes—your place does seem to be a deceptive one for trackers to focus on."

"I've tried to make it so," said Bradshaw, opening the door. "And it helps that I'm a dead man."

"I reckon," said Kootie, following him outside.

Parrots fluttered past overhead, shouting raucously, and the mocking-birds on the telephone lines had learned the two-note chirrup that car alarms emitted when they were activated by the key-ring remotes, and which always sounded to Bradshaw like the first two notes of the "Colonel Bogie March."

Bradshaw was remembering the early days of working on "Ghost of a Chance," in '55 and '56. CBS had filmed the show's episodes on a couple of boxy sets on a soundstage at General Service Studios, and in spite of the depth-and-texture look that Ozzie Nelson had pioneered for "The Adventures of Ozzie and Harriet," the director at General Service had held to the old flat look of early television—bright lighting with minimal shadow and background.

During the show's tightly scheduled first two years, Nicky Bradshaw had seemed to spend most of his waking hours on those sets, and it had been a deepening and expanding of his whole world when CBS had given the job of filming the show to Stage 5 Productions in 1957. The Stage 5 director had used a series of sets that had been built for Hitchcock's "The Trouble with Harry," and often filmed scenes at local parks, and occasionally at the beach.

His world had gone flat again when the show was finally canceled in 1960, a year after his godfather's death. (He hurried Kootie toward the office—he must do this thing before his godfather's ghost arrived.) And then it had flattened to the equivalent of sketchy animation in a flip-book after his own death in 1975.

Most of all—more than sex, more than food—he missed dreams. He had not allowed himself to sleep at all in the last seventeen years, for if he were to have a frightening dream while he wasn't consciously monitoring the workings of his dead body, he wouldn't be able to wake himself up—and the inescapable trauma would surely be strong enough to cause him to throw ghost-shells in his fright . . . and, since he had continued occupying his body past the end of his lifeline, the ghosts would have no charged line to arc back to.

They would collide, collapse into jarring interference, implode in fearful spiraling feedback.

He knew of several cases in which a person had suffered a profound trauma *only a few moments* after unacknowledged death, and had burst into flames. Bradshaw had accumulated *seventeen years.*

But he could still remember laying his weary body down and closing his eyes and letting sleep take him, remember awakening in darkness and seeing by a luminous clock face that there were hours yet to sleep, remember drifting to wakefulness on sunny mornings with the images of dreams still dissolving before his eyes as he stretched and threw back the covers.

After seventeen years, he wasn't sure he remembered what dreams were, any more than he really remembered what the sensations of taste had been like. Dreams had been . . . visions, it seemed to him now, like vivid daydreams over which one had little or no control; scary sometimes, it was true—but also, as he recalled, sometimes achingly erotic, sometimes luminous with a wrenching beauty that seemed to hint of some actual heaven somewhere. And in dreams he had been able to talk and laugh again with people he'd loved who had died.

His hand was on Kootie's bony shoulder, propelling the boy toward the main building.

When they had both stepped up into the dark office, Bradshaw ducked into the kitchen to fetch Elizalde's pint bottle of tequila, which was still more than half full.

"You're how old?" he asked gruffly.

"Eighty-four," said Kootie.

"Old enough to have a drink." Bradshaw actually took an involuntary breath. "If you'd like one."

"A shot won't hurt the boy," assented Kootie. "It seems I've acquired a taste for the stuff, since my expiration."

You ghosts always do, thought Bradshaw as he poured a liberal slosh of the yellow liquor into a Flintstones glass.

"You're not going to have any?" asked Kootie alertly.

"Oh," said Bradshaw, "sure. I've just got to find a cup for myself." On a bookshelf he found one of the coffee cups from which he'd been drinking his Eat-'Em-&-Weep Balls tea, and he poured an ounce of tequila in on top of the red stickiness.

Kootie raised his glass, but waited until Bradshaw had tipped up his coffee cup and taken a mouthful of the tequila.

What do I do now, thought Bradshaw—swallow it?

He glanced up at Kootie, who hadn't even taken a sip yet. Bradshaw sighed and swallowed, feeling the volatile coldness in his throat and trying to remember what tequila tasted like. Pepper and turpentine, as far as he could recall.

That will do, he thought. I suppose that stuff will just sit in my stomach until it . . . evaporates? Soaks into my dead tissues like a marinade? For the next day or two, he thought seriously, I'll have to be careful about burping around any open flame.

Flame, he thought, and he remembered those cases of "spontaneous combustion" that had occurred when a newly dead person experienced an emotional trauma. In a number of the cases, the person had been drinking alcohol.

He put down the cup. "I'm too old for tequila," he said. He inhaled, feeling again the chill of the fast-evaporating alcohol in his mouth. "I'll be regretting even just that one sip."

Edison took another swallow from his glass. "Well, I'm eighty-four years old, but I'm working with an eleven-year-old stomach. The boy will probably sleep through until morning, so another drink or two will do no harm. I've got something to celebrate anyway."

Too weary to speak, Bradshaw raised his eyebrows.

"I received a Bachelor of Science degree on Sunday."

Bradshaw couldn't imagine what Edison was talking about, but he nodded ponderously as he reached for the bottle to refill Kootie's glass. "That's good." He sucked air into his lungs. "A college degree can make all the difference in the world."

There was a broader lake in a shallow green meadow on the north side of the cemetery lane, and its water was still enough that Sullivan could clearly see the vertical reflections of the tall palms on the far shore. There were two more palm trees reflected in the water than there were standing on the shore.

Marble benches stood here and there on the grass slope, and there seemed to be figures sitting on every one. Some stared at Sullivan and Elizalde, while others silently went through the motions of talking or laughing, and a couple were bent over notebooks, perhaps writing poetry. Sullivan supposed that one or two of them might be living people who saw this place as solitary.

Past the urns and markers and statues he hurried, holding Elizalde's free hand as they made their way down the slope. Around the north curve of the shore, only a few hundred feet ahead, he could see another rectangle of broken white stones, and he was sure that his father's grave was very near there.

He and Elizalde were striding along the shoreline now to stay away from the ghosts on the slope, though the animate palm fronds swam in closer to them, creaking woodenly in eerily good imitation of the grumble of ducks. Rope-wide grooves were curled and looped across the muddy bottom of the shallow lake, as if big worms had been foraging earlier in the day.

Sullivan blinked around at the marble-studded slopes, and he sniffed the chilly jasmined air—then realized that it was a *sound* that he had become aware of, a low vibration as if a lot of people hiding behind the nearer stones and trees were humming the same bass note.

Clustered red water lilies hid the lake floor at this north end of the lake, and his father's grave was just on the far side of a bushy gray-green juniper that overhung the water.

"Got to go back up the slope for just a few steps," he said tightly, "to get around this shrubbery."

"I'd rather wade across," whispered Elizalde.

He thought about the worm tracks, and for a moment he wondered if there even *was* a bottom right here, under the blanket of water lilies. "It's just a few steps," he said, tugging her uphill around the juniper. Two ghosts were pirouetting on the Cecil B. DeMille crypts, but no one was paying any evident attention to Sullivan and Elizalde.

Back down beside the water on the far side, he saw that a knee-high white statue of the Virgin Mary had been propped up on the rectangle of white stones, with red flowers in the little stone hands and a black cloth hood tied around the head.

Jayne Mansfield's etched pink cenotaph lay at the feet of the stone Virgin; the surface of the marker had apparently once had a reproduction of Mansfield's face bonded to it, but the image had been crudely chipped off. In the shadows under the juniper Sullivan could see a couple of empty cans of King Cobra malt liquor and a dozen white candles in a clear plastic bag.

Off a few steps to the east of Mansfield's marker lay a low black-marble square that, from the way its placement jibed with his thirty-three-year-old memories, must be the one that would have his father's name on it.

Kootie's head seemed to be bobbing in time to a slow pulse, and Bradshaw stood up and fetched a jar from the kitchen. It was a Smucker's orange-marmalade jar, scraped nearly empty.

"How're you doing," he said as he plodded back into the office with it. "Mr. Edison."

Kootie was frowning intently, and the expression made him even look like an old man, in the dim sunlight that filtered in through the lantana branches clustered outside the windows. "I'm afraid," he said with evident care, "that I've stuck poor Kootie with . . . what I trust will be . . . the first hangover of his life."

Bradshaw knew that if his flesh had still been alive, his hand would have trembled as he held out the marmalade jar. "Best thing for the boy would be," he said. There was no heartbeat in his chest, but it should have been knocking. "For you to get sick now, while the booze is still. Undigested. Cough yourself out into this jar. The boy will feel better for it."

"There never has been a vacuum produced in this country that approached anywhere near the vacuum which is necessary for me," said Edison, articulating each syllable meticulously with Kootie's mouth. "A hundred-thousandth of an atmosphere was enough to let the filament burn. I need to find my vacuum."

"This jar is evacuated," said Bradshaw. "Hop in. You've had too much to drink. Carry the hangover into the jar. To free the boy."

"Physicists and sphinxes in majestical mists. Nothing wrong with my . . . sibilant syllables." Kootie's eyes were half closed.

"Dammit," said Bradshaw. "Mr. Edison. *Exhale yourself. Get in the jar.*"

But Kootie's chin wobbled downward, lifted once with a questioning whine, then dropped to his chest. A hoarse snore blew out through the boy's lips, but Bradshaw knew it was just breath, not Edison's ghost.

"Mr. Edison," said Bradshaw, his voice droning flatly as he tried to speak louder. "Wake up. It's just a hop, skip, and a sigh. To bed."

Kootie was unconscious, though, and didn't stir even when Bradshaw reached out to nudge his head with the empty jar.

Bradshaw's face was immobile, but a red tear ran down his gray cheek as he set the jar carefully on the cleared-off desk.

Horribly, there still was something he could do.

ARTHUR PATRICK SULLIVAN
"And flights of angels sing thee to thy rest"
1898–1959

Sullivan waved a circling gnat away from his face and stared down at his father's gravestone. He was tightly holding Elizalde's hand.

His father's stone had a picture attached, too; a playing-card-sized greened-brass plaque with an engraving of the old man's face etched on it. Sullivan recognized the smiling likeness; it was from a Fox Studios publicity still taken in the forties.

The breeze paused, and when it came back it was chillier. The palm-frond swans scudded away toward the ring of fountain jets that stuck up above the surface of the water; Sullivan had at first glance thought the nozzles were a cluster of baby ducklings, and perhaps they still appeared so to the creaking frond-birds.

Sullivan released Elizalde's hand, crouched, and touched the inset plaque—and it was loose, simply resting in the shallow rectangular recess in the stone. He pried it out with a fingernail and stood up again, tucking it into his shirt pocket and retaking hold of Elizalde's hand.

Sullivan's mouth was dry and tasted of pennies. When he began to speak, he found that his voice had a rusty flippancy: "So where are you, Dad?" he asked, aware that Elizalde was listening. "We want to be on the road before the evening traffic gets heavy."

The breeze twitched at his hair, and then a small voice in his ear said, *"Call me Fishmeal."*

Sullivan didn't move. The voice might be that of any random ghost. He seemed to remember that the line was from the beginning of *Moby Dick.*

"On the freeways," the voice went on, *"there you feel free."*

Sullivan's heart was suddenly beating hard enough to shake his shoulders. *That* phrase was familiar—it was something his father had always said to the twins, though the old man had only lived to see the earliest of the Southern California superhighways—the 110 to South Pasadena, and the one that he had always stubbornly gone on calling the Ramona Freeway, though it had been renamed the San Bernardino Freeway four years before he died.

Sullivan's mouth opened, but all the things there were to say overwhelmed him, and he just exhaled a descending "Ssshhhhh."

"You're a good boy," said the tiny buzzing voice, *"and I know you won't slap me, even though I* am *an insect."*

Sullivan's hand was cold and shaking in Elizalde's, and he guessed that she was looking at him in concern, but he held his head still.

"What kind of insect?" he whispered.

"Good, then you don't—" began the voice—

But it was interrupted by the wailing hyena laughter from the shadowy trees.

Elizalde's free hand gripped his, hard. "It's that laughing bag," she whimpered. "The thing Kootie and I saw today—the thing that spoke on the phone."

"Swing south," buzzed the voice, *"past Fairbanks to the Paramount wall, there's a tunneling effect there, the field of the movies overlaps a bit and blurs things; then just cut north to the entrance."*

"Back the way we came," said Sullivan, pulling Elizalde away from the juniper bush and the stone Virgin. "But we can go around this other side of the lake."

"What about your father?"

"He's in my ear," Sullivan told her. And he remembered the scene in the railway carriage in *Through the Looking-Glass*, and he added with weary certainty, "He's a gnat."

Elizalde obviously hadn't understood what he had said, but let herself be hurried along up the east shore of the lake.

Trying to run smoothly so as not to jar his head and possibly dislodge his father, Sullivan nevertheless kept glancing across the lake, toward the setting sun. The figures on the far-side slope were beginning to fragment; an old woman would take a tottering step and then abruptly be a child running, and a figure on a bench would close a book and stand up and suddenly be two figures. One pedestrian became a motorcycle and rider, and silently sped away over the grass, bounding over gravestones as if they were hurdles.

Up by the Cathedral Mausoleum, Sullivan and Elizalde crossed the grass through a cluster of stones with Armenian names, each of which had an unlit candle in front of it and a dish for burning incense, and then they had sprinted across the road and were hurrying past the west side of the mausoleum, toward the stairs above the lake grave of Douglas Fairbanks.

"Scuttle fast and low through the little valley past these stairs," Sullivan whispered, "and then when we're among the trees—"

A sudden, shocking racket from the west slope of the Douglas Fairbanks lake made them both instantly crouch and bare their teeth—it was a loud metallic squealing drowned out by idiot laughter.

A thing was flapping toward them from the trees beyond the road to the west, about ten feet above the grass and muscling its way rapidly through the twilight air; it flexed through a slanting beam of golden sunlight, and Sullivan saw that it had long metal wings but its body was a swinging burlap bag with a baseball cap bobbing on top.

Elizalde's razory scream seemed to shake leaves out of the overhanging willow branches, and she let go of Houdini's plaster right hand—and it disappeared.

Sullivan's hand was abruptly empty too; but when he glanced down he saw that he was wearing a black formal jacket with white shirt cuffs just visible at his wrists.

And then he felt the sleeves of the jacket snap loose above the elbows when the jacket and pants twisted him to his left, toward the stone stairs that led down to the lake.

"Whoa, Nellie!" buzzed Sullivan's father in his ear.

Elizalde too had turned toward the stairs. She was shorter suddenly, and plump, and her hair was up in a wide bun above the high collar of her lacy white blouse; but the eyes in the unfamiliar round face were Elizalde's brown eyes, and white showed all the way around the irises.

"It's the mask," said Sullivan jerkily as he found himself scuffing down the stone steps toward the water. "Relax and go with it—I think we're about to start wading."

His unfamiliar shoes stepped right off the bottom step into the warm water, and sank to the ankles in silt; then his long shirtsleeves pulled his arms forward and he was diving.

He braced himself to land flat and not strike his knees or elbows on the bottom—but there was no bottom, and he was swimming breathlessly in choppy *cold* water. Cold *salt* water.

He gasped in sudden shock, stiff with vertigo even though he was supported by the water. He didn't know where he was, or even if he was still conscious and not hallucinating.

The splashing of his clumsy strokes was echoed back to him by a close wall which was not the wall of the Cathedral Mausoleum but, only yards away, the vertical black steel hull of a ship too vast to be comprehended from way down here.

Someone on a deck far above cried, "Get out of town!"

Sullivan could hear Elizalde splashing along next to him, but in the quickly lowering darkness he couldn't see her. Some current kept bumping him against the steel hull of the ship and bumping Elizalde against him, even when they both swam sharply out away from it—and then he heard a metallic boom as Elizalde collided with a wall on *her* side; apparently the two of them were now swimming through some narrow channel.

And the walls were sharply concave now, curling up around him. The light was gone, and Sullivan's knees had somehow got jammed up under his chin by the rounded metal that was now underneath him too.

He was shivering violently at the speed and force of whatever was happening—but then it stopped, and he was encapsulated underwater, in darkness.

He could feel the struggling bony pressure of Elizalde crowding hard at his back, and he knew that she was being tightly constricted by the wall on her side. They were completely submerged in solid water now, with no smallest pocket of air.

A metal floor was shoved up against Sullivan's shoes, and the echoes of his scraping soles told him that there was a lid very close over his head. He and Elizalde had got trapped inside some kind of closed cylinder full of water. Sullivan's ear canals chugged and bubbled as they were icily filled, and his heart hammered at the mental image of his father lost again under seawater.

Sullivan reached out to push against the wall in front of his face, and he felt tightly ratcheted handcuffs cut into the skin of his wrists. Elizalde was thrashing furiously against his back.

With her shaking him, he couldn't even get his legs under himself to batter his head against the lid, and he was about to lose the breath that was clenched inside his lungs by blowing it all out in a helpless scream—when he became aware that his hands were busy.

His right hand had dug in the kinky hair over his ear and pulled free something that felt like a hairpin; and his fingers now worked carefully as they straightened the bit of wire. He knew that they were working more slowly and carefully because one finger was now missing.

He managed to nudge Elizalde in the back of her ribs with his left elbow, hoping the gesture conveyed, *Hold still!*

Then the fingers had deftly poked the wire into the receiver slot of the left cuff, between the close cowl and the knurled outer side of the swing arm, and, without letting go of the wire, his fingers had gripped the sides of the cuff and compressed it painfully tighter—and a moment later the swing arm had sprung back out, and his left wrist was freed. His left hand took the wire then, and, with all of its fingers to work with, freed his right wrist even more quickly.

He pushed Elizalde back and braced his feet. Now his hands thrust up past his head, scraping his elbows against the claustrophobically close metal walls, and pressed strongly upward against the metal lid—and *twisted*. The forceful torque released a catch, and then he was turning the whole lid and the upper edge of the cylinder, bracing his feet against the floor. He straightened his legs, and he was lifting the lid off of them, pushing it up with his hands, which were out in rushing cold air to the wrists—and only then did Sullivan realize that he and Elizalde had been upright rather than lying horizontally.

And then *up* abruptly became *down*, and both of them were falling headfirst out of the narrow can while air bubbles clunked and rattled past them; Sullivan's shoulders jammed in the narrower neck for a moment, but the water and a lot of loose metal disks coursing past him pushed him free—

And he fell through sunlit air and splashed heavily into shallow water, twisting his neck and shoulder against a muddy bottom and catching Elizalde's knee hard in the small of his back.

When he struggled up to a sitting position the water was rocking around his chest and his eyes were blinking in the golden light of late afternoon. He was leaning back against vertical stone, wheezing and panting, and through the sopping tangles of his hair he could see two branching tree trunks standing up from the shadowed brown water a couple of yards away from where he sat, and, a couple of yards beyond them, a low cement coping and a hedge; a few of the top leaves shone golden green in the last rays of sunlight.

His hands were spasmodically clawing in the silty mud under him, trying to find a tree root to grip in case the world was going to turn upside down again.

Elizalde sat up in the water beside him and held on to his shoulder while she coughed out muddy water and whoopingly sucked air into her lungs. Her mud-matted hair was long again, and the lean, tired face was her own. When he could see that she would be able to breathe, Sullivan cautiously leaned his head back and looked up. He was sitting against a square marble pillar that supported a marble crosspiece far overhead. He and Elizalde were apparently in the south corner of the lake, in the tail-end lagoon behind the marble walls of the Douglas Fairbanks monument.

The world was holding still, and he began to relax, muscle by muscle.

There was a twisting itch in his ear then, and he nearly thrust his finger into it; but the buzzing voice said, *"You've got to get to the Paramount wall—but first grope around in the water and get Houdini's hands."*

"Okay, Dad."

Sullivan pushed away from the pillar and slowly waded on his knees out across the pool, his face bent so closely over the water that his harsh breaths blew rings onto the surface, and he swept his hands through the velvety silt. Elizalde was just breathing hoarsely and watching him.

Faintly he could hear a rapid creak of metal and quacking laughter, but the sounds were distant and not drawing closer.

The silt was thick with pennies and nickels and dimes, but he tossed them aside—Elizalde inhaled sharply when she saw the first handful of them—and at last he found the plaster hand with the missing finger and silently handed it to her, and then a few moments later he found the other.

"Up this far slope to the service road," he whispered to Elizalde, "and then turn right and hug the wall all the way back west. The car is—"

"You were *in* there, *with* me," interrupted Elizalde tensely, "right? The can was full of *salt water* this time, wasn't it?"

Sullivan sucked the elastic cuff of his leather jacket; and he thought that it still tasted of salt. "I don't know if it really *happened* or not," he said, "but I was in there with you."

In Sullivan's ear the voice resonated again: *"At the end there, that was Houdini's famous escape from the padlocked milk can. Big news in the teens and twenties."*

Sullivan helped Elizalde stand up in the yielding mud, and then he waded to the coping, stepped up onto it, and threw one leg over the hedge. "My dad says that was Houdini's famous escape from the milk can," he said quietly.

"This time it was ours," Elizalde said, reaching up from the water for Sullivan to give her a boost. "Happy birthday."

Nicholas Bradshaw had shambled slowly out across the shadow-streaked parking lot to Pete Sullivan's shrouded van, and by the back bumper he crouched to pick up the little magnet they'd taken out of the telephone. Before turning his steps toward one of the garages, he put the magnet in his mouth.

I wonder, he thought stolidly, if you're held entirely accountable for sins you commit after you're dead. Kids before the age of reason aren't considered capable of knowing right from wrong, so if a five-year-old kills a playmate, he's not blamed. Or not much. He's just a little kid, after all. So what about adults past the age of . . . expiration? We're just *dead* guys, after all.

He thought of the "beasties," the solid ghosts who wandered up from the beach in the evenings and hung around outside his office door, waiting for Bradshaw to set out paper plates with smooth pebbles on them. The poor old creatures could be vindictive—they sometimes pulled license plates off parked cars, and once or twice had got into incomprehensible squabbles among themselves and left broken-off fingers and noses to be swept up in the morning along with the usual litter of rocks and beer cans—but it would be folly to assign *blame* to them. "Wicked" was too concrete an adjective to be supported by the frail nouns that they were.

He tugged open the creaking garage door, and dug out a folded tarpaulin and a big paint tray from behind the dusty frame of a '55 Chevy. He carried them outside and pulled the door back down.

When he had lugged everything across the lot and up into the office, Kootie was still snoring heavily in the Naugahyde chair by the desk.

Bradshaw dropped his burdens and stumped into the kitchen and shook a steak knife free of the litter in one of the cabinet drawers.

He would work without thinking—he would spread the tarpaulin out across the rug and lay the paint tray in the middle of it; then he would lift Kootie out of the chair . . .

But he himself was *not* one of those mindless solid ghosts. He couldn't honestly take refuge in that shabby category. He was dead (through no fault of his own), but his soul had not ever vacated his body.

His face was cool, and when he brushed his hand across his forever-unstubbled jowls, it came away wet. Tears or sweat, it was Eat-'Em-&-Weep juice either way.

Bradshaw would, he was determined that he would, simply lean over the boy's face and, with the telephone magnet between his teeth, inhale the boy's dying breath.

Bradshaw would thus get Edison. And Edison could monitor Bradshaw's body during the long nights aboard the boat, so that Bradshaw himself could sleep, and dream—just as Kootie had been able to sleep while the old ghost walked and spoke and looked out for him.

I've never eaten a ghost, Bradshaw thought; well, why *would* I, none of the average run of ghosts could responsibly *watch the store* while I slept. But Thomas Edison could.

Thomas Edison is probably the *only* ghost that I'd do this to get, he thought, and certainly the only very powerful one *I'll* ever get a shot at; the only one that could let me safely dream. I wouldn't . . . *sell my soul*, ever, except for this. It's God's fault, really, for putting this within my reach.

He remembered the boy saying, *I won't be any trouble, mister.*

Bradshaw stood over the snoring boy, staring at the pulse under his ear; and then he looked down at his right hand, which was gripping the steak knife.

For the first time since his death in 1975, his hand was trembling.

Hunching along through the shadows under Paramount Studios' corrugated aluminum back wall that was streaked with rust stains and gap-toothed with broken windows, Sullivan thought of the broad sunny lanes and parking lots and white monolithic soundstages on the other side. When he had last been on the Paramount lot, in about 1980, there had even been a dirt-paved street of Old West buildings under a vast open-air mural of a blue sky.

"We made a hundred and four pictures there in 1915," said his father's tiny voice in his ear, *"back when it was Lasky, DeMille, and Goldfish in charge, and we'd moved everything here from the barn at Vine and Selma. Sixteen frames a second, the old Lumiere standard. Now because of sound reproduction it's twenty-four frames a second,*

ninety feet a minute, and nobody needs to know how to read in order to see a movie, and the purity of the silent silver faces is gone. For us, the graveyard extends all the way south to Melrose."

Sullivan glanced back through the trees toward the Douglas Fairbanks lake. "Keep your voice down, Dad."

"Keep *your* voice down," whispered Elizalde, who of course couldn't hear what his father was saying.

Gravestones stood in thickly clustered ranks outside the Beth Olam Mausoleum, and Sullivan felt as though he and Elizalde and his father were hiding behind a crowd. The shadowy human-shaped figures that stood among the stones seemed to be facing away almost vigilantly, as though guarding Arthur Patrick Sullivan's retreat, and the multitudinous bass humming was louder.

"You got a lot of friends here, Dad?" Pete Sullivan whispered.

"*Oh, sure,*" said the voice in his ear. "*Go up to the doors there, and rap* shave-and-a-haircut."

"Just a sec," Sullivan told Elizalde, and then he sprinted up the steps to the locked door of the mausoleum and rapped on the glass: *knock, knock, knock-knock, knock*

From inside came the answering *knock, knock.*

Elizalde was smiling and shaking her head as he rejoined her and they began walking north along the broad straight lane; receding perspective made the curbs seem to converge in the distance, and on the blue hills above the implicit intersection point stood once again the familiar white letters of the HOLLYWOOD sign. Why, Sullivan thought, can't I get away from it?

"*It's a gravestone, too,*" said Sullivan's father.

For a minute they trudged along in silence through the gathering twilight. A couple of cars were parked ahead, and real people were opening the doors and climbing in; Sullivan no longer felt that he and Elizalde were conspicuous intruders.

As they walked up to Bradshaw's car Sullivan thought he heard laughter in the remote distance, but there was no triumph anymore in the cawing; and, from some radio or tape player a bit closer, he heard the opening notes of Al Jolson's "California Here I Come."

I been away from you a long time . . . Sullivan thought.

They climbed in and closed the doors gently. Sullivan started the engine, and as they drove out onto Santa Monica Boulevard and turned right, making oncoming cars swerve because of the way the Nova's skewed front end seemed to be about to cross the divider line, Sullivan said, impulsively, "Dad, I don't know if you knew it or not, but I didn't swim out, to help you."

Elizalde was looking out the window at the Chinese restaurant they were passing.

"I knew it," buzzed the gnat in his ear. *"And we both know it wouldn't have done any good if you had swum out, and we both know that isn't an excuse you'll look at."*

Sullivan hiked up a pack of Marlboros from the side pocket of his jacket and bit one cigarette out of it. "Did Sukie—Elizabeth—tell you that Kelley Keith is gunning for you?"

"I knew she'd be waiting for me. So I came ashore hidden inside a sea monster. Grounded and damped to a flat magnetic line."

Sullivan pushed in the cigarette-lighter knob. "What . . . brings you to town?" he asked, unable to keep the defensive flippancy out of his tone. He didn't look at Elizalde.

"Why, I got a free ticket to the coast," droned the gnat's voice, possibly trying to imitate Sullivan's tone, *"and I thought I'd look you kids up."* The voice was silent, then said, *"A big one was switched on here, and all of us were sympathetically excited by it. I came out of the ocean, after God knows how long; to find that the broken stragglers of Elizabeth had joined me, and that you had never—"* The voice lapsed again.

"Had never what, Dad?" Sullivan asked softly, looking almost across Elizalde to see where he was going through the windshield. "Stopped running? Away from the surf, that would be, Angelica." His smile was stiff. "I didn't want to look back, that's for sure. 'I said to Dawn: Be sudden—to Dusk: Be soon,' remember that, Dad? Francis Thompson poem. I've always tried to . . . what, to have nothing permanent, leave nothing behind that would, like, *hang around.* I always hated things to be . . . etched in stone."

"Uh," said Elizalde hesitantly, "I think the car's on fire."

Smoke was trickling, then billowing, from the slots on the top of the dashboard. "Shit," said Sullivan—he snatched the cigarette lighter out of its slot, and blinked for a moment at the flaming, gummy wad on the end of it; then he gripped the wheel with his free fingers while he cranked down the driver's-side window with his left hand, and he pitched the burning thing out onto the street. "That *was* the cigarette lighter, wasn't it?" he asked angrily.

Elizalde bent over to look at the still-smoking ring in the dashboard. "Yes," she said. "No—it's a cigar lighter. Wait a minute—altogether it says, L.A. CIGAR—TOO TRAGICAL. What the hell does that mean?"

Sullivan waved caramel-reeking smoke away from his face, and he was remembering the tin ashtray that had briefly burst into flame at Los Tres Jesuses on Wednesday morning. "Let's remember to ask Nicky."

"Freeway coming up," said Elizalde.

*   *   *

And so, thought Nicholas Bradshaw as he tucked the still-clean knife back in the kitchen drawer, *I* don't get the renewal, *I* don't get a rebirth. I have heard the candy-colored clowns they call the sandmen singing each to each—I do not think that they will sing to me.

Cinnamon tears were still running down his slack cheeks, and his hands were still trembling, but, when he had plodded back into the office, he crouched and picked up Kootie's limp, breathing body and straightened up again with no sense of effort. He even stood on his bad right ankle long enough to hook the outside door open with the left, and felt no twinge of pain.

Shutting down, he thought.

The boy whined in his sleep as the chilly evening air ruffled his sweat-damp hair. Every step Bradshaw took across the shadowed asphalt seemed to be the snap of a television being turned off, the slam of a door in an emptied building, the thump of a yellowed copy of *Spooked* being tossed out of a vacated apartment onto a ruptured vinyl beanbag chair in an alley. I am unmaking myself, he thought. I am looking at a menu and pointing past the flowing script on the vellum page, past the margin and the deckle edge, right off the cover of the menu, at, finally, the crushed cigarette butts in the ashtray.

"I believe I feel like Death Warmed Over this evening," he said out loud.

Aside from a remote sadness that was almost nostalgia, he had no feelings about his decision not to kill Kootie and inhale the Edison ghost: not guilt at having considered doing it, nor satisfaction at having decided not to. He had held the knife beside the boy's ear for several minutes, knowing that he could hide the body in one of the several freezers in the garages, and that Pete Sullivan and the Angelica woman would believe him when he told them that the boy must have run away; knowing too that he would be able thereafter to sleep again, and dream.

Had it been the thought of the sort of dreams he might have had, that had made him finally pull back the knife? He didn't think so. Even if the dreams had proved to be uniformly horrible—of the day he learned of his stepfather's death, for example, or the summer-of-'75 week he had spent drunk and freshly dead inside the refrigerator on the Alaskan trawler in the Downtown Long Beach Marina, or whatever detail-memories the murdering of Kootie would have given him—he still thought he could have *lived* with them.

In the end he just hadn't been able to justify extending the mile-markers of his personal highway by reducing this living boy to one of them.

At the apartment door now, he set the boy upright against the wall, and held him in place with one hand while he opened the door with the other. Then he got his arms under the boy's arms and knees again and carried him inside.

Bradshaw knelt to lay Kootie on the floor where he had been napping earlier. The boy began snoring, and Bradshaw got to his feet and left the apartment, being sure that the door was locked behind him.

Back in his office he sat down on the couch without bothering to turn on any lights. The desk was bare—the components of the telephone had been disassembled and laid in a cardboard box, and Bradshaw had not brought the television set back in. His charred pigs, relieved of their malignant batteries, lay in a heap in the corner. Distantly he wondered if he would ever again marshal his warning systems.

He reached around behind the arm of the couch and pulled free the broom, then clutched the straw end and boomed the top of the stick twice against the ceiling.

Tomorrow, he thought, I'd like to drive to the Hollywood Cemetery myself, and lie down on one of those green slopes and just sleep. But I've been dead for seventeen years—God knows how bad it might be. The explosion might knock half the mausoleums off their foundations.

He heard Johanna's door slam upstairs, and then in the quiet night he could hear the faint ringing of the metal stairs. There was silence when she had got down to the asphalt, and then came a knock at the door.

"Come in," he said. "It's not locked."

Johanna pushed the door open and stepped inside. "Not by accident?" she said in a concerned voice. "Always you lock it. And won't you get your pigs and TV back up?"

"I don't think, so," he said. "Sweetie-pie." He inhaled, and then made words of the sigh: "Bring me a can of snuff, would you please? *(Gasp)* And then sit here by me."

The couch shifted when she sat down. "And no lights," she said.

"No." He took the snuff can from her extended hand and twisted the lid. "Tomorrow is Halloween," he said. "All these things we've had up through this night—will be broken up and lost. Like a rung bell finally stopping ringing—but. When dawn comes. Find it a sweet day, Johanna. Find it a blessed day. Live in the living world. While it lasts for you. I hope it may see you happy, and not hungry. Not hurt, not crying. Every one of me will be watching over you. To help, with all of whatever I'm worth then."

He tapped a little pile of snuff out onto his knuckle and sniffed it up his nose. Almost he thought he could smell it.

Johanna had tucked her head under his jaw, and her shoulders were shaking. "It's all right if I cry now," she whispered.

He tossed the little can out onto the dark rug and draped his arm around her. "For a while," he said.

After a time he heard the crunch of the Nova's tires on the broken pavement outside, and he kissed her and stood up. He knew it must have got cold outside by now, and he went to the closet to put on a shirt.

CHAPTER 41

"—then you don't like all *insects?" the Gnat went on, as quietly as if nothing had happened.*

"I like them when they can talk," Alice said. "None of them ever talk, where I come from."

"What sort of insects do you rejoice in, where you *come from?" the Gnat inquired.*

"I don't rejoice *in insects at all," Alice explained, "because I'm rather afraid of them . . ."*

—Lewis Carroll,
Through the Looking-Glass

In spite of their muddy clothes, Sullivan and Elizalde had stopped to buy a couple of pizzas and a package of paper plates and an armload of Coke and Coors six-packs, and when they had turned on the chandelier light in the apartment living room Sullivan carried the supplies to the open kitchen. He was glad of the heat being on so high in the apartment. "Wake up Kootie," he called, "he'll want some of this."

Elizalde crouched over the boy and shook him, then looked up blankly. "He's passed out drunk, Pete. Tequila, by the smell."

Sullivan had unzipped his sodden leather jacket, and now paused before trying to pull his hands through the clinging sleeves. "How did he—? Could he be a drunk already, at his age?"

"I suppose. Did you bring the bottle back here?"

"No, didn't think of it." He worked his arms free and tossed the jacket into a corner, where it landed heavily.

They had left the front door open, and now Nicky Bradshaw spoke from the doorstep. "I gave it to him," he said. "He was Edison. We were talking, and he said he could have a couple."

Elizalde stood up, obviously furious. "That's . . . *criminal!*" she said.

"Edison should have had more sense. He's *in loco parentis* here—I wonder if he let his own kids drink hard liquor." She squinted at Bradshaw. "You should have known better too."

"I wasn't watching him pour," Bradshaw said. "Can I come in?"

"*Nicky!*" buzzed the gnat in Sullivan's ear, and then it was gone.

"Yeah, come in," Sullivan said. "Where's Johanna?"

"She's fixing her makeup." Bradshaw stepped ponderously in, creaking the floorboards. "Did you find—" His hand jerked up toward his head, then stopped, and suddenly his weathered face tensed and his eyes widened. "Uncle Art!" he said softly.

Sullivan looked down at Elizalde, who was still crouched over Kootie. "My father flew over to him," he explained. "How is Kootie?"

"I think he's waking up. You've got instant coffee in your van? Could you go get it?"

"Sure." She had carried in Houdini's hands and laid them by the door, and he hefted one up as he stepped outside, but though the night breeze chilled him in his damp clothes he didn't feel peril in it, here. He walked shivering across the lot to the van and lifted the parachute to get at the side doors with his key; in the total darkness inside, he groped like a blind man, finding the coffee jar and a spoon and a couple of cups by touch, with Houdini's hand tucked under his arm.

Before he climbed down out of the van, he stood beside the bed and sniffed the stale air. He could smell cigarette smoke, and the faintly vanilla aroma of pulp paperback books, and the machine-oil smells of the .45 and the electrical equipment he had bought today. It occurred to him that it was unlikely that the van would ever be driven again, and he wondered how long this frail olfactory diary would last. On the way out he carefully pulled the doors closed before lifting the parachute curtain to step away from the van.

Kootie was awake and grumbling when Sullivan got back inside, and Bradshaw was sitting against the wall in the corner, muttering and laughing softly through pink tears. Sullivan pursed his lips and narrowed his eyes, but didn't go over to where Bradshaw and his father were talking, instead striding on to the kitchen. Elizalde stood up from beside Kootie to help Sullivan unpack the supplies.

They took turns washing their hands in the sink, then opened the pizza boxes. "Edison says he doesn't want any," Elizalde said as she lifted a hot slice of pepperoni-and-onion pizza onto a paper plate, "but I think he will when he sees it."

Sullivan had measured a spoonful of powdered coffee into one of the cups, and now he turned to frown at the water he had left running in the sink. "I wonder if this is even connected to a hot pipe," he said, putting a finger into the cold stream from the tap.

"You could always make it from the back of the toilet," she said. "That's plenty hot. And it's what Edison deserves."

"Kootie *is* still in there?" Sullivan asked quietly.

"Yes. It was him that first woke up. Edison's planning to 'go into the sea' tomorrow, and I think it's doing Kootie good to have him run things in the meantime, so Kootie can get a lot of sleep."

"You're the doctor." The water was still running cold, so Sullivan put down the coffee cup, jacked a Coors out of one of the six-pack cartons, and popped the tab on top. "Do you figure you've laid Frank Rocha?" He stepped back before her sudden hot glare. "What I mean is, you know, is the ghost laid. Is he R.I.P. now? Can we just . . . buy some kind of old car and leave California?"

"You and me and Kootie?"

"Kootie? Is he part of the family?"

"Are we a family?" Her brown eyes were wide and serious.

Sullivan looked away, down at the pizza. He lifted another triangle of it onto a paper plate. "I meant partnership. Is he part of the partnership?"

"Is your father?"

"Jesus, is this what you psychiatrists *do*? Take the night off, will you?" He looked across the room just as Johanna stepped up to the front door. "Here, Johanna, you want a piece of pizza?"

"And a beer, please," she said, walking in. Her blue eye shadow looked freshly applied, but her eyes were red, and she was wearing a yellow terry-cloth bathrobe.

Sullivan pushed the paper plate across the counter to her and opened her a beer. He didn't want to talk to Elizalde; he was uncomfortable to realize that he *had* meant the double entendre about laying Frank Rocha, though he had acted surprised and innocent when she had glared at him. Was he jealous of her? He knew he was jealous of Bradshaw's easy conversation over in the corner with his father, though he didn't want to take Bradshaw's place.

Then abruptly his ear tickled, and his father's tiny voice said, *"Nicky's got to go to some other building here. Let's you and me walk along. Your girl can talk to Nicky's girl."*

My *girl*, thought Sullivan. "That's not how it is," he said. He was sweating in spite of his clinging, wet clothes—for his father would want to talk seriously now—and he picked up the can of Coors.

"Your sister went on to drink a lot, didn't she?"

Sullivan paused, with the beer halfway to his mouth. "Yes," he said.

"I could tell. Do you know why I came back, out of the sea? There goes Nicky, follow him."

Bradshaw was at the open doorway. "Nick," said Sullivan, putting down the beer and stepping past Elizalde out of the kitchen area. "Wait up, I'll—we'll—walk you there."

"Thank you, Pete," said Bradshaw. "I'd like that."

Bradshaw began clumping heavily across the dark lot toward the office, and Sullivan walked alongside, his hands in his pockets. "Nick," he said. "What does 'L.A. cigar—too tragical' mean?"

"Damn it," said Bradshaw in his flat voice. "Did you burn up the car?" He stepped up to his office door and pushed it open.

"No, but I threw your cigarette lighter out onto Santa Monica Boulevard." Sullivan followed him inside to the kitchen, where Bradshaw opened a cupboard to pry a finely painted china plate out of a dusty stack.

"It's a . . . mercy thing," said Bradshaw, not looking at him. "That some people do. It's a hippodrome, where it reads the same forwards as backwards. I don't know who started it, or even who else does it. But you write it around . . . *(gasp)* . . . ashtrays, and lighters, and chimneys. I've seen little shops on Rosecrans, where you. Can buy frying pans with it written. Around the edge." He had opened a drawer and lifted out a handful of shiny pebbles. "The hippodrome words attract new ghosts. They hang around—trying to figure it out how the end can be the same as the beginning. And then when the fire comes. They get burned up." He spread the pebbles on the china plate, and then carried it back out through the dark office and right outside to the parking lot.

"Beasties!" he called in a harsh whisper. "Din-din, beasties!" He put the plate down on the pavement. "It's a mercy thing," he said again. "They're better off burned up and gone. If they hang around, they're likely to get caught by people like Loretta deLarava. That's Kelley Keith, Uncle Art, what she calls herself now. Caught, and digested, to fatten the parasite's bloated, pirated personality. And if they *don't* get caught by somebody . . ."

He stepped back, almost into the doorway of the office, and Sullivan joined him in the shadows.

From around behind an upright old car hood on the other side of the yard, a lumpy figure came tottering uncertainly into the glow of the parking-lot light. It was wearing a tan trench coat over its head, with apparently a broad-brimmed hat under that to hold the drapery of the coat out to the sides like a beekeeper's veil. Its groping hands looked like multi-lobed sweet potatoes.

And from the overgrown chain-link fence on the other side of the lot came a rattling and scuffling, and Sullivan saw more shapes rocking forward out of the darkness.

Bradshaw turned and walked into the dark office, and when Sullivan had followed him inside he closed the door. "They're shy," Bradshaw said. "So's your dad. I'll be back at the party."

"Nicky, wait," said Sullivan quickly. When the fat old man turned his impassive face toward him, he went on almost at random, "Have you got copies of the Alice books? *Alice in Wonderland, Through the Looking-Glass?*"

Bradshaw walked around to his desk and opened one of the drawers. After rummaging around, he looked up and called, "Catch," and tossed a paperback toward Sullivan.

Sullivan did catch it, and he tilted it toward the light from the kitchen; it was both of the Alice books published together. "Thanks," he said, tucking it into his hip pocket.

Bradshaw left the building through the kitchen so as not to disturb the timid ghosts at their pebble buffet, and Sullivan sank cautiously into the Naugahyde chair in the middle of the office floor.

"You still got that brass plate from my gravestone?" said the tiny voice of his father.

Sullivan slapped the front of his damp shirt, and felt the heavy angularity still there. "Huh! Yes."

"Don't lose it, I'm tethered to it. It's my night-light. If I stray far from it, I'll get lost."

Sullivan took it out of his pocket, then began unbuttoning his shirt.

"Do you know why I came back, out of the sea?" his father's voice said.

"Because Thomas Edison lit up the sky here Monday night." Sullivan slipped the brass plate down inside the soaked front-side wallet of his scapular and buttoned his shirt up again.

"That's how I was able to find my way back. That's not why."

Sullivan was shivering, and the cinnamon-and-rot smell of the office seemed to be infused with the smells of suntan lotion and mayonnaise. "Okay," he whispered to the insect in his ear. "Why?"

"Because I . . . abandoned you and Elizabeth. I was a white-haired old fool showing off like a high-school Lothario, trying to impress this thirty-three-year-old girl I had married! With three-score and ten, I would have had nine more years with the two of you, seen you reach sixteen. But I had to be Leander, swimming . . . a Hellespont that turned out to be . . . well, I only just this week got back to shore."

Sullivan's eyes were closed, but tears were running down his cheeks. "Dad, you're allowed to go swimming—"

"And I hoped that . . . that it would have been okay, that Kelley would have taken care of you two, and that you'd have grown up to be happy people. I hoped I would come ashore and find you both with . . . normal lives, you know? Children and houses and pets. Then I could have relaxed and felt that I had not done you any real harm by dying a little sooner than I should have."

"I'm sorry we weren't able to show you that."

Sullivan was thinking of Sukie, drunk and grinning wickedly behind dark sunglasses in a late-night bar, perhaps singing one of her garbled songs; he thought of the way the two of them had watched out for each other through the lonely foster-home years, each always able to finish the other's interrupted sentence; and he thought of the two of them running away from the sight of their father's intolerable wallet on the Venice pavement in '86, running away separately to live as solitary shamed fugitives. And he imagined Sukie at forty years of age (he hadn't even seen her since they'd both been thirty-four!) hanging up a telephone after having called Pete to warn him about deLarava's pursuit—and then putting a gun to her head.

"Kelley Keith was to have been our stepmother," Sullivan said aimlessly. "And she did . . . *adopt* us, in a way, after we got out of college." He wondered if he meant to hurt his father by saying it; then he knew that he did, and he wondered why.

The gnat was just buzzing wordlessly. Finally it said, *"What can I do, what can I do? I've come back, and Elizabeth's killed herself, she's in the house of spirits with all the other restless dead, idiots jabbering over their pretend drinks and cigarettes. You're a rootless bum. I gave you kids a mother that was—that was nothing more than a child herself, a greedy, mean, selfish child, and then I* left *you with her. And it's wrecked you both. Why did I come back? What the hell can I do?"*

Sullivan stood up. "We've got to get back to the party." He sighed. "What you can do . . . ? Sukie and I let you down, even if you don't see it that way, even if it plain *is not* that way. Tell us . . . that you don't hold it against us; that there are no hard feelings. I bet Sukie will hear you too. Tell us that you . . . l-love us anyway."

"I love you, Pete, and not 'anyway.' Don't hold it against me, please, that I left you, that I abandoned you to that woman."

"We never did, Dad. And we always loved you. We still do."

The thing in his ear was buzzing indistinctly again, but after a moment it said, *"One last favor for your old man?"*

Sullivan had crossed to the door, and paused with his hand on the knob. "Yes. Anything."

"See that I get back in the ocean tomorrow, on Halloween. Say good-

*bye to me willingly and at peace, and I'll do the same. That's the way
we'll do it this time. And then—Lord, boy, you're forty years old! Stop
running, stand your little ground.''*

"I will, Dad," Sullivan said. "Thanks."

He opened the door. The humped ghosts were crouched around the
plate, clumsily picking up pebbles, and they shifted but didn't flee as
Sullivan stepped around them and strode back toward the apartment.
"You asked why you came back," he said, "remember? I think you
came back so that we could finally get this done."

When they got back to the apartment, the pepperoni pizza was gone
and everyone had started on the sausage-and-bell-pepper one. Sullivan
took a piece of it with good enough grace, and he retrieved his beer.

Bradshaw and Johanna were standing by the window. Elizalde was
sitting with Kootie and they were talking amiably; either it was Kootie
animating the boy's body now, or she had got finished yelling at Edison
for getting the boy drunk.

"Join you two?" said Sullivan shyly, standing behind her with his
beer and his paper plate. His father had flown away when they had
reentered the hot apartment; Sullivan had seen the flicker of the gnat
looping away toward Bradshaw, but he was no longer jealous.

"The electrical engineer!" said Kootie. Apparently he was still Edison.

Elizalde looked up at Sullivan with a rueful smile. "Sit down, Pete,"
she said. "I'm sorry I got into my psych mode there."

"I asked for it," he said, folding his legs and sitting next to her.
"And your questions were good. I've got answers to 'em, too."

"I'd like to hear them later."

"You will, trust me."

Sullivan guessed that Edison was still a bit drunk; the old man in the
boy's body resumed telling some interrupted story about restoring com-
munications across a fogged, ice-jammed river by driving a locomotive
down to the docks and using the steam whistle to toot Morse code across
the ice to the far shore, where somebody finally figured out what he
was up to and drew up a locomotive of their own so that messages
could be sent back and forth across the gap. "Truly wireless," Edison
said, slurring his words. "Even electricless. We're like the people on
the opposite banks, aren't we? The gulf is torn across all our precious
math, and it calls for a very wireless sort of communication to get our
emotional accounts settled." He blinked belligerently at Sullivan. "Isn't
that right, electrical engineer? Or did I drop a decimal place
somewhere?"

"No, it sounds valid to me," Sullivan said. "We're . . . lucky, I guess, that you were there with a whistle that could be heard . . . across the gap.''

After an hour or so, Kootie's body curled up asleep again, and Sullivan boxed up the remaining pizza and declared the party over. They all agreed to meet again early in the morning for a walk down to the beach, and then Bradshaw and Johanna plodded away toward the main building, hand in hand, and Elizalde told Sullivan to lock the door, and went into the bathroom to take a shower. When Sullivan leaned the Houdini hands against the closed door, he noticed that the broken finger had been glued back on. Elizalde must have borrowed glue from Johanna.

Sullivan took the Alice book out of his hip pocket and leaned against the kitchen counter to start reading it. When Elizalde came out of the steamy bathroom, wearing her relatively clean jumpsuit, she switched off the living-room chandelier and lay down on the floor near Kootie.

"Will this kitchen light keep you awake?" Sullivan asked quietly.

"An arc-welder wouldn't keep me awake. Aren't you . . . coming to bed?"

He raised the book. *"Alice in Wonderland,"* he said. "I'll be along after a while, when I'm done with my homework."

She stretched on the floor and yawned. "What were your answers to my pushy questions?"

He was tired, and the paperback book was jigging in his trembling fingers. He laid it facedown on the counter. "Here's one. We are a family, rather than a partnership, if you would like us to be."

She didn't say anything, and her face was indistinct in the dark living room. Sullivan got the impression that his answer had surprised her, and pleased her, and frightened her, all at once.

"Let me sleep on that," she said finally.

He picked up the book again. "I'm not going anywhere."

He stared at the page in front of him, but he wasn't able to concentrate until she had shifted around to some apparently comfortable position, and her breathing had become regular and slow with sleep.

EPILOGUE

Burn Rubber,
Sweet Chariot

If they go faster than my machine, I will be able to go downhill as fast as they dare to and for hill climbing the electric motor is just the thing, so I will beat them there. On rough roads they will not dare to go faster than I will; and when it comes to sandy places, I am going to put in a gear of four to one which I can throw in under such circumstances, and which will give me 120 horse power of torque, and I will go right through that sand and leave them way behind.

—Thomas Alva Edison,
Electrical Review, August 8, 1903

CHAPTER 42

"I mean," she said, *"that one ca'n't help growing older."*
"One ca'n't, perhaps," said Humpty Dumpty; *"but two can. . . ."*
—Lewis Carroll,
Through the Looking-Glass

The morning air was raucous with the cries of the parrots that were swooping like livid green Frisbees from the telephone wires to the branches of the shaggy old carob trees along the Twenty-first Place curb, but when one of the apartment doors finally opened, the gray-haired fat man who came shuffling out ignored the clamoring exotic birds as though he were blind and deaf. He was clutching a sheaf of white business-size envelopes, and he tucked them into a rack under the bank of mailboxes out front.

The old man's punctual in paying his bills, thought J. Francis Strube. The first of November isn't until tomorrow, but tomorrow will be a Sunday, with no mail pickup.

Strube's dark blue BMW was idling almost silently a hundred feet away from the apartment building, and certainly wasn't blowing any telltale smoke out of the exhaust, but still he slid down a little in the leather seat, just peeking over the dashboard at the old man.

And he wasn't sure. This fellow fumbling with the mail was about the right age, but Nicky Bradshaw had been athletically slim—and *healthy.* This man . . . he didn't look well at all; he moved slowly and painfully, squinting up and down the street now with impotent ferocity. Strube slid down even lower in his seat.

The old man by the apartment building was plodding back along the walkway toward the door he had come out of; but he paused halfway there, and just stood, staring down toward his feet.

Strube's lower back was cramping, and he sat up a little straighter in the seat.

And the old man curled one arm over his head and stretched the other out with his fingers spread, and turned on his heel in a 360-degree circle; then he paused again, let his arms fall to his sides, and opened the door and went back inside.

Strube had steamed the inside of his windshield by whispering a deep, triumphant "Hah!"

That had been the Spooky Spin, and even someone like himself, who had only seen reruns of the old "Ghost of a Chance" show, had to remember the way the Spooky character had always executed that move just before the primitive stopped-camera trick photography had made him seem to disappear into thin air.

Strube was whistling the "Ghost of a Chance" theme music—*dooo-root-de-doodly-doot-de-doo!*—as he punched into the telephone the Find Spooky number. Probably no one would be answering the line until nine or so, but he couldn't wait.

It rang twice, and then, to his surprise, someone did answer. "Have you seen Spooky?" a woman asked with practiced cheer.

"Yes," said Strube. "I've found him."

"Well, congratulations. If we verify that it really is Nicky Bradshaw, you'll be getting two complimentary tickets to the filming of the reunion show. Where is he?"

"It's him. My name is J. Francis Strube, I'm a Los Angeles–based attorney, and I worked for him as a legal secretary when he had an office in Seal Beach in the mid-seventies. Also, I just this minute *saw* him do the Spooky Spin, if you're familiar with the old show."

After a pause, the woman said, "Really? I'm going to transfer you to Loretta deLarava." The line clicked, and then Strube was listening to a bland instrumental version of "Mr. Tambourine Man."

I should think so, Strube thought, sitting back in the seat and smiling as he kept his gaze locked on Bradshaw's door. I imagine Loretta deLarava will have room for a quick-witted attorney on her staff.

"This is Loretta deLarava," said a harsher woman's voice now, speaking over background static. "I understand you're the clever person who has found our missing Spooky! Where is he?"

"Ms. deLarava, my name is J. Francis Strube, and I'm an attorney—"

"An attorney?" There was silence on the scratchy line. Then, "Are you *representing* him?" deLarava asked.

"Yes," said Strube instantly. Spontaneity wins, he thought nervously. Trust your instincts.

"Where is he?"

"Well, we want certain assurances—"

"Look, Mr. Strube, I'm on the E Deck loading dock of the *Queen Mary* right now." Good God, Strube thought, she's hardly two miles away across the harbor! "I'm doing a Halloween-related shoot about famous ghosts on board the ship today, and I had been hoping to find Bradshaw in time to at least get him in a couple of shots there, film him doing his trademark Spooky Spin on the Promenade Deck, you know?" She was sniffling. "You're not going to take a piss, are you?"

Strube assumed this was some showbiz slang, meaning *be an obstruction* or something. *Rain on my parade.* "No, of course not, I just—"

"So what? Do you want us to interview you, too? It'd be a cinch. Prominent local attorney, right? 'The man who tracked down Spooky.' And then we could discuss your client's possible role in the reunion show later. How does that sound?"

Strube didn't like her tone, or her apparent assumption that he was motivated by a desire for publicity; and he wished he could say something coldly dismissive to her.

But of course he couldn't. "That sounds good," he said. Then, despising himself, he went on, "Do you promise?"

"You have my word, Mr. Strube. Now where is he?"

"Well—in Long Beach, in the Twenty-first Place cul-de-sac by the beach." Strube read her the address from the stenciled numerals on the curb. "I'll be there too," he said, "and I'm confident—"

"Good," she interrupted. "I knew somebody was confident. I should have guessed it'd turn out to be a lawyer."

And the line went dead.

I guess she'll be here soon, Strube thought timidly.

The shouting of the parrots made Sullivan open his eyes. He knew that he had been very nearly awake for some time; he remembered having dreamed of Venice Beach sometime during the night, but he couldn't remember now if it had been Venice of 1959, 1986, or 1992, and it didn't seem important.

A faint *thwick* from the kitchen made him lift his head—Kootie was sitting cross-legged on the kitchen counter, looking at Sullivan over the top of the Alice paperback, a page of which he'd just turned. Kootie touched a finger to his lips.

Sullivan turned his head sideways, and his neck creaked, and Elizalde opened her eyes and smiled sleepily.

"I guess we're all awake, Kootie," Sullivan said, speaking quietly just because it was the first remark of the day. He rolled over, got stiffly to his feet, and stretched. "How are you feeling?"

"Fine, Mr. Sullivan—Pete, I mean. Could I have cold pizza and Coke for breakfast?"

Maybe Edison is sleeping off the hangover, Sullivan thought. "Sure. I think I'll pass, though. We'll probably be leaving here in an hour or two, after a . . . a walk down to the beach. You sure you wouldn't like to wait, and get something hot?"

"I like cold pizza. We hardly ever have pizza at home."

"Tear it up then." Sullivan yawned and walked into the kitchen to turn on the hot-water tap. He couldn't remember now whether the water had ever got hot last night; well, there *was* always the hot water in the toilet tank.

"Uh," said Kootie. "Could you help me down? My cut hurts if I stretch. I was halfway up here before I knew I couldn't climb up."

"Sure," Sullivan said.

"Kootie," said Elizalde, who had got up and now hurried over to the counter, "didn't I tell you not to put any strain on it?"

"No, miss," the boy said.

"Oh. Well, once we get you down from there—"

Suddenly a fourth voice spoke, from the bedroom doorway. "Leave him where he is."

Sullivan spun, and then froze. A man was standing there, pointing at them a handgun made from a chopped-down double-barreled 12-gauge shotgun. Focusing past the gun, Sullivan saw that the man had only one arm; then that he was wearing baggy camouflage pants and a stained windbreaker, and that his round, pale face was dewed with sweat. His gaze crawled over Sullivan's face, to Elizalde's, and to Kootie's, like a restless housefly.

"*Harry Houdini* made a call from Long Beach last night," the man said in a high, calm voice, "and as it happens I'm a big Houdini fan. But when I came down here I kept getting deflections, I couldn't get any consistent directional for him. So I remembered this dead spot by the beach, like the wood where Alice lost her name. And then you all had a party last night. A man went to an Armenian restaurant, because his friends told him to order the herring; when it was served, it was alive, and the herring opened its eye and looked at him. He left, but his friends told him to go back the next night, so he did, and he ordered the herring again. But on the plate it opened its eye again, and he ran away. The next night he went to a Jewish restaurant instead, and ordered herring, and when the waiter brought him his plate the herring opened its eye and looked at him and said, 'You don't go to the Armenian place anymore?' "

Sullivan felt a drop of sweat roll down his ribs under his shirt, and he kept staring at the sawn muzzles of the gun, each barrel looking big enough for a rat to crawl down it. Elizalde had stepped in front of Kootie, but now none of them were moving.

"What do you want?" asked Sullivan in an even voice.

"I want to speak to Thomas Edison."

"This is the guy that stabbed me," whispered Kootie; then he shivered, and in a louder voice he said, "You have my attention. What did you want to talk about?"

"Unplug me," the man said. "The rotten ghost is jammed in my mind, and I can't . . . eat. When you did this to me in '29, I cleared it inadvertently, by injecting a quick ghost into a vein in my arm; that worked, but it blew my arm off. I can't afford to do that again, even if I could be sure the ghost would only blow off another limb, and not detonate inside my heart. You did this, you must know how to undo it." His wheezing breath was a hoarse roar, punctuated with little whistles that sounded like individual cries in an angry crowd.

"And then you'll stab me again, right?" said Edison with Kootie's voice. "Or just blow out my middle with that scattergun and catch the boy and me both, when we breathe our last breath. It's a Mexican standoff." Kootie looked up at Elizalde. "No offense, Angelica."

Elizalde rolled her eyes in angry frustration. "For God's sake, Edison!"

"I won't," said the one-armed man. Distant voices shouted in his lungs. "I'll leave you alone, and subsist on ordinary ghosts. How can I assure you of this?"

Sullivan saw Elizalde's eyes glance across the room, and he looked in that direction. The .45 was lying against the wall where she had slept. He knew she was thinking that a dive in that direction would make the one-armed man swing the shotgun away from Kootie and himself.

But she couldn't possibly get the gun up and fire it before the shotgun would go off; and the shotgun wouldn't have to be aimed with any precision for the shot pellets to tear her up. He spread his fingers slowly, to avoid startling the gunman, and closed his hand firmly on Elizalde's forearm.

A whining buzz tickled Sullivan's ear, and he restrained his free hand from slapping at it.

"*What the hell is this?*" said the tiny voice of Sullivan's father's ghost. "*I can't get to the beach by myself—I'm tethered to my grave portrait, and it's way too heavy for me to carry.*"

Sullivan looked anxiously back at the one-armed man—but the man was apparently unaware of the ghost in Sullivan's ear.

The barrels of the shotgun wobbled. "Well?" The man's tiny eyes were fixed on Kootie's face.

"I could write the procedure down," said Kootie's voice thoughtfully, "after you let us go, and leave it in some preagreed place. You'd have to trust me to do it, though."

"Which," said the one-armed man, "I don't." He kept his little eyes fixed on Kootie, but he rocked his head back and *sniffed* deeply. "There's another ghost in here. If you tell me how to get unjammed, I'll just eat *it*. That'll keep me alive until I can go get more."

"No good," said Kootie's voice, "that's Pete's dad, and Pete's sentimental about it. Besides, the procedure involves a bit of work on your part." The boy's face kinked in a crafty grin. "It's not just crossing your eyes and spitting."

The one-armed man stared impassively at the boy sitting on the counter. Finally he sighed. "Let me tell you a parable," he said. "A man had a new hearing aid, and he was telling a friend how good it was. 'It cost me twenty thousand dollars,' the man with the hearing aid said, 'and it runs on a lithium battery that's good for a hundred years, and it's surgically implanted right into the skull bone and the nerve trunk at the base of my brain.' And his friend said, 'Wow, what kind is it?' and the man with the hearing aid looked at his watch and said, 'Quarter to twelve.'"

Sullivan wished the story had been longer. Surely Nicky would . . . would somehow come along soon, and perceive this, and put a stop to it. The shotgun was steady, and the man was standing just obviously too far away for Sullivan to have any hope of leaping forward and knocking the short barrels aside before the gun would be fired.

"I'll give you twenty thousand dollars," the one-armed man said. "I'll take that automatic that's against the wall there, I can hold that on you without being conspicous. We'll go out and get the money, and you can tell me then, once I've handed it over to you. We'll be out in public, I won't be eager to shoot you out in a street. Once I'm unjammed, I can kill *anybody* and eat 'em, I won't need you."

Kootie's head swung back and forth. "No. You'd still want Thomas Edison."

The man's pale face puckered in a derisive smile. "For that much money you'd have told me. You don't even *know* how to do it, do you?" He shifted his stance and raised the gun slightly.

"Yes he does!" said Elizalde shrilly.

Kootie turned on her, scowling. "Damn it, Angelica, I *do* know how this fellow can do it. You don't need to think you're . . . helping some old *fool* run a *bluff*."

"No, no," said the one-armed man. "You might have known once—but you're senile now. Hell, you're what, a hundred and fifty years old?" He snickered. "I can *see* that you're wearing a big set of those geriatric diapers right now."

Kootie's hands flew to the buttons on his shirt. "I can—damn you—*prove* you're wrong." He was smiling tensely, but his face was red. "This is an electric belt, urine would short it out!" His shaky fingers were making no progress at undoing the buttons. "You're talking to someone who understands electricity, believe me! I recently received—"

"He's just taunting you, Edison!" said Elizalde urgently. "Don't let him get you excited. It's not worth—"

"You just *hired* people who understood electricity," the man with the shotgun interrupted, shaking his head with evident good humor. "*You* were always just doing dumb stuff like . . . what was it, trying to make tires out of milkweed sap? *That's* proved to have been a real breakthrough, hasn't it?"

"It happens I recently received a B.S.—"

"Oh really? Where's your diploma?" The man laughed. "B.S. is right. Bullshit. Why don't you go ahead and add a Ph.D.? 'Piled higher and deeper.' "

Kootie was squirming furiously. "It's not a, a '*dip*shit *dip*loma,' you ignorant—"

"So how do I *do* it, then, if you're so smart?"

"Edison, don't—" said Elizalde quickly—

But Kootie's mouth was already open, and with it Edison said, "I already told you—cross your eyes and spit."

And now the one-armed man was doing just that. His eyes crossed until the irises had half disappeared in the direction of his nose, as if the pupils might *touch* each other behind his nose, and his mouth opened wide.

The barrels of the stumpy shotgun lifted and swung back and forth, and Sullivan pressed himself back against the kitchen counter. He glanced at Kootie, who just shrugged, wide-eyed.

It was as if the one-armed man had a speaker surgically implanted in his larynx—men's angry voices, crying children, laughing women, a chaotic chorus was shouting out of his lungs.

He might have been trying to spit. His lower jaw rotated around under his nose, and his tongue jerked—and finally one of the voices, a woman's, shrill and jabbering as if speeded up by some magical Doppler effect, rose and became louder and clearer.

And the one-armed man *spit*—and then gagged violently, convulsing like a snapped whip—

—As a glistening red snake shot out of his mouth. It was smoking even before it slapped heavily onto the floor, and the instant reek of ammonia and sulfur was so intense that Sullivan, who had involuntarily recoiled from its abrupt appearance, now involuntarily flinched from its fumes. And a chilly, laughing breeze punched past him and instantaneously buckled the blinds and shattered out the window.

Everyone was moving—Kootie had leaped from the counter and was colliding with Elizalde out on the floor in the direction of the broken window and the .45, the red snake-thing was slapping and hopping in front of the one-armed man, who was hunched forward with a rope of drool swinging from his mouth, and Sullivan made himself push off from the kitchen counter and vault over the spasming snake-thing to kick the hand that held the chopped shotgun.

Both shells went off, with a crash like a far-fallen truck slamming through the ceiling. Sullivan had jumped with no thought of anything beyond kicking the gun, and the air compression of the shotgun blasts seemed to loft him further—his knee cracked the one-armed man's head and then Sullivan's shoulder and jaw hit the bedroom doorframe hard, and he bounced off and wound up half-kneeling on the floor.

The room was full of stinging haze, and through squinting, watering eyes he could see Elizalde and Kootie. They were up, moving, opening the front door, in the ringing silence of stunned eardrums. Unable to breathe at all, Sullivan crawled around the wet red snake, which was already splitting and falling apart, and scuttled painfully on his hands and knees toward the daylight and the promise of breathable air. His hands bumped against Houdini's plaster hands, and he paused to grab them—but they disappeared when he touched them.

He hopped and scrabbled out through the door into the fresh air, rolling over the doorstep onto his back on the chilly asphalt. The breeze was cold on the astringent sweat that spiked his hair and made his shirt cling to him.

Nicky Bradshaw, wearing a sail-like Hawaiian shirt, was standing on the sidewalk, looking down at him with no expression on his weathered old face. Behind Bradshaw were two tensely smiling men in track suits—and each of them held a semiautomatic pistol.

Some kind of the new 9-millimeters, Sullivan thought bleakly; Beretta or Sig or Browning. Ever since Mel Gibson in *Lethal Weapon*, everybody's crazy about 9-millimeters. He looked down past his belt buckle, and saw Elizalde slowly crouching to place his old .45 on the pavement, watched closely by another of the smiling, trendily armed young men.

Sullivan's nostrils twitched to a new smell—the burning-candy reek of clove-flavored cigarettes. And when a woman's voice spoke, barely audible over the ringing in his ears, Sullivan didn't even need to look to know whose it was. She had, after all, been his boss for eleven years.

"I'm glad they've come without waiting to be asked," said Loretta deLarava. "I should never have known who were the right people to invite! Cuff 'em all," she added, "and get 'em into the truck, fast. Nicky and Pete I recognize, and this must be the famous Koot Hoomie Parganas, found at last—but I want all of them. Get anybody who's inside. Find Pete's van, and search it and this apartment for my mask. You know what to look for."

Sullivan at last rocked his head around to look up at her. Pouches of pale flesh sagged under her bloodshot eyes, and her fat cheeks hung around her sparking cigarette in wrinkly wattles.

"Hi, stepmother," he gasped, hardly able to hear his own voice. He hadn't wanted to speak to her, or even look at her, but it was important to let the ghost of his father know who this was. He wasn't sure how well the ghost could see, and in any case Loretta deLarava didn't look anything like the Kelley Keith of 1959.

DeLarava frowned past him, sucking hard on the cigarette, and didn't reply.

On one of the second-floor balconies, a white-bearded man in jeans and a T-shirt was looking down at this crowd in alarm. "Sol!" he yelled. "What's going on? Was that a gunshot? What's that terrible stink?"

"You're the manager here, Nicky?" said deLarava quietly. "I don't want your people to get hurt."

Bradshaw squinted up at his alarmed tenant. "Health-code enforcement," he grated. "Stay inside. These new renters have some kind of. Bowel disorder."

"Jesus, I'll say!" The man disappeared from the balcony, and Sullivan heard a door slam.

More by vibration in the pavement under his back than by hearing, Sullivan became aware of someone else striding up now, from the direction of the street. "Ms. deLarava?" a man said brightly. "My name is J. Francis—" The voice trailed off, and Sullivan knew without looking that he had noticed the guns. "I'm an attorney. I think somebody here is going to need one."

"Cuff that asshole too," said deLarava.

CHAPTER 43

*"Consider what a great girl you are. Consider what a long way you've come
today. Consider what o'clock it is. Consider anything, only don't cry!"*
                                            —Lewis Carroll,
                                            Through the Looking-Glass

A couple of deLarava's men hustled the handcuffed attorney to a new
Jeep Cherokee at the curb out front; three others opened the back of a
parked truck and tossed about a thousand dollars' worth of red and black
cable coils and clattering black metal light doors out onto the street to
make room for the rest of her captives: Kootie, Sullivan, Elizalde, the
one-armed man, and Bradshaw. Sullivan noted that Johanna had eluded
capture, and he wondered if Nicky had in some sense anticipated this,
and sent her safely away; if so, Sullivan wished Nicky had conveyed
his misgivings to the rest of them.

A Plexiglas skylight cast a yellow glow over the interior of the truck.
The captives were arranged along the truck's right wall, with their
cuffed wrists behind them; each pair of ankles was taped together and
then taped at two-foot intervals onto a long piece of plywood one-by-
six, which was then screwed into the metal floor with quick, shrill bursts
of a Makita power screwdriver. The one-armed man wasn't cuffed—
deLarava's men had simply taped his right arm to his body, with his
hand down by his hipbone.

And deLarava stayed in the back with the captives when the truck
door was pulled shut, leaning against the opposite wall while her driver
backed and filled out of the cul-de-sac and then made a tilting right turn
onto what had to be Ocean Boulevard.

"Nicky," she said immediately, "remember that you've got an innocent woman and child in here with you. If you feel any kind of . . .
psychic crisis coming on, I trust you'll be considerate enough to let me

know, so that my men can transfer you to a place where you won't harm anyone.''

''Nothing ever excites me when I'm awake,'' said Bradshaw, who was slumped below some light stands up by the cab. ''And I'm not feeling sleepy.''

''Good.'' She reached into the bosom of her flower-patterned dress and pulled out a little semiautomatic pistol, .22 or .25 caliber. ''If anyone wants to scream,'' she said, sweeping her gaze back and forth over the heads of her captives, ''this will put a fairly quick stop to it, understood?''

''Lady,'' said the one-armed man weakly, ''I can help you. But I need to eat a ghost, bad. I just threw a couple of pounds of dead ectoplasm, *and* a *good* ghost, and I'm about to expire.'' He was sitting next to Sullivan, against the door, and each one of his wheezing breaths was like a Wagnerian chorus.

DeLarava's mouth was pinched in a fastidious pout, but without looking down at him she asked, ''Who *are* you, anyway?''

The man was shaking, his right knee bumping Sullivan's thigh. ''Lately I've been calling myself Sherman Oaks.''

''How can Sherman Oaks help me?''

''I can . . . well, I can tell you that the boy there is carrying the ghost of Thomas Alva Edison.''

DeLarava gave a hiccuping laugh. ''That I already knew,'' she said, greedily allowing herself to actually stare at Kootie.

Sullivan looked angrily past Elizalde at Kootie. ''Why in hell did you tell him how to unclog himself, anyway?''

Kootie flinched, and said defensively, ''Mr. Edison didn't tell him *exactly* how. He—'' Kootie choked and spat. ''I can speak for myself, Kootie. He did *more* than what I *told* him, Pete. He kicked the rotted one out by throwing out a good one.''

''After you told him the right . . . posture to assume,'' said Sullivan.

''Pete,'' said Elizalde, ''let it go, it's done.''

Meaning, Sullivan thought, don't torment a senile old man who made a mistake out of wounded vanity.

''What do you all mean by 'unclogged'?'' asked deLarava, still staring at Kootie.

Sullivan looked up at her, and realized that Kootie and the one-armed man were looking at her too. This might conceivably be a bargaining chip, he thought.

''When you suck in a ghost that has rotted in an opaque container,'' said Sherman Oaks, ''your ghost-digestion gets clogged. Impacted, blocked. You can't eat any more of them, and the ghosts already inside you get rebellious. I was that way. Now I know how to get clear of it, how you can Heimlich yourself. *Ptooie*, you know?''

''Could we refer to them as 'essences'?'' said deLarava stiffly. ''And use the verb 'enjoy'?''

''Where are we going?'' asked Elizalde in a flat voice.

DeLarava squinted at her as if noticing her for the first time. ''Pete's Mex gal! One of my boys tells me you're the crazy psychiatrist who's been on the news. We're all going to the *Queen Mary*.''

Sullivan's leather jacket had been left back at the apartment, probably still balled up on the floor from having served as a pillow; and now through his thin shirt he felt fingers fumbling weakly at his left shoulder.

He looked at the man next to him, surprised that Oaks could have freed his single arm from the tape—and he saw that Oaks' hand *wasn't* free, was in fact still strapped down against his right hip; but Oaks was hunched around toward Sullivan, as if miming the act of reaching toward him with the arm that wasn't there.

Breath hissed in through Sullivan's teeth as he jerked away from Oaks in unthinking fright.

''What—'' snapped deLarava, convulsively switching her little pistol from one hand to the other, clearly startled by his sudden move. ''What is it?''

Sullivan realized that she hadn't once looked directly at him, and that she apparently didn't even want to speak his name. She plans to kill me at some point today, he thought; and because of that she's too fastidious to *acknowledge* me.

He turned back to look at Sherman Oaks, and the tiny eyes returned his gaze with no expression; but the man now sniffed deeply.

You smell my father's ghost, Sullivan thought. You know he's in here with us.

At least the phantom fingers had moved away from him. ''My shoulders are cramping up something terrible,'' Sullivan said, deliberately, still staring at Oaks. *Have we got a deal?* he thought into the little eyes. *I won't tell her you've got a ''hand'' free if you won't tell her about the ghost.*

''Any discomfort is regretted,'' said deLarava vaguely.

Sullivan looked back at the old woman. She was blinking rapidly, and her eyes, again fixed on the wall over the captives' heads, were bright with tears.

''They could only find the thumb,'' said deLarava hoarsely, looking right up at the skylight now. ''Where are the hands?''

''Lost in the Venice canals,'' said Sullivan at once. ''I tried to fish them out, but they dissolved in the salt water like . . . like Alka-Seltzer.''

Jammed behind him, his left hand was digging in his hip pocket; all that was in there was his wallet—containing nothing but ID cards and a couple of twenty-dollar bills—and his pocket comb.

"*Why* are we going to the *Queen Mary*?" asked Elizalde.

"To enjoy—" began deLarava; but her hair abruptly sprang up into a disordered topknot, drawing startled gasps from Kootie and Elizalde. And deLarava began to sob quietly.

Sullivan was aware of an itch in his right ear, but his father's ghost didn't say anything.

The Jeep Cherokee was leading the procession, and when it turned left off Ocean onto Queen's Way the two trucks followed.

J. Francis Strube didn't dare hunch around in his seat, for the man in back was presumably still holding a gun pointed at him, but he could peer out of the corners of his eyes. They had driven past the new Long Beach Convention Center on the left, and past Lincoln Park on the right, and now they were cruising downhill toward a vista of bright blue lagoons and sailboats and lawns and palm trees. Out across the mile-long expanse of the harbor he could see the black hull and the white upper decks of the *Queen Mary* shining in the early-morning sunlight.

The car radio was tuned to some oldies rock station, and the driver was whistling along to the sad melody of Phil Ochs's "Pleasures of the Harbor."

For the past five minutes Strube had been remembering how cautious Nicholas Bradshaw used to be, when Strube had worked for him in 1975—refusing to say where he lived, never giving out his home phone number, always taking different routes to and from the law office. Maybe, Strube thought unhappily, I should have taken his paranoia more seriously. Maybe I was a little careless today, in the way I blundered into this thing. "Are we actually going to the *Queen Mary*?" he asked in a humbled voice.

The driver glanced at him in cheerful surprise. "You've never been on it? It's great."

"I've been there," Strube said, defensively in spite of everything. "I've had dinner at Sir Winston's many times. I meant, are we really going there now."

"DeLarava's scheduled a shoot there today," the driver said. "I understood you were to be interviewed, along with that Nicky Bradshaw fellow. He was the actor who played Spooky, the teenage ghost in that old show. You must have seen reruns. He's to do some kind of dance, was my understanding."

Strube was squinting against his bewilderment as if it were a bright light. "But why am I *handcuffed*? Why all the guns?"

The man chuckled, shaking his head at the lane markers unreeling ahead of him. "Oh, she can be a regular Von Stroheim, can't she? What's the word? Martinet? I mean, you wanna talk about *domineering*? Get outta here!"

"But—what are you saying? What happened back there at that apartment building? You people threw all those wires and metal shutters out of the truck onto the street! And what was that awful smell?"

"Ah, there you have me."

Strube was dizzy. "What if I try to get out, at the next red light? Would this man behind me *shoot* me?"

"Through the back of the seat," said the driver. "Don't do it. This isn't a bluff, no, if that's what you're asking. The new automatics are ramped and throated so they have no problem feeding hollow-points, and it might not even make an exit wound, but it would surely make a hash of your vital organs. You don't want that. In fact—" He slapped the wheel lightly and nodded. "In fact, if Sir Winston's is open for lunch, we might be able to get her to spring for a good meal!"

"Never happen," said the man in the back seat gloomily.

After they had been driving for about ten minutes, stopping and starting up again and making some slow turns, Sullivan felt the truck stop and then reverse slowly down a ramp; and the skylight went dark, and he could hear the truck's engine echoing inside a big metallic room. Then the engine was switched off.

Car doors chunked in the middle distance, and he could feel the shake of the truck's driver's-side door closing; footsteps scuffed across concrete to the truck's back door, and the door was unlatched and swung open. The chilly air that swept into the truck's interior smelled of oiled machinery and the sea.

"E Deck," called a young man who was pulling a wheeled stepladder across the floor of the wide white-painted garagelike chamber. "We chased off the ship's staff for the moment, and we've got guys around to whistle if they come back. They say they've turned off the power in the circuit boxes on the Promenade and R Decks, and the gaffers are off to patch in and get the Genie lifts and the key lights set up for the first call at ten."

Test it with a meter anyway, thought Sullivan as his constricted left hand fingered his pocket comb. You don't want to be hooking your dimmer-board to the lugs if somebody forgot, and there's still a live 220 volts waiting for you in the utility panel.

Behind the fright that was dewing his forehead and shallowing his breathing, he was vaguely irritated at his suspicion that these efficient-looking young men might be better at the job than he and Sukie had been.

DeLarava was still sniffling as she clumped heavily down from rung to rung of the stepladder. "Get a couple of runners to take . . . the kid, and the old guy up by the front, and Pete Sullivan, he's the guy in the white shirt . . . to that room they're letting us use as an office. Gag the woman and the one-armed guy and leave them where they are for now."

Sullivan looked at the one-armed man seated awkwardly beside him. Sherman Oaks seemed to be only semiconscious, and his breathing was a rattling, chattering whine, like a car engine with a lot of bad belts and bearings. But the fabric of the man's baggy brown-and-green trousers was bunching and stretching over the left thigh, as if kneaded by an invisible hand.

Does he have fingernails on that hand? wondered Sullivan. If so, are they strong enough to peel off the tape that's holding down his flesh-and-blood arm? If he frees himself, and he's left in here with Angelica, he'll surely kill her to eat her ghost.

Should I tell deLarava about Oak's unbound—unbindable!—hand? If so, he might in return tell her that my father's ghost is on my person, and she'd fetch in some kind of mask and eat the old man with no delay.

Elizalde was sitting at Sullivan's right, her taped ankles screwed down next to his, and he rocked his head around to look at her. Her narrow face was tense, her lips white, but she crinkled her eyes at him in a faint, scared smile.

"I'd bring Dr. Elizalde too," Sullivan said. He was peripherally aware of an increasing ache in his left forearm; his fingers seemed to be nervously trying to pry the thick end-tooth off of his comb, which was a useless exercise since the comb was aluminum.

"Why would I want to bring Dr. Elizalde?" deLarava mused aloud.

"She's a medical doctor as well as a psychiatrist," Sullivan said, at random.

Sherman Oaks was singing in a whisper with each scratching exhalation now, without moving his lips at all, and his voice seemed to be a chorus of children: ". . . *Delaware punch, tell me the initials of your honey-bunch, capital A, B, C-D-E . . .*"

"In that case bring them all!" cried deLarava; though Sullivan thought it was Oaks's eerie singing rather than his own suggestion that had changed the old woman's mind. "Put cats in the coffee," she sang wildly herself, "and mice in the tea, and welcome Queen Kelley with thirty-times-three!"

Sullivan recognized the bit of verse—it was from the end of *Through the Looking-Glass*, when Alice was about to be crowned a queen.

DeLarava kept her little pistol pointed at her captives, as a runner hopped up into the truck and knifed the tape off of everyone's ankles.

"You want that lawyer that's in the Cherokee?" the man asked.

"Leave him where he is," deLarava said. "Lawyers are for after."

The fingers of Sullivan's left hand suddenly strained very hard at the end of the aluminum pocket comb, and with a muffled snap it broke, cutting his thumb knuckle. He palmed the broken-off end when the runner hopped down from the truck and began hauling Oaks's legs out over the bumper.

After Oaks had been propped upright against the side of the truck it was Sullivan's turn, and when he had been lifted down he stepped back across the floor to make room for Elizalde and Kootie—and Bradshaw, the shifting of whose bulk across the truck floor required the summoning of a second runner.

Down on the deck at last, Bradshaw hopped ponderously to shake the legs of his shorts straight. "I bet those guys were gay," he muttered.

"Don't try to shuffle away, Pete!" said deLarava sharply; and Sullivan was tensely sure that this direct address meant that she intended to kill him very soon indeed.

"Not me, boss," he said mildly.

When at last Bradshaw was standing next to Kootie and Elizalde on the concrete deck, deLarava pirouetted back, then mincingly led the way down a white hallway while the runners prodded the captives along after her. "O Looking-Glass creatures," called deLarava shrilly over her shoulder, "draw near. 'Tis an honor to see me, a favor to hear."

Sullivan managed to catch Elizalde's glance as they fell into step, and he gave her an optimistic wink.

It wasn't completely an empty gesture—it had just occurred to him that the hands sticking out of his shirt cuffs might well be Houdini's. The mask wasn't complete—he wasn't wearing the jacket with the detachable sleeves—but that was probably because he didn't have the whole outfit, he wasn't carrying the magician's dried thumb; nevertheless the plaster hands had disappeared when he had touched them, back there in the fumy apartment, and now *somebody's* left hand was clutching a bit of broken metal.

Lurching along up at the head of the procession, Sherman Oaks was tall enough to have to duck under a couple of valves connecting the pipes that ran along under the low ceiling, but the room deLarava led them into was as roomy as a TV studio. Fluorescent lights threw a white glow over two low couches against the walls, and a metal desk out in the middle of the floor, and rolls of cable on stacked wooden apple-boxes in a corner; deLarava waved toward one of the couches and then crossed ponderously to the desk and lowered her bulk into the chair behind it.

To the pair of her employees who had herded her captives into the room, deLarava said, "Loop a cable through their cuffs—under the arm of the one-armed fellow—and sit them down on the couch and tie the cable where they can't reach it."

As soon as Sullivan had been tethered and pushed down onto the couch, again sitting between Elizalde and Oaks, he felt his thumb begin to pry at one of the narrow comb-teeth that had broken away with the thick end-tooth. To explain any muscular shifting of his shoulders, he leaned forward and looked to his right—Elizalde and Kootie were whispering together, and Bradshaw, at the far end of the long couch, was just frowning and squinting around at the walls as if disapproving of the paint job.

DeLarava waved the runners out of the room with her little gun. From the floor behind the desk she lifted a big leather purse, and with her free hand she shook it out onto the desktop. Three cans of Hires Root Beer rolled out, two of them solidly full and one clattering empty; and then a brown wallet thumped down beside the cans, followed by a ring of keys.

"You recognize these, Pete?" deLarava asked, staring down at the items on the desk.

CHAPTER 44

*. . . and she had a vague sort of idea that they must be collected at once
and put back into the jury-box, or they would die.*
                                            —Lewis Carroll,
                                                Alice's Adventures in Wonderland

Sullivan didn't answer. He took a deep breath—and thought he
caught a whiff of bourbon on the air-conditioned breeze.

"And I've got an electromagnet," deLarava went on, "and some very
specific music, and a schizophrenic who's a better mask than you and
your sister ever were. I don't want a *glut* today, just your father—and,
as long as they're here, Thomas Alva Edison and Koot Hoomie Parganas." She lifted her pouchy face and stared right into Sullivan's eyes.
"And, wherever he is, Apie will come when I call him," she said. "Did
you know that he and your mother had their honeymoon aboard the
Queen Mary, in 1949?"

"No," said Sullivan. Their father had never liked to talk to the twins
about their mother, who had died in 1953, when they were a year old.

His left hand had broken off one of the narrow comb-teeth, and his
fingers were prodding the tiny sliver of metal into the gap between the
hinged single-blade swing-arm and the pawl housing of the cuff on his
right wrist.

Sullivan was trying to remember what he'd read last night about
Alice's coronation party; he wished he could lean across Elizalde and
ask Kootie, who'd been reading the book this morning. Sullivan's fingers were still pushing the comb-tooth against the cuff, and, recalling
the trick his hands had done yesterday inside the magically projected
milk can in the cemetery lake, he tried to help—and immediately the
tooth sprang out of his grip, and was lost forever down between the
couch cushions.

A young man who was apparently the second assistant director leaned in at the doorway. "That producer guy, Neal Obstadt, is here," he said. "He says you're—Jesus!—expecting him!" the young man finished as a burly man in a business suit pushed right past him into the room. The newcomer's iron-gray hair was clipped short, and the cut of his jacket didn't conceal broad shoulders that Sullivan guessed were probably tattooed.

Sullivan's heart beat faster at the thought that this intrusion might mean rescue—but the surge of hope died when the tanned cheeks spread back at the sight of deLarava's five captives, baring white teeth in a delighted smile.

"Why, Kelley!" he said. "I don't see how that boy there could be anyone but the famous Koot Hoomie Parganas! What a thoughtful," he added, frowning abruptly, "tithe." He glared across the room at her now. "You've been eating ghosts for years, right? You know how it works?"

"That will be all, Curtis," deLarava said hastily to the young man in the doorway, who seemed relieved to be able to hurry away.

Neal Obstadt waved at the captives. "They're secured?"

"Cuffed to a cable," said deLarava.

"And I assume," he went on, "that all five of your guests here will be dead before sundown?"

DeLarava rolled her eyes. "If you insist on subverting the civilized circumlocutions of—"

"You gonna kill 'em or not? I don't have all day, and neither do you, trust me."

"Fuck you, Neal. Yes."

"I can talk freely then. Some smoke dealer named Sherman Oaks sold me a dead ghost. Well, they're *all* dead, aren't they? But this one had gone rotten, and now it's stuck in my head; it's *in the way*, and I can't eat any more ghosts. All that happens when I try is that I get the nitrous oxide—but I don't get a life. The *life* in the dose just gets exhaled away. Does me no good. Have you run into this problem?"

"I've heard of it, yes," deLarava began.

"I know how to undo it," said Sherman Oaks—surprising Sullivan, who had thought the ragged one-armed man was nearly unconscious.

"So do I," said Sullivan and Kootie in quick unison.

"My name is Sherman Oaksssss . . ." said the one-armed man.

He went on exhaling past the end of his sentence, and the breath didn't stop, but kept whistling out of him as if his mouth were an opening in a windy canyon; and on that wind came the chanting voices of half a dozen little girls:

> *"There was a man of double deed*
> *Sowed his garden full of seed.*
> *When the seed began to grow,*
> *'Twas like a garden full of snow."*

Obstadt had reached into his jacket and smoothly drawn a stainless-steel .45 semiautomatic, cocked and locked. Sullivan blinked helplessly at Elizalde and nodded. *Same kind of gun,* he thought. *God help us.*

"When the snow began to melt," the girls' voices chanted on out of Sherman Oaks's slack mouth,

> *" 'Twas like a ship without a belt;*
> *When the ship began to sail,*
> *'Twas like a bird without a tail."*

Behind Sullivan's back, the strong fingers of his left hand quickly broke another narrow tooth off the comb-end, and again began working the end of it into the handcuff housing, in under the pawl wheel. This time he didn't try to help his hands.

> *"When the bird began to fly,*
> *'Twas like an eagle in the sky;*
> *When the sky began to roar,*
> *'Twas like a lion at the door."*

"The fuck is he doing?" shouted Obstadt. He pointed the pistol at Oaks and yelled, "Shut up!" Sullivan could see that the safety lever was down now.

The voices continued, with the businesslike diligence of a child's jump-rope ritual; and Oaks's mouth was slack, and his throat wasn't visibly working, as the soprano syllables stitched his outrushing breath:

> *"When the door began to crack,*
> *'Twas like a stick across my back;*
> *When my back began to smart,*
> *'Twas like a pen-knife in my heart;*
> *When my heart began to bleed,*
> *'Twas death and death and death indeed."*

Oaks's eyes were crossed sharply together behind his nose. He was frowning and shaking his head, and Sullivan was sure this performance wasn't voluntary; Sullivan guessed that it was some kind of after-effect of the unclogging the man had done back in the apartment.

DeLarava had stood up, and now Sullivan looked away from Oaks at her. Her face was as pale as bacon fat, and her mouth was trembling. "My little girls!" she screamed suddenly. "That's them! He's the one who ate my little birth day girls!"

Then she was end-running around the desk, her blubbery arms swinging horizontally and her belly jumping under the flowered dress, and she flung herself onto her knees in front of Oaks and planted her lips over his still-exhaling mouth.

And the wind out of Oaks must have increased, for deLarava's head was flung aside, and she teetered and windmilled her arms for a moment before sitting down heavily on the deck—and a smell of flowers and green grass tickled Sullivan's nose, and the room was full of flickering shadows and quick tapping and anxious little cries.

All at once Sullivan could see several skinny little girls in white dresses—or it might have been one, very quick, skinny little girl—flashing around the room, like a carousel of hologram photographs spinning under a strobe light; then the apparition was gone, and he heard sobbing and laughter and light fluttering footsteps receding away down the hallway beyond the door, away from the direction of the trucks, farther into the maze of the ship.

Sullivan felt the tiny metal blade trip the pawl inside the cuff mechanism, and then the fingers of his left hand squeezed the cuff tight, and released it—and his left hand was free.

"You can have the Parganas," wheezed deLarava as she rolled over onto her hands and knees and began dragging one big knee, and then the other, under herself, "kid. And Oaks." She raised her obese body to her feet in one steady straightening, though the effort sent bright blood bursting out of her flaring nostrils and down the front of her dress. "Leave me the others."

Then she took a deep breath and went charging out the door after the girl-ghosts. "Wait," she was bellowing hoarsely as she clumped and caromed down the hall, "wait, I'm one of you too! Delaware punch! Tell me the—goddammit—"

Obstadt was still pointing the .45 at Sherman Oaks's round face, but his finger was out of the trigger guard and he was looking after de-Larava.

"Like that," said Oaks in a frail voice.

Obstadt looked down at him over the sights. "What?"

"What I just did. That's how you do it. I just now spit out those ghosts. To get cleared of the rotten one, hike one of your quick ones up to the top of your mind. Cross your eyes, hard, so you can *see* the quick one standing there on the diving board of your mind, and then exhale and *spit.* The live one goes, and knocks the rotten one out with it.''

Sullivan was still sure that Oaks's latest seizure had been involuntary, and that the little girl-ghosts had simply forced their way out of him, past the now-compromised containment of his will; Sullivan guessed that the one-armed man was simply incontinent now, and would leak ghosts whenever he so much as sneezed. Nevertheless, Sullivan was a little surprised that Oaks would give the crucial information away with no security.

Sullivan had got his toes well back in under the couch, and he was watching Obstadt intently.

Obstadt stepped back, leaned against the desk, and crossed his eyes.

Sullivan heard a creaking from down the couch to his right, and when he glanced that way he saw Bradshaw squinting and gathering himself as if for a rush, as if he'd forgotten that he was tethered. Sullivan caught the old man's eye and frowned hard, shaking his head slightly.

Obstadt exhaled, leaning forward with the .45 pointing at the deck, and coughed; and he shook spasmodically, and his shoulders went up and his chin dropped onto his chest, then his shoulders fell and his head snapped forward and a black cylinder with ribs or folded legs ridging its sides came inflating out from between his gaping jaws, balanced for a moment on his teeth, and then fell and slapped onto the floor, where it flexed muscularly. The irregularities on its sides separated and proved to be legs that waved uselessly in the fouled air.

Sullivan had flinched at the sight and the smell of the thing's sudden appearance, but before Obstadt could straighten up Sullivan had sprung from the couch and whipped his right hand down in a fast arc past Obstadt's jaw, so that the freed cuff cracked solidly against the back of the man's head. Sullivan's bar-time jolt of surprise, halfway through the move, had only made him hit harder.

The .45 went off with an eardrum-hammering bang and blew the black thing to wet fragments, and the ricochet rang around the metal room and punched a hole in the couch where Sullivan had been sitting; Obstadt was on his hands and knees, and from somewhere a fist malleted the back of his bloodied head, sending Obstadt's face snapping down to the deck like a smacked croquet ball. Wind and a man's shouting voice were blowing out of his mouth now.

Sullivan looked up—Oaks had freed himself from the gaffer's tape, and it had been he that had punched Obstadt.

Sullivan's right arm was paused across his body from the follow-through of his blow, and now he lashed it back up hard at Sherman Oaks's face, which was looming over his own; the cuff just tore Oaks's cheek, for Sullivan's fingers had snatched at the chain, but Sullivan followed the blow with a solid kick of his left knee into Oaks's groin, and the one-armed man convulsed double and fell over sideways into the stinking mess that had been the buglike expelled ghost. The other ghost Obstadt had exhaled, the one with a man's voice, whirled gasping around the room and cycloned away in the hall.

Sullivan took one hitching half-breath, and the instant sting in his lungs made him decide not to breathe. He fished his comb out of his pocket and broke off another tooth, and when he had freed his right wrist he crouched to ratchet one cuff tightly around Oaks's wrist and the other around Obstadt's left ankle.

Then he tried to pick up the .45—but his fingers had suddenly gone limp, and all he could do was to push the weapon around clumsily; even by pressing the heels of both hands together, he couldn't get a grip on the gun. *Fuck it*, he thought in despair, straightening up.

Still not breathing, though his eyes were watering from the harsh fumes of the sizzling, evaporating ghost, he reeled back to the couch, and his hands were suddenly strong and dextrous again as he leaned behind Elizalde and then Kootie and then Bradshaw and sprang free the left wrist of each of them.

He expelled the last exhausted air in his lungs in croaking to Elizalde, *"Get the gun!"*

Her nostrils were whitely pinched and her eyes were teary slits, but she nodded and quick-stepped to crouch by where Obstadt and Oaks, linked, were writhing in the wet, smoking mess. Elizalde snatched up the .45 without difficulty and tucked it into the waistband of her jeans, pulling the untucked sweatshirt hem over it.

"Out," she barked, leading the way out the door and into the hallway.

Sullivan couldn't tell how much of the screaming racket in his ears was external and how much was just the internal overload-protest of his eardrums, but at least the appalling smell seemed to be keeping de-Larava's employees back at the garage end of the hall.

Then he did hear something, from back in the direction of the garage—a familiar wailing laugh.

Elizalde was hurrying down the hall away from the garage, in the direction deLarava had gone, and Sullivan and Kootie and Bradshaw went stumbling hastily after her.

The Jeep had been parked well in, right up against the inboard bulkhead of the garage area, and the trucks had parked behind it. At the boom-

and-echoes of the gunshot, Strube's guards had climbed out and rushed toward the hall; but they had been stopped by the fumes, and had joined the general rush out into the fresh air on the sunlit loading dock. Some men in undershirts had come inside from the dock carrying a burlap sack with a baseball cap on it and something thrashing inside it, and they hurried into the vacated hall.

Strube didn't mind the smell. He hiked his left arm behind himself until he could reach the door handle with his right hand, and when he had timidly opened the door and stepped down to the deck, he wandered down the hall himself—slowly, so that any of deLarava's men who might see him would be likelier to yell at him than shoot.

But apparently no one saw him. He walked past an open doorway and glanced in at two men rolling in a black puddle. The odd smell was strongest here, and one of the struggling men had only one arm, but Strube wasn't curious. If he kept walking, he was sure to find an elevator or stairway that would lead him up to the tourist decks, where he could surely get someone to call the police for him; maybe he would be able to get a security guard to unlock the handcuffs.

And then what? He could refuse to press charges, and take a cab back to Twenty-first Place, where he had left his car. Then he would drive back to his office, to think. His venture into show-business law was proving to be more difficult than he had anticipated.

CHAPTER 45

"If that there King was to wake," added Tweedledum, *"you'd go out—bang!—
just like a candle!"*

—Lewis Carroll,
Through the Looking-Glass

By the fluorescent tubes overhead, Sullivan could see that the hallway
broadened out ahead of Elizalde—the port walls slanted outward with
the hull, and were riveted steel with vertical steel crossbeams welded
on, and the edges of the empty doorways on the inboard side were
knobby from having been cut with torches—and in the far bulkhead,
beyond a row of wheeled aluminum carts, he saw a tiny recessed booth
with accordion bars pulled across it.

"Whoa, Angelica!" he called. "That's an elevator."

Elizalde nodded and skidded sideways and sprinted to the elevator.
By the time she had pulled back the bars from the little stall, Sullivan
was right behind her, and he took her arm as the two of them stepped
into the telephone-booth-like box.

The walls were paneled in rich burl elm that was dinged and scratched
at the tray-level of the wheeled carts. He folded up a hinged wooden
seat and flattened himself against the elevator wall to make room for
Kootie; and over the boy's head he saw Bradshaw shuffling slowly
across the deck.

"Come *on*, Nicky," Sullivan called, thinking of the winged bag that
had flown after them in the cemetery yesterday. "Hurry!"

"I don't," said Bradshaw, scuffling to a stop. "Feel so good. Motion
sickness. I'd throw up in there. I'll meet you. Later."

The ringing in Sullivan's ears had decreased to a shrill whining . . .
and he was suddenly aware of an airy absence. He slapped his chest,

feeling the angular hardness of the brass grave-portrait plaque, still in his scapular. "My father!" he said. "Is he with you, Nicky?"

Bradshaw paused, then shook his head. "But I'll watch for him," he said. "Go on now."

Sullivan bared his teeth and clenched Houdini's fists. His father might be anywhere down here. *DeLarava* might be anywhere down here. "Nicky, get in the elevator!"

Bradshaw smiled. "You know I won't, if I say I won't."

"—Okay." There's nothing I can do, Sullivan thought. "Okay. *Vaya con Dios, amigo.*"

"*Y tu tambien, hermano,*" said Bradshaw.

Sullivan pulled the folded gate out again across the gap until it clanged shut, and said, "We've got to go down a deck."

"*Down?*" panted Elizalde. Her breaths were frightened sobs. "No, Pete—up! Sunlight, normal people!"

"I should have thought of this before," said Sullivan. "Kootie, do you remember how Alice's coronation ceremony got wrecked?"

The boy's brown eyes blinked up at him. "The food at the banquet came to life," he said, "and it didn't want to be eaten."

"Right, the leg of mutton was talking and laughing and sitting in the White Queen's chair, and the pudding yelled at Alice when she cut it, and—and the White Queen dissolved in the soup tureen, remember? The *bottles* even came to life, and took plates for wings and forks for legs. And Queen Alice was knocked right out of the Looking-Glass world." He punched the button that had a downward-pointing arrow on it. "We've got to find the after steering compartment."

The little booth shook, and then with a hydraulic whine the deck outside started to move upward; before his vision was cut off by this ascending fourth wall, Sullivan heard the sirenlike laugh again, closer, and he saw Bradshaw shift heavily around to face the way they had come.

The bare bulb in the shelved, inlaid elevator ceiling made the faces of Kootie and Elizalde look jaundiced and oily, and Sullivan knew he must look the same to them.

Elizalde was shaking. "Goddamn you, Pete, what's in this after steering compartment?"

"The degaussing machinery," said Sullivan, trying to speak with conviction. "They'd have had to install it when the *Queen Mary* was a troopship during the war, to keep her hull from attracting magnetic mines, and there's no way they'd have gone to the trouble of tearing it out, afterward. And the after steering room is the electrical spine of any ship—there'd have been a diesel engine there to run a sort of power-steering pump, so they could steer the ship from down there if the bridge was blown away. It's the backup bridge, in effect, and I don't suppose they're using the real one for anything at all now, with tourists dropping snow cones all over everything. There'll be live power down below still.'' It's certainly possible, he thought.

"So what?" Elizalde was leaning against the back of the car, her sunken eyes watching the riveted steel of the elevator shaft rising beyond the frail bars of the gate, and she spoke quietly in the confined space. "What the hell good is this old anti-mine stuff going to do us? Jesus, Pete, tell me you know what you're doing here!"

"How did this apparatus keep the ship from attracting magnetic mines?" asked Kootie.

Sullivan looked down at the boy. "The mines had a specific magnetic polarity," he said. "Once that was known, it was easy enough to forcibly reverse the ship's own natural magnetic field by passing a current through a set of cables around the hull."

"But it's turned off now?"

"Sure, it'll be disconnected, but it'll still be there."

"And you think there'll still be power there too. So you're planning to reconnect it and crank up a big magnetic field; and," it was Kootie's little-boy cadences that went on, "you're gonna wake up every dinner aboard."

"It'll draw 'em out," Sullivan agreed. From the walls, he thought, from the closets in the old staterooms, from the deck planks weathered by three decades of sunny summer cruises and North Atlantic storms. "And none of 'em will want to be eaten. It'll be a mass exorcism." Once drawn out, he thought, they'll dissolve away in this alien Long Beach air. He remembered Bradshaw's explanation of the L.A. CIGAR traps, and he hoped the dim old ghosts might somehow understand that this was . . . rescue? Liberation? Finishing the job of dying, say.

A breeze on his ankles made Sullivan look down past Kootie, and he saw that an edge of the elevator shaft had appeared down by their feet; the gap below it rode up until he could see another deck, dimly lit by electric lights somewhere. The elevator floor clanged against the painted steel deck, and he pulled the accordion gate aside. The bulkheads of the silent old corridors were ribbed and riveted, painted gray below belt-height and yellowed white above.

"This has got to be as close to water level as you can get," he said, instinctively speaking quietly down here so close to the sanctum sanctorum of the vast old liner. "It'll be right behind us, directly over the rudder."

"Get these cuffs off us," said Kootie.

"Oh, yeah." Sullivan took out his comb, broke off another narrow tooth, and quickly opened the handcuff that was still on Kootie's right wrist; then he did the same for Elizalde.

"Where did you learn that?" Elizalde asked as the cuffs clanked to the floor and she massaged her freed wrist.

Sullivan held up his hands, palms out, and wiggled the fingers at her. "If you hadn't glued that plaster finger back on, I'd be missing one right now." He started down the corridor toward the stern. "Come on."

Ancient bunks, with brown blankets still tumbled on them, were bolted on metal trays to the steel bulkheads down here, and as he led Elizalde and Kootie past them Sullivan shuddered at the thought of coming back this way if he got the field up and at maximum intensity.

"That's serious electrical conduit," said Kootie, pointing at the ceiling.

Sullivan looked up, and saw that the boy was right. "Follow it," he said.

A few steps farther down the hall the conduit pipes curved into the amidships bulkhead over a dogged-shut oval door, and Sullivan punched back the eight dog clips around the door's perimeter; the door rattled in the bulkhead frame, and Sullivan realized that the rubber seal had rotted away. He prayed that he wasn't the first person to open this door since the ship was docked here in Long Beach in 1967.

But there were lights burning inside the twenty-foot-square room beyond the door when he pulled it open; and they were new fluorescent tubes, bolted up alongside the very old lights, which were hung on C-shaped metal straps so that the recoil of the big wartime guns on the top deck wouldn't break the filaments.

A diesel engine the size of a car motor sat on a skid supported by two I-beams laid down near the left bulkhead, with two banked rows of square batteries on shelves behind it; and Sullivan saw a new battery charger bolted to the bulkhead over them.

"They're live!" he said, his shoulders slumping with relief. "See? This must be the ship's backup power supply now, in case the AC from ashore goes funny. UPS for their computers, uninterrupted power supply so they don't lose their data."

"Groovy," said Elizalde. "Hook it up and let's get out of here."

"Right." Sullivan looked around and identified the reduction-gear box and the steering pump and the after steering wheel to his left, and so the three-foot-by-four-foot box on the right-hand bulkhead had to be the degaussing panel. He walked past it and began unlooping heavy coils of emergency power cable from the rack riveted to the bulkhead.

Sullivan was remembering another exorcism he had helped perform, at the Moab Nuclear Power Station in Utah in 1989.

The Public Utilities Commission had claimed that it would be cheaper to produce power elsewhere than to spend the millions needed to bring the reactor up to current safety standards—but the real reason had been that the site had become clogged with ghosts attracted to the high voltage. The things had clustered around the big outdoor transformers, and some had got solid enough to fiddle with the valves and switches and steal the employees' cars.

The power line from the degaussing panel had been cut, just beyond the breaker, disconnecting the panel from the rest of the ship; but a post stuck out above the hacksawed conduit, and Sullivan pulled the dusty canvas cover off the emergency power three-phase plug on the end of the post.

"They call these things biscuits," he told Elizalde defiantly.

"Call it a muffin if you like," she said, "today I'm not arguing."

He picked up one end of the cable and separated the inch-thick wires protruding from the end of it. The red one he shoved into the positive hole in the biscuit, and the black one he shoved into the negative hole. They fit tightly enough to support the weight of the cable. He would be getting direct current from the batteries, so he let the white wire hang unconnected.

The Moab station had in its time produced more than fifty billion kilowatt hours, enough power to light half a million homes for a quarter of a century. But he had stood in the control room and watched the dials as the power had fallen from fifty to twenty to three percent of capacity, and then a voice on the intercom had said, "Turbine trip," and Sullivan's gaze had snapped to the green lights on the control panel in the instant before they flashed on, their sudden glow indicating that the circuit breakers were open and no electricity was being produced.

And as the superintendent reached for the switch that would drive the cadmium rods into the reactor core, killing the uranium fission, Sullivan alone among the technicians in the control room had heard the chorus of wails as the resident ghosts had faded into nothing.

He was setting up the same devastation now. The current he would shortly be sending through the degaussing coils in the length of the hull would wake up all the dormant, undisturbed ghosts aboard the ship; focused, they would venture timidly out of their housekeeping-tended graves, only to evaporate into nothingness when the drain on the batteries outstripped the ability of the recharger to counter it, and the magnetic field collapsed.

Perhaps sensing his unhappiness, Kootie and Elizalde wordlessly stepped aside as he dragged the other end of the cable across the painted steel deck to the stepped ranks of batteries against the left bulkhead.

Steel bars connected the terminals of each battery in a row to the next, and he wedged the inch-thick end of the red wire under the bar on the first battery in the top row, then did the same with the black wire to the first battery on the bottom row. He had now hooked up the degaussing panel, at the expense of the the diesel engine's starter motor.

As he straightened up, he softly whistled, in slow time, the first notes of reveille.

He walked back across the deck to the panel and, with a sigh, pushed the master switch up into the on position. There was a muffled internal click.

The needle of the first DC voltmeter on the face of the panel jumped to 30, but that one was only indicating full power from the batteries. Then he took hold of the rubber-cased rheostat wheel and started turning it clockwise; the second voltmeter's needle began to climb across the dial toward 30, as the needle on the ammeter next to it moved more slowly up toward 150. For the first time in more than forty years, current was coursing through the wartime degaussing cables that ribbed the hull all the way from back here by the rudder to the bow a thousand feet north of him.

The deck had begun to vibrate under his feet, and a droning roar was getting louder; when he had cranked the wheel all the way over as far as it would go clockwise, the noise was so loud that Elizalde had to shout to be heard.

"What are you doing?" she yelled. "You've turned something on!"

"My God," said Kootie, loudly but reverently, "that's the noise of the screws. You've waked up the ghost of the ship herself!"

CHAPTER 46

"What matters it how far we go?" his scaly friend replied. "There is another shore, you know, upon the other side."
—Lewis Carroll,
Alice's Adventures in Wonderland

O h," Elizalde moaned, "let's get *out* of here!"

Sullivan backed away from the panel, and even Houdini's hands were trembling. "Yes," he said.

Sullivan led the way out of the after steering compartment and back down the corridor toward the elevator. The hallway reeked of sweaty bodies now, and he could hear a scratchy recording of Kitty Kallen singing "It's Been a Long, Long Time" echoing from somewhere ahead of them.

Bony figures were shifting among the blankets on the bulkhead-hung bunks as Sullivan and Elizalde and Kootie hurried past; hands still translucent groped at Elizalde, and voices blurred by unformed mouths mumbled amorously at her.

The elevator motor was buzzing and rattling when they rounded the corner, but the car was coming down to this deck—and through the bars Sullivan saw the burlap sack with the black Raiders baseball cap on it slumped on the elevator floor, shifting furiously and yowling as if it were filled with cats.

Before he could grab Kootie and Elizalde and run, the cat noises stopped and the front flap of the bag fell away, and as the car clanked down to the deck a naked young woman, slim and dark-haired, stood up in it and blinked through the bars at Sullivan and beyond him. Her body wasn't solidified yet—ribs showed faintly through the white softness of her breasts, and her loins were a wash of shadow.

Her eyes were bewildered brown depths, and already solid enough for Sullivan to see tears on the lashes. *"Es esto infierno?"* she asked.

Elizalde pulled back the gate. *"Esto es ninguna parte,"* she said. *"Y esto pasara pronto."*

Is this hell? the ghost-woman had asked; and Elizalde had told her that this was nowhere, and would soon pass. Sullivan stared at the woman nervously, remembering the thing that had flown over the grass at the cemetery yesterday, laughing and clanking metal wings—and she stared back at him without any recognition, her imprinted malice having fallen away with the burlap sack under her bare feet.

The woman stumbled out of the elevator car, looked blankly around, and then walked uncertainly back toward where the bunks were hanging, and Sullivan paused as if to stop her or warn her; but Elizalde grabbed his arm and pulled him into the car.

"Tumble a bunch of old books together," she said. "Books so old and fragile that nobody can read them anymore. The pages will break off and get mixed up. Does it matter?"

Sullivan was sweating as he stepped into the car, crowding the wall to make room for Elizalde and Kootie. These limitless dim lower decks, with all their forgotten alcoves and doors and passageways, were suddenly potent, and darkly inviting, and he pushed the up button hard. "Let's go all the way to the top," he said hoarsely.

"Amen," said Elizalde.

J. Francis Strube had found a carpeted hallway and he had started running downhill along it, past silent doors recessed in the wood-paneled walls. The hallway curved up ahead of him to disappear behind the gentle bulge of the glossy ivory ceiling, as if he were sprinting around the perimeter ring of a very elegant space station, and he had assured himself that somewhere between here and the eventual bow he must run across someone who could help him.

But a grinding roar had started up under the carpet and the whole ship had *moved* slightly, as if flexing itself, and he had lost his footing and fallen headlong; his hands had still been cuffed behind him, and though he had managed to take the first hard impact on his shoulder, his chin and cheekbone had bounced solidly off the carpeted floor.

Now he was up again, and walking, but he had to step carefully. Perhaps it was some Coriolis effect that made walking so difficult; he had to plant his feet flat, with the toes pointed outward, to keep from rolling against the close walls.

Over the droning vibration from below the deck he could presently hear children laughing, and when he came to a gleaming wooden staircase he saw a little girl with blond braids come flying down the banister; she rebounded from the floor and the wall like a big beach ball, and her long white dress spread out in an air-filled bell to let her sink gently to the carpeted landing.

Another girl came zooming down right behind her to do the same trick, and a third simply spun swan-diving down through the vertical space of the stairwell, graceful as a leaf.

"Up, up!" cried girl voices from the landing above, and when Strube stepped forward to tilt his head back and peer in that direction, he saw three more blond little girls stamping their feet with impatience.

All six of the girls seemed to be identical—sextuplets?—and to be about seven years old. How could they be doing these impossible acrobatics? They were a little higher up than he was—was the gravity weaker up in that ring? When he counted them all again, he got seven; then five; then eight.

"Girls," he said dizzily; but the three or four on his level were holding hands and dancing in a ring, chanting, "*When* the *sky* be*gan* to *roar*, 'twas *like* a *lion* at the *door!*" and the three or four above went on calling, "Up, up!"

"Girls!" he said, more loudly.

The several who had been dancing dropped their hands now and stared at him wide-eyed. "He can see us!" said one to another.

Strube was dizzy. His neck was wet, and he couldn't shake the notion that it was wet with blood rather than sweat, but with his hands cuffed behind him he couldn't reach up to find out.

"Of course I can see you," he said. "Listen to me. I need to find a grown-up. Where's your mother?"

"We don't think we have a mother," said one of the girls in front of him. "Where is *your* mother, please?"

This was getting him nowhere. "What are your names?"

One of the girls at the landing above called down, "We're each named Kelley. We all became friends because of that, and because we couldn't sleep, even though it was pitch dark."

"In most gardens," spoke up a girl in front of Strube, "they make the beds too soft, so the flowers are always asleep."

"We came from a hard, noisy garden," put in one who was sliding slowly down the banister. "We've got to go up," she told her companions. "If there isn't the sun, there'll be the moon."

"Who is taking *care* of you?" Strube insisted. "Who did you come here with?"

"We were thrown out of a dark place," said one of the girls above.

The four or five below were climbing the stairs now with graceful spinning hops. "Again," put in another.

At least they seem to be well cared for, Strube thought. Then he looked more closely at a couple of them and noticed their pallor and their sunken cheeks, and he saw that their dresses were made of some coarsely woven white stuff that looked like matted cobwebs.

"Where do you *live*?" asked Strube, speaking more shrilly than he had meant to. His heart was pounding and his breath was fast and shallow; he realized that he was frightened, though not of these girls, directly.

"We live in Hell," one of the Kelleys told him in a matter-of-fact tone. "But we're climbing out," one of her companions added.

Strube wasn't able to think clearly, and he knew it was because of the bang his head had taken against the floor back up the hallway. His stomach felt inverted; he would have to find a men's room soon and throw up. But he felt that he couldn't leave these defenseless, demented children down here in these roaring, flexing catacombs.

"I'll lead you out of here," he said, stepping up the stairs after them. He had to hunch his left shoulder up and stretch his right arm to hold on to the banister, for the ship was rolling ponderously. "We've all got to get out of here."

The girls looked down at him doubtfully from the landing. One of them said, "Would you know the sun, or the moon, if you saw either of them?"

Jesus, thought Strube. "Yes. Definitely."

"What if it's just another painted canvas?" one of the girls asked.

"I'll tear it down," Strube said desperately. "The real one'll be up there, trust me."

"Come on, then," a Kelley told him, and the girls whirled and leaped around him as he climbed on up the stairs. The gravity did seem to be weaker as one ascended higher, and he had to restrain himself from dancing with them.

A lift attendant had abruptly appeared in the elevator, cramping things terribly. He was an elderly man in a white shirt and black tie, and in a fretful English accent he demanded to know what class of accommodations Sullivan and Kootie and Elizalde had booked.

Sullivan glanced bewilderedly at Elizalde, and then said heartily, "Oh, first-class!"

"All the way!" added Kootie.

The old man stared at their dirty jeans and disordered hair, and he said, "I think not." He pushed the button for R Deck, and a moment later the elevator car rocked to a stop. "The Tourist Class Dining Saloon is down the hall ahead of you," he said sternly as he leaned between Sullivan and Kootie to slide open the gate, "just past the stairs. See that you go no higher up."

Sullivan hesitated, and considered just throwing the old man out of the car and resuming their upward course; but he and Kootie and Elizalde were deep in the ghost world now, and they might well find the solid ghosts of security guards from the 1930s waiting for them on the higher decks.

"I think we'd better play along," he said quietly to Elizalde. "We're in good cover so far, and I doubt that Edison's field shows up at all in this chaos." He stepped out of the car onto a carpeted hallway.

After an agonized, tooth-baring whine, Elizalde followed him out, tugging Kootie along by the hand.

Behind them the gate slid closed, and the car began to sink away down the shaft.

The ship was alive with voices now, and Sullivan and his companions seemed to have left the rumble of the screws below them.

Many of the room doors were open, and laughter and excited shouting shook the tobacco-scented air, but when they peeked into the lighted staterooms they passed, they could see only empty couches, and mirrored vanity tables, and paneled walls with motionless curtains over the portholes.

At the open, polished burl walnut stairway they could hear children's voices ascending from below; but the dining-room doors were ahead of them, and a steamy beef smell and a clatter of cutlery on china was accompanying the voices from beyond the closed doors, and Sullivan led the way around the stairs and pushed the doors open.

The noises were loud now, but the tables and chairs set across the ship's-width hardwood floor were empty; though a chair here and there did occasionally shift, as if invisible diners were turning their attentions from one companion to another.

Sullivan took Elizalde's cold hand, while she took Kootie's, and he led them between the noisy tables toward the service doors in the far bulkhead; and though there were no diners visible, Sullivan tried to thread his way exactly between the tables, and not violate the body spaces of any ghosts.

They exited the dining room through the starboard service door, and now, among the kitchens, they saw people.

Nearly solid men in white chef's hats were pushing carts in and out of open kitchen doorways, apparently oblivious of the unauthorized intruders; the dishes on the carts were covered with steel domes, and, since the kitchen staff didn't seem able to see Sullivan and he hadn't eaten at all today, he reached out and touched one of the covers on a cart that had been momentarily left against the hallway bulkhead. The cover handle was warmly solid, and he lifted the dome away.

From a bed of baby carrots and asparagus, a woman's face was smiling up at him. Her eyes were looking directly into his, and when her lips opened to puff out a bourbon-scented whisper of *"Hi, Pete,"* he recognized her as Sukie.

Elizalde tugged at his arm, but he pulled her back, feeling the relayed shake as Kootie was stopped too.

"Hi, Sukie," he said; his voice was level, but he was distantly surprised that his legs were still holding him up. He glanced sideways at Elizalde's face, but she was looking down at the plate, and then at him, in frowning puzzlement.

"I guess she can't see me," said Sukie's face. "You've spilled it all out onto the floor, haven't you? How long can this magnetic charge last? Who's your chick, anyway? She's the one who was on the phone last night, isn't she?"

"Yes." Sullivan squeezed Elizalde's hand. "The charge—I don't know. An hour?"

"When I consider how my light was spent! And then I'll be gone, and you'll probably be sorry, but not near sorry enough. You're in love with her, aren't you? How do I look in a halo of vegetables? I'll see if I can't wish you something besides misery with her; no promises, but I'll see what I can muster up. Haul your ass—and hers, too, I guess— and you got a kid already?—up to the Moon Deck. We also serve who only stand and gaff."

Elizalde barked a quick scream and her hand tightened on Sullivan's, and then the face was gone, and all that was on the plate was steaming vegetables.

"You saw her, didn't you?" said Sullivan as he hurried on down the kitchen corridor, pulling Elizalde and Kootie along.

"Just for a second," said Elizalde, having to nearly shout to be heard over the feverish clatter of pots and pans, "I saw a woman's *face* on that plate! No, Kootie, we're not going back!" To Sullivan, she added, "You were . . . *speaking* to her . . . ?"

"It was my sister." Sullivan saw a door in the white bulkhead at the end of the corridor, and he tugged Elizalde along more quickly. "She says I'm in love with you. And she says she'll try to wish us something besides misery."

"Well," said Elizalde with a bewildered and frightened grin, "this *is* your *family*, after all—I hope she tries hard."

"Yeah, me too, in spite of everything." They had reached the door.

"Catch up, Kootie, I think we've got another dining room to pass through." He pushed open the door.

This dining room too was as wide as the ship, but the ornate rowed mahogany ceiling was fully three deck-heights overhead; ornate planters and huge, freestanding Art Deco lamps punctuated the middle height—and there were visible diners here.

All the men at the tables were wearing black ties and all the women were in off-the-shoulder evening dresses. The conversation was quieter in this vast hall, and the air was sharp with the effervescence of champagne. On the high wall facing them across the length of the dining room, a vast mural dominated the whole cathedral chamber; even from way over here Sullivan could see that it was a stylized map of the North Atlantic, with a clock in the top of it indicated by radiating gold bars surrounding the gold hands, which stood at five minutes to twelve.

"I'm not dressed for this," said Elizalde in a small voice.

Sullivan looked back at her, and grinned at how humble she looked, framed in the glossy elm burl doorway, in her jeans and grimy Graceland sweatshirt. Kootie, peering big-eyed from behind her, looked no better in his bloodstained polo shirt, and Sullivan found that he himself was sorry he hadn't found time to shave yesterday or today.

"Probably they can't see us," he told her. "Come on, it's not that far."

But as they strode out across the broad parquet floor, a white-haired gentleman at one of the nearer tables caught Sullivan's glance, and raised an eyebrow; and then the man was pushing back his chair and slowly standing up.

Sullivan looked away as he hurried past the table and pulled Elizalde along, glad to hear Kootie's footsteps scuffing right behind her.

Men were standing up at other tables, though, all looking gravely at Sullivan and his two companions as they trotted through the amber-lit vista of white tablecloths and crystal wineglasses, and now the women were getting to their feet too, and anxiously eyeing the shabby intruders.

"Halfway there," gritted Sullivan between his teeth. He was staring doggedly at the mural above and ahead of them. Two nearly parallel tracks curved across the golden clouds that represented the Atlantic, but only one track had anything on it—one miniature crystal ship, all by itself out in the middle of the metallic sea.

How could there be a room this big in a *ship*? he thought as he strode between the tables, tugging Elizalde's hand. Polished wooden pillars, the vaulted ceiling so far away up there, and it must be a hundred tables spread out on every side across the floor to the distant dark walls recessed at the lowest level. . . .

Someone among the standing ghosts began clapping; and more of them took it up, and from somewhere the full-orchestra strains of "I'll Be Seeing You" began to play. All the elegantly dressed ghosts were standing and applauding now, and every face that Sullivan could see was smiling, though many were blinking back tears and many others openly let the tears run down their cheeks as they clapped their hands.

When he was close to the far doors, a crystal goblet of champagne was pressed into Sullivan's hand, and when he glanced back, his face chilly with sweat, he saw that Elizalde and Kootie each held a glass as well. The applause was growing louder, nearly drowning all the old familiar music.

Elizalde hurried up alongside Sullivan and turned her head to whisper in his ear: "Do you think it's poison?"

"No." Sullivan slowed to a walk, and he lifted the glass and sipped the icy, golden wine. He wished he were a connoisseur of champagnes, for this certainly seemed to be first-rate. He blinked, and realized that he had tears in his own eyes. "I think they're grateful at being released."

At the door, on an impulse, he turned back to the resplendent dining room and raised his glass. The applause ceased as every ghost raised a glass of its own; and then the rich tawny light faded as the lamps on the Art Deco pillars lost power, and the music ceased (with, he thought, a dying fall), and finally even the background rustle of breathing and the shifting of shoes on the parquet floor diminished away to silence.

The dining hall was dark and empty now. The tables were gone, and a lot of convention-hotel chairs were nested in stacks against the bulkheads.

Sullivan's lifted hand was empty, and he curled it slowly into a fist. "The field is beginning to fail already," he said to Elizalde. "We'd better get upstairs fast." He pushed open the door at his back.

Across a broad foyer was a semicircular bronze portal like the entry to a 1930s department store. Its two doors were open wide, and on the broad mother-of-pearl ceiling within Sullivan could see the rippling reflection of brightly lit water, and hear splashing and laughter; these doors apparently led to a balcony over the actual pool, which must have been one deck-level below. Sullivan thought the swimmers must be real people, and not ghosts.

Elizalde looked in the same direction and whispered, "Good Lord, stacked like a slave ship!"

An imposingly broad mahogany stairway opened onto the foyer to their left, and Sullivan waved Elizalde and Kootie up—the stairs were wide enough for all three of them to trot up abreast, though Kootie was stumbling.

"Did you see some bathing beauty in there?" Sullivan asked Elizalde as he hurried up the stairs, pulling Kootie along by the upper arm. " 'Stacked' I get, but 'like a slave ship'—is that good or bad?"

"I meant those bunks," she panted, "you pig. Stacked to the ceiling in there, with soldiers all crammed in, trying to sleep. I didn't notice any—damn *'bathing beauty.'* "

"Oh . . . ? What I saw was a balcony over a swimming pool," he told her. Apparently the field *hadn't* yet collapsed, but was out of phase. "What did you see, Kootie?"

"I'm looking nowhere but straight ahead," said the boy, and Sullivan wondered which of the personalities in Kootie's head had spoken.

Maybe one or more of the degaussing coils *have* been disconnected, Sullivan thought uneasily, at the substations along the length of the ship. I've got a big wheel spinning—is it missing some spokes? Is it going to fly apart?

"All we can do is get out of here," he said. "Come on."

They jogged wearily up two flights of the stairs, and then paused just below the last landing. Peering around the newel pillar, Sullivan assessed the remaining steps that ascended to the broad Promenade Deck lobby area known as Piccadilly Circus.

From down here he could see the inset electric lights glowing in the ceiling up there, and he could hear a couple of voices speaking quietly. Far up over his head on the other side, on the paneled back wall of the stairwell, hung a big gold medallion and a framed portrait of Queen Mary.

"Up the stairs," he whispered to Elizalde and the boy, "and then fast out the door to the left. That'll lead us straight off the ship onto the causeway bridge, across that and down the stairs to the parking lot. Ready? Go!"

They stepped crouchingly across the landing, then sprang up the last stairs and sprinted wildly across the open floor, hopping over loops of cable to the wide open doorway out onto the outdoor deck—and then all three of them just stopped, leaning on the rail.

The rail had no gap in it, and the causeway to the parking-lot stairs was gone. The stairs, the parking lot, all of *Long Beach* was gone, and they were looking out over an empty moonlit ocean that stretched away to the horizon under a black, star-needled sky.

CHAPTER 47

*"I wish I hadn't cried so much!" said Alice, as she swam about, trying to
find her way out. "I shall be punished for it now, I suppose, by being
drowned in my own tears!..."*

—Lewis Carroll,
Alice's Adventures in Wonderland

For a long moment the three of them just clung to the rail, and Sullivan, at least, was not even breathing. He was resisting the idea that he and Elizalde and Kootie had died at some point during the last few seconds, and that this lonely emptiness was the world ghosts lived in; and he wanted to go back inside, and cling to whoever it was whose voices they had heard.

He heard clumsy splashing far away below, and when he looked down he thought he could see the tiny heads and arms of two swimmers struggling through the moonlit water alongside the *Queen Mary*'s hull. The sight of them didn't lessen the solitude, for he guessed who they must be.

Hopelessly, just in case the cycle might be breakable, he filled his lungs with the cold sea breeze and yelled down to the swimmers, *"Get out of town tonight!"*

He looked at Elizalde, who was half-kneeling next to him, stunned-looking and hanging her elbows over the rail. "Maybe," he said, "I'll listen to me this time."

She managed to shrug. "Neither of us did yesterday."

The spell broke when sharp, heavy footsteps that he knew were high heels on the interior deck approached from behind Sullivan, and he didn't need to smell a clove cigarette.

He grabbed Elizalde's shoulder and Kootie's collar and shoved them forward. "Wake up!" he shouted. "Run!"

They both blinked at him, then obediently began sprinting down the deck toward the lights of the bow, without looking back; he floundered along after them, his back chilly and twitching in anticipation of a shot from deLarava's little automatic.

But the big silhouette of deLarava stepped out of a wide doorway *ahead* of Elizalde and Kootie, and deLarava negligently raised the pistol toward them.

They skidded to a halt on the worn deck planks, and Sullivan grabbed their shoulders again to stop himself. He looked behind desperately—

And saw deLarava standing back there too.

"I'm not seeing a railing at all," called both the images of deLarava, in a single voice that was high-pitched with what might have been elation or fright. "To me, you're all standing straight out from the Promenade Deck doorway. From your point of view, you can walk here by coming forward or coming back. Either way, get over here right now or I'll start shooting you up."

Elizalde's hand brushed the untucked sweatshirt at her waist. The night sea breeze blew her long black hair back from her face, and the moonlight glancing in under the deck roof glazed the lean line of her jaw.

"No," whispered Sullivan urgently. "She'd empty her gun before you half drew clear. Save it." He looked at the forward image of deLarava and then back at the aft one. "Tell you what, you two walk forward, and I'll walk back."

"And I'll be in Scotland afore ye," whispered Kootie. Sullivan knew the remark was a bit of bravado from Edison.

As Elizalde and Kootie stepped away toward the bow, Sullivan turned and walked back the way they had run; and as he got to the open Piccadilly Circus doorway he saw that Elizalde and Kootie were stepping in right next to him, both blinking in exhausted surprise to see him suddenly beside them again. The soft ceiling lights and the glow of another freestanding Art Deco lamp kindled a warm glow in the windows of the little interior shops at the forward end of the lobby.

DeLarava had stepped back across the broad inner deck, and she was still holding the gun on them; though Sullivan could see now that the muzzle was shaking.

"Do you know anything about all this, Pete?" deLarava asked in an animated voice. "There's some huge magnetic *thing* going on, and it's broken the ship up, psychically. Right here all the ghosts have waked up, with their own stepped-up charges, and they've curved their bogus space all the way around us, and this lobby area of this deck is in a . . . a closed loop—if you walk away from it, you find yourself walking right b-b-back into it." She sniffed and touched her scalp. "Goddam-mit."

The only other person visible in the broad lobby was a white-haired little old fellow in a khaki jacket, though the area had at some time been set up for a shoot—a Sony Betacam SP sat on a tripod by the opposite doorway, and the unlit tic-tac-toe board of a Molepar lamp array was clamped on a sandbagged light stand in the corner next to a couple of disassembled Lowell light kits, and power and audio cables were looped across the deck, some connected to a dark TV monitor on a wheeled cart. Nothing seemed to be hot now, but Sullivan could faintly catch the old burnt-gel reek on the clove-scented air.

It seemed to him that the ceiling lights had dimmed from yellow down toward orange, in the moments since he had stepped in from the outside deck.

With her free hand, deLarava snicked a Dunhill lighter and puffed another clove cigarette alight. "Is Apie here, Joey?" she asked.

Sullivan nervously touched the brass plaque under his shirt.

The old man in the khaki jacket was grimacing and rocking on his heels. "Yes," he said. "And he can no more get out of here than we two can. We toucans." He sang, *"Precious and few are the mo-ments we toucans sha-a-are . . ."* Then he frowned and shook his head. "Even over the side—that's not the real ocean down there now. Jump off the port rail and you land on the starboard deck."

"I think he tried it," whispered Kootie bravely, "and landed on his head."

Sullivan nodded and tried to smile, but he was glancing around at the pillars and the stairwell and the dark inward-facing shop windows. *Keep your head down, Dad,* he thought.

The ceiling lamps were definitely fading and the lobby was going dark—but reflections of colored lights were now fanning above the wide throat of the open stairwell on the aft side of the lobby, gleaming on the tall paneled back wall and the big gold medallion and the framed portrait, and from some lower deck came the shivering cacophony of a big party going on.

DeLarava stumped across the glossy cork deck to the top of the stair-well—a velvet rope was hung doubled at the top of one of the stair railings, and she unhooked one brass end, walked across to the other railing with it, and hooked the rope there, across the gap.

"Nobody go near the well," she said, her voice sounding more plead-ing than threatening. "Joey—*where is Apie*?"

The Piccadilly Circus lobby was almost totally dark now, the lamps overhead glowing only a dull red, and Sullivan could see reflections of moonlight on the polished deck.

Then, with the echoing clank of a knife switch being thrown, the white-hot glare of an unglassed carbon-arc lamp punched across the lobby from the forward corridor between the shops, throwing deLarava's bulbous shadow like a torn hole onto the paneling of the stairwell's back wall.

The lamp was roaring because of working off alternating current, but from the darkness behind and beyond the cone of radiance, a strong, confident voice said, "I'm here, Kelley."

DeLarava had flung her hand over her face, and now reeled away out of the glare, toward the doorway that led out onto the starboard deck, on the opposite side of the lobby from Sullivan.

He spun away from the glaring light toward Elizalde and Kootie—and stopped.

Angelica Elizalde was still standing where she'd been, her hair backlit now against the reflected glare from the stairwell wall, but a portly old man stood between her and Sullivan, where Kootie had been a moment before, and Kootie was nowhere to be seen. Sullivan blinked at the old man, wondering where he had appeared from, and who he was.

Sullivan opened his mouth to speak—then flinched into a crouch a moment before a hard *bang* shook the air, and he felt the hair twitch over his scalp.

He let his crouch become a tumble to the deck, and he reached for Elizalde's ankles but she was already dropping to her hands and knees. The old man who'd been standing between them had stepped forward into the glare, the tails of his black coat trailing out behind him as if he were walking through water.

Sullivan's father's voice boomed from the forward darkness behind the light. "Step forward, Kelley!"

"Fuck you, Apie!" came deLarava's shrill reply. "I just killed your other precious stinking kid!"

Sullivan grabbed Elizalde's upper arm and pulled her into the deeper penumbra behind the cone of light. "Where's Kootie?" Sullivan hissed into her ear as they crawled toward the wall.

"*That's* him," Elizalde whispered back, waving out at the old man in the center of the deck. Sullivan looked up, and noticed two things: the old man's jowly, strong-jawed face, which in this stark light even looked like a figure in a black-and-white newsreel, was instantly recognizable from the photos he'd seen of Thomas Alva Edison; and the shadow the old man cast on the far aft wall above the stairs was the silhouette of a young boy.

This was the Edison ghost out and solid, and Sullivan knew deLarava would not want to damage it. "Give me the gun," he whispered to Elizalde.

The two of them had scrambled forward, to the wall below one of the little interior windows on the port side, and Elizalde sat down on the deck and pulled the .45 from the waist of her jeans and shoved it toward him.

His hands wouldn't close around it. "Shit," he whispered, panting and nearly sobbing, "Houdini must have been a fucking pacifist! I guess he didn't want his mask to be able to *kill* anybody! Here." He pushed it back to her with the heels of his limp hands. "You've got to do it. Shoot deLarava."

He looked up and squinted, trying to see the old woman on the far side of the pupil-constricting glare. Then a movement above the stairwell, out across the deck to his right, caught his attention.

A rapid clicking had started up, and the light narrowed to a beam as if now being focused through the lens of a projector.

In a wide, glowing rectangle of black and white and gray on the stairwell wall, Sullivan saw an image of the corner of a house, and a fat man frustratedly shaking the end of an uncooperative garden hose; Kootie's shadow-silhouette had been replaced with a projected image of a boy, who was standing on the lush gray lawn with one foot firmly on the slack length of the hose behind the fat man. The man scratched his head and looked directly into the nozzle—at which point the boy stepped off the hose, and a burst of water shot into the man's face.

"Plagiarism!" called the ghost of Edison, which, though solidly visible in the light, was itself now throwing no shadow at all. "That's my 'Bad Boy and the Garden Hose,' from 1903!"

"Lumiere made it first, in 1895," called Sullivan's father's ghost from the blackness behind the carbon-arc radiance to Sullivan's left. "Besides, I've improved it."

In the projected movie scene, the water was still jetting out of the hose, but the figure holding the nozzle was now a fat woman, and the gushing flow was particulate with thousands of tiny, flailing human shapes, whose impacts were eroding the fat woman's head down to a bare skull.

Across the deck, deLarava screamed in horrified rage—then another gunshot banged, and the light was extinguished.

"Is that supposed to be sympathetic magic?" deLarava was screaming. "I'm the one that's going to walk out of here whole, Apie! And everything will be what *I* say it is!"

"*Shoot* her, goddammit!" said Sullivan urgently, though Elizalde surely couldn't see any more than he could in the sudden total darkness.

"I *can't*," said Elizalde in a voice tight with anger, "*kill* her."

Sullivan jumped then, for someone had tugged on his shirt from the forward side, away from Elizalde; but even as he whipped his head around that way he smelled bourbon, and so he wasn't wildly surprised when Sukie's voice said, "Get over here, Pete."

"Follow me," he whispered to Elizalde. He grabbed the slack of her sweatshirt sleeve and pulled her along after the dimly sensed shape of Sukie, stepping high to avoid tripping over cables, to the narrow forward area behind where the light had been.

Sukie proved to be solid enough to push Sullivan down to his knees on the deck, and into his ear she whispered, "Not hot."

He groped in the darkness in front of his face, and his fingers touched a familiar shape—a wooden box on the end of a stout cable, open on one face with a leather flap across the opening. It was a plug box of the old sort known as "spider boxes" because of the way spiders tended to like the roomy, dark interiors of them. Like the carbon-arc lamp, this was an antique, and had surely not been among deLarava's modern equipment. The spider-box devices had been outlawed at some time during the mid-eighties, when he and Sukie had still been deLarava's gaffers, because of the constant risk of someone's putting their hand or foot into one and being electrocuted.

But Sukie had said *Not hot*, so he pulled back the leather flap with one hand, then rapped the box with the other hand and held it out palm up.

Sukie slapped one of the old paddle plugs into his hand, and he tipped it vertical and shoved it firmly into the grooves inside the box. Then he let the flap fall over it and pulled his hands back.

"Set," he said.

"Hot," said Sukie, "now."

And again a knife-switch clanked across a gap, right next to him now, and another carbon-arc lamp flared on with a buzzing roar, the sudden light battering at Sullivan's retinas.

By reflected light he could see his father standing over him; Arthur Patrick Sullivan looked no more than fifty, and his hair was gray rather than white. He glanced down at Pete Sullivan, who was crouched over the spider box, and winked.

"I think we need a gel here," said Pete's father; and the old man reached around in front of the lamp and laid his palm over the two arcing carbon rods in the trim clamps.

Sullivan winced and inhaled between his teeth, but the hand wasn't blasted aside; instead it shone translucently, the red arteries and the blue veins glowing through the skin, and his father was looking down the length of the room and smiling grimly.

On the stairwell wall another scene was forming—this time in color. (Flakes falling from the ceiling sparked and glowed like tiny meteors as they spun down through the beam of light.)

Glowing tan above, blue below—the bright rectangle on the wall coalesced into focus, and Sullivan recognized Venice Beach as seen from the point of view of a helicopter *(though no helicopter had been in the sky on that afternoon).*

In the colored light it was just Kootie standing and blinking in the middle of the deck; the boy shaded his eyes and glanced wildly back and forth.

"This way, Kootie!" called Elizalde, and the boy ran to her through the rain of flakes and crouched beside her, breathing fast.

In the projected image on the stairwell wall at the other end of the lobby, Sullivan could see the four tiny figures on the beach; three were staying by the patchwork rectangles of the towels spread on the sand, while the fourth, the white-haired figure, strode down to the foamy line of the surf.

One of the flakes from the ceiling landed on the back of Sullivan's hand, and he picked it up and broke it between his fingers; it was a curl of black paint (and he remembered his father describing how Samuel Goldwyn's glass studio had been painted black in 1917, when mercury-vapor lamps superseded sunlight as the preferred illumination for filming, and how in later years the black paint had constantly peeled off and fallen down onto the sets like black snow).

Loretta deLarava was clumping out into the light now from the far side of the lobby, her face and broad body glowing in shifting patches of blue and tan as she took on the projection.

"Nobody but me is getting out of here alive, Apie," she said, pointing her pistol straight at the glowing hand over the light. "Prove it all night, if you like, to this roomful of ghosts."

The white-haired little image in the projection had waded out into the surf, and now dived into a wave.

Just then from down the stairs behind deLarava came a young man's voice, singing, *"Did your face catch* fire *once? Did they use a* tire iron *to put it out?"* It was a tune from some Springsteen song—and Sullivan thought he should recognize the voice, from long ago.

A movement across the lobby caught Sullivan's eye—five or six little girls in white dresses were dancing silently in the open doorway on the starboard side, against the black sky of the night.

Now something was coming up the stairs; it thumped and wailed and rattled as it came. DeLarava glanced behind her down the stairwell and then hastily stepped back, her gun waving wildly around.

Even way over on the forward side of the lobby, Sullivan flinched away from the spider box when a lumpy shape with seven or eight flailing limbs hiked itself up the last stairs onto the level of the deck and knocked the velvet rope free of its hooks.

Then Sullivan relaxed a little, for he saw that it was just two men, apparently attached together; they were both trying to stand, but the wrist of one was handcuffed to the ankle of the other. He thought they must be Sherman Oaks and Neal Obstadt, but the man cuffed by a wrist had two arms with which to wrestle his companion, had one fist free to pummel against the other man's groin and abdomen, two elbows with which to block kicks to the face.

Behind them, as if shepherding them, a young man stepped up the stairs to the deck, into the projected glare; he was broad-shouldered and trim in a white turtleneck sweater, with blond hair clipped short in a crew cut.

"Kelley Keith," said this newcomer in a resonant baritone, and from childhood memories and the soundtrack of the old TV show Sullivan belatedly recognized the youthful voice of Nicky Bradshaw. "Listen to the hookah-smoking caterpillar—this mushroom's for you. And it won't pass away."

The carbon-arc lamp over Sullivan's head was roaring, and the paint flakes were falling more thickly, and, down the length of the lobby, projected right onto the blood-spattered fabric of deLarava's broad dress now, the little figure in the surf was waving its tiny arms.

Crouching up forward by the spider box, Sullivan was clasping Elizalde's hand in his right hand, and Sukie's in his left.

"It's not the real moon!" cried several of the little girls visible through the open doorway out on the starboard deck. "It's painted! We're still in Hell!"

"No, look!" shouted a man at the rail behind them. "It's crumbling! The real sun is out there!" By the now-rumpled business suit and necktie and the blood-streaked white shirt, Sullivan recognized him as the lawyer whom deLarava's men had driven away in the Jeep Cherokee; the man's hands were still cuffed but he had got them in front of him, and he was holding a long broom that he was waving over his head as high as he could reach. Black paint chips fell down onto him like confetti.

"My baby ghosts!" screamed deLarava; she started ponderously out of the projected light toward the half-dozen little girls, but the man with the broom had swept a hole in the night sky out there, and a beam of sunlight (cleaner and brighter, Sullivan thought, than a 3200 Kelvin lamp through a blue gel) lanced down to the deck. The girls flocked to it, then broke up and dissolved in white mist and breathless giggling, and were gone, in the moment before deLarava ran through the spot where they had been and collided with the still-shadowed rail.

The carbon-arc lamp, working off AC and no doubt a choke coil or a transformer, was flickering and glowing a deepening yellow. Sullivan's father's ghost lifted his hand away from the carbon rods, and the beam of light now just threw a featureless white glow down the lobby onto the far wall. Sullivan felt Sukie reach off to the side, and with an arcing snap the light went out, the carbon rods abruptly dimming to red points.

In the sudden silence the fat old woman backed across the exterior deck from the starboard rail, and in the open doorway she turned around to face the dark Piccadilly Circus lobby.

Her dress still glowed with the image that had been projected onto it, and the tiny white-haired swimmer, carried on her dress right out of the rectangle that had shone on the stairwell wall, was floundering below the shelf of her breasts.

She stomped slowly back in through the doorway and started across the lobby floor. "I will at least have Edison," she said.

CHAPTER 48

Come, hearken then, ere voice of dread,
With bitter tidings laden,
Shall summon to unwelcome bed
A melancholy maiden!
We are but older children, dear,
Who fret to find our bedtime near.
— Lewis Carroll,
Through the Looking-Glass

From aft by the stairs, the ankle-cuffed man stepped forward (dragging his flailing companion) into the dim glow projected by deLarava's dress, and Sullivan saw that he *was* the gray-haired Obstadt. "No, Loretta," Obstadt said hoarsely, kicking at the man attached to his foot, "you said I could have him. You work for *me* now. Get back—"

And, crouched on the floor, the two-armed man who must neverthe-less have been Sherman Oaks was jabbering urgently in what sounded to Sullivan like Latin.

DeLarava shoved her little gun at Obstadt's belly and fired it. The *bang* was like a full-arm swing of a hammer onto the cap of a fire hydrant, and Obstadt stopped and bowed slightly, his mouth working. The man on the floor took the opportunity to lash his free fist twice, hard, into Obstadt's groin, and Obstadt bowed more deeply.

Beams of sunlight lanced into the lobby from behind Sullivan, re-flecting off the floor to underlight deLarava's jowls, and he realized that the night sky was breaking apart on the port side too.

"Koot Hoomie Parganas," said deLarava, moving forward again. Her dress still glowed in surging fields of tan and blue, and the tiny swimmer was waving its arms under her breasts.

Sullivan glanced past Elizalde at Kootie, who was sitting cross-legged in a nest of cables, his hair now backlit by reflected daylight. The boy seemed to have been forsaken by Edison—his wide eyes gaped in horror at the approaching fat woman, and his lips were trembling.

Elizalde stood up from her crouch beside Sullivan. "No," she said loudly, stepping in front of the boy, "*Llorona Atacado.* You won't replace your lost children with this boy." And she jabbed her hand in the air toward deLarava's face, with the first and little fingers extended. "*Ixchel se quite!* Commander Hold-'Em take you," she said, and she spit.

The saliva hit the deck between them, but deLarava reeled back, coughing and clutching the glowing fabric over her stomach as if the tiny drowning figure were sinking into her diaphragm. She blinked up at Elizalde from under her bushy eyebrows, and the barrel of the little automatic came wobbling up.

Sullivan was on his feet now, and he could see that Elizalde was not even going to think of raising the .45.

DeLarava's gun was pointed from less than two yards away at the center of Elizalde's Graceland sweatshirt—and as Sullivan leaned forward to grab Elizalde and yank her out of the way, his scalp contracted with the bar-time advance-shock of deLarava's gun going off.

And so instead of trying to pull Elizalde back, he made his forward motion a leap into the space between the two women (in the moment when both of his feet were off the deck he whiffed suntan oil and mayonnaise and the cold, deep sea—and, faintly, bourbon), and then the real gunshot punched his eardrums and hammered his upper arm.

The impact of the shot (and bar-time anticipation of the second) spun him around in midair to face the glowing figure of deLarava, and her second shot caught him squarely in the chest.

His feet hit the deck but he was falling backward, and as he fell he heard the fast *snap-clank* of the .45 at last being chambered; and as his hip thudded down hard and he curled and slid and the needlessly ejected .45 round spun through the air, he saw Elizalde's clasped hands raise the weapon toward deLarava, her thumbs safely out of the way of the weapon's slide; the .45 flared and jumped, and the gunshot in the enclosed lobby was like a bomb going off.

Sullivan's knees were drawn up and his right arm was folded over his chest, but his head was rocked back to watch deLarava's fat body fly backward, sit boomingly on the deck, and then tumble away toward the starboard doorway in a spray of blood—

—Sullivan slid to a tense halt, staring—

But deLarava was at the same time still standing in front of Elizalde, and still holding the little automatic, though her arm was transparent; she was looking from Elizalde to the automatic in puzzlement, and the weight of the gun was pulling her insubstantial arm down toward the deck.

Then the top of her head abruptly collapsed from the eyebrows up, as the rubber bands imploded the frail ectoplasmic skull.

Sullivan's chest felt split and molten, but he rolled his head around to scan the sunlight-spotted deck for a glimpse of his own freshly dead body. Surely deLarava's chest-shot had killed him, and he was now a raw ghost about to blessedly dissolve into the fresh daytime air that was streaming in through the cracking night sky; after all, he wasn't able to breathe—his lungs were impacted, stilled, and the only agitation in him was the thudding heartbeat that was jolting his vision twice every second. . . .

My heart's beating! he thought, with a shiver of dreadful hope. Suddenly he realized that he wanted to live, wanted to get away from here with Elizalde and Kootie and live. . . .

DeLarava's grotesquely pinheaded ghost was staring at its arm, which had been stretched all the way down to the deck by the weight of the little automatic. The translucent figure stumbled away forward toward where the carbon-arc light had been, and her arm lengthened behind her as the automatic slid only by short jerks after her across the polished cork deck.

Obstadt had reeled out through the open lobby doorway to the starboard rail. Beyond him, the induced black sky was breaking up, and Sullivan could see whole patches of luminous distant blue showing through it.

Obstadt's tethered companion was up and hunching along beside him like a wounded dog—now the companion only had one arm, and Sullivan realized that it had certainly been Sherman Oaks all along, with his missing arm only temporarily provided by the ship's degaussing field, which had been so magically stepped-up in this one segment of the ship. Oaks was wheezing like a hundred warped harmonicas, and his windbreaker and baggy camouflage pants were rippling and jumping and visibly spotting with fresh blood, as though a horde of starved rats were muscling around underneath.

The battered-looking lawyer who had been standing with the little girls was still holding the broom and staring stupidly up at the fragmenting sky—and Obstadt's right hand lashed out and caught the man by the necktie. Obstadt strongly pulled him along the rail toward himself and opened his mouth wide over the lawyer's throat.

But Nicky Bradshaw lumbered over to them and pulled Obstadt away.

Bradshaw's crew cut had lengthened messily in the last few seconds and was shot with gray now, and his turtleneck sweater was beginning to stretch over his belly, but he grabbed Obstadt's coat lapels with both hands and boosted him up until the wounded man was nearly sitting on the rail; and then he braced his feet and pushed Obstadt over backward.

With a tortured roar and a useless flailing of arms and legs, Obstadt tumbled away out of sight below the deck, and Sherman Oaks was abruptly dragged upright and slammed belly-first against the rail, his single arm stretched straight downward as it took Obstadt's pendulous weight.

"Nicky," Oaks wheezed, "I worked with you at Stage 5 Productions in '59! I can get you a ghost that'll make you young again! *Thus from infernal Dis do we ascend, to view the subjects of our monarchy!*"

In the brightness of the sunlight that was shining over there Sullivan saw tears glisten on Bradshaw's cheek—

But Bradshaw took hold of Oaks's belt and lifted him over the rail— Oaks kicked, but had no free hand with which to grab anything, and howled, though all his voices seemed to have lost the capacity to form words—and Bradshaw effortfully tossed the tethered pair away into the brightening abyss.

Away on the other side of the Piccadilly Circus deck, Sullivan cringed at the receding scream of a thousand voices.

Sullivan couldn't roll over, but he saw Kootie look back toward the port deck to see if Obstadt and Oaks would land there—but there was no sound of impact from that direction. The supernaturally amplified magnetic field was obviously breaking down, and the two men had certainly fallen all the long way down into the walled lagoon that lay like a moat around the ship.

Sullivan heard Elizalde gasp, and looked across the lobby again—to see that Bradshaw had now climbed right up onto the starboard rail outside and was standing erect, balanced on it, with his arms waving out to the sides.

Bradshaw's recently youthful and trim body was visibly deteriorating back into the gross figure of Solomon Shadroe, and with every passing second it became a more incongruous sight to see the fat old man tottering up there.

Bradshaw squinted belligerently down at the disheveled attorney, who had lurched back across the narrow section of outdoor deck and was leaning in the Piccadilly Circus doorway, panting. The attorney had evidently wet his pants.

"You okay, Frank?" asked Bradshaw gruffly.

The lawyer blinked around uncertainly, then goggled up at the fat old man standing on the rail; and he seemed to wilt with recognition. "Yes, Mr. Bradshaw. I—I brought all this—"

"Good." Bradshaw blinked past him into the shadows of the Piccadilly Circus lobby. He was probably unable to see in even as far as where deLarava's gorily holed body lay tumbled on the polished cork floor, but he called, "Pete, Beth—Angelica, Kootie—" The freshening breeze ruffled his gray hair, and he wobbled on his perch. "—Edison. I don't want to spoil the party, so I'll go. This here just won't last much longer."

He might have been referring to the psychically skewed magnetic field, but Sullivan thought he meant his control over his long-dead body and his long-held ghost; and nervously Sullivan thought of the descriptions of the way Frank Rocha's body had finally gone.

Then Bradshaw's face creased in a faint, self-conscious, reminiscent smile—and he curled one hand over his head and stuck his other arm straight out, and he spun slowly on the rail on the toe of one foot; and, almost gracefully, he overbalanced and fell away out into empty space and disappeared.

Sullivan found himself listening for a splash—irrationally, for the water was a good hundred feet below, and Sullivan was sprawled on the other side of the Piccadilly Circus lobby, closer to the port rail than the starboard one from which Bradshaw had just fallen—but what he heard three seconds later was a muffled *boom* that vibrated the deck and flung a high plume of glittering spray into the morning sunlight up past the starboard rail.

The lawyer seemed to be sobbing now, and he ran away aft, his footsteps knocking away to silence on the exterior deck planks, and the footsteps didn't start up again from some other direction.

Sullivan discovered that he was able to sit up; then that he could get his legs under himself and get to his feet. Elizalde hurried around to his right side and braced him up, and at last he dared to look down at his chest.

A button hung in fragments on his shirtfront and a tiny hole had been raggedly punched through the cloth, but there was no blood; and then with a surge of relief he remembered the brass plaque from his father's gravestone, tucked into his scapular, over his heart.

"Your arm's bleeding," said Elizalde. "But somehow that seems to be the only place you're hit." Her face was pale and she was frowning deeply. Sullivan could see the lump of the .45 under the front of her sweatshirt.

He looked down at his left arm, and his depth perception seemed to flatten right down to two dimensions when he saw that his shirtsleeve was rapidly blotting with bright red blood. "Hold me up from that side," he said dizzily, "and maybe no one will notice. You're a doctor, Angelica—can you dig out a bullet?"

"If it's not embedded in the bone, I can."

"Good—Jesus—soon." He took a deep breath and let it out, feeling as disoriented as if he'd had a stiff drink and an unfiltered Pall Mall on an empty stomach. "Uh . . . where to?"

"The bridge is there again," said Kootie anxiously, "the one that leads to the stairs and the parking lot. Let's get off this ship while we can."

Sullivan looked up, across the wide lobby. DeLarava's body was still sprawled out there in the middle of the deck, but the lights and camera gear at the forward end of the room were all her modern equipment again. The little old man in the khaki jacket was crouched over one of the Lowell light kits, busily packing away the scrims and light-doors, and humming. He didn't look up when Kootie ran back there, snatched up a half-used roll of silvery gaffer's tape, and hurried back to Sullivan and Elizalde.

"Kootie's right," said Elizalde, scuffling back around to Sullivan's left side and hugging his bloody arm to her breast. "Let's get back to Solville before people are able to wander in here and find this mess."

"Joey," said a frail voice behind Sullivan, *"stop them."*

Sullivan looked back at the film equipment and saw that deLarava's fat ghost was leaning on the tripod, her translucent chin resting on the black Sony Betacam. Her head ended right above the eyebrows, constricted to a short, stumpy cone by the rubber bands; and her translucent ectoplasmic right arm was still stretched out for yards across the deck, the limp fingers of the ghost hand twitching impotently on the grip of the automatic pistol.

The old man by the light kit looked up. "Oh, I've seen these before," he said cheerfully, speaking toward the ghost. "I should pop it into a marmalade jar, so somebody can sniff it. Crazy. No more point to it than catching somebody's shadow by slapping a book shut on it. *If* you ask *me.*"

"Joey," said the ghost in a peremptory but birdlike tone, *"you work for me. You gentlemen—why, you* all *work for me. Joey, I seem to have dislocated my wrist—take the gun from my hand and kill those three."*

"I hear a voice!" exclaimed Joey, smiling broadly. "A blot of mustard or a bit of undigested beef, speaking to me! A sort of food that's bound to disagree—not for me.'' He stood up and bowed toward Kootie, who was nervously holding the roll of gaffer's tape. ''Thanks a lot, boy,'' Joey said, ''just the same.''

DeLarava's ghost was fading, but it straightened up and drifted across the floor straight toward Sullivan, and its eyes, as insubstantial as raw egg-whites, locked onto his. *''Come with me, Pete,''* the ghost said imperiously.

Sullivan opened his mouth—almost certainly to decline the offer, though he was dizzy and nauseated at the hard sunlight, and giving a lot of his weight to Elizalde's right arm—but the breath that came out between his teeth was sharp with bourbon fumes, and it whispered, *''What number were you trying to reach?''*

DeLarava's ghost withered before the fumy breath, and the gossamer lines of the fat face turned to Kootie. *''Little boy, would you help an old woman across a very wide street?''*

''Physicists and sphinxes in majestical mists,'' came the old man's voice out of Kootie's mouth. *''I will go right through that sand and leave you way behind.''*

The smoky shred that was deLarava's ghost now swung toward Elizalde, and the voice was like wasps rustling in a papery nest: ''You *have no mask.*''

The bloody fabric of the sweatshirt over Elizalde's breasts flattened, as if an unseen hand had pressed there, and then a spotty handprint in Sullivan's blood appeared on the sweatshirt shoulder, and smeared. Elizalde cocked her head as if listening to a faint voice in her ear, and then said, almost wonderingly, ''Yes, of course.''

Sullivan felt the bourbon-breath blow out of his mouth again. *''This one is my family, too,''* the voice said softly.

Then Elizalde's shoulder twitched as if shoved.

—And out of Sullivan's mouth Sukie's ghost-voice added, *''A.O.P., kids.''*

As quick as an image in a twitched mirror, deLarava's ghost folded itself around past Kootie and stood between the three of them and the roofed causeway off the ship. *''No one passes,''* it whispered.

Kootie looked back at Sullivan fearfully; and in spite of his own sick-making pain, Sullivan noticed that the boy's curly black hair needed washing and combing, and he noticed the dark circles under the haunted brown eyes; and he vowed to himself, and to the ghosts of his father and sister, that he would make things better.

''There's no one there, Kootie,'' he said. ''Watch.'' He stepped forward, away from Elizalde's arm, and faintly felt the protesting outrage as deLarava's fretful substance parted before him like cobwebs and blew away on the strengthening sea breeze.

Kootie and Elizalde hurried after him. Kootie looked up at Elizalde with a strangely lost look, and he waved the roll of gaffer's tape he had snatched off the deck. He held it gingerly, as if he didn't want to get any more of the glue on his fingers than he could help. "When we get to the stairs," he said, "I figured you could tape Pete's arm with this."

Elizalde looked startled. "Of course. That's a good idea . . . Edison?"

"No," said Kootie, trotting along now between the two grown-ups. "Me."

Halfway across the elevated walkway, Sullivan paused and began unbuttoning his shirt. "One last stop," he said hoarsely.

He fished out the front-side wallet of his scapular and pried free of the torn plastic sleeve the brass portrait-plaque that he had taken off of his father's gravestone yesterday evening. DeLarava's bullet, a .22 or .25, had deeply dented the center of the metal plate, and the engraved portrait of his smiling father was almost totally smashed away.

Sullivan rubbed his own chest gingerly, wondering if the blocked gunshot had nevertheless cracked his breastbone; and he held the brass plate between the thumb and forefinger of his right hand.

"Goodbye, Dad," he said softly. "I'll see you again, after a while—in some better place, God willing."

The piece of brass was warm in his hand. He hefted it and looked down at the shadowed water between the dock and the ship.

"I'll take that," said a whisper from behind Kootie.

Sullivan whipped his head around in exhausted alarm, but it was the ghost of Edison who had spoken, a smoky silhouette hardly visible out here in the breezy sunlight; the hand the old ghost was extending was so insubstantial that Sullivan doubted it could hold the brass plate, but when he held the plate out and let go of it, Edison supported it.

"I'll take him, and go, at last," Edison said faintly. *"I hope it may be very beautiful over there."* Sullivan thought the ghost smiled. *"On the way,"* it whispered, *"your father and I can talk about the . . ."* and then Sullivan couldn't tell whether the last word was *silence* or *silents.*

Kootie wanted to say goodbye to Edison, but was shy to see the ghost standing out away from himself, tall and broad in spite of being nearly transparent.

But the ghost bent over him, and Kootie felt a faint pressure on his shoulder for a moment.

In his head he faintly heard, *"Thank you, son. You've made me proud. Find bright days, and good work, and laughter."*

Then the Edison ghost stepped right through the railing and, still holding Peter Sullivan's piece of brass, began to shrink in the air, as if he were rapidly receding into the distance; the image stayed in the center of Kootie's vision no matter which direction he looked in—down at his feet, toward the buildings and cranes on the shore, or up at the mounting white decks and towering red funnels of the ship—so he turned to the walkway rail and gripped it and stared at the glittering blue water of the harbor until the image had quite shrunk away to nothing there.

And at last he stepped back, and took Peter Sullivan's hand in his left hand and Angelica Elizalde's in his right, and the three of them walked together to the stairs that would lead them down to the parking lot and away, to whatever eventual rest, and shelter, and food, and life these two people would be able to give him.

EARTHQUAKE WEATHER

PROLOGUE

The Dolorous Stroke

LAS VEGAS—A small earthquake rattled Boulder City on New Year's morning, and workers at the nearby Hoover Dam reported feeling the shock.

—Associated Press,
January 2, 1995

CHAPTER 1

PANDARUS: . . . she came and puts me her white hand to his cloven
             chin—
CRESSIDA: Juno have mercy; how came it cloven?
                                          —William Shakespeare,
                                          Troilus and Cressida

A pay telephone was ringing in the corridor by the rest rooms, but the young woman who had started to get up out of the padded orange-vinyl booth just blinked around in evident puzzlement and sat down again, tugging her denim jacket more tightly around her narrow shoulders.

From over by the pickup counter her waiter glanced at her curiously. She was sitting against the eastern windows, but though the sky was already a chilly deep blue outside, the yellow glow of the interior overhead lighting was still relatively bright enough to highlight the planes of her face under the disordered straw-blond hair. The waiter thought she looked nervous, and he wondered why she had reflexively assumed that a pay-phone call might be for her.

The counter seats were empty where the half-dozen customers who lived in town usually sat chugging coffee at this hour—but the locals could sleep in on this New Year's Day, and they'd be right back here tomorrow at dawn. This morning the customers were mostly grumpy families who wanted to sit in the booths—holiday-season vacationers, drawn in off of the San Diego Freeway lanes by the spotlit billboards beyond the Batiquitos Lagoon to the north or the San Elijo Lagoon to the south.

The woman sitting in the dawn-side booth was almost certainly a waitress somewhere—when he had taken her order she had spoken quickly, specified all the side-order options without being asked, and she had sat where she wouldn't be able to see into the kitchen. And she was hungry, too—she had ordered scrambled eggs *and* poached eggs, along with bacon and cottage fries, and coffee and orange juice and V-8.

. . . And now she had set something on fire at her table.

The waiter clanked her plates back down on the counter and hurried across the carpet toward her booth, but he quickly saw that the smoking paperback book on the table was just smoldering and not actually flaming, and even before he got to the table the woman had flipped open the book and splashed water from her water glass onto the . . . *cigarette butt!* . . . that had ignited the pages.

The pay telephone was still ringing, but the overhead lights had gone dim for a moment, and a waitress back by the electronic cash register was cussing under her breath and slapping the side of the machine, and nobody else had happened to notice the briefly burning book; and the blond woman, who was now folding the soggy thing closed again, had gone red in the face and was smiling up at him in embarrassed apology—she couldn't be thirty years old yet—and so he just smiled cautiously back at her.

"Yesterday you'd have been legal," he said sympathetically; then, seeing that she was confused, he added, "Seven hours ago there'd have been ashtrays on the table, you wouldn't have had to hide it."

She nodded, pushing the book away across the tabletop and frowning as though she'd never seen the object until it had started smoldering in front of her. "That's right," she said to him sternly. "No smoking in restaurants at all in California now, as of midnight last night." She looked past him now, with a forgiving, we'll-say-no-more-about-it air. "Where are your public telephones?"

"Uh . . ." He waved in the direction of the ringing telephone. "Where you hear. But your breakfast is coming right up, if you want to wait."

She was hitching awkwardly forward out of the booth and levering herself up onto her feet. "All I ordered was coffee." The waiter watched as she walked away toward the telephone. Her left leg swung stiff, not bending, and he was uneasily sure that the dark, wet spot on the thigh of her jeans must be fresh blood.

She picked up the telephone receiver in mid-ring.

"Hello?" Again the restaurant's lights dimmed for a moment, and the woman's face hardened. In a harsher, flatter voice than she'd used before, she said, "Do I know you, Susan? Sure, I'll tell him. Now, I don't mean to be abrupt, but I've got a call to make here, don't I?"

She hung up and dug a handful of litter out of a jacket pocket and dumped it onto the shelf below the telephone; from among these match-books and drywall screws and slips of paper and bits of broken green stucco she selected a quarter, thumbed it into the slot, and then punched in a local number.

After ten seconds of standing with the receiver to her ear, "Hi," she said, still speaking in her rough new voice. "Is this the Flying Nun?" She laughed. "Gotcha, huh? Listen, Susan says to tell you she still loves you. Oh, and what I called about—I'm going to assume the Flamingo, you know what I mean?" She listened patiently, and with her free hand picked up one of the fragments of green-painted stucco. "Potent pieces of it . . . persist in percolating in the . . . what, pasture? Can you spell alliteration? What I'm trying to say, sonny boy, is that even though they did tear it down, I've got a chunk of it, and your ass is grass. Don't waste time chasing the long stories on the front page this morning—skip right to the funny papers."

After hanging up, she smacked her lips and frowned as if she'd eaten something rancid, then stepped across to the ladies' room door and pushed it open.

She dug a little bottle of Listerine out of another jacket pocket as she crossed the tile floor to the sink, and by the time she was standing in front of the mirror she had opened the bottle and taken a swig; she swished it around in her mouth, looking down at the chrome faucets rather than into the mirror, and she spat out the mouthwash with a grimace.

She re-capped the bottle and hurried back to her table.

Already the sky had brightened enough outside the window to cast dim shadows from the steaming plates and glasses that now sat on her table, and as she slid carefully into the booth she frowned at the elaborate breakfast. From her open purse she lifted a waitress's order pad and another, larger bottle of the mouthwash, and for the next half hour, as she ate, she flipped through the pages of the pad, frowning over the inked notes that filled nearly every leaf, and paused frequently to swallow a mouthful of Listerine. She held her fork in her left hand to eat the scrambled eggs, but switched it to her right to eat the poached eggs. The cash register on the other side of the room kept on spontaneously going into its cash-out cycle, to the frustration of the cashier.

When the first ray of sunlight from over the distant Vallecito Mountains touched a pastel painting on the far wall of the restaurant, the blond woman lifted her right hand and made a fist in the new daylight; then she packed up her order pad and mouthwash bottle, got up out of the booth, and tossed a twenty-dollar bill onto the table next to the soggy, blackened old paperback copy of Ian Fleming's *On Her Majesty's Secret Service*.

The waiter was Catholic, so he caught what she was muttering as she hurried past him: "In the name of the Father, the Son, the Holy Ghost." Then she had pushed open the glass front door and stepped out into the chilly morning sunlight.

Through the glass he watched her hobble out to a little white Toyota in the dawn-streaked parking lot; then he sighed and told a busboy to bring along a towel and a spray bottle of bleach to that booth, because there was probably blood on the seat. "The booth where Miss Chock Full o' Nuts was sitting," he told the busboy.

She drove west on Leucadia Boulevard, past old bungalows set back under pines and fig trees away from the new, high pavement, and then crossed a set of railroad tracks; the street descended sharply, and she made a right turn onto a wide street with big old eucalyptus trees separating the north and south bound lanes; after driving past a few blocks of dark surfboard shops and vintage clothing stores she turned left, up into one of the narrow lanes that climbed the bluff beyond which lay the sea. Fences and closed garage doors batted back the rattle of her car's engine.

A long fieldstone wall with pepper trees overhanging it hid a property on the seaward side of Neptune Avenue. At the entrance of the private driveway, by a burly pine tree that was strung with flowering orange black-eyed Susans, the woman pulled over onto the gravel shoulder and switched off the engine. The dawn street was empty except for a couple of dew-frosted cars parked tilted alongside the road, and silent—no birds sang, and the surf beyond the bluff was just a slow subsonic pulse.

Her face was set in a hard grin as she got out of the car, and when she had straightened up on the gravel she began unbuckling the belt on her jeans; and she kept whispering, "Just in the leg, that's all, settle down, girl! Just in the leg as a *warning*, and anyway he stabbed himself in the leg already one time, just to have something to talk to some lady about—and he shot himself in the foot before that, with this here very spear. No big deal to him, I swear." She unzipped her jeans and pulled and tugged them down to her ankles, exposing white panties with SUNDAY embroidered in red on the front, and exposing also a two-foot-long green-painted trident that was duct-taped to her knee and thigh.

It was a short aluminum speargun spear, with three barbless tips at the trident end and three diagonal grooves notched into the pencil-diameter shaft. The tan skin of her thigh was smeared red around several shallow cuts where the points were pressed against her, and it was with a harsh exhalation of relief that she peeled off the tape and lifted the spear away. Gripping it with her elbow against her ribs, she wrapped one length of the tape back around her thigh, covering the cuts, and then she pulled her pants back up and re-buckled her belt.

She stuck the spear upright through the gravel into the loam underneath, and then leaned into the car and hoisted out of the back seat a Makita power screwdriver and a yard-square piece of white-painted plywood with black plastic letters glued onto it. She fished two screws out of her pocket and, with an abrupt shrill blasting of the Makita's motor, screwed the sign to the trunk of the pine tree.

The sign read:

> REST IN PEACE
> "THE LITTLE LAME MONARCH"
> LATE OF LEUCADIA;
> PREVIOUSLY OF SAN DIEGO, SONOMA, LAS VEGAS
> AND REMOTER PARTS.

For a moment she just stood there on the dew-damp gravel, with the Makita in her hand still harshly stitching the dawn air with its shrill buzz, and she stared at the sign with a look of blank incomprehension. Then her fingers relaxed and the machine crunched to the gravel, quiet at last.

She plodded over to the upright spear, plucked it free, and strode around the pine tree and down the unpaved private driveway, away from the street.

Fifteen minutes later and two hundred and fifty miles to the northeast, an earthquake shook the deep-rooted expanse of Hoover Dam, forty-five million pounds of reinforcing steel and four million cubic yards of concrete that stood braced across Black Canyon against the south end of Lake Mead as it had stood for sixty years; morning-shift engineers in the powerhouse wings below the dam thought that some vast vehicle was traversing the highway at the top, or that one of the gigantic turbines had broken under the weight of water surging down through the penstocks buried inside the Arizona-side mountain. Vacationers aboard houseboats on the lake were shaken awake in their bunks, and in the nearby city of Boulder more than two hundred people called the police in a panic.

* * *

Dawn-patrol prostitutes and crack dealers on Hollywood Boulevard reeled and grabbed for walls or parking meters as the sidewalk pavement, already sagging lower than normal because of shoddy tunneling being done for the Metro Rail line, abruptly dropped another inch and a half.

Just across the highway from Colma, the gray little cemetery town on the San Mateo Peninsula to which all the evicted burial plots of neighboring San Francisco had been relocated, a pregnant woman wrapped in a bedsheet and screaming nonsense verses in French ran out into the lanes of the 280 Highway.

Along Ocean Beach on the west coast of San Francisco a sudden offshore gale was chopping up the surf, blowing the swells at chaotic angles and wrecking the long clean lines of the waves. The couple of surfers out past the surf line who had been riding the terrifying winter waves gave up and began struggling to paddle back in to shore, and the ill-at-ease men who had been clustering around the vans and pickup trucks in the Sloat Boulevard parking lot cheered up and assured each other that they had stayed out of the water just because it had been obvious that the weather was going to change this way.

Similar abrupt gales split and uprooted trees as far north as Eureka and as far south as San Diego, all on that same morning.

And in a bedroom in a run-down old apartment building in Long Beach, south of Los Angeles, a fourteen-year-old boy was jolted awake—out of a dream of a woman running madly through rows of grapevines and clutching in her hand an ivy-wrapped staff that somehow had a bloody pinecone stuck on the end of it.

Koot Hoomie Sullivan had sat up in bed at the shock of the vision, and now he swung his bare feet out from under the blankets onto the wooden floor. His heart was still pounding, and his left hand had gone numb though his watchband was comfortably loose.

He glanced out the window, past the lantana branches that pressed against the glass; the carob trees and the parachute-draped van outside were casting long shadows across the broken concrete, and he could hear wild parrots shouting in the tree branches. It could hardly be seven o'clock yet—he was certainly the first person awake in the apartment—but the warm interior air was heavy with the smell of burning coffee.

"Call me Fishmeal," he whispered, and shivered. He had not smeared mud on the foot of his bed at all this winter, and he had eaten several slices of rare London broil for dinner last night—he had even been allowed to drink a glass of champagne at the stroke of midnight!—but nevertheless he was again, clearly, experiencing the sense of being nearly able to *see* the whole American West Coast in some off-the-visible-spectrum frequency, as if with eyes underground as well as in the sky, and almost *hear* heartbeats and whimpers and furtive trysts and betrayals as if through the minute vibrations of freeway-shoulder palm trees and mountain sage and urban-lot weeds. And below the conscious level of his mind, faintly as if from distances remote beyond any capacity of natural space, he thought he could hear shouts and sobs and laughter from entities that were not any part of himself. When he had felt this sense of expanded awareness before, it had generally been in breathless dreams, or at most in the hypnagogic state between sleep and waking, but he was wide awake right now.

He stood up and got dressed, quickly but thoughtfully—Reeboks, and comfortable jeans, and a loose flannel shirt over the bandage taped onto his ribs; and he made sure the end of his belt was rotated into a Möbius twist before he buckled it.

He blinked as he let his gaze drift over the things in his room—the tasco 300-power reflector telescope in the corner, the framed black-and-white photograph of Thomas Edison on the wall, the coin-collection folders, the desk with clothes and a pair of in-line skates piled carelessly on it.

He jumped in surprise, and an instant later a woman's voice mournfully exclaimed *"Oh hell!"* somewhere in the parking lot outside the window.

"It's bar-time showtime, folks," Kootie whispered self-consciously, and he opened the bedroom door and stepped out into the hallway that led to the open kitchen and the living room.

He could hear someone moving around in his adopted-parents' bedroom, but he wanted to have something specific to say before he talked to them—so he hurried to the front door and unhooked the feather-fringed chain and unbolted the door.

The woman who was the property owner was just walking around the corner of the building from the parking lot as Kootie shuffled across the threshold and pulled the front door closed behind him; and her brown face was streaked with tears. "Oh, Kootie," she said, "all the beasties are dead!"

They were already dead, Kootie thought—but he knew what the woman must mean. The morning air was sharply chilly in his curly, sweat-damp hair, but the breeze was still scented with the night's jasmine, and he felt ready to deal with this particular crisis. "Show me, Johanna," he said gently.

"Over by the trash cans and Mr. Pete's van." She was plodding heavily back the way she had come, her bathrobe flapping around the legs of her burst spandex tights. Over her shoulder she said, "I gave them some new gravel last night—could that have poisoned them?"

Kootie remembered his dreamed vision of the woman in the vineyard with the bloody, ivy-wrapped staff, and as he followed Johanna around the corner into the slantingly sunlit parking lot, he said, "What killed them was nothing that happened around here."

He trudged after her across the broken checkerboard of asphalt and concrete, and when he had stepped around the back end of the parachute-shrouded van he stopped beside her.

The beasties were *obviously* dead now. Three of them were sprawled on the pavement and in the ice plant here, their gnarled old hands poking limply out of the thrift-store shirt cuffs, their mouths gaping among the patchy gray post-mortem whiskers, their eyes flat and sheenless behind the scavenged spectacles.

Kootie shook his head and clumsily ran the still-numb fingers of his left hand through his curly black hair. "Terrific," he said. "What are we going to *do* with them?"

Johanna sniffed. "We should give them a burial."

"These people died a long time ago, Johanna," Kootie said, "and these aren't their bodies. These aren't *anyone's* bodies. The coroner would go nuts if he got hold of these. I doubt if they've got any more internal organs than a sea-slug's got . . . and I always thought their skeletons must be arranged pretty freehand, from the way they walk. Walked. I doubt they've even got fingerprints."

Johanna sighed. "I'm glad I got them the Mikasa glass candies at Christmas."

"They did like those," Kootie agreed absently. Her late common-law husband had got into the habit of feeding the shambling derelicts, and for the last three Christmases Johanna had bought decorative glass treats for the things, in his memory. They couldn't eat organic stuff because it would just rot inside their token bellies, but they had still liked to gobble down things that *looked* like food.

"Good God," came a man's voice from behind Kootie; and then a woman said, softly, "What would *they* die *of?*"

Kootie turned to his adopted parents with a rueful smile. "Top of the morning. I was hoping I'd be able to get a tarp over 'em before you guys got up, so I could break it to you over coffee."

His adopted mother glanced at him, and then stared at his side. "Kootie," she said, her contralto voice suddenly sharp with alarm, "you're bleeding. Worse than usual, I mean."

Kootie had already felt the hot wetness over his ribs. "I know, Angelica," he said to her. To his adopted father he said, "Pete, let's get these necrotic dudes stashed in your van for now. Then I think we'd better go to Johanna's office to . . . *confer.* I believe this is going to be a busy day. A busy year."

He nearly always just called them "Mom" and "Dad"—this use of their first names put a stop to further discussion out here, and they both nodded. Angelica said, "I'll get coffee cooking," and strode back toward the building. Pete Sullivan rubbed his chin and said, "Let's use a blanket from inside the van to lift them in. I don't want to have to touch their 'skin.' "

Angelica Sullivan's maiden name had been Elizalde, and she had the lean face and high cheekbones of a figure in an El Greco painting; her long, straight hair was as black as Kootie's unruly mane, but after she put four coffee cups of water into the microwave in Johanna's kitchen, and got the restaurant-surplus coffee urn loaded and turned on, she tied her hair back in a hasty ponytail and hurried into the manager's office.

A television set was humming on the cluttered desk, but its screen was black, and the only light in the long room was the yellow glow that filtered in through the dusty, vine-blocked windows high in one wall. A worn couch sat against the opposite wall, and she stepped lithely up onto it to reach the bookshelves above it.

She selected several volumes from the shelves, dropping them onto the couch cushions by her feet, and took down too a nicotine-darkened stuffed toy pig; then she hopped down, sniffed the air sharply, and hurried back into the little kitchen—but the coffee was not burning.

A sudden hard knock at the door made her jump, and when she whirled toward the door she saw Kootie's face peering in at her through the screened door-window; and then the boy opened the door and stepped in, followed by Johanna and Pete.

"You're not on bar-time, Mom," said Kootie, panting. "You jumped *after* I knocked on the door; and Dad jumped *after* I flicked cold hose-water on his neck."

Pete's graying hair was wet, and he nodded. "Not *much* after."

Johanna was staring at Kootie without comprehension, so he told her, "Bar-time is when you react to things an instant *before* they actually happen, like you're vibrating in the *now* notch and hanging over the sides a little. It's . . . 'sympathetically induced resonation,' it means somebody's paying psychic attention to you, watching you magically."

He looked at Pete and Angelica. "*I've* been on bar-time since I woke up. When Johanna found the beasties, I jumped a second before she yelled, and when we went back to the apartment to wash our hands just now, I reached for the phone an instant before it started ringing.''

Kootie led the three of them out of the kitchen into Pete's long dim office.

"It was one of your clients on the phone," Pete told Angelica, "Mrs. Perez. She says her grandparents' ghosts are gone from the iron pots you put them in; the pots aren't even magnetic anymore, she says. Oh, and I noticed that your voodoo whosis is gone from the cabinet by *our* front door—the little cement guy with cowrie shells for his eyes and mouth.''

"The Eleggua figure?" said Angelica, collapsing onto the couch. "He's—what, he's the Lord of the Crossroads, what can it mean that he's *gone?* He must have weighed thirty pounds! Solid concrete! I didn't forget to *propitiate* him last week—did I, Kootie?''

Kootie shook his head somberly. "You spit rum all over him, and I put the beef jerky and the Pez dispenser in his cabinet myself.''

Pete was sniffing the stale office air. "Why does everywhere smell like burning coffee this morning?''

"Kootie," said Angelica, *"what's going on here today?"*

Kootie had hiked himself up to sit on the desk next to the buzzing black-screened television set, and he pulled his shirt up out of his pants—the bandage taped to his side was blotted with red, and even as they looked at it a line of blood trickled down to his belt. "And my left hand's numb," he said, flexing his fingers, "and I had to rest twice, carrying the dead beasties, because I've got no strength in my legs.''

He looked up at his adopted mother. "We're in the middle of winter," he went on, in a tense but flat voice. "This is the season when I sometimes dream that I can ... sense the American West Coast. This morning—" He paused to cock his head: "—*still,* in fact—I've got that sense while I'm awake. What I *dreamed* of was a crazy woman running through a vineyard, waving a bloody wand with ivy vines wrapped around it and a pinecone stuck on the end of it.'' He pulled his shirt back down and tucked it in messily. "Some balance of power has shifted drastically somewhere—and somebody is *paying attention* to me; somebody's going to be coming here. And I don't think the Solville foxing measures are going to fool this person.''

"Nobody can see through them!" said Johanna loyally. Her late husband, Solomon "Sol" Shadroe, had bought the apartment building in 1974 because its architecture confused psychic tracking, and he had spent nearly twenty years adding rooms and wings onto the structure, and re-routing the water and electrical systems, and putting up dozens of extraneous old TV antennas with carob seed-pods and false teeth and old radio parts hung from them, to intensify the effect; the result was an eccentric stack and scatter of buildings and sheds and garages and conduit, and even now, more than two years after the old man's death, the tenants still called the rambling old compound Solville.

Pete Sullivan was the manager and handyman for the place now, and he had dutifully kept up the idiosyncratic construction and maintenance programs; now his lean, tanned face was twisted in a squinting smile of apprehension. "So what is it that you sense, son?"

"There's a—" Kootie said uncertainly, his unfocused gaze moving across the ceiling. "I can almost see it—a chariot—or a . . . a gold cup? Maybe it's a tarot card from the Cups suit, paired with the Chariot card from the Major Arcana?—coming here." He gave Johanna a mirthless smile. "I think *it* could find me, even here, and *somebody* might be riding in *it,* or carrying *it.*"

Angelica was nodding angrily. "This is the *thing,* isn't it, Kootie, that was all along going to happen? The reason why we never moved away from here?"

"Why we stopped running," ventured Pete. "Why we've been . . . standing our little ground."

"Why Kootie is an *iyawo,*" said Johanna, sighing and nodding in the kitchen doorway. "Why this place was first built, from the earthquake wreck of that ghost house. And the—"

"Kootie is not an *iyawo,*" Angelica interrupted, pronouncing the feminine Yoruba noun as if it were an obscenity. "He hasn't undergone the *kariocha* initiation. Tell her, Pete."

Kootie looked at his adopted father and smiled. "Yeah," he said softly, "tell her, Dad."

Pete Sullivan pulled a pack of Marlboros out of his shirt pocket and cleared his throat. "Uh, 'it's not a river in Egypt,' " he told his wife, quoting a bit of pop-psychology jargon that he knew she hated.

She laughed, though with obvious reluctance. "I know it's not. *The Nile, denial*—I know the difference. How is this denial, what I'm saying? *Kariocha* is a very specific ritual—shave the head, cut the scalp, get three specially initiated drummers to play the consecrated *bata* drums!—and it just *has not been done* with Kootie."

"Not to the letter of the law," said Pete, shaking out a cigarette and flipping it over the backs of his fingers; "but in the . . . spirit?" He snapped a wooden match and inhaled smoke, then squeezed the lit match in his fist, which was empty when he opened it again. "Come on, Angie! All the formalities aside, basically a *kariocha* initiation is putting a thing like an alive-and-kicking ghost inside of somebody's head, right? Call it a 'ghost' or call it an 'orisha.' It makes the person who hosts it . . .

what, *different*. So—well, *you* tell *me* what state Kootie was in when we found him two years ago. I suppose he's not still an *omo,* since the orisha left his head, voluntarily . . . but it did happen to the boy.''

"I saw him when he was *montado,*" agreed Johanna, "possessed, in this very kitchen, with that *yerba buena y tequila* telephone. He had great *ashe,* the boy's orisha did, great luck and power, to make a telephone out of mint and tequila and a pencil sharpener, and then call up dead people on it." She looked across at the boy and smiled sadly. "You're not a virgin in the head anymore, are you, Kootie?"

"More truth than poetry in that, Johanna," Kootie agreed, hopping down from the desk. "Yeah, Mom, this does feel like *it.*" His voice was unsteady, but he managed to look confident as he waved his blood-spotted hand in a gesture that took in the whole building and grounds. "It's why we're here, why I'm what I am." He smiled wanly and added, "It's why your Mexican wizard made you give a nasty name to this witchery shop you run here. And this *is* the best place for us to be standing when it meets us. Solville can't *hide* us, but it's a fortified position. We can . . . receive them, whoever they might be, give them an audience."

Angelica was sitting on the couch, flipping through the pages of her battered copy of Kardec's *Selected Prayers.* Among the other books she had tossed onto the couch were Reichenbach's *Letters on Od and Magnetism,* and a spiral-bound notebook with a version of Shakespeare's *Troilus and Cressida* hand-copied into it, and a paperback copy of Guillermo Ceniza-Bendiga's *Cunjuro del Tobaco.*

"How far away are they?" she snapped, without looking up. "Like, are they coming from Los Angeles? New York? Tibet? Mars?"

"The . . . thing is . . . on the coast," said Kootie with a visible shiver. "Sssouth? Yes, south of here, and coming north, like up the 5 Freeway or Pacific Coast Highway."

CHAPTER 2

Our doctors say this is no month to bleed.
—William Shakespeare,
Richard II

The caged clock high on the green-painted wall indicated exactly eleven, and most of the patients were already filing out the door to the yard for their fifteen-minute smoking break, following the nurse who carried the Bic lighter, and Dr. Armentrout was glad to leave the television lounge in the care of the weekend charge nurse. The big, sunny room, with its institutional couches and wall-mounted TV sets, looked as though it should smell of floor wax and furniture polish, but in fact the air was always redolent with low-rent cooking smells; today he could still detect the garlic-and-oil reek of last night's lasagna.

The common telephone was ringing behind him as he puffed down the hallway to his office; each of the patients apparently assumed that any call must be for someone else, and so no one ever seemed to answer the damned thing. Armentrout certainly wasn't going to answer it; he was cautiously elated that he hadn't got his usual terrible dawn wake-up call at home today—the phone had rung at his bedside as always, but for once there had been, blessedly, only vacuous silence at the other end—and for damn sure he wasn't going to pick up any ringing telephones that he didn't *have* to answer. Resolutely ignoring the diminishing noise, Armentrout peeked through the wire-reinforced glass of the narrow window in his office door before turning the key in the first of the two locks, though it was nearly impossible that a patient could have sneaked inside; and he saw no one, and of course when he had turned the key in the second lock and the red light in the lockplate came on and he pulled the door open, the little room was empty. On the weekends the intern with whom he shared the office didn't come in, and Armentrout saw patients alone.

He preferred that.

He lowered his substantial bulk into his desk chair and picked up the file of admission notes on the newest patient, with whom he had an appointment in less than a quarter of an hour. She was an obese teenager with a dismal Global Assessment Score of 20, diagnosed as having Bipolar Disorder, Manic. Today he would give her a glass of water with four milligrams of yellow benzodiazepine powder dissolved into it; instantly soluble and completely tasteless, the drug would not only calm her down and make her suggestible but also block the neurotransmissions that permitted memorization—she would remember nothing of today's session.

A teenager! he thought as he absently kneaded the crotch of his baggy slacks. Obese! Manic! Well, she'll be going home in a few days, totally cured and with no manic episodes in her future; and I will have had a good time and added some depth-of-field and at least a few minutes to my lifespan. Everybody will be better off.

With his free hand he brushed some patient's frightful crayon drawings away from the rank of instant-dial buttons alongside the telephone. When the girl arrived he would lift the receiver and punch the button to ring the telephone in the conference room, where he had left good old reliable Long John Beach jiggling and mumbling in a chair by the phone—though it was possible that Armentrout wouldn't *need* Long John Beach's help anymore, if this morning's reprieve from the hideous wake-up call was a sign of the times, a magical gift of this new year.

The ringing of *this* telephone, the one on his desk, snapped him out of his optimistic reverie; and under his spray-stiffened white hair his forehead was suddenly chilly with a dew of sweat. Slowly, his lips silently forming the words *no, please, no*, he reached out and lifted the receiver.

"Dr. Armentrout," he said slowly, hardly expelling any breath.

"Doc," came a tinny voice out of the earpiece, "this is Taylor Hamilton? Desk sergeant at the San Marcos County Sheriff's branch? I'm calling from a pay phone in the back hall."

Armentrout's chin sagged into his jowls with relief, and then he was smiling with fresh excitement as he picked up a pen. For the past several years he had been alerting police officers and paramedics and psych techs all over southern California to watch for certain kinds of 51-50, which was police code for involuntary-seventy-two-hour-hold psychiatric cases.

"Taylor Hamilton," noted Armentrout, consciously keeping the eagerness out of his voice as he wrote down the man's name on a Post-it slip. "Got it. You've got a good one?"

"This lady seems like just what the doctor ordered," said Hamilton with a nervous laugh. "I bet you anything that she turns out to have gone AWOL from your place yesterday."

Armentrout had already pulled down an escape-report form from the shelf over the desk, and he now wrote *12/31/94* in the date box.

"I'll bet you," Hamilton went on, "*one thousand dollars* that she's a runaway of yours."

Armentrout lifted the pen from the paper. "That's a lot of money," he said dubiously. A thousand dollars! And he hated it when his informants made the arrangement sound so nakedly mercenary. "What makes you think she's . . . one of mine?"

"Well, she called nine-one-one saying that she'd just half an hour earlier killed a guy in a field above the beach in Leucadia this morning, like right at dawn, stabbed him with a *speargun spear*, if you can believe that—but when the officers had her take them to where it supposedly happened and show them, there was no body or blood at all, and no spear; in fact they reported that the field was full of blooming flowers and grapevines and it was obvious nobody had walked across it for at least the last twenty-four hours. She told them it was a *king* that she killed there, a *king* called *the Flying Nun*—that's solid ding talk, isn't it? The officers are convinced that her story is pure hallucination. She hasn't stopped crying since she called nine-one-one, and her nose won't stop bleeding, and she says some guy rearranged her teeth, though she doesn't show any bruises or cuts. And listen, when they first tried to drive her back here, for questioning?—the black-and-white wouldn't start, they needed a jump; and when we've been talking to her in here the lights keep dimming and my hearing aid doesn't work."

Armentrout was frowning thoughtfully. The electromagnetic disturbances indicated one of the dissociative disorders—psychogenic amnesia, fugue states, depersonalization. These were the tastiest maladies he could cure . . . short of curing somebody of their very *life*, of course, which was ethically problematic and in any case contributed too heavily to the—

He shied away from the memory of the morning telephone calls.

But *a thousand dollars!* This Hamilton fellow was a greedy pig. This wasn't really supposed to be about *money*.

"I don't," Armentrout began—

But she did go crazy on *this morning*, he thought. She might very well have been reacting to the same thing, whatever it might be, that saved me from my intolerable wake-up call. These poor suffering psy-

ch*os* are often psych*ic,* and a dissociative, having distanced herself from
the ground state of her core personality, might be able to sense a wider
spectrum of magical effects. By examining her I might be able to figure
out what the hell *has* happened. I should call around, in fact, and tell
all my sentries to watch especially for a psychosis that was triggered
this morning.

"—see any reason not to pay you a thousand dollars for her," he
finished, nevertheless still frowning at the price. "Can I safely fax you
the AWOL report?"

"Do it in . . . exactly ten minutes, okay? I can make sure nobody else
is near the machine, and then as soon as your fax has cooled off I'll
smudge the date and pretend to find it on yesterday's spike."

Armentrout glanced at his watch and then bent over the police-report
form again. "Name and description?"

"Janis Cordelia Plumtree," said Hamilton. "She has a valid driver's
license, and I Xeroxed it. Ready? DOB 9/20/67 . . ."

Armentrout began neatly filling in the boxes on the escape-report
form. This morning a manic teenager on benzodiazepine, and, soon, a
dissociative who was strong enough to interfere with both AC and DC
. . . and who might also provide a clue to why Armentrout had been, at
least for this morning, freed from the attention of all the resentful ghosts
and ghost fragments!

This was already shaping up to be a fine year, though it was only
eleven hours old.

When he finally hung up the telephone he looked at his watch again.
He had five minutes before he should send the fax or expect the bipolar
girl to be brought in.

He got his feet firmly under the chair and stood up with a grunt, then
crossed to the long couch that couldn't be seen through the door window,
and lifted off of the cushions a stack of files and a box of plastic Lego
bricks. Clearing the field, he thought with some anticipation, for the cul-
tivation of the bipolar girl's cure. The plowing and seeding of her recov-
ery. And it *would* be a real cure, as decisive as surgery—not the dreary,
needlessly guilt-raising patchwork of psychotherapy. Armentrout saw no
value in anyone dredging up old guilts and resentments, ever.

Finally he unlocked the top drawer of the filing cabinet and rolled it
partway out. Inside were only two things, two purple velvet boxes.

One box contained a battered but polished .45-caliber derringer for
which he had paid a hundred thousand dollars a year and a half ago, its
two stubby barrels chambered to take .410 shot shells as well as Colt
.45 rounds; some spiritualist medium had found the blocky little gun on
Ninth Street in downtown Las Vegas in 1948, and there was documen-

tation to suggest that the gun had been used to castrate a powerful French occultist there; and Armentrout knew that a woman had killed herself with it in Delaware in October of 1992, shortly before he had acquired it. Probably it had inflicted injuries on other people at other times. The tiny gun was alleged, with some authority, to be able to shoot straight through magical protections that would deflect a bullet shot from a mundane gun: the French occultist had been heavily warded, but the person who had shot him had been his wife and the mother of his children, and so she had been inside his guard and able to wound him— and the gun had thus definitively shared in her privileged position, and was now reputedly capable of shooting the equivalent of supernatural-Teflon rounds.

Armentrout had never fired it, and certainly he wouldn't be needing it for the bipolar teenager.

The other velvet box he lifted out of the file drawer.

He carried it to the low coffee table carefully. Inside the box were twenty cards from a tarot deck that had been painted in Marseilles in 1933. Armentrout had paid a San Francisco bookseller *four hundred thousand* dollars for the cards in 1990. Twenty cards was less than a third of the complete tarot deck, and the powerful Death and The Tower cards were not among this partial set—but these twenty cards were from one of the fabulously rare Lombardy Zeroth decks, painted by a now-disbanded secret guild of damagingly initiated artists, and the images on the cards were almost intolerably evocative of the raw Jungian archetypes.

Armentrout had used the contents of *this* box on *many* occasions— he had awakened catatonics simply by holding the Judgment card in front of their glassy eyes, realigned the minds of undifferentiated schizophrenics with a searing exposure of The Moon, settled the most conflicted borderlines with the briefest palmed flash of The Hanged Man; and on a couple of occasions he had *induced* real, disorganized schizophrenia by showing a merely neurotic patient the Fool card.

For the bipolar girl today he would try first the Temperance card, the winged maiden pouring water from one jug to another.

And he would avoid looking squarely at any of the cards himself. When he had first got the deck he had forced himself to scrutinize the picture on each card—enduring the sea-bottom explosions they seemed to set off in his mind, clenching his fists as alien images arrowed up to his conscious levels like deep-water monsters bursting up into the air.

The experience had, if anything, only diminished his personal identity, and so he had not been in danger of attracting the notice of his . . . of any *Midwest ghost* . . . but locally he had been a clamorous maelstrom in the psychic water table, and for the next three days his phone had rung at *all* hours with southern California ghosts clamoring on the line, and after a few weeks he had noticed that his hair was growing out completely white.

And like a lock of unruly hair, he thought now as he picked up the escape-report form and turned his chair toward the fax machine, this teenage girl's mania will be drawn out tight by the urgent attraction of the image on the card, and I will snip that bit off of her—

—and swallow it into myself.

She was at the door; he took the telephone receiver off the cradle, pushed the instant-dial button, and then stood up ponderously to let her in.

In the Long Beach apartment building known as Solville, Angelica Sullivan had been having a busy morning; she wanted to hover protectively over Kootie, but she had found that there were other demands on her time.

Over the rental-office door that faced the alley, she had last year hung up—reluctantly, for the business name had not been of her choosing—a sign that read TESTÍCULOS DEL LEÓN—BOTÁNICA Y CONSULTORIO. And it seemed that every client who had ever consulted her here had come blundering up to that rental-office door today, or at least called on the telephone; they were mostly Hispanic and black, dishwashers and motel maids and gardeners, on their lunch breaks or off work or out of work, and nearly all of them were jabbering with gratitude at having been abruptly relieved, at about dawn, of the various afflictions that had led them to seek out Angelica's help in the first place. Most mentioned having been awakened by an earthquake, though the radio news station that Angelica had turned on hadn't yet mentioned one.

Many of her people had felt that this deliverance needed to be formalized with ritual thanks, and so, with help from Kootie and Pete and Johanna, Angelica had harriedly tried to comply. In her role as a *curandera* she had got pots of mint tea brewing, and served it in every vessel in the place that would do for a cup, and Johanna had even dug out some of her late husband's old coffee cups, still red-stained from the cinnamon tea that Sol Shadroe had favored; as a *maja*, Angelica had lit all the *veladores*, the candles in the glass tumblers with decals of saints stuck to the outsides; as a *huesera* she had got sweaty massaging newly painless backs and shoulder joints; and out in the parking lot, to perform a ritual *limpia* cleansing, six men in their undershorts were now crowded into a child's inflatable pool that Kootie had filled with honey and bananas and water from the hose.

Cures of impotence, constipation, drug craving, and every other malady appeared to have been bestowed wholesale as the sun had come up, and in spite of Angelica's repeated protests that she had done nothing to accomplish any of it, the desk in Pete's office was now heaped with coins; whatever amount the pile of money added up to, it would be divisible by forty-nine, for forty-nine cents was the only price Angelica was permitted by the spirit world to charge for her magical services.

A few of her clients, like the one who had called Pete first thing in the morning, were unhappy to find that the spirits of their dead relatives were gone from the iron containers—truck brake drums, hibachis, Dutch ovens—in which they had dwelt since Angelica had corralled and confined them, one by laborious one over the last two and a half years; the candies left out for these spirits last night had apparently not been touched, and the rooster-blood–painted wind chimes that hung from the containers had rung no morning greeting today. Angelica could only tell these people that their relatives had finally become comfortable with the notion of moving on to Heaven. That explanation went down well enough.

Others with the same kind of problem were not so easily mollified. Frantic *santeros* from as far away as Albuquerque had telephoned to ask if Angelica, too, had found that her orisha stones had lost all their *ashe*, all their vitality—she could only confirm it bewilderedly, and tell them in addition about the total disappearance of the cement Eleggua figure that she had kept by her front door; and as the sunlight-shadows in the kitchen had touched their farthest reach across the worn yellow linoleum and begun to ebb back, Angelica began to get the first news of gang warfare in the alleys of Los Angeles and Santa Ana, skirmishes ignited by the absence today of the *palo gangas* that served as supernatural bodyguards to the heroin and crack cocaine dealers.

"Were those ghosts too?" asked Pete as he carried a stockpot full of small change into the kitchen and heard Angelica acknowledging the latest such bulletin.

"The *gangas?*" said Angelica as she hung up the phone for the hundredth time and brushed back stray strands of her sweaty black hair. "Sure. The *paleros* get some human remains into a cauldron, and it's their slave as long as it stays under their control. That thing that was hassling us in '92 was one, that thing that laughed all the time and talked in rhyming Spanish."

"The canvas bag full of hair," said Pete, nodding, "with the Raiders cap stapled on the top." He grunted as he hoisted the pot up and dumped the coins in a glittering waterfall into the oil drum he'd dragged in an hour ago, which was now already a third full of coins. "I call it a good day, when things like that are banished."

The kitchen, and the office and even the parking lot now, smelled of mint and beer and sweat and burning candle-wicks, but under it all was still the aroma of burning coffee. Angelica sniffed and shook her head doubtfully; she opened her mouth to say something, but a white-haired old grandmother bustled into the kitchen just then, reverently holding out a quarter and two dimes and four pennies in the palm of her hand.

"*Gracias, Señora Soollivan,*" the old woman said, pushing the coins toward Angelica.

Angelica couldn't remember now what service this old woman was grateful for—some haunting ended, some bowel disorder relieved, some recurrent nightmare blessedly forgotten.

"*No,*" said Angelica, "I haven't—"

But now a man in a mechanic's uniform blundered into the kitchen behind the old woman. "Mrs. Sullivan," he said breathlessly, "your *amuletos* finally worked—my daughter sees no devils in the house now. I got the *cundida* at work this week, so I can give you two hundred dollars—"

Angelica was nodding and waving her hands defensively in front of herself. She knew about *cundidas*—a group of people at a workplace would contribute some amount of each paycheck to the "good quantity" fund, and each week a different one of them got the whole pool; among the new-immigrant Hispanic community, to whom bank accounts were an alien concept, the *cundidas* were the easiest way to save money.

"I didn't *do* anything," she said loudly. "Don't pay *me* for your blessings—somebody else has paid the price of it."

And who on earth can that have been? she wondered.

"But *I* need to pay," the man said quietly.

Angelica let her shoulders droop. "*Okay,*" she said, exhaling. "If I run into your benefactor, I'll pass it on. But you can only give me forty-nine cents."

During Christmas week in 1993, Angelica had—finally, at the age of thirty-five—flown alone to Mexico City and then driven a rented car more a hundred miles southeast to a little town called Ciudad Mendoza. Members of her grandfather's family were still living in the poor end of the town, known as Colonia Liberación, and after identifying herself to the oldest citizens and staying with some of her distant relatives until after Christmas, she had got directions to the house of an old man called Esteban Sandoval, whom she was assured was the most powerful *mago* south of Matamoros. In exchange for the rental car and the cut-out hologram bird from one of her credit cards, Sandoval had agreed to complete and formalize and sanction her qualifications for the career she had fallen into a year earlier.

For three months Sandoval had instructed her in the practices of the ancient folk magics that are preserved as *santería* and *brujería* and *curanderismo;* and on the night before he put her on the bus that would take her on the first leg of her long journey back to her new American family, he had summoned several orishas, invisible entities somewhat more than ghosts and less than gods, and had relayed to her from them her *ita,* the rules that would henceforth circumscribe her personal conduct of magic. Among those dictates had been the distasteful name that she was to give to her business, and the requirement that she charge only forty-nine cents for each service.

Pete Sullivan accepted the exact change from the two people and walked over to toss it too into the barrel of coins.

Kootie was at the open kitchen door now, silhouetted against the spectacle of Angelica's colorfully dressed clients dancing under the sun-dappled palm trunks outside, and his eyes were wide and the hand he was pressing to his side was spotted with fresh blood.

"Mom—Dad—" he said. "They're here, nearly—block or two away."

Pete pushed the old woman and the mechanic out of the kitchen, into the crowded office room, and when he turned back to Kootie and Angelica he lifted the front of his untucked shirt to show the black Pachmayr grip of the .45 automatic tucked into his belt.

It was, Angelica knew, loaded with 230-grain hollow-point Eldorado Starfire rounds that she had dipped in an *omiero* of mint and oleander tea; and Pete had carefully etched L.A. CIGAR—TOO TRAGICAL in tiny letters onto the muzzle ring of the stainless-steel slide.

"Take it, Angelica," he said tensely. "I could hardly even pick it up this morning. My Houdini hands are on extra solid today."

Angelica stepped forward and pulled the gun out of Pete's pants, making sure the safety catch was up and engaged. She tucked it into her own jeans and pulled her blouse out to cover it.

Kootie nodded. "We'll receive them courteously but carefully," he said.

Through the open kitchen door, from the street, Angelica could now hear an approaching discordant rumble, like bad counterpoint tempo beaten out on a set of *bata* drums that the orishas would surely reject for being perilously tuned; and when she stepped outside, striding resolutely across the sunlit walk and onto the driveway, she saw a big, boxy red truck turn in from the street and then slowly, boomingly, labor up the gentle slope toward where she stood. Peripherally she noticed that Kootie was now standing at her left and Pete at her right, and she reached out and clasped their hands.

The red truck rocked and clattered to a halt a couple of yards in front of them. It was streaked and powdered with dust, but its red color shone through lividly; and she noticed that an aura like heat waves shimmered around it for a distance of about a foot, and that the leaves of the carob trees on the far side of the driveway looked gray where she viewed them through the aura.

The truck's driver's-side door clanked and squeaked open, and a rangy man of about Pete's age stepped down to the pavement; his worn boots and jeans seemed only deceptively mundane to Angelica, and his lean, tanned face, behind a ragged mustache the color of tobacco and ashes, was tense with care.

"What *seeems* to be the problem?" he drawled, and there was at least some exhausted humor in his voice and his squinting brown eyes.

The passenger-side door was levered open now, and a pregnant woman in a wrinkled white linen sundress stepped down onto the driveway-side grass. She too looked exhausted, and her blond hair was pulled back, like Angelica's black hair, into a hasty, utilitarian ponytail—but Angelica thought she was nevertheless the most radiantly beautiful woman she had ever seen.

"Any problem here," said Pete levelly, "is one you've brought with you. Who are you?"

"Good point," said the man with the mustache, nodding judiciously. "About us bringing it with us. Sorry—my name's Archimedes Mavranos, and this lady is Diana Crane." He looked past Angelica's shoulder and raised an eyebrow. "And we sure do apologize to be interrupting your party."

Angelica glanced behind her, and realized how odd the crowd in the parking lot must look—the kneeling old women giving thanks, the men and women appearing to pantomime swimming and goose-stepping and traffic-directing as they flexed various freshly pain-free limbs, and the six apparently naked men crowded into the Little Mermaid inflatable pool.

"We're humbly looking," Mavranos went on seriously, "for a man with a wound in his side that won't quit bleeding."

After a moment, Kootie let go of Angelica's hand; he held up his blood-reddened palm, and then, as slowly as a surrendering man showing a gun to a policeman, lifted his shirttail to show the bloody bandage.

"A kid!" said Mavranos with an accusing glance toward Pete. He peered more closely at Kootie, then stepped forward. Angelica let her right hand brush the hem of her blouse over the .45, but the man had only knelt before Kootie and taken the boy's left wrist in his gnarled brown hand. "You've Möbiused your watchband?" he said gently. "That won't work anymore, son. *Now* when you do that you're just insulating yourself from your own *self.*" He had been unbuckling the watch strap as he spoke, and now he tucked the watch into Kootie's shirt pocket. "If you follow me. Oh, and the same with your belt, hey?

That I'll let *you* fix. Lord, boy," he said, shaking his head as he lithely straightened up again, "both legs and your left hand! You must have been weak as a kitten all day."

Kootie seemed embarrassed, as though he'd blundered into a girls' rest room by mistake. The boy quickly unbuckled his belt, straightened out the twist, and re-buckled it; then he pointed at the truck and asked gruffly, "Why is your truck the color of blood?"

The pregnant woman by the truck closed her eyes, and Mavranos crossed his arms and nodded several times. "The hard way, of course. You take the low road and I'll crawl in the goddamned dirt, right? That's the spirit. Oh, that was the wrong *question*, boy!"

He turned and walked back to the still-open driver's-side door, and for a moment Angelica hoped these two people, and whatever they might have brought with them in the truck, would now just go away; but Mavranos only leaned in to hook out a can of Coors beer, which, from the way it swung in his hand as he trudged back to where he had been standing, was already half-emptied.

He took a sip from it before speaking. "But since you ask. This lady and a friend painted it red on Ash Wednesday of 1990, in Las Vegas, to elude detection by the police—like the blood of the lamb over the doorposts in Egypt, right?—and ever since then the truck spon-*tane*-eously turns red every year during Holy Week. Ordinarily it's blue."

"This isn't Holy Week," ventured Pete. "This is New Year's Day."

"Oh, the error of it hadn't eluded me, honest," Mavranos said. He looked again at Kootie, and frowned. "You were a street beggar in L.A. a couple of years ago, weren't you? With an old black guy and a dog? Didn't I give you five bucks?"

Kootie's eyes widened, and then narrowed in a slow, shy smile. "Yeah, you did. And it *was* a blue truck."

"Sure," Mavranos said. "I remember now I saw room for the crown on your head even then. I should have *figured* it would be you we'd find today." After crouching to put his beer can down on the pavement, he straightened and spat in the palm of one hand and then struck it with his other fist; the spit flew toward the kitchen, and he looked up at the crazy old building for the first time.

He was staring at the sign over the door. "I *met* Leon," he said softly; "though he had lost his *testículos* years before."

On top of her anxious tension, Angelica was now embarrassed too. "It means 'Testicles of the *Lion*,' " she said. "All *consultorios* have animal valor names—Courage of the Bull, Heart of the Leopard, things like that. It's . . . a custom."

Mavranos looked down at her, and his eyes were bright until he blinked and resumed his protective squint. "We're in the choppy rapids of custom every which way you look, ma'am. Now, the random . . . *trajectory* of my spit has indicated your building. Will you give permission for my party to come inside?"

Party? Angelica was suddenly certain that there was a third person in the old red truck—a person, *the* person, central to all this—sick or injured or even dead; and suddenly she very strongly didn't want any of these strangers inside the buildings of Solville. Apparently permission would have to be given for that to happen—and she opened her mouth to deny it—

But Kootie spoke first. "I am the master of this house," the boy said. "And you have my permission to bring your party inside."

Angelica wheeled on Kootie, and she could feel her face reddening. *"Kootie, what are you—"* Then she stopped, and just exhaled the rest of her breath in helpless frustration.

Under the tangled curls of his black hair, Kootie's face looked leaner, older now; but the apologetic smile he gave her was warm with filial affection, and sad with a boy's sadness.

Mavranos's grin was flinty. "Just what you were about to say yourself, ma'am, I know," he growled. "Oh well—now that the boy's got the strength in his limbs back, maybe he could help me and this other gentleman with the carrying." He picked up his beer can and drained it, then tossed it onto the grass. Perhaps to himself, he said, softly, "But why couldn't the boy have asked me *whose truck it was?*"

Again Angelica opened her mouth to say something, but Mavranos waved her to silence. "Moot point and rhetorical question," he said. "It always happens this way, I guess."

"At least give me forty-nine cents!" Angelica said. If these people pay me and thus become clients of mine, she thought, if I'm following my *ita* in my dealings with them, we can be protected by the orishas; if there are any orishas left out there, if my *ita* still counts for anything, after whatever it is that has happened today.

Mavranos grinned sleepily and dug a handful of change out of his jeans pocket. "Look at that," he said. "Exact." He dropped the quarter and two dimes and four pennies into her shaky, outstretched palm. He looked past her at Kootie and Pete, and called, "You fellas want to give me a hand? Let me get the back of the truck open."

He plodded back toward the truck, his hand rattling keys in the pocket of his old denim jacket, and Kootie and Pete exchanged a nervous glance and then stepped forward to follow him.

BOOK ONE

To the Boats

The likeness passed away, say, like a breath along the surface of the gaunt pier-glass behind her, on the frame of which, a hospital procession of negro cupids, several headless and all cripples, were offering black baskets of Dead Sea fruit to black divinities of the feminine gender . . .

—Charles Dickens,
A Tale of Two Cities

TROILUS: *Fear me not, my lord;*
I will not be myself, nor have cognition
Of what I feel.

—William Shakespeare,
Troilus and Cressida

CHAPTER 3

"In short," said Sydney, "this is a desperate time, when desperate games are played for desperate stakes. Let the Doctor play the winning game; I will play the losing one . . ."

—Charles Dickens,
A Tale of Two Cities

Where Janis Cordelia Plumtree finally wound up was in a chair in the TV lounge.

She had visited people in hospitals where the lines on the linoleum floors *led* you somewhere—"Follow the yellow line to OB" or something—but the black lines in the gray floors of Rosecrans Medical Center just led around in a big dented loop, with frustrating gaps where hallways crossed. Maybe the point was that you were free to pick your own destination . . . the TV lounge, or the meds station, or your "room" with two unmade beds in it and no bath or shower and a door that couldn't lock.

There were wire-reinforced windows in the halls and the lounge, but the views were only of fenced-in courtyards, shadowy in the late-afternoon sunlight and empty except for picnic tables and dome-topped swing-door trash cans; and you generally couldn't get out there anyway.

The pictures on the walls—vapid reproductions of watercolor flowers—had rectangles of Plexiglas over them in the frames, rather than real breakable glass. She couldn't remember how she knew this, she didn't recall having touched one in the . . . *nine* days she'd been living here.

"I think he's like you," Dr. Armentrout went on. The rotund white-haired psychiatrist had dragged up a chair next to the one she'd collapsed into after finally stepping off the floor-line circuit and wobbling into the TV lounge. He had been talking to her for a minute or two now, but she was looking past him.

On the TV, hung behind a clear Plexiglas shield up above head-height on the wall beyond Armentrout, Humphrey Bogart was showing his teeth, talking mean and ruthless as he told the fat man, "We've got to have a fall guy." There were no colors—all the figures, the Fat Man and Bogart and Joel Cairo and "the gunsel," were in black-and-white, like a memory for someone else.

Plumtree shifted on the vinyl chair and tucked her denim skirt more tightly around her knees but didn't take her eyes off the screen. Murder had been done, apparently, and a scapegoat would have to be . . . *turned over.*

"What a flop," she said; then added, absently, "Who's like me?"

"This man Cochran, who's being transferred here from Metro in Norwalk," said Armentrout. "His wife was killed last Sunday, New Year's Day, at dawn—dressed herself up in a bedsheet and tied ivy vines in her hair and ran out into traffic on the 280, up in San Mateo County." Plumtree didn't look at the doctor or speak, and after a few seconds he went on, "She was pregnant, and the fetus died too, do you suppose that's important? Last week he flew her ashes back to her family estate, in France. He appears to have had a delusional episode there, and another when he got off the plane at LAX, in Los Angeles."

"Rah rah rah," said Plumtree.

"What happened on that Sunday morning?" he asked, as casually as if he hadn't been asking her that question every day.

"This guy's wife was run over by a bus," Plumtree said impatiently, "according to you. Cockface."

The doctor's voice was tight: "What did you call me, Janis?"

"Him, not you. Wasn't that what you said his name was?"

"Coch*ran.*"

The vinyl seat of Armentrout's chair croaked as he shifted, and Plumtree grinned, still watching the movie.

"Cochran," Armentrout repeated loudly. "Why do you say it was a bus? I didn't even say she was hit by a vehicle. Why should it have been a bus?"

The TV screen went dark, and then flared back on again.

It was a Humphrey Bogart movie; apparently *The Maltese Falcon*, since Plumtree saw that Elisha Cook and Mary Astor and Sidney Greenstreet were in it too. She was surprised to see that it was in color, but quickly reminded herself that they were colorizing all those old movies now.

She couldn't remember how long she might have been sitting here watching it, and was startled when she glanced to the side and saw Dr. Armentrout sitting in a chair right next to her. She unfolded her legs and stretched them out, with the heels of her sneakers on the floor and the toes pointed upward.

"So what do you say, Doctor?" Plumtree said brightly. Partly to delay further talk, she dug a little plastic bottle of Listerine out of her shirt pocket, twisted off the cap, and took a sip of it.

On the screen on the wall, Bogart had agreed to Peter Lorre's proposal that the Mary Astor character be turned over to the police. "After all," Bogart said, "she *is* the one who killed him." He mumbled something about miles, and an archer. Had the murdered person been killed from a distance, with an arrow? Hadn't it been up close with a spear?

But Plumtree had seen this movie before, and this was not how this scene went; they were supposed to pick the Elisha Cook character to "take the fall." Perhaps this was an alternate version, a director's cut or something.

Plumtree looked around for something to spit in, then reluctantly swallowed the mouthwash. "I'm sorry if I haven't been paying attention," she said to Armentrout. She glanced again up at the screen, and added, "I love Bogart movies, don't you?"

Armentrout was frowning in apparent puzzlement. "Why should it have been a bus?" he said.

"Why ask why?" said Plumtree merrily, quoting last year's Budweiser ad slogan.

All the characters in the movie were startled now by a knock at the door. Plumtree recalled that the story took place in San Francisco—a knock at the door could be anything. She held up one finger for quiet, and watched the screen.

The colorized Bogart got up and opened the door—and it was Mary Astor standing in the hallway, apparently playing a twin of herself. Clearly this was some peculiar alternate version of the movie. Perhaps it was well known, perhaps there were alternate versions of all sorts of movies. The Mary Astor twin in the open doorway was wearing a captain's cap and a peacoat spotted with dried blood, and her face was stiff and white—she was obviously supposed to be dead; but she opened her mouth and spoke, in a sexless monotone: "Forgive me. Madame has forgotten that we agreed to play in partnership this evening."

Bogart stood frozen for only a moment, then turned and lifted up in both hands the newspaper-wrapped bundle that had lain on the altar-like table; Greenstreet and Lorre didn't say anything as Bogart handed it to the dead Mary Astor—*they* certainly didn't want it, the severed head of a murdered king. The live Mary Astor was just sitting on the couch, staring wide-eyed at her dead double in the doorway.

Plumtree's new wristwatch beeped three times. She didn't even glance at it.

Armentrout chuckled. "Are you being paged, Janis?"

Plumtree turned to him with a smile. "That's my *zeitgeber*," she said. "Dr. Muir gave it to me. *Zeitgeber* means 'time-giver' in German. Dr. Muir suspects that—"

"He's not a doctor, he's just an intern. And he's not your primary, I am." Dr. Armentrout leaned forward abruptly, staring at Plumtree's legs. "Is Muir also the one who strapped a *mirror* to your knee, Janis?" His good cheer was gone. "Is that so he can look up your *skirt*?"

Plumtree paused, and the TV picture flickered; but a moment later she gave him a reproachful smile. "Of course not, silly!" She reached down to unbuckle the plastic band that held the two-inch metal disk to her bare knee. "I had a *dozen* of these on this morning, I must have forgotten to take this one off. It's for the—" She paused, and then recited proudly, "the Infrared Motion Analysis System. Dr. Muir has me sit at a computer and take a test, and while I'm doing that the computer measures how much I . . . move around. I move fifty milli-meters a second sometimes! Doct—Mr. Muir suspects that my *circadian rhythms* are out of whack. The *zeitgeber* watch is set to beep every fifteen minutes; it's to keep me aware of the . . . the time. When's *now*."

Armentrout leaned back in his chair. "When's now," he repeated. After a moment he waved at the television. "You're missing your Bo-gart movie, talking."

"That was the end," she said.

He opened his mouth, then apparently changed his mind about what he was going to say. "But you've had these zeitgebers all along, Janis. I've noticed that you bring the front page of the newspaper to bed with you, so you'll know in the morning what day it is; and you hardly answer a 'howdy do' without looking around for a clock, or sneaking a look at that waitress pad you keep in your purse."

Her watch beeped again, and the television set went dark.

Plumtree sat stiffly; somehow her *watch* was . . . making a noise; she could feel the vibration on her wrist. She didn't touch the watch, or look at it. Maybe it was *supposed* to be making a noise. She would watch for cues.

Dr. Armentrout was sitting beside her, looking at her speculatively. "So," he said, "do you feel that you've been making progress, now that you've been a patient here for two years?"

Her stomach went cold, but a deep breath and a fast blink kept tears from flooding her eyes. It's okay, she told herself. It's like Aunt Kate's funeral again, that's all. "I reckon I have," she said stolidly.

"I was lying, Janis," Armentrout said then. "You've been here only nine days. You believed me, though, didn't you?"

"I thought you said . . . 'with your fears,' " she whispered. Her watch was still beeping. The doctor wasn't remarking on it. Maybe all the patients had been given these stupid noisy watches today, as part of some bird-brain new therapy. *What* a flop!

At last Armentrout was looking away from her, past her, over her shoulder. "Here's our Mr. Cochran now," he said, getting laboriously to his feet and smoothing the skirt of his long white coat. "Just in time for the self-esteem group. Maybe he'll have some funny stories about his visit to France." Without looking down, he said, "Have you ever been to France, Janis?"

She shrugged. "I wouldn't be surprised."

She shifted around in her chair and squinted at the man standing with Dr. Muir by the nursing station. The new patient looked a bit like Bogart, it seemed to her; a hassled Bogart, tall but stooped, and gangly and worried-looking, with his dark hair combed carelessly back so that it stood up in spikes where it was parted.

She smiled, and the television came back on, and she wondered who the stranger by the nursing station was. Were they expecting a new patient? Would he be staying here?

"I wouldn't be surprised," she said, dimly aware that she was echoing a statement someone had made here very recently.

Scant?" said Dr. Armentrout.

Cochran sat up in his chair and blinked at the doctor, who was seated at the desk and leafing through the file of Cochran's transfer notes from Norwalk Metro.

At first Cochran had followed him to what the doctor had described as the conference room, which had proved to be just a back office cluttered with stacked plastic chairs and a blackboard and a bulky obsolescent microwave oven; but the patient sitting at the table in there, a bald, round-faced old fellow with only one arm, had just grinned and begun quoting dialogue from the tea-party scene in *Alice in Wonderland* when Armentrout had asked him to leave, so the doctor had given up on it and led Cochran down a hall to this locked office instead.

Now Armentrout raised his bushy eyebrows and tapped the stack of transfer notes. "Why does it say 'Scant' here?"

"Oh—it's a nickname," said Cochran. "From when I broke my leg as a kid."

"So is that leg . . . *shorter* than the other?"

"No, Doctor." Armentrout was staring at him, so Cochran went on, helplessly, "Uh, I limp a little in bad weather."

"You limp a little in bad weather." Armentrout flipped a page in the file. "You don't seem to have been limping on Vignes Street Sunday. After you broke the liquor store window, you took off like an Olympic runner, until the police managed to tackle you." He looked up at Cochran and smiled. "I guess it wasn't bad weather."

Cochran managed to return a frail grin. "Mentally it was. I thought I saw a man in that liquor store—"

"You probably did."

"I mean this man—a man I met in Paris. A couple of days earlier. *Mondard,* his name was . . . unless I hallucinated that whole thing, meeting him and all. And he changed into a bull—that is, he had a bull's head, like the minotaur. I imagine it's all in those notes, I told the doctor at Metro the whole story. And I thought that policewoman was—" He laughed unhappily. "—was going to kill me, that is tear me to pieces, and take my head back to him." He took a deep breath and let it out. "How is she?"

"You knocked out two of her teeth. Hence the Ativan and Haldol . . . which I'll leave you off of, if you behave yourself."

"I'll tell you the truth, Doctor, I don't *know* if I'll behave myself. I didn't mean to go crazy on Vignes Street, Sunday."

"Well, you left the airport during your layover. You were supposed to catch a connecting flight back up to San Francisco, right? And you ditched all your ID."

"It . . . seemed urgent, at the time. I guess I thought he might find me . . . he *did* find me, at that liquor store."

Armentrout nodded. "And you had seen this man before."

"In France, right. In Paris. On Friday."

"No, I mean . . . where is it." The doctor flipped back a couple of pages. "Four years ago last April, in 1990. *Also* on Vignes Street— hmm?—right after you had a 'breakdown' on your honeymoon."

Cochran's heart was pounding, and he wanted to grip the arms of his chair but his hands had no strength. *"That was him too?"* he whispered. "He had a wooden mask on then, that time. But—yeah, I guess that was him, that time. Big." He shook his head. "Wow," he said shakily. "You guys are good. And I didn't remember that it was on the same L.A. street. I guess the police report's in there from that time too, right?"

"What happened on your honeymoon?"

"I . . . went crazy. We got married on the sixth of April in '90, at a place on the Strip, and—"

"The Strip? You mean on Sunset?"

"No, the Las Vegas Strip, Las Vegas Boulevard. We—"

"*Really?* Well well well! And here I'd been assuming you were married in Los Angeles!"

"No. Las Vegas. And—"

"At the Flamingo?"

"No." Cochran blinked at the doctor. "No, a little place called the Troy and Cress Wedding Chapel—"

"Oh, better still!" exclaimed Armentrout happily. The fat doctor looked as though he wanted to clap his hands. "But I should shut up. Do go on."

"I'm not making that up. It's probably in your file."

"I'm sure you're not making it up. Please."

Psychiatrists! thought Cochran, trying to put a tone of brave derision into the thought. "*And*—at dawn the next day, it was a Saturday, I guess a car honked its horn right outside our motel-room door, a *loud* car horn; the chapel was a motel too, see, with rooms out in the back. They told me later that it was just a car horn. But I was hungover, or still drunk, and in my dream it was the man in the mask, very big, roaring like a lion, and blowing up a building he'd been locked up in, just by the force of his will. A *loud noise.* And he was loose, and he might do anything."

Armentrout nodded and raised his eyebrows.

"So . . . we left Vegas. I was in a panic." He looked at the psychiatrist. "Having a panic attack," he ventured, hoping that conveyed it more forcefully. "I made Nina drive back, across the Mojave Desert." He held up his right hand. "I was afraid that if I drove, we'd go . . . God knows where. And then when I *did* go ahead and drive, after we'd got all the way back to California, we wound up in L.A.—on, I guess, Vignes Street."

"Where you *saw* him."

"Right. On the other side of the street. Right. He was wearing a wooden mask, and . . . *beckoning,* like Gregory Peck on Moby Dick's back." Cochran looked up, and saw that the psychiatrist was staring at him. "In the movie," he added.

"And you punched a store window that time too, and cut your wrist on the broken glass. Intentionally, the police thought, hence your 51-50. Standard with suicide attempts."

"I wasn't trying to kill myself," said Cochran defensively. "This was nearly five years ago, and I don't really remember, but I think I was trying to cut off my right hand.''

''Oh, is that all.''

Armentrout put down his file and got up and crossed to a filing cabinet against the far wall. He pulled open the top drawer and came back to the desk carrying a spiral notebook and two fancy purple velvet boxes. He sat down again and put the boxes down by his telephone, well out of Cochran's reach, and then flipped open the notebook.

''You were married on the sixth of April,'' he said.

''Ri-ight,'' said Cochran, mystified.

''That's very interesting! A week later a lot of people went crazy there. Well, at Hoover Dam, which is nearby. Most of them recovered their senses by the next day, though two gentlemen fell to their deaths off the after-bay face of the dam.'' He sat back and smiled at Cochran. ''We've got a woman on the ward here who also had a nervous breakdown in Las Vegas in April of 1990—on the fifteenth, Easter Sunday.''

''Uh . . . did she also go crazy in L.A.?''

''Yes! Or nearly. In Leucadia, which is . . . well, it's almost to San Diego. But she called the police nine days ago and told them that she'd killed a man. She said he was a king, and that she killed him with a speargun spear. Do you believe in ghosts?''

''Shit, no,'' snapped Cochran impatiently. He shook his head. ''Sorry—I thought you'd be showing me Rorschach ink-blots here, or having me interpret proverbs, like they did at Metropolitan in Norwalk. No, I don't believe in ghosts.''

''Have you ever seen anything that seemed to be supernatural?''

''Well, I saw a man turn into a bull, on Vignes Street, day before yesterday.''

Armentrout stared at him for several seconds with no expression. ''You're getting hostile.''

''No, I'm sorry, I—''

''You were being cooperative a few moments ago. You may be too labile right now to participate usefully in group.''

''Too what?'' Cochran wondered if he meant lippy.

''The charge nurse showed you your room? Where the cafeteria is, where you shower?''

''Yes.''

''That was your roommate, the one-armed man I couldn't roust out of the conference room. John Beach—we all call him Long John. It's almost certainly not his real name; I think he chose it just because he was found in *Long Beach*, get it? He's been with us since November of '92.''

Cochran felt empty, and hoped the one-armed old man didn't recite from *Alice in Wonderland* all the time, at all hours.

"He'll be in group. So will Janis Plumtree—she's the one who had the breakdown in Vegas in '90, and who believes she killed a king nine days ago. You may as well participate. I'll ask you to leave if you start acting out or getting too gamy."

Gamy? thought Cochran, involuntarily picturing tusked and antlered animal heads on the stone floor of an old smokehouse.

Armentrout led him back up the hallway to the TV lounge, but Cochran hung back in the entry when the doctor strode out across the shiny waxed floor and lowered himself into one of the upholstered chairs around the conference table near the window. Four men and two women were already seated around the table, visible only in silhouette from the hall entry—Cochran thought it must almost be time for the lights to come on, or curtains to be pulled, for the evening sun was throwing horizontal poles of orange light into the room through the shrubbery that waved outside the reinforced glass.

"My civil rights are being violated," a young woman at the table was saying harshly. "I haven't signed anything, and I'm being held here against my will. What's nine days' impound fees on a car in the San Diego County municipal lot? I bet it's more than my car's worth, it's just an '85 Toyota Celery, but I need it for my job, and I'm holding you people, you soy dissant doctors, responsible."

"It was a Toyota *Cressida*, Janis," said Armentrout, and the backlit blob of his head turned either toward Cochran or toward the window. "Unless you're thinking of some other vehicle. Perhaps a bus?"

"Fuck you, Doctor," the woman went on, "you're not scaring me away. It was legally parked, and—"

"Janis!" interrupted another man sharply. "Personal attacks are not permitted, that's non-negotiable. If you want to stay, be good." He raised his head. "Are you here for the self-esteem group?"

Cochran understood that he was being addressed, and he shuffled forward uncertainly.

"Come in and sit down, Sid," said Armentrout. To the group he said, "This is a new patient, Sid Cochran."

Cochran broadened his stride, squinting as he walked through the brassy sunbeams to the nearest empty chair, which was at the end of the table, next to the angry young woman, with the windows to his right and slightly behind him.

"Hi, Sid," said the man who had rebuked the angry woman; he was wearing a white coat like Armentrout's, and seemed to be another doctor. "How are you?"

Cochran stared into the man's youthful, smiling face. "I'm fine," he said levelly.

"Ho ho!" put in Armentrout.

"Well, my name is Phil Muir," the younger man went on, "and we're here this evening to address problems of self-esteem. I was just saying that you have to love yourself before you can love someone else—"

The young woman interrupted: "And I was just saying, 'Fuck you, Doctor.' " She pointed at Armentrout. "To him. *'Ho . . . ho.'* You big fat fag."

Cochran looked at her in alarm—then found himself suppressing a grin. Under the disordered thatch of blond hair her sunburned face had a character he could only think of as *gamin*, with a pointed chin and wide mouth and high cheekbones, and the humor lines under her eyes and down her cheek made her outburst seem childishly valiant, just tomboy bravura.

Hoping to prevent her from being ejected from the group, he laughed indulgently, as if at an off-color joke.

But when she whipped her head around toward him, he quailed. Her pupils were tiny black pinpricks and too much white was showing around her irises, and the skin was tight and mottled on her cheeks—

Abruptly an old man who a moment ago had seemed to be asleep hunched forward and hammered a frail fist onto the table. *"The . . . rapist!"* he roared as the pieces of a forgotten dominoes game spun across the tabletop. "That's what it spells! Don't pronounce it *ther*apist! You've raped me with your needles!" He twisted in his chair and suddenly smacked both of his palms around Muir's throat.

Muir was able to struggle to his feet with the old man's weight on him, but he wasn't succeeding in prying the hands free of his throat, and tendons were standing up like taut cables under his straining chin.

"Staff!" roared Armentrout, shoving back his chair and thrashing to his feet. *"Code Green! Help, get a chemical here!"*

The nursing-station door banged open and two nurses came sprinting out, and with the help of a couple of the patients who had leaped up from the table they pulled the old man off Muir and wrestled him face down to the floor.

"I'll be snap-crackling pork chops with Jesus!" the old man panted, his cheek against the linoleum tiles. "You sons of bitches! Bunch of Heckle and Jeckles!"

Armentrout was standing beside the table. "Thorazine," he told the charge nurse, "two hundred milligrams I.M., stat. Put him in four points in the QR till I tell you different." Two uniformed security guards hurried in from the outer hallway; after taking in the scene, they slung their nightsticks and knelt on the old man so that the patients could return to their seats. The overhead fluorescent lights had come on at some point during the commotion, and as the doctors and patients sat down again the group seemed to be only now convening.

Cochran felt a touch on his shirt cuff, and he jumped when he realized that it was the woman Janis; but when he looked at her, she was smiling. She couldn't, he thought, be as much as thirty years old.

"With his hands and feet tied down," she said, "at the *four points* of a mattress, in the Quiet Room, he'll be back to himself in no time."

Cochran smiled back at her, touched that she had worded her remark so that he would understand the psychiatrist's jargon without having to admit ignorance; though in fact he himself had spent time in four points in a QR back in 1990.

"Ah," he said noncommittally. "I hope so."

Two mental-health workers had rolled a red gurney into the room, and the old man was lifted onto it and strapped down. Cochran saw a nurse walking away with an emptied hypodermic needle.

Muir was kneading his throat. "And I think Janis—" He looked across the table at her and stopped. "Janis," he said again; "maybe you'll be good now."

"I do apologize to everybody," she said. She watched the gurney being wheeled out of the room. "I hope Mr. Regushi is going to be all right . . . ?"

"He just flipped out," said Armentrout shortly, settling into his chair. "Very uncharacteristic."

"We feel vulnerable, threatened," said Muir hoarsely, "and we get defensive and lash out—when we don't *feel good about ourselves.* We feel like bugs on a sidewalk, like somebody's going to step on us." He gave the patients a wincing smile. "Janis, I think your recurrent dream of the sun falling on you from out of the sky is indicative of this kind of thinking. How do you feel about that?"

Cochran braced himself, but the woman was just nodding seriously.

"I think that's a valuable point," she said. "I've always been frightened, of everything—jobs, bills, *people.* I've wasted my whole life being afraid. My only constellation is that I'm finally getting good, caring, state-of-the-art help now."

"Well," said Muir uncertainly. "That's good, Janis." He looked at Cochran. "I've, uh, looked at your file, Sid, and I think you're afraid of being hurt. I noticed that when poor Mr. Regushi attacked me, you didn't get up to help. I suspect that this is characteristic of you—that you're afraid to reach out your hand to people."

Cochran shifted uncomfortably in his chair. "Reach out your hand, you get it cut off, sometimes."

Belatedly he noticed old Long John Beach at the other end of the table. The one-armed man bared his teeth, and a domino on the table in front of him quietly flipped over . . . as if, it seemed to Cochran, he had flipped it with a phantom hand at the end of his missing arm.

No one else had noticed the trick, and Cochran quickly looked back at Muir. Long John probably tied a hair to it, Cochran thought, and yanked on the hair with his real hand. He's probably got a dozen such tricks. And he's my roommate! And now I've probably offended him with my get-it-cut-off remark. Swell.

Muir had apparently followed Cochran's brief glance. "Long John can't remember how he lost his hand," he said. "His whole arm, that is. But he's okay with that, aren't you, John?"

"In *some* gardens," said Long John Beach in a thoughtful tone, as if commenting on what had been said before, "the beds are so hard that the flowers can't even put down roots—they just *run around*—right out into the street."

"The dwarves in *Snow White,*" put in Janis, "came home every night—because their little house was fixed up so nicely. Snow White made them keep it *just so.*"

Cochran thought of his own little 1920s bungalow house in South Daly City, just a few miles down the . . . *the 280* . . . from Pace Vineyards on the San Bruno Mountain slope; and he reflected with bitter amusement that these doctors would probably consider it "valuable" for him to "share" about it here, ideally with hitching breath and tears. Then all at once he felt his face turn cold with a sudden dew of sweat, as if he were about to get sick, for he realized that he *wanted* to talk about it, wanted to tell somebody, even these crazy strangers, about the tiny room Nina had fixed up in preparation for the arrival of the baby, about the teddy bear wallpaper, and the intercom walkie-talkie set they had bought so as to be able to hear the baby crying at night. Their whole lives had seemed to stretch brightly ahead of them; and in fact he and Nina had even bought adjoining plots at the nearby Woodlawn Cemetery, just on the other side of the highway—but now Nina's ashes were in France, and Cochran would one day lie there alone.

Janis touched his hand then, and he impulsively took hold of her hand and squeezed it—but his vision was blurring with imminent tears, and Armentrout was probably staring at him, and the mark on his knuckles was itching intolerably; he released her hand and pushed his chair back and stood up.

"I'm very tired," he managed to pronounce clearly. He walked out of the room with a careful, measured stride—not breathing, for he knew his next breath would come audibly, as a sob.

He blundered down the hall to his room and flung himself face-down onto the closer of the two beds, shaking with bewildered weeping, his hands and feet at the corners of the mattress as if he were in four points again himself.

She's DID," said Muir to Armentrout. He was sipping coffee and still absently massaging his throat. The two of them were standing by the supervision-and-privilege blackboard in the nursing station, and Muir waved his coffee cup toward Janis Plumtree's name, beside which was just the chalked notation SSF—supervised sharps and flames—which indicated that she, like most of the patients, was not to be entrusted with a lighter or scissors.

"Degenerate Incontinent . . . Dipsomaniac," hazarded Armentrout. He wished the pay telephone in the lounge would stop ringing.

"No," said Muir with exaggerated patience. "Haven't you read the new edition of the diagnostic manual? 'Dissociative identity disorder.' What we used to call MPD."

Armentrout stared at the intern. Muir had been resentful and rebellious ever since they'd heard the news about the overweight bipolar girl Armentrout had treated and released last week; the obese teenager had apparently hanged herself the day after she had gone home.

"Plumtree doesn't have multiple personality disorder," said Armentrout. "Or your DID, either. And I don't appreciate you running tests on her circadian rhythms, and giving her . . . *zeitgeber*s? That silly watch that beeps all the time? You're not her primary, I am. I'm on top of her—"

"The watch is a grounding technique," interrupted Muir. "It's to forcibly remind her that she's here, and now, and safe, when flashbacks of the traumas that fragmented her personality forcibly intrude—"

"She's not—"

"You can practically *see* the personalities shift in her! I think the patients have even caught on—did you hear Regushi mention Heckle and Jeckles? I think he was trying to say Jekyll and Hyde . . . though I can't figure out why he seemed to *resent* her."

"She's not a multiple, damn it. She's depressed and delusional, with obsessive-compulsive features—her constant demands to use the shower, the days-of-the-week underwear, the way she gargles mouth-wash all the time—''

"Then why haven't you got her *on* anything? Haloperidol, clomipra-mine?'' Muir put down his coffee cup and crossed to the charge nurse's desk.

To Armentrout's alarm, the man picked up the binder of treatment plans and began flipping through it. ''You don't know enough to be second-guessing me, Philip,'' Armentrout said sharply, stepping forward. ''There are confidential details of her case—''

''A shot of *atropine,* after midnight tonight?'' interrupted Muir, reading from Plumtree's chart. He looked up, and hastily closed the binder. ''What for, to dilate her pupils? Her pinpoint pupils are obviously just a conversion disorder, like hysterical blindness or paralysis! So is the erythema, her weird 'sunburn,' if you've noticed that. My God, atropine won't get her pupils to *normal,* it'll have 'em as wide as garbage dis-posals!''

Armentrout stared at him until Muir looked away. ''I'm going to have to *order* you, *Mister* Muir, in my capacity as Chief of Psychiatry here, to cease this insubordination. You're an intern—a student, in effect!—and you're overstepping your place.'' The pay telephone in the patients' lounge was still ringing; in a louder voice he went on, ''I've been prac-ticing psychiatry for nineteen years, and I don't need a *partial* recitation of the effects of *atropine,* helpful though you no doubt meant to be. Shall I . . . *dilate!* . . . upon this matter?''

''No, sir,'' said Muir, still looking away.

''How pleasant for both of us. Were you going home?''

''. . . Yes, sir.''

''Then I'll see you—you're not working here tomorrow, are you?''

''I'm at UCI in Orange all day tomorrow.''

''That's what I thought. You're going to miss our ice-cream social! Well, I'll see you Thursday then. Bright-eyed and bushy-tailed, right?''

Muir walked out of the nurses' station without answering.

Armentrout looked after him for a moment, then made his way around the cluttered desks to the window and looked out into the TV lounge at the patients, who couldn't be bothered to answer the telephone. Plum-tree and Long John Beach had stayed at the conference table after the foolish self-esteem group had broken up—Armentrout favored the quick ''buying the pharm'' attitude toward mental illness over the long, tor-menting, dangerous routines of psychotherapy—and he saw that Sid Cochran had got over his sulk and rejoined them. They appeared to be playing cards.

You've got a busy day tomorrow, he told himself; coordinating the paperwork on the nurse anesthetist and the attending nurses, and then dealing with Plumtree after she recovers from the procedure. A busy day, and you'll be lucky to get a few hours of sleep tonight. But tomorrow you may very well find out what happened on New Year's Day, and learn how to make it happen again.

Atropine, Philip—you fool—is used for more than just dilating eye pupils; it also dries up saliva and nasal secretions, which is desirable in the administration of . . . of what the patients sometimes call "Edison Medicine."

At first they had tried to play for cigarettes, but after Long John Beach had twice *eaten* the pot, snatching the Marlboros and shoving them into his mouth and chewing them up, filters and all, Cochran and Plumtree decided to play for imaginary money.

They were playing five-card stud, listlessly. To make up for the tendency of any sort of showing pair to automatically win in this short-handed game, they had declared all queens wild; and then Long John Beach had proposed that the suicide king be taken out of the deck.

"I second that emotion," Janis had said.

"What's the suicide king?" Cochran had asked.

The one-armed old man had pawed through the deck, and then flipped toward Cochran the King of Hearts; and Cochran saw that the stylized king was brandishing a sword blade that was certainly meant to be extending behind his head, but, with the token perspective of the stylized line drawing, could plausibly be viewed as being stuck right *into* his head.

"Sure," Cochran had said nervously. "Who needs *him?*"

Janis had just won a "multi-thousand-dollar" pot with two queens and a king, which according to the rules of this game gave her three kings; Cochran had folded when she was dealt a face-up queen, but Long John Beach idiotically stayed to the end with a pair of fives.

"Hadda keep her honest," the old man mumbled.

"I almost dropped out when you raised on third street, John," Janis told him. "I was afraid you'd caught a set of dukes." Cochran realized that her doubletalk was a charitable pretense of having seen shrewdness in the old man's haphazard play.

Of course Beach couldn't shuffle, and Cochran had dealt that hand, so Janis gathered in the cards and shuffled them—expertly, five fast riffles low to the table so as not to flash any cards—and then spun out the three hole cards.

"Have you had your PCH scheduled yet?" she asked Cochran.

"That's probable cause hearing," she added, "to authorize the hospital to keep you for longer than two weeks."

"*Longer* than two weeks?" said Cochran. "Hell no, not *even.*" He had an eight down and an eight showing, and decided to keep raising unless a queen showed up. "No, I'm just in on a 51-50, seventy-two hours observation, and that's up late tomorrow night, which I suppose means they'll let me go Thursday morning. I don't know why anybody bothered to have me transferred here from Norwalk. I've got a job to get back to, and Armentrout hasn't even got me on any medications."

"I bet a thousand smokes," said Long John Beach, who was showing an ace. The tiny black eyes in his round face didn't seem to have any sockets to sit in, and they were blinking rapidly.

"We're playing for imaginary dollars now, John," Janis told him, "you ate all the cigarettes, remember?" To Cochran she said, "Has he *talked* to you yet? Dr. Armentrout?"

"For a few minutes, in his office," said Cochran. "She calls," he told Long John Beach, "and I raise you a thousand."

"She calls," echoed the old man, still blinking.

"He'll want to talk to you more," Plumtree said thoughtfully. "And he'll probably give you some kind of meds first. Do cooperate, tell him everything you know about—your problems, so you'll be of no further use to him. He—he *can* keep anybody he wants, for as long as he wants."

"I been here two and a half years," said the old man. "My collapsed lung's been okay for so long now it's ready to collapse again."

Collapsed brain, you mean, Cochran thought. But he stared out the window, and shivered at the way the spotlights on the picnic tables in the fenced-in courtyard only emphasized the total darkness of the parking lot beyond, and he thought about the wire mesh laminate that would prevent him from breaking that glass, if he were to try, and about the many heavy steel, doubly locked doors between himself and the real world of jobs and bars and highways and normal people.

The telephone was still impossibly ringing, but Cochran was again remembering the intercom he and Nina had bought to be able to hear their expected baby crying, and remembering too Long John Beach's hollow echo of *She calls,* and he wasn't tempted to answer it.

"Have you," he asked Plumtree, "had *your* . . . PCH, yet?"

"Yes." A rueful smile dimpled her cheeks. "A week ago, right in the conference room over yonder. You're allowed to have two family or friends from outside, and my mom wouldn't have come, so my roommate Cody came. Cody hasn't got any respect for anybody."

"Oh." The one-armed old man had not called Cochran's raise, but

Cochran didn't want to say anything more to him. "What did Cody do?"

Plumtree sighed. "*I* don't know. She apparently *hit* the patient advocate—the man had a bloody lip, I recall that. I think Dr. Armentrout was teasing her. But!—the upshot!—of it all was that I'm now 53-53 with option to 53-58—the hospital was given a T-con on me, a temporary conservatorship, and I might be here for a year ... or," she said with a nod toward the distracted Long John Beach, "longer. I'm sure my waitress job, and my car, are history already."

"That's ... I'm sorry to hear that, Janis," Cochran said. "When I get out, I'll see if there's anything I can do—" He could feel his face turning red; the words sounded lame, but at this moment he really did intend to get her out of this hospital, away from the malignant doctor. He reached across the table and held her hand. "I'll get you out of here, I swear."

Plumtree shrugged and blinked away a glitter of tears, but her smile was steady as she looked into Cochran's eyes. " 'All places that the eye of heaven visits,' " she recited, " 'Are to a wise man ports and happy havens.' "

Cochran's arms tingled, as if with returning circulation, and he laced his fingers through Plumtree's. Those lines were from *Richard II*, from a speech his wife Nina had often quoted when she'd been feeling down, and he knew it well. The lines immediately following referred to being exiled by a king, and Cochran recalled that Plumtree had been committed for having claimed to have killed a king; so he skipped ahead to the end of the speech: " 'Suppose the singing birds musicians,' " he said unsteadily, " 'The grass whereon thou tread'st the presence strewed, the flowers fair ladies, and thy steps no more than a delightful measure or a dance—' "

Long John Beach opened his mouth then, and his harsh exhalation was a phlegmy cacophony like the noise of a distant riot; and then, in a *woman's* bitterly mocking voice, he finished the speech: " 'For gnarling sorrow hath less power to bite the man that mocks at it and sets it light.' "

—And then Cochran was standing on the linoleum floor several feet back from the table, shaking violently, his chair skidding away behind him and colliding with the wall—the woman's voice had been *dead Nina's* voice, and when Cochran had whipped his head around he had seen sitting beside him a massive figure wearing a wooden mask, and the golden eyes that stared at him out of the carved eye-holes had had horizontal pupils, like a goat's—and Cochran had instantly lashed out in an irrational terror-reflex and driven his right fist with all his strength into the center of the mask.

But it was Long John Beach who now rolled across the floor off of his overturned chair, blood spraying from his flattened nose and spattering and pooling on the gleaming linoleum.

Plumtree was out of her own chair, and she ran around the table to kneel by the old man—but not to help him; she drew her fist up by her ear and then punched it down hard onto a puddle of the blood on the floor. The *crack* of the impact momentarily tightened Cochran's scalp with sympathetic shock.

"Jesus!" came a hoarse shout from the nurses' station. "Staff! Code fucking Green, need a takedown!"

Plumtree had time only to meet Cochran's frightened gaze and smile before the hallway doors banged open and an upright mattress was rushed into the room, carried by two of the security guards; then the guards had used it to knock Plumtree over backward on the floor, and had jumped onto it to hold her down.

"She," choked Cochran, "*she* didn't hit him, *I* did!"

Armentrout was hurrying in, and he glanced angrily at Cochran. "Look at her," he snapped.

Plumtree's bloody fist was thrashing free of the mattress for a moment, then one of the guards had grabbed her wrist and pressed her hand to the floor.

"And what hand did *you* hit him with?" Armentrout asked sarcastically.

Cochran held out the back of his right hand and saw, with a sudden chill in his belly but no conscious awareness of surprise, that the skin of his knuckles was smooth and unbroken, the old ivy-leaf discoloration not distended by any swelling at all.

"*No chemicals for her,*" called Armentrout sharply to the charge nurse, who had sprinted into the room with a hypodermic needle. "Not tonight, she's, uh, due for a dose of atropine in a couple of hours. Don't argue with me! Put her in four points in the QR for tonight, with five-minute checks."

One of the security guards looked up at him desperately. "You're not gonna *sedate* her?" he asked, rocking on the mattress as he held down Plumtree's spasming body.

"*I'm* the one who hit the old man!" shouted Cochran. "*She* didn't do it, I did!"

"You've bought yourself a meds program," Armentrout told him, speaking in a conversational tone but very fast, "with this . . . display of childish gallantry. *No*," he called to the guard. "PCP tactics. You're going to have to just wrestle her in there."

"Terrific," the man muttered. "Get hold of her other arm, Stan, and I'll get this busted hand in a hard come-along."

"Watch she don't bite," cautioned his partner, who was groping under the mattress. "I got her hair too, but she's in a mood to tear it right out of her scalp."

The guards dragged Plumtree to her feet. Her teeth were bared and her eyes were squinting slits, but the come-along hold on her wounded hand was effective—when the guard who held it rotated her wrist even slightly, her knees sagged and her mouth went slack. The three of them shuffled carefully out of the room. The charge nurse had got Long John Beach into a chair, where he sat with his face hanging between his knees and dripping blood rapidly onto the floor, while she talked into a telephone on the counter.

"Do you remember the way to your room?" Armentrout asked Cochran. "Good," he said when Cochran nodded, "go there and go to sleep. Your roommate is apparently going to be a bit late coming in."

Cochran hesitated, not looking the doctor in the eye—his first impulse had been to tell Armentrout that he had just had a recurrence of the hallucination that had landed him in the state's custody, but now he was glad that Armentrout hadn't let him speak. Any shakiness he exhibited now would be considered just a response to this noisy crisis.

For his self-respect, though, he did permit himself to say, just before turning obediently away toward the hall, "I swear, on the ashes of my wife and unborn child, I'm the one that hit him."

"I will heal you, Sid," he heard the doctor say tightly behind him. "That's a promise."

The door to the Quiet Room was open, and Cochran waited until the yawning psych tech had glanced in and then walked away down the hall before he stepped out of his own room and tiptoed to the open door. It would be five minutes before the man would be back to look in on Plumtree again.

She was lying face-up on a mattress in the otherwise empty room; and she rolled her head over to look at him when he appeared in the doorway.

"Mr. Cochran," she said wearily, "of the dead wife. Rah rah fucking rah. You *did* hit him, didn't you?"

"Yes," said Cochran. "I had to sneak in here and thank you for taking the blame, but I—I can't let you do it. I tried to tell Armentrout tonight what really happened; I'll make him . . . *get* it, tomorrow. Even though it'll probably mean *I* get a—'' What did she call it, he thought nervously, the highway through Laguna and Newport, ''—a PCH. My God, Janis, your poor hand! You shouldn't have done that, not that I don't—not that I'm not grateful—I *do*.'' I'm not making sense, he thought. But how can they leave her tied down on the floor like this? ''But I meant what I said, earlier—even if they keep me for two weeks, I'll get you out of here one way or another. I promise.''

''I punched the *floor,* didn't I? For *you*. Shit. You'd *better* get me out, I hope you can pull strings and you're not just a, like a burger-flipper somewhere. And see you do tell 'em what really happened—first thing tomorrow, hear? I've got troubles enough, in the name of the Father, the Son, the Holy Ghost. They're gonna give me some kind of *shot* here in a couple of hours, Christ knows what for.'' Her mouth was working, and he wondered if she was about to start crying. ''This is *just* like twit Janis, to fall for some dorky tuna in the *nut hatch*.'' She opened her mouth and licked her lower lip, and flexed her arms uselessly against the restraints. ''You want to have been of some use on Earth? Scratch my chin for me, it's itching like to drive me . . . sane.''

Cochran stepped into the room and knelt by her head, and the lights dimmed for a moment. He reached out, with his trembling *left* hand, and gently drew his fingernails over the side of her chin she had apparently been trying to reach with her tongue.

She surprised him by lifting up her head and kissing his palm. ''I was sorry to hear about your wife's death,'' she whispered. ''How long were you married?''

''. . . Nearly five years,'' Cochran said. He had stopped scratching her chin, though his fingertips were still on her cheek.

''How did you meet her?''

''She . . . fell down some steps, and I caught her.'' He pulled his hand back self-consciously. ''I'm a cellarman at a vineyard up in San Mateo County, by Daly City, Pace Vineyards, and she was visiting from France, touring all the Bay Area vineyards. Her family's in the wine business in the Bas Médoc—the Leon family, they've been there since the Middle Ages. And she was looking at the casks of Zinfandel, in fact she was just in the act of tasting the young vintage with a *tâte-vin,* thing like a ladle, and at that moment the big earthquake of '89 hit—5:04 in the afternoon—and she fell down the steps.''

''And you caught her,'' Plumtree said softly. ''I remember that earthquake. Poor Sid.''

''He,'' exhaled Cochran, finally nerving himself up to broach the point of this midnight visit, ''the old one-armed man, he—I thought he talked with her voice, there, when we were quoting the Shakespeare.

My dead wife's voice. And then he looked like a, a man who chased me in Paris. That's why I hit him, it was just a shocked reflex. But it *was* her voice, it was *her*—unless I'm a whole lot crazier than I even thought.''

"I'm sure it *was* her. He can channel dead people like a vacuum cleaner, and you were sitting right by him." She glanced at the open doorway, and then back at Cochran. "You'd better go. I'm not supposed to have visitors here."

He managed to nod and stand up, though he was even more disoriented now than he'd been when he'd walked in. As he turned toward the door, she said quietly behind him, "I love you, Sid."

He hesitated, shocked to realize that he wanted to say that he loved her too. It *wasn't* possible, after all: he had met this woman only a few hours ago, and she did seem to be some genuine variety of crazy— though that only seemed to be something the two of them shared in common, actually—and in any case *Nina had been dead for only ten days.* And her . . . *ghost* might be . . .

He forced that thought away, for now.

"My friends call me Scant," he said, without turning around; then, though he was aching to say something more, he made do with muttering, "I'm as crazy as you are," and hurried out of the room.

CHAPTER 4

"All sorts of people who are not in the least degree worthy of the pet, are always turning up," said Miss Pross. "When you began it—"
"I began it, Miss Pross?"
"Didn't you? Who brought her father to life?"

—Charles Dickens,
A Tale of Two Cities

At dawn they awoke Plumtree by sticking another hypodermic needle into the vein on the inside of her elbow—this shot contained a potent mix of Versed and Valium, and she had only ten bewildered seconds to curse and swear at the two nurses and Armentrout, and strain uselessly against the damp canvas straps of the four-point restraints, before she collapsed into unconsciousness. After the nurses unstrapped the rubber tourniquet from around her biceps and unbuckled the restraints, Armentrout crouched beside her and held her swollen hand in both of his, rolling the bones under his thumbs and prodding between the knuckles with his fingertips; then gently, almost tenderly, he lifted the young woman's limp body onto the gurney.

The ECT clinic was at the other end of the building, and Armentrout was pleased to see that the hallway lights didn't dim as Plumtree was wheeled along under them. One of the nurses striding alongside was holding a black rubber Ambu face mask over Plumtree's nose and mouth and rhythmically squeezing the attached black bag to assist the comatose woman's weakened breathing.

The nurse anesthetist who was waiting for them in the fluorescent-lit treatment room was a bearded young man Armentrout had worked with many times before, and the man leaned back against a counter and frankly stared as the nurses unzipped Plumtree's jeans and pulled them down past her hips and then unbuttoned her blouse and lifted her up into a sitting position to tug her limp arms back and pull the blouse free; Armentrout allowed himself only a glimpse—for now—of Plumtree's pale breasts when the nurses removed her bra. When they had laid her back down, positioning her head carefully on the perforated plastic cushion, the anesthetist stepped forward.

"What happened to her hand?" the man asked as he looped a Velcro blood-pressure cuff around her left upper arm and then inserted an Intercath needle into the back of her bruised right hand and taped it down. The blush of red blood that backed up in the IV tube cleared instantly when he opened the valve to full flow.

"She punched a guy," said Armentrout shortly. "Just soft-tissue damage to her hand, no crepitation."

"I hope he's not pissed off—very shortly now she won't remember doing it." He taped onto Plumtree's right forefinger the pulse oxymeter that would shine a white light through her fingertip and monitor her oxygen level by changes in the ruby red color of her flesh.

"This guy can't remember his own name," absently remarked the nurse who was peeling the backs off of the wire-tethered plastic disks that were the heart-monitor EKG electrodes. She began pressing the disks sticky-side-down onto Plumtree's skin at each shoulder and hip and then in a cascade pattern around Plumtree's left breast.

"Get her on the ventilator," snapped Armentrout.

The anesthetist obediently pried open Plumtree's mouth and pushed in past her teeth the steel shaft of a laryngoscope that was guiding a balloon-tipped plastic tube into her throat; and when he had got the tube far down her trachea and inflated the cuff to get an occlusive seal, the ventilator began chugging and sighing as it forced oxygen in and out of her lungs.

"And inflate the blood-pressure cuff," Armentrout said; "it's time to get the succinylcholine running." Armentrout was hunched over Plumtree's head now, ruffling the thatch of her blond hair and at measured intervals poking down into her scalp the tiny needles of the EEG electrodes that would measure her brain-wave activity.

Plumtree's semi-nude body shivered under the monitor wires as the succinylcholine hit, then relaxed totally—Armentrout knew that the motor end plates of all of her voluntary muscle fibers had now subsided in depolarization, and only the insistence of the ventilator was even keeping her lungs flexing.

A nurse now leaned over the unconscious woman to fit a bifurcated foam-rubber bite block around the endotrachial tube and between the teeth of Plumtree's upper and lower jaws.

Finally Armentrout smeared conducting jelly on the steel disks that

would deliver the voltage, and he carefully stuck one onto each of Plumtree's temples—this would be a full bilateral square wave procedure,
not one of the wishy-washy unilaterals with one of the disks stuck onto
the forehead. Armentrout knew it wouldn't damage her—he had undergone a series of full bilateral-wave ECTs himself, when he had been
just seventeen years old, after his mother's death.

"Low voltage tracing," said the nurse who was watching the EEG
monitor; "huh!—with some intermittent sleep spindles at about fourteen
hertz."

"That's to be expected," said Armentrout, not looking at the anesthetist. "You'll see some biphasics, too, if we make a loud noise." He
looked at his watch—it had been two full minutes since the muscle-
disabling succinylcholine had gone coursing down the IV tube.
"Clear!" he called, and everybody stepped back from Plumtree's elec-
trode-studded body. For a moment Armentrout let his eyes play over
her breasts, the exposed nipples erect in the chilly air of the treatment
room, and the wisp of blond pubic hair curling above the elastic waistband of her TUESDAY-stitched panties, and then he twisted the dial on
the plastic monitor box to two hundred and fifty joules, took a deep
breath, and flipped the toggle switch.

Instantly Plumtree's left hand twitched and clenched in a fist, for the
tight constriction of the blood-pressure cuff had effectively prevented
the neuromuscular blocking drug from getting into her forearm.

"Total chaos," calmly said the nurse who was watching the EEG
monitor. Plumtree's brain waves on the screen were a forest of tight,
wildly disordered peaks. "A ten on the Richter scale."

Then, slowly, the middle finger of Plumtree's tight-clenched left hand
unfolded and extended out straight.

The anesthetist noticed it and laughed. "She's flipping you off, Richard," he told Armentrout. "I've never seen *that* happen before."

Armentrout kept his face impassive, but his belly had gone cold and
his heart was knocking in his chest. I can't believe that's not involuntary, he thought—but—*who the hell* are *you, girl?*

"Me either," he said levelly.

Cochran put on yesterday's clothes when he got out of bed—Long John
Beach was in the other bed now, black-eyed and snoring like a horse
behind a metal brace taped to his nose, and Cochran was careful not to
wake him—but when he had sneaked out of the room he got one of the
psych techs to let him rummage for fresh clothes in "the boutique," a
closet full of donated clothing; and twenty minutes after he had got a
nurse to unlock the shower room and give him a disposable Bic razor,

he shambled into the windowless cafeteria, freshly bathed and shaved and with his wet hair combed down flat for the first time in twenty-four hours, wearing oversized brown-corduroy bell-bottom trousers and a T-shirt with A CONNECTICUT PANSY IN KING ARTHUR'S SHORTS lettered on it. All the other shirts had been too narrow for his shoulders or were women's blouses that buttoned right-over-left. He didn't think the crazy people, or even the staff, would read the lettering, and he nervously hoped Janis Plumtree might be able to find it funny.

But when he took a tray and got into the line for oatmeal and little square milk cartons and individual-size boxes of cereal, he looked around the tables and saw that Plumtree wasn't in the cafeteria.

He carried his tray to an unoccupied table and sat down, and began eating his cornflakes right out of the box, like Crackerjacks, ignoring the little carton of milk. He was breathing shallowly, and dropping as many cornflakes onto his lap as he got into his mouth.

He was wondering just how bad an infraction it was to break the nose of another patient; and he was giddily alarmed at his determination, even stronger this morning than it had been last night, to keep his promise to Janis Plumtree and get the true story across. Eventually Armentrout would be on the ward, and Long John Beach would be up to corroborate the facts. Cochran might very well even have to admit to having had another hallucination, and he supposed that would surely guarantee him a "PCH," an unfavorable one—which would mean not being able to see the *real* PCH, Pacific Coast Highway, for at least two weeks—but Cochran would be able, finally, to . . . *take the blame.*

And she loves me, he thought as he licked his trembling finger to get the last crumbs out of the corn flakes box; or she did last night; or she said she did last night. I will take her out of this place.

But neither Plumtree nor Armentrout appeared in the cafeteria, and just as Cochran was reluctantly getting up to investigate the TV lounge, and brushing corn-flake fragments off the crotch of his ludicrous corduroy pants, a young woman in a white lab coat came striding up to his table.

"Sid Cochran?" she said brightly. "Hi, I'm Tammy Eddy, the occupational therapist, and if you're free I'd like to get your dexterity tests out of the way. Kindergarten stuff, really—the patients are always asking me if I majored in basket-weaving!"

Cochran managed to return her smile, though her cheer seemed as perfunctory to him this morning as the HAVE A NICE DAY admonition printed on the "moist towelette" package on his tray, and she didn't notice his shirt.

He opened his mouth to tell her that he had something important to say to Dr. Armentrout first—but instead relaxed and said, "Okay."

"Let's go to the conference room, shall we?"

Maybe we'll meet him on the way, Cochran told himself defensively.

But there was no one in the sunny TV lounge as the young occupational therapist led him through it—Cochran noticed that the blood had been cleaned up, and the floor was a glassy plane again—and she had to fetch out her keys and unlock the conference room, for no one had been in it yet today.

"Sit down, Sid," the woman said, waving at a chair by the table. "Can you find a patch of clear space there? Good, yeah, that'll do. Today you're going to get a lesson in—" She had been moving things on a shelf over the microwave oven, and now turned around and laid on the table in front of him two five-inch square pieces of blue vinyl with holes around the edges, and a blunt white plastic yarn needle and a length of orange yarn. "Can you guess?"

"Knitting," said Cochran carefully, abruptly reminded of the book he'd read on the flight home from Paris three days ago.

"That's close. *Stitching.* This is called the Allen Cognitive Levels test, and it's just me showing you different ways to sew these two vinyl squares together. Here, the needle's already threaded—you go ahead and sew them together any way you like."

Cochran patiently laced the things together as if they were the front and back covers of a spiral-bound book, and when he was done she beamed and told him that he'd just figured out the "whipstitch" all on his own. She took back the squares and unlaced them and began showing him a different stitch that involved skipping holes and then coming back around to them, but though his fingers followed her directions, his mind was on the book he'd read on the plane.

The disquieting thing was that he had read Dickens' *A Tale of Two Cities* before; and though that had been a long time ago, he had eventually become aware that this book he was reading in the airplane seat by the glow of the tiny overhead spotlight—a Penguin Classics paperback, wedged between his cigarettes and the several little airline bottles of Wild Turkey bourbon—was a different text.

The variances hadn't been obvious at first, for he'd only been able to read the book fitfully, especially the Parisian scenes; he had still been shaky from his encounter the day before—in the ancient narrow streets south of the river Seine, by Notre Dame cathedral, where fragrant lamb koftes turned on spits in the open windows of Lebanese restaurants—

with the man who had called himself Mondard . . . and who had shortly stopped seeming to be a man, to be a human being at all . . .

Cochran forced himself to concentrate on pushing the foolish plastic needle through the holes in the vinyl—not knitting, stitching—

The woman in the book had been knitting, *and* stitching, weaving into her fabrics the names of men who were to die on the guillotine. He'd remembered her name as having been something like Madame Laphroaig, but in this text all the French revolutionaries called her Ariachne—a combination of the names *Arachne* and *Ariadne*, given to her because she was always knitting and was married to the "bull-necked" man who owned the wineshop. The notes in the back of the book explained that it was a *nom de guerre* of the revolution, like the name *Jacques* that was adopted by all the men. Cochran recalled that during the French Revolution they had even re-named all the calendar months; the only one he could remember was Thermidor, and he wondered what the others could have been. Fricassee? Jambalaya? Chowder?

He smiled now at the thought; and he tried to pay attention to the occupational therapist's cheery explanation of how to do a "single cordovan" stitch, and not to think about the book.

But he realized now that the story he'd read on the airplane must have started to diverge from the remembered text very early on. In the scene in the Old Bailey courthouse in London, for example, in which the Frenchman Charles Darnay was on trial for treason, Cochran seemed to remember having read that the court bar was strewn with herbs and sprinkled with vinegar, an apparently routine precaution against "gaol" air . . . but in this text the bar was twined in living ivy, and splashed liberally with red wine.

And just because of the rhyme he had remembered "Cly the spy," whose death had been a hoax and whose coffin had proved to contain only paving stones—but he had remembered Cly as a *man*, and certainly the name had not been short for *Clytemnestra*.

His hand shook as he pushed the needle through the holes. In the book he'd read on the plane, Madame Ariachne's cloth had flexed and shivered as she had forced each new, resisting name into the fabric.

"You're not quite getting the hang of that one, are you?" said Tammy Eddy.

Cochran looked up at her. "It's hard," he said.

"Hard to remember what I said?"

"Hard to remember anything at all. But I can do it."

He thought of the scene at the end of the book as he had read it years ago, in which the dissolute Englishman Sidney Carton redeemed himself by sneaking into the Conciergerie prison to switch places with his virtuous double, the Frenchman Charles Darnay who was condemned to die the next morning; and then Cochran made himself remember the scene as he had read it on the airplane three days ago—

In that variant version it had been a woman who furtively unlocked the cell door—the woman Clytemnestra, who was somehow the classical Greek Clytemnestra from Aeschylus' *Oresteia,* come to atone for having killed the high king Agamemnon.

And in this crazy version the prisoner was a woman too, though still the visitor's mirror-image double; and when she demanded to know the reason for this visit, this exchange of places, Clytemnestra had said, "Forgive me. Madame has forgotten that we agreed to play in partnership this evening."

Tammy Eddy was speaking sharply to him—and he realized that she had been repeating herself for several seconds. He looked up at her, and saw that she had retreated to the door and pulled it open. "Put," she said, obviously not for the first time, "the needle . . . *down,* Sid."

"Sorry. Sure." He opened his fingers and the needle dropped to the tabletop. "I wasn't listening." He looked at the vinyl squares and saw that he had stitched them together and then with the blunt needle *torn a hole* in the center of each square. "I guess I wrecked your . . . your test," he said lamely. And no doubt failed it, he thought. She'll probably testify at my PCH.

"They're not expensive. That'll be all for today, Sid." She stepped back a yard into the TV lounge as he pushed his chair back and sidled around the table to the door. "What," she asked him as he walked past her toward the cafeteria, "were you making, there at the end?"

He stopped for a moment but didn't look back at her. "Oh, nothing," he said over his shoulder. "I just got bored and . . . distracted."

Perhaps she nodded or smiled or frowned—he kept his eyes on the cafeteria door as he strode forward. He might or might not tell Armentrout, but would certainly not tell this woman, that he had been unthinkingly making a frail mask in which to face the mask that the big bull-headed man would be wearing.

Probably because of his having hit Long John Beach the night before, the knuckles of his right hand stung, and he alternately made a fist and stretched his fingers as he walked through the cafeteria and back out into the lounge without having seen Plumtree or Armentrout—Tammy Eddy was nowhere to be seen now either—and then started down the hall, past the Dutch door of the meds room, to the wing of patient rooms.

At every corner and intersection of hall there was a convex mirror attached to the ceiling, so that anyone walking through the unit could see around a corner before actually stepping around it. At L-corners the mirror was a triangular eighth of a globe wedged up in the corner, and at four-way crossings it was a full half-globe set in the middle of the ceiling. Cochran didn't like the things—they seemed to be *whole* spheres, only part-way intruded here and there through temporary violations of the architecture, like chrome eyes peering down curiously into the maze of hallways, and he couldn't shake the irrational dread of rounding a turn and seeing two of them in the wall ahead of him, golden for once instead of silver, with a single horizontal black line across each of them—but he did reluctantly glance at a couple of them to get an advance look around corners on the way to Plumtree's room.

But when he finally arrived at her room he saw that her door, in violation of the daytime rules, was closed. He shuffled up to it anyway, intending to knock, and then became aware of Plumtree speaking quietly inside; he couldn't hear what she said, but it was followed by Armentrout's voice saying, "So which one of you was it that took the shock?"

The question meant nothing to Cochran, and he was hesitant about interrupting a doctor-and-patient therapy session; and after a few moments of indecisive shuffling, and raising his hand and then lowering it, he let his shoulders slump and turned away and plodded back down the hall toward the TV lounge, defeatedly aware of the wide cuffs of his bell-bottom trousers flapping around his bare ankles.

Somebody went flatline ten seconds after the shock," Armentrout went on when Plumtree didn't immediately answer. "We dragged the Waterloo cart into the treatment room, but your heart started up again before we had to put the paddles on you." He was smiling, but he knew that he was still shaky about the incident, for he hadn't meant to call it a "Waterloo cart" just now. Waterloo was the brand name of the thing, but it was known as a crash cart, or a cardiac defibrillator; the incident would probably have been *his* Waterloo, though, as soon as the idealistic Philip Muir heard about it, if Plumtree had died undergoing electroconvulsive therapy with forged permissions while just on a temporary conservatorship. Muir was surely going to be angry anyway, for ECT was not a treatment indicated for multiple personality disorder—or dissociative identity disorder, as Muir would trendily say.

And Armentrout couldn't pretend anymore that he didn't know she was a multiple—the ECT had separated out the personalities like a hammer breaking a piece of shale into distinct, individual hard slabs. Armentrout could have wished that it was a little less obvious, in fact; but perhaps the personalities would blend back together a little, before Muir saw her tomorrow.

"Valerie," said the woman in the bed. "She always takes intolerable situations. It caught Cody by surprise."

"And who are you?"

"I'm Janis." She smiled at him, and in the dim lamplight her pupils didn't seem notably dilated or constricted now.

"How many of you are there?"

"I really don't know, Doctor. Some aren't very developed, or exist just for one purpose . . . like the one called—what does he call himself?—'the foul fiend Flibbertigibbet!' What a name! He got it . . . from Shakespeare, according to him. Is there a play called *Leah*? He claims to have been a Shakespearean actor. I—don't want to talk about him, he's who we've brought up when we've had to fight, to defend our life. He makes our teeth hurt like we've got braces on, and he gives us nosebleeds. I don't want to talk about him." She shivered, and then smiled wryly. "We're like the little cottage full of dwarves in *Snow White*—each of us with a job to do, while the poisoned girl sleeps. I used to sign my high-school papers 'Snowy Eve White' sometimes."

"Snow White, Eve White—you've seen the movie *The Three Faces of Eve*? Or read the book?"

She shook her head. "No, I've never heard of it."

"Hmm. I bet. And one of you is a man?"

She blinked—and Armentrout could feel the hairs standing up on his arms, for the woman's face changed abruptly, as the muscles under the skin realigned themselves; her mouth seemed wider now, and her eyes narrower.

"Valerie says you had all my clothes off," she said in a flat voice. "I'd be pissed about that if I didn't know you're a total queer. What did you hit me with?"

"Cody," said Armentrout in cautious greeting, suddenly wishing Plumtree had been put back in restraints. She had recovered from the succinylcholine amazingly fast, and she didn't seem to be dopy and blurry, as patients recovering from ECT generally were for at least the rest of the day.

"You're the one," he went on, "speaking of hitting, who hit Long John Beach last night, aren't you, Cody?"

"I don't know. Probably." Plumtree's forehead was dewed with sweat, and she was squinting. "Was this while I had my clothes off? He probably asked for it, he's got a frisky spirit hand to go with the flesh-and-blood one. And I saw that Cockface guy's hand—I don't like his birthmark. A lot of tricky hands around here, and this place is a stinking flop."

She was breathing through her open mouth, and she looked pale.

Altogether she was acting like someone with a bad hangover, and it occurred to Armentrout that the Janis personality had been unimpaired because it had been Cody who had taken the shock treatment. Cody was the one who had given him the finger. Ten seconds had gone by before the Valerie personality, the one who took "intolerable situations," had taken over. He leaned forward to look at Plumtree's face, and he saw that her pupils were as tiny as pores. She definitely looked dopy and blurry now.

"What we're going to try to do is achieve *isolation,* Cody," he said. "We'll decide which personality is most socially viable, and then bring that one forward and . . . cauterize the others off." This was hardly a description of orthodox therapy, but he wanted to draw a reaction from her. She didn't seem to be listening, though.

"How many of you are there, Cody?" Armentrout went on. "I've met you and Janis, that I know of, and I've heard about Valerie."

"God, I am still in the psych hospital, aren't I?" she mumbled, rubbing her eyes. "I suppose a cold beer is out of the question. Shit. But no hair of *that* dog, thank you—that was the goddamn Wolfman."

"That was ECT," Armentrout said, leaning back in the chair beside the bed and smiling at her, "electroconvulsive therapy—shock treatment, Edison Medicine." He smiled reminiscently and said, "Generally a course of treatment is six or twelve shock sessions, three a week."

All the worldly weariness disappeared from her face, and for a moment Armentrout thought the Cody personality had gone away and been replaced by a little girl, possibly the core child; but when she spoke it was in response to what he had just said, so it was probably still Cody, a Cody for once frightened out of her sardonic pose.

She said, "*Again?* You want to do that to me *again?*"

A genuine reaction at last! "At this point I'm undecided." Armentrout's heart was beating rapidly, and a smile of triumph kept twitching at his lips. "I'll make up my mind after our conference later today."

"Don't you need . . . my permission, to do that?"

"One of you signed it," he said with a shrug. She would probably believe that, even if shown the bogus signature. "How many of you are there?"

"Oh, sweet Jesus, there's a lot of kids on the bus," she said wearily, leaning back against the pillows and closing her eyes, "all singing 'Row, Row, Row Your Boat,' and crying, with a smashed-up crazy man holding a gun on the driver."

Armentrout recognized the image—it was from the end of the Clint Eastwood movie *Dirty Harry,* when the battered and hotly pursued serial killer hijacked a schoolbus full of children.

"Where is the . . . the 'foul fiend Flibbertigibbet' sitting?"

Plumtree's eyes were still closed—her eyelids were as wrinkled and pale as paper wrappers bluntly accordioned off drinking straws—but she managed to put derisive impatience into the shake of her head. *"He* isn't *sitting,"* she said.

Then she was snoring through her open mouth. Armentrout reached out and switched off the lamp, then got up and opened the door to the hallway.

His belly felt hollow with anticipation as he pulled the door closed behind him—We'll surely get some tasty therapy done, he told himself smugly, in our therapy session at three.

An hour after lunch Cochran stood in the fenced-off picnic yard, smoking his third-to-last Marlboro, which the charge nurse had lit for him with her closely guarded Bic lighter when she had let the patients out here for the hourly smoke break. The afternoon sunlight shone brightly on the expanse of asphalt and the distant palm trees outside the iron-bar fence, and Cochran was squinting between the bars at two men in the parking lot who were using jumper cables to try to start a car, and he was envying them their trivial problems.

Long John Beach was leaning on the fence a couple of yards to Cochran's right, gingerly scratching the corner of one swollen eye under the silvery nose brace. Cochran remembered the old man *eating* nine cigarettes last night, and he tried to work up some resentment over it; and then he tried to be grateful that the one-armed lunatic seemed to have no memory of, nor even any interest in, how his nose had been broken; but these were just frail and momentary distractions.

Cochran threw the cigarette down and stepped on it. "Nina," he said, loud enough for Long John Beach to hear but speaking out toward the parking lot, "can you hear me?"

The old man had jumped, and was now craning his neck around to peer across the sunny lot at the men huddled under the shade of the car hood. "You'll have to shout," he said. "Hey, was I snoring real bad last night? I got coughing when I woke up, thought I'd cough my whole spirit out on the floor like a big snake."

Cochran closed his eyes. "I was talking to my wife," he told the old man. "She's dead. Can you . . . hear her?" After a moment he looked over at him.

"Oh—" Long John Beach shrugged expansively. "Maybe."

Cochran made himself concentrate on her bitter voice as he had heard it last night.

"Nina," he answered her now, as awkwardly as a long-lapsed Catholic in the confessional; he was light-headed and sweating, and he had to look out through the fence again in order to speak. "Whatever happened, whatever—I love you, and I miss you terribly. *Look*, goddammit, I've lost my *mind* over it! And—Jesus, I'm sorry. Of course you were right about the Pace Chardonnays—" He was talking rapidly now, shaking his head. "—they are too loud and insistent, and they do dominate a meal. Show-off wines, made to win at blind tastings, you're right. I'm sorry I called your family's wines flinty and thin. Please tell me that it wasn't that silly argument, at the New Year's Eve thing, that—but if I am to blame—"

He paused; then glanced sideways at his attentive companion.

Apparently aware that some response was expected of him, Long John Beach shuffled his feet and blinked his blackened eyes. "Well . . . I was never much of a wine man," the old man said apologetically. "I just ate smokes."

Cochran was clinging to a description of lunatics a friend had once quoted to him—*One day nothing new came into their heads*—because lately he himself seemed to be able to count on at least several appalling revelations every day.

" 'Think not the King did banish thee,' " he said unsteadily, quoting the lines he'd skipped last night, " 'but thou the King.' "

Long John Beach opened his mouth, and the voice that came out was not his own, but neither was it Nina's; and it was so strained that Cochran couldn't guess its gender. " 'The bay trees in our country are all withered, and meteors fright the fixed stars of heaven,' " the voice said, clearly quoting something. " 'These signs forerun the death or fall of kings.' "

"Who are you?" Cochran whispered.

" 'I am bastard begot,' " the eerie voice droned on, perhaps in answer, " 'bastard instructed, bastard in mind, bastard in *valor*, in everything illegitimate.' "

Cochran was dizzy, and all at once but with no perceptible shift the sunlight seemed brassy amber, and the air was clotted and hard to push through his throat. "Where is my wife?" he rasped.

" 'Her bed is India; there she lies, a pearl.' "

"Wh—*India?* Are you—talking to me? Please, what do you mean—" He stopped, for he realized that he was looking *up* at Long John Beach, and the base of his spine stung. He had abruptly sat down on the pavement beside one of the picnic tables.

There had been a startled shout from out in the parking lot, and the power lines were swinging gently far overhead. When Cochran peered out at the men, he saw that the car hood had fallen onto one of them;

the man was rubbing his head now and cussing at his companion, who was laughing.

"Whoa!" said Long John Beach, also laughing. "Did you feel that one? Or are you just making yourself at home?"

Cochran understood that there had been an earthquake; and, looking up at the power lines and the leaves on the banana tree in the courtyard, he gathered that it was over. The sunlight was bright again, and the jacaranda-scented breeze was cold in his sweaty hair.

He got to his feet, rubbing the seat of his corduroy pants. "I suppose you've got nothing more to say," he told Long John Beach angrily.

The one-armed man shrugged. "Like I say, I was never a wine man."

The charge nurse was standing in the lounge doorway, waving. The smoking break was apparently ended.

Cochran turned to trudge back to the building. "You don't know what you've been missing," he said.

When the two of them had shuffled up to the door, the nurse said, "Dr. Armentrout wants to see you."

"Good," said Cochran stoically. "I want to talk to him."

"Not you," the nurse said. "Him." She nodded toward the one-armed old man.

Long John Beach was nodding. "For the Plumtree girl," he said. "He wants me on the *horn*. On the *blower*."

"The usual thing," said the nurse in obvious agreement as she flapped her hands to shoo the two men inside.

Armentrout knew it wasn't Cody that knocked on his office door at three, because when he peeked out through the reinforced glass panel he saw that Plumtree had walked down the hall and was standing comfortably; Cody would have needed the wheelchair he had told the nurses to have ready.

He unlocked the door and pulled it open. "Come in . . . Janis?"

"Yes."

"Sit down," he told her. "Over on the couch there, you want to relax."

The tape recorder inside the Faraday cage in the desk was rolling, and the telephone receiver was lying on the desk, with Long John Beach locked into the conference room on the other side of the clinic, listening in on the extension—Armentrout was psychically protected, masked. Beside the receiver on the desk was the box that contained the twenty Lombardy Zeroth tarot cards, along with a pack of Gudang Garam clove-flavored cigarettes and a box of strawberry flavor-straws, so he was ready to snip off and consume at least a couple of Plumtree's supernumerary personalities—escort some of the girls off the bus, he thought with nervous cheer, kidnap a couple of Snow White's dwarves. *The better to eat you with, my dear.* And if Cody chose to step out and get physical, he had the 250,000-volt stun gun in the pocket of his white coat. A different kind of Edison Medicine.

When she had sat down on the couch—sitting upright, with her knees together, for now—he handed her the glass of water in which he had dissolved three milligrams of benzodiazepine powder.

"Drink this," he said, smiling.

"It's . . . what?"

"It's a mild relaxant. I'll bet you've been experiencing some aches and pains in your joints?"

"In my hand, is all."

"Well . . . *Cody* will appreciate it, trust me."

Plumtree took the glass from his hand and stared at the water. "Give me a minute to think," she said. "You've jumbled us all up here."

Armentrout turned toward the desk, reaching for the telephone. "Never mind, I'll have them give it to you intravenously."

The bluff worked. She raised her bruised hand in a *wait* gesture and tilted up the glass with the other, draining it in four gulps; and if the desk lamp had flickered it had only been for an instant.

She now even licked the rim of the glass before leaning forward to set it down on the carpet; and when she straightened up she was sitting forward, looking up at him with her chin almost touching the coat buttons over his belt buckle.

"This is a highly lucrative position," she said. "But I guess nobody can see us right here, can they?"

"Well," said Armentrout judiciously, glancing from the couch to the door window as if considering the question for the first time ever, "I suppose not." The drug couldn't possibly be hitting her yet.

She reached out with her right hand and winced, then with her left caught his left hand and pressed it to her forehead. "Do you think I have a fever, Doctor?"

She was rubbing his palm back and forth over her brow, and her eyes were closed.

His heart was suddenly pounding in his chest. Go with the flow, he told himself with a jerky mental shrug. Without taking his hand away from her face he sat down on the couch beside her on her left. "There are," he said breathlessly, "more reliable . . . areas of the anatomy . . . upon which to manually judge body temperature. From."

"Are there?" she said. She pulled his palm down over her nose and lips; and when she had slid it over her chin and onto her throat she breathed, "Tell me when I'm getting warmer, Doctor."

He had got his fingers on the top button of her blouse when the desk lamp browned out and she abruptly shoved his hand away.

"Shouldn't there be a nurse present for any physical examination?" she said rapidly.

He exhaled in segments. "Janis."

"Yes."

"Who . . . was that?"

"I believe that was Tiffany."

"Tiffany." He nodded several times. "Well, she and I were in the middle of a, a useful dialogue."

"Valerie has locked Tiffany in her room."

"In the . . . dwarves' cottage, that would be?"

Plumtree smiled at him and tapped the side of her head. "Exactly." She had begun shifting uncomfortably on the couch, and smacking her lips, and now she said, "Could I go take a shower?"

Of course there was no tone of innuendo at all in the remark. "Your hair's damp right now," Armentrout told her shortly. "I bet you took a shower since lunch. You can take one after we're done here." He slapped his hands onto his knees and stood up, and crossed to the desk. With shaky fingers he fumbled a clove cigarette out of the pack and lit it with one of the ward Bics. He puffed on it, wincing at the syrupy sweet smoke, and then flipped open the purple velvet box.

"Well!" he said, spilling the oversized tarot cards faceup onto the desktop, though not looking directly at them. "I did want to ask you about New Year's Day. You said you killed a man, remember? A king called, somehow, the Flying Nun? A week later Mr. Cochran saw a man who had a bull's head, in Los Angeles. On *Vignes* Street, that means 'grapevines' in French; there used to be a winery there, where Union Station is now." Pawing through the cards and squinting at them through his eyelashes and the scented cigarette smoke, he had managed to find the Sun card, a miniature painting of a cherub floating over a jigsaw-edged cliff and holding up a severed, grimacing red head from which golden rays stuck out like solid poles in every direction.

Now he spun away from the desk and thrust the card face-out toward her. "Did your king have a bull's head?" He sucked hard on the cigarette.

Plumtree had rocked back on the couch and looked away. And Armentrout coughed as much from disgust as from the acrid smoke in his lungs, for there was no animation, no identity, riding the smoke into his head—he had missed catching the Janis personality, the Plumtree gestalt had parried him.

"Hi, Doctor," Plumtree said. "Is this a come-as-you-are party?" She stared at him for a moment, and appeared to replay in her head what had last been said. "Are you talking about the king we killed? Look, I'm being cooperative here. I'll answer all your questions. But—trust me!—if you hit us with the . . . Edison Medicine again, none of us will tell you anything, ever." Her shoulders had slumped as she'd been talking. "No, he didn't have a bull's head. He was barefooted, and had long hair down to his shoulders, and a beard, like you'd expect to see on King Solomon or Charlemagne." She rubbed her hand over her face in an eerie and apparently unwitting re-enactment of what she had done with Armentrout's hand. "But I recognized him."

Armentrout knew his shielded tape recorder would be getting all this, but he tried to concentrate on what the woman was saying. You let that Tiffany girl get you all rattled, he told himself; you don't *want* to eat the *Janis* personality, you idiot, she's the one you want to leave *in* the body, to show how successful the integration therapy was. You're *lucky* you didn't get her, in the clove smoke. "You . . . say you recognized him," he said, nodding like a plaster dog in the back window of a car. "You'd seen him before?"

"In that game on the houseboat on Lake Mead in 1990. Assumption—it's a kind of poker. He was dressed as a woman for that, and the other players called him the Flying Nun. Our mental bus navigator Flibbertigibbet was trying to win the job Crane was after, the job of being the king, which is why he had us there, playing hands in that terrible game; and he didn't succeed—and he went flat-out crazy on Holy Saturday when Crane won . . . *it*, the crown, the throne."

"Crane?"

"Scott Crane. I didn't know his name until we all got talking together today; I thought Flying Nun was, like, his *name*, it might be a Swedish name, right, like Bra Banning? He was a poker player in those days."

"I remember another man who wanted to be this king," said Armentrout thoughtfully, "a local man called Neal Obstadt. He died in the same explosion that collapsed Long John Beach's lung, two and a half years ago. And Obstadt was looking for this Crane fellow back in '90—had a big reward offered." He looked at her and smiled. "You know, you may *actually have* killed somebody, ten days ago!"

"What good news," she said hollowly.

"Whatever you did could be the *cause* of everything that's been different since New Year's Day—I thought you were just delusionally *reacting*, the way Mr. Cochran almost certainly is." He held up one finger as though to count off points of an argument. "Now, you couldn't have got through all of Crane's defenses, and abducted his very *child*, as you say you did, without powerful sorcerous help; you'd need virtually another *king*, in fact. Who could that be?"

"You got me."

"I thought you said you'd be honest with me here. We can schedule another ECT *tomorrow*."

"I—I'm being honest. I was alone. I don't *know* whose *idea* the whole thing was."

"One of you might have been acting on someone's orders, though, right? On someone's careful instructions." He was sitting on the desk now, drumming his fingers excitedly on the emptied velvet box. "There was a boy around, a couple of years ago, living in Long Beach somewhere. *He* was a sort of proto-king, as I recall." Armentrout wished he had paid more attention to these events at the time—but they had been other people's wars in the magical landscape, and he had been content to just go on eating pieces of his patients' souls on the sidelines. "His name was something goofy—Boogie-Woogie Bananas, or something like that. *He* could probably kill a king, or bring one back to life, even, if he wanted to. If he's kept to the disciplines. Somebody, your man Crane, probably, brought the gangster Bugsy Siegel back to life, briefly, in 1990. You've seen the Warren Beatty movie, *Bugsy*? Siegel was this particular sort of supernatural king, during the 1940s. Yes, this kid would be fifteen or so now—he could be the one that sent you to kill Crane. Does a name like Boogie-Woogie Bananas ring any bells?"

Plumtree visibly tried to come up with a funny remark, but gave up and just shook her head wearily. "No."

"His party had a lawyer! Were you approached by the lawyer? He had a pretentious name, something *Strube*, like J. Submersible Strube the third."

"*I* never heard of *any* of these people." Plumtree was pale, and perspiration misted her forehead. "But *one* of us went to a lot of trouble to kill Crane. Obviously."

Armentrout pursed his lips. "Did you say anything to him, to Crane?"

"Sunday before last? Yeah. I wasn't going to hurt his kid, this little boy who couldn't have been five years old yet—God knows how I lured him out of the house, but I had the kid down on his back in this grassy meadow above the beach, with the spear points on his little neck—I suppose Flibbertigibbet *would* have killed the kid!—and when I found myself standing there after losing some time, I looked at the kid's *father* standing there, Crane, and I just said, almost crying to see what a horrible thing I was in the middle of, I said, 'There's nothing in this flop for me.' " There were tears in Plumtree's eyes right now, and from the angry way she cuffed them away Armentrout was sure that she was Cody at the moment. "And," she went on hoarsely, "Crane said, 'Then pass.' He must have been scared, but he was talking gently, you know?—not like he was mad. 'Let it pass by us,' he said."

"And what did you say?"

"*I* lost *time* then. When *I* could see what was going on again, Crane was lying there dead, with the spear in his throat, sticking up through his Solomon beard like a fishing pole, and the kid was gone." Plumtree blinked around at the desks and the couch and the foliage-screened window. "Why did Janis leave, just now? You made her peel off, didn't you?" Her expression became blank, and then she was frowning again. "And she's crying in her bus seat! What did you do to her?"

Armentrout held up the card. "I just showed her this."

But Plumtree looked away from it. And when she spoke, it was in such a level voice that Armentrout wondered if she'd shifted again: "Strip poker, we're playing here?" She looked past the card, focussing into his eyes, and Armentrout saw that one of her pupils was a tiny pinprick, as was usual with her, but the other was dilated in the muted office light. The mismatched eyes, along with the downward-curling androgynous smile she now gave him, made him think of the rock star David Bowie. "I can be the one that wins here, you know," she said. "I can rake in *your* investment, or at least toss it out into the crowd. Strip poker. How many . . . *garments* have *you* got?"

Armentrout was annoyed, and a little intrigued, to realize that he was frightened. "Are you still Cody?" he asked.

"Largely." Plumtree struggled up off of the couch to her feet, though the effort made drops of sweat roll down from her hairline, and she stumbled forward and half fell onto the desk. She was certainly still Cody, who had taken the succinylcholine and the electroconvulsive therapy at dawn this morning. Armentrout hastily slid the delicate old tarot cards away from her.

She shook out a Gudang Garam cigarette and lit it.

"This phone is your mask, right?" she gasped through a mouthful of spicy smoke, grabbing the telephone receiver and holding it up. "Your nest of masks? What's your name?" Armentrout didn't answer, but she read it off the name plaque on his desk. "Hello?" she said into the telephone. "Could I speak to Richard Paul Armentrout's mom, please?"

Armentrout was rocked by the counter-attack—she was trying to get a handle on his *own* soul! *That* handle! What personality in her was it that knew how to do this?—but he was confident that Long John Beach was psychotically diffractive enough to deflect this, and many more like it. "I t-took a vial of your blood," Armentrout said quickly, "when you were first brought in here, because I thought I might put you on lithium carbonate, and we have to do a lot of blood testing to get the dosage right for that. I never did give you lithium, but I've still got the vial of your blood." He was breathing rapidly, almost panting.

"That's a big ace," Plumtree allowed, "but you've lost one garment now, and I've only lost my . . . oh, call her one silly hat."

Armentrout looked down at the cards under his hands, and his pelvis went quiveringly cold, followed a moment later by a bubbly tingling in his ribs, for he had no time here to squint cautiously sidelong at the distressing things, and was looking at them squarely. He snatched up the Wheel of Fortune card, the miniature Renaissance-style painting of four men belted to a vertical wheel—*Regno*, Latin for "I reign," read the word-ribbon attached to the mouth of the man on top; the ones to either side trailed ribbons that read *Regnabo* and *Regnavi,* "I shall reign" and "I reigned"—and he shoved the card into Plumtree's face as he took a cheek-denting drag on his cigarette.

The bulb in the desk lamp popped, and shards of cellophane-thin broken glass clinked faintly on the desk surface; the room was suddenly dimmer, lit now only by the afternoon sunlight streaking in golden beams through the green schefflera leaves outside the window.

Again Armentrout had got nothing but a lungful of astringent clove smoke. And he wasn't facing Cody anymore. Plumtree had twitched away the card-concussed, vulnerable personality before he could draw it into the barrel of his flavored cigarette, had swept the stunned Cody back to one of the metaphorical bus seats or dwarf-cottage bunks, and rotated a fresh one onstage.

"Hello?" said Plumtree into the telephone again. "I'm calling on behalf of Richard Paul Armentrout—he says he owes *somebody* there a tre-*men*-dous apology." The coal on her cigarette glowed in the dimness like the bad red light that draws loose souls in the underworld in the Tibetan *Bardo Thodol.*

Armentrout dropped the card and fumbled in his coat pocket for the stun gun. I think I've got to put an end to this, he thought; punch her right out of this fight with 250,000 volts and try again tomorrow, after another ECT session in which I'll give her a full 500 joules of intracranial juice. If she really can summon, from across the hundreds of miles of mountain and desert wilderness, my m—or *any* of my potent old guilt ghosts, and lead them all the way in past Long John Beach's masks *to* me, they could attach, and collapse my distended life line, *kill* me.

They're all still out there, God knows—I've never had any desire for the Pagadebiti Zinfandel, *confiteor Dionyso.*

Nah, he thought savagely, that one-armed old man is a better sort of Kevlar armor than to give way under just two shots—and I *will have* this woman. The damp skin of his palm could still feel her chin, and the hot slope of her throat. *Tell me when I'm getting warmer, Doctor.*

He snatched up one of the tarot cards at random with one hand and the lighter with the other, and he spun the flint wheel with the card blocking his view of the upspringing flame; the card's illuminated face was toward her, while he saw only the backlit rectangle of the frayed edge. Gaggingly, and fruitlessly, he again sucked at the limp cigarette—sparks were falling off of it onto the desk like tiny shooting stars.

"Let me talk to *your* m-mom," he wheezed, knowing that multiples generally included, among their menagerie, internalized duplicates of their own abusive parents. Surely Plumtree's distorted version of her mother wouldn't be able to maintain this fight!

Plumtree's body jackknifed forward off the desk and tumbled to the carpet. "Behold now," she gasped in a reedy voice, "I have daughters which have not known man." Armentrout recognized the sentence—it was from Genesis, when Lot offered the mob his own daughters rather than surrender the angels who had come to his house. "Name the one you want, Omar," Plumtree's strained voice went on, clearly not quoting now, "and I'll throw her to you! Just don't take *me* again!"

Armentrout was confident that he could consume *this* one, this cowardly, Bible-quoting creature—but this was only Plumtree's approximation of her mother, not a real personality; so he said, "Give me . . . Tiffany."

"Tiffany," said the woman on the floor.

And when Plumtree got back up on her feet and leaned on the desk with one hand while she pushed her tangled blond hair back from her sweaty forehead with the other, she was smiling at him. "Doctor!" she said. "What bloody hands you have!"

Armentrout glanced down—he had cut his hand on a piece of the broken light bulb in grabbing for the lighter, and blood had run down his wrist and blotted into his white cuff.

"With you, Miss Plumtree," he panted, managing to smile, "strip poker is something more like flag football." I can have sex with her now, he thought excitedly. Janis snatched Tiffany away from me before, but Janis is off crying in her dwarf bunk now; and I routed Cody too, and whoever that third one was; and the mother personality has outright *given* Tiffany to me!

"Strip poker?" she exclaimed. "Ooh—" She began unbuttoning her blouse. "I'll raise you!"

The clove cigarette was coming to pieces in Armentrout's mouth, and he pulled it off his lip and tossed it into the ashtray and spat out shreds of bitterly perfumy tobacco. He wouldn't be able to consume any of her personalities this session, it looked like, but he could at least relieve the aching terror-pressure in his groin.

"Sweeten the pot," he agreed, fumbling under his chin to unknot his necktie.

The close air of the office smelled of clove smoke and overheated flesh, and the skin of his hands and face tingled like the surface of a fully charged capacitor. This psychic battle had left him swollen with excitement, and he knew that the consummation of their contest wouldn't last long.

She reached out and tugged his cut hand away from his collar, and again she pulled his palm down across her wet forehead and nose and lips—her eyes were closed, so he couldn't see whether her pupils were matched in size or not—

And then she sucked his cut finger into her mouth and *bit* it, and in the same instant with her injured hand she grabbed the bulging crotch of his pants and *squeezed.*

Armentrout exhaled sharply, and the heel of one of his shoes knocked three times fast against the side of the desk as his free hand clenched into a fist.

Gotcha, Doctor," said a man's voice flatly from Plumtree's mouth. "I got the taste of your blood now, and the smell of your jizz. In voodoo terms, that constitutes having your ID package."

Plumtree had stepped lithely away from the desk, and now stared down at Armentrout with evident amused disgust as she wiped her hands on the flanks of her jeans.

When Armentrout could speak without gasping, he said, "I suppose you're . . . the foul fiend Flibbertigibbet, is that right?"

Plumtree frowned. "That's what I've told the girls to call me. You were just talking to their mom, weren't you? Playing 'Follow the Queen.' "

"Your name's Omar," Armentrout said. "What's your last name?" He was still sitting on the desk, but he straightened his white coat and frowned professionally. "I can compel you to tell me," he added. "With ECT and scopolamine, just for example."

"I reckon you could. But I ain't scared of a little white-haired fag like you anyway. My name's Omar Salvoy.'' Plumtree's pupils were both wide now. She picked up the telephone receiver, then smiled and held it out toward the doctor.

From the earpiece a faint voice could be heard saying, *''Let me up, Richie darling! Pull the plug!''*

With a hoarse whimper, Armentrout grabbed the receiver and slammed it into its cradle, and then he opened the second velvet box—but Plumtree had stepped around the desk and crouched by the chair.

''*You* got a *gun* in the box there, haven't you?'' said the Salvoy personality jovially while Plumtree's hand fumbled under the desk. ''Think it through, old son. You kill us and you've got some fierce ghosts on your ass—we got your *number* now, no mask is gonna protect you from us. Call your momma back and ask *her* if I ain't telling you the truth.''

Armentrout's heart was hammering in his chest like a jackhammer in an airplane hangar, and he wondered if this was capture, death. No, he thought as he remembered to breathe. No, she can't have—got a *fix* on me—in that brief moment, with Long John Beach diffracting my hot signal.

After a moment, Armentrout let go of the derringer and closed the box. Had he been planning to shoot Plumtree, or himself?

''And I'll bet this button right *he-ere,''* Plumtree went on, her arm under the desktop, ''is the alarm, right?''

An instant later the close air was shaken by a harsh metallic *braaang* that didn't stop.

Still too shaken to speak, Armentrout stood up from the desk and fished his keys out of his pocket to unlock the door and swing it open. Security guards were already sprinting down the hall toward the office, and he waved his bleeding hand at them and stood aside.

CHAPTER 5

No fight could have been half so terrible as this dance.
—Charles Dickens,
A Tale of Two Cities

His little boy may have *watched* me kill him,'' said Janis Plumtree in a quiet, strained voice.

A waterproof Gumby-and-Pokey tablecloth had been spread on the big table in the TV lounge, and she and Cochran were standing in line, each of them holding a glossy little cardboard bowl and a napkin that was rubber-banded around a plastic spoon.

"*You* didn't kill him," whispered Cochran earnestly. "Cody did." He looked nervously at the patients on either side of them, but the old woman ahead of Plumtree and the morose teenager behind Cochran were just staring ahead, anxiously watching the ice cream being doled out.

Plumtree had been escorted to the Quiet Room again, directly after her conference with Dr. Armentrout this afternoon, and confined there for an hour, and when she had found Cochran afterward she had told him about the morning's costly discovery of her multiple personalities, the "dwarves in Snow White's cottage." He had listened with unhappy sympathy, withholding judgment but taking the story as at least a touching apology for her occasional rudenesses, which supposedly had all been the doing of the ill-natured "Cody personality." Apparently there was no Cody-the-roommate, really.

The appalling thing, the stark fact that still misted his forehead every time he thought of it, was that she had actually undergone shock therapy this morning; he was clinging to her insistence that it had been scheduled for her even before Long John Beach had been hit, and he was happy to be talking about topics that had nothing to do with the hospital, for he had not yet found a chance to tell Armentrout what had really happened last night.

"Well," Plumtree said now, "Cody didn't kill him either, directly. But we all knew we were going to that Leucadia estate to do somebody harm. Old Flibbertigibbet kept saying that we were just going to stab somebody in the leg. But we all knew what he could do, what he probably *would* do, and we all cooperated. We didn't care." She sighed shakily. "We do what he wants, ever since we got him to . . . *kill* a man in '89."

Cochran was inclined to doubt that; and he was fairly sure that she hadn't killed anybody on this last New Year's Day, either, for she'd surely be in a prison ward somewhere right now if the police or the doctors had found any reason to take her story seriously.

But *she* clearly believed these things, and was troubled by them—and Armentrout had given her *shock therapy* this morning!—so he said, with unfeigned concern, "Poor Janis! How did that happen?"

They had got to the front of the line, and a nurse scooped a ball of vanilla ice cream into Plumtree's bowl and tucked a wafer cookie alongside it. Plumtree waited until Cochran had been served too, and then they sidled off to the window-side corner, by unspoken agreement choosing the far end of the room from where Long John Beach sat blinking and licking a spoon. At their backs, beyond the reinforced glass, a half-moon shone through the black silhouettes of the palm trees outside the courtyard.

"We were in a bar in Oakland," she said quietly when the two of them had sat down on the linoleum by the nursing-station-side wall, "and Cody got real drunk. I was twenty-two, and Cody was drinking a lot in those days, though I always stayed sober to drive home. And we lost time—or maybe Cody had an actual alcoholic blackout!—and when *I* could see what was going on again, I was on my back in a van in the alley parking lot, and the boyfriend I was at the bar with was trying to pull my clothes off. Cody had passed out, and he figured he could do what he wanted with an unconscious woman. This was only . . . well, it was five-oh-four in the afternoon, wasn't it? Across the bay, you were just about to catch your wife, wife-to-be, when she fell down the winery stairs. Anyway, this guy gave me a black eye but I was able to fight him off because he hadn't expected me to . . . *wake up.* I scrambled out of the van, with him still grabbing at me and me not able to run, with my clothes all hiked up and down. I probably could have got away from him then with no trouble, 'cause I was awake and outside and I think he was apologizing as much as anything; but I . . . *got so mad* . . . at him thinking he could do that to me when I was passed out that way, that I called a real serious *sic 'im!* in my head. You know? Like you would to a pit bull that was real savage but was *yours*. I can see now that all of us, even drunk Cody, helped call it. We hadn't ever been *that mad* before. We knew it was bad, and that it would cost us, but we called anyway. And we woke up Flibbertigibbet.''

Cochran recalled that this was another of her supposed personalities, a male one. Janis had told him that she didn't know much of what had happened at the therapy session with Armentrout today—she'd said she had ''lost a lot of time'' after he had showed her some miniature painting that she couldn't bear to look at—but that she was pretty sure Flibbertigibbet had been out. Probably Flibbertigibbet had been the one who had reportedly broken the doctor's desk lamp and bitten his finger, earning Plumtree her most recent stay in the Quiet Room. She had said that she was grateful that Flibbertigibbet hadn't done anything worse.

''And . . . Flibbertigibbet—'' Cochran was embarrassed to pronounce the foolish name. ''—killed the guy?''

She shivered. ''He sure did. The big earthquake hit right then, and I suppose the cops thought it was falling bricks that smashed his head that way. It was never in the papers, anything about a guy being murdered there. I ran to my car, and it took me two hours to drive the ten miles home. Nobody at my apartment building, what was left of it, said anything about the blood on me—a lot of people were bloody that day.''

''. . . I remember.''

The Franciscan shale of San Bruno Mountain hadn't shifted much in that late-afternoon quake, and only a couple of Pace Vineyards' oak casks had fallen and burst, spilling a hundred gallons of the raw new Zinfandel like an arterial hemorrhage across the stone floor of the cellar, which Cochran had eventually had to mop up; but when he and a couple of the maintenance men had immediately driven one of the vineyard pickup trucks down to the 280 Highway, they had found cars spun out and stalled across the lanes, and in the little town of Colma hillsides had toppled onto the graves in the ubiquitous cemeteries, and he remembered stunned men and women standing around on the glass-strewn sidewalks, many of them in blood-spattered clothes and holding bloody cloths to their heads. Paramedic vans had been slow and few, and Cochran had driven several people to the local hospital in the back of the pickup truck before eventually returning to the vineyard. The visitor from France, young Mademoiselle Nina Gestin Leon, had been stranded there, and had stayed for the subdued late dinner in the Pace Vineyards dining room. They had all drunk up innumerable bottles of the '68 late-harvest Zinfandels from Ridge and Mayacamas, he remembered; the night had seemed to call for big, wild reds, implausibly high in natural alcohol content and so sharp with the tea-leaf taste of tannin that Cochran had thought the winemakers must have left twigs and stems in the fermenting must.

"I had blood and wine on my clothes when I went to bed that night," he said now.

"Cody's more of a vodka girl," said Janis. She leaned back against the TV lounge wall and sang, "*You can always tell a* vodka *girl . . .*"

"That's the tune of the old Halo Shampoo ads," Cochran said. "That's before your time, isn't it? *I* barely remember that."

"Geber me no zeitgebers," she said shortly. She looked at the nearest of the other patients—poor old Mr. Regushi a dozen yards away, eating his ice cream with his hands—and then she said quietly, "We've got to escape out of this place."

"I think it'd be better to get *released* out of here," Cochran said hastily. "And I do think we can do it. I have a lawyer up in San Mateo County—"

"Who couldn't get us out before tomorrow dawn, could he? Dr. Armentrout is going to give me the electroconvulsive therapy again tomorrow—I can tell, I was told not to eat anything after ten tonight. He says he's elected *me*, Janis, to be the dominant personality inside this little head, and he's going to . . . *cauterize* Cody away, like you would a wart."

Cochran opened his mouth, wondering what he should say; finally he just said, "Do you *like* her?"

"Cody? No. She's a, a *bitch* is the only word for it, sorry. She thinks I'm crazy to be—well, she doesn't like you. And I think her story about being a security guard somewhere at nights is a lie—I think she does *burglaries.*"

"Well . . . I hope not. But if you don't like her, why not *let* Armentrout . . . do that?" He could feel his face reddening. "I mean, he *is* a doctor, and you certainly don't need—"

"She's a real person, Scant, as real as me. I don't like her, but I can't just stand by and let *her* get killed too." Her lips were pressed together and she was frowning. " 'Cause it would be the death penalty for her, and that without an indictment or jury or anything. Do you see what I mean?"

Cochran doubted that Cody was any more real than a child's imaginary playmate, much less as real as Janis. But, "I follow your logic," he said cautiously. Then, recklessly, he added, "I'm ashamed of myself for saying just now to let Armentrout do it again. I can't bear thinking that it happened to you even once."

"I'm sure he's got something planned for you, too," she told him. "You and me and Long John Beach—we're not specimens he's going to let go of."

Cochran still hoped that he could get some rational planning done here. "This lawyer of mine—"

"This what? This *lawyer?* You think old Dr. Trousertrout hasn't got lawyers? He'll sneak some meds into your food that'll make you such a five-star skitz you'll be running around naked thinking you're Jesus or somebody, or even easier just show you a few tarot cards to do it." She glanced around, then looked back at him and noticed, and stared at, his T-shirt. "A Connecticut Pansy? Unbelievable. Unbelievable! Hell, *you* he could probably just show the *instruction* card to." She flexed her jaw and winced. "My teeth hurt. I hope I'm not gonna have a nosebleed."

One of the nurses had brought a portable stereo out and set it on the table and was now trying to get all the patients to sing along to "Puff the Magic Dragon." Plumtree was humming something different in counterpoint, and after a moment Cochran recognized it as "Row, Row, Row Your Boat." "Listen," she said suddenly, "—what we've got to do?—is escape—tonight."

Cochran was still sure that his lawyer would be able to secure his release, and very possibly Janis's too, with some routine legal maneuver; and the man might even be able to get some kind of stay-of-shock-therapy for her tonight, if Cochran could get him on the phone. He slapped the pockets of his corduroy bell-bottoms and was reassured to feel the angularity of coins.

"I'm going to call this lawyer—" he said, bracing himself to stand up.

Plumtree grabbed his upper arm with her good hand. "It won't work, we've got to escape—"

"Janis," he said irritably, "we *can't*. Have you seen the doors, the locks? How quick the security guards show up when there's trouble? Unless your Mr. Flibbertigibbet can come up with another earthquake—"

Her hand sprang away from his arm, and she was gaping at him. "Has he . . . *called* you?"

The group sing-along was already getting out of hand—Long John Beach was improvising lyrics at the top of his lungs, and the other patients were joining in with gibberish of their own, and the nurse had switched the music off and was now trying to quiet everyone—but Cochran was staring at Plumtree in bewilderment.

"Who?" he said, having to speak more loudly because of the singing and his own alarmed incomprehension. "Flibbertigibbet? No, you told me about it, how you were in that Oakland bar on October seventeenth—"

"I never did, not that *date, none* of us would!" She was shaking. "Why would we?"

"Wh—Jesus, Janis, because I told you I met my wife that day, she fell down some steps when the earthquake hit, and I caught her. What's the matter—"

"My God, not *this* way!" She blinked, and Cochran saw tears actually squirt from the inner corners of her eyes. Her pupils were tiny, hardly discernible. "Why did you mention him, you fucking idiot? I can handle locks—in the name of the Father, the Son, the Holy Ghost! Rah rah rah, you Connecticut pansy, I hope you get in his way!"

Cochran wasn't listening to her—he had scrambled to his feet, and now he reached down and pulled Plumtree up too. "Get ready to run," he told her. "I think we're going to have a riot in here."

Long John Beach and a couple of other patients had grabbed the window side of the table, lifted it, and, still singing raucously, now pushed it right over; the bowls and spoons and ice cream cartons tumbled as the colorful tablecloth flapped and billowed, and then the tabletop hit the floor with an echoing knock.

"Pirate ships would bloom with vines," the one-armed man was singing, *"When He roared out his name!"*

"Code Green!" yelled a nurse. "Hit the alarm!"

Cochran could hear a roaring now, a grinding bass note that seemed to rumble up from the floor, from the very soil under the building's cement slab foundation. He had to take a quick sideways step to keep his balance.

"Aftershock," he said breathlessly, "from the one this afternoon." He glanced at Plumtree, and took hold of her forearm, for her face was white and pinched with evident terror, and he was afraid she would just bolt. "Stay with me," he said to her loudly. The fluorescent lights on the ceiling flickered.

"Code Green, code fucking Green!" shouted the nurse, retreating toward the hallway door.

The building was shaking now, and from the nursing station and the conference room echoed the crashes of cabinets and machinery hitting the floors.

"—the magic flagon," sang Long John Beach, whirling the tablecloth like a bullfighter's cape, *"lived by the sea, and frolicked in the Attic mists in a land called Icaree!"*

And all the lights abruptly went out. Glass was breaking inside the building somewhere, beyond the waving and thrashing shapes dimly visible in the reflected moonlight in the room, but Cochran spun toward the reinforced window, yanking the unseeing Plumtree with him.

The window was glittering like the face of the sea, for silvery cracks were spreading across it like rapid frost and shining with the captured radiance of the moon—and a cloud of plaster dust curled and spun at the far corner.

"Get me Cochran and Plumtree!" came Armentrout's panicky call through the shouting, lurching bodies jamming the room. "Stun guns *and* Ativan!"

Cochran looked back toward the hall doorway. The fat, white-haired doctor was standing just inside the room, waving a flashlight in random circles that momentarily silhouetted clawed hands and tossing heads and vertical siftings of plaster dust; two men Cochran had never seen before were standing closely on either side of the doctor, with their arms around his shoulders—and of the whole chaotic, crashing scene, the one element that chilled Cochran's belly was the sight of those two blank-faced men swivelling their heads back and forth in perfect unison, and flapping their free arms in swings that were awkward and disjointed but as perfectly synchronized as the gestures of a dance team.

Cochran bent down to shout in Plumtree's ear, "Don't move, stay right where you are—we're getting out of here." And he let go of her arm and lifted one of the upholstered chairs in both hands.

The floor was still flexing and unstable but he took two running steps toward the far corner of the window, muscling the chair around him in a wide loop, and then he torqued his body hard, at the expense of keeping any balance at all, and slammed the chair with all his strength into the reinforced glass at that end.

The window *bent*, like splintering plywood, popping out of its frame at that corner.

"*One dark night it happened,*" the voice of Long John Beach roared on somewhere behind him, "*Paki Japer came no more—*"

Cochran's full-tilt follow-through had thrown him headfirst against the buckling sheet of glass, tearing it further out of its frame, and tumbled him to the gritty floor; but he scrambled to his feet and wobbled back to where Plumtree stood dimly visible in the roiling, flashlight-streaked dimness, and he pulled her toward the window. "Both of us hit the glass with our shoulders," he gasped, "and we're out of here. Keep your face turned away from it."

But a hand gripped Cochran's right hand strongly, and he was jerked around against the solid restraint of the big hard fingers clenched on his knuckles and wrist. He looked back—and whimpered aloud when he saw that there was no one anywhere near him. Then in a flicker of the flashlight beam he saw Long John Beach a dozen feet away, staring at him and hunched forward to extend his amputated stump.

Cochran tugged hard, and the sensation of clutching fingers was gone; Long John Beach recoiled backward into the crowd.

A number of the patients had lifted the table over their heads like a float in a parade, all of them singing now, and Cochran and Plumtree were able to step away from the wall and get a running start toward the bent sheet of glass.

It folded outward with a grating screech when they hit it, and then the two of them had fallen over the sill and were rolling on the cold cement pavement outside. Plumtree had hiked up her legs as she'd hit the glass, and had landed in a controlled tumble, but Cochran's knees had collided with the sill and he had jackknifed forward to smack the pavement with his outstretched hands and the side of his head, and in the moment when his legs flailed free and he was nearly standing on his head he was sure that his spine was about to snap.

But then he had fallen over and Plumtree had dragged him to his feet, and he was able to limp dizzily forward across the dark courtyard, pulling her after him; the exterior spotlights had gone out too, and Plumtree kept whispering that she couldn't see at all, but the dim shine of the half-moon was bright enough for Cochran to avoid the wooden picnic tables as he led her to the parking-lot fence, where he and Long John Beach had stood talking six hours ago.

"Grape leaves fell like rain . . ." came a wail through the broken window behind them.

The winter night air was as harsh as menthol cigarette smoke in Cochran's nose, but it cleared his head enough so that he could lift one of the picnic-table benches and prop it firmly against the spike-topped iron fence; and though he saw two of the security guards furiously pedalling their bicycles across the lot from the main hospital building, they were clearly heading for the clinic entrance, and no one shouted or shined a light at Cochran as he boosted Plumtree up the steeply slanted boards of the bench seat.

The fingers of her good hand caught the top edge, and with a fast scuffling she was at the top, and leaping; and Cochran was already scrambling up the bench when her sneakers slapped the pavement. Then he had jumped too, and though he almost sat down when he landed, he was ready to run when he straighened up.

But Plumtree caught his shoulder. "Don't be a person in a hurry," she said breathlessly. She linked her arm through his, wincing as her swollen knuckles bumped his elbow. "It's lucky we're a couple. Just be a guy out for a stroll by the madhouse with his girlfriend, right?"

"Right." With his free hand he reached back through the bars of the fence and pushed the bench away; the clatter of it hitting the cement pavement in the yard was lost in the crashing cacophony shaking out through the sprung window. "What's my girlfriend's name?" he asked as they began walking—a little hurriedly, in spite of her advice—along the tree-shadowed fence toward the lane that led out to Rosecrans Boulevard.

"I'm Janis again. Cody came back just now like somebody fired out of a cannon, so don't tell me what happened—okay?—or you'll just have Valerie on your hands. It's enough to know that you agreed about escaping, and that we've done it." She gave him a frightened smile. "Let's make like a tree, and leave."

He nodded, and though his breathing was slowing down, his heart was still knocking in his chest. "Put an egg in your shoe and beat it," he responded absently. He could see the corner of the fence ahead, and it was all he could do not to walk even faster. "I did agree, in the end."

He was remembering a pair of shoes Nina had bought for him, actually leather hiking boots. They were only about an eighth of an inch bigger than his ordinary shoes at any point, but he had constantly found himself catching the sides of them against furniture, and tripping on the tread edges when he'd go upstairs, and generally kicking things he hadn't realized were in his way; and it had occurred to him that in his ordinary old shoes, as he had routinely walked through each day, he must have been only narrowly missing collisions and entanglements with every thoughtless step.

What size shoe am I wearing now? he thought giddily. I'm not walking any differently, but lately I've collided with a man who can talk with my dead wife's voice, and who can reach out and grab you across a room with a hand he hasn't got; and I've run afoul of a doctor who wants to keep me locked up in a crazy ward and give electroshock treatments to a woman I . . . am growing very fond of; and *she* claims to actually be several people, one of whom doesn't like me and another of whom is reportedly a man, who can—

He took a shuddering breath and clasped her arm tighter, for he was afraid he might fling it away and just run from her.

—who apparently can, he went on, finishing the thought, call up actual earthquakes at will.

Maybe I'm not wearing any shoes at all now, he thought, in that manner of speaking. It's mostly barefoot people that break their toes.

"You've . . . seen this stuff too, right?" he said softly. "Ghosts? And—" She didn't want to hear about the earthquake right now. "—supernatural stuff?" He had spoken haltingly, embarrassed to be talking about the very coin of madness; but he needed to know that he really did have a companion in this scary new world.

"Don't make me lose time here, Scant."

"Sorry." Her abrupt reply had brought heat to his face, and he tried to keep any tone of hurt out of his voice. "Never mind." Don't be *disturbing* her, he told himself bitterly, with talk of something distasteful that might be *important* to you, like your mere *sanity*.

"I'm sorry, Scant," she said instantly, hugging his arm and leaning her head on his shoulder, "I was afraid you'd say something more— something specific!—that would drive me away from you here. You and I can't have misunderstandings between us! Yes—I've seen this stuff too, undeniably. Sometimes it's hard for me to tell, because even normal things . . . *change*, if I take my eyes off them. I never cross the street on the green light, because an hour—a week!—might have gone by between the moment I saw the WALK sign flash and the moment I step off the curb; I always cross with people, almost hanging on to their coats. When I was twelve, my mother took me to her sister's funeral, and halfway through the ceremony I found out that it was her *mother's* funeral, and I was *fourteen!* I think if she hadn't ever brought me to another funeral at that same cemetery, so I could recognize it, I wouldn't have found my way back at all, ever, to this day!"

She laughed helplessly. "But I've seen ghosts, too, sure. I *attract* them, they come to me crying, often as not, telling me they're lost and want help finding their mothers, these transparent little . . . *cellophane bags,* like cigarette-pack wrappers! Or they're . . . feeling romantic, and whisper nasty things in my ear, as if they could *do* anything about it. But they can't grab me, I always just lose time. And Cody and Valerie have different birthdates from me, so each of us that comes up is a fresh picture, and the ghosts slide off, can't get a grip." He felt her shudder through his arm. "I think they'd hurt me, I think they'd *kill* me, if they *could* get a grip."

Cochran kissed the top of her head. "Why are they attracted to you?"

"Because I have 'wide unclasped the table of my thoughts.' Don't ask me about that," she added hastily, "or you'll be kissing Valerie's head." She smacked her lips. "I wish I'd brought my mouthwash."

They had rounded the fence corner now, and they were walking on a sidewalk under bright streetlights. Cars were driving by, and he could see the traffic signal for Rosecrans Boulevard only a hundred yards ahead of them.

"I think I could call my lawyer now," he said, "when we find a Denny's, somewhere we can sit down and they have a pay phone. I've got change for the call, and I think I can slant the story a little to make sure he'll wire us money and then legally get us out of Armentrout's control.''

''A Denny's would be nice,'' Plumtree agreed, ''I've got a twenty in my shoe, and Ra only knows when I last ate. But we don't need your lawyer—Cody can get us money and a place to stay, and we've got . . . things to do, locally, people to see.''

Cochran could imagine nothing now but getting back to his house in South Daly City up in San Mateo County as quickly as possible. ''People?'' he said doubtfully. ''What, family?''

''No. I'll tell you when we've got drinks in front of us. Don't most Denny's serve liquor?''

''I don't know,'' Cochran said, suddenly very happy with the idea of a shot of lukewarm Wild Turkey and an icy Coors for a chaser. ''But most bars sell food.''

CHAPTER 6

"Tell me how long it takes to prepare the earthquake?"

"A long time, I suppose."

"But when it is ready, it takes place, and grinds to pieces everything before it. In the meantime, it is always preparing, though it is not seen or heard. That is your consolation. Keep it."

—Charles Dickens,
A Tale of Two Cities

Do you know about 'making amends'?'' Plumtree asked as she led him across a dark parking lot in the direction of the white-glowing façade of a fast-food ice-cream place called the Frost Giant. Cochran thought she sounded a little uneasy.

"I suppose," he said, trudging along beside her and wondering when they would get their drinks and talk. The night air was chilly, and he wished he'd been wearing a jacket when they had escaped from the mental hospital, and he wanted to get someone in San Mateo County to wire him some money tonight, or at least use a credit-card number to get him a motel room. That should be feasible somehow. "Restitution," he said. "Taking the blame, if you deserve it; paying back people you've cheated, and admitting you were the villain, and apologizing." He smiled. "Why, did that guy in the 7-Eleven give you too much change?" They hadn't bought anything at the convenience store three blocks back, but Plumtree had cajoled the clerk into giving her seventeen one-dollar bills and a double fistful of assorted coins in exchange for the crumpled twenty-dollar-bill that had been in her shoe. When they had got outside, she had made Cochran give her four quarters from his pants pocket.

"No. The thing is, making amends is . . . good for your soul, right?"

He shrugged. "Sure."

"But before you can *do* it, you've got to cheat somebody."

"I—" He laughed as he exhaled. "I guess. If you want the sacrament of Confession, you do have to have some sins."

"Whatever." She gave him a blank, tired look in the white glow. "Don't speak, here, okay? Do you know any foreign languages, besides plain old Mexican?"

"Oui, mademoiselle—je parle Français, un peu."

"That's French, right? Cool, you be a Frenchman. They'll figure you don't know what your stupid shirt says."

She pulled open the glass door of the Frost Giant, and a puff of warm, vanilla-scented air ruffled Cochran's hair.

There was only one customer in the brightly lit restaurant, a woman in a Raiders sweatshirt in a booth by the far window. Plumtree scurried to the counter, and she was laughing with evident embarrassment as she dumped her pile of bills and change onto the white formica.

"Could you do me a *big* favor?" she asked the teenage boy who was the cashier. "My friend paid me back twenty dollars he owed me, but he doesn't understand about American money—I can't fit all this in my pockets! Could you *possibly* give me one twenty-dollar bill for all this?"

"I—don't think so, lady." The young cashier smiled nervously. "Why don't you get rid of some of it by buying some ice cream?"

A muted crack sounded from the far booth, and the woman in the sweatshirt said, "Shit. You got any spoons that are any damn good?"

Plumtree gave the young man a sympathetic smile as he fetched another white plastic spoon from under the counter and walked around to give it to the woman.

"I understand," Plumtree said when he was back behind the counter, "and we can come back tomorrow and buy some. But my friend here doesn't speak any English at all, and he thinks all Americans are stupid—especially me. I told him I could get this money changed into one bill, and if you don't do it, he'll call me a, a *haricot vert* again. That means damn fool. You can tell he's thinking it already, look at him." She waved at Cochran. *"Momentito, Pierre!"*

"Ce n'était pas ma faute," said Cochran awkwardly. *"Cet imbecile m'est rentre dedans."* It was a bit he remembered from the Berlitz book: *It wasn't my fault, this imbecile crashed into me.*

The name badge on the cashier's shirt read KAREN, and Cochran, perceiving him as a fellow-victim of ludicrous men's wear, sympathetically wondered when the boy would notice that he had put on the wrong badge. "Well," said the young man, "I guess it'd be okay. We could use the ones, I guess."

"Oh, thanks so much," said Plumtree, helpfully spreading the bills out on the counter for him to count.

The young cashier opened the register drawer and handed her a twenty-dollar bill, his eyes on the ones and the change.

"What are you giving me this for?" asked Plumtree instantly.

The bill in her outstretched hand was a one-dollar bill.

The young man stared at it in evident confusion. "Is that what I just gave you?"

"Yeah. I wanted a *twenty*. You must have had a one in your twenty drawer."

"I . . . don't think that's what I just gave you."

"You're gonna take all my money and just give me a dollar?" wailed Plumtree in unhappy protest.

The woman in the Raiders sweatshirt broke her spoon again. "Hey, shithead!" she yelled. "You'd think with all the money you make cheatin' folks, you could afford decent spoons!"

After a tense pause, the young man took back the dollar and pulled a twenty out of the drawer. He stared at it hard for a moment before looking up.

"I really hope," he said quietly as he handed the twenty to her, "we're not twenty short at cashout. You seemed nice."

Cochran's teeth were clenched, and he could feel his face heating up. This was abominable. He knew he should make Plumtree give back the other twenty-dollar bill, the one she had palmed, but all he could think of was getting *out* of this place. "Uhh," he said, feeling a drop of sweat run down his ribs. "*Merde.*"

"I'll come back tomorrow and make sure," said Plumtree, pocketing the fresh twenty and hurrying away from the counter. She took Cochran's elbow and turned him toward the door. "Thanks again!"

Cochran was dully amazed that she could maintain her cheery tone. When they were outside again, he tried to speak, but she shook his arm, and so he just pressed his lips together. His foolish shirt was clammy with sweat now, and he was shivering in the chilly breeze.

At last she spoke, when they had scuffled away out of the radiance of the Frost Giant. "Now we've got a clear twenty for food and drink." Her breathing was labored, and she was sagging against him, as if the conversation in the ice-cream place had exhausted her.

"The kid's right," he said tightly. "You *did* seem nice. He'll probably lose his job."

"He might lose his job," she said flatly, apparently agreeing with him. "I'll understand—I'll respect it!—if you decide you don't want anything to eat, anything that's bought with this money." She frowned at him. "Is that what you're saying?"

"No. Now that it's done—"

"I could go back." She straightened and stepped away from Cochran, though she still seemed sick and wobbly on her feet. "Do you want me to give it back to him?"

Cochran shivered, and as he shoved his cold hands into his pants pockets he wondered how energetically the police might be looking for Plumtree and himself, and how easy or difficult it might actually be to get money "wired" to him from the Bay Area at this hour. Where would he go to pick it up? Wouldn't he need a driver's license or something? And he was very hungry, and he desperately wanted the warm relaxation and comfortable perspective that a couple of shots of bourbon would bestow. "Well—no. I mean, now that it *is* done—"

"Right," she interrupted dryly. "You're just like Janis."

"I hear you're not really a security guard," he said—absently, for he had noticed a red neon sign ahead of them, on the same side of Rosecrans, that read MOUNT SABU—COCKTAILS. "I hear what you really do is burglaries."

"She just tells you every damn thing, doesn't she?"

A mirror-studded disco ball was turning under the ceiling over the dance floor in Mount Sabu, but none of the people in the bar was dancing— possibly because the stone dance floor was strewn with sand as if for a soft-shoe exhibition. Even over here on this side of the long room, by the street door, Cochran could feel grit under his shoe soles as he led Plumtree to an empty booth under a lamp in the corner. The warm air smelled of candle wax and mutton.

"Hi, Scant," Plumtree said when they had sat down. "Are we going to have a drink? What—" She paused, staring at his T-shirt. "Stand up for a minute, will you?"

He slid back out of the booth and stood up, and she started laughing.

"A Connecticut pansy in . . . King Arthur's *shorts!*" she gasped. "I love it! By Marky 'Choo-Choo' Twain, I suppose."

Cochran managed a sour grin as he sat back down, but her obviously spontaneous reaction to the shirt had shaken him. He had to ask: "Do you, uh, happen to feel like dancing?"

"Sure!" she said brightly. "Is that why we came in here?"

"No." He sighed. "No, and I don't want to dance, actually. A shot of Wild Turkey, please, and a Coors chaser," he said to the dark-haired woman who had walked up to the booth with a tray. "And . . . ?" he added, turning to Plumtree.

"A Manhattan, please," Plumtree said.

"And a couple of menus," put in Cochran.

The waitress nodded and clunked down a fresh ashtray with some slogan printed around the edge of it before striding back toward the bar, her long skirt swishing over the sandy floor. Two men in rumpled business suits were playing bar dice for the price of drinks, banging the leather cup on the wet, polished wood.

"What does Cody drink," asked Cochran, "besides vodka?"

"Budweiser." She smiled at him. "This is fun! She's letting me sit and talk to you. Usually I just get to go to the bathroom—over and over again, throwing up there sometimes, while Cody gets to sit and talk to the man, and she never has to get up and leave him at all."

"Well, she doesn't like me, you said. And," he added, still shaken by the realization, "she seemed exhausted, a few moments ago. *She* wouldn't have wanted to dance."

Plumtree nodded. "That treatment this morning hit her hard. She might appreciate a drink or two herself, before we leave here."

Cochran thought of mentioning how they would be paying for the drinks and eventual food, but decided he didn't want to break Janis's cheerful mood.

A frail electronic beeping started up, and he remembered that her watch had made a noise like that when she had been talking the 7-Eleven clerk into giving her all the ones and change for her original twenty-dollar bill. "What do you have that set for?" he asked.

"Oh, this silly thing. You have a watch, don't you? I think I'll just leave this one here. One of the doctors gave it to me—it's supposed to keep me in *now,* and not in the past . . . or future, I suppose." She had unstrapped the watch as she'd been speaking, and now held it up by one end, as if it were a dead mouse. "It's my last link with that stupid hospital. If I leave it behind, I'll bet I can leave all of their depressive-obsessive doo-dah with it. They *want* you to be sick, in hospitals. I bet I won't even have my old nightmare as much, away from that place."

In spite of himself, Cochran said, "About the sun falling out of the sky?"

"Right *onto* me, yeah." She shook her head sharply. "Filling up the sky and then punching me flat onto the sidewalk. I was in the hospital when I was two, and I guess there was no window in my room, 'cause I somehow got the idea that the sun had died. My *father* died right around that time, and I was too young to grasp what exactly had happened." She frowned at her fingernails. "I still miss him—a lot—even though I was only two when he died."

The waitress had returned, and she set their drinks down on the tablecloth and then handed Cochran and Plumtree each a leather-bound menu. "Could I borrow a pen?" Cochran asked her. When he raised his hand and made doodling motions in the air the woman smiled and handed him a Bic from her tray. Cochran just nodded his thanks as the woman turned away and strode back toward the bar.

"Prassopita," said Plumtree, reading from the menu. "Domatosoupa. This is a Greek restaurant." She took a sip of her drink and audibly swished it around in her mouth before swallowing.

"Oh." Cochran thought of Long John Beach singing *frolicked in the Attic mists . . . ,* and then remembered that Janis hadn't experienced that part of the evening. "I guess that's all right." He opened his own menu and stared at the unfamiliar names as he took a sip of the warmly vaporous bourbon. Finally he looked squarely at her. "I believe you, by the way," he began.

"We're not talking about the menu now, are we?"

"That's right, we're not. I mean I believe you about you being a genuine multiple personality." He took several long gulps of the cold beer. "*Whew!* You obviously hadn't noticed my dumb shirt before a minute ago, and Cody saw it back at the hospital; and she didn't get that it was a joke about a Mark Twain book title."

"You should believe it, it's true. I don't think Cody's much of a reader. I am—and I love books about King Arthur, though I've never been able to read *One Flew Over the Cuckoo's Nest.*" She rolled her eyes. "You're taking a whole crowd of girls out to dinner!"

Cochran decided not to ask what she thought *One Flew Over the Cuckoo's Nest* had to do with King Arthur. A slip of paper with daily specials on it was clipped to the inside of the menu, and he tugged it free and poised the pen over the blank back side of it. "Who all are you? Just so I'll . . . know what names to write on the thank-you card."

"Oh, Cody's paying for dinner, eh? I don't want to hear about it. Well, you know me and her . . . and there's Tiffany . . ." She paused while Cochran wrote it down. "And Valerie . . ." she added.

He wrote it down the way it was generally spelled, but she leaned over and tapped the paper with her finger. "It's spelled with an *O*— Val*o*rie."

Cochran smiled at the idiosyncrasy. "Like *calorie.* If you had an overeater in there, you could call her Calorie, and they could be twins."

Plumtree bared her teeth in a cheerless grin. "Valorie isn't a twin of anybody." She stared at the names on the paper. "Then there's *him.* Just write 'him,' okay? I don't like his name being out, even on paper."

As he wrote the three letters, it occurred to Cochran that this Flibbertigibbet character was probably as real as Cody and Janis . . . and might very well actually have killed a man in Oakland, a little more than five years ago.

And then he wondered about the king that Plumtree claimed to have killed ten days ago.

"That's a birthmark," Plumtree said, "not a tattoo—right?"

Cochran put down the pen and flexed his right hand, and the ivy-leaf-shaped dark patch below his knuckles rippled. "Neither one. It's . . . like a powder-burn, or a scar. Rust under the skin, I suppose, or even stump-bark dust. I was seven years old, and I got my hand between a big set of pruning shears and a stump-face. I guess I thought it was an actual, live face, and I tried to block this field worker from cutting the old man's head off."

Plumtree was frowning over the rim of her glass. "What?" she said when she'd swallowed and put it down.

Cochran smiled. "Sorry—but you obviously didn't grow up in the wine country. It's as old as 'Ladybug, ladybug, fly away home,' or the Man in the Moon. *Le Visage dans la Vigne*, Froissart called it. The Face in the Vine Stump. See, in the winter, when it's time to prune back the grape vines, sometimes the lumpy budwells in the bowl of an old head-trained vine look like an old man's face—forehead, cheekbones, nose, chin. People used to be real superstitious about it, like in France in the Middle Ages—they'd uproot the one that looked most like a real face, and take it out on a mountaintop somewhere and burn it. In the middle of winter, so spring would come. The old man had to die." Throw out the suicide king, he thought.

" 'As long as you do not die and live again, you are a stranger to the dark earth,' " Plumtree said, obviously quoting something. "Don't ask me what that's from, I don't even know which of us read it. Have you ever thought of having the mark removed? Doctors could do that now, I bet."

"No," said Cochran, making a fist of the hand to show the mark more clearly, "I'm kind of proud of it, actually—it's my winemaker's merit badge, an honorable battle scar."

Plumtree smiled and shook her head. "I think I'll get this Arni Kapama thing, if I can chew it."

Cochran looked at the menu. "Lamb cooked with sugar and cinnamon? Yuck. I guess I'll go with the Moskhari Psito. At least that's beef, according to this. I wish they had plain old cheeseburgers."

"Well, yeah. We don't have all night. Are you still set on calling *your* lawyer? What is it you'd be wanting him to *do?*"

The waitress came back then, and they placed their orders; Cochran ordered another bourbon and beer chaser, too, and Plumtree ordered another Manhattan.

"I'd want the lawyer," he said when the woman had gone sweeping away, "to . . . *wire me some money* . . . so that I could get back home. And I"—he looked straight into her tiny-pupiled eyes—"I hope you'd be willing to come with me, Janis. The lawyer would be able to work for you better if you were up there, and you'd be that much farther away from Armentrout."

Plumtree sang, *"I'll take you home again, Kathleen . . ."* and then sighed. "What's the hurry? About you getting back home?"

Cochran blinked at her. "Isn't that song about a girl who's going to die?"

"I forget. So what is the hurry?"

Cochran spread his hands. "Oh . . . a paycheck."

"What's the work, in January, in a vineyard?"

He barked out two syllables of a laugh, and flexed his right hand again. "Well—pruning. It's winter. Get our guys to cut each vine back to two canes, with two buds per cane, and save what they call a goat-spur, a water-sprout relacement spur, closer to the stump for fruit a year or two from now—and then drive around to the vineyards we buy off-premises grapes from, and see how they're pruning their vines. If they're leaving three or four canes, and a lot of buds, for a water-fat cash crop, I'll make a note not to buy from them come harvest." He looked at the gray ivy-leaf mark on the back of his otherwise unscarred hand, and he remembered the vivid shock-hallucination that had accompanied the childhood injury, and it occurred to him that he didn't want to be there for the pruning—not this year. *Grape leaves fell like rain . . .* "Why, what's on your agenda?"

Plumtree eyed her cola-colored drink as the electric light over their heads flickered, and then she waved at the waitress. "Could I get a Budweiser here?" she called. "Two Budweisers, that is?"

Cochran heard no reply, just the continuing thump and rattle of the bar dice.

After a few moments he spoke. "Janis mentioned that you might want a couple of drinks," he said, levelly enough. He was annoyed to see that his hand trembled as he lifted his beer glass. He made himself look squarely at her, and the skin of his forearms tingled as he realized that he could *see* the difference, now that he knew to look for it; the mouth was wider now, the eyes narrower.

"My agenda," said Cody. "I've got a lawyer of my own to look up. His name is Strube. He'll be able to lead me to a boy who's about fifteen now, a boy-who-would-be-king, apparently, named something like Boogie-Woogie Bananas.''

Cochran raised his eyebrows as he swallowed a mouthful of beer and put his glass down. "Uhh . . . ?''

"This boy apparently knows how to restore a dead king to life. What's that you're drinking?''

"Wild Turkey and Coors.''

"Coors. Like screwing in a canoe. Oh well.'' She reached across the tablecloth and lifted his glass and drained it in one long swallow. "And two more *Coorses* too,'' she called without looking away from Cochran.

"You can afford it,'' he said.

"*Fuck you!*'' yelled a woman in the booth by the door; and for a second Cochran was so sure that she had been yelling at him that his face went cold. But now a man in the same booth was protesting in shrill, injured tones, and when Cochran looked over his shoulder he saw the blond woman who had shouted shaking her head and crying.

" 'Nuff said,'' remarked Plumtree.

If Long John Beach's crazy lyrics for "Puff the Magic Dragon'' had not still been jangling in his head, if Beach had not clasped Cochran's hand tonight with a hand that he didn't have, if the bang and rattle of the dice-players at the bar hadn't been emphasizing the fact that nobody in this bar had seemed to speak above whispers until the woman had shouted, Cochran would never have thought of what he said next; and if he hadn't downed the bourbon on a nearly empty stomach he would not have spoken it aloud; but,

"You *throw* it, don't you?'' he said wonderingly to Plumtree. "Anger. Like, it can't be created or destroyed, but it can be *shifted.*'' Over the aromas of lamb and mint and liquor, the humid air was sharp with the smell of wilted, chopped vegetation, like a macheted clearing in a jungle. "Is that part of your *dissociative* disorder, that you can stay calm by actually throwing your anger off onto somebody nearby? The lady who kept breaking her spoon in the ice-cream place, and cussing, when the kid wouldn't give you a twenty . . . and Mr. Regushi jumping up to strangle Muir yesterday, when Armentrout pissed you off.'' He was dizzy, and wished the waitress would hurry up with the beer.

"*What gives you the right—!*'' choked the blond woman by the door.

Cochran exhaled, and gave Plumtree a frail, apologetic smile. "Nothing, I guess,'' he said.

"You still got any quarters?'' asked Plumtree calmly.

Cochran squeezed his thigh under the table. "At least one.''

"Let's go make a call.''

They stood up out of the booth and crossed the sandy floor to the

pay telephone by the rest rooms in the far corner, and after Plumtree
had hoisted the white-pages telephone book up from a shelf under the
phone and flipped through the thin leaves of it, she said, "No Strube
listed. Not in L.A."

Cochran was peering over her shoulder at the STR page. "There's a
. . . 'Strubie the Clown,' " he noted. "He's listed twice, also as 'Strubie
the Children's Entertainer.' "

She nodded. "It's a good enough flop for a call. Gimme your quarter."

Cochran dug it out for her, and she thumbed it into the slot and
punched in the number. After a few seconds of standing with the receiver to her ear, she said, "It's a recording—listen."

She leaned her head back and tilted the receiver, and Cochran pressed
his chin to her cheek to hear the message with her. His heart was pounding, and he let himself lay his hand on her shoulder as if for balance.

"*. . . and I can't come to the phone right now,*" piped a merry voice
from the earpiece. "*But leave your name and number, and* Strubie *will
right back to* you *be!*" A beep followed, and Plumtree hung up the
phone and shook off Cochran's arm.

"He's, uh, not home, I guess," said Cochran to cover his embarrassment as they scuffed back to the booth. Their dinners had been
served—two plates sat on the tablecloth, the meat and vegetables piled
on them steaming with smells of garlic and lamb and onion and cinnamon, along with another Manhattan and a fresh shot glass of bourbon
and five fresh glasses of beer.

"Where *would* we be without you to figure these things out?" Plumtree said acidly as she slid into the booth.

Cochran sat down without replying, and as he began hungrily forking
up the mess of onions and tomatoes and veal on his plate he looked
around at the bar and the other patrons rather than at Plumtree. He hoped
she'd be Janis again soon; and he resolved to catch her if she got up to
go to the ladies' room.

The bartender was a woman too, and as Cochran watched she drew
a draft beer for one of the men who had been playing bar dice. The
man pulled a little cloth bag from his coat pocket and shook from it a
pile of yellow-brown powder onto the bar. The bartender scooped the
powder up with a miniature dustpan and disposed of it behind the bar.

Gold dust? wondered Cochran with the incurious detachment of being
half-drunk. Heroin or cocaine, cut with semolina flour? Either way, it
seemed like an awful lot to pay for one beer.

A black dwarf on crutches was laboriously poling his way out of the
bar now, and when he had braced the door open to swing his crutches

outside, Cochran caught a strong scent of the sea on the gusty cold draft that made the lamps flicker in the moment before the door banged shut behind the little man. And under the resumed knock and rattle of the dice he now heard a deep, slow rolling, as if a millwheel were turning in some adjoining stone building.

He became aware that his food was gone, along with the bourbon and a lot of the beer, and that Plumtree had a cigarette in her mouth and was striking a match. Cochran's cigarettes were still back at the madhouse.

When she threw the match into the ashtray it flared up in a momentary flame; an instant later there was just a wisp of smoke curling over the ashtray, and a whiff of something like bacon.

"Brandy in the ashtrays?" said Cochran, in a light tone to cover for having jumped in surprise. "What's the writing on it say? 'No smoking near this ashtray'?"

Plumtree was startled herself, and she reached out gingerly to tilt the ashtray toward her. "It says—I think it's Latin—*Roma, tibi subito motibus ibit amor*. What does that mean?"

"Lemme see." Cochran tipped the warm ashtray toward himself. "Uh . . . 'How romantic, to be . . . submitting . . . in a motor bus, having . . . a bit! . . . of love.' "

"You liar!" She actually seemed frightened by his nonsense. "It doesn't say that, does it? In a motor bus? You're such a liar."

Cochran laughed and touched her arm reassuringly. "No, I don't know what it says." He took a sip from one of the beer glasses, and to change the subject he asked, "Why did you say Coors is like screwing in a canoe?"

"Because it's fuckin' near water. *Ho ho.* Let's get out of here. Strubie the Clown ought to be home by now. I'll go copy down the address listed for him and call us a cab." She had got out of the booth and was striding away toward the telephone before he could protest.

"Strubie the goddamn *Clown* . . . ?" he muttered to himself. "It won't be the right guy, not this lawyer you want. Tonight?"

He at least managed to finish the bourbon and the beers before she got back and pulled him up onto his feet; but when she had marched him to the door and pulled it open—there was no sea scent on the breeze now—she hurried back inside so that she could speak to the blond woman who had been shouting, and who by this time was very drunk and crying quietly.

When Plumtree rejoined him and pushed him out across the Rosecrans sidewalk, she immediately began looking anxiously up and down the street. "I hope the cab gets here quick," she muttered.

"Oh hell. Me too," said Cochran, for he saw that she was now holding a purse.

Strubie the Clown's house was a little one-story 1920s bungalow off Del Amo and Avalon in the Carson area of south Los Angeles, and after the taxi dropped them off Cochran and Plumtree hurried out of the curbside streetlight's glare, up the old two-strip concrete driveway to the dark porch.

No lights seemed to be on inside the house, but Plumtree knocked on the door. Several seconds went by without any sound from inside, and Cochran blinked around at the porch.

A wooden swing hung on chains from a beam in the porch roof, and Cochran wobbled across the Astroturf carpeting and slumped into it— and instantly one of the hooks tore free of the overhead beam, and the swing's streetside corner hit the porch deck with an echoing bang.

"Christ!" hissed Plumtree; she reeled back and bumped a ceramic pot on the porch rail, and it tipped off and broke with a hollow thump and rattle on the grass below. Cochran had rolled off the pivoting and now-diagonal swing, but his arm was tangled in the slack chain, and it took him several seconds to thrash free of it. The fall had jolted him. His face was suddenly cold and damp, and his mouth was full of salty saliva; beside the front door sat a wide plastic tray heaped with sand and cat turds, and he crawled over and began vomiting into it, desperately trying to do so quietly.

"You shithead!" Plumtree gasped. "We're wrecking his place!"

Cochran was aware of the sound of a car's engine idling fast out at the curb as if it was shifted out of gear, and then the noise stopped and he heard a car door creak open and a moment later clunk shut.

"He's home," whispered Plumtree urgently. "Stop it! And get up!"

Cochran was just spitting now, and he got his feet under himself and straightened up, bracing himself on the wall planks. " 'Scuse me," he said resentfully with his face against the painted wood. " ' 'Scuse the *fuck* out o' *me.*" He pulled his shirt free of his pants and wiped his mouth on it, then turned around to lean his back against the wall.

"Who's there?" came a man's frightened voice from the front yard.

"Oh," muttered Plumtree, "I got no time for this flop." A moment later she turned toward the front steps. "Mr. Strube?" she said cheerily. "My friend and I need your help."

"Who are you?"

Cochran pushed the damp hair back from his face and peered out into the yard. The figure silhouetted against the streetlight glare wore baggy pants and a tiny, tight jacket, and great tufts of hair stood out from the sides of the head. The shoes at the ends of the short legs were as big as basketballs.

"We're people in trouble, Mr. Strube," Plumtree said. "We need to find a boy whose name sounds like . . . well, like *Boogie-Woogie Bananas*. He'll be able to help us."

"I . . . don't know anybody whose name sounds . . . even remotely like that." The clown walked hesitantly up to the porch steps, and his gaze went from Plumtree to Cochran to the broken swing. "Is he a clown? I know all the local clowns, I think—"

"No," said Plumtree. "He's . . . a king, or a contender for some kind of throne . . . it's supernatural, a supernatural thing, actually. . . ."

Strubie's bulbous rubber nose wobbled as he sniffed. "Did you two get sick here? Are you drunk? What have you done here? I'm going to have to ask you to leave. I'm in the entertainment business, and my schedule . . ."

Cochran jumped then, for suddenly a *man's* voice came grinding out of Plumtree's mouth, gravelly and hoarsely baritone: "Frank, you got a show-biz friend in the bar here!" the voice drawled amiably. "Nicky Bradshaw, his name is. Shall I tell him where you live?"

Cochran gaped at Plumtree, totally disoriented. There had been a TV star called Nicky Bradshaw—he had starred in some situation comedy in the fifties. Was this voice Flibbertigibbet talking? Cochran was pretty sure that Nicky Bradshaw had died years ago. What *bar* was Flibbertigibbet talking about?

"Bradshaw doesn't . . . blame me," said the clown quietly, "for his death."

Again the man's voice boomed out of Plumtree's throat: "Then you don't mind if I tell him where you live, right?"

The clown sighed shakily. "Don't do *anything*." He clumped up the steps to the porch, digging a set of keys out of the pocket of his baggy trousers, and he unlocked the front door. "Come inside, if you've got to talk about these things."

Plumtree followed the clown into the dark house, and after a light came on inside Cochran stepped in too, pulling the door closed behind him.

The green-carpeted living room was bare except for some white plastic chairs and a long mahogany credenza against the far wall; impressionistic sailboat prints and unskilled oil paintings of clowns hung in a cluster over it, as if Strubie had once, briefly and with limited resources, tried to brighten the empty expanses of mottled plaster walls.

Plumtree sat down in one of the plastic chairs and crossed her legs. Her jeans were tight, and it made Cochran dizzy to look at her legs and at the same time remember the voice she had just now been speaking with.

In the glare from the lamp on the credenza, the clown was hideous; the white face-paint was cracked with his anxious frown, and the orange tufts of hair glued onto the bald wig above his ears emphasized the exhausted redness of his eyes.

He didn't sit down. "Who are you?" he asked, shakily pulling off his white gloves.

"That's not important," said the man's voice from Plumtree's throat. A sardonic grin made her cheekbones and the line of her jaw seem broader, and Cochran had to remind himself that it *was* a woman's face.

Strubie cleared his throat. "Who's your friend, then?" he asked, nodding toward Cochran, who, daunted by this attention, let himself fold into one of the chairs.

"I'll tell you the truth, I don't know." Plumtree's face turned toward Cochran, and the wide-pupilled eyes squinted at him. "I gotta say I don't much like the look of him. However, he may kiss my hand, if he likes."

Cochran shook his head and licked beads of sweat off his upper lip.

Strubie took a deep breath, and then hugely startled Cochran by reaching both hands behind his ears and peeling the white scalp, with the tufts of orange hair still attached to it, forward and right off of his head. "Who is this bananas person," the clown asked wearily, "and how can he help you out of whatever trouble it is that you're in?" He tossed the white bald wig onto the wooden floor. His thinning hair was gray and tangled, and the inch of unpainted forehead below his hairline was the color of oatmeal.

The light dimmed out, then brightened.

And when Plumtree spoke, it was in a woman's voice: "Don't tell him," she said. "You didn't tell him yet, did you?" Cochran glanced at her quickly, but was unable to guess which personality was up at the moment.

"Tell who," said the clown, "what?"

"The . . . the man who was speaking through me," she said. "Valorie has blocked him, for now. Did you tell him how to find the boy?"

"No," said Strubie.

"Good. I'll go away, and you'll never hear from . . . that man, again. Or me." Cochran thought it was Cody speaking. "Tell me how to find the boy, and no harm will come to him, I promise."

Strubie laughed softly, exposing yellow teeth in the white-painted face. "I used to be a divorce lawyer," he said. "I've hurt enough children. Today I try to . . . give them some moments of joy, if only in a frail, half-assed way. It's what I can do. How do I know you're not going to go hurt this boy, or kill him? Other people have wanted to, in the past.''

Plumtree spread her hands. ''I need to find him because he can restore a dead king to life. I killed . . . or at least, the man you were just listening to, I helped *him* kill . . . a king, and I need to make it right.''

''A king,'' echoed Strubie. ''And if I tell you nothing . . . ?''

''Then I'll hang around. I'll be back tomorrow. The bad man will get it out of you one way or another, and incidentally you'll have a terrible time. Everybody will.''

''God help everybody,'' said Strubie softly.

Strubie reached under the lapel of his midget's jacket and slid out of an inner pocket a flat half-pint bottle of Four Roses whiskey; he unscrewed the cap and took a deep swig of the brown liquor; his long exhalation afterward was almost a whistle.

''The boy's name is Koot Hoomie Parganas,'' he said hoarsely. ''His parents were murdered just before Halloween in '92, because they were in the way. The Parganas boy had another person inside his head with him—you should be able to empathize!—and a lot of ruthless people *wanted* that person, wanted to *consume* it into themselves. For them to do that, incidentally, would have involved killing the boy.''

He sat down on the credenza and lowered his face into his hands. ''The last I heard of him,'' came his muffled voice, ''he was living in an apartment building in Long Beach. I don't remember the address, but it's a big old rambling three-story place on the northwest corner of Ocean and Twenty-first Place, run-down, with a dozen mailboxes out front, and he was living there with a man named Peter Sullivan and a woman named Angelica Elizalde.'' He raised his head and pried off his bulbous red nose; his real nose was textured and scored with red capillaries. ''The building used to belong to Nicholas Bradshaw, the man who played the Spooky character in the old 'Ghost of a Chance' TV show—he owned the building under the alias Solomon Shadroe—but it was quit-claimed to his common-law wife, who had some Mexican last name.''

''Valorie's got all that,'' said Plumtree. ''Do you owe this Koot Hoomie any money?''

''Owe him—?'' said Strubie, frowning. ''I don't think so. No. In fact, I got gypped out of a reward, when I led the bad people there; they were offering a reward to whoever could find Bradshaw, find the Spooky character, and I used to work for Bradshaw when he was a lawyer, after he quit being an actor, so I was able to track him down there. I never got—''

"It sounds like you made Koot Hoomie's life harder, doing that," said Plumtree. "Would you like me to take any money to him, from you, as a token of restitution?"

The clown put down his bottle and stared at her out of his red, watery eyes. "I couldn't," he said finally, stiffly, "give you more than a hundred dollars. I swear, that's the absolute—"

"I think that'll do," said Plumtree.

The clown stared at her for another few seconds, then wearily got to his feet and shuffled out of the room in his blimp shoes. Cochran could hear him bumping down an uncarpeted hall, and then a door squeaked and clicked shut.

Cochran exhaled through clenched teeth. "This is very damned wrong, Cody," he whispered. "This poor man can't afford your . . . extortion, or protection, or whatever it is. Hell, I'm sure that lady in the bar couldn't afford to lose her purse! I'm going to—first chance I get, I'm going to pay these people back—"

"Talk the virtuous talk, by all means," Plumtree interrupted. "Janis can give you tips on it. I'll make my own restitutions, like always. In the meantime, I don't need to hear *your* estimates of how much cash is *enough* to finance the resurrection of a dead king." Her lip curled in a smile. "No offense, pansy."

Cochran shook his head. "Janis is right about you. Did you know she escaped to save your life?"

"Well sure. She needs me a whole lot more than I need her."

The door down the hall creaked open again, and the clown soon reappeared with a sheaf of crumpled bills in his hand.

"I'm paying not to see you people again," he said.

"We'll see you get your money's worth," Plumtree told him, standing up and taking the bills. She even counted them—Cochran could see that it wasn't all twenties, that there were at least a couple of fives in the handful.

Strubie crouched with an effortful grunt, and picked the latex bald wig up off the green carpet; and when he had straightened up again he tugged it back over his hair, and retrieved the rubber nose from where he had set it down on the credenza and planted it firmly on his face again. "You've stirred old ghosts tonight," he said hoarsely. "I'll sleep in my full mask."

"Let's for Christ's sake go," said Cochran, struggling back up onto his feet.

Plumtree pushed the bills into the newly acquired purse and strode to the door.

When she and Cochran had stepped out onto the devastated dark porch, and then made their unsteady way down the driveway to the halo of streetlight radiance at the curb, Cochran squinted back at the house: and in spite of everything that had gone before he jumped in surprise to see five—or was it six?—thin little girls in tattered white dresses perched like sickly cockatoos on the street edge of the roof, their skinny arms clasped around their raised knees. They seemed to be staring toward Plumtree and him, but they didn't nod or wave.

"Look at me!" said Plumtree in an urgent whisper. When Cochran had jerked his head around toward her, she went on, "Don't look them in the eyes, you idiot. You want to be bringing a bunch of dead *kids* along with us? And *you're* not even *masked!* You'd just flop down dead, right here. Those are Strubie's concerns, whoever they might once have been, not ours."

Cochran's head was ringing in incredulous protest, but he didn't look back at the girls on the roof.

Plumtree had started scuffling along the street in the direction of the gas-station and liquor-store lights of Bellflower Boulevard, and he followed, shivering and pushing his hands into the pockets of his corduroy pants.

Cochran forced himself to forget about the ragged little girls and to focus on Plumtree and himself. "We've got plenty enough money for a motel," he said. "To sleep in," he added.

"Maybe it's a motel we'll wind up at tonight," Plumtree allowed, "but it'll be in Long Beach, I think. We need to find another cab."

Cochran sighed, but broadened his stride to keep up with her. Perhaps because of Long John Beach's upsettingly wrong lyrics to "Puff the Magic Dragon," misunderstood rock lyrics were now spinning through Cochran's head, and it was all he could do not to sing out loud,

> *Had a gold haddock,*
> *Seemed the thing to do,*
> *Let that be a lesson,*
> *Get a cockatoo,*
> *Wooly bully . . .*

Plumtree called for a taxi from a pay phone at an all-night Texaco station on Atlantic, and when the yellow sedan rocked and squeaked into the shadowed area of the lot where the phone was, out by the air and water hoses, Cochran and Plumtree shuffled across the asphalt and climbed into the back seat. The driver had shifted into neutral when he had stopped, but even so the car's engine was laboring, and it stalled as Plumtree was pulling the door closed; the driver switched off the lights, cranked at the starter until the engine roared into tortured life again, and then snapped the lights back on and clanked it into gear and pulled out onto the boulevard before either of his passengers had even spoken.

"Long Beach," said Plumtree flatly. "Ocean and Twenty-first Place." She was gingerly rubbing the corners of her jaw with both hands.

"It'll be costly," observed the driver in a cheerful voice. Cochran saw that the man had a full, curly beard. "That's a lo-o-ong way."

"She can afford it," muttered Cochran, feeling quarrelsome. He was breathing deeply; the interior of the car smelled strongly of roses, and he was afraid he might get sick again.

"Oh," laughed the driver, "I wasn't doubting your reserves. I was doubting mine." The man's voice was oddly hoarse and blurred, and over the reek of roses Cochran caught a whiff of the wet-streets-and-iodine smell of very dry red wine. Their driver was apparently drunk.

"What," Cochran asked irritably, "are you low on gas?"

"What gas would that *be?*" the man asked in a rhetorical, philosophical tone. "Hydrogen, methane? Not nitrous oxide, at least. An alternative fuel? But this is an electric car—I'm running on a sort of induction coil, here."

"Swell," said Cochran. He looked at Plumtree, who was sitting directly behind the driver, but she was holding a paper napkin to her nose and staring out the window. She's missing some scope for her sarcasm here, Cochran thought. "You *can* find Long Beach, though, right?"

"Easy as falling off a log, believe me."

Plumtree was still sitting up rigidly on the seat and staring out at the dark palm trees and apartment buildings as if desperate to memorize the route, and Cochran slumped back in the seat and closed his eyes. The tires were thumping in an irregular drumming tempo, and he muttered sleepily, "Your tires are low on air."

The driver laughed. "These are experimental tires, India rubber. Hard with hard vacuum. Has to be a very hard vacuum, or I'd combust."

The driver's nonsense reminded Cochran of Long John Beach's remark this afternoon: *Her bed is India; there she lies, a pearl.* Cochran frowned without opening his eyes, and didn't make any further comments. In seconds he had fallen asleep.

CHAPTER 7

*"My credentials, entries, and memoranda, are all comprehended in the one
line, 'Recalled to Life;' "* . . .

—Charles Dickens,
A Tale of Two Cities

Dogs were howling out in the alleys and dark yards of Long Beach,
and unless the ringing air was particularly distorted—which Koot
Hoomie reflected that it might very well be—they were howling out on
the beach sand too, possibly mistaking the electric glow of the *Queen
Mary*'s million lights across the harbor for the moon, or a close-passing
comet.

Kootie stepped out onto the front porch and pulled the door closed
behind him. Or, he thought as the night breeze swept the echoes of
amplified wailing around from the parking-lot side of the old apartment
building, maybe the dogs are tired of our music. The tenants in the
neighboring complexes would probably have come to complain about
it a week ago if they could locate the source.

For ten days now, all day and all night, there had been some person
or other dancing in the Solville parking lot; Elizalde's clients had spontaneously conceived and taken on the eccentric task, and many of them
had missed work to do their individual four-hour shifts, each successive
businessman or tattooed *cholo* or portly matron dutifully hopping and
scuffing to the music banging out of the portable stereo that was connected by extension cords to an outlet in the kitchen. On Sunday and
Monday of last week it had been a randomly eclectic sequence of sixties
rock, mariachi, rap, and Country-Western musics, but by this last weekend they had somehow found and settled on one song—a hoarse, hag-
gardly persevering thing called either "Lay Down" or "Candles in the
Wind," by Melanie, recorded more than a decade before Kootie had

been born—and Arky Mavranos had dubbed a cassette of nothing but that song, repeated over and over again, for the dancers to play endlessly.

And his foster dad and Arky Mavranos had located and busted open an old fireplace behind the drywall in the bathroom down the hall from the office, and had climbed up on the roof and knocked the layers of tar paper off the obscured chimney, and so a fire of pine and oak logs had been kept continuously burning. There were enough people in residence to keep the fire tended, but Mavranos had in recent days begun to complain about having to drive all over town for more wood, and Kootie was afraid he would soon insist that they cut down one of the shady old carob trees around the parking lot.

Ten days so far on this deathwatch, and not even a whiff of decomposition yet. Kootie wondered if they would be able to keep on maintaining all these observances even until the weekend.

Kootie sighed, staring out at the dark rooftops.

And whenever the old king *did* begin to show some sign of decay, and could thus be formally acknowledged as dead, Kootie would apparently . . . be the next king. His poor naive dead parents had raised him to be some kind of Indian holy man, the new Krishnamurti, the *jagadguru,* and that discipline had been close enough to what was required here, what with all the well-remembered fasts and the meditations and the sacramental meal of smoked salmon and whitefish at Canter's Jewish delicatessen on Fairfax, one Friday in 1988—and he was a virgin, physically, and he had the perpetually bleeding wound in his side.

That was why Arky Mavranos and Diana were here—to transfer the mantle, to pronounce *Le Roi c'est mort, vive le Roi.*

These recent mornings—in the sunny cool-breeze moments between waking and getting out of bed, when he seemed to thrill to the vertiginous flights of crows all over the L.A. basin, and flex with the powerful iron tides roaring along the San Diego and Harbor and Pomona freeways, and be able to just tap his feet in rhythm with the heartbeat of the continent—he found himself very much wanting this job the people in the red truck had brought for him; it was only after the sun had gone down over the smokestacks of the *Queen Mary* a quarter mile away across the harbor that he seemed to catch the tang of fresh blood and stale beer on the taste buds of the broken asphalt, and cramp with the hopeless hunger and unknown withdrawals in the mazes of cracked plaster and parking garages and electric rainbows in glass on street corners, and shiver with the grinding of fast, shallow panting, or of some subterranean *gnawing,* that invisibly agitated all the pavements.

Kootie would soon have to either accept it, or refuse it; and he couldn't get rid of the thought that he would be accruing some debt either way—that a consequence, a price, would be demanded of him at some future time.

Tonight he just wanted to be Kootie, the fourteen-year-old boy who lived in Long Beach and studied astronomy and went in-line skating down the sidewalks of Bluff Park in the afternoons.

He leaned back against the clapboard wall and closed his eyes, and he cautiously let his attention expand just to include the building here. Most strongly he felt the presence of Scott Crane, the still-undecaying dead man in the kitchen, robed in white now and laid out across a dining-room table, with the sawed-short spear segment standing up from his shut-down, pulseless throat; but Kootie was also aware of his foster mom Angelica and the pregnant, bald-headed Diana lady fussing over the big pot of bouillabaisse on the stove near the dead man's bearded head, and of his foster dad Pete crouching by the television set in the long office room, talking to Diana's two sons, Scat and Oliver; and of Johanna, who owned the buildings that were Solville, sitting out on the back steps drinking Tecate beer and eating homemade enchiladas with the girlfriend of the teenage boy who was currently keeping the dance going.

Now Pete had straightened up and was looking for Kootie—but it was probably just to ask about the pans full of bean sprouts, and Kootie didn't bother to open his eyes or step away from the shadowed wall. After Angelica had been convinced that these uninvited houseguests had to stay, and that in some vague but compelling way they needed and merited Kootie's cooperation, she had done some research into their problem and come up with, among other troublesome measures, her "Gardens of Adonis"—five shallow aluminum pans with half an inch of damp dirt and a handful of beans in each of them; the things had sprouted and quickly died again and had to be re-sown twice already, and Kootie knew that Pete was of the opinion that this third crop had about had it too. Let this lot go one more day, Dad, Kootie wearily thought now.

But Pete had leaned out the back door and spoken to Johanna, and had walked back through the office and was now striding up the hall toward the front door.

Kootie stepped away from the wall and opened the door just as Pete was reaching for the inside knob.

Kootie smiled. "Let 'em go till tomorrow, Dad."

"You're talking about those beans, aren't you?" said Pete Sullivan impatiently. "To hell with the beans. We've got a line on the TV."

"Oh. Okay." Kootie followed his foster father back into the hall, and made sure to slide the feather-hung security chain into the slot on the inside of the door.

The hallway, and the office when they walked in there and stood beside the television set, smelled strongly of burnt coffee again. The smell had been untraceably hanging around the whole place for the last ten days, generally stronger at night, even with all the windows open and people cooking for a crowd and smoking and often not having bathed; Arky Mavranos had only joined in the general puzzled shrug when people remarked on the odor, but privately he told Kootie that when Scott Crane's first wife, Susan, had died of a heart attack in 1990, she'd been drinking a cup of coffee, and it was unfinished and still hot after the paramedics had taken her body away—and that Crane, unable to bear the thought of it too eventually cooling off, had put the cup in his oven over the lowest heat setting, and that it had baked dry in there, apparently filling the house with the burned smell. After a while, Arky had said, a crippled and malevolent facet of the wine god Dionysus had come to Crane in the apparition of Susan's ghost, incongruously heralded by the hot coffee reek. All this had apparently happened before Crane had become . . . *king of the west* . . . on Holy Saturday of 1990.

Tonight the coffee smell had a sharper edge to it, like hot, vapory Kahlua.

Kootie ignored the smell for now, and stared at the television on the desk. For the past ten days the set had been left on, with the brightness control turned down far enough to dim the screen to black. Now, though, a steady horizontal white streak bisected the black screen.

"Well," Kootie said slowly, "it's a ghost, somewhere nearby. According to Sol Shadroe, the guy that used to own this place, disembodied personalities are an electromagnetic commotion in the fifty-five-megahertz range—which is roughly the frequency of Channel Two, which this set is tuned to." He breathed a shallow, hitching sigh and ran his fingers through his hair, then glanced nervously at the bookshelves on the back wall, where the weather-beaten stuffed-toy pig sat on the top shelf. "Has the line got brighter since you first saw it?"

"Yes," said Diana's son Scat, who was Kootie's age, and who liked to sit in front of the TV even though the screen was generally blank. "Uh . . . twice as bright already, in this minute or so since it first showed up."

"Then it's getting closer."

Diana's first son, Oliver, was a year older than the other two boys, but the eyes in his tanned face were wet as he looked up at Kootie. "Our dad," he said, "our stepfather, I mean, he took all the ghosts with him, when somebody . . . killed him. The ghosts are *gone*." He said it proudly, as though Scott Crane had gone down under an on-slaught of ghosts, and only after heroically decimating their ranks.

"The local ones, yeah," Kootie agreed gently, "whatever 'local' means, exactly, in this business." He sighed, and went on, almost to himself, "It's hard to judge their distance, just from their apparent brightness here, like trying to figure the absolute magnitude of stars. This here ghost could be one that was insulated—clathrated—when the king died, or it could be a visitor from outside the local area. Or of course it could be the ghost of somebody that died in this week-and-a-half *since*."

For several moments no one spoke, and the only noise in the room was the steady plink and splash of water from the leaking ceiling falling into the pots and buckets around the couch, though it was not raining outside. Then Kootie heard a clatter and footsteps from the kitchen, and at the same instant a loud, mechanical burping started up behind and above him. He looked toward the kitchen doorway, though he did dart a glance down at Oliver, who was crouched on the floor, and say, "That's the pig, right?"

"The toy one on the shelf," said Oliver steadily, "right. Burping."

"There's an old man out front," snapped Angelica, wiping her hands on a kitchen towel. "He's caught in the pyrocantha bushes." She glared across the office at the bookshelf. "Of course this would be when the pig decides to put in its two cents' worth."

"Two cents' worth . . ." echoed Kootie, catching an urgent thought from outside the building's walls; then it was gone. "Get Arky Mavranos, will you, Oliver?"

"Right." Oliver straightened up lithely and sprinted out toward the back parking lot.

Diana, the pregnant wife of the dead man in the kitchen, said, "Is this a ghost, out front?"

She was standing beside Angelica; Kootie was getting used to her appearance—all the hair on her scalp had fallen out during the first night the dead king's company had spent in Solville, the first night after the king's murder. Probably her sudden baldness was an extreme re-action to grief and loss, but at times Kootie had uneasily wondered if it was instead somehow a consequence of his having asked the wrong question, when their party had driven up in the red truck ten days ago. *Why is your truck the color of blood?* he had asked, instead of *Who does it serve?* Damn all this magical minefield, he thought.

"Probably," he answered her. "Tangled in the bushes—he sounds like one of what Johanna calls the 'beasties'—the old ghosts that don't dissipate, and accumulate substance from bugs and spit and cigarette butts and stuff, and then walk around panhandling money for liquor. Snips and snails and puppydog tails. He doesn't sound like being . . . whoever it is we've been waiting for.''

"The Three Kings," said Scat. "With gold and frankincense and myrrh.''

Arky Mavranos had stepped into the office from the back yard, followed by Oliver. "And *they're* supposed to show up on Epiphany," Mavranos said gruffly, "to venerate the new king. They're five days late already." He took a sip from the can of Coors beer in his hand, leaving foam on his salt-and-pepper mustache. "You got a line on the TV and a ghost out in the bushes by the driveway, is how I hear it." He glanced disapprovingly at the stuffed pig on the bookshelf, which was still noisily retching. "Ollie, take the batteries out of that suffering beast, will you? Kootie, let's you and I go out and talk to this ghost, see if he's got any news for us."

"Do you want to bring him anything?" asked Diana, who was still holding the ladle from the pot of bouillabaisse.

"Keep a plate of rocks ready," said Kootie, "in case he hasn't had dinner yet."

Mavranos was laughing at that as he and Kootie walked down the hall to the front door; by unspoken agreement they had avoided the quicker route, through the kitchen and the presence of the dead, bearded king.

The dogs were still howling, and the breeze off the ocean was colder, when Kootie undid the chain and opened the door; and when the two of them had trudged around to the driveway, Kootie jumped back with an involuntary yelp at the sight of the old man who was thrashing in the pyrocantha bushes.

In the fragmentary yellow light from the kitchen window the old man appeared to have a lot of long insect legs or antennae waving in the air around him, as if he were a gigantic daddy-longlegs spider. Then Kootie got a clearer look at the white-bearded figure in the middle of the tangle, and he saw with relief that the waving, flexing filaments were metal, and were attached to the old man's belt.

"Shit, I *know* this guy," said Mavranos, striding forward. "And he's still wearing his silly damn curb-feelers. Easy, there, Joe," he said to the old man, "you're just making it worse. Hold still." Mavranos pulled the old man out of the bushes and began yanking the metal filaments free of the branches. Twigs and leaves spun across the driveway pavement. "This guy ain't a ghost. I don't *think*—you didn't, like, *die,* did you, Joe?"

"Fuck you," sputtered the old man, thrashing his hands against the bushes as if to help free himself. "No, I'm not dead. Are *you* dead? If you know me, then I must have found the right place, so there's a dead guy here *somewhere,* right?"

"Yeah, but inside, we don't keep him out here in the shrubbery. Where's Booger?"

The old man was panting but standing still now, letting Mavranos pull him free. "*She* died," he said harshly. "She walked out into the desert, the day after your Easter of 1990. I went after her, calling—but I'm blind, and she was mute. Somebody found her body, after a while."

"I'm truly sorry to hear that," Mavranos said. He tugged the last filament free, and now old Joe was swaying on the driveway in the middle of his cluster of bobbing antennae, like, thought Kootie, a sea urchin left here by a high tide, or a big old dandelion seed carried here by the night wind.

From the dark street at Kootie's back came a shrill whisper: "*You ask them.*"

Kootie spun toward the voice, peripherally aware that Mavranos had quickly turned that way too.

A lanky, dark-haired man in a T-shirt was shuffling up the driveway, visibly shivering in the breeze. "Excuse me," he said, "but—" His gaze fell on the old man, and he took a quick step backward. Then, after peering more closely, he exhaled hard, took another breath, and went on: "Sorry. Why not? 'Specially tonight, huh? We're—" He barked a nervous, mirthless laugh and spread his hands. "—looking for a boy named Koot Hoomie Parganas. He lived here, at one time."

A slim blond woman had sidled up behind the man, and was peering wide-eyed over his shoulder. Now she nodded.

"Kootie's living in Pittsburgh these days—" began Mavranos, but Kootie interrupted.

"I'm Koot Hoomie Parganas," he said.

Abruptly Kootie could feel the old man whom Mavranos had called Joe staring at him, and Kootie glanced sideways at him in surprise— and the old man *was* obviously blind, his eyelids horribly sunken in his dark, furrowed face—but nevertheless the old man was suddenly paying powerful attention to him.

Kootie looked back at the man and woman shivering on the driveway.

Kootie heard footsteps rapping down the steps from the kitchen door, and he sensed that it was Angelica. "*¿Tiena la máquina?*" he asked, without looking around: *Do you have the machine?*

"*Como siempre,*" came Angelica's voice coldly in reply. *As always.*

"No need for your *máquinas,*" said the blond woman, stepping out from behind her companion. Her tight jeans emphasized her long slim legs, and her flimsy white blouse was bunched up around her breasts as she hugged herself against the cold. "Sorry, I can't have been listening. Did you all say Koot Hoomie Parganas is here, or not?" She laughed, rocking on the soles of her white sneakers. "Have we even *asked* yet?"

"*I'm* him," Kootie said, irritated with himself for being distracted by her figure. "What did you want me for?"

"I—well, short form, kiddo, I need you to tell me how to find a dead king and restore him to life. Does this make any sense to you? Could we talk about it inside?"

"No," said Angelica and Mavranos in unison; but a moment later Mavranos muttered, "Restore him to *life?*"

Kootie gave the woman a quizzical smile. "Why is it *your* job," he asked quietly, "to restore this dead king to *life?*"

She tossed her head to throw her thatch of blond hair back from her face, and she stared at Kootie. "Amends," she said in a flat voice. She raised her hands, palms out, as if surrendering. "These are the hands that killed him."

Kootie's heightened senses caught not only the rustle of Angelica's hand sliding up under her blouse, but also the tiny *snick* of the .45's safety being thumbed off.

Kootie glanced sideways and caught Mavranos's eye, and nodded.

"You two don't appear to be armed," Mavranos said cheerfully, "but we are. I reckon you can all come in, but keep your hands in sight and move slow."

Plumtree didn't pull her injured hand away when Cochran gently took it, and the two of them followed the boy with the funny name across the dark lawn to the apartment building's open front door. Cochran was walking slowly and keeping his free hand open and away from his body—he had glimpsed the black grip of the automatic under the blouse of the tall, dark-haired woman who had come out of the kitchen, and he was suddenly sober, and taking deep breaths of the cold night air to keep his head clear.

We've blundered into some kind of crazy cult, he thought, and Janis—or Cody, probably—has got them mad at us. Watch for a chance to grab her and sneak out, or find a phone and call 911.

His heart was pounding, and he wondered if he might actually have to try to prevent these people from injuring Janis, or even killing her.

"How did you find this place?" called the man with the graying mustache from behind them as they stepped up to the front door and began walking up a carpeted hall. The place smelled like some third-world soup kitchen.

Cochran decided to protect poor Strubie, who had paid them the hundred dollars to keep out of this. "A psychiatrist at Rosecrans Medical Center gave us the address—" he began.

The hall opened into a long room with a couch against the near wall and a desk with a TV set on it against the opposite wall. The TV set's screen was glowing a brighter white than Cochran would have thought possible, and as the others crowded in behind him one of the two teenage boys on the couch leaped up and snatched the plug out of the wall socket.

"Thanks, Ollie," said the man who had followed them in. "The ghost that was torquing the TV is apparently the deceased wife of my old pal Spider Joe here, this old gent with the curb feelers on his belt." He now stepped to the bookshelves behind the couch and reached down a stainless-steel revolver, which he held pointed at Cochran's feet. "Everybody sit down, hm? Plenty of room on the floor, though the carpet's wet in spots. And don't move those pots, they're catching leaks."

The old man who was apparently called Spider Joe shambled across the threadbare carpet and slid down into a crouch beside the kitchen doorway, and the antennae standing out from his belt scraped the wall and knocked a calendar off a nail; and as Cochran sat down beside Plumtree in front of the desk he wondered if the ghost of the old man's wife might be snagged on one of the metal filaments. The woman with the automatic and the boy with the funny name stood beside the couch.

"Let's get acquainted," said the man holding the revolver. "My name's Archimedes Mavranos, and the lady in the kitchen is Diana, the guy beside her is Pete, and this lady with the *máquina* is Pete's wife Angelica. The boys on the couch are Scat and Ollie. Kootie you know." He raised his eyebrows politely.

Cochran had resolved to give false names, but before he could speak, Plumtree said, "I'm Janis Cordelia Plumtree, and this is Sid *Cochran.*" She pronounced his name so precisely that Cochran knew she had restrained herself from saying *Cockface* or something. For God's sake behave yourself, Cody, he thought. The long room was hot and smelled of garlic and fish and Kahlua, and he could feel sweat beading on his forehead.

Water was thumping and splashing into a saucepan by his feet, and he looked up at the mottled, dented, dripping ceiling, wondering how heavy with water the old plaster was, and whether it might fall on them. "It's, uh, not raining," he said inanely. "Outside."

"It's raining in San Jose," spoke up a heavy-set woman who had stepped up to an open door at the far side of the room. She spoke shyly, with a Spanish accent.

"Oh," said Cochran blankly. San Jose was three hundred and fifty miles to the north, up by Daly City and San Francisco. "Okay."

"And that's Johanna," said Mavranos, "our landlady. I wasn't asking how you got this address," he went on, "just now, but how you physically *got* here."

"In a taxi," said Plumtree. When Mavranos just stared at her, she added, "We were in Carson. We told the driver the address, and he . . . drove us here."

"Dropped us at the corner," put in Cochran. "He didn't want to drive up to the building."

"So much for our *protections* here," said the pregnant woman in the kitchen doorway. Cochran focussed past the bobbing antennae of Spider Joe to get a look at her, and was startled to see that she was completely bald.

"No," said Kootie, "the space is still bent, around this building. The driver must have *been* somebody." He stepped forward now, and leaned down to extend his right hand to Cochran. "Welcome to my house, Sid Cochran," he said.

Cochran shook his hand, and the boy turned to Plumtree. "Welcome to my house, Janis Cordelia Plumtree."

Plumtree gingerly reached up with her swollen right hand, and the boy clasped it firmly; but Plumtree's cry was one of surprise rather than pain.

"It doesn't hurt!" she said. She held up her right hand after the boy released it, and Cochran could see that the swelling was gone. She flexed the fingers and said, "It doesn't hurt anymore!"

Cochran made himself remember the hard *crack* of her fist hitting the linoleum floor last night, and how this evening her knuckles had just been dimples in the hot, unnaturally padded flesh of her hand. He looked from Plumtree's metacarpal bones, now visible again under the thin skin on the back of her hand as she bunched and straightened her fingers, to the face of the boy standing in front of him, and for a moment in the garlic-and-Kahlua reek the boy was taller, and the brown eyes under his curly hair seemed narrowed as if with Asian epicanthic folds, and the unregarded blur of his clothing had the loose drapery of robes. Cochran's abdomen felt hollow, and he thought, This is a Magician. A real one.

"No," said Kootie to him softly, once more just a teenage boy in blue jeans and a flannel shirt, "something different than that."

Cochran closed his own right hand, still warm from the boy's grip; and he relaxed a little, for he no longer believed that these people meant to harm him or Plumtree.

Kootie looked past him. "Ah, my dinner," he said. "I hope you all don't mind if I eat while we talk." He patted the flannel shirt over his left ribs. "I'm bleeding, and I've got to keep up my strength." He hiked himself up onto the desk and crossed his legs like a yogi. "If any of you are hungry, just holler—we've got lots."

The bald woman was carrying in a steaming, golden bowl cast in the form of a deeply concave sunfish, and the rich smell of garlic and fish broth was intensified; Angelica followed her back into the kitchen, and reappeared with a bottle of Mondavi Chardonnay and a bowl of some sauce for Kootie, while Diana brought steaming ceramic bowls for the two teenage boys who were sitting on the far end of the couch. Kootie was pouring the wine into a gold goblet that was shaped like a wide-mouthed fish standing on its tail.

Had a gold haddock, thought Cochran. "What is it?" he asked.

"Bouillabaisse," Kootie answered, stirring some orange-colored sauce into his bowl. "According to old stories, a bunch of saints named Mary—Magdalen, Mary Jacob, Mary Salome, maybe the Virgin Mary too—fled the Holy Land after the crucifixion and were shipwrecked on the French Camargue shore, at a place that's now called Les-Saintes-Maries-de-la-Mer, and the local fishermen served them pots of this. Ordinarily I just have grilled sole or tuna sandwiches or H. Salt or something, but—" He waved his spoon toward Diana and the two boys on the couch. "—it's the traditional restorative dinner for fugitive holy families."

"I heard you can't make real bouillabaisse in this country," said Plumtree. "There's some fishes that it needs that you can only get in the Mediterranean."

"Rascasse," Kootie agreed, "and conger eel, and other things, yeah. But there don't seem to be *any* kinds of loaves and fishes that can't show up in the back of Arky's old red truck after he's driven it around town."

"This lady," Mavranos broke in, waving his revolver in the direction of Plumtree without quite pointing it at her, "says she's the one who killed Scott Crane."

In the silence that followed this statement Cochran stared down at the carpet, wishing he had a glass of Kootie's wine. He could feel the shocked stares of the bald lady and the teenagers on the couch and the Mexican lady in the back doorway, and he knew they were directed at Plumtree and not at him; and he found himself thinking about the twenty dollars Plumtree had swindled from young "Karen" at the ice-cream place, and the purse she had stolen from the lady at the bar, and wishing he weren't sitting next to Plumtree here.

"Benjamin, our four-year-old," said bald Diana softly, "did say it was a woman, at first. He says it was a man that did it, but that it was a woman who walked up, and then changed into a man."

"Benjamin's my godson," said Mavranos, "but he's a . . . chip off the old block. Half of what he *sees* is more like stuff that's going on in some astral plane than stuff going on in any actual zip code. Still, he did say that. *And,*" he went on, "Miss Plumtree claims that she's come here *now* to . . . restore the king to *life.*"

"*Is that possible?*" asked Diana quickly. Cochran suddenly guessed that Diana was this Scott Crane person's widow, and in vicarious shame he kept his eyes on the carpet.

"Well, I want to listen to what she has to say," said Mavranos, "but I'm pretty sure it's not, no. Sorry. Scott's gone on to India, we established that right away—obviously there's no pulse or respiration, and there are no reflexes, and the pupils are way abnormally dilated and don't respond at all to light. And he's cold. And the spear is in his *spine.* We haven't been able to do an EEG for brain-wave activity, but the electron brush-discharge in Pete's carborundum bulb doesn't flicker when the body is wheeled past it with nobody else in the room, and the Leucadia place isn't sustained anymore, not even the rose garden—his *ashe* is completely gone. And he hasn't risen on the third day or anything."

Johanna spoke from the back doorway: "Did you try to call up his ghost?"

"Any *ghost* of him wouldn't be *him,*" Mavranos said wearily, stepping back and rubbing his eyes with his free hand, "any more than a— goddammit, an old video or tape recording, or a pile of holograph manuscript, or an old pair of his pants, would be him."

"I was possessed by the ghost of Thomas Alva Edison for a week in '92," said Kootie, looking up from his golden bowl, "and that ghost was as lively as they come; and I have some understanding now of what the king is . . . what he does, what he monitors. And I've got to say that even *Edison's* ghost wouldn't have had the *scope* for the job."

"Jesus, lady," Mavranos burst out, "if you *are* the one that killed him, how did you *get* to him? He was castled!"

"A knight's move," said Plumtree flatly. "I'm not the same person, necessarily, from moment to moment, so I can't be psychically tracked if I don't want to be. And I approached from around below the grounds, from the beach, with the whole half-globe of the Pacific's untamed water at my back. And I used a spear that was already inside his defenses— I was told that he had injured himself with it, once before—and my own blood was on the spearpoints, so I was in the position of overlapping his aura." She frowned. "And I—there was something about a phone call—he was in a weakened state. And it was midwinter, the shift of one year to the next—the engine of the seasons had the clutch out, coasting." She looked up at Mavranos and shrugged. "*I*—this person talking to you now—I didn't set it up, or *do* it. *I* just . . . cooperated, went along with somebody else's plan. And I don't know who that 'somebody else' was."

"He accidentally shot himself in the ankle with a speargun, in '75," said Diana. She visibly shifted her weight from one foot to the other, as if in sympathy. "I remember it."

"So," said Mavranos, "did you have any . . . *ideas,* about how you'd go about bringing the king back to life?"

"Yes," Plumtree said. "And then I was told that Koot Hoomie Parganas could probably do it too. I came looking for him—figuring he could at least help me, somehow. See, I don't know *exactly* how I'll go *about* it."

"How did you *plan* to do it?" Mavranos asked with heavy patience. "Approximately."

"Where is the body?" Plumtree countered.

"Do you need the body, to do your trick?"

She shivered. "I hope so. But I suppose not."

"If you even reach out toward his foot," Mavranos told her, "I'll shoot you away from him, please trust me on that." He gestured toward the kitchen doorway with the revolver, which Cochran estimated was at least .38 caliber, and which appeared to be fully loaded—he could see the holed noses of four hollow-point bullets in the projecting sides of the cylinder.

"Let's adjourn to the next room," Mavranos said.

Cochran stood up when Plumtree did, and followed her into the fluorescent-lit kitchen.

The white-robed body of a powerfully built, dark-bearded man was lying on a long dining-room table in there. A three-inch metal rod stood up out of his beard above his throat.

"Shit!" exclaimed Cochran. "Is this *him,* is this guy *dead?*" His mouth was dry and his heart was suddenly pounding. Forgetting Mavranos's threat to Plumtree, he stepped forward and touched the figure's bared forearm—the flesh was impossibly cold, as cold as an ice pack, and he stepped back quickly. "You can't keep a dead guy in here. Have you called the police? Jesus! Are you all—"

Angelica had walked up to him, and now put her hands on his shoulders and pushed down hard. His knees buckled, and he sat down abruptly on a chair that Diana had slid behind him a moment before.

"He is dead," Angelica said to him clearly. "The only symptoms he doesn't show are livor mortis, which is the discoloration caused by blood settling in the lowest areas of the body, and any evidence of decomposition. These *may* be signs that your girl *can* do something. Take a deep breath and let it out—would you like a drink?"

"No! I mean—hell yes."

Cochran heard a clink behind him, and then Diana was pressing a glass of amber liquid into his shaking hand. It proved to be brandy.

"*Do* something?" he said breathlessly after he'd drunk most of it and helplessly splashed the rest onto the front of his T-shirt. "What you can *do* is call the—the coroner. All this supernatural talk is just—entertaining as hell, but it's all *crap,* you've got—"

"This is *all* supernatural," said Pete Sullivan loudly, overriding him. "From this undecaying body here all the way down to the TV in the other room. It's all real, independent of whether you believe it or not."

Pete smiled tiredly and went on in a quieter voice. "Hell, we had a—a piece of string!—here, that an old man in Mexico gave to Angelica; it couldn't be severed. Just ordinary cotton string, and you could have cut it or burned it in two with a match, or just pulled it apart in your hands—if you could have got *around* to it! But somehow every time you'd try, something would interrupt—the phone would ring, or you'd cut yourself with the scissors and have to go get a Band-Aid, or the cat would start to throw up on some important papers, or you'd accidentally drop the string down behind the couch. I suppose if you really cornered it and forced it, you'd find that you'd suffered a stroke or a heart attack, or got knocked down by a random bullet through the window—and the piece of string would be on the floor somewhere, still whole." He shook his head. "None of these things make logical sense, but they're true *anyway.* If you insist on the world being *logical* at every turn, you'll eventually be forced to retreat all the way into genuine insanity, I promise you."

"Bring *me* the goddamn piece of string," said Cochran loudly. "I'll break the son-of-a-bitch for you!"

Angelica stood back and crossed her arms. "We lost it."

After a tense moment Cochran let his shoulders slump; he sighed and rubbed his face with both hands. "I suppose he's really a king, too. What's he king *of,* what *was* he king of?"

"The land, for one thing," said Kootie, who had followed them into the kitchen, "the American West. If he's well, the land is well—right now he's dead, and we're in winter and having earthquakes all over. God knows what the spring will be like, or if there'll even be one."

Cochran raised his head and stared at the dead man's strong, bearded face. It was pale, and the eyes were closed, but Cochran could see humor and sternness in the lines around the eyes and down the cheeks. "How could *he* have been . . . in 'a weakened state'?" he asked softly.

Mavranos was frowning, and he passed the revolver from his right hand to his left and back again; Cochran could hear the bullets rattle faintly in the chambers. "We didn't know how. He and Diana were having healthy babies—though this last couple of years the kids were getting bad fevers in the winter—and the land was yielding several crops a year! But there were signs—the phylloxera—"

"The phylloxera had nothing to do with anything," snapped Diana angrily from behind Cochran.

"Okay," Mavranos said. "Then I haven't got a clue."

"What the hell's a phylloxera?" asked Plumtree.

"It's not important," Diana said. "Don't talk about it."

Cochran said nothing—but he knew what phylloxera was. It was a plant louse that in the 1830s had inadvertently been brought from America to Europe, where it had eventually nearly wiped out all the vineyards—the fabulous old growths in Germany, and Italy, and even France, even Bordeaux. The louse injected a toxin that killed the roots, six feet under, so that the vine and the grapes up on the surface withered away and died; the eventual desperate cure had been to graft the classic old European *vitis vinifera* grapevines, everything from Pinot Noir and Riesling to Malvasia and the Spanish Pedro Ximenez, onto phylloxera-resistant *vitis riparia* roots from America. But now, just since about 1990, a new breed of phylloxera had been devastating the California vineyards, which were mostly grown on a modern hybrid rootstock known as A×R#1. Most of Pace Vineyards' vines were old Zinfandel and Pinot Noir on pre-war *riparia* rootstocks, so the subterranean plague hadn't hit them, but Cochran knew personally a number of winemakers in San Mateo and Santa Clara and Alameda Counties who were facing bankruptcy because of the expense of tearing out the infested A×R#1 vines and replanting with new vines, which wouldn't produce a commercial crop for three to five years.

He thought of what Kootie had said—*If he's well, the land is well.* And he thought of the billions of minute phylloxera lice, busily working away . . . *six feet under.* The land, Cochran thought, has not been truly well for several years.

"And he was always . . . less powerful, in winter," Mavranos said, shrugging, "and stronger in summer. One of the tarot cards that represents him is *Il Sole,* the Sun card."

"This really is Solville," said Angelica quietly, "while he's here."

Kootie pointed at the withered bean sprouts in Angelica's Gardens of Adonis pans on the counter by the door. "Solville in eclipse," he said.

"Not runnin' a carny peep-show here," said Mavranos gruffly. "Back into the office, now."

"Wait a minute," mumbled old Spider Joe, who had been peering in blindly through the doorway. "I've got to . . . put in my two cents' worth." He pushed his way into the kitchen now, his projecting curb-feelers dragging noisily through the doorframe and then twanging free to wave and bob over the dead man's bare feet. One of the metal filaments whipped across Plumtree's cheek, and she whispered "Shit, dude!" and batted it away.

The white-bearded old blind man dug two silver-dollar-size coins out of the pocket of his stained khaki windbreaker, and for a moment he held them out on his outstretched palm. They appeared to be dirty gold, and were only crudely round, with bunches of grapes stamped in high relief on their faces, along with the letters TPA.

"Trapezus, on the Black Sea," exclaimed Kootie, "is where those are from. Those are about two thousand years old!"

Spider Joe closed his hand, and when he opened it again the coins were United States silver dollars. "These are what he paid me with, nearly five years ago, for the tarot-card reading that led him to the throne."

"I remember," said Mavranos quietly.

"Well, he's gonna need them again, now, isn't he?—to pay for passage across the Styx, and for the drink of surrender from the Lethe River, over on the far side of India." In spite of being blind, the old man shuffled forward, reached out and accurately laid one of the coins on each of the dead man's closed eyelids.

Mavranos's face was stiff. "We okay now? Right, everybody out."

They all began shuffling and elbowing their way through the doorway back into the office, while Mavranos hung back with the revolver; a couple of Spider Joe's antennae hooked one of Angelica's bean pans off the counter and flung it clattering to the floor, spilling dirt and withered bean sprouts across the linoleum.

CHAPTER 8

Mark, silent king, the moral of this sport:
How soon my sorrow hath destroyed my face.
                                   —William Shakespeare,
                                      Richard II

Kootie was back up on the desk beside the inert television, sitting cross-legged and finishing his fish stew. When everybody had resumed their places, he refilled his wine cup and said, "Who was this person who gave you my name and address?"

"And when did he give 'em to you?" added Mavranos.

"Dr. Richard Paul Armentrout, at Rosecrans Medical Center in Bell-flower," said Plumtree, who was sitting on the floor beside Cochran in front of the couch now. "This afternoon." Apparently she too was respecting Strubie the Clown's hundred-dollar bid to be left out of this picture.

Mavranos frowned, his high cheekbones and narrowed eyes and drooping mustache making him look like some old Tartar chieftain. "He *sent* you here?"

"No," Plumtree said. "Sid and I broke out of the hospital, when the earthquake hit, a couple of hours ago. Armentrout didn't even believe there *was* a king, much less that I had . . . helped to kill him, until he talked to me this afternoon. Then he said, 'Oh, you must have had help, from somebody who was practically a king himself, like this kid from a couple of years ago.' " She looked up past Cochran at Kootie. "Which was you."

Kootie put the bowl aside and took a sip of the wine. "Why did you escape?"

"Armentrout wants to find out what happened on New Year's Day," Plumtree told him, "and he wasn't going to let us go until he was totally satisfied that he'd found out everything, using every kind of strip-mining therapy that his operating room and pharmacy have available; and even then I don't think he'd have wanted us to be able to talk, after. He wouldn't have killed us, necessarily, but he'd have no problem fucking up our minds so bad that between us we couldn't string together one coherent sentence. This afternoon, just as a warm-up, he tried to break off and . . . *consume* a couple of my personalities.''

"Your personalities,'' said Angelica.

"I've got MPD—that's multiple—''

"I know what it is,'' Angelica interrupted. "I don't think the condition *exists,* I think it's just a romanticizing of post-traumatic stress disorder, best addressed with intensive exploratory psychotherapy, but I do know what it is.''

"My wife was a psychiatrist,'' remarked Pete, "before she became a *bruja.*"

Plumtree gave Angelica a challenging smile. "Would you advise Edison Medicine for the condition?''

"ECT? Hell no,'' snapped Angelica, "I've never condoned shock therapy for *any* condition; and I can't imagine *anyone* prescribing it for PTSD, or a hypothetical MPD.''

"Edison Medicine,'' came Kootie's wryly amused voice from above Cochran. "It knocked *me* right out of my own head—and killed my dog.''

One of Spider Joe's antennae popped up from the carpet with a musical twang, making Plumtree jump against Cochran's shoulder. He put his arm around her, and in the moment before she shrugged it off he noticed that she was trembling. Well, he was too.

"Whatever,'' said Pete, who had sat down on the couch. To Plumtree he went on, "You say he tried to eat some of your personalities. Was he masked, when he did this?'' He absently tapped a Marlboro out of a pack and flipped the cigarette into the air; it disappeared, and then he reached behind his ear and pulled out what might have been the same cigarette, lit now, and began puffing smoke from it. "Like, did he have a . . . a *pair of twins* present, or a schizophrenic?''

"He had a crazy guy on the extension phone, listening in,'' spoke up Cochran. To Plumtree he said, "The old one-armed guy, Long John Beach.''

For a moment no one spoke, and the only sound was the chaotic drumming of water splashing into the pots on the floor. Then, "A one-armed guy,'' said Kootie steadily, looking hard at Pete Sullivan, "named after a local city.''

"I—I thought he died,'' said Angelica, who was standing beside the desk. "You mean the one who called himself Sherman Oaks, who wanted to kill you so he could eat the Edison ghost out of your head?"

"Right, the smoke-fancier." Kootie glanced at Plumtree. "Ghosts are known as 'smokes' to the addicts who eat them, and he used to eat a lot of them."

"Shit, he still does," put in Cochran. "Though he's down to Marlboros these days."

"I thought he was dead," insisted Angelica. "I thought he blew up along with Nicky Bradshaw, when they both fell off the *Queen Mary* two years ago."

"With 'a local man called Neal Obstadt,' right?" said Plumtree. "Who was looking for Scott Crane in 1990? Armentrout mentioned this. The explosion killed the Obstadt person, according to him, but just collapsed a lung of this Long John Beach, or Sherman Oaks." She grinned, breathing rapidly between her teeth. "I wonder what other names he's used. Wes Covina. Perry Mount."

Cochran was embarrassed by her incongruous merriment, and nudged her. She nudged him back, hard, in the ribs.

"Or in drag, as Beverly Hills," Pete agreed absently. Then he stood up abruptly and looked around the room. "Well, he's been here before—he knows the way here, too. We'd better get ready for him, and for this psychiatrist."

Angelica visibly shivered, and she touched the gun under her blouse. "We should just run, right now."

"We need to know *where* to run, first," Pete told her. He stepped to the television set and clanked the channel switch a couple of notches clockwise. "Could you plug this thing in again, Oliver? We need some readings, Angie. Pennies, I'd think, for a fine-grain closeup-type picture. What year was Crane born in?"

"Nineteen forty-three," said Diana.

The tanned teenager hopped up off the couch and plugged the TV set's cord into the wall while Angelica pulled open a desk drawer and bumped glass jars around in it. "Pennies," she muttered. "Nineteen . . . forty . . . three, there we are." She lifted one of the little jars out and sat down on the couch. The set's screen had brightened, and a woman in a commercial was talking about some new Ford car. Cochran and Plumtree hiked themselves forward on the carpet to be able to see the screen.

Angelica shook the jar, and the half-dozen old pennies in it rattled and clinked—and the TV picture shifted to a newscaster reading the day's winning lottery numbers. She shook the jar again, and now they were watching the portly, bearded figure of Orson Welles sitting at a restaurant table, waving a glass of wine and quoting the Paul Masson slogan about selling no wine before its time.

Pete Sullivan caught Cochran's glance and smiled. "Plain physics so far," Pete said. "This is an old set, from the days when the remote controls used ultrasound frequencies to change channels and turn the sets on and off. The remote was a tiny xylophone, in effect, too high in frequency for anybody but dogs and TVs to hear. Nowadays the signals need to carry more information, and they use infrared."

"I get it," said Cochran, a little defensively. He was still shaking, still enormously aware of the dead man on the table in the kitchen. He nodded. "The TV thinks her jingling pennies are a remote. Who are you, uh, hoping to consult, here?"

Pete shrugged. "Not who—what. Just . . . the moment; right now, right here. The pennies she's shaking are a part of now with a link to Crane's birth year, and the pictures they'll tune the TV to will be representative bits of now in the same field of reference—just like a piece of a hologram contains the whole picture, or a drop of your blood contains the entire physical portrait of you. It's what Jung called synchronicity."

"Synchronicity!" sneered Angelica, who was shaking the jar again and staring at the screen. She stepped back and sat down on the couch, still shaking the pennies.

"Angie thinks there are actual, sentient entities behind this sort of thing," said Pete. "A querulous old woman, in this case—the same party that's behind the Chinese I Ching, according to her."

"A straitlaced and disapproving old party," said Angelica without looking away from the screen. "Sometimes I can almost smell her lavender sachet. Ah, we're online."

Cochran peered at the screen curiously, but it was just showing a grainy black-and-white film of a blond woman brushing her hair.

"It always starts with this," said Pete, visibly tenser now. "That's Mary Pickford, the old silent-movie star. A guy name Philo T. Farnsworth was the first guy in the American West to transmit images with a cathode-ray tube, in San Francisco in 1927, and he used this repeating loop of Mary Pickford as a demo." He sighed shakily. "This isn't a real-world, 1995 broadcast—we're into supernatural effects now, sorry."

"You were getting spook stuff even *before,*" said young Oliver nervously. "Paul Masson hasn't aired that Orson Welles ad for *years.*"

"I think he's right," murmured Angelica from the couch.

Spider Joe had been sitting silently against the kitchen wall, but now he reared back, and half a dozen of his antennae sprang up from the carpet. "Who just came in?" he barked, the sunken eyelids twitching in his craggy brown face.

Cochran glanced fearfully at the open back door, but there was no one there; and Plumtree and Diana and Angelica had been craning their necks down the hall and toward the kitchen, but there was no sign or sound of any intruder.

Kootie had directed an unfocussed stare at the ceiling, and now he lowered his head. "There's no one new on the whole block."

Mavranos cleared his throat. "But, uh . . . your *Mary Pickford* has changed into a *negro.*"

"And she got older," noted the teenager who had been introduced as Scat, and who hadn't taken his eyes off the screen since they'd all trooped back in from the kitchen.

On the TV screen, the figure was in fact a thin old black woman in a high-necked dark dress now, sitting at a mirrored vanity table and brushing her hair—and though her jawline was strong and unsagging, her kinky hair now looked more white than blond.

As if in response to Angelica's hard shaking of the penny jar, the grainy black-and-white picture sharpened in focus, and an open window with a row of eucalyptus trees beyond it was visible in the wall behind the old woman; and sounds were audible—a faint, crackling susurration as the old woman drew the brush through her hair, an insistent knocking of the raised window shade bar against the window frame, and a clanging bell from outside.

"The knocking, and the bell, those are to confuse ghosts," said Plumtree.

Angelica was shaking the jar harder, as if trying to drive the image off the TV screen, and she seemed irritated that the pennies weren't doing it, were instead just jangling in rhythmic counterpoint to the bell.

"It's San Francisco, all right," said Pete. "That's a cable-car bell in the background."

"This film clip is seventy years old," panted Angelica. "Everyplace probably had streetcars then."

"It isn't the old clip anymore," objected Pete. "This here has got sound."

"Pete," said Kootie loudly as he clanked his empty bowl down beside the television set, "dig out the Edison telephone and get it hooked up again. We're in a new game now, with this restoration-to-life talk, and even an idiot shell of Scott Crane might have something to say worth hearing. And I reckon Janis Plumtree should be enough of a link for us to reach him, her being his own personal murderer."

"And his wife," said the bald Diana from the kitchen doorway. "You've got his wife here, too."

"Right," said Kootie hastily. "Sorry, Diana—I was thinking in terms of the new arrivals. I meant *murderer* now *too.*"

Angelica finally leaned forward and set the jar of 1943 pennies down on the carpet. "I'm not dealing with the I Ching old lady here," she said, wiping her hands on her jeans as she leaned back against the couch cushions. "And it's not being run by just your *synchronicity* either, Pete. It's . . . I sense some *other* old woman."

Cochran saw Mavranos glance at Spider Joe. Clearly he was wondering if the crazy old blind man's dead wife might be taking over the show here. Cochran wondered if Booger had been a black woman.

"If you say so, Kootie," said Pete. "Scat, Ollie—you guys can help me carry some boxes in from the garage."

After Diana's two boys had followed Pete out the back door, Angelica Anthem Elizalde Sullivan stared resentfully at the Plumtree woman sitting in front of the desk with her drunk Connecticut pansy boyfriend. MPD, thought Angelica scornfully. I didn't even think that was a hip diagnosis anymore, I thought everybody was busy uncovering suppressed memories of childhood sexual abuse these days.

"Kootie," Angelica called, "toss me my *Lotería* cards."

Her adopted son twisted around on the desk and dug through a pile of utility bills and check stubs, then tossed over the heads of Cochran and Plumtree a little deck of cards held together with a rubber band.

Angelica caught the bundle and pulled the rubber band off the cards. "Miss Plumtree," she said, having forgotten the woman's first name, "come sit by me on the couch here and chat."

Plumtree stared back at her. "Why should I answer your questions, lady?"

Angelica smiled at her as she deftly shuffled the cheap paper cards. "I know about . . . *making amends* to people you've allowed to die; people you're linked with by chains of guilt, hm? *Real* guilt and shame, the kind you've got to go back and *fix,* not just 'get past' or 'put behind you' or get 'okay with.' You think you can do it without help, but that's like thinking one hand can fix what it took two hands to break. If that dead man in the kitchen *can* be resurrected, it might be some thing you can tell us that'll help us all to get the job done." She looked around the room affectionately. "I wonder if we've got even one person here who doesn't believe, with some validity, that he or she is directly responsible beyond any excuse for the death of someone."

"Shee-it," snarled Plumtree; but she struggled wearily to her feet and shambled over to the couch, which thumped the floor with an uneven leg when she dropped onto it beside Angelica. Her boyfriend, Cochran, got to his feet and leaned attentively on the corner of the desk.

Angelica scooted back and spread the cards messily facedown on the couch cushion between them; the blurry black-and-white plaid patterns on the backs of the cards blended together so that it seemed to be one puddle on the cushion. In Mexico these cards were used to play a gambling game similar to bingo, but Angelica had long ago found that the mundane pictures on the fronts of them were useful for eliciting free association from patients. "Pick me three of them," Angelica said.

Pete and the boys came clomping back in, carrying cardboard boxes, as Plumtree carefully drew three of the cards out of the pile; and Angelica leaned forward to be heard over the clanking of telephone and radio parts being lifted out of the boxes and spread out on the desk. "Now flip one of them faceup," she said.

With a trembling hand Plumtree turned over . . . card 51, El Pescado, a picture of a red fish upside down in smoky water, holding a tethered hook in its mouth.

"I guess you know what that one indicates," Angelica said in a carefully confident and dismissive tone.

" 'I'll bite' is what it . . . *means,* " Plumtree said, nodding. "But if this is a reading of me, it's wrong. I won't bite. Maybe it's a warning for me, huh? Don't let yourself get pulled out into the air, get separated from the school—off the school bus!—get cooked and eaten and digested by somebody out there. 'Full fathom five my father lies.' "

Angelica just nodded, but she was surprised—she had expected that this serendipitous picture would evoke some mention of the Fisher King, whom Plumtree claimed to have killed.

Angelica looked up and made a *ch-ch!* sound; Kootie had climbed down from the desk, but instantly looked around toward her.

"St. Michael the Archangel," Angelica told him, "with High John the Conqueror ready."

The boy nodded and pulled open one of the desk drawers; he lifted out two aerosol spray cans and handed the purple one across to his foster mother.

"Your father's in the other direction, then," Angelica said to Plumtree, hefting the can, "from whoever's dangling the line into the water, is that right? Tell me about your father."

"Well, he's dead. Is that Scotchgard? I wasn't going to piss on your couch, lady." When Angelica didn't reply or change her expression, Plumtree sighed and went on. "He died when I was two, but I was in the hospital, so they didn't tell me about it right away, about him being dead. Janis doesn't remember him any more than I do, but she claims to miss him real bad. All she knows about him is what she's heard from Valorie.''

"Valorie's older?''

"Yes," said Plumtree tightly. "Valorie's been—around from the beginning.''

"She remembers a lot of stuff?''

"She remembers everything. But all her memories,'' Plumtree added, glancing at the TV set, "are in black and white, and always with some drumming or banging going on in the background.''

"Can I talk to Valorie?''

Plumtree shifted uncomfortably and shot a nervous glance toward Cochran. "Not unless she wants to talk to you.''

"What were you in the hospital for? When you were two?''

"I don't remember. Measles? Stress? Some kid thing.''

Pete had unplugged the TV set and was lifting it down off the desk to make room for the Ford coil box and the battered old field frequency modulator. "I hope mice haven't got into all this stuff in these two years,'' he muttered to Kootie.

"It'd be *ghosts* of mice that'd be attracted to it,'' said Kootie, who was still holding the other spray can.

"How did he die?'' Angelica asked Plumtree. "Your father.''

"Jesus, lady!'' said Plumtree tightly. "You're just *asking* to have me lose time here.''

Angelica held up the purple spray can and let Plumtree look at the picture on the label, a crude drawing of a winged, sword-wielding angel kicking a bat-winged devil into a fiery pit. The directions advised, *Spray all areas of your surroundings. Make the sign of the Cross.* "This is just air-freshener, really,'' Angelica said, "but the chlorofluorocarbons in it, and this groovy *label,* repel ghosts. After I spray it around us, you can talk freely.''

Angelica held the can over Plumtree's head and pushed the button on the top of it; a mist that smelled like bus-station rest rooms hissed out, drifting over Plumtree and Angelica both.

Plumtree took a deep breath and let it out. "Well!'' she said when Angelica had lowered the can. "He fell off a building, is what happened, in San Francisco, one of the old wino buildings south of Market. *Soma,* they used to call that area, from *south* of *Mar*ket, get it? *In Soma's realm are many herbs, and knowledge a hundredfold have they.* That's from the Rig-Veda. I hope you're right about that spray stuff. He was the chief of a hippie commune, like the Diggers, you know? A group that fed homeless runaways. My father's commune was called the Lever

Blank, they're mentioned in a couple of the books about the Manson family. I suppose the name meant *vote-for-nobody* or something. My mom left the commune a couple of years after he died, and she always said that they killed him, because it was the summer solstice and he had failed to become this king of the west at Easter. '69 was a competition year for it, just like '90 was.''

Pete had sent Ollie back outside to fetch a car battery from one of the Solville vehicles, and was now brushing the dust off the pencil lines and screw holes still in the wood surface of the desk from the time they had set up this telephone in October of 1992.

"Okay," Angelica said cautiously. She pointed at the two cards that were still facedown. "Hit me again."

Plumtree turned over the second card, and it was the unnumbered El Borracho card, The Drunk—a picture of a man in laborer's white clothing walking bent-legged and carrying a bottle, with a dog snapping at his heels.

"That was you, tonight," Plumtree said to Cochran, picking up the card and showing it to him.

Cochran peered at the picture on it, then jerked his head back, frowning. "I may have been drunk," he said, "but I wasn't *bestial.* That there is more like who Long John Beach was singing about." He rubbed his hand clumsily over his face, and Angelica noticed a leaf-shaped birthmark on his knuckles. "And who was it that drank the Manhattans," he went on, "and all the Budweisers?"

"We're talking about *you,* here," Angelica told Plumtree. "How do you feel about this picture?"

"I hate drunks," said Plumtree. "I'd never let Janis get involved with one." Apparently to end discussion of the Borracho card, she reached down and flipped over the third card.

It was number 46, El Sol, a drawing of a bodiless round red face encircled by a jagged gold corona.

Plumtree's eyes slammed shut and she flung herself back hard against the couch cushions, with her fingers clawed into the disordered thatch of her blond hair; her nostrils were tensely white as she whistlingly inhaled a deep breath, but her face was reddening visibly even under her sunburn—and fleetingly Angelica wondered how a patient in a mental hospital could acquire a sunburn. Plumtree was whispering some rapid-cadenced phrase over and over again.

From long practice Angelica resisted the impulse to participate in her patient's panic. "I think we'd better titrate up our St. Michael dosage," she said calmly, raising the purple can and spraying two more long bursts of the stuff over their heads.

Pete and Kootie had paused in their phone-assembly work to stare at Plumtree, and Mavranos was frowning and tapping the revolver barrel against his thigh.

Now Angelica could hear what Plumtree was whispering: "—Ghost! In the name of the Father, the Son, the Holy Ghost! In the name of—"

"What is it that this *reminded* you of?" Angelica asked the woman in a voice just loud enough to override the frantic whispering. "Whatever it is, it's not *here*. Only this little drawing is *here*."

"Let me," said Cochran. He stepped forward and knelt beside the stiff, shaking Plumtree. "Janis," he said to her, "this is 1995, the eleventh of January, Wednesday, probably getting on for midnight. You're in Long Beach, and you're twenty-eight years old." He looked at the Sol card that was still faceup on the couch cushion; he turned it face down, and then he glanced up at Angelica. "She has a recurrent nightmare, of the sun falling out of the sky onto her, knocking her flat."

Plumtree's eyes opened and she lowered her hands, and she blinked around at everyone staring at her. "I'm sorry," she said. "Was I yelling?"

Angelica smiled at her. This, she thought, must be one of her other *personalities*. How I do love the histrionics and theatricalities of dissociatives. "No," Angelica said patiently. "The gentlemen were wanting help with their telephone." Plumtree's mention of herbs a few moments ago actually had reminded her of a crucial part of the telephone; she looked over at Johanna and said, "You remember the mix we cooked on the stove, two years ago? You'd better get a pot of it going—Pete would have forgotten it, being all wrapped up in his hardware. The mint—the *yerba buena* leaves—you can pick out back by the garage, and there's tequila in the cupboard, unless Arky's drunk it all up."

"It's your bourbon I drank up," Mavranos said defensively. "I don't touch tequila."

Angelica clasped her hands and turned back to Plumtree. As casually as she could, she asked, "Do you remember much about the hospital you were in, when you were two? Did it have . . . lawns, playrooms, a cafeteria? Try to picture it."

"I only remember the room I was in," Plumtree said. "There were get-well cards on the table by the bed," she added helpfully.

"Close your eyes again, but this time relax." When Plumtree complied, Angelica went on, "you'll find you can remember details very clearly, especially from when you were young, if you clear your mind of every distraction and just *relax*. And you're safe here with us, so you *can* relax, can't you?"

Without opening her eyes, Plumtree said, "You're right here, Scant?"

Cochran clasped her shoulder. "Right here."

"Then I can relax."

"So . . . remember the hospital room," said Angelica. "What did it smell like?"

". . . Fresh-peeled adhesive tape," Plumtree said dreamily, "and laundry baskets, and the woody taste of Fudgsicle sticks once you've sucked all the ice cream off, and shampoo."

"And what did the room look like?"

"There was a window—there *was* a window!—with metal venetian blinds to my left, but I could only see part of a tree branch through it; the wallpaper was lime green, and there were dots, little holes, in the white tiles on the ceiling—"

Plumtree's eyes were still closed, and Angelica permitted herself a faint nod and a tiny mild smile of triumph. "Why," she asked in a voice she forced to sound careless, "couldn't you see anything more out the window?"

"I didn't go over to it, to look out."

"Were you . . . *afraid* to?"

"No, it was on the ground floor. I just didn't get out of bed at all, even to go to the bathroom. I had to use a bedpan, though I was certainly not wearing diapers anymore, by then."

"Can you see the room? All the details?"

"Sure."

"Look at yourself, then, at your arms and legs. Why didn't you get out of bed?"

"I—I couldn't!—not with a cast on my leg and my arm in a sling—!"

Plumtree's eyes sprang open, and it was all Angelica could do to maintain her gentle smile—for she was abruptly, viscerally certain that it was an entirely different person now behind the Plumtree woman's eyes. Angelica made herself go on to note the physical indications—the tightened cast of the woman's mouth and jaw, the wider eyes, the newly squared shoulders—but the conviction had come, indomitably, first.

Plumtree turned her head to look at Cochran, who flinched slightly but kept his hand on her shoulder.

"How're you taking all this?" he asked her nervously.

"Upon my back," Plumtree said in a flat voice, "to defend my belly; upon my wit, to defend my wiles; upon my secrecy, to defend mine honesty; my mask, to defend my beauty; and you, to defend all these. And at all these wards I lie, at a thousand watches."

"Now who just *left?*" demanded Spider Joe from the corner.

"Wow," said Angelica humbly.

Plumtree had lowered her face into her hands, and now she looked up, squinting. "Wha'd I miss?" she asked irritably. "Do you people have such a thing as a *beer* around here?"

The woman has shifted again, Angelica thought. I may talk myself out of it eventually, but right now I'm a believer in MPD.

"Yes," she said, just to get away from this woman who was such an affront to her professional convictions. "Right. A beer. I'll get one of Arky's for you." But she was still too shaken by what she had deduced about Plumtree's condition to stand up right away; and she was wondering if the telephone call would even be possible with Plumtree here on the premises.

"Coors, that means," sighed Plumtree.

"This stuff on the desk here is the antenna," Pete was telling Scat and Oliver, "but we can't be in the room with it, or the carborundum bulb and the rectifying lens will just pick up on our living auras. Let's set up the actual telephone receiver in the laundry room. That used to be the kitchen, before one of our remodeling campaigns, and it's where we did it before."

And you don't want to do it in the current kitchen, right in the presence of the dead king, Angelica thought as she finally stood up, dizzily, from the couch. Well, neither do I.

She paused in the kitchen doorway, standing back against the doorframe to avoid getting tangled in Spider Joe's arching antennae. "How are you planning to scramble the call?" she asked Pete. "Even if Sherman Oaks and this bad psychiatrist already know where we are, there's no use in lighting a beacon for every *other* smoke-fancier in the L.A. area, if we can help it."

Pete held up his hands and made dialling motions with his forefingers. "I've still got antique hands."

"Yeah," said Angelica uncertainly, "but they're *yours* now."

Pete lowered his hands. "I guess you're right. I've even put a few new scars on 'em in the last two years."

"You do hand transplants, lady?" Plumtree asked Angelica. "You sound more like Dr. Frankenstein than Dr. Freud."

"Yeah," said Mavranos, frowning like someone having health-insurance billing explained to them, "what's all this Beast-With-Five-Fingers talk?"

"Sorry," said Pete. "The magician Houdini had a customized mask made in the twenties, see, sort of a decoy with a magical spell on it, to make it look like he was where he wasn't. It was plaster casts of his hands, and his actual cut-off dried thumb, and if you were carrying the lot when bad magicians focussed on you, you'd suddenly take on the physical appearance of Houdini—short stature, dinner jacket with break-away sleeves, curly hair, the whole outfit. And—''

Plumtree's boyfriend made a suppressed snorting sound.

''I wish we did still have that magical string from Mexico,'' Angelica told him scornfully; ''I'd love to see you suddenly notice that your goddamn *shoes* were on fire, or you suddenly had a live *bat* in your hair, when you tried to snap it.''

''On Halloween day of '92,'' Pete went on, ''we were dragged out of our apartment here at gunpoint by the people who wanted the Edison ghost that was in Kootie's head then—you got any problems with *that*, mister?—and the dried thumb was somewhere else, the bad guys found that; but I grabbed the plaster hands—and they disappeared—and suddenly I had *Houdini's* hands.'' He held his hands up and wiggled the short, strong fingers. ''And I've had 'em ever since. They won't hold a weapon—I guess Houdini didn't want his decoy hurting anyone—and I'm more comfortable now writing with a fountain pen, and shaving with a straight razor; but at least I can do lots of parlor-magic stunts.'' He clenched the hands into fists. ''Angie's right, though—they are mine now. They wouldn't disguise the source of the call.''

For a moment no one spoke, and the drumming of water falling from the leaky ceiling into the pots and pans was the only sound.

Then, ''Arky has the dried eyeball of a dead Fisher King,'' said Kootie. ''That would be a fine scrambler.''

''Make it two beers,'' called Plumtree, ''if I gotta sit here and listen to all this creepy shit.'' Angelica could hear the tremor of fear under the woman's bravado.

Angelica decided that she would have a beer herself; and maybe some of the tequila, which she could now smell heating up in the kitchen, if there was any still left in the bottle. She rocked her head back against the doorway frame with a firm knock. ''I suppose you really do have that,'' she said wearily to Mavranos. ''And I suppose a one-time Fisher King's ghost might not have been banished by the current Fisher King's death, because of standing *behind* the shotgun, as it were.'' She sighed. ''An eyeball. So is it *activated* at all, in any sense? I mean, is there any *ashe* in it, any vitality? How far away is the *rest* of this . . . dead Fisher King? If his body is real far away, or under water, then your . . . *dried eyeball* . . . won't be a whole lot of use.''

''Oh well,'' said Mavranos, shrugging and shaking his head, ''as a matter of fact, I think the rest of him is in Lake Mead. And I think he's used up anyway.''

''Oh well,'' agreed Angelica, and she strode into the kitchen and walked around the dead king's feet to the refrigerator. Johanna was stirring the aromatic pot of mint leaves and tequila on the stove, and the sharp smell of it reminded Angelica to snag a beer for herself along with the two for Plumtree.

She heard Pete ask Mavranos, "Who was it?"

"Bugsy Siegel," came Mavranos's rueful answer. "The eye was shot out of his head when he was killed in '46, and Scott's father had it stashed away in a hidey-hole in the basement of the Flamingo Hotel in Vegas. Scott's father was king, from '46 until '90."

"No shit? Hey, Angie!" called Pete then. "We're in business after all."

CHAPTER 9

The wine was red wine, and had stained the ground of the narrow street in the suburb of Saint Antoine, in Paris, where it was spilled. It had stained many hands, too, and many faces, and many naked feet, and many wooden shoes. The hands of the man who sawed the wood, left red marks on the billets; and the forehead of the woman who nursed her baby, was stained with the stain of the old rag she wound about her head again. Those who had been greedy with the staves of the cask, had acquired a tigerish smear about the mouth; and one tall joker so besmirched, his head more out of a long squalid bag of a night-cap than in it, scrawled upon a wall with his finger dipped in muddy wine-lees—BLOOD.

—Charles Dickens,
A Tale of Two Cities

And now they're all drinking, thought Cochran, and cooking up a pot of some kind of noxious mint-and-tequila punch; and young Boogie-Woogie—*Kootie*—has refilled his wine cup at least once; and if there's a crazier brand of bullshit being talked in California tonight, it's gotta be in a loony bin for far worse cases than any at Rosecrans Medical. But *I'm* supposedly the one who's the *drunk*.

"Bugsy Siegel's ashes are in the Beth Olaum Mausoleum at the Hollywood Cemetery on Santa Monica, only about twenty miles from here," the man called Pete was saying now. "His ghost was a pal of my dad's ghost—Angie, you remember, it was Siegel's ghost that rapped back *knock-knock* when I rapped *knock, knock, knock-knock, knock*, when we were there to pick up my dad's ghost, day before Halloween in '92."

"I do remember that," allowed the woman who was coming back from the kitchen with three cans of Coors. Two for Cody and none for me, Cochran thought. He thought of going into the kitchen and fetching a couple for himself, but couldn't face the thought of seeing the dead man again.

And he was still unsettled by the picture on the card that Cody had shown him—with the comment *This was you tonight*—the fat, bearded, idiot face of the drunken figure in the drawing, the crown of roses that seemed to conceal horns, the animal-skin cloak, the sketchy legs that bent the wrong way like a goat's and ended in sketchy stumps like hooves!

Kootie had lifted out of one of the cardboard boxes an electric pencil sharpener, and now the boy carefully unsnapped its wood-grain printed plastic cowl. Underneath, instead of the crossed grinders of a pencil sharpener's works, a thick stick of yellow chalk was attached to the rotor.

"This middle section is pretty deeply grooved from the last time," Kootie said, peering at the chalk. "But we can attach the spring to a different section, closer to the motor, and I remember how Edison set it up."

"I'm not sure Edison himself knew what he was doing," said Pete.

"I remember how he set it up," said Kootie.

"Fine," said Pete. "Good." He glanced at Cochran and smiled. "That's our speaker, our receiver—that pencil sharpener. Most speakers use induced changes in the field of a magnet to wiggle the diaphragm; we can't do that, because an actual physical magnet would draw ghosts the way a low spot on a pavement collects rainwater. If we did this a lot, I'd hook up a piezoelectric quartz, or an electrostatic setup with perforated condenser plates, but this arrangement actually does work well enough. We'll soak the chalk with water, and then attach the diaphragm spring to the surface of the chalk, which will be spinning when we turn on the pencil sharpener—wet chalk is toothy and full of friction ordinarily, see, but it gets instantly slick when there's an electric current going through it. The changes are variable enough and rapid enough to get decent low-quality sound out of the attached diaphragm."

Cochran understood that the man was sociably trying to let him in on what was going on, so he returned the smile, jerkily, and nodded. "Clever," he said.

"It was better sound quality than a lot of the headphones out there," said Kootie.

"I'm not dissing your old orisha, son," Pete said mildly. In one hand he picked up a rack of glass tubes and in the other a glass cylinder that had a little metal rod rattling in it like a bell clapper. "I'm gonna take the vacuum pump out to the kitchen and hook it to the faucet to evacuate the Langmuir gauge. You might get everybody crowded into the laundry room, Kootie, or out in the back yard. Out of this room, anyway.''

''While you're in the kitchen,'' spoke up Cochran, trying not to speak with passion, ''could you get me one of those beers?''

Behind him Plumtree snickered. Pete looked at Kootie, who shrugged and nodded.

''Okay,'' Pete said.

Young Oliver was leaning against the couch, and now he hesitantly spoke. ''You're gonna call our father's ghost, now? Not him, himself, but his ghost?'' The boy's face was stiff, but Cochran could see the redness in his eyes.

''That's right, Oliver,'' said Mavranos. ''You're the man of your family now, you can be there for it, if you like.''

Oliver shook his head. ''No,'' he whispered. ''It'd—''

''It'd just be him dead in that room too,'' said his brother Scat solemnly. ''Like it is in the kitchen.'' He looked at Oliver and then said, ''We'll wait in the back yard.''

Their mother, Diana, just bit her knuckle and nodded.

Cochran followed Plumtree and Angelica and Diana into the flower-wallpapered little laundry room, and he sat down beside Plumtree at the foot of a sink in the corner. Kootie had climbed up on top of the washing machine, which was one of the heavy-duty commercial kind that had a push-in slot for quarters; the pencil sharpener sat on a shelf beside his shoulder, attached now to the frame of a disassembled pasta machine with a spring and a paper loudspeaker cone attached to it.

Pete had set up a TV table and a lawn chair in the middle of the linoleum floor, and almost ceremoniously had placed on the table an old black Bakelite rotary-dial telephone that was connected with phone cords trailing one way to the pencil sharpener and strung along the linoleum floor the other way to the assembly on the table out in the office. Johanna had stayed in the present-day kitchen to keep an eye on the pan of mint-and-tequila, though the astringent smoke from it was making Cochran's eyes water. Probably she just forgot about it, he thought, and went outside to listen to the music some more, and the pan's on fire. He sipped his freshly opened beer cautiously, not having any idea how long this procedure might take; crazy old Spider Joe had elected to join the boys outside in the yard, where the music was, and Cochran was wishing he had gone along with the old blind man.

''Can I have the . . . eye?'' Pete asked Mavranos, who was standing by the washer and puffing on a Camel cigarette as if to drive away the burning mint smell. With the hand that wasn't holding the gun, Mavranos dug a wad of tissue paper out of his shirt pocket and passed it across to him. "And," Pete said as he carefully unwrapped it, "we've got Crane's . . . murderer, and his wife, here, which should one way or another work as a homing beacon. Kootie, start up the speaker; and Angie, would you do the honors in the next room?" He looked at Cochran as Angelica sidled past the TV table out into the office. "We're out past physics again," he said. "She's got to light some candles, and pronounce certain Spanish rhymes, and splash *Vete de Aquí* oil over the door lintel." He looked at Diana, who was standing beside Mavranos. "I need Crane's full name, and his birthdate. I realize it seems like bad security, to be dealing in his real psychic locators, but we can't have any masks at all in the way, for this."

"Scott Henri Poincaré Leon Crane," said Diana—who, even in the harsh electric light from the single naked bulb dangling from the ceiling, looked to Cochran's befuddled gaze like a luminous preliminary Boticelli painting of Venus, before the hair was brushed in. "February 28, 1943."

The pencil sharpener was spinning the wet chalk cylinder now, and a featureless hiss was rasping out of the paper speaker. Angelica hurried back into the little laundry room, wiping her hands on her blouse and exposing for a moment the grip of the automatic pistol in her waistband.

Pete grimaced as he lifted out of the tissue paper an angular black lump like an oversized raisin; but he sat down in the lawn chair and started to dial.

But even before he had carefully pulled the 7 hole of the dial around to the stop, a buzzing sounded from the speaker; it stopped, then started up again.

"Uh . . . that's an incoming call," Angelica said helplessly. "You may as well answer it."

Pete picked up the receiver. "Umm . . . hello?"

The frail voice of an old woman came shaking out of the paper speaker cone: "Pirogi," it said. "That's a bayou boat, barely big enough for a body to kneel in. It's a thing you can cook, too, looks like a boat— stuff an eggplant with *seafood* once you've gouged away the . . . the *core* of the vegetable like a dugout canoe. If he hollers, don't let him go, right? You all need to come here, I can guide your boats. I betrayed the god, I desecrated his temple, but this is my day of atonement. Today is January the eleventh, isn't it?"

For several seconds nobody spoke, then Kootie said, "Yes, ma'am."

"Ninety-one years ago today," rasped the old woman's disembodied voice, "I died. Three Easters and three days later he came for me, out of the sea, and he knocked down all the buildings and took all the other ghosts to himself, burned them up. *Yerba buena*, burning.''

The telephone speaker hissed blankly for nearly half a minute, and at last Angelica said, ''Well, she's right, the *yerba buena* does smell like it's burning. Johanna,'' she called through the doorway, *''atenda a lo fuego!''* Then she looked at Pete. ''You're getting the party-line effect. Hang up and try again.''

''You are to come and fetch me,'' insisted the old woman's amplified voice, ''and another dead lady, too, who is hiding in a tight little box.''

''I—I think it's the old black lady,'' ventured Kootie. ''Who was on the TV.''

''I think it is too,'' said Angelica. ''Will you hang *up*, Pete? We don't need help from stray ghosts drawn by the electromagnetic field here, wanting to celebrate their *deathdays*. Fetch two old women ghosts!—it sounds like a sewing circle. Hang up, and dial Crane's number.''

''Rightie-o,'' said Pete flatly, hanging up the receiver. He leaned forward again with the dark lump—which was apparently someone's eye!—and used it to rotate the dial. ''And I'm enough of a mathematician to know how to spell *Poincaré*.''

Altogether, for Crane's name and birth date, Pete dialled thirty-four numbers into the phone. ''It's very long distance,'' muttered Kootie, which got a smothered laugh from Plumtree.

Again from the speaker sounded the measured buzz that apparently indicated ringing, and then a click sounded. Pregnant Diana's hands clenched into fists against the tight fabric of her jeans.

''Hello,'' came a man's baritone voice from the pencil-sharpener apparatus, ''you've reached Scott Crane, and I'm not able to come to the phone right now. But if you leave your name and number and the time that you called, I'll get back to you as soon as possible.''

''The woman who killed you,'' said Diana loudly, ''says she can restore you to life. Cooperate in this, Scott! And do give us a call, if you can.''

At the first syllables of the man's voice, Plumtree's elbow had bumped Cochran's knee; he glanced at her now and saw that though she was still sitting slumped against the pipes below the sink she had gone limp, her hands open and palms-up on the linoleum floor and her head bowed forward so that her blond hair had fallen over her face. He didn't bother to try to rouse her.

''Nearly midnight, Scott,'' called Mavranos, ''on the eleventh of January,'95; Arky and Diana, and some allies; and we'll have to try you again somehow, or you'll have to catch us at some pay phone we might be near, okay?—I don't think we're gonna be by this phone much longer.''

Now that he had sat down again, Cochran found that he was hardly able to keep his eyes open. The voices of these strangers, and his cramped posture, and his nervous exhaustion, all strongly called to mind the sleepless twelve-hour flight home from Paris four days ago—he could almost hear again the faint brassy big-band music that had seemed to whisper perpetually from some forgotten set of earphones several rows ahead; and his eyes were aching now as they had when he had kept trying to read *A Tale of Two Cities*, while fatigue had been persistently casting faint, hallucinatory green bands across the bottoms of the pages; and he squinted in the glare of this laundry-room lightbulb and remembered how the horizontal white light of dawn over the north Atlantic had lanced in through the 747's tiny windows, and been reflected in wobbling flickers onto the white plastic ceiling by the compact-mirrors of ladies fixing up their slept-in makeup.

When the jet had landed at LAX in Los Angeles, he had got off and walked right out of the airport, abandoning his luggage.

Summoning all his strength now, he struggled to his feet and mumbled, ''Which way to the head?''

Mavranos, still holding the revolver, pursed his lips and scowled at him. ''Hold tight, sonny,'' he said. ''Your bladder won't pop.''

''You're not Speedy Alka-Seltzer,'' agreed Pete absently as he hovered over the phone, ''you won't dissolve.''

''It's not—'' Cochran swayed in the smoky air. ''I think I'm gonna puke again.''

''Oh hell,'' Mavranos said, glancing for reassurance at the unconscious Plumtree. ''Down the hall to the right. If I see you turn left, toward the kitchen, I'll shoot you, okay?''

''Okay.''

Cochran stepped carefully over the telephone cords to the doorway, and glanced at the ivy-leaf mark on the back of his right hand to make sure he didn't turn the wrong way by mistake.

He followed his hand sliding along the wallpaper to the hallway corner. As he had done at the airport, he was forcing himself not to think about the consequences of this course of action; all his concentration was on the immediate tasks: step quietly down the side hall, unchain the street door, and then hurry away into the night, away from the dead body in the kitchen and *everybody* here, never looking back.

But when he had shambled around the hallway corner he froze.

Instead of the remembered narrow hall through which he and Plumtree had entered the building, with its threadbare carpeting and low, flocked ceiling—

—he was in a broad, dark entry hall, at the foot of a spiral staircase that curled away upward for at least two floors; rain was drumming on a skylight far overhead, and drops were free-falling all the long way down the stairwell to splash on the parquet floor at his feet. In the taut, twanging moment of astonished vertigo he rocked his head forward to look at the floor, and saw in the wood a stain that he was viscerally certain was old blood.

Then he had no choice but to look behind him.

A gilt-framed mirror hung on the panelled wall, and in the mirror, behind the reflection of his own wide-eyed face, stood the man he had met in the streets of Paris five days ago, who had called himself Mondard.

Cochran whirled to face the man, but there was no one there; he was still alone in the empty baroque hall; and so he had to look back into the mirror.

The man in the reflection had the same curly dark beard he'd had when Cochran had first spoken to him in the courtyard of the Hotel L'Abbaye, around the corner from the Church of St. Sulpice, but now it reminded Cochran of the bearded dead king who lay somewhere behind him; and these liquid brown eyes had shone with this same perilous joy even when they had stared at Cochran from a living bull's head on the man's shoulders, later that same morning in the narrow medieval Rue de la Harpe; and when Cochran had fled, stumbling over ancient cobblestones past the Lebanese and Persian restaurants with whole lambs turning on spits in the windows, the thing that had pursued him and finally tripped him up on the Quai Saint Michel pavement by the river had been a man-shaped bundle of straw, with dried ivy for hair and split and leaking grapes for eyes.

In the hotel courtyard the man had introduced himself as Monsieur Mondard, having to lean close to be heard over the glad baying of the dog in the lobby, and he had frightened Cochran by speaking of the dead Nina and offering him an insane and unthinkable "surcease from sorrow"—and as Cochran stared again now into the reflection of those horizontally pupiled eyes, he knew from their unchanged hot ardor that Mondard was still holding out the same offer.

"Donnes moi le revenant de la femme morte," Mondard had said, *"buvez mon vin de pardon, et debarrassez-vous d'elle." Give the dead woman's ghost over to me, drink my wine of forgiveness, and be free of her.*

In that old Paris courtyard, under the marbled winter sky, Cochran had believed that the man could do what he offered: that he could actually relieve him of the grief of Nina's death by taking away Cochran's memories of her, his useless love for her.

And he believed it again now. The figure in the mirror was holding a bottle of red wine, and in the reflection the letters on the label were something like I BITE DOG AP but Cochran couldn't read it because of the sudden swell of tears in his eyes. Why *not* take a drink of the sacramental wine, and by doing it give over to this creature his intolerable memories of Nina—give to this thing that called itself Mondard his now cripplingly vestigial love for his killed wife?

When he looked up into Mondard's face, the goat-pupilled eyes were looking past him, over Cochran's shoulder; a moment later they were warmly returning his gaze, and he knew that Mondard was promising to provide the same solace, the same generously ennobling gift, when Cochran's grief would be for the death of Plumtree.

And Cochran wondered exactly *how* Nina had come to run out into the lanes of the 280 Freeway at dawn, ten days ago; had she been chased? . . . Lured?

Nina was dead, and Cochran was suddenly determined not to betray his love for her by disowning it; and Janis was alive, and he was not going to sanction her death, abandon her to this thing, even implicitly.

The bottle of wine, "Biting Dog" or whatever it was called, gleamed in the long-nailed hand in the mirror's reflection, and on the back of the hand was a mark that might have corresponded to the mark on Cochran's hand—but Cochran shook his head sharply, and turned away and blundered back the way he had come.

CHAPTER 10

"You know that you are recalled to life?"
"They tell me so."
"I hope you care to live?"
"I can't say."
"Shall I show her to you? Will you come and see her?"
                                    —Charles Dickens,
                                      A Tale of Two Cities

Plumtree was still huddled under the sink when Cochran stepped carefully back into the stark yellow light of the laundry room, but she was blinking and looking around now and Angelica was crouched beside her, talking to her.

Pete was hunched over the telephone, tapping the hang-up button; the paper speaker cone on the shelf was silent in the instants when the phone was hung up, but always came back again with the same noise, which was distant mumbling and laughter and vitreous clinking, as if the phone at the other end had been left unattended in a crowded bar somewhere. Perched up on the washing machine, Kootie was frowning in the mint-and-tequila smoke from the kitchen, and holding his bleeding side.

As Cochran stepped over the telephone and electric cords to get back to his place beside the sink, he found that he was straining to hear, among the slurred babble crackling out of the speaker, the rattle-and-bang of someone playing bar dice.

"Oh, Scant!" said Plumtree when he sat down beside her. "I was afraid you ran out on me."

Cochran managed to smile at her. "Decided not to," he said shortly.

Angelica glanced at him, and then stared at him. He wondered what his expression looked like. "Good," she said. "Did you get . . . *lost*, at all, looking for the bathroom?"

Cochran realized that he'd been holding his breath, and he let it out. "Yes," he said. "Never did—find it." Now that he had resumed breathing, he was panting, as if he had run a long distance back here.

"Big Victorian halls?" Angelica asked him in a neutral tone. "Rich-looking?"

Cochran caught his breath with a hiccup, both relieved and frightened to learn that she knew about the hall he had found himself in, that he had not been hallucinating. "Yes," he admitted. "Grand once—decrepit now."

Angelica was nodding. "For the last week and a half," she said slowly, "we've been getting print-through, here, overlay, overlaps, of two other houses, old Victorians. One's dark and mildewy, and the other's clean and got electric lights. This building was put up in 1923, partly constructed of lumber salvaged from the Winchester House in San Jose. The top couple of floors of that house collapsed in the big earthquake in 1906—"

"When *he* came for the black lady's ghost, out of the sea," said Janis in a helpful tone, "and knocked down all the buildings. Valorie told me that part."

"Oh, do be quiet, girl," whispered Angelica, closing her eyes for a moment. "The Winchester House is still standing, of course," she went on to Cochran, "big haunted-house tourist attraction on the 280 south of San Fran . . . but lately when it's raining in San Jose, the roof leaks here."

"It was—leaking there, too," panted Cochran. "Through a sky-light." He didn't feel able to tell her about the man he'd seen in the mirror.

"Talk to Kootie about it, he's seen—"

A clunking sounded from the speaker, then breathing; clearly some-one at the unimaginable other end had picked up the telephone.

"*Whooo* wawnts it?" came a man's drawling voice from the speaker. "Your daddy's home, baby! That bad old doctor wanna play *strip poker*, I'll see he gets his ashes hauled for real." A high, razory whine had started up in the background.

Cochran's face went cold, for he was certain that this was the voice that had come out of Plumtree's mouth at Strubie the Clown's house.

Plumtree had sat up and stiffened. "That *is* my daddy!" she said hoarsely, her voice seeming to echo faintly out of the speaker. "Daddy, can you hear me? I'm so *sorry* I let you die, I tried to catch you—"

"Course I can hear—"

The whine grew abruptly louder and shriller, as if Dopplered by the source of the carrier-wave signal accelerating toward them at nearly the speed of light; a blue glow was shining now in the dark office beyond the laundry-room doorway, and the drumming of water into the pots out there was a barrage; then the speaker abruptly went silent and the blue glow was extinguished. Cochran couldn't hear the roof dripping in the other room at all now.

In the silence, Pete pushed back his chair and shuffled carefully to the doorway and looked into the office.

"The carborundum bulb *exploded,*" he said, turning back into the brightly lit little room. He gave Plumtree an empty, haggard stare. "Your dad's ghost is one muscular son of a bitch."

"He's not a ghost," said Angelica in a shaky tone as she lithely straightened her legs and stood up. "And it wasn't Spider Joe's dead wife that whited out the TV. Let's go in the other room and get the *Vete de Aquí* oil splashed around."

Cochran knew enough Spanish to understand that the phrase meant, roughly, *Go Away;* and in spite of his recent resolve to stay with these strange people, he forlornly wished he could rub some of that oil onto the soles of his shoes.

I've got to make a couple of ordinary phone calls before we settle down again," said Angelica when everybody had filed back into the office and turned the lights back on and Johanna and Kootie had begun shaking yellow oil from tiny glass bottles onto the doorframes and the windowsills. Angelica hurried into the kitchen, and Cochran heard a pan clank in a sink, and then running water and the sudden hiss of steam. Pete had unplugged the electrical cords and was twisting the clamps off the terminals of the car battery that was sitting on the desk.

"I'll bet he's an angel," Plumtree was saying, "if he's not a ghost. I'll bet he's my guardian angel."

Cochran drained the last third of his can of beer in several deep swallows. Has she not even *considered,* he wondered, the likelihood that her father's personality is the famous Flibbertigibbet?—who battered the would-be rapist to death in 1989 on October the unforgettable seventeenth? An angel, maybe, Cochran thought, but one with a harpoon rather than a harp.

The thought of a harpoon reminded him of the sawn-off spear in the neck of the dead king in the kitchen; he darted a nervous glance in that direction, and then peered up at Kootie, who had climbed back up onto the desk and was sitting cross-legged among the wires and radio parts.

Kootie was looking at him. "Call me Fishmeal," the boy said, softly and not happily.

Cochran blinked at him. "Uh . . . sorry, you said what?"

"Never mind," sighed Kootie.

Angelica came striding back into the office from the kitchen, her dark hair swinging around her pale, narrow face. "Your Bugsy Siegel eye worked," she told Mavranos. "The two L.A.-area *santeros* I just called were aware of some powerful ghost agitations a few minutes ago, but Alvarez in Venice registered it as northeast of him, and Mendoza in Alhambra clocked it as just about exactly west."

"The Hollywood Cemetery . . . ?" ventured Pete.

"Unmistakably," said Angelica. "So we're no more vulnerable than we were before. At least."

She threw herself down on the couch and stared hard at Plumtree, who was sitting on the floor beside Cochran. Impulsively Cochran put his arm around Plumtree's shoulder; and she leaned back against him, which led him to believe that she was currently Janis.

"And I'm pretty sure I've got you diagnosed, girl," Angelica said to her, "though I'd love it if you could have brought your admission notes with you from the madhouse." She looked around at the other people in the long, smoky room—just Cochran and Kootie and Mavranos and Diana—and she said, "I'm afraid I'm going to be violating doctor-patient confidentiality in what I say here. But everybody here is concerned in this—and anyway, you never paid me forty-nine cents."

Angelica shook her head and smiled then, though she was frowning. "You know, when I was a practicing psychiatrist, I learned real quick that the regular doctors, the surgeons and all, were cowards when it came to giving their patients bad news. They'd call one of us shrinks over to their wing of the hospital to 'consult' on a case, and it always just meant . . . 'Would you explain to my patient that his cancer is fatal? Would you tell his family?' So a lot of times I had to be the one to tell some stranger that his leg had to be amputated, or tell some girl her father had died. I always felt bad to be the one breaking the news." She coughed out two syllables of uncomfortable laughter. "I'm rambling, aren't I? What I mean is, I don't want to say what I've got to say now—though in a way I've got the opposite sort of news." Plumtree must have opened her mouth to speak, for Angelica held up her hand. "Let me talk, Miss Plumtree. You are, genuinely, a multiple personality," Angelica said, "but that's not all that's . . . peculiar about you. How do I start? For one thing, I'm just about sure that you were present when your father . . . well, let's call it *died.*"

Cochran belatedly noticed that Angelica had brought a glass of something with her from the kitchen, tequila probably, and he watched her take a solid gulp of it now. "I think," she went on, "that you were standing on the pavement below the building he fell from—I think he partly *landed on you,* which is why you were in the hospital with broken bones. And it was almost certainly a sunny day, because you seem to have identified him with the sun, hence your dream of the sun falling out of the sky onto you, and hence too your no doubt stress-triggered hysterical sunburn and constricted pupils. Conversion disorders, we call that class of physical symptoms.''

Angelica leaned forward—but her head was now over one of the drip-catching pots, and the next drop spattered on her scalp. She leaned back again on the couch. "That much is orthodox—Angelica Anthem Elizalde the doctor talking. Now it's *Bruja Angelica, del 'Testículos del León':* I think that in the instant before his body died, when you were both lying there on the sidewalk or whatever, he managed to look into your eyes, and then he . . . *jumped across the gap,* threw his soul into your two-year-old body.'' She was frowning deeply, staring at the liquor in her glass. "So at the tender age of two you lost your psychic virginity, in what must have been a traumatic violation of your *self.* I doubt that your home life in the hippie cult-commune was real conducive to mental health, but this virtual rape by your own father was undoubtedly the event that triggered your multiplicity.''

"I'm still here," said Plumtree cautiously. "Valorie hasn't made me lose time. So this must not be bad news.''

"We-ell," said Angelica, raising her eyebrows, "the news is that your father is discorporate, but he's in you; like one of those flanged wedges they use to split logs into several pieces. And he's *alive,* he's not a ghost; he never did die, never did experience the psychic truncation of death. He *is,* though, almost certainly the person that killed Scott Crane.''

"My father is alive," said Plumtree, clearly tasting the thought. "I *didn't* let him die! I *did* catch him—save him!''

And he's Flibbertigibbet, thought Cochran nervously. Don't lose sight of that, Janis.

A jangling metallic screech at the back door made Cochran jump and almost shout; Spider Joe was coming back inside, and the long, stiff wires that projected from his belt were scraping paint chips from the doorframe. "Goddammit," the blind old man was muttering. Once through the narrow doorway he plodded across the floor, as Mavranos stepped out of his way and the antennae bunched and snagged the carpet and whipped through the air, and finally he sat down heavily on the floor beside the couch. Perhaps self-consciously, he groped around until he found Angelica's deck of *Lotería* cards, and began shuffling the frail cards in his brown-spotted hands.

Angelica turned back to Plumtree. "Do you know what those lines were that you quoted a few minutes ago?'' she asked Plumtree sharply. ''A list of defenses, all provisional and makeshift-frail—'Upon my back, to defend my belly,' and so forth?''

''Don't say any more,'' said Plumtree hastily, ''please. No, I don't even recall quoting anything.''

''Well, they happen to be from *Troilus and Cressida,*'' Angelica said, ''a Shakespeare play that isn't considered one of his good ones, mainly because it doesn't seem to make a whole lot of sense. But some spiritualists, mediums, *brujas y magos*—the real ones—are very aware of the play.''

''What's it about?'' asked Cochran—in a strained voice, for it had been at the Troy and Cress Wedding Chapel in Las Vegas that he had married Nina Gestin Leon—his beloved dead Nina—and had next morning had his first debilitating hallucination of the big, masked man.

Angelica sighed and finished her drink. ''Only a few people know what I'm about to tell you,'' she said. ''See, Shakespeare didn't write the play for the general public—its only intended performance was for a small, sorcerously hip audience in London in 1603—and in the published version he had to add four or five lines to the end of the first scene, tacked on after the rhyming couplet that originally ended it, in order to take away the real point of the play—which is that Troilus didn't go out and fight, but got his wound at home—fatally, by his own hand. Hardly anybody knows, anymore, that it's really a play about ghosts.''

She glanced at Plumtree, with what might have been sympathy. ''I'll have to re-read it, but it takes place during the Trojan War—you know? like in Homer?—and it's about a Trojan girl, Cressida, who is being prepared to be a vehicle for the ghost of her dead father. The Greeks who are besieging the city have got hold of the ghost, and they want to use it against the Trojans, but they've got to get the ghost into a living body that's both compatible with it and not a virgin, psychically. It's a dirty-pool move, like using biological warfare, and some of the Greeks such as Ulysses don't approve of the tactic; the Greek soldiers are suffering disorientation from the powerful ghost's proximity, and they're using masking measures—'emulation,' Ulysses calls it—to insulate themselves. So anyway, a traitor spiritualist in Troy is talking Cressida into having sex with the ghost of her dead *boyfriend,* Troilus, who near-decapitated himself with his sword before the action starts. In the play it's never outright stated that Troilus is dead, a suicide ghost, but his very name should have been a clue to the theater-going public, really—in Homer's *Iliad*, the Troilus character is dead long before this point in the story, though Homer doesn't say he killed himself out of unrequited love of Cressida, as Shakespeare secretly has it. Anyway, a trade is set up—the clueless Trojans agree to turn over Cressida in exchange for some VIP prisoner-of-war Trojan, and the spiritualist manages to get Cressida into bed with Troilus's ghost just barely before she's got to leave the city. And, of course, the Greek scheme works: Troy falls, the noble prince Hector is killed. Though," she added, visibly restraining herself from glancing toward the kitchen doorway, "Apollo and Aphrodite preserved Hector's body from corruption."

Mavranos was still holding the revolver. He looked across the room at Plumtree and asked, "What was your plan for reviving Scott Crane?"

She shivered under Cochran's arm and muttered, "In the name of the Father, the Sun, the Holy Ghost." The lights flickered; then she squinted at Mavranos. "Okay, sorry—what did you say?"

"I asked you how you planned to restore Crane to life."

"A time for hard questions." She took a deep breath and let it out. "I believed a *living* king would be able to restore him. A king in a living body. I knew he was a, a magic guy, and I figured he knew how to do shit like that. So I wanted to find the Flying Nun's—Crane's—presently disembodied spirit, and let him take my body, so he'll *be* occupying a living body—*this* one—and he'll be able to do the magical trick, whatever it involves. *I know* how to . . . open myself up, 'wide unclasp the table of my thoughts,' step aside and let another personality take control of my body—I do it a hundred times a day. And he wouldn't be compromising himself by violating my spiritual virginity—I'm a regular Grand Central Station for personalities passing through this little head. So far they've all been homegrown, as far as I know, but I'm confident that any . . . psychic hymen! . . . is long gone."

Truer than you yet know, Cody, thought Cochran. *You should have been here for what Angelica said about your father a minute ago.*

Plumtree was still holding Mavranos's gaze, though Cochran could see the glitter of tears in her eyes. "And," she went on steadily, "if he can't manage the trick of getting himself back into his own body—even though it *does* happen to be so perfectly preserved *right here* in your kitchen!—then he can simply, God, simply stay in mine, *keeep* it. Mine's not perfect, and it's the wrong sex, but it's young, and it's all I have to give him, by way of atonement." She wiped her eyes impatiently on her shirtsleeve. "That was my plan. Dr. Armentrout said Koot Hoomie Parganas might know a way to do it, maybe another way." She looked up at the boy on the desk. "Hanging around here tonight, I get the idea you *don't*, in fact, know a way to do it. Is that . . . true?"

Angelica spoke up in answer, angrily. "Of course it's true! If Kootie could revive the dead king, do you think he wouldn't have done it?"

After staring at Kootie for another second or two, Plumtree turned a tired smile on Angelica. "No, lady," she said quietly.

Mavranos swivelled his bleak gaze to Angelica. "Now I know how you feel," he said hoarsely, "delivering the bad news to people." He cleared his throat, but when he spoke again his voice was still as gritty as boot soles on sandstone: "I think Miss Plumtree's plan might work."

Angelica was visibly tense. "Who is that bad news for?"

"*You* all, goddammit. You and Pete and Kootie. Shit. What Diana and I meant to do by coming here was to confer the kinghood onto the man with the bleeding wound in his side. That office, the kinghood, would have carried with it a lot of protections—Miss Plumtree can tell you again how much work she had to do to get through the defenses to Crane. *But*—if Crane can be revived, even though he's dormant and powerless right now, then Kootie doesn't become the king after all. There are no protections. And you people are fatally compromised— you've invited us in, you've voluntarily taken the dead king's very *body* in, given it shelter and respect! You've eaten bread and drunk wine in his corpse's presence, you've declared allegiance and fealty to his reign, like it or not. The bad guys know your address, this bad psychiatrist and—" He glanced at Plumtree, "—and other villains. And they won't let you live, you all being sworn-in soldiers in the routed side's army now, and knowing what you know. These two," he said, waving at Plumtree and Cochran, "found you tonight—hell, their *taxi driver* found you. And old Spider Joe had no problem, apparently, and he's *blind*. By morning you may have armored assault vehicles pulling up out front. You've blown your mask-gaskets by letting us in, and I don't even think you could run and hide somewhere else, now, and stay effectively hidden for long."

Angelica had stood up from the couch during this, and paced to the kitchen doorway and back. "Then annoint Kootie," she said. "Make Kootie the king, as you originally planned. We'll have the protections of the true living king then."

Mavranos reached up to the side and laid the revolver on the bookshelf beside the inert stuffed pig, and he wiped the palm of his hand on his jeans. "I deliberately killed a man once, at Hoover Dam, to protect my friends, and it has weighed cruel hard on me ever since. I won't—I *won't* kill a living person to protect a *dead* man; especially a living person I've become indebted to. You can march into the kitchen there and, I don't know, chop Scott's head off with a carving knife, if you like. I won't shoot you, Angelica. Kootie would become king then, even without the blessings of me and Diana, which it would damn sure *be* without. But Kootie will have become king by being an accessory to the murder of his predecessor . . . as, in fact, most of the previous kings have done. And his will be—trust me!—a reign poisoned at its root.''

Cochran thought of the phylloxera lice, killing the sunny grapevines from the darkness six feet under.

''I . . . won't do that,'' said Kootie softly.

''Then I take back our invitation!'' shouted Angelica. ''I hereby annul it! *I* never invited you in, and all we did for your damned *king* was lay him out on the kitchen table! Pete and Kootie will carry him right back out to your abracadabra truck—and you can wipe your fingerprints off the doorknobs and take your kids and your toothbrushes and get out of here—take a broom with you and sweep your footsteps off the walkway as you leave!'' She looked at Pete and lifted her open hand, and caught the little bottle of *Vete de Aquí* oil that he obediently tossed across the room to her.

''Go,'' said Plumtree with a giddy wave, ''and never darken our towels again.''

Mavranos smiled sadly at Angelica. ''You took my forty-nine cents, that first day.''

''Cheerfully refunded!'' Angelica stamped to the desk, pulled open the top drawer, and pawed through a pile of scattered change. Then she turned and threw seven coins at Mavranos.

The coins tumbled to a Wiffle-ball halt in mid-air; and they seemed to pop there, silently, like big grains of puffed rice; and then they fluttered away on dusty white wings toward the dripping ceiling.

Cochran watched them, and cold air on his teeth made him aware that his mouth was hanging open. The coins had turned into live luna moths, and a chilly draft had sprung up in the room.

Angelica was panting audibly as she dug seven more coins out of the drawer, and she flung them too toward Mavranos.

Again the coins dragged to a halt in mid-air, and twitched and puffed out in the moment that they hung suspended, and became live white moths that fluttered away in all directions. The long office room was cold now.

Pete stepped forward then, and he caught Angelica's wrist as she was scrabbling in the drawer for more coins; and she collapsed against him, sobbing. ''Why did you people have to . . . *come* here?'' she wailed, her hot breath steaming in the chilly air.

Mavranos spread his hands. ''Why did Kootie have to be the one with the qualifications, the unhealing cut in his side?''

Blind Spider Joe held up two of Angelica's *Lotería* cards; Cochran leaned forward to peer at them, and saw that they were a pair, two copies of a picture of a woman in a narrow canoe, labeled LA CHALUPA.

"Nobody's brailled these cards for me," the old man said irritably. "What are these?"

"They're both the same," said Kootie. "A lady in a little boat. She's got, uh, baskets of fruit and flowers by her knees, jammed in the bow."

"Two boats," Spider Joe said. "You were in a boat on a boat, a boat aboard a boat, when you got wounded, boy, isn't that right? And you had a guide who protected you through the ordeal, somebody like Merlin, or Virgil who escorted Dante through the Inferno. That was a *rite de passage*—he didn't just save you, he saved you *for* something. That's when you swung around to point here, to this."

"When my side got cut?" said Kootie. "Not boats—I was in a van that some bad guys had driven up inside a truck, on Slauson, by the L.A. trainyards. I was being kidnapped. And the ghost of Thomas Edison saved my life."

"And you had been prepped," Spider Joe went on, "like a piece of amber rubbed with a cloth, charged—fasting and observances as a child, that's obvious, and then you were violently severed from that life, and then you must certainly have renounced your name and your race; and you were a passenger, helpless. And what's a little charged boat floating aboard a boat?" asked Spider Joe. "It's a compass. You've got to get to the boats now, point north, find a new Merlin or Virgil—or Edison. An *intercessor*."

Pete Sullivan was squinting at the old man, and now he looked at Mavranos. "You know this old guy, Arky. Is there value in this?"

Mavranos opened his mouth and closed it, and shrugged. "He seemed to give Crane some good advice, before the big poker game on the houseboat on Lake Mead."

"It sounds like the old black lady's boat, her pirogi," said Diana. She glanced at Angelica. "Do you still think she was just a . . . random ghost drawn by your telephone?"

"This is the blind leading the blind," Angelica said.

Cochran stood up, though he had to lean on the desk, and he crossed his arms to hide the foolish writing on his T-shirt. "You tried to get your man Crane on the phone, and he wasn't there," he said. "North, says the, the *oracular* Mr. Spider Joe here; and you said that TV signal originated in San Francisco, and the old black lady's ghost was talking about San Francisco—obviously she was talking about the 1906 earthquake and fire, and she said 'Yerba Buena burning,' and Yerba Buena isn't just the Spanish term for mint, it was the original name for San Francisco, because of all the wild mint that used to grow on the northshore dunes there. Your very *house* leaks because it's raining in *San Jose*, which is next door to San Francisco. And she said, 'You all need to come here, and I'll guide your boats,' remember?'' And back up in the Bay Area, he thought yearningly, I can get my bearings, get to my house and get some *clothes,* pick up a paycheck, talk to my lawyer. ''For all sorts of reasons, none of us wants Crane to just *keep* Janis's body. We all have a stake in him getting his own back.'' Or, better, him just going untraceably *away,* he added to himself. ''And Mr. Mavranos points out that we can't stay here. If we all leave now, we can be at the Cliff House in San Francisco for breakfast.''

''To the boats,'' said Plumtree gaily.

CHAPTER 11

PANDARUS: . . . Is it not birth, beauty, good shape, discourse,
             manhood, learning, gentleness, virtue, youth, liberality,
             and such like, the spice and salt that season a man?
CRESSIDA: Ay, a minced man; and then to be baked with no date in
             the pie, for then the man's date is out.
                                          —William Shakespeare,
                                              Troilus and Cressida

As Johanna was banging around in the reeking steamy kitchen, insistently making snacks to sustain the travellers during the proposed long drive, Archimedes Mavranos was standing in the middle of the office floor and giving orders. He had taken his revolver down from the shelf again, and with his finger outside the trigger guard was now slapping his thigh with the barrel to emphasize his points.

"Diana," he said, "you take one of the Sullivans' cars and go back to Leucadia with the boys—Nardie and Wendy will be tired of taking care of all the young'uns by themselves. Mr. King-Arthur's-Shorts and Miss Plumtree can sit up in the front seat of the truck with me, and Kootie and Pete and Angelica can sit in the back seat, with Angelica holding—"

"*Kootie* certainly won't go along," interrupted Angelica, who had sat down on the couch and crossed her arms. "And Pete and I aren't cowards, but I don't see why we should go along either." She blinked around belligerently. "And you can't take one of our cars. Pete or I can drive Diana and the boys back to Leucadia."

"I thank you for the offer," said the woman Cochran had begun to think of as the cue-ball madonna, "but we'll take a bus. I would be honored to die with you, Angelica, if it were necessary, but I wouldn't let my boys or my unborn baby go anywhere with someone who was targeted to die.''

Angelica drummed her fingers on the arm of the couch. ''Why,'' she asked Mavranos, ''would you even think of bringing a fourteen-year-old boy?'' One of the moths fluttered past her face, and she waved it away impatiently.

''He's more than that, Angelica,'' Mavranos said. ''He's an apprentice king—no, a *journeyman* king; he can see and sense things we can't. And if we fail, he's *the* king—he should be up to speed for that, be able to land running. And I'll tell you another bit of bad truth, I'm not at all sure that this restoration-to-life will work, without him.''

''*Meaning what?*'' Angelica demanded.

''*I* don't know at *all* what it means,'' said Mavranos, baring his teeth. ''But he's *here,* he's *empowered,* as you shrinks like to say. He's a uniquely potent soldier in the king's meager army.'' He shrugged. ''*But,* if the boy doesn't want to go, I certainly won't try to compel him.''

Cochran couldn't help sneaking a sidelong glance at Kootie.

The boy was frowning and holding his wounded side. ''My mom and dad will die if this doesn't succeed,'' he said carefully.

Angelica leaped lithely to her feet. ''Kootie, that's not—''

''*Or* hide real damn low,'' assented Mavranos. ''Moving frequently, not keeping souvenirs. For the rest of their lives.''

''What have we *been* doing but hiding real damn low?'' Pete said to Kootie. ''The cops have been looking for us since '92, and for your mom since before that. Kootie, we don't—''

''Well what about *him?*'' Mavranos said, turning to face Pete Sullivan. ''Kootie himself? He was brought up to be king, groomed for it— by the plain *universe,* apparently, if not by any specific person. Weren't you listening to Spider Joe at all? Even if Kootie never gets to take the crown, the ambitious guys will want him dead, like a valid pretender, and his is a soul they'll want to eat; they'll want it bad. You think he can keep his belt and his watchband Möbiused all his life, one edge and one side, get along forever with half his strength?''

''I *will* go with them,'' said Kootie. He had picked up the bottle of Mondavi Chardonnay from the back corner of the desk, and now refilled his gold fish-cup. He smiled at Angelica. ''And I won't insult you and dad by asking whether or not you'll come along.''

The bald woman's lower lip was pulled away from her teeth in what might have been profound relief or pity, or both; and she hurried into the kitchen and came back with a ratty pale-yellow baby blanket. ''Kootie,'' she said hoarsely, ''this belonged to my mother, who was . . . such a successful avatar of the Moon Goddess that she was killed for it in

1960, at the order of Scott's natural father, when *he* was king. Spider Joe could tell you about it. Carry it with you, and she'll help you do . . . whatever it might be that you have to do.''

Kootie started to say something, then wordlessly took the little blanket and began slowly folding it.

"Okay," said Mavranos. "Good. We'll have Crane's body in the back of the truck, like under a tarp, and Angelica will be sitting just forward of that, in the back seat, with a gun: Miss Plumtree is our tool for restoring Crane, but at the same time she's a potential Trojan Horse, she *contains* the man that *killed* him—so Angelica has to be ready to shoot her if her father should take over and try to mess things up."

Plumtree was nodding absently, shaking a cigarette out of a pack from her purse.

"If I *shoot* her," noted Angelica shakily, "she won't be much use in restoring Crane."

"You might not *kill* her," said Mavranos.

"And even if you did," put in Kootie, who seemed tensely distracted as he tucked the folded-up baby blanket into his hip pocket, "we might find another way."

Angelica opened her mouth as if to demand an explanation of that, but Cochran overrode her. *"She!*—came here *voluntarily!"* he said loudly. His face was hot, and he was trying not to stutter. "At some peril to herself." He turned to stare into Angelica's hostile brown eyes. "You're Spanish," he said breathlessly. "Okay, that counts. But I'm Irish. If you decide to kill her, or hurt her, you'd be smart to kill me first."

"Noted," said Mavranos stolidly. "Joe, do you need a ride anywhere that's along the 101 north? We won't want to take a route that strays too far inland—I think proximity to the sea is part of what's been sustaining Crane's corpse." He grinned at Angelica. "Along with Apollo and Afro-Dydee, natch." He stared toward where Spider Joe sat on the floor beside the couch, then turned to Pete.

"The, uh, 'beasties,' " Mavranos went on. "Those strange dead guys that you had stacked in your trashed old van last week—we're gonna have to delay long enough to rip up the turf again over where we planted 'em."

Pete Sullivan frowned with evident distaste. "What the hell for? I let all the air out of the old Chevy Nova's tires after we parked it over them; and those were old tires, they might not take air again."

"All of us together can push it," said Mavranos softly, "even on a flat or two." He had been steadily slapping his thigh with the gun barrel, and now he struck himself hard enough with it to make Cochran wince.

"Shit," Mavranos said in an almost conversational tone. "The thing is, Pete, we gotta . . . well, a Dumpster in back of some gas station wouldn't be right; we do owe Spider Joe a *burial*."

Cochran watched everybody else turn to stare toward the couch before he looked away from Mavranos's stony face.

Spider Joe's head was rolled back, and above his slightly opened mouth the sightless eye sockets gaped at the ceiling; and the metal filaments that stood out from his belt were bent double, folded back across his khaki shirt like a dozen crossed fencing foils.

"He did traverse afar," said Mavranos, "to bring his gifts to the king—to return those two silver dollars."

"Poor old fucker," said Plumtree quietly. "You got lots of dead guys around here, huh."

For a long moment the dripping in the pans was the only sound. Cochran's teeth ached with the desire to be away from this building.

"Go with my blessings, Spider Joe," said Kootie softly, "whoever I may be in this."

After a pause, "His wife was the one who lured my mother to her death," said Diana. "I wonder if I—" She shook her head. "His last words," she went on, "were, 'Get to the boats, point north, find a new Merlin or Virgil or Edison. An *intercessor*.'" She had been rubbing her eyes as she spoke, and now looked tiredly around at the others in the steamy, smoky room; drops of water fell from the ceiling and plunked in idiot drumming into the various pots, and the moths were bumping against the shade of the lamp on the desk. "An intercessor is for dealing with somebody else—a person more powerful. Who," she asked, "do you imagine *that person* would be?"

"Wake up and smell the Kahlua," said Mavranos. "That person would be nobody else but Dionysus."

"Ah, God," said Angelica softly. "I was really hoping it wouldn't be. I didn't want this to involve the Bay Area—that country's all . . . *vineyards*."

The word *vineyards* caroled in Cochran's head, echoed by the syllables of *Vignes;* and insistent memories flooded his mind—of the predawn rolling clatter of the stainless-steel Howard winepress cylinder during the October crush, always run before daylight to elude *las moscas,* the flies and bees and whatever influences they might carry into the wine; of the fresh, sharp smell of new wine fermenting in a two-hundred-gallon redwood tank when he would pump the awakening juice over the cap of grape skins, the new-born red vintage splashing and spurting out of the hose and flinging up spray; and of the cathedral silence in the eight-foot-wide lanes between the vines, roofless holy aisles carpeted with yellow mustard-weed flowers in the spring, plowed under in the fall and sown with the yeast-rich pomace of spent grape skins to assure continuity of benevolent wild-yeast strains on the skins of the next season's grapes.

And he lifted his right hand now and stared at the gray ivy-leaf mark on the back of his knuckles . . . and reluctantly he called up his impossible childhood memory of what had happened on the day his hand was cut.

"I think he's right," Cochran said hollowly. "I think it is Dionysus." He looked at Plumtree, and had no idea who might be behind her eyes at the moment. "When they were talking about shooting you, just now," he said to her, "did you . . . do your stay-calm trick, did you throw your anger over onto me?"

"No," Plumtree said. "They weren't insulting me, I wasn't mad. That was all *you*—but hey, I gotta say I liked your style."

"Well, good for me. But a person can throw other things, anybody can. What I mean is, you can throw away grief for dead people you loved, if you're willing to disown along with it all you have of them, all your memories and all your—all the feelings you had about them . . . which are arguably of no use to you anymore anyway, they're just stuff in your head that there's nothing to be done with anymore, like a collection, a very damn *costly* collection, of eight-track tapes after all the stereos are gone that ever played 'em."

"Yeah," said Plumtree quietly, "they just make you unhappy. All you could do would be dust off the big old cassettes; whistle the tunes from memory and try to remember the instruments, and the vocals."

Pete closed his eyes for a moment and shook his head. "This is all just—deep and moving as hell, you know, but it's near midnight and—"

"Let the guy talk," said Mavranos.

"You can disown the dead person," Cochran went on, "but not just into a void; I suppose that'd . . . like, violate the law of conservation of grief, right? The god wants you to give it all to *him.*" He smiled, but didn't dare look at anyone but the dead body of Spider Joe. "And it's a gift, that the god takes it—in exchange he gives you 'surcease from sorrow.'"

"Euripides?" said Mavranos.

"That's what the tailor says," put in Plumtree with hectic cheer, "when you bring in a torn pair of pants; and then *you* say, 'Eumenides!'"

"That's mighty funny," said Mavranos patiently. "But Euripides wrote a play that deals with what Mr. Cochran is talking about." He glanced at Angelica. "It's another play with a secret hidden in it, like your *Troilus and Cressida.*"

Cochran sighed, with a shiver at the bottom of his lungs. "This would be *Les Bacchants,* wouldn't it," he said. This soaked ceiling may as well fall in on me, he thought; everything else is.

"I guess so," said Mavranos. "That's French? I mean what in English they call *The Bacchae,* this ancient play about a guy named Pentheus, who was king of Thebes, and his mom, Agave, who cut his head off and brought it to town."

"Agave is the cactus they make tequila from," noted Plumtree. "Often enough I've felt like it cut *my* head off."

"I never read the play," Cochran told Mavranos. He yawned, creaking his jaw and tipping tears from the corners of his eyes. "But as a matter of fact my in-laws were reading bits of it to me just last week, in France."

Cochran wished for another cold American beer, to chase away the palate-memory of the flinty claret with which Monsieur Leon had kept topping up his glass—the family's most prized *vin de bouche,* the old 1945 vintage, picked from vines that had gone unpruned during the Nazi occupation—while Madame Leon had droningly read page after leisurely, age-yellowed page of the old play; and he remembered how his weary brain had eventually stopped struggling to translate the French sentences, and had begun simply letting the syllables come through as random near-miss English, and how it had all seemed then to be phrases of idiot obscenity, both childish and shocking at the same time. There had been some moral the elderly couple had wanted him to derive from the play, and though he had come to their fifteenth-century farmhouse in Queyrac to turn over to them the urn that contained the ashes of their daughter and unborn grandchild, it had soon become clear that they were trying to get him into bed with their other, younger daughter, the slow-witted Marie-Claire. The thought that had sent him running from the house to his rented car and speeding away down the D-1 across the low country of the Bas Médoc toward distant Paris was *It's only January—they want a second try at a grandchild crop out of me in this thirteen-moon year.*

"At the start of the play," said Mavranos, "Dionysus comes to Thebes disguised as a stranger from Phrygia, but he gets all the local women to go dancing off into the hills in his honor, wearing animal skins and waving these staffs that are wrapped in ivy and topped with pinecones—"

"Easy on the *vino* there, Kootie," interrupted Angelica.

But the boy didn't put the bottle down until he had refilled his gold cup; and when he spoke, it was to Mavranos: "Was there blood on these staffs too?"

"After a while, there was," Mavranos told him. "The old retired king, Cadmus, he puts ivy vines in his hair and goes out to honor Dionysus too; but the present king, Pentheus, disapproves of all this crazy behavior and has the stranger arrested and thrown in jail. But since the stranger is really the god Dionysus, it's no problem for him to conjure up an earthquake and blow the jail to bits and get out. Pentheus asks him who set him free, and the stranger says, 'Him who provides mortal man with the grapevine.' And Pentheus says something argumentative back, which makes the stranger laugh and say, 'That's hardly an insult to Dionysus!' "

Dutifully, Cochran asked him, "What did Pentheus say?"

"Well, officially that line has been lost. In all the modern editions the editors have put in something like, 'The god who makes men and women act like lunatics.' But Scott Crane's dad had a real old copy, in Latin, and in this old version the original line's still there—and it translates to 'An unjust gift—that lets men forsake their wronged dead.' Then the stranger talks Pentheus into putting on a dress so he can go spy on the women, disguised as one of them. Pentheus is like somebody with a concussion at this point—he's seeing double, and he asks the stranger, 'Were you an animal a minute ago? You've got a bull's head now.' "

Cochran could feel Plumtree's gaze on him, but he didn't glance at her; instead he strode into the kitchen and managed to fumble three cans of Coors out of the refrigerator without looking squarely at the dead man on the table. Perceived only in his peripheral vision, the body seemed huge.

"Sorry," he said when he had stepped back into the office and popped open one of the cans. He took a deep sip of the stinging cold beer and gasped, "Do go on."

"Well," Mavranos said, "the women aren't fooled by Pentheus's disguise, and they chase him down and just tear him apart. His own mom, Agave, is the worst—she's, like, delirious, and doesn't recognize him, she thinks they've caught a mountain lion or something, and she cuts off his head and carries it back to town, real pleased with herself. Old Cadmus, who's her dad, *he* sees that this is his grandson's head, and he talks her out of her delirium so that she sees it too; they're both horrified at what she's done—and then there's another missing section, a whole couple of pages. Modern editors have put in made-up speeches from Cadmus and Agave saying what a terrible thing this is and how bad they feel. And then when the old, real text picks up again, Dionysus is condemning Cadmus and his wife to be turned into snakes, and sending Agave off into destitute exile.''

"Is that how it ends?'' asked Plumtree. "Downer play, if you ask me.'' Angelica closed her eyes and sighed, obviously weary of Plumtree's remarks but reluctant to snap at her.

"Well, yeah,'' Mavranos agreed. "You do wonder why the god treats 'em so rough, when they were apparently just doing what he wanted 'em to do. It doesn't make sense—the way it's published these days. But in the original version, after Cadmus and Agave realize what she's done, the god offers them a sacramental wine, called the debt-payer; he tells them that if they drink it, they will lose all memory of Pentheus, and therefore all guilt and unhappiness and grief over his bloody murder. They'll be turning over Pentheus's ghost to the god, and in return he'll give them forgetfulness and peace. And the reason the god is being so harsh to them at the end of the play is that in the last bit of the omitted section they *refuse* his offer, his gift—they can't bear to renounce their love of Pentheus, can't make themselves disown him, even though he's dead.''

Angelica was frowning, and looked as though she was ready to spit. "Dionysus wants to take grief, and then more of it—and he won't wait for it to occur accidentally.'' She visibly shivered. "We *don't* want to deal with him face-to-face, visit him where he lives—if we've got to deal with him at all, we want to deal with his borders.''

Pete was half-sitting against the desk, and he looked up at Angelica with raised eyebrows. "He takes in boarders?''

Diana had sat down on the couch and was holding her distended belly. "It doesn't sound like Dionysus will want to help us, does it?'' she asked. "We want to do the *opposite* of renounce Scott.''

"That's why we need an intercessor, I reckon,'' said Mavranos. He squinted at Cochran. "How did you get that mark on the back of your hand?''

"I was—'' Cochran began.

"Jesus!'' yelled Pete Sullivan suddenly, leaping away from the desk. "Angie! Get me the can of brake-parts cleaner!''

Angelica had jumped when he shouted, and now she spoke angrily. "No. What is it, a wasp?''

Kootie had scrambled down from the desk, so fast that his forgotten bouillabaisse bowl flew off too and hit the carpeted floor with an echoing clang and a spray of tepid fish broth.

"Yes!'' said Pete without looking away from the lamp. "Your goddamn moths are turning into wasps. Get me the goddamn brake-parts cleaner, this wasp's as big as my head!''

Angelica was just staring at him, and frowning impatiently. "It's not that big."

"It is! Will you hurry!"

"Well, it's not as big as a *normal* person's head."

"If a normal person comes in here we can check. Get me the goddamn brake-parts cleaner!"

"I'll get it," said Kootie. Before stepping into the kitchen, the boy grinned nervously up at Cochran. "Best thing for killing bugs, brake-parts cleaner spray is."

"I bet," said Cochran to his receding back. Absently he licked fish broth off his shaking fingers.

Plumtree took Cochran's other hand and led him away from the confusion, past Spider Joe's corpse to the far end of the couch; then, while Pete and Angelica went on arguing about the wasp, Plumtree stepped quietly into the entry hall, pulling Cochran along after her.

The wasp must have made a break for it, or else another one had manifested itself, for Cochran heard renewed banging and cursing from the office behind them; but Plumtree calmly used the noise as cover while she drew back the chain in the doorframe slot and pulled the heavy door open.

The cold night air was potent with the briny smell of the wild sea as the two of them sprinted down the walk and across the lamplit asphalt to the corner of Ocean Boulevard; and when they had dashed through a gap in the surging headlights across the lanes of Ocean, Plumtree dragged Cochran around a parking lot to a set of iron stairs that led downward toward the beach sand. The majestic old liner *Queen Mary* was moored permanently as a hotel now at the Port of Long Beach peninsula a quarter-mile away across the dark harbor water, and her yellow lights glittered on the low waves like a windy lane of incandescent flowers.

Plumtree's blond hair was blowing around her face as she stepped off the last of the iron stairs onto the sand. "Untamed water," she said, waving at the sea. "They won't be able to sense us here, even if they've got time to look. Which they don't. They're crazy even to think of delaying long enough to bury the poor old buggy man."

Now that they were below the seaside cliffs, Cochran could see a couple of fires down the beach, a hundred yards or so to the south, and he wondered uneasily who might be sustaining them out here in the middle of this night. Faintly on the breeze he could hear drumming.

"Uh," he said, shivering, "where to?"

"Frisco," Plumtree said. "Why the Cliff House?"

"It's—" he said with a shrug, "—a nice place for breakfast. Tourist spot, good cover.'' He shoved his hands into his pockets and tried to figure out why the Cliff House had seemed such an obvious place for them all to reconnoiter. ''I don't know, Cody, it just came to me. It's right by the ruins of the old Sutro Baths, and that's a good area to talk, down on the plain among the ruins, right by the water, the *untamed* water, because you can see anybody coming a long way off; nobody could eavesdrop, and the wind and the sea would even fox a shotgun microphone; and—'' He laughed self-consciously. ''And on the cliffs of Sutro Heights Park, there used to be rows and rows of Grecian statues. They're all buried in the park somewehere now. I guess I was thinking they'd be a, a protective influence. All the stone people, to distract attention from us.''

He glanced to the side at her shadowed face, wondering if she would make fun of him, but she was just nodding. ''Why did they bury 'em?''

''It was during World War Two,'' he said. ''The government was afraid they'd draw the attention of Japanese submarines.''

''Sure,'' she said absently as they trudged through the loose sand north, away from the fires. ''Guy at the periscope sees a bunch of naked white guys standing on the cliffs in the middle of the night—'This mussa be Flisco, Captain-san!' ''

Cody's crude witticism depressed Cochran, and he hoped Janis would be up again soon. ''For this,'' he said stiffly, ''I think we could call my lawyer, and have him wire us some money. We could rent a car then—''

''And leave a paper trail for Armentrout to follow,'' she said, nodding again. ''Fuck that noise, as the poet said. I'll get us a car.''

Armentrout had never stayed this late on the ward. The patients had all long since been put to bed, and the lights in the common rooms were dimmed; after the final clang of the door closing behind the last of the staff who would not be staying all night, the silence was whole, and tense—the occasional breathless, yiping scream, or raucous laugh, was a welcome collapse-to-one of the standing wave that seemed to fill all the rooms and corridors when the silence was unbroken.

Armentrout was sitting in one of the upholstered chairs at the re-righted table in the TV lounge. The television screen overhead was an opaque dark green, and he knew that the view of the courtyard behind him was blocked by the two broad sheets of plywood that had been bolted over the window through which Cochran and Plumtree had escaped.

The *views*, the extensions to the outside world, were truncated. The pay phone had stopped its incessant ringing, and he was afraid that if he were to get up and cross to it and lift the receiver, he wouldn't even hear a dial tone.

Every couple of minutes he slapped his pants pockets, and twice in the last couple of hours he had actually had to dig out his keys and look at them to reassure himself that he could leave this locked ward if he wanted to. So far he was resisting the impulse to *try* the key in the door; what if it should fail to fit the lock, and none of the nurses or staff admitted to knowing who he was? What if they made him take off his white coat and put on clothes from the boutique closet, and forced him to take some subsistence-pharmer dose of meds, and showed him a bed in one of the rooms and told him it was his? What if it *was* his? He *had* been a patient in a place like this, in Wichita, at the age of seventeen. . . .

Atropine again for Richie. . . .

The charge nurse had given him a bewildered look when he had burst into the demented ice-cream social, hours ago, wearing his awkward two-figure mannikin appliance. He had mumbled something about it being a tool to reintegrate dissociatives—well, he could stick with that. He might *try* it on a dissociative sometime!

But he had needed the masking effect of the contraption. Long John Beach had been dangerously preempted during that ice-cream-social bedlam, and Armentrout had needed every masking measure he could put on, what with the god apparently *right in here,* breaking the place up with an earthquake and freeing inmates from their captivity.

Armentrout rocked his head back to look up at the raw cracks in the ceiling.

All at once he stood up, shuddering. His fully charged cellular telephone was a weight in his jacket pocket, but suddenly he couldn't bear being in the TV lounge any longer. He waved at the night charge nurse through the station window as he hurried past.

Plumtree and *Cochran,* Armentrout thought as he strode down the dark hall toward his closed office door. Why would the god have freed Cochran *too?*

Armentrout wondered uneasily if he ought to have paid more attention to the deluded widower. How *had* the man come to have that ivy-leaf mark on the back of his right hand? Cochran hadn't reported having any delusional episodes—or visitations—while he was here; Armentrout would have been alerted by anything like that; but was the dreary fellow more than just psychically sensitive, could he have some *link* with the god?

Armentrout's key unlocked his office door, but he was too distracted to be pleased by the little vindication. I should have had him on hard meds, he thought as he blundered across the linoleum floor and sat down at the desk; hell, I should have given *him* benzodiazepine and ECT! I lost more than I gained, working them out on Plumtree, even if my— even if no distant ghost got a fix on me.

I got the taste of your blood now, and the smell of your jizz. In voodoo terms, that constitutes having your ID package. True, Armentrout thought now. But I do have a vial of your blood, Mr. Salvoy.

He stared at the two-figure mannikin appliance that was canted against the couch. With shirts, jackets, trousers, and shoes hung and hooked onto the aluminum poles, and the pair of clothing-store mannikin heads stuck on the swivelling neck-posts, the thing did look like two blandly smiling men with their arms around the shoulders of an invisible third man in the middle; and when he strapped the framework onto his own shoulders, Armentrout would become the third man, the man in the middle. A lever in the chest of the left-hand dummy permitted him to work the mechanical outside arms, and one in the right-hand dummy let him swivel the heads this way and that. And he had cored out holes in the backs of the Styrofoam heads, under the Dynel wigs, and stuffed into the holes dozens of paper towels spotted with patients' blood samples. The thing weighed about twenty pounds and was awkward to wear, and in public it drew *far* too much derisive attention, but on several occasions it had proven to be an effective multi-level psychic scrambler, a terrifically refractive and deflecting mask. Even some moron with a plain old *gun*, Armentrout thought, would be likely to hit the wrong head.

The telephone on his desk rang, making him jump in his chair, and in the instant before he realized that the vibration in his ribs was just his cellular phone ringing too, he thought he was having some sort of cardiac arrest.

"Yes?" he said into the receiver when he had fumbled it up to his ear. Not long-distance, he thought fervently, please. Let it just finally be the cop.

And, thankfully, it *was* the cop.

"Doctor?" came the man's voice. "Officer Hamilton here. Sorry it's so late, I called as quick as I could after I got off work. Got a pencil? I've got the location of the place where your Appleseed girl said she killed the Flying Nun king."

Armentrout shakily wrote down an address on Neptune Avenue in Leucadia. "And did you come up with anything about Neal Obstadt's death two years ago?"

"More or less. Something damn peculiar was going on that week, and the L.A. cops are still trying to figure it out. Obstadt's body was found in the water off the ocean side of the *Queen Mary* after some kind of bomb went off in the water there, on October 31 of '92, though no traces of any kind of explosive chemicals were found in the water, and no bomb fragments at all were recovered; he was blown to pieces, but they found a small-caliber bullet in his guts too. And the body of a film producer named Loretta deLarava was found up on one of the tourist decks with a *.45* slug in her heart. She was filming some kind of TV special there, and we questioned a lot of her employees. Apparently deLarava had brought six people aboard *at gunpoint, as handcuffed prisoners.* One was that one-armed amnesiac nut you took charge of, who still had a pair of cuffs hanging from his wrist when they found him half-dead on the shore of the lagoon. And I've got the names of the other five, if you want 'em.''

"Yes, please.''

"Okay. Nicholas Bradshaw—he was the actor who played Spooky the ghost in that old TV show, 'Ghost of a Chance,' which was cancelled in 1960; a lawyer named J. Francis Strube, who spoke to detectives only through a lawyer of his own and basically had nothing useful to say; an itinerant electrical engineer named Peter Sullivan, whose twin sister had killed herself in Delaware five days previous; a lady psychiatrist who's been wanted on manslaughter charges since November of 1990, named Angelica Anthem Elizalde; and an eleven-year-old kid named Koot Hoomie Parganas, whose parents were torture-murdered the same night Sullivan's twin sister killed herself. All these people got free of their handcuffs, as if one of 'em had a key or was an escape artist.''

Hamilton sighed over the line. "Bradshaw and Sullivan and Elizalde and the Parganas kid haven't been found since," he went on, "even though they're seriously wanted for at least questioning. DeLarava was offering a big reward for the fugitive Parganas boy, and the boy apparently called nine-one-one on the evening of the 27th, but the call was interrupted, and *I* think he's probably dead; and the Elizalde woman apparently shot at a woman in the Westlake area on the 28th. And then after Halloween the LAPD was deluged with calls about all this—from *psychics!* Unhelpful.''

Elizalde! thought Armentrout with a stir of remembered admiration. What a deluded pioneer that woman was! And a dark, long-legged beauty, too—I used to see her a lot when she was on the staff at the County Hospital in Huntington Park in '88 and '89.

But the mention of one-armed Long John Beach had reminded him that the crazy old man was presently in ''three-points'' in the Quiet Room, and that if he was going to have to take Beach out of the hospital, it would be far easier with just the night staff to get past.

"So, have there been," Armentrout asked, knowing that this was his main question, and not at all sure what answer he wished for, "any of the peculiarities I asked about, going on at the Leucadia address, or near it?" *Do I get to go home now and catch a few hours of sleep, and visit the Neptune Avenue place at my leisure and alone,* he thought—*or must I rush off there now, bringing all my cumbrous psychic-defense impedimenta along?*

"Well," said Hamilton, "nobody's *reported* any 'sudden growth of vegetation' to the cops . . . nor the opposite . . . but they wouldn't hardly, would they?"

"I suppose not," said Armentrout with a smile, beginning to relax and think of his bed.

"But there've been a *whole* lot of calls about crazy teenagers driving through the neighborhood honking their horns and shooting off firecrackers—guns too, we've found ejected shells on the street. And either them or some other crowd of teenagers has been dancing on the beach at all hours, real noisy. You did mention 'other disturbances.' And," Hamilton added, chuckling through a yawn, "you didn't ask about this, but *two separate people* have called the *Union Tribune* to announce that Elvis Presley is going to be coming to town to stay with them for a few weeks. Oh, and you know the way evangelists are always saying the world's about to end? Well, a nut Bible church on the 101 there, one of the charismatic-hysterical types that rent space in failed laundromats, has announced that the world *already* ended, on New Year's Day. We're all living in some kind of delusional Purgatory right now, they say."

While the man had been talking, Armentrout had abandoned all thought of going home to bed, and was now wearily planning how he would get Long John Beach and the two-figure appliance out of the clinic past the security guards.

"These . . . teenagers," Armentrout said, just to be sure, "are they . . . dressed nice? Seem to have money?"

"Not in particular. But hey, their cars all look like solid gold! They drive anything at all, Volkswagens, beat old Fords, Hondas, see—but a whole lot of them are painted metallic gold, and they've got wreaths of flowers hung over the license plates; even on the back plates, which is a violation. The neighborhood residents say it'd look like a parade if they weren't tearing through so fast. The kids on the beach, it's hard to tell—get this, they bring big pots of *white clay,* and smear themselves up with it for their dancing. Can't even tell what race they are, I gather."

Armentrout sighed. "Thank you, Officer Hamilton. I think that will be all."

"Okay, Doc. Say, how's your crazy girl working out? Was her name Figleaf? I hope she was worth the money."

Armentrout thought of telling Hamilton that the woman had escaped, then discarded the idea. I don't really want the cops in on this now, he thought. "Miss Figleaf has been a valuable addition to our team," he said vaguely.

"Softball league, sounds like. Well, if you use electric scoreboards, nobody'll know when you lose—right?—with her playing for you."

Armentrout agreed absently and hung up the phone. "And if the referee's got a pacemaker, he'd better not declare her out," he said softly, to no one but the Siamese-twin mannikins leaning against the couch.

Well, she really did kill the king, he thought, our Miss Plumtree, our Miss Figleaf . . . who certainly held tight to her fig leaf while she was here. And a new king is apparently in readiness. Those people expecting Elvis sense it—*the undying King is coming here!*—and the gangs of teenagers are clearly some kind of spontaneous embodiment of the Maruts who are mentioned in the Rig-Veda: noisy, armed youths from a culture so primitive that dance served the purpose of devout prayer, who—helpfully in this instance, while the king is temporarily out of the picture—aggressively embody fertility; and they're assuming too the role of the Cretan Kouretes, who hid the vulnerable infant Zeus from his murderous father Kronos by performing their Sword Dance around the baby, and masked his crying with the noise of their clashing weapons.

It's in Leucadia that I'll get a line on the new king, Armentrout thought, whoever it turns out to be. I wonder if dawn is close enough yet for Venus to be shining like a star in the eastern sky.

The telephone rang again. Armentrout assumed Hamilton had forgotten some detail, and he picked up the receiver. "Hello?"

And then his lungs seemed to freeze—because over the phone he was hearing once again, for the first time in eleven days, the familiar phantom bar sounds, laughter and clinking glass and moronic jabbering. Then a well-remembered voice came on the line—loud, as the very fresh ones always were: "Doctor?" whined the teenaged bipolar girl who had killed herself last week. "I walk all crooked now—where's the rest of me?"

He hung up the phone without saying anything. There was no use talking to ghosts anyway, and he didn't want to give the thing the confirmation of having found him.

But she *had* found him, and no doubt would again. Hers was the first local death for which he'd been responsible since the mysterious and apparently one-shot amnesty that had been granted at dawn on New Year's Day. How long could it possibly, reasonably be before he would need to send more people—or even just idiot mumbling fragments of people, which would clump together—to that uncorporeal bar?

As he stood up and crossed to the file cabinet to fetch out the two purple velvet boxes and the unrefrigerated blood sample from Plumtree, he was mentally rehearsing his imminent departure from the clinic. I can avoid some carrying-hassle by strapping the two-figure appliance right onto Long John Beach, he thought; he's already established as crazy.

I'll write him a pass, say we're going on a field trip . . . to early-morning mass at some Catholic church. I'll tell the guards that the old man thinks he's the Three Wise Men, overdue at Bethlehem.

CHAPTER 12

My father hath a power; inquire of him,
And learn to make a body of a limb.

—William Shakespeare,
Richard II

Watch for a Mobil station,'' said Plumtree, leaning back in the driver's seat and squinting through cigarette smoke at the onrushing dark pavement of Highway 101.

Cochran nodded and peered through a wiped-clean patch of the steamy windshield, though there was nothing at the moment to see but the endless ellipsis of reflective orange lane-marker dots and the perilously close night-time fog hanging on the road shoulder. They were north of Oxnard, out of L.A. County, and had just driven past the exit for something called Lost Hills Road. *Why would anyone take that exit?* Plumtree had wondered aloud. *If* hills *get lost out there, they'd certainly lose* you.

''The Jenkins woman's not gonna be cancelling her credit cards till ten,'' Plumtree went on now, ''at the earliest. Hell, the way she was knocking back the margaritas, she probably won't get up before noon.''

Jenkins had proven to be the name of the woman whose purse Plumtree had stolen at the Mount Sabu bar. After searching the Belmont Shore area for an older-model car, and then finding and quickly hot-wiring a '69 Ford Torino that had been parked off Redondo Avenue, Plumtree had used the Jenkins woman's Visa card in an all-night Ralph's market to buy a carton of cigarettes and a dozen cans of soup and a can opener and a fistful of Slim Jim packages and two twelve-packs of Coors and two bottles of Listerine and three 750-milliliter bottles of Popov vodka. A vodka bottle was opened now, wedged between her thighs and occasionally rattled by the bumps on the steering wheel when she changed lanes.

One of the lane changes was a sharp enough swerve to press Cochran against the passenger-side door and make him drop his cigarette, and Plumtree only remembered to click on the turn signal after she was in the left lane and yanking the car back straight. The vodka bottle had rattled like a mariachi band's percussion gourd. "You want me to drive?" Cochran asked, fumbling on the floor for his cigarette.

"You're drunk," said Plumtree. "And don't . . . *point out to me* . . . that I'm drinking. Alcohol makes me a better driver, keeps me alert. We need an alert driver, for this fog."

Cochran sat back in the passenger seat and hoped she was right. Certainly he wasn't sober . . . and at least they both had their seat belts on. He didn't want to have to stop and get out of the car, anyway—the car had a heater, and Plumtree had blessedly turned it up to full blast.

Past her silhouetted head he could faintly see the line of the surf glowing gray as it silently rose and fell out past the State Beach, under stars haloed by the incoming fog so that they looked like the stars in Van Gogh's *Starry Night.*

"I wonder if the dead king's crowd has even got started yet," he said.

"All the dead king's horses and all the dead king's men . . ." Plumtree said softly.

Couldn't put Scott Crane together again, Cochran mentally finished the rhyme.

"I think—" Plumtree began; then she went on quickly, "this car runs pretty smooth, doesn't it? I'd like to have done a compression check before we took off on an eight-hour drive, but I don't hear any bad lifters or rocker arms."

Cochran bent over to reach into the bag between his feet, and he tore open the top of one of the beer cartons and lifted a can out. "*What* do you think?" he asked casually as he popped the top and took a leisurely sip.

"You may as well start working on those," said Plumtree with a nod, "they'll only warm up, sitting down there by the heater vent." She hiked up the vodka bottle and took a hearty gulp. "I think *I* turned those moths into wasps."

The lights and exit ramps of Ventura had swept past now, but Cochran hadn't noticed a Mobil sign. Oh well, he thought, Santa Barbara is coming up fast, and—he peered at the lighted dashboard—we're only a little under a quarter tank. "Really?" he said, his voice quiet but not skeptical. "Good enough so they could actually sting?"

"Well, I don't know if they could really *sting*. And it would be Valorie that did it, not actually this here *me*. But I think it was because that Mavranos guy asked you about the mark on your hand, and I— we—didn't want him to find out about it. Is that a birthmark?"

"I—told Janis about it," Cochran whispered hoarsely after another gulped sip. "She and I don't speak to each other much."

Cochran sighed. "In 1961, when I was seven, I thought I saw a face, a whiskery little old head, in an old Zinfandel stump that was being pruned back for the winter, and, without thinking, I shoved my hand out to stop the shears from cutting the old man's head off." The steady green glow of the instrument-panel dials was a cozy contrast to the night and the fog and the rushing lane markers outside, and he took another sip of the cold beer, secure in the knowledge that there were twenty-three more full cans between his ankles. The coal of his cigarette glowed as he inhaled on it, and a moment later exhaled smoke curled against the windshield.

"*Actually,*" he said slowly, then paused; "I think it's old rust or bark dust, under the skin. Like a powder-burn. Anyway, it's not a birthmark."

Plumtree nodded and had another couple of swallows from the vodka bottle. "Actually what?" she asked.

Her question forced a short, awkward laugh out of Cochran. It made him dizzy to realize that he was teetering on the brink of telling this Plumtree woman—*this* one!—a secret he had kept for thirty-three years; and to realize too that, in the warm nest-like secrecy of this anonymous car flying along in the middle of cold dark nowhere, he *wanted* to; so he choked down a big impulsive mouthful of beer and used the sudden dizziness to get himself over the hump.

He spoke rapidly: "Actually—as I remember it, anyway, maybe I'm confusing it with dreams I had later—the shears cut right through my hand, cut it most of the way *off*. No kidding—there was blood squirting everywhere, and the vineyard worker with the shears was in shock, looking like . . . like his face was carved out of bone, with a big bullet-hole for a mouth." He tilted up the can to finish the beer in three deep gulps. "Then, about one full second later, there was an almighty bang— a, a crash like you dropped a Sherman tank from thirty thousand feet onto the roof of the Astrodome—and when I could *think* again, maybe another second or two later, my hand was fine, whole, not a scratch, and not a drop of blood anywhere—my hand didn't even have this mark on it yet; that was there when I woke up one morning about exactly a year later—but the old vine was standing there in full, bushy, *impossible* summertime bloom.'' Jerkily he leaned forward again to put the empty can onto the floor mat and tug another can free of the carton.

''Mobil station,'' he said briskly when he had straightened up again and looked out through the windshield. ''Next exit, it looks like,'' he added, nodding and squinting like a navigator. He popped the can open, but just held it. ''And,'' he went on gently, shaking his head, ''it had ripe grape bunches hanging all over it, but also . . . pomegranates, and figs, and I don't know what all else. This was in the *dead* of winter.'' He took a deep breath and let it out, then glanced at Plumtree with a wry smile. ''You'd better let me deal with pumping the gas, and paying for it. You're gonna reek of liquor.''

''That's Santa Barbara,'' Plumtree said, switching on the turn-signal indicator and scuffing her tennis shoe from the gas pedal to the brake. ''After this we turn inland at Gaviota. The fog'll be worse then. Vodka doesn't have half the smell that beer's got. You probably stink like an old bar towel. What did the guy with the shears do, the vineyard worker?''

''He got very damn drunk.''

Plumtree nodded as she steered off the highway and rattled across an intersection on a green light. ''That shows respect.''

The left-side tires bounced up over the curb when she swung the big old Ford into the white-lit Mobil station, but she managed to park it next to one of the pumps. Cochran had dropped his cigarette again, but he just stomped it out on the floorboards. Before he could remark on the way she'd handled the driveway, she said, ''I gotta disconnect the coil to turn this off. That's good, though—a modern car, with the ignition in the steering column, I'd have had to bust it out, and cops look for that, in parking lots, and then . . . they wait for whoever to come back to the car. Who's driving it.''

She enunciated the syllables as carefully as if she were pushing silver dollars out of her mouth one at a time, and Cochran realized that she herself was very drunk; and when he levered open the passenger-side door and stood up and took several deep breaths of the icy air, he was so dizzy that he had to hang on to the door to keep his balance.

He swung his unwieldy gaze over the car's roof, and watched Plumtree shuffle to the front bumper, frowning and holding on to the vibrating fender with both hands. When she had hoisted up the hood and pulled free the wire that connected the coil to the battery, the engine shook twice and then wheezed to a halt; and in the silence he said, ''I think we should . . . let Janis drive.''

''She'd get lost,'' said Plumtree shortly. ''I'm gonna go give the man the card, sign for it—you pump the gas when I wave.'' She wobbled across the damp asphalt toward the glass door, then halted and looked back at him. "On the Torinos the gasp cap is behind the rear licempse plate."

Cochran squeaked the license plate down, unscrewed the gas cap, and shoved the nozzle of the premium pump into the filler hole, and then he leaned heavily on the trunk as he held the aluminum trigger squeezed and numbly watched the wheels behind the little gas pump window roll around to, finally, fifteen dollars and sixty cents. The aromatic reek of gasoline on the cold night air did nothing to sober him up.

He had hung up the nozzle but was still trying to get the cap threaded back on when Plumtree reattached the coil wire and jumped the solenoid again to start the engine. When he heard the hood slam down he just dropped the cap and let the license plate snap up over it, and then hurried to the passenger-side door and got in, glad of the interior warmth even if they were both about to die in a Driving-Under-the-Influence one-car crash in the foggy canyons beyond Gaviota.

She clanked the engine into gear and drove right over the curb onto Milpas Street, swinging wide in a chirruping left turn to get back to the 101.

"Oh, *okay,*" she said, and the engine missed for a moment, coming back strongly when she fluttered the gas pedal. "Whoops! When do I turn?"

"Take that on-ramp on the right," said Cochran through clenched teeth, pulling the seat belt across himself. "101 north."

She glanced at him after she had made the turn. "Scant! What day is it?"

He relaxed a little, and didn't attach the seatbelt. "It's the morning of the twelfth by now," he said cautiously, "of January. It's been a couple of hours since we left Solville."

"My father is alive," she said. "I *did* catch him!"

"That's . . . right, I guess. According to that Angelica woman." He tried to remember when it had been that Janis had last been up.

She leaned back in the seat now, straightening her arms and flexing her fingers at the top of the wheel. "This is disorienting—I don't have to watch for cues, I can just *ask* you! How did we get away from there? I don't think they wanted us to just leave."

"No—we snuck out. They were talking about—holding a gun on you. We're still working with them, I guess, but at arm's length."

She was gingerly licking her lips and grimacing. "I'm glad to get away from that burnt-liquor stink. Nobody got hurt, I hope?"

"Oh no." He let the seat belt reel back up into the slot above the door, and finally sat back and let himself exhale. "Well, not *hurt*—but that old man with the windshield wipers all over him died. But it was just, like, a heart attack, I guess. Nothing to do with us. And then in the confusion Cody just grabbed my hand and we walked out. And stole us this car.''

"My father spoke to me over the telephone.''

Cochran thought of someone who had to maintain a '69 Torino, going out to work on a Thursday morning and finding the car gone; but at least Janis was a sober driver. She hadn't had anything to drink since . . . what? A Manhattan or two at dinner, hours and hours ago. Of course it was the same bloodstream, really, but it did seem that Cody had taken the alcohol away with her.

"Yes," he said. "I heard him."

She was still smacking her lips, and now she said, "Did Cody get mouthwash?''

"As a matter of fact, she did. A big bottle of Listerine.''

"Could you pass it to me?''

Cochran did, and she unscrewed the cap and took a swig of the mouthwash; she swished it around audibly in her mouth for a few seconds, then rolled down the window to spit it outside.

"We're going to San Francisco, aren't we?'' she said as she rolled the window back up.

"Yes." Cochran blinked in the new Listerine fumes, trying to remember whether Janis had still been on when San Francisco had first been proposed. He was sure she had not, that Cody had already been in control then. "How did you know that?''

"That's where he . . . fell off the building. And I caught him.''

"We're going there because it's where they all—you all—hell, *we* all, can get Scott Crane restored to life." According to a crazy old dead black lady, at least, he thought.

"They're bringing his body along, I hope?'' It seemed to Cochran that she spoke anxiously.

He thought of the vague plan Cody had described for getting Crane back into his own undecayed body—or, failing that, into hers permanently; and he discarded the idea of asking her about it, for she would probably just lose time if he did ask, and leave the drunk Cody to drive.

"They said they were," he told her. "We're probably going to be meeting them at a place called the Cliff House Restaurant, on the northwest shore.''

"I'll be hungry by then—Cody ate most of my dinner. Did she pick up any snacks?''

"Some Slim Jims," said Cochran, trying to remember if he had been as unconcerned as this when he had learned that Spider Joe was dead; of course he had actually seen the body, and Janis had not.

"Could I have a pack?"

Cochran leaned down and dug a Slim Jims package out of the bag; and he got out too another beer for himself. He opened the can, and, before he took the first sip, he said, "Here's to poor old Spider Joe. May he rest in peace."

Plumtree nodded, staring ahead. "His wife died, though, right? Recently?"

"They did say that," agreed Cochran. He took another, deeper sip.

At the gas-station-and-motel town of Gaviota the 101 curled sharply to the east, inland, and soon they were climbing through the dark canyons of the Santa Ynez Mountains. The fog was a blurry wall close ahead of them, glowing gray with the diffracted radiance of the headlights, and the short patch of pavement that was visible in front of the fog seemed to Cochran's tired eyes to be stationary, so that the black lines of skid marks were standing waves shimmying in place, and the point-of-impact of a long-ago dropped can of white paint seemed to be the beak of a diving white bird. They passed big semi-trailer trucks that were stopped on the shoulder, visible through the fog only by yellow lights along their roofs; and the lights seemed to Cochran to trace the rigging of tanker ships more remote in the night than the trucks could possibly really be.

Cones of light, luminous triangular shapes in the darkness, resolved themselves into spotlit billboards, or steep hillside shoulders with headlights approaching from the other side, as he watched them gradually materialize out of the night; and rotating spoke-like fingers of light would turn overhead when an unseen car in the southbound lanes approached behind invisible tree branches. Sometimes Plumtree would change lanes to get around the ghostly red eyes of brake lights ahead of them, and in those transitional moments when the tires were thumping across the lane-divider bumps the turn-signal lights would strobe deeply into the fog on the shoulder, illuminating a bottle or a weed or a shoe for a brief, startled instant.

From time to time Cochran glimpsed moonlit forests off to the side, and the sterile extents of deserts, but it wasn't until he twice saw a vast castle in the remote distance, with rows of yellow- and green-lit windows, and then saw that it was only a reflection of the instrument panel lights in the close window glass, that he realized that nothing he saw beyond a distance of about six feet could be genuine. The realization didn't stop his weary, smoke-stung eyes from registering new wonders;

in fact it seemed to free his optic nerves to present him with wilder things, ships and towering siege engines and dirigibles.

The old Ford's engine had begun to cough when they were driving past the isolated lights of the Madonna Inn in San Luis Obispo, but began to run smoothly again after that—and Plumtree, who for some miles had been folding her left leg and straightening it again and scooting forward and back in her seat as if trying to stay awake, reached out to the side and squeezed Cochran's leg just above the knee.

"Do we have any more cigarettes?" she asked.

"A—whole carton," Cochran said, suddenly very aware of the close flex of her legs in the tight jeans. He gripped his current beer between his thighs and bent forward to grope by his feet for a fresh pack of Marlboros.

But when he straightened up she glanced at it and shook her head. "I meant More, the brand name. I suppose Cody just thought of herself, and got just the Marlboros." Her fingers were curled around his leg now, palpably brushing against the dashboard-facing side of the beer can, and her thumb was absently rubbing the top of his thigh. "And I don't suppose she bought any Southern Comfort."

"No," said Cochran. "Just beer and vodka." He stubbed out his cigarette in the ashtray and then, as if for a sip of beer, lifted away the impeding can. Her hand slid halfway up his thigh, her fingers kneading the worn secondhand corduroy.

"All alone in the middle of nighttime nowhere," she said, barely loud enough for him to hear. "Some people would consider this a highly lucrative situation."

Cochran didn't see how some people would, but he shifted closer to her and put his arm around her shoulder to stroke her coarsely cut blond hair. She rolled her head back against his forearm, and her right hand slid up his leg until her little finger was brushing the tight fabric over his crotch.

"We should," he said hoarsely, "probably pull over and park on the shoulder for a while. Till the fog clears a bit." His heart was thudding in his chest, and he wished there was somewhere he could put down the beer he was holding in his right hand. And I should try to get a slug of that mouthwash, he thought.

Her kneading hand was fully on his crotch now, and he simply let go of the beer can; it thudded to the carpeted floorboard as he reached across to cup the unfamiliar hot softness of her left breast through the thin fabric of her blouse.

"Nobody can interrupt us out here," she whispered, and snapped the turn signal lever up to indicate a lane change. "Nobody knows where we are.'' The right tires were rumbling on the shoulder, and Plumtree's leg flexed as she pressed the brake pedal. ''There's no phone here, so nobody can say we should have taken the time to call anyone.''

''You're a big girl,'' Cochran agreed dizzily. ''You don't have to call your mother and let her know where you are.''

''Ah!'' she said, and her voice sounded sad; then she had whipped her right hand up so hard that it struck the head liner and nearly broke his elbow. Her foot slammed onto the gas pedal, and the back tires screeched and burned rubber as she steered the bucking old Ford back out into the slow lane.

''Fog, take it easy!'' Cochran yelled, clasping his elbow.

She hit the brake hard enough to throw him forward against the padded black dashboard. He could hear his dropped beer can rolling on the floor.

''I will drive this car straight into a wall if you try to touch me, Omar!'' Plumtree said loudly. ''In arousing ways! Jesus will not blame me—He will take me into His bosom, and throw *you* into the fires of Gehenna! You know I will, and you know He will!''

''Fine!'' Cochran gasped. ''Drive normal! What's the matter with you, Janis?''

She straightened the wheel, and though the engine was coughing again she quickly accelerated the car to a steady twenty miles an hour, glancing harriedly from the road to the rear-view mirror and back. ''I'm sorry, Scant!'' she said. ''I must have dozed off! God, I might have got us killed! Okay, fog still, okay. Did I hit anything? God, my arms are shaking! Are you all right?''

''Well you nearly broke *my* arm,'' he said harshly. ''Jesus, girl!'' He could see that there had been at least one personality shift, and that the erotic moment was long gone. ''No, you didn't hit anything.'' He leaned down and yanked a fresh beer out of the box. The floorboard carpeting was marshy under the soles of his tennis shoes, and the hot air was fetid with the smell of the spilled beer. ''Who's Omar?''

''That's my father's name! Be careful now, Scant, I don't want to lose time with you—but—was *he* here?''

''No,'' Cochran said. Thank God, he added mentally. He popped the tab on the beer can. ''Another woman—did I . . . ? Do you, uh, recall putting your hand on my leg?''

''Oh, God, Tiffany,'' she said ruefully. ''That would be Tiffany, I bet. She made a pass at you, right? And you thought it was me! Poor Scant!''

He had been panting, but now began to relax. ''I wouldn't mind,'' he said cautiously, ''if it was you.''

"It will be, Scant, I promise you, soon, and not in the back of an old car, either." She patted at the seat around her legs. "Did she eat my Slim Jim? God, that woke me up, at least—I could feel that I was slipping in and out, back there. I guess Tiffany was slipping out and in."

Her guileless last couple of lines were echoing in his head, and he tilted up his fresh can of beer for a distancing, objectivity-inducing mouthful.

"If you get sleepy again," he said, "just pull over. You can catch a nap on the front seat, and I'll do the same in the trunk."

"Did Cody get a key to the trunk?"

He sighed. "I was kidding. And no, she didn't—she hot-wired the car somehow."

"She is mechanically inclined," Plumtree allowed, diligently watching the road. Her mouth was working, and she rolled down the window; cold night air blew into the car and twitched Cochran's sweaty hair. "My mouth's full of Tiffany's spit," Plumtree said, her voice frailer with the open window beyond her. "Could I have the mouthwash?"

Cochran passed it to her, and again she swished a sip of the sharp-smelling stuff and spat it out the window. He was glad when she rolled the window up again, though the sudden scents of diesel exhaust and spicy clay and the dry-white-wine smell of the fog had been a relief from the warm-beer fumes.

"You okay to drive?" he asked.

"Oh, sure. I kind of did catch a nap there, I guess, while she was on. Besides, you're a little—you're more than point-oh-eight blood alcohol, I'd guess."

"Technically, I suppose, yeah," he said. "We'd better," Cochran went on steadily, "take the 280, to the city, rather than follow the 101 all the way up. We can stop at my house, and I can pick up some clothes and money." And think all this over, soberly, he thought. And check the phone messages, and take in the mail. And clip the holstered .357 onto the back of my belt, if I decide we should indeed go on and meet the others.

"Tell me when to turn," Plumtree said.

"Oh, it won't be for hours yet."

"Won't it . . . bother you, seeing the place where you lived with your wife?"

Cochran took a long drag on his cigarette. "I suppose so. Sure it will. Gotta be done, though. Faced."

Plumtree shivered. "It must be scary, not having anyone you can turn the wheel over to, in bad situations."

Cochran smiled bleakly. "I never—"

Both of them jumped when for an instant a big brown owl swooped into the flickering headlight glow and then disappeared over the roof.

Cochran forced a laugh, embarrassed to have been so startled but pleased that he had not dropped his cigarette. "I wonder what owls think of this highway of lights running through the middle of their mountains."

"They're hoping for a crash, a fire that'll drive the mice and rabbits out of hiding."

After a moment, he said, "A plausible answer, Cody, but I was talking to Janis."

She exhaled as if trying to whistle. "Listerine! Who else was on?"

"Somebody called Tiffany. And then—"

"You pig." She rocked on the seat and then brushed the fingers of one hand from the buttons of her blouse to the fly of her jeans. "What did you two *do* with me?"

"Nothing." He tried to say it as though he had resisted Tiffany's advances. This was a disorienting basis for conversation, and it occurred to him that it might be difficult to manage any intimacy even with Janis, without Cody objecting and interfering in humiliating ways. "Anyway, she was interrupted by somebody else, a woman who cussed me out— called me Omar." He wondered how much Cody might have sobered up in the time she was gone, and he half-hoped something he said might drive her away and let Janis back on.

"Follow the Queen, you were playing," said Plumtree. "You must have mentioned our . . . female parent, right? She comes up sometimes when somebody even just mentions her, and *always* when somebody *asks* for her. You ever play Follow the Queen?"

"The poker game? Sure—seven-card stud, where the next card dealt faceup, after a faceup queen, is wild."

"Wild, right—that is, it's *whatever you declare it to be*. And when our parent-of-the-fair-sex is up, the next girl is whoever you ask for. Who did you ask for? Not me, Mom doesn't do the mouthwash bit."

"I guess I called for Janis."

"Not Tiffany? That was noble of you. Of course you didn't understand the rules yet. Do you *swear* you two didn't do anything with me?"

Cochran realized, to his surprise, that he didn't want to swear to a lie. "I swear there was no kiss," he said, "and not a button was undone or a zipper unzipped."

"Oh, you pig. I bet you groped me. I bet you were ready to go all-in on that flop."

"Flop," said Cochran, thinking in poker terms now, and remembering that she had used the word several times before this. "That's what the three communal cards are called, in Hold-'Em: the flop. You hope they make some good hand, combined with your two personal down-cards. Sometimes you just pass even if you've got ace-king down, if the flop is all the wrong suit,'cause *somebody's* surely got two of the flop's suit, for a flush."

"When it's . . . *real life* . . . you can't pass," she said grimly, "it's like you're the perpetual Big Blind, gotta make the bet whether you want to or not."

Cochran remembered Janis telling him, just a few moments ago, that he must find it "scary" not to be able to turn a bad situation over to another personality; and he laughed softly with dawning comprehension. "You girls are like a . . . squad, a relay-team, at the big Poker Table of Life, though, aren't you? If a flop comes that's no good to Cody's hole-cards, Janis or Tiffany or somebody will be holding two different cards, ones that'll make a flush or a full boat or something. And so the girl with the playable cards steps in."

"It still calls for some hard bluffing sometimes. But so far they haven't dealt us a flop *one* of us couldn't play."

Cochran tilted up his beer to get the last swallow, and sleepily wondered whether to bother opening another. And he thought again about Janis's remark: *Won't it bother you, seeing the place where you lived with your wife?*

"Must be convenient, though," he said now, "nevertheless. 'Somebody yelling at me? I got a headache? I'll split, and be back when it's been taken care of.' "

Plumtree's vodka bottle was on the seat between them, and he impulsively picked it up and unscrewed the cap. "*I—I* had to go identify my wife's run-over pregnant body," he said, suddenly speaking loudly, "in the morgue. She was *pregnant.* We bought stuff for the kid-to-be— the stuff's in that house now, that I'm gonna be breaking a window to get into in a few hours—a crib, goddammit, teddy-bear wallpaper. And Nina and I had adjoining plots, in a cemetery there, we picked out a spot we liked and paid for it—but I had to have her cremated and take her ashes to France, so I'll be buried there alone." He gulped a mouthful of the warm, scorching liquor and burningly exhaled through his nose. "*I* haven't had the option of *going away* during *any* of this. *I've* got to *pay* for what I take, sometimes as much as all I've got. I've got to, like *most* people, I've got to take the wounds and then just keep playing, wounded, shoving all my chips out with one hand while I—hold my burst guts in with the other." The fumes in his nose were making his eyes water. "My hole cards are two dead people, and the, the *flop* I'm

facing is—is those three merciless ladies in Greek mythology who measure out life and fucking cut it off.''

"Clotho, Lachesis, and Atropine,'' said Plumtree blandly, watching
the road. "Let's play a game—I'll name a paper product, and you guess
what it is.''

Cochran's heart was hammering, and his mouth was dry and hot in
spite of the vodka, but he didn't go on shouting. "What?'' he said, his
voice cracking. "That doesn't make any sense.''

"Why don't you take a nap, then, champ? It might sober you up, and
I'll be ready to be spelled off, come dawn.'' She glanced at him and
smiled. "Little man, you've had a busy day.''

"... Maybe I will.'' His anger had evaporated as quickly as it had
come, leaving him deflated. Slowly he screwed the cap back on the
bottle. "You want some of this?''

"I'm fine for now. Leave it on the seat there, in case of emergencies.''

Cochran stretched his feet out and leaned his head against the cool,
damp window glass. "You did that trick just now, didn't you?'' he said
emptily, closing his eyes. "What I said made you mad, and you threw
the anger over onto me. I—I'm sorry if I hurt your feelings.'' Though
as I recall, he thought, everything I said was true.

"Go to sleep. You can say anything you want, and yeah, if it pisses
me off I'll just throw it back at you. 'I'm rubber, you're glue, whatever
you say bounces off me and sticks to you.' All I care about is looking
out for Number One.'' She laughed softly. "I'm just trying to figure
out who that is.''

Cochran's last thought before he went to sleep or passed out was that
her remarks about his interval with Tiffany must not, after all, have
represented real anger.

Mad as a March herring,'' observed Kootie, agreeing with Mavranos's
assessment of Janis Cordelia Plumtree. They were sitting in the front
seat of Mavranos's truck, barrelling along at a steady seventy miles per
hour north on the 101 out past Oxnard, with the surf a rippling line far
away in the darkness on their left. Mavranos's view of the right lane
was partly blocked by a new Buddha-like stone statue on the dashboard,
but he was getting used to that.

"That would be the technical term, yes,'' said Angelica Sullivan from
the back seat, where she was loading a stack of extended-round .45
ACP magazines—pressing each Eldorado Starfire hollow-point bullet
down against the spring pressure with the forefinger of her left hand

while she tucked the next into the cleared top of the magazine with the fingers of her right.

Mavranos could see her working in the rear-view mirror. She must have loaded a dozen of those illegal twelve-round magazines by now, he thought. Even with her .45 Marlin carbine, handily built to take the same size magazine, that's a whole lot of back-up ammo.

She looked up, and in the mirror he could see a glint of highway light reflect from her eye. "You think I'm over-preparing?" she asked.

Mavranos shrugged. "Better than under."

Pete Sullivan lifted three of the loaded magazines and tucked them into the canvas knapsack at his side. "And these bullets have each got a drop of a rust-based *omiero* soup in the tip," he said, "—my pacifist Houdini hands have been capable of that much work, at least—so these'll stop a ghost as readily as a live human."

"Good thing," said Mavranos, watching the traffic ahead and wondering what sort of vehicle Plumtree and Cochran might be driving in. "For the Plumtree woman you'd want both functions. I know, Angelica, you already said her murderer father's actually not a ghost—but I swear there's a ghost in that blond head *too*." He glanced at the dashboard. "We're gonna need gas again, next chance—maybe switch in one of the fresh batteries too."

"We should have taken one of the Solville cars," said Pete Sullivan; saying it in fact for about the sixth time since they'd buried Spider Joe in the parking lot behind the Solville buildings.

"We need this truck," said Kootie.

"*Why*, exactly?" asked Pete.

"It's—" Kootie sighed, and Mavranos caught the boy's brief, frail grin out of the corner of his eye. "Because when I sensed it coming north to us, Sunday before last, I sensed it as a cup, a chalice. And when Arky takes it to town, it always comes back full of as much food as we're needing—all this last week and a half, there's been enough tortillas and bananas and fishes and ground beef and cheese and beer and all, when we unload it, for all the people who've been coming over, even though we don't know in advance how many there'll be."

"And it turns red during Holy Week, or any local equivalents," said Mavranos. "And," he added ruefully, "so many ghosts are drawn to it and sucked into the air cleaner and burned up in the carburetor that their cast-off charges screw up the electrical system."

"And it's used to serve the king," said Kootie quietly, as if that settled it.

*   *   *

Right now, thought Mavranos as he glanced in the rearview mirror at the draped tarpaulin in the back, it's being used to *carry* the king.

Mavranos remembered another time Scott Crane had lain stretched out in the back of the truck while Mavranos drove. It had been very nearly a year ago, on January 19th of last year.

Scott had been wearing sweatpants for that painful mid-morning trip up the 405 to Northridge, with not even a bit of twine for a belt, but still his legs had been as weak and racked with cramps as if he'd been wearing a Möbius-twisted belt during a solar eclipse; and he had been as sick—vomiting blood, seeing double, hearing voices—as if he had eaten a rare steak cooked in an iron pan on a Friday in Lent.

He had been that way for two days—ever since 4:31 in the pre-dawn morning of January 17th, when the Northridge earthquake had struck Los Angeles with a force of 6.4 on the Richter scale and 6.7 on the more modern moment-magnitude scale. It had been one of the newly recognized "blind thrust faults," punching the land upward from a previously unsuspected subterranean fault line.

Mavranos had even noticed several white strands in the coppery bushiness of Scott's beard.

Scott had been too weak to talk loudly enough for Mavranos to hear him up in the front seat of the rackety truck, and the intercom set they had brought along for the purpose was drowned in the static-fields of thousands of ghosts awakened to idiot panic by the quake, and so they had stopped at a Carl's Junior hamburger place on the way and put together a string-and-paper-cup "telephone."

Mavranos had specially "stealth-equipped" the truck for the trip, with sea-water in the windshield-washer reservoir and clumps of anonymous hair from a barbershop floor taped onto the radio antenna supplementing the usual tangle of ultrasonic deer-repelling whistles glued in conflicted patterns on the roof and hood, and he was sure they couldn't be traced while they were in the moving vehicle; but he was uneasy about Scott's determination to struggle out of the truck and walk around among the fractured and concussed buildings.

"It's the *date*, Pogo," Mavranos had finally said, turning his head to speak into the paper cup while keeping the string taut, "that makes me nervous about this. It seems like a . . . almost a warning." Mavranos had routinely addressed Scott by the name of the possum character in the Walt Kelly comic strip.

"Today is the 19th," had come Scott's faint, buzzing answer through the cup.

"Sure it is," Mavranos had replied impatiently, "but the earthquake was on the 17th. St. Sulpice and all that."

Scott hadn't answered right away, but even through the unvibrating string Mavranos had been able to feel the ill king's irritation. Mavranos still believed that his point had been relevant, though.

A Vietnamese woman who lived at the Leucadia estate had been given the job of tracing historical events having to do with the secret history of the Fisher Kings and their rivals, and she had discovered a peculiar reactionary vegetation-king cult that had appeared in Paris in 1885, four years after a special congress in Bordeaux had, reluctantly but officially, advised grafting all French grapevines onto imported American rootstocks, which were resistant to the phylloxera louse that looked likely otherwise to obliterate all the vineyards of Europe. The dissenting cult had centered around the seminary and cathedral of St. Sulpice in the St. Germaine district of Paris, and had included among its members the writers Maurice Maeterlinck and Stéphane Mallarmé, the composer Claude Debussy, and eventually the writer and film-maker Jean Cocteau—but it appeared to have been started by a village priest from a parish in the rural Languedoc Valley south of Carcassonne. The priest, Berenger Sauniere, had in 1885 uncovered some documents hidden in the foundation stones of his church, which stood on the site of an ancient Visigoth winery dating back at least to the sixth century, and of a Roman mysteries-temple before that; Sauniere's discoveries had led somehow to his getting substantial payments from the French government and a Hapsburg archduke; and Sauniere had suffered a stroke on January 17th of 1917, and died five days later, after an attending priest had found it impossible to give the dying man the sacraments of confession and Extreme Unction. January 17th was the feast day of St. Sulpice.

The Vietnamese woman, a one-time cabdriver and casino night manager called Bernardette Dinh, had flagged this particular cult because it had shown signs of continuing well into the twentieth century in several splintered branches. In the Bibliothèque Nationale in Paris she had traced a network of obscure items published from the late 1950s through the 1970s—pamphlets, and issues of a rare magazine called *Circuit*, and a privately printed booklet called *Le Serpent Rouge*, which had been published on January 17th of 1967 and whose three authors were found hanged at separate locations less than two months later. All of these publications mentioned the cathedral of St. Sulpice and contained cryptical essays on the science of multi-generational, almost genealogical, viticulture and vine-grafting. Some researchers had evidently considered that *Le Serpent Rouge* dealt with a long-preserved bloodline, but Dinh had speculated that it referred to a secretly cultivated varietal, snaking its way in concealment down through the centuries, of *red wine*.

One branch of the cult survived in the village of Queyrac in the Bas Medoc, and another had taken the name of a fifteenth-century Dionysiac cult called L'Ordre du Levrier Blanc and appeared to have relocated to the American west. In all the branches—and in fact in many other cultures, from the Estonians on the Baltic Sea who sacrificed sheep and oxen on that date, to the Egyptian Copts who observed the day as the anniversary of the death of the tormented visionary St. Anthony—January 17 was a date to be both celebrated and feared.

"At least," Scott had said finally, his voice humming in the paper cup linked to where he had lain in the back of the truck on that day, "if I have a stroke, I won't have any trouble remembering some sins to tell the priest."

"I can help you out there," Mavranos had agreed; and the tense moment had passed, but they had still been driving north toward the wounded city.

Traffic on the 405 had slowed to a stop near the intersection with the Ventura Freeway, northwest of Los Angeles, and Mavranos had got off onto the crowded surface streets; plywood covered many shop windows along these sunlit blocks, and hasty curtains of chain-link fencing had been hung across the breezeways of several of the apartment buildings they passed, and finally on a side street off Reseda and Roscoe he had simply let the truck engine's idle-speed drift them to a parking space at the curb, where he stepped on the brake and, almost as an afterthought, switched off the ignition.

His attention sprang out to the surroundings when the clatter of the engine subsided into silence, and he heard Crane hiking himself up to look out too.

The opposite curb was crowded with empty cars parked bumper-to-bumper, glittering in the bright midwinter sunlight; and the roof of every one of the cars was crushed in, the windshields twisted and white with crazed cracking, the side windows just gone. Beyond the block-long line of Bronco and Jetta and Eldorado hulks, across a lot somehow already brown with dead grass, stood the ruptured apartment complex from whose collapsed carports these cars had been extricated—the outer walls had sheared away, exposing interior rooms and doors, and when Mavranos cranked down the driver's-side window he could smell the faint strawberry tang of garbage on the breeze.

Mavranos had got out and swung open the back of the truck to help Scott down, uneasily noting the fresh blood blotting Scott's shirt from the unhealing wound in his side, and though Mavranos had been afraid that they'd be arrested as looters, Scott had insisted on hobbling across the empty street and inspecting the damage.

They had climbed in among the apartments, picking their way over the drywall and joist beams and aluminum window frames that had fallen across beds and couches, and shuffled carefully across springy, uneven floors, and stared at the body counts spray-painted by rescue workers on the pictureless walls.

When they had clambered outside again, Scott had sat down on the metal box of a fallen air-conditioning unit. Harsh, shouting rap music echoed from some open window on the other side of the street. "My lands are in disorder," Crane said. "Broken."

"From underneath," said Mavranos stolidly. He had agreed with Dinh that the resurgent phylloxera plague in the north California wine country was a bad sign for Scott's reign, a message of discontent "from six feet under."

Scott squinted toward the far side of the empty street. "Sitting on a, an air-conditioning unit, weeping again the king my father's wreck, this music gibbered by me upon the pavement." He laid his bare wrist on a torn edge of metal. "So what am I *not doing?* Just five weeks ago the old Flamingo building in Las Vegas was torn down—that was my father's castle, when he was king, before I killed him—wasn't that a victory? Las Vegas is turning into a family place now, a kid's place. And Diana and I have had four children, and we . . . get three crops a year at the Leucadia place. . . ."

"Why don't you ever prune back the grapevines, in the winter?"

"They don't *need* it. . . ." He looked up at Mavranos and gave him a wasted grin through his disordered beard. "Well, they *don't,* you know. But okay, that's not the reason. I *did* prune 'em back, in that first winter after Las Vegas, but later I—I dreamed about it. In the dreams, the branches *bled* where they were cut; and I dreamed about Ozzie, turned to dust at the touch of Death and blowing away across the desert."

Mavranos just nodded, and wished he'd brought along one of the beers from the truck. Scott and Diana weren't related, but they had both been informally adopted by the same man, an old-time poker player named Oliver Crane but known in the poker world as Ozzie Smith. He had disappeared in the desert outside Las Vegas during the tumultuous Holy Week of 1990, and Scott had always maintained that the old man had died in saving Scott from a murderous embodiment of Dionysus and Death that had taken the physical form of Scott's dead wife Susan.

"Maybe you're *s'posed* to dream about Death, Pogo," Mavranos said. "It's one of the Major Arcana in the tarot deck, and I get the idea that in your dreams you practically go *bar-hopping* with the rest of that crowd."

"I humanize them," Scott said. "A perfect Fisher King wouldn't just have a wounded side, he'd have no left arm or leg or eye, like the *santería* orisha called Osain—*his* other half was the land itself. I take the archetypes into myself, and they stop being just savage outside influences like rain or fire, and start to be allies—family, blood relations— a little."

"Poor old Death sounds like the bad witch in Sleeping Beauty," said Mavranos. "Pissed off because she was the only one not invited to the christening."

"You haven't . . . *been* there, Arky. Death isn't a . . . it doesn't embody a characteristic that shows up in humans, the way the others do, so you can't *relate* to it at all. There's no common ground. It has no face—and I can't just arbitrarily assign the face of, say, poor Susan to it, 'cause that was just my own personal closest death mirrored back at me; anybody else there would have seen some face from *their* past." He coughed weakly and shook his head. "In the court of the tarot archetypes, Death's just a blobby black hole in the floor."

Mavranos had taken a deep breath then—and he wondered if he could bring himself to say what he thought he had to say here, for Scott Crane was his closest friend, and Mavranos was godfather of Scott and Diana's first child—but he made himself say it: "Seems to me there *is . . . one* face you could put on Death."

Crane sat there on the air conditioner and stared at the dead grass and didn't speak, and Mavranos wondered if he had heard him. Then Crane shifted, and coughed again. "You mean the fat man in the desert," he said softly. "My father's bodyguard, my father's emotionless hired assassin. And *I* killed *him,* in cold blood—the first shot was in self-defense, to save you as much as me, but he was still alive after that. The last five shots, when he was lying in the gully below the road, were to make sure he didn't wind up recovering in a hospital."

Mavranos nodded, though Crane couldn't see the gesture. The fat man had at some time become a localized embodiment of one of the oldest, possibly pre-human archetypes, a cold figure of almost Newtonian retribution which showed up spontaneously in desert swap-meet legendry and country-western songs and insane-asylum artwork and even, as a repeating obese silhouette, in certain iterative mathematical equations on the complex number plane. Diana's mother had been an avatar of the Moon Goddess, and the fat man had killed her outside the Sands Hotel in Las Vegas—"shot the moon in the face"—when Diana had been an infant, in 1960. Mavranos had not been sorry when Crane had killed the fat man, but that homicide was surely Crane's letter of introduction, his indenture, to the kingdom of death.

"No," said Crane finally. "It can't be done. It doesn't *need* to be done."

Mavranos had thought of reminding him of the phylloxera, had considered mentioning the many species of tropical fish that had recently stopped being born with any distinct sexes, and the rapid decline in the sperm count of modern male humans—even the slow, progressive collapse of Hollywood Boulevard down into the catacombs being dug for the MTA Metro Rail—but at that point an unkempt middle-aged couple and their two blank-eyed children had come shuffling up through the brown grass to where the bearded king sat, and had hesitantly asked Scott if everything was going to be okay. They were living in their car, they told him, and had hung curtains in the windows, and were wondering if they shouldn't simply keep living in those cozy quarters forever, even after the houses had been put back up again.

Scott had wearily told them that he would do what he could; and they had showed no surprise, only sympathetic gratitude, when Scott had pushed his own wrist down onto the jagged piece of metal and then held out his hand so that his blood dripped rapidly onto the dry dirt.

Mavranos had muttered a panicky curse and sprinted to the nearby truck for the first-aid kit. And he had noted bleakly, after he had tied a bandage around Scott's wrist and helped him up for the walk back to the truck, that no flowers had sprung up from where the king's blood had fallen.

It's what Nardie Dinh calls the Law of Imperative Resemblance," said Mavranos to Angelica and Pete now.

Fog was beginning to roll in off the ocean, and Mavranos knew that it would be getting worse as the night wore on toward dawn and their route led them inland at Gaviota; maybe he'd get Pete to drive for a while. "There are eternal potent *forms* out there," Mavranos went on, "idiosyncratic outlines, and if you take on enough characteristics of one of the forms, if you come to resemble it closely enough, knowingly or not, you find that you're wearing the whole damned outfit—you've *become* the thing. It *arrives* upon you."

"Like critical mass," said Kootie sleepily, rocking on the passenger seat.

"Well, *hijo mío*," said Angelica sternly to the boy as she went on loading her .45 magazines, "*you're* not going to be taking communion at this Mass."

CHAPTER 13

The bay trees in our country are all withered,
And meteors fright the fixed stars of heaven,
The pale-faced moon looks bloody on the earth,
And lean-looked prophets whisper fearful change;
Rich men look sad, and ruffians dance and leap,
The one in fear to lose what they enjoy,
The other to enjoy by rage and war.
These signs forerun the death or fall of kings.

— William Shakespeare,
Richard II

Bernardette Dinh, known as Nardie to her few close friends, was perched crouched on a dead peach-tree limb, staring down the flagstone steps that led away between rows of dead grapevines to the beach and the dawn-gray sea. Five years ago she had got into the habit of climbing a tree when she was very scared or disoriented, and during these last eleven days she must have spent nearly a full day's worth of hours up in the branches of this or that dead carob or apple or avocado tree in different corners of the Fisher King's Leucadia estate, in the periods when she could get Wendy to keep an eye on the kids.

Twenty years ago, when Nardie had arrived at Clark Air Base in Manila on the rainy morning of April 29 in 1975, airport personnel and travellers alike had exclaimed over her and the other passengers that got off the plane with her: *Oh, thank God you're safe!* She had then learned that the Saigon airport had been heavily shelled at 5 A.M., just four hours after her plane had taken off; but rockets had been shelling Saigon for two months before her American father had got her a ticket, and for the whole ten years of her life to that point, as she recalled it now, there had always been the background noise of planes and bombings. Her luggage had been mailed ahead, but never did show up anywhere—when she finally arrived at Camp Pendleton in Southern California, all she had had was the clothes she'd been wearing and the cellophane-thin sheets of gold leaf her father had managed to stuff into her pockets.

California had been bewildering, even with the help of other immigrant Vietnamese; *Here the poor eat beef every day,* she had been told, *and the rich people are all vegetarians.* And when her new American half-brother had taken her to a modern shopping center in Costa Mesa, the thing that had most struck her had been the pennies and nickels and even quarters scattered in the pool around an indoor fountain; she had struggled with the two ideas of it: that people had tossed the coins in there, and that other people didn't climb in to get them out.

Nardie was thirty now—but since the first of this month, when Scott's dead body had been found in the canted meadow down here between the house and the beach, she had been dreaming of those days again. But the fountains in her dreams were dry and bare, and the rockets came plummeting out of the night sky before the airliner she was in could take off.

The last time Nardie had seen Scott Crane alive, he had been trudging away barefoot down these flagstone steps to rescue his four-year-old son, Benjamin; Scott had got some kind of formal threatening challenge over the telephone only ten minutes earlier, and when he had hastily awakened and summoned to the atrium everybody that lived here at the compound—Arky and Wendy and their two teenage daughters, and Diana's two teenage sons by her first marriage, and Nardie herself, and Diana and the four young children she and Scott had had together—Benjamin had proved to be missing, and the three-year-old girl had said that a black crow had flapped down onto Benjamin's bedroom windowsill and told the boy that a magical woman in the meadow needed to see him right away.

It was a woman, on the phone just now, Scott had told Nardie and Arky and Diana in the kitchen as he'd pulled off his shoes and tugged his still-dark-brown hair out of the rubber-banded ponytail and let it fall loose onto his shoulders; *she claimed to have spoken to the ghost of my first wife, Susan, who was the embodiment of Death in the Las Vegas desert five years ago; and she knows I was called the Flying Nun in the big game on Lake Mead, and she said she was going to "assume the Flamingo," which must mean that she's some "jack," some rival, from the game five years ago, when the Flamingo Hotel was still the king's bunker-castle. I told her that it had been torn down, but I guess she's got a piece of the physical building—and that* would *be a potent . . . charm, talisman. She must have a lot of other things, too, protections and masks and even maybe a tethered ghost or two, to have got in here past our wards without showing up as a consistent, solid intruder. And we have to assume that she's got Benjamin now. I've got to go meet her alone, or it's too likely that she'll kill him.*

Arky Mavranos had tried to insist that it was his own clear duty to go and rescue the child—*I'm Benjamin's godfather, Scott,* he had said forcefully, *and* I'm *not* wounded.

Scott Crane had refused to let Arky go, and had then had to flatly forbid the man's offers of "armed back-up support, at least."

And so Scott had gone padding down that set of steps alone, to the tilted meadow below the house . . . and a few minutes later Benjamin had come running back, sobbing about a woman who had knocked him down and held a spear to his throat, and who had changed into a man. *Daddy stayed to talk to the man,* the boy had said. *It's a very bad man.*

At that moment the pans had begun rattling in the cupboards, and the overhead light had begun swinging on its chain.

Arky Mavranos and Diana had simply bolted outside then, and skipped and hopped down the shaking steps after Scott . . . and by the time they had got to the slanting meadow, the earthquake had stopped, leaving only smoke-like clouds of raised dust hanging over the cliffs to mark its passage, and they had found Scott's supine body on the grass, speared through the throat.

They had half-carried and half-dragged the body back across the meadow to the steps before going to get Nardie to help carry, and apparently blood had fallen copiously from Scott's torn throat, like holy water shaken from a Catholic priest's aspergillum—

—And, from every point where the blood drops had hit the grass, a spreading network of flowers and vines had violently erupted up out of the soil in a ripping spray of fragmenting dirt clods, as if in some kind of horticultural aftershocks—so that Arky and Diana had in effect been shuffling along at the advancing, upthrusting edge of a dense thicket of vibrant grape and ivy and pomegranate. An hour later Nardie had seen a couple of uniformed police officers escorting a blond woman around the edge of the newly overgrown meadow, but they had gone away again without even ringing the bell at the outer gate.

Mavranos had lifted Crane's body into the back of the—tragically, prematurely!—*red* truck, in preparation for driving away with Diana to search in the north for *another* man who would have an unhealing wound in his side: the man whom they would acknowledge and bless as the next Fisher King.

Nardie had given Mavranos a baseball-sized white stone statue of Tan Tai, the Vietnamese god of prosperity, to put on the truck's dashboard; and only after the truck had gone creaking and rattling away down Neptune Avenue did she recall that her half-brother had given her one very like it, back in the brightly familial days before he had tried to break her spirit and mind to further his own bitter Fisher Kinghood ambitions. Arky Mavranos had had to *kill* her half-brother eventually, at Hoover Dam during the terrible Holy Week in 1990—Nardie hoped now that her gift had not been an unwitting expression of some lingering subconscious resentment. She had never . . . *blamed* poor, staunch Arky for the death of her only blood sibling.

All the magical new plants had wilted and withered during the following week, along with all the other plantings on the whole sprawling estate; and now the grounds were drifted with dry leaves—among which, if she looked closely, she could discern husks of perished bees and the stiffened, lifeless forms of the million earthworms that had come corkscrewing up out of the ground on that morning—and Nardie could only hope that a new good king would somehow be appointed before the Tet celebration at the end of the month.

Crane had kept a rose garden near the house, and when all the red petals had fallen to the brick pavement last week, they had looked to Nardie like the exploded scraps of firecracker paper that used to litter the Saigon pavements on Tet Nguyen Dan, the festival of the first day of the Vietnamese New Year. She had put a photograph of Scott Crane on her Tet altar, and now she whispered a prayer to the Kitchen God, a humble entreaty for, somehow, prosperity and health for her friends during this disastrous new year.

All she could see ahead of her, in the notch between the brown grapevines, was a triangle of the distant gray sea . . . but now she heard the scuffle of someone, possibly several people, climbing the cement stairs that led up the sloping cliff from the beach sand to the slanting meadow. Nardie watched the flagstone steps, but the visitors were probably just more of the white-clay dancers, come to solemnly jump rope with trimmed lengths of kelp for a while in the blighted meadow below the steps—though generally the unspeaking white figures kept that softly drumming vigil at the end of the day, when the red sun was disappearing below the remote western horizon.

At her back she could often hear the cars of the crazy local teenagers racing up the street, and she heard at least one screeching past now, and heard too the *pop-pop-pop* of automatic weapons fire. In this last week and a half she had sensed a kind of vigilant protection in their constant racket, but an impatience too. Absently, Nardie touched the angular weight in her sweater pocket that was her ten-ounce Beretta .25 automatic.

The dry leaves on the peach-tree branches rattled in the chilly wind from the sea, and Nardie caught the familiar wild strains of the music from the beach. Arky had telephoned the Leucadia estate several times from pay phones, and he had laughed once—dryly—when she had described the music to him, and he had told her the name of the constantly repeated song: ''Candles in the Wind,'' by somebody called Melanie. Apparently the disattached people near where the killed king was were spontaneously playing the same song as were the disattached people near the king's broken castle. Nardie wondered if the ones near wherever the killed king was had covered themselves with white mud, too.

Definitely there was more than one person in the meadow—Nardie could hear excited voices.

The white-clay dancers had never spoken.

Silently Nardie swung down from the branch, and her tennis shoes crackled only faintly in the dry grass as she landed and then stole to the top of the steps and looked down.

At the edge of the new wilderness of dead vines in the meadow, by the top of the stairs that led down to the beach, four figures stood silhouetted against the vast gray sea. Three stood together with their arms around each other, though the effect was more as if they were handcuffed that way than comradely; the fourth figure, standing apart, was an old man who had only one arm.

The middle figure of the trio, whose styled hair was white, reached out toward a dead pomegranate bush—and when his two dark-haired companions twisted their heads up toward her and clumsily grabbed their crotches in perfect unison Nardie shivered and bared her teeth, for she understood abruptly that only the middle figure was a real person, and that the outer two were some kind of mobile mannikins.

As if following the gaze of the two artificial heads, the one-armed old man looked up the slope at Nardie.

''Heads up, Doc, all three,'' the old man said, loudly enough for Nardie to hear. ''The homegrown Persephone yonder don't want you triflin' with her *seed pods.*''

Nardie realized that she had drawn her tiny gun, so she lifted it and pointed it down the steps toward the two living men and the two dummies, though she kept her finger outside the trigger guard.

The one-armed man turned his shoulder stump to her, as if hiding behind the upraised, missing arm; and the trio shifted position, so that one of the dark-haired mannikins was blocking her view of the white-haired man in the middle—who now shakily reached out and plucked the dried gourd of a dead pomegranate from the bush.

Then, in a crackling of trodden dry leaves, all four of the figures in the meadow were lurching away back toward the stairs that led down to the beach, the two mannikins waving their free arms in perfect synchronization, like, Nardie thought giddily, a couple of Gladys Knight's Pips.

Her teeth stung as she sucked in the cold sea air. Should I shoot at him? she wondered. What, she thought then, for stealing a *pomegranate?* A *dead* one? And at this range with this stubby barrel, I'd be doing well to put the bullet in the meadow at all, never mind hitting a head-size target. And she remembered Arky's assessment of her weapon: *A .25's a good thing to have in a fight, if you can't get hold of a gun.*

The four figures tottered away down the beach stairs, the mannikin arms waving in spastic unison over the two fake heads.

Nardie straightened up when they had descended out of her sight, and she smiled derisively at herself when she noticed that she was standing hunched, and looking around for cover between nervous glances at the sky. The rockets fell a *week and a half* ago, she told herself; and you're *living* in the dry, coinless fountain.

She pocketed her little gun and turned to trudge back uphill toward the house. She'd have to tell Arky about these intruders, whenever he next called from wherever he was.

She really did hope Arky was safe.

Tan Tai be with you, she thought blankly.

The dozen white dancers who appeared to be made out of clay had been high-stepping around in a solemn ring on the flat sand a hundred yards to the south when Dr. Armentrout and Long John Beach had originally walked up the beach to the Crane estate's stairs, but now they were skipping and hand-clapping back this way. The dawn wind was cold, but Armentrout felt a drop of sweat roll down his ribs under his shirt as he scuffed down from the last cement step onto the sand.

"Keep walking," Armentrout whispered to Long John Beach as he began plodding away north under the weight of the two-mannikin appliance, "back to the stairway that'll take us up to the Neptune Avenue parking lot, and don't look back at those . . . those white people."

The one-armed old man immediately turned to gape at the figures following, and his eyes and mouth were so wide that Armentrout turned around to look himself, fearing that the dancers might be silently running at them, perhaps armed with some of the smooth black stones that studded the marbled black-and-gray sand.

But the white figures, though closer, were just walking purposefully after Armentrout and Long John Beach now, and staring at them with eyes that seemed yellow and bloodshot against the crusted white faces. The clay plastered onto their swimsuit-clad bodies made them seem to be naked sexless creatures animated out of the wet cliffs.

Armentrout let go of the lever that controlled the mannikins' heads, in order to reach into his jacket pocket and grip the butt of the .45 derringer. The Styrofoam heads now nodded and rolled loosely with every jouncing step toward the cement pilings of the wooden municipal stairway that led up to the parking lot, and to the car, and away from this desolate shoreline.

But Long John Beach stopped and pointed back at the advancing mud-people. "No outrageous thing," he cried, his voice flat and un-echoing in the open air, "from vassal actors can be wiped away; then kings' misdeeds cannot be hid in clay."

For a moment Armentrout considered just leaving the crazy old man standing here, as a cast-off distraction to occupy the dancers while he himself trotted away to the car; but he knew now that he needed to find Koot Hoomie Parganas, and he would need every scrap of mask for that.

So Armentrout stopped too, and he turned to face the advancing animated statues; and with deliberate slowness he tugged the fist-sized gun free and let them see it. He gripped the ball-butt tightly, for he remembered that the little derringer tended to rotate in his hand when he pulled the hammer back against the tight spring, and now he cocked it with a crisp, ratcheting click.

"What business," Armentrout said, "*exactly,* do you have with us?"

One of the figures, breastless and so probably a young man, stepped forward. "You took something," came a high voice, "from up the stairs."

"I did? What did I take?"

The figure's blue eyes blinked. "You tell me."

"Answer my question first. I asked you what *exactly* your business is here."

The stony figures shuffled uneasily on the wet black-veined sand, and Armentrout suppressed a smile; for these were young people whose random propensities for music and dancing and the beach had happened to constitute a compelling resemblance to an older, mythic role in this season of insistent definition—but they *were* just San Diego County teenagers of the 1990s, and when they were challenged to *explain* their presence here, the archaic hum of the inarticulate purpose was lost beneath the grammar of reason.

"No law against dancing," the figure said defensively.

"There *is* a law about concealed weapons," another piped up.

The modern phrases had dispelled the mythic cast—they were now thoroughly just modern kids on a beach, with mud all over them.

"Scram," said Armentrout.

The white figures began to amble away south with exaggerated nonchalance. Armentrout put the gun away and turned toward the stairs. A blue sign on the railing said,

WARNING
Stay Safe Distance
Away From Bluff Bottom
FREQUENT BLUFF FAILURE

Not today, Armentrout thought with satisfaction as he shooed Long John Beach ahead of him up the stairs.

In the parking lot between landscaped modern apartment buildings, Armentrout unstrapped the two-mannikin appliance and stowed it in the back seat of his teal-blue BMW.

Then he opened the passenger-side door and pushed Long John Beach inside. "Belt up," he said breathlessly to the old man.

" 'The purest treasure mortal times afford,' " the one-armed old man wailed, the strange and eerily flat voice echoing now between the white stucco walls, " 'is spotless reputation; that away, men are but gilded loam or painted clay.' "

"I said *belt up*," hissed Armentrout between clenched teeth as he hurried around to the driver's side and got in. "Anyway," he added in shrill embarrassment as he started the engine, "there's no *hope* anymore for our reputations in *this* town."

As he drove back down Neptune Avenue, in the southbound lane this time, Armentrout could see a plywood sign attached to a pine tree beside the gates of the fieldstone wall on his right. Black plastic letters had been attached to it once, but weather or something had caused most of them to fall away; what remained was accidental Latin:

E   T   IN
ARC
ADIA
EGO

Et in Arcadia ego.

And I am in Arcadia, he thought, tentatively translating the words; or, *I am in Arcadia, too;* or, *Even in Arcadia, I am.*

Armentrout reflected uneasily that the word Arcadia—with its resonances of pastoral Greek poetry and balmy, quiet gardens—probably had applied to this place, before Our Miss Figleaf had come here and killed the king; but who was the *Ego* that was speaking?

Even when he had got back on the 5 Freeway, heading north through the misty morning-lit hills below the Santa Ana Mountains, Armentrout found himself still noticing and being bothered by signs on the shoulder. The frequent GAS-FOOD-LODGING 1 MI AHEAD signs had stark icons stenciled on them for the benefit of people who couldn't read, and though the stylized images of a gas pump and a knife-and-plate-and-fork were plain enough, the dot-dash figure of a person on a long-H bed looked to him this morning disturbingly like a dead body laid out in state; and while he was still south of Oceanside he saw several postings of a sign warning illegal Mexican immigrants against trying to sprint across the freeway to bypass the border checkpoint—the diamond-shaped yellow sign showed a silhouetted man and woman and girl-child running hand-in-hand so full-tilt fast that the little girl's feet were off the ground, and under the figures was the word PROHIBIDO. Armentrout thought it seemed to be a prohibition of all fugitive families.

And when he became aware that his heartbeat was accelerated, he recognized that he was responding with defiance, as if the signs were reproaches aimed at him personally. *I* didn't kill any king, he thought; *I* haven't uprooted any families. I'm a *doctor,* I—

Abruptly he remembered the voice of the obese suicide-girl as he had heard it over the telephone a few hours ago: *Doctor? I walk all crooked now—where's the rest of me?*

But I certainly didn't mean *that* to happen, he thought, her *killing* herself. I don't give anyone a treatment I haven't undergone and benefited from myself; and from my own experience I know that cutting the problem right out of the soul, rather than laboring to assimilate it, really does effect a cure. And even when these misfortunes do result— goddammit—aren't I allowed some sustenance? I genuinely do a lot of good for people—is it wrong for me to sometimes take something besides money for my payment? Does this make me a, a *sicko?* He smiled confidently—*Not . . . at . . . all.* The whole notion of intrinsic consequences of "sin" is just infantile solipsism, anyway: imagining that in some sense you are everybody and everybody's you. Guilt and shame are just the unproductive, negative opposites of self-esteem, and I feel healthily good about everything I do. That's *okay* today.

Then he thought of what it was he now planned for his patient Janis Cordelia Plumtree, whenever he might catch up with her, and for Koot Hoomie Parganas, if the boy was still alive—and he heard again the flat howl that had burst from Long John Beach's throat: *gilded loam or painted clay.*

It occurred to him, with unwelcome clarity, that the idealistic dancers on the beach had carried the rainbow of living flesh on the *inside*, and dry, cracked clay on the *outside.*

And so he was nearly driven to pull out his derringer and fire it at the sign on the tailgate of the sixteen-wheel trailer rig that cut him off near San Onofre, after Long John Beach pointed at the sign and said, "Hyuck hyuck—that's addressed to you, Doc." The sign read: INSIDE HEIGHT 10'—NOSE TO REAR 110'.

Armentrout's forehead was suddenly chilly at the thought that his hand had actually brushed the derringer's grip in his unthinking reflexive rage—but still!—*"nose to rear"? How was* he supposed to take that?

His cellular telephone buzzed, and he fumbled it up from between the seats and flipped open the cover. "Yes?" he said furiously after he had switched it on.

"Get your *toes* aft of the *white line*, please," drawled a man's humorous voice, "and sit your ass down in one of the seats! I'm in control of this bus, and you're upsetting the children!"

In his first seconds of confusion Armentrout knew he recognized the voice, but he seemed to remember it as disembodied—a ghost?—and this was clearly not a ghost call. The voice and the background breeze-hiss were *real,* unlike the eternal clattering busy-ness of the group-projected ghost-bar.

"You was comin' on to my *daughter,* man," the voice said now; "you can't blame me for having got a bit *testy,* now can you?" Before Armentrout could stammer out anything, the voice went on: "This is Omar Salvoy, and I can't talk for long. Listen, you and I each got a gun pointed at the other, haven't we? Mexican standoff. I think we can work together, both eat off the same plate. Here's the thing—you'd like to get Koot Hoomie Parganas locked up in your clinic, wouldn't you, in a coma and brain-dead, on perpetual life-support? Or haven't you thought it through that far?"

It made Armentrout dizzy to hear this voice on the phone speaking his recent, somewhat shameful, thought aloud. "Y-yes," he said, glancing sideways at Long John Beach and then in the rear-view mirror at the two placid Styrofoam heads. "What you describe is . . . it could, I guess you've figured out that it could, benefit you and me both. But not *yet*—it would have to be after he had been induced to, uh, officially . . . *take the crown,* if you know what I mean. I was just at the Fisher King's castle, this morning, and it's very evident from the look of things there that no new king has been consecrated yet. But after that's occurred, I could set things up so that you and I could both benefit. As you know, I'm uniquely able to set up that scenario, just as you describe it.''

"Ipse dipshit. Now the girls have got some cockamamie idea about restoring the dead king, the *old* one, to life—I gotta monkeywrench that scheme, that guy is really *old,* he's hardened in his thought-paths and likely to be resistant, not like the kid would be.''

"All ROM and no RAM,'' agreed Armentrout, though he didn't see how any of this would matter in a brain-dead body.

"Rom? Ram? Gypsies, sheep? Easy on the mystical, there, Doctor, I want you for *science.* You do know about how the spirit-transfer thing works, knocking a personality out of somebody's head?''

"Uh.'' Armentrout wiped his forehead and blinked sweat out of his eyes to be able to watch the freeway lanes. "Yes.'' I wasn't being mystical, he thought—doesn't Salvoy know anything about computers? Oh well, give him the science. "The force that, that holds them *in,* works the opposite of forces like gravity and electromagnetism and the strong nuclear force, which all get weaker as the, the *satellite,* say, moves further away from the primary; ghost personalities are more strongly *restrained,* the further they get out, especially in sane people, but feel no clumping-together force at all if they stay within the mind's confines. It's much the same situation as is theorized for the quarks that make up subatomic particles—if they stay close together, they experience what's called asymptotic freedom—''

"Speaking of which, I'm gonna have to pick up my ass and tote it out of here. I'm at a pay phone—we've stopped for gas in King City, and her boyfriend has just ducked off to visit the gents' and pump the gas. You'd better get up here, right now; and then on to San Fran, apparently—this thing will go a lot smoother if we've got a real licensed psychiatrist along, for authority-figuring in case any locals should object to anything. Wave the stethoscope, flourish the prescription pad. I'll make a point of getting out here again and calling you with more specific directions as we proceed, so take your telephone with you, you can do that, can't you?''

"King City? San Francisco? Certainly, I've got the phone with me now. Obviously. But the P—the boy—he's alive, I gather? Is *he* in San Francisco? We need—''

"He's alive, and on his way there. Gotta go—stay by the phone.''

The line was dead, and Armentrout clicked the phone off, closed the cover, and wedged it carefully between the seat and the console. He would have to dig out of the trunk the phone-battery recharger that could be plugged into the cigarette lighter.

His lips were twitching in a brittle, almost frightened grin. There's no reason why this shouldn't work, he thought. When the king died eleven days ago, his death opened a temporary drain in the psychic floor locally, so that all my vengeful old California ghosts, at least, were sucked away, leaving me with their abandoned memories and strengths intact and harmless. I was *fifty miles away,* and my ghosts were banished! That drain has since closed up—but imagine if I could be *in the same building* with a flatline Fisher King! If we can get the new king on perpetual brain-dead life-support, the drain could be held propped open for . . . for decades. I'll be able to outright *terminate* patients, consume their whole lives, without fear of being hassled by their outraged ghost personalities afterward. And Omar Salvoy will be able to—what? I suppose to evict all the girls from Plumtree's head, so that he'll have that youthful body all to himself, to live in.

It'll be the best of both worlds, Armentrout thought, nodding and smiling twitchily. All the forgiveness that Dionysus's *pagadebiti* wine offers, but with the profit from the sin retained intact too!

He glanced again at Long John Beach and the two heads in the backseat. I may be able to outright *ditch* the three of you in San Francisco, he thought.

Who were you calling?'' asked Cochran, frowning.

They hadn't found a Mobil station here in King City, and so they were using some of the Jenkins woman's cash at this Shell station, and apparently the Torino's tank hadn't had room for a whole twenty's worth of gas—Cochran was stuffing a couple of ones into the pocket of his corduroy bell-bottoms. He must have bought the cheapest gas.

Plumtree blinked at him around the aluminum cowl of the pay telephone. There was only a dial tone to be heard from the thoroughly warmed earpiece of the receiver she held in her hand. Cochran looked tired and bed-raggled, she noted, in the cold morning sunlight, and she could see strands of white hair among the disordered brown locks tangled over his forehead.

"It was ringing," she said, in the old reflexive dismissal of a patch of lost time. "Nobody on when I picked it up." She reflected that this *might* be the literal truth; but she wasn't happy to find herself reverting to the helpless shuck-and-jive evasions, the poker-table calls that were bluffs because she didn't know what her hole cards were, so she went on spontaneously, "Let's get breakfast now, there's a Denny's a block back—we can just have coffee with the others at the Cliff House place—and maybe a dessert, if they have some kind of sweetrolls there. And listen, if there's a Sav-On or someplace open in this town, I'd like to buy some fresh underwear—these panties I've got on still say Tuesday on 'em—and *Tiffany's* been wearing them."

". . . Okay."

They got back into the beer-reeking warmth of the car and drove around, but didn't find any open store at all in the whole town, and so eventually she had to go into the ladies' room in Denny's, pull off her jeans, and wash the panties in the sink—with hand soap, wringing them halfway dry in a sheaf of paper towels after she'd rinsed them out— and then shiveringly pull them back on.

Now she was eating scrambled eggs and shifting uncomfortably on the vinyl booth seat, bleakly sure that the dampness must be visibly soaking through the seat of her jeans, and remembering reading *On Her Majesty's Secret Service* in another restaurant booth eleven days ago. She had had the aluminum spear taped to her thigh during that breakfast, the points of it cutting her skin.

"I can't ever sit comfortably in restaurants," she complained. She remembered that a telephone had started ringing then, too, on that morning, right in the restaurant; it was Janis's job to answer telephones, and Cody recalled flipping her lit cigarette into the open paperback book, intending to slam the cover firmly closed and extinguish the coal, since there had been no ashtray on the table and Janis didn't smoke. But Janis had come on more quickly than usual, apparently, and hadn't known about the lit Marlboro between the pages.

Cody grinned sourly now. *Excu-u-se* me!

At least my teeth don't hurt much right now—not any worse than usual, anyway. And I certainly don't have a nose-bleed! If Flibbertigibbet was on, it wasn't for very long.

She looked up. Across the table, Cochran was smiling at her gently, out of his tired, red eyes. "Who were you calling?" he asked again.

Okay—perhaps the gas-station pay phone had *not* already been ringing when she had picked it up, and Cochran knew it. Okay. "I call time," she said, "a *lot*. That's UL3-1212 everywhere. In England they call it 'the speaking clock,' which always makes me picture Grandfather Clock, from the 'Captain Kangaroo' TV show, remember? *Wake up, Grandfather!* Even when I have a watch on. Those liquid-crystal displays, you can't ever be—"

He was still smiling tiredly at her.

"I—" She exhaled and threw down her fork with a clatter. "Oh, fuck it. *I* don't know, Sid. The receiver was warm, we must have been talking to somebody. My teeth *are* hurting, but we *do* call time a lot.''

"Not for extended conversations, though, I bet." He took a sip from his glass of V-8, into which he'd shaken several splashes of Tabasco. "In this hippie commune you grew up in," he said; "what was it called?''

"The Lever Blank. My mom and I lived at their farm commune outside of Danville for another couple of years after my father died.''

"Did they let you watch a lot of TV?''

Plumtree stared at him. "This was mandala yin-yang hippies, Sid! Organic vegetables and goat's milk. Old mobile homes sitting crooked on dirt, with no electric. My father was the only one that even read *newspapers.*''

"So how did you ever see 'Captain Kangaroo'? And Halo Shampoo ads? And I'm not sure, but it seems to me that neither one of those was still being aired in '71. I'm an easy ten years older than you, and *I* hardly remember them.''

Plumtree calmly picked up her fork and shovelled a lump of scrambled egg into her mouth. "That's a, a terrible point you make, Sid,'' she remarked after she had swallowed and taken a sip of coffee. "And I don't seem to be losing time over it, either, do I? This must be my flop. Do you think I'm an alcoholic? Janis thinks so.''

"Of course not,'' he said, with a laugh. "No more than I am.''

"Oh, *that's* good, *that's* reassuring. Jesus! The reason I ask is, I need a drink to assimilate this thought with. Let's pay up and get out of here.''

"Fine,'' Cochran said, a little stiffly.

Oh, *sorree,* Plumtree thought, restraining herself from rolling her eyes.

As Cochran took their bill to the cashier, Plumtree walked out of the yellow-lit restaurant to the muddy parking lot. The sky had lightened to an empty blue-gray vault, but she felt as though there were the close-arching ceiling of a bus overhead, and that the battered madman who had hijacked the bus and cowed the driver had now turned and begun to advance on the hostage children, all the brave little girls.

The chilly dawn wind was throwing all sounds away to the south, and she was able to hum "Row, Row, Row Your Boat'' until Cochran had come out of the restaurant and shuffled up to within a yard of her, before she had to stop humming for fear he might hear.

North of King City they were driving up through the wide Salinas Valley, with green fields of broccoli receding out to the far off Coast

Range foothills. Long flat layers of fog, ragged at the top, hung over the ruler-straight dirt roads and solitary farmhouses in the middle distance, and Cochran began to notice signs for the Soledad Correctional Institute. Don't want to be picking up any hitch-hikers around there, he thought. We've got enough of them aboard right now. Neither he nor Plumtree had spoken since getting back into the car in the parking lot of the Denny's in King City, though she had taken a quick, bracing gulp of the vodka after she had started the engine, and, after a moment of resentful hesitation, he had shrugged and opened one of the warm beers. The sky had still been dark enough then for her to turn on the headlights, but she reached out now and punched the knob to turn them off.

"Smart thinking," he said, venturing to break the long silence. "We'd only forget to turn them off, once the sun's well up."

"And it's cover," she said, speaking indistinctly through a yawn. "You can tell which cars have been driving all night, because they've still got their lights on. Everybody with their lights *out* is a local." She yawned again, and it occurred to Cochran that these were from tension as much as weariness. "But we can't hide—*I* can't, anyway—from my father. Those are *his* memories, those TV things. Captain Kangaroo, that shampoo. He was born in '44." A third yawn was so wide that it squeezed tears from the corner of her eye. "If we're compartmentalized, in this little head, then he's leaking into my compartment. I wonder if he's leaking into the other girls' seats too."

Seats? Cochran thought.

"Like in a bus," she said. "*You* could step off, you know, Sid. Like the driver in that movie, *Speed,* who got shot, remember? The bad guy let him get off the bus, because he was wounded. When we stop at your house. I could drop you off at some nearby corner, in fact, so Flibbertigibbet won't even know where you live."

After a long pause, while he finished the can of warm beer and reached down to fetch up another, "No," Cochran said in an almost wondering tone; "no, I reckon I'm . . . along for the ride."

Plumtree laughed happily, and began drunkenly singing the kid's song, "Row, Row, Row Your Boat." After she had finished the trite lyric and started it up again, frowning now and waving at him, his face heated in embarrassment as he gave up and joined in, singing the lyric in the proper kindergarten counterpoint. And until he put out his hand to stop her, the vodka bottle between her knees was rhythmically rattled as she swung the wheel back and forth, swerving the big old car from one side of the brightening highway lane to the other in time to their frail duet.

CHAPTER 14

... blood, like sacrificing Abel's, cries
Even from the tongueless caverns of the earth
To me for justice and rough chastisement ...
                              —William Shakespeare,
                                      Richard II

After *a more distant sort of* pop-pop-pop *sounded from the cliffs above the plain of ruins, and while echoes of the rapid knocks were still batting away between the old broken walls, Plumtree swung her ponderous gaze to Cochran, and she saw his face change from the robust color of damp cement to an ashier gray. It was certainly an external noise, she reasoned. It must have been gunfire. Cody always springs away at sudden dangerous sounds—telephones, gunfire.*

Plumtree skipped lightly ahead down the muddy path, almost tap-dancing in instinctive time to the constant hammering noise in her ears, and she beckoned Cochran forward, downhill, toward the ruins and the wide, still lagoons that were separated by eroded walls from the crashing sea beyond. The lush, steel-colored vegetation on either side of the path shook in the ocean breeze.

"Further down?" she heard him say. His voice was shrill and uncertain. "Toward the baths?"

"A seething bath," Plumtree pronounced, "which yet may prove against strange maladies a sovereign cure."

"Valorie," he said as he hurried after her.

The clatter and thump that rang ceaselessly in her head increased its tempo, and she knew that an emotion was being experienced. "She that loves her selves," she called, "hath not essentially, but by circumstance, the name of Valorie." The emotion was something like shame, or cowardice—or fear of those.

On an impulse but resolutely, she halted and pulled from the pocket of her jeans the object she had prepared at Cochran's house, when they had stopped there earlier this morning; and she held it out to him in a hand that shook with the rhythmic cracking in her head. "This form of prayer can serve my turn," she said: " 'Forgive me my foul murder.' "

Still glancing up at the cliffs and the road, Cochran took the folded cardboard from her hand.

And Cochran paused to stare obediently at the green-and-tan 7-Eleven matchbook Plumtree had handed him, but it was just a matchbook. "Thanks, Valorie," he said, "but could I talk to Janis?" Neither Janis nor Cody, he reflected fretfully, had ever mentioned that Valorie was crazy. *"Jan-is,"* he repeated.

He shifted impatiently from one foot to the other, grateful, in this chilly mist or sea spray, for the jeans and boots and flannel shirt and London Fog windbreaker he had changed into at his house; and he was nervously reassured by the angular bulk of the holstered .357 Magnum clipped onto his belt in the back.

"Scant!" Plumtree exclaimed; and then she stared around at the vast, fog-veiled amphitheater into which they had by now halfway descended. "Wow, I'm glad I don't have to pretend with you, Scant! Are we still in California, at all?"

"Yes," he said, taking her arm and hurrying her forward. "San Francisco—that building up on the promontory behind us is the Cliff House Restaurant, Cody and I were just in there. It's only been a few hours since you were last up. But let's get . . . *behind a wall,* okay? I swear I heard gunfire up on the highway—not a minute ago."

She trotted along beside him, and he was tensely glad that the bouncing blond hair and the lithe legs were Janis's again, and that the deep blue eyes that blinked at him were those of his new girlfriend, in this strange landscape under this rain-threatening gray sky.

He could see why she had doubted that they were still in California. The Sutro Baths had only burned down in 1966, but these low, crumbled walls and rectangular lagoons—all that was left of the baths, overgrown now with rank grass and calla lilies—fretted the plain in vast but half-obliterated geometry between the steep eastern slope and the winter sea like some Roman ruin; long gray lines of pavement cross-sections, broken and sagging, showed in the hillsides in the misty middle distance, and every outcrop of stone invited speculation that it might actually be age-rounded masonry. Fog scrimmed the cliffs to the north and south to craggy silhouettes that seemed more remote than they really were, and made the green of the wet leaves stand out vividly against the liver-colored earth.

"Who was just up?" Plumtree panted. "Were you going to light a cigarette for somebody?"

A low roofless building with ragged square window gaps in its stone walls stood a few hundred feet ahead of them, where the path broadened out to a wide mud-flat, and Cochran was aiming their plodding steps that way. "Valorie," he said shortly. "No, she gave me these matches." He flipped the matchbook open, and then he noticed fine-point ink lettering, words, inscribed on the individual matches.

"She's *written* something on 'em," he said; and he felt safe in stopping to squint at the carefully printed words, for the popping from the highway had been distant and hadn't been repeated. He read the words off each of the matches in order, aloud: " *'Si bene te tua laus taxat, sua laute tenebis.'* Latin, again."

"Again?"

"There was some Latin writing on the ashtray last night, in that bar, Mount Sabu—"

"Scant!" she interrupted, seizing his arm and staring at the top of the northern cliff wall. "God, you almost lost me, almost got Valorie back!"

Cochran had spun to look up that way, his right hand brushing the back of his belt; but he could see nothing up on the fog-veiled cliff top.

"What?" he said tensely, stepping sideways to catch his balance on the slippery mud. "Should we run?"

"There was a wild man up there, looking down here!"

"Shit. Let's—let's get inside this," he said, stepping up onto the undercut foundation of the roofless stone structure and crouching to fit through one of the square window gaps. Grass and gravelly sand covered any floor there might have been inside, and when he had glanced around and then helped Plumtree in, they both crouched panting against one of the graffiti-painted walls. Cochran had pulled the revolver free of the holster, and he belatedly swung the cylinder out and sighed with relief to see the brass of six rounds in the chambers.

"What's a wild man?" he asked, snapping the cylinder closed.

"Bearded and naked! In this weather!"

"A *naked* guy?" Cochran shook his head. "I don't know how scared we've got to be of a *naked* guy."

"I looked away. I didn't want to look at his face."

"Didn't want to look at his face," Cochran repeated tiredly. He stared up into the gray sky that from where he sat was bisected by low stone crossbeams. "I wonder when the others will show up here. I wonder *if* they will. I did give the hostess at the restaurant ten bucks to tell them we'd meet 'em down here, in the ruins.''

'' 'If'? You said they would, Scant!'' She glanced up wide-eyed at the ragged top of the wall close above their heads—as if, Cochran thought, she was afraid her wild man might have bounded down from the cliff and be about to clamber right over the wall. ''They're bringing the king's body, right?'' she asked.

''Yes.''

''And it's still okay? They didn't drop it on its head or anything?''

Cochran smiled. ''It's still apparently inhabitable, Janis.''

''Good. I did help kill him, and I do owe him his life back, but . . . I'd just as soon get to keep my own life afterward, not let him just *have* me . . . even though that's what I *deserve.*'' She shivered visibly and, after another fearful glance at the close top of the wall, leaned against Cochran. ''Of *all* things,'' she said in a small voice, ''I don't want what I *deserve.*''

''None of us wants that,'' he agreed quietly.

He draped his left arm around her shoulders, and he wondered if she might be mixing up the death of Scott Crane, for which she *had* been to some extent responsible, with the death of her father. A question for Angelica to wrestle with, he thought; though in fact Angelica, and now Janis, don't believe Janis's father died at all. Somehow.

Her shoulder was pressing into his ribs the tape cassette he'd taken from the telephone answering machine in his house a couple of hours ago, and he shifted his position—not to relieve the jabbing, but to keep the cassette in his pocket from possibly being broken.

When he had punched in his kitchen-door window with an empty wine bottle that had been standing on his back porch, he had heard his wife's voice speaking inside the house—''. . . *and we'll get back to you as quickly as posseebl' . . .*''—and even though his mind had instantly registered the fact that the voice was coming from an electronic speaker, his spine had tingled with shock, and his hands had been clumsy as he had unlatched the chain and pushed the door open.

Whoever had called had not stayed on the line to leave any message.

He had gone to the telephone answering machine and popped the cassette out of it, without letting himself think about why he was taking it; and then he had gone to her sewing room to find a sample of Nina's handwriting. Cody had followed him, and in a surprisingly humble tone had asked if she might ''borrow'' some of Nina's clothes. Cochran had curtly assented, and as Cody had gone through Nina's closet and dresser, he had pulled out the drawers of her desk. And while Cody carried away underwear and jeans and blouses and a couple of jumpsuits and sweaters, Cochran took from one of the desk drawers an old French-language Catholic missal, on one page of which Nina had written a lot of presumably important dates, including their wedding day; several snapshots, with Nina's inked notes on the back, were tucked in between the missal's pages, and he tamped them in firmly before tucking the book into his jacket pocket. And from the bedroom he had retrieved the gun and half a dozen twenty-dollar bills and Nina's wallet.

Cochran had driven the stolen Torino out into the back yard and parked it between the garage and the greenhouse, and then draped a car cover over it.

He and Plumtree had driven the rest of the way up the 280 to San Francisco in Cochran's '79 Ford Granada. Getting off the freeway onto Junipero Serra Boulevard, and then driving past the lawns of the San Francisco Golf Club and Larsen Park, had made him think of his many bygone trips to the city in this car with Nina sitting beside him, and he had been glad that the car had no tape player, for he might not have been able to resist the temptation to play Nina's phone-machine greeting over and over again.

Allo—you 'ave reached Sid and Nina, and we are not able to come to ze phone right now . . .

From far away up the amphitheater slope, someone was whistling a slow, sad melody. Cochran recognized it—it was the theme music from the movie *A Clockwork Orange*. And that had been some old classical piece, a dirge for the death of some monarch. . . .

Cochran straightened up, still holding the black rubber Pachmayr grip of the revolver, and he peeked over the top of the crumbling wall.

Arky Mavranos was plodding down the path from the road above, with Kootie hopping and scrambling along behind him. The two of them looked like a father and son out for a morning stroll, the father whistling meditatively—but Mavranos's right hand was inside his denim jacket, and even at this distance Cochran could see the man's eyes scanning back and forth under the bill of the battered blue Greek fisherman's cap.

"They're here," Cochran told Plumtree. He lifted the revolver and clicked the barrel twice against a stone that protruded from the top of the wall.

The sound carried just fine in the foggy stillness; Mavranos's gaze darted to the structure in which Cochran stood, and he nodded and turned to speak to Kootie.

"We'll negotiate with them," Cochran said quietly to Plumtree. "They'd like to have you in captivity, but we'll make it clear that's not an option. We can get a motel room, and have him give us a phone number where we can reach them. Go on meeting like this, on neutral ground.''

''My aims don't conflict with theirs,'' she said bleakly. ''If you'll come with me, I don't mind being in captivity, for the . . . duration of this. All of us are here, their friend is dead, because of what I did, what I let happen. *Mea maxima culpa.* I'm just ashamed to meet them.''

It's not entirely why *I'm* here, Cochran thought, aware of the angularities of the cassette and the French missal in his pockets. ''Well—let me do the talking, okay?''

''What?''

''I said, let me do the talking.''

''Oh, blow me.'' She looked around at the roofless stone walls. ''What are we paying for this room?''

Cochran bared his teeth. ''We're in San Francisco, Cody, and Mavranos and the Kootie kid are walking up. I've got a gun, and so does Mavranos, but if you don't do anything stupid here we won't have to all shoot each other, okay?''

''Was it him that was shooting at us before? I guess I dove for cover.''

''No, that wasn't him, I don't know who that was.'' Cochran peered again over the wall. Mavranos was close enough now to be eyeing the stone structure for a place to step up. ''I don't *think* it was him.'' To Mavranos, he called, ''I've got a gun.''

''So does everybody this morning, seems like,'' Mavranos said. He used both hands to climb up onto the exposed foundation ledge a few yards to Cochran's left, and Cochran noted the deepened lines around the man's eyes and down his gaunt cheeks. ''We got shot at, on the road up there, as we were driving up to that restaurant—maybe you heard it. Semi-auto, definitely, because of how fast the shots came; looks like nine-millimeter, from the holes. We drove on past the restaurant, eluded 'em with some magical shit and some *return fire* in the numbered streets east of here and parked in an alley off Geary, and Kootie and I took a cab back here.'' He noticed Plumtree crouched below him on the inner side of the wall, and touched the bill of his cap. ''Mornin', Miss Plumtree.''

''Was the king's body hurt?'' she asked.

''It—yeah, it was shot in the thigh.'' He rubbed one brown hand across his face, leaving a streak of mud down his jaw. ''Live blood was leaking out, till we bandaged it tight. I mean, it was purple venous blood, but it turned bright red in the air. Got oxygenated, according to Angelica. It's a good sign, that the blood is still vital. Not so good that he's got a bullet in his leg now.''

Cochran glanced down at Kootie, who was still standing on the mud-flat. The boy's face under the tangled black curls was tired and expressionless.

"Who was it that shot at you?'' Cochran asked.

"Local jacks,'' spoke up Kootie. "Boys who would be king. The world's been twelve days without a king, and it's getting impatient. If we wait long enough, the *trees* will be trying to destroy Crane's body. The *rocks* will be.''

"Kootie's . . . *sensory apparatus* works better up here,'' said Mavranos. Plumtree had stood up to be able to see over the top of the wall, and he squinted belligerently at her. "You still up for the restoration-to-life stunt, girl?''

Plumtree gave him an empty look.

And down on the ground Kootie stepped back, his face suddenly paler, and he glared at Plumtree. *"Don't,''* he said, almost spitting, *"ever . . . do that to me again.''* He took a deep breath and let it out. "Just because neither of us is a virgin, psychically, doesn't make both of us . . . *sluts.''*

Cochran glanced at Plumtree. She was looking down now, and she said, "Well, you just tell your fucking pal—oh, hell, I'm sorry, kid! But Mavranos just now asked me—with a straight face!—if I wasn't a coward and a liar and a cheat, on top of being a, a murderer. Murderess. 'Are you still up for it, girlie!' After I came to you people.''

"And then ran out,'' added Mavranos stonily.

Cochran caught on that Cody had thrown her anger to Kootie—who had instantly known where it had come from! "If she was really trying to 'run out,' '' Cochran said to Mavranos reasonably, "we wouldn't have come here to meet you, would we? Let's not waste time. What do we do next, now that we're in San Francisco?'' How, he thought, does a restoration-to-life *work?*

Mavranos reached into one of the outer pockets of his denim jacket, and Cochran tightened his grip on his own gun—but what Mavranos pulled out was a can of Coors, which he popped open one-handed. "Okay. Angelica says we gotta call up that black lady that talked to us on the phone, the one who was brushing her hair on the TV. She's our *intercessor,* though Angelica doesn't totally trust her, doesn't want her taking over. And Angelica brought along a lot of . . . beacons and landing lights, for Dionysus's remote attention as well as Crane's soul: those two silver dollars Spider Joe brought, and a gold Dunhill lighter that some hired assassin gave Crane one time—Angelica says the guy was a representative of Death, so it's a significant gift—and a bunch of myrtle-bush branches from the back garden. What other stuff we may need we'll—"

Plumtree interrupted him with a sharp, startled laugh—she was staring over the edge of the wall in the direction of the north cliff—and then she shivered and closed her eyes; Cochran glanced where she'd been looking, and his eyes widened in surprise to see a powerfully built naked man standing on the mud a couple of hundred feet away, facing them, with shoulder-length brown hair and a curly reddish beard that fell over his chest.

And Cochran's rib-cage went cold, for he recognized the man. "That's our taxi driver!" he exclaimed. "The guy that drove us to Solville!"

"That's Scott Crane," said Mavranos hoarsely. "Or his ghost."

"Catch him in a bottle," said Kootie.

Cochran stifled a nervous laugh at the foolishness of the boy's unconsidered remark—but then the naked man turned away, toward the cliff, and suddenly the distance and perspective were problematic. The man seemed to be smaller, tiny, as if he were some kind of elf standing on the rim of the wall a yard in front of Cochran's face, and a moment later he seemed to be immensely far away, and huge; and when he moved—away, presumably, for his form appeared to shrink—he shifted without any apparent contact with the ground. For one instant he seemed to jump from side to side like a figure in patchy animation—and Cochran grabbed one of the shoulder-height stone crossbeams, viscerally certain that the figure had been holding still and that it had been the whole world that had jumped.

Cochran's straining eyes focussed by default on the cliff face, and he noticed that a deep shadow at the base of it was the mouth of a cave; and when the naked figure flickered away out of sight it seemed to disappear into the shadowed opening.

Mavranos was sprinting away around the coping of a sunken mud lagoon, toward the cliff and the cave.

"It's just his ghost," yelled Kootie, starting after him.

"It's the ghost of my friend!" Mavranos shouted back.

Cochran shoved his revolver into his belt, then crouched to climb back out through the crusted-stone window hole. "Come on," he gasped at Plumtree, "we should go along."

She wailed softly as she followed him out. Then, "He drove our *taxi?*" she said as she hopped down after him from the foundation ledge to the mud. "He must have *known who I was!* I held a fucking *spear* to his baby boy's *throat!*" Even though she was Cody, she took his hand as the two of them trotted after Mavranos and Kootie. "If it comes to *facing* him, I think it'll have to be Valorie. She's the one who plays intolerable flops."

The cave opened into a roughly straight tunnel, high enough for a person to walk upright in. The passage appeared to be natural, floored with wet gravel and bumpy with stone outcroppings on the rounded walls and ceiling, though Cochran could dimly see a metal railing installed along part of the seaward wall, halfway down the shadowed tunnel. By the time Cochran and Plumtree had come scuffing and panting into the broad entrance, Kootie was a dark silhouette far down the length of the tunnel and Mavranos stood in chalky daylight out beyond the far side, perhaps thirty yards distant. Reflected gray sky glittered in agitated puddles that filled low spots of the floor, and the moist breeze from the vitreous corridor was heavy with the old-pier smell of tide pools.

"Come on," Cochran said, tugging Plumtree's cold hand as he stepped into the darkness.

"Take Valorie," she said tightly, "I hate caves."

Cochran thought about the dead-eyed woman Plumtree had been right after the hollow knocking of the gunshots, and he shuddered at the prospect of walking through this dim, wet tunnel with her. "I'd rather have you along, Cody," he said, "actually."

She shrugged irritably and stepped forward, her sneakers crunching in the wet gravel. "I'm here at the moment."

The mushy rattle of their shoes on the yielding humped floor echoed from the stone walls, but Cochran could hear too the hissing rise and gutter of contained surf—and when he and Plumtree had trudged to where the metal railing stood against the seaward wall, he saw that two jagged holes opened out from floor level to the outer air, where waves could be seen foaming up over rocks that glittered in the gray daylight outside.

A seething bath, he thought, *which yet may prove against strange maladies a sovereign cure.*

Up ahead, Kootie too was out in the leaden light now, and Mavranos's voice came reverberating down the tunnel: "Get your girlfriend out here."

"Come on, girlfriend," Cochran said.

She yanked her hand free of his, and hurried past him so that he had to splash along after her.

"Wait for moron Tiffany, asshole," she called back to him.

He touched the lump in his jacket that was the cassette tape from the telephone answering machine. Tiffany, he thought, or someone else.

*   *   *

There was only a wide ledge under the open sky at the other end of the tunnel, and no way to go farther without climbing over wet, tilted boulders.

Cochran blinked around in the relative glare when he was standing out there beside Kootie and Mavranos and Plumtree, and he pointed at the tan boulder nearest to them, across a narrow gap that had sea water sloshing in it. "That one looks like George Washington," he said, inanely. It did, though—the broad face turned out to sea in profile, the nose and the jawline and even the edge of the wig, were all rendered in weather-broken stone.

"The father of our country," said Plumtree brightly.

Kootie was peering down into the water, staring at the foamy scum on the waves. "He's gone," he said.

Cochran frowned at Plumtree to stop her from asking if he meant George Washington.

Mavranos was squinting up at the northern cliff face and then out across the huge tumbled stones. "He's not corporeal," he said, speaking loudly to be heard over the waves crashing on the rocks farther out. "That's good, right? He's not one of the solidified ghosts, like those 'beastie' things your dad had in his van."

"He wasn't corporeal just *now*," Kootie said. "And I think it generally takes a fresh ghost a while to firmly gather up enough . . . spit and bubble gum and bug blood and plaster dust . . . to form a reliably solid body. Still, he . . ." Kootie yawned widely. "Excuse me. Did Crane *drink* a lot?"

"Drink, like alcohol?" Mavranos scowled at the boy. "Well, he used to. He cut back hard after Easter in '90—since then it's been a glass or two of wine, with the bread and fish he has for breakfast, lunch, and dinner. Why?"

In a fruity, affected voice, Plumtree said, "I *enjoy* a *glass of wine* with my *meals*."

Ignoring her, Kootie said, "I think ghosts of drunks solidify faster. And then they keep drinking, buying cheap wine with money they get panhandling—but they can't digest the alcohol, and it comes bubbbling out of their skin like sweat. It's like the *habit* is what animates them." He turned a cold gaze on Plumtree. "Do *you* drink a lot?"

"Well," she said, "one's not enough and a thousand is too many, as they say. Why do you ask?"

"If he *was* your taxi driver," the boy said, "he must have had some substance for that. Turning the steering wheel, pushing the pedals. You met him then, and you were the first to see him today. Sometimes a ghost clings to the person responsible for his death, especially if the person has a lot of guilt about the death. Al—Thomas Edison—he had a couple of 'em hanging on him, at one time and another.''

''You're saying what, exactly?'' said Plumtree quickly.

''I'm saying your dad may have had help screwing up our TV set. I'm pretty sure you've got the ghost of Scott Crane riding in your head like . . . like a bad case of lice. And you're only making the ghost develop faster by drinking all the time.''

Cochran couldn't tell if Plumtree relaxed or tensed up at this statement; then her mouth opened and she droned, ''Sometimes she calls the king, and whispers to her pillow, as to him, the secrets of her overcharged soul: and I am sent to tell his majesty that even now she cries aloud for him.''

''Valorie,'' Cochran said.

''She that loves her selves,'' Plumtree said woodenly, ''hath not essentially, but by circumstance, the name of Valorie.''

Cochran shivered in the chilly ocean breeze, and he was glad Mavranos and Kootie would be accompanying him and Valorie back through the tunnel to the ruins and the mud-flats and the long zigzagging path back up to the normal-world San Francisco highway; for this was the same thing Valorie had said half an hour ago, when he had mentioned her name, and it had just now occurred to him that the Valorie personality was to some extent a kind of reflex-arc machine . . . dead.

Mavranos had been nodding rapidly while Plumtree spoke, and now he said, ''Groovy. Scott sure picked a well-ventilated head to *occupy*.'' He turned a pained look on Kootie. ''But in fact *he* doesn't know anything about it, does he?''

''Right,'' said Kootie. ''Crane *himself* is . . . somewhere else. Wherever the actual dead *people* go. Somewhere I guess only Dionysus has the key to. This . . . 'beastie,' this naked thing we saw today, it's like a ROM disk. Not useless, if we could talk to it, but hardly more a real person than the Britannica on CD-ROM would be. No, Crane himself wouldn't know about this thing we followed down here, any more than the real Edison knew about the ghost I had in my head two years ago.''

''No doubt.'' Mavranos stared at Cochran. ''So are you and Miss . . . Miss Tears-On-My-Pillow coming with us?''

Cochran touched the butt of his revolver. ''No.'' His heart was beating fast. ''No, we're gonna get a motel room somewhere. You and Angelica can cook up the restoration procedure, and we'll join you for that. You go get a place to stay, and meet me tomorrow at . . . Li Po, it's a bar on Grant Street. At noon. If you forget the name, just remember where we are right now—the street entrance to the bar is stuccoed up to look like a natural cavern. You can give me, then, the phone number of whatever place you're staying at, and we can set up a time and place where Janis and I can meet you all.''

Mavranos smiled. ''You don't trust us.''

''Somehow I just don't,'' Cochran agreed, struggling to keep his voice level. ''I think it must have something to do with,'' he added with a jerky shrug, ''you all discussing *shooting* Janis, last night.''

''That's noble,'' Mavranos said. ''But she just did one of her personality changes right now, didn't she?'' He smiled at Plumtree. ''You're Dr. Jeckyll, or Sybil, or the Incredible Hulk now, right?'' To Cochran he went on, ''Any time you leave her alone—hell, any time at all—she could change into her father, who murdered Scott Crane. Do you think he wouldn't kill you?''

Cochran quailed inwardly when he remembered the man who had spoken out of Plumtree's body last night at Strubie the Clown's house; but aloud he said, ''I'll take my chances.''

''You'll be taking all of our chances,'' said Kootie.

Cochran jumped when Plumtree spoke again, but the flat voice was still that of the Valorie personality: ''How chances mock, and changes fill the cup of alteration with diverse liquors!''

And Cochran remembered the bottle of wine that the Mondard figure had generously offered him in the hallucinated mirror last night. *Biting Dog,* or something, the label had seemed to read, in the reflection. And he thought too about Manhattans, and Budweisers and vodka, and Southern Comfort; and about flinty French *Graves* wine thoughtlessly disparaged at a New Year's Eve party.

Mavranos had already shrugged and started slogging back down the tunnel; Kootie followed him, after shaking his head and saying, ''Liquor, again.''

Cochran took Plumtree's elbow and led her after them. And all he was thinking about now was the—admittedly warm—twelve-pack of Coors he had transferred from the stolen Torino to his Granada, parked now just up the hill.

BOOK TWO

Diverse Liquors

O God! that one might read the book of fate,
And see the revolution of the times
Make mountains level, and the continent,—
Weary of solid firmness,—melt itself
Into the sea! and, other times, to see
The beachy girdle of the ocean
Too wide for Neptune's hips; how chances mock,
And changes fill the cup of alteration
With divers liquors! O! if this were seen,
The happiest youth, viewing his progress through,
What perils past, what crosses to ensue,
Would shut the book, and sit him down and die.
                                   —William Shakespeare,
                                   Henry IV, Part II

CHAPTER 15

It was an inconsistent and ubiquitous fiend too, for, while it was making the whole night behind him dreadful, he darted out into the roadway to avoid dark alleys, fearful of its coming hopping out of them like a dropsical boy's-Kite without a tail and wings. It hid in doorways too, rubbing its horrible shoulders against doors, and drawing them up to its ears, as if it were laughing.

—Charles Dickens,
A Tale of Two Cities

For five days now the skirts of the storm clouds had swept across the fretted hills and smoky lowlands of San Francisco. At the northeast corner of the peninsula the intermittent downpours had saturated the precipitous eastern slope of Telegraph Hill, loosening wedges of mud that tumbled down onto the pavement of Sansomme Street, where old wooden cottages still stood from before the 1906 earthquake, having been saved from the subsequent fire by bucket brigades of Italians who had doused the encroaching flames with hundreds of gallons of home-made red wine; and the rain had swelled the waters of Stow Lake in Golden Gate Park, making a marsh of the playground to the south and completely submerging the strange old stones that edged the lake's normal boundaries; and in the southeast corner of the city the rain had frequently driven customers out of the open-air Farmer's Market on Alemany Boulevard, and kept the Mexican children from playing in the streets of the Mission District east of Dolores. In the blocks of run-down post-war housing in Hunter's Point, east of the 101, gunfire from passing cars was more common than usual.

In fact, incidents of random gunfire had increased all over the city in the five days since a burst of semi-automatic weapons fire had startled tourists outside the Cliff House Restaurant on the northwest shore, on the morning of January 12th. Of less general concern, the wild monkeys that lived in the sycamore trees on Russian Hill had begun a fearsome screeching every evening at sunset, and in the sunless dawns vast flocks of crows wheeled silently over the old buildings at the south end of the Embarcadero by the China Basin. The *Chronicle* ran a brief human-interest article about the spontaneous street-dancing that had started in these South-of-Market streets and alleys around the French restaurant whose name translated as *I Am Starving;* the rain-soaked dancers were described as neo-Beatnik youths and unreconstructed old hippies, and the dance was supposed to be a revival of the French *carmagnole,* and the preferred dance music appeared to be the 1970 Melanie song "Candles in the Wind."

The newspaper had noted that the *carmagnole* dancers liked to toss lit strings of firecrackers around their feet as they stamped and spun in the ferocious dance, but to Archimedes Mavranos, standing now on the second-floor balcony of the apartment he had rented on Lapu Lapu Street in the shadow of the elevated Bay Bridge Freeway, the staccato *pop-pop-pop* sounded like volleys of full-auto machine-gun fire.

He was tapping his current can of Coors on the wet iron balcony rail. "I don't like it," he said over his shoulder.

"Duh," said Kootie from the living room behind him.

After frowning for another moment down at the shiny car roofs trundling by on the wet pavement, Mavranos smiled and turned back to the room. "I guess I have made it clear that I don't like it," he allowed. "But dammit, it *is* the day the earthquake blew up L.A. The one-year anniversary."

Kootie was sitting against the door of the unfurnished room, holding a red-blotted face-cloth to his side, and Pete and Angelica Sullivan stood over the old black-and-white television set they had brought along from Solville. It was sitting on top of another TV set, newer but non-functioning, that they had found in the street.

"We drove up there too, a day or so later, to Northridge," said Pete, without taking his eyes from the images on the working screen, which were just a modern Ford ad at the moment, "to look at the wreckage. Kootie insisted."

"Of *course* the seventeenth of January is a day to be scared of," Kootie said to Mavranos. "I saw what happened to L.A. But that would be why the French people you told us about made such a big deal *of* it. How could Dionysus's mid-winter death-day be anything *but* scary?" He smiled unhappily. "He's the earthquake boy, right?"

"Our pendulum stuck over the thirty-first, too," pointed out Angelica—wearily, for she had pointed it out many times already. "Tet."

"Our *pendulum*," said Mavranos in disgust as he drained his beer and strode in through the living room to the kitchen, which fortunately had come with a refrigerator. "Our *scientific apparatus*," he called derisively as he took a fresh can from the refrigerator's door-shelf.

Angelica had brought along several jars of pennies to shake at the TV, and over the last five days the old black woman had several times been induced to intrude on the TV screen here in San Francisco, though the reception of her inserts was scratchy here with some unimaginable kind of static. And she had spoken, too, though her opening words each time had been just an idiot repetition of the last phrases spoken on the ,real channel before her image had crowded out the normal programming.

At first the old woman had said that they must find her house, and "eat the seeds of my trees," so that one of their party could be "indwelt," which apparently meant inhabited by the old woman's ghost. The disembodied image on the television had insisted that this was the only way she could properly guide the dead king's company.

Angelica had vetoed that. *We have no hosts to spare,* she had said. *This is just identity-greed, she wants a body again, and she probably would cling. She can* advise *us just fine from the TV screen, and do her interceding from there.*

And the old black woman had had a lot to say, even just from the television speakers. She had babbled—uselessly, Mavranos thought—about being a penitential servant now of Dionysus, whose chapel she had apparently desecrated during her lifetime; she had said that they needed to call the god beside untamed water, and had talked uncertainly about some banker friend of hers who had drowned himself "near Meg's Wharf." Pete had gone to the library and established that her drowned friend had been William Ralston, who had founded the Bank of California, and who had drowned near *Meigg's* Wharf in 1874 after his bank went broke. And she had said that a calendar would have to be consulted with "a plumb line" to determine a propitious date.

Angelica had called on her *bruja* skills and made a pendulum of hairs from Scott Crane's beard, weighted with the gold Dunhill lighter a professional assassin had once given to Crane; and, after Mavranos had been sent out to buy a calendar, Kootie had dangled the makeshift pendulum over the January page.

The glittering brick-shaped lighter had looked like some kind of Fabergé Pez dispenser with its mouth open, for Angelica had had to open the lid to knot the hair around it—and the lighter had visibly been drawn to the square on the calendar that was the seventeenth, continuing to strain toward it, as if pulled magnetically, even after Kootie's hand had moved an inch or so past it. And, as Angelica had noted, the swinging lighter had been tugged toward the thirty-first, too, which was the Vietnamese Tet festival and the Chinese New Year. The Year of the Dog was ending, the Year of the Pig due to start on the first of February—and *that* date was the first day of Ramadan, the Moslem holy month of fasting.

Mavranos drank the fresh beer in three very big swallows, then popped open another can to carry with him into the living room.

"The thirty-first would probably work," he told Angelica stolidly. "I'm with you, I like it better; for one thing, we might be able to get more of a showing from this dead lady that's supposed to be our *intercessor*. But the thirty-first is two weeks from now. The seventeenth is tomorrow. We've been in San Francisco five days today. Scott's body is still in the back of the truck, and we'll be getting warm weather eventually. And as Kootie says, if we're going to ask Dionysus for a favor, it does make sense to do it on his own . . . terrible . . . day."

He looked out the window at the gray concrete pillars of the elevated 101, and he remembered the newspaper photos of the collapsed double-deck I-880 in Oakland, after the big quake in October of '89; and he remembered too the flattened cars he and Scott Crane had viewed in Los Angeles a year ago. "Shit," he said mildly. "I guess we do have to try it tomorrow, intercessor or no intercessor. You should have picked up a football helmet for each of us, along with your skeleton wine."

"And some Halloween masks," said Kootie quietly, with a somber glance at Marvranos. "Two or three apiece, ideally."

Mavranos returned the boy's look, and thought, *You've known all along how this will have to go, haven't you, kid? And you came along anyway, to save your parents.* Aloud, he said, "Yeah, they're probably real cheap this time of year."

Angelica darted a suspicious look from her foster-son to Mavranos. "That Plumtree woman had *better* still be willing to go through with this," she said. "Does Cochran say anything about her, what she's been *doing* for four days? I don't suppose he'll bring her along today."

"No chance of that," said Mavranos. "Just like I haven't, for example, been bringing Scott's body along when I've met Cochran at the bar. They-all and us-all don't trust each other; he thinks I'll try to shoot Plumtree, and I think Plumtree's dad will try to finish the job on Scott's body." He took a sip of the beer and licked foam off his graying mustache. "I bet Cochran takes as *circuitous* a route back to wherever he's staying as I do when I come back here."

"Wherever *he's* staying?" spoke up Angelica. "Isn't she staying with him?"

"Well, I assume," Mavranos began; "he tells me that she is—" Then he exhaled and let himself sit down cross-legged on the wooden floor. "I think she ran away from him, actually," he admitted in a level voice, "and he doesn't want to tell me. I think Cochran doesn't have any clue where she is. Sorry. I think her father came on sometime, and just . . . ran away with her body."

Cochran had been visibly drunk at their last two noon meetings at the Li Po bar, and too hearty in his assurances that Plumtree was still eager to get the dead king restored to life; and Mavranos had got the uneasy impression that Cochran was hoping to hear that *Mavranos* had somehow heard from her.

Kootie winced as he got to his feet. "Consider phlebotomy," he said.

" '—Who was once as tall and handsome as you,' " added Mavranos, automatically making a pun on the line in T. S. Eliot's *The Waste Land* about Phlebas the drowned Phoenician sailor.

Angelica's face was suddenly pale as she whirled to glare at Kootie, and her voice was low: "*I forbid it absolutely.* We've got money— we're going home. Or somewhere. To hell with this king."

Pete Sullivan was blinking at the woman and the boy in alarm. Clearly no one had got Mavranos's pun, not that it mattered. "What?" said Pete. "Lobotomy? For who?"

"*Phle*-botomy," said Angelica, still scowling at her foster son. "Venesection, bloodletting; from Crane's body into a, a wine glass, I suppose. You are simply *not* going to let the, that *dead man who we don't even know,* occupy your head, Kootie! You're not going to let him have *your* body! Pete, tell him that we—"

"Mom," said Kootie stonily. "*Angelica.* We've *all known,* we haven't talked about it but we've all known—come on!—that the king would probably have to take *my* body to do this, not that woman's." His eyes glistened, but he seemed even angrier than Angelica. "Look at my qualifications—I'm a *male,* for one thing. I'm not a virgin, psychically; and I *am* a virgin, physically, which Plumtree probably is not; and I've been living the king's discipline, fish and wine, and rituals, and visions! Call me fucking Fishmeal, excuse me. I've got to be . . . served to him." His shoulders relaxed, and he rubbed the face-cloth across his eyes, leaving a brushstroke of fresh blood on his cheek. "And who knows, it might work out just the way the Plumtree woman said— he might just use my body to do the magical stuff that'll let him get back into his own."

"His own?" shouted Pete. "His own is over fifty years old! And two weeks dead! You've been *planning* this? Your mother's right. Even if he *wanted* to, the Fisher King probably *couldn't* shift back out of an adolescent body into an old one! Any more than water can run uphill! How would this 'bloodletting'—"

" 'Even if'—?" Mavranos interrupted harshly; then he took a deep breath and started again. " 'Even if he wanted to'? You—goddammit, you didn't know the man, so I guess I got no right to take offense. But you know *me*, and I'm telling you now that he wouldn't, ever, save his own life at the expense of somebody else." He glared at the TV. "Hey, turn it up—our lady's on again."

Angelica gave the screen a startled look, then twisted the volume knob.

In the grainy black-and-white picture, the old black woman was standing beside her chair now, and staring directly out of the screen. "Gotta get the *bugs* out of your *house,*" she quavered, apparently reciting the tail end of some exterminator commercial she had interrupted. Mavranos hoped she wouldn't, this time, go on for several minutes with the parroted recitation.

"But I didn't—I wasn't even shaking the pennies," said Angelica softly.

A crackling had started up inside the dead TV set that they were using as a table for the working one.

"The bugs that work six feet under," said Kootie in a tense voice.

Mavranos couldn't tell if the boy was responding to what the old woman had said, or was sensing something nearby, or was speculating on the source of the noise in the dead TV; and he realized that his heart was pounding.

"Too late!" said the old black woman. "The bugs win this round! *You* get out."

It's not an exterminator ad, thought Mavranos.

Black smoke abruptly began billowing up from the back of the bottom television set; but its speakers came to booming life, croaking right along with the top TV set's, when the old woman shouted, "Boy-king, witch, escape artist and family retainer, I am speaking to you all! *Get out now*. They're coming up the stairs, the ones who hate the California vines! You four go out the window—I will distract the intruders with conversation and difficult questions."

Before she was finished speaking Mavranos had dropped his beer and stepped forward, and he grabbed Kootie and Angelica by their shoulders and propelled them stumbling across the floor toward the balcony. Pete Sullivan had reached through the black smoke to snatch the car keys off the top TV set, and he stepped along after his wife and foster son.

"There's a fire escape on the right side," Mavranos said, trying not to inhale the sharp-smelling smoke. He paused to grab his leather jacket and Angelica's purse, because their handguns were in them, and then he was standing on the balcony beside Angelica and Pete, taking deep breaths of the fresh air; he shoved the purse at Angelica with one hand while he flexed his free arm into the sleeve of the jacket. "You got a live one in the chamber?" he gasped.

She nodded, frowning.

"Take the time to aim," he said, boosting Kootie over the railing.

Behind them, a knock shook the hallway door. As if jolted to life by the knocking, the room's smoke alarm finally broke into a shrill unceasing wail.

"Who is it?" demanded the old woman's voice loudly from the two sets of speakers. "Be damned if I'm lettin' any *bug men* into my home!"

Kootie was halfway down the iron ladder now, but Angelica had only swung one leg over the rail, and Pete was standing behind her, uselessly flexing his hands.

Mavranos's mouth was dry, and he realized that he was actually very afraid of meeting whoever it might be that the old woman was referring to as bug men. "Pete," he said gruffly, "we're only on the second floor here."

Pete Sullivan gave him a twitchy grin. "And it's muddy ground below."

Both men clambered over the long rail of the balcony and hung crouched on the outside of it—like, thought Mavranos, plastic monkeys on the rims of Mai Tai glasses—then kicked free and dropped.

After a windy moment of free-fall Mavranos's feet impacted into the mud and he sat down hard in a puddle, but he was instantly up and limping to the curb, his hand on the grip of the .38 in his pocket as he stared back up at the balcony. "Keep 'em off to the side of me," he called to Pete, who had got to his feet behind him.

Over the distance-muted siren of the smoke alarm Mavranos could hear the loud, cadenced voice of the old woman—she seemed to be shouting poetry, or prayers.

Kootie had hopped down onto a patch of wet grass, and as soon as he had sprinted to the sidewalk Angelica sprang away from the ladder and landed smoothly on her toes and fingertips. As she straightened up and followed Kootie to the sidewalk, she caught her swinging purse with her left hand and darted her right hand into it.

Pete herded them down the sidewalk past a tall bushy cypress tree and a brick wall; Mavranos followed, but stopped to peek back through the piney branches of the cypress.

Across the lawn and above him, wisps of black smoke were curling out of the open balcony doorway and being torn away by the rainy breeze, but he saw no people up there; and he was about to step away and hurry after his companions when all at once three figures shuffled clumsily out onto the balcony, and from the second-floor elevation looked up and down Lapu Lapu Street. The middle figure, a white-haired man in a business suit, was clearly holding a weapon under his coat; but it was the pair of men flanking him that made Mavranos's belly go cold.

The two figures were bony and angular inside their identical lime-green leisure suits, and their bland faces swung back and forth in perfect unison—and though they didn't appear to say anything, and their theatrically raised hands didn't move to touch the white-haired man, Mavranos was certain that the pair had somehow perceived him. And at the same time he was sure that they were inanimate mannikins.

Mavranos turned away and ran; but by the time he had caught up with Pete and Angelica and Kootie he had reined in his momentary panic and was able to plausibly force his usual squint and grin. The old red truck with Scott Crane's tarpaulin-covered body in the back of it was at the curb in front of them, and there was no use in spooking these people—though before long he would have to tell them what he had seen.

Not right now, though—not for several minutes, several miles, at least. Whatever it is, it's what Nardie saw in Leucadia last week.

"It looks like we *all* go meet Cochran today," he panted as he held out his hand to Pete for the car keys. "And," he added in a voice he forced to be level, "I hope there aren't any bug men at Li Po."

In an upstairs room at the Star Motel in the Marina district of the city, Sid Cochran was sitting on the bed, gently nudging a clean glass ashtray across the back of a yellow enameled-metal National Auto Dealers Association sign he had salvaged two days ago from a gas-station Dumpster at Lombard and Octavia.

The sign was lying face down on the bedspread, but he knew that the front of it read NADA, and he found that oddly comforting. On this blank side he had inked the twenty-six letters of the alphabet and numbers from 0 to 9, in a bow-and-string pattern like what he remembered seeing on Ouija boards. Up by the pillows, next to an ashtray full of cigarette butts, lay half a dozen sheets of paper covered with lines of lettering tentatively divided into words by vertical slashes.

He had been trying for some time now to conduct a lucid conversation with the ghost of his wife.

Now the ashtray appeared to have stopped moving again, and he sat back and wrote down the last letter it had framed, and then he stared uneasily at the latest answer the ashtray had spelled out for him: *CETAITLEROIETPUISSONFILSSCOTTETAITLEROI.*

After driving away from the Sutro Bath ruins on Thursday in his old Granada, and then looping around and around the blocks of the Marina district until he was sure they were not being followed, Cochran and Plumtree had checked into this motel on Lombard Street. Cody had used Nina's Visa card, signing "Nina Cochran" on the credit-card voucher.

Plumtree had stayed up all that night and into Friday the thirteenth, watching television with the sound turned low enough so that Cochran could at least try to sleep; Cochran's only clue as to which personality might be up at any time had been the choice of programs. Cochran had gone sleepily stumbling out to meet Mavranos at noon, and when he had got back to the motel at about two in the afternoon, Plumtree had been gone. Cochran had slept until nearly midnight, by which time she had not reappeared.

And he had not seen her since. Twice on Saturday the telephone had rung, but when he had answered it there had been only choked gasping on the line.

On both of the days since her disappearance he had gone out to meet Arky at the Chinese bar at noon, and a couple of times a day he had trudged to the deli on Gough for coffee and sandwiches and bourbon and beer, but he had spent most of his time drunkenly studying the French Catholic missal he had found in Nina's sewing room when he and Plumtree had stopped at his house early on Thursday morning.

One page of the little volume was clearly a family tree. Cochran learned that Nina had not been the first of her family to have emigrated to the United States—a grand-uncle, one Georges Leon, had moved to New York in 1929, and then onward west to Los Angeles in 1938, and had had a son in 1943. Old Georges had apparently been a black sheep of the Leon family, had *n'avait pas respecte le vin,* disrespected the primordial French rootstocks. In tiny, crabbed script someone had declared that, precisely because the Bordeaux wines were terrible from 1901 through 1919, these were the times when all true sons of *père Dionysius Français* should show their loyalty, not go running off to *les dieux étrangers,* strange gods.

In fact, just about all of the notes in the missal concerned viticulture and wine-making. On the *dates importantes* page, 1970 was noted because Robert Mondavi of California's Robert Mondavi Winery had in that year met with Baron Phillipe de Rothschild of Bordeaux—in Honolulu, of all the remote places. 1973 was listed just for having been the year in which the Baron's Chateau Mouton Rothschild claret was finally promoted to the official list of First Growth Bordeaux wines; this development was apparently viewed as bad news by Nina's family because of the Baron's association with the Californian Robert Mondavi. One marginal scrawl described the two men as acolytes of the damnable California Dionysus.

Some of the notes were too brief and cryptic for him to make any sense of at all. For 1978 was just a sentence which translated as, "Mondavi visits the Medoc—failure." The following year was pithily summarized with the French for "Answered prayers! The new phylloxera."

For 1984 was simply the words *Opus One,* but because of his profession he did know what that must refer to.

"Opus One" was the '79 vintage California wine that Mondavi and Phillipe de Rothschild had finally released in 1984 as a joint venture between their premier Californian and French vineyards. It had been a fifty-dollar-a-bottle Cabernet Sauvignon with some Cabernet Franc and Merlot blended in, to soften the roughness imparted by the Napa hot spell in May of '79, fermented in contact with the skins for ten days and aged for two years in Nevers oak casks at Mouton, in the Medoc. Cochran remembered the Opus One as having been a subtle and elegant Cabernet, but the person who had scribbled the notes in the missal didn't approve of it at all: *le sang jaillissant du dieu kidnappe,* she called it, "haemorrhage blood of the kidnapped god."

The 1989 entry was on the next page, and it was just *J'ai recontre Adrocles, et c'est le mien*—"I have met Androcles, and he is mine."

A photograph of Sid Cochran was laid in at that page.

Sitting drunk in the Star Motel room, Cochran had taken some comfort from the fact that Nina had treasured his picture this way . . . until he noticed that in it he was posed with his chin on his right fist, and the ivy-leaf mark on the back of his hand was in clearer focus than his face was.

And so he had improvised the makeshift Ouija board.

Using the glass ashtray as a planchette, he had spelled out a call for Nina's ghost, and then had let the ashtray drift of its own accord from one letter to another after he had spoken questions aloud to it.

To his shivering nausea and breathless excitement, the device had appeared to work. The indicated letters, which he had painstakingly copied down one by one on sheets of Star Motel stationery, had been resolvable into French words.

The very first words had told him that he was indeed the "Androcles" the missal note had referred to—and his initial suspicion that he had unknowingly propelled the planchette himself, just subconsciously spelling out what he'd wanted to read, had been dispelled when further words appeared: *TU TEXPOSES AU DANGER POUR SAUVER LE DIEU DANGEREUX,* "You put yourself in danger to save the dangerous god." That part made no sense to him.

Twice he had told his wife's ghost—aloud, in stammering self-conscious syllables—that he loved her; and both times the slowly indicated letters had advised him to turn all his feelings for her over to the god who died for everyone. The wording had been exactly the same both times, and he had been reminded of the repetitive answers he had got from Plumtree's Valorie personality.

In spite of that, he had carefully wrapped the cassette from the telephone answering machine in a clean sock and stashed it in the bedside table drawer, beside the Gideon Bible—and he had stayed here at the motel, running up Nina's credit-card debt, in the hope that Plumtree would come back here, ready to do her mind-opening trick. He had called Pace Vineyards and got them to agree to let him have an unspecified amount of vacation time.

Yesterday morning he had got around to asking the Ouija board about one of the missal notes that had puzzled him—and then, in horrified alarm, he had chosen to regard the resulting answer as delusional, a fever-dream notion induced in the unimaginable sleep of death.

He'd had no choice: for in answer to his question about the unspecified "failure" during Mondavi's 1978 visit to the Medoc, the planchette had given him the letters *JAI ESSAYE MAIS JAI MANQUE A TUER LHOMME DE CALIFORNIA,* which worked out to spell, "I tried but failed to kill the man from California" in French.

After getting that answer on Sunday morning, he had stayed away from the planchette all the rest of that day—he had spent most of the gray daylight hours on a long, agitated walk among the incongruously peaceful green lawns of nearby Fort Mason. Nina would have been only fourteen years old in 1978—he had assured himself that the Ouija-board statement could not be anything more than a sad, morbid fantasy.

But this morning he had nevertheless helplessly found himself consulting the NADA sign and the ashtray once again, and a few minutes ago, at lonely random, he had got around to asking about her disgraced grand-uncle Georges Leon.

The answering string of letters that he had just copied down was easily translatable as, "He was the western king, and then his son Scott was the western king."

And he now remembered Pete Sullivan dialling out Scott Crane's full name on the old rotary telephone in the laundry room in Solville, six days ago—Cochran had noticed at the time that one of the two last names had been Leon.

It could hardly be a coincidence—apparently the dead king in the back of Mavranos's truck was some remote cousin of Cochran's dead wife.

Abruptly there was a hard knock at the motel-room door, and Cochran jumped so wildly that both ashtrays sprang off the bed; then he had dived to the closet and fumbled up the .357 with hands so shaky that he almost fired a bullet through the ceiling.

"Who is it?" he demanded shrilly. He hoped it was Plumtree at last, or even Mavranos—and not the police, or Armentrout with a couple of burly psych-techs and a hypodermic needle, or whoever it had been that had shot at Mavranos by the Sutro ruins last week.

"Is that you, Sid?" came a woman's hoarse voice from outside.

Carrying the gun, Cochran hurried to the door and peeked out through the little inset lens. It was Plumtree's flushed face staring at him—in fact, in spite of the apparent sunburn and the tangled blond hair across her face, he could recognize her as being specifically Cody. And even through the peep-hole he could see dried blood on scratches below her jaw and at one corner of her mouth.

He pulled the chain free of the slot and swung the door open. "Cody, I'm damn glad to—" he began, but guilt about his recent schemes stopped his voice.

She limped in past him and sat down heavily on the bed. She was wearing clothes he hadn't seen before, khaki shorts and a man's plaid flannel shirt, but she smelled of old sweat, and her bare legs were scratched and spattered with mud and burned a deep maroon. As he closed the door and reattached the chain, Cochran remembered dully that the Bay Area sky had been solidly overcast this whole past week.

Plumtree was shaking her head, swinging her matted hair back and forth, and she was mumbling, perhaps to herself, "How do I *hang on,* how do I *keep him down?* I feel like I've been stretched on the *rack!* Even Valorie can only pin him down *sometimes.*" She looked at the gun in Cochran's hand, and then her bloodshot eyes fixed on his. "Shooting me might be the best plan, that Mavranos guy's no idiot. But right now you better tell me you've got something to drink in here." She sniffed and curled her grimy lip. "Jeez, it stinks! Talk to the school nurse about *hygiene,* would you?"

"*I—*" Cochran stopped himself, and just tossed the gun down on the bed and fetched the current pint bottle of Wild Turkey from the windowsill. After he had handed it to her he hesitantly picked the gun up again and tucked it into his belt.

Plumtree tipped the bottle up and took several messy swallows, wincing as the whiskey touched the cut at the corner of her mouth; but she nodded at him over the neck of the bottle as she drank, and when she had lowered it and gingerly wiped her mouth, she wheezed, "Don't be shy about it," breathing bourbon fumes at him. "Put one through my thigh if you've got the leisure and elbow room, but—if I turn into my dad?—you *stop* me." The bottle had been half full when he'd handed it to her, but there was only an inch or so left when she gave it back to him. "How long have I been gone?" she asked. "Not too long, I guess, if you're still here. I was afraid you wouldn't be—that, like, everything happened a year ago, and the king was dead past recall."

"Today is Monday the sixteenth," he said, "of January, still. You've been gone . . . two full days." He thought of wiping the neck of the bottle, then just tilted it up for a sip. The whiskey will kill any germs, he thought. "Where *were* you?" he asked after he had swallowed a mouthful of the vapory, smoldering liquor.

"You're a gentleman, Sid. Where *was* I? I—" She inhaled sharply, and then she was sobbing. She looked up at him and her eyes widened. "*Scant!* You found me!" She clawed the bedspread as if the room might begin tossing like a boat; then she grabbed his arm and pulled him down beside her, and buried her face in his shirt. "God, I hurt all over—my teeth feel like somebody tried to pull them all out—and I'm a mess," she said, sniffling. "Hold on to me anyway. Don't let me run away again! You might have to handcuff me to the plumbing in the bathroom or something." He had both his arms around her now, and felt her shaking. "But don't—Jesus, don't *hurt* him, if he comes out."

He patted her dirty hair and kissed the top of her head. I've got to just throw away that cassette from the phone-answering machine, he thought. Even if it *would* serve as a potent lure, how could I possibly have thought of—pushing this woman out of her own head, in order to get Nina back?—or even just compounding Janis's problems by adding one more ghost to her sad menagerie? And Nina is *dead,* she'd only be what Kootie called a ROM disk, like Valorie. I swear I will *not* settle for that!

The bottle was in his right hand, behind her, and he wished he could get it up to his mouth.

"Where have you been, Janis?" he asked softly.

"Where—?" She shuddered, and then shoved him away. "Right back to me, hey?" she said. "Janis can't face this flop? Or did you have Tiffany here, is that why you're on the bed? How much time's gone by *now?*"

Cochran stood up. "It was Janis," he said wearily, "and just for a few seconds. Cody, I wish you—never mind. So *where were* you all?"

"*I was*—well, I was out in the hills. *I've* got to remember this, huh?

Out in the woods with people wearing hoods, killing goats.'' Tears spilled down her cheeks, and smeared the grime when she cuffed them away, but when she went on her voice was animated, a parody of vivacity: "One of the goat heads wound up on a, a *pole,* and I was on for just a couple of heartbeats when it was in the middle of *speaking* to us, in what I think was Greek. The goat head was speaking, in a human language. Goats have horizontal pupils because they look from side to side, mostly, and cats have vertical pupils because they're always looking up and down. My pupils are . . . staying after school for detention. I don't know who the hooded people were." She nudged the NADA sign with her hip. "Whaddaya got, a Ouija board? Ask *it* who they were." She smiled at him. Her nose had begun bleeding. "The hooded people.''

Cochran glanced at the clock radio on the bedside table. He still had an hour and a half before he was to meet Mavranos. In the last couple of days he had got into the habit of walking up Russian Hill on Lombard to Van Ness and catching the cable car down to California Street and then taking another one west to Chinatown, but today he could drive the old Granada, and hope to find a parking place. He might even get Cody to drop him off at a corner near Grant and Washington. No, she'd be way too drunk—maybe Janis could drive him.

"Okay," he said. He stepped into the bathroom and hooked a facecloth off the towel rack, then tossed it to her as he bent down beside the bed to retrieve the clean ashtray. "Your nose is bleeding, Cody," he said, placing the ashtray on the metal sign. "Put pressure on it." He sat down on the bed and laid his fingertips on the round piece of clear glass. "Who has . . . Miss Plumtree been with, during these last few days?" he asked.

As soon as he spoke, it occurred to him that Cody should be touching the ashtray too, and that he should have cleared the ghost of Nina off the line; but the ashtray was already moving.

"Write down the letters as they come," he told Plumtree nervously.

"I can remember 'em," she said, her voice muffled by the towel.

"Will you please—here we go." The ashtray had paused over the L, and now moved sideways to the E.

"Letterman," mumbled Plumtree. "I knew it. I was with David Letterman."

When the ashtray planchette had spelled out L-E-V-R, Plumtree inhaled sharply and stumbled back to the Wild Turkey bottle and took a gulp from it, wincing again. "Fucking Lever Blank," she gasped as blood spilled down her chin, "that's what I was afraid of. Goddamn old monster, he can't leave that pagan hippie cult alone, even though they threw him off that building in Soma.''

"It's not 'lever,' dammit,'' interrupted Cochran loudly without looking up from the metal sign. "Will you please write this stuff down? It's L-E-V-R, with no second E. And now an I, and an E . . . get the goddamn pencil, will you?'' He glanced quickly at her. "And you're bleeding all over the place.''

"Okay, okay, sorry. Just, my hands feel like I've got arthritis.'' The alcohol was visibly hitting her already—she was weaving as she walked back to the bed, as if she were on a ship in choppy water. She fumbled at the paper and pencil. "What . . . ?''

"L-E-V-R-I-E-R-B,'' he spelled out. "And another L—and an A.''

She was goggling blearily at the board now. "And N . . . and C . . .'' she noted, painstakingly writing the letters.

After several tense seconds, Cochran lifted his fingers from the ashtray. "That's it. What, Levrierble . . . ?''

"Levrierblanc.'' She held out the blood-spattered sheet of paper and gave him a scared, defiant glare. "That's still Lever Blank, if you ask me. The French version.'' She pressed the towel to her nose again.

"My wife is French,'' he said, nodding, realizing even as he spoke that it was an inadequate explanation. "Was.''

"I know. Sorry to hear she died, dirty shame.'' She snapped a dirty fingernail against the paper, spiking the blood drops on it. "It's two words. Blanc's the second word, like Mel Blanc.''

Cochran nodded. Obviously she was right—and he suspected that if Nina hadn't been their . . . *operator* here, it would have come out in plain English as *LEVERBLANK.*

"A goat head,'' he said, "speaking Greek.'' In his mind he heard Long John Beach's crazy lyrics again: . . . *and frolicked in the Attic mists in a land called Icaree.* "I think you'd better write down everything you can remember about this Lever Blank crowd.'' He glanced again at the clock radio. "Not right now. I've got to meet Mavranos in a little over an hour. Let's get Janis to drop me near the place, she—'' isn't falling-down drunk, he thought; "—isn't having a nose-bleed, and then you can come back here and—''

"Janis drive? Fuck that. I can drive, and I'm meeting Marvos—dammit—*Mavranos* with you, too. We'll get this *done.* I don't want to have that little kid's dad's blood on my hands one hour more than I have to.'' Her own blood was running down her wrist. "He just wants, my father, he wants to become king, like he failed to do when he was in a body of his own. A *male* body, he needs. If we can get Crane solidly raised from the dead, I think my father will have no reason to hang around, he'll just go back into hibernation, like a case of herpes in remission. You don't have herpes, do you?"

Cochran blinked at her. "No."

"Tiffany does. You should know. I won't even drink out of a glass she's used. How far away is it, where you're meeting Marvy-Arvy?"

"Oh—no more than twenty minutes, if we drive. Of course if we've got to find a place to *park the car,* I don't know how long that might take. No, I really think it's too dangerous for you to be there, Cody— if Mavranos gets hold of you, he's liable to do something like—"

"Nothing I'll object to. Nothing I won't deserve. I got his friend killed." She struggled up from the bed, still pressing the bloody face-cloth to her nose. "You got coffee? Good. Make me a cup, and pour the rest of that bourbon into it. I'm gonna," she said with a sigh, as if facing a painful ordeal, "take a shower."

"Could I talk to Janis about all this?"

"No. And what do you mean, 'she doesn't have a nosebleed'? It's her nose too, isn't it?"

Cochran opened his mouth to point out some inconsistencies in the things she'd said, but found that he was laughing too hard to speak; tears were leaking from the corners of his eyes, and his chest hurt. "I'll," he managed to choke, "have the coffee ready when you . . . get out of the shower."

Her mouth twitched. "Laugh it up, funny boy," she said mockingly, then lurched into the bathroom and closed the door with a slam. From the other side of the door he heard her call, "And don't be peeking in here to see if Tiffany's on!"

Cochran was still sniffling when he pulled open the bedside table drawer, and he lifted out the cassette and stared at it.

Two full seconds over a lit match would destroy the thing.

But, *It's her nose too, isn't it?*—and, if it comes to that, *his*, too. Her terrible father's. A lot of jumping around, re-shuffling and discarding, might happen before we all get out of San Francisco.

He tucked the cassette carefully into his shirt pocket.

CHAPTER 16

Besides that all secret men are men soon terrified, here were surely cards
enough of one black suit, to justify the holder in growing rather livid as he
turned them over.

—Charles Dickens,
A Tale of Two Cities

Dr. Armentrout knew he was lucky to have got out of the smoky apartment building and back down to the street, and his car, and to Long John Beach, before encountering this . . . *very shifty* woman.

The day had started propitiously, but this last half hour had been a rout.

Late last Thursday his teal-blue BMW had finally limped off the 280 at Junipero Serra Boulevard and sputtered up Seventh to Parnassus to the UCSF Medical Center, where he had got a couple of colleagues to make some telephone calls for him; the upshot was that he had been allowed to take over house-sitting duties at the nearby Twin Peaks villa of a neurologist who was on sabbatical in Europe.

The first thing he had done at the empty house was to change the phone-answering message. Then, very quickly, he had made a photocopied blank sheet of letterhead from the nearby Pacifica minimum-security psychiatric facility, and he'd altered the phone and fax numbers on it to those of the absent neurologist's house; he had addressed the sheet to Rosecrans Medical, and typed on it a transfer for Long John Beach, along with a request for Beach's records—to make it look plausible he had had to ask for everything: nursing progress reports, psychosocial assessment, treatment plan, financial data, the legal section. He hoped the neourologist was in the habit of keeping a lot of paper in his home fax printer. Long John Beach was 53-58, on a full conservatorship, but the old man's "conservator" had been a fictitious entity from the start, so there'd been no risk in signing the remembered made-up name.

Then Armentrout had telephoned Rosecrans Medical and peremptorily announced his application for immediate administrative leave. He'd explained that he was temporarily working as a consultant at UCSF Medical, and pointed out that he was entitled to six weeks a year of vacation, and had never taken any of it. He had named one of the other doctors, an elderly Freudian, to serve as acting chief of staff in his absence. Nobody had argued with him, as he had known they would not—a chief of psychiatry could pretty well do as he liked in a clinic.

To his surprise, he had felt bad about violating their trust, breaking the rules—and not just because he would lose his career and probably be charged with a felony if he were to be caught. He had pursued a psychiatric career largely out of gratitude for his own long-ago deliverance from guilt and shame, and he regretted the necessity of this dishonesty far more than he had ever regretted the killing of a patient.

While waiting vainly to hear from Plumtree's Omar Salvoy personality on the cellular telephone, Armentrout had printed up a flyer and posted it in various bars and surf shops and parks around the city; REWARD FOR INFORMATION, the flyer had read, followed by a picture of Koot Hoomie Parganas—an old school photo, the same one that had been on billboards in Los Angeles when the boy had dropped out of sight in '92—and one of Angelica Anthem Elizalde, also from that year, blown up from a newspaper photo, and unfortunately showing her with her mouth open in surprise and her eyes closed. He had printed the absent neurologist's phone number at the bottom, and let the answering machine take all calls to it.

There would have been no point in listing the number of his cellular phone—it rang all day long now, with apparently every idiot ghost in the country wanting to threaten him or weep at him or beg him for money or rides to Mexico. He had to answer it every time, though, because it was the line Salvoy would call in on; and at times during this last couple of days, tired of Long John Beach's insane ramblings, Armentrout had even stayed on the line and had disjointed conversations with the moronic "ghostings," as the old writers had referred to the things. They certainly were more gerund than noun.

The woman he was facing now, though, seemed to deserve a noun.

This morning a call had come in on the neurologist's line, and Armentrout had picked it up after hearing a few sentences. It was an old man calling from a pay phone at the Moscone Convention Center, and he was excitedly demanding the reward money. Armentrout had driven over there and paid him fifty dollars, and the man had then told him that the woman and boy on the flyer, and two other men, were living in an upstairs apartment on Lapu Lapu, a block away.

And probably the old informant had been right. When Armentrout had burst into the indicated apartment, wearing his clumsy two-figure mannikin appliance, the occupants had apparently just fled out the window. Two smoking television sets sat one atop the other in the middle of the room, chanting crazy admonitions at him like Moses' own burning bush. He had shambled past them out onto the balcony before fleeing the room, but, though the two mannikins he was yoked with had seemed to twitch spontaneously as he had stood out there in the rainy breeze, he had seen no one on the street below.

And so he had shuffled sideways back down the stairs and outside to the car. Fortunately Long John Beach had got tired of waiting in the back seat and had got out to urinate on the bumper—for Armentrout had no sooner opened his mouth to yell at the one-armed old man than he became aware of someone standing only a yard away from Long John Beach and himself.

Armentrout had jumped in huge surprise, the two mannikins strapped to his shoulders twitching in synchronized response, for there had been no one standing there a moment earlier. The impossible newcomer was a lean dark-skinned woman in a ragged ash-colored dress, and her first words to him were in French, which he didn't understand. In the gray daylight her face was shifting like an intercutting projection, from bright-eyed pubescence in one instant to eroded old age in the next. Armentrout knew enough not to meet her eyes.

"No habla Français," he said hoarsely. This is a ghost, he told himself. A real one, standing beside my car on this San Francisco sidewalk. His shirt was suddenly clammy, and the heads and arms of the mannikins yoked on either side of him were jiggling because his hands were shaking on the control levers inside the jackets of their green leisure suits.

"No habla Français," echoed Long John Beach, stepping forward and shoving his still-swollen nose against the outside ear of the right-hand mannikin, "today. No grandma's cookies, so de little mon say. Madame has forgotten that we agreed to play in partnership this evening."

The flickering woman goggled at the four heads in front of her—teeth were appearing and disappearing inside her open mouth—and clearly she was uncertain as to which head was which. Armentrout was careful to look away from her eyes, but as her gaze brushed past him he felt his attention bend with the weight of her unmoored sentience, and he shuddered at the realization that he had come very close to dying in that instant—in a group therapy session once he had seen a patient meet the eyes of a ghostly figure that had been loitering out on the lawn for several days after an in-house suicide, and the ghost figure had disappeared in the same moment that the patient had toppled dead out of his chair.

Now Long John Beach raised the amputated stump of his left arm, and the two Styrofoam mannikin heads began nodding busily. Armentrout wasn't doing it—he could feel the control lever in his nerveless right hand jiggling independently of him.

"If she hollers, let her go," Long John Beach chanted as the heads bobbed, "my momma told me to pick this ver-ry one, and out . . . goes . . . *you.*"

He sneezed at the woman, and her face imploded; and with a disembodied wail of *"Richeee!"* she all at once became nothing more than a cloud of dirty smoke tumbling away down the sidewalk.

"G-good work, John," stammered Armentrout, spitting helplessly as he spoke. The ghost-woman's final cry had sounded like Armentrout's *mother's* voice—invoked by Long John Beach saying *my momma?*— and he was afraid he was about to wet his pants; well, if he did, he could switch trousers with one of the mannikins, and people would think the Styrofoam-man had wet *his* pants. That would work. But then Armentrout would be wearing lime green pants with a gray tweed jacket.

He assured himself that what he feared was impossible. How *could* his mother's ghost be here? He had left his loving mother in that bathtub in Wichita thirty-three years ago, drunk, *dead* drunk; and then intensive narcohypnosis and several series of ECT had effectively severed that guilt-ghost from him, way back in Kansas. "John, what do you suppose—"

"We better motate out o' here," interrupted the one-armed old man. "That was several girls in one corset. I sneezed a ghost at 'em to knock 'em down, but they'll be back soon, with that ghost glued on now too."

"Right, right. Jesus." Armentrout was blinking tears out of his eyes. "Unstrap me, will you?"

With the deft fingers of his one hand—or maybe, it occurred to Armentrout now, with help from his phantom hand—Long John Beach unbuckled the two-mannikin appliance, and Armentrout shrugged it off and tossed it into the back seat and got in behind the wheel and started the car. After the old man had gone back to the bumper to finish pissing, and had finally got in on the passenger side, Armentrout drove away through the indistinct shadow of the elevated 80 Freeway.

"Let me tell you a parable," said Long John Beach, rocking in the passenger seat. "A man heard a knock at his door, and when he opened it he saw a snail on the doorstep. He picked up the snail and threw it as far away as he could. Six months later, he heard a knock at his door again, and when he opened it the snail was on the doorstep, and it looked up at him and said, 'What was *that* all about?' "

Armentrout was breathing deeply and concentrating on traffic. "Don't *you* start getting labile and gamy on me, John," he said curtly.

He was driving north on Third Street, blinking through the metronomic windshield wipers at the lit office windows of the towers beyond Market Street. Beside him Long John Beach was now belching and gagging unattractively.

"Stop it," Armentrout said finally, as he made a left turn and accelerated down the wet lanes southeast, toward Twin Peaks and the neurologist's house. "Unroll the window if you're going to be sick."

In a flat, sexless voice, Long John Beach said, "I would be blind with weeping, sick with groans, look pale as primrose with blood-drinking sighs, and all to have the noble king alive."

Armentrout blinked at the man uneasily. Ghosts were harmless in this form, channelled through the crazy old man, but their arrival often made the car's engine miss—it had stalled almost constantly on the drive up here—and he worried about what the ghosts might overhear and carry back to the idiot bar where they seemed to hang out—"India," the old writers had called that raucous but unphysical place. And this particular ghost, this sexless one that seemed to quote Shakespeare all the time, had been coming on through Long John Beach frequently lately, ever since their visit at dawn last Thursday to the beach below Scott Crane's Leucadia estate.

There was something oracular about this ghost's pronouncements, though, and Armentrout found himself impulsively blurting, "That last cry, from that ghost out on the sidewalk—that might have been my mother."

"My dangerous cousin," came the flat voice from Long John Beach's mouth, "let your mother in: I know she is come to pray for your foul sin."

"*My* foul sin?" Armentrout was shaking again, but he forced a derisive laugh. "And I'm no cousin of yours, ghosting. Don't bother holding a chair for *me*, in your . . . moron's tavern."

"Most rude melancholy, Valerie gives thee place."

"Shut up!" snapped Armentrout in a voice he couldn't keep from sounding petulant and frightened. "John, come back on!" The one-armed figure was silent, though, and just stared at the streaks of head-lights and neon on the gleaming pavement ahead; so Armentrout picked up the telephone and switched it on, meaning to punch in some null number and talk to whatever random ghost might pick up at the other end.

But someone was already on the line—apparently Armentrout had activated it in the instant before it would have beeped.

"Got no time for your ma nowadays, hey Doc?" came a choppy whisper from the earpiece. "She's back here crying in her drink, com-plaining about you sneezing in her face. Shall I put her on?"

The cellular phone was wet against Armentrout's cheek. "No, please," he said, whispering himself. He knew this caller must be Omar Salvoy, Plumtree's ingrown father, and Armentrout had no decent de-fenses against the powerful personality. The tape recording he had made last Wednesday had been magnetically erased by Salvoy's field—even in the Faraday cage inside his desk!—and the vial of Plumtree's blood had come open in Armentrout's briefcase, and soaked the waxed-paper wrapper of a sandwich he'd stowed there for lunch; he couldn't imagine how he could use a dried-out bloody sandwich as a weapon against the Salvoy personality. "You need my clinic," he ventured weakly. "You need my authority for commitment of the boy, and ECT treatment, and maintenance on life-support."

"I don't need this black dog," came the whisper. "When it barks, the whole India bar shakes out of focus. Is this your dog?"

In the passenger seat beside Armentrout, Long John Beach rocked his gray old head back against the headrest and began jerkily *whining* up at the head-liner, in an eerily convincing imitation of a dog.

"Stop it!" Armentrout shouted at him, accidentally swerving the BMW in the lane and drawing a honk from a driver alongside.

"Take it slow, Daddy-O," Salvoy said through the telephone. "I only got a minute, boyfriend is in the shower, and anyway I'm not . . . *seated* properly here, I'm steering from the back seat and can't reach the ped-als—*as it were.* Valerie is surely gonna kick me out again any time now. This isn't the Fool's dog, is it? *Get away!* Listen, my *girl* got away from me hard today, and that's bad because tomorrow is a Dionysus death-day, it's their best day to do the restoration-to-life trick with Scott Crane's body. And my girl Janis tells me that they were talking last week to a ghost black lady in the Bay Area who claimed to have died in like 1903; that can only be this old voodoo-queen ghost known as Mammy Pleasant, who's been screwing with TV receptions around here ever since there's been TVs to screw with. If the Parganas crowd is still in touch with Pleasant, they might be getting some real horse's mouth. Better than half-ass goat head. It'll be by the water, in any case, at dawn—oh shit, stay by the phone."

With a click, the line went dead. Then, seeming loud in contrast to Salvoy's whispering, a girl's nasal voice from the earpiece said, "Doctor, I'm eating broken glass and cigarette butts! Is this normal? I eat till I jingle, but I can't fill myself up! Won't you—"

Armentrout flipped the phone's cover shut and slammed it back into its cradle. That last speaker had probably been the obese bipolar girl who had killed herself last week—but who was the flat-voiced one who had spoken through Long John, the one who seemed always to quote Shakespeare and who apparently called herself Valerie? Could it be *Plumtree's* Valerie personality, astrally at large and *spying* on him? Good God, he had told her about his mother!

And the voice on the sidewalk *had* been his mother's—Salvoy had said she'd been in the bar weeping about someone sneezing in her face.

Armentrout sighed deeply, almost at peace with the realization that he would have to perform a seance, and an exorcism, today.

Long John Beach had hunched forward over the dashboard now, sniffing in fast puffs punctuated by explosive exhalations.

It was so convincing that Armentrout almost thought he could smell wet dog fur. Long John had been doing this sort of thing periodically for the last couple of days, sniffing and whining and gnawing the neurologist's leather couch—was the crazy man channeling the ghost of a *dog?*

This isn't the Fool's dog, is it?

It occurred to Armentrout that in most tarot-card decks the Fool was a young man in random clothes dancing on a cliff edge, with a dog snapping at his heels; and certainly Long John's crazy speech, his "word-salad" as psychiatrists referred to skitzy jabbering, did sometimes hint at a vast, contra-rational wisdom.

But surely the crazy old man couldn't be in touch with one of the primeval tarot archetypes! Especially not *that* one! The Fool was a profoundly *chaotic* influence, inimical to the kind of prolonged unnatural stasis that Armentrout needed to establish for the life-support confinement of the Parganas boy.

Could the old man possibly channel someone—or something—that big?

A Dionysus death-day.

Armentrout remembered the catastrophic ice-cream social at Rosecrans Medical Center last week. Long John Beach had seemed to be channeling—had seemed to be *possessed* by—the spirit of the actual Greek god *Dionysus* on that night. It was hard for Armentrout to avoid believing that Dionysus had somehow been responsible for the earth-quake that had permitted Plumtree and that Cochran fellow to escape.

Armentrout thought he knew now why the death of the Fisher King had eliminated all the ghosts in the Southern California area. Murdered in the dead of winter, the slain Fisher King had become compellingly identical to the vegetation-god Dionysus, whose winter mysteries cele-brated the god's murder and devourment at the hands of the Titans and his subsequent return from the kingdom of the dead. Being a seasonal deity of death and the underworld—and incarnate this winter in this killed king—the god had taken all the local ghosts away with him, as a possibly unintended entourage, just as the death of summer takes away the vitality of plants, leaving the dried husks behind. In the case of the ghosts, it was their memories and strengths that had lingered behind, while their lethal, vengeful *sentiences* were conveniently gone.

If you like dead leaves, Armentrout thought as he drove, it's good news to have a dead Fisher King; and I like dead leaves. I *sustain myself spiritually* on those dear dead leaves.

But eventually, he thought, if nature follows her cyclical course, Di-onysus begins his trek back from the underworld, and a Fisher King again becomes evident; and the plants start to regain their life, and the ghosts—quickly, it seems!—are again resistant, dangerous presences. The god wants to *rake up* the dead leaves, he wants to gather to himself not only the ghosts but all the memories and powers and loves that had accrued to them . . . which scraps I don't want to let him have. He wants us to figuratively or literally drink his *pagadebiti* Zinfandel, and let go of every particle of the cherished dead, give them entirely to him . . . which I don't want to do.

When Armentrout and Long John Beach had finally got off the 280 Freeway last Thursday, the crazy old man had suddenly and loudly insisted that they take a right turn off of Junipero Serra Boulevard and drive five blocks to a quiet old suburban street that proved to be called Urbano; and in a grassy traffic circle off Urbano stood a gigantic white-painted wooden sundial on a broad flat wheel with Roman numerals from I to XII around the rim of it. After demanding that Armentrout stop the car, Long John Beach had got out and plodded across the street and walked back and forth on the face of the sundial, frowning and peering down around his feet as though trying to read the time on it—but of course the towering gnomon-wedge had been throwing no shadow at all on that overcast day. The passage of time, as far as this inexplicable sundial was concerned, was suspended.

And if Armentrout could succeed in getting the new Fisher King maintained flatline, brain-dead, on artificial life-support in his clinic, Dionysus's clock would be stopped—at the one special point in the cycle that would permit Armentrout to consume ghosts with *impunity*— with no fear of consequences, no need for masks.

The two-mannikin framework shifted and clanked in the back seat now as Armentrout drove fast through the Seventeenth Street intersection, the car's tires hissing on the wet pavement. Market Street was curving to the right as it started up into the dark hills, toward the twin peaks that the Spanish settlers had called *Los Pechos de la Chola,* the breasts of the Indian maiden.

"There was still *time,*" Long John Beach said, in his own voice.

"For what?" asked Armentrout abently as he watched the red brake lights and turn-signal indicators reflecting on the wet asphalt ahead of them. "You wanted to get something to eat? There's roast beef and bread at the house—though I should feed you in the driveway, the way you toss it around." He passed a slow-moving Volkswagen and sped up, eager to put more distance between himself and that shifting maternal ghost on Lapu Lapu Street. "I should feed you Alpo."

"I mean there *was* still *time,* even though I couldn't see it. It doesn't stop because you have something blocking the light. If we coulda seen in infrared," he went on, pronouncing the last word so that it rhymed with *impaired,* "the shadow woulda been there, I bet you anything." The BMW was abruptly slowing, because Armentrout's foot had lifted from the gas pedal, but the old man went on, "Infrared is how they keep patty melts hot, in diners, when the waitress is too busy to bring 'em to you right when they're ready."

"Stay," said Armentrout in a voice muted to a conversational tone by the sudden weight of fear; he took a deep breath and made himself finish the sentence, "out . . . of . . . my . . . mind. God damn you." But his thoughts were as loud and rapid as his heartbeat: You can't read *my* mind! You can't start channelling *me!* I'm not dead!

Long John Beach shrugged, unperturbed. "Well, you go around leaving the door open . . ."

From the backseat came a squeak that could only have been one of the Styrofoam heads shifting against the other as the car rocked with resumed acceleration—but to Armentrout it sounded like a hiccup of suppressed laughter.

Tall cypresses hid from any neighboring houses the back patio of the neurologist's villa on Aquavista Way, and the green slope of the northernmost Twin Peak mounted up right behind the pyrocantha bushes at the far edge of the lawn. After Armentrout had parked the car in the garage and made Long John Beach carry the two-mannikin appliance out to the patio, he fixed a couple of sandwiches for the one-armed old man and then carefully began scouting up paraphernalia for a seance and exorcism in the back yard.

The neurologist's house didn't afford much for it—Armentrout found some decorative candles in glass chimney shades, and a dusty copper chafing dish no doubt untouched since about 1962, and a bottle of Hennessy XO, which was almost too good to use for plain fuel this way. *Popov vodka* would be more appropriate to his mother's—

He hastily drank several mouthfuls of the cognac right from the bottle as he made himself walk around the cement deck of the roofed patio, shakily lighting the candles and setting them down in a six-foot-wide circle. Then he picked up a hibachi and walked around the circle shaking clumped old ash in a line around the perimeter; after he tossed the hibachi out onto the lawn, where it broke like glass, he walked around the circle again, stomping and scuffing the ash so that the line was continuous and unbroken. The chafing dish he set on a wooden chair inside the circle, and, needing both hands to steady the bottle, he poured an inch of brandy into it.

Then for several minutes he just stood and stared at the shallow copper pan while the morning hilltop breeze sighed in the high cypress branches and chilled his damp face. I *can* face her, he told himself firmly; if it's for the last time, and if she's concealed behind the idiot shell-masks of Long John Beach's broken mind, and if I'm armed with the Sun card from the monstrous Lombardy Zeroth deck—and there's brandy to lure her, and then burn her up.

A hitch that might have been a sob or a giggle quivered in his throat. Will this mean I'll have committed matricide *twice?*

He shivered in the cold wind, and took another big gulp of the brandy to drive away the image of the old face under the surface of the water, the lipsticked mouth opening and shutting, and the remembered cramps in his seventeen-year-old arms.

He looked up at the gray sky, and swallowed still another mouthful, and mentally recited the alphabet forward and backward several times.

At last he felt steady enough to go back inside and fetch out from under the bed the two purple velvet boxes.

"Finish your sandwich and get out here," he told Long John Beach as he carried the boxes through the kitchen to the open back door. "We've got a . . . a call to make."

When Long John Beach came shambling out of the house, absently rubbing mustard out of his hair and licking his fingers, Armentrout had to tell him several times to go over and stand inside the circle, before he finally got the old man's attention. "And step *over* the ash line," he added.

At last the old man was standing inside the circle, blinking and grinning foolishly. Armentrout forced himself to speak in a level tone: "Okay, John, we're going to do our old trick of having you listen in on a call, right? Only this time, you're going to be the telephone as well as the eavesdropper. 'Kay?"

Long John Beach nodded. "Ring ring," he said abruptly, in a loud falsetto.

Armentrout blinked at him uncertainly. Could this be an *incoming* call? But this couldn't start *yet*, he hadn't lit the brandy yet! "Uh, who is this, please?" he asked, trying to sound stern so that the old man wouldn't laugh at him if he'd just been clowning around and this *wasn't* a real call.

"Dwayne," said Long John Beach.

Armentrout tried to remember any patient who had ever had that name. "Dwayne?" he said. "I'm sorry—Dwayne who?"

"Dwayne the tub, I'm dwowning!"

Armentrout reeled back, gasping. It wasn't his mother's voice, but it had to be a sort of relayed thought from her ghost.

"J-John," he said too loudly, fumbling in his pockets for a match or a lighter, "I want you to light the brandy—light the stuff in that pan there."

He found a matchbook and tossed it into the circle, then fell to his knees on the wet grass beside one of the purple velvet boxes. I can't *shoot* him, he thought, it wouldn't stop her, she's just passing through Long John's train-station head.

He flipped open the other box and spilled the oversized cards out onto the grass, squinting as he pawed through them until he found the Sun card.

When he looked up, Long John Beach had lifted the copper chafing-dish pan in his one hand and was sniffing it. And now it *was* Armentrout's mother's voice that spoke from the old man's mouth: *"Oh, how I wish I could shut up like a telescope!"*

"Put that down," Armentrout wailed.

The pan tipped up toward the old man's mouth.

"Mm—" Armentrout choked on the word *mom,* and had to make do with just shouting, "Don't drink that! John! Kick out that woman's ghost for a minute and listen to me!"

Suddenly, from the gate by the garage, a man's voice called, "Dr. Armentrout?"

"Get out of here!" Armentrout yelled back, struggling to his feet. "This is private property!"

But the gate clanged and swung open, and it was the young intern from Rosecrans Medical Center, Philip Muir, who stepped out onto the backyard grass. He didn't have his white coat on, but he was wearing a long-sleeved white shirt and a tie. "John!" he exclaimed, noticing the one-armed old man standing in the ash circle on the patio. Long John Beach was noisily drinking the brandy now, and slopping a lot of it into the white whiskers that bristled on his cheeks and neck these days. Muir turned to Armentrout. "He's supposed to be at Pacifica."

"I—have him out on a day pass," Armentrout panted. "This is none of your—"

"*Richie!*" called Armentrout's mother's voice from Long John Beach's throat, bubbling around the last gulp of the brandy. "*Can you hear me under water? I've got a* beard*! Did they have to give me . . .* hormones*? Pull the plug, darling, and let me breathe! Where's some more of this whiskey?*"

Muir sniffed sharply. "And you're giving him whiskey? Doctor, I—"

"It's not whiskey," babbled Armentrout, "it's brandy, she doesn't know the difference—"

Muir was frowning and shaking his head. " 'She'? What's the matter with you? Have you got Plumtree and Cochran up here too? I know Cochran is in the area, he telephoned the vineyard he works at—"

Armentrout interrupted him to call out, "I'll get you more liquor in a moment! Just—*wait* there!"

But Long John Beach blinked at him and spat. "I was never a liquor man," he said. "I just ate smokes."

Armentrout sighed deeply and sank down cross-legged beside the two velvet boxes. At least his mother was gone, for now. But Muir surely intended to report this, and investigate Beach's transfer, and end Armentrout's career. "Come over here, Philip," he said huskily, lifting the lid of the box that contained the derringer. "I think I can show you something that will explain all of this."

"It's not me you need to be explaining things to. Why on earth did you give Plumtree ECT? What the hell happened during the ice-cream social last Wednesday? Mr. Regushi swallowed his *tongue!*"

Armentrout again got wearily to his feet, one hand holding the box and the other gripping the hidden derringer. "Just look at this, Philip, and you'll understand."

Muir angrily stepped forward across the grass. "I can't imagine what it could be."

"I guess it's whatever you've made it."

The flat, hollow boom of the .410 shot-shell was muffled by the cypresses and the hillside.

CHAPTER 17

TROILUS: *What offends you, lady?*
CRESSIDA: *Sir, mine own company.*
TROILUS: *You cannot shun yourself.*
CRESSIDA: *Let me go and try.*
                    —William Shakespeare,
                    Troilus and Cressida

Cochran said he's been walking and taking the cable cars to get down here into Chinatown," said Archimedes Mavranos. "Maybe the cable cars were full today, and he's gotta hike the whole way."

Shadows from a slow ceiling fan far overhead swept rhythmically over the red Formica tabletop.

"He might have sold us out," said Kootie. "Maybe bad guys are just about to come busting in here." He had asked for a straw with his Coke, and now he glanced over his shoulder; the bartender was looking at the television in the corner above the bar, so Kootie stuck his straw into Angelica's glass of Chardonnay and took a sip of it. "It's sacramental," he explained to his foster-mother when she frowned at him. "The king needs a sip at noon, especially if bad guys are due."

"I don't need Coke in my wine," Angelica said.

"If bad guys want to open a hand in a no-limit game like this," said Mavranos with more confidence than he felt, touching the front of his denim jacket and glancing at Angelica's purse, "they're liable to see some powerful raises."

Pete Sullivan was sitting beside Angelica at the table by the stairs that led down to the restrooms, and he was deftly, one-handed, cartwheeling a cigarette over the backs of the knuckles of his right hand; it had been unlit, fresh from the pack, when he'd started, but the tip was glowing when he flipped it into the air off his last knuckle and caught it by the filter in his lips.

"Wow," said Mavranos.

"Yeah, wow," agreed Pete irritably as he puffed smoke from the cigarette. "Magic tricks. But if I try to hold a *weapon,* my hands are no good at all. Even a pair of scissors I drop, if I think about stabbing somebody." He wiggled his fingers. "Houdini made sure his mask wouldn't be capable of hurting anybody."

Kootie grinned wanly. "He can't even play video games," the boy told Mavranos. "The hands think he's really trying to shoot down enemy pilots."

Mavranos opened his mouth to say something, then focussed past Kootie toward the front door of the bar. "Heads up," he said.

Sid Cochran had just stumbled in from the street, and Mavranos felt his face tighten in a smile to see the blond Plumtree woman lurching along right behind him.

Mavranos pushed his chair back and stood up. "I was afraid we weren't ever going to see you again, ma'am," he said to Plumtree.

Plumtree's hair was wet, and Mavranos thought she looked like someone going through heroin withdrawal as she collapsed into the chair beside Kootie. There were cuts under her chin and at one corner of her mouth, and her face had a puffy, bruised look. "Shove it, man," she said hoarsely. "I'm an accessory to a murder today. More than anything else in the world, I want *not* to be. Soon, please God."

"A murder *today?*" asked Kootie.

Plumtree closed her eyes. "No. I'm *still,* today, an accessory to Scott Crane's murder. Is what I meant. But tomorrow I might not be."

"Tomorrow you might not be," Mavranos agreed.

"She insisted on coming," said Cochran nervously as he took the chair opposite her, next to Pete Sullivan. "We're laying our cards on the table here, but we can see yours too. We saw your truck in the Portsmouth Square parking structure, and saw what had to be your, your *dead* guy under a tarp in the back of it. If we'd wanted to screw this up, we'd have put a bullet through Crane's head right then."

Plumtree was blinking around now at the gold-painted Chinese bas-reliefs high up on the walls, and she squinted at a yard-wide, decorated Chinese paper lantern hanging from a string above the bar. An old Shell No-Pest Strip dangled from the tassel at the bottom of the lantern.

"Can I get a drink in this opium den?" she asked. "What is all this shit? The entrance to this place looks like a cave."

Mavranos could smell bourbon on her breath right across the table.

"It's named after a famous eighth-century Chinese poet," he told her. "The pictures painted on that lantern are scenes from his life."

"What'd he do to earn the No-Pest Strip?" she asked. "Somebody get me a Bud, hey?"

I guess there's no need for her to be sober, thought Mavranos; he shrugged and leaned over to pick up his own beer glass, which was empty.

"I'll have a Singapore Sling," Cochran said. He glanced at Plumtree. "They make a good Singapore Sling here."

"Said the Connecticut Pansy," remarked Plumtree absently. "Did flies kill him?" she asked Mavranos. "Your eight-cent poet, I mean— that yellow plastic thing is to kill flies, if you didn't know."

"*Las moscas,*" said Cochran, and Mavranos realized that he wasn't totally sober either. "That's what they call flies at a vineyard. They can get into the crush, if you do it after sunup—the Mexican grape-pickers think flies will carry little ghosts into the fermenting must, make you dizzy and give you funny dreams when you drink the wine, later. I suppose you might die of it, if enough ghosts had got into the wine."

"I'm sure each of us has a funny story about flies," said Mavranos patiently, "but right now we've got more important . . . *issues at hand.*" He turned away toward the bar, then paused and looked back at Plumtree. "The poet is supposed to have drowned—the story is he fell out of a boat, drunk, in the middle of the night, reaching for the reflection of the moon in the water."

"Rah rah rah," said Plumtree.

When Mavranos got back to the table with the three drinks and sat down, Plumtree greedily took the glass he pushed across to her and drank half of it in one long, wincing sip. "I should have told you to get two," she said breathlessly when she had clanked the glass back down. "Do you people have a set of handcuffs? My father took over control of my body three days ago, and I just this morning got free of him; and I feel like he spent the whole time body-surfing in avalanches. But he might come back on at any time." She opened her mouth and clicked her teeth like a monkey.

Mavranos stared at her. We should just ditch these two losers, he thought. Get back to the truck now, and just drive away.

"No, Arky," said Angelica sharply. She was glaring at him. "*She's* the one that's going to do the . . . that's going to let Crane assume her body."

Plumtree glanced at their faces. "Well, *yeah.* What, were you—" Her bloodshot eyes widened in sudden comprehension. "My God, you were gonna have the *kid* do it! Shit, did you people even consider the possib-lil—*possibil*ity that Crane might not be able to get back *into* his old body, afterward?—that he might have to *keep* the one he takes for this?''

"We did consider that," said Kootie. "*I* did consider that. But we're *all* gonna get *killed* if this doesn't get settled. Our TV burned up today, and—well, you had to be there. And," he added with a scared glance at Mavranos, "I'm taking Arky's word that Crane won't keep my body, if he can help it at all."

"Well, he won't get a chance," Plumtree told him with a haggard but possibly kindly meant smile. "*I'm* going to do it."

"Damn right," said Angelica.

"Kootie's correct," said Mavranos, "in saying that we've got to settle this situation—we've got to collapse this probability wave, let the daylight into Schrödinger's shitty cat box. As long as there's no real king working, we're all exposed—hell, *spotlighted*—and pretty near totally defenseless. You're staying at a motel or something?''

"Ye-es," said Cochran cautiously.

"Well congratulations, you now have four houseguests. I hope the management won't mind. We're gonna do this thing tomorrow at dawn, it looks like, this *restoration-to-life,* so there's no point in us getting a different room at the same motel. We just this morning got rousted out of our place by some kind of walking department-store dummies, and—''

Cochran choked on his Singapore Sling. "Did they," he said after he'd wiped his mouth redly on his sleeve, "move in synch, like they were puppets working off the same strings?''

"They did," said Mavranos stolidly. "And suddenly I don't like the idea of Scott's body sitting out there in the truck, you know? Let's finish up here, and get to your motel. With you and me and Pete, we should be able to get Scott into the motel room. And then we've got some preparations to make."

Kootie nodded, and Angelica scowled at him.

"Finish every drop of your drinks," said Plumtree with a ghastly, exhausted gaiety, "there's poor people sober in China."

Chinese New Year was still two weeks off, but Asian boys on ribbon-decked bicycles tossed strings of lit firecrackers ahead of the six of them, as they walked south on the Grant Street sidewalk under the red-and-gold pagoda-roofed buildings, so that their ears rang with the staccato popping, and their noses burned with the barbecued-chicken smell of gunpowder, and Kootie was treading on fragments of red paper that crumpled and darkened on the wet pavement underfoot like fallen rose petals; and when they trudged across the wet grass of Portsmouth

Square, the hoboes and winos hobbled out of their path and seemed to bow, or at least nod, as they passed.

And when they had piled into the two vehicles—Plumtree riding in the front seat of Mavranos's truck, and Pete riding in the Granada with Cochran, for mutual trust as much as to make sure both parties knew the way to the Star Motel—crows and mockingbirds swooped over them as the old car and truck labored up Van Ness, the darting birds seeming to be fighting in the gray sky.

At Lombard Street at the top of Russian Hill, where a right turn would have led them down the ornamental, brick-paved "crookedest street in the world," they turned left instead, and drove down the straight lanes between bars and car-repair shops and liquor stores and motels, and after three blocks both vehicles ponderously turned left up the driveway into the Star Motel parking lot.

When they'd parked and all climbed out onto the asphalt, Angelica and Plumtree crowded around the tailgate of Mavranos's dusty red truck to block the view as Pete and Cochran and Mavranos slid Scott Crane's body out from beneath the tarpaulin. The body was dressed now in jeans and a white shirt, though with no shoes or socks, and Cochran tried not to look at the bloody bandage knotted around the thigh, over the denim.

The body was limp, not stiff, but they managed to tilt it into an upright posture and march it right past the ice and Coke machines and up the stairs to Cochran's room; Plumtree had got her key out and scrambled ahead of them, and had got the door open by the time they had carried the dead king to the room.

They flopped Scott Crane down onto the bed that didn't have Cochran's homemade Ouija board on it, and Mavranos straightened the body's arms and legs and unlooped the graying beard from the sawn-off stump of spear that stood up from the throat. The room was still humid from Plumtree's and Cochran's showers this morning, and smelled like old salami and unfresh clothing.

"Just like Charlton Heston in *El Cid*," said Kootie bravely. "Dead, but leading the army."

"He is d-damn cold," panted Cochran as he stood back and flapped his cramping hands. His heart was pounding more than the couple of minutes of effort could justify, and he was shivering with irrational horror at having touched the dead man again. "How can you—*think* he—" His voice almost broke, and he turned toward the TV set and just breathed deeply.

"Your place—could use some airing," said Angelica, smoothly calling everyone's attention away from his momentary loss of control.

"Kootie, see if you can't open the windows, while I go back down to the truck for our witchy supplies."

"Don't blame me for this pigpen," said Plumtree, "I been away."

"Witchy supplies," put in Cochran in a carefully neutral tone. He gave Plumtree a resentful glance, very aware of the cassette tape in his shirt pocket and the French-language missal in the bedside table drawer. Kootie had ducked under the curtains and was noisily yanking at the aluminum-framed window.

Mavranos had his hands in the pockets of his denim jacket as he stared at Cochran. "I got to ask you to give me your gun," he said. "I almost apologize, since we're all really on the same side here and my crowd is taking over your place this way, for tonight—but Miss Plumtree said herself that her dad came on three days ago and she just this morning came back to herself; and you appear to have a . . . loyalty to her. I can't justify—"

"Sure," said Cochran, speaking levelly to conceal his reflexive anger. Slowly, he reached around to the back of his belt and tugged the holster clip free. Then he tossed the suede-sheathed gun onto the bathroom-side bed.

Mavranos leaned forward to pick it up with his left hand, keeping his right in his jacket pocket. "Thanks," he said gruffly. "If we run into outside trouble, I'll give it back to you."

Cochran just nodded. *I can see his point*, he insisted to himself. *I'd do the same, in his place.*

Angelica came tromping back upstairs lugging a green canvas knapsack, and Cochran had to move his NADA sign and papers as she began unpacking its contents onto the bedspread.

She lifted out some springy shrub branches that smelled vaguely of eucalyptus, held together by a rubber band. "Myrtle," she said. "Sacred to Dionysus, the books say. And a bottle of wine for us all to drink from, to show him respect."

With shaky fingers Cochran took from her the bottle she had dug out of the knapsack. It was, he saw, a Kenwood Vineyards 1975 Cabernet Sauvignon, and the stylized picture at the top of the label was of a skeleton reclining on a grassy hillside.

Cochran's ears seemed to be ringing with a wail that he was afraid he might actually give voice to, and for the moment he had forgotten the dead king and his confiscated gun. "This—was never released," he said, making himself speak slowly. "This label, I mean, with this picture on it. I remember hearing about it. David Goines originally did one of a nude woman on the hill, and the BATF rejected it because they said it was indecent, so he did this one of the same woman as a skeleton;

and they rejected *it* because of fetal alcohol syndrome or something. Finally Goines did one of just the hillside, and that got okayed, and Kenwood printed it.'' He looked up into Angelica's concerned gaze, and let himself relax a little. ''But this was never released, this label was never even printed!—except, I guess, for this one. Where the hell did you find it? And why did you get *it?* I mean, it's a twenty-year-old Cab! There must have been cheaper ones.''

Angelica opened her mouth, then closed it. ''I,'' she said finally, ''don't remember what it cost. But I got change back from a twenty, and we got ice and some canned green beans in the same purchase, I remember. This was the only fancy wine they had, at this little place called Liquor Heaven in the Soma neighborhood—Arky, you drove us there and waited in the truck, remember?—the only other wine was one of those bum's-rush specials, Hair-of-the-Dog or some name like that.''

Mavranos had been watching Plumtree and Cochran, but now he slowly turned to Angelica. ''. . . Bitin Dog?'' he asked.

Cochran sat down on the bed, heedlessly crushing Angelica's myrtle branches, and he was remembering the Mondard figure in the mirror in the vision he'd had last week in Solville. ''That's how it looks in a reflection,'' he said dizzily. ''You must have been in Looking-Glass Land. The right-way name is something like *pagodetibi.*''

''Get your butt off the boughs of holly,'' Plumtree told him.

''No,'' said Mavranos, ''stay where you are, Dionysus probably likes it a bit crushed, like cats do catnip. Miss Plumtree, you sit beside him. You got your *máquina,* Angelica?''

Angelica touched the untucked tail of her blouse. ''Yes, Arky,'' she sighed.

''Stand over here and keep your hand on it, and watch those two. Pete and I gotta go to the truck, drag up some of our *scientific apparatus,* more of our *high-tech defensive hardware.*''

Kootie sniffed the air after Arky and his foster-dad had shuffled outside and pulled the door closed behind them. He sensed at least a couple of fragmentary personalities buzzing clumsily around the room.

''The king's body is drawing ghosts,'' he told his foster-mom. ''A couple got in when Arky opened the door just now.'' He sniffed again. ''Just little broken-off bits, probably shells thrown off of somebody who didn't even die of it.''

Kootie knew that people, especially very neurotic people whose personalities spun in wide and perturbed orbits, often threw ghost-shells in moments of stressfully strong emotion. Kootie could feel the insistent

one-note resonance of these, and his hands were shaky and he wasn't
able to take a deep breath.

He found himself staring at Janis Plumtree's loose blouse and tight
jeans, and he snorted and shook his head to dispel the induced lust. Easy
to guess what the unknown source-person was up to, he thought, when
he shed *these* . . . psychic snakeskins! And the man must have been left
bewildered and abruptly out-of-the-mood after they'd broken away.

The vibrations of the ghost fragments did have a strongly male cast;
Kootie wondered what his own response would have been if the source-
person had been a woman—would he have found himself looking at
. . . at *Cochran?*—or would he have been so out-of-phase with them
that he wouldn't have sensed their presence at all?

"I'm okay," he told Angelica, who had taken her eyes off Cochran
and Plumtree long enough to give Kootie a raised eyebrow. "I hope
Arky's bringing up the St. Michael and High John the Conqueror
sprays."

"I packed 'em," she said.

In spite of himself, Kootie was staring at Plumtree again. She was
clearly nervously excited—she had pulled a little order pad out of her
pocket and was flipping through the pages, nodding and mumbling to
herself.

She looked up and caught his gaze, and her sudden smile made his
heart thump. "Tomorrow," she said through her teeth, "no matter what
it may cost me, I *won't* be a murderer anymore!"

Her companion seemed less happy about the idea—Cochran was
frowning as he shook a cigarette out of a pack and flipped open a book
of matches. Probably he's worried that this attempt tomorrow will work
the way she thinks it will, Kootie thought, and his girlfriend's body will
suddenly have a fifty-two-year-old *man* in it.

Talk about out-of-phase!

Kootie wasn't aware of the ghost fragments now—probably his lust-
ful response had blunted his latent Fisher King ability to sense them.
As if I took a long sniff of a rare hamburger that was cooked in an iron
pan, he thought ruefully, or spent the day at the top of a modern high-
rise building, far up away from the ground, or gargled with whiskey on
a Friday in Lent.

Cochran struck a match—and the matchbook flared in a gout of flame,
and Cochran had dropped it and was stamping it out on the carpet.

Cochran and Plumtree both exclaimed "Son of a bitch!" and Plumtree went on to add, "You clumsy stupid shit!"

But Kootie had caught a whiff of cooked bacon on the stale, humid air, and he said, "I think you burned up the ghosts, Mr. Cochran. Toss me the matches, would you?"

Cochran bent over, pried the matchbook from the carpet, and tossed it to Kootie, who juggled the hot thing around in the palm of his hand to look at it.

The moment of flame had not obliterated the letters inked onto each match. Kootie read the words carefully, then looked up at Cochran. "The match you lit has *'tenebis'* written on it, doesn't it?"

Cochran bent down again and brushed his hand over the carpet until he had found the match he had struck; then he straightened and stared at it.

" *'Tenebis,' "* Cochran read. He looked at Kootie. "You've seen this inscription before? It's Latin, right?"

"I suppose it's Latin," Kootie said. "I've never seen it before, but I can tell what the missing word must be—'cause it's a palindrome. See?" He tossed the matchbook back to Cochran. "The letters read the same backward as forward."

"On a matchbook," said Angelica with a wry smile. "That's like the people who letter *L.A. Cigar—Too Tragical* around chimneys and frying pans—or gun muzzles," she added, touching the grip of the automatic in her belt. "Ghosts are drawn to palindromes, and these tricks burn 'em up—dispel 'em into the open air, unlike in the coal of a cigarette, which sends their broken-up constituent pieces straight into your lungs, for a nasty predatory high. The palindrome torchers send them safely on past India."

This seemed to jar Cochran. "What exactly the hell do you people mean by 'India'?" he asked.

A measured thumping sounded at the motel-room door, and Kootie could hear Arky Mavranos impatiently call something from outside.

"Peek out before you unlock it," Angelica said as Kootie stepped toward the door.

"Right, Ma." Kootie peered out through the lens, then said, "It's just them," as he snapped back the bolt and pulled the door open.

Mavranos came shuffling in carrying one of his spare truck batteries in both hands; Pete Sullivan followed, carrying a stack of boxes balanced on top of the ice chest. An electric plug dangled from one of the boxes.

"On the table by the window," said Mavranos to Pete. "Hook up the charger to the battery, a quick charge on the ten-amp setting—if it's not too dead you might have time to drag one of the others up here and charge it too."

"What's India?" insisted Cochran.

"Uh—ghosthood," said Angelica, frowning at the boxes Pete was putting down. Then she glanced at Cochran and apparently noted the man's anxious squint. "In Shakespeare's time," she went on patiently, "*India* was sorcerously hip slang for a sort of overlap place, a halfway house between Earth and Heaven-or-Hell. It's the antechamber to Dionysus's domain—the god was supposed to have come to Thebes by way of Phrygia from northern India, around Pakistan."

"*Paki Japer came no more,*" sang Plumtree, to a bit of the tune of "Puff the Magic Dragon."

Mavranos barked out two syllables of a laugh at that, wiping black dust off his hands. "I'm gonna—" he began.

"So what would it mean," Cochran interrupted shakily, "to say . . . 'Her bed is India, there she lies, a pearl'?"

Angelica was frowning at him with, Kootie thought, puzzled sympathy. "That's a line from *Troilus and Cressida*," Angelica said. "It would mean 'she' is in that India space—a ghost associating with a living person, or vice versa. The overlap, see? And the 'pearl' reference would probably mean she's accreting stuff from the other category—physical solidity, if she was a ghost to start with, or ghosts, if she was a living person. The Elizabethan slang for ghosts was 'ghostings'—by way of folk etymology from 'coastings,' meaning coastlines, outlines, silhouettes; traced replicas—and later in the play—"

"I'm gonna go trace the coastline here," said Mavranos, "the north coast, from Fort Point by the bridge to where those three old ships are moored at the Hyde Street Pier: the area where the wild mint used to grow, that gave the city its original name of Yerba Buena. I've got a *piedra iman,* and a—"

"A *magnet?*" said Angelica, turning toward Mavranos. "But that's only good for drawing *ghosts*, Arky, you don't want Crane's *ghost*—"

"Why aren't you gonna check west of the bridge?" demanded Plumtree. "The Sutro Baths ruins is where we saw his naked ghost, last week, and that's west of the bridge. I think you should—"

"But you don't *want* his ghost—" Angelica went on; and Kootie was interrupting too: "We should see what the old black lady has to say about it—"

Arky had lifted one of Angelica's weather-beaten stuffed toy pigs out of the box Pete had carried in, and now he shoved a C battery into the compartment in its rear end; and the pig's sudden, harsh mechanical burping silenced the two women and Kootie.

After three noisy seconds Mavranos pulled the battery out, and the croaking stopped. "I'm not gonna look for his ghost," he said clearly, "nor where we saw his ghost. What I want to do first is search around the area where your old black lady's banker friend drowned, back in 1875; that's near the Hyde Pier. And I'm gonna use the magnet *along with a magnetic compass*—I figure that when the compass needle ignores both the magnet and the real magnetic north pole, I'll have found the spot where we can yank Scott back here from the far side of India. Wherever the spot is, it's got to be a regular *black hole* for plain-old ghosts, and they've got to add up to a pre-emptive magnetic charge—especially now, on the eve of Dionysus's day." He bared his teeth in a smile. *"Okay?"*

"Just asking," said Angelica.

"I have no idea how long this'll take," Mavranos went on. "I'm gonna walk it, and leave you people the truck. If I get no readings at all, I'll just come back here, well before dawn, and we can do the restoration-to-life right at the spot where the banker jumped in." He swivelled an unreadable stare from Kootie to Angelica to Plumtree. "You all are gonna want to figure out your tactics. Don't go out—order a pizza delivered, and if you need beers or something, send Pete. Angelica," he added, with a nod toward where Cochran and Plumtree sat on the bed, "if they try anything at all, don't you hesitate to—"

"I know," said Angelica. "Shoot our hosts."

"Right," agreed Mavranos. He slapped the pocket of his denim jacket and nodded at the solid angularity of his revolver. Then he was out the door, and the clump-clop of his boots was receding down the stairs.

"What happens," asked Plumtree bleakly, "if you untie that bandage from around Crane's leg?"

"He bleeds," said Angelica. "He's got no pulse, but fresh blood leaks out of him."

"Not forever," Plumtree said. "Where we stabbed him . . . his throat stopped bleeding after a while, right? I mean, I doubt they tied a tourniquet around his neck, then." She sighed hitchingly, and ran her fingers through her disordered hair. Her lips were turned down sharply at the corners. "Tilt a few good slugs of his blood into that empty Wild Turkey bottle. Tomorrow I'll—probably have to—" Her eyes widened in evident surprise and her face went pale. "Scant! Why am I—"

Plumtree stood up and wobbled to the bathroom then, barely managing to slam the door behind her before Kootie heard her being rackingly sick in there.

"Who's in the mood for a pizza?" he asked brightly.

"Hush," said Angelica quietly. She opened her mouth as if to say more, then just repeated, "Hush."

* * *

At sunset the entirely discorporate spirit of Scott Crane stood on a cliff over a sea, and it was no longer possible for him to overlook his sin of omission. The call of the one neglected tarot archetype could no longer be drowned out in the busy distractions of life. It had been beckoning during three winters—whispering from six feet under in the agitation of the lice that blighted the vineyards, wheezing in the fevered lungs of Crane's young children in the winter months, and roaring like a bull in the cloven earth under Northridge a year ago tomorrow. And on New Year's Day of this year it had come to his house.

It had worn many faces—that of Crane's first wife, and that of his adopted father, and a hundred others; but today it wore the face of the fat man he had shot to death in the desert outside Las Vegas in 1990. A bargain had been made, and his part had not been fully paid.

CHAPTER 18

"Afraid?"
   "It's plain enough, I should think, why he may be. It's a dreadful remembrance. Besides that, his loss of himself grew out of it. Not knowing how he lost himself, or how he recovered himself, he may never feel certain of not losing himself again. That alone wouldn't make the subject pleasant, I should think."

                                    —Charles Dickens,
                                     Tale of Two Cities

The sky beyond the curtains had been dark for hours, and the clock on the bedside table read 10:30, when the traditional Solville knock sounded on the door: *rap-rap-rap, rap,* in the rhythm of the Rolling Stones' "Under My Thumb."

Angelica was sitting on the carpet in front of the television, and she put down her jar of pennies. "Peek out anyway," she told Kootie as she straightened her legs and stood up. It was a relief to be able to look away from the grotesque, distressing images on the screen.

Kootie hurried to the door and peered out through the lens. "It's him," he said as he unchained the door, "alone." He pulled the door open.

Mavranos brought in with him the smells of crushed grass and cold pier pilings, and Angelica thought she could see the stale room air eddy behind him as he strode to the ice chest and crouched to lift out a wet can of Coors.

"I found our place," Mavranos said shortly, after popping the top and taking a deep sip. "It's hardly more than walking distance from here. I found it at sunset, but I've spent all this time making sure I wasn't followed back here. There was a lot of local hippies dressed up as druids there—or druids dressed as hippies?—and I kept on *seeing* them after I left the place.''

He finished the can and crouched again to get another. ''I'd see 'em on *rooftops,* and in passing *buses,* but each of 'em was looking at *me,* I swear, with no expressions at all on their faces, under the hoods. I finally lost 'em by buying a—hah!—a Jiminy Cricket latex rubber mask in Chinatown, and then *wearing* it while I rode the cable cars Washington-to-Mason-to-Jackson-to-Hyde in a windshield circle for about an hour.'' He glanced at Angelica. '' 'Windshield'—the olden-times word was 'widdershins.' '' He twirled a finger in the air. ''It means moving counterclockwise, to elude magical pursuit.''

''I know what widdershins is,'' said Angelica. *''Contra las manecil-las.* So where is this place? Is it where the banker drowned?''

''No, it's—well, you'll see it tomorrow at dawn. It's out at the end of the peninsula at the Small Craft Harbor, on the grounds of some yacht club; I had to step over a 'No Admittance' sign on a chain. It looks like an old ruined Greek or Roman temple. I asked about it at the yacht club—apparently the city planners had a whole lot of cemetery marble left over after they cleared out all the graveyards in the Rich-mond District in the thirties, transplanted the graves south to Colma, and so somebody set up this pile of . . . steps and seats and pillars and patchwork stone pavements . . . out at the end of the peninsula. Very windy and cold—and the compass needle had no time for my magnet or the north pole; I swear I could feel that compass twisting in my hand, so the needle could point *straight down.''*

His eyes moved past Angelica to the body on the bed, and when he gasped and darted a glance toward the Plumtree woman, Angelica knew he had seen the fresh blood smeared on Scott Crane's jeans.

''She go messin' with him?'' Mavranos demanded. ''Did her dad, I mean?''

Angelica took hold of his arm. ''No, Arky. We decanted some of Crane's blood into a bottle. We think she'll have to—''

''Phlebotomy,'' put in Kootie.

''Right,'' Angelica agreed nervously; ''it looks like she'll probably have to, to *drink* some of Crane's blood, to summon Crane, to draw him into her body tomorrow.''

Mavranos's nostrils widened in evident distaste at the thought, and Angelica sympathetically remembered how the poor Janis personality had found herself suddenly in a body that was convulsing with nausea, after the Cody personality had first proposed the idea and then fled.

Mavranos glared around the room and ended up staring at the television, which for the last five minutes had been insistently showing some French-language hard-core pornographic movie.

"So you decided to distract yourself with some T-and-A," he said sourly. "You psychiatrists figure this is wholesome entertainment for fourteen-year-old boys, do you?"

"T and . . . ?" echoed Angelica. "Oh, tits and ass, right? Sorry—to me T-and-A has always been tonsillectomy-and-adenoidectomy." With a shaky hand she brushed a damp strand of hair back from her forehead. "No, damn it, we've been trying to get this *off* the screen—we had the old black lady, for a few seconds—but now shaking the pennies and even pushing the buttons on the set won't shift us from this channel." She glanced at Kootie, who was studiously looking away from the screen but who had clearly been upset—even haunted, she thought— when the desperate, contorting figures had first appeared on the screen.

From far away out in the chilly darkness came the metronomic two-second moan of a foghorn.

"I been hearing that all day, seems like," Mavranos said absently. "It's the horn on the south pier of the Golden Gate Bridge. Two seconds every twenty seconds." He sat down on the carpet and put down his beer can so that he could rub his eyes. "Okay," he said with a windy sigh, "so did the old black lady have anything useful to say? She's supposed to be our *intecessor*, and she's been awful scarce."

"She," Angelica began; then, "No," she said. I'll tell you later, Arky, she thought. "Cochran and Plumtree have been working his homemade Ouija board, though, and—"

But Kootie spoke. "She said, 'The debt-payer is always a virgin, and must go to India still a virgin.' "

Angelica could feel her face go slack with exhaustion; she was certain that this was a verbatim recollection of the old woman's words. Then she made herself raise her head and put on a quizzical expression. "Yes," she said briskly, "that's what she said." Oh, it won't be you, Kootie, she thought. I won't *let* it be you, don't worry. Oh, why the hell are we even—

"*Damn* this garbage!" she burst out, and she sprang to the wall and yanked the television's plug right out of the wall socket.

And then she just blinked from the cord in her hand to the television screen, on which the sweaty bodies still luminously strained and gasped. Her chest went suddenly hollow and cold a full second before she was sure she had pulled out the right plug.

Mavranos had got to his feet and stared at the wall behind the dresser the television sat on, and now he even waved his hand across the back of the set as though verifying a magic trick.

"Lord," he said softly, "how I do hate impossible things. Pete, let's carry this abomination down to the truck, and—"

But at that moment the screen went mercifully dark at last.

"Bedtime for the satyrs and nymphs," Mavranos said. "And for us too, I think." He looked toward Plumtree and Cochran. "What did the Ouija board say?"

Plumtree shifted on the bed. "We asked to talk to anyone who knew about this . . . situation of ours, and—well, you tell them, Scant."

Cochran reached behind Plumtree to pick up one of the many sheets of Star Motel stationery. " 'Canst thou remember a time before we came unto this cell?' " he read. " 'I do not think thou canst, for then thou wast not out three years old.' "

"I do think that's your subconscious speaking," Angelica said to Plumtree. "Or the core-child, the traumatized personality: the poisoned comatose girl in your Snow White scenario, or the battered lady bus driver in Cody's *Dirty Harry* version." Angelica looked at Mavranos and shrugged. "God knows why it's in that Shakespearean language— Pete's pretty sure it's from *The Tempest*, the exiled king Prospero talking to his daughter Miranda."

"Valorie always talks that way," said Cochran. "She's the oldest personality, and I think she may be—" He hesitated, and then said, "I think she may be the core-child."

You were going to say dead, *weren't you?* thought Angelica. *You were right to keep that idea from her, whether or not it's true.*

Quickly, so as not to let Plumtree think about Cochran's momentary hesitation, Angelica asked him, "Why does Janis call you Scant?"

Cochran glanced at the back of his right hand and laughed uncomfortably. "Oh, it's a childhood nickname. I grew up in the wine country, doing odd jobs around the vineyards, and when I was ten I was in a cellar when one of the support beams broke under a cask of Zinfandel, and I automatically stepped forward and tried to hold it up. It broke my leg. The support beams are called scantlings, and the cellarmen told me I was trying to be a proxy scantling."

"*Atlas* would have been a good name, too," remarked Kootie.

"Or *Nitwit,*" said Mavranos, stepping away from the television. "Angelica, you and Miss Plumtree can sleep on the Ouija-board bed by the bathroom after you clear the pizza boxes off it, with her on the bathroom side, away from Crane's body; and we'll tie a couple of cans to her ankle so as to hear her if she gets up in the night. Cochran can sleep on the floor on that side, down between the bed and the wall. Kootie can sleep over by the window, and Pete and I will take turns staying awake with a gun; well, I'll have a gun, and Pete can wake me up fast. At about five we'll get up and out of here.''

"If that TV comes on again during the night," said Kootie in a small voice. He sighed and then went on, "Shoot it.''

"I bet my hands would let me do that, actually," said Pete.

Valorie's perceptions and memories and dreams were always in black-and-white, with occasional flickers of false red and blue shimmering in fine-grain moiré patterns like heat waves; and always there was a drumming or knocking, which she understood was an amplification of some background noise present in the soundtrack—or, if there was no actual sound to exaggerate, was simply imposed arbitrarily on the scene. Her dreams never had any fantastic or even inaccurate elements in them, aside from the constant intrusive percussion—they were just re-run memories—and her default dream was always the same, and all the Plumtree personalities experienced at least the last seconds of it whenever she did:

Her mother was wearing sandals with tire-tread soles, but in the dream they rang a hard clack-clack *from the sidewalk concrete, and Plumtree's little shoes and shorter steps filled in the almost reggae one-drop beat.*

"They've painted a big Egyptian Horus eye on the roof," said her mother, pulling her along by the hand. "Signaling to the sun god, Ra, he says. All the time Ra Ra Ra! But he blew his big play at Lake Mead on Easter, and nobody can pretend anymore that he's gonna be any kind of king."

Plumtree couldn't see the men dancing on the roof of the building ahead of them, but she could see the bobbing papier-mâché heads that topped the tall poles they carried.

The sun burned white like a magnesium tire rim, straight up above them in the sky, at its very highest summer-solstice point.

"You stay by me, Janis," her mother went on. "He'll want to do the El Cabong bang-bang, but he won't try anything with me today, not if his own baby daughter is watching. And—listen, baby!—if I tell you to run along and play, you don't *go, hear? He won't hit me, not with you there, and he can't . . . well, not to talk dirty, let's just say he* can't— okay?—*unless he's knocked me silly, kayoed me past any ref's count of ten. As close to dead as possible. I never even* met *him before he— I didn't even* meet *him during, I was in a* coma *when he—when you stopped being just a glitter in your daddy's evil eye. Dead* would've *been better, for him, but if you knock 'em dead you can't knock 'em up, right? Never mind."*

On the sidewalk in front of the steps up to the door her mother stopped. "And what do you say," her mother demanded, "if he says, 'Baby, do you want to leave with your mother?' "

Plumtree was looking up at her mother's backlit face, and the view blurred and fragmented—that was because of tears in her eyes. "I say, 'Yes,' " Plumtree said obediently, though the cadence of her voice indicated an emotion.

Plumtree's eyes focussed beyond her mother—above her. Way *above her.*

This was the part of the dream that the other Plumtree personalities always remembered upon awakening.

There was a man in the sky, his white robes glowing in the sunlight for a moment; then he was a dark spot between the girl on the pavement and the flaring sun in the gunmetal sky. Plumtree opened her eyes wide and tried to see him against the hard-pressure glare of the sun, but she couldn't—he seemed to have become *the sun. And he was falling.*

"Daddeee!"

Plumtree pulled her hand free of her mother's, and ran to catch him. The clattering clopping impact drove her right down into the ground.

Cochran was jolted out of sleep and then rocked hard against textured wallpaper in the darkness, and his first waking impression was that a big truck had hit whatever this building was.

Carpet fibers abraded his face, and a mattress was jumping and slamming on box springs only inches from his left ear; he couldn't see anything, and until he heard shouting from Mavranos and abruptly remembered where he was and who he was with, Cochran was certain he was back in the honeymoon motel room behind the Troy and Cress Wedding Chapel in Las Vegas in 1990, again enduring the tumultuous escape-from-confinement of the big man in the wooden mask.

"Earthquake!" someone was yelling in the pitch blackness. Cochran sat up, battered by the mattress that was convulsing beside him like a living thing, and then he scrambled forward on his hands and knees until his forehead cracked against some unseen piece of furniture—the dresser the television had been sitting on, probably. The pizza boxes tumbled down onto his head, spilling crumbs and crusts.

"Mom!" yelled Kootie's voice. "Mom, where are you?"

Two shrill voices answered him: *"Here!"*

Light flooded the room, just yellow electric lamplight but dazzling after the darkness. Squinting, and blinking at the trickle of blood running down beside his nose, Cochran saw that Angelica was standing beside the door with her hand on the light switch, and that Mavranos was crouched between the beds holding his revolver pointed at the ceiling. Kootie and Pete Sullivan stood beside Angelica, staring at the bed with Plumtree on it.

The bed was still jumping, the bedspread flapping like manta-ray wings, and Plumtree's body was tossing on it like a Raggedy Ann doll— even though the rest of the room had stopped shaking.

"Omar!" grated a shrill, keening voice from between Plumtree's clenched teeth. "Damn your soul! Stop it, take one of the girls, Tiffany or Janis, just let me go!" The three empty beer cans that Mavranos had wired to her ankle with a coat hanger were shaking and clattering.

Kootie has provoked the Follow-the-Queen sequence, Cochran thought; he did it when he yelled for his mother. Next card up is wild, whatever you declare it to be. Dizzy and light-headed, Cochran opened his mouth.

"Nina!" he called hoarsely.

"Omar, I will kill any child conceived in this way!" screamed the voice out of Plumtree's mouth. "God will not blame me!"

It hadn't worked.

Cochran's bruised forehead was chilly with sweat. "J—" he began; then, "Cody!" he called.

At first he wasn't sure the card he had declared would be honored, for though Plumtree's eyes sprang open she was now gasping, "In the name of the father, the sun, the holy ghost!" Then she had rolled off the spasming mattress and scrambled across the carpet to the front door, the beer cans snagging in the carpet and hopping behind her.

"Whoa," said Mavranos.

The mattress flopped down flat and stopped moving.

Mavranos stared at the bed with raised eyebrows. "I," he said, as if speaking to the bed, "was talking to Miss Plumtree."

Cochran half-expected the bed to start jumping again at this explanation, but it just lay sprawled there, the mattress at an angle now to the box springs and the pillows and blankets tumbled in disorder.

"Get back by boyfriend," Mavranos told Plumtree.

Somewhat to Cochran's surprise Plumtree had no rude retort, but just obediently stepped back toward the bed; though she did shake her ankle irritably, rattling the attached cans. She was smacking her lips and grimacing. "Jeez, was my *female parent* on? I hate her old spit. I gotta gargle, excuse me." She hurried past Cochran into the bathroom, and he could hear her knocking things over on the sink.

The light in the room was flickering, and when Cochran looked around he saw that the television had come on again, possibly because of having been jolted in the earthquake. Again the screen showed a

glowing nude man and woman feverishly groping and sucking and colliding.

Mavranos stepped back to see behind the set, and frowned; clearly
the cord was still unplugged.

"Could you get me a beer, Angelica?" he said, holding out his left
hand and not taking his eyes off the television. He was gripping the
revolver in his right hand, and Cochran wondered if he might actually
shoot the TV set, and if he'd think of muffling the shot with a pillow.

Angelica leaned over the ice chest and fished up a dripping can; she
popped it open and reached over to slap it into his open palm.

"Thanks." Mavranos tilted the beer can over the ventilation slots on
the back slope of the television set, and after a few seconds of beer
running down into the set's works the picture on the screen abruptly
curdled into a black-and-white pattern like a radar scan, with a blobby
figure in one corner that looked to Cochran like a cartoon silhouette of
a big-butted fat man with little globe limbs, and warts all over him; and
the sound had become a roaring hiss that warped and narrowed to mimic
whispered words: *et . . . in . . . arcadia . . . ego . . .*

Then it winked out and was dark and inert, a wrecked TV with beer
puddling out from the base of it. Mavranos absently drank the rest of
the beer and clanked the can down on the dresser.

For several seconds no one spoke, and the distant foghorn moaned
out in the night.

Mavranos raised the gun barrel for silence while he stared at the
watch on his left wrist.

Cochran began to let the muscles in his shoulders relax, and he gently
prodded the bloody bump on his forehead.

The foghorn sounded again, and Mavranos lowered his arms. His face
was expressionless. "What time is it?" he asked.

"You were just staring at your watch!" said Angelica.

"Oh yeah." Mavranos looked at his watch again. "Quarter to five,
apparently that's showtime." He sighed shakily and rubbed his left hand
over his face. "Let's mobilize. Angelica, get your witchy shit together
and have Pete carry it downstairs and into the truck while you cover
him with your .45, and don't forget to bring that Wild Turkey bottle
with Scott's blood in it. Don't put stuff in the back bed, though—we'll
be carrying Scott down and putting him back there. I'll drive the truck,
and Pete can drive Mr. Cochran's Granada—"

Plumtree had stepped out of the bathroom, and Cochran could smell
the Listerine on her breath from a yard away, though he was ashamed
to meet her eye. She dug in the pocket of her jeans and pulled out a
bundle of bills.

"Kid," she said to Kootie. When he looked up, she thrust the bills out toward him. "This is yours. A hundred bucks—long story, don't ask. I want to give it to you now, in case we get . . . in case we don't quite meet again." Cochran thought there was gruff sympathy in her voice. "No hard feelings."

Kootie was holding the little yellow blanket that bald-headed Diana had given him back in Solville, but he reached across the bed with his free hand and took the money. "Thank you, Janis Cordelia Plumtree," he said.

"And Janis Cordelia can ride shotgun in the Granada," Mavranos went on rapidly, "with Angelica behind her ready to shoot. Come on, everybody, up! I want us out of here in five minutes."

Angelica snatched up her knapsack and grabbed the Wild Turkey bottle. "What's the hurry, Arky?" she asked irritably. "Sunrise isn't for another hour or so, and you said the place is walking distance from here."

Mavranos had peered through the peek hole and now unchained the door and pulled it open. "That foghorn, just now—it's sounding every *fifteen* seconds, not twenty, and it's a different tone. It's a different foghorn."

Pete was squeezing the battery charger's clamps off the terminals of one of Mavranos's car batteries and then lifting the battery in both hands. "So?" he asked breathlessly. "Maybe the wind's from a different direction."

"They don't vary that way, Pete," said Mavranos impatiently, "or they wouldn't be any good as foghorns, would they? We're—we're Scott's army, this king's army, and in that sense we won't truly exist until the potential of his resurrection becomes an actuality. Our waveform has to shake out as *one* rather than as *zero*. And I think—this wrong foghorn makes me think—that we're a fragmented waveform right now, that psychically we're *somewhere else* too, as well as here in a motel on Lombard Street."

"So," said Angelica, spreading her hands, "what do we *do?*"

"What are you asking *me* for?" Mavranos snapped. "All *I* can think of is for us to go to this crazy cemetery temple on the peninsula, in the wrong gear and without even our TV-star intercessor, and hope we can catch up to ourselves." He darted a glance around the room. "Where'd Kootie go?"

"He's right outside," said Angelica. "He waved his hand in front of his face like he wanted fresh air, and he stepped out." She hurried to the door, calling, "Kootie?"

She leaned around the doorjamb to look, and then she had lunged outside, and Cochran heard her voice from out on the railed walkway: "A note!" she yelled. "Shit—*'Can't be with you for this—sorry—'* Pete, he's run away!"

Kootie had already tiptoed down the stairs and sprinted across the dark parking lot to the Lombard Street sidewalk, and was now hurrying to a cab that had pulled in to the curb after he had, without much confidence, waved to it. He levered open the back door and scrambled in. Better than hiding behind a Dumpster somewhere, he thought nervously, and I can *afford* this now, thanks to Miss Plumtree. He hiked up on the seat to stuff Diana's baby blanket into his hip pocket.

The cab driver was an elderly black man who stared at him dubiously over his shoulder. "You okay, kid?"

"Yes," panted Kootie. "Drive off, will you?"

"I don't like hurry." As if to prove the point, he cocked his head to listen to a dispatch on his radio. "And I don't like driving people who turn out to not have any money," he went on finally. "Where did you want to go?"

Kootie bared his teeth in impatience and tried to remember the name of any place in San Francisco. "Chinatown," he said.

"You better give me ten dollars up front, kid—I'll give you the change when we get there."

Hurriedly Kootie dug out of his pocket the money Plumtree had just given him, and he held the bills up to the window to be able to see the denominations by the glow of the nearest streetlight. He peeled off two fives and thrust them over the top of the front seat to the driver.

At last the driver shifted the car into gear and accelerated away from the curb. Kootie pressed his lips together and blinked back frightened tears, but he didn't look out the back window.

Angelica trudged back up the stairs from the parking lot. Many of the motel rooms had their lights on after the earthquake, and the doorway at which Mavranos stood wasn't the only one that had been opened.

"No sign of him," she told Mavranos when she had stepped inside and closed the door. "There was a taxi driving away—he might have been in it, or not, and I couldn't see what company it was anyway." She gave Plumtree a look that was too exhausted to be angry. "Thanks for giving him getaway money."

Plumtree narrowed her eyes, then visibly relaxed and just pursed her lips. "He was going anyway—read the rest of the note!—and if the money did let him take a cab, you should be glad he's not walking, in this neighborhood at this hour."

"Gimme the note."

Pete Sullivan wordlessly passed to Angelica the piece of Star Motel stationery that had been weighted down with a motel glass on the walkway outside the room, and Angelica forced her tired and blurring eyes to focus on the clumsy ballpoint-ink letters:

> MOM & DAD & EVERYBODY—I CAN'T BE WITH YOU FOR THIS. I'M SORRY. I KNOW ID HAVE TO DO THE BLOOD DRIKING—HOPE YOU CAN READ THIS, I DON'T TURN ON THE LIGHT—JESUS I HOPE TV STAYS OFF—I'D HAVE TO DRINK THE BLOD, & I CANT DO IT AGAIN: LET SOMEBODY HAVE ME—& ME BE OUT OF MY HEAD. EDISON IN 92, NEVER AGAIN, ID GO CRAZY. I ~~HAVE~~/HAVE NOT TAKEN THE TRUCK. I DO ~~NOT~~ HAVE A KEY TO THIS ROOM BUT I'LL BE BACK AFTER. I'VE GOT ~~A LITTLE~~ MONEY, ENUFF. I LOVE YOU DONT BE MAD KOOTIE

Angelica looked up at Mavranos. "I've got to stay here."

Mavranos started to speak, but Pete Sullivan overrode him. "No, Angie," he said loudly. "We've got to go through with this thing, this morning. We've got Plumtree, and we've got the dead king—and we need a *bruja*. And Kootie knows where we'll be, he heard Arky describe the place—if he wants to find us, that's where he'll go, not here."

"Just what I was gonna say myself," growled Mavranos.

Plumtree had sat down on the bathroom-side bed, and was untwisting the coat-hanger wire from around her ankle. "You don't mind if I get rid of the house-arrest hardware now, do you? Me, I'm glad the kid's out of it."

She tossed the wired pair of beer cans aside and straightened up, then looked around and chuckled softly. "Do you all *realize* what we've done to this room? Burnt the rug and now stomped old pizza crusts into it, blasted the bed, poured beer in the TV—at least Janis made it to the toilet to puke last night. There's even a lot of shed black *dog hair* on the beds! I'm glad it's no credit card of mine this is on." For a moment her face looked very young and lost, and Angelica thought of the little girl who had been hospitalized because the sun had fallen out of the sky onto her. "Get your Wild Turkey bottle and let's go," Plumtree whispered. "And please God I still be here by lunchtime, and Crane be alive again."

"All of us still alive at lunchtime," said Mavranos, nodding somberly. "Amen."

CHAPTER 19

I would be blind with weeping, sick with groans,
Look pale as primrose with blood-drinking sighs,
And all to have the noble duke alive.
　　　　　　　　　　—William Shakespeare,
　　　　　　　　　　Henry VI, Part II

The pavement of the yacht club's empty parking lot was wet with sea spray and pre-dawn fog, and the low overcast looked likely to drop actual rain soon. The clouds were moving across the sky from the direction of the Golden Gate Bridge, but the eastern horizon was still open sky—a glowing pearl-white, making black silhouettes of the long piers at Fort Mason a mile away.

In spite of the dim light, Angelica Sullivan was wearing mirror sunglasses—*Standard precaution,* she had told Cochran curtly when she and Plumtree had climbed out of Cochran's Ford Granada; *the mirror surface throws ghosts back onto themselves, prevents 'em from being able to fasten on your gaze. Don't* you *look squarely at* anything.

Cochran remembered the half-dozen little girl ghosts he had glimpsed on the roof of Strubie the Clown's house in Los Angeles, and how Plumtree had yelled at him for looking at them. Right, he thought. I won't look at anything.

Driving the Granada with Cochran and Plumtree and Angelica in it, Pete had followed Mavranos's red truck up Divisadero to Marina and Yacht Road, and the two vehicles were now parked side by side in the otherwise empty lot. Beyond the curb and a short descending slope of tumbled wet boulders, the gray sea of the San Francisco Bay looked as rolling and wild as open ocean.

On a shoulder strap under her tan raincoat Angelica was carrying a compact black Marlin .45 carbine, its folding stock swivelled forward to lie locked against the left side of the trigger guard; and as she stepped away from the Granada she pulled back the rifle's slide-lever and let it snap back, chambering a live round. The extended base of a twelve-round magazine stuck out from the magazine well, and back in the motel room Cochran had seen her stuff a couple of extra magazines in the pocket of her jeans and a couple more in the raincoat's left pocket. *You expecting an army?* he had asked her.

I want to have plenty of the ghost-killer hollow-points, she had answered in a flat, singsong voice, as if talking to herself, *but I want hardball too, full-jacket, 'cause if I shoot off the first magazine's dozen rounds and need more, I'm likely to be shooting at a distance after that, or through car doors, and hardball's more reliable for that kind of thing; and adrenaline's likely to make me shaky, loosen my grip, and hollow-points don't feed through smoothly sometimes if the gun's not being braced firmly. Hardball in the raincoat, hollow-point* omieros *in the jeans.*

You've given it thought, Cochran thought now as he watched her pull the raincoat around herself and loosely tie the belt in front.

Plumtree was wearing a cranberry-colored cashmere sweater of Nina's, and she was huddled against the Granada's front bumper beside Cochran and blowing into her cupped hands. "I don't see any of Mavranos's hippie druids," she said quietly.

"With luck they don't get up this early," said Cochran. I hope nobody does, he added to himself. Mavranos said we'll be trespassing, going on out to the end of this peninsula.

And what about coming back? Is it really conceivable that Scott Crane will be *walking back* here with us? Limping, I guess, with the bullet in his thigh now. And—

"My God," he said; then, speaking more loudly, "Angelica? You're gonnna remember to pull the spear out of his throat, right? It'd be no good if he *did* come back to life, if—"

He saw two reflections of his own pale face in Angelica's mirror sunglasses when she smiled at him. "We've thought of that, Sid. Thanks, though." She looked past him. "Arky? How wide is the path to the cemetery temple place? I think you should just back the truck right out to it."

Mavranos had opened the back of the truck and was kneeling on the tailgate. "*Back* it out there?" he said, squinting over the Granada's roof at her. "Well, it would mean we don't have to *carry* Scott's body. . . ."

"Nor the rest of the crap," Angelica agreed. "And I like the truck's exhaust—with the muffler all fucked up the way it is, it's kind of a spontaneous *bata* drumbeat, and it's the pulse of the king's vessel."

"There's a chain across the path," Mavranos went on. "Probably padlocked."

"What's another dent? What's some more scratches in your paint?"

"Quicker exit afterward, too," allowed Mavranos. "That's worth a lot. Okay." He hopped down to the pavement and hoisted the lower half of the tailgate shut, though he left the top half raised. "Pete will walk backward ahead of me, waving directions so I don't go off into the water; Plumtree and Cochran ahead of Pete, so I can keep an eye on 'em over Pete's shoulder; Angelica behind, watching for pursuit."

"I should have my gun," said Cochran.

Mavranos frowned at him. "Actually, I suppose you should. Okay." He walked around to the open driver's-side door and leaned in, then walked back to the rear of the truck with Cochran's holstered revolver. "Just keep it away from Miss Plumtree," he said as he handed it to Cochran. "And put it away for now."

Cochran reached behind himself with both hands to clip the holster to the back of his belt.

Mavranos pointed to the northeast corner of the parking lot. "The path starts behind that building, as a paved service road. All of you meet me there."

He got into the driver's seat and closed the door, started the engine again, and audibly clanked it into reverse; the truck surged backward out of the parking space and began yawing away across the asphalt in a broad circle.

"After you two," said Angelica to Cochran and Plumtree, punctuating the request by letting the hidden rifle barrel briefly tent the tan fabric of the raincoat in front of her knee.

They all began trudging after the receding red truck. When Plumtree took his hand, Cochran glanced at her in surprise, for Cody had been on a moment before; but then he saw that it was still Cody—by now he could recognize her stronger jaw and the deeper lines around her flinty eyes.

Her nostrils flared as she inhaled deeply. "Kahlua," she said, "burning."

Cochran too had caught a whiff of hot-coffee-and-alcohol on the cold sea breeze. "Just like down in Solville."

She squeezed his hand. "I guess that means *something* is gonna happen."

He looked at her again, but the humble and subdued voice had still been Cody's.

*   *   *

The battering exhaust of Mavranos's truck rolling along at idle speed in reverse behind them set the pace of their walk.

"Don't fall over the chain here, Pete," called Cochran over his shoulder.

After Plumtree and Cochran stepped over the chain with the rusty NO ADMITTANCE sign hanging from it, their shoes were crunching in sandy red dirt, and they could see a cluster of low, rectangular stone structures and an iron light pole a hundred yards ahead of them at the end of the narrow spit of land; and a few seconds later they heard the chain creak and snap and then thrash into the dry wild-anise bushes that fringed the road.

"What chain?" came Pete Sullivan's voice from behind them, speaking loudly to be heard over the indomitable drumming of the truck's exhaust.

Cochran and Plumtree kept walking along the dirt path, their hands in their pockets now because of the chill. Puddles in the road reflected the gray sky, and the red dirt was peppered with fragments of brick and marble.

They were close enough to see the structures ahead now—Cochran and Plumtree were already walking past ornate broad capitals of long-gone Corninthian columns that sat upside-down on the dirt like heroic ashtrays, and spare blocks of carved and routed granite that lay at random among the weeds; but though the low walls and stairs and tomb-like alcoves ahead had been cobbled together out of mismatched scavenged brick and marble, the site had a unified look, as if all these at-odds components had come to this weathered, settled state together, right here, over hundreds of years.

A motorboat had been crossing the choppy water of the yacht harbor to their right, between the peninsula and the distant white house-fronts on Marina Boulevard; it had rounded the tip of the peninsula and was coming back along the north side, several hundred feet out, and now Cochran heard a rapid hollow knocking roll across the waves.

And behind him, much closer, he heard the rattling pop of car-window glass shattering. Brick fragments exploded away from a stairway head in front of them even as he had grabbed Plumtree's forearm and yanked her forward into a sliding crouch behind a low marble wall.

He looked back—Pete was running back toward Angelica, who had flung open her raincoat and raised the short pistol-grip rifle, and the open back end of the red truck was jumping on its old shock absorbers as it picked up speed.

Angelica fired three fast shots, then quickly unfolded the stock and had it to her shoulder and fired two more even as the ejected brass shells of the first three were bouncing on the red dirt. Out here under the open sky the shots sounded like sharp hammer blows on a wooden picnic table.

The truck ground to a halt with its back bumper rocking only a couple of yards from where Cochran and Plumtree were crouched, and two more hard gunshots impacted the air—Cochran realized that Mavranos was now shooting at the boat through the hole where his passenger-side window had been.

The motorboat had paused, out on the gray water; but now its engine roared, and its bow kicked up spray as it turned north and began curving away from the peninsula, showing them nothing but wake and a bobbing transom.

Pete and Angelica came sprinting up as Mavranos hopped down out of the truck.

"Let's get him out," Angelica gasped, "and down these stairs to that cobblestone lower level there. I should have had hardball rounds first up. You all carry him, I'll fetch the *bruja* stuff."

Cochran stood up, and realized that he had drawn his revolver at some point during the confrontation, and that it was cocked; and after he had carefully lowered the hammer he had to touch the cold barrel to be sure he hadn't fired it. His right hand was shaking as he reached around behind him and stuffed the gun back into its holster. He brushed a buzzing fly away from his ear, and then, with huge reluctance, stepped toward the truck.

Robed and whole and in some sense still barefoot, the spirit of Scott Crane stood beside the lapping gray water. It wasn't precisely where Mavranos and the Plumtree woman and the two silver coins were—he was just as immediately aware of the capering naked ghost of himself that was flickering like a hummingbird at the ruins by the sea, where the foghorn moan came for two seconds every fifteen seconds—but what confronted him either way was the water, the obligation to cross the cold, unimaginable water.

Obligation but not inevitability. He could with only moderate difficulty blunt and truncate himself enough to animate the ghost, become no more than the ghost but at least be wholly that, and stay here, with real physical mass; free to shamble around in the familiarity of noisy human streets, and bask in the earthly sun, and pour the coarsening common short-dog wine down his shabbily restored throat. He would be a poisoned and diminished quantity, but still a real quantity.

Or he could take the two silver dollars that Spider Joe had brought back to him, at such cost, and spend them on the oblivion that the

Greeks had represented as Charon's ferry over the River Styx—and then drink from what the Greeks had called Lethe, the river of forgetfulness and surrender.

No guarantees of anything there, that way, not even of nothing. Total abject and unconditional surrender, to whoever or whatever it might ultimately be behind the busy, clustering gods and archetypes that humanity had tried to hold up to it for size. He could hope for mercy, but there would certainly be justice, a justice older and more implacable than the forces that kept the suns shining and the galaxies wheeling in the nighttime sky.

Sitting in the steamy BMW idling in the Star Motel parking lot, Long John Beach turned to the two-mannikin appliance in the back seat. "Let me tell you a parable," he said.

"Talk to *me*, goddammit," said Armentrout hoarsely, gripping the sweat-slick steering wheel. *They were here during the Marina 3.2 earthquake last night,* one of the motel guests had told him. *They were all yelling at each other, and yelling, "Where's Kootie?" They carried a guy down the stairs to a truck, and drove away, some of 'em in the truck and some in a beat old brown Ford.*

"I'll tell you all," Long John said equably. "A man's car drove over a cliff, and in midair he jumped out, and caught hold of a tree stump halfway down the cliff. Below him is only fog, and he can't climb up or down. He looks into the sky and says, 'Is there anybody up there? Tell me what to do!' And a big voice says, 'Let go of the tree.' So after a few seconds the guy says, 'Is there anybody *else* up there?' "

Armentrout nodded impatiently, and finally turned to Long John. "So? What did he do?"

The one-armed man shrugged. "That's the end of the story."

Down a set of mismatched brick-and-marble stairs, under the shadow of a scrollwork-roofed marble alcove that looked as if it should shelter the carved effigy of a dead king, a broad cobblestone-paved crescent with a raised stone edge-coping projected out over the sea like an ancient dock.

At the moment the only dead king present was laid out on the pavement below the alcove, his jeans and white shirt blotting up moisture and grime from the puddles between the uneven paving stones; and all that was on the broad table-like slab under the alcove roof was a couple of sheets of corrugated cardboard, bedding for some absent transient.

In the direction of the peninsula point and the iron light pole another set of steps led back up to road level from this stone floor, flanked against the open gray sky by a bench that was a marble slab laid across two broken granite half-moons. Cochran realized that he badly wanted to feel that this shelter was an enduring, solid edifice—but it was too obvious that what distinguished this place from a real, old ruin was the fact that all the stone edges here, even the ones fitted up against each other as part of some wall or seat, were broken and uneven. A line from some poem was tolling in his head: *These fragments I have shored against my ruins* . . .

Plumbing pipes projected up out of the muddy ground at every shelf and wall-top, their open-mouthed ends bent horizontal to project the echoing sound of sea water rising and falling in their buried shafts, a deep twanging like slow-fingered ascending and descending slides on slack bass-guitar strings. Cochran's thudding heartbeat and his shallow panting seemed to provide a counterpoint, and it was only Plumtree's evident, valiant desperation to accomplish the task at hand, and his own queasy shame at having called for Nina's ghost during the Follow-the-Queen episode, that kept him from wading out into the cold sea on the Marina side and trying to swim to shore.

His face was chilly with sweat, and not just because of having had to help carry the cold dead body a few moments ago. In his mind he was again seeing the carbine jolting in Angelica's fists and flinging out ejected shell casings, and the brick stairway-top exploding into dust and high-speed fragments, and he was shaking with a new, visceral comprehension of velocity and bullets and human mercilessness. He couldn't help but be glad that he hadn't fired his own gun.

Angelica had fetched her canvas knapsack from the truck while Mavranos and Pete and Cochran had been carrying Scott Crane's body down the steps, and now she was spreading out on the damp stones her paltry-looking tools—there was, along with the assorted garage-sale litter he'd seen last night in the motel room, an empty H. Upmann cigar box, a can of Ronsonol lighter fluid, a pair of pliers, a Star Motel postcard . . . Cochran shook his head in bewilderment.

Mavranos cussed and slapped at his own neck. "No hippie druids this morning," he said, "but we got flies up the butt."

"Here, at this hour," said Angelica in a strained voice, "those can't be anything but ghost-flies; *las moscas,* little essences of dead people, either brought in on us or already here. Ordinarily they'd just be an implicit cloud, but they're condensed to individuality this morning by the sudden low pressure of having the dead king right here." She glanced up, frowning. "Try not to breathe them—and if any of you have got any bleeding cuts, cover them."

She handed Mavranos the bottle of '75 Kenwood Cabernet. "You hold this, Arky," she told him; "open it when I tell you."

"Go ahead and do this thing right," Mavranos said, "but as much on fast-forward as you can, okay? Those guys in the boat will be back, or their friends."

"Right, Arky," Angelica said, "but it's important for this procedure that all the minds present understand what's going on, assent to it." Speaking to all of them, she went on rapidly, "See, we're gonna be doing a kind of ass-backward honoring-of-the-dead here. Usually the procedure is to have a heavily masked guy, a Lucumi *ogungun,* let himself be taken over by the ghost of the deceased; it's to let the ghost see the funeral and mourners and flower displays and all, and everybody being sorry, so that the ghost can go away, can dissipate happily and not hang around and cause trouble."

While she'd been talking she had laid the cigar box on the stones and draped it with a white linen handkerchief, and now she set on it a water glass from the motel. As she hoisted a plastic bottle of Evian water out of the knapsack and began twisting off the cap, she said, in a formal tone, "This is an altar, a *bóveda espiritual.*" It seemed to be a declaration, and she poured the glass half full of water as she spoke.

She looked up at Plumtree then, and her mirror glasses were lozenges of glowing gray sky. Cochran could see the butt of the slung carbine under her open raincoat. "The way it ordinarily works," Angelica went on at her previous quick pace, "is you set out a glass of some nice kind of water, and everybody dabs some on their hands and temples, as a kind of cleansing, so the guest-of-honor ghost will have a transparent medium to focus on but won't *fixate* on anybody." She took the Wild Turkey bottle out of the canvas sack and twisted out the cork. "But," she said hoarsely, "we don't *want* his *ghost,* we want *him.* And we want to make sure that he *does* fixate, that retreat is not even an option for him."

She poured the still-liquid red blood into the water, about three tablespoons, and then covered the glass with the Star Motel postcard to keep the ghost-flies out of it. "So you're going to *drink* this."

Plumtree was biting her lip, but she nodded. "This has to work," she was whispering, "please let this work, this has to work . . ." The sunburn was spotty over her cheekbones, as if the skin was stretched tight, and Cochran guessed that her hands would have been trembling if she had not been clenching them tightly together, as if in prayer.

Cochran remembered the note Kootie had left, when he had run away last night. *I can't do it again . . . me be out of my head . . . I'd go crazy.* This woman, Cochran thought, underwent electroconvulsive therapy six days ago this morning. She was knocked out of her own head, and has been evicted again several times since then by her terrible father . . . most recently for more than two whole days, and she got herself back just yesterday morning. Cochran remembered her saying yesterday, in a falsely, bravely cheerful voice, *The goat head was speaking, in a human language* . . . But she's here, doing this, voluntarily. *Assenting*, and then some.

He stepped closer to her and reached out and squeezed her hand. Without glancing away from the glass of streaky red water on the draped cigar box, Plumtree shook her hand free of his.

"No offense," she said faintly. "This is our flop."

Cochran took a step back. Over the wavering drone of the flies he heard a faint pattering on the stones behind him, and when he turned he saw Mavranos brushing tiny cubes of truck-window glass out of his hair.

"I could drive back for coffee and doughnuts," Mavranos said.

"We're almost ready here," said Angelica.

She now laid the myrtle branches on the stones and squirted them with the Ronsonol lighter fluid; and she laid out as well the gold Dunhill lighter and the two silver dollars that Spider Joe had brought to Solville.

At last Angelica straightened up, with a visible shudder, and elbowed the slung carbine back behind her hip. "Okay, Arky," she said, "open that skeleton-label wine. We're each going to take a sip of it, and then I'm going to light the myrtle. This stuff will get—God help us!—it'll get the attention of Dionysus, his *remote* attention, I trust, and that will give us a line-of-sight link to the underworld."

"And from the underworld right back to us, here," said Mavranos stolidly as he twisted the corkscrew of his Swiss Army knife into the cork. "Pogo?" he called loudly into the gray sky. He yanked the cork out with a frail pop. "That's a sound you ought to recognize, old friend."

He tipped the bottle up to his lips, and after a couple of bubbles had wobbled up inside it he lowered it and passed it to Pete Sullivan, who also drank from it.

"Plumtree last," said Angelica, taking the bottle from her husband and handing it to Cochran. The harbor breeze was tossing her black hair around her face. "And out of the glass."

Cochran raised the cold bottle and took several deep gulps, and he was so hungry for the blurring effect of alcohol on his empty stomach, on this terrible morning, that he had to force himself to hand it back without swallowing more.

"Thirsty boy," said Angelica bleakly. "You're not through yet, by the way.'' She drank a token mouthful herself, then crouched again by her little altar and, flicking the postcard away, topped up the water glass with purple Cabernet. She clanked the bottle down on the stones and lifted the glass, and straightened up and handed it to Plumtree.

"Not quite yet,'' Angelica said to her. "You,'' she told Cochran, "hold up that right hand of yours, toward the water, with that birthmark facing out.''

Cochran's ears were ringing, and he distinctly felt a drop of sweat roll down his ribs under his shirt. "Why?'' he whispered. I won't, he thought. He heard again what he had said in the self-esteem group at Rosecrans Medical Center, on that first day: *Reach out your hand, you get it cut off, sometimes.* And he remembered seeing the red blood jetting from his chopped wrist, when he had put his hand between the old Zinfandel stump and the pruning shears thirty-three years ago. He was about to say *I won't* out loud, but Mavranos spoke before he could:

"I got no affection for your girlfriend,'' Mavranos said gruffly, "but I gotta say that she's bought a lot of . . . plain cold admiration, in my rating. Not that she cares, I'm sure. What she's ready to do . . . I don't think I *could* do. None of the rest of us can claim our part's too hard, in this, compared to hers.''

"That mark on your hand is some kind of Dionysus badge,'' Angelica said gently, "isn't it?''

Le Visage dans la Vigne, Cochran thought. The Face in the Vine Stump. "I suppose it is,'' he said helplessly, and then in his mind he heard again the hard *crack* of Plumtree's fist hitting the bloody madhouse linoleum floor, right after he had punched Long John Beach in the nose. His teeth ached now as he took a deep breath of the sea air and let it out in shaky segments. "I'm . . . with you. Okay.'' Slowly he lifted his right arm, with the palm of his hand turned back.

"Okay,'' echoed Angelica. To Plumtree she said, "Now when I get the myrtle burning, you call to—damn it, you brought this on yourself, you know, girl, I'm so sorry, but—call to Scott Crane; and then drink—'' She shook her head quickly and waved at the glass of rusty-colored liquid in Plumtree's hand, then whispered the last word, "—it.''

Cochran noticed that the peak of the alcove roof and the top of the marble stair were shining now in the cold pink light of dawn. Mavranos stood on tiptoe and looked back down the peninsula.

"Sun's coming up,'' he said, "over Fort Mason.''

"Get the pliers,'' Angelica told him. "Pull the spear out of his throat.''

Mavranos swallowed visibly, but his face was impassive as he nodded. "Happy to.'' He picked up the pliers and then knelt beside Scott

Crane's body, with his back to the others; Cochran saw his shoulders flex under the denim jacket, and then he was straightening up, holding the closed pliers out away from himself, and the red-stained three-pointed spearhead quivered between the pliers' jaws.

"Can I pitch it into the ocean?" he asked hoarsely.

"You have to," said Angelica, nodding and not looking at the thing.

Mavranos reached back over his shoulder and then snapped his hand forward, letting the pliers spring open at the last moment, as if he were casting a fishing fly. The little bloody metal fork spun away, glittering for a moment in the horizontal sunlight, and then disappeared behind a wave.

Cochran looked back at the body of Scott Crane. A spatter of fresh red blood stood out on the dark beard, but the pale, lined face was as composed and noble as before, and he reminded himself that at the moment Crane was incapable of feeling pain.

The two silver dollars were lying on the stones near Scott Crane's bare feet. "Aren't you gonna put the coins on his eyes?" Cochran asked.

"No," snapped Angelica. "They're his fare *over*. We want him to come *back*."

Then why have them here at all? thought Cochran defensively. His raised arm was getting tired.

Angelica crouched to pick up the myrtle branches and the gold cigarette lighter, and she opened the lighter's lid and flicked the striker; the myrtle caught and burned with an almost invisible flame, though Cochran could smell the incense-like smoke.

Angelica nodded to Plumtree.

Plumtree faced the now-glittering gray water, and when she had lifted the glass she paused. "Not even Valorie?" she asked in a quiet voice, clearly not addressing any of the others present. "This is *mine?*"

Standing to the side of her with his arm stiffly raised, Cochran could see wind-blown tears streaming back across her cheek.

"*Scott Crane!*" she called strongly out toward the waves and the glowing fog. "*I know you can fucking hear me! Come into me, into this body of your murderer!*" And she tipped the glass up and drank it down in three convulsive swallows.

With a drumming roar like the sound of a forest fire, sudden solid rain thrashed down onto the peninsula, flinging up a haze of splash-spray over the stones and blurring the surface of the sea. The sudden haze of flying water was lit by two rapid white flares of lightning, and the sudden hard crash of close thunder battered at the marble walls and rocked Cochran back on his heels.

Plumtree's hair was instantly soaked, and it flew out like snakes when she flung her head back and shouted out three syllables of harsh laughter.

"Four-and-twenty blackbrides baked in a pie!" roared the voice of Omar Salvoy from her gaping mouth. *"When the pie was opened, the brides began to sing! Wasn't that a dainty dish to set before the king!"*

Cochran had lost his footing, and he twisted as he fell so that his knees and elbows knocked against the wet stones.

He could see the remains of Scott Crane, only a couple of feet in front of his face. It was a bare gray skull that now lolled above the collar of the shirt, and the already-wet fabric was collapsed against stark ribs and no abdomen at all, and the hands that spilled from the cuffs were long-fingered gray bone.

Plumtree turned away from the sea, and even through the dimness and the retinal afterglare from the lightning Cochran could see the white of her bared teeth, and he knew this was Plumtree's father, Omar Salvoy. He might have been looking straight at Cochran.

"Moth-er!" Cochran yelled, and though he was only trying to induce the Follow-the-Queen effect in her, to his surprise the wail powerfully evoked his own dormant childhood fear of being heartbreakingly lost and monstrously found, and he was glad that the rain would hide the tears he felt springing from his eyes. For his self-respect more than from any particular hope of its efficacy, he shouted, *"Janis's mom!"*

Perhaps it had worked—at any rate the figure that was Plumtree was allowing itself to be hustled back up the stairs by Mavranos, and Angelica was now crouched on the other side of the dressed skeleton, hastily folding the stick-like arms and legs.

Angelica looked up at him over the arch of the cloth-draped breastbone. "Get the Wild Turkey bottle!" she said.

Cochran nodded, and crawled across the stones and snatched up the pint bottle in the moment before Pete Sullivan grabbed him under the arms and hauled him to his feet. Cochran had almost dropped the bottle in surprise—it was as hot as if scalding coffee had just been poured out of it, and he shoved it into the pocket of his windbreaker.

Another flare of lightning lit the weathered stones through the thick haze of rain, and the instant bomb-blast of thunder fluttered the wet hair on the back of Cochran's head.

Things like beanbags were falling out of the sky and hitting the stones all around him—he squinted at a couple of them as Pete hurried him across the pavement, and he saw that they were dead seagulls. Over the roar of the rain battering the pavement he could hear bestial groans and howls shaking out of the mouths of the deeply moored pipes now.

He and Pete followed Angelica up the slippery stone steps to the roadway mud, and after Angelica had unceremoniously dumped the armful of clothes and bones in through the open back window of Mavranos's truck they all scrambled around to the side doors and piled in, kicking out old clothes and McDonald's take-out hamburger wrappings.

Cochran and Plumtree and Pete were all wedged uncomfortably in the back seat; but Cochran relaxed a little when he heard Plumtree muttering about Jesus. Apparently the Follow-the-Queen invocation had worked, and this was the personality of Plumtree's mother.

Mavranos had started the truck and levered it into gear before they had got the doors shut, and he clicked the headlights on as the truck rocked forward along the dirt path back toward the yacht-club parking lot. Tools and frying pans clanked in the truck bed, and Cochran wondered if Crane's skeleton was being broken up back there.

Then he leaned forward over the back of the front seat to peer ahead past the squeaking whips of the windshield wipers. Translucent human figures waved and grimaced out on the road in the yellow headlight glare, and stretched or sprang away to the sides as the massive bumper and grille bulled through them.

Angelica was crouched in the front passenger seat with her carbine across her knees. "I see lights, ahead," she said, speaking loudly to be heard over the rain and wind that were thrashing in through the broken window by her right elbow. "Don't waste time focussing on these ghosts."

"Motorcycles," said Mavranos, squinting through the streaming windshield. He took his right hand from the steering wheel long enough to draw the revolver from under his belt and lay it across his lap. "They're on Yacht Road, turning into the parking lot." He tromped on the accelerator, and the old truck bounced violently on its shocks, clanging the tools and pans in the back. "I'm gonna stop," he called, "sudden, when we're past the Granada. You all jump out and get into it— I'll use this truck to clear a path through these guys."

"No, Arky—" Angelica began, but then the truck had slammed down over a curb and had passed the parked Granada, and was braking hard and slewing around to the right on the wet asphalt. Cochran was pressed against the back of the front seat, but he shoved the right-side door open while the truck was still rocking from side to side, its left side facing the oncoming glare of motorcycle headlights.

He dragged Plumtree out onto the pavement after him, and he was fumbling in his pants pocket for the Granada's keys. Pete had followed him out and had opened the truck's front passenger door, but Angelica was arguing with Mavranos and wouldn't get out.

"I'll shoot ahead while you drive," she was yelling. "Pete, go get in the Ford! Arky, *drive us out of here!*"

Over the stadium-roar of the rain Cochran heard several hard bangs, and the truck's long right rear window became an opaque spiderweb in the moment before it fell out onto the asphalt in a million tiny pieces.

He saw Mavranos lunge up and across the front seat, blocking Angelica from the gunfire; "Angelica," Mavranos was yelling, "get down, get back to—"

Five more fast bangs hammered at the truck, and Angelica tumbled backward out of the truck and sat down hard on the puddled pavement. As Pete Sullivan ran toward her, Cochran spun away, toward the Granada. He frog-marched Plumtree around to the passenger side, opened the door, and shoved her into the back seat; then he ran around the front and got in behind the wheel and started the engine.

Angelica was on her feet, and Pete was hurrying her to the passenger side of the Granada. They got in, and Cochran shifted the engine into low gear.

"Don't go!" Angelica was yelling in his ear as he stepped on the gas, "Drive into them, Arky's been shot, we've got to get him—"

"He's driving," Cochran told her. He took his eyes off the advancing pavement ahead for just long enough to give her a quick up-and-down glance, but he didn't see any obvious blood on her rain-soaked jeans and blouse. Apparently she had not been hit.

Ahead of them the truck had surged around and roared forward, and with an audible slam a motorcycle headlight beam whirled up across the dark sky as the truck rocked right over the fallen machine and rider; Cochran swerved his lower-slung car around the body and the spinning, broken motorcycle, and then he tromped on the accelerator to keep up with the racing truck as it sped out of the parking lot. Dead seagulls thumped under the tires.

The motorcyles were behind them now, their headlights slashing the walls of rain as they turned around, and Angelica was lying across Pete's lap to hold the carbine outside of the car, its black plastic stock wedged against the still-open passenger door.

She pulled the trigger five times—the concussions of the shots were stunning physical blows inside the confined cab of the car, and the flashes of hard yellow muzzle-flare made it impossible to see anything more than the truck's taillights in the dimness ahead, but the headlights behind didn't seem to be gaining on them, so Cochran just bit his lip and hummed shrilly and kept squinting through the rain-blurred wind-shield.

Over the ringing in his ears and the roaring of the engine, he became aware that Plumtree was shouting in a quacking voice in the back seat. "You can't kill him with bullets," he dimly heard her say. "Even when his Lever Blank acolytes threw him off a building in Soma, he didn't die. He is the Anti-Christ."

"Oh hell," he whispered. Who to call up, he thought—not Janis nor Cody, there's no point in breaking the bad news to them yet. *"Valorie!"* he shouted.

At least it shut her up. Angelica had pulled the door closed and folded the stock of her carbine, but now she had popped out the old magazine and rammed a new one in—hardball rounds, Cochran guessed—and had rolled down the window and was sitting on Pete's knees with her head and shoulders, and the rifle, out the window.

She fired six measured, presumably aimed shots—the explosions rang the car roof, but were much less assaulting than the previous five had been—and then she hiked herself back inside and rolled the window back up. Cochran glanced at the rear-view mirror and couldn't see any headlights back there.

"Arky's shot," Angelica said breathlessly. "He got shot in the head."

Cochran nodded at the truck ahead of them, which had just caught the tail end of a green light and turned left onto Marina Boulevard. "He's driving fine." Cochran sped up and honked his car horn to catch the yellow light and stay behind the truck; the tires squealed on the slick asphalt but didn't lose traction.

Angelica rubbed her fist on the steamy inside surface of the wind-shield and peered out through the glass. "I don't *see* him, though—do you see his *head* at all, if he's driving?"

Cochran tried to see details of the truck in the moments when the windshield wipers had swept aside the blobs and streams of rain. "No," he admitted finally, "but he might be sitting real low." With the feed-back-like ringing in his abused eardrums he had no idea how loud he might be talking.

"But—" he went on shakily, in a louder voice. Hadn't Pete or Angelica noticed? "But the truck is blue, now."

"It's—?" Angelica stared expressionlessly at the boxy truck bobbing in the lane ahead of them. Even in the dim gray light, the truck's color was unmistakably a dusty navy blue. "And it's—that's him, that's the same truck, we haven't taken our eyes off it." She sat back between Pete and Cochran, looking all at once small and young behind the wet black metal of the gun in her arms. "The local Holy Week is over, that means—and nobody rose from the dead. We really did fail here today."

Plumtree wailed in the back seat, and for a moment Cochran thought the mother personality was still on; then she spoke, in the flat cadence of Valorie: *"What would you have me be, an I be not a woman? Manhood is called foolery, when it stands against a falling fabric. And tell the pleasant prince this mock of his hath turned his balls to gun-stones."*

For a moment no one spoke; then, "I reckon Kootie was right," said Pete. "I guess the receiver had to be somebody of the same sex."

Cochran's right shoe sole squeaked back and forth between the brake and the gas pedal, and the engine roared and slacked, roared and slacked, as he swerved from one to another of the eastbound lanes to keep the speeding truck in sight ahead of them, and the word *sex* hung in the steamy air.

CHAPTER 20

*The night wore out, and, as he stood upon the bridge listening to the water
as it splashed the river-walls of the Island of Paris, where the picturesque
confusion of houses and cathedral shone bright in the light of the moon, the
day came coldly, looking like a dead face out of the sky. Then, the night, with
the moon and the stars, turned pale and died, and for a little while it seemed
as if Creation were delivered over to Death's dominion.*

—Charles Dickens,
A Tale of Two Cities

Though he couldn't see her in the shadowy alley ahead of him, Kootie
sensed that the woman in the hooded white raincoat had found the *other*
mouth of this interminable unroofed passage, and was picking her way
down the rain-slicked cobblestones toward him, patient as a shadow.

Even if there had not been wooden crates full of cabbage heads and
big green onions stacked against the ancient brick walls, the alley would
have been too narrow for any car to drive down it; and the scalloped
eaves of the pagoda-style roofs were four or five stories overhead, and
Kootie was certain that even on clear days the sunlight had never at
any season slanted all the way down to these wet paving stones, which
had probably not been dry of rain water and vegetable juices and spit
and strange liquors since the pavement was laid—and Kootie giddily
thought that must have been before the 1906 earthquake.

If that earthquake ever even happened, he thought, here.

He was crouching in the deeper shadows under an iron stairway, and
all he was doing was breathing deeply and listening to his own heartbeat, which for several minutes now had been alternating between scary
rapid bursts and even scarier three-second dead stops. Like bad-
reception images on a TV, every object he looked at seemed to have a
faint twin half-overlapping it to one side, and he suspected that the

rainbow-edged twins weren't precisely identical to the actual objects; and the cold, oily air seemed to be shaking with big dialogues he couldn't quite *hear,* like the faint voices you can catch on a turned-up stereo in the moments between tracks.

He wasn't at all sure he was still entirely in the real, San Francisco Chinatown.

When he had first noticed the Chinese woman in the white hooded raincoat he had been standing out of the downpour under an awning in an alley called Street of Gamblers; and he had ducked through a touristy souvenir shop to evade her, hunching through aisles of woks and wisdom hats and plastic back-scratchers, and when he had pushed through the far door and stepped out into the rain again, he had sprinted right across the narrow neon-puddled street, between the idling, halted traffic, into the dark slot of this alley. He hadn't looked back, for when he had caught the woman's eye in the Street of Gamblers she had for one hallucinatory moment seemed to be the globular black silhouette that had showed up on the motel TV screen this morning in the instant after Arky had poured beer into the set; and he had guessed that, whoever she was, she had assumed a psychic posture that had made her compellingly identical to one of the wild archetypes.

He had hurried down this alley—jogging past inexplicable open-air racks of whole barbecued ducks, under ornate balconies and indecipherable banners and clotheslines crazily hung with dripping squid, and stared at by ancient women smoking clay pipes in open doorways—and he had skidded to a panting halt here when it had finally occurred to him that no real alley in San Francisco could stretch this far without crossing a street.

He hadn't eaten anything since a few slices of delivery pizza late yesterday afternoon, and he had been wearing this now-wet flannel shirt for twenty-four hours. He was dizzy, and exhausted without being at all sleepy, and he knew by the aching fractures in his mind that something awful had happened this morning. Something besides industrial pollution and dead sparrows was coming down hard with this rain, and the cooked ducks and raw squids were, he thought, probably being exposed to it intentionally, for some eventual bad sacramental purpose.

He jumped in surprise—and a moment later,

"You caught me," came a high, lilting voice from close by.

He looked up to his left, and there she was, smiling down at him where he crouched under the stairs.

He had been startled a moment before she had spoken. He was on bar-time again, experiencing events a moment before they actually happened. That meant that she, or somebody, was paying a magical sort of attention to him—but he had bleakly guessed that already.

Her face under the white plastic hood was younger than he had thought, and the faint aura he saw off to one side of her was rainbow-colored now, and was clearly just a reiteration of her real shape.

He noticed that her feet were bare on the wet stones, and that the long black hair that trailed across her chest between the lapels of her raincoat seemed to be clinging to bare skin, rather than to any clothing.

He hiked himself forward and stood up in what he now thought of as the duck-and-squid-basting rain; and he opened his mouth to say something, but she spoke first:

"What are you looking for?" she asked.

Kootie thought about that. "Shelter, I guess," he said. "Food, rest." He glanced fearfully up and down the alley, clenching his fists against another burst of rapid heartbeat. "Real streets," he added breathlessly.

"Go to this place," she told him, pulling a folded sheet of white paper out of the raincoat pocket and handing it to him. Her fingertips were as cold as the rain.

Then she had hurried past him and away, and the wings of her rain-coat spread out wide in the rainy wind, so that she was a white triangle receding away with eerie speed between the close, dark walls.

Kootie unfolded the piece of paper, trying to shield it from the rain with one shaky hand. It was a poorly photocopied line drawing of a scowling Chinaman with tiny smudged images of ships and animals all over his shirt and trousers. In the bottom margin of the paper, ballpoint-ink numbers were arranged unevenly:

$$60$$

31 10, 78 53:
    49 80, 86/100 90 91.

$$—12$$

Kootie looked after the vanished woman. He understood this code, but he wondered how she had known that he would. It was the Cuban *charada china*, a lottery and rebus system that had been brought to Havana by Chinese contract laborers in the mid-nineteenth century. Originally of thirty-six characters, it had been expanded during the twentieth century to include a hundred symbols.

This reproduction of the famous drawing was so poorly copied that not even the little images on the *chino's* clothing, much less the tiny numbers beside each one, could be made out—but Kootie's foster-mother Angelica had done so much divination work with the antique system that Kootie effortlessly remembered what picture or pictures each number traditionally referred to.

Now he tried to read the indicated images as a message, a letter to him, and after a few moments he had mentally arranged them into phrases, filling in gaps with words that seemed probable:

> (On this day of) *dark sun*
> *Deer Big Fish, Bishop of* (Thomas Edison's) *electric light:*
> (Look for a, you'll find a) *drunk physician* (or *physician for drunks*), (at the) *hotel* (or *convent*) (where you saw the) *big mirror and the old man,* (by the) *gemstone tortoise.*

> —*Saintly woman* (or *prostitute*)

How long, Kootie wondered, was she following me? Right around sunrise, when the dead sparrows fell out of the sky with the sour rain, I *did* see an old man propping up a big gilt-framed mirror against a brick wall and staring at me in the reflection. I think he was in front of a Chinese restaurant, though, not a hotel or a convent—though in fact this was right next to a shop called . . . *Jade Galore*, with a big jade tortoise in the display window. It had been near the Street of Gamblers . . . Washington and Stockton.

Even as he wondered how he might find his way back to the normal San Francisco streets, he heard the rippling throb of car tires on wet pavement; and when he stepped forward and looked to his left, he saw the muted colors of cars moving past across the alley from left to right. A real street!—ask and ye shall receive, he told himself.

He thought about the old man he'd seen with the mirror . . . and about the woman in the white raincoat.

Saintly woman (or *prostitute*).

Angelica would see danger in this invitation, spiritual peril even more than phsyical peril. *Not everybody that uses magic is bad,* she had told him more than once over the past two years, *but it's always bad for them—even if you're masked and working for the good of others or in self-defense, it coarsens and blunts your soul.*

Kootie was trudging toward the cross-street ahead, not taking his eyes off the vision of the passing cars, but he was very aware of the paper crumpled in his hand. Angelica would expect him to run away from whatever it was that this letter offered—run to a Catholic church, or to the police, even; ideally, of course, she would expect him to run to her and Pete, if he could find them.

But he knew what his psychically concussed symptoms this morning meant. As Mavranos had pointed out, Kootie was a member of Scott Crane's magical army now—and he knew, in his guts and his spine and the primitive base of his brain, that their army had within the last hour suffered the equivalent of a nuclear strike.

All he could sense with his stunned powers was injury and absence. The attempt to restore Scott Crane to life had palpably failed. Mavranos and Plumtree and Cochran were very likely dead.

Kootie's thoughts just exploded away into chaos whenever he tried to think about his foster-parents. He couldn't believe that Pete and Angelica were dead, but he knew too that his individual capacity for belief wouldn't affect whatever *was*. His natural parents had been tortured to death only a little more than two years ago; and now the fugitive couple who had taken him in, and had loved him and cared for him and been loved by him, might very well be dead too.

He could only postpone that thought, for now.

For now, Kootie was alone and conspicuous in a hostile, awakened city.

49 80, he thought. *12.*

He had emerged at last from the dimness of the alley—his sneakers were scuffing on the wet cement of the street sidewalk now, and the passing cars were so obviously real that he could see the momentarily clear tread-prints of their tires on the puddled asphalt as they rolled past, and so close that he could see faces behind the rain-beaded window glass. This street was Stockton. Washington should be the next street down to his left.

He shoved the crumpled paper into his jeans pocket. His legs were shaky, and he had to actually glance down at his belt to make sure he had not buckled it in a Möbius twist—he had not—but he sighed and began shuffling south, toward Washington Street.

The blue truck hadn't been stopping for red lights as it led the Granada on a swerving, skidding chase through the dawn streets of the Richmond district. The truck had braked for cross-traffic, but then gunned through the rainy intersections as soon as a gap between oncoming cars appeared, as if the red lights were just yield signs. Cochran had been hard-pressed to keep the vehicle in sight through the slapping windshield wipers, and even so he had had to run a couple of red lights himself, cursing and sweating as he did it. He had told Angelica to stash her gun under the seat in case they were pulled over by a cop.

On the long westbound stretch of Geary Street, Cochran had briefly been able to pull up in the left lane alongside the racing blue truck, and Pete had hiked himself up nearly to a standing position in the Granada's passenger seat, with his head and shoulders out the window; and when he had slumped back down in the seat and looked across Angelica at Cochran, his rain-wet face was pale.

"He's lying across the seat," Pete had said flatly. "Face down, with blood on the seat by his head."

Cochran had hissed angrily as the truck had edged ahead again. Both vehicles had at times reached speeds of at least fifty, probably sixty—at green lights flying right across the stepped intersections and clanking the abused shock absorbers on the downhill slopes—and he'd been glad these Chinese restaurants and secondhand clothing shops weren't open yet, and that traffic was sparse. "So who's *driving?*" he'd demanded.

"Nobody is," Pete had said. "The truck is."

"I don't mean to be—" Cochran had begun. "Damn it, do you mean the *truck* is driving? Driving *itself?*"

"That's what he means," Angelica had told him, chewing her knuckles. "If he'd stop—if *it* would stop—at a red light, Pete could get out and get behind the truck's steering wheel."

"No chance of that, it looks like," Cochran had said grimly. "Maybe the thing'll run out of gas."

Now the truck and the car were on the Great Highway, headed south along the western coast under the lightening gray sky, having screeched through the twisting promontory lanes of Point Lobos Avenue and gunned past the Sutro Bath ruins and the Cliff House Restaurant.

Last week we saw Crane's naked ghost on the seaside rocks down there, Cochran had thought as he had leaned the speeding car around that bend of the highway. Today we're chasing a runaway truck with Crane's skeleton dumped in the back of it, and the Kootie kid is gone and Mavranos is probably dead. The king's army has been pruned back right down to the dirt.

The open lanes of the Great Highway stretched straight ahead, with the slate-colored sea to the right and the massive greenery of Golden Gate Park and the stumpy tower of an old windmill rolling past to the left beyond the northbound lanes. Ahead of the Granada the truck was barrelling along, staying in its lane.

Pete Sullivan was sweating. "Pull up right behind him," he told Cochran, "and kill the wipers. We left the back window of the truck's tailgate open, see?"

Cochran switched off the windshield wipers and carefully edged up behind the truck, watching its close bumper rock nearer by inches as the two engines roared on and the lane markers whipped past under the wheels. The raised horizontal window at the back of the truck bobbed on its struts.

"Hope he don't brake," said Cochran through clenched teeth, "or—"

"What the hell are you going to do, Pete?" interrupted Angelica. "You can't!"

"*I* can't," said Pete Sullivan, flexing his hands and staring at the close back of the truck through the rain-stippled windshield, "but I bet Houdini can." He glanced at Angelica. "Arky might be dying in there."

"Or *dead*," she told him shrilly, "and *you* might be dying right on this highway! Under the wheels of this very car I'm driving in! Pete, *you can't.* You may have Houdini's hands, but you haven't got his . . . the *rest* of his body!" Out of the corner of his eye Cochran saw her pat Pete's knee, as if the subject were closed. "We'll wait for the truck to run out of gas." To Cochran she said, "Hey, back off, you're gonna run right up his tailpipe. And turn the wipers back on."

The seat jerked hard then as Plumtree grabbed it from behind, and Cochran lifted his foot away from the gas pedal to keep from being jolted into accidentally ramming the truck. Plumtree seemed to be trying to climb over the seat—and then she was clawing at the open passenger-side window as if she intended to climb right out of the speeding car.

"*Take these rats thither,*" she was saying loudly, "*to gnaw their garners. Worshipful mutineers, Valorie puts well forth; pray, follow.*"

Pete Sullivan pried her wet hands loose from the window frame. "I'll go," he said, speaking distinctly into her blank face. "*I will go.* You stay." He pushed her backward against evident resistance until she was again sitting stiffly in the back seat.

In the rear-view mirror Cochran saw her lean back in the seat, watching Pete steadily.

"Catch up," Pete told Cochran as he turned around in the front seat and again peered out through the rain-blurred windshield. "Get closer. Angie, what you can do is say a prayer to . . . Ogun, right?" He was panting, almost laughing. "Isn't he the orisha of iron—Detroit iron, I hope!—and the guy who takes people who die in traffic accidents? Tell him to hold off, here."

Angelica held up the hand she'd been chewing on, and Cochran saw blood on her knuckles. "I've been," she said. "There's iron in blood. But—Kootie needs you! *I* need you, goddammit!"

Pete rocked his head toward the back seat. "Imagine the scene in here if I don't. Anyway it's gonna work."

Angelica was nodding, and biting her knuckle again. She took her bloody hand away from her face long enough to say, "I can see you're going to do it. If you die—listen to me!—if you die here I *will not* forgive you.''

Pete dragged his knees up until he was crouching on the seat. "I'm not gonna die.'' He threw a bright glance at Cochran and said, "Watch me, and the truck. Compensate.''

Cochran was dizzy with the realization that there was no way out of this. "Get it over with,'' he said tightly, gripping the wheel and gently fluttering the gas pedal to keep the car's bumper close to the truck's. He didn't dare glance away from the truck's horribly close back window to look at the speedometer, but the lane markers were hurtling past and he knew the two vehicles must be doing sixty miles per hour.

Pete hiked himself up to sit on the windowsill, with his whole upper body out of the car, out in the battering rain; then he raised his left knee outside and braced the sole of his shoe against the doorpost. He leaned forward against the headwind, and peripherally through the windshield Cochran saw his right hand grip the base of the radio antenna; then Cochran was aware of the fingertips of Pete's left hand pressed against the top edge of the windshield glass.

"Fucking lunatic,'' Cochran whispered absently. The steering wheel and the gas pedal seemed to be living extensions of himself, aching with muscular tension, and he felt that he was using the car to reach out and *hold* the speeding truck.

And he was balanced in the driver's seat, ready for it, when Pete jackknifed forward and slammed prone against the outside of the windshield; Cochran just raised his head to be able to see over the blur of Pete's shoulder against the glass, and the speeding car didn't wobble in the lane.

Angelica was muttering syllables in which Cochran heard the name *Ogun* several times; and in one corner of his mind he realized that the words droning in his own head were the Lord's Prayer.

Outside the glass, Pete's hands were braced out to the sides and in front of him as he slowly drew in his feet and edged forward across the car's hood on his knees. His weight was on his fingertips, and it seemed to be his hands that were maintaining his balance.

Houdini's hands, Cochran thought.

Now the fingers of Pete's right hand were curled over the front edge of the car hood, and the left hand slowly lifted in the rushing headwind . . . and beckoned.

Cochran increased the pressure of his foot on the gas pedal by an infinitesimal degree; and he felt a nevertheless solid clang shake the car as its bumper touched the truck's.

And in that instant Pete's hands had both lifted away from the hood, and his legs had straightened as he lunged forward in a dive.

Angelica exhaled sharply, and Cochran could only guess at the control it had taken for her to make no greater sound.

But now Pete's shoes were clearly visible kicking in dark gap under the raised back window of the truck. He had gone into the truck rather than under the car's wheels.

Cochran was shouting with hysterical laughter as he snatched his foot off the gas pedal and trod on the brake, and Angelica was laughing too, though the sudden deceleration had thrown her against the dashboard.

"He must have landed *right on* Crane's skeleton!" Cochran yelled delightedly.

"He'll come up wearing the skull like a hat!" agreed Angelica.

"A *skullcap!*" crowed Cochran, and then he and Angelica were both laughing so hard that he had to slow down still more to keep from weaving in the lane.

"A kamikaze yarmulke," choked Angelica. "Catch up, catch up, you don't want to lose 'em now. And turn the windshield wipers back on."

Cochran's hands were shaking on the wheel now, and the tires thumped over the lane markers as the car drifted back and forth. When he switched the windshield wipers back on, he could see the dim silhouette of Pete Sullivan inside the truck, clambering over the seats.

When Pete seemed to have got up to the driver's seat the truck wobbled visibly and then backfired like a cannon-shot, with two flashes of bright yellow flame at the exhaust pipes by the back wheels.

Then Cochran saw Pete Sullivan's hand wave out of the driver's-side window, and the truck swayed smoothly back and forth in a clearly deliberate S-pattern.

Angelica exhaled. "He's got control," she said softly. "He'll be pulling over real quick."

"Not here," said Cochran, "there's no shoulder." He let himself finally take his eyes off the truck and look around at the landscape. The gray surf still streaked the sea beyond the fence to the right, but at some point they had passed the green forest wall of Golden Gate Park, and now it was low pastel-colored apartment buildings and bungalows that fretted the gray sky to the left. "He'll want to turn inland to find some place we can park," he said, and he clicked his left-turn indicator to give Pete the idea.

Pete steered the blue truck in a careful left turn onto Sloat Boulevard, and then drove slowly through half a dozen residential blocks of old white-stucco houses to the parking lot at the South Sunset Playground.

There were no other cars in the lot as Cochran swung the Granada into the parking space next to the truck, and Angelica was out of the car before he had even come to a full stop. When Cochran turned off the ignition and got out, she was already standing at the opened passenger-side door of the truck. The rain had stopped and the clouds were breaking up in the east, and the mirror lenses of Angelica's sunglasses flashed as she leaned into the truck cab over Mavranos.

"Can you push against Pete's hands with your feet?" she was saying to Mavranos. "Both feet? Good! Open your eyes, Arky, I want to check your pupils." She looked up toward Pete, who was still behind the wheel of the truck. "We'll need to get him to a hospital, stat. He's conscious, with no bleeding from the ears or nostrils, and this isn't a bullet wound, but . . . he *was* knocked out, it *is* a concussion."

She doesn't want to say *possible subdural hematoma,* thought Cochran nervously. Mavranos is probably in shock, and doesn't need to hear that there might be blood leaking inside his skull, lethally pressing against the brain.

Plumtree had climbed out of the back of the car now, and she was leaning on the front fender, blinking around at the lawns and swing sets and the two vehicles. "Did it work?" she asked hoarsely.

"Not a bullet wound?" said Cochran, reluctant to answer Plumtree. He could see that the truck's windshield was starred with cracks radiating from a hole low down on the passenger side. "What is it then?"

Angelica turned her mirror lenses toward him, then held out a fragment of polished white stone. "A bullet hit this statue he had on his dashboard—some kind of Buddha—and part of *it* hit him, to judge by the fragments in his scalp. A glancing blow to the back of the head, above the occipital region." She turned back to Mavranos, whose head Cochran could just see on the truck seat. "Arky," she said. "Open your eyes for me."

"Did it fucking *work?*" Plumtree demanded. "Is Scott Crane alive now?"

Cochran bared his teeth in irritation and pity. "No, Cody. It—failed, I'm sorry."

"I think the truck was heading back to Leucadia," said Pete, who had opened the driver's-side door and had one foot down on the pavement. "I think it would have driven all the way back there, like a horse that knows the way home—if somebody would have filled the gas tank every hour."

Plumtree had taken a wobbling step back across the asphalt. "Did it work?" she asked. "Where's Scott Crane?"

"Radioactive!" Mavranos seemed to say, loudly but in a slurred voice.

"No, Janis," Cochran said. "I'm sorry, but it didn't work." It occurred to him that Plumtree was sounding like a concussion victim herself.

"Look at me," Angelica said to Mavranos.

"You're upside-down," Mavranos said in a high, nasal voice, "but I'll look at you all you want." To a tune that Cochran recognized as some old Elvis Costello song, Mavranos sang, "You better listen to your radio." But he slurred the last word, so that it seemed to be *ray-joe*.

Angelica had jerked back against the open door, her forehead wrinkled above the sunglasses. "You—your pupils are normal," she said uncertainly. "But we've got to get you to a hospital, Arky, you've got a—"

"Bitch broke my nose!" Mavranos braced himself on his elbow and sat up, feeling his face. "Is my traitor sister here?" He blinked at Angelica. "Who the hell are you people? My nose *isn't* broken! Am I—did I do it, am I the king?"

Angelica held out the white stone fragment. "This was a statue of a, a fat Buddha," she said, and Cochran could tell that she was trying to keep her voice level. "Do you—recognize it?"

"Buddha," said Mavranos in his new, high voice, "it's not Buddha, it's Tan Tai, gook god of prosperity. I gave her one like it once, when she was still my loyal half-sister."

Angelica stepped slowly away from the truck, glancing worriedly at Cochran and Plumtree. "Look only at me please," she said to them in a quiet, professional tone. "Pete? Eyes front. We won't be going to a hospital after all, unless I see a deterioration in Arky's vital signs."

Cochran could feel goose bumps rasping the fabric of his damp shirt-sleeves, and not because of the dawn chill. He understood now that a ghost had got punched into Mavranos's head back there; and he wondered if it was one of the ones that had clustered ahead of the truck on the drive back from the ruins at the end of the yacht-club peninsula, or if it was one that Mavranos had been carrying with him all along, like an old intolerable photo in a sealed locket.

To Cochran, Angelica said, "You're a local boy—where is there water nearby? Tamed water, contained water. With—we need to get Arky and me into a boat, very quick."

"A *boat?*" echoed Cochran, trying not to wail in pure bewilderment.

"Okay. Well! Golden Gate Park, I guess. Stow Lake. You can rent boats, I think."

"Close by?" asked Angelica.

"Two or three miles back the way we came."

"It's not—famously *haunted* or anything, is it?"

Cochran rocked his head uncertainly. "There's supposed to be druid stones on the island in the middle of the lake," he said, "and I heard that there were stones from a ruined Spanish monastery around the shore; but my wife and I went looking for this stuff a couple of years ago, and couldn't find any of it. Anyway, no, I've never heard of any hauntings or murders or anything."

Remotely, as if from some previous life, he remembered the picnic he and Nina had unpacked on the Stow Lake island one sunny weekday morning, and how in the bough-shaded solitude at the top of the island hill they had soon forgotten the sandwiches and overturned the wine as they had rolled around on the dewy grass. They had made a sort of bed of their cast-off clothing, and when they had finally collapsed, spent, Nina had said that it had been as if they'd been trying to *climb through* each other.

And now he jumped, for Plumtree had slid her hand up the clinging seat of his wet jeans.

"Can we go?" she asked quietly. "Did they get the dead man back alive again?"

"No," Cochran said, blinking away tears of exhaustion, "Tiffany. It failed. The dead man is—deader than he was before."

Her hand was snatched away, but he didn't look at her to see who she might be now; he just stepped to the side to block her view of Mavranos and said, rapidly, "Remember the little girls we saw on the roof of that clown's house? I think we're in the same sort of situation now. Look only at Angelica. Do you follow me?"

"Mirrors can ricochet," she said bleakly, in the voice he now recognized as Cody's. "I'm looking no higher than the ground."

Angelica gently pressed the truck door closed until it clicked, as if to keep from waking someone up. "You lead the way to this lake," she told Cochran as she pulled open the truck's back door to get in. "And when we get there, you walk ahead of us and buy the tickets or whatever."

"Right." Cochran turned back to the Granada, jerking his head at Plumtree to follow.

"What's left for us?" Plumtree asked dreamily as she got in on the passenger side and Cochran started the engine again. "After this?" Perhaps she was talking to herself.

"Getting drunk," he said anyway, clanking the shift lever into reverse. "What did you think?"

"Oh," she said, nodding. "Right. Of course."

"Boats first."

"To the boats," she said, emptily.

CHAPTER 21

CRESSIDA: . . . he is himself.
PANDARUS: Himself? Alas, poor Troilus, I would he were.
CRESSIDA: So he is.
PANDARUS: Condition, I had gone barefoot to India.
                                    —William Shakespeare,
                                        Troilus and Cressida

At the corner of Stockton and Washington, Kootie had found only the Chinese restaurant he remembered having passed at dawn, next door to the Jade Galore shop; the restaurant wasn't open, and the old man who had been peering into a mirror propped against the restaurant wall was gone now, and the big old gilt-framed mirror too. Someone had even swept up the dead sparrows. Kootie had turned away toward the wet intersection, stepping to the curb and mentally cursing the Chinese woman who had given him the useless message, when he sensed a change in the light from behind him.

And when he turned around, the restaurant was gone.

In its place stood a three-story plaster-fronted building with narrow arched windows. At a wrought-iron gate to an enclosed patio garden, the woman in white stood staring out at him, and behind her he could see the big framed mirror, propped now against a knotty tree stump in the rainy garden. On a white sign over the gateway arch, plain black letters spelled out, PLEASANT BOARDING HOUSE.

Oh, this is magic, Kootie thought, his spine suddenly tingling with a chill that wasn't from the cold rain. I should run away.

Run away to what place, he asked himself bitterly then, that hasn't been conquered? To what people, that haven't been defeated and probably killed?

His breath was hitching and catching in his throat.

The Chinese woman beckoned with constrained urgency, and touched a finger to her lips. Kootie noticed that though she was still draped in white, it was a frail linen robe she was wearing now, and the fabric appeared to be dry.

At least she's offering shelter, he told himself as he shrugged and stepped back across the sidewalk from the edge of the curb. His sneakers squished on the pavement, and he could feel cold water spurting between his toes.

The woman tugged the gate open on hinges that made no sound over the clatter of the rain, and then pushed it closed again after Kootie had stepped through onto the round paving stones laid out across the patio mud. "What is this place?" he whispered to her.

Her face was tense as she shook her head again and pressed her cold lips to his ear. "Later," she breathed, and at least her breath was warm. "Don't wake up the master of the house." As she pulled her face back she nodded out toward the garden without looking that way.

Kootie had to look. He glanced over his shoulder as the woman took his elbow and hurried him toward a pair of windowed doors ahead—but all he saw in the walled garden, aside from the dripping ginger stalks and rose vines on the far side of the rain-stippled puddles, was the tree stump with the mirror leaning against it.

Squinting against the rain, he saw that the stump was a gnarled and hairy old grapevine, a full yard thick, with jagged, chunky outcrops where old canes had been pruned back. A soggy animal fur had been draped around two of the truncated woody limbs as if around shoulders, and to Kootie the bumpy bark between the cane stumps looked, in the moment before the woman pulled him through the doors into a dry, pine-floored hallway, like the whiskery gray face of an aged man.

The woman in the white robe was leading him quickly toward a set of polished black wood stairs that led upward. "What is this place?" Kootie whispered again.

"It's his boardinghouse," she whispered back. He takes in boarders? Kootie thought. "It's not here all the time," she went on, "but it's always here on January seventeenth, for people with the right kind of eyes—and with this bad checkmate rain, the place would certainly have been here today in any case—or else this rain couldn't have happened except on this day, St. Sulpice's Day. If you're a fugitive, you're welcome here." They had reached a shadowy upstairs corridor with narrow gray-shining windows along one wall, and she led Kootie by the hand to an open interior door.

"Are you hungry?" she asked. "I've cooked you a king's breakfast."

Kootie could smell some kind of spicy roasting meat on the musty air. "Hungry as a bedbug," he said, quoting an old Solville line that had somehow evolved from *Don't let the bedbugs bite.*

"Me too!" she said with a breathless laugh as she stepped into the dimly lit room. "This Death-card rain will bring out a *lot* of fugitive places in the city, like toadstools, that won't be there anymore after the sun comes out again. But the eating is best here."

Kootie followed her into the room, and quickly stepped across onto a knitted rug so as not to drip rain water onto the polished wood floor. There were no windows in the room, but flames in oil lamps on the walls threw a soft illumination across dark old tapestries and a battered white make-up table and a huge, canopied bed. A black-brick fireplace took up most of the far wall, and though there were no logs on the grate, a tiny brass brazier stood on the broad hearthstone, with coals glowing under a grill draped with strips of sizzling, aromatic meat. A basket of thick black bread slices stood on a carpet nearby.

"The Loser's Bar is surely out there somewhere today," the woman said as she tossed her head back, freeing her long black hair from the linen hood, "serving pointless seafood today—though they might as well be serving cooked sandals and baseball caps, for all the good it can do anyone on a day like this."

Her hair was lustrously dry now, and Kootie wondered how she could have dried it, and changed her clothes, and prepared this food, in the few minutes since he had seen her in the long alley off the Street of Gamblers. And he remembered how her silhouette had seemed for a moment to be the knobby round figure that had shown up briefly on the motel television.

I don't care, he thought. I can take care of myself. He saw a bottle of dark wine by the mirror on the make-up table, and he was able to cross to it and pick it up without stepping on bare floor.

The label just said, BITIN DOG.

"I shouldn't," he said uncertainly, "be eating . . . meat." Or drinking alcohol, he thought.

"Here's a dry robe for you," she said. "You don't want to meet the lord of this house in those clothes anyway. Take them off and get warm." She looked at the bottle in his hand and smiled at him. "You can have a drink of that . . . after. It's the wine of forgetfulness, you know. And it's all right—*it* you can swallow with impunity, as much as you like, the whole bottle." She knelt in front of him and began prising loose the knots in his soaked sneaker laces. She looked up at him. "You'd like some of that, wouldn't you? Impunity?"

"God," said Kootie softly, "yes." *After,* he thought. After what?

"The peppered venison is still raw in the middle," she said. "We can eat it, too, after."

"Okay," he said, and began unbuttoning his shirt with shaking fingers. He hoped the cut over his ribs wasn't bleeding through the bandage.

Fleetingly to his mind came an image of himself buttoning his shirt as he stumbled sleepily out of his Solville bedroom, sniffing onions and eggs and coffee on jasmine-scented morning air, yawning and replying *As a bedbug!* to Angelica's cheery *Are you hungry?*

Goodbye to all that, he thought despairingly.

The boathouse in Golden Gate Park was locked up and the boats were inert and chained to the dock when the five bedraggled figures trudged across the lake lawn to the shuttered rental window, but the two teen-aged park employees who'd been banging around inside agreed to open early after Angelica made Cochran offer them a hundred dollars; and by the time the sun was coming up over the cypresses, two electric boats were buzzing slowly out across the glassy surface of Lake Stow—Pete and Angelica and the distracted Mavranos in one, and Cochran and Plumtree closely pacing them in the other.

The boats were small, with not quite enough room on the padded benches for three people to sit comfortably. A toggle switch on the right side by the steering wheel turned the electric motor of each boat on and off, and with no windshield the long flat hood was a sort of table. Cochran wished they could have stopped to get beer—in addition to his hundred dollars, he had paid twenty-six dollars for the minimum full hour for two boats, and it looked as though it would take the tiny engines the whole hour to coax the boats all the way around the wooded island in the middle of the lake. The unrippled water ahead was studded with ducks and seagulls who all might have been asleep. Cochran remembered the dead birds that had fallen out of the sky after Crane had turned into a skeleton, and so he was relieved when a couple of these ducks awoke and went flapping away across the lake, their wing tips slapping rings in the water like skipped stones.

The boat with Angelica and Pete and Mavranos in it buzzed along at a dog-paddle pace only two yards to the right of Cochran's elbow, which hung out over the low gunwale of the boat he shared with Plumtree.

"Angie, shouldn't we be going the other way around?" asked Pete Sullivan in a near-whisper. "This is clockwise, not . . . windshield."

"I wish we could," Angelica muttered. "But that's an evasion measure, we don't dare—we might wind up losing the wrong one." She shook her head. "God, this is slow! The motor on this boat sounds like a *sewing machine*."

Cochran thought of the woman who had been called Ariachne in the version of *A Tale of Two Cities* that he had read on the plane home from Paris a week and a half ago—the woman who sewed into her fabrics the names of people who were to be beheaded on the guillotine.

Angelica sighed and squared her shoulders. "What's your name?" she said now, speaking to Mavranos. Her voice was clear in the still air.

"Ray-Joe Pogue," Mavranos said quietly. "I'm not okay, am I? I remember now—I fell off of Hoover Dam. I was blind, and a man told me it was the *water* below me, Lake Mead, but he lied. It was the *other* side of the dam below me, the tailrace, the power station roof—way, way down, with a hard, hard landing."

"It's the water below you now, though," Angelica said gently. "You can see it, can't you?" She dipped her hand in the water, lifted a palmful and let it trickle back into the lake.

"I'm seeing two of everything," said Mavranos. He looked at Angelica. "There are two bulls in your glasses! Did you have animals in your glasses before? You do now." He was visibly shivering.

"Now you're seeing as you should be seeing," said Angelica. "The pairs will get farther apart—like bars in a prison—until you can escape between them." She smiled. "But you should lose some weight! Tell me how your sister betrayed you."

Cochran remembered Angelica's description of a conventional honoring-of-the-dead ritual. Clearly she was trying now to lift the ghost away from Mavranos's mind, over this giant cup of relatively transparent water so that the ghost wouldn't . . . *fixate*. And, in asking the ghost to talk about itself, she was apparently trying to get it to relax its psychic claws out of *Mavranos's* mind and memories. It probably helped that Mavranos's mind was still concussed and disorganized—that must have been why she'd been in such a hurry to get here.

"Nardie Dinh," came the high, nasal voice from Mavranos's mouth. "*Bernardette* Dinh. She was my half-sister, our dad married a Vietnamese woman after he divorced my mom. I was supposed to become the king, at the succession in '90, and Nardie was supposed to be my queen. I kept her a virgin, until I should take the crown, the crown of the American West . . . but she rebelled against me, she was ungrateful for what I had made her into, with diet and discipline and exposure to the gods behind the Major Arcana tarot cards . . . she *killed* the woman I had placed her with, *escaped* me. Nardie threw in her lot with the Scott Crane faction—"

All at once, with a chill, Cochran remembered Mavranos saying back in Solville that he had once killed a man at Hoover Dam.

"—and she hit me in the nose, broke my nose, five days before Easter. Swole up, black eyes. I couldn't become the king with the injury, and for sure there wasn't time for it to heal. I drove out to the dam to stop the succession, use magic to throw it off for another twenty years . . . and she sent—this man!—" Mavranos's hand touched his face. "—to kill me."

Mavranos's head rocked back to stare into the overhanging alder branches against the sky. "It's true," he said in a harsher voice, "that I killed you. On purpose, knowing what I was doing—because you would have killed my friends, if I hadn't. But Nardie didn't want me to do it."

He inhaled hitchingly, and when he spoke again it was in the nasal voice: "But she thanked you for doing it. I was aware of that." And Mavranos's natural voice said, "It's true."

Angelica's mouth was open and she was frowning, as if she wanted to convey a message to Mavranos without letting the Pogue ghost hear; and Cochran wondered if Mavranos had ruined Angelica's plan by awakening now and conversing with the ghost; but Mavranos was speaking again in his own voice:

"Ray-Joe Pogue, the bars are nearly wide enough apart for you to leave, to jump, and it *is* water below you, this time. I've carried you, in guilt, for five years, nearly—and Nardie has too, I've seen it pinch her face when people talk about . . . *family.* I bet we've both thought of you every day, your death has been a, like a bad smell that I can't get rid of, that I notice just when I've started to forget about it and have a nice time." Mavranos yawned, or else Ray-Joe Pogue did. "Before you go free," Mavranos said, "can you forgive us?"

"Do you want that?" came the other voice from his throat.

Angelica dipped her hand into the water again.

Mavranos inhaled to be able to reply. "Yes. We do both want that— very badly."

"Mess with the bull, you get the horns," said the high voice. "It's enough to know that you do want it."

Mavranos sighed deeply, and his head rocked forward—and Angelica whipped her hand across and slapped him in the face with a handful of water.

"*Now,* Arky!" she said urgently. "What's my name? Where were you born? Who's president of the United States?"

Mavranos was spitting. "Angelica Sullivan, goddammit. Muscoy, San

Bernardino County, California, in 1955, okay? And William Jefferson Airplane Clinton.''

Both boats had stalled in the water.

''Get these boats moving out of here,'' said Angelica sharply, ''the ghost is off him, but it'll be a standing wave here for a while. Everybody lean out and paddle, if you have to.''

Cochran flipped the toggle switch on his boat off and on again, and the motor resumed its buzzing and his boat surged slowly ahead of Angelica's until she copied his move and got hers running again too.

Pete Sullivan exhaled as though he'd been holding his breath. ''Good work, Angie.''

Angelica pushed her hair back from her face, and Cochran saw that she was sweating. ''He might have forgiven you, Arky,'' she panted, ''but I had to swat him off right then—he had let go of your mind for a moment, in something like real serenity, but he might have gripped on again at any moment, and clung. It would have killed you.'' She looked around, and spun the steering wheel to avoid tangling the boat in the arching branches of an oak tree that had fallen from the island bank into the water. ''Sorry, if I was too hasty.''

Mavranos cleared his throat and spat mightily out past the bow. ''I'll ... get along without it,'' he said hoarsely. ''Damn, I can still taste his ghost. Motor oil and and *Brylcreem.*''

Plumtree spoke up from beside Cochran. ''You want people to *forgive* you?''

Cochran steered the boat ponderously out toward the middle of the water. ''Some people want that, Cody.''

''I'm Janis. I'd rather buy a new tire than drive on one with a patch.''

The boats were trundling around the east end of the island in the middle of the lake. Seagulls wheeled above a waterfall that poured over tall stone shelves on the island, and closer at hand Cochran saw some kind of Chinese pavilion on the shore, among the green flax stalks that crowded right down into the water. At the top of the island hill he could see the trees around the clearing where he and Nina had made love, so terribly long ago.

''We're going to watch you closely, Arky,'' said Angelica. ''If your pupils start to act funny, or your pulse, or if your speech gets slurred or disconnected—'waxing and waning mentation'—then you *are* going into a hospital, and we can do our level best to keep you masked in there. But you've—right now you'd be much better off out of such a place.''

Mavranos nodded grimly, touching the cut in the back of his scalp. His hair was spiky with bourbon as well as blood, for Angelica had sterilized it with a few hasty splashes from a pint bottle Mavranos had kept in his glove compartment, promising to put a proper bandage on it as soon as the wound had been "thoroughly aired out." Presumably it had been, now.

"Nardie Dinh gave me that statue I had on the dashboard," Mavranos said. "She probably did mean something by it, even after all these years, though she loves me like a—like a brother. Damn sure she didn't mean it to be shot into my head." He looked at Angelica. "But it was. And I think you mean ghosts would be attracted to me in a hospital . . . now."

"There are a lot of scared, lonely, hungry ghosts hanging around in hospitals," Angelica said, staring ahead. The boats had rounded the eastern end of the island, and were now buzzing irresolutely in the direction of a double-arched stone bridge.

Mavranos laughed weakly. "Keep your eyes on the course, by all means," he said. "Lose control of this torpedo and we're liable to plow right up onto the bank. What I mean is, I'm *particularly* vulnerable right now, aren't I?"

"*Yes,*" said Angelica. She gave Plumtree a haggard stare. "What did you mean, Janis, about a new tire?"

"Oh, I meant like a . . . relationship that's been . . . fractured," Plumtree said. "I wouldn't try to patch it up, I'd just move on and meet somebody new, somebody who didn't yet have any disappointments with me."

"Or cobble up a new personality out of some of the unused lumber of your soul," Cochran said tiredly, "one that hasn't even met the other person yet. Fresh start all around."

Plumtree nodded. "My father hath a power; inquire of him, and learn to make a body of a limb."

That had sounded like Shakespeare. "Valorie?" Cochran asked.

"Janis," Plumtree said, glancing at him impatiently. "I told you that, Sid."

A lot of the tall oaks had fallen into the water on this side of the island, and the interior wood at the split stumps was raw and pale, and the leaves on the water-spanning branches were still green; clearly these trees had been felled in the storms that had battered the whole California coast two weeks ago, at dawn on New Year's Day . . . when Scott Crane had been killed.

"Don't say anything specific," Plumtree said hastily, "about why we're here, or you *will* have Valorie in the boat with you. But even in what we were trying to do, I—I wanted *him* to be *alive* again, but I didn't want his *forgiveness*. I didn't want one bit more of his attention on me than would have been necessary! And even that, Valorie would have taken." There were tears in her eyes, and she let Cochran put his arm around her.

"Not your flop," he said.

She buried her face in the shoulder of his damp windbreaker, and when his hand slid down to her waist his palm was on her bare, cool skin where Nina's sweater had hiked up away from her jeans; and he found himself remembering Tiffany's hand caressing him half an hour earlier—and the steamy sweater smelled of Nina's rose-scented perfume, blended once again here with the wild odors of pine sap and lake water, and for just a reflexive moment, before instant shame actually pulled his lips back from his teeth, he wondered if the rain had ruined the cassette in his shirt pocket.

None of them spoke as the boats buzzed quietly under the island-side arch of the old stone bridge. Cochran noticed one, then several, then dozens of black turtles perched motionless on the unnaturally horizontal branches of the felled trees—but as soon as he started to watch for them, all the dark ovals he focussed on proved to be pinecones.

He lifted his left arm from around Plumtree so that he could steer the boat with that hand; his right hand, with the ivy-leaf mark on the back of it, he stuffed into the pocket of his windbreaker.

To the left, beside the park road, a particularly big redwood tree had fallen this way across the lakeside footpath, and a segment as broad as the path had been sawed out of the six-foot-thick log so that strollers and bicyclists could pass unimpeded. Perhaps the tree was too heavy to move, and would stay there forever as a randomly placed wall, while its water-arching branches would eventually be overgrown by ivy and form a sort of new, hollow bank. After a while, like the cemetery construction on the yacht-club peninsula, it might look like part of the original plan.

With that thought Cochran looked ahead—and at last saw the carved stones of the Spanish monastery.

They were set low into the lakeside mud as an irregular segmented coping between the park grass and the water, each placed so that a broken-stone face was turned upward; only from this vantage point, low and out on the water, could the fretted and fluted carved sides be seen.

"Nina and I didn't search from out in a boat," he said wonderingly. When Angelica gave him a weary, questioning look, he went on, "There's the stones from the old monastery—from here you can see what they are."

Mavranos blinked ahead uncomprehendingly. "What are they?" He had still been unconscious when Cochran had mentioned them before.

"William Randolph Hearst bought a medieval Spanish monastery," Cochran said, quoting what Nina had told him, "and he had it dismantled and shipped to America to reassemble over here—but the crates and plans burned up, and nobody knew how to put the building back together again. And after a while the park maintenance guys began using the stones for . . . odd little landscaping projects, like *that*." He pointed ahead, at the half-submerged bits of forgotten pillars and porticoes.

"And you said there are druid stones on the island," said Pete Sullivan. "Maybe the monastery stones *counter* those, balance 'em—net zero."

"A monastery building would have been formally blessed," Mavranos muttered, nodding. "Sanctified."

"I'm glad you were along," Angelica told Cochran. "This lake *was* a perfectly balanced place to shake off the ghost."

"Not the job those stones thought they'd have," Mavranos went on, "when they were carved up so pretty, I bet—just sitting here in the water, not even looking different from plain old fieldstones to anybody walking by 'em. But there's this purpose they can serve. Even broken. *Because* they're broken."

Again Cochran thought of walls made of chance-fallen trees, and stairs and benches and pavements made of scavenged pieces of derelict cemetery marble.

"There's the dock," said Pete, pointing ahead and to the right. "Our tour's up. Where to now? Back to the Star Motel, see if Kootie's waiting for us there?"

"Not yet," said Angelica. "And not in the truck with Crane's skeleton in it. We—"

Plumtree jumped in the seat beside Cochran. "His *skeleton's* in the truck? How did he—" She blinked around. "What? What scared Janis?"

Cochran turned to her, wondering if he was about to summon Tiffany here, and if so, what he'd tell *her*. "Crane's skeleton is in the truck, Cody."

She blinked at him. Then, "Fuck me!" she said, and in spite of himself Cochran smiled at the idea that he might take the exclamation as evidence of Tiffany's presence; but in fact he could see that this was still Cody. "I'm still *on?*" she said angrily. "How come *I'm* the one that gets to stay with all the horrible flops lately? His *skeleton?* Goddammit, Valorie's supposed to take the intolerable stuff!"

"I guess you can tolerate more than you imagine," said Cochran gently.

"They say that God won't hit you with more than you can handle," said Mavranos in a faint, shaky voice, possibly to himself. "Like, if He made you so you can just take a hundred pounds per square inch, He won't give you a hundred and one."

"We're still too hot," Angelica went on. "Magically, I mean. There's been a lot of fresh—" Her breath caught in her throat. "—fresh blood spilled, this morning. I think plain *compasses* will point at us for a while after all this stuff—and we can't be certain we haven't been followed, either. On the drive down here, we were all looking ahead at the truck, not back. If Kootie *is* at the motel, he'll wait for us, he's got a key. And I guess he's . . . *the king,* now. He'll have the protections that come with the office." She looked around among the trees at the the anonymous pastel Hondas and Nissans that had begun to drive slowly past on the park road. "We should drive somewhere, aimless, watching behind, and just sit for an hour or so. Give ourselves time to fall back to our ground states."

"I'm a, a *citizen* of the ground state," said Plumtree. "And our— *community hall*—is a bar. I need a drink like a Minnie needs a Mickey."

"The truck can go where it likes," Cochran declared. "The Ford is going to the first bar we find."

"I'd be interested in finding something to chase that cabernet with," ventured Pete.

"I *don't think,*" said Angelica judiciously, "that I can stay sane for very long, right now, without a drink, myself." She sighed and clasped her elbows. "Arky, I guess you can have one, but you'd better stay sober. Doctor's orders."

Mavranos didn't seem to have heard any of the discussion. "But can we really imagine," he went on quietly, "that He'd give you anything less than ninety-nine-point-nine?"

Angelica frowned at Mavranos's disjointed rambling, probably thinking about *waxing and waning mentation.* "If Kootie's at the motel," she said again, absently, "he'll wait for us. And he'll be safe. He's the king now."

When he had tugged off his shirt and jeans and kicked his soaked sneakers heedlessly away across the gleaming floor, the woman had kissed Kootie, her arms around his neck and her robe open on nothing but bare, hot skin against his cold chest. Her tongue had slid across his teeth like an electric shock.

They had fallen across the quilt on the huge, canopied bed, and Kootie had been feverishly trying to free his hands to pull the robe off of her and tug his own damp jockey shorts off as she kissed his neck and chest—when he'd heard what she had been whispering.

"Give me you," she'd been saying hoarsely, "you're not a virgin—
fill me up—you're so big—you can spare more than I can take—and
not near die."

Die? he had thought—and then her teeth had begun gently scoring
the skin over the taut muscle at the side of his neck.

If she had been drawing any blood at all it had been from no more
than a scratch, and the sensation had been only pleasurable . . .

But he had suddenly been aware that his psychic attention and self
was wide open and strainingly extended, and that with all the strength
of her own mind she was trying to *gnaw off a piece of his soul.*

*—In an instant's flash of intolerable memory he was again duct-taped
into a seat in a minivan that had been driven up inside a moving truck
in Los Angeles—"a boat in a boat"—while a crazy one-armed man
with a hunting knife was stabbing at his ribs, trying to cut out his soul,
and consume it—*

Abruptly the room seemed to tilt, and grow suddenly darker and hot-
ter, and he was unreasoningly sure that he was about to fall bodily into
her furnace mouth, which in this moment of virtiginous nightmare panic
seemed to have become the gaping black fireplace below his feet.

He felt himself sliding—

And with all the psychic strength that the events of this terrible morning had bequeathed to him, he lashed out, with such force that he was
sure he must have burst a blood vessel in his head.

He hadn't moved at all, physically, and only a second had passed,
when he realized that her skin was impossibly cold and that her bare
breasts were still—she was not breathing.

He tugged his arms out from under her chilly weight and scrambled
off the bed. Sobbing and shaking, he clumsily pulled his jeans and shirt
on, and he was thrusting his feet back into his sodden sneakers, when
the hallway door was snatched open.

An old woman was standing silhouetted in the doorway.

"Call nine-one-one," Kootie blubbered, "I think she's—"

"She's dead, child," the old woman said sternly. "Both the telephones downstairs are still ringing themselves off their hooks with their
poor magnets shaking, and the god's big mirror has got a crack right
across it. She's dead and flung bodily right over the spires of India like
a cannonball. What-all did the poor woman want, one little bit of the
real you, and you couldn't spare it? Child, you don't know your own
strength." She shook her head. "He can't meet you now, with or without the humble-pie breakfast, the wine and the venison. Later, and probably not affording to be as polite as it would have been now. You've
clouded yourself beyond his sight here today."

Kootie cuffed the tears from his eyes and blinked up at her—and then clenched his teeth against a wail of pure dismay. The figure scowling down at him was the old woman he and his parents had seen so many times on the magically tuned black-and-white television. Now he could see that her eyes were of different colors, one brown and one blue.

"I'm Mary Ellen Pleasant," she told him. "You may as well call me Mammy Pleasant, like everybody else. Now, boy, don't you fret about what you've done here, bad though it damn well is—hers won't be the first dead body I've disposed of in secret. Right now you get your clothes in order, and come down and talk to me in the kitchen."

She stepped back out into the hall, mercifully leaving the door open. As her footsteps receded away along the wooden floor outside, Kootie stood up. Without looking toward the nearly naked body on the bed, he crossed to the make-up table and picked up the bottle of Bitin Dog wine.

You'd like some of that, wouldn't you? he remembered the woman saying. *Impunity?*

The humble-pie breakfast . . .

Cochran had said, "Couldn't have asked for a better place," and swung the Granada across momentarily empty oncoming lanes into the uneven parking lot of a bar-and-restaurant that seemed to be a renovated cannery from the turn of the century, the walls all gray wood and rusty corrugated iron. Over the door nearest where he parked was a sign that read THE LOSER'S BAR, but Plumtree pointed out a sign over the main building: SEAFOOD BOHEMIA.

"Fine," Cochran said as they left the car unlocked and hobbled to the bar door, "we can have bohemian seafood for lunch, if they take plastic here."

The dusty blue Suburban was out in the center divider lane of Masonic Avenue, its left blinker light flashing.

Cochran plodded up the wooden steps, hiking himself along with his hand on the wet wrought-iron rail, and he held the bar door open for Plumtree.

She took one step into the dim interior, and then stopped and looked back over her shoulder at him. "Sid," she said blankly, "this place—"

He put one hand on her shoulder and stepped in past her.

The mirror-studded disco ball was turning over the sand-strewn dance floor, but again there was no one dancing. The air still smelled of candle wax, but with a strong accompaniment of fish-reek this time instead of mutton. Two men in rumpled business suits, conceivably the same men as before, stood at the bar and banged the cup of bar dice on the wet, polished wood.

The dark-haired waitress in the long skirt smiled at them and waved toward a booth near the door.

"We shouldn't stay," whispered Cochran. He was still holding the door open, and he glanced nervously back out at the car and the parking lot and the Suburban, which was now turning into the lot.

"You think if you go in and shut the door, we'll walk out and be on Rosecrans again?" asked Plumtree. "Down in Bellflower?"

"It's possible," he said, his voice unsteady. "If it's possible for this place to be *here* at all."

"Wait in the car, if you like." She stepped away from his hand, into the dimness of the bar. "I'll try to sneak you out a beer from time to time. *I* need a *drink.*" She was shaking, but clearly not because of the weird bar.

"—No," he said. "I'm with you."

They both stepped inside, and as the door squeaked shut behind them they scuffed across the sandy wooden floor to the indicated booth and sat down, with Plumtree facing the front door. Cochran noticed two aluminum crutches propped on the seat of the booth beyond theirs, but neither he nor Plumtree were inclined to be peering around at their surroundings, and they just humbly took the two leather-bound menus the waitress handed them.

"Two Budweisers," said Plumtree. She was breathing deeply, like someone hoping not to be sick.

"And I'll have two Coorses, please," said Cochran. "Oh, and there are three more in our party," he added, holding up three fingers. The waitress nodded, perhaps understanding, and strode away back to the bar, her long skirt swirling the patterns of sand on the floor.

Plumtree had opened her menu, and now pried a slip of paper from a clip on the inside cover. She frowned. "Do you remember if the specials were all fish things, before?"

"No, I don't," said Cochran. "I ordered off the printed menu that time."

"I didn't look at the specials either, then." She read, "*Barbunya, Morina, Levrek*—mullet, cod, bass—this is all fish. And it seems more Middle Eastern now, than Greek. If it was Greek before."

"Then maybe this *isn't* the same place, because I do remember you saying it was—" he began; then he paused, for she had flipped the specials sheet over and then pushed it across the table toward him.

On the back of the sheet, in his own handwriting in ballpoint ink, was written: CODY, JANIS, TIFFANY, VALERIE, HIM. The E in VALERIE had been crossed out, with an O written in above.

"Do you remember writing that?" she asked.

In spite of everything that had happened to him during this last two and a half weeks, Cochran's first impulse was to look around at the other people in the bar, to see who had set up this hoax; then he sagged, remembering how random and unconsidered had been their route to this place today.

"Sure," he said dejectedly. "It was only a week ago, and I wasn't that drunk." His heart was thudding in his chest, and he stared at the paper and wondered if he was more angry or scared. "I guess this is more . . . *magic,* huh."

Plumtree tapped the word HIM. "I can't," she said, "ever have *him* come on again." She touched her face and her throat. "Do you see these cuts? Razor nicks! I think *he* was *shaving.*" Behind Cochran the front door squeaked.

He opened his mouth, but Plumtree had looked past him, toward the front door, and now held up her hand to cut him off. "The rest of the losers have arrived," she said loudly; then she leaned toward him and whispered quickly, "I think he *had* to!"

Mavranos and Pete and Angelica slid into the booth from Cochran's side, so that Pete Sullivan was now crowding him against Plumtree.

"Scott's skeleton is all busted to shit," said Mavranos.

"Valorie says Pete jumped on it," said Plumtree.

"Somebody should bury it," said Mavranos, "back at the Leucadia compound."

"You can do that yourself, Arky," said Angelica. "Oh hell—a tequila *añejo,* neat, with a Corona chaser," she said to the waitress, who had walked up with a tray and begun to shift full beer glasses onto the table, "and a—Coors Light, Pete?—for this gentleman, please. Arky? Dr. Angelica Elizalde says you can have one beer."

Mavranos heaved a windy sigh. "A club soda for me," he said. " 'That which I greatly feared hath come upon me.' "

"What, sobriety?" said Pete Sullivan. "I don't think that's a decision you should make right after a concussion."

"At Spider Joe's trailer, out in the desert north of Las Vegas in 1990," Arky said, "the Fool archetype took possession of everybody in the room, except me. *I* knocked the tarot cards onto the floor, broke the spell. I couldn't . . . have a personality in my head that wasn't me."

Angelica touched his scarred brown hand. "He's gone, Arky," she said. "I'd tell you he was inhabiting one of those ducks on that lake now, if I wasn't sure he went right on past India."

Mavranos nodded, though Cochran got the feeling that Angelica hadn't addressed the man's real concern. "I'll stick with water," Mavranos said. "It probably should be salt water, for the *leaching* properties."

"Carthage cocktail," came a gravelly voice from the table behind Cochran, away from the front door. "In the winter and spring, surfers taste fresh water in the San Francisco Bay sometimes, from the Sacramento River."

Cochran shifted around to see the speaker, and at this point he was only a little surprised to recognize the black dwarf who had made his way on crutches out of the Mount Sabu bar down in the Bellflower district of Los Angeles, when Cochran and Plumtree had been . . . had been here, there; and Cochran recalled now that when the dwarf had opened the door then the draft from outside had smelled of the sea.

The little man's aluminum crutches stood on the seat next to him, the cushioned ends leaning against the electric light sconce over his gleaming bald head. An iron wok sat incongruously on the table in front of him, red-brown with rust and filled to near the rim with a translucent reddish liquid that seemed to be wine.

Cochran had braced his right hand behind Plumtree's shoulders, and now the black man was staring at the back of Cochran's hand. He met Cochran's eyes and exposed uneven teeth in a smile, then rang the rim of the wok with an oversized spoon. Ripples fretted the surface of the wine, for that's what it was—Cochran could smell it now, a dry domestic Pinot Noir or Zinfandel.

Plumtree on his right and Pete on his left were leaning forward, leaving Cochran to talk to the stranger.

"My name is Thutmose?" said the black man. "Known as Thutmose the Utmos'? This year the surfers haven't tasted fresh water yet." He ladled some of the wine into a glass with the spoon. "Do you think they will?"

Cochran had already gulped down half of one of his beers, and he could feel the dizzying pressure of it in his head. "No," he said, thinking of the failure at dawn. "I reckon they won't, this year."

"That's the wrong attitude," said Thutmose. "Will you drink some of my wine? It's decent store-bought Zinfandel right now, and it *could* be . . . *sacramento.*"

"No, I've—I'm working on beer," said Cochran. His neck was aching from being twisted around toward the dwarf, and he was irritably aware that the others at his table were now talking among themselves.

Thutmose seemed disconcerted. "Do you know where Zinfandel

came from?'' he snapped. The whites of his glittering eyes were as red as the wine.

"What, originally?'' Cochran closed his tired, stinging eyes for a moment, then opened them. "Sure, a guy named Count Haraszthy brought it to California from Hungary in the 1850s.'' He was trying to keep track of both conversations—behind him he heard Angelica say, "I picked up the lighter, but the two silver dollars were just gone.'' And Plumtree helpfully said, "Well, the lighter's worth a lot more than two bucks.''

"It showed up in the eastern Mediterranean in 1793,'' declared Thutmose, "right after the revolutionaries up in Paris desecrated Notre Dame cathedral—they deliberately stored *grain* there, in the place that had already been holy to the vine for thousands of years before any Romans laid eyes on the Seine River—and then they—filled the gutters of Paris!—with the blood of the aristocrats who had been using the holy wine's debt-payer properties too freely. 'It is not for kings and princes to drink wine, lest they drink, and forget the law.' Proverbs 13. So the Zinfandel grape all at once appeared and started growing wild in all the god's old places, in Thebes, and Smyrna, and Thrace, and Magnesia. The Yugoslavian Plavac Mali grape is a strayed cousin of it. And the disrespected vine took its new Zinfandel castle right across the water to America, tossing the bad root-lice behind it like the Romans sowed salt in Carthage. A *mondard* of the *new* world now.''

Halfway through the little man's speech, long before even the word *mondard*, Cochran had nervously realized that Thutmose was somehow involved in the season's Fisher King contentions, and that he must be here at the Loser's Bar for reasons related to those of Cochran's party; clearly too the dwarf had at least guessed that Cochran and his friends had been concerned in it.

As if confirming Cochran's thought, Thutmose said, "You're the people who had the red truck, and the undead king.''

But it's all over now, Baby Blue, Cochran thought helplessly. The red truck's blue now, and the undead king is deader than a mackerel. Kootie will be king now, and Kootie isn't here.

"Do you know what *sin-fan-dayl* means, in classical Greek?'' Thutmose went on, in a wheedling tone now. "'A sieve, washed clean and bright and joyous in the noonday sun.' Drink the sacramental Zinfandel and *become* the sieve—all your loves fall right through you to the god, and you're cleansed and cheered in the process—you're refreshed, even under the harsh eye of the sun. 'Give wine unto those that be of heavy hearts.'" The little man was practically declaiming now, and Cochran hoped Plumtree hadn't heard the bit about the eye of the sun.

Again the dwarf rang the wok with his spoon, and it dawned on Cochran that Thutmose wanted him to acknowledge the rusty bowl, refer to it.

It's a half-ass Grail, Cochran thought suddenly; and Thutmose is some sort of near-miss, fugitive, underworld Fisher King—crippled by God-knows-what unhealing injury, and clearly hoping for some kind of vindication, some salvific Wedding-at-Cana miracle, from Dionysus. This terrible New Year has probably brought hundreds like him to San Francisco. And now he's seen the "Dionysus badge" on my hand—maybe he even saw it when we were in this place back in L.A., and he's somehow found me again.

At the Li Po bar on Sunday, Mavranos had told Cochran how Kootie had asked the wrong question when first confronted with the red Suburban truck—*Why is it the color of blood?* instead of *Who does it serve?*

"Why," asked Cochran gently now, "is your bowl the color of blood?"

Thutmose the Utmos' sighed, and seemed to shrink still further. "When he was a baby-god, Dionysus was laid in a winnowing fan. You're being a dog in the manger." He shook his head, and there were tears in his red eyes and the word *dog* seemed to hang in the air. "It's rust, what did you think? Goddammit, I'm an ex-junkie, trying to turn my life around! I used wine to get off the smack, and now I just want to find the god's own forgiveness wine." He tapped the wok with the spoon again, miserably. "A heroin dealer used it to mix up batches, step on the product. When it got too rusty for him to use, he gave it to me. I scraped some of the red crust off and cooked it up in a spoon, and I slammed it, even though I was sure I'd get lockjaw. It did do something bad to my legs—but I didn't die, and this red bowl kept me well for months."

"None of us here can do anything for each other," interjected Plumtree. Cochran saw that she had shifted around and was listening in. "If we could, we'd be in a place called the Glad Boys Bar, or something, not here." She slid out of the booth now and stood up. "Come talk to me over by the phones," she told Cochran.

Glad to get away from the unhappy dwarf, Cochran got up and followed her across the sandy floor.

Cochran hadn't heard the front door squeak while he'd been listening to Thutmose, but there were a lot of people in the long barroom now, though they were all talking in low whispers. Cochran thought they looked like people tumbled together at random in an emergency shelter—he saw men in dinner jackets or denim or muddy camouflage, women in worn jogging suits and women in inappropriately gay sundresses—and none of them looked youthful and they all looked as if they'd been up all night. Cochran reflected that he and his friends must look the same way.

As he and Plumtree passed the bar, Cochran saw a man pay for a drink by shaking yellow powder out of a little cloth bag—and before the lady bartender carefully swept the powder up, Cochran was able to see that it was some kind of grain, perhaps barley.

We walked in here through a door in Los Angeles once, he thought, and now through a door in San Francisco—how old *is* this place, and from what other places has that door opened, perhaps on leather hinges, over the centuries and even millennia? Boston, London? Rome, Babylon, Ur?

Cochran was relieved to see that the pay telephones were the same modern push-button machines he and Plumtree had used to call Strubie the Clown.

"Listen," said Plumtree hoarsely. "What we've got to do? Is escape."

"Okay," said Cochran. "From what? To where?"

"You remember," said Plumtree in a near-whisper, "who the *he* on the menu-specials paper referred to, right? After he was on in '89, I ached in all my joints, and had nosebleeds. And in Holy Week of '90, when he tried to win the kinghood in that poker game on Lake Mead, he was on for a day and a half, and I had a nervous breakdown so I can't remember *what* I *felt* like. But this time, ending yesterday morning, he had me for almost three full days, and I could hardly even walk, yesterday and today." She touched her jaw and the corner of her mouth. "And I swear he *shaved* while he was in this body!"

Cochran winced, and nodded. "Probably meaning—like you said—that he had to."

"Right. He's not a ghost, he's not dead—he imposes his natural form on this body when he's in it for any length of time, so it's . . . like I'm taking steroids. I grow fucking *whiskers*, and I'm sure he screws up my period." She was blinking back tears, and Cochran realized that she was frightened, and possibly struggling to stay on for this flop. "I think if he was to occupy me for too long—" She slapped her chest. "—this would turn all the way into a man's body—a clone of *his* body, the one that got smashed when it fell partly *on* me, on the Soma pavement in 1969."

Cochran spread his hands. "What can you *do?*"

"God, I don't know. Figure out a way to *kill* him, don't tell Janis. Hide out, in the meantime, and stay away from that Kootie kid—*he* is very interested in that Kootie kid."

"We can go to my house," Cochran said. "You remember it, you were on when we were there last week."

She pushed back her ragged blond bangs and stared at him. "You don't mind living with a murderess? Or even maybe one day a mur-der*er*?"

Cochran stared into Cody's frightened, squinting eyes—and admitted to himself that in these last eight nightmare days this rough-edged young woman had become, for better or worse, a part of his life. The jumpy infatuation he had initially felt for Janis was gone, but at this moment he couldn't imagine a life for himself that didn't abrasively and sur-prisingly include Janis Cordelia Plumtree.

"I think," he said with a weary grin, "we're partners, by now."

"Shake on it."

He shook her cold hand.

"Let's hit the road," she said.

"Okay. But let's have lunch first." He smiled. "And then you can help me get rid of a stolen car in my back yard, when we get there."

"I can deal with that," she said. "I hadn't forgotten it."

Thutmose didn't look up from his bowl when Cochran and Plumtree returned to the booth. The waitress was just taking orders for food, and Cochran quickly asked for carp in wine while Plumtree frowned over the menu and grumpily settled for stuffed mussels.

By the time the food arrived, Cochran had finished both his beers and ordered two more. The fish tasted like pier pilings and the wine sauce was featureless acid and he hadn't realized the dish would have raisins in it.

All the people in the bar were still talking in whispers, and after his fourth beer Cochran noticed that the whispering was in counterpoint unison—a fast, shaking chant that took in the bang-and-rattle of the bar dice as punctuation. The exhausted-looking men and women were all jerkily walking back and forth and between each other, and after staring in befuddled puzzlement for a few moments Cochran saw that their spastic restlessness was a dance. The dancers didn't appear to be en-joying it, perhaps weren't even doing it voluntarily. Beneath the rapid shaking whispers and the noise of the dice there was a deep, slow roll-ing, like a millwheel.

Plumtree leaned toward him. "Let's hit the road," she whispered. "And . . . *to a-void com-plications* . . . let's just walk out without saying anything."

It was easy enough to slide out of the booth again and walk away across the gritty floor—in the booth behind them Angelica was clearly avoiding her own appalling recent memories by talking consolingly to Mavranos, and Pete Sullivan was waving his empty glass and trying to catch the waitress's eye—and soon Cochran and Plumtree had made their ducking, sidestepping way, helplessly participating in a few shuffling steps of the joyless group dance, to the front door.

Outside, in the fresh wet-greenery-and-topsoil breeze from Golden Gate Park, the sun had broken through the morning's overcast and glittered in the raindrops that still speckled the brown Granada and the blue Suburban. Oddly, there were no other vehicles in the lot.

As Cochran opened the Granada's passenger-side door for Plumtree, she paused by the back end of the truck to peer in through the dusty glass. Cochran had carefully avoided looking at that window at all, not wanting to see the tumbled, broken skeleton of Scott Crane.

Now Plumtree shuddered visibly, and stepped back to catch her balance; but a moment later she again stepped up to the back of the truck and looked in.

And again she staggered, and it was a blank look she gave him as she finally shuffled forward and got into the Granada.

"You okay?" he said as he got in himself and started the engine.

"Fine," she said. "Don't talk. On the way to—on the way—stop for some cigarettes and booze. Mores regular, and Southern Comfort."

Cochran had said "Okay," before remembering that she had asked him not to talk. He nodded; and, because he was drunk, it was easy for him to think only about how he would get from here over to Mission Street, which would take him south to the 280, seven miles down which he would find South Daly City—right across the highway from the little transplanted-cemetery town of Colma—and his empty, empty house.

Neither of them spoke at all as Cochran steered the old car down the straight, narrow lanes over South San Francisco and then looped west past San Bruno Mountain, with its highway-side Pace Vineyards Tasting Room billboards; and, even with a wordless stop while he ducked into a strip-mall liquor store, it was only twenty minutes after leaving the Loser's Bar parking lot that he pulled into his own driveway and switched off the car motor.

Plumtree had her arm around his waist and her head on his shoulder as they trudged up the walkway to the front door; and when he had unlocked the door and led her in, then handed her the liquor-store bag and locked the door again behind them, it seemed only natural that they should both shuffle into the bedroom. The bureau drawers were still pulled out and disordered from their hasty visit five days earlier.

Plumtree twisted the cap off the bottle of Southern Comfort and poured several big splashes of the aromatic liqueur into the glass on the bedside table, and drained it in one swallow. Then as she unbuttoned her blouse with one hand, she touched his lips with the forefinger of the other. "No talk," she whispered.

Cochran nodded, and sat down on the bed to take off his muddy shoes.

CHAPTER 22

I would not deprive Col. Haraszthy of a moiety of the credit due him as the first among the first grape culturists of this state, but an investigation of the subject forces the conclusion, that the glory of having introduced [the Zinfandel grape] into the state is not among the laurels he won ... To who is the honor of its introduction due? To an enterprising pioneer merchant of San Francisco, the late Captain F. W. Macondray, who raised the first Zinfindal wine grown in California in a grapery at his residence, on the corner of Stockton and Washington streets, San Francisco.

—Robert A. Thompson,
San Francisco Evening Bulletin,
May 1885

With no key to the motel room, Angelica and Pete and Mavranos just sat in the blue truck for an hour in the Star Motel parking lot. Mavranos hadn't eaten anything at the Loser's Bar, and at one point he got out and trudged across the street to get a tuna sandwich, but he came back to the truck to eat it, and when he had tossed the wrappers onto the floorboards there was still no sign of Cochran and Plumtree, nor of Kootie. Every five minutes or so one of them would impatiently get out and climb the stairs to knock at the room door, but there was never an answer.

They had driven back up here in a roundabout route that had taken them through the green lawns of the Presidio, with Pete at the wheel and Angelica watching behind to be sure they weren't followed. Cochran and Plumtree had sneaked out of the bar and driven away with Angelica's carbine still under the front seat of their car, but she still had her .45 handgun, and Mavranos's .38 was on the truck seat now, under an unfolded Triple-A map.

Angelica's flesh quivered under the .45 that was now tucked into her belt.

*The full-throated bang, and after the blue-white muzzle flash faded
from her retinas she saw one less motorcycle headlight in the dawn
dimness behind the racing Granada . . . and then she had steadied the
jumping rifle sights on another headlight . . .*

"What's two times twelve, Arky?" she asked quickly.

Mavranos sighed and wiped the steamy inside surface of the windshield. "Twenty-four, Angelica."

"It's *your* mentation that's waxing and waning, Angie," said Pete
irritably from the back seat. "You were saving our lives. If my stupid
hands could hold a gun, it would have been *me* shooting out of the car
window."

"Oh, I know you would have, Pete," she said miserably, "and you
came back for me both times when they were shooting at us. I'm glad
it *wasn't* you. I wouldn't wish this on you."

Mavranos was squinting at her sideways with what might have been
knowing sympathy.

"Twice thirteen," she snapped.

"Twenty-six," said Mavranos. "You told me you shot a lady on the
Queen Mary two years ago, after you thought she had killed Pete. Today
you thought these boys had killed me. Both times the bad people *would*
have killed us, if you hadn't stopped them, if you hadn't killed them.
What's half of two?"

"Oh," she said with a sudden, affected breeziness, "less than one,
if it's me and Pete. Or even me and you, I guess." She had been looking
past Mavranos, and now she lowered her head and rubbed her eyes.
"How long has that turquoise BMW been parked over there? Its engine
is running. See the steam?"

Pete shifted around in the back seat to peer. "Four guys in it," he
said after a moment. "The two in the back look . . . funny."

Mavranos had not taken his eyes from the Lombard Street sidewalk.
"There's Kootie," he said suddenly.

Angelica whipped her head around—and the thin, scuffling figure
walking down the sidewalk from beyond the motel office was indeed
Kootie. She yanked open the truck door and hopped down to the asphalt,
and as she began sprinting toward the boy she heard behind her the
truck's other two doors creaking open as Pete and Mavranos followed.

She also heard a car engine shift into gear from idle, and then accelerate.

The Green Ripper, Kootie had been thinking insistently as he had trudged
up the Octavia Street sidewalk toward Lombard—he was afraid to think
about his foster parents, and whether or not he might find them still alive

after this ruinous morning—*the Green Giant, the Green Knight. I owe him a beheading. The Green Ripper, the Green Giant . . .*

Hours earlier, in the upstairs room of the magical boardinghouse that had appeared at Stockton and Washington, Kootie had picked up the bottle of Bitin Dog in both shaking hands—and he had wondered helplessly how he could possibly keep from drinking it right there. He was sure that the dead woman on the bed had been telling the truth: that the bottle contained real impunity, that if he were to drink it he would simply *lose,* lose *track* of, the enormous sin that made even taking each breath seem like the shameful act of a horrifying impostor. Kootie had despairingly thought that *especially* if his foster-parents were still alive he should drink it—if they were somehow not dead, he couldn't encompass the thought of going back to them with the mark of a murder on his soul. Angelica would see it on his face as clearly as she would a tattoo.

But he knew that if he drank it, he would forget about them too. In good faith the wine would take all his loves along with all his guilts—and because he would be drinking it in this stolen, unsanctioned moment, the wine would certainly not ever give any particle of them back. It was a kind of maturity that the wine had to offer, which was to say that it was a renunciation of his whole youth—he would be a man if he drank it, but he would be the wine's man.

After what could only have been a few seconds, really, he had lifted the bottle past his shoulder and flung it into the cold fireplace. It disappeared in that darkness without any sound at all, and he thought that the house had reabsorbed it, and not with disapproval or offense. Only afterward did he fully and fearfully comprehend that he had chosen to remain Koot Hoomie Sullivan—the wounded foster-son of Pete and Angelica Sullivan—the fourteen-year-old who had committed a murder this morning.

That knowledge was like a boulder in the living room of his mind, so that his thoughts had to crawl over it first before they could get anywhere.

He had carried this new and all-but-intolerable identity downstairs, where the old black woman had prepared him a different sort of meal than the peppered venison that was cooking to cinders upstairs. It was a spicy hot salmon that Mammy Pleasant set out for him on the kitchen table, served with the fish's tail and sunken-eyed head still attached; he forked up mouthfuls of it hungrily, and though it blunted no memories it reinvigorated him, made him feel implausibly rested and strong.

And as he had eaten it, he had learned things.

With some evident sympathy, Mammy Pleasant had told him her own story—and, in this impossible building on this catastrophic day, Kootie found that he had no capacity for disbelief left.

She told him that she had been born a slave in Atlanta in the winter of 1815, her mother a voodoo queen from Santo Domingo. At the age of ten Mary Ellen had been sold to a merchant who had placed her in the Ursuline convent in New Orleans, to be brought up by the nuns— but a Catholic convent had *not* been any part of the god's plan for her. The merchant soon died, and she was eventually sent to be a servant for a woman who ran a yardage and crockery store way up north in New England, on remote Nantucket Island.

In New England in those days a new variety of wine grape had appeared, brought in obscurely on the transatlantic schooners and cultivated in American greenhouses. Something terrible had already begun to devastate the great old European vineyards of the Herault and the Midi, but in America this new wine from across the sea flourished aggressively. It was variously known as the Black Lombardy and the Black St. Peter's, but in 1830, at the Linnaean Botanic Gardens on Long Island, it was tentatively dubbed the Black Zinfardel.

On wintry Nantucket Island the teenaged Mary Ellen had discarded the Caribbean voodoo systems her mother had taught her, and had begun giving her allegiance to an older god, a wild deity of woods and ivy. As a teenager she learned to tie strips of pine bark to the bottoms of her shoes, so as to mask her footprints when she stole fruit from neighboring farms at night, and she had only been caught when she had used the trick to steal exotic Brazilian peanuts.

The woman storekeeper had taught Mary Ellen how to ferment and bottle the new wine—and when Mary Ellen was twenty-four, and still a virgin, the store had caught fire and burned, and the storekeeper had died of shock, or possibly fright, after staring too intently at the tall, wildly dancing flames. Mary Ellen inherited hundreds of the miraculously undamaged bottles.

The new variety of wine was also called *pagadebiti,* Italian for debtpayer, and Mary Ellen had understood that the god had come to her in it, and that he was generously holding out to her the duty to drink it and become his American Ariadne, rescued by him from abandonment on a bleak island. She knew that the god was Dionysus, and that he was offering to take all her debts, past and future, in exchange for her individual will.

But her will had prevailed—she had *sold* the wine, for profane cash, to a local importer who had a lifetime of old crimes to forget.

A Hungarian emigrant called Agoston Haraszthy had arrived in America in that same year, 1840, and by 1848 had taken on the role of secret king of the American West in distant San Diego—the first of the New World kings—but Mary Ellen had already unfitted herself to be his destined queen, and his reign would now be unbalanced and obstructed.

For sheer concealment she went through the rituals of conversion to Roman Catholicism, and then married a man who owned a tobacco plantation in Charles Town, Virginia. She poisoned him with arsenic, and shortly after that married the plantation overseer in order to sacramentally take the man's fortuitous last name: *Plaissance,* which derived from the French *plaisant:*—a jester, a joker. It was a name that was virtually a motley mask in itself.

She took her new husband back to New Orleans. Though ostensibly Catholic now, Mary Ellen bore little resemblance these days to the girl who had scampered through the halls of the Ursuline convent in muslin dresses and ribbon-tied sandals—she took up the bloody practice of real voodoo, under the tutelage of the infamous Marie Laveau, who got for Mary Ellen a high-paid position as cook for the household of a planter in nearby Bayou St. John.

Mary Ellen was a sincerely ardent abolitionist, and she used her priveleged position to make contacts with negro slaves throughout the New Orleans area; and she managed to spirit away such a number of them to freedom through "the Underground" that the authorities began looking for the light-skinned negro woman who always seemed to attend somehow at the escapes—and this slave-stealing woman was too-accurately described as tall and thin, with mismatched eyes.

And so one night Mary Ellen had fled, leaving behind in her bed a bolster wrapped in her nightdress with a wig on it. Marie Laveau booked steamship passage for her to San Francisco, by way of Cape Horn.

Mary Ellen arrived in San Francisco on April 7, 1852—but Agoston Haraszthy himself came to the city only a few months later to establish his kingdom in nearby Sonoma; and of course he had brought with him cuttings of the god's New World wine, which by this time had already reached the Bay Area and was known, properly at last, as *Zinfandel.*

The god would still have forgiven her, on some basis—but she fought him.

She quickly got employment as a gourmet cook, serving Cajun *pirogis* and shrimp *remoulade* and exotic spicy *jambalaya* to the bankers and gold-dealers of San Francisco—and she made contact with escaped slaves and was able to find jobs for them in the households of affluent families; and then she used her beneficiaries as spies to garner valuable particulars of scandal . . . murders, illicit births, embezzlements, abortions. Soon she owned several laundries, but blackmail was her real business.

"My life," she had told Kootie ruefully this morning at the kitchen table, "was based on the very *opposite* of any divine *pagadebiti*."

In her voodoo procedures she didn't hesitate to *use* the power of alcohol, and even of wine, but always in spitefully broken or vitiated forms. The founder of the mercantile firm F. W. Macondray & Company had erected a grapery, a greenhouse-chapel to the god's holy vine, at the corner of Stockton and Washington—and so in 1866 Mary Ellen Pleasant, as she now called herself, bought the property and sacreligiously converted it to the boardinghouse whose kitchen she and Kootie were now sitting in; and to the bankers and steamship owners who dined at her boardinghouse she served hot raspberry vinegar, and cowslip wine, and double-distilled elderberry brandies. When in 1892 she finally killed the man who had been her main benefactor in San Francisco, she first hobbled his ghost by serving him wine from which she had boiled off all the alcohol . . . and then after she had pushed him over a high spiral stair railing she hurried down to where his body lay on the parquet entry-hall floor and pulled the hot brains out of his split skull, so that the ghost would be sure to dissipate in confused fragments.

"A surer trick than those ashtrays with *Madam, I'm Adam* or some such nonsense written around them," Mammy Pleasant had told Kootie this morning.

"I bet," Kootie had said hoarsely.

"But at the turn of the century the god caught up with me," she had said, taking Kootie's empty plate to the sink, "and took everything away—my great house on Octavia Street, my servants, my money— until at the last I was a plain homeless charity case, shambling around the Fillmore district like . . . like a bolster with an old wig on it, in a nightdress. I had only one companion left by then, a negro giant who was actually my captor and guard, known to people as *Bacus*—" She spelled it out for Kootie. "—because people didn't ever see it spelled right, which would have been B-A-C-C-H-U-S. He—it—was a sort of idiot fragment of the god's attention. And finally, on January eleventh of 1904, in the spare room of a mere Good Samaritan acquaintance, I died."

Kootie looked past her. He thought the strings of garlic and dried red peppers hung in the high corner of the ceiling had lost some of their color in the last few minutes, even become a bit transparent, but he wished forlornly that he could just forget his life and become one of the boarders here.

The old woman went on softly, perhaps talking to herself: "For a while after that I just drifted in the gray daguerreotype-plate ghost-world version of the city, lost, mostly on the beaches by Sutro's Cliff House and Point Lobos and Land's End. It was a time of cleansing exile for me, like Ariadne abandoned on Naxos by her false human lover Theseus. At last, three Easters and three days after I died, the god mercifully did come back for my ghost, and he knocked down Yerba Buena when he came.''

She looked up at Kootie, and her mismatched eyes were again sharp. ''For me,'' she said, ''January eleventh is the open door of the revolving year, and on that day I was able to call out to you people, to try to tell you all what you had to do. And I was interceding for you all with the god—he broke your two friends out of the madhouse on that night, and allowed the king's ghost to be called and drive them right to where you were, where his body was. You had every species of help.''

''I don't know that we've done very well,'' said Kootie.

''You've all done very badly,'' she agreed, ''and amassed huge debts.''

From a shelf stacked with old gray cookbooks and account ledgers she now pulled down a jarringly modern oversized paperback book with garish red and green swirls and the word FRACTALS in big red letters on the slick cover. She flipped it open to an inner page and showed Kootie a color picture of flames or ferns or octopus tentacles boiling away from a warty, globular black shape.

''Have you seen this silhouette before?'' she asked gently, pointing to a clearer picture of the five-lobed silhouette, which resembled a fat person with a little round head and stumpy arms and round buttocks.

Kootie could only look away from the picture and nod and close his throat against sudden nausea. It was the silhouette that had appeared on the television screen in the motel this morning after Arky had poured beer into the set, and it was, too, the shape he had momentarily seen overlapping the pretty Chinese woman when he had first glimpsed her today in the Street of Gamblers.

Mammy Pleasant sighed and shook her head. ''Oh, it's death, child, the person of the god's unholy trinity that's retributive death, and you can testify yourself that it does love to have people enter into its terrible bargain. *It* was the person of the god that came for me *first*, on that cold January eleventh morning, demanding payment for chopping down the vine in Macondray's grapery—dethroning the vine god, killing the vegetation king, beheading the Green Knight. In olden-days history it was called the Quinotaur, and it gave power to the Frankish king Merovee in the Dark Ages—it came to him in the form of a talking bear, and Merovee cut its head off—and it came back under the name of''—

she tapped the page—"Pepin the Fat, to kill Merovee's greatly-greatly-grandson Dagobert, and that ended the Merovingian line of kings in that long-ago time. And it's been known as Bertilak of the High Desert, the Green Knight, who met Sir Gawain at the Green Chapel on New Year's Day, a year after Gawain had cut off Bertilak's head, to collect on that debt. Other folk, meaning to or not, have let the Quinotaur take over themselves to some degree, and always they come back to demand payment-in-kind for their murders."

Mammy Pleasant seemed to relax, though she was still frowning. "You should go now, child. The New Year is close at hand. The Quinotaur doesn't always *take* the life he's owed—the Green Knight didn't behead Gawain, just nicked his neck, because he showed courage. Show courage yourself."

"Courage," echoed Kootie, and the word reminded him of the Cowardly Lion of Oz. The memory of watching that innocent movie on television in Solville, in the contented days before the red truck had arrived, before Kootie was a murderer, brought tears to his eyes.

She tugged a bookmark out of the volume's back pages, and handed it to Kootie. "You people should have come to me for this before. Your king is the suicide king now, you've got to keep him in your deck—he's unconditionally surrendered, you see, and is waiting for his instructions, any orders at all. But the god is merciful sometimes—these commandments haven't changed." She handed Kootie the paper—he glanced at it, but it seemed to be poetry in Latin, which he couldn't read. "You bring your people back here," the old woman went on, "and take me away with you. The god still looks with favor on your king, and wants you all to succeed in restoring him to life: the god owes a good turn to one of your king's company. But it will cost each of you much more, now, than it would have once. Child, it can't any longer be your *king* who comes under your curly-haired roof—and your *king* will have to come somewhere else."

Mammy Pleasant put down the book and then moved some jars away from a breadbox on the counter, scattering dust and tearing cobwebs. Kootie looked around and saw that the kitchen had deteriorated in the last few moments—the windows were blurred with greasy dirt now and blocked by vines clinging to the outside of the glass, and the paint was flaking off of the sagging shelves. The old woman tugged open the lid of the breadbox, breaking old rust deposits—and then she lifted out of it Diana's yellow baby blanket. She reached across the warped table to hand it to him.

Kootie wordlessly took it and tucked it into the back pocket of his jeans. He knew it must have fallen out of his pocket in the bedroom upstairs, not an hour ago; and he couldn't even bring himself to wonder how it had wound up here.

Mammy Pleasant blinked around at the iron sinks and the cutting boards and the wire-mesh pantry doors, as if for the last time. "This place won't stay visibly wedged into your electric new world much longer," she said. "I'll show you out."

She led him out of the kitchen—into a huge shadowy Victorian hall, clearly once elegant but now dark and dusty and empty of furniture. A spiral stairway receded away up toward a dim skylight several floors above, and when Kootie looked down at his feet he saw a dark stain on the parquet floor.

"We're in my house on Octavia Street now," Pleasant told him as she led him to a tall, ornate door at the end of the passage, "not as it was in my arrogant days, and anyway *it* won't last much longer here either. You all come back here and get me. Look to the trees, you'll see how." She twisted the knob and pushed open the door. "Go left," she said from behind him, "up the street. Don't look back for a few blocks."

Kootie blinked in the sudden gray daylight. Splintery old wooden steps led down to a yard choked with brown weeds, and beyond a row of eucalyptus trees he could see a street, with a cable car trundling up the middle of the pavement and ringing its bell.

He remembered this cable-car bell from the first time they had got Pleasant on the television in Solville, and he recalled Thomas Edison's ghost telling him once that streetcar tracks were a good masking measure—"the tracks make a nice set of mirrors." *For a while,* Kootie thought now as he stuffed the piece of paper into his pocket. *Not forever.*

Obediently he walked down the steps and across the overgrown yard to the sidewalk, where he turned left, kicking his way through the drifts of acorn-like seeds that had fallen from the eucalyptus trees.

He was sweating in the cold morning air, and he wasn't tempted to look back as he walked away from the house; he didn't even want to look around, for there were no traffic lights at all visible between the corniced buildings bracketing the narrow intersection ahead of him, and aside from the receding cable car all the vehicles on the street were horse-drawn carriages, and though he was aware of the clopping of the horses' hooves and the voices of the quaintly dressed people that he passed, he was aware too of breezy *silence* in the background. The air smelled of grass and the sea and wood smoke and horse manure.

After he had walked two blocks, the noise of the modern world abruptly crashed back in upon him: car engines, and radio music, and the sheer roaring undertone of the modern city. His nostrils dilated at the aggessive odor of diesel fumes.

Oh, this is magic, he thought, for only the second time in that whole morning.

Between the traffic lights swung a metal street sign—he was at the intersection of Octavia and California, and Lombard Street and the Star Motel lay a dozen steep blocks ahead of him.

If my mom and dad are still alive, I'll meet them there, he thought. If they're not, if they've been killed because I ran away this morning—

Recoiling away from the thought, and from a suspense that could not possibly be resolved either way without grief, he began a loud chanting in his head to drown out all thoughts as he strode north on the Octavia Street sidewalk: *The Green Ripper, the Green Giant, the Green Knight. I owe him a beheading. The Green Ripper, the Green Giant, the Green Knight . . .*

CHAPTER 23

Angelica glanced jerkily back over her shoulder—the bumper of the turquoise BMW was scooping fast across the motel parking lot pavement toward her—no, it would miss her—it was accelerating straight at Kootie.

She tried to run faster toward the boy, and she managed to suck enough air into her lungs to yell to him, *"Get out of the way!"*

Kootie just stood and stared; but Mavranos was ahead of her now, his arms and knees pumping and his dark hair flying as he lashed himself across the lot. As the low BMW roared past her, painfully clipping her left elbow with the passenger-side mirror and nearly spinning her off her feet, she saw Mavranos bodyblock Kootie right off his feet into a driveway-side planter as the car screeched to a halt where Kootie had been standing. The two heads in the rear seat flopped forward and back as if yanked by one string.

Mavranos had rolled over Kootie and was struggling to his hands and knees on the sidewalk past the planter, and Angelica saw a clenched hand poke out of the BMW's driver's-side window. A stubby silver cylinder was squeezed in the fist, and it was pointed toward where Kootie lay thrashing weakly among the flowers.

The icy recognition of *It's a gun* shrilled in Angelica's head, but as she sprang forward again she also thought, imperatively, *but he's!—the king now!—he's got protections against plain guns!*

The fist was punched back out of sight by the recoil, and the *pop* was loud enough to set her ears ringing and deafen her to the roaring of her panting breath and the hard scuff of her sneaker soles on the pavement.

Long John Beach tried to hold on to the seat-back with his phantom left hand, but when Armentrout stood on the brake the psychic limb snapped like taffy and his head smacked the windshield; still, he was able to peer out the open driver's-side window as the doctor frantically contorted his own arm to get the little gun extended outside the stopped, rocking car.

Even in the passenger seat on the far side of the console, Long John Beach was only a couple of yards from the boy who was lying on his back among the pink geraniums . . . and in the instant before the gun flared and cracked back against the doorframe, their eyes met, and Long John Beach and the boy recognized each other.

The rangy man in denim who had shoved the boy out of the car's path was on his feet, and he lunged at the car and slammed a tanned fist against the windshield hard enough to flash silvery cracks across it. Then he was reaching in through the open window and had grabbed a handful of the doctor's white hair—

But wailing Armentrout stamped on the gas pedal, and though his head was yanked violently back the car had slewed out into the lanes of Lombard Street; horns were honking but there were no audible collisions, and in a moment Armentrout had wrestled the wheel into line and was steering the car fast down the eastbound left lane.

"That was the boy," Armentrout was whispering rapidly, "I *know* that was the boy! He was older, but the face was the same as the one in the picture."

"That was Koot Hoomie Parganas," said Long John Beach.

Peripherally he could see Armentrout glance at him, but Long John had seized on an *old* memory, and had no attention to spare for the doctor. The sight of the boy in the flowers had reminded him of some *old* event.

He nearly never remembered anything of his life before Halloween of 1992, when he had been found on the shore rocks beside the permanently moored *Queen Mary* in Long Beach. When the police and paramedics had found him he had had a ruptured spleen and a collapsed lung, with "pulmonary hemorrhages"—as well as a set of handcuffs dangling from his bloody right wrist. He had spent weeks in a hospital, at first with a chest tube inserted between his fifth and sixth ribs. Apparently he had been in the lagoon around the old ship when an under-water explosion had occurred. The doctors had speculated that he must have been exhaling in the instant of the blast, and curled up into a ball, and that that was why he hadn't been killed; another man in the water *had* been killed . . . and must have lost at least his shoe and all the skin off his left foot, for . . . for somebody had previously handcuffed Long John Beach's wrist to the man's ankle!

But Long John Beach had been going by another name, then—another makeshift name based on a city he had found himself in.

Like a whisper the old name came to him: *Sherman Oaks.*

He had been hunting for Koot Hoomie Parganas in that long-ago season, and so had the man who had died in the underwater explosion . . . and so had a fat woman who had been some kind of movie producer. Each of them had wanted to get hold of the Parganas boy, and kill him, and inhale the powerful ghost that the boy contained—the ghost of Thomas Alva Edison.

Sherman Oaks had failed, and of course the man who'd died in the explosion had failed. Perhaps the fat lady had succeeded in inhaling Edison.

No—she couldn't have, because that would have involved killing the boy, and Long John Beach had just seen the boy a minute ago, alive.

The boy's face, when the haunted brown eyes had locked on to Long John Beach's gaze just now, had been pale and gaunt, and openmouthed with surprise and apprehension—but the sick wrinkles around the eyes spoke of some iminent punishment feared but *expected,* even accepted. The expression was one of fearful guilt, Long John Beach thought.

The boy's face had been younger when Beach had first seen it, but it had worn that same look of pathetically anticipating and deserving punishment.

The Parganas boy had apparently run away from home one night in October of '92, directly after stealing the Edison ghost from whatever shielded hiding place his parents had kept the thing in. Long John Beach—Sherman Oaks, rather—had tracked the ghost's intense field to the boy's Beverly Hills home, and he had duct-taped the boy's mother and father into chairs and tortured them to find out where the ghost had gone. But they hadn't *known* where, and he had wound up killing them in a fury of hungry impatience, finally even gouging out their sightless eyes.

And then later that night the boy had come back home, repentant and sorry, visibly ready to take his punishment for having run away and stolen whatever glass container had held the ghost.

It had been Sherman Oaks, not his parents, who had awaited him;

but the boy had eluded Oaks, and had run out of the house . . . *right through the room in which sat his dead mother and father.*

And then a few days later Sherman Oaks had succeeded in briefly capturing the boy, in a van in the back of a moving truck—and after terrifying him nearly to madness Oaks had tried to kill him, and had in fact managed to stab him in the side with a hunting knife.

Long John Beach had never, since Halloween of '92, had much awareness of himself as a distinct person. The Edison ghost had lashed out at him somehow and broken something in his mind, so that he'd been left with nothing but the useless ability to channel stray ghosts, as inertly and promiscuously as a tree harbors birds. But now, in this swerving, speeding car, that tortured boy in the flowers back there was connected to his self. The boy's evident unhappiness was not—Long John Beach flexed the hoardings of his mind to be sure, and it was true—was not separable from the admittedly dim and decayed entity that was Long John Beach's own self.

He knew that as Sherman Oaks, and probably as other personalities before that one, he had killed people; and he remembered that in those old days he had been addicted to inhaling ghosts, consuming them rather than just channelling them, strengthening his own soul by eating those poor dissolving "smokes"—but suddenly it was Koot Hoomie Parganas, whom he had not even killed, that was an intolerable weight on his frail mind.

There was no new sound in the humming BMW, and Long John Beach saw nothing but the drab motels of western Lombard Street through the windshield, but he was suddenly aware of a *change.*

A personality that wasn't a ghost, and might not even have been human, lifted him like a wave under a foundering ship; cautiously, still clinging to the prickly husk that was his identity, he nevertheless let the new person partway into his mind.

All at once he was speaking. "I always have a dog," Long John Beach found himself saying. "For now he barks all night at the end of his tether. Chancy measures at the bowsprit of the million-dollar hot-air balloon, what you might call an exaltation of barks if you had to spit-shine a wingtip hanging upside down by one ankle." He was laughing excitedly now. "Just imagine! Shouting out of your liver and lights to hand-deliver these parables—pair-o'-bulls!—to the momma's boy who wants to put the salmon in the freezer."

"You and your dog." Armentrout was blinking rapidly at the traffic ahead, and breathing through his mouth. "It doesn't matter now," he whispered. "It's all cashed out, I *killed* the boy back there."

Long John Beach gathered back the shreds of his mind and pushed himself away from the big inhuman personality—and he got a quick impression of a young man in patchwork clothes, with a bundle over his shoulder, dancing at the edge of a cliff. He recognized the image—it was one of the pictures in the doctor's set of oversized tarot cards, the one the doctor called The Fool.

The doctor was afraid of that one. And Long John Beach was not ready to surrender himself to The Fool. The one-armed old man's identity was nothing more than a limp threadbare sack, angular at the bottom with the fragments of broken poisonous memories and short, rotted lengths of intelligence, but it was all he had.

In spite of his uneasiness with the memories of the Koot Hoomie Parganas boy, he was not ready to surrender himself to The Fool.

Kootie was sobbing and trying to get up when Angelica tumbled to her hands and knees in the muddy planter beside him; Pete slid to an abrading stop against the cement coping beside her.

Mavranos was kneeling on the other side of the boy, and holding him down with hands that were red with fresh blood. "Let your ma look at you, first," Mavranos said irritably, and then he squinted up into Angelica's face. "He was rolling over when the bullet hit him—I don't think it was a direct hit."

"Mom!" Kootie wailed. "I thought you were all dead!"

"Check it out as a doctor, Angie," said Pete breathlessly.

"*Hit* him?" she panted. "We're fine, Kootie, we're—all just fine." To Pete she snapped, "It can't have *hit* him." Gently but irresitibly she pushed Kootie down on his back in the snapping geranium branches and pulled his shirt up, and the familiar old unhealed knife cut over his left ribs was now a raw long gash with blood runneling down his side and pattering onto the green leaves.

Angelica's peripheral vision cringed inward so that all she could see was this gleaming red rip in Kootie's white skin; but she replayed what Pete had said and forced herself to look at it professionally. "You're right, Arky—it's shallow, no damage at all to the muscle layer and hardly even scored the corium, the deeper skin layer—not life-threatening." She grinned at the boy as confidently as she could, and gasped out, "Welcome back, kiddo," but she knew the look she then gave Mavranos must have been stark. "Get the truck here right now. I don't want my boy in a hospital like this."

"Right." Mavranos scuffled to his feet and sprinted heavily away.

"Let's get you moving, Kootie," Angelica said, grunting as she and Pete helped the boy stand up. Bright drops of blood spilled down the left leg of his jeans, and she mentally rehearsed grabbing the first-aid kit that Mavranos kept in a box beside the back seat. "That must have been a magical gun—" she began. Then she looked into his eyes. "You're not hurt anywhere else, are you? Physically?"

"No." But Kootie was crying, and Angelica knew it was about something that had happened before this shooting . . . and after he had run away in the pre-dawn darkness this morning.

"Tell your dad and me about it when we get clear of this," she said gently.

"And I thought," the boy sniffled, "that I got you killed, by running away. I just *ran away* from you! I'd give anything if I could go back and do that different."

"We're just fine, son," said Pete, hugging the boy against himself. "It's okay. And now you're back. We're all *alive* for our . . . reconciliation here, and that's a very big thing."

Angelica remembered Pete making a very similar apology to *his* father's *ghost,* on the night before Halloween in '92—Pete too had run away once, when it counted—and she winced in sympathy and opened her mouth to say something; but the shrill whine of the truck engine starting up stopped her.

The truck came grinding up behind her and squealed to a halt, and Angelica helped Pete hustle Kootie around the front bumper to the back door. As soon as they had boosted him in onto the back seat and clambered aboard themselves, Pete in the front seat and Angelica in the back seat with Kootie, Mavranos gunned the dusty blue truck out of the parking lot; Kootie sprawled across the seat, and Angelica, crouched on the floorboards beside him, had to lean out over the rushing pavement to catch the swinging door handle and pull the door shut.

Then she hiked the first-aid kit down with one hand while she raised her other hand over the back of the front seat; and Pete had already opened the glove compartment, and now slapped into her palm Mavranos's nearly empty bottle of Jack Daniel's bourbon.

Kootie was lying on his back, and Angelica knelt over him and popped open the first-aid kit. "This'll hurt," she told him as she tore open a gauze pad envelope and spilled bourbon onto the cotton.

"Good," said Kootie. Then he said, "The old guy in the passenger seat of that BMW—it was Sherman Oaks, the one-armed guy who killed my natural mom and dad. I recognized him. And he recognized me."

Angelica suppressed a worried frown, and just pressed the wet bandage onto his wound. "Drive right out of the city, Arky," she called over her shoulder, "in whatever direction you're heading. To hell with whatever we left in that motel room. When we're—"

"No," said Kootie through clenched teeth. "First we've got to go to Octavia Street—uh, two blocks south of California Street."

"Tell me which," growled Mavranos from the driver's seat.

"Why, Kootie?" asked Pete, hunching around to look back at the boy. "If that Sherman Oaks guy is here in town—"

"We've got to do it *right* this time," said Kootie hoarsely. "We've got to *fetch* Mammy Pleasant. She's the old black lady from the TV, and her house is on Octavia there."

"Oh, honey, that—didn't work out," Angelica said as she peeled adhesive tape off a roll. She restrained herself from glancing over his head toward the bed of the truck. "That's all over."

"It's not," Kootie said, closing his eyes as Angelica pressed the strip of tape tightly over the bandage. "He can still come back. To life. Dionysus *wants* him to."

"South on Van Ness," announced Mavranos as the truck leaned into a right-hand turn. "I'm going straight on down to the 101 south unless somebody convinces me to do different."

"*Arky,*" Kootie wailed, "get over to Octavia! We won't ever be okay until we've paid this thing off. Does it look like we're done, here? Does it look like I'm the king now? *He can still be restored to life.*"

"You don't know the whole story, Kootie," said Pete. "We do. Trust me, there's no way—" He paused, for Mavranos had swung the truck into another hard right turn at Filbert, and the battering exhaust was echoing back from the close garage doors alongside the narrow, steep street. "Arky—? The 101 is—"

"Talk to me, Kootie," said Mavranos. "If he *can* still come back, it can't be into his own body anymore. That turned into a skeleton, and got all busted up."

"And it won't be into yours," said Angelica, peeling off another strip of tape. "I will sabotage any effort at that, I promise. So don't even—"

"No," said Kootie, "it *would* have been that way, if we'd done it right, and then he would have shifted back into his own. Arky and the Plumtree woman were right about that. But we were doing it wrong, we didn't get Mammy Pleasant to guide us like she told us to, and then I ran away—" He sniffed. "Mammy Pleasant gave me a message for Crane, some Latin poetry on a piece of paper, from Dionysus."

Angelica felt a thump through the front seat at her back, and she looked up—Mavranos had thrown his injured head back, though he was still squinting furiously ahead. "So how *will* it work out?" he asked in a gravelly voice. "Now?"

"I don't know at all," said Kootie. His eyes were wide and he was staring up at the rust-spotted bare metal roof. "I think we might all die, if it works out right this time."

"Let's see this message," said Pete.

Luckily Kootie had stuffed it into his right-hand pocket; he was able to dig it out without putting any strain on his bandaged side. "Here," he said, handing it to Angelica, who passed it over the seat to Pete.

Pete read it aloud, slowly:

> *"Roma, tibi subito motibus ibit Amor,*
> *Si bene te tua laus taxat, sua laute tenebis,*
> *Sole, medere pede: ede, perede melos."*

He handed it back to Angelica, who returned it to Kootie. "It's a palindrome," Pete said thoughtfully, rocking in his seat as the truck continued to climb the narrow street. "Three palindromes, that is. Latin, and I don't read Latin." He yawned. "Palindromes draw ghosts."

"I'd like to know what it means," said Angelica defiantly.

"I think we better go pick up the old lady's ghost in the meantime," sighed Mavranos. "I'll stop at a pay phone on the way and read Kootie's note to Nardie Dinh; she'll be able to puzzle it out for us, if we give her time to go through her books—and she owes me one."

At a tiny corner liquor store on the corner of Gough and Filbert, Mavranos found a parking space and then copied the text of Kootie's note onto the back of his car registration. Finally he got out of the truck, leaving it in park with the engine running.

After he closed the driver's door he leaned in the open window to say, "Pete, if you see a blue-green BMW, you just ram it and then drive away, and meet me at Li Po at sunset."

He trudged across the tiny lot into the liquor store, slapping his pockets for coins for the pay phone by the beer cooler.

He strode up to the phone and dropped a quarter into the coin slot, and then punched in the well-remembered Leucadia number; and after a recorded voice asked him to deposit another dollar and thirty cents, and he impatiently rolled six more quarters into the slot, he heard ringing, and then Nardie's voice saying, cautiously, "Hello?"

"Nardie," he said, "this is Arky, still up in San Fran, with—apparently!—still no conclusions." His forehead was damp; he had almost said *concussions.* He wanted to touch the back of his head, and to ask her about the dashboard statue she had given him. But, *She didn't do it,* he told himself, and he only said, "I got some Latin for you to translate, if you got a pencil—"

"It means, 'And in Arcadia, I—' " came Nardie Dinh's voice. "It's an unfinished sentence, like the story's not over, okay? I think the speaker is supposed to be Death, so it's like Death hasn't made up his mind yet what he'll do, here. Where have you seen it?"

Mavranos blinked, and discovered that the telephone cord was long enough for him to open the beer cooler and pull out a can of Coors. "What?" he said. "But it's longer than that. And where did *you* find it?"

Nardie Dinh paused. "This is something that's lettered on a sign somebody put up on the big pine tree out front, by the driveway. *Et in Arcadia ego.* What Latin have *you* got?"

"Jeez. Well, mine's longer. Have you got a pencil?"

"Shoot," she said.

He winced, and his finger hovered over the tab on the beer can, but he knew the owner was watching him and would throw him out if he opened it in the store.

He read her the three palindromes slowly, spelling the words out.

"I'll have a translation for you in an hour," she said. "I suppose you're not at a phone I'll be able to call you at?"

"No," he told her, "I'll call you." He shifted his weight from one foot to the other, and he wished he could open the beer, for his mouth was dry. "Nardie, your brother—"

"Oh, Arky!" Her voice was startled and not happy. "Do let it lie, please!"

"I—well, I discover I *can't.* Anymore. I know *he* doesn't forgive me, but I do have to ask you—ask you—" He was sweating. "I have to tell you that I'm—sorry, for it." He coughed, and though his eyes were squeezed tightly shut, his voice was almost casual: "Always have been."

"I know you are, Arky. Don't still trouble yourself about it—whatever my feelings were for my brother, or are now, I love you—" She laughed awkwardly. "I was going to say 'I love you anyway,' but there's no 'anyway' to it; you did what you had to do, for all of us. So I'll just say, I love you."

Mavranos discovered that he hadn't been inhaling or exhaling, and he let his breath out now in a long sigh. "Thank you, Nardie. I love you too. Call you back in an hour or so."

He remembered to pay for the can of beer before he walked out of the store, and he popped it open as he walked across the asphalt to the truck, which was still idling where he'd left it. In spite of his undiminished dreads of what was to come, his step was lighter, and after he had got back in and taken a deep sip of the beer, he wedged the can between his thighs and said, with a fair imitation of hearty cheer, "Now we're off to pick up Kootie's old lady."

In the rear-view mirror he saw the boy close his eyes.

Mavranos drove right by the place, because Kootie wasn't sure whether it had been two or three blocks he had walked up to get to California Street, and none of these office and apartment buildings looked familiar to him—and it was only after they had driven past the Bush Street intersection that he realized that the six huge, shaggy eucalyptus trees they had just passed must be all that was left of the long row of trees he had seen when he had walked out of Mammy Pleasant's run-down Victorian mansion an hour ago.

"Back," he said. "Her house is gone, but those six eucalyptuses are where it was."

"She say meet you by the trees?" asked Mavranos as he signalled for a right turn to go around the block.

"She said 'Look to the trees, you'll see how.' To pick her up. And last week on the TV she said 'Eat the seeds of my trees.' " He shifted uncomfortably. "She's just a ghost, remember—I don't think we'll have to make much room for her in here."

Mavranos looped around Sutter and Laguna to Bush, and then turned right onto Octavia again and parked at the curb, putting the truck into park but leaving the engine running. Where Pleasant's dry-brush yard had been was now a walkway-transected green lawn out in front of a Roman-looking two-story gray stone building.

"It's a . . . a pregnancy counseling center," said Angelica, staring at the big white sign out front as she opened the door and climbed down to the sidewalk. "That's a . . . pleasant . . . use for the property." Pete got out of the passenger side and stood beside her as she shaded her eyes to look up and down the street. Finally she stared down at the pavement and scuffed some leaves aside. "There's a stone plaque inset in the sidewalk here—it says something about—" She frowned as she puzzled out the letters. *"Mary Ellen Pleasant Memorial Park,"* she read aloud. *". . . mother of civil rights in California . . . supported the western terminus of the underground railway for fugitive slaves . . . legendary pioneer once lived on this site and planted these six trees."* Angelica looked up. "And it says she died in 1904. You were—here today, Kootie?"

Kootie was half sitting up in the back seat, staring out through the open back door.

"Her old house was still standing when I was here," called Kootie, "an hour ago, by my clock. There were more trees then, and they weren't so big and shaggy."

"I should have had more respect for her ghost," said Angelica. "She sounds like she was a fine woman."

"She had her faults," said Kootie shakily. "Like us all, I—" he let the sentence hang unfinished. "Do any of the trees . . . look funny?"

"Funny," echoed Angelica out on the sidewalk. "Well, they've all got strips of bark hanging off 'em . . . and got bright green moss around their feet."

"Around their *roots*," Pete corrected her, standing by the truck bumper. "Their *feet* are way up in the air." He was standing by the second one from the corner, looking up at its thick, bifurcated trunk. "This one looks like somebody buried head-down up to the waist, with their legs sticking up. Wasn't there a place in Dante's *Inferno*, where the damned souls were stuck head-downward?"

"In the Eighth Circle," called Mavranos from the driver's seat. He was looking down, fumbling with both hands among the papers on the front seat, and Kootie heard a faint metallic rattle. "The Simoniacs, who sold ecclesiastical offices and indulgences and forgivenesses. *Sold* is the key word there. But in the book they were stuck head-down in baptismal fonts." Kootie heard the cylinder of the revolver click closed. "Hurry up," Mavranos said loudly. "I haven't reloaded since this morning." He sat back, not looking at Kootie. "I've been . . . distracted," he said quietly.

Though she gave a deprecating laugh, Angelica had taken a step back from the gnarled old tree with its two bulky, skyward-stretching limbs. "For what god is a *hole in the ground* a baptismal font?"

"The god of woods," said Kootie, though probably only Mavranos could have heard him. He was remembering Mammy Pleasant's confession of having sold a fabulous cache of the *pagadebiti* Zinfandel for money, way back in her youth on Nantucket Island. More loudly, he called, "Gather up some of those acorns or chestnuts or whatever they are, from around that tree. And peel off some strips of the bark; she can't go barefoot."

A minute later Pete and Angelica climbed back into the truck, Angelica with two pockets full of the seeds and Pete with an armload of musty-smelling damp bark strips.

Mavranos clanked the engine into gear and steered out away from the curb. "Out of town, now?" he asked.

"Yes," said Angelica, "but not by the 101." She smiled. "Take the 280 south."

CHAPTER 24

TROILUS: *O, let my lady apprehend no fear; in all Cupid's pageant*
there is presented no monster.
CRESSIDA: *Nor nothing monstrous neither?*

—William Shakespeare,
Troilus and Cressida

After he got out of the hot shower Cochran wiped the steam off the medicine-cabinet mirror and thoroughly brushed his teeth, and as he stared at the reflection of his haunted face he kept thinking about Nina's green toothbrush hanging in its slot only inches behind the hinged mirror; and he decided not to open the medicine-cabinet door again to get out his razor. When he had fumbled out his own toothbrush he hadn't thought to note how dry Nina's must be, and he didn't want to now.

Plumtree had been asleep under the sheet when he had got out of bed to come in here. The shower, and now the shock of a mouthful of Doctor Tichenor's mouthwash, had sobered him up, and he was profoundly disoriented to realize that a naked blond woman whom he had met one week ago was at this moment inertly compressing the springs of the bed he and Nina slept in.

He was remotely glad that the cassette from the phone-answering machine was in the pocket of his shirt on the back of the dressing-table chair—he didn't want to know what his response would be if someone were to call now, and Nina's recorded voice were to speak from the machine.

Plumtree would certainly sleep for at least a couple of hours. Cochran hadn't been watching the bottle of Southern Comfort, but she must have refilled her glass half a dozen times, before, between, and after. His thoughts just slid away from memories of the details of their lovemaking; all he could really bring himself to remember right now—and even that shakily—was Plumtree's hot, panting breath, flavored with More cigarette smoke and the peach-liqueur-and-bourbon taste of Southern Comfort.

He spat in the sink, and rinsed out his mouth with cold tap water scooped up in his hand because the bathroom glass was in the other room, sticky with liqueur. He had closed the bathroom door when he had come in here, and now he paused before opening it again; and after a moment of indecision he picked up his jeans and pulled them on and zipped the fly before he turned the damp doorknob and stepped out onto the bedroom carpet.

And he blinked in surprise—Plumtree was sitting up in bed, anxiously holding the sheet up to her chin.

Her shoulders slumped when she saw him. "Oh, *you,* Scant?" she wailed. "Oh, why? I *told* you I'd go to bed with you, if you'd wait! I was *sure* it was going to be a *stranger* that would walk out of that bathroom! I was just waiting to see what sort of—creep!—it would be, so I'd know who to give this flop to! Oh, Sid—*Tiffany?''* She buried her face in the sheet, and her muffled voice went on, "I loved you! And I thought you loved *me.''*

Cochran could feel his face get instantly hot, and at the same time chilly with evaporating sweat, for he suddenly had to fully admit to himself that what he was about to say was a lie. "Janis," he said, too shrilly, "I thought it was you! Are you saying that it *wasn't* you? Good God, I'm sorry, how was I—"

"You *stole*—me! It's as if you had sex with me while I was knocked out, unconscious, like when I nearly got raped in the van behind that bar in Oakland. At least *that* guy didn't ... *have* me." She shook her head furiously. "How could I ever *give* myself to you now?"

"Janis, it was a, a horrible mistake, I swear I really thought we—you were *conscious,* for God's sake—we were both drunk—"

"I said 'as if.' You *knew.* Oh, God, I've lost you." She lifted her tear-streaked face and stared at him; then she looked down at the sheet over her body, and flexed her legs. Finally she smacked her lips. "Oh, you horny son-of-a-bitch. Do you have any idea how badly you've hurt her? She was in *love* with you, you asshole!"

"Oh, I know, Cody," he said miserably. "But goddammit, we *were* both drunk, and you *do* all look exactly alike!"

Cody was scowling at him with evident disgust. "You're saying you didn't know it was Tiffany? Didn't even suspect it might be? Are you honestly telling me that?"

"I—" He sighed. "No." He lifted his shirt from the chair and slid his numb, leaden arms through the sleeves. "No, I guess not—not the *didn't even suspect* part, anyway, I guess. You're right—she's right—I wasn't *thinking* about who it was, I was just . . . what you said." He could feel the fabric of the shirt clinging to his chest already. "Jesus, Cody, I'm not being flippant, and I am sorry. You all deserved way more . . . respect? consideration? . . . from me. God, what can I—"

"Try getting out of here, so I can get dressed."

"Okay. Of course." He gave her a fragile smile as he buttoned the shirt. "I'm asking for an insult here, and I deserve it—but I've got to say I hope you won't leave. I hope you'll stay, somehow." He stepped toward the hallway door. "I'll be in the kitchen, making some coffee."

At least she didn't say anything as he walked out.

At the kitchen sink he filled the glass coffeepot with water and poured it into the back of the coffee machine; the action reminded him of that Mavranos guy pouring beer down the back of the Star Motel TV set, and he remembered that the room had been on Nina's credit card. Five nights, plus a wrecked TV set. God knew what it would cost.

As he spooned ground coffee into the filter he wondered who Tiffany might be, how complete a person—whether she was anything more than the Plumtree sex function, with no character details besides the sketched-in tastes for More cigarettes and Southern Comfort. Maybe she had been provided with one or two other props he hadn't discovered—some surface preferences in movies, or food. The ideal girlfriend, some sophomoric types would probably say with a snigger. He wondered if he had ever been shallow enough to say something like that. Well, he'd been shallow enough to *act* on it, today, which had to be worse.

He slid the filter funnel into the coffee machine and clicked it on and opened the cabinet to snag down a couple of cups. His hands were still shaking. Sugar was on the table, and he opened the refrigerator and took out a half-full carton of milk.

Plumtree was like a family of sisters—with a scary, seldom-seen father, and a crazy mother. Cochran had been initially attracted to the nice sister, and now he had gone to bed with the nymphomaniac one; but the one he had come to rely on and even admire was the . . . the tough one.

He tweaked open the milk carton and sniffed the contents. The weeks-old milk smelled cheesy, and he sighed and poured it down the sink. There was a jar of Cremora in the cabinet, he recalled.

The coffee machine had just started to sputteringly exhale air when Plumtree stepped into the kitchen from the hall. She was wearing her jeans and white blouse again, though she was still barefoot, and she was tugging one of Nina's hairbrushes through the disordered blond thatch of her hair.

"Coffee sounds good," she said. "I think spiking it would be a bad idea."

"I think we've had enough to drink for today," Cochran agreed cautiously.

"Well," she said, pulling out one of the chairs at the kitchen table and sitting down heavily, "as for the whole *day,* I don't know. I kind of picture a glass or two of something at around sundown." When Cochran had set a cup of steaming coffee in front of her, she added, "Bring that milk over here."

"It's empty," he said, turning back to the cabinet. "I've got Cremora, though."

"Cremora," she echoed, stirring sugar into the coffee. "What do you keep the milk carton around for?"

"I just now poured it out, it was bad." He glanced at the milk carton, thinking he might save it for the garden. "At the vineyard we put half-gallon milk cartons around young vines," he added absently as he poured his own cup. "It keeps the rabbits from getting at them, and prevents sunburn, and makes the shoots grow straight, up toward the light at the top." He carried his cup to the table and sat down across from her, and stared out the window at the roof of the greenhouse as he sipped it. "They'll be putting out the new seedlings soon, at Pace, in the couple of acres down by the highway." He used the Italian pronunciation for the vineyard name, *pah-chay.*

At last he looked at her. Plumtree seemed to be listening, and so he let himself go on about this neutral topic. "And," he said, "the malo-lactic fermentation will be starting up soon in the casks of last year's wine—that's a second fermentation that happens at about the same time that the new year's leaves are budding out, as if they're in communication; it's bacteria, rather than yeast, and it converts the malic acid to lactic acid, which is softer on the tongue. You want it to happen, in the Zinfandels and the Pinot Noirs." He smiled faintly, thinking about the vineyard. "When I left for Paris, the grape leaves were all in fall colors—you should see it. The Petite Sirah leaves turn purple, the Chardonnays are gold, and the Cabernet Sauvignon leaves go red as blood."

"You miss the work," said Plumtree. "Do you make good wine there?"

"Yeah, we do, actually. These last few years we've been having ideal marine-influence weather, and we're picking later in the season, and our '92 and '93 Zinfandels, not bottled yet, are already showing perfect old-viney fruit, with tannin like velvet." He shrugged self-consciously. "But, hell, since 1990, everybody in California's been making good wines, it seems like. Not just the names you've heard of, like Ridge and Mondavi, but Rochioli in the Russian River Valley and Joel Peterson's Ravenswood in Sonoma; everybody's producing spectacular harvests and vintages, in spite of the phylloxera bugs. It's almost as if the world-scale has to stay balanced—Bordeaux, all of Europe, in fact, have been getting way too much rain in these growing seasons, and *they've* been consistently *mediocre* since '90.''

"Well, Scott Crane became king in 1990. I bet '95 will be a terrible year.''

"That Kootie kid might be a good king. Maybe we'll be able to tell if he's okay, by how the wine turns out.''

Plumtree tasted the coffee and grimaced. "Did your wife like wine? Just because I'm talking to you doesn't mean I've stopped thinking you're a heartless dickhead.''

He gave her a constricted nod to show that he understood. "Nina,'' he said, clearing his throat. "Actually, she seemed to resent the big, vigorous California wines—''

Plumtree's mouth opened. "Why should the god favor this coast on the wrong side of the world? Where none of the *Appellation Controlee* commandments are even being observed! Here you are free to mechanically irrigate, if no rain comes! And you may produce . . . three, four, six tons of grapes per acre, with no penalty! In the Médoc our *vandangeurs* hold to the god's old laws, making no more than thirty-five hectoliters of wine from each hectare of land, and we nurture the sacred old Cabernet Sauvignon and supplicate the god to make it into his forgiving blood, as he did in the centuries before the Revolution—and for our pains we scarcely get a wine that's fit to drink with dinner! It's rejected like Cain's sacrifice. Here in barbaric California the desecrated Cabernet is turned into wines like, like cathedrals and Bach concertos, and *it's* not even the wine he *blesses*—he consecrates this unpedigreed upstart interloper *Zinfandel*.''

Cochran had stopped breathing, for this was Nina's voice. He could see his shirt collar twitching with his heartbeat, and he hardly dared to move, fearing that any motion might startle her ghost away.

He realized that he should speak. "Uh, not always,'' he said in a quiet, placating tone, peripherally reminded of poor Thutmose with his rusty grail full of Zinfandel that he craved to have transformed into the *pagadebiti*. "Most Zinfandel is just red wine.''

"You called me,'' said Nina's voice. She looked around at her own kitchen. "When I was on the *lit marveil,* the jumping bed, in the room with all the people in it.'' She shifted her chair back from the table and peered out the window at the midday glare on the greenhouse roof. "When was that?''

Cochran remembered having called *Nina!* when Plumtree's mother had been controlling her body, right after the pre-dawn earthquake. "That was this morning, early," he said steadily. He had been ashamed of calling her name, immediately after he'd done it, and he didn't want to look squarely at the action now. "I didn't think you heard me."

"I had a long way to come, to answer." She was frowning thoughtfully, and Cochran felt goosebumps rise on his forearms as he recognized the top-of-the-nose crease of Nina's characteristic frown, on Plumtree's sunburned face. "I was in a—unless it was a dream?—a *bar,* with a lot of very drunk people." She visibly relaxed, and smiled at him. "But I'm home now."

This isn't *her,* he told himself as his heart hammered behind his ribs, it's just her ghost. Wherever the real Nina is—*her bed is India; there she lies, a pearl*—she has no part in this. Still, this is a ghost of *her,* this is *her* ghost. Could she stay? Sleep in the bed, dampen the toothbrush? She was building a stone fountain in the garden, when she died; could she finish building it now?

But there was something wrong—something subtly but witheringly grotesque—about the idea of dead-reflex, mimic hands finishing the living woman's interrupted garden work.

And would the unborn *baby's* ghost come back, sobbing inconsolably in the darkness late some night?

And could he do this to Cody?

He lifted his coffee cup and stood up and crossed to the sink, pausing by the refrigerator to pry off of its door one of the little flat promotion-giveaway magnets stamped to look like a miniature bottle of Pace Zinfandel. "I've decided to have the mark on the back of my right hand removed," he said over his shoulder as he dumped the half-cup of lukewarm coffee into the sink. He was speaking carefully. "Laser surgery, get it done in a couple of out-patient sessions."

"Ce n'est pas possible!" she exclaimed, and he heard Plumtree's shoes scuff on the floor as she stood up. "It is your Androcles mark! The lion owed Androcles an obligation after Androcles merely pulled the thorn from the lion's paw—but you at some time put out your hand to injury to save the god! I've never spoken of it; but the mark is for only the god to take away, as it was for him to bestow it. I would never have—I would not have your child, if its father were not marked by *him.* My family didn't send me here simply to—" She gripped his shoulder with Plumtree's strong hand. "Tell me you won't do it, Scant."

"Okay," he said gently. "Sorry. I won't do it."

He filled the coffee cup with cold tap water and carried it back to the table. "Sit down," he told her, placing the cup of tap water on the table between them and stirring it with the forefinger of his right hand. After she had resumed her seat, he asked, "What . . . happened, on New Year's Day?" He touched his forehead with his wet fingertip. Then he took the cassette from the phone-answering machine out of his shirt pocket.

"In the morning, at dawn," said Nina's voice with Plumtree's lips. "I thought it might be him again, this morning, when you called me on the leaping bed. I was thrown awake at dawn on New Year's Day, and I knew he was calling me, from outside the house. My . . . I was married to him, through you. And he was freed that morning, when the earth moved and the trees were all knocked down. I wrapped myself in a bedsheet, and tied ivy in my hair, and I ran out to meet him, down the backyard path to the highway. And I—did?—it was loud, and it hurt— but I knew that was how he would come." She was staring into the clear water in the cup, and she sighed deeply.

Cochran felt empty. "What's your name?" he asked, in a voice that he tried to keep from being as flat as a dial-tone.

Slowly, he slid the little bottle-shaped magnet back and forth over the cassette.

"Nina Gestin Leon. Ariachne." Plumtree's blue eyes met his. "I see two of you, Scant. I *died* that morning, it seems to me now. Didn't I?"

"Yes, Nina." Fighting to conceal the aching bitterness in his throat, he said hoarsely, "You died that morning. I flew your ashes back to the Bas Medoc, to Queyrac, and I talked to your mother and father. We were all very sorry that you were gone, none sorrier than me. I loved you very much." He pushed the erased tape away, until he felt it tap against the coffee cup.

She shivered visibly, and blinked away tears. "Where do I go now?"

Her peace is the important thing here, he told himself wonderingly, not your betrayed love, not your pride. Let her rest in what peace there is to be had. "To your real husband at last, not just to a symbol any-more." He couldn't tell if the quaver in his voice was from rage or grief. "I imagine you'll find the god . . . in the garden."

The frown unkinked from Plumtree's forehead, leaving her sunburned face expressionless; and Cochran closed his eyes and slowly lowered his face into his hands. He was panting, his breath catching in his throat each time he inhaled, and when he felt hot tears in his palm he realized that he was weeping.

He heard the lifeless voice of Valorie: "O he is even in my mistress' case, just in her case!" A cold finger touched his cheek. "Stand up, stand up! Stand an you be a man."

He raised his head and dragged his shirtsleeve across his wet eyes. And then it was recognizably Cody who sat across from him now, blinking at him in bewildered sympathy.

"Sid," she said. "There's a car pulling into your driveway."

He pushed his chair back and stood up. He had left his revolver in the bedroom, and he started down the hall—but then, in the moment before the engine in the driveway was switched off, he recognized the sound of the rumbling exhaust.

He padded barefoot to the front door and squinted through the peephole.

The old Suburban in his driveway was bright blood red. An aura like heat waves was shimmering around it for a distance of about a foot, and the green box hedge on the far side of the driveway shone a brighter green through the aura band.

Pete and Angelica Sullivan were climbing out on this side, and he could see Arky Mavranos getting out from the driver's side. Kootie's head was visible in the back seat, and there was no one else with them.

Cochran unlocked the door and pulled it open, and the ocean-scented breeze was chilly on his wet face.

Pete and Angelica were helping Kootie step down from the back seat, but Mavranos plodded around the front of the truck and up the cobblestone walkway.

"Congratulations," Mavranos said from the bottom of the porch steps. "You've got four houseguests." He looked over Cochran's shoulder and smiled tightly, and Cochran realized that Cody must have followed him to the door. "It looks like the trick can still be done—somehow—on new terms that no one's got a clue about." His smile broadened, baring his white teeth. "I hope you're still feeling up for it, girl."

"Oh, shut up, Arky," Cody said. She stepped past Cochran, out onto the porch. "Is Kootie hurt?"

"Somebody shot him," said Mavranos. "Probably your psycho doctor. But the boy's apparently gonna be okay."

Cody gave a hiss of concern and hurried down the steps, past Mavranos, to help Pete and Angelica.

In Cochran's living room Angelica stitched up Kootie's wound with dental floss from a freshly opened box, Pete kneeling alongside to hand her scissors and cotton, while Mavranos paced back and forth at the front window with his revolver in his hand, watching the road. Cochran and Plumtree retreated into the kitchen, where they threw together in a stockpot a big stew of canned clam chowder, crabmeat, chopped green onions, cheap Fume Blanc and curry powder. When it was hot, the aroma apparently convinced everyone that the late breakfast at Seafood Bohemia hadn't been adequate, and in half an hour all of them, even Mavranos, were sitting around Cochran's dining-room table mopping the last of the makeshift chowder out of their soup bowls with stale sourdough bread. By unspoken common consent they were all drinking Pellegrino mineral water.

Cochran had to remind himself that these people had treated him rudely—and abused his credit card—and got him into the middle of an actual *gunfight,* in which people had probably been *killed*—for he found that he was unthinkingly warmed to have the Sullivans and Kootie and Mavranos come fussing and suffering into his life again, somehow especially after his humiliations with Plumtree and Nina's ghost. Despite all their bickering and crisis, they always brought with them an urgent, sweaty sense of purpose.

"How long were you people planning to stay here?" Cochran asked now, forcing his voice to be flat and uncompromising. "Overnight?"

Mavranos gave him a bland stare and Pete and Angelica Sullivan looked uneasy, but it was Kootie who answered: "Until the end of the month," the boy said diffidently. "Until the Vietnamese Tet festival, or maybe the start of the Moslem fast, Ramadan. That's February the first. Our pendulum—"

"Two weeks?" protested Cochran. "I've got a job! I've got neighbors! I've got—furniture that I don't need wrecked."

"It's not *quite* two weeks," said Kootie. "Uh . . . eleven days."

"I saw Scott Crane's skeleton," said Plumtree. "How is it supposed to work this time? He takes me forever?" She raised her eyebrows. "He takes *Kootie* forever?"

"Neither, I think," said Kootie. Cochran noticed that the boy didn't seem happy to be exempted—in fact he looked haunted and sick. "I don't know—we have to ask Mammy Pleasant. She's the old black lady from the TV."

Angelica snorted. "She's been no help up to now."

"Maybe Crane will just . . . *materialize* a body," ventured Plumtree.

"No," said Pete, "where will he get *stuff* from? He'll need protoplasm, like a hundred and sixty or so pounds of it!"

"Edison conjured up a sort of body," said Kootie quietly, "a mask, at least, when he took me over, in '92; he used the flesh of a dog I was friends with. I've dreamed of it, since. In one second, Fred—the dog—was suddenly just a bloody skeleton, and Edison had a flesh head and hands of his own, and even a furry black overcoat." He gulped some of the mineral water. "But the flesh was killed in the rearrangement. I'm sure it just rotted, after we shed it."

Jesus, thought Cochran.

Angelica nodded. "So he'll not only need protoplasm, but *unkilled* protoplasm. Are we supposed to bring some homeless guy along? A bunch of dogs?"

"Pigs are supposed to be very like humans, physically," said Plumtree. "Maybe we should bring a couple of good-size pigs."

Mavranos was pale, and looked as though he wanted to spit. "Kootie *talked* to old Pleasant today. Her ghost, but in person, not on a TV. She's apparently sort of an indentured servant, or prisoner serving out hard-labor time, of Dionysus, and she's—and the god is too—trying to help us. Apparently. She gave Kootie a message for Crane, some kind of summons and commandment, and it's in the form of a Latin palindrome. I don't like that, 'cause it's *ghosts* that are drawn to palindromes, and Crane's *ghost* is a naked imbecile running around at the Sutro ruins."

"Is it the Latin thing I burned up the matchbook with," asked Cochran, "in the motel room? And there was another Latin bit that Cody and I saw, on an ashtray in L.A. I don't remember what it was."

Mavranos hiked his chair back to dig a car registration slip out of his jeans pocket. He unfolded it, and read:

> "*Roma, tibi subito motibus ibit Amor.*
> *Si bene te tua laus taxat, sua laute tenebis.*
> *Sole, medere pede: ede, perede melos.*"

"That first line is definitely the thing that was on the ashtray in L.A.," said Plumtree.

Cochran could feel hairs stirring on the back of his neck. "After I read that line out loud, there, Crane's ghost showed up as our taxi driver. And after I read out the second one, in the Sutro ruins, his crazy naked ghost appeared *there*."

"Don't speak the third one now," said Mavranos. "A naked guy banging around in your kitchen would only upset the ladies. Wouldn't do me any good, either, seeing a semblance of my old friend in that totally bankruptious state." He sighed, then glared at Cochran. "Okay if I use your phone? I should see if Nardie's got the damn thing translated."

"There's a speakerphone in the kitchen," Cochran said. "Talk to her on that, so we can all hear it."

* * *

In the sunny kitchen, Cochran and Plumtree resumed their seats at the table, while Pete and Angelica leaned on the counter by the sink. Kootie slumped into a third chair, but looked at the counter as if he'd have liked to climb up on it if he hadn't had fresh stitches in his side. Cochran recalled that Kootie had sat up on a washing machine when they had tried to call Crane's ghost in Solville, and he wondered why the boy wanted to be distanced from the ground when important calls were being made.

Mavranos had walked straight to the telephone on the wall and punched in the eleven digits of the long-distance number, and now tapped the speakerphone button.

"Hello?" came a young woman's cautious voice out of the speaker; Cochran had seldom used the speakerphone function, and he now reflected ruefully that the sound wasn't as good as what Kootie's chalk-in-the-pencil-sharpener speaker had produced.

"Arky here, Nardie," said Mavranos, "with all the king's horses and all the king's men listening in. Whaddaya got?"

"Okay, your three palindromes are a pentameter followed by a hexameter followed by a pentameter," said the woman called Nardie. "That's a natural alternation in Roman lyric verse, like in Horace and Catullus. This could be very damned old, you know? And the lines do seem to relate to your—our—situation. You got a pencil?"

Mavranos pulled open a drawer under the telephone and pawed through it. "Yes," he said, fumbling out an eyeliner pencil and Cochran's January gas bill.

"Okay," said Nardie's voice from the speaker, "*Roma,* with a comma after it, is in the vocative case, addressing Rome, which our context pretty clearly makes 'spiritual power on Earth,' like a rogue version of the Vatican, okay? *Tibi subito* is 'to you, suddenly, abruptly.' *Motibus* is in the ablative case, indicating in what manner, so it means something like 'with dancing motion,' though Cicero uses it in the phrase *motus terrae,* which means an earthquake."

"You told me *motibus* was 'motor bus,' " Plumtree whispered to Cochran. She seemed relieved.

He nodded tightly and waved at her to be quiet.

"*Ibit,*" Nardie was saying, "is the third-person future tense of 'to go.' Of course *amor* is 'love,' but the capital *A* makes me think it's a person, like some god of love; and in this suddenness-and-earthquake context very likely a harsh one."

Cochran was thinking of the god who had awakened him with an apparent earthquake in the Troy and Cress Wedding Chapel in Las Vegas nearly five years ago, and of Nina, who had preferred that god's fatal love to his own.

"In the second line," Nardie went on, "*taxat* is a first-declension verb, *taxo, taxare,* meaning 'hold, value, esteem.' Literally, it's 'if your praise values you well,' but in English that'd be 'if you value your praise well.' *Sua* is a possessive pronoun—it has to be in the nominative case, though I'd have liked *suam* better; anyway, it's feminine, agreeing with the feminine *laus*, which is 'praise' or 'fame.' I think 'your fame' here is supposed to be actually, literally feminine in relation to this *Amor* person, who is fairly emphatically masculine. *Laute* is 'gloriously.' *Tenebis* is a second-declension verb: 'to hold, to arrive at.' "

Mavranos was impatiently waving the eyeliner pencil in front of his face. "Nardie, what does the goddamn thing *mean?*"

A shaky sigh buzzed out of the speaker. "I'm explaining why I think it means what I'm gonna tell you, Arky, okay? Now listen, the last line really does flicker between alternate readings; I just finished untangling this a few minutes ago. *Sole,* with a comma after it, is like *Roma* in the first line, it has to be the vocative of *sol,* direct address for 'sun,' as in 'O Sun.' *Medere* is an infinitive or a gerund—or, as we've got here, an imperative—of 'cure, remedy'; it's not so much 'to cure' or 'curing' as it is an *order,* see—'fix it!' or 'remedy it!' *Pede* is 'louse,' the singular noun, as in Pliny's use of *pediculus* or the English word 'pediculosis,' which means an infestation of lice. Now the verb *Ede* is very interesting here; it's either from *edo, edere, edi, esum,* which is the usual Latin verb for 'devour, consume, eat away'—or else it's another verb, *edo, edere, edidi, editum,* which means 'breathe one's last, bring to an end,' or at the same time 'give birth to,' or 'give forth from oneself.' Either verb works here, though the long *e* imposed by the trochaic meter makes me favor the second one. *Perede* is emphasis, emphatic repetition of the previous verb, whichever that is. And *melos* is generally translated as 'song,' but it's a Latinized Greek word—obviously, from the suffix, right?—and the Greek for *melos* can also be 'limb.' As a Latin word it could be either nominative or accusative here, but with the Greek form it's got to be accusative, a direct object."

"What," said Mavranos, speaking with exaggerated clarity, "does— *the-damn-thing-mean?*"

"Okay. In my interpretation, it means: 'O spiritual power on Earth, the god of love will come to you suddenly and abruptly,' either 'with dancing movements' or 'as an earthquake'—or as both, conceivably. 'If you value your praise highly you will hold it'—or 'arrive at it'—'gloriously. O Sun, remedy the louse: give forth from yourself, and give forth from yourself again, your limb.' And with the confusion of the two *edo* vebs, there's the implication of 'your *devoured* limb.' "

"Leave the suicide king in the deck," said Plumtree.

Mavranos frowned at her, but nodded. "I think I tried to tell Scott that, when we went to Northridge after the earthquake a year ago. The subterranean phylloxera lice were a summons from . . . under sanctified ground."

"He never could bear to cut back the grapevines, in the midwinter," said Nardie's voice from the speaker, "after that first year. Even when the babies started to get fevers and pulmonary infections in the winters, and he had to eat No-Doz all day long, and his fingernails bled." There was a pause while she might have shrugged. "He was still strong in the summers."

Cochran was remembering putting out his hand to keep the face in the stump from being beheaded. "What we do next," he said, glancing at everyone but finally fixing his gaze on Angelica, "is what?"

Angelica gave him a tired smile. "Thank you for the 'we,' " she said. "We won't ask you for your gun again. What we do next," she said, stepping away from the counter and stretching, "can't be anything else but summon Kootie's silly old black lady, I guess." She dropped her arms and looked at Plumtree. "We've got to talk to her in person."

"In *this* person, you mean," said Plumtree, though only in a tone of tired resignation. "Jeez, if my own genetic *father,* imposed on me, gives me toothaches and nosebleeds, God knows what this strange old woman will be like."

"No," said Kootie, "your father never died, but Mammy Pleasant did. She's a ghost. When Edison had possession of me, there was nothing like that afterward. Ghosts don't have the, the *psychic DNA* of a body anymore, they've got no vital structure to impose on the living body that hosts them."

"Cool," sighed Plumtree. "Not really my idea of a fun date *anyway,* to tell you the truth, but I guess that's neither here nor there." She stood up from the table. "Tell me what I've got to do."

"I'm Bernardette Dinh," came the voice from the speaker, "at the king's overthrown Camelot in Leucadia."

"I'm Janis Cordelia Plumtree, and my *compadre* here is Sid Cochran. I hope we can all meet in person one day, in the presence of the king."

"Back in Solville," said Kootie hesitantly, "Mammy Pleasant told us, 'eat the seeds of my trees.' "

Angelica now reached into the pocket of her denim jacket and pulled out a fistful of what looked like angular gray acorns. She dropped them onto the kitchen table, and their rattling was nothing like bar dice. "We picked these up this morning, at the foot—sorry, at the *waist*—of one of her suffering trees. Koala bears eat this stuff, so it's probably not poison,'' she said. ''I figure we can make an infusion in wine with some of 'em, and grind up some others to mix with flour and make bread.''

BOOK THREE
Gout de Terroir

The vine by nature is apt to fall, and unless supported drops down to the earth; yet in order to keep itself upright it embraces whatever it reaches with its tendrils as though they were hands.
—Marcus Tullius Cicero

CHAPTER 25

"I am afraid of it," she answered, shuddering.
"Of it? What?"
"I mean of him. Of my father."
　　　　　　　　　—Charles Dickens,
　　　　　　　　　A Tale of Two Cities

In the Salinas and Santa Clara and Livermore valleys, on the jade green slopes that stretched away from the highways up to where the Santa Cruz Mountains in the west and the Diablo Range in the east met the gray sky, the newly head-pruned grapevines stood in rows like gnarled crucifixes, as if a tortured god hung at endlessly reiterated sacrifice in the cold rain.

The work in the vineyard cellars in late January was racking the wines, pumping the new vintages from one cask to another to liberate them from the freshly thrown sediments of dead yeast cells, and fining them with egg whites to precipitate cloudiness out. In the Pace cellars on San Bruno Mountain the suspension-cloudiness in the casks was heavy this year, and bentonite clay as well as egg whites were both needed to bring the wine to clarity, and the *"goût de terroir,"* the flavor of earth, was especially pronounced. On the slopes outside, tractors dragged harrows and cultivators through the old-standard eight-foot aisles between the rows, and this year the blades and disks were soon blunted to uselessness by the rocky soil and had to be replaced after having served only half of their expected life spans.

During the long days Sid Cochran oversaw the washing out of the drained casks with soda ash and hot water so that the wines could be racked back into them, and in the evenings he was kept busy in the lab, chilling some samples of the adjusted new wines to test for tartaric acid stability and heating others to provoke any incipient protein hazing.

After his twelve days off, which the payroll clerk had listed as compassionate leave following the death of a family member, Cochran had now worked for seven days straight, as much for relief from his five houseguests as for catching up on the uncompromising vineyard chores and getting in some justifiable overtime pay.

Six or seven houseguests, he thought on Saturday afternoon as he steered the Granada up into his driveway and switched off the engine; at least. Though admittedly only five at any particular moment.

Mavranos's truck was parked at the top of the driveway. The new pair of tan car covers, weighted down with bricks, concealed the truck's red color, but did nothing to hide its boxy shape.

Cochran got out of the car and walked toward his 1960s ranch-style house across the lawn rather than on the stepping-stones, for Kootie had covered them with chalk detection-evasion patterns he'd apparently learned from Thomas Alva Edison two years ago; and up on the porch Cochran brushed aside Angelica's wind chimes of chicken bones and old radio parts, avoided stepping in the smears of pork-fat-and-salt that Mammy Pleasant had carefully daubed onto the concrete, then ignored the brass keyhole plate below the doorknob and crouched to fit his housekey into the disguised lock Mavranos had installed at the base of the door.

The warm air in the entry hall smelled of WD-40 spray oil and stewing beef and onions, and Cochran could hear Bob Dylan's "It's All Over Now, Baby Blue" from the *Subterranean Homesick Blues* album playing on the stereo in the living room. The music told him that Mavranos was in the house, and the pair of treebark-soled Ferragamo pumps by the door indicated that Mammy Pleasant was not currently occupying the Plumtree body.

"Cody?" he called as he shrugged out of his rain-damp windbreaker.

"She's out working on the Torino," came Pete Sullivan's voice from the kitchen. "How goes the bottle?" He was sitting at the kitchen table, leaning over a couple of half-dismantled walkie-talkies with a screwdriver.

"Aging." Yesterday Cochran had replied, *Cobwebby.* He stepped into the kitchen and tossed his windbreaker onto the counter and then opened the refrigerator to get one of Mavranos's beers. Freshly scratched into the white enamel of the refrigerator door were the numbers *1-28-95;* during this week of frustrating waiting Plumtree had got into the habit of key-scratching the current day's date on any surface that would show a gouge—wood tabletops, drywall, book spines. When he had protested after finding the first few examples, last weekend, she had doggedly told him that she had to do it, that it was like the hospital

surgery-ward policy of inking *NO* on limbs that were not to be "ecto-
mied," cut off. And she had been using a black laundry-marking pen
to letter the name of each day on whatever blouse of Nina's she was
wearing. Probably she was doing the same to her underwear; Cochran
was sleeping on the living-room couch these days, and didn't know.

Cochran carried his beer out through the laundry room to the back
door, the window of which was still broken from the morning two weeks
ago when he and Plumtree had let themselves in by breaking the glass
with a wine bottle. When he unlocked the door and pushed it open
against the cold outdoor breeze, the woman standing by the raised hood
of the '69 Torino looked at him, and was clearly Cody.

"You've got to talk to Janis," Cody said.

Cochran walked up to the old car. Cody had taken the carburetor and
the distributor cap off of the engine, and had laid out wrenches and a
timing-light gun on a towel draped over the fender.

"I've tried to," he said.

Several times at their noisy buffet-style breakfasts he had noticed
Plumtree eating poached or fried eggs, holding the fork in her right
hand, and he had caught her eye—but each time her face had changed,
and it had been Cody who had given him a blank, questioning look as
she switched the fork to her left hand and reached for the bowl of
scrambled eggs; and once Plumtree's posture, as she had stood on tiptoe
to reach a volume of Edna St. Vincent Millay down from a high bookshelf, had clearly been Janis's shoulders-back stance—but, when he had
called to her, Cody had blinked impatiently at the book and paused only
long enough to dig her set of car keys out of her pocket and scratch the
date into the cover before putting it back.

"She's avoiding me," Cochran said.

"Well I wonder why." Plumtree laid down a screwdriver she'd been
twisting the idle screw with and held out her black-smeared left hand.
"Can I have your beer? I'm too dirty to be touching your doorknobs
and refrigerator handles."

Cochran handed it to her, without even taking a last sip of it. "And
I'll get you another if you want, just to save you the walk," he said,
"but *mi casa es su casa,* Cody. Mess up anything you want."

Plumtree took the beer with a grin. After a deep sip, she exhaled and
said, "Thanks, but Mammy Pleasant will make me clean up any messes
I make. Have you *seen* those lists of chores she leaves for me? Not just
shopping and cleaning—sometimes she tells me to go buy or sell
houses! But I called about a couple, they're all pre-1906 addresses. It's
a good thing she doesn't know the 1995 prices I'm paying for her

groceries, she'd think I was embezzling. And in the notes she's always calling me Teresa.''

Cochran nodded. Cody and Mammy Pleasant were both strong presences in the household, and managed to get on each other's nerves in spite of the fact that they could never meet, taking turns as they did at occupying the same body. But Cochran had several times talked directly to the old-woman personality, and she seemed to be as senile as Kootie said most ghosts were. The Teresa person had evidently been a servant she'd had when she'd been alive.

The Mammy Pleasant ghost had first arrived upon Plumtree last Sunday, after Cody had consented to eat bread baked with ground Octavia Street eucalyptus seeds in it and drink wine in which the split seeds had sat soaking overnight. For an hour after taking the dubious sacrament, Plumtree had just sat on the living-room couch, flushing her mouth with vodka to kill the taste of the eucalyptus and watching the news—

And then she had blinked and reared back, staring with clear recognition into the faces of Kootie and Pete and Angelica and Cochran through eyes that momentarily seemed to Cochran to be mismatched in color. After a few seconds she had looked back at the television, and said in a strong, deep voice, "I was talking to you people through that thing, wasn't I?"

"Yes, ma'am," said Kootie, looking away from her.

"Courage, boy!" she said. "Remember Gawain."

"Yes, ma'am," said Kootie again.

Angelica had begun asking the old woman questions, but Mammy Pleasant had immediately demanded to know if they had brought any eucalyptus bark from her tree; and, when she'd been assured that they had, that a pair of shoes be soled from the bark for her. And when Pete and Kootie had cut out bark soles and heels and Superglued them onto a pair of Nina's low-heeled Ferragamo pumps—Pleasant had haughtily dismissed the notion of using a pair of Reeboks after getting a look at them—the old woman had put the shoes on and walked outside in the crackling, fragmenting footwear, straight to the greenhouse.

Scott Crane's disordered skeleton was laid out in there on a shelf between Nina's orchids and a crowd of potted fuchsias, and the Plumtree hands were shaky as they touched the broken skull. "He himself will lead you to the god's wine," she had said. "And by then you'll have learned where to go with it, and what to do."

She hadn't said very much more about Crane's restoration to life than that—then or in the six days since. She generally came on within an hour to either side of noon, though the sun was seldom visible through the overcast, and often she seemed absentminded, or senile, or even drunk—which, Mavranos noted, was only to be expected in a servant of Dionysus. She kept finding jobs around the house for "Teresa" to do, and had to leave notes because she could never find the girl; and Plumtree had begun leaving notes in return, suggesting that the old woman clean the floors and windows herself. When Kootie or Angelica stopped the old woman and try to get information about the procedure they were supposedly going to perform on the day of the Tet Festival, Pleasant's drunkenness would seem to become more pronounced—and she would just insist that Crane would presently tell them what to do. Adding to the confusion was the fact that she generally slurred the name to *Cren*, and frequently pronounced it with a stutter, *C-cren*, so that she seemed to be referring to Cochran. Even her pronunciation of *Scott* sometimes seemed to slur nasally toward *Scant.*

Cochran now watched Cody spraying the carburetor with some very flammable-smelling aerosol.

"Janis is avoiding me," he said again.

"Don't light a cigarette right now," Cody said. "I don't blame her. But I think she should talk to you." She put down the spray can and squinted up at him, her face shadowed by the raised car hood. "I saw into her dream for a couple of seconds last night. You were in both of our dreams, and the . . . figure of you, your outline, must have sort of matched up and spun around at the partition between her mind and mine—like one of those secret bookshelf-walls in old movies, that rotate on a pivot when you pull on the right book." Cody took another gulp of the beer. "Her dream was in color, but barely—it looked fake, like a black-and-white photo touched up with watercolors, and the backgrounds were plain gray. And there was music, the dwarf music from *Sleeping Beauty*, but I could hardly hear the melody because the drumming was so hard and loud. It sounded like soldiers marching fast on an iron deck."

Cochran bared his teeth unhappily. He couldn't forget the image of Janis valiantly punching the linoleum floor at the Rosecrans Medical Center nearly three weeks ago; nor her look of despairing hurt in his bed last Tuesday, when he had last spoken to her. "What does that mean?" he asked Cody.

"*Valorie's* memories are in black-and-white, and always have drumming going on. I think Janis is draining away into Valorie."

But Valorie's dead! he almost said. "Can . . . that happen?"

"As far as we're concerned, Sid, *anything* can happen. We went to a funeral once when we were twelve, and by the time the minister was done talking it was somebody else's funeral and we were fourteen; and what we thought was the emotion of rage turns out to be our male parent, who's alive and crouching inside our head; and I have to look at whatever I last scratched the date on to be sure—'' She glanced at fresh scratches in the greasy curve of the manifold valve cover. ''—to be sure that the goddamn Edison Medicine that broke us all into separate pieces, all finally *aware* of each other, happened only seventeen days ago!''

Cochran smiled with half of his face. ''I see what you mean. The word 'impossible' isn't what it used to be, for any of us.'' Cody was holding out the beer can toward him; he took it to throw away for her, but it was still more than half full, so he gratefully tilted it up for a sip and then handed it back to her. ''What can I say to Janis besides that I'm sorry? Besides that I know I was the bad guy and that she deserved better from even a total stranger, never mind from somebody she had got herself into bad trouble to protect?''

Cody laughed. ''Besides those things?'' Then she sobered. ''I honestly don't *know,* but it might save her if you told her you love her.'' She shook her head. ''My . . . it's not sister; my *other half?* . . . seems to be evaporating, *dying.*''

''I *could* tell her that, I suppose, if it would help,'' he said cautiously. He glanced back at the kitchen door. ''But if it did help, and she came back, even though I'd—I mean, she'd be able to tell—''

Cody raised an eyebrow. ''You don't love her?''

''No.''

''Huh. She seems to me like the ideal woman, everything I'm not. So do you love *anybody?*'' She coughed. ''I mean, anybody who's alive?''

At first Cochran thought he wouldn't be able to look at her. Then he did meet her eyes, though his voice was incongruously light when he answered, ''Yes.''

It was Cody that looked away. ''I don't think that's very smart.'' She coughed again, rackingly. ''Well, go ahead and lie to her, and we can worry about the consequences once she's herself again. Better a car that's gonna let you down halfway home than one that won't run at all.''

Cochran considered, then rejected, the idea of drinking a couple of beers first. ''I don't know what I'll say. But go ahead—call her up.''

''I can't, she won't come voluntarily. *You've* got to call her up.''

''How am I supposed to—oh. Follow-the-Queen.''

''Right. Wait right here, I'll . . . get my stupid parentess.'' Plumtree closed her eyes. ''Mother!'' she called.

Instantly her eyes sprang open, and she stepped back away from Cochran after grabbing up a screwdriver from the fender. ''You tell him,'' she said, ''that if he comes out of that house I'll drive this straight into my own heart. He'll know I mean it.'' The skin of her neck was suddenly looser, and her eyes seemed closer together.

''He's nowhere around here, Mrs. . . . Plumtree,'' said Cochran awkwardly. Why was he talking to this personality? According to Angelica it wasn't her real mother, nor even a real ghost, just an internalized version of her parent patched together from memories and overheard conversations. ''I do know who you mean,'' Cochran went on. ''We're hiding from him.'' He felt as though he had dialed six digits of Janis's number, and was afraid to dial the last one. ''We're protecting your daughter from him.''

''You can't *hide*, you can't *protect* anyone, from Omar Salvoy,'' said the querulous voice, though her fist relaxed around the screwdriver handle. But Cochran's stomach was cold, and he wished she had not mentioned Salvoy's name. ''*Especially* you can't protect *her*. He wants to have a child by a dead woman. I was nearly dead when he had intercourse with me, I was—unconscious!—in a coma!—after a head injury!''

Cochran thought of his afternoon with Tiffany, then drove the horrifying parallel out of his mind.

The mother personality almost put Plumtree's eye out as she reached up to rub her eyes with the hand holding the screwdriver. ''Listen to me,'' she went on. ''He studied the old books of the Order of the Knights Templar, and one of their secret mystery-initiation stories was about a man who dug up a dead woman out of her grave and had intercourse with her cold body; and after he had raped the corpse and buried it again, a voice from the earth told him to return in nine months and he would find a divine son. He came back then, and when he dug her up this time he found a, a blinking, grimacing little black *head* lying on her thigh-bones. And the voice from the earth told him to guard it well, for it would be the source of all forgiveness. And so he took it away, and guarded it jealously, and he prospered with impunity.'' There were tears in her eyes as she glared at Cochran. ''My baby died when he fell on her. There's some kind of . . . *kaleidoscope* girl that's grown up in there, in her head, but my *baby* died that day in Soma.'' She was shaking her head violently and drawing the screwdriver blade across her chest. ''But she can still, my *dead daughter* can still become pregnant, if Omar is in a male body. He can become the father of the god.''

Cochran knew that it was his vision, and not the sky, that had darkened; but with a shaking hand he reached out and and then suddenly, firmly, gripped the blade of the screwdriver.

''Don't kill her,'' he whispered. Was this the same god? he wondered;

was the horrible little homunculus she'd described the same person as the deity of groves and grapevines that offered the *pagadebiti?* The *mondard* that had spoken to him in Paris with such fatherly affection, before turning into a bull-headed thing and then into a tumbled straw effigy? The god that had made the Agave woman in Mavranos's Euripides play cut off her son's head? What kind of primordial proto-deity could be all these things?

He thought of the endless rows of gnarled crucifixes dripping out on the surrounding hills in the rain.

"Don't kill her," he repeated. "I'll protect her, I'll save her from him. I love her." I love the *real* one, he thought, even if you don't know which that is.

Plumtree shook her head in evident pity. "She'll come to the point where she'll tear you to pieces just for the honor of being able to bring your head to him. Who are *you* to the *god?*"

Cochran abruptly pulled the screwdriver out of her hands. Then, slowly, he turned his hand around to show her the mark below his knuckles. "When I was a boy," he said, "I put out my hand to save him from the pruner's shears."

Plumtree had gasped, and now nodded slowly. "Send her away into the sea," she said. "She belongs in India, not here, not being the mother of the god. The god himself couldn't want that, to have an incarnate aspect of himself in filial obligation to a monster." The smile she gave him was one he had not seen before on Plumtree's face, but it was brave. "I love her too."

"I'll do what's right," he said, "for her." Then he took a deep breath and said, gently, "Janis."

Plumtree's features pinched in anxiety. "Oh, it's Scant," she said; then her voice quickened: "Was *he* here? I can feel his name still on my tongue! *Daddy?*" she called, glancing around at the yard and the greenhouse. "I'll never ditch you, Daddy! I'll always catch you! Listen to me! Where I go, you go, I swear on my life!"

"Shut up, Janis, please!" Cochran hissed, spinally aware of the vineyards and of the skeleton in the greenhouse. "He wasn't here. I have to talk to you, Janis. You don't have to forgive me, but you do have to know that, that *I* know I was totally in the wrong, and I'm terribly sorry and ashamed of myself." He smacked his fist against his thigh, angry with himself for saying this badly. "All my excuses were lies, Janis. You were right about me, but I want to make it up to you, to whatever extent I can. Will you come back to us, please? Cody needs you. *I* need you. I—"

"To be or not to be, that is the question," said Plumtree.

Cochran faltered. "Valorie?"

"No . . . no, I'm Janis, still."

I should have known, Cochran thought, that it wouldn't be Valorie quoting the only Shakespeare line that everyone in the world knows. "Janis, I—"

"Don't, Scant mustn't, I'll make myself deaf to him—we can do that. Leave me alone, if he wants to do something for me, he can leave me alone!" She hurried away across the concrete patio deck to the kitchen door, yanked it open, and slammed it behind her.

Cochran thought seriously for a moment about pursuing her. Then he sighed, picked up Cody's abandoned beer, and leaned against the car fender. Maybe, he thought, I should tell it all to dead *Valorie,* and let *her* explain it to Janis.

What damn good is this person that's me? he thought, glancing from the kitchen door to the mark on the back of his hand. How in hell am I supposed to play this flop, when I'm gambling with so many people's bankrolls? And he remembered Kootie telling him, at the Sutro ruins two weeks ago, *You'll be taking all our chances.*

Omar Salvoy found himself in a bedroom with a telephone in it.

He knew he would have to be careful in what he said to Dr. Richard Paul Armentrout, and he crossed his arms under his daughter's breasts— *A divine offspring for you to nurse during this thirteen-moon year, baby, I promise,* he thought—and paced up and down the rag rug in front of the bedside table. *Bye, baby bunting, Daddy's gone a-hunting, gone to get a leopard-skin to bury baby bunting in.*

In his youth Salvoy had only wanted to find a king to serve. He had been a theater major at Stanford University, specializing in Shakespeare and finding startling clues in some of the obscurer plays, and living in a shabby little apartment in Menlo Park.

In May of 1964, when he had been nineteen, Salvoy had gone with a friend to the La Honda house of Ken Kesey, out in the redwood forests at the south end of State Highway 84. Kesey's *One Flew Over the Cuckoo's Nest* had been published only two years earlier.

And, in Kesey, Salvoy thought he had found his king. The burly, balding Oregonian had gathered a whole tribe together at his remote hillside ranch in the canyon, and he spoke of the new drug LSD as the almost sacramental key to "worlds that have always existed." Hi-fi speakers boomed and yowled on the roof of the house, shattering the silence of the ancient redwood forest, and weird wind chimes and crazy paintings were hung on all the trees. Omar Salvoy had begun visiting the place on his own, driving his old Karmann Ghia down the 84 over the Santa Cruz Mountains to the La Honda ranch every weekend.

One day out in the woods someone had found a dozen oversized wooden chessmen, weathered and cracked, and Kesey's tribe had spontaneously begun improvising a dialogue among the figures—it had had to do with a king threatened with castration, and a girl with "electric eel tits that ionized King Arthur's sword under swamp water"—and though the impromptu play was just a cheerful stoned rap from a bunch of distracted proto-hippies, Salvoy had believed he had heard mythic, archetypal powers manifesting themselves in the lines. When Kesey had set his people to painting random patterns in Day-Glo paint all over the 1939 International Harvester school bus he had just bought, Salvoy had climbed up to the destination sign over the windshield and painted on it the name ARTHUR.

That night he had managed to catch Kesey for a few minutes away from his followers, and he had told him about the magical kingdom of the American West, and how the current king—a castrated transplanted Frenchman!—could surely be overthrown when that cycle came around again, at Easter in '69, five years hence. And he had told Kesey about the supernatural power he would have if he took the throne, how he would be able to shackle and control the god of earthquakes and wine as the present king was doing, and raise ghosts to do his errands, and live forever. Omar Salvoy would be King Kesey's advisor.

But Kesey had just laughed and, as Salvoy recalled, had said something like, "And if I jump off a cliff, angels will bear me up lest I dash my foot against a stone, right?"—and he had walked away. Salvoy believed it had been a quote from the New Testament, when Jesus was refusing to be tempted by Satan. *One Flew Over the Cuckoo's Nest* had been full of Christ-figure imagery. Salvoy had driven home over the mountains in a humiliated rage, and never returned. Later he had seen a photograph of Kesey's bus in *Life* magazine—someone had painted *FU* over his *A* on the destination sign, so that it now just read, idiotically, FURTHUR.

Salvoy had abandoned college, though he'd kept studying the plays of Shakespeare, and he began to sample the strange cults that were springing up in the Bay Area in the mid-sixties. From a splinter group of the Order of the Knights Templar he learned about the uses of the Eye of Horus symbol, the *udjat* eye that looked like a profile falcon, in countering the influences of the feminine Moon Goddess; and that it was possible actually to become the human father of a living, absolving fragment of the god who died with the grapevines every winter and was reborn in them every spring, by impregnating a dead woman; and for a few months he traveled up and down the coast on Highway 1, from Big Sur to the state beaches between Santa Barbara and Ventura, with the agricultural human-sacrifice cult that was then still calling itself the Camino Hayseeds, not for two decades yet to be internally reorganized and have its name changed to the Amino Acids.

And then toward the end of the year he had found the Danville-area commune known as the Lever Blank, whose secret and very old real name was L'Ordre du Levrier Blanc, which meant The Order of the White Greyhound. The name had apparently been chosen as long ago as the thirteenth century as a repudiation of the dog that appeared on the Fool card in the tarot deck, which was always a mongrel and generally black. The Lever Blank grew vegetables and marijuana on part of its land, and dispensed food to indigent street people, and talked a lot about harmony with nature and celebrations of life; but the Levrier Blanc was concerned with the grapes that grew on the rest of the commune land, and with re-establishing the carefully preseved old pre-phylloxera vines that had borne Dionysus's sacramental wine before the French Revolution, and with the supernatural kingdom of the American west which Salvoy had already perceived. Salvoy had decided to join them and become the king, the earthly personification of the sun-god, himself. And, based on what he had learned from the Order of the Templars, he had resolved too to father an incarnate piece of the earthbound, annually dying vegetation god.

He had failed at all that, then. This year he would do it.

But it would be a risky and probably one-shot procedure. He would have to learn from Armentrout how to exit a body without hurting it—he wanted to leave the Plumtree body alive, healthy, and fertile. The Koot Hoomie boy would have to be comatose, flat-line brain-dead; Salvoy would take the ventilator out of his throat and then lean over the boy and jump across the gap in a moment when Koot was, ideally, inhaling. At that point, with no tenant-mind to overcome, Salvoy would simply *have* Koot Hoomie's body.

And Salvoy would quickly have to kill Armentrout, whose goal in all this was to have a *perpetually* flatline brain-dead king. If Armentrout were actually present, Salvoy would have to remember to put a gun or a knife into the boy's limp hand before throwing himself out of the Plumtree body into Koot Hoomie.

He punched the doctor's number into the telephone, and when the querulous voice said, hoarsely, "Hello?" Salvoy forgot diplomacy and just said, "You tried to kill Koot Hoomie, you fat freak!" He did remember to keep his voice down.

"But I failed," said the doctor quickly. "My mother—Muir—my

ghosts are *still around*, they haven't been banished! The boy must still be alive—healthy, even!—I've been searching for him with the shadow of a pomegranate, but there's been so little sun—''

"Yeah, he's alive. He's with us, still. I'm in the same house with him right now! But I ain't tellin' you dick if you're just gonna try and kill him again.'' He bared the Plumtree teeth and spat out, ''You fucking block, you stone, you worse than goddamn senseless thing!''

"No, I won't, I was desperate that day—of course I want to, we both want to, get him onto the perpetual life-support arrangement, brain-dead—but, try to understand this, my *mother's ghost* had found me! I was desperate—I was only thinking about—if I killed him outright it would at least get rid of *her*.''

"You fucking dumb—didn't you think *Koot Hoomie's* ghost would come after you?''

"It would have been a reprieve—and he's the king, and I think the king's ghost would have bigger concerns than to go after his murderer. Crane didn't come after your girls, did he? Anyway, I *didn't kill the boy*.''

"Well, you're on my shit-list, ipso fatso. The good news is that they did the restoration-to-life trick *all wrong*, and this Koot Hoomie boy is the king if anyone is. Anyway, nobody else is. Look, I'll cut the boy out of the pack here, but before I let you anywhere near him, you're gonna have to tell me everything you know about transferring a person from one body to another.''

"Why would you need to know that? All you need to know is that a dead Fisher King is a heat-sink.'' Armentrout giggled breathlessly. "He takes the heat.''

"Tell you what, why don't I just go find another doctor? There's gotta be more than one psychiatrist in this country who'd like to have in his clinic an engine for . . . for eliminating the spiritual consequences of sin.'' Salvoy clunked the receiver against the wall as if about to hang up—and then he heard a knock at the bedroom door.

It was recognizably Cody who pulled open the bedroom door after Cochran's knock, and she was holding the telephone receiver to her ear against the spring-tension of the stretched-out cord. Her face was spotty, and she touched a finger to her tight bloodless lips as she held the receiver out toward him.

Cochran twisted his head to listen, with her—and he heard Dr. Armentrout's unmistakable fruity voice coming out of the earpiece: ''—can hear you breathing! You need *me*, Salvoy, don't kid yourself! What other psychiatrist is going to *know* that mind-shifting trick you want? Hah?

Asymptotic freedom, remember? How to pick up your *ass and tote it* out of there? I'll tell you how to do it—I'll *help* you do it, I was just curious why you wanted to, that's all. And I'm her physician-of-record!'' Armentrout was panting over the phone. "You're listening, right? So tell me where you are, where *he* is.''

Cochran ventured to make a gravelly "Hmm,'' sound.

"You say they did the restoration-to-life trick all wrong,'' said Armentrout, catching his breath. "Are you afraid they might do it again, and do it *right* this time? I don't know why you should care about that, but if you want to screw them up, I can certainly help you, you know. You could *use* the physician-of-record being present. Is that Cochran guy there too?''

Nervous sweat itching under his eyes, Cochran replied with a careful whistling sigh.

"Oh shit,'' whispered Armentrout. "Janis?'' he said then, strongly. "Cody? This is your doctor. Please tell me where you're staying.''

Cochran saw Plumtree put her top teeth into her lower lip as though preparing to say a word that started with *F,* but instead she shook her head and stepped back to the phone to rattlingly hang up the receiver.

"Smart not to say anything,'' Cochran said when the connection had been broken. "This way he can't be *sure* it wasn't . . . your father. I'm sorry I spooked him, there, at the end—''

"No,'' she said, staring at the telephone as if she thought it might manifest some dire noise or light that would give them only seconds to flee the room, flee the house; "you had to make *some* response, and that first *hmm* got a couple of extra sentences out of him.'' When she looked up at him her pupils were pinpricks and her jawmuscles were working. "Janis let him on. *Damn* her, it makes me *sick* to think of him—'' She spread her fingers and then closed her hands into tight fists, "*in here,* in me.'' He mouth worked, and then she spat on the rug. "I need Listerine. At least he wasn't on for long enough to give me a nosebleed or hurt my teeth much—and he didn't tell Armentrout where we are.'' She glanced at the black plastic ten-dollar watch she'd bought to replace the hospital *zeitgeber* watch. "How long ago was it that I called up my mother for you?''

"Oh—five minutes?''

Plumtree tossed her head in exasperation. "Five minutes at the end for *some* of them,'' she said sternly, "but *they've* got to be sautéed *too,* and added in with the ones that have been cooking all along. You want onions that're still toothsome, surely, but others should be nearly melting, they've been in there so long.''

You saved me from a reproach, Mammy, Cochran thought after his

first instant of puzzlement. "Whatever you say, Mrs. Pleasant." In fact
the old-woman personality had unexpectedly proven to be a terrific
cook, and during the past week had prepared a couple of black-*roux*
jambalayas that had even drawn enthusiasm from the preoccupied
Mavranos. Cochran now remembered smelling onions cooking when he
had come into the house. "Are you talking about what you've got sim-
mering in there now?"

"Yes, a *beef bourguignonne*, and eggplant *pirogis*," she said. Plumtree's eyes had a heavy-lidded, almost Asian cast when Mammy Pleasant was on. "You've got three pirogis," she went on. "Do you know
how they are to be filled?"

He knew she was no longer talking about dinner—and he was fairly
sure of what she meant. "I think I know how to fill *one*," he said
bleakly, "temporarily, at least. I hope somebody else suggests it—I
hope *she* thinks of it, herself!—so I won't have to."

"Partly you're here to think of things," came the old woman's strong
voice out of Plumtree's mouth; "yes, partly each of you has been chosen
for your wits and cleverness. But each of you has a specific task as
well. Each of you, like the three wise men, has brought a gift to your
helpless king in this January season of Epiphany. Do you know what
gift it is you've brought him, Scant Cochran? Do you know what it is
that you're to give away?"

Cochran thought about that. Nina's ghost, his now objectless and
always deceived love for her? Well, yes, the god did appear to want
that, but that couldn't be his purpose here. "Something to do," he said,
"with the mark on my hand."

Plumtree's blond head nodded. "If all goes well this time, if you all
generously do what the god generously asks, King Crane will be alive
at midsummer, and you will no longer have in hand the god's marker."

Cochran realized that his mouth was open; he closed it, and then said,
"That's why I'm here, involved in this? To give away the—" What
had Angelica called it at the broken temple on the end of the yacht-
harbor peninsula? "—the Dionysus badge?"

"Boy, it's the only reason you were allowed to volunteer to get the
mark in the first place."

"*Allowed* to—?" Cochran could feel his face heating up. In the
Mount Sabu bar in Bellflower, when Janis had asked him why he didn't
get the mark removed, he had told her, *I'm kind of proud of it . . . it's
my winemaker's merit badge, an honorable battle scar.* And he remembered Nina's ghost telling him that when he had put his hand out to
injury to save the god, thirty-four years ago, he had been like Androcles
daring to pull the thorn from the lion's paw in the old story; the lion

had thereafter owed Androcles a debt of gratitude. And Cochran was surprised now at the hurt of learning that in his own case he had apparently only been meant to hold the golden beast's favor for someone else, someone more highly esteemed—that it had never been for him. Like my wife's love, he thought.

"So all along the god meant," he said, forcing his voice not to hitch ludicrously, "for me to just hold the obligation in trust for Scott Crane? Why didn't the god let f—let precious Crane earn the obligation himself, get his *own* hand half cut off?"

"The god, and Scott Crane too, was yoked in the harness of another king then, a bad king. The god had to incur the debt outside the king's control but still within his own—that is, in a remote vineyard. I think that, as much as anything, you were chosen because of the similarity of your name to that of the favored boy who would one day be king." She smiled at him, with no evident malice or sympathy. "As if the god needed a sign even to remember you. And later, it was probably just so that you would get a name closer to *Scott* that he broke your leg under a cask of his wine." She reached out and gently touched his marked hand. "To be used by him—yes, even to ignominious destruction—is to be loved by him. You should be honored to have been judged worthy of being deceived and cheated in this way."

Cochran let the hurt run out of himself as his shoulders relaxed. Spider Joe brought the two coins, he thought, and an oracular reading of Angelica's cards; and died to do it, and ended up buried under an old Chevy Nova in a Long Beach parking lot. "And Cody brought her father," he said dully.

"Yes. The king had to die, so that he would no longer be a stranger to the dark earth."

Cochran frowned into the blue eyes that seemed for the moment to be of two slightly different colors. "I meant for what we've got to do next: make him tell us what we did wrong, what we should have done differently, last week. I didn't mean—my God, woman, are you saying that Dionysus not only wants Crane restored to life, but wanted him to die too?"

"He's no real king, no real representative of the god, if he doesn't spend the pruning season of each year in the kingdom of darkness. Few kings have been thorough enough in their observations of the office to *do* that—to actually die, each year—but the god does love Scott Crane."

"To Crane's misfortune. To the misfortune of all of us."

"Yes," she agreed, "the god loves all of us, in spite of our rebellions and failures.'' She blinked around the room then. ''I'm too alert—I'll draw attention. Where are my penance shoes?''

''By the front door where you left 'em.''

She nodded and shuffled past him, her shoulders, too, slumped in unsought humility. ''I'll probably forget, once I've got them on—but the dinner will be ready to serve at sundown.''

And I'll have something to serve to poor Cody, Cochran thought as he followed the old woman out of the bedroom. A flop that even Valorie might quail at. *It makes me sick to think of him in here, in me.*

Angelica had taken a bus into the city early that morning, and had spent the day consulting *magos* and *santeros* in the run-down Mission and Hunter's Point districts south of Market Street. She came plodding back up the driveway just at sundown, and grabbed a beer from the refrigerator and slumped on the couch in the living room while the others ate Mammy Pleasant's beef bourguignonne. Angelica had had a late lunch of pork tamales and menudo and Tecate beer, and couldn't now face a plate of steaming, vinous beef stew and a glass of room-temperature Zinfandel.

My poor people, she thought as she sipped the beer and stared out through the back window at the darkening greenhouse, *who have nothing.*

When Kootie and Pete had begun clanking the emptied dishes together and carrying them out to the kitchen sink, Angelica got to her feet and walked into the dining room.

She hadn't looked behind the door when she had come in, to see if the eucalyptus-soled shoes were leaned against the wall, but by now she could recognize Cody Plumtree.

''Our supernatural escrow is about to close,'' Angelica said, loudly enough for Pete and Kootie to hear in the kitchen. ''Tet is only three days off, and we have no clue about what we're supposed to do, this time. My people in the *barrios* and ghettos are getting signs of something big cooking, but for all their painted bells and chicken blood they don't know what or where. Our crazy old lady keeps saying that Crane or *C-cren* will direct us when the time comes—but the old lady's just a ghost.''

''Sid,'' said Cody Plumtree, ''speak up.''

Sid Cochran pushed his chair back. ''*C-cren* has got a, a horrible proposal,'' he said, ''which as far as I'm concerned anybody here can veto—especially Cody.''

Angelica glanced at Cody, who was sitting across from Cochran in the corner against the kitchen-side wall and had just lit a cigarette—and she got the feeling that Cody knew what Cochran was going to say, and hated it, but was not going to interrupt now, nor veto later.

"Omar Salvoy," said Cochran, "that's Cody and Janis's dad, who killed Scott Crane, came on today, here—he was talking on the phone to our Dr. Armentrout."

Armentrout! thought Angelica. That's the man who shot Kootie! She darted a fearful glance toward the front door as she touched the .45 automatic at her belt and opened her mouth to speak.

But Cochran had held up his hand. "Wait. Salvoy faded off while they were speaking, and Cody and I heard Armentrout going on talking; Salvoy had *not* told the doctor where we are. But—" Cochran paused and shook his head. "But, from what Armentrout was saying, it was pretty clear that Salvoy knows what we did wrong, when we tried to bring Crane back to life last week." He glanced at Cody, who just stared straight back at him. "I think," Cochran went on stolidly, "we've got to do the Follow-the-Queen trick to talk to Omar Salvoy."

Angelica whistled a descending note.

"Why should he tell us anything?" interrupted Pete from the kitchen doorway.

"Valorie can make him, I bet," said Cody. "She could be on with him, if you call her, like a second file showing in split-screen on a computer monitor." Once again Angelica found herself admiring the woman. "It's a—goddammit, it's a good idea. My father probably *would* know. He knew enough to nearly become the king, twenty-five years ago, and from the day he exited his smashed body he's had one foot in India."

"And I think I could effectively threaten him," said Kootie quietly from behind Pete.

Angelica stared at her adopted son warily. "With what, *hijo mío?*"

Ever since the seventeenth, when he had run away from the Star Motel before dawn and reappeared in the afternoon, having spent some part of the morning talking with Mammy Pleasant in her boardinghouse kitchen, Angelica thought Kootie seemed somehow far older than his fourteen years. All he had told Pete and herself about that morning was that he had killed someone, but Angelica had known that much when she had simply met his eyes as he'd lain shot and bleeding in the planter outside the Star Motel office—behind the physical shock that had paled his face and constricted his pupils, independent of that injury, dwarfing it, the new horror and guilt had been clearly evident to her.

"In '92," said Kootie, "when Sherman Oaks or Long John Beach tried to eat the Edison ghost out of me, he had to lure it up toward the surface of my mind first. This was when we were in the 'boat on the boat,' the van inside the truck. And from what Miss Plumtree has said about her psychic striptease session with that doctor, he was trying to draw a personality to the surface, to bite it off. The one on top is the one that's vulnerable." The boy bared his teeth in a humorless smile. "It seems like a personality brought up by this Follow-the-Queen trick is . . . stuck in the *on* position for at least a little while. I think I could validly threaten to . . . *bite him off.*"

Angelica's ears were ringing. "But," she said, "no, you can't—it's like slamming bad heroin, Kootie, you'd have his memories in you like heavy metal—his poisonous life force—" Much worse than whatever you're carrying now, she thought helplessly, trust me.

"Besides," said Pete Sullivan, staring in obvious dismay at his adopted son, "*he's* not a *ghost.* He's a full-power person. You'd—you'd probably blow up!"

"I said *validly threaten.*" Kootie sat down in the dining-room chair next to Plumtree, where Pete had been sitting. "If *I* can't be sure I can't do it, neither can he. And I think I *could kill* him, depending on how strong he is—swat him off the top of Miss Plumtree's mind like driving a golf ball off a tee."

Oh, don't be flippant and proud of it, Kootie, thought Angelica unhappily; and she would have said it out loud but for the knowledge that they might in fact need him to do it, and if so she didn't want to hamper him in advance.

"Without killing 'Miss Plumtree'?" asked Cochran, his voice hoarse and his eyes wide with skepticism.

Kootie raised his eyebrows and squinted across the table at him—then peripherally caught Angelica's anguished, vicariously mortified gaze; and the boy instantly looked down at the tablecloth, his face reddening. "I don't know," he whispered. "I don't know if he isn't stronger than me, even. He's older than me, and meaner, so he might be." He looked up, clearly abashed. "But—see?—I can believably *threaten* him with it."

"Just don't kill me before he's said what to do," said Plumtree with what Angelica recognized as hollow, exhausted bravado. Plumtree held up her hands, and her voice skidded up and down the scale as she said, "Sid, do you have some duct tape?"

Kootie looked nauseous.

"We won't do it tonight," Angelica said hastily. Plumtree was like a flexed piece of tempered glass, and Angelica was afraid one measured tap might actually shatter her mind into a *thousand* tiny personalities, no one of them more sentient than an infant. And Kootie wasn't looking much better himself. "Not if he's already been out once today," Angelica went on in her most self-assured doctor-tone. "Tomorrow will be plenty of time."

Both Kootie and Plumtree sagged in what looked like uncomfortable relief.

"Then for God's sake right now get me a drink," said Plumtree in a husky voice. "Sid, you got vodka?"

"Got vodka," said Cochran, getting up out of his chair like an old man.

"Got a lot of it?"

Cochran just nodded as he shambled into the kitchen.

He paused by the sink before reaching up to the liquor cabinet overhead, and stared at the glittering white mound of tiny soap bubbles that stood motionless above the dish-filled sink. And he experienced a vivid memory-flash of how Nina had looked, so many times, wearing an apron and leaning over this sink; and all at once, silently except for a nearly inaudible hissing, the soap foam diminished away to nothing, leaving the dishes exposed poking out of the surface of the gray water.

Her ghost is gone, he thought giddily as he reached up for the vodka bottle, but my memories of her apparently still have some palpable force.

We're not . . . *finished,* yet.

CHAPTER 26

I'll hide my silver beard in a gold beaver . . .
—William Shakespeare,
Troilus and Cressida

Cochran woke up in his own bed, alone, roused by the gunning of the Torino engine in the back yard. From the gray light filtering into the bedroom through the lace curtains, he muzzily judged that it must be about seven in the morning. He had sat up drinking with Plumtree until after midnight; and when at last he had got up unsteadily and announced his intention of retiring to the couch, Plumtree had told him to take the bed. *I'll sleep on the couch,* she had said, enunciating carefully. *I can see it from here, so I know I'll be able to find it.*

As much as anything, they had been discussing immortal animals. Cody had insisted that carp never died naturally, and survived the winter frozen solid in pond ice; and Cochran had told her about toads that had been found alive in bubbles in solid rock. When the animals in question began to be imaginary ones from children's books and science-fiction movies, like the Pushmi-pullyu and E. T., Cochran had just followed the drift of the conversation, and talked about Reepicheep the mouse in the Narnia books, and the bread-and-butter-flies from *Through the Looking-Glass.* Plumtree's voice had changed several times, and she had vacillated sharply between skepticism and credulity—but since Cochran was the only other person in the room she had not had to address him by name, and the nearest electric light that was on had been the one in the kitchen and Cochran couldn't tell when it might have flickered, and their talk had been abstract and speculative enough to keep him from guessing who he might have been talking to at any particular moment. He hadn't been aware of any obvious archaisms that would have indicated lines quoted from Shakespeare, though he hadn't by any means caught everything she had said; and if Tiffany had been on, she had been subdued, and content with vodka.

He got into a fresh shirt now and pulled his jeans back on and opened the bedroom door. The car noise had evidently awakened the Sullivans too—he could hear Kootie and Pete talking quietly behind the closed door of the spare bedroom.

Mavranos was sitting at the dining room table frowning over the Saturday *San Francisco Chronicle.* In front of him a cup of coffee sat steaming, and on the opposite side of the table stood fourteen mismatched cups and tumblers. Cochran padded over barefoot and peered at them; each had a grainy white sediment puddled in the bottom.

"You better pick up some more Alka-Seltzer when you go out," said Mavranos quietly; "a big bottle. I guess each of the girls had a hangover, and couldn't stomach drinking out of another one's used glass."

Cochran stared at the cups and glasses on the table. *"Fourteen?"* he whispered in awe.

"Each one for a different bad flop, I reckon," Mavranos said with a shrug. "Like chopping up a starfish." He lifted his coffee cup in both hands to take a sip. "I kind of admire her restraint in having only fourteen, after twenty-seven years. If I had the option, I'd be splitting off all the time." Softly he sang a line Cochran believed was from a Grateful Dead song: " 'I need a *mir*acle *ev*-ery day.' "

Cochran began carrying the cups and glasses into the kitchen, gripping three with the fingers of each hand; and when he came back from carrying the first six out of the dining room, Kootie was wordlessly picking up four more.

When they had brought the last of the cups and glasses out to the counter, the Torino hood audibly slammed down outside; and after Cochran had rinsed out two of the cups and filled them with fresh coffee and carried them back to the dining-room table for himself and Kootie, he heard Plumtree come battering in through the kitchen door and run more water in the sink. A moment later she shuffled into the dining room with a steaming McDonald's mug and slumped down into the chair beside Kootie. She was clearly Cody, and her T-shirt was correctly marked SUNDAY in crude black letters.

"You're awake," she observed as she lit a Marlboro.

"Somehow," agreed Cochran.

"The Torino's running again, a lot better than before. Let's get this thing done." She squinted at Kootie. "Your mom and dad up yet?"

"I think they are," said Kootie nervously. "I think they'll be out in a minute."

"Sid," said Cody, "if this goes real wrong, leave the Torino parked somewhere it's sure to be towed, will you? And leave the registration on the front seat. Oh, and the Jenkins purse is in the trunk—first mail that to the Jenkins woman."

"I—won't hurt you," said Kootie.

"It's not you I'm scared of, kiddo—but thanks."

Pete and Angelica Sullivan came in then, and Angelica sat down at the table while Pete went into the kitchen.

"This chair is no good," said Plumtree, wiggling the arms of her dining-room chair. "My snips-and-snails parent could bust it to kindling. Let's go out back and use one of the iron patio chairs." She had one more sip of her coffee and then stood up.

"What," said Angelica, wide-eyed, "right now? Before breakfast?"

"Well I'm just not hungry, somehow," said Plumtree. "And the sooner we get my job done, the sooner you can have your old lady in the wooden shoes cook you up some fucking *gumbo* or something, right?"

"Sorry," said Angelica.

"Shit," said Plumtree. "If her nose isn't bleeding too bad for her to cook, by then."

Five minutes later Mavranos, Angelica, Pete, Kootie, and Cochran were sitting, uncomfortably like judges, on one side of the long picnic table under the patio roof between the kitchen and the backyard greenhouse, facing the chair in which Plumtree now sat confined by strips of duct tape wrapped tightly around her wrists and waist and ankles. The sky was low and gray behind the pepper trees that overhung the yard; and though the breeze was chilly, Cochran knew that wasn't why Plumtree was visibly shivering. Inside Mavranos's open denim jacket Cochran had seen the checkered wooden grip of the revolver tucked under the man's belt.

For a few moments Plumtree waited blankly, relaxed enough for her teeth to chatter; then she rolled her head back to stare up at the beams of the patio roof, and she whispered, "Valerie, whatever you make at your job, you're overpaid." She took a deep breath, and Cochran did too. "Mom!" called Plumtree hoarsely.

Then she lowered her head to stare at the five people sitting across from her at the table, and her shoulder muscles flexed under her T-shirt. At last her gaze fixed on Cochran. "Are we near the sea?" she asked him in the shriller voice of Plumtree's mother. "Are you going to call her up now, and send her to India?"

"No," Cochran said. "We need to learn some things Omar Salvoy knows. We're going to call *him* up, and question him. You can see that he'll be restrained.''

"I can *see* a car,'' protested Plumtree's mother, "and I can *smell* the ocean! Are you too squeamish to kill her body? You said you loved her!''

At the same time Angelica was leaning forward from between Mavranos and Pete to say, quietly, "Sid, this isn't even a ghost of her mother, this is just a, an 'internalized perpetrator,' why are you talking to it—''

"As far as Cody's concerned,'' Cochran interrupted, "it's her mom.'' He looked back at Plumtree taped into the chair. "Trust me,'' he said, "I won't let him have her.''

"We won't let him have her,'' Mavranos agreed.

"Oh, Jesus,'' said the mother's voice. She looked back to Cochran. "I hope you're a lot smarter than you look, mister.'' She sighed shakily. "Go ahead, and God be with you.''

"Omar Salvoy,'' said Cochran, and he felt Kootie tense beside him.

Plumtree's eyes hadn't left Cochran's face, but now it was an amused, crafty, almost reptilian gaze. Again the arms flexed, but the tape held, even though the muscles had bulked out more. "*Hell*-lo, baby!'' said the man's voice from Plumtree's mouth. Cochran's nerves were twanging with the impulse to run, but his muscles felt as loose as wet cement.

"Valerie,'' said Cochran then, breathlessly.

One of Plumtree's pupils visibly tightened down to a pinprick. *Split-screen,* thought Cochran.

Like a pole-vaulter visually picking out each spot his feet would touch on the run to the bar, Cochran prepared his words; then, carefully, he spoke: "What did we do wrong twelve days ago, when we tried to get Scott Crane restored to life?''

"Oh, eat me.'' The childish taunt rode incongruously on the deep, vibrating voice.

"I will, if you don't tell us,'' spoke up Kootie. "I can.''

"Ay,'' came a new, flat voice from Plumtree's lips, speaking to Kootie, "sharp and piercing, to maintain his truth; whiles thy consuming canker eats his falsehood.'' The face contorted and gasped for breath, and the man's voice added, "Dammit, that's *Henry the Sixth, Part One*! Valerie, you traitorous bitch! Who do you think you got all your lines from, anyway? Do you remember *Love's Labour's Lost*? 'We to ourselves prove false, by being once false for ever to be true to those that make us both—fair ladies, you.' ''

"Valerie is on our side," said Kootie, "and she'll know it if you lie."

Plumtree's gaze fixed on Kootie, and her teeth were bared.

Kootie's shoulder jumped against Cochran's arm, and then the boy leaned tensely forward—

—The air was suddenly colder, and Cochran thought the pepper trees shook in no breeze—

And in the same instant Plumtree's head was rocked back as if from a physical blow. "Easy, kid!" gasped the man's voice. "Unless you want all the fair ladies dead!"

"I bet you can tell I pulled that punch," said Kootie. His voice was calm and level, though Cochran could feel the boy shivering. "I *have* used it full strength, before today. And I don't believe that punching you dead out of that head would hurt any of the Plumtree ladies."

"You haven't yet seen *any* of *my* strength, boy." Salvoy's voice seemed to vibrate in Cochran's ribs. "That was a love-pat a moment ago. I *killed* your king, and I did *not* flinch when I did it. But I don't want you to be hurt." The teeth were still bared, and now the lips curled in a smile. "I'm prob'ly the only one here who doesn't want you to kill yourself."

Angelica started to say something, but a rumbling, liquid growl from Plumtree's throat stilled her.

"You're the one with the wound in your side, boy," the man's voice went on, loudly and almost anguished. "It's always been you that would have to drink the real *pagadebiti,* even supposing you assholes could ever find a bottle of the stuff. It's *you,* Baby Gawain, that would have to be possessed by the actual god, abandon yourself to his . . . bestial mercies. You sure you're up for that, Gumby Gunslinger?"

Cochran heard elbows shift on the wooden table somewhere to his right, and guessed it was Angelica.

Plumtree's gaze swung toward Angelica, and the flat Valorie voice said, "Pardon me, madam: little joy have I to breathe this news; yet what I say is true."

"Were we at the right *place,* at least?" asked Mavranos insistently. "Out at those ruins by the yacht club? Mammy Pleasant was talking about a spot out on that shore."

"You were in the right place," said Omar Salvoy, "but you didn't have the right wine, and I'm glad to say I don't even know where you would get—" Abruptly Plumtree choked; and then Valorie's voice said, "Upon my soul a lie, a wicked lie. Touching this dreadful sight twice seen of us—you may approve our eyes, and speak to it. Looks it not like the king? Thou art a scholar; speak to it." And immediately Salvoy's voice shook breathlessly out of the mouth: "Valerie, when I have you alone under me—"

"At those other ruins, she means," said Kootie, "the ruins of the baths, by that restaurant. That's where we saw Crane's ghost. And it was the second time Plumtree had seen it."

The Plumtree body leaned back in the chair and took a deep breath.

"You all were so embarrassed by that, I bet," said Salvoy, grinning. "Your exalted king, probably babbling nonsense and dressed like a bum, right? Or naked, looking like a crazy man. Brought down in the world, and how. Dizz-gusting! And you sensible folks probably just ran away from him. Think how pleased he must have been with his *friends.*"

"I," stammered Mavranos, "ran after him—!"

"The palindrome should have been a clue," Pete Sullivan interrupted, making a chopping gesture at Mavranos. "The Valorie personality gave Cochran one line of that, at the ruins, and we knew that palindromes were good for nothing but drawing ghosts."

"Palindrome?" said Salvoy. "What palindrome?"

"Sit on a potato pan, Otis," Kootie told him.

"And that foghorn was a clue," said Mavranos. "I bet the foghorn we heard in that motel room at dawn was the one you'd hear out at the Sutro Baths ruins. Shit, I even *noticed* it."

Plumtree's face was red and twitching, but in a mockingly conversational tone Salvoy asked, "Is one of you ready to *die?* That's part of it, you know. To get a life back, the god wants one in exchange. Even to repay an old debt-of-honor," he said, with a scorching glance at Cochran, "he can't violate his own math. And blood—fresh blood has got to be spilled. Splintered bone, torn flesh, before he'll consider it consummated. Ask apple-o'-my-eye Valorie if you think I'm lying about this." Plumtree's head rocked back, and the Valorie voice said, "That this is true, father, behold his blood. 'Tis very true." Her head came down and Salvoy's furious gaze swept across them. "And what *body* is your king going to take, now? Some bum's? That's another death, in addition to the god's bargain!" He gave a harshly jovial laugh, and then Plumtree's eyes squeezed shut. "I'm fading out, thank Ra. Think about what I've said, Koot Hoomie—and any of the rest of you that care—"

Plumtree's chin fell forward onto her chest, and for a moment she just panted. Then she looked up, in blank puzzlement; but when her eyes darted to Cochran she looked away again quickly. "Oh, it's Scant," she said. "I can't stay here." She flexed her arms and legs and then said again, in a voice shrilling with panic, "I can't stay here! Arky, what's going on?" She smacked her lips. "Was my *father* just here?"

"Can I talk to Cody?" said Cochran, standing up from the table. He was aware now that his shirt was clinging to his back with sweat.

"Nobody can talk to anybody, please," said Plumtree quickly. Her hands were fists. "Arky, get me *out of this!*"

Mavranos had stood up too, and was opening his lockback pocket-knife one-handed as he strode around the table to the chair. "Relax, Janis," he was saying gruffly, "you're gonna hurt yourself. Here." He crouched in front of her iron chair to swipe the knife blade through the duct tape on her wrists and ankles, then got up and went around to the back of the chair to cut the strips that bound her waist. "Sorry about this imposition," he said to her as he helped her struggle to her feet. "*Inquistion,* even. We can explain it whenever you want to hear about it."

"I just want to get inside," she muttered quickly, "away from him."

Cochran wondered which *him* she meant as he watched her shakily peel cut flaps of duct tape from her wrists. She was limping past him toward the kitchen door, with one hand on Mavranos's shoulder, and she looked at her wristwatch and then raised her elbow and tilted her head to hold the watch to her ear.

But of course it was a black Casio quartz watch, with a liquid-crystal display. Her gesture reminded Cochran of old black-and-white Timex ads on TV, and in his head he heard the old shampoo-ad song: *You can always tell a* Hal*o girl* . . .

When, Cochran wondered, did I last see anybody with a watch that *ticked?*

Oh, Jesus, she's still *split-screen!*

But her mismatched eyes had been watching him, and caught his instant comprehension, and as he opened his mouth now she was snatching the revolver from Mavranos's belt and lunging, smashing the barrel and butt of the gun like brass knuckles into Cochran's belly.

Then Plumtree had danced back away as Cochran folded and sat down jarringly hard on the concrete, and she slapped both hands to her face, her left palm covering her eyes and her right hand pointing the gun up at the patio roof.

And she pulled the trigger. The *bang* was a ringing impact in Cochran's ears, and Plumtree's head smacked the stucco wall at her back.

But an instant later the gun barrel was horizontal, the muzzle pointed at Mavranos's chest. Mavranos stepped back, his hands open and out to the sides.

"Mom," Cochran choked, not able to get air into his lungs. "Janis's . . . mom." Fragments of wood and tar paper spun down from the new hole in the roof.

Angelica understood what he was doing, and called "Janis's mom! Mother!''—before visibly wilting with the realization that Plumtree was deaf now.

As Mavranos shuffled backward across the patio deck, the gun muzzle swung toward Angelica. To Cochran's tear-filled eyes it seemed to leave a rippling wake in the air. "Koot Hoomie," said Salvoy, much too loudly, "pick up the roll of duct tape and come here—or I put a big hole in your mom. Scant-boy—reach slow into your pants pocket and throw me the car keys." Plumtree wasn't looking at Kootie directly.

Cochran thought he could feel ruptured organs inside himself ripping further open as he dragged his legs up under his torso and crawled across the concrete to Plumtree; he even had to reach out and brace himself with one hand on Plumtree's blue-jeaned thigh as he hitchingly got up onto his knees. His lungs were chugging in his rib cage, but he still wasn't able to draw any breath down his throat, and his vision had narrowed to a tunnel.

Plumtree had her back against the house wall, so she couldn't retreat; Cochran was looking up at her, and his dizzy focus shifted effortlessly outward from the ring of the .38-caliber muzzle to her eyes. Both of her eyes were wide and staring at him, the tiny-pupiled one and the dilated one, and at the bottom of his vision he could still blurrily see down the rifled barrel of the gun.

"Troilus, farewell!" hissed Valerie as Plumtree's body shook with internal conflict against the stucco wall. The finger lifted out of the trigger-guard ring. "One eye yet looks on thee, but with my heart the other eye doth see." Then the Salvoy voice grated, "No," and the finger wobbled back down onto the trigger, and whitened.

Abruptly a youthful brown right hand sprang into Cochran's narrow field of vision and closed over the muzzle, and from above him Kootie's voice said, "You want this to be *your* right hand one day, don't you? Will you shoot it off?"

Plumtree couldn't have heard what the boy had said, but her eyes lifted. And Kootie's gaze must have caught hers, for she suddenly convulsed sideways across the wall onto the projecting hose faucet as Kootie crouched along with her and violently twisted the gun in her hand.

Cochran threw himself onto her back as she rolled off the faucet and thudded heavily to the concrete, and he too was grabbing for the gun—and when he saw the hammer jump back he got his thumb in under it as it came down.

At last Kootie yanked it away, tearing a gash in the base of Cochran's thumb. Cochran was breathing at last, in abrading gasps.

With a solid boom Mavranos rebounded off the wall then and fell to his knees on Plumtree's right arm, and the roll of duct tape shrilled as he tore a long strip free and wrapped it around her wrist; then he had grabbed her other arm and wrapped tape around that wrist too.

Her back was rising and falling as she panted, and after a moment she rolled her head so that she could squint up sideways at Cochran. "How'd it," she gasped with a bloody rictus of a smile, "go?"

Her nose was bleeding, though Cochran couldn't guess whether it was from the physical stresses of Salvoy's visitation or from having collided with the concrete deck. *"Can you hear me?"* he managed to croak loudly.

Cochran's heart ached to see how wrinkled her eyelids were as she closed her eyes.

"Yes, Sid, oh, shut up!" She was gasping for breath and her bloody upper lip was twitching away from her teeth. "God, Sid, I hurt! Did I fall off the roof? What the fuck *happened?*"

"Cut her loose, Arky," choked Cochran, in horror, as he braced his hands on the concrete deck and carefully climbed off her legs.

"She may still be split-screen," came Angelica's voice from behind him.

"Not—Cody." Cochran reached out his jigging, bleeding hand and gently touched Plumtree's shoulder. "We can—trust Cody."

And in fact Mavranos was already knifing the tape off of her wrists.

CHAPTER 27

Her bed is India; there she lies, a pearl.
Between our Ilium and where she resides
Let it be called the wild and wand'ring flood,
Ourself the merchant, and this sailing Pandar
Our doubtful hope, our convoy, and our bark.
　　　　　　—William Shakespeare,
　　　　　　　Troilus and Cressida

Angelica wanted to look at Plumtree's bashed ribs and possibly sprained hand, but when Cochran and Mavranos had helped Plumtree to her feet and walked her into the house, she shook them off.

"Leave me be," she said irritably, leaning over the kitchen sink while blood dripped from her nose. "It's just a spell of the spasmodics." She grabbed a dishtowel and pressed it to her face. "Get Teresa to fetch me a cup of Balm Tea," she said through the towel, "with some gin in it." Then she blinked around at the low-ceilinged white kitchen she was standing in, with its blocky white refrigerator and the gleaming black box of the microwave oven. "I mean, a glass of Z-Zinfandel," she amended querulously. "And my bark-soled penance shoes."

"No," said Cochran sharply, "not yet. Sit down, Mrs. Pleasant. Have some coffee. Arky, get her a cup of coffee. Listen, we've learned some things about Crane's resurrection."

He felt goose bumps tickle against the sleeves of his shirt then, for when the woman looked at him, her forehead and high cheekbones seemed for a moment to be patrician with age, and momentarily her blond hair appeared white in the shine of the overhead fluorescent lights; then it was Plumtree's face, with both eyes the same shade of blue, though the eyelids were still full and vaguely Asian. She sat down in one of the kitchen chairs stiffly, dabbing at her nose with the bloody towel. Her nose wasn't bleeding anymore, and the Mammy Pleasant personality didn't appear to feel any pains in her ribs.

Raindrops began tapping against the window over the sink.

"I tried to tell you people everything," said Mammy Pleasant's cautious voice, "right from the first, well in time for you to have done it correctly on St. Sulpice's Day. I was supposed to be your intercessor—I told you then that I would have to indwell one of you, but you thought I just wanted a body to take the fresh air in."

"We're listening now," said Angelica. "And you've got the body now."

"I'll tell you nothing, *now*," said Pleasant's voice. "Your Chinaman holiday isn't until the day after tomorrow. Ask me about it then, respectfully, and I might tell you what to do, and I might not. At any rate I can have wine for one more day, and my shoes."

Kootie had started toward the hall, but Cochran said, "Don't get the shoes, Kootie. They apparently work as a damper to keep her personality from being conspicuous, from being a beacon to this house—maybe she seems to be a *tree,* to psychic radar, when she's wearing 'em—but I think they're also a damper on her intelligence. I think they're like dope."

"Now I will *assuredly* tell you nothing."

"But you've said that the god's purpose is your purpose too," said Angelica in a tone of sympathetic concern. She knelt beside Plumtree. "And that the god's purpose is to bring Crane back, as king. We need to know what to do." Cochran guessed that Angelica was already resolved to ditch this whole enterprise, and every person that resided in the Plumtree head, and simply wanted to find out as much as possible before fleeing; but he had to admit that she projected sincerity. Doctors are trained to do that, he thought.

"The god's *purpose,*" said Pleasant, stubbornly shaking Plumtree's tangled blond hair. "You're to take two old women to the sea, and throw them in, because the god's *purpose* doesn't include poor frightened old ghosts trying to sleep in some frail shelter out of the rain." She turned to Angelica, blinking rapidly. "What if we *did* fight him? Who *won?*"

Two old women? thought Cochran. She mentioned another old woman right at the first, on the Solville TV—Angelica said it sounded like a sewing circle. Who's the other one? Plumtree's phantom mother?

"Could I have insisted?" the old woman went on. Plumtree's eyes were blinking rapidly. "I tried to insist! Through your, your 'boob tube'! You *could* have accomplished it then, on St. Sulpice's Day, if you had listened to me."

"And if I hadn't run away," said Kootie

"We were well down the wrong track already, by that morning," Mavranos told the boy gruffly. "Going to the wrong shore, with the wrong wine . . ." To Plumtree's sunburned face, he said, "You could have told us more. We might not have listened, but . . ."

"I needed to be in a body! I told you that much! How could I *think*, without a *brain?*" Plumtree's eyes were blinking rapidly.

Mavranos's nostrils were flared and the corners of his mouth were drawn down. "You wanted a body to take the fresh air in," he said flatly.

Rain was drumming now against the window over the sink, and Cochran could see the bobbing stems of Nina's window-box basil outside. The back door was open, and the cold draft smelled of wet clay.

"I wanted some time to *rest,*" Mammy Pleasant said in a near-whisper, perhaps agreeing with him. "This little time, these little days sitting with the orchids in the greenhouse, and cooking for people again! I don't see how anybody can describe *total oblivion* as *rest*—you couldn't even call it losing yourself, because for losing to go on there has to be a loser, and there wouldn't be even that. Oh, believe me, the god's purpose has only been delayed."

"And made . . . costlier," said Mavranos, very quietly. His brown hands were clenched in fists against his thighs.

"Let me tell you about Omar Salvoy's purpose," Cochran said, leaning back against the refrigerator. "According to Plumtree's mom, he wants to get into the right male body and become this Fisher King, and then get Plumtree pregnant—specifically, get *Valorie* pregnant. Valorie is evidently the core child inside Plumtree, and she's apparently dead. Salvoy believes that if he can father a child by a dead woman—well, not a whole child; I gather it would be just a sort of deformed, unconnected head—that partial child will be a living, obligated piece of Dionysus."

"Jesus!" exclaimed Angelica, looking away from Plumtree to gape up at him.

Kootie was hugging himself, grasping his elbows; and Cochran thought that this revelation had somehow stirred the boy's memories of whatever devastating thing it was that he had done twelve days ago, after he had run away from the motel on Lombard Street before dawn.

For several seconds no one spoke.

Plumtree's head was bowed. "Yes," she whispered finally, "if he was the king, he could force that. If he had the body with the wounded side, and if he made a mother of Death, he could stand *in loco parentis* to the god. Other kings have sometimes achieved degrees of domination over the god, in other ways."

"*Loco* parentis is right," said Mavranos hollowly.

Plumtree's head snapped back, throwing her blond locks back from her forehead. "The god, in that form," she said, "and that king, would have uses for a couple of old ghost ladies." Her face was impassive, but tears spilled down her cheeks. "Thank you, Scant Cochran, for making me understand that the oblivion in the sea is one of the god's mercies. I do thank him for the offered gift of ceasing to exist. And I'm grateful, too, that it must be the last of his gifts to me."

Cochran opened his mouth to speak, but Mammy Pleasant rapped Plumtree's knuckles on the kitchen table. "I will speak, now, and you all will listen," she said. "When your king's castrated father was king, he ruled in Las Vegas. And your king ruled and may rule again in the place that rhymes with Arcadia. But there was a king who cultivated the miraculous Zinfandel vine in San Diego until 1852, and who then castled to Sonoma, north of San Francisco, where he grew the vines in the Valley of the Moon, between Sonoma Mountain and Bismark Knob. The god originally intended me to be queen to this king, but I had irretrievably rebelled against the god a dozen years earlier."

"This was . . . Harass-thee," said Kootie.

"Haraszthy," said Plumtree, subtly correcting the boy's pronunciation. "Agoston Haraszthy, who took the title of 'Count' for the grandeur in it. In 1855 he was made assayer and melter and refiner of gold at the United States Mint at Mission Street, south of Market; and the furnaces burned all day and all night, and after he quit, the roofs of the surrounding houses were all deeply stained with misted gold." The reminiscent smile on Plumtree's face somehow implied lines and creases that weren't actually there. "That was a kingly thing, if you like! But, like most of the men who attain the throne, he refused to submit to real death in the winter. And so in the thirteenth year of his reign, 1861, the worst winter floods in the history of California devastated Haraszthy's precious grapevines; and in 1863, the surviving vines withered in the worst drought in twenty-five years. I was happy to help in undermining this king's power, and in 1868 I bought the Washington Street property that had housed the original greenhouse-shrine devoted to the Zinfandel in California, and I tore out the sacred old vines and converted the place to a boardinghouse."

She stared curiously around at the kitchen, as if to fix the details of it in her memory. "After that sacrilege," she went on, "Haraszthy was getting no spiritual power from the god at all, no psychic subsidy, and so he just abandoned his ordained throne and the American West altogether, and he fled south all the way to Nicaragua—to distill *rum,* from unsanctified *sugarcanes!"* She laughed gently and shook her head. "He was hiding from Dionysus, who was without a king now, and therefore not as close to human affairs. I decided to put them both out of my picture—and so on the night of June 24th of the next year, on St. John's Eve, I celebrated the very first voodoo ceremony to be held in the American West, and in the woods out along the San Jose Road my people danced and drummed and drank rum and worshipped Damballa the Great Serpent, and I conveyed my prayers to him. And twelve days later, down in Nicaragua, the Dionysus who was no longer very human found his faithless king—Haraszthy was eaten by an alligator, which was Sebek-Re, a very crude, early Egyptian personification of the fertility-and-death god."

Cochran looked away from the ophidian eyes and the somehow distinctly Egyptian-seeming smile, and saw that his companions too were avoiding looking into Plumtree's face. He thought of the broken skeleton out in the greenhouse in the rain, and he wished someone would close the back door.

"I did not know, at first," Mammy Pleasant's voice went on carefully, "that the kinghood had rebounded like a snapped rope when Haraszthy fled this continent in 1868. Dionysus," she said, with a look that Cochran could feel on the skin of his face, "places great stock in names, in clues and similarities in names; and a weapons manufacturer back East who was known as 'the rifle king,' and who, among other fortuitous resemblances, had the middle name 'Fisher,' became the unintended and unknowing and unsanctified focus of the kinghood. A . . . measurable westward deflection! . . . of my magics, made me aware of the obstruction of him, and in 1880 I held another voodoo ceremony—this time in the basement of my grand house on Octavia Street. Again my people drummed and danced to the Great Serpent, and in the December of that year this poor misplaced king-apparent died. He had a middle-aged son, and in the following March the son died too, of consumption, leaving behind a childless forty-one-year-old widow. They had had one child, a daughter, who had perished of the marasmus back in '66 at the age of a month-and-a-half.''

"Is she the . . . other old-woman ghost?" asked Cochran.

Plumtree's head nodded. "And she's a rebel, like me, now. She wasn't always—right after her husband died, she consulted a spiritualist, who told her that she was obligated to the god for the attentions he had so generously paid to her family, and that in return she must use her inherited fortune to build an infinite chapel: a gateway for straying ghosts to leave this world through, and go on to the next. And she did, only a couple of years after her precious husband had died. She set about building an enormous house designed to attract ghosts, and then not let them get out; construction of it never stopped for nigh forty years, there was hammering and sawing day and night, and new doors and halls every day—doors and stairways that led nowhere, windows in the floors, faucets way up where no one could reach—and about the only way the ghosts could get out was to be unmade and sent off to the god through one of the fireplaces. She had forty-seven fireplaces there, before she died.''

''I thought hammering repelled ghosts,'' said Cochran.

''No,'' snapped Angelica, ''banging, hammering sounds, the racket disorients 'em. It jolts them out of the groove, resets their controls back to zero—cashes out bets they'd have wanted to let ride.'' She looked at Pete. ''Of course we know what this crazy house is.''

''And who the old lady was,'' Pete Sullivan agreed. ''It's the Winchester House, a few miles down the 280 from here.''

''Winchester,'' said Pleasant's voice out of Plumtree's mouth. ''Yes. And like me she was chosen to be a caretaker and communicant of the god's *pagadebiti* wine—the consecrated Zinfandel. But one night in 1899, even while I was being evicted from my own overthrown house and taken into custody by the idiot god-fragment known as Bacus, Winchester found a black handprint on the wall of her chapel, in the wine cellar, and she knew that she was being called upon to give over to the god her own husband's ghost . . . and she couldn't bring herself to obey *that,* to forget *him.* And, even while knowing that she'd be punished, she rebelled: she *walled up the wine cellar.* When the god came to take charge of my wandering ghost three days after Easter in 1906, he struck her too, *en passant,* with the earthquake of his arrival—the top floors of her house fell onto her bedroom, and she was trapped in there for hours. But she didn't repent her rebellion—after her servants freed her, she boarded up that whole wing of the house, and spent six months living on water, aboard a houseboat called *The Ark,* in the south bay here by the Dumbarton Bridge.''

''And the scrap lumber,'' said Pete, ''from the collapsed upper floors, was used to build a maternity hospital in Long Beach in the 1920s; probably because of the ghost-confusion influences in it.'' He looked at Cochran. ''That hospital eventually became our apartment building—Solville.''

''When Winchester returned to her house,'' Pleasant went on, ''she was masking herself against the god as well as the ghosts now. And when she eventually died, she left instructions that her ghost was to be caught, and hidden. And so it was, and now the god wants you to bring her, and me, to him. You'll need to find a guide.''

Mavranos was rubbing his forehead.

"Omar Salvoy says that someone will have to die, probably more than one person, for our king to come back to life," said Cochran. "He says there will have to be bloodshed."

"Of course," said Pleasant.

Angelica straightened up beside Pleasant's chair. "And he says that Kootie, the boy here, has to be possessed by Dionysus."

"Everybody does, eventually," said Pleasant calmly.

"Well, that's simply *out,* I'm afraid," said Angelica, shaking her head. "I don't know what's *going* to happen, but that's the thing that's *not* going to happen. We've got nearly two clear days to run away."

Plumtree's shoulders bobbed with tired laughter. "Don't try Nicaragua," said Pleasant's voice.

"No, Mom," said Kootie. "What, should I save myself for Omar Salvoy?" He was speaking softly, not looking at any of the others in the kitchen. "If the, the god, is offering me his debt-payer wine, I'm very damn ready to take a drink." He went on even more quietly, "And I do owe a beheading. He might not *take* it, but I *owe* it."

"We'll see about that," said Angelica, but her voice was too loud, and Cochran thought she looked lost and scared.

"How do we get a guide?" asked Mavranos.

Angelica threw him a surprised, hurt look. "Arky, Kootie is *not*—"

"On the resurrection day," said Pleasant, "you are to give a ride to a hitch-hiker. In your motor-car. I have now told you this. And this woman," she said, touching Plumtree's forehead, "is to carry with her, at all times, that gold cigarette lighter. I have now told you this." She nodded virtuously.

And of course you'd have told us two weeks ago, thought Cochran angrily, if we'd simply asked: *Should we be picking up hitch-hikers? Should Plumtree hang on to that Dunhill lighter?*

"Go ahead and get her goddamn shoes, Kootie," he said. He crossed to the back door and pushed it closed, not looking out through the broken glass; he was afraid he might see the naked figure of Scott Crane's ghost out there, sitting in the wet grass and possibly even mournfully looking this way.

Cody came back on just as the sun was redly silhouetting the northern-most peaks of the Montara Mountains. Cochran was in the driveway, walking around the shrouded Suburban with a tire-pressure gauge, when through the open living-room window he heard a cry and a thudding fall.

He let the gauge clatter to the driveway pavement and just sprinted across the grass to the window, punched in the screen, and pulled the curtains up.

Plumtree was lying on her side on the carpet, huffing furiously and struggling up to a sitting position, trying to get traction with the crumbly eucalyptus-bark soles of Pleasant's penance shoes. Mavranos and Pete scuffed and bumped to a halt in the hall doorway a moment after Cochran leaned in the window.

"This is like the—end of the—fucking *Wizard of Oz*," Cody panted, blinking away tears. "Everybody leaning in to see if the—little girl is okay. After her knock on the head." She was sitting up on the floor now, hugging her side and breathing deeply. "She was—dancing! I came on in the middle of some—kind of goddamn pirouette, off balance. Don't help me up!" she said in a wheezing voice to Mavranos, who had hurried across the room to her. "My ribs are like broken spaghetti in a cellophane bag. I'll get up on my own. In a minute." She looked up at Cochran. "She was dancing around in here, all by herself! *How* old is she?"

"Hundred and something," said Mavranos.

"And now I bet I've got a broken hip, too," Plumtree said, "from falling on whatever she put in my pocket." Bracing herself on an old overstuffed easy chair, she fought her way to her feet, then reached into the hip pocket of her jeans.

"Look at that," she said, holding out the gold Dunhill lighter. "The old dame was stealing the lighter!"

Cochran swung one leg over the windowsill and climbed into the room, thrashing out from under the curtain like, he thought sourly, a rabbit from under a magician's handkerchief.

"No she wasn't, Cody," he said. "That's *supposed* to be in your pocket."

"We discover," added Mavranos.

"Have Angelica earn her keep," said Plumtree, "and tape up my ribs or something. And for God's sake get me something to drink."

Cochran started toward the hall. "You want your mouthwash?"

"No," she said, "ghosts don't seem to have spit. I want vodka." She squinted belligerently from Pete and Mavranos and Cochran to the window beyond the flapping curtain. "The day's over, it looks like. Is it possible for you to tell me what's been going on?"

"We can try," said Cochran. He took her arm, and she let him lead her down the hall toward the dining room. "Have something to eat, with your vodka,'' he said gently. ''The old lady made a fine-looking shrimp remoulade this afternoon, and I was going to make some sandwiches.'' He was nodding solemnly. ''I think if we all take our time, and don't interrupt each other, we can actually explain what's gone on today.''

''Well don't goddamn strain yourselves,'' she said, leaning on Cochran.

''Oh, well,'' he said, his voice suddenly quivering with an imminent, mirthless giggle, ''I don't know that we can do it without straining ourselves.''

''It really calls for mood music,'' said Pete from behind them. His voice too was tense with repressed hysteria. ''Wagner, I think, or Spike Jones.''

Mavranos gave a harsh bark of laughter. ''And I better make some hand-puppets,'' he said.

Even Plumtree was snorting with nervous merriment as they came lurching and cackling into the living room, drawing puzzled stares from Angelica and Kootie.

Cochran made ham and pepper-jack cheese sandwiches, and Plumtree switched from vodka to beer when they ate, then went back to vodka after the dinner dishes were cleared away; and the occasional pauses in the tense and unhappy conversation were punctuated by horns and sirens wailing past on the highway at the bottom of the sloping backyard, the 280.

And seven miles to the northeast, in the Li Po bar in Chinatown, Richard Paul Armentrout sat at a table under the high, slowly rotating fans and nervously rolled the rattling pomegranate shell around the ashtray and the club-soda glasses. The two Lever Blank men had frisked him in the downstairs men's room, but after a quick, whispered conference between themselves they had decided to let him keep the pomegranate. Lucky for them that they did, Armentrout thought defiantly. I wouldn't be talking to them if they'd taken it, and on their own they would never figure out how to find the king with it.

Now they were sitting on the other side of the table from Long John Beach and himself. Armentrout was sure they had guns concealed under their tailored Armani suit coats somewhere. Plumtree had told him about the commune she had grown up in, and he was finding it difficult even to believe that these two gray-haired businessmen had been leaders of a Bay Area hippie cult in the sixties, much less that they were still somehow involved in it.

''We tried,'' said the balding one who had introduced himself as

Louis, "to stop the resurrection out at the St. Francis Yacht Club on the seventeenth of this month; some field men of ours did interfere, and in fact the attempted resurrection did fail. We would have acted more decisively if Mr. Salvoy had approached us sooner, and if there had not been unavoidable delays in establishing that the . . . apparent young woman *was* Mr. Salvoy; that required summoning entities we don't usually hold congress with, and procedures, out in the remote hills around Mount Diablo, that the ASPCA wouldn't approve of."

The other man, Andre, leaned forward. "Had to kill some goats," he said. "Needed their heads, for the entities to speak through."

"Let me tell you a parable," said Long John Beach.

"Not now, John," said Armentrout in embarrassment.

Armentrout knew that these two men wanted to intimidate him; and he *was* intimidated, but not by what *they* were saying. He forced himself not to focus on the television screen above and behind the men, and he tried not to listen to the two voices buzzing out of the television speaker.

"I gather," said Louis, "that you don't precisely *represent* Mr. Salvoy. You and he are not partners."

"No," agreed Armentrout. "Our interests have overlapped, but my main goal right now is to get a drink of the—"

Andre coughed and held up his hand. "No need to say it, we know you're not talking Thunderbird."

On the television screen above the bar, Armentrout's mother said, "I bet I swallowed gallons of that bath water." She and Philip Muir were sitting in vinyl-looking padded chairs in front of a blue backdrop with big red letters on it that spelled out AFTERHOURS. She was wearing the same housedress she had been wearing when seventeen-year-old Armentrout had held her under the bath water in 1963, and the dress was still soaked, dripping on the studio floor; but she was opaque and casting a shadow, and when she spoke her teeth glinted solidly between the twisting red-painted lips. Muir, never a heavy drinker and only recently dead, was still a bit translucent, and his eyes were still very protuberant and his forehead visibly blackened in pseudosomatic response to the gunshot that had killed him. "Thanks for sharing," he croaked. Armentrout remembered greeting cards that audibly produced the syllables of *happy birthday* or *merry Christmas* when a thumbnail was dragged down an attached strip of textured plastic; Muir's voice reminded him of them. "I can hold my breath for hours now," Muir went on. "In fact, I can't breathe." Armentrout's dripping mother reached across the low table that separated the chairs and imploded Muir's shoulder with a sympathetic pat. "Why would you want to breathe when everything smells so bad?" she said.

"Mr. Salvoy did good work for us," said Louis, "a long time ago—though he was unsuccessful in becoming the king, in 1969, and had to be retired."

Andre winked at Armentrout.

"We would be happy to take Mr. Salvoy on again," Louis said, "in this new *persona*, on the basis of his achieving the kinghood this time, and his being willing to comply with the harsher requirements of the office." He took a sip from his glass of club soda. "But when he spoke to us on the sixteenth he didn't tell us *quite all* about the Koot Hoomie boy. He simply indicated that there was a healthy young body he was ready to assume. If we had known that the boy was virtually the king already, we would not have risked harming him; a plain bullet wouldn't have been able to hurt the true king, but the truck could have rolled into the sea, and the king could drown in sea water. But as it happens the boy wasn't present, at that attempt at the yacht club. Our only urgency then was preventing the undesirable Scott Crane kinghood from being renewed."

Andre spread his hands. "We'll be happy with either one of them, Salvoy or Koot Hoomie, in the boy's body. We just want a king, an emissary to the god."

"A cooperative king," added Louis. "The boy alone might actually be easier to work with. He'd probably be more malleable."

"Well," said Armentrout, carefully not looking at the pomegranate and trying to project easy confidence, "I've got a sort of *psychic dowsing rod* that's leading me to the boy, and Salvoy is committed to keeping me apprised of his own whereabouts by telephone. I can lead you to both of them."

"A rabbi in a synagogue," said Long John Beach, "told his congregation, '*I* am . . . *nothing!*' And after the service, a prosperous businessman from the congregation shook the rabbi's hand and said, with feeling, nodding and agreeing with the rabbi, '*I* am . . . *nothing!*' "

"I'll tell you frankly," Louis said to Armentrout, "we haven't been able yet to ferment the real sacramental . . . beverage you want, though we've preserved and cultivated the very oldest strain of *vitis sylvestris* vine, untouched by the phylloxera louse plague, and we do press a vintage from it every autumn; waiting for the year when the god will see fit to answer our prayers."

Armentrout didn't follow all this—he only knew that if he should not be able to kill Koot Hoomie, his sole hope for immunity from the two ghosts who were now on the television screen would be to take a drink of the fabulous *pagadebiti* wine: disown the ghosts, let Dionysus have all of Armentrout's memories of them. But he hoped it wouldn't come to that, for the god might take *all* of the ghosts, and pieces of ghosts, that he had consumed over the course of his psychiatric career; and Armentrout wasn't sure he could mentally or even physically survive that loss. But it's just a back-up, last-ditch measure, Armentrout told himself reassuringly; I'll almost certainly find an opportunity to kill the boy.

"And the custodian came up," went on Long John Beach, "and he said, real earnestly, '*I* am . . . *nothing!*' And the businessman jerked his thumb at this guy and said to the rabbi, 'Look who thinks he's nothing!' "

Armentrout was looking intently into Louis's eyes, but from the television he heard imbecilic laughter.

"But bottles of it do survive," said Louis, a little impatiently. "We still have several that were bottled on the Leon estates in the Bas Medoc in the early eighteenth century. And when the Scott Crane contingent tries to do their resurrection ritual again on Tet, they may very well have got hold of a bottle themselves. Bottles of it are around, especially in the Bay Area. We can make sure that you are given a drink of the god's forgiving blood, one way or the other."

Andre said cheerfully, "I imagine we'll have our people retire the whole party, except for the Koot Hoomie boy and, at least for a while, the Plumtree woman."

"Certainly the one called Archimedes Mavranos," agreed Louis. "His commitment to restoring Scott Crane appears to be so strong that he would try to impede the coronation of anyone else."

Armentrout had to force himself to comprehend that these men were talking about *killing* Cochran, Plumtree, and the Sullivan couple and Mavranos. Not therapeutically, nor as a regrettable necessity for personal sustenance, as he himself had sometimes had to do, but just because these people were inconvenient, in the way; and for a moment he was profoundly sickened at his alliance with them.

How, he wondered forlornly, and when, did I become indistinguishable from the bad guys?

When Louis and Andre had introduced themselves, they had told Armentrout that they were in the children's products business these days, and owned a controlling interest in the White Greyhound brand of toys. Armentrout had remembered the White Greyhound Solar Heroes action figures and the Saturn's Rings carnival set; and he had been unhappy to learn, in conversation this evening, that the toys had been designed to intiate children at least a little way into the Dionysian mysteries. Armentrout had learned that the toy figures in the carnival set had been designed to subliminally embody the Major Arcana figures from the tarot deck: with The Magician as the ticket seller, The Lovers on the Ferris Wheel of Fortune, Death as the janitor, and so forth; the White Greyhound people had carefully not included anything to represent The Fool, but they had had to stop production of the set anyway, because by 1975 children all over the country were spontaneously adding a Clown of their own, and suffering bad dreams at night and even banding together during the day to elude the hideously smiling painted figure of random madness that their consensual credulity had nearly brought into real, potent existence.

Louis and Andre had told him with satisfaction that their original five-year-old consumers were now in their late twenties, and as a segment of American society were beginning to show valuable symptoms.

These men are monsters, Armentrout thought. They've trekked much farther out into the dark than I ever have, and abandoned items from the original spiritual kit that I could not ever abandon.

And he might have spoken—but now Louis and Andre had hiked their chairs around and were staring at the television over the bar.

On the screen, Muir and Armentrout's mother had got to their feet and were doing an awkward dance around the studio floor; his dripping mother was making swimming motions, and Muir had pulled up his diaphanous pants cuffs and was walking on his heels. They were both staring right into the hypothetical camera, right out at Armentrout—he avoided looking squarely into their phosphor-dot eyes, even though he doubted that they could get a handle on his soul through the television screen—and they were chanting in unison, *"Why so stout, Richie Armentrout? Let 'em all out, Richie Armentrout!"*

Louis's face was pale as he turned back to stare at Armentrout, and his voice was actually shaky: "They're . . . talking to *you?*"

"Leftovers from the old Dale Carnegie days," Armentrout said hoarsely as he shoved his own chair back and stood up. "We've got a deal—let's get out of here."

Outside, the Grant Street pavement glittered with reflected neon, and rippled like sketchy animation with the constant rearrangement of the falling raindrops.

CHAPTER 28

Brethren and sisters of the hold-door trade,
Some two months hence my will shall here be made.
It should be now, but that my fear is this,
Some galled goose of Winchester should hiss.
> —William Shakespeare,
> *Troilus and Cressida*

The rain kept up all night, and into the morning.

In spite of Mammy Pleasant's wish for as much on-time as she might still be able to have, she didn't appear at all throughout the gloomy morning, and Pete Sullivan wound up making lunch—tacos of fried ground beef and chopped ortega chilis, with the corn tortillas heated in the grease and a hot red salsa splashed liberally over it all. There had been only one Alka-Seltzer cup on the table this morning, and at lunch it was just Cody who sweated and scowled as she ate the restoratively spicy Mexican food and washed it down with a succession of cold beers. She was wearing one of Cochran's dress white shirts, with MONDAY freshly inked over the pocket.

After Kootie had cleared away the dishes and Angelica had taken the ads from the *San Francisco Chronicle* out to the living-room couch, Cochran stood at the back door and looked out across the wet yard at the Torino, which for all of Cody's work still shook as its engine was gunned.

Cody herself had shambled back to bed right after lunch, declaring that she needed to rest the cracked ribs and sprained hand that Angelica had diagnosed and taped up yesterday evening; it was Arky Mavranos who was out revving the car engine in the rain—pointlessly, for the Torino was blocked in by the Granada that was parked behind it.

"He's near used-up," said Pete quietly, standing with a freshly opened can of beer beside Cochran and looking too out the window. "I don't know what his part in this thing tomorrow is supposed to be, but it better not call for liveliness. He doesn't even drink beer anymore, and he doesn't eat, either, except for rice and beans and tortillas. That shrapnel-hit to his skull, or else that ghost that was on him . . ." he said, shaking his head, "broke him down."

"At least the engine's in park now," said Cochran. "A few minutes ago when I ran out there he had it in drive. I told him there's a mud track that curls down the slope to the 280 at the back of the yard, but that he'd have to drive right through the greenhouse to get to it." He tossed his cigarette out through the hole in the door window onto the patio. "Now I think of it, I'm glad he didn't just *do* that."

"No chance," said Pete with a faint, sad smile. "He wouldn't run over Scott Crane's skeleton. And he wouldn't have the heart to move the bones, either." He finished his beer and visibly thought better of throwing it out the window after Cochran's cigarette.

"*Morituri emere*, or something," he said, stepping into the kitchen. " 'We who are about to die go shopping.' Angie and I are going to take the Suburban truck out to fill the tank and check the oil in preparation for whatever it is that's going to befall tomorrow, on resurrection day—and Angie's made a list of *bruja* items to shield Kootie with, so we're going to stop at a grocery store. Oils, candles, chalk, batteries for the stuffed toy pigs. Anything you want? Beer's already on the list."

"A Kevlar suit and hat," said Cochran absently, still staring out at the unhappy man sitting alone in the roaring, smoking car. "A squirt gun full of holy water. A home skitz-testing and lobotomy kit."

He turned away from the broken door-window and walked into what he still thought of as Nina's kitchen, littered now with Coors twelve-pack cartons full of empty cans, the shelves crowded with Angelica's morbid herb bundles and saint-decal candles. "No, if you've got beer on the list, I guess I—" He sagged; all at once the whole house was too depressing to bear. "Oh hell, I don't appear to be going to work today, and I'll just get in a fight with Mammy Pleasant if I hang around here. I'll go with you."

"Oh." Pete picked up his denim jacket from the pile of damp clothes and scarves on the kitchen table. "Okay. We've told Kootie to stay away from Plumtree, and it looks like she's down for the day anyway. Angie'll want to leave him her .45, but she'd do that even if you were staying." He pulled on his jacket and then lifted down one of Angelica's stuffed pigs from on top of the refrigerator. "Get you fitted for a battery," he said to it.

Kootie stepped into the kitchen now from the front hall, and Cochran could smell wine on the boy's breath. "Is Mammy Pleasant planning on making dinner?" Kootie asked. "I'd rather order in a couple of big American pizzas, actually, than have another Creole thing." He shrugged. "I believe tomorrow I'm gonna be eating in India."

Cochran and Pete stared at him, and Pete began to stammer a response, waving the stuffed pig.

"I hear they have a New Delhi," Kootie added hastily.

Pete exhaled. "Here comes your mother. Don't upset her unless it's necessary, okay?"

Angelica stepped into the hall, carrying her stainless-steel .45 automatic in one hand and tucking a shopping list into the hip pocket of her jeans with the other. "Good deal on Coors at Albertson's," she said. "Are you coming along, Sid?"

"Thought I would, instead of going to work."

"Here, Kootie," she said, handing the gun to the boy. "Cocked and locked. Sid, we've got the carbine in the truck, but why don't you bring your .357 too."

Pete took the truck keys from a hook by the door as Cochran nodded and hurried back into the living room to get his revolver out of the locked strongbox on the bookshelf. "We should be back in an hour," Pete told Kootie. "If Pleasant shows up, tell her we're getting pizza. Tell her she might like it."

Freed of the two car covers, the red truck was in good enough condition to drive. Last week Mavranos had pulled out the holed, starred windshield and sealed a new windshield in place, and scraped the broken glass out of the rear panel windows and replaced them with sawn pieces of plywood. Mavranos himself had not driven the vehicle since parking it in Cochran's driveway thirteen days ago, possibly because it would agitate the fragments of Scott Crane's skeleton that were scattered among the cubes of broken window glass in the truck bed.

Angelica got into the back seat, so Cochran climbed into the front and sat in the passenger seat while Pete started the engine and let it warm up. The truck interior smelled of fresh plywood and old beer. Cochran had just settled back in the seat against the hard bulk of the revolver at the back of his belt, and lit a cigarette, when through the rain-blurred new windshield he saw the front door of his house pulled open, and saw Plumtree step out.

She was wearing his old leather jacket now, and sneakers—and when she stared across the driveway at the truck, Cochran's face chilled in the instant before he consciously recognized the narrower face and higher shoulders.

"I guess Cody wants to come along too," observed Pete, moving the stuffed pig so that Cochran could scoot over.

Cochran ground his cigarette out in the ashtray. "It's Janis," he said.

He stared toward her, and their eyes met with an almost palpable reciprocation through the glass; and Cochran was peripherally aware that a big raindrop rolling down the outside slope of the windshield stopped at the top edge of their linked gaze as if at an invisible barrier, then wobbled off to the side and ran on down to the black rubber gasket without having crossed between their eyes.

Then Janis was hurrying across the wet pavement with her head down and her hands in the pockets of the leather jacket, and she opened the front door and climbed in beside Cochran, who shifted to the middle of the long seat to give her room.

"Janis," he said, "I'm glad you—"

She touched her ear and shook her head. "I'm deaf, Scant," she said in a loud, droning voice.

"Oh." All he could do then was look into her eyes and nod, as Pete clanked the gearshift into reverse and backed the truck around on the wide driveway, then drove down the road to Serramonte Boulevard and made a right turn onto the southbound lanes of the 280.

"Janis's mom!" said Angelica sharply from the back seat. And when Janis just kept looking ahead at the rainy highway lanes for several seconds, Angelica said, "I guess she really is deaf."

"Don't . . . *tease* her," said Cochran, "even if she . . . can't know you're doing it."

Janis had seen him speaking, and looked at him; he looked into her eyes and lifted his right hand, and then held it raised even though after the first few seconds he thought Pete must be expecting him to thumb his nose at the traffic ahead. At last Janis brought up her unbandaged left hand and clasped his, creaking the sleeve of the leather jacket. For several seconds she squeezed his hand hard; then she had released it and looked away, out at the road shoulder rushing past outside.

"I wasn't teasing her," said Angelica quietly. "And I'm glad she's along. I wasn't thrilled to be leaving her back there with Kootie, and just poor Arky."

Beyond the window glass the livid green San Mateo County hills swept past under the low gray sky, with pockets of fog visible in the hollows, and columns of steam standing up like white smoke from behind the middle-distance hills.

Black crows were flapping low across the rainy sky, and for a panicky moment Cochran couldn't see any buildings or signs, and there appeared to be no other cars on the highway.

Then Janis spoke loudly: "Why would someone be hitch-hiking on a day like this?"

The truck's engine seemed to roar more loudly after Pete had lifted his foot from the gas pedal. Obscurely reassured by a glimpse of a couple of cars passing the truck on the left, Cochran leaned forward to peer out between the slapping windshield-wiper blades—there was a lone figure in flapping white clothing on the misty highway shoulder a hundred yards ahead, trudging south, the same way they were going, with its highway-side left arm extended.

"Well, it can't be the hitch-hiker the old lady told us about," said Angelica matter-of-factly, "today's not the day. *Tomorrow's* Tet."

Pete was pressing the brake. "I'm not risking any more carelessness."

"How far are we from Soledad?" protested Angelica. She was leaning forward across the seat, her breath hot on the back of Cochran's neck. "That's probably an escaped prisoner!"

"Do they dress them in bedsheets?" asked Pete quietly.

The right-side tires were now hissing and grinding in the muddy shoulder gravel, and the mournful squeal of the brakes made the walking figure stop.

"We're a hundred miles north of Soledad," said Cochran.

The hitch-hiker was barefooted and wearing a sort of stiff, blue-patterned white poncho, and when Cochran made out the letters ARLI on the fabric and looked more closely, he realized that the garment was a big painted-canvas banner from one of the roadside garlic stands down in Gilroy. The person was still facing away from them.

"Long dark hair," said Angelica. "Is it a man or a woman?"

"There's a beard," said Pete.

The figure had turned its head in profile to look back at the vehicle, and Cochran recognized the high forehead and chiselled profile. "It's—" he began.

Beside him, Plumtree jumped violently. "The Flying Nun!" she wailed.

"—Scott Crane," said Angelica, after giving Plumtree a startled glance. "I remember the face from when he was stretched out dead on my kitchen table down in Solville. Well, we're really in the animal soup now." She levered open her door, and the sudden chilly breeze inside the truck carried the earthy smells of wet grass and stone. "Uh . . . hop in," she called over the increased hissing of the rain, squinting as she leaned out of the still slowly moving truck. Obvious fright made her speak too loudly. "Where you headed?"

With shaking hands, Plumtree cranked down the passenger-side window, and Cochran flinched at the damp wind in his face.

Scott Crane's ghost turned to face them—it might have been naked under the makeshift poncho, but it was decently covered at the moment. Its beard and long hair were dark and ropy with rain water. "Jack and Jill went up the hill," the figure called back, "to fetch a chalice of *aquamort*. To the grail castle, to take away the container of the god's reconciling blood." Its voice was baritone but faint, like a voice on a radio with the volume turned down. "I will brook no . . . trout," the ghost said.

"Before its time," agreed Plumtree. The voice was Cody's, and fairly level, though Cochran could hear the edge of hoarse strain in it. "We can drive you there," she cried. "But you got to tell us where to turn."

Can we get there by candlelight? thought Cochran, quoting the old nursery rhyme; *aye, and back again.*

"And we might need to stop for gas," said Pete shakily.

Cochran was shifted around with his right elbow down the back of the front seat now, and he saw Angelica visibly consider climbing into the back of the truck or even over the front seat and right onto his lap; but by the time the king's ghost had limped to the truck's side door she had simply slid all the way over to the left.

The ghost was as solid as a real person as it climbed in—the truck even dipped on its shocks—and when the dripping bony face turned toward the front, Cochran could feel cold breath on his right hand. "What gas would that be?" the ghost asked. "Not nitrous oxide, at least. I'm running on a sort of induction coil, here." Its eyes squinted ahead through the rainy windshield. "Straight on south," the ghost said, pulling the door closed with a slam. The thrashing of the rain on the highway shoulder was shut out, and there was just the drumming on the truck's roof.

"I know the way," said Cochran nervously as he shifted back around and clasped his hands in his lap, "and we won't need to stop for gas, if it's the Winchester House in San Jose." He was breathing fast, but he wasn't panicking; and it occurred to him that Crane's ghost wasn't nearly as scary as his dead body had been.

"Find the green chapel," said the ghost. "Take what you've dished out; there's a New Year's Eve party coming that'll square all debts."

When Scott Crane's ghost directed Pete to take the Winchester Boulevard off-ramp, following the signs meant to lead tourists to the "Winchester Mystery House," Cochran nodded. "Be ready to take a left onto Olsen," he told Pete quietly. "The parking lot's right there."

Cody pointed at a bleak hamburger-stand marquee sign that read STEAK SAN/PASTRAMI. "I think we're supposed to go to the San Pastrami Mission," she whispered to Cochran. He could feel her shivering next to him.

But, "Take a left onto Olsen," said the ghost in the back seat. Its voice was deeper now, and louder. "The parking lot's right there."

Cochran remembered that ghosts tended to be repetitive. And the same thought might have occurred to Cody, for beside him she whispered, "I never need mouthwash, after Mammy Pleasant has been on. Ghosts don't have spit." Cochran looked at her in time to see teardrops actually fly out from the inner corners of her eyes.

"Valorie never has spit—I—never have to gargle, after Valorie."

"I don't think you need to—" Cochran began.

"Valorie's dead!" said Cody wonderingly. "Isn't she?"

Cochran took her hand. "It's—it's not," he stammered, "I mean, you—" The truck interior was steamy since the dead king had got in, and Cochran was sweating under his windbreaker. He wanted to say, *If it works, don't worry about it.* "Whatever Valorie's status is, Cody," he said finally, "*you're* certainly not dead."

"But she's the oldest of us!" Cody gripped his hand, hard, as if the truck was tipping over and she might fall out. "All the rest of us are at least two years younger! *She's* the one who has our, our *birth!*"

Angelica leaned forward across the dead king's ghost to squeeze Plumtree's shoulder. "Cody," she said strongly, "*lots* of people are divided from their births by some kind of fault-line. Most of them aren't fortunate enough to know how it happened, or even *that* it happened—they're just aware of a pressure-failure back there somewhere." She paused, obviously casting about for something else to say. "Plants often can be safely severed from their original taproots, if they've developed newer roots further along the vine."

Cody was hurting Cochran's gashed thumb, and even her bandaged right hand was pulling on the door handle so hard that Cochran thought the handle must be about to break off. Her feet were braced against the slippery wet floorboards. "But *have* I, have any of us?" she whispered. "Janis is deaf now, and her dreams were fading to black-and-white even on Friday night! Tiffany, Janis, Audrey, Cody, Luanne . . . are we all going to slide into the, the booming black-and-white *hole* that's Valorie?"

The king's ghost spoke now, clearly addressing Cody: "In the midsummer of this year," said the deep voice, gently but forcefully, "you and I will be standing in happy sunlight on the hill in the lake."

Cochran looked back at him—and didn't jump in surprise, only ex-

perienced a dizzying emptiness in his chest, to see that the ghost was
draped in a white woolen robe now, apparently dry, conceivably the
same robe Crane's body had worn when it had been lying in state in
Solville. The full, King Solomon beard was lustrous and dry.

The truck rocked as Pete steered it into a parking space and tromped
on the brake. "The grail castle," he said. "The green chapel." A tall
hedge blocked the view of the estate from here, but they could see a
closed gate, and signs directing tourists toward the low, modern-looking
buildings to the right.

Pete Sullivan led the way across the parking lot, but he took his four
bedraggled companions toward the locked gate instead of in the direction of the little peak-roofed booth and the Winchester Products Museum beyond it.

He had pulled his comb out of his pocket, and he appeared to be
trying to break the end of it off. "I suppose they count the guests, on
the guided tours," he said to Cochran over the hiss of the rain.

"Yes," Cochran told him. "Even *one* couldn't sneak away, let alone
five. And I bet they wouldn't let a barefoot guy go anyway."

"I don't expect anybody's looking this way," Pete said, "but the rest
of you block the view of me; act like you're taking pictures of the
house."

Cochran took Plumtree's elbow and stood to Pete's left, pointing
through the gate and nodding animatedly. "I'm pretending to be a tourist," he told her when she frowned at him. "Play along."

Pete's comb was metal, apparently stainless steel, and he had broken
two teeth off one end of it and bent kinks into them. Now he had tipped
up the padlock on the gate and was carefully fitting the teeth into the
keyhole.

Cochran stared between the bars of the gate at the house. Past a low
row of pink flowering bushes he could see the closest corner of the vast
Victorian structure, a circular porch with a cone-roofed tower turret over
it. Through the veils of rain beyond it he could see other railed balconies
and steeply sloped shingle roofs, and dozens of windows. Lights were
on behind many of the windows, and he hoped Pete's hands could work
quickly.

"When I say *three,*" said Pete as he twiddled with the comb teeth
in the lock mechanism, "we'll all go through the gate and then walk
fast to the corner of that box hedge by the porch. I can see a sign on a
post, I think tourists are allowed to be there."

"Yeah," said Cochran, "it's part of the garden tour—that's self-guided. But they may not have the gardens open, on a rainy day like this.''

"Great. Well, if anybody comes up to us," Pete said grimly, "smile at 'em and talk in a foreign language, like you wandered out here through the wrong door. And then—'' He looked down at his busy, pacifist hands. "Sid, you'll have to cold-cock 'em.''

Cochran thought of Kootie and Mavranos back at his house, ready to risk their lives, and of the Sullivans, who had reluctantly committed themselves to this, and of Plumtree, hoping to undo the murder of the ghost that was standing right behind them. He looked back at the bearded figure, and noticed without surprise that the king's ghost was now wearing a sort of tropical white business suit, though still barefoot. The ghost, as apparently solid as any of them, looked like a visiting emperor.

"I can see the necessity of that," Cochran said to Pete. "Let's hope nobody notices us."

Pete nodded, and Cochran heard the snap of the lock. "One, two, *three.*" Pete was lifting the gate as he swung it open, and the wet hinges didn't squeal; then Cochran took hold of the elbow of Plumtree's leather jacket again and they were hurrying across the cobblestone driveway to the sign. Behind him Cochran heard the gate clink closed again, and Pete's footsteps slapping up to where the rest of them now stood.

They halted there, rocking, and Cochran stared fixedly at the lettering on the waist-high sign while he tensed himself for any evidence of challenge; but the only sound was the timpani drumroll of the rain on the cobblestones and the smack of bigger drops falling from the high palm branches that waved overhead, and his peripheral vision showed him no movement on the shadowed porches or the walkways or hedged lawns.

Plumtree had actually read the sign. "That iron cap in the ground is to the coal chute," she told him. "And those windows up on the second floor there to the left are where the old lady's bedroom was. 'The Daisy Bedroom'—huh!''

"We're supposed to," panted Pete, "find the Winchester woman's ghost—and, I guess, a—container?—of the *pagadebiti* wine.'' He turned to the ghost. "You can do those things?''

The tall, bearded ghost was looking at Cochran when it echoed Pete's last sentence: "You can do those things," it said hollowly.

"I guess that'll do," sighed Pete. "Up onto the porch there, everybody, and I'll unlock us a door."

*   *   *

They found a modern-looking glass door with an empty carpeted hall visible inside. A decal on the glass read PLEASE NO ADMITTANCE EMPLOYEES ONLY, but Pete was able to pop back the bolt with a contemptuous fiddle-and-twist of his kinked comb-teeth.

"We should hear a tour-party, if one's nearby," whispered Cochran as he stepped inside. Angelica was leading the king's ghost by the hand, and Plumtree had sidled in ahead of them and was now carefully standing on the other side of Cochran from the ghost. "We'll hear the guide talking, and the footsteps. Move the *other way* if we do, right?"

They hurried down the corridor toward the interior of the great house, and soon the corridor turned left and they were in a broad, empty Victorian entry hall lit by electric lights that mimicked gas lamps. Polished carved mahogany framed the windows and doors and the corners of the ceiling, and panelled the walls from the wainscot down; and the floors were a sort of interlocking-plaid pattern of inlaid maple and walnut. The panes in the two front doors were hundreds of carved quartz crystals arranged in fanciful flower and fleur-de-lis patterns, set in webs of silver and lead and bronze.

"How many rooms did the old lady build here?" asked Angelica in a whisper.

"I don't know," said Cochran. "Two hundred."

"Can we—*call* her ghost, somehow? We can't search every damn room!"

"The goose of Winchester can't hear to hiss," said the king's ghost. "A bolt-hole, a hidey-hole, is where she is—hidden, escaped from Dionysus like a possum hidden in its own pouch." He touched the glossy, deeply imprinted white wallpaper.

"Swell," said Cody. "Let's move on."

They hurried down the hall, and found themselves in a vast, dark ballroom. Even in the shadowy dimness Cochran could see that the floor, and the framed and panelled and shelved walls, and the very ceiling way up above the silver chandelier, were of glossy inlaid wood. Far out across the floor on one side was a pipe organ like a cathedral altar, and in the long adjoining wall a fireplace was inset between the two tall, narrow windows that let in the ballroom's only light.

Cochran could faintly hear the muffled creak and knock of footsteps on the floor above, and he looked around helplessly at the huge, high-ceilinged room. He was aware of nearly inaudible creaks and rustles from the far, dark corners of the room, and realized that he'd been hearing these soft flexings ever since they had entered the house; and he had steadily felt attention being paid to him and his companions, but it felt childish and frightful, nothing like a tour-guide or a security guard.

Could the ghost of Mrs. Winchester be looking at them now from some remote shelf or alcove, flitting along after them from room to room? He flexed his right hand—but got no sense of help from the god.

"Let's just goddamn keep going," he whispered.

"Sid—!" gasped Plumtree. "Look at the stained-glass windows!"

Cochran focussed his eyes on the panes of leaded glass that glowed with the gray daylight outside, and he noticed that they each portrayed a long banner curling around ivy-vine patterns. And there was stylized lettering, capitals, on each banner—WIDE UNCLASP THE TABLES OF THEIR THOUGHTS, read the one in the left-hand window, and on the banner in the right was spelled out THESE SAME THOUGHTS PEOPLE THIS LITTLE WORLD.

"The left one's the *Troilus and Cressida* quote," said Angelica softly, "though 'tables' isn't supposed to be plural. And the right one is from *Richard II,* when the king is alone in prison, and conjuring up company for himself out of his own head." She shook her head. "Why the hell would Winchester have put *them* up here? The *Troilus and Cressida* one is from a speech where Ulysses is saying what a promiscuous ghost-slut Cressida is!"

Plumtree's cold left hand clasped Cochran's, and was shaking.

"It'd get a raised eyebrow from any Shakespeare-savvy guest," agreed Pete.

"Is that a *clue,* is she in *here?*" snapped Cochran, looking from the windows to the ghost in the white suit.

"Probably not in a room with a fireplace," said Pete. "Fireplaces would be the . . . portals for ghosts to get broken up in and sent to the god, like the ashtrays you see with palindromes lettered around the rims."

"She was talking to *me,*" said Plumtree flatly. "Those windows were put there as a message for . . . for the person who looks like is turning out to be me, all these years later. This little *head.* Shit, she must have been, voluntarily or *in*voluntarily, a multiple-personality herself."

"So what's the message?" asked Angelica.

"She—she didn't want to go smoking away up one of the chimneys," said Plumtree.

"Sail on," said Scott Crane's ghost, with a chopping wave toward the rest of the house.

They found a broader hall and tiptoed along it, instinctively crowding against one panelled wall after another, and darting quickly across the wide, gleaming patches of hardwood floor between. The electric lights were far apart, but the open rectangular spaces were all grayly lit by the dozens of interior windows and arches and skylights. In fact the

layout of the rooms was so open and expansive that the sprawling scope
of the house was evident at every turn, from every obtuse perspective;
at no point could one fail to get the visceral impression that the house
was infinite in every dimension, like a house in an Escher print—that
one could walk forever down these broad, carpeted halls, up and down
these dark-railed stairs from floor to ever-unfamiliar floor, without once
re-crossing one's path. And Cochran remembered Mammy Pleasant saying that the place had been built to attract, and trap, and dispatch to the
afterworld, wandering ghosts reluctant to go on to the god.

"It looks open," whispered Angelica at one point, "but she's made
the geometry in here as complicated as the mazes in the Mandelbrot
set; there are patches of empty air in here that might as well be steel
bulkheads. You'd never know because you could never quite manage
to *get* to 'em."

Cochran found a stairway, but it ran uselessly right up against the
ceiling, with not even a trap-door to justify it; then he led his party up
another set of stairs that switchbacked seven times but only took them
up one floor, for each step was only two inches tall; and he led them
through galleries with railed-off squares to keep one from stepping into
windows that were set in the floor, and through a broad hall or series
of open-walled rooms in which four ornate fireplaces stood nearly side
by side; and they shuffled past mercifully locked windowed doors that
opened onto sheer drops into kitchens and corridors below.

"More a house for birds," said Cody at one point, "or monkeys,
than for people."

"Aerial manlike entities," agreed Angelica with a glance at the dead
king.

"Smoking away up the chimneys," said the bearded figure, drawing
a frown from Plumtree.

At last they found themselves in a room with an open railed balcony
on the fourth floor, unable to climb higher. The room was unfinished,
with bare lath along one wall; an exposed brick chimney, with no fireplace, rose from the floor to the ceiling in the left corner.

Pete stepped toward the balcony, crouching to peer out over the green
lawns and red rooftop peaks without being seen from below.

"It's infinite," he said, hopelessly. "I can't even see an end to the
house, from here. You'd think I could see the freeway, or a gas-station
sign, or something."

"This place is still a supernatural maze," said Angelica. "It's got to
be drawing ghosts like a candle draws moths, still. I swear, down in
those endless galleries and halls I could feel all their half-wit attentions
on us. Old lady Winchester 'wide unclasped the table of her thoughts'—

her patterns of thoughts, her accommodating masks—to every footloose ghost in the West, she was no virgin, psychically; and 'these same thoughts people this little world.' Except it doesn't look so little, from inside.'' She shook her head violently and then startled Cochran by spitting on the floor. ''They're all around us right now, like spiderwebs. These fireplaces should be running full-blast, twenty-four hours a day.''

''She probably assumed they'd be used, in the winter at least,'' said Cody. ''After her death.''

Cochran looked away from Angelica, toward the corner of the room.

''This chimney is like the first stairway we tried,'' he said, ''look. There's no hole in the ceiling for it.''

Pete Sullivan walked over and reached up with both hands to hook his fingertips over the uneven row of bricks at the top edge of the chimney, which did end several inches short of the solid ceiling planks. ''My hands are twitchy,'' Pete said, ''like they want to . . . *participate* with it. Did Houdini ever do an escape from a chimney?''

The white-clad ghost strode over and, taller than Pete, was able to slide its whole hand into the drafty space between the bricks and the ceiling planks.

''Clean, uncarboned brick,'' the ghost said solemnly; ''and gold. I can smell gold on the draft.''

''Gold?'' echoed Cochran, disappointed that they had apparently found some old treasure instead of the old woman's ghost.

''Well now, gold would damp out her wavelengths,'' said Pete, lowering his hands and brushing brick dust off on his jeans. ''Ghosts are an electromagnetic agitation, so she'd have to be locked up in something shielding, to be hidden. People used to make coffins out of lead, to keep the ghost in, contained and undetectable. Gold's not quite as dense as lead, but it'd certainly do.''

''And,'' said Cochran, nodding, ''if chimneys generally destroy ghosts, if that's common knowledge, then you certainly wouldn't ever *look* for a ghost to be *hiding* in one.''

''Not unless you knew it was a dummy chimney,'' agreed Angelica. ''And with a hundred *real* fireplaces and chimneys around the place, who'd notice that *one* was a fake?''

The ghost's white sleeve disappeared behind the top row of bricks . . . and Cochran noticed that the figure was leaning braced against the chimney with one knee, for the other leg appeared now to be just a hanging, empty trouser leg, its cuff flapping over an empty white shoe.

''The chimney is like the hole Alice fell down,'' said the ghost softly. ''Tiny shelves all the way down, with papers and locks of hair and rings and stones and dry leaves.'' After another moment, the ghost said, ''Ah.''

Then the trouser leg filled out and the cuff lowered to cover the shoe, which shifted as weight visibly settled into it again.

A clunking, scraping noise at the top of the chimney made Cochran look up—and the ghost was trying to rock something out of the chimney, apparently struggling to angle it out through the narrow gap between the bricks and the ceiling planks.

The hard object was not coming out. ''Break away a brick or two,'' suggested Cochran, looking nervously toward the stairs. He could hear voices now, and the knocking of footsteps. ''I think a tour's coming.''

Pete reached his own hand in next to the ghost's, and then shook his head. ''It's not that it won't fit out,'' he said through clenched teeth, ''it's just *stopping,* in mid-air, like the thin air turns rubbery, like we're trying to push two big magnets together at their positive ends.''

Cochran could definitely hear voices mounting from below now. ''What *is* it?'' he asked anxiously. ''If it's just an old magnet or something, drop it and let's go!''

''It's rectangular,'' gasped Pete, ''heavy.''

Plumtree stood by the chimney and jumped up, peering into the gap. ''You've got a gold box,'' she said when her sneaker soles had hit the floor again.

''Dead woman's gold,'' said Angelica, ''she's probably got the geometry of the chimney-boundary magicked to not let it pass.''

''Let's see if the chimney can tell the difference between that and a dead *man's* gold,'' said Plumtree. She dug the gold Dunhill lighter out of her pocket and tossed it up in a glittering arc toward the gap.

The lighter knocked against the wooden ceiling and disappeared behind the bricks, down inside the chimney, and then Pete jackknifed backward and sat down hard on the wooden floor, holding in his lap a metal box that gleamed gold under a veil of cobwebs.

Scott Crane's ghost had leaped back, or *flickered* back like an image in a jolted mirror; and when Cochran heard a scuffling flutter behind him he spun around to see a white-painted canvas banner settling onto the floor. The word GARLIC was painted on it in cursive blue letters, and the king's ghost was gone.

Cochran looked back at Angelica and Plumtree, who were staring wide-eyed at the empty canvas. Cochran shrugged at Plumtree. ''You tossed his lighter,'' he said.

''Good,'' she said with a visible shiver.

''Is there somebody up there?'' came a voice from the stairs at the back of the room.

Plumtree grabbed the dusty, cobwebby box from Pete and took a long step toward a doorway that led away from the stairs. She jerked her head for the others to follow.

Cochran helped Pete to his feet and followed Angelica and Plumtree down this unexplored hallway. Let the tour-guide explain the garlic banner, he thought: *Damn ghosts!—leaving their goofy shit around everywhere.*

They hurried on through a hastily glimpsed kaleidoscope of architecture, with skylights below them and stairways curling around them and interior balconies and windows receding away at every height in the patches of electric lamp-glow and lancing columns of gray daylight.

At the top of one white-painted stairway Cochran's right hand was suddenly tugged diagonally out and down. He crouched and made a *ch-ch!* sound, and then started hopping down the stairs before his hand could pull him off balance and send him tumbling down them. He could hear the others following behind him, but he didn't dare lift his eyes from the crowding-up stair-edges to look back.

The stairway continued down past the next floor, but was bevelled dark wood now, and the walls and doors and ceilings were framed in carved mahogany. Cochran's hand was pulled out horizontally away from the landing and down a hall, and he almost thought he could feel a warm, callused hand clasping his palm and knuckles, and a deeply jarring pulse like seismic temblors.

Helplessly Cochran led his companions through a wide doorway, and his first impression was that they had come to another unfinished section—but a closer look at the walls showed him that the wide patches of exposed lath were edged with broken plaster and torn wall fabric.

"This must be the earthquake-damaged section," Cochran whispered to Plumtree, who was holding the gold box in both hands.

She stepped carefully over the uneven floor to the windows, which were panes of clear glass inset at the centers of stained-glass borders.

"We're in the, what was it, the Daisy bedroom," Plumtree said breathlessly, peering out at the grounds, "or near it. You can see the sign we reconnoitered at, down there to the left. This here would be where she was sleeping on that night in 1906, when Dionysus knocked down the tower onto her."

Cochran flexed his hand, then waved it experimentally in the still air; and it seemed to be free of any supernatural tether now.

"It must be here," he said, "whatever we're supposed to find."

Two big, framed black-and-white photographs were hung on one raggedly half-plastered wall. Still hesitantly holding his hand out to the side, Cochran walked over to the pictures, and saw that they were views of the house as it had stood in the days before the top three stories had fallen; and the additional crenellations and pillars and balconies, and the peak-roofed tower above it all, ashen and fortress-like and stern in the old gray photographs, made the structure's present-day height and red-and-beige exterior seem modest by comparison.

"The House of Babel," said Plumtree, who had walked up beside him with her hands in the pockets of the leather jacket. "I guess that's how the god looked at it."

"There was a fireplace over here," called Pete softly from the other side of the room, "at one time."

He was standing beside a chest-high square gap in the wall, through which the exposed floor joists of another room were visible on the far side. Pete crouched and looked up at the underside of the gap. "You can see the chimney going on upward."

A piece of white-painted plywood had been neatly fitted in to cover the spot where the hearth would have been, and Cochran crossed to it and then knelt down on the floor beside Pete's knees to take hold of the edge of the board. Pete stepped back.

"I'm certain this must be bolted down," Cochran said softly.

"Think of young King Arthur," said Angelica behind him, "with the sword in the stone. You're the—the guy with the Dionysus mark on his hand."

Cochran yanked upward on the board, and nearly fell over backward as it sprang up in his hands. He shuffled his feet to regain his balance, and leaned against the board and pushed it forward onto the floor joists of the next room; then for several seconds he just peered down into the rectangular brick-lined black hole he had exposed. He dug a penny out of his pocket and held it over the hole for a moment, then dropped it; and he waited, but no sound came back up.

At last he stood up and quickly stepped away from the hole. Instead of stepping over to look for themselves, Angelica and Pete and Plumtree stared at him.

"Well," Cochran said, "there's—it's very fucking dark down there, excuse me. But there's *rungs,* starting a yard or so down."

"Rungs." Angelica quickly crossed to one of the windows and stared out at the shaggy palm trees nodding out in the rain. "Damn it, we were just going to get . . . *gas,* and *beer,* and *batteries,*" she said harshly. "Kootie's ordering a *pizza.* I'm not—hell, I'm not even *dressed* for climbing down into some goddamn—unlit—spidery *catacombs* in a *haunted house.*" She turned around and glared at Plumtree. "If *only,*" she cried out, "you hadn't killed Scott Crane!"

Plumtree opened her mouth and blinked, then snarled, "And who did *you* kill, lady? *'If only'!* Back in your shanty house in Long Beach, you told me that each of you was responsible for the death of somebody, and had guilty amends to make. You told me you can't get rid of the guilt and shame without help, that that'd be like thinking one hand could fix what it took two to break, remember? I've had stinking *beer cans* wired to my ankles, and I've been taped into a chair and then thrown onto a backyard faucet hard enough to crack my ribs, and, and I get the idea that it's a big honor for me to be allowed to *eat* with you all.'' Her voice was shaking, and her lip was pulled back to expose her lower teeth as she went on, ''So tell me, bitch—who did *you* kill?''

Angelica stared at Plumtree blankly. Then she said, ''Fair enough. Okay. I was a psychiatrist in private practice, and I used to perform fake Wednesday-night seances to let my patients make peace with dead friends and relatives; and five Halloweens ago one of the seances, right in the middle of it, stopped being fake. A whole lot of real, angry ghosts showed up, and among other things the clinic caught fire. Three patients died, and five more are probably still in mental hospitals to this day.'' She took a deep breath and let it out, though her face was still expressionless. ''One of the ones that died was in love with me; I wasn't in love with him, but I—didn't really discourage him. Frank Rocha. I killed Frank Rocha, through carelessness in the expertise I was trained for, the expertise he had paid me to use. His ghost troubled me for two years, and the police have been looking for me ever since.'' She smiled tiredly and held out her right hand. ''I do apologize, Cody. Are we friends?''

Plumtree was shaking her head, but apparently more in bewilderment than denial. She took Angelica's hand and said, ''I never had a friend before.''

''It's a tricky flop,'' said Cochran shortly. He could feel a jumpy restlessness in his right hand, and he knew it wanted to point toward the brick chimney hole in the floor. Climb down before it pulls you down, he thought. ''Somebody give me a . . . a Bic lighter or something, since we don't have the Dunhill anymore.'' He sighed and ran his hands through his hair, patted the gun under the windbreaker at the back of his belt, then walked over to the hole and sat down on the floor beside it, swinging his legs into the dark empty space.

Plumtree pulled a red Bic out of the leather jacket pocket. ''Here, Sid—and I'm right behind you.''

''So are we, so are we,'' sighed Angelica.

Cochran slid himself forward, down into the hole, so that his toes and the seat of his jeans were braced against opposite brick surfaces and most of his weight was on his elbows. The angular bulk of the holstered .357 jabbed him over his right kidney.

"Just a bit lower than you'd like," he said breathlessly through clenched teeth, "there's a rung you can get a foot onto. Then I guess you just drag your back as you go down until you've gone far enough to get your hands onto the rungs."

He heard several sighs behind and above him, and then Pete's voice said, "I'll go last, and pull the plywood cover back over the hole."

CHAPTER 29

Roma, tibi subito motibus ibit Amor . . .
—Sotades of Maroneia in Thrace,
c. 276 B.C.

The shaft was wide for a chimney, but the rough brick sides kept snagging the elbows of Cochran's windbreaker no matter how carefully he kept them tucked in against his ribs, and after Pete pulled the board over the top of the shaft there was no light at all, and the close amplification of panting breath and the gritty scuff of feet on iron rungs emphasized the constriction; Cochran was terribly aware that even if he unhooked his gun holster and pressed his back flat against the wall behind him he would not have had room to bring his knee up to his chest.

Bits of mud dislodged from Plumtree's sneakers tapped his head and face and hands in the total blackness, and he thought about pausing to strike the lighter; but the strong clay-scented draft from below would probably have extinguished the flame instantly, and anyway he wasn't sure he wanted to *see* how close in front of his face the bricks were, and *see* the narrow space overhead blocked by the shoe-soles of only one of the three people whose bodies clogged the way back up to air and light and room to move.

When his right elbow swung free in a side opening, Cochran's eyes had been in total darkness long enough for him to detect a faint gray glow from the side tunnel, which slanted downward at roughly a forty-five-degree angle. Faintly he could hear voices coming up through it.

"Side chute to one of the fireplaces," he whispered upward. "Don't take it—keep going—straight down."

He heard Plumtree relaying the message up to Pete and Angelica as he resumed abrading himself down the angular stone esophagus.

After a dozen more rungs he knew he must be well below the level of the ground floor—and when he had hunched a few yards farther down he was sure that he heard far-distant music from the impenetrable darkness below his feet, and that the upwelling draft was elusively scented with hints of cypress and coarse red wine and crushed night-time grass.

He thought of whispering *Getting close now,* but told himelf that the others would detect it too.

He didn't realize that he'd been nervously bouncing the heel of each shoe off the back wall between rung-steps until the moment he swung one foot back and it met no wall; and he almost lost his grip in surprise. But then he noticed that the scuff of his feet wasn't tightly amplified anymore, either, and soon he felt the bottom edge of the scratchy brick surface at his back scrape up across his shoulders and then ruffle the hair at the back of his head. He could stretch out away from the iron ladder in the darkness now, and the sound of his breathing scattered away behind him with no echoes.

And, though it was only the dimmest ashy diffraction, there was light—Cochran could see the backs of his hands as faint whitenesses bravely distinct from the background blackness.

Soon came a moment when his left foot reached down and instead of swinging through empty air struck a gritty, powdery ground, jolting his spine. He got his other foot down onto the ground too, but he whispered for the others to stop, and then spent several seconds pawing around with his shoe soles and flexing his knees, before he dared to unclamp his hands from the last rung. He flicked the lighter then, and, looking away from the dazzling flame, saw that he was standing on a patch of soot that covered this corner of a broad dirt floor. Stone walls and a low stone ceiling receded away into shadows, but he could see an arched doorway at the far end of the room. The distantly musical and sylvan breeze was even more remote now, but seemed to be coming to him through the arch.

He cupped his free hand around the lighter flame until his three companions had climbed all the way down out of the chimney shaft and joined him on the sooty patch of dirt, and by that time he was able to look directly into the flame without squinting. When he let it snap off to cool his thumb the darkness seemed absolute again by contrast.

"There's an arch ahead of us," he whispered.

"No . . . presences," whispered Angelica; "I don't sense ghosts down here."

At that moment Cochran jumped and gasped in pure panic, for he had the clear but visually unverifiable impression that a big, warm hand had clasped his right hand, and was gently tugging him forward out across the dirt floor. "Follow me!" he choked urgently to the others as he stumbled forward.

By the echoes of his panting breath he knew when he was passing through the stone arch—and then the dim gray light was strong enough for him to see his empty hand stretched out in front of him. And as soon as he could see that no other hand held his, the sensation of it vanished. He lowered his arm, aware now that his heart was pounding rapidly, and as the sweat cooled on his face he blinked around at the racks and knobs that covered the closest wall.

The racks were wine racks, and the knobs were the foil-sheathed necks of bottles lying horizontally in them. "We're in the wine cellar!" he whispered. He remembered Mammy Pleasant telling them yesterday that Mrs. Winchester had walled up the wine cellar after seeing the black handprint of her dead husband on the wall.

He flicked the lighter again, and by the sudden yellow glare he walked over and lifted one of the dusty bottles out of the nearest rack, and wiped the label on his windbreaker—and when he had peered at it he shivered and glanced around in suspicious fright, for what he held was a bottle of the fabulous 1887 Inglenook Cabernet Sauvignon, the very same California vintage that Andre Simon had described in 1960 as "every bit as fine as my favorite pre-phylloxera clarets."

He heard a rattling knock from behind him, and Angelica yelped, "Jesus, a skull! There's a goddamn *skull* on the floor here!"

Cochran turned around, still holding the bottle; Angelica was standing stiffly by the arch, her feet well back from what did appear to be a human skull lying on the dirt. Focussing on the dim corners around the room, he now saw pale curls and ribby clusters that might be other bones.

"At least one other skull," whispered Pete through an audibly tight throat, "over here. And—an antique revolver."

"They're old," Cochran said to Angelica. "They may have been down here a hundred years."

"I know, I know," she said, obviously embarrassed at having been frightened.

"Sid," called Plumtree softly from the opposite wall, "bring your lighter over here a second." She was standing beside a section of plain white plastered wall, pointing at a shadowed spot down by her knee.

Still holding the gas-release lever down, Cochran carefully carried the light over to where she was pointing, and crouched to illuminate the spot.

It was an old mark, in still faintly adhering soot, of a tiny hand.

Angelica had hurried up beside Cochran, and now she bent over to look at the handprint. "Ah!" she exclaimed sharply, stepping back. "The baby! It wasn't her dead *husband's* ghost that the god finally asked Mrs. Winchester to give over to him! Mammy Pleasant had that wrong. It was the ghost of Winchester's dead *baby daughter!*" And Cochran saw the *bruja* of Solville make the Catholic sign of the cross. "She couldn't bring herself to do *that,* just as Agave couldn't disown the ghost of her killed son, in Arky's Euripides play!"

"And she entombed the wine," said Pete Sullivan shakily, "but she left a chimney air shaft to link this cellar with her bedroom. I'll bet she never permitted any fires in any of the fireplaces that connect with that chimney, after she walled up the cellar."

Cochran let the lighter flame go out, and he handed the hot lighter to Plumtree while he walked back to the rack to reluctantly replace the legendary Inglenook. And after he had put the bottle back, his hand twitched to the side—

—*and in his nose was the sagebrush-and-dry-stone smell of the Mojave Desert outside Las Vegas, and the acid perfume of Paris streets after rain, and the hallucinated mildewy staleness of the Victorian hall in which he had seen Mondard in a mirror—*

—and his fingers were pressed firmly around another bottle. He lifted it out carefully and carried it over to Plumtree, who struck the lighter.

The label on the bottle was Buena Vista, Count Haraszthy's old Sonoma vineyard; and below the brand name and a statement of limited bottling was the date, 1860, and the single word PAGADEBITI.

"I've got the wine," he whispered. "Let's *esplitavo.*"

"God," said Angelica, "back up that chimney?"

The dirt floor shook then, and Cochran was so careful not to drop the bottle that he fell to his knees cradling it. Plumtree had let the lighter snap off, and when she flicked it on again there were vertical streaks of dust sifting in the air below the stone ceiling. And through the arch behind them came the echoing rattle of bricks and iron clattering down in the old chimney shaft.

"*No,*" said a new, deep voice.

Again Plumtree let the lighter go out—and when the flint-wheel had stutteringly lit the flame again, Cochran jumped in surprise to see a tall, broad-shouldered black man standing in the open arch. Even in the frail lighter glow, this newcomer seemed *solider* than Cochran and his companions—glossier because of reflecting the light more strongly, his feet more of a weight on the dirt floor, the very air seeming to rebound more helplessly from his unyielding surfaces.

The man, if it was a man and not some sort of elemental spirit, was wearing a spotted animal skin like a toga, and leafy vines were tangled

in his long braids; in his hand was a staff wrapped with vines and capped
with a pinecone.

"I am the guardian of the god's blood," the figure said. The voice
shook the streaks of dust that hung in the air, and his breath seemed to
carry the faint music and the forest smells. *"Did you think there would
be no guard? Nobody takes the god's blood out of the tabernacle past
me."* He shifted the staff to his right hand, and it gleamed in the frail
light now, for it had become a long, curving sword, and muscles flexed
in the strong black arm to hold the weapon's evident new weight.

"Well I say god*damn!"* burst out Plumtree. The lighter was jiggling
wildly in her hand, and Angelica took it from her and re-lit it.

"The," said Pete Sullivan quickly, "the god wants us to take the
wine. He *led* us here, to get it!"

"So these others claimed," said the black man, rolling his obsidian
head around at the bones without looking away from the four intruders.
*"Did you think there would be no guard? Nobody takes the god's blood
out of the tabernacle past me."* When he inhaled, Cochran yawned
nervously, expecting his eardrums to pop.

Cochran held up the back of his right hand. "This is the god's mark,
given to me when I put out my hand to save the god's vine from being
cut back!" He made a fist. "The god led me into this room, *by* this
hand, half a minute ago!"

"So these others claimed," repeated the tall black man, again rocking
his head.

Cochran realized that the figure was not listening to what they said;
perhaps didn't even have the capacity to understand objections. It was
some kind of idiot *genius loci,* an apparently unalterable part of the
god's math, as implacable and unreasoning as an electrified fence. With
his free hand Cochran reached around under the back of his windbreaker
and, though hollowly aware that the "antique revolver" had apparently
been of no use to one long-ago intruder, nevertheless unsnapped his
holster.

Beside him, Plumtree shivered.

"If I—put the wine back—" Cochran began hoarsely.

All at once the supernatural guard stamped far forward into the room,
sweeping the sword in a fast horizontal arc—the blade whistled as it
split the quivering air—

—Hopping back, Cochran snatched the Pachmayr grip and yanked
the gun out of the holster, and despairingly pointed the muzzle into the
center of the broad chest—

And in the same instant Plumtree stepped forward so that a backswing from the sword or a shot from the gun would hit her; and Mammy Pleasant's imperious voice said, "Bacchus!"

The curved sword blade paused behind the black man's left shoulder like the rising crescent moon behind a mountain, and Cochran tipped the gun barrel upward.

"Don't you recognize me, Bacchus?" spoke the old woman's voice from Plumtree's mouth. "I'm Mary Ellen Pleasant, the poor old woman you took *custody* of, in '99! You were there when I died, five years later—and you were there too when the god came breaking down Yerba Buena for my ghost, three Easters after that."

"*I—do recognize you,*" said the solid black figure.

"Am I, like you, a totally surrendered servant of the god?"

"*You are.*"

"I am," said Pleasant as Plumtree's blond head nodded. "And I tell you that the god has sent me to fetch out this wine, and bring it to the king." Without looking away from the creature's eyes, she held out one hand toward Cochran. He carefully laid the bottle in her palm.

For several long seconds the tall black figure stood motionless. Cochran kept the gun pointed at the ceiling but didn't take his finger out of the trigger guard.

Then the apparition tossed the sword through the eddying air to its left hand, and the sword again became a vine-wrapped staff with a pinecone on it.

The figure waved it and said, *"Pass."*

Again the ground shook, and this time the bottles on the walls clinked and clicked like castanets and temple bells, and didn't stop rattling; and Cochran didn't fall to his knees this time, but just crouched like a surfer to keep his balance on the gyrating floor.

While the floor was still shifting, Plumtree turned and began dancing like a tightrope-walker into the darkness at the far end of the cellar, away from the arch and the supernatural guard. Angelica let the lighter go out as she went hopping and skipping after her, and Pete and Cochran were bounding along at her heels.

And, over the bass drumming of the earth, Cochran thought as he ran that he could hear distant pipes playing, unless that was just some whistling overtone of his panicky panting breath as he followed the sounds of Pete and Angelica through the rocking pitch blackness.

Soon they were able to see slanting gray light ahead of them and hear the crackle of rain, and when they had hurried to the muddy end of the tunnel, and climbed up over tumbled masonry out onto wet grass in a battering showery wind, they could see that they were in some kind of park. Cochran hastily shoved his revolver back into its holster, and pulled the back of his windbreaker down over it.

The rain quickly made runny black mud of the soot that smeared their backs and knees, and by unspoken agreement they didn't run for the shelter of the corrugated metal roof over some nearby picnic tables, but plodded through the cleansing shower straight across the grass toward the nearest visible road.

When Plumtree glanced at him, Cochran saw that she was Cody again. "I guess I look as shitty as you do," she said through chattering teeth.

"I guess you do," he said stolidly.

She touched the angular bulge at the bottom of the zipped leather jacket, right over her belt, and Cochran realized that it must be the gold box from the chimney. "I swear I can feel her kicking in there," she said.

CHAPTER 30

Hades and Dionysus, for whom they go mad and rage,
are one and the same.

—Heraclitus

The road proved to be called Tisch Way, and they trudged a quarter of a mile west along its gravel shoulder through the downpour to the intersection of Winchester Boulevard, with the rushing lanes of the 280 visible now just past a chain-link fence on the other side of the road.

When they had wearily got back into the red truck and wedged the bottle of *pagadebiti* securely in the glove compartment, Pete started the engine and drove out of the Winchester Mystery House parking lot, but then just made a left turn onto Olsen Drive and an immediate right into the parking lot of a big new shopping center; he drove up to the empty Winchester Boulevard end of the rain-hazed lot and pulled into a parking space under a towering three-panel movie-theater sign and turned off the engine. The rain drummed on the truck roof, and every five seconds a drop collected on the rusty underside and fell soundlessly onto the soaked thigh of Plumtree's jeans.

She was sitting in the back seat beside Cochran, and she fumbled the gold box out from under the soaked leather jacket. It was no bigger than a couple of decks of cards stuck together back-to-back, and its lid appeared to be an unhinged plate held in place by six gold screws.

"Find me a screwdriver, Pete," she said. "A flat-tip one."

"No," said Cochran, "don't open it. We're supposed to pitch it into the ocean."

"Not still shut up tight, though, right? Or she might as well have stayed in the chimney—there'd be no difference between the box sitting there or sitting still-sealed at the bottom of the bay. She's gotta be broke open, like an egg into a frypan.'' Plumtree leaned back in her seat and closed her eyes. Her wet hair was plastered to her head and streaked with black. "Is Mammy Pleasant going away voluntarily? Or are you just gonna be shoving her in?''

"Voluntarily," Cochran said. "She's going along, anyway. She appears to be resigned to it.'' The interior of the truck felt warm and close after the gusty chill outside, and he wrinkled his nose against the remembered childhood smell of doused campfires.

"That's what I thought." Plumtree fitted her thumbnail into one of the screw slots and twisted gently, but it didn't move.

"I don't know if ghosts really have a whole lot of capacity for voluntary action, actual *volition,*'' said Angelica from the front seat; and immediately she frowned, as if ashamed to have had the thought.

"These *are* dead people, Cody," Pete said.

"Like Valorie," Plumtree agreed, nodding expressionlessly. "Where's that screwdriver?''

Pete sighed and bent forward to grope under the front seat.

"If you let her out," said Angelica, clearly nettled but not quite ready to interfere, "she'll be gone as quick as a puff of steam.''

Pete had dragged a black metal toolbox onto the seat, and unsnapped the catches and opened it. Wordlessly he passed a screwdriver over the back of the seat.

"I don't think she will," said Plumtree. "Obviously I wasn't busted out of the madhouse and made a part of this company just so you'd be able to question my father . . . and hell, I've already hosted Mammy Pleasant.''

". . . Oh," said Angelica, humbly. "I—I see. Cody, I do think you could get away with not doing it.''

Plumtree had already used the screwdriver to back one of the screws out of the box. "Look at that," she said, holding the screw up. "*All* gold, not just the head.''

"I don't imagine she'd scrimp," said Cochran bitterly, "on what she thought would be her eternal resting place.'' He knew he wouldn't be able to talk Cody out of hosting the old woman's ghost, if it was still viable in there, and he only hoped Winchester wouldn't get her into any trouble, or hurt her ribs or her hand. "I wonder when she decided to have this box and these screws made.''

"After 1899, I guess," said Angelica, "if that's when her daughter's handprint showed up. The old lady was apparently a loyal servant of Dionysus before then.''

"Call her *Mrs. Winchester,*'' said Plumtree. "I've got three of the screws out, she may be able to hear you.'' Plumtree was rocking slightly on the truck seat, and Cochran could just hear what she was humming: *Row, row, row your boat* . . . She peered out the windows at the agitated puddles on the asphalt. "Don't tell me, if it's too horrible, but how did we get away from the big black genie-guy?"

"Mammy Pleasant knew him," said Pete. "I think he was a bit of the god's remote attention, not able to make many decisions—like a horse's tail, swatting flies while the horse looks at something else. But he recognized her, and he let us get out with a bottle of the super-Zinfandel." He stared out the window at the rain that was splashing up in waves of mist across the parking lot. "Poor Johanna," he said quietly. "The roof in Solville must be leaking like six firehoses."

Plumtree had unthreaded the last screw and lifted it out of the hole. Now she slid the cover off the gold box, and lifted from a nest of ribbon-tied locks of smoky-fine hair and folded strips of newsprint a corked but apparently empty glass test tube.

"Careful you don't just *eat* her, the way Sherman Oaks or your Dr. Armentrout would," said Angelica nervously.

"I didn't *eat* old Pleasant, did I?" Plumtree lifted the tube and stared through it. "I've got plenty of practice at just standing aside and making room for an incoming personality, like when the phone rings."

She frowned slightly, and Cochran knew she must be thinking of Janis, whose job it always was to answer telephones.

"Wide unclasp," she said then, perhaps speaking to the glass tube. "I'm the one who got the message in the stained glass. Meet the ones that people *this* little head." And with one motion she bit out the cork and inhaled strongly over the open tube.

The cork fell out of her lips and she sat back in the seat.

"Oh my Lord," she said then, exhaling and staring wide-eyed at the three people in the truck with her, "has found me, hasn't he?" The voice was strong but higher in pitch than Cody's or Pleasant's.

"No," said Cochran, "we're—well, yes, I suppose so. We're sort of contract labor for him, I guess."

Tears gathered in Plumtree's eyes, and spilled down her sunburned cheeks.

"You don't have to go," said Angelica suddenly, "if you don't want to. We can . . . I don't know. Damn it! Is there a way to . . . hide you again, hide you better?"

Beside her, Pete looked as though he wanted to object, but he just pressed his lips together and rolled his eyes to the rusty ceiling.

Plumtree's eyebrows went up. "No, there's not." She raised Plumtree's hands and flexed them in front of her face. "I'm . . . out now! . . . and bound for the god, bound for the sea; and I'll take my baby's ghost with me, at least, dry dust though she is. Lord, I did think we'd have to spend eternity in that box. I ran out of thoughts after only a few hours, I believe, and even my dreams were just of being in the box. The memories of her that I kept, defiantly kept, were just black dust after all. Nothing but soot. I should have known.'' The eyebrows went up even further when she looked down at the soaked leather jacket and jeans she was wearing. ''I'm . . . grateful to this person for a little interval time in which to breathe fresh air.''

Hardly very fresh, thought Cochran. He yawned from sheer nervousness, anxious to have Cody back on again.

''What,'' asked Mrs. Winchester as Cody's body seemed to brace itself, ''is the date, today?''

''Monday the thirtieth of January,'' said Pete, ''uh, 1995.''

The news appeared to alarm Mrs. Winchester, and Cochran thought it was learning what day of the month it currently was, rather than that seventy-odd years had passed since her death, that had upset her. ''When is the Chinese New Year?'' she asked quickly.

''Tomorrow,'' Cochran told her. ''The Year of the Pig.''

''And today's already dark? How is it that you've dawdled so? We can't wait around through the passage of another *year,* before we get consumed! We're far past stale already, my poor shred of a daughter and I. Has the god chosen a king?''

''Yes,'' said Pete and Cochran and Angelica simultaneously.

''Go to where he waits, then, and stop wasting time. Go quickly— this *is* some species of *automobile*, isn't it? Has one of you taken a drink of the wine?''

''No, ma'am,'' said Pete in a harried tone, turning around to face the dashboard and twist the key in the ignition.

''Ah, one of you should have!—back in my house, if that's where you found me, if it's still standing. You *do have* the wine, don't you? The god will take some host for himself, for the ceremony, but first one of you must thus . . . formally *invite* him. You've got to awaken him, and bring him.'' She peered in bewilderment out the side window at the shopping-center parking lot. ''Find a grove, wooded groves are still implicitly sacred to him—or a cemetery, a quiet cemetery with trees.'' Softly, perhaps to herself, she added, ''I can remain rational through this final event, if it happens soon.'' Then she looked around quizzically at the three people in the old truck with her. ''I don't know you people, but I presume you know each other. It should be obvious who is to take the drink.''

''I guess,'' Pete said through clenched teeth as he gunned the engine and then clanked it into gear, ''we could draw straws—''

"It's me," said Cochran, "it's me." His heart was pounding, but like Mrs. Winchester he somehow didn't seem able to find the prospect of cooperating with the god totally repellent. "Dionysus led me by the hand into the wine cellar, so I guess I should be the one to lead him by the hand to the Sutro ruins. And I do have to . . . finish giving somebody over to him; I know which cemetery. It's right on the way, just off the"—the monstrous, he thought, the merciless—"the 280." I might as well have taken the drink of forgetfulness when Mondard first offered it to me, he thought defeatedly, in the courtyard of the Hotel de l'Abbaye in Paris.

He remembered what Nina's ghost had told him, in the kitchen of their house two weeks ago, when he had said he wanted to have the mark removed from his hand: *I would never have—I would not have your child, if its father were not marked by* him. *I was married to him, through you.*

"It's me," he repeated. But he remembered too the vision he'd had in the Solville hallway, of the Mondard in the mirror, and he remembered his apprehension then that the fatally loving god would next ask him to give over his memories of a deceased Plumtree. "But he will take only one woman from me."

"He'll welcome into his kingdom whomever you love," flatly said the old woman out of Plumtree's lips, "unless he so loves you that he welcomes you first."

As Pete steered the truck away from the tall theater sign, Cochran noticed the titles of the movies that were showing in the three theaters: *Legends of the Fall*, *Murder in the First*, and *Little Women*.

Cochran's South Daly City house was just on the other side of the 280 from Colma, but the little town was in the area he always thought of as "north of south and south of north"—when he was travelling to or from Pace Vineyards or San Francisco he used the John Daly Boulevard exit north of the town, and when he had business in Redwood City or San Jose he used the Serramonte Boulevard exit south of it; and so, though he knew the rest of the peninsula cities well, the peculiar little town that he could see across the highway lanes from his back yard was almost totally unfamiliar to him.

The last time he had visited the place had been two years ago, when he and Nina had driven straight across the highway to pick out adjoining plots at the Woodlawn Cemetery. And now Nina and their unborn baby had been cremated, and he had acceded to her parents' wishes and taken the urn to France, where it would stand forever on the mantle in their house in Queyrac in the Bas Médoc; and the grass grew undisturbed on the plot in Colma.

Colma was the town to which all the graves of San Francisco had been transplanted; until 1938, nearly a third of the Richmond district of San Francisco, from Golden Gate Park north to Geary and from Park Presidio east to Masonic Avenue, was still occupied by cemeteries, as the whole of the district had been before 1900. Colma, six miles to the south, had taken the evicted dead, and on the day Cochran and Nina had gone to buy the plots, Nina had remarked that the town's dead residents outnumbered the living ones seven hundred to one.

Cochran had Pete steer the truck off the 280 at Serramonte Boulevard, but had him turn east, away from his house, to El Camino Real; and as they drove up the weaving, rain-hazy road, past roadside "monument" shops and misty rolling green hills studded with white grave markers, Cochran tried not to remember the sunny, gaily mock-morbid drive he and Nina had taken along this same road.

Following Cochran's directions, Pete turned left up the sloping drive-way of Woodlawn and parked at the curb, in front of the grim stone tower that stood between the two stone arches opening onto the grounds. The four dishevelled travellers pushed open the truck doors and climbed out, and walked through the south arch and then trudged uphill along the gravel lane that led to the graves.

Cochran was carrying the bottle of *pagadebiti*, and in his pocket he now had Mavranos's bulky key ring with its attached Swiss Army knife. The tall palm trees and twisted cypresses that stood at measured inter-vals across the green hills gave him no clues as to what spot he and Nina had chosen on that long-ago sunny day, and the gray roads curved around with no evident pattern.

He had kept glancing at Plumtree during the drive up from San Jose, but the woman who had looked apprehensively back at him each time had clearly been Mrs. Winchester, blinking and shivering in the unfa-miliar body in the big leather jacket; and so he was profoundly glad when Plumtree took his hand now and he looked at the face under the wet blond bangs and recognized Cody.

"I see by our outfits that it's the same day-o," she said quietly, glancing back at Pete and Angelica; "but what are we doing in a cem-etery?"

"I—" he began; but she had gasped and squeezed his hand.

She was staring at the grassy area to their left, and he followed her gaze.

They were next to what he recalled now was the children's section of the cemetery, and on a pebble-studded slab of concrete on the grass stood eight painted plaster statues, one of them two feet tall and the others half that. They were the Disney-images of Snow White and the Seven Dwarves; and behind them, on a truncated section of decoratively carved and pierced marble, stood a verdigrised brass plaque on which he could make out the raised letters,

SUFFER LITTLE CHILDREN
TO COME UNTO ME

" 'Suffer, little children,' " Plumtree read aloud, in a panicky voice. "Sid, *who are we here to bury?*"

"My dead wife," he told her hastily, knowing that she was thinking of Janis. "Or not *bury,* so much as *disown.* Give to the god." He waved the bottle of antique wine, idiotically wondering if he was stirring up sentiment in it. "I've got to drink some of the *pagadebiti,* to summon Dionysus."

Her hand had relaxed only a little in his. "Oh, Sid, don't—your wife—I'll do it, I'll drink it."

"You—" he said, then paused. *You would probably lose Valorie,* he thought; *and we might need her.* "You don't have to," he finished. "I can do it—she's dead, and her ghost is gone, and—actually, my wife was, was more married to the god than to me, even when she was alive." Only after he'd begun speaking had he decided to tell her that, and he was remotely surprised now at how difficult it had been to say.

Cody bared her teeth and nodded. "And we *might* need *her.*"

Cochran knew she meant Valorie, and he wondered if she had actually read his mind or simply knew him well enough to guess his thoughts.

"My wife and I bought a pair of plots," Cochran said, loudly enough for Pete and Angelica to hear too; "further uphill somewhere, across this road. That would be the place where I should drink it."

On the lawn to their left, isolated stone angels and Corinthian pillars stood on pedestals above clustered ranks of upright black marble slabs with gold Chinese ideographs and inset color photo-portraits on their faces, while the lawns stretching away to the right were dotted with rows of flat markers like, thought Cochran, keys on a vast green key-board. The gray weight of the spilling sky seemed to be held back by the brave yellow and red spots of flower bouquets around many of the headstones; and in the children's section behind them, silver helium balloons and brightly colored pinwheels had made an agitated confetti glitter against the carpet of wet grass.

They stepped up to the curb, over cement water-valve covers that looked at first glance like particularly humble little graves, and plodded out across the grass.

Far up the hill they came upon a scene almost of ruin. To the right, the grass had been stripped away from a broad area, leaving puddles and hillocks of mud around the stranded stone markers; an iron sign on a pole indicated that the grounds were being renovated for installation of a new sprinkler system and would be reseeded, and warned passersby that WOODLAWN WATERS ITS LAWNS WITH NONPOTABLE WELL WATER. And to the left, farther away across the marble-studded grass, a gigantic oak tree had fallen over in the direction away from them, probably during the storms that had ravaged the California coast on New Year's Day; where the base of the tree had erupted out of the ground, the uplifted knotty face of dirt-caked roots was a monument taller than any of the carved marble ones, an abrupt black section of natural wall whose bent topmost crown-spikes stiffly clawed the sky far higher up than a man could reach. As he and Plumtree walked hand-in-hand around the fallen giant, he saw a thick carpet of fresh green grass still flourishing on the once-horizontal surface far overhead, as if in defiance of the piles of orange sawdust and the vertical saw-cuts visible farther along the trunk, evidences of toiling attempts to dispose of the gigantic thing.

And sheets of rain-darkened plywood had been laid across the grass to form a wheelbarrow's road toward an open freshly dug grave; the mound of mud beside the hole was the same orange color as the sawdust. For a moment Cochran thought the grave had been dug in one of the plots he and Nina had bought, and he quailed at the thought of standing on the grass verge and staring down into the hole; then he noted the position of two nearby palm trees relative to the road and realized that his plots were on the far side of the open grave.

"Over here," he said, stepping up onto the plywood walk and striding along it. Plumtree was beside him, and he could hear the drumming of Pete's and Angelica's footsteps behind.

Nina's ghost was gone, exorcised over a coffee cup full of tap water in his kitchen two weeks ago. Today he was going to relinquish whatever might be left of his love for her, of his possession of her.

I caught you in a wine cellar, he thought bewilderedly as cold water ran down his heated face, and now I'm going to drop you out of my heart, beside an open grave, with a swallow of wine. I really only interrupted your fall, didn't I—delayed your impact by four-and-something years.

And, he thought, fathered a companion for you to take with you. Was that death a part of your plan, of the god's plan? How can I be giving to the god someone I was never allowed to know?

He didn't know or care if tears were mingling with the rain water on his face.

"This will do," he said harshly, stepping around a winch-equipped trailer with a big rectangular concrete grave-liner sitting on the bed of it. There were of course no markers to indicate which patches of grass were his plots, so he just stood on the grass with the open grave at his back and clasped the bottle under his arm as he pulled Mavranos's key ring out of his pocket and pried out the corkscrew attachment.

Rain thumped on his scalp and ran in streams from his bent elbows as he twisted the corkscrew right through the frail old lead foil on the bottle; and when the corkscrew was firmly embedded in the cork, he paused and looked at Plumtree.

"I don't want to love her anymore," he said breathlessly; "and I was never permitted to love the child."

Plumtree might not have heard him over the thrash of the rain; at any rate she nodded.

He tugged at the red plastic knife handle, and with no audible pop the cork came out all in one piece in spite of its age.

Abruptly the wind sighed to a halt, and the last drops of rain whispered to the grass, and even the drops of water hanging from the cypress branches seemed to cling for an extra moment to the wet leaves so as not to fall and make a sound. In that sudden enormous silence Cochran would have tapped the knife handle against the glass of the bottle to see if his ears could still hear, except that he knew he was not deaf, and except that he didn't dare violate the holy stasis of the air.

He tipped the bottle up, and took a mouthful of the *pagadebiti*.

At first it seemed to be cool water, so balanced were the tannins and the acids, the fruit so subtle as to be indistinguishable from the smells of grass and fresh-turned earth in his nostrils. Then he swallowed it, and like an organ note rising from total silence, that starts as a subsonic vibration too low even to feel and mounts mercilessly to a brazen chorus in which the very earth seems to take part, bringing tears to the listener's eyes and standing the hairs up on his arms, the wine filled his head with the surge of the spring bud-break on the burgeoning vines, the bursting slaughter of ripe grapes in the autumn crush, the hot turbulent fermentation in the oaken casks as the soul of the god awoke in the crucible of fructose and malic acid and multiplying yeast. And Cochran was able to see as if from a high promontory the track of the god's endlessly repeated deaths and resurrections, through the betrayed vineyards of the Gironde and Loire valleys, back to sacred Falernum on the very slopes of slumbering Vesuvius, and the trellised vine gardens at Nebesheh and below the White Wall of Memphis on the Nile, eastward through Ara-

bia, Media, Phrygia and Lydia, and the terraced temple vineyards on
the ziggurats of the Babylonians and Sumerians, dimly all the way back
to the primeval *vitis vinifera sylvestris* vines of lost Nysa in the mountains above Nineveh at the source of the Tigris River.

And then he was looking out through a crudely cut earthen doorway
at the gray sky; no, he was lying on his back, and the ringing in his
head and the jolt throughout his frame was from having fallen backward
into the opened grave. The breath had been knocked out of him, and
until his lungs began to heave and snatch at the cold air it seemed that
his identity had been knocked out of him too.

Now three faces appeared around the edges of the grave, peering
down at him; Plumtree was standing closest, leaning over, and he could
see that she was holding the bottle of *pagadebiti*, apparently having
taken it from him in the first transported moments.

"He's killed," said Angelica.

"No, he's not," said Plumtree angrily. "Sid, get out of there." The
voices of both of them were oddly muffled and ringing, as if the women
were embedded in crystal.

"I'm . . . not killed," Cochran said. He rolled over and got to his
hands and knees, and then, hitchingly, straightened all the way up to a
standing posture, bracing his hands on the back-hoed clay walls; and
the color of the exposed dirt darkened from orange clay toward black
topsoil as he painfully hiked himself erect. "Pete," he said, trying to
pitch his voice so that it would carry in the changed air, "give me a
hand." He tossed the Swiss Army knife up onto the grass by Plumtree's
feet.

Pete and Plumtree both leaned over so that he could grasp their wrists,
while their free hands extended back to Angelica, who clasped them
firmly and braced herself. With a heave from above, Cochran was able
to walk up the side of the grave and take two balance-catching steps
out across the grass.

I don't feel any different, he thought cautiously. I swear I don't. If
the god's riding on me now, he's riding lightly.

Pete had bent to pick up Mavranos's knife, and now he twisted the
cork off the corkscrew and held the cork out to Plumtree, who shoved
it into the open mouth of the bottle as if hoping to stifle some shrill
sound.

But in fact it was the *silence* that Cochran wished would stop. The
plywood sheets thumped underfoot as he followed Plumtree and the
Sullivans to the gravel road and hurried down it toward the distant front
gate, but the sound of their footsteps seemed to agitate the air only very
close by. No rain fell, and Cochran couldn't shake the notion that all

the raindrops were hanging suspended under the clouds, like rocks in a Magritte painting.

As he reeled past the Snow White and the Seven Dwarves statues, Cochran was nervously ransacking his memory. He had forgotten something here today—he had known the wine would make him forget it. But what had it been? Then he remembered saying to Cody, *My dead wife;* and, *my wife was more married to the god than to me.* Apparently he had been married, and the wife was dead. He had to concentrate to keep the idea from sliding out of his mind, like thoughts that occur late at night in bed when the light has been turned out. I was, he thought— what? Somebody was more married to the god than to me. When was anybody ever married to me . . . ? Married to the god—to Dionysus? I must have been thinking of the woman in that strange version of *A Tale of Two Cities*, Ariachne. Something about a Dickens novel . . . ? I can't remember.

Finally he was just aware that he had forgotten something; but the awareness carried no anxiety. It didn't have the mental flavor of importance. If it was important, he thought, I'll no doubt be reminded of it.

He remembered vividly the climb down the chimney in the Winchester House, and the supernatural black man in the wine cellar, and Mrs. Winchester's occupation of Plumtree's body, and her insistence that they perform the resurrection soon, today, now.

Twice—once as they passed under the stone gate, and once as Pete pulled open the driver's-side door of the red truck—Cochran got the impression that Mrs. Winchester had come on; both times Plumtree gasped, and blinked around in a terror that was not Cody's, and then only a moment later recognizably *was* Cody, catching her balance and gripping the bottle and counting her companions.

They had all got into the truck and pulled the doors closed, but Pete was still fumbling with the key ring, when the engine roared to life. Pete stared at the empty ignition keyhole, then stared at Angelica beside him. With a shrug he put the key into the ignition anyway, and turned the switch into the on position.

Slowly he clanked it into reverse gear, and then tugged at the wheel as he backed out of the parking space; the truck wobbled obediently. "I was afraid it was going to drive itself again," he muttered, "like it did when Arky got shot."

"Don't speak," choked Angelica. "Get us—out of here."

Pete steered the truck in a back-and-fill star pattern to drive back down to El Camino Real. A car going north squealed to a halt and honked twice as Pete turned south, and the brake lights flared redly at the back of the shiny new white car in front of the truck.

"What are these white Saturns," said Pete.

Cochran was already frightened—the wine he had drunk was making him dizzy, and he had the crazy impression that the action and speech around him were subtly happening at the wrong speed, as if somebody had filmed cars and actors moving and speaking too rapidly, and then projected it at a slowed-down speed to make it all appear normal—but with the gaps between the frames subliminally perceptible now—and Pete's remark about Saturns seemed to carry huge portent.

"There's another," said Angelica, her finger repeatedly bumping the windshield as she pointed toward the oncoming lane; and though her voice was if anything shriller than normal, Cochran thought he could hear every click and release of her vocal cords.

"This flop is all face-down," said Plumtree hoarsely—her voice too was muffled and fragmented, and even though he was sitting right beside her in the back seat Cochran could hardly make out her words—

Abruptly a harsh animal roaring shattered the stale air inside the truck, and the physical shock of it peeled Cochran's lips back from his teeth and jerked his right hand to the small of his back, where his revolver was holstered. Squinting against the stunning noise, Angelica fumbled the stuffed toy pig up from the front seat—and Cochran realized that the bestial clamor was coming from the pig. But, he thought in real, angry protest, it hasn't even got a battery in it!

In the center of the cavernous roaring, Angelica was frenziedly bashing the toy against the dashboard, to no apparent effect—the toy pig was smoking, and Cochran could see bright dots of tiny burning coals in its pink nylon fur—

Out one of the windows—in the confusion Cochran somehow couldn't tell if it was through one of the side windows or through the windshield—Cochran glimpsed a glittering golden vehicle, and in it a carved wooden mask; and an instant later he was deafened by a tremendous metallic crash, and the truck was halted, rocking violently as its passengers rebounded from seat-back and dashboard.

Cochran had wrenched open the door and reeled out onto the pavement, and the smoking pig bounced past him, rolling toward the gutter. The rain was coming down again like a battering avalanche, and the car behind the truck—a white Saturn—had stopped, and a portly white-haired man had opened the passenger-side door and stepped out.

Cochran waved at him. *"Cet ivrogne m'est rentre dedans!"* he shouted over the roar of the rain. He stopped speaking, wanting desperately to run to the side of the road and throw himself down on the wet grass; what he had just said was French, meaning, *This drunkard crashed into me.* "Do you," he shouted, listening to his own words to be sure he was speaking English, "have a cellular—"

The man standing by the other car was staring at him, in obvious surprised recognition. Cochran cuffed rain water from his eyes and peered at the man . . . and with a sudden cold hollowness in his chest recognized Dr. Armentrout.

Someone was tugging at Cochran's sleeve, and shouting; he turned and saw that it was Cody, and that she didn't seem to be injured. "The truck started again!" she was yelling. "It's not hurt, nobody's hurt, we didn't even hit anything—get back in!"

She hadn't noticed Armentrout. Cochran nodded at her and put one foot up on the truck floor as she climbed back inside—but he saw Armentrout getting back into the Saturn.

The truck was shaking as Pete gunned the engine; it did seem to be capable of driving.

But so was the Saturn. And all Cochran could remember now was Armentrout saying to him three weeks ago, *I will heal you, Sid. That's a promise.* Still perceiving all the motions and sounds as discrete fragments, Cochran fumbled under the back of his sopping windbreaker and pulled out his muddy revolver; and he aimed it at the white hood of the Saturn, between and just behind the headlights, and pulled the trigger.

The flare was dazzling, but the noise of the gunshot was just a thud against his abused eardrums. He fired again, and then Plumtree had leaned out of the truck and closed her fist in the fabric of his shirt. The truck was moving, slowly. Cochran flailingly pulled the trigger again, and one of the Saturn's headlights exploded; and then he threw the gun onto the truck floor and lunged inside.

Pete must have floored the accelerator then, for Cochran was tumbled into the seat half across Plumtree's lap, and the door slammed shut without his help. The interior of the truck was dark in the renewed rainstorm.

"—*the fuck were you doing—!*" Pete was shouting, and Cochran yelled back, overriding him, "*It was Dr. Armentrout!*" In the instant of silence this news caused, Cochran sat up and added, "In that car. He would have followed us. He shot Kootie, remember?"

The roar of the engine rose and fell as Pete swerved from lane to lane to pass slower-moving cars. He had switched on the headlights, and the road ahead was only dimly visible behind a glittering curtain of rain.

"Good," panted Angelica, "that was good, you were right to shoot him." She was glancing around wildly, wide-eyed. "What the fuck *hit* us, Pete? How can the truck be running? We should be—"

"The god hit you," said Mrs. Winchester from the shadows beside Cochran, in a quavering voice that seemed to carry a trace of satisfaction, "a good deal less hard than he hit my house in 1906."

"I didn't shoot *him,*" said Cochran loudly, "I shot the *car,* the *radiator.*"

"We've got to cross the 280 and pick up Kootie and Arky," said Pete.

"No," said Angelica, "there were other white Saturns driving around back there, and Armentrout's still fucking alive. We might lead them to Kootie—and this truck's a beacon, magically and plain-old visually. And turn off your headlights."

"These are sorcerous bad guys, Angie," said Pete, nevertheless reaching forward to switch off the lights. "What do you think they were *doing* down here? Following *us?* I bet they were tracking the new king, which is Kootie. They might be zeroing in on Cochran's house right now."

"Ah, you're right, you're right," said Angelica desperately. "Get on the freeway, get right over in the fast lane to draw any pursuit, and then cut off hard at the first off-ramp, hard enough to send 'em on past it, if they are following us. We'll call Kootie from a pay phone."

"It's getting late, you must let this *Kootie* person fend for himself," said Mrs. Winchester's voice. "I *heard* that!" added Cody; "they'd surely kill the boy, and anyway we need his help, and Arky's, to get this thing done." And then Valorie's flat voice said, "O, what form of prayer can serve my turn? 'Forgive me my foul murder.' "

"A pay phone at a gas station," said Pete, his wet shoe sole squeaking from the gas pedal to the brake and back. "We're gonna need gas."

Pete followed Angelica's directions so exactly that Cochran thought they were all going to be killed. From the fast far left-hand lane of the northbound 280, while a scatter of anonymous headlight-pairs bobbed behind them at hard-to-judge distances, Pete cut the wheel sharply to the right, and the truck veered across the shiny black lanes like a banking surfboard, booming over the lane-divider dots in brief staccato bursts, finally half-missing the exit and throwing Cochran onto Plumtree again as the two left wheels slewed on the shoulder.

Then he had straightened the wheel, braked down to about twenty miles per hour without quite making the tires squeal, and pulled sedately into a Chevron gas station, steering the truck around to the back by the rest rooms and pay phones. The headlights were still switched off.

He pushed the gearshift lever over into neutral. *"No—"* he began, but his voice was squeaky; "nobody's followed us here," he said in a deeper tone.

"Guess not," said Angelica faintly. Then she stirred herself and pushed open the door. "Let's call . . ."

She froze with one leg extended out into the rain, and Cochran followed the direction of her gaze to the cone of light around the pay telephone.

At first glance he thought the light was full of moths; then he saw that the fluttering streaks of light were rain-gleams on transparent figures: the streak of a contorted jawline here, the squiggle of a flexed limb there, invisible wet lips working in imbecilic grimaces.

"Something's got all the ghosts worked up this evening," Angelica said. "They're drawn by the magnets in the phone, or they each want to call somebody and haven't got any quarters." She gave Pete a stricken look over her shoulder. "I'm not masked enough for this. Breathing, *talking on the phone,* in that stew? My voice—and Arky might say my name! I couldn't hide my—my psychic locators, my name, my birthday—from all of them. At least a couple of them would be into my head like piranhas in five seconds."

" 'These same thoughts people this little world,' " said Mrs. Winchester confidently out of Plumtree's mouth; to which Cody added, "All us kids on the bus got bogus birth-dates and somebody else's picture on our IDs," and the flat voice of Valorie said, "I shall play it in a mask, and you may speak as small as you will."

"Oh, thank you—!" said Angelica to Plumtree, clearly at a loss as to what name to use. "Give her a quarter, Pete," she added as Cochran opened the truck's back door and stepped down into the rain. "Speak this: tell Kootie and Arky to get out of there," she told Plumtree urgently. "Tell 'em don't take the Granada, we were driving that when I shot at the bikers out at the yacht club, they might remember it. Tell 'em to take the old Torino out back."

"And bad guys might be out in front of the house, nervous about our guns and waiting for reinforcements," added Pete. "Tell Arky to drive right out *through* the greenhouse, like Cochran said this morning— there's apparently a mud road that leads down the backyard slope right to the 280."

Cochran could see that Plumtree had to do this, but after she had stepped wearily down out of the truck he grabbed her unbandaged hand and said, "Would it help to have another person beside you? I can concentrate on *you,* and not pay attention to the ghosts."

The tired lines in her face lifted in a wan smile. "I'd like that, Sid.

Yeah, you'll be safe enough if you just don't speak a word, and look nowhere but at me.''

"That's my plan." He was nervously pleased to be speaking coherently, after having drunk the *pagadebiti*; and he was reminded of a time an unidentified snake had bitten him on a hike, and how he had monitored himself for the rest of the day, watching for slurred speech or numbness or any other symptoms of poisoning.

Plumtree took a quarter from Pete, and then she and Cochran walked hand-in-hand across the pavement to the cone of rain-streaked and ghost-curdled light around the telephone.

The ghosts were whispering and giggling in Cochran's ears, and though he tried not to listen he heard faint, buzzing sexual propositions, pleas for rides to other states, demands for money, offers to wash his car windows for a dollar.

Cochran kept his eyes on Plumtree. Her face was shifting in response to it all, like a fencer parrying in different lines, and once Cochran got a broad wink that he thought must have been from Tiffany. She reached through the contorting forms as if through cobwebs to drop the quarter into the slot, and punched his home number into the keypad as if emphasizing points by poking someone repeatedly in the chest.

After a few moments she tensed and said, ''Hi. It's me, the girl-of-a-thousand-faces. Use the old king's eye as a scrambler to call me back at this number.'' And she read off the number of the pay phone and hung up the receiver.

"Good thinking," said Cochran through slitted lips.

"Don't talk!—they could get down your throat. They do but jest, poison in their jest; no offense i' the world."

At last the telephone rang, and Plumtree snatched up the receiver. ''Hello? *Hello?*'' She took the receiver from her ear and knocked it against the aluminum cowl around the phone. ''I'm deaf!'' she said loudly. Into the phone she said, ''Kootie, Arky, I hope you can hear me. I'm deaf, so just listen!'' Her voice softened. ''Arky, you've got the cutest butt. *Out!*'' Cody yelled, apparently at Tiffany. ''Listen, you've both got to get *out* of there, right now—take the—''

She looked at Cochran in panic, and he knew that it had just occurred to her that *Janis was listening,* and could relay their plans to Omar Salvoy, in her mental Snow White cottage. ''The way Sid told Arky this morning, *exactly* that way, are you following me?''

She flipped the receiver around in her hand and *bit* the earpiece—and Cochran realized that she was hearing by bone conduction. She fumbled the receiver back to her ear. ''Good, don't say anything more, we're being overheard here in spite of your scrambler, it's enough that

I know I'm not just talking to somebody who likes calling pay phones. Listen, we're going, *right now*, to—to George Washington's head.''

Cochran nodded. Janis hadn't been on when they had hiked through the tunnel at the Sutro Bath ruins and seen the boulder that Kootie had said looked like Washington; and Cody wasn't saying that this was *the big event,* happening today instead of tomorrow as they had all expected. Janis could relate all of this to her father without his knowing where Kootie and Mavranos would be going.

"Tell me you understand," Cody said, and again bit the receiver. Then she said into the mouthpiece, "Good. Oh, and Kootie better bring that . . . that little yellow blanket that the bald lady gave him, if he's still got it." She sighed. "Go," she added, and she hung up the chewed and spitty receiver. Cochran faintly heard one of the ghosts say that the telephone was for calling room service to order food, that one didn't eat the telephone.

Plumtree took Cochran's elbow and led him out of the swarm of idiot ghosts, and neither of them inhaled until they had got back to the truck.

"That was Kootie," Plumtree panted, "and then Arky. They understood, and I didn't hear either of 'em say anything that would clue anybody. They'll meet us there." She looked nervously at Cochran. "I can hear the rain, now, but I don't know about voices. You say something."

He smiled at her. *"Vous êtes très magnifique,"* he said, and he was sure that it had been his own deliberate decision to speak in French.

She laughed tiredly. "Thank you very kindly, sir, now I hear you clearly."

"Back in the truck," said Pete, "everybody. I don't want Kootie to get there before we do. Sid, you got a ten for gas?"

CHAPTER 31

Yes. Like the mariner in the old story, the winds and streams had driven him within the influence of the Loadstone Rock, and it was drawing him to itself, and he must go.

—Charles Dickens,
A Tale of Two Cities

The secret switchboards of the city logged dozens of calls in the ordinarily slow witchery-and-wonders categories, as reports of supernatural happenings were phoned in from Daly City south of town up to the Sunset area around Ocean Beach and the Richmond district north of Golden Gate Park—accounts of brake-drums singing in human voices, root beers and colas turning into red wine in the cans, and voices of dead people intruding on radio receptions in unwelcome, clumsy karaoke. In Chinatown, under the street-spanning banners and the red-neon-bordered balconies and the white-underlit pagoda roofs, hundreds of nests of firecrackers were set hopping on the puddled sidewalks, clattering like machine-gun fire and throwing clouds of smoke through the rain, and the lean young men noisily celebrating the new year frequently paused below the murals of dragons and stylized clouds to listen to the storefront radio speakers, out of which echoed an Asian woman's voice predicting earthquakes and inversions and a sudden high-pressure area locally.

Old Volkswagens and Chevrolets and Fords, painted gold and hung with wreaths at the front and back bumpers, roared with horns honking north through the hospital glare of the Stockton tunnel, to emerge in Chinatown at Sacramento Street still honking, the passengers firing handguns out the windows into the low sky. Police and paremedics' sirens added to the din, and under the gunpowder banging and the electric howls was the constant hiss of the night rain, and the unending echoing rattle of the cables snaking at their steady nine-miles-an-hour through the street-pavement slots.

On the Bay Bridge, from remote Danville in the hills over on the east side of the bay, three white Saturns passed over the Coast Guard Reservation on Yerba Buena Island on their way in to the China Basin area of the Soma district; and two more were moving west up Ocean Avenue toward the Great Highway and Ocean Beach.

Dr. Armentrout had had to insist, almost tearfully, that the driver of the lead car get off the 280 at Ocean instead of continuing toward Chinatown.

Armentrout was sitting in the back beside Long John Beach and the two-figure mannikin appliance, but the Lever Blank man in the front passenger seat shifted and said, "It's the pomegranate." He turned around. "What does it do, point?" When Armentrout just gripped the dry gourd and stared belligerently, the man added, "We won't take it from you, if you tell us where we can get another one."

"I picked it from a bush in the meadow where Scott Crane was killed," Armentrout muttered finally, "at his compound in Leucadia." He held the thing up and shook it, and dry seeds rattled inside. "In daylight, even such daylight as you get up here, its shadow is perceptibly displaced toward the king, which is the Koot Hoomie boy, I think. I've been—*shadowing* him." He choked back a frightened giggle, and sniffed; he was still shaking, and his shirt was more clammy from sweat than from rain. "And," he added, "tonight it . . . even *tugs* a little." He nodded toward the windshield. "That way."

Armentrout had hysterically demanded that the two-figure mannikin appliance be brought along in this car too, and now it was sitting ludicrously in Long John Beach's lap beside him. Armentrout wondered if Long John Beach too found the two figures *heavier* lately than they used to be.

"The royal tree," said Long John Beach from behind the two Styrofoam heads, in what Armentrout had come to think of as the Valerie-voice, "hath left us royal fruit."

"It led us to the red truck," said the driver, "back there in Colma where we had to switch cars. Was the boy in the truck?"

"I don't know," said Armentrout. "I don't think so." *Sid Cochran and Janis Plumtree* were in the truck, he thought. And Sid Cochran, who I heedlessly let slip through my net back at Rosecrans Medical, shot a *gun* at me! "I think they were all staying somewhere in the area, and we just ran across the truck before we found the boy. But they must have gone to him after they evaded you people, or else they called him." He shook the pomegranate again, and felt its inertial northward pull.

"The primary is certainly northwest of us now. I can't imagine why Salvoy didn't *call* me—we could have been waiting for the boy right now, at whatever place they're going to, instead of just chasing him this way."

The radio on the dashboard clicked, and then an amplified voice said, "I thought we were going to where the Macondray chapel used to be."

The driver unhooked a microphone from the console. "The—" He smiled at Armentrout in the rear-view mirror. "—*dousing rod* is apparently indicating the west coast," he said. "Tell the brothers coming in from Danville not to waste time circling the Washington and Stockton site. Straight west on Turk to Balboa, tell them, and link up with us probably somewhere below the Cliff House."

"Aye aye," said the man in the following car, and clicked off; and Armentrout thought *eye-eye*, and remembered the tiny pupils of Plumtree's eyes.

"The woman who pulled . . . the gunman back into the truck," Armentrout said, "was Janis Plumtree, the one with your man Salvoy in her head. I'd like to . . . *have* her, after Salvoy has moved on." Moved on to his eternal reward, ideally, he thought.

"Everybody except the king has got to be retired, sorry," said the man in the front passenger seat. "But we do have to wait until we figure out who the king *is*, and what body he's in." He reached out and unhooked the microphone. "Andre," he said, "tell the field men not to go shooting anybody until the subjects are out of the vehicles, and even then no women or boys. Got it?"

The driver was shaking his head. "Crisis of faith!" he said quietly.

"Nix," came the voice from the radio. "The field men understand that the true king can't be hit with a casual bullet."

"But he might not be in his chosen body yet!" protested the man in the front seat. "You can tell 'em that, can't you? It's nothing but the truth."

"Better we don't introduce the complication," insisted the voice from the radio; "and hope for the best."

The man replaced the microphone and fogged the window with a sigh. *"Field men,"* he said. "Manson-family rejects."

"Knuckleheads, panheads, and shovelheads," agreed the driver. "Look, the Koot Hoomie body *is* the *king,* and it'll deflect bullets. All we stand to lose is old Salvoy in the Plumtree, and that might not be altogether a bad thing."

Armentrout touched the little lump in his jacket pocket that was the derringer. No casual bullet, he thought. But nothing fired from this gun is casual, and I've got a couple of very serious .410 shot-shells in it.

That's the way this has got to work out—these Lever Blank boys kill the Plumtree body and everybody in it, and I kill the Parganas boy. And then stay well clear of the zealot field men.

On the long straight stretch of the Great Highway with the black-iron sea to the west, a relayed spot of darkness moved up the coast as each of the sodium-vapor streetlights went out for a moment when the red truck sped past on the pavement below.

Pete Sullivan was driving, and beside him Angelica was irritably drying off the .45 carbine with a handful of paper towels. The knapsack with the spare magazines had been under the seat too, and was also soaked by the rain water that had puddled on the floorboards.

She laid the gun down on the seat, then snapped open the glove compartment; and when she shifted around to look back at Cochran and Plumtree, she was holding the *pagadebiti* in her hands. "I never brought the . . . the hardware into your house," she said to Cochran. "I think the Wild Turkey bottle that had Crane's blood in it is behind you, in the hub of Arky's spare tire."

Cochran winced, for he'd been able to feel Plumtree shivering beside him, even through the soaked leather jacket she was wearing, ever since they'd stopped to call Mavranos and Kootie, and this reminder of the stressful failure two weeks ago wasn't likely to cheer her up. But he rocked his head back to peer into the truck bed. "Voilà," he said. "Still there," he added shortly.

He had been mentally reciting the multiplication tables to monitor his own alertness, and now he had forgotten his place.

"Here," said Angelica, handing the wine bottle over the back of the front seat. "Pour some of this *pagadebiti* wine into it, and swish it around and then pour it back." When he just stared at her, she added, "I say that in my capacity as the king's ad hoc *bruja primera*."

Cochran took it from her. "O-*kay*." He hiked one knee up onto the seat to be able to reach back with his free hand to the Wild Turkey bottle. Sitting back down again, he gripped the wine bottle and the pint bourbon bottle between his thighs, and pulled the corks out.

"When I close my eyes," said Plumtree in a voice that was shaky but recognizably Cody, "I'm in a bus seat, and the crazy smashed-up man is standing at the front and holding a gun on the driver. *Row, row, row your boat.*"

Cochran carefully lifted the wine bottle and tilted it over the pint bottle and poured a good four ounces of dark wine into it. He re-corked the little bottle and shook it up, then uncorked it and poured its foaming contents back into the bottle of *pagadebiti*.

"*So* far," said Angelica to Plumtree judiciously, "you're better off keeping your eyes open, then. But, any time now, that vision might be preferable to what's actually going on outside your eyelids."

"Oh, *that's* helpful," snapped Cochran as he shoved the corks back into the bottles and reached around to drop the Wild Turkey bottle onto the wet truck-bed floor behind his seat. He wiped his hands on his damp jeans, glad that he had taken his own sip of the wine before this adulteration.

The truck was moving up a grade now, and angling to the left. Cochran peered out through the rain-streaked window and saw concrete barriers on the right shoulder, with yellow earth-moving machines and black cliffs beyond it.

"Cliff House coming up on the left," said Pete. "I'll go on past and park in the Sutro Heights lot, up the hill. Rainy walk back down, but I guess we can't get any wetter than we are."

"Sorry," Angelica told Cochran. Then she said brightly to Plumtree, "Of course nothing bad will happen to any of us. As soon as we're done with this, we could all take Scott Crane to dinner at the Cliff House Restaurant, even." She snapped her fingers. "Oh, except that we're drenched in black mud!"

Plumtree gave a hitching laugh. "And Crane'll p-probably be wearing that garlic banner again," she said. "And some restaurants," she added quietly, "don't like you bringing your own wine."

Pete turned in to the Sutro Heights Park driveway, and drove slowly up the hill with the headlights off and parked the truck against a dark grassy bank with overhanging elms. The nearest parking lot light dimmed but didn't go out—and Cochran was glad of it as he climbed out of the truck carrying the wine bottle, for the overcast sky was already winter-night-time dark. There were many other cars in the lot, and they all seemed to have wreaths hung on them, but Cochran didn't see any other people.

The wind sweeping up the cliffs from the sea was cold, and his wet clothing was no protection at all. He was glad that Plumtree at least had the leather jacket.

Angelica had stepped out onto the wet pavement, but now she leaned back in and tore the woven blue seat cover off the front seat, yanking on it to break the strings that tied it to the struts, and when she had dragged it out and shaken dust and cigarette butts out of it she wrapped up her short rifle in it; the stock was folded forward, and the bundle was no more than a yard long, with the ends flapping loose over the pistol grip. She laid it on the truck hood while she shouldered on the sopping knapsack.

"You've got what, three rounds left?" she asked Cochran as she picked up the bundled rifle.

Taking the question as a fresh test of his mental acuity, Cochran called up the details of his shooting at the Saturn. "That's right," he told her firmly.

"I've got seventy rounds of mixed hardball and hollow-point, but the magazines have been sitting in greasy water for a couple of days. Oh well—I've heard .45s will even fire underwater."

"I hope the *omiero* hasn't washed off of the hollow-points," said Pete as he slammed the door on his side and walked around the back of the truck.

"I imagine the ghosts will all be gone, at least," said Plumtree, "after what's-his-name shows up, old Dickweed McStump."

"What?" said Angelica. "Who?"

"This famous Greek god. What's his name?"

"Dionysus," said Cochran with an apprehensive glance at the bottle in his left hand. "This isn't the night to be dissing him, Cody."

"Whatever," said Plumtree. "It sounds like he takes ghosts away with him. The big trick," she added, "will be seeing to it that he doesn't wind up taking any of *us* along in that crowd."

"Well, *that's* cleared it up," said Cochran. "You've put your finger on it, all right."

"I'll put my finger in your *eye*, if you don't shut up," she told him; but she linked her shivering arm through his as they began trudging down the park driveway. Cochran was holding the *pagadebiti* bottle with both hands.

When they got to Point Lobos Avenue, they had to walk south along the shoulder for a couple of hundred feet, and almost didn't dare to cross at all, for cars with no headlights on were hurling their dark bulks around the corners from north and south, so fast that the tires yiped, and their passengers were leaning out of the windows and firing guns into the air as they swooped past. But finally there was a quiet gap, and Cochran and his companions sprinted wildly across the lanes and sprang over the far curb onto the sidewalk.

Leaning on the wet iron railing on the seaward side of the highway, they could see, through the marching curtains of rain, patches of bright flame on the dark plain below them. Dots of yellow fire that must have been torches bobbed and whirled on the line between the vast rectangular pool of water and the open sea beyond, and Cochran realized that people must be out dancing along that narrow concrete wall. And even

way up here on the highway ridge he could hear distant drumming over
the roar of the rain.

"Damballa!" said Plumtree huskily; then, "The sounds of hammering and sawing must not cease."

"It's good, the drumming's good," agreed Angelica nervously.

"Scott Crane is down there somewhere," whispered Plumtree. "Tonight I'll face *him,* not his ghost."

The statement seemed to click a switch in her head, and at long last
Valorie had no choice but to remember New Year's Day. After dawn,
first:

*Trucks and cars on the road behind the gas-station telephone booth
had been drumming their tires over a step in the asphalt, and Plumtree
had had to hold her free hand over her ear to hear the 911 operator.
"You killed him with a speargun?" the voice said.*

*"No," said Plumtree in a harsh voice. Cody had been the one who
had taken this flop, this early-morning telephone call, and an emotion
had been interfering with her speech. "A spear from one. I stabbed him
in the throat. He was stabbed with it before, in 1990."*

"You stabbed him in 1990?"

"No, this morning, an hour ago."

"He was known as . . . the Flying Nun?"

"I don't know. That's how I was thinking of him."

*Valorie had been aware of Cody's guess that the 911 operator was
just keeping her talking, keeping her on the line . . .*

*And a police car had soon come chirruping up behind her, and po-
licemen with drawn guns had shouted at her: "Drop the phone! Let us
see your hands!" One had wanted to shoot her; then he'd wanted to
mace her. "Take it easy." another had said, "She's just a ding."*

*They had handcuffed her with her hands in front. "Let's go. Show
us where you killed him."*

*But when they had driven her to the slanting meadow above the
beach, and got out of the car, the field was silvery bright with fresh
vines and grasses and fruit; and since there had been only the cries of
wild parrots in the meadow on that morning, Valorie's memory now
had to make the birdcalls loud and harsh and poundingly rhythmic.*

*The policemen said it was obvious that no one had stepped across
the grass in the last day, and so they had marched her back into the
car, and driven here to the jail and put her into a cell with mattresses
looped over the white-painted steel bars and steady clanging from one
of the other cells. Lunch had been hot dogs and sauerkraut, and when*

*they had offered to let her make a call, Cody had declined, but asked
if she could have the twenty cents anyway, or a cigarette.*

And then, finally, Valorie let herself remember the actual dawn:

*In her father's voice, Plumtree's body had called to the bearded man
who had stepped barefoot into the meadow: "Get over here, Sonny
Boy."*

*But when the man had walked closer, her father had abruptly re-
ceded, and it had been Cody who found herself standing over the little
boy who was lying on his back on the dirt. Plumtree was holding the
spear with the points at the little boy's throat.*

*She looked up at the tall bearded king, and her vision was blurry
with tears as she said, "There's nothing in this flop for me."*

*"Then pass," said the king in a quiet voice. "Let it pass by us."
After a moment he nodded at her, almost smiling, and said. "In the
midsummer of this year, you and I will be standing in happy sunlight
on the hill in the lake."*

*"I don't think so," said the reintruded father, breathing in a choked
way while the little boy shivered at his feet, "I'll call—I called you this
morning!—and I raise you the kid." Plumtree's eyes darted down to
the pale child under the spearpoints. "That's a raise you don't dare
call, right?" Tight laughter shook Plumtree's throat. "This flop . . . finally! . . . gives me a king-high flush in spades. It's the first day of the
new year, and you've got to face the Death card—the suicide king."*

*The bearded man stepped back. "I've—seen you before." he said.
"Where?"*

*"I'm—I'm putting the clock on you, here, no more time—and I won't
give you any psychic locators on me—"*

*"You're shaking," said the living king. "Throw the spear away.
Don't tell me anything, I'll let you take back your bet."*

*"You think I'm afraid of you? Now? It was in a poker game on Lake
Mead, almost five years ago. You were disguised as a woman, and the
other players called you 'the Flying Nun.' "*

*The king was frowning. "And you failed then, didn't you? You failed
to assume the hand, assume the Flamingo, take the throne. You'll fail
this time, too, I swear to you, even if you ruin everyone in trying. You
flinched away just now, when I approached you. Let it pass." He raised
one hand toward the road. "Go away now, in peace."*

*"Lest you dash your foot against a stone. Don't patronize me, you,
you kings." Plumtree's hands gripped the spear shaft more tightly. "Do
you call?"*

Through clenched teeth, the king said, "No, I do not."

"Then step closer," hissed the father in Plumtree. And when the king had walked up beside them, her father said, "See you in the funny papers," and snatched the spear away from the child and drove it into the king's throat.

Plumtree let go of the iron railing as if it might collapse, and clung to Cochran's arm so tightly that he nearly dropped the bottle. Cochran thought it must have been Janis, or even Tiffany, but the sharp profile was clearly Cody, and she was staring down at the fires on the plain.

"What?" he snapped, his knees shaking at the thought of dropping the *pagadebiti* now.

"Nothing," she said, shaking her head. "Just remembering why I'm here. Let's get it over with."

Angelica seemed to agree. "Let's get down there before Kootie does," she said.

They found the gate in the chain-link fence and started down the path that led between high dark hedges and ivy-covered mounds, and after the first few steps Cochran felt as if they had left the highway and all of San Francisco, even the twentieth century, far behind. The night wind in the bending cypresses, the monotonous distant drumming weaving in and out of the boom of the surf, the bonfires and waving torches, and the smells of ocean and wet leaves on the cold wind, all made him think of some pre-Christian Mediterranean island, with mad, half-human gods demanding worship and sacrifice.

He was looking to the left, out across the broad dark slope of the basin, when the whole quarter-mile from the Cliff House to remote Point Lobos was lit in glaring white, halting raindrops as shotgun patterns of dark stippling against the marble undersides of the clouds; and when the instant explosion of thunder threw the raindrops against his face and extinguished the light, he carried on his retinas a vision of the slope as a ruined amphitheater, the collapsed walls and sagging foundations undisguised beneath the froth of wild vegetation.

By the yellow glitter of flame reflected in the lake-like puddles, he could see that the path levelled and broadened out ahead of them, and he could make out the low stone building in which he and Plumtree had first met up with Mavranos and Kootie again after fleeing Solville. The uneven windows and the top of the roofless wall were silhouetted by fires on the sand floor within, and he could see apparently naked figures dancing on the wall rim.

Half a dozen torch flames were bobbing toward Cochran and his party now across the mud-flats, and he reached around with his right hand to touch the grip of his revolver as he squinted at the approaching forms.

He was able to see that they were people by the bronze glare of the torches many of them were waving, but their bodies and staring-eyed faces were plastered with wet pale mud, so that they seemed to be figures of animated earth, naked and sexless. There were more of them than there were torches, and many carried fist-sized stones. Two or three even had pistols.

Angelica had raised her seat-cover bundle, and Cochran drew his revolver and held it out away from him, pointed at the ground for now. His ears were ringing and his breath was short with the thought of raising the gun, of firing it at these people.

He opened his mouth to speak, but the mud-figures had halted a dozen feet away; and now the torches dipped as they all got down on their bare knees in the mud.

A hot wave of relief rippled up from Cochran's abdomen—but when he glanced at his right hand he saw that it wasn't the gun, or even the bottle of wine in his left hand, that had cowed them.

The night seemed suddenly less dark—variations of grays—in contrast to the ivy-leaf mark on the back of his right hand; it shone with such an intense, absolute blackness that his first, spinal impulse was to somehow instantly cut it off.

Far out in the rainy basin, out among the ruined buildings and crumbled pool copings and the ledge where the tunnel mouth gaped against the firelight, the drumming became louder, and faster.

"We knew you'd come," called one of the figures hoarsely.

"From Phrygia," wailed one of them in a woman's voice, "from Lydia, from *India!*"

To his horror, Cochran's right hand twitched and clenched and *raised;* he was able to push it up still further in the instant before it fired the gun, so that the bullet flew away over the top crags of Point Lobos, but the sound and flash of the shot were lost in another simultaneous blast of white light and ground-jolting thunder, and as the echoes rolled away to shake the trees on the slopes he hastily fumbled the gun back into its holster.

The mud-people might not even have been aware of the gunshot; or they might have *expected* their god to greet his worshippers by trying to murder one of them out of sheer love; they bowed their heads, and began doing a fast, counterpoint hand-clapping that jangled Cochran's thoughts the way drumming was supposed to confuse ghosts.

"And here is your king!" shouted one of the sexless clay people, pointing behind Cochran and his companions.

Cochran turned, half expecting to see Scott Crane restored already— but what he saw through the driving rain was a tall figure and a shorter one reeling down the path from the highway; they were hardly a dozen yards away, and after a moment he recognized Mavranos and Kootie.

The recognition was soon mutual: Kootie's eyes widened and he hurried forward toward Pete and Angelica, and Mavranos trudged up and called, with forced and haggard panache, "What *seeems* to be the problem?"

"What's going on?" yelled Kootie over the noise of the storm. "We drove the car right through the greenhouse in low gear, right over Scott Crane's skeleton!"

"This is it," Plumtree told him shrilly. "We picked up Scott Crane's ghost hitchhiking, and he led us to the devil's wine!" The boy had stumbled closer across the splashing mud now, and she was able to speak in an almost conversational tone when she added, "And we picked up the other old lady ghost, too." She tapped the side of her head. "It looks like we're doing it right this time!"

Kootie and Mavranos were bundled up in raincoats, and Mavranos was wearing his Greek fisherman's cap while Kootie had on an old felt fedora of Cochran's.

"But Chinese New Year isn't until tomorrow!" protested Mavranos, staring at the blackly blazing mark on Cochran's right hand. "Not until midnight, at the soonest! They can't just change it this way! I haven't had time to think—"

"Midnight?" said Pete. "Is that standard time or daylight savings?" He waved at the rain-swept dark sky. "This day is over."

Kootie was blinking at the bottle of wine in Cochran's left hand. "Yeah," he said bleakly, "the sun's down. I guess there's debts you don't carry into the new year."

Mavranos scowled around at the kneeling clay people in the guttering torchlight. "Are you people *volunteers?*" Mavranos roared at them, and Cochran thought there was a note of desperate hope in the man's voice. "Do you *mean* to put yourselves in the way of what's happening here?"

"We're here of our own will, which is the god's will," called one of the figures.

Mavranos nodded, though he was still frowning and squinting as if against the glare of the vanished lightning. "If this cup may pass away," he muttered. Then, more loudly, he said, "Let's get to the cave."

Plumtree took Cochran's right hand, and the two of them set off across the marshy plain, with the others following; the mud-people did appear to be allies, but when Cochran glanced back he saw that Angelica with her bundle of soaked fabric, and Mavranos with his hand in the pocket of his raincoat, were hanging back a few paces to watch the roofless building and the landward slopes and the path behind.

Cochran was suddenly, viscerally sure that not all of the king's company would survive this night; and he was still dizzy from his mouthful of the forgiveness wine, and wondering what memories and loves it had taken from him . . . and if it might soon take more.

"This is like in a chess game," he said to Plumtree through clenched teeth, "when all the castles and bishops and knights are focussed on one square, and there's like a *pause,* before they all start charging in and knocking each other off the board." He walked faster, pulling her along the slope up toward the cave mouth, so that several yards of thrashing rain separated them from Pete and Kootie.

"I don't care what—" he said to her, "well, I do, I care a lot—but *whatever* you think, whatever your feelings are, I've got to tell you—" He shook his head bewilderedly. "I love you, Cody."

She would have stopped, but he pulled her on.

"Me?" she said, hurrying along now. "I'm not worth it, Sid! Even if I love *you*—"

He glanced at her sharply. *"Do* you?" he asked, leaning his head toward hers to be heard, for his heart was thudding in his chest and he couldn't make himself speak loudly. *"Do* you love me?"

She laughed, but it was a warm, anxious laugh. "How do I love thee?" she said. With her free hand she pulled her soggy waitress pad out of her jeans pocket. "Let me read the minutes."

From far away behind them, somewhere on the overgrown terrace paths above this plain but below the highway, came two hard pops that were louder than the drumming; and Cochran was still wondering if they had been gunshots when several more echoing knocks shivered the rain, and then the dark basin behind them was a hammering din of gunfire.

He looked back, crouching and stepping in front of Plumtree. Mavranos had his revolver out as he backed fast across the mud, and Angelica had thrown away the bundle of cloth and was holding the pistol-grip .45 carbine in both hands. Cochran could see winking flashes now on the distant ruined buildings and along the sea-wall; most of the shooters seemed to be firing into the air, and perhaps this whole barrage was just a live-ammunition variation on the Chinatown firecrackers.

But Cochran drew his own revolver again, hollowly reflecting that he now had only two rounds left in the cylinder.

"I'm still here," said Cody wonderingly as the two of them scrambled on up the muddy slope. *"Gunfire,* a *lot* of it, and I haven't passed the hand."

CHAPTER 32

False eyebrows and false moustaches were stuck upon them, and their hideous countenances were all bloody and sweaty, and all awry with howling, and all staring and glaring with beastly excitement and want of sleep.

—Charles Dickens,
A Tale of Two Cities

Dr. Armentrout and Long John Beach had jumped off the muddy path to the left after his first reflexively answering shot had provoked so much return fire, and the two of them had tumbled over an old ivy-covered stone wall, with the two-mannikin appliance flailing wildly on Armentrout's shoulders, and then they tumbled and spun down a mud slope in darkness, away from the torches up on the path. He believed at least one of the Lever Blank men had been shot.

When they had still been in the car, the pomegranate had been pulling hard enough to jump away from his hands when he had let go of it, and so he had made sure to grip it tightly as they had climbed out of the Saturn in the parking lot up the hill—he could imagine the thing getting away from him and rolling off into the night to find the king by itself. He had ordered Long John Beach to strap the heavy two-man appliance onto him, and he had held the pomegranate tightly in each hand while sliding the other through the arm loops—even when the left-hand-side Styrofoam head had nuzzled his cheek in an eerie similitude of affection or attack.

With the mannikins flanking him, the leisure-suited aluminum-pole arms around his shoulders, there had seemed to be six people who ran across the drag-strip highway and started down the path toward the Sutro Baths ruins, and they must have been conspicuous; before Armentrout and Long John Beach and the two Lever Blank men had walked ten yards, their way had been blocked by torch-bearing figures of a sort Armentrout had seen before, on the Leucadia beach.

And tonight again he had stared at the human eyes in the clay faces, and again he had used his most authoritative doctor's voice as he'd said, "What, precisely, is your business here? Get out of our way, please."

An earthen hand pointed at the pomegranate he held, and a red mouth opened on teeth that glittered in the close orange torchlight: "*That's* what you took," said an adolescent voice, "from up the stairs at the Leucadia Camelot."

With his free hand Armentrout pulled the little derringer out of his inside jacket pocket. He levered the hammer back, and then confidently raised the gun and pointed it at the center of the breastless, clay-smeared chest. "Get out of our way, please," he said again.

And then a ringing explosion flared in the ivy to the right, and Armentrout was tugged around in that direction by a punch to his right-side mannikin.

His instant twitch of astonishment clenched his fists—the hollow pomegranate crumpled in his left hand, and his right hand clutched the little gun—

—and then his wrist was hammered by the impact of the wooden ball-grip being slammed into his palm, and the muzzle-flash burned his retinas—but not so dazzlingly that he wasn't able to see the clay-smeared figure step back and then sit down abruptly in the mud, with a ragged golf-ball-sized hole in its chest.

The shrubbery had seemed to erupt in glaring flashes and deafening bangs then, and Armentrout and Long John Beach had vaulted over the ivy on the downhill side of the path. In the ensuing tumbling slide, Armentrout just tried to let the aluminum bodies and the grunting mannikin heads take the abrasions and knocks, while he kept his hands clamped on the gun and the broken pomegranate.

When they had rolled to a halt in a rainy pool down on the plain, Armentrout sat up in the water and squinted sideways at the Styrofoam head on his right shoulder. A great red flare of afterimage hung in the center of Armentrout's vision, but he could see that the Styrofoam man had been shot squarely through the forehead—and then he looked away again quickly, because for just an instant the blank white features had been the face of Philip Muir, pop-eyed and gaping as it had been after Armentrout had put a point-blank load of .410 shot between Muir's eyes.

All he could hear down here, through the ringing in his ears, was a rapid drumming—and then he became aware of a whole siege of popping, spattering gunfire, none of it very close. Peering out through the curtains of cold rain, he saw blinks and flashes of light all along the walls and paths on the plain.

The Maruts, he thought almost in awe; the militant youths described in the Rig-Veda, springing up spontaneously on this western American shore, armed with guns now instead of swords and spears, and wearing earthen rather than golden armor. And they're embodying the Cretan Kouretes, too, protecting the new king by making a distracting racket with their weapons.

The pomegranate was still pulling in his hand, though it was cracked now and bright little seeds were popping out of it and flying away toward the dark cliffs of Point Lobos on the far side of the lagoons and the low stone buildings. "We have to find the king," he gasped to Long John Beach as he struggled painfully to his feet and thrust the leaking pomegranate into his pocket. "Come on!"

Long John Beach pushed himself up with his one arm—and then, without falling back, impossibly lifted the arm from the water to push his sopping white hair back out of his face while he was still propped up at an angle out of the pool.

Then he had got his feet under himself and stood up, and the tiny miracle was over. "I do stand engaged to many Greeks," the old man said in the dead Valerie-voice, "even in the faith of Valerie, to appear this morning to them." Then he blinked at the three heads on Armentrout's shoulders as if all of them were alive; and after staring attentively at the one beside Armentrout's left shoulder, he looked the doctor in the eye and said, "Your mother, in most great affliction of spirit, hath sent me to you."

In the moment it took Armentrout to remember that he now had only one .410 shell left unfired in the magical gun, he was ready to shoot Long John Beach; then he tried to speak, but all that came out of his mouth was a hoarse stuttering wail like a goat's. Frightened and angry, and desperate to be once again free of all the demanding dead people, Armentrout just tucked the gun too into his pocket and shoved Long John Beach forward toward the cliffs.

Cochran and Plumtree had scrambled up to the ledge road, and the cave was only a dozen feet to their left.

Cochran wasn't aware that he had been hearing idling engines until the headlights came on, up the slope to the right—single headlights, motorcycles—and at the same moment he heard the whirring clatter of Harley-Davidson engines throttling up. Cochran clutched the wine bottle to his ribs with his left hand and cocked the hammer of his revolver with his right. Because he had been half thinking in French all evening, he was able to recognize the chorus of yells from the riders: *Vive le Roi! Vive le Roi!*

The flashes of the first cracking gunshots were aimed toward Pete and Kootie, in the middle of the group; Cochran raised his revolver and saw, in razory tunnel-vision over the gun sights, a bearded and wild-haired rider swinging a pistol left-handed toward Angelica and Mavranos.

And Cochran touched the trigger. Blue flames jetted out in an X from the gap where the cylinder met the barrel, and the hammer-blow of sound rocked him as much as the recoil did, but he glimpsed the rider rolling over backward as a booted leg kicked out and the motorcycle's wheels came up and the bike went down in a plowing slide.

A second motorcycle rode down into the fallen one and then stood up on end and somersaulted forward, tossing its rider tumbling across the mud to within a yard of Cochran's feet as the heavy bike clanged away downhill through the curtains of rain; Cochran was aiming now at two more riders who had banked down toward Pete and Kootie.

But Angelica's carbine and Mavranos's .38 were a sudden jack-hammer barrage, flaring like a cluster of chain-lightning, and then the motorcycles wobbled past as Kootie dived one way and Angelica leaped in the other direction—one of the machines crashed over sideways, throwing its rag-doll rider to the ground, while the other bounded straight over a low wall into the big rectangular lagoon with an explosive hissing splash.

Cochran spun to the man who had fallen at his feet—and saw Plumtree straightening up from the man's bloody, sightless face and tossing away a wet rock; raindrops splashed on a stainless-steel automatic that lay in the man's limp hand. Plumtree's eyes were bright, and she cried, "It's still me, Sid!"

And not Salvoy, he thought, remembering the story of the would-be rapist in Oakland in '89. Cochran's right hand was twitching, re-experiencing the hard recoil of the gun, as if his very nerves wished the action could still be cancelled; and he cringed for Cody's sake, at the thought that she had now been permitted to commit homicide for herself.

A fresh volley of gunfire erupted from down the slope, and stone splinters whistled through the air as bullets hammered into the cliff face to his left and behind him and ricochets twanged through the rain. Then someone had grabbed Cochran's arm and yelled into his ear, "Back—Arky's been shot, and there's bikers in the cave."

Cochran threw his arm around Plumtree's shoulders and pulled her away from the dust-spitting cliff face, back down the mud slope toward the fires. He realized that it was Pete who had seized him, and he glimpsed more moving headlights up the slope on the right. The cold rainy air was fouled now with the smells of motor oil and cordite.

"This isn't aimed at us!" yelled Pete over the banging din.

"*Gooood!*" wailed Cochran, gritting his teeth and trying to block Plumtree from at least one quarter of the banging, flashing night. The two of them stumbled and slid back down the slope after Pete; squinting against the battering rain, Cochran could see Mavranos being half-carried back toward the roofless stone building by one of the naked-looking clay-people, with Angelica and Kootie hunching along after. The flames that boiled up from within the stone walls were huge now, throwing shadows across the mud-flats and clawing the night sky, seeming even to redly light the undersides of the clouds.

"The men on m-motorcycles," said Pete, speaking loudly to be heard, "think-kuh Kootie is the khing, but they want him to be-be *their* king. They'll—kill—everyone else, if they *cannn*."

Sound was becoming jerky and segmented again, and Cochran again felt that he was experiencing time in fast but discrete frames—the unceasing rattle and pop of gunfire near and far began to be *paced,* in a fast, complicated counterpoint tempo like the hand-clapping of the clay people—

—Cochran was stumbling, suddenly feeling very drunk, with the taste of the *pagadebiti* wine blooming back into his throat and expanding his head—

—Clumsily he pushed the revolver back into the holster at the back of his belt so that he could hold the bottle with the black-stained hand too—

—And then in an instant all the noise *stopped,* with one last distant rebounding echo to deprive him of the consolation of believing that he had gone deaf; and as if the stunning racket had been a headwind he'd been leaning against, the abrupt cessation of it pitched him forward onto his knees in the mud.

The cork popped out of the bottle's neck, and Cochran thought he could hear the *smack* of it hitting the mud a moment later.

Even the rain had stopped—the air was clear and cold, with no slightest breeze, and the fire in the stone building convulsed overhead for another moment and then stood up straight, a towering yards-wide brushstroke of golden glare against the black night.

Cody Plumtree was on her hands and knees beside him, panting. "When the shooting started," she whispered, "the other girls fell back, and I was on the bus alone, in the driver's seat, driving away from them." Her voice was faint, but in the silence Cochran could hear every sound her teeth and lips and breath made. "But the man standing beside me in the vision wasn't the broken lunatic anymore—it was Scott Crane, all strong and excellent and wise, guiding me; and we sped up and leaped the bus right over the gap in the freeway, and landed whole on the other side."

From *Dirty Harry* to *Speed*, thought Cochran. That's good, I guess. "Kootie did say," he whispered cautiously, "when we were here two or three weeks ago, that you're probably carrying Crane's ghost on you."

"Tonight he gets washed off."

Cochran remembered the motorcyclist she had killed, and the automatic in the man's limp hand. "Cody," he said, "you saved my life."

"Old Chinese proverb," said Plumtree hoarsely. " 'Whoever saves another person's life should dig two graves.' "

Kootie came plodding up to where Cochran and Plumtree knelt. And the boy's splashing footsteps in the mud awoke a wind from over the eastern slopes—the gusty breeze swept down the bowl of the vast amphitheater, bending trees and rippling the ponds, and twitched at Cochran's wet hair as it stepped over him and his companions and moved out over the dark ocean. The air smelled of dry wine and fresh tree sap.

"Give me the wine," said Kootie, his raincoat flapping in the breeze. He had lost Cochran's hat at some point.

Cochran looked past Kootie. The tall flame was curling and snapping again, and by its yellow glow he could see Angelica standing close behind Kootie, and next to her Mavranos with his left arm around Pete's shoulders and his right hand pressed to his side. Cochran lifted the bottle over his head with both hands and the boy took it.

"Now I think Dionysus . . . *set me up* to kill that woman, meant me to do it, in his boarding house," the boy said quietly. The firelight made deep shadows of his cheeks and his eye sockets. "But I did kill her— I do still have to offer my neck to the Green Knight's blade." Angelica would have said something, but Kootie raised his hand. "We won't be able to get into the cave, until I do—and I know the god will kill us all here tonight if I don't. Remember the end of that play Arky told us about, the one where the people refused to drink the god's wine."

"The Bacchae," said Mavranos through clenched teeth.

A deep, hollow drumbeat rolled down the strengthening breeze; then after a few seconds came another. Like two very slow steps.

"Get up," Kootie told Cochran and Plumtree. "Let's go over by the water—"

Cochran struggled to his feet and helped Plumtree up, and with Angelica and Pete and Mavranos they followed the boy down the slope toward the black water beside the stone building. The heat from the flames was a sting on the right side of Cochran's face.

They passed half a dozen of the mud-smeared youths, all of them kneeling; several of them, and many others on the plain, were facing away, toward the Point Lobos cliff, and holding pistols and even rifles at the ready. *Bikers in the cave*, Cochran remembered. Four ragged figures were trudging at a labored pace down from the highway-side slope into the light; one was limping, evidently supported by two of his companions.

The drumbeat had continued as the wind strengthened, and was now thumping a little faster. At least two other drums, at other points across the dark basin, had joined the first one in the same rhythm. White patches showed in the eastern sky, where the moon was breaking through the wind-riven clouds.

But it can't be the moon, thought Cochran. The moon has been waning for a week, it was full on the first of the month—it should be totally dark tonight.

The ground sloped right down into the water here, any original wall long gone, and Kootie halted with his boots a yard from the water. He dug a fluttering paper out of his raincoat pocket and passed it carefully to Cochran. It was a car-registration slip.

"Arky wrote the palindrome on that," Kootie told him. "When I give you a nod, read the last line aloud."

"Right," Cochran said, in a rusty voice. When I read each of the two previous lines aloud, he thought, Crane's ghost showed up; first as our taxi driver after I read the Latin on the ashtray at the Mount Sabu bar, and then as a naked flickering image right here, after I read the next line from Valorie's matchbook.

"When are you going to drink the wine?" asked Angelica with badly concealed urgency. Her wet black hair was blowing in tangles across her lean face.

"When we get back up to the cave," Kootie told her firmly.

The drumbeat was pounding exactly in time with Cochran's pulse now, and he intuitively knew that his companions were experiencing the same synchronization.

Quickly, before Angelica or Pete could react, Kootie raised the wine bottle and tipped it up to his lips; and when he lowered it, Mavranos quickly reached out and took it out of his hands.

"Aaah!" Angelica's wail was snatched away over the sea by the wind, and Cochran knew that she had intended to stop the boy, and that Kootie had known it too.

The boy reeled back across the mud, away from the water, but he didn't fall; well, thought Cochran, *he* wasn't standing next to an open *grave.*

Kootie reached jerkily into an inside pocket of the raincoat and yanked out the dirty little yellow blanket that he had been given by the Diana woman, Scott Crane's widow. For a moment Cochran thought he was going to throw it away. Then the boy pulled it around his shoulders, and he was suddenly closer, or taller, and the blanket seemed to be a spotted yellow fur. Cochran was having trouble focussing on him in the light of the gusting fire.

Cochran shoved the wet car registration into his pocket. His right hand was still flexing, and he was trying to focus his eyes clearly on anything—the low stone walls that stretched away in the darkness, Plumtree's face, his own hands—and he found that he couldn't make out the exact shape of the black hole in the back of his twitching right hand, no matter how he blinked and narrowed his eyes—

The drumbeats were coming more rapidly—the mud-smeared people had got to their feet and were milling around uneasily, swinging their rifles and pistols—and now fast-thudding footsteps from behind were matching the drum's strokes.

Cochran turned, and flinched even as his right hand sprang once again toward the holster at the back of his belt.

The fire-lit figure rushing straight at them across the mud looked at first like some hallucinatory three-headed Kali with four waving arms, and Cochran's abdomen momentarily turned to ice water; then he saw that it was a portly white-haired man, with a pair of life-size gesticulating mannikins attached to his shoulders; and as Cochran fumbled the gun out of the holster he recognized the muddied, grimacing face—it was Dr. Armentrout, and one of the doctor's hands clutched a tiny silver pistol.

But another man was running up behind Armentrout, and now caught the doctor; and he must have punched him between the shoulder blades, for Armentrout's head rocked back sharply and he plunged forward face-down into the mud. The little pistol flew out of his hand and bounced once off the mud and splashed into the dark water.

Before the doctor's encumbered form had even stopped sliding, his pursuer had leaped onto his shoulders, and Cochran saw that it was Long John Beach. The one-armed old man was gripping the back of Armentrout's neck—the two artificial white heads were splayed out to the sides in the mud, their aluminum neck-poles bent, and between them the doctor's head was jerked violently to the side each time Long John Beach's shoulder stump flexed over him.

Cochran was pointing his revolver at the pair, into the middle of the spider-cluster of mismatched arms and heads, but the muzzle wavered. He was aware of Plumtree standing beside him, breathing fast.

Without halting his invisible beating of the doctor, Long John Beach raised his round white-whiskered face, and his little eyes seemed to be squinting fearfully up at Kootie. "A three-headed dog—on your altar," he said, panting as his shoulder spasmed metronomically and blood began to blot through the doctor's snapping white hair. "Your way," he gasped, "is—clear." Then he leaned down over the doctor's limp, jerking form, and a woman's voice cawed, *"Can you breathe, Richie dear? Say something if you can't breathe."* The voice must have come from Long John Beach's throat, but Cochran thought the left-side mannikin head had been jerking in time to the words.

A dozen drums were pounding in rapid unison now, and though it was no longer synchronized with even his presently very fast heartbeat, Cochran thought the drums were matching some other rhythm inside him—an ancient, savage brain-frequency that made thought impossible. His open mouth was fluttered by the wind, and his nose was full of the wine and sap smells.

A warm, strong hand gripped Cochran's shoulder—and he found himself helplessly pointing his revolver at the two jolting figures on the mud in front of him, and then he pulled the trigger—but he must have miscounted his previous shots, for the gun didn't fire.

He was dizzily ready to crouch beside Armentrout and begin pounding on all three of the twitching heads with the pistol grip; but the hand on his shoulder pulled him back and gave him a shockingly hard shove that spun him around twice before he was able to flailingly catch his balance. In the fire-lit wheeling blur he had glimpsed a wooden mask on broad, fur-caped shoulders, but the urgency was now somewhere else; Cochran was still off-balance, somehow.

The clay-smeared people had all stood up at once from the mud around him, and were walking, then striding, toward the Point Lobos cliff. And in a moment they had opened their mouths in a shrill, ululating chorus, and they were running. Cochran let himself start to fall in the same direction.

And then Cochran and Plumtree were running too, right with them, and Cochran didn't even know if he was joining in the predatory yelling as his feet thudded in the mud and flames whirled around him and Plumtree. No particular sound in the shaking din told him that the struck bullet in the gun he was carrying had belatedly fired into the ground, just the jolt in his hand and the flare at his thigh; he didn't even look down, just flipped the gun around in his hand so that it would be a better club.

He did hear shots from up the slope ahead—a rapid-fire stutter that conveyed desperation and panic—and over the close tossing clay dreadlocks Cochran could see muzzle-flashes from the mouth of the cave. None of the sprinting youths appeared to be shooting back—like Cochran they were waving their firearms overhead like clubs, or just tossing them away.

Cochran and Plumtree leaped over wall sections and fallen naked bodies, and then he had lost the gun and they were scrambling up the mud slope toward the cave, imitating the naked earth-people around them in hunching forward to pull themselves up with their hands as well as push themselves along with their feet. All the torches and even the guns had been dropped and left behind, and it seemed to be a pack of four-legged beasts rushing up the path to the cave.

The gunshots were just sporadic punctuation to shrill screams now, and the cave was packed with straining, clawing forms streaked only with reflected moonlight. Cochran was breathing fast through his clenched teeth as he fought to get through the press of bodies to the prey; until a heavy, hairy ball rolled over the shoulders in front of him and fell into his empty hands.

He stared at it. For one transfigured moment it was the head of a lion, shining gold—then it was a human head in the silver moonlight, bearded and gap-toothed and wide-eyed, leaking slick hot blood onto his hands. The nose and ears were torn and bent and tangled in the bloody hair, and an actual thought appeared in Cochran's fevered mind: This was *twisted off* of its body.

He stumbled back and shook the thing free of his hands, and it fell into a tangle of vines at his feet.

Looking up, he saw Plumtree backing away, dragging her right shoulder across the clustered fluttering leaves that covered the cliff face, while her left shoulder was jostled by the muddy, sexless figures. She was biting her knuckles and staring toward where Cochran had dropped the severed head; and her face was bone white in the moonlight, but when she looked up at him she was recognizably still Cody.

Cochran dodged his way over to where she stood, and he started to hold out his hand to her; then he saw that it was gleaming black with blood.

But she clasped it anyway, and he leaned beside her against the leaf-covered unevenness of the cliff.

The clay-smeared youths were dancing away from the cave now, whirling and leaping out of the tunnel and waving over their dreadlocked heads pieces of human bodies as they whirled away back down the slope to the wild beat of the drumming.

And the bounding dancers didn't pause, but the crowd of them split widely around a figure that was striding up the slope now.

Angelica and Pete, supporting the limping Mavranos, were following it.

It wore no mask, and of course it was Kootie—but the boy was taller, and the skirted raincoat and the blanket around his shoulders flapped like robes in the driving wind, and his stern face was dark and Asian in the moonlight. Cochran remembered that the boy's last name was something from India.

The clay-smeared youths were dancing and running around the fire in the roofless structure now; but other figures, clothed and wet and limping, were toiling across the mud-flats toward the cliff; one was as short as a child, and poling itself forward on crutches.

The impossibly full moon was a white disk hanging over the waving trees at the top of Sutro Park above the highway, and by its light Cochran could see that the whole Point Lobos cliff behind himself and Plumtree was covered with vines; and bunches of grapes swung heavily in the wine-reeking wind.

Cochran and Plumtree stepped back and lowered their eyes as the tall figure that was at least partly Koot Hoomie Parganas stepped up to the broad ledge; tracks of motorcycle tires, and swirling gouges left by motorcycle footpegs and handlebars, stood out in starkly shadowed relief in the mud, but Kootie's boots sank deeper, and the holes of his bootprints quickly filled with dark liquid.

The god just walked past you, Cochran told himself; Dionysus, walking the Point Lobos cliffs on this broken night.

But the thought was too big to grasp, and slid off his mind, and he could only look away, down the slope.

CHAPTER 33

Soon wild commotions shook him and made flush
All the immortal fairness of his limbs;
Most like the struggle at the gate of death;
Or liker still to one who should take leave
Of pale immortal death, and with a pang
As hot as death's is chill, with fierce convulse
Die into life . . .

—John Keats,
Hyperion

Mavranos's head was lowered, but he was thrusting himself up the slope strongly with his good left leg; the right leg of his jeans was dark with blood. The faces of Pete and Angelica on either side of him were strained and expressionless with the work of supporting his weight as they climbed the slope. Angelica had apparently lost her carbine, but she was gripping the bottle of *pagadebiti* in her free hand.

When the path levelled out, Mavranos lifted his head, and his stony gaze swept down across the vine-covered cliff to Cochran. "Are there any of the," Mavranos said through clenched teeth, "mud-kids still in the tunnel?"

Kootie had already disappeared into the tunnel, and Cochran plodded carefully to the cave mouth, stepping out wide of it and peering. The tunnel was nearly as dark as the mark on his hand, but beyond the tall, slowly receding silhouette that was Kootie he could see moonlit rock surfaces beyond the arch of the far opening, and no other people.

He shambled back to where Pete and Angelica and Mavranos stood swaying before he answered, for he didn't want to seem to be calling down the tunnel.

"Nobody at all, but Kootie," he said. "They all ran back to the fires, after they—when they—"

Angelica nodded. "We saw what they were carrying."

"Then," said Mavranos in an anguished voice, *"who?"*

"Sid," said Angelica, "help Pete carry Arky."

Cochran stepped up beside Mavranos, and Angelica got out from under Mavranos's left arm and draped its weight around Cochran's shoulders. And then Angelica went sprinting to the cave mouth and disappeared inside, still carrying the bottle. Drops of the wine splashed out onto the mud, and fresh leafy vines curled violently up out of the ground where they had struck, like convulsing snakes.

"I'll watch her," said Plumtree to Pete, and she hurried into the cave after Angelica. Cochran gritted his teeth, remembering that Cody hated caves.

"Come on," said Pete, starting forward strongly; Cochran braced his right arm around Mavranos's ribs and followed, and the two of them were in effect *carrying* Mavranos into the gravel-floored cave, in spite of occasional help from Mavranos's one good leg.

Cochran could feel the short hairs standing up at the base of his neck at the sharp metallic smell that filled the tunnel, and when he realized that it was the smell of fresh blood he made sure to breathe only through his mouth.

Their footsteps crunched and sloshed along the puddled gravel floor, and over the hooting whistle of the wind Cochran could hear sea water crashing and guttering on rocks in the holes below the remembered iron railing that was invisible in this darkness.

"Crowd your wall," he gasped to Pete, for the railing had been on the left.

Then he could see the iron railing below Mavranos's dangling left hand, silhouetted against the luminous foam of the waves outside, beyond the rock wall. *A seething bath,* he recalled Valorie saying here, *which yet may prove against strange maladies a sovereign cure.*

As his shoes deeply furrowed the unseen wet gravel, he twice felt the brief entanglement of strips of cloth, and once he kicked a boot that rolled away too loosely to still have a foot in it—his feet didn't bump anything that felt like flesh and bone, but he was still breathing through his mouth.

When Kootie had stepped out into the diffuse moonlight on the ledge over the water, and the hurrying silhouettes of Angelica and Plumtree had brightened with detail as they shuffled outside too, Cochran could hear footsteps rattling the gravel some distance behind him; but he couldn't free his head to look around. Pete must have heard the steps as well, for he joined Cochran in striding along at a quicker pace.

At last the three of them stumbled out into the relative brightness of the moonlit cloudy sky. Kootie was standing at the seaward lip of the ledge, staring out at the dark Pacific Ocean. He was clearly taller than Plumtree now, who was braced against the seaward rock face beside Angelica, and he even seemed through some trick of moonlight and perspective to be bigger than the great stone profile, across the splashing gap to the right, which was itself staring out to sea in the same direction.

Cochran had to look away; an aura played about Kootie's fur-draped shoulders, and Cochran's eyes hurt when he tried to focus on the boy. He was aware of heat radiating from that side of the ledge, and he wondered helplessly if apotheosis might cause Kootie to spontaneously combust.

Mavranos pushed himself away from Cochran and Pete and stood swaying by himself, blinking around at the stone head and the other huge boulders and tumbled stones piled against this side of the Point Lobos cliffs.

Free of the heavy arm on his shoulders, Cochran quickly turned to look back down the tunnel. At least two silhouettes were trudging this way up the wet stone windpipe; and he was sure that the one struggling along on crutches could be no one but Thutmose the Utmos', the dwarf junkie he had met at the Seafood Bohemia bar, apparently still desperate for a sip of the forgiving wine.

Cochran hurried across to stand beside Plumtree. "We got," he gasped, "company."

The figure in the aura at the seaward side of the ledge turned ponderously, rippling the gusty air, and through the optical distortions the inhumanly calm wooden mask nodded at Cochran. There was respectful greeting in the gesture, possibly even a blessedly remote affection, but there was also command.

Pete was braced against the wall beside Angelica, and now appeared to be holding her back from rushing at the god.

Cochran dug his cold-numbed fingers into his pocket and pulled out the soggy car-registration form.

The light was far too dim for him to read any words off the water-darkened paper; and in sudden abysmal panic he realized that he couldn't remember one word of the Latin.

He lifted his right hand toward his face to rub uselessly at his eyes—and then noticed that the black mark on his knuckles seemed to radiate darkness, so that the letters on the paper shone clearly with the same intense, reflected blackness.

He took a deep breath of the cold wine-and-blood-scented sea air.

"*Sole,*" he read, calling loudly to be heard over the wind whistling in the tunnel at his back, "*medere pede: ede, perede melos.*" And now he remembered the translation the woman had given them: *O Sun, remedy the louse: give forth from yourself, and give forth from yourself again, your devoured limb.*

The masked figure that was no longer recognizable as Kootie was shaking, and Cochran could feel heat on his eyes. He stepped back, raising his hand to throw a cool shadow across his face, and saw Long John Beach shamble out onto the ledge.

Cochran tensed and stepped around in front of the man to grab Plumtree's arm; but the old man was cowering, and his single arm was shaking as he pointed behind and above Cochran.

The waves of the sea glittered silver as a wash of bright moonlight swept in from the horizon toward the shore with eerie speed, and then the full moon was suddenly above the cliffs, shining down onto the rocks, and Cochran could see a naked, bearded man, seeming to stand as tall as Michelangelo's *David*, on the top of the George Washington boulder.

Cochran shivered, flinching in the moonlight. Dionysus *and* the Moon Goddess, for this, he thought. It must have been Diana's baby blanket that called *her.*

The tall figure in the wooden mask shifted ponderously around to face the boulder, and Cochran's eyes narrowed against the radiant heat.

"No!" shouted Long John Beach into the eddying wind. "Wait, listen to this person!" Still cowering before the mask and the moon, he nevertheless shambled out across the ledge toward the masked god. "Look who thinks he's nothing," he said in a whimper; "but the voice from the sky said, 'Let go of the tree.' " More loudly, he called to the expressionless mask, "Now *you're* killing the boy! Take—take *this* body—it's presumed to do a lot of your proper work, in its time—and it's . . . pruned."

Long John Beach hunched forward across the slanted ledge in the stark moonlight—against evident resistance, as if he were weighed down and struggling uphill; Angelica started to push herself away from the cliff to stop him, but Plumtree and Pete both caught her and pulled her back out of the wind.

Cochran was sure that the wind or magnetic repulsion or tilted gravity was going to topple Long John Beach impotently over backward—

—the one-armed man slid back a yard, away from the god—

"*Okay!*" howled the one-armed old man to the sky, and the wetness on his haggard face had to be tears, "I do it, I let go, I—I surrender everything!"

All at once the old man was laughing, and just for an instant another figure seemed to be superimposed on him, out of scale and suspended as if in mid-dance-step above the stone ledge—a young man in patch-work clothing, with two arms, and a pack over his shoulder and a dog snapping at his heels—and then he was just lone, haggard old Long John Beach again, but standing now right in front of the Dionysus figure.

The lone arm stretched out, and one of the old man's fingers reached through the rippling aura and touched the mask.

And then Long John Beach spun around to face the naked figure up on the top of the boulder, and he seemed to Cochran's aching eyes to have spun a number of times, just too fast to catch. And now he was taller, broader-shouldered, and draped in a flapping silver leopard-skin, and it was *his* face that was hidden by the mask.

Kootie collapsed off to the side in his floppy raincoat, and Angelica and Plumtree both caught him and fell to their knees to lower him gently to the puddled stone surface; Angelica had dropped the bottle, and it had bounced off her foot and was rolling on the ledge, spurting dark wine onto the wet rocks. For a moment Kootie was struggling weakly in the arms of both women, the raincoat collar half hiding his face, and then Plumtree disengaged herself and snatched up the bottle.

Scott Crane's ghost was flickering up on top of the boulder, like a figure badly projected on a drive-in movie screen—and now Kootie was shaking violently in Angelica's arms, in the same rhythm.

Mavranos took a step forward, and his right leg folded under him and he fell to his knees in front of Plumtree. "Oh, it *will* be Kootie," he gasped, "if *I* don't do it. I hoped one of the killer clay-kids would volunteer to do it, that this cup wouldn't be for me, but—ahh God."

He reached up and grabbed the bottle from Plumtree—and then he tilted it to his mouth, and Cochran could see his throat working as he swallowed gulp after gulp of the bloody wine. Cochran winced in sympathy, remembering what Mavranos had said at their first attempt, out on the yacht-harbor peninsula: *What your girlfriend is ready to do . . . I don't think I could do.*

A wail echoed from the mouth of the tunnel behind them, and Thutmose the Utmos' came skittering and thrashing out onto the ledge in a tangle of aluminum crutch-poles. "For me! The holy blood—I've worked harder—"

Mavranos lowered the bottle and scowled, and the dwarf subsided into silence. "I was—dying of cancer!" shouted Mavranos through the rain, staring at his empty left hand, "when I met Scott Crane! And what he did cured me!'' He made a fist, and when he went on it was in a voice almost too low for Cochran to hear: "This five years has been gravy. Tell Wendy and the girls that I . . . paid my debts. Tell them they had a husband and father they could be proud of.''

He stood up, not wincing as he put weight on his right leg, and he walked across to stand balanced on the seaward rim of the ledge, nearly eclipsed by the tall masked god whose outlines roiled beside him. Mavranos squinted the other way, up at the towering naked bearded figure on the rock, and he called out strongly, *"Scott! Pogo, do you hear me? Jump this way, old friend, I'll—catch you!''*

And Cochran raised his marked right hand against the wind.

Cochran made himself stare across the ledge into the carved, placid features of the wooden mask that he had seen on Vignes Street in Los Angeles and in the mental hospital in Bellflower; and to it he called, *"I'm Scant Cochran—extend to Scott Crane the favor you owe me.''*

Dionysus swept down one muscular arm and punched Mavranos off the ledge—Mavranos threw his arms out to the sides as he fell away toward the sea, and then he was gone, the bottle spinning away with him.

Thutmose the Utmos' sprang howling away from the wall and covered the length of the ledge in three slithering hops, and then he had dived off the rocky rim and disappeared after Mavranos.

A crash of thunder like a basso-profundo shout from the cliffs themselves shook the air, and in the same instant a blast of white buckshot abraded the cliff face and punched Cochran solidly into Plumtree, and his first thought was that the rushing moon had exploded; but when the blast struck again, and then was followed by sheets of battering rain, Cochran looked down at the white pellets rolling on the stone surface by his shoes and saw that the white buckshot had been BB-sized hailstones.

Cochran forced his head around against the whipping onshore wind, and through tearing, narrowed eyes saw that there was no figure up on the George Washington head now; and the corner of the ledge was empty where Long John Beach or Dionysus had stood.

We failed at it again, he thought incredulously. He clung to Plumtree as tears were blown out of the corners of his eyes and his shoulders heaved. All of us have about killed ourselves, and Arky *has* killed himself, and we've failed.

Suddenly Plumtree gripped his upper arms hard.

Over the racket of the storm, someone was roaring, or screaming, out in the ocean; and through the rain the cliffs echoed with the baying of a hound.

And the ledge was shaking.

Cochran crouched and pulled Plumtree down, and then he reached past her and tugged hard at Kootie's raincoat, trying to help Pete Sullivan to drag both the boy and Angelica toward the tunnel. Boulders were moving out in the curtains of rain, and rocks were toppling from the crests of the cliffs and spinning down through the air to crack and rumble in pieces into the churning sea; and some kind of water main must have broken in the core of Point Lobos, for solid arching streams were shooting out far above the boulders and being torn to spray by the wind.

"Get inside!" Cochran yelled at Angelica. "Rock fall!"

"Wait for him!" she screamed back.

Cochran was panting in pure fright as he clung to the heaving ledge over the boiling sea; his tears were flying away past his ears, and the spray in his open mouth was fresh water. He turned around with his hands splayed flat on the wet shifting stone, and shouted to Plumtree, "Get in the tunnel!"

A falling rock impacted so hard with the ledge rim in the moment of shattering like a bomb that the very concussion of the air stunned him and he thought his wrists were broken just from the jolt through the stone.

Two weeks ago the shooting at the ruins on the yacht-club peninsula had shocked him with the facts of velocity and human mercilessness; now his mind was seized-up with a cellular comprehension of force and physical mass and Nature's mercilessness. Hail and gravel and rain lashed like chains at his back, and he tried to block Plumtree from it as he pulled her toward the tunnel. The ledge had shifted under his knees, and he was sure it was within moments of breaking away and falling into the sea.

But Plumtree grabbed his chin in her cold hand and yelled, "Look!"—and she stared past him, toward Pete and Angelica and Kootie.

Feeling as though he were turning himself inside-out, Cochran tore his eyes from the close darkness of the stone tunnel and twisted his head around to look toward the open sea.

A man was climbing up out of the waves onto the shaking ledge, clutching each new, bucking handhold with bunched muscles and straining tendons. He was shirtless, and a thick dark beard, sopping wet, was matted across his broad chest. When he had hauled himself up and got one knee onto the shelf, Cochran saw that he was naked, and that a wound in his right side was bleeding; Kootie pushed himself away from Angelica and began unbuttoning his raincoat.

A big black dog, wet as a seal, was scrambling up the rocks on the side of the ledge closer to the George Washington boulder, and Kootie paused to scream *"Fred!"* over the howling of the storm.

The dog clawed the stone and got its legs under itself and then bounded to the boy, water flying from its weakly wagging tail.

Cochran met the dark eyes of the bearded man—

And with a sudden hollowness in his chest he recognized Scott Crane, alive in a living body at last.

Blood was streaming away in the rain from the man's nose and mouth and ears, but he smiled through evident pain; and then he braced himself and straightened his legs and stood up. Blood ran down his right leg from the gash below his ribs.

Cochran was sure the man would just be blown right back off the ledge and broken to pieces on the rocks—but the wind rocked to a halt as if Scott Crane had put his aching shoulders under it, and the cliffs stopped shaking under the weight of his bloody bare feet.

In spite of the glad leaping of the dog, Kootie had managed to shrug out of the raincoat, and he knelt forward to hold it up toward Crane. The bearded man took it and slowly pulled it on and belted the yellow sash, and at once he no longer appeared to Cochran to be some sea god risen from the waves—just a robed king, barefoot and wounded.

The rain was falling vertically out of the sky onto the surfaces of stone now, and the arching streams of water had stopped gushing from the cliff. Scott Crane's gaze travelled from Pete and Angelica and Kootie and the dog to Cochran and, finally, to Plumtree. Cochran wasn't touching her, but he could feel her flexed tension, and he thought he heard a high, keening wail.

Crane smiled at her, and nodded in recognition.

Then Crane's great bearded head turned as he looked around at the surrounding boulders and the tunnel opening. "Where is Arky?" he said, and his low voice cut effortlessly through the hiss and spatter of the rain. "He called me, all the way from Persephone's shore, beyond India."

Plumtree was on her hands and knees, but now she cautiously stood up, bracing herself with one hand against the rock wall. "The gunshot wound in your side," she wailed, "is all that's left of him. He gave you his body—and you've transformed it into your own." She was shaking against the stone, and Cochran realized that she was sobbing. *"He* restored you to life."

The bearded king was visibly shaken by this. "Is this true?" he asked hollowly.

Cochran realized that it must be, and he nodded even as Kootie said, "Yes."

Crane raised his bearded head and stretched his arms out to the sides—as Mavranos had when he had fallen into the sea—and he roared a wordless yell that echoed back from the cliffs, and fell to his knees.

"How can I take this?" he said loudly. "Is this how Dionysus gives his favors?"

"Yes," said Cochran, and he was aware that he and Plumtree had spoken the word in unison.

"Yes," echoed Kootie.

"*Medere pede,*" said Crane, quietly but clearly; "*ede, perede, melos.* I heard that and assented to it—I came back, on those terms. And there's more blood owed on the account, shamefully proxy blood, still. But after this dawn I can make sure it's only *me* that pays, every winter." He exhaled a long, harsh *aah*. "But what can my kingdom be, without . . . loyal, old, Archimedes Mavranos?" Still kneeling, Scott Crane looked across the ledge at Kootie. "You're the . . . young man who held the crown."

"Fumbled it," called Kootie miserably over the rain. He was hugging the big black dog. "I ran away, on the morning of Dionysus's day. And I . . . can't remember what I did then, but . . ."

"My family," said Crane. "My son Benjamin, my wife—do you know if they're all right?"

"They're fine," said Plumtree. Cochran believed that she needed to talk to Crane now, in spite of her guilt—that she needed to keep on establishing that the man really had returned to life. "According to a woman called Nardie Dinh," Plumtree went on, "who's taking care of your place."

"Nardie," said Crane hoarsely. "That's good."

Again Crane got to his feet, smoothly but with pain evident in the stiffening and sudden pallor of his face. "Stand up," he said. "You five constitute my army and my field marshals." Bloody teeth showed through the soaked curls of his beard as he gave them a clenched but resolute smile. "Have you got a car?"

"A Torino," said Kootie, glancing at Cochran and Plumtree.

"Which is stolen," said Plumtree. "We've got Arky's truck."

Crane winced, either at the evident pains of his transfiguration or at the mention of Mavranos's old Suburban. "Take me to it, and one of you drive," he said. He stared into Plumtree's eyes then, making her flinch. "We've got two poor bankrupt old women to see off at the cemetery dock."

"Im—immediately?" asked Cochran, trying to make his voice neutral. All of them had been soaked with cold rain in cold wind for hours, and he had been passionately looking forward to a car heater and a hot shower and then enough to drink so that he could drive out of his mind the image of a severed head in his hands.

Then he glanced at Crane, naked under the raincoat and drenched in sea water and wounded, too, and he was ashamed of having asked. "Not that I—"

"I reckon it'll be immediate by the time we get there," said Crane, "yep. We've got to go to the cemetery marble temple, out at the end of the peninsula. I think you've been there before."

And been shot at, thought Cochran. "Yes," he said.

There appeared to be nothing more to say. Plumtree and Cochran led the way back down the tunnel to the slope that descended to the amphitheater plain. The full moon had disappeared behind the clouds, and the fire in the roofless stone structure had died down to a height hardly above the ragged walltops, and the dancers were moving in rings now, waving their torches in unison to the quieter drumming.

It was just a Bacchanalian revel now, no longer a Dionysian hunt. The gods were no longer present.

CHAPTER 34

Ghosts all! The ghost of beauty, the ghost of stateliness, the ghost of elegance, the ghost of pride, the ghost of frivolity, the ghost of wit, the ghost of youth, the ghost of age, all waiting their dismissal from the desolate shore, all turning on him eyes that were changed by the death they had died in coming here.

—Charles Dickens,
A Tale of Two Cities

Like a bruise all over,'' said Plumtree intently as Scott Crane labored up the steep driveway toward the Sutro Heights parking lot, ''isn't it? Like you've been hammered with a meat tenderizer, especially on the insides.''

''It is—like that,'' panted Crane. ''Who—*are* you?''

''Cody. Cody Plumtree.''

They were skirting the illuminated patch of asphalt under one of the park light poles, and Cochran looked back at the king. The man had refused any help from him or Pete, and he was striding along steadily, but the moisture on his bearded face was clearly as much sweat, and perhaps tears, as cold rain. Kootie and the black dog were running on ahead and then running back, staying in sight.

''Ch-ch-changes,'' said Plumtree. ''At least you're not changing your sex.''

''I can imagine,'' Crane said, nodding stiffly, ''that that would be rough.''

Cochran could see the red truck under the overhanging elms ahead, still parked among the nondescript but gold-painted old sedans and station wagons. ''Don't be bothering him, Cody,'' he whispered.

''I'm not bothering him. Am I bothering you?''

''The climb up the rocks,'' said Crane, ''took a lot out of me. I made hard use of a lot of—rearranged muscles that were still too shocked to register their initial pain yet.''

Pete had fumbled out Mavranos's key ring with the Swiss Army knife on it, and was trying to find the key. Kootie and the black dog were already standing by the front bumper.

"Could you open the tailgate?'' asked Crane. "I'd be more comfortable lying down in the back. I've travelled back there before, when the winter was a bad one.''

More recently than you know, thought Cochran, feeling his face stiffen at the idea of the living man riding back there where his corpse, and then his wrecked skeleton, had been carried around for a week.

"Sure,'' said Pete.

"Jeez, we should sweep it out,'' said Plumtree in an awed voice. "There might still be bits—''

Cochran silenced her with a wide-eyed look behind Crane's back.

After Crane had sweatingly but without help climbed up into the truck bed and stretched out, Pete closed the tailgate and then got in behind the wheel next to Kootie and Angelica, while Cochran and Plumtree got into the back seat, with the dog sitting up panting on the seat between them. When the doors had all been chunked shut, Pete started the engine and backed the truck around, then drove slowly down to the coast highway with the windshield wipers slapping aside the steady streams of rain, and turned right. Everyone seemed to be on the point of saying something, chin and eyebrows raised, but no one spoke as the truck swayed and grumbled through the landscape of gray woods and rock outcrops, looping around the curves of Point Lobos Avenue to the north and then straightening out onto Geary Boulevard, heading east.

The little restaurants and stucco houses on Geary were all dark behind the rain-veiled streetlights, and Cochran wondered what time it could be. If the impossibly full moon had been moving in real time, it might be nearly dawn now. At least the truck's heater was on full, blowing out hot air that smelled of tobacco and stale beer and dispelled the dog's odor of sea water and wet fur.

Plumtree had dozed off against the left side window, and though she whimpered and twitched in her uneasy sleep, Cochran had thought it kinder not to wake her; but as the truck was passing a gold-domed cathedral she abruptly hunched forward and spat. Cochran shifted to peer at her past the wakeful, whining dog.

"Just let me talk,'' Plumtree whispered. "A condemned . . . person should get to make a last statement, especially when there's gonna be no trial before the execution.''

"Cody!'' said Cochran sharply, thinking she was still in the middle of a dream. "We're in the truck, and the restoration-to-life worked this time, remember?"

Plumtree looked up at Kootie, who was peering back from the front seat; he looked startled, and might have been asleep a moment ago himself. "Then you're not the king anymore," she whispered, "but will you give me permission to talk, to be heard?"

"Uh," said Kootie, clearly mystified, "sure."

"Okay," came the whisper; then Omar Salvoy's voice said, "Plumtree is gonna have to die. A death is still owed in this math, and blood and shattered bone. Your Mavranos just died to provide the *body*. Somebody's still gotta pay Dionysus for return of the king's *soul*." Salvoy smiled, and the face wasn't Cody's anymore. " 'For me, the ransom of my bold attempt shall be this cold corpse on the earth's cold face,' as the Valerie one would say. Ask *the king* if I'm making this up." Plumtree's body shifted over against the far window, as if Salvoy didn't like contact with the dog.

I thought you were deaf, thought Cochran helplessly; then he remembered that Janis had taken on the deafness.

After a moment of silence except for the roaring of the engine and the rippling hiss of the tires on the pavement outside, Scott Crane said, wearily, "He's right." Behind them he sat up and shifted around in the bed of the truck. "Even if I—were to kill myself, Dionysus will demand a payment for the fact of this night's resurrection." He sighed. "I get the idea you people—didn't *know* this?—before you undertook to call me back from Erebus."

"It'll be poor gallant Plumtree," said Salvoy, shaking Plumtree's head, "if nobody else volunteers." Plumtree's eyes darted warily to Angelica, who had opened her mouth. "The boy said I could talk!"

"I'll volunteer," Cochran found himself saying.

"Of course," Salvoy went on, ignoring him, "I wonder if it really shouldn't be somebody with a cold-blooded murder to atone for, somebody who is already owed a stroke from the Green Knight's axe. Kootie? What *did* you do, that morning at Mammy Pleasant's boardinghouse?"

"I—can't remember," said Kootie. "But I do remember saying— something?—about the Green—"

"It'll be 'poor gallant Plumtree,' " interrupted Angelica loudly, "and *you,* mister. I like Cody, but all of you in there committed or abetted the murder of—". She waved at the bearded man sitting up in the back of the truck. "—of *him,* and if somebody's got to die for it, take the fall for it, it's the Plumtree crowd."

"Dionysus will decide," said Scott Crane. "It's his show."

"Scant here volunteered," said Salvoy, speaking faster. "Let me talk, Kootie's not a child! You could kill him, Kootie, just assist in his voluntary suicide, and become the king yourself—Crane is old, and doesn't have his strength back yet—let *him* go home and tend to his *rose*-bushes—and then you could forget that killing, and *all* your sins!—with the *pagadebiti*. The king can always score a bottle of that. Don't talk, listen! Think of it—you must have experienced a taste of it, while Crane was dead—the sensory-neural awareness of the whole American West: cracking your joints and stretching with the sun-warmed mountains and freeway bridges at dawn, drinking the snow-melt from the granite keeps in the Sierra Nevada through the Oroville dam, inhaling and exhaling all the millions of suffering births and deaths!" Salvoy's voice was strained. "Work with me, boy!"

Cochran could see Kootie's lower lip pulled away from the teeth, and could see the glitter of tears in the boy's eyes; and he was suddenly afraid that Salvoy would abandon this dangerous gambit of dialogue and switch deaf Janis on at any moment.

Cochran silently drew a deep breath, but before he could speak, Kootie looked away from Plumtree to the dog and said, clearly, *"Mom!"*

The dog licked his face, and Angelica hugged him.

Plumtree's face had started to kink into Janis's puzzled frown even as the boy had spoken, and for several moments her face twitched with conflicting personalities; then it was recognizably the mother's voice that said, triumphantly, "Hah! I am out in the world!" The eyes that seemed closer-set blinked at Cochran. "Are we going to the sea? Are you going to send her past India at last?"

"Oh, *Cody,*" Cochran groaned.

Plumtree cringed back in the seat, but the Follow-the-Queen trick had worked—it was Cody's voice that said, "God, it was *him,* wasn't it?" She spat again. "Don't let me sleep any more. Get to the goddamn temple on the peninsula and let's get this *paid off.*"

Cochran realized as he put his arm around her stiff shoulders that she had known all along that a death would be owed in payment.

But he was resolved that it would be his own.

The dark clouds were breaking up, and the sky was clear and molten red over the long piers of Fort Mason nearly a mile away to the east when Pete drove the truck slowly down the service road behind the yacht club; when they had passed the end of the asphalt and the tires were grinding in sandy mud, Cochran saw that the chain with the NO ADMITTANCE sign hanging from it had been hung across the path again.

"What's another dent," said Angelica hollowly.

"We won't be getting shot at, this time," said Pete.

"Ideally," put in Cochran.

"Sometime," came Scott Crane's hoarse voice from the back of the truck, "I will need to hear about all this." He spoke absently, blinking and squinting as he tried to look at the red sky ahead. "My first dawn," he said. "It's very bright." Tears were rolling down over his prominent cheekbones now, possibly from trying to stare at the dawn.

Pete clanked the engine into low gear, and Cochran heard the groan and snap of the chain breaking, and then the rustle as the broken ends sprang away into the shrubbery.

Cochran had rolled down the window, and in spite of the dawn chill he was taking deep breaths of the sea air. He could smell flowers and fresh-turned loam on it too, and he saw that the roadside anise bushes that had been brown and dry when they had been out here two weeks ago were now brightly green and bursting with tiny white flowers.

Pete brought the truck to a slow, squeaking halt a few yards short of the descending stone stairway, up which Angelica had carried Crane's skeleton in the rain two weeks ago, when dead birds had been falling out of the sky. And Cochran thought he could see a slowly rocking shimmer beyond the stone walls.

Cochran's face was wet and his mouth was dry, and he was breathing shallowly; and his thoughts were chasing each other around in his head without becoming complete sentences: *We'll all step down there, but not all of us will—me, rather than her, but I hope—think, will you, there must be some way to—but me rather than her, me rather than her—*

He didn't fumble in levering open the door, and when he stepped down onto the gravelly sand he was steady enough not to be knocked over when the big black dog bounded out and collided with his legs. He reached up and took Plumtree's hand as she hopped out of the truck, and they could hear the rusty squeal as Pete swung the tailgate down.

Plumtree was staring south across the narrow inlet at the white house-fronts of the Marina district—the windows were dark, but a few bicyclists were distantly visible on the sidewalks of the Marina Green.

"My male parent probably told you I'll die here," Plumtree said quietly, "and that may be true. I think I wouldn't mind that—I knew that might be part of the price of undoing our murder—if I hadn't met you, Sid."

Cochran opened his mouth, but couldn't think of anything to say. If he did manage to pay for the murder himself, he and Cody would still not be together.

"I—feel the same way" was all he could come up with.

There was faint music on the gentle breeze from over the water, distant bells and strings tracing a melody he knew he had loved long ago: bright and almost sprightly, wafting with forlorn insouciance around a core of nostalgic despair. At each moment he could almost anticipate the next note—could almost have hummed along, if his throat had not been choked with grief—and he knew this was only the bridge, that the melody would soon be returning to the valiantly, uselessly brave tragedy of the main theme.

Scott Crane had walked to the head of the white marble stairs, and stood for a moment looking down toward the cobblestone-paved dock. Then he sat down on a broken Corinthian pillar and lowered his head into his hands. Blood was still running from his ears, and his bare right foot shone red in the strengthening light.

Cochran took Plumtree's hand and walked across the crunching sand to the head of the stairs. He could hear the others following him, and the pad and panting of the dog.

At the top of the stairs he stopped, staring down at the dock-like pavement below.

At first he thought a stray patch of fog had clung to this corner of the choppy bay water; then his eyes shifted their perspective in some way . . .

And a crystal boat rocked in the gray water under a glassy mast, and smoky transparent forms sat at the thwarts; they became fleetingly clear when he looked squarely at them, then flickered away in a kaleidoscope tumble of diaphanous faces and hands, and he saw that they were frail shells of people, ghosts, blinking around in the dawn. He recognized old blind Spider Joe, who still wore the daddy-longlegs filaments around his waist, and thought he saw Thutmose the Utmos', though without crutches now; and then he saw, clearly, Archimedes Mavranos standing up by the bow. Mavranos was looking back at the people on the dirt above the dock stairs, and Cochran thought he was smiling and waving.

The faint distant music paused for a full second, like a dancer on tiptoe; then it swept back, stronger—gracious and smiling and evoking sun-dappled streets and old walled gardens even as it bade farewell to all things and bowed to oblivion.

Plumtree pulled her hand free of his; there was a finality to the gesture that chilled him, and he spun toward her.

And as if she stood in the center of a ring of mirrors, he saw more than a dozen of her, opaque enough so that where several overlapped he couldn't see the red of the truck through them.

Then he saw that two were still solid—no, it was only one, but it was alternately Cody and then Janis, and Plumtree appeared to shift her

position against the distant buidings as she changed from one to the
other, as if he were helplessly looking at her first through one eye and
then through the other. Her ragged blond hair gleamed or was backlit
in the dawn's glow.

"I'll take this flop," said Cochran hastily. "I'll pay the life."

"You didn't kill him, Sid," said Cody. "I'll go. I've loved you, Sid,
and that's a real magic trick—that was never a part of me—"

She shifted, backlit against the brightening sky, and "No," came one
voice that was both Janis and Valorie speaking; " 'madame has forgot-
ten that we agreed to play in partnership this morning.' " It was clearly
Janis who went on, "That's James Bond to Tracy di Vicenzo, in *On
Her Majesty's Secret Service*, when he volunteers to cover her gambling
losses. You wouldn't remember it, Cody—you set the book on fire."
The Janis figure clenched her fists, as if against an internal struggle.
"I'll never ditch you, Daddy—where I go, you go, I swear on my life!"
Then she sagged, and it was a lifeless face that swung from the boat to
the brightening dawn behind the distant piers, and back. "See how the
morning opes her golden gates, and takes her farewell of the glorious
sun!"

There were two Plumtree bodies now; Cody was clearly standing
away from the figure that was Janis and Valorie; and that figure was
fading.

Janis's bright eyes in Valorie's dead face turned on Cochran as the
face became transparent. "And so farewell," said the figure that was
now just one more ghost, "and fair be all thy hopes, and prosperous be
thy life!"

The ghost spun in a casual pirouette, and gathered into its insubstantial self all the other Plumtree ghosts; and Cody was left standing solidly
on the sand beside Cochran. He seized her hand, both to be sure she
was a living human being and to prevent her from following the ghost,
which was now gliding down the marble stairs and across the cobblestone dock toward the boat; and for a moment now the faint music
seemed to be the strains of "I'll Take You Home Again, Kathleen."

"But I'll be alone!" wailed Cody, in a voice that shook with absolute
loss.

"No, you won't," said Cochran strongly. He gripped her shoulders
and said again, looking into her face, "No—you won't."

"No," she agreed brokenly, "I won't." She fell forward against him,
and he hugged her tightly.

Omar Salvoy's words were echoing in his head: *A death is still owed
in this math.* But that was it, Cochran thought shrilly; poor Janis just

died, along with Omar Salvoy at last, and Tiffany and the rest of them. Wasn't that death enough for the god?

And the rest of what Salvoy had said . . .

Then Plumtree stiffened in his arms, and he felt her ribs clench as she screamed. A moment later Pete and Angelica yelled in alarm, and the dog was barking.

Cochran wheeled around, crouching and dizzied.

If he had not seen Dr. Armentrout running at them last night like a spidery Vedic demon, he would not have recognized the battered monster that had clambered out of the bay to his right and was now rushing at Scott Crane; and even so his chest emptied for a moment in cold horror.

The two figures that were attached to Armentrout's shoulders were twisted and draped with seaweed, and their grimacing fleshy heads were canted outward like the leaves on a fleur-de-lis; but Armentrout's right hand held the muddy derringer that had bounced into the lagoon last night, and the bloodshot eyes in Armentrout's swollen purple face were fixed on Scott Crane.

Cochran leaned into the monster's path, stretching out his right leg and hand. The mannikin heads were yelling suddenly—*"Feel good about yourself!"* one was cawing, and the other was shrilling, *"Pull the plug, let me up!"*

The little gun was coming up in the pudgy hand as Armentrout took another running step—Scott Crane had lifted his head and turned on the pillar, but he would not be able to dive out of the way—Pete and Kootie had started forward, and the black dog's forelegs were raised in a leap— and Angelica had drawn the .45 automatic clear of her belt, but Armentrout would have time to fire the derringer before she would be able to swing the heavy gun into line.

In Cochran's memory the silvery edges of the pruning shears plunged toward the old king's face, and Cochran instinctively blocked the thrust with his right hand.

The flat, hollow *pop* of the .410 shell deafened him, and he lost his footing as his right hand was punched away upward. The marble-and-brick-peppered sand plunged up at him and he twisted his left shoulder around to take the jarring impact as he slammed against the ground. With a ringing crystalline clarity Cochran saw drops of his own blood spattering down onto the wet sand around the truck's front tires.

Then he rolled his head down to look at his right hand, and his vision narrowed and lost all depth—for above his wrist was just a glistening red wreckage of torn skin and splintered white bone, and blood was jetting out into the air.

The rest of what Salvoy had said flickered through his stunned consciousness—*Blood and shattered bone—*

Later Cochran learned that Fred the dog had hit Armentrout and knocked him over backward, so that Armentrout had dropped a broken dry pomegranate that he had been carrying in his left hand—it had rolled uphill to Scott Crane's foot, onto which it had spilled clinging red seeds like blood drops—and that after trying to shoot the emptied gun at the dog that was tearing at his four arms Armentrout and his two attached figures had gone stumbling back down over the wet tumbled rocks into the sea to get away.

But all Cochran saw when he swivelled his shock-stiffened face away from his ruined hand, toward the yelling that was so loud that he was able to hear it even through the ringing in his ears, was Armentrout standing thigh-deep in the shallow sea and doing something strenuous with two people: one was a heavy-set old woman in a sopping housedress, and the other was a slim young man with protuberant eyes and a blackened ragged wound in his forehead.

The dog kept running back and forth between Cochran and the water, and everyone behind him was shouting too. Somehow it didn't occur to the stunned Cochran that the three figures out in the water were *fighting*—Armentrout's companions appeared instead to be forcibly giving him something like a full-immersion baptism, dunking him under the water and then hauling him up to shout at him, and then doing it again, and the white-haired doctor did seem to be responding with denials and oaths and genuflexions. It was violent, certainly, but to Cochran it seemed that all three were trying to get an important job done.

Angelica was kneeling beside him on the wet sand, urgently saying things he couldn't hear and tightly tying a leather belt around his right wrist. But finally a moment came in which it dawned on Cochran that the woman and the pop-eyed young man had held Armentrout under the waves one last time and would not ever be letting him up at all.

"They've killed him!" Cochran yelled, struggling to get up.

Behind and above him he heard Angelica say, "Is that a bad thing, Sid?"

Out in the water the old woman and the young man with the holed face seemed to merge, and then become a shape *superimposed on* the seascape instead of *in* it: the stylized black silhouette of a fat man with stubby limbs and a warty round head. And as it shrank, or receded in some non-spatial sense so that it didn't disappear into the water, it flickeringly seemed to be a very fat naked white man with tattoos all over him, and a middle-aged Mexican man, and a pretty Asian woman, and others . . .

Then it had faded to nothing like a retinal glare-spot, and the sea was an unfeatured expanse of rippled silver all the way across to the Marina.

"No," Cochran said. A death *was* still owed in the math, he thought. A physical heart had to literally stop. "No," he said again.

Cochran was lying on his back. He twisted his head to look up at Angelica, and then he focussed past her. Two transparent old women stood above and behind her, and their milk-in-water eyes were fixed on the puddle of blood on the dirt below Cochran's tourniquetted wrist. Their hands were reaching toward the blood, and their fingers were stretching like old cobwebs disturbed by a solid person's passage.

Up the slope by the stairs, Scott Crane had at some point got to his feet. His beard had dried enough to be lustrous and full, so that seen from below this way he looked like a schoolbook picture of Solomon or Charlemagne; and in a voice so deep and resonant that it cut through the shrilling in Cochran's impacted eardrums, Crane said, "Hot blood is what you're leaving behind forever now, ladies. Get aboard the boat now; the tide is about to ebb, and you have to go."

The ghosts of Mrs. Winchester and Mammy Pleasant swirled away to the steps and down toward the insubstantial boat, and then the first rays of the rising sun touched the iron lamp-post at the end of the peninsula. Cochran thought he could hear distant voices singing.

He was sagging with fatigue, and he wondered that he was able to hold his head up; and then he realized that Cody Plumtree was sitting on the sand behind him and cradling his head in her lap. Kootie was kneeling white-faced behind Plumtree, with his arms around the black dog's neck. Blood was trickling down Kootie's own neck from a long, shallow cut below his ear, where a stray shot-pellet had evidently nicked him.

Cochran rolled his eyes to look back out at the water of the bay, but it was still empty—the blobby black figure had certainly gone.

The Green Knight gave the boy just a token cut, Cochran thought; and he settled his head more firmly against Cody's warm, solid legs. The retribution-aspect of Dionysus was merciful, this morning.

Pete was behind the wheel of the truck, and now started up the rackety old engine; and just because of the new noise Cochran became aware that at some point violin-pure voices had begun singing out of the pipes that stood up from the masonry, a high solemn wordless chorus that now coaxed Cochran's sluggish pulse to meet the vibrant cadences implicit in the new dawn.

"Get up, Sid," said Plumtree, and Angelica added, "On this morning you can go to a hospital, with no fear of ghosts."

Cochran got dizzily to his feet, leaning heavily on the two women as he shambled up the slope toward the shaking truck.

White seagulls, luminous in the new daylight, were circling high overhead against the blue of the clean sky, whistling and piping in the open, unechoing air as if calling out the news of the soon-returning spring.

EPILOGUE:

"In the Midsummer of This Year . . ."

All, all is yours,
The love I owed my father, who is dead,
The love I might have given to my mother,
And my poor sister, cruelly doomed to die.
All yours now, only yours.
                    —Aeschylus,
                    The Libation Bearers

Cupped at the very top of the steep green hill, above the lake that encircled the island and above the fenced-in reservoir that fed the waterfall, was a little lake surrounded by cherry laurel trees and standing green and orange stones. The lake water was so still that every tree branch against the blue sky was reflected motionless in the water.

Cody Plumtree had run up the steps of half-buried railway ties ahead of the others, and now she carefully lifted the hem of her white linen skirt and stepped up onto the altar-like rock at the east end of the little lake. This rock looked as if it were once a source for a waterfall into this lake, and it also looked as if it had been the site of fires in remote times. She remembered Sid saying that these moss-green stones were druid stones, magically counterweighted by the monastery stones around the lake below. Sid might not remember that now, but he would know it if she told him about it and then made sure to tell him about it again a few times.

It was a topic that was connected to his memories of his dead wife, and all those memories really had disappeared. He knew these days that he had been married, and he could even recognize photographs of the Nina woman, but he was like an amnesia victim—except that an amnesia victim would probably want to learn about the lost past. Along with the memories, Sid had lost any interest in what they had been of.

Cody didn't mind, and she would probably not remind him of the history of the stones.

The two of them had been living in Sid's South Daly City house for five months now, but somehow—like, she thought helplessly, the Solville piece of string that couldn't ever quite be cut—it had consistently been a celibate relationship. That would change after this ceremony today, she was certain.

Cody had not lost any memories at all, and she still dreamed of the other girls that had occupied her head with her. On some nights she even dreamed of the day the sun fell on her, the day—twenty-six years ago now to the day, perhaps to the hour—when her father was thrown off the building in Soma; it was a harrowing dream, but she was glad to experience it, especially since she saw it in *color*—it indicated that she had absorbed, taken as her own, those earliest memories that had been in the sole custody of dead Valorie.

And last night she had dreamed of driving the bus, speeding up and jumping across the wide empty gap in the freeway to land safe on the other side, and the man standing beside her had been Sid Cochran.

Two miles away to the southeast she could see the tall X-shaped TV tower on Mount Sutro; and when she shifted around, she could see the two distant piers of the Golden Gate Bridge, appearing in foreshortening to be standing next to each other on the horizon.

The other people were scuffing up the steps now—and she saw Scott Crane come striding lightly across the grass first, tall and brown and smiling through his lustrous coppery beard; he was fifty-two years old now, but hardly looked thirty-five, and on this midsummer's day his wound didn't make him limp at all. He wasn't dressed as any kind of priest, though that was the function he would be serving here today; he wore a navy blue suit with a white shirt, and his long hair was tied back in a ponytail secured, she had noticed on the walk over the bridge, with a gold Merovingian bee.

The others from the Leucadia compound were right behind him, led by lithe Nardie Dinh and Diana with her three-inch thatch of radiant blond hair. Arky's widow, Wendy, was leading their two teenage daughters; Plumtree had been afraid to meet them at first, and then had been surprised by their unaffected friendliness and their eagerness to hear stories about Arky's last month. Diana's boys Scat and Oliver appeared next, herding the children up into the clearing. Behind them she could hear a barking dog, which meant that the Solville contingent was coming right up.

With the Valorie-memories which were now her own, Cody called across the hilltop glade to Crane, "Standing in happy sunlight on the hill in the lake!"

Crane laughed quietly, and the sound seemed to shake the green leaves and send ripples across the little lake.

Through the green branches overhead, the sky was a cloudless, deep blue. It was a good day for a wedding.

*   *   *

Sid Cochran was glad now that he hadn't acceded to the advice of the other sales representatives at Pace and worn some kind of tuxedo. His suit was formal enough, and in these wooded sunlit groves the affected pretension of a tuxedo would have been ludicrous. In the same spirit, he had left his prosthetic hand in the car's glove compartment, and was just wearing a white sock over the stump of his right wrist.

Behind him Fred was bounding along the cinder path on a leash, for Angelica hadn't wanted him jumping up on people's nice clothes, and Kootie was kept as busy as a fishing boat trying to stay over a powerful marlin, with the dog wanting to sniff at the mossy stones along the path and go loping and barking across the grass. Kootie had left his sport coat in the Solville van, and Cochran could see that there was no bandage anymore under the boy's white shirt. Angelica had told him that Kootie's two-year-old wound had finally healed up within a week of their return to Long Beach.

"And the cement *Eleggua* figure was back in its cabinet, when we got back home," said Angelica now, striding along between Cochran and Pete Sullivan.

"With a bunch of snapshots in the cabinet with him," added Pete. "Pictures of the Eleggua statue in front of Stonehenge, and at the Great Pyramid, and at Notre Dame cathedral . . ."

Cochran glanced sharply at him, but Pete's face was resolutely deadpan and Cochran couldn't quite decide if he was kidding or not.

Cody had kept in touch with Angelica during these five months, and the two of them had cautiously agreed that there appeared to have been, so far, no legal or psychic or underworld repercussions from their arduous January. Cochran and Plumtree had heard nothing from Rosecrans Medical—possibly because, according to the newspapers, Dr. Armentrout had run off with a number of patient files before allegedly murdering intern Philip Muir at the borrowed house of an absent neurologist, and then disappearing for parts unknown—and Cody had anonymously, and grumblingly, sent money to the people whose purse and car she had stolen, as well as twenty dollars to the Frost Giant ice-cream shop and a hundred to Strubie the Clown; and Angelica was still safely doing underground-occult consulting work among the Long Beach poor, though she no longer corralled ghosts for clients, and nobody had come looking for Spider Joe, who would ideally rest in peace forever beneath the Solville back parking lot.

The newspapers had reported that Richard Paul Armentrout had apparently been a victim of childhood incest at the hands of his alcoholic single mother, and that he had been committed to a men's psychiatric hospital and had undergone electroconvulsive therapy at the age of seventeen, after killing her.

That bit of news had obscurely upset Cody, and she had spent a good part of the afternoon sitting in the bone-strewn ruins of the backyard greenhouse, uncommunicatively drinking vodka; Cochran had eventually got her to come inside, and they had got stoically drunk together.

With the loss of his hand, Cochran had become unfitted for his cellar-and-vineyard work, and now was working out of the office as a sales representative; the change had been disorienting at first, but he had really had no choice, for along with his hand he had lost too his instinctive understanding of the soil and the vines and the slow pulse of the wines maturing in the casks.

Above him the path levelled out between the descending green slopes, and the trees were farther apart.

They had reached the clearing at the top of the hill, and Cochran could see his bride-to-be standing with Scott and Diana Crane on the far side of the little lake, talking with them and the Nardie Dinh woman and Mavranos's widow, while a gang of children climbed around on the rocks. Cochran had seen Cody's white skirted suit when she had got into the blue truck from Leucadia, but when he looked at her now, standing over there straight and slim and softly laughing, her blond hair in a long pageboy cut, he thought she looked even more beautiful than Diana Crane.

Scott Crane had seen the newcomers step up onto the level grass, and he held up one hand—and then walked down the shallow slope and waded several steps out into the lake, until the water was above his ankles. Fred barked at the spectacle, until Kootie shushed him.

With his beard and broad shoulders, Crane still seemed taller than everyone else. "This is a balanced place," he said in his deep, rolling voice, "and we want to maintain that and not be showing up as a spike in anyone's charts." Diana and Mavranos's widow seemed to be the only ones who knew what he was doing—Diana was looking away, down the grassy slope toward the surrounding lake, and Wendy was staring thoughtfully at Crane.

Crane went on, slowly, "When I came back, five months ago—through the self-sacrifice of my best friend—I accepted certain terms, the terms stated in that palindrome. I expect now to spend the January of every year in Erebus, as I did this winter—but with my lifeless body in Leucadia, and not requiring strenuous help to come *back* to life, each time. Three representatives of Death, two ghosts and one murderer who was shortly to die, brought me the requisite sacrament."

He held up a lumpy little brown ball that seemed from this distance to be cracked. "A pomegranate," he said, "which Nardie tells me was brought all the way from my own back garden . . . appropriately." He broke it and let most of it fall into the water, but held up something tiny between a thumb and forefinger. "One seed," he said. "Like what Persephone ate." And he put it into his mouth, and swallowed.

The children had paid attention when he had walked out into the water, but had lost interest when he had paused to talk; Kootie had dropped Fred's leash, and now the children and the dog were happily climbing around on the rocks in the dappled sunlight.

Scott Crane had seemed to go pale for a moment, but he inhaled deeply in the flower-scented air, and smiled toward the oblivious children. "This *is* a happy day," he said, "all of us obedient to our proper places in the seasons. And," he went on, looking into Cochran's eyes for a moment, "summer is the season for weddings."

He turned and walked back out of the lake, the cuffs of his pants flinging bright drops of water out onto the grass.

"Cody Plumtree," said the king, holding out his left hand to her, "who wide unclasped the table of your thoughts, so that intercessors of one sort and another could help me through all the houses of the year."

Cody stepped up to where he stood and took his hand with her right hand.

"And," called the king, now holding out his right hand and looking across the lake, "Sid Cochran, who reached out your hand twice to save the old king, and selflessly held the god's favor to give to me."

Everyone, even the children and the dog, was looking at Cochran; and he was sweating and awkward and he wanted to put the stump of his right wrist into his pocket. This hilltop clearing and lake, with the ring of leaning old laurels and redwoods around the perimeter, looked oddly familiar to him. He thought he might have been here once before, a very long time ago . . . happily . . . ?

"Go to your bride," muttered Pete Sullivan, nudging him in the back.

And Cochran met Cody's blue eyes across the lake, and she was smiling at him—and he smiled back at her, and walked straight toward her, down the bank and into the lake and striding through the clear, cleansing water all the way across while the children laughed delightedly and the dog barked, though the water rose to his waist in the middle of the lake and was cold down around his toes and ankles, striding finally up the far bank and stepping up onto the sunlit grass beside her and the king to take his vows, profoundly glad.